Elizabeth Gaskell

by Lacey Belinda Smith

2

Contents

Cranford   5

Ruth   116

The Grey Woman   379

Curious If True   411

Six Weeks At Heppenheim   421

Libbie Marsh's Three Eras   445

Christmas Storms And Sunshine   462

Hand And Heart   470

Bessy's Troubles At Home   482

Disappearances   495

Sylvia's Lovers. Vol. III   501

The Half-Brothers   604

The Manchester Marriage   611

GASKELL, ELIZABETH CLEGHORN (1810-1865), English novelist and biographer, was born on the 29th of September 1810 in Lindsay Row, Chelsea, London, since destroyed to make way for Cheyne Walk. Her father, William Stevenson (1772-1829), came from Berwick-on-Tweed, and had been successively Unitarian minister, farmer, boarding-house keeper for students at Edinburgh, editor of the *Scots Magazine*, and contributor to the *Edinburgh Review*, before he received the post of Keeper of the Records to the Treasury, which he held until his death. His first wife, Elizabeth Holland, was Mrs Gaskell's mother. She was a Holland of Sandlebridge, Knutsford, Cheshire, in which county the family name had long been and is still of great account. Mrs Stevenson died a month after her daughter was born, and the babe was carried into Cheshire to Knutsford to be adopted by her aunt, Mrs Lumb. Thus her childhood was spent in the pleasant environment that she has idealized in *Cranford*. At fifteen years of age she went to a boarding-school at Stratford-on-Avon, kept by Miss Byerley, where she remained until her seventeenth year. Then came occasional visits to London to see her father and his second wife, and after her father's death in 1829 to her uncle, Swinton Holland. Two winters seem to have been spent in Newcastle-on-Tyne In the family of William Turner, a Unitarian minister, and a third in Edinburgh. On the 30th of August 1832 she was married in the parish church of Knutsford to William Gaskell, minister of the Unitarian chapel in Cross Street, Manchester, and the author of many treatises and sermons in support of his own religious denomination. Mr Gaskell held the chair of English history and literature in Manchester New College.

Henceforth Mrs Gaskell's life belonged to Manchester. She and her husband lived first in Dover Street, then in Rumford Street, and finally in 1850 at 84 Plymouth Grove. Her literary life began with poetry. She and her husband aspired to emulate George Crabbe and write the annals of the Manchester poor. One poetic "Sketch," which appeared in *Blackwood's Magazine* for January 1837, seems to have been the only outcome of this ambition. Henceforth, while in perfect union in all else, husband and wife were to go their separate literary ways, Mrs Gaskell to become a successful novelist, whose books were to live side by side with those of greater masters, Mr Gaskell to be a distinguished Unitarian divine, whose sermons, lectures and hymns are now all but forgotten. In her earlier married life Mrs Gaskell was mainly occupied with domestic duties—she had seven children—and philanthropic work among the poor. Her first published prose effort was probably a letter that she addressed to William Howitt on hearing that he contemplated a volume entitled *Visits to*

Remarkable Places. She then told the legend of Clopton Hall, Warwickshire, as she had heard it in schooldays, and Howitt incorporated the letter in that book, which was published in 1840. Serious authorship, however, does not seem to have been commenced until four or five years later. In 1844 Mr and Mrs Gaskell visited North Wales, where their only son "Willie"died of scarlet fever at the age of ten months, and it was, it is said, to distract Mrs Gaskell from her sorrow that her husband suggested a long work of fiction, and *Mary Barton* was begun. There were earlier short stories in *Howitt's Journal*, where"Libbie Marsh's Three Eras" and "The Sexton's Hero" appeared in 1847. But it was *Mary Barton: A Tale of Manchester Life* that laid the foundation of Mrs Gaskell's literary career. It was completed in 1847 and offered to a publisher who returned it unread. It was then sent to Chapman & Hall, who retained the manuscript for a year without reading it or communicating with the author. A reminder, however, led to its being sought for, considered and accepted, the publishers agreeing to pay the author £100 for the copyright. It was published anonymously in two volumes in 1848. This story had a wide popularity, and its author secured first the praise and then the friendship of Carlyle, Landor and Dickens. Dickens indeed asked her in 1850 to become a contributor to his new magazine *Household Words*, and here the whole of *Cranford* appeared at intervals from December 1851 to May 1853, exclusive of one sketch, reprinted in the "World's Classics" edition (1907), that was published in*All the Year Round* for November 1863. Earlier than this, indeed, for the very first number of *Household Words* she had written "Lizzie Leigh." Mrs Gaskell's second book, however, was *The Moorland Cottage*, a dainty little volume that appeared at Christmas 1850 with illustrations by Birket Foster. In the Christmas number of *Household Words* for 1853 appeared "The Squire's Story," reprinted in *Lizzie Leigh and other Tales* in 1865. In 1853 appeared another long novel, *Ruth*, and the incomparable*Cranford*. This last—now the most popular of her books—is an idyll of village life, largely inspired by girlish memories of Knutsford and its people. In *Ruth*, which first appeared in three volumes, Mrs Gaskell turned to a delicate treatment of a girl's betrayal and her subsequent rescue. Once more we are introduced to Knutsford, thinly disguised, and to the little Unitarian chapel in that town where the author had worshipped in early years. In 1855 *North and South* was published. It had previously appeared serially in *Household Words*. Then came—in 1857—the*Life of Charlotte Brontë*, in two volumes. Miss Brontë, who had enjoyed the friendship of Mrs Gaskell and had exchanged visits, died in March 1855. Two years earlier she had begged her publishers to postpone the issue of her own novel *Villette* in order that her friend's *Ruth* should not suffer. This biography, by its vivid presentation of the sad, melancholy and indeed tragic story of the three Brontë sisters, greatly widened the interest in their writings and gave its author a considerable place among English biographers. But much matter was contained in the first and second editions that was withdrawn from the third. Certain statements made by the writer as to the school of Charlotte Brontë's infancy, an identification of the "Lowood" of*Jane Eyre* with the existing school, and the acceptance of the story of Bramwell Brontë's ruin having been caused by the woman in whose house he had lived as tutor, brought threats of libel actions. Apologies were published, and the third edition of the book was modified, as Mrs Gaskell declares, by "another hand." The book in any case remains one of the best biographies in the language. An introduction by Mrs Gaskell to the then popular novel, *Mabel Vaughan*, was also included in her work of this year 1857, but no further book was published by her until 1859, when, under the title of *Round the Sofa*, she collected many of her contributions to periodical literature. *Round the Sofa* appeared in two volumes, the first containing only "My Lady Ludlow,"the second five short stories. These stories reappeared the same year in one volume as *My Lady Ludlow and other Tales*. In the next year 1860 appeared yet another volume of short stories, entitled *Right at Last and other Tales*. The title story had appeared two years earlier in *Household Words* as "The Sin of a Father." In 1862 Mrs Gaskell wrote a preface to a little book by Colonel Vecchj, translated from the Italian—*Garibaldi and Caprera*, and in 1863 she published her last long novel, *Sylvia's Lovers*, dedicated "to My dear Husband by her who best knows his Value." After this we have—in 1863—a one-volume story, *A Dark Night's Work*, and in the same year *Cousin Phyllis and other Tales* appeared. Reprinted short stories from *All the Year Round*, *Cornhill Magazine*, and other publications, tend to lengthen the number of books published by Mrs Gaskell during her lifetime. *The Grey Woman and other Tales* appeared in 1865.

Mrs Gaskell died on the 12th of November 1865 at Holyburn, Alton, Hampshire, in a house she had just purchased with the profits of her writings as a present for her husband. She was buried in the little graveyard of the Knutsford Unitarian church. Her unfinished novel *Wives and Daughters* was published in two volumes in 1866.

Elizabeth Gaskell—selected works

CRANFORD

CHAPTER I - OUR SOCIETY

In the first place, Cranford is in possession of the Amazons; all the holders of houses above a certain rent are women. If a married couple come to settle in the town, somehow the gentleman disappears; he is either fairly frightened to death by being the only man in the Cranford evening parties, or he is accounted for by being with his regiment, his ship, or closely engaged in business all the week in the great neighbouring commercial town of Drumble, distant only twenty miles on a railroad. In short, whatever does become of the gentlemen, they are not at Cranford. What could they do if they were there? The surgeon has his round of thirty miles, and sleeps at Cranford; but every man cannot be a surgeon. For keeping the trim gardens full of choice flowers without a weed to speck them; for frightening away little boys who look wistfully at the said flowers through the railings; for rushing out at the geese that occasionally venture in to the gardens if the gates are left open; for deciding all questions of literature and politics without troubling themselves with unnecessary reasons or arguments; for obtaining clear and correct knowledge of everybody's affairs in the parish; for keeping their neat maid-servants in admirable order; for kindness (somewhat dictatorial) to the poor, and real tender good offices to each other whenever they are in distress, the ladies of Cranford are quite sufficient. "A man," as one of them observed to me once, "is *so* in the way in the house!" Although the ladies of Cranford know all each other's proceedings, they are exceedingly indifferent to each other's opinions. Indeed, as each has her own individuality, not to say eccentricity, pretty strongly developed, nothing is so easy as verbal retaliation; but, somehow, good-will reigns among them to a considerable degree.

The Cranford ladies have only an occasional little quarrel, spirited out in a few peppery words and angry jerks of the head; just enough to prevent the even tenor of their lives from becoming too flat. Their dress is very independent of fashion; as they observe, "What does it signify how we dress here at Cranford, where everybody knows us?" And if they go from home, their reason is equally cogent,"What does it signify how we dress here, where nobody knows us?" The materials of their clothes are, in general, good and plain, and most of them are nearly as scrupulous as Miss Tyler, of cleanly memory; but I will answer for it, the last gigot, the last tight and scanty petticoat in wear in England, was seen in Cranford - and seen without a smile.

I can testify to a magnificent family red silk umbrella, under which a gentle little spinster, left alone of many brothers and sisters, used to patter to church on rainy days. Have you any red silk umbrellas in London? We had a tradition of the first that had ever been seen in Cranford; and the little boys mobbed it, and called it "a stick in petticoats." It might have been the very red silk one I have described, held by a strong father over a troop of little ones; the poor little lady - the survivor of all - could scarcely carry it.

Then there were rules and regulations for visiting and calls; and they were announced to any young people who might be staying in the town, with all the solemnity with which the old Manx laws were read once a year on the Tinwald Mount.

"Our friends have sent to inquire how you are after your journey to-night, my dear" (fifteen miles in a gentleman's carriage);"they will give you some rest to-morrow, but the next day, I have no doubt, they will call; so be at liberty after twelve - from twelve to three are our calling hours."

Then, after they had called -

"It is the third day; I dare say your mamma has told you, my dear, never to let more than three days elapse between receiving a call and returning it; and also, that you are never to stay longer than a quarter of an hour."

"But am I to look at my watch? How am I to find out when a quarter of an hour has passed?"

"You must keep thinking about the time, my dear, and not allow yourself to forget it in conversation."

As everybody had this rule in their minds, whether they received or paid a call, of course no absorbing subject was ever spoken about. We kept ourselves to short sentences of small talk, and were punctual to our time.

I imagine that a few of the gentlefolks of Cranford were poor, and had some difficulty in making both ends meet; but they were like the Spartans, and concealed their smart under a smiling face. We none of us spoke of money, because that subject savoured of commerce and trade, and though some might be poor, we were all aristocratic. The Cranfordians had that kindly *esprit de corps* which made them overlook all deficiencies in success when some among them tried to conceal their poverty. When Mrs Forrester, for instance, gave a party in her baby-house of a dwelling, and the little maiden disturbed the ladies on the sofa by a request that she might get the tea-tray out from underneath, everyone took this novel proceeding as the most natural thing in the world, and talked on about household forms and ceremonies as if we all believed that our hostess had a regular servants' hall, second table, with housekeeper and steward, instead of the one little charity-school maiden, whose short ruddy arms could never have been strong enough to carry the tray upstairs, if she had not been assisted in private by her mistress, who now sat in state, pretending not to know what cakes were sent up, though she knew, and we knew, and she knew that we knew, and we knew that she knew that we knew, she had been busy all the morning making tea-bread and sponge-cakes.

There were one or two consequences arising from this general but unacknowledged poverty, and this very much acknowledged gentility, which were not amiss, and which might be introduced into many circles of society to their great improvement. For instance, the inhabitants of Cranford kept early hours, and clattered home in their pattens, under the guidance of a lantern-bearer, about nine o'clock at night; and the whole town was abed and asleep by half-past ten. Moreover, it was considered"vulgar" (a tremendous word in Cranford) to give anything expensive, in the way of eatable or drinkable, at the evening entertainments. Wafer bread-and-butter and sponge-biscuits were all that the Honourable Mrs Jamieson gave; and she was sister-in-law to the late Earl of Glenmire, although she did practise such "elegant economy."

"Elegant economy!" How naturally one falls back into the phraseology of Cranford! There, economy was always "elegant,"and money-spending always "vulgar and ostentatious"; a sort of sour-grapeism which made us very peaceful and satisfied. I never shall forget the dismay felt when a certain Captain Brown came to live at Cranford, and openly spoke about his being poor - not in a whisper to an intimate friend, the doors and windows being previously closed, but in the public street! in a loud military voice! alleging his poverty as a reason for not taking a particular house. The ladies of Cranford were already rather moaning over the invasion of their territories by a man and a gentleman. He was a half-pay captain, and had obtained some situation on a neighbouring railroad, which had been vehemently petitioned against by the little town; and if, in addition to his masculine gender, and his connection with the obnoxious railroad, he was so brazen as to talk of being poor - why, then, indeed, he must be sent to Coventry. Death was as true and as common as poverty; yet people never spoke about that, loud out in the streets. It was a word not to be mentioned to ears polite. We had tacitly agreed to ignore that any with whom we associated on terms of visiting equality could ever be prevented by poverty from doing anything that they wished. If we walked to or from a party, it was because the night was *so* fine, or the air *so* refreshing, not because sedan-chairs were expensive. If we wore prints, instead of summer silks, it was because we preferred a washing material; and so on, till we blinded ourselves to the vulgar fact that we were, all of us, people of very moderate means. Of course, then, we did not know what to make of a man who could speak of poverty as if it was not a disgrace. Yet, somehow, Captain Brown made himself respected in Cranford, and was called upon, in spite of all resolutions to the contrary. I was surprised to hear his opinions quoted as authority at a visit which I paid to Cranford about a year after he had settled in the town. My own friends had been among the bitterest opponents of any proposal to visit the Captain and his daughters, only twelve months before; and now he was even admitted in the tabooed hours before twelve. True, it was to discover the cause of a smoking chimney, before the fire was lighted; but still Captain Brown walked upstairs, nothing daunted, spoke in a voice too large for the room, and joked quite in the way of a tame man about the house. He had been blind to all the small slights, and omissions of trivial ceremonies, with which he had been received. He had been friendly, though the Cranford ladies had been cool; he had answered small sarcastic compliments in good faith; and with his manly frankness had overpowered all the shrinking which met him as a man who was not ashamed to be poor. And, at last, his excellent masculine common sense, and his facility in devising expedients to overcome domestic dilemmas, had gained him an extraordinary place as authority among the Cranford ladies. He himself went on in his course, as unaware of his popularity as he had been of the reverse; and I am sure he was startled one day when he found his advice so highly esteemed as to make some counsel which he had given in jest to be taken in sober, serious earnest.

It was on this subject: An old lady had an Alderney cow, which she looked upon as a daughter. You could not pay the short quarter of an hour call without being told of the wonderful milk or wonderful intelligence of this animal. The whole town knew and kindly regarded Miss Betsy Barker's Alderney; therefore great was the sympathy and regret when, in an unguarded moment, the poor cow tumbled into a lime-pit. She moaned so loudly that she was soon heard and rescued; but meanwhile the poor beast had lost most of her hair, and came out looking naked, cold, and miserable, in a bare skin. Everybody pitied the animal, though a few could not restrain their smiles at her droll appearance. Miss Betsy Barker absolutely cried with sorrow and dismay; and it was said she thought of trying a bath of oil. This remedy, perhaps, was recommended by some one of the number whose advice she asked; but the proposal, if ever it was made, was knocked on the head by Captain Brown's decided "Get her a flannel waistcoat and flannel drawers, ma'am, if you wish to keep her alive. But my advice is, kill the poor creature at once."

Miss Betsy Barker dried her eyes, and thanked the Captain heartily; she set to work, and by-and-by all the town turned out to see the Alderney meekly going to her pasture, clad in dark grey flannel. I have watched her myself many a time. Do you ever see cows dressed in grey flannel in London?

Captain Brown had taken a small house on the outskirts of the town, where he lived with his two daughters. He must have been upwards of sixty at the time of the first visit I paid to Cranford after I had left it as a residence. But he had a wiry, well-trained, elastic figure, a stiff military throw-back of his head, and a springing step, which made him appear much younger than he was. His eldest daughter looked almost as old as himself, and betrayed the fact that his real was more than his apparent age. Miss Brown must have been forty; she had a sickly, pained, careworn expression on her face, and looked as if the gaiety of youth had long faded out of sight. Even when young she must have been plain and hard-featured. Miss Jessie Brown was ten years younger than her sister, and twenty shades prettier. Her face was round and dimpled. Miss Jenkyns once said, in a passion against Captain Brown (the cause of which I will tell you presently),"that she thought it was time for Miss Jessie to leave off her dimples, and not always to be trying to look like a child." It was true there was something childlike in her face; and there will be, I think, till she dies, though she should live to a hundred. Her eyes were large blue wondering eyes, looking straight at you; her nose was unformed and snub, and her lips were red and dewy; she wore her hair, too, in little rows of curls, which heightened this appearance. I do not know whether she was pretty or not; but I liked her face, and so did everybody, and I do not think she could help her dimples. She had something of her father's jauntiness of gait and manner; and any female observer might detect a slight difference in the attire of the two sisters - that of Miss Jessie being about two pounds per annum more expensive than Miss Brown's. Two pounds was a large sum in Captain Brown's annual disbursements.

Such was the impression made upon me by the Brown family when I first saw them all together in Cranford Church. The Captain I had met before - on the occasion of the smoky chimney, which he had cured by some simple alteration in the flue. In church, he held his double eye-glass to his eyes during the Morning Hymn, and then lifted up his head erect and sang out loud and joyfully. He made the responses louder than the clerk - an old man with a piping feeble voice, who, I think, felt aggrieved at the Captain's sonorous bass, and quivered higher and higher in consequence.

On coming out of church, the brisk Captain paid the most gallant attention to his two daughters.

He nodded and smiled to his acquaintances; but he shook hands with none until he had helped Miss Brown to unfurl her umbrella, had relieved her of her prayer-book, and had waited patiently till she, with trembling nervous hands, had taken up her gown to walk through the wet roads.

I wonder what the Cranford ladies did with Captain Brown at their parties. We had often rejoiced, in former days, that there was no gentleman to be attended to, and to find conversation for, at the card-parties. We had congratulated ourselves upon the snugness of the evenings; and, in our love for gentility, and distaste of mankind, we had almost persuaded ourselves that to be a man was to be "vulgar"; so that when I found my friend and hostess, Miss Jenkyns, was going to have a party in my honour, and that Captain and the Miss Browns were invited, I wondered much what would be the course of the evening. Card-tables, with green baize tops, were set out by daylight, just as usual; it was the third week in November, so the evenings closed in about four. Candles, and clean packs of cards, were arranged on each table. The fire was made up; the neat maid-servant had received her last directions; and there we stood, dressed in our best, each with a candle-lighter in our hands, ready to dart at the candles as soon as the first knock came. Parties in Cranford were solemn festivities, making the ladies feel gravely elated as they sat together in their best dresses. As soon as three had arrived, we sat down to "Preference,"I being the unlucky fourth. The next four comers were put down immediately to another table; and presently the tea-trays, which I had seen set out in the store-room as I passed in the morning, were placed each on the middle of a card-table. The china was delicate egg-shell; the old-fashioned silver glittered with polishing; but the eatables were of the slightest description. While the trays were yet on the tables, Captain and the Miss Browns came in; and I could see that, somehow or other, the Captain was a favourite with all the ladies present. Ruffled brows were smoothed, sharp voices lowered at his approach. Miss Brown looked ill, and depressed almost to gloom. Miss Jessie smiled as usual, and seemed nearly as popular as her father. He immediately and quietly assumed the man's place in the room; attended to every one's wants, lessened the pretty maid-servant's labour by waiting on empty cups and bread-and-butterless ladies; and yet did it all in so easy and dignified a manner, and so much as if it were a matter of course for the strong to attend to the weak, that he was a true man throughout. He played for threepenny points with as grave an interest as if they had been pounds; and yet, in all his attention to strangers, he had an eye on his suffering daughter - for suffering I was sure she was, though to many eyes she might only appear to be irritable. Miss Jessie could not play cards: but she talked to the sitters-out, who, before her coming, had been rather inclined to be cross. She sang, too, to an old cracked piano, which I think had been a spinet in its youth. Miss Jessie sang, "Jock of Hazeldean" a little out of tune; but we were none of us musical, though Miss Jenkyns beat time, out of time, by way of appearing to be so.

It was very good of Miss Jenkyns to do this; for I had seen that, a little before, she had been a good deal annoyed by Miss Jessie Brown's unguarded admission (*à propos* of Shetland wool) that she had an uncle, her mother's brother, who was a shop-keeper in Edinburgh. Miss Jenkyns tried to drown this confession by a terrible cough - for the Honourable Mrs Jamieson was sitting at a card-table nearest Miss Jessie, and what would she say or think if she found out she was in the same room with a shop-keeper's niece! But Miss Jessie Brown (who had no tact, as we all agreed the next morning) *would* repeat the information, and assure Miss Pole she could easily get her the identical Shetland wool required, "through my uncle, who has the best assortment of Shetland goods of any one in Edinbro'." It was to take the taste of this out of our mouths, and the sound of this out of our ears, that Miss Jenkyns proposed music; so I say again, it was very good of her to beat time to the song.

When the trays re-appeared with biscuits and wine, punctually at a quarter to nine, there was conversation, comparing of cards, and talking over tricks; but by-and-by Captain Brown sported a bit of literature.

"Have you seen any numbers of 'The Pickwick Papers'?" said he. (They we're then publishing in parts.) "Capital thing!"

Now Miss Jenkyns was daughter of a deceased rector of Cranford; and, on the strength of a number of manuscript sermons, and a pretty good library of divinity, considered herself literary, and looked upon any conversation about books as a challenge to her. So she answered and said, "Yes, she had seen them; indeed, she might say she had read them."

"And what do you think of them?" exclaimed Captain Brown. "Aren't they famously good?"

So urged Miss Jenkyns could not but speak.

"I must say, I don't think they are by any means equal to Dr Johnson. Still, perhaps, the author is young. Let him persevere, and who knows what he may become if he will take the great Doctor for his model?" This was evidently too much for Captain Brown to take placidly; and I saw the words on the tip of his tongue before Miss Jenkyns had finished her sentence.

"It is quite a different sort of thing, my dear madam," he began.

"I am quite aware of that," returned she. "And I make allowances, Captain Brown."

"Just allow me to read you a scene out of this month's number,"pleaded he. "I had it only this morning, and I don't think the company can have read it yet."

"As you please," said she, settling herself with an air of resignation. He read the account of the "swarry"which Sam Weller gave at Bath. Some of us laughed heartily. *I* did not dare, because I was staying in the house. Miss Jenkyns sat in patient gravity. When it was ended, she turned to me, and said with mild dignity -

"Fetch me 'Rasselas,' my dear, out of the book-room."

When I had brought it to her, she turned to Captain Brown -

"Now allow me to read you a scene, and then the present company can judge between your favourite, Mr Boz, and Dr Johnson."

She read one of the conversations between Rasselas and Imlac, in a high-pitched, majestic voice: and when she had ended, she said, "I imagine I am now justified in my preference of Dr Johnson as a writer of fiction." The Captain screwed his lips up, and drummed on the table, but he did not speak. She thought she would give him a finishing blow or two.

"I consider it vulgar, and below the dignity of literature, to publish in numbers."

"How was the *Rambler* published, ma'am?" asked Captain Brown in a low voice, which I think Miss Jenkyns could not have heard.

"Dr Johnson's style is a model for young beginners. My father recommended it to me when I began to write letters - I have formed my own style upon it; I recommended it to your favourite."

"I should be very sorry for him to exchange his style for any such pompous writing," said Captain Brown.

Miss Jenkyns felt this as a personal affront, in a way of which the Captain had not dreamed. Epistolary writing she and her friends considered as her *forte*. Many a copy of many a letter have I seen written and corrected on the slate, before she "seized the half-hour just previous to post-time to assure" her friends of this or of that; and Dr Johnson was, as she said, her model in these compositions. She drew herself up with dignity, and only replied to Captain Brown's last remark by saying, with marked emphasis on every syllable, "I prefer Dr Johnson to Mr Boz."

It is said - I won't vouch for the fact - that Captain Brown was heard to say, *sotto voce*, "D-n Dr Johnson!" If he did, he was penitent afterwards, as he showed by going to stand near Miss Jenkyns' arm-chair, and endeavouring to beguile her into conversation on some more pleasing subject. But she was inexorable. The next day she made the remark I have mentioned about Miss Jessie's dimples.

CHAPTER II - THE CAPTAIN

It was impossible to live a month at Cranford and not know the daily habits of each resident; and long before my visit was ended I knew much concerning the whole Brown trio. There was nothing new to be discovered respecting their poverty; for they had spoken simply and openly about that from the very first. They made no mystery of the necessity for their being economical. All that remained to be discovered was the Captain's infinite kindness of heart, and the various modes in which, unconsciously to himself, he manifested it. Some little anecdotes were talked about for some time after they occurred. As we did not read much, and as all the ladies were pretty well suited with servants, there was a dearth of subjects for conversation. We therefore discussed the circumstance of the Captain taking a poor old woman's dinner out of her hands one very slippery Sunday. He had met her returning from the bakehouse as he came from church, and noticed her precarious footing; and, with the grave dignity with which he did everything, he relieved her of her burden, and steered along the street by her side, carrying her baked mutton and potatoes safely home. This was thought very eccentric; and it was rather expected that he would pay a round of calls, on the Monday morning, to explain and apologise to the Cranford sense of propriety: but he did no such thing: and then it was decided that he was ashamed, and was keeping out of sight. In a kindly pity for him, we began to say, "After all, the Sunday morning's occurrence showed great goodness of heart," and it was resolved that he should be comforted on his next appearance amongst us; but, lo! he came down upon us, untouched by any sense of shame, speaking loud and bass as ever, his head thrown back, his wig as jaunty and well-curled as usual, and we were obliged to conclude he had forgotten all about Sunday.

Miss Pole and Miss Jessie Brown had set up a kind of intimacy on the strength of the Shetland wool and the new knitting stitches; so it happened that when I went to visit Miss Pole I saw more of the Browns than I had done while staying with Miss Jenkyns, who had never got over what she called Captain Brown's disparaging remarks upon Dr Johnson as a writer of light and agreeable fiction. I found that Miss Brown was seriously ill of some lingering, incurable complaint, the pain occasioned by which gave the uneasy expression to her face that I had taken for unmitigated crossness. Cross, too, she was at times, when the nervous irritability occasioned by her disease became past endurance. Miss Jessie bore with her at these times, even more patiently than she did with the bitter self-upbraidings by which they were invariably succeeded. Miss Brown used to accuse herself, not merely of hasty and irritable temper, but also of being the cause why her father and sister were obliged to pinch, in order to allow her the small luxuries which were necessaries in her condition. She would so fain have made sacrifices for them, and have lightened their cares, that the original generosity of her disposition added acerbity to her temper. All this was borne by Miss Jessie and her father with more than placidity - with absolute tenderness. I forgave Miss Jessie her singing out of tune, and her juvenility of dress, when I saw her at home. I came to perceive that Captain Brown's dark Brutus wig and padded coat (alas! too often threadbare) were remnants of the military smartness of his youth, which he now wore unconsciously. He was a man of infinite resources, gained in his barrack experience. As he confessed, no one could black his boots to please him except himself; but, indeed, he was not above saving the little maid-servant's labours in every way - knowing, most likely, that his daughter's illness made the place a hard one.

He endeavoured to make peace with Miss Jenkyns soon after the memorable dispute I have named, by a present of a wooden fire-shovel (his own making), having heard her say how much the grating of an iron one annoyed her. She received the present with cool gratitude, and thanked him formally. When he was gone, she bade me put it away in the lumber-room; feeling, probably, that no present from a man who preferred Mr Boz to Dr Johnson could be less jarring than an iron fire-shovel.

Such was the state of things when I left Cranford and went to Drumble. I had, however, several correspondents, who kept me *au fait* as to the proceedings of the dear little town. There was Miss Pole, who was becoming as much absorbed in crochet as she had been once in knitting, and the burden of whose letter was something like, "But don't you forget the white worsted at Flint's" of the old song; for at the end of every sentence of news came a fresh direction as to some crochet commission which I was to execute for her. Miss Matilda Jenkyns (who did not mind being called Miss Matty, when Miss Jenkyns was not by) wrote nice, kind, rambling letters, now and then venturing into an opinion of her own; but suddenly pulling herself up, and either begging me not to name what she had said, as Deborah thought differently, and *she* knew, or else putting in a postscript to the effect that, since writing the above, she had been talking over the subject with Deborah, and was quite convinced that, etc. - (here probably followed a recantation of every opinion she had given in the letter). Then came Miss Jenkyns - Deborah, as she liked Miss Matty to call her, her father having once said that the Hebrew name ought to be so pronounced. I secretly think she took the Hebrew prophetess for a model in character; and, indeed, she was not unlike the stern prophetess in some ways, making allowance, of course, for modern customs and difference in dress. Miss Jenkyns wore a cravat, and a little bonnet like a jockey-cap, and altogether had the appearance of a strong-minded woman; although she would have despised the modern idea of women being equal to men. Equal, indeed! she knew they were superior. But to return to her letters. Everything in them was stately and grand like herself. I have been looking them over (dear Miss Jenkyns, how I honoured her!) and I will give an extract, more especially because it relates to our friend Captain Brown:-

"The Honourable Mrs Jamieson has only just quitted me; and, in the course of conversation, she communicated to me the intelligence that she had yesterday received a call from her revered husband's quondam friend, Lord Mauleverer. You will not easily conjecture what brought his lordship within the precincts of our little town. It was to see Captain Brown, with whom, it appears, his lordship was acquainted in the 'plumed wars,' and who had the privilege of averting destruction from his lordship's head when some great peril was impending over it, off the misnomered Cape of Good Hope. You know our friend the Honourable Mrs Jamieson's deficiency in the spirit of innocent curiosity, and you will therefore not be so much surprised when I tell you she was quite unable to disclose to me the exact nature of the peril in question. I was anxious, I confess, to ascertain in what manner Captain Brown, with his limited establishment, could receive so distinguished a guest; and I discovered that his lordship retired to rest, and, let us hope, to refreshing slumbers, at the Angel Hotel; but shared the Brunonian meals during the two days that he honoured Cranford with his august presence.

Mrs Johnson, our civil butcher's wife, informs me that Miss Jessie purchased a leg of lamb; but, besides this, I can hear of no preparation whatever to give a suitable reception to so distinguished a visitor. Perhaps they entertained him with 'the feast of reason and the flow of soul'; and to us, who are acquainted with Captain Brown's sad want of relish for 'the pure wells of English undefiled,' it may be matter for congratulation that he has had the opportunity of improving his taste by holding converse with an elegant and refined member of the British aristocracy. But from some mundane failings who is altogether free?"

Miss Pole and Miss Matty wrote to me by the same post. Such a piece of news as Lord Mauleverer's visit was not to be lost on the Cranford letter-writers: they made the most of it. Miss Matty humbly apologised for writing at the same time as her sister, who was so much more capable than she to describe the honour done to Cranford; but in spite of a little bad spelling, Miss Matty's account gave me the best idea of the commotion occasioned by his lordship's visit, after it had occurred; for, except the people at the Angel, the Browns, Mrs Jamieson, and a little lad his lordship had sworn at for driving a dirty hoop against the aristocratic legs, I could not hear of any one with whom his lordship had held conversation.

My next visit to Cranford was in the summer. There had been neither births, deaths, nor marriages since I was there last. Everybody lived in the same house, and wore pretty nearly the same well-preserved, old-fashioned clothes. The greatest event was, that Miss Jenkyns had purchased a new carpet for the drawing-room. Oh, the busy work Miss Matty and I had in chasing the sunbeams, as they fell in an afternoon right down on this carpet through the blindless window! We spread newspapers over the places and sat down to our book or our work; and, lo! in a quarter of an hour the sun had moved, and was blazing away on a fresh spot; and down again we went on our knees to alter the position of the newspapers. We were very busy, too, one whole morning, before Miss Jenkyns gave her party, in following her directions, and in cutting out and stitching together pieces of newspaper so as to form little paths to every chair set for the expected visitors, lest their shoes might dirty or defile the purity of the carpet. Do you make paper paths for every guest to walk upon in London?

Captain Brown and Miss Jenkyns were not very cordial to each other. The literary dispute, of which I had seen the beginning, was a "raw," the slightest touch on which made them wince. It was the only difference of opinion they had ever had; but that difference was enough. Miss Jenkyns could not refrain from talking at Captain Brown; and, though he did not reply, he drummed with his fingers, which action she felt and resented as very disparaging to Dr Johnson. He was rather ostentatious in his preference of the writings of Mr Boz; would walk through the streets so absorbed in them that he all but ran against Miss Jenkyns; and though his apologies were earnest and sincere, and though he did not, in fact, do more than startle her and himself, she owned to me she had rather he had knocked her down, if he had only been reading a higher style of literature. The poor, brave Captain! he looked older, and more worn, and his clothes were very threadbare. But he seemed as bright and cheerful as ever, unless he was asked about his daughter's health.

"She suffers a great deal, and she must suffer more: we do what we can to alleviate her pain; - God's will be done!" He took off his hat at these last words. I found, from Miss Matty, that everything had been done, in fact. A medical man, of high repute in that country neighbourhood, had been sent for, and every injunction he had given was attended to, regardless of expense. Miss Matty was sure they denied themselves many things in order to make the invalid comfortable; but they never spoke about it; and as for Miss Jessie! - "I really think she's an angel," said poor Miss Matty, quite overcome. "To see her way of bearing with Miss Brown's crossness, and the bright face she puts on after she's been sitting up a whole night and scolded above half of it, is quite beautiful. Yet she looks as neat and as ready to welcome the Captain at breakfast-time as if she had been asleep in the Queen's bed all night. My dear! you could never laugh at her prim little curls or her pink bows again if you saw her as I have done." I could only feel very penitent, and greet Miss Jessie with double respect when I met her next. She looked faded and pinched; and her lips began to quiver, as if she was very weak, when she spoke of her sister. But she brightened, and sent back the tears that were glittering in her pretty eyes, as she said

"But, to be sure, what a town Cranford is for kindness! I don't suppose any one has a better dinner than usual cooked but the best part of all comes in a little covered basin for my sister. The poor people will leave their earliest vegetables at our door for her. They speak short and gruff, as if they were ashamed of it: but I am sure it often goes to my heart to see their thoughtfulness." The tears now came back and overflowed; but after a minute or two she began to scold herself, and ended by going away the same cheerful Miss Jessie as ever.

"But why does not this Lord Mauleverer do something for the man who saved his life?" said I.

"Why, you see, unless Captain Brown has some reason for it, he never speaks about being poor; and he walked along by his lordship looking as happy and cheerful as a prince; and as they never called attention to their dinner by apologies, and as Miss Brown was better that day, and all seemed bright, I daresay his lordship never knew how much care there was in the background. He did send game in the winter pretty often, but now he is gone abroad."

I had often occasion to notice the use that was made of fragments and small opportunities in Cranford; the rose-leaves that were gathered ere they fell to make into a potpourri for someone who had no garden; the little bundles of lavender flowers sent to strew the drawers of some town-dweller, or to burn in the chamber of some invalid. Things that many would despise, and actions which it seemed scarcely worth while to perform, were all attended to in Cranford. Miss Jenkyns stuck an apple full of cloves, to be heated and smell pleasantly in Miss Brown's room; and as she put in each clove she uttered a Johnsonian sentence. Indeed, she never could think of the Browns without talking Johnson; and, as they were seldom absent from her thoughts just then, I heard many a rolling, three-piled sentence.

Captain Brown called one day to thank Mist Jenkyns for many little kindnesses, which I did not know until then that she had rendered. He had suddenly become like an old man; his deep bass voice had a quavering in it, his eyes looked dim, and the lines on his face were deep. He did not - could not - speak cheerfully of his daughter's state, but he talked with manly, pious resignation, and not much. Twice over he said, "What Jessie has been to us, God only knows!"and after the second time, he got up hastily, shook hands all round without speaking, and left the room.

That afternoon we perceived little groups in the street, all listening with faces aghast to some tale or other. Miss Jenkyns wondered what could be the matter for some time before she took the undignified step of sending Jenny out to inquire.

Jenny came back with a white face of terror. "Oh, ma'am! Oh, Miss Jenkyns, ma'am! Captain Brown is killed by them nasty cruel railroads!" and she burst into tears. She, along with many others, had experienced the poor Captain's kindness.

"How? - where - where? Good God! Jenny, don't waste time in crying, but tell us something." Miss Matty rushed out into the street at once, and collared the man who was telling the tale.

"Come in - come to my sister at once, Miss Jenkyns, the rector's daughter. Oh, man, man! say it is not true," she cried, as she brought the affrighted carter, sleeking down his hair, into the drawing-room, where he stood with his wet boots on the new carpet, and no one regarded it.

"Please, mum, it is true. I seed it myself," and he shuddered at the recollection. "The Captain was a-reading some new book as he was deep in, a-waiting for the down train; and there was a little lass as wanted to come to its mammy, and gave its sister the slip, and came toddling across the line. And he looked up sudden, at the sound of the train coming, and seed the child, and he darted on the line and cotched it up, and his foot slipped, and the train came over him in no time. O Lord, Lord! Mum, it's quite true, and they've come over to tell his daughters. The child's safe, though, with only a bang on its shoulder as he threw it to its mammy. Poor Captain would be glad of that, mum, wouldn't he? God bless him!" The great rough carter puckered up his manly face, and turned away to hide his tears. I turned to Miss Jenkyns. She looked very ill, as if she were going to faint, and signed to me to open the window.

"Matilda, bring me my bonnet. I must go to those girls. God pardon me, if ever I have spoken contemptuously to the Captain!"

Miss Jenkyns arrayed herself to go out, telling Miss Matilda to give the man a glass of wine. While she was away, Miss Matty and I huddled over the fire, talking in a low and awe-struck voice. I know we cried quietly all the time.

Miss Jenkyns came home in a silent mood, and we durst not ask her many questions. She told us that Miss Jessie had fainted, and that she and Miss Pole had had some difficulty in bringing her round; but that, as soon as she recovered, she begged one of them to go and sit with her sister.

"Mr Hoggins says she cannot live many days, and she shall be spared this shock," said Miss Jessie, shivering with feelings to which she dared not give way.

"But how can you manage, my dear?" asked Miss Jenkyns; "you cannot bear up, she must see your tears."

"God will help me - I will not give way - she was asleep when the news came; she may be asleep yet. She would be so utterly miserable, not merely at my father's death, but to think of what would become of me; she is so good to me." She looked up earnestly in their faces with her soft true eyes, and Miss Pole told Miss Jenkyns afterwards she could hardly bear it, knowing, as she did, how Miss Brown treated her sister.

However, it was settled according to Miss Jessie's wish. Miss Brown was to be told her father had been summoned to take a short journey on railway business. They had managed it in some way - Miss Jenkyns could not exactly say how. Miss Pole was to stop with Miss Jessie. Mrs Jamieson had sent to inquire. And this was all we heard that night; and a sorrowful night it was. The next day a full account of the fatal accident was in the county paper which Miss Jenkyns took in. Her eyes were very weak, she said, and she asked me to read it. When I came to the "gallant gentleman was deeply engaged in the perusal of a number of 'Pickwick,' which he had just received," Miss Jenkyns shook her head long and solemnly, and then sighed out, "Poor, dear, infatuated man!"

The corpse was to be taken from the station to the parish church, there to be interred. Miss Jessie had set her heart on following it to the grave; and no dissuasives could alter her resolve. Her restraint upon herself made her almost obstinate; she resisted all Miss Pole's entreaties and Miss Jenkyns' advice. At last Miss Jenkyns gave up the point; and after a silence, which I feared portended some deep displeasure against Miss Jessie, Miss Jenkyns said she should accompany the latter to the funeral.

"It is not fit for you to go alone. It would be against both propriety and humanity were I to allow it."

Miss Jessie seemed as if she did not half like this arrangement; but her obstinacy, if she had any, had been exhausted in her determination to go to the interment. She longed, poor thing, I have no doubt, to cry alone over the grave of the dear father to whom she had been all in all, and to give way, for one little half-hour, uninterrupted by sympathy and unobserved by friendship. But it was not to be. That afternoon Miss Jenkyns sent out for a yard of black crape, and employed herself busily in trimming the little black silk bonnet I have spoken about. When it was finished she put it on, and looked at us for approbation - admiration she despised. I was full of sorrow, but, by one of those whimsical thoughts which come unbidden into our heads, in times of deepest grief, I no sooner saw the bonnet than I was reminded of a helmet; and in that hybrid bonnet, half helmet, half jockey-cap, did Miss Jenkyns attend Captain Brown's funeral, and, I believe, supported Miss Jessie with a tender, indulgent firmness which was invaluable, allowing her to weep her passionate fill before they left.

Miss Pole, Miss Matty, and I, meanwhile attended to Miss Brown: and hard work we found it to relieve her querulous and never-ending complaints. But if we were so weary and dispirited, what must Miss Jessie have been! Yet she came back almost calm as if she had gained a new strength. She put off her mourning dress, and came in, looking pale and gentle, thanking us each with a soft long pressure of the hand. She could even smile - a faint, sweet, wintry smile - as if to reassure us of her power to endure; but her look made our eyes fill suddenly with tears, more than if she had cried outright.

It was settled that Miss Pole was to remain with her all the watching livelong night; and that Miss Matty and I were to return in the morning to relieve them, and give Miss Jessie the opportunity for a few hours of sleep. But when the morning came, Miss Jenkyns appeared at the breakfast-table, equipped in her helmet-bonnet, and ordered Miss Matty to stay at home, as she meant to go and help to nurse. She was evidently in a state of great friendly excitement, which she showed by eating her breakfast standing, and scolding the household all round.

No nursing - no energetic strong-minded woman could help Miss Brown now. There was that in the room as we entered which was stronger than us all, and made us shrink into solemn awestruck helplessness. Miss Brown was dying. We hardly knew her voice, it was so devoid of the complaining tone we had always associated with it. Miss Jessie told me afterwards that it, and her face too, were just what they had been formerly, when her mother's death left her the young anxious head of the family, of whom only Miss Jessie survived.

She was conscious of her sister's presence, though not, I think, of ours. We stood a little behind the curtain: Miss Jessie knelt with her face near her sister's, in order to catch the last soft awful whispers.

"Oh, Jessie! Jessie! How selfish I have been! God forgive me for letting you sacrifice yourself for me as you did! I have so loved you - and yet I have thought only of myself. God forgive me!"

"Hush, love! hush!" said Miss Jessie, sobbing.

"And my father, my dear, dear father! I will not complain now, if God will give me strength to be patient. But, oh, Jessie! tell my father how I longed and yearned to see him at last, and to ask his forgiveness. He can never know now how I loved him - oh! if I might but tell him, before I die! What a life of sorrow his has been, and I have done so little to cheer him!"

A light came into Miss Jessie's face. "Would it comfort you, dearest, to think that he does know? - would it comfort you, love, to know that his cares, his sorrows" - Her voice quivered, but she steadied it into calmness - "Mary! he has gone before you to the place where the weary are at rest. He knows now how you loved him."

A strange look, which was not distress, came over Miss Brown's face. She did not speak for come time, but then we saw her lips form the words, rather than heard the sound - "Father, mother, Harry, Archy;" - then, as if it were a new idea throwing a filmy shadow over her darkened mind - "But you will be alone, Jessie!"

Miss Jessie had been feeling this all during the silence, I think; for the tears rolled down her cheeks like rain, at these words, and she could not answer at first. Then she put her hands together tight, and lifted them up, and said - but not to us - "Though He slay me, yet will I trust in Him."

In a few moments more Miss Brown lay calm and still - never to sorrow or murmur more.

After this second funeral, Miss Jenkyns insisted that Miss Jessie should come to stay with her rather than go back to the desolate house, which, in fact, we learned from Miss Jessie, must now be given up, as she had not wherewithal to maintain it. She had something above twenty pounds a year, besides the interest of the money for which the furniture would sell; but she could not live upon that: and so we talked over her qualifications for earning money.

"I can sew neatly," said she, "and I like nursing. I think, too, I could manage a house, if any one would try me as housekeeper; or I would go into a shop as saleswoman, if they would have patience with me at first."

Miss Jenkyns declared, in an angry voice, that she should do no such thing; and talked to herself about "some people having no idea of their rank as a captain's daughter," nearly an hour afterwards, when she brought Miss Jessie up a basin of delicately-made arrowroot, and stood over her like a dragoon until the last spoonful was finished: then she disappeared. Miss Jessie began to tell me some more of the plans which had suggested themselves to her, and insensibly fell into talking of the days that were past and gone, and interested me so much I neither knew nor heeded how time passed. We were both startled when Miss Jenkyns reappeared, and caught us crying. I was afraid lest she would be displeased, as she often said that crying hindered digestion, and I knew she wanted Miss Jessie to get strong; but, instead, she looked queer and excited, and fidgeted round us without saying anything. At last she spoke.

"I have been so much startled - no, I've not been at all startled - don't mind me, my dear Miss Jessie - I've been very much surprised - in fact, I've had a caller, whom you knew once, my dear Miss Jessie" -

Miss Jessie went very white, then flushed scarlet, and looked eagerly at Miss Jenkyns.

"A gentleman, my dear, who wants to know if you would see him."

"Is it? - it is not" - stammered out Miss Jessie - and got no farther.

"This is his card," said Miss Jenkyns, giving it to Miss Jessie; and while her head was bent over it, Miss Jenkyns went through a series of winks and odd faces to me, and formed her lips into a long sentence, of which, of course, I could not understand a word.

"May he come up?" asked Miss Jenkyns at last.

"Oh, yes! certainly!" said Miss Jessie, as much as to say, this is your house, you may show any visitor where you like. She took up some knitting of Miss Matty's and began to be very busy, though I could see how she trembled all over.

Miss Jenkyns rang the bell, and told the servant who answered it to show Major Gordon upstairs; and, presently, in walked a tall, fine, frank-looking man of forty or upwards. He shook hands with Miss Jessie; but he could not see her eyes, she kept them so fixed on the ground. Miss Jenkyns asked me if I would come and help her to tie up the preserves in the store-room; and though Miss Jessie plucked at my gown, and even looked up at me with begging eye, I durst not refuse to go where Miss Jenkyns asked. Instead of tying up preserves in the store-room, however, we went to talk in the dining-room; and there Miss Jenkyns told me what Major Gordon had told her; how he had served in the same regiment with Captain Brown, and had become acquainted with Miss Jessie, then a sweet-looking, blooming girl of eighteen; how the acquaintance had grown into love on his part, though it had been some years before he had spoken; how, on becoming possessed, through the will of an uncle, of a good estate in Scotland, he had offered and been refused, though with so much agitation and evident distress that he was sure she was not indifferent to him; and how he had discovered that the obstacle was the fell disease which was, even then, too surely threatening her sister. She had mentioned that the surgeons foretold intense suffering; and there was no one but herself to nurse her poor Mary, or cheer and comfort her father during the time of illness. They had had long discussions; and on her refusal to pledge herself to him as his wife when all should be over, he had grown angry, and broken off entirely, and gone abroad, believing that she was a cold-hearted person whom he would do well to forget.

He had been travelling in the East, and was on his return home when, at Rome, he saw the account of Captain Brown's death in *Galignani*.

Just then Miss Matty, who had been out all the morning, and had only lately returned to the house, burst in with a face of dismay and outraged propriety.

"Oh, goodness me!" she said. "Deborah, there's a gentleman sitting in the drawing-room with his arm round Miss Jessie's waist!" Miss Matty's eyes looked large with terror.

Miss Jenkyns snubbed her down in an instant.

"The most proper place in the world for his arm to be in. Go away, Matilda, and mind your own business." This from her sister, who had hitherto been a model of feminine decorum, was a blow for poor Miss Matty, and with a double shock she left the room.

The last time I ever saw poor Miss Jenkyns was many years after this. Mrs Gordon had kept up a warm and affectionate intercourse with all at Cranford. Miss Jenkyns, Miss Matty, and Miss Pole had all been to visit her, and returned with wonderful accounts of her house, her husband, her dress, and her looks. For, with happiness, something of her early bloom returned; she had been a year or two younger than we had taken her for. Her eyes were always lovely, and, as Mrs Gordon, her dimples were not out of place. At the time to which I have referred, when I last saw Miss Jenkyns, that lady was old and feeble, and had lost something of her strong mind. Little Flora Gordon was staying with the Misses Jenkyns, and when I came in she was reading aloud to Miss Jenkyns, who lay feeble and changed on the sofa. Flora put down the *Rambler* when I came in.

"Ah!" said Miss Jenkyns, "you find me changed, my dear. If can't see as I used to do. I Flora were not here to read to me, I hardly know how I should get through the day. Did you ever read the *Rambler*? It's a wonderful book- wonderful! and the most improving reading for Flora" (which I daresay it would have been, if she could have read half the words without spelling, and could have understood the meaning of a third),"better than that strange old book, with the queer name, poor Captain Brown was killed for reading - that book by Mr Boz, you know- 'Old Poz'; when I was a girl - but that's a long time ago - I acted Lucy in 'Old Poz.'" She babbled on long enough for Flora to get a good long spell at the "Christmas Carol," which Miss Matty had left on the table.

CHAPTER III - A LOVE AFFAIR OF LONG AGO

I thought that probably my connection with Cranford would cease after Miss Jenkyns's death; at least, that it would have to be kept up by correspondence, which bears much the same relation to personal intercourse that the books of dried plants I sometimes see ("Hortus Siccus," I think they call the thing) do to the living and fresh flowers in the lines and meadows. I was pleasantly surprised, therefore, by receiving a letter from Miss Pole (who had always come in for a supplementary week after my annual visit to Miss Jenkyns) proposing that I should go and stay with her; and then, in a couple of days after my acceptance, came a note from Miss Matty, in which, in a rather circuitous and very humble manner, she told me how much pleasure I should confer if I could spend a week or two with her, either before or after I had been at Miss Pole's; "for," she said, "since my dear sister's death I am well aware I have no attractions to offer; it is only to the kindness of my friends that I can owe their company."

Of course I promised to come to dear Miss Matty as soon as I had ended my visit to Miss Pole; and the day after my arrival at Cranford I went to see her, much wondering what the house would be like without Miss Jenkyns, and rather dreading the changed aspect of things. Miss Matty began to cry as soon as she saw me. She was evidently nervous from having anticipated my call. I comforted her as well as I could; and I found the best consolation I could give was the honest praise that came from my heart as I spoke of the deceased. Miss Matty slowly shook her head over each virtue as it was named and attributed to her sister; and at last she could not restrain the tears which had long been silently flowing, but hid her face behind her handkerchief and sobbed aloud.

"Dear Miss Matty," said I, taking her hand - for indeed I did not know in what way to tell her how sorry I was for her, left deserted in the world. She put down her handkerchief and said -

"My dear, I'd rather you did not call me Matty. She did not like it; but I did many a thing she did not like, I'm afraid - and now she's gone! If you please, my love, will you call me Matilda?"

I promised faithfully, and began to practise the new name with Miss Pole that very day; and, by degrees, Miss Matilda's feeling on the subject was known through Cranford, and we all tried to drop the more familiar name, but with so little success that by-and-by we gave up the attempt.

My visit to Miss Pole was very quiet. Miss Jenkyns had so long taken the lead in Cranford that now she was gone, they hardly knew how to give a party. The Honourable Mrs Jamieson, to whom Miss Jenkyns herself had always yielded the post of honour, was fat and inert, and very much at the mercy of her old servants. If they chose that she should give a party, they reminded her of the necessity for so doing: if not, she let it alone. There was all the more time for me to hear old-world stories from Miss Pole, while she sat knitting, and I making my father's shirts. I always took a quantity of plain sewing to Cranford; for, as we did not read much, or walk much, I found it a capital time to get through my work. One of Miss Pole's stories related to a shadow of a love affair that was dimly perceived or suspected long years before.

Presently, the time arrived when I was to remove to Miss Matilda's house. I found her timid and anxious about the arrangements for my comfort. Many a time, while I was unpacking, did she come backwards and forwards to stir the fire which burned all the worse for being so frequently poked.

"Have you drawers enough, dear?" asked she. "I don't know exactly how my sister used to arrange them. She had capital methods. I am sure she would have trained a servant in a week to make a better fire than this, and Fanny has been with me four months."

This subject of servants was a standing grievance, and I could not wonder much at it; for if gentlemen were scarce, and almost unheard of in the"genteel society" of Cranford, they or their counterparts- handsome young men - abounded in the lower classes. The pretty neat servant-maids had their choice of desirable "followers";and their mistresses, without having the sort of mysterious dread of men and matrimony that Miss Matilda had, might well feel a little anxious lest the heads of their comely maids should be turned by the joiner, or the butcher, or the gardener, who were obliged, by their callings, to come to the house, and who, as ill-luck would have it, were generally handsome and unmarried. Fanny's lovers, if she had any -and Miss Matilda suspected her of so many flirtations that, if she had not been very pretty, I should have doubted her having one - were a constant anxiety to her mistress. She was forbidden, by the articles of her engagement, to have "followers"; and though she had answered, innocently enough, doubling up the hem of her apron as she spoke, "Please, ma'am, I never had more than one at a time,"Miss Matty prohibited that one. But a vision of a man seemed to haunt the kitchen. Fanny assured me that it was all fancy, or else I should have said myself that I had seen a man's coat-tails whisk into the scullery once, when I went on an errand into the store-room at night; and another evening, when, our watches having stopped, I went to look at the clock, there was a very odd appearance, singularly like a young man squeezed up between the clock and the back of the open kitchen-door: and I thought Fanny snatched up the candle very hastily, so as to throw the shadow on the clock face, while she very positively told me the time half-an-hour too early, as we found out afterwards by the church clock. But I did not add to Miss Matty's anxieties by naming my suspicions, especially as Fanny said to me, the next day, that it was such a queer kitchen for having odd shadows about it, she really was almost afraid to stay; "for you know, miss," she added,"I don't see a creature from six o'clock tea, till Missus rings the bell for prayers at ten."

However, it so fell out that Fanny had to leave and Miss Matilda begged me to stay and "settle her" with the new maid; to which I consented, after I had heard from my father that he did not want me at home. The new servant was a rough, honest-looking, country girl, who had only lived in a farm place before; but I liked her looks when she came to be hired; and I promised Miss Matilda to put her in the ways of the house. The said ways were religiously such as Miss Matilda thought her sister would approve. Many a domestic rule and regulation had been a subject of plaintive whispered murmur to me during Miss Jenkyns's life; but now that she was gone, I do not think that even I, who was a favourite, durst have suggested an alteration. To give an instance: we constantly adhered to the forms which were observed, at meal-times, in "my father, the rector's house." Accordingly, we had always wine and dessert; but the decanters were only filled when there was a party, and what remained was seldom touched, though we had two wine-glasses apiece every day after dinner, until the next festive occasion arrived, when the state of the remainder wine was examined into in a family council. The dregs were often given to the poor: but occasionally, when a good deal had been left at the last party (five months ago, it might be), it was added to some of a fresh bottle, brought up from the cellar. I fancy poor Captain Brown did not much like wine, for I noticed he never finished his first glass, and most military men take several. Then, as to our dessert, Miss Jenkyns used to gather currants and gooseberries for it herself, which I sometimes thought would have tasted better fresh from the trees; but then, as Miss Jenkyns observed, there would have been nothing for dessert in summer-time. As it was, we felt very genteel with our two glasses apiece, and a dish of gooseberries at the top, of currants and biscuits at the sides, and two decanters at the bottom. When oranges came in, a curious proceeding was gone through. Miss Jenkyns did not like to cut the fruit; for, as she observed, the juice all ran out nobody knew where; sucking (only I think she used some more recondite word) was in fact the only way of enjoying oranges; but then there was the unpleasant association with a ceremony frequently gone through by little babies; and so, after dessert, in orange season, Miss Jenkyns and Miss Matty used to rise up, possess themselves each of an orange in silence, and withdraw to the privacy of their own rooms to indulge in sucking oranges.

I had once or twice tried, on such occasions, to prevail on Miss Matty to stay, and had succeeded in her sister's lifetime. I held up a screen, and did not look, and, as she said, she tried not to make the noise very offensive; but now that she was left alone, she seemed quite horrified when I begged her to remain with me in the warm dining-parlour, and enjoy her orange as she liked best. And so it was in everything. Miss Jenkyns's rules were made more stringent than ever, because the framer of them was gone where there could be no appeal. In all things else Miss Matilda was meek and undecided to a fault. I have heard Fanny turn her round twenty times in a morning about dinner, just as the little hussy chose; and I sometimes fancied she worked on Miss Matilda's weakness in order to bewilder her, and to make her feel more in the power of her clever servant. I determined that I would not leave her till I had seen what sort of a person Martha was; and, if I found her trustworthy, I would tell her not to trouble her mistress with every little decision.

Martha was blunt and plain-spoken to a fault; otherwise she was a brisk, well-meaning, but very ignorant girl. She had not been with us a week before Miss Matilda and I were astounded one morning by the receipt of a letter from a cousin of hers, who had been twenty or thirty years in India, and who had lately, as we had seen by the "Army List,"returned to England, bringing with him an invalid wife who had never been introduced to her English relations. Major Jenkyns wrote to propose that he and his wife should spend a night at Cranford, on his way to Scotland - at the inn, if it did not suit Miss Matilda to receive them into her house; in which case they should hope to be with her as much as possible during the day. Of course it *must*suit her, as she said; for all Cranford knew that she had her sister's bedroom at liberty; but I am sure she wished the Major had stopped in India and forgotten his cousins out and out.

"Oh! how must I manage?" asked she helplessly. "If Deborah had been alive she would have known what to do with a gentleman-visitor. Must I put razors in his dressing-room? Dear! dear! and I've got none. Deborah would have had them. And slippers, and coat-brushes?" I suggested that probably he would bring all these things with him. "And after dinner, how am I to know when to get up and leave him to his wine? Deborah would have done it so well; she would have been quite in her element. Will he want coffee, do you think?" I undertook the management of the coffee, and told her I would instruct Martha in the art of waiting- in which it must be owned she was terribly deficient - and that I had no doubt Major and Mrs Jenkyns would understand the quiet mode in which a lady lived by herself in a country town. But she was sadly fluttered. I made her empty her decanters and bring up two fresh bottles of wine. I wished I could have prevented her from being present at my instructions to Martha, for she frequently cut in with some fresh direction, muddling the poor girl's mind as she stood open-mouthed, listening to us both.

"Hand the vegetables round," said I (foolishly, I see now- for it was aiming at more than we could accomplish with quietness and simplicity); and then, seeing her look bewildered, I added, "take the vegetables round to people, and let them help themselves."

"And mind you go first to the ladies," put in Miss Matilda. "Always go to the ladies before gentlemen when you are waiting."

"I'll do it as you tell me, ma'am," said Martha;"but I like lads best."

We felt very uncomfortable and shocked at this speech of Martha's, yet I don't think she meant any harm; and, on the whole, she attended very well to our directions, except that she "nudged" the Major when he did not help himself as soon as she expected to the potatoes, while she was handing them round.

The major and his wife were quiet unpretending people enough when they did come; languid, as all East Indians are, I suppose. We were rather dismayed at their bringing two servants with them, a Hindoo body-servant for the Major, and a steady elderly maid for his wife; but they slept at the inn, and took off a good deal of the responsibility by attending carefully to their master's and mistress's comfort. Martha, to be sure, had never ended her staring at the East Indian's white turban and brown complexion, and I saw that Miss Matilda shrunk away from him a little as he waited at dinner. Indeed, she asked me, when they were gone, if he did not remind me of Blue Beard? On the whole, the visit was most satisfactory, and is a subject of conversation even now with Miss Matilda; at the time it greatly excited Cranford, and even stirred up the apathetic and Honourable Mrs Jamieson to some expression of interest, when I went to call and thank her for the kind answers she had vouchsafed to Miss Matilda's inquiries as to the arrangement of a gentleman's dressing-room - answers which I must confess she had given in the wearied manner of the Scandinavian prophetess-

"Leave me, leave me to repose."

And *now* I come to the love affair.

It seems that Miss Pole had a cousin, once or twice removed, who had offered to Miss Matty long ago. Now this cousin lived four or five miles from Cranford on his own estate; but his property was not large enough to entitle him to rank higher than a yeoman; or rather, with something of the "pride which apes humility," he had refused to push himself on, as so many of his class had done, into the ranks of the squires. He would not allow himself to be called Thomas Holbrook, *Esq.*; he even sent back letters with this address, telling the post-mistress at Cranford that his name was *Mr* Thomas

Holbrook, yeoman. He rejected all domestic innovations; he would have the house door stand open in summer and shut in winter, without knocker or bell to summon a servant. The closed fist or the knob of a stick did this office for him if he found the door locked. He despised every refinement which had not its root deep down in humanity. If people were not ill, he saw no necessity for moderating his voice. He spoke the dialect of the country in perfection, and constantly used it in conversation; although Miss Pole (who gave me these particulars) added, that he read aloud more beautifully and with more feeling than any one she had ever heard, except the late rector.

"And how came Miss Matilda not to marry him?" asked I.

"Oh, I don't know. She was willing enough, I think; but you know Cousin Thomas would not have been enough of a gentleman for the rector and Miss Jenkyns."

"Well! but they were not to marry him," said I, impatiently.

"No; but they did not like Miss Matty to marry below her rank. You know she was the rector's daughter, and somehow they are related to Sir Peter Arley: Miss Jenkyns thought a deal of that."

"Poor Miss Matty!" said I.

"Nay, now, I don't know anything more than that he offered and was refused. Miss Matty might not like him - and Miss Jenkyns might never have said a word - it is only a guess of mine."

"Has she never seen him since?" I inquired.

"No, I think not. You see Woodley, Cousin Thomas's house, lies half-way between Cranford and Misselton; and I know he made Misselton his market-town very soon after he had offered to Miss Matty; and I don't think he has been into Cranford above once or twice since - once, when I was walking with Miss Matty, in High Street, and suddenly she darted from me, and went up Shire Lane. A few minutes after I was startled by meeting Cousin Thomas."

"How old is he?" I asked, after a pause of castle-building.

"He must be about seventy, I think, my dear," said Miss Pole, blowing up my castle, as if by gun-powder, into small fragments.

Very soon after - at least during my long visit to Miss Matilda - I had the opportunity of seeing Mr Holbrook; seeing, too, his first encounter with his former love, after thirty or forty years' separation. I was helping to decide whether any of the new assortment of coloured silks which they had just received at the shop would do to match a grey and black mousseline-delaine that wanted a new breadth, when a tall, thin, Don Quixote-looking old man came into the shop for some woollen gloves. I had never seen the person (who was rather striking) before, and I watched him rather attentively while Miss

Matty listened to the shopman. The stranger wore a blue coat with brass buttons, drab breeches, and gaiters, and drummed with his fingers on the counter until he was attended to. When he answered the shop-boy's question, "What can I have the pleasure of showing you to-day, sir?" I saw Miss Matilda start, and then suddenly sit down; and instantly I guessed who it was. She had made some inquiry which had to be carried round to the other shopman.

"Miss Jenkyns wants the black sarsenet two-and-twopence the yard";and Mr Holbrook had caught the name, and was across the shop in two strides.

"Matty - Miss Matilda - Miss Jenkyns! God bless my soul! I should not have known you. How are you? how are you?" He kept shaking her hand in a way which proved the warmth of his friendship; but he repeated so often, as if to himself, "I should not have known you!" that any sentimental romance which I might be inclined to build was quite done away with by his manner.

However, he kept talking to us all the time we were in the shop; and then waving the shopman with the unpurchased gloves on one side, with"Another time, sir! another time!" he walked home with us. I am happy to say my client, Miss Matilda, also left the shop in an equally bewildered state, not having purchased either green or red silk. Mr Holbrook was evidently full with honest loud-spoken joy at meeting his old love again; he touched on the changes that had taken place; he even spoke of Miss Jenkyns as "Your poor sister! Well, well! we have all our faults"; and bade us good-bye with many a hope that he should soon see Miss Matty again. She went straight to her room, and never came back till our early tea-time, when I thought she looked as if she had been crying.

CHAPTER IV - A VISIT TO AN OLD BACHELOR

A few days after, a note came from Mr Holbrook, asking us - impartially asking both of us - in a formal, old-fashioned style, to spend a day at his house - a long June day - for it was June now. He named that he had also invited his cousin, Miss Pole; so that we might join in a fly, which could be put up at his house.

I expected Miss Matty to jump at this invitation; but, no! Miss Pole and I had the greatest difficulty in persuading her to go. She thought it was improper; and was even half annoyed when we utterly ignored the idea of any impropriety in her going with two other ladies to see her old lover. Then came a more serious difficulty. She did not think Deborah would have liked her to go. This took us half a day's good hard talking to get over; but, at the first sentence of relenting, I seized the opportunity, and wrote and despatched an acceptance in her name - fixing day and hour, that all might be decided and done with.

The next morning she asked me if I would go down to the shop with her; and there, after much hesitation, we chose out three caps to be sent home and tried on, that the most becoming might be selected to take with us on Thursday.

She was in a state of silent agitation all the way to Woodley. She had evidently never been there before; and, although she little dreamt I knew anything of her early story, I could perceive she was in a tremor at the thought of seeing the place which might have been her home, and round which it is probable that many of her innocent girlish imaginations had clustered. It was a long drive there, through paved jolting lanes. Miss Matilda sat bolt upright, and looked wistfully out of the windows as we drew near the end of our journey. The aspect of the country was quiet and pastoral. Woodley stood among fields; and there was an old-fashioned garden where roses and currant-bushes touched each other, and where the feathery asparagus formed a pretty background to the pinks and gilly-flowers; there was no drive up to the door. We got out at a little gate, and walked up a straight box-edged path.

"My cousin might make a drive, I think," said Miss Pole, who was afraid of ear-ache, and had only her cap on.

"I think it is very pretty," said Miss Matty, with a soft plaintiveness in her voice, and almost in a whisper, for just then Mr Holbrook appeared at the door, rubbing his hands in very effervescence of hospitality. He looked more like my idea of Don Quixote than ever, and yet the likeness was only external. His respectable housekeeper stood modestly at the door to bid us welcome; and, while she led the elder ladies upstairs to a bedroom, I begged to look about the garden. My request evidently pleased the old gentleman, who took me all round the place and showed me his six-and-twenty cows, named after the different letters of the alphabet. As we went along, he surprised me occasionally by repeating apt and beautiful quotations from the poets, ranging easily from Shakespeare and George Herbert to those of our own day. He did this as naturally as if he were thinking aloud, and their true and beautiful words were the best expression he could find for what he was thinking or feeling. To be sure he called Byron "my Lord Byrron," and pronounced the name of Goethe strictly in accordance with the English sound of the letters- "As Goethe says, 'Ye ever-verdant palaces,'"&c. Altogether, I never met with a man, before or since, who had spent so long a life in a secluded and not impressive country, with ever-increasing delight in the daily and yearly change of season and beauty.

When he and I went in, we found that dinner was nearly ready in the kitchen - for so I suppose the room ought to be called, as there were oak dressers and cupboards all round, all over by the side of the fireplace, and only a small Turkey carpet in the middle of the flag-floor. The room might have been easily made into a handsome dark oak dining-parlour by removing the oven and a few other appurtenances of a kitchen, which were evidently never used, the real cooking-place being at some distance. The room in which we were expected to sit was a stiffly-furnished, ugly apartment; but that in which we did sit was what Mr Holbrook called the counting-house, where he paid his labourers their weekly wages at a great desk near the door. The rest of the pretty sitting-room - looking into the orchard, and all covered over with dancing tree-shadows - was filled with books. They lay on the ground, they covered the walls, they strewed the table. He was evidently half ashamed and half proud of his extravagance in this respect. They were of all kinds - poetry and wild weird tales prevailing. He evidently chose his books in accordance with his own tastes, not because such and such were classical or established favourites.

"Ah!" he said, "we farmers ought not to have much time for reading; yet somehow one can't help it."

"What a pretty room!" said Miss Matty, *sotto voce*.

"What a pleasant place!" said I, aloud, almost simultaneously.

"Nay! if you like it," replied he; "but can you sit on these great, black leather, three-cornered chairs? I like it better than the best parlour; but I thought ladies would take that for the smarter place."

It was the smarter place, but, like most smart things, not at all pretty, or pleasant, or home-like; so, while we were at dinner, the servant-girl dusted and scrubbed the counting-house chairs, and we sat there all the rest of the day.

We had pudding before meat; and I thought Mr Holbrook was going to make some apology for his old-fashioned ways, for he began -

"I don't know whether you like newfangled ways."

"Oh, not at all!" said Miss Matty.

"No more do I," said he. "My house-keeper *will* have these in her new fashion; or else I tell her that, when I was a young man, we used to keep strictly to my father's rule, 'No broth, no ball; no ball, no beef'; and always began dinner with broth. Then we had suet puddings, boiled in the broth with the beef: and then the meat itself. If we did not sup our broth, we had no ball, which we liked a deal better; and the beef came last of all, and only those had it who had done justice to the broth and the ball. Now folks begin with sweet things, and turn their dinners topsy-turvy."

When the ducks and green peas came, we looked at each other in dismay; we had only two-pronged, black-handled forks. It is true the steel was as bright as silver; but what were we to do? Miss Matty picked up her peas, one by one, on the point of the prongs, much as Aminé ate her grains of rice after her previous feast with the Ghoul. Miss Pole sighed over her delicate young peas as she left them on one side of her plate untasted, for they *would* drop between the prongs. I looked at my host: the peas were going wholesale into his capacious mouth, shovelled up by his large round-ended knife. I saw, I imitated, I survived! My friends, in spite of my precedent, could not muster up courage enough to do an ungenteel thing; and, if Mr Holbrook had not been so heartily hungry, he would probably have seen that the good peas went away almost untouched.

After dinner, a clay pipe was brought in, and a spittoon; and, asking us to retire to another room, where he would soon join us, if we disliked tobacco-smoke, he presented his pipe to Miss Matty, and requested her to fill the bowl. This was a compliment to a lady in his youth; but it was rather inappropriate to propose it as an honour to Miss Matty, who had been trained by her sister to hold smoking of every kind in utter abhorrence. But if it was a shock to her refinement, it was also a gratification to her feelings to be thus selected; so she daintily stuffed the strong tobacco into the pipe, and then we withdrew.

"It is very pleasant dining with a bachelor," said Miss Matty softly, as we settled ourselves in the counting-house. "I only hope it is not improper; so many pleasant things are!"

"What a number of books he has!" said Miss Pole, looking round the room. "And how dusty they are!"

"I think it must be like one of the great Dr Johnson's rooms,"said Miss Matty. "What a superior man your cousin must be!"

"Yes!" said Miss Pole, "he's a great reader; but I am afraid he has got into very uncouth habits with living alone."

"Oh! uncouth is too hard a word. I should call him eccentric; very clever people always are!" replied Miss Matty.

When Mr Holbrook returned, he proposed a walk in the fields; but the two elder ladies were afraid of damp, and dirt, and had only very unbecoming calashes to put on over their caps; so they declined, and I was again his companion in a turn which he said he was obliged to take to see after his men. He strode along, either wholly forgetting my existence, or soothed into silence by his pipe - and yet it was not silence exactly. He walked before me with a stooping gait, his hands clasped behind him; and, as some tree or cloud, or glimpse of distant upland pastures, struck him, he quoted poetry to himself, saying it out loud in a grand sonorous voice, with just the emphasis that true feeling and appreciation give. We came upon an old cedar tree, which stood at one end of the house -

"The cedar spreads his dark-green layers of shade."

"Capital term - 'layers!' Wonderful man!" I did not know whether he was speaking to me or not; but I put in an assenting "wonderful," although I knew nothing about it, just because I was tired of being forgotten, and of being consequently silent.

He turned sharp round. "Ay! you may say 'wonderful.' Why, when I saw the review of his poems in *Blackwood*, I set off within an hour, and walked seven miles to Misselton (for the horses were not in the way) and ordered them. Now, what colour are ash-buds in March?"

Is the man going mad? thought I. He is very like Don Quixote.

"What colour are they, I say?" repeated he vehemently.

"I am sure I don't know, sir," said I, with the meekness of ignorance.

"I knew you didn't. No more did I - an old fool that I am! - till this young man comes and tells me. Black as ash-buds in March. And I've lived all my life in the country; more shame for me not to know. Black: they are jet-black, madam." And he went off again, swinging along to the music of some rhyme he had got hold of.

When we came back, nothing would serve him but he must read us the poems he had been speaking of; and Miss Pole encouraged him in his proposal, I thought, because she wished me to hear his beautiful reading, of which she had boasted; but she afterwards said it was because she had got to a difficult part of her crochet, and wanted to count her stitches without having to talk. Whatever he had proposed would have been right to Miss Matty; although she did fall sound asleep within five minutes after he had begun a long poem, called "Locksley Hall,"and had a comfortable nap, unobserved, till he ended; when the cessation of his voice wakened her up, and she said, feeling that something was expected, and that Miss Pole was counting -

"What a pretty book!"

"Pretty, madam! it's beautiful! Pretty, indeed!"

"Oh yes! I meant beautiful" said she, fluttered at his disapproval of her word. "It is so like that beautiful poem of Dr Johnson's my sister used to read - I forget the name of it; what was it, my dear?" turning to me.

"Which do you mean, ma'am? What was it about?"

"I don't remember what it was about, and I've quite forgotten what the name of it was; but it was written by Dr Johnson, and was very beautiful, and very like what Mr Holbrook has just been reading."

"I don't remember it," said he reflectively. "But I don't know Dr Johnson's poems well. I must read them."

As we were getting into the fly to return, I heard Mr Holbrook say he should call on the ladies soon, and inquire how they got home; and this evidently pleased and fluttered Miss Matty at the time he said it; but after we had lost sight of the old house among the trees her sentiments towards the master of it were gradually absorbed into a distressing wonder as to whether Martha had broken her word, and seized on the opportunity of her mistress's absence to have a "follower." Martha looked good, and steady, and composed enough, as she came to help us out; she was always careful of Miss Matty, and to-night she made use of this unlucky speech -

"Eh! dear ma'am, to think of your going out in an evening in such a thin shawl! It's no better than muslin. At your age, ma'am, you should be careful."

"My age!" said Miss Matty, almost speaking crossly, for her, for she was usually gentle - "My age! Why, how old do you think I am, that you talk about my age?"

"Well, ma'am, I should say you were not far short of sixty: but folks' looks is often against them - and I'm sure I meant no harm."

"Martha, I'm not yet fifty-two!" said Miss Matty, with grave emphasis; for probably the remembrance of her youth had come very vividly before her this day, and she was annoyed at finding that golden time so far away in the past.

But she never spoke of any former and more intimate acquaintance with Mr Holbrook. She had probably met with so little sympathy in her early love, that she had shut it up close in her heart; and it was only by a sort of watching, which I could hardly avoid since Miss Pole's confidence, that I saw how faithful her poor heart had been in its sorrow and its silence.

She gave me some good reason for wearing her best cap every day, and sat near the window, in spite of her rheumatism, in order to see, without being seen, down into the street.

He came. He put his open palms upon his knees, which were far apart, as he sat with his head bent down, whistling, after we had replied to his inquiries about our safe return. Suddenly he jumped up -

"Well, madam! have you any commands for Paris? I am going there in a week or two."

"To Paris!" we both exclaimed.

"Yes, madam! I've never been there, and always had a wish to go; and I think if I don't go soon, I mayn't go at all; so as soon as the hay is got in I shall go, before harvest time."

We were so much astonished that we had no commissions.

Just as he was going out of the room, he turned back, with his favourite exclamation -

"God bless my soul, madam! but I nearly forgot half my errand. Here are the poems for you you admired so much the other evening at my house." He tugged away at a parcel in his coat-pocket. "Good-bye, miss," said he; "good-bye, Matty! take care of yourself." And he was gone.

But he had given her a book, and he had called her Matty, just as he used to do thirty years to.

"I wish he would not go to Paris," said Miss Matilda anxiously. "I don't believe frogs will agree with him; he used to have to be very careful what he ate, which was curious in so strong-looking a young man."

Soon after this I took my leave, giving many an injunction to Martha to look after her mistress, and to let me know if she thought that Miss Matilda was not so well; in which case I would volunteer a visit to my old friend, without noticing Martha's intelligence to her.

Accordingly I received a line or two from Martha every now and then; and, about November I had a note to say her mistress was "very low and sadly off her food"; and the account made me so uneasy that, although Martha did not decidedly summon me, I packed up my things and went.

I received a warm welcome, in spite of the little flurry produced by my impromptu visit, for I had only been able to give a day's notice. Miss Matilda looked miserably ill; and I prepared to comfort and cosset her.

I went down to have a private talk with Martha.

"How long has your mistress been so poorly?" I asked, as I stood by the kitchen fire.

"Well! I think its better than a fortnight; it is, I know; it was one Tuesday, after Miss Pole had been, that she went into this moping way. I thought she was tired, and it would go off with a night's rest; but no! she has gone on and on ever since, till I thought it my duty to write to you, ma'am."

"You did quite right, Martha. It is a comfort to think she has so faithful a servant about her. And I hope you find your place comfortable?"

"Well, ma'am, missus is very kind, and there's plenty to eat and drink, and no more work but what I can do easily - but -" Martha hesitated.

"But what, Martha?"

"Why, it seems so hard of missus not to let me have any followers; there's such lots of young fellows in the town; and many a one has as much as offered to keep company with me; and I may never be in such a likely place again, and it's like wasting an opportunity. Many a girl as I know would have 'em unbeknownst to missus; but I've given my word, and I'll stick to it; or else this is just the house for missus never to be the wiser if they did come: and it's such a capable kitchen - there's such dark corners in it - I'd be bound to hide any one. I counted up last Sunday night - for I'll not deny I was crying because I had to shut the door in Jem Hearn's face, and he's a steady young man, fit for any girl; only I had given missus my word." Martha was all but crying again; and I had little comfort to give her, for I knew, from old experience, of the horror with which both the Miss Jenkynses looked upon "followers"; and in Miss Matty's present nervous state this dread was not likely to be lessened.

I went to see Miss Pole the next day, and took her completely by surprise, for she had not been to see Miss Matilda for two days.

"And now I must go back with you, my dear, for I promised to let her know how Thomas Holbrook went on; and, I'm sorry to say, his housekeeper has sent me word to-day that he hasn't long to live. Poor Thomas! that journey to Paris was quite too much for him. His housekeeper says he has hardly ever been round his fields since, but just sits with his hands on his knees in the counting-house, not reading or anything, but only saying what a wonderful city Paris was! Paris has much to answer for if it's killed my cousin Thomas, for a better man never lived."

"Does Miss Matilda know of his illness?" asked I - a new light as to the cause of her indisposition dawning upon me.

"Dear! to be sure, yes! Has not she told you? I let her know a fortnight ago, or more, when first I heard of it. How odd she shouldn't have told you!"

Not at all, I thought; but I did not say anything. I felt almost guilty of having spied too curiously into that tender heart, and I was not going to speak of its secrets - hidden, Miss Matty believed, from all the world. I ushered Miss Pole into Miss Matilda's little drawing-room, and then left them alone. But I was not surprised when Martha came to my bedroom door, to ask me to go down to dinner alone, for that missus had one of her bad headaches. She came into the drawing-room at tea-time, but it was evidently an effort to her; and, as if to make up for some reproachful feeling against her late sister, Miss Jenkyns, which had been troubling her all the afternoon, and for which she now felt penitent, she kept telling me how good and how clever Deborah was in her youth; how she used to settle what gowns they were to wear at all the parties (faint, ghostly ideas of grim parties, far away in the distance, when Miss Matty and Miss Pole were young!); and how Deborah and her mother had started the benefit society for the poor, and taught girls cooking and plain sewing; and how Deborah had once danced with a lord; and how she used to visit at Sir Peter Arley's, and tried to remodel the quiet rectory establishment on the plans of Arley Hall, where they kept thirty servants; and how she had nursed Miss Matty through a long, long illness, of which I had never heard before, but which I now dated in my own mind as following the dismissal of the suit of Mr Holbrook. So we talked softly and quietly of old times through the long November evening.

The next day Miss Pole brought us word that Mr Holbrook was dead. Miss Matty heard the news in silence; in fact, from the account of the previous day, it was only what we had to expect. Miss Pole kept calling upon us for some expression of regret, by asking if it was not sad that he was gone, and saying -

"To think of that pleasant day last June, when he seemed so well! And he might have lived this dozen years if he had not gone to that wicked Paris, where they are always having revolutions."

She paused for some demonstration on our part. I saw Miss Matty could not speak, she was trembling so nervously; so I said what I really felt; and after a call of some duration - all the time of which I have no doubt Miss Pole thought Miss Matty received the news very calmly - our visitor took her leave.

Miss Matty made a strong effort to conceal her feelings - a concealment she practised even with me, for she has never alluded to Mr Holbrook again, although the book he gave her lies with her Bible on the little table by her bedside. She did not think I heard her when she asked the little milliner of Cranford to make her caps something like the Honourable Mrs Jamieson's, or that I noticed the reply -

"But she wears widows' caps, ma'am?"

"Oh! I only meant something in that style; not widows',of course, but rather like Mrs Jamieson's."

This effort at concealment was the beginning of the tremulous motion of head and hands which I have seen ever since in Miss Matty.

The evening of the day on which we heard of Mr Holbrook's death, Miss Matilda was very silent and thoughtful; after prayers she called Martha back and then she stood uncertain what to say.

"Martha!" she said, at last, "you are young"- and then she made so long a pause that Martha, to remind her of her half-finished sentence, dropped a curtsey, and said -

"Yes, please, ma'am; two-and-twenty last third of October, please, ma'am."

"And, perhaps, Martha, you may some time meet with a young man you like, and who likes you. I did say you were not to have followers; but if you meet with such a young man, and tell me, and I find he is respectable, I have no objection to his coming to see you once a week. God forbid!" said she in a low voice, "that I should grieve any young hearts." She spoke as if she were providing for some distant contingency, and was rather startled when Martha made her ready eager answer -

"Please, ma'am, there's Jem Hearn, and he's a joiner making three-and-sixpence a-day, and six foot one in his stocking-feet, please, ma'am; and if you'll ask about him to-morrow morning, every one will give him a character for steadiness; and he'll be glad enough to come to-morrow night, I'll be bound."

Though Miss Matty was startled, she submitted to Fate and Love.

CHAPTER V - OLD LETTERS

I have often noticed that almost every one has his own individual small economies - careful habits of saving fractions of pennies in some one peculiar direction - any disturbance of which annoys him more than spending shillings or pounds on some real extravagance. An old gentleman of my acquaintance, who took the intelligence of the failure of a Joint-Stock Bank, in which some of his money was invested, with stoical mildness, worried his family all through a long summer's day because one of them had torn (instead of cutting) out the written leaves of his now useless bank-book; of course, the corresponding pages at the other end came out as well, and this little unnecessary waste of paper (his private economy) chafed him more than all the loss of his money. Envelopes fretted his soul terribly when they first came in; the only way in which he could reconcile himself to such waste of his cherished article was by patiently turning inside out all that were sent to him, and so making them serve again. Even now, though tamed by age, I see him casting wistful glances at his daughters when they send a whole inside of a half-sheet of note paper, with the three lines of acceptance to an invitation, written on only one of the sides. I am not above owning that I have this human weakness myself. String is my foible. My pockets get full of little hanks of it, picked up and twisted together, ready for uses that never come. I am seriously annoyed if any one cuts the string of a parcel instead of patiently and faithfully undoing it fold by fold. How people can bring themselves to use india-rubber rings, which are a sort of deification of string, as lightly as they do, I cannot imagine. To me an india-rubber ring is a precious treasure. I have one which is not new - one that I picked up off the floor nearly six years ago. I have really tried to use it, but my heart failed me, and I could not commit the extravagance.

Small pieces of butter grieve others. They cannot attend to conversation because of the annoyance occasioned by the habit which some people have of invariably taking more butter than they want. Have you not seen the anxious look (almost mesmeric) which such persons fix on the article? They would feel it a relief if they might bury it out of their sight by popping it into their own mouths and swallowing it down; and they are really made happy if the person on whose plate it lies unused suddenly breaks off a piece of toast (which he does not want at all) and eats up his butter. They think that this is not waste.

Now Miss Matty Jenkyns was chary of candles. We had many devices to use as few as possible. In the winter afternoons she would sit knitting for two or three hours - she could do this in the dark, or by firelight - and when I asked if I might not ring for candles to finish stitching my wristbands, she told me to "keep blind man's holiday." They were usually brought in with tea; but we only burnt one at a time. As we lived in constant preparation for a friend who might come in any evening (but who never did), it required some contrivance to keep our two candles of the same length, ready to be lighted, and to look as if we burnt two always. The candles took it in turns; and, whatever we might be talking about or doing, Miss Matty's eyes were habitually fixed upon the candle, ready to jump up and extinguish it and to light the other before they had become too uneven in length to be restored to equality in the course of the evening.

One night, I remember this candle economy particularly annoyed me. I had been very much tired of my compulsory "blind man's holiday," especially as Miss Matty had fallen asleep, and I did not like to stir the fire and run the risk of awakening her; so I could not even sit on the rug, and scorch myself with sewing by firelight, according to my usual custom. I fancied Miss Matty must be dreaming of her early life; for she spoke one or two words in her uneasy sleep bearing reference to persons who were dead long before. When Martha brought in the lighted candle and tea, Miss Matty started into wakefulness, with a strange, bewildered look around, as if we were not the people she expected to see about her. There was a little sad expression that shadowed her face as she recognised me; but immediately afterwards she tried to give me her usual smile. All through tea-time her talk ran upon the days of her childhood and youth. Perhaps this reminded her of the desirableness of looking over all the old family letters, and destroying such as ought not to be allowed to fall into the hands of strangers; for she had often spoken of the necessity of this task, but had always shrunk from it, with a timid dread of something painful. To-night, however, she rose up after tea and went for them - in the dark; for she piqued herself on the precise neatness of all her chamber arrangements, and used to look uneasily at me when I lighted a bed-candle to go to another room for anything. When she returned there was a faint, pleasant smell of Tonquin beans in the room. I had always noticed this scent about any of the things which had belonged to her mother; and many of the letters were addressed to her - yellow bundles of love-letters, sixty or seventy years old.

Miss Matty undid the packet with a sigh; but she stifled it directly, as if it were hardly right to regret the flight of time, or of life either. We agreed to look them over separately, each taking a different letter out of the same bundle and describing its contents to the other before destroying it. I never knew what sad work the reading of old-letters was before that evening, though I could hardly tell why. The letters were as happy as letters could be - at least those early letters were. There was in them a vivid and intense sense of the present time, which seemed so strong and full, as if it could never pass away, and as if the warm, living hearts that so expressed themselves could never die, and be as nothing to the sunny earth. I should have felt less melancholy, I believe, if the letters had been more so. I saw the tears stealing down the well-worn furrows of Miss Matty's cheeks, and her spectacles often wanted wiping. I trusted at last that she would light the other candle, for my own eyes were rather dim, and I wanted more light to see the pale, faded ink; but no, even through her tears, she saw and remembered her little economical ways.

The earliest set of letters were two bundles tied together, and ticketed (in Miss Jenkyns's handwriting) "Letters interchanged between my ever-honoured father and my dearly-beloved mother, prior to their marriage, in July 1774." I should guess that the rector of Cranford was about twenty-seven years of age when he wrote those letters; and Miss Matty told me that her mother was just eighteen at the time of her wedding. With my idea of the rector derived from a picture in the dining-parlour, stiff and stately, in a huge full-bottomed wig, with gown, cassock, and bands, and his hand upon a copy of the only sermon he ever published - it was strange to read these letters. They were full of eager, passionate ardour; short homely sentences, right fresh from the heart (very different from the grand Latinised, Johnsonian style of the printed sermon preached before some judge at assize time). His letters were a curious contrast to those of his girl-bride. She was evidently rather annoyed at his demands upon her for expressions of love, and could not quite understand what he meant by repeating the same thing over in so many different ways; but what she was quite clear about was a longing for a white "Paduasoy"- whatever that might be; and six or seven letters were principally occupied in asking her lover to use his influence with her parents (who evidently kept her in good order) to obtain this or that article of dress, more especially the white "Paduasoy." He cared nothing how she was dressed; she was always lovely enough for him, as he took pains to assure her, when she begged him to express in his answers a predilection for particular pieces of finery, in order that she might show what he said to her parents. But at length he seemed to find out that she would not be married till she had a "trousseau"to her mind; and then he sent her a letter, which had evidently accompanied a whole box full of finery, and in which he requested that she might be dressed in everything her heart desired. This was the first letter, ticketed in a frail, delicate hand, "From my dearest John." Shortly afterwards they were married, I suppose, from the intermission in their correspondence.

"We must burn them, I think," said Miss Matty, looking doubtfully at me. "No one will care for them when I am gone." And one by one she dropped them into the middle of the fire, watching each blaze up, die out, and rise away, in faint, white, ghostly semblance, up the chimney, before she gave another to the same fate. The room was light enough now; but I, like her, was fascinated into watching the destruction of those letters, into which the honest warmth of a manly heart had been poured forth.

The next letter, likewise docketed by Miss Jenkyns, was endorsed, "Letter of pious congratulation and exhortation from my venerable grandfather to my beloved mother, on occasion of my own birth. Also some practical remarks on the desirability of keeping warm the extremities of infants, from my excellent grandmother."

The first part was, indeed, a severe and forcible picture of the responsibilities of mothers, and a warning against the evils that were in the world, and lying in ghastly wait for the little baby of two days old. His wife did not write, said the old gentleman, because he had forbidden it, she being indisposed with a sprained ankle, which (he said) quite incapacitated her from holding a pen. However, at the foot of the page was a small "T.O.," and on turning it over, sure enough, there was a letter to "my dear, dearest Molly,"begging her, when she left her room, whatever she did, to go *up*stairs before going *down*: and telling her to wrap her baby's feet up in flannel, and keep it warm by the fire, although it was summer, for babies were so tender.

It was pretty to see from the letters, which were evidently exchanged with some frequency between the young mother and the grandmother, how the girlish vanity was being weeded out of her heart by love for her baby. The white "Paduasoy" figured again in the letters, with almost as much vigour as before. In one, it was being made into a christening cloak for the baby. It decked it when it went with its parents to spend a day or two at Arley Hall. It added to its charms, when it was "the prettiest little baby that ever was seen. Dear mother, I wish you could see her! Without any pershality, I do think she will grow up a regular bewty!" I thought of Miss Jenkyns, grey, withered, and wrinkled, and I wondered if her mother had known her in the courts of heaven: and then I knew that she had, and that they stood there in angelic guise.

There was a great gap before any of the rector's letters appeared. And then his wife had changed her mode of her endorsement. It was no longer from, "My dearest John;" it was from "My Honoured Husband." The letters were written on occasion of the publication of the same sermon which was represented in the picture. The preaching before "My Lord Judge," and the "publishing by request," was evidently the culminating point - the event of his life. It had been necessary for him to go up to London to superintend it through the press. Many friends had to be called upon and consulted before he could decide on any printer fit for so onerous a task; and at length it was arranged that J. and J. Rivingtons were to have the honourable responsibility. The worthy rector seemed to be strung up by the occasion to a high literary pitch, for he could hardly write a letter to his wife without cropping out into Latin. I remember the end of one of his letters ran thus: "I shall ever hold the virtuous qualities of my Molly in remembrance, *dum memor ipse mei, dum spiritus regit artus*," which, considering that the English of his correspondent was sometimes at fault in grammar, and often in spelling, might be taken as a proof of how much he "idealised his Molly;" and, as Miss Jenkyns used to say, "People talk a great deal about idealising now-a-days, whatever that may mean." But this was nothing to a fit of writing classical poetry which soon seized him, in which his Molly figured away as "Maria." The letter containing the *carmen* was endorsed by her, "Hebrew verses sent me by my honoured husband. I thowt to have had a letter about killing the pig, but must wait. Mem., to send the poetry to Sir Peter Arley, as my husband desires." And in a post-scriptum note in his handwriting it was stated that the Ode had appeared in the*Gentleman's Magazine*, December 1782.

Her letters back to her husband (treasured as fondly by him as if they had been *M. T. Ciceronis Epistolae*) were more satisfactory to an absent husband and father than his could ever have been to her. She told him how Deborah sewed her seam very neatly every day, and read to her in the books he had set her; how she was a very "forrard,"good child, but would ask questions her mother could not answer, but how she did not let herself down by saying she did not know, but took to stirring the fire, or sending the "forrard" child on an errand. Matty was now the mother's darling, and promised (like her sister at her age), to be a great beauty. I was reading this aloud to Miss Matty, who smiled and sighed a little at the hope, so fondly expressed, that "little Matty might not be vain, even if she were a bewty."

"I had very pretty hair, my dear," said Mist Matilda; "and not a bad mouth." And I saw her soon afterwards adjust her cap and draw herself up.

But to return to Mrs Jenkyns's letters. She told her husband about the poor in the parish; what homely domestic medicines she had administered; what kitchen physic she had sent. She had evidently held his displeasure as a rod in pickle over the heads of all the ne'er-do-wells. She asked for his directions about the cows and pigs; and did not always obtain them, as I have shown before.

The kind old grandmother was dead when a little boy was born, soon after the publication of the sermon; but there was another letter of exhortation from the grandfather, more stringent and admonitory than ever, now that there was a boy to be guarded from the snares of the world. He described all the various sins into which men might fall, until I wondered how any man ever came to a natural death. The gallows seemed as if it must have been the termination of the lives of most of the grandfather's friends and acquaintance; and I was not surprised at the way in which he spoke of this life being "a vale of tears."

It seemed curious that I should never have heard of this brother before; but I concluded that he had died young, or else surely his name would have been alluded to by his sisters.

By-and-by we came to packets of Miss Jenkyns's letters. These Miss Matty did regret to burn. She said all the others had been only interesting to those who loved the writers, and that it seemed as if it would have hurt her to allow them to fall into the hands of strangers, who had not known her dear mother, and how good she was, although she did not always spell, quite in the modern fashion; but Deborah's letters were so very superior! Any one might profit by reading them. It was a long time since she had read Mrs Chapone, but she knew she used to think that Deborah could have said the same things quite as well; and as for Mrs Carter! people thought a deal of her letters, just because she had written "Epictetus," but she was quite sure Deborah would never have made use of such a common expression as "I canna be fashed!"

Miss Matty did grudge burning these letters, it was evident. She would not let them be carelessly passed over with any quiet reading, and skipping, to myself. She took them from me, and even lighted the second candle in order to read them aloud with a proper emphasis, and without stumbling over the big words. Oh dear! how I wanted facts instead of reflections, before those letters were concluded! They lasted us two nights; and I won't deny that I made use of the time to think of many other things, and yet I was always at my post at the end of each sentence.

The rector's letters, and those of his wife and mother-in-law, had all been tolerably short and pithy, written in a straight hand, with the lines very close together. Sometimes the whole letter was contained on a mere scrap of paper. The paper was very yellow, and the ink very brown; some of the sheets were (as Miss Matty made me observe) the old original post, with the stamp in the corner representing a post-boy riding for life and twanging his horn. The letters of Mrs Jenkyns and her mother were fastened with a great round red wafer; for it was before Miss Edgeworth's "patronage" had banished wafers from polite society. It was evident, from the tenor of what was said, that franks were in great request, and were even used as a means of paying debts by needy members of Parliament. The rector sealed his epistles with an immense coat of arms, and showed by the care with which he had performed this ceremony that he expected they should be cut open, not broken by any thoughtless or impatient hand. Now, Miss Jenkyns's letters were of a later date in form and writing. She wrote on the square sheet which we have learned to call old-fashioned. Her hand was admirably calculated, together with her use of many-syllabled words, to fill up a sheet, and then came the pride and delight of crossing. Poor Miss Matty got sadly puzzled with this, for the words gathered size like snowballs, and towards the end of her letter Miss Jenkyns used to become quite sesquipedalian. In one to her father, slightly theological and controversial in its tone, she had spoken of Herod, Tetrarch of Idumea. Miss Matty read it "Herod Petrarch of Etruria," and was just as well pleased as if she had been right.

I can't quite remember the date, but I think it was in 1805 that Miss Jenkyns wrote the longest series of letters - on occasion of her absence on a visit to some friends near Newcastle-upon-Tyne. These friends were intimate with the commandant of the garrison there, and heard from him of all the preparations that were being made to repel the invasion of Buonaparte, which some people imagined might take place at the mouth of the Tyne. Miss Jenkyns was evidently very much alarmed; and the first part of her letters was often written in pretty intelligible English, conveying particulars of the preparations which were made in the family with whom she was residing against the dreaded event; the bundles of clothes that were packed up ready for a flight to Alston Moor (a wild hilly piece of ground between Northumberland and Cumberland); the signal that was to be given for this flight, and for the simultaneous turning out of the volunteers under arms - which said signal was to consist (if I remember rightly) in ringing the church bells in a particular and ominous manner. One day, when Miss Jenkyns and her hosts were at a dinner-party in Newcastle, this warning summons was actually given (not a very wise proceeding, if there be any truth in the moral attached to the fable of the Boy and the Wolf; but so it was), and Miss Jenkyns, hardly recovered from her fright, wrote the next day to describe the sound, the breathless shock, the hurry and alarm; and then, taking breath, she added, "How trivial, my dear father, do all our apprehensions of the last evening appear, at the present moment, to calm and enquiring minds!" And here Miss Matty broke in with -

"But, indeed, my dear, they were not at all trivial or trifling at the time. I know I used to wake up in the night many a time and think I heard the tramp of the French entering Cranford. Many people talked of hiding themselves in the salt mines - and meat would have kept capitally down there, only perhaps we should have been thirsty. And my father preached a whole set of sermons on the occasion; one set in the mornings, all about David and Goliath, to spirit up the people to fighting with spades or bricks, if need were; and the other set in the afternoons, proving that Napoleon (that was another name for Bony, as we used to call him) was all the same as an Apollyon and Abaddon. I remember my father rather thought he should be asked to print this last set; but the parish had, perhaps, had enough of them with hearing."

Peter Marmaduke Arley Jenkyns ("poor Peter!" as Miss Matty began to call him) was at school at Shrewsbury by this time. The rector took up his pen, and rubbed up his Latin once more, to correspond with his boy. It was very clear that the lad's were what are called show letters. They were of a highly mental description, giving an account of his studies, and his intellectual hopes of various kinds, with an occasional quotation from the classics; but, now and then, the animal nature broke out in such a little sentence as this, evidently written in a trembling hurry, after the letter had been inspected:"Mother dear, do send me a cake, and put plenty of citron in." The "mother dear" probably answered her boy in the form of cakes and "goody," for there were none of her letters among this set; but a whole collection of the rector's, to whom the Latin in his boy's letters was like a trumpet to the old war-horse. I do not know much about Latin, certainly, and it is, perhaps, an ornamental language, but not very useful, I think - at least to judge from the bits I remember out of the rector's letters. One was, "You have not got that town in your map of Ireland; but *Bonus Bernardus non videt omnia*, as the Proverbia say." Presently it became very evident that "poor Peter" got himself into many scrapes. There were letters of stilted penitence to his father, for some wrong-doing; and among them all was a badly-written, badly-sealed, badly-directed, blotted note:- "My dear, dear, dear, dearest mother, I will be a better boy; I will, indeed; but don't, please, be ill for me; I am not worth it; but I will be good, darling mother."

Miss Matty could not speak for crying, after she had read this note. She gave it to me in silence, and then got up and took it to her sacred recesses in her own room, for fear, by any chance, it might get burnt. "Poor Peter!" she said; "he was always in scrapes; he was too easy. They led him wrong, and then left him in the lurch. But he was too fond of mischief. He could never resist a joke. Poor Peter!"

CHAPTER VI - POOR PETER

Poor Peter's career lay before him rather pleasantly mapped out by kind friends, but *Bonus Bernardus non videt omnia*, in this map too. He was to win honours at the Shrewsbury School, and carry them thick to Cambridge, and after that, a living awaited him, the gift of his godfather, Sir Peter Arley. Poor Peter! his lot in life was very different to what his friends had hoped and planned. Miss Matty told me all about it, and I think it was a relief when she had done so.

He was the darling of his mother, who seemed to dote on all her children, though she was, perhaps, a little afraid of Deborah's superior acquirements. Deborah was the favourite of her father, and when Peter disappointed him, she became his pride. The sole honour Peter brought away from Shrewsbury was the reputation of being the best good fellow that ever was, and of being the captain of the school in the art of practical joking. His father was disappointed, but set about remedying the matter in a manly way. He could not afford to send Peter to read with any tutor, but he could read with him himself; and Miss Matty told me much of the awful preparations in the way of dictionaries and lexicons that were made in her father's study the morning Peter began.

"My poor mother!" said she. "I remember how she used to stand in the hall, just near enough the study-door, to catch the tone of my father's voice. I could tell in a moment if all was going right, by her face. And it did go right for a long time."

"What went wrong at last?" said I. "That tiresome Latin, I dare say."

"No! it was not the Latin. Peter was in high favour with my father, for he worked up well for him. But he seemed to think that the Cranford people might be joked about, and made fun of, and they did not like it; nobody does. He was always hoaxing them; 'hoaxing' is not a pretty word, my dear, and I hope you won't tell your father I used it, for I should not like him to think that I was not choice in my language, after living with such a woman as Deborah. And be sure you never use it yourself. I don't know how it slipped out of my mouth, except it was that I was thinking of poor Peter and it was always his expression. But he was a very gentlemanly boy in many things. He was like dear Captain Brown in always being ready to help any old person or a child. Still, he did like joking and making fun; and he seemed to think the old ladies in Cranford would believe anything. There were many old ladies living here then; we are principally ladies now, I know, but we are not so old as the ladies used to be when I was a girl. I could laugh to think of some of Peter's jokes. No, my dear, I won't tell you of them, because they might not shock you as they ought to do, and they were very shocking. He even took in my father once, by dressing himself up as a lady that was passing through the town and wished to see the Rector of Cranford, 'who had published that admirable Assize Sermon.' Peter said he was awfully frightened himself when he saw how my father took it all in, and even offered to copy out all his Napoleon Buonaparte sermons for her - him, I mean - no, her, for Peter was a lady then. He told me he was more terrified than he ever was before, all the time my father was speaking. He did not think my father would have believed him; and yet if he had not, it would have been a sad thing for Peter. As it was, he was none so glad of it, for my father kept him hard at work copying out all those twelve Buonaparte sermons for the lady - that was for Peter himself, you know. He was the lady. And once when he wanted to go fishing, Peter said, 'Confound the woman!' - very bad language, my dear, but Peter was not always so guarded as he should have been; my father was so angry with him, it nearly frightened me out of my wits: and yet I could hardly keep from laughing at the little curtseys Peter kept making, quite slyly, whenever my father spoke of the lady's excellent taste and sound discrimination."

"Did Miss Jenkyns know of these tricks?" said I.

"Oh, no! Deborah would have been too much shocked. No, no one knew but me. I wish I had always known of Peter's plans; but sometimes he did not tell me. He used to say the old ladies in the town wanted something to talk about; but I don't think they did. They had the *St James's Chronicle* three times a week, just as we have now, and we have plenty to say; and I remember the clacking noise there always was when some of the ladies got together. But, probably, schoolboys talk more than ladies. At last there was a terrible, sad thing happened." Miss Matty got up, went to the door, and opened it; no one was there. She rang the bell for Martha, and when Martha came, her mistress told her to go for eggs to a farm at the other end of the town.

"I will lock the door after you, Martha. You are not afraid to go, are you?"

"No, ma'am, not at all; Jem Hearn will be only too proud to go with me."

Miss Matty drew herself up, and as soon as we were alone, she wished that Martha had more maidenly reserve.

"We'll put out the candle, my dear. We can talk just as well by firelight, you know. There! Well, you see, Deborah had gone from home for a fortnight or so; it was a very still, quiet day, I remember, overhead; and the lilacs were all in flower, so I suppose it was spring. My father had gone out to see some sick people in the parish; I recollect seeing him leave the house with his wig and shovel-hat and cane. What possessed our poor Peter I don't know; he had the sweetest temper, and yet he always seemed to like to plague Deborah. She never laughed at his jokes, and thought him ungenteel, and not careful enough about improving his mind; and that vexed him.

"Well! he went to her room, it seems, and dressed himself in her old gown, and shawl, and bonnet; just the things she used to wear in Cranford, and was known by everywhere; and he made the pillow into a little - you are sure you locked the door, my dear, for I should not like anyone to hear - into - into a little baby, with white long clothes. It was only, as he told me afterwards, to make something to talk about in the town; he never thought of it as affecting Deborah. And he went and walked up and down in the Filbert walk - just half-hidden by the rails, and half-seen; and he cuddled his pillow, just like a baby, and talked to it all the nonsense people do. Oh dear! and my father came stepping stately up the street, as he always did; and what should he see but a little black crowd of people - I daresay as many as twenty - all peeping through his garden rails. So he thought, at first, they were only looking at a new rhododendron that was in full bloom, and that he was very proud of; and he walked slower, that they might have more time to admire. And he wondered if he could make out a sermon from the occasion, and thought, perhaps, there was some relation between the rhododendrons and the lilies of the field. My poor father! When he came nearer, he began to wonder that they did not see him; but their heads were all so close together, peeping and peeping! My father was amongst them, meaning, he said, to ask them to walk into the garden with him, and admire the beautiful vegetable production, when - oh, my dear, I tremble to think of it - he looked through the rails himself, and saw - I don't know what he thought he saw, but old Clare told me his face went quite grey-white with anger, and his eyes blazed out under his frowning black brows; and he spoke out - oh, so terribly! - and bade them all stop where they were - not one of them to go, not one of them to stir a step; and, swift as light, he was in at the garden door, and down the Filbert walk, and seized hold of poor Peter, and tore his clothes off his back - bonnet, shawl, gown, and all - and threw the pillow among the people over the railings: and then he was very, very angry indeed, and before all the people he lifted up his cane and flogged Peter!

"My dear, that boy's trick, on that sunny day, when all seemed going straight and well, broke my mother's heart, and changed my father for life. It did, indeed. Old Clare said, Peter looked as white as my father; and stood as still as a statue to be flogged; and my father struck hard! When my father stopped to take breath, Peter said, 'Have you done enough, sir?' quite hoarsely, and still standing quite quiet. I don't know what my father said - or if he said anything. But old Clare said, Peter turned to where the people outside the railing were, and made them a low bow, as grand and as grave as any gentleman; and then walked slowly into the house. I was in the store-room helping my mother to make cowslip wine. I cannot abide the wine now, nor the scent of the flowers; they turn me sick and faint, as they did that day, when Peter came in, looking as haughty as any man - indeed, looking like a man, not like a boy. 'Mother!' he said, 'I am come to say, God bless you for ever.' I saw his lips quiver as he spoke; and I think he durst not say anything more loving, for the purpose that was in his heart. She looked at him rather frightened, and wondering, and asked him what was to do. He did not smile or speak, but put his arms round her and kissed her as if he did not know how to leave off; and before she could speak again, he was gone. We talked it over, and could not understand it, and she bade me go and seek my father, and ask what it was all about. I found him walking up and down, looking very highly displeased.

"'Tell your mother I have flogged Peter, and that he richly deserved it.'

"I durst not ask any more questions. When I told my mother, she sat down, quite faint, for a minute. I remember, a few days after, I saw the poor, withered cowslip flowers thrown out to the leaf heap, to decay and die there. There was no making of cowslip wine that year at the rectory - nor, indeed, ever after.

"Presently my mother went to my father. I know I thought of Queen Esther and King Ahasuerus; for my mother was very pretty and delicate-looking, and my father looked as terrible as King Ahasuerus. Some time after they came out together; and then my mother told me what had happened, and that she was going up to Peter's room at my father's desire - though she was not to tell Peter this - to talk the matter over with him. But no Peter was there. We looked over the house; no Peter was there! Even my father, who had not liked to join in the search at first, helped us before long. The rectory was a very old house - steps up into a room, steps down into a room, all through. At first, my mother went calling low and soft, as if to reassure the poor boy, 'Peter! Peter, dear! it's only me;' but, by-and-by, as the servants came back from the errands my father had sent them, in different directions, to find where Peter was - as we found he was not in the garden, nor the hayloft, nor anywhere about - my mother's cry grew louder and wilder, Peter! Peter, my darling! where are you?' for then she felt and understood that that long kiss meant some sad kind of 'good-bye.' The afternoon went on - my mother never resting, but seeking again and again in every possible place that had been looked into twenty times before, nay, that she had looked into over and over again herself. My father sat with his head in his hands, not speaking except when his messengers came in, bringing no tidings; then he lifted up his face, so strong and sad, and told them to go again in some new direction. My mother kept passing from room to room, in and out of the house, moving noiselessly, but never ceasing. Neither she nor my father durst leave the house, which was the meeting-place for all the messengers. At last (and it was nearly dark), my father rose up. He took hold of my mother's arm as she came with wild, sad pace through one door, and quickly towards another. She started at the touch of his hand, for she had forgotten all in the world but Peter.

"'Molly!' said he, 'I did not think all this would happen.' He looked into her face for comfort - her poor face all wild and white; for neither she nor my father had dared to acknowledge - much less act upon - the terror that was in their hearts, lest Peter should have made away with himself. My father saw no conscious look in his wife's hot, dreary eyes, and he missed the sympathy that she had always been ready to give him - strong man as he was, and at the dumb despair in her face his tears began to flow. But when she saw this, a gentle sorrow came over her countenance, and she said, 'Dearest John! don't cry; come with me, and we'll find him,' almost as cheerfully as if she knew where he was. And she took my father's great hand in her little soft one, and led him along, the tears dropping as he walked on that same unceasing, weary walk, from room to room, through house and garden.

"Oh, how I wished for Deborah! I had no time for crying, for now all seemed to depend on me. I wrote for Deborah to come home. I sent a message privately to that same Mr Holbrook's house - poor Mr Holbrook; - you know who I mean. I don't mean I sent a message to him, but I sent one that I could trust to know if Peter was at his house. For at one time Mr Holbrook was an occasional visitor at the rectory - you know he was Miss Pole's cousin - and he had been very kind to Peter, and taught him how to fish- he was very kind to everybody, and I thought Peter might have gone off there. But Mr Holbrook was from home, and Peter had never been seen. It was night now; but the doors were all wide open, and my father and mother walked on and on; it was more than an hour since he had joined her, and I don't believe they had ever spoken all that time. I was getting the parlour fire lighted, and one of the servants was preparing tea, for I wanted them to have something to eat and drink and warm them, when old Clare asked to speak to me.

"'I have borrowed the nets from the weir, Miss Matty. Shall we drag the ponds to-night, or wait for the morning?'

"I remember staring in his face to gather his meaning; and when I did, I laughed out loud. The horror of that new thought - our bright, darling Peter, cold, and stark, and dead! I remember the ring of my own laugh now.

"The next day Deborah was at home before I was myself again. She would not have been so weak as to give way as I had done; but my screams (my horrible laughter had ended in crying) had roused my sweet dear mother, whose poor wandering wits were called back and collected as soon as a child needed her care. She and Deborah sat by my bedside; I knew by the looks of each that there had been no news of Peter - no awful, ghastly news, which was what I most had dreaded in my dull state between sleeping and waking.

"The same result of all the searching had brought something of the same relief to my mother, to whom, I am sure, the thought that Peter might even then be hanging dead in some of the familiar home places had caused that never-ending walk of yesterday. Her soft eyes never were the same again after that; they had always a restless, craving look, as if seeking for what they could not find. Oh! it was an awful time; coming down like a thunder-bolt on the still sunny day when the lilacs were all in bloom."

"Where was Mr Peter?" said I.

"He had made his way to Liverpool; and there was war then; and some of the king's ships lay off the mouth of the Mersey; and they were only too glad to have a fine likely boy such as him (five foot nine he was), come to offer himself. The captain wrote to my father, and Peter wrote to my mother. Stay! those letters will be somewhere here."

We lighted the candle, and found the captain's letter and Peter's too. And we also found a little simple begging letter from Mrs Jenkyns to Peter, addressed to him at the house of an old schoolfellow whither she fancied he might have gone. They had returned it unopened; and unopened it had remained ever since, having been inadvertently put by among the other letters of that time. This is it:-

"MY DEAREST PETER, - You did not think we should be so sorry as we are, I know, or you would never have gone away. You are too good. Your father sits and sighs till my heart aches to hear him. He cannot hold up his head for grief; and yet he only did what he thought was right. Perhaps he has been too severe, and perhaps I have not been kind enough; but God knows how we love you, my dear only boy. Don looks so sorry you are gone. Come back, and make us happy, who love you so much. I know you will come back."

But Peter did not come back. That spring day was the last time he ever saw his mother's face. The writer of the letter - the last - the only person who had ever seen what was written in it, was dead long ago; and I, a stranger, not born at the time when this occurrence took place, was the one to open it.

The captain's letter summoned the father and mother to Liverpool instantly, if they wished to see their boy; and, by some of the wild chances of life, the captain's letter had been detained somewhere, somehow.

Miss Matty went on, "And it was racetime, and all the post-horses at Cranford were gone to the races; but my father and mother set off in our own gig - and oh! my dear, they were too late - the ship was gone! And now read Peter's letter to my mother!"

It was full of love, and sorrow, and pride in his new profession, and a sore sense of his disgrace in the eyes of the people at Cranford; but ending with a passionate entreaty that she would come and see him before he left the Mersey: "Mother; we may go into battle. I hope we shall, and lick those French: but I must see you again before that time."

"And she was too late," said Miss Matty; "too late!"

We sat in silence, pondering on the full meaning of those sad, sad words. At length I asked Miss Matty to tell me how her mother bore it.

"Oh!" she said, "she was patience itself. She had never been strong, and this weakened her terribly. My father used to sit looking at her: far more sad than she was. He seemed as if he could look at nothing else when she was by; and he was so humble - so very gentle now. He would, perhaps, speak in his old way - laying down the law, as it were - and then, in a minute or two, he would come round and put his hand on our shoulders, and ask us in a low voice, if he had said anything to hurt us. I did not wonder at his speaking so to Deborah, for she was so clever; but I could not bear to hear him talking so to me.

"But, you see, he saw what we did not - that it was killing my mother. Yes! killing her (put out the candle, my dear; I can talk better in the dark), for she was but a frail woman, and ill-fitted to stand the fright and shock she had gone through; and she would smile at him and comfort him, not in words, but in her looks and tones, which were always cheerful when he was there. And she would speak of how she thought Peter stood a good chance of being admiral very soon - he was so brave and clever; and how she thought of seeing him in his navy uniform, and what sort of hats admirals wore; and how much more fit he was to be a sailor than a clergyman; and all in that way, just to make my father think she was quite glad of what came of that unlucky morning's work, and the flogging which was always in his mind, as we all knew. But oh, my dear! the bitter, bitter crying she had when she was alone; and at last, as she grew weaker, she could not keep her tears in when Deborah or me was by, and would give us message after message for Peter (his ship had gone to the Mediterranean, or somewhere down there, and then he was ordered off to India, and there was no overland route then); but she still said that no one knew where their death lay in wait, and that we were not to think hers was near. We did not think it, but we knew it, as we saw her fading away.

"Well, my dear, it's very foolish of me, I know, when in all likelihood I am so near seeing her again.

"And only think, love! the very day after her death - for she did not live quite a twelvemonth after Peter went away - the very day after - came a parcel for her from India - from her poor boy. It was a large, soft, white Indian shawl, with just a little narrow border all round; just what my mother would have liked.

"We thought it might rouse my father, for he had sat with her hand in his all night long; so Deborah took it in to him, and Peter's letter to her, and all. At first, he took no notice; and we tried to make a kind of light careless talk about the shawl, opening it out and admiring it. Then, suddenly, he got up, and spoke: 'She shall be buried in it,' he said; 'Peter shall have that comfort; and she would have liked it.'

"Well, perhaps it was not reasonable, but what could we do or say? One gives people in grief their own way. He took it up and felt it: 'It is just such a shawl as she wished for when she was married, and her mother did not give it her. I did not know of it till after, or she should have had it - she should; but she shall have it now.'

"My mother looked so lovely in her death! She was always pretty, and now she looked fair, and waxen, and young - younger than Deborah, as she stood trembling and shivering by her. We decked her in the long soft folds; she lay smiling, as if pleased; and people came - all Cranford came - to beg to see her, for they had loved her dearly, as well they might; and the countrywomen brought posies; old Clare's wife brought some white violets and begged they might lie on her breast.

"Deborah said to me, the day of my mother's funeral, that if she had a hundred offers she never would marry and leave my father. It was not very likely she would have so many - I don't know that she had one; but it was not less to her credit to say so. She was such a daughter to my father as I think there never was before or since. His eyes failed him, and she read book after book, and wrote, and copied, and was always at his service in any parish business. She could do many more things than my poor mother could; she even once wrote a letter to the bishop for my father. But he missed my mother sorely; the whole parish noticed it. Not that he was less active; I think he was more so, and more patient in helping every one. I did all I could to set Deborah at liberty to be with him; for I knew I was good for little, and that my best work in the world was to do odd jobs quietly, and set others at liberty. But my father was a changed man."

"Did Mr Peter ever come home?"

"Yes, once. He came home a lieutenant; he did not get to be admiral. And he and my father were such friends! My father took him into every house in the parish, he was so proud of him. He never walked out without Peter's arm to lean upon. Deborah used to smile (I don't think we ever laughed again after my mother's death), and say she was quite put in a corner. Not but what my father always wanted her when there was letter-writing or reading to be done, or anything to be settled."

"And then?" said I, after a pause.

"Then Peter went to sea again; and, by-and-by, my father died, blessing us both, and thanking Deborah for all she had been to him; and, of course, our circumstances were changed; and, instead of living at the rectory, and keeping three maids and a man, we had to come to this small house, and be content with a servant-of-all-work; but, as Deborah used to say, we have always lived genteelly, even if circumstances have compelled us to simplicity. Poor Deborah!"

"And Mr Peter?" asked I.

"Oh, there was some great war in India - I forget what they call it - and we have never heard of Peter since then. I believe he is dead myself; and it sometimes fidgets me that we have never put on mourning for him. And then again, when I sit by myself, and all the house is still, I think I hear his step coming up the street, and my heart begins to flutter and beat; but the sound always goes past - and Peter never comes.

"That's Martha back? No! *I'll* go, my dear; I can always find my way in the dark, you know. And a blow of fresh air at the door will do my head good, and it's rather got a trick of aching."

So she pattered off. I had lighted the candle, to give the room a cheerful appearance against her return.

"Was it Martha?" asked I.

"Yes. And I am rather uncomfortable, for I heard such a strange noise, just as I was opening the door."

"Where?' I asked, for her eyes were round with affright.

"In the street - just outside - it sounded like" -

"Talking?" I put in, as she hesitated a little.

"No! kissing" -

CHAPTER VII - VISITING

One morning, as Miss Matty and I sat at our work - it was before twelve o'clock, and Miss Matty had not changed the cap with yellow ribbons that had been Miss Jenkyns's best, and which Miss Matty was now wearing out in private, putting on the one made in imitation of Mrs Jamieson's at all times when she expected to be seen - Martha came up, and asked if Miss Betty Barker might speak to her mistress. Miss Matty assented, and quickly disappeared to change the yellow ribbons, while Miss Barker came upstairs; but, as she had forgotten her spectacles, and was rather flurried by the unusual time of the visit, I was not surprised to see her return with one cap on the top of the other. She was quite unconscious of it herself, and looked at us, with bland satisfaction. Nor do I think Miss Barker perceived it; for, putting aside the little circumstance that she was not so young as she had been, she was very much absorbed in her errand, which she delivered herself of with an oppressive modesty that found vent in endless apologies.

Miss Betty Barker was the daughter of the old clerk at Cranford who had officiated in Mr Jenkyns's time. She and her sister had had pretty good situations as ladies' maids, and had saved money enough to set up a milliner's shop, which had been patronised by the ladies in the neighbourhood. Lady Arley, for instance, would occasionally give Miss Barkers the pattern of an old cap of hers, which they immediately copied and circulated among the elite of Cranford. I say the *élite*, for Miss Barkers had caught the trick of the place, and piqued themselves upon their "aristocratic connection." They would not sell their caps and ribbons to anyone without a pedigree. Many a farmer's wife or daughter turned away huffed from Miss Barkers' select millinery, and went rather to the universal shop, where the profits of brown soap and moist sugar enabled the proprietor to go straight to (Paris, he said, until he found his customers too patriotic and John Bullish to wear what the Mounseers wore) London, where, as he often told his customers, Queen Adelaide had appeared, only the very week before, in a cap exactly like the one he showed them, trimmed with yellow and blue ribbons, and had been complimented by King William on the becoming nature of her head-dress.

Miss Barkers, who confined themselves to truth, and did not approve of miscellaneous customers, throve notwithstanding. They were self-denying, good people. Many a time have I seen the eldest of them (she that had been maid to Mrs Jamieson) carrying out some delicate mess to a poor person. They only aped their betters in having "nothing to do" with the class immediately below theirs. And when Miss Barker died, their profits and income were found to be such that Miss Betty was justified in shutting up shop and retiring from business. She also (as I think I have before said) set up her cow; a mark of respectability in Cranford almost as decided as setting up a gig is among some people. She dressed finer than any lady in Cranford; and we did not wonder at it; for it was understood that she was wearing out all the bonnets and caps and outrageous ribbons which had once formed her stock-in-trade. It was five or six years since she had given up shop, so in any other place than Cranford her dress might have been considered *passée*.

And now Miss Betty Barker had called to invite Miss Matty to tea at her house on the following Tuesday. She gave me also an impromptu invitation, as I happened to be a visitor - though I could see she had a little fear lest, since my father had gone to live in Drumble, he might have engaged in that "horrid cotton trade," and so dragged his family down out of "aristocratic society." She prefaced this invitation with so many apologies that she quite excited my curiosity. "Her presumption" was to be excused. What had she been doing? She seemed so over-powered by it I could only think that she had been writing to Queen Adelaide to ask for a receipt for washing lace; but the act which she so characterised was only an invitation she had carried to her sister's former mistress, Mrs Jamieson. "Her former occupation considered, could Miss Matty excuse the liberty?" Ah! thought I, she has found out that double cap, and is going to rectify Miss Matty's head-dress. No! it was simply to extend her invitation to Miss Matty and to me. Miss Matty bowed acceptance; and I wondered that, in the graceful action, she did not feel the unusual weight and extraordinary height of her head-dress. But I do not think she did, for she recovered her balance, and went on talking to Miss Betty in a kind, condescending manner, very different from the fidgety way she would have had if she had suspected how singular her appearance was. "Mrs Jamieson is coming, I think you said?" asked Miss Matty.

"Yes. Mrs Jamieson most kindly and condescendingly said she would be happy to come. One little stipulation she made, that she should bring Carlo. I told her that if I had a weakness, it was for dogs."

"And Miss Pole?" questioned Miss Matty, who was thinking of her pool at Preference, in which Carlo would not be available as a partner.

"I am going to ask Miss Pole. Of course, I could not think of asking her until I had asked you, madam - the rector's daughter, madam. Believe me, I do not forget the situation my father held under yours."

"And Mrs Forrester, of course?"

"And Mrs Forrester. I thought, in fact, of going to her before I went to Miss Pole. Although her circumstances are changed, madam, she was born at Tyrrell, and we can never forget her alliance to the Bigges, of Bigelow Hall."

Miss Matty cared much more for the little circumstance of her being a very good card-player.

"Mrs Fitz-Adam - I suppose" -

"No, madam. I must draw a line somewhere. Mrs Jamieson would not, I think, like to meet Mrs Fitz-Adam. I have the greatest respect for Mrs Fitz-Adam - but I cannot think her fit society for such ladies as Mrs Jamieson and Miss Matilda Jenkyns."

Miss Betty Barker bowed low to Miss Matty, and pursed up her mouth. She looked at me with sidelong dignity, as much as to say, although a retired milliner, she was no democrat, and understood the difference of ranks.

"May I beg you to come as near half-past six to my little dwelling, as possible, Miss Matilda? Mrs Jamieson dines at five, but has kindly promised not to delay her visit beyond that time - half-past six." And with a swimming curtsey Miss Betty

Barker took her leave.

My prophetic soul foretold a visit that afternoon from Miss Pole, who usually came to call on Miss Matilda after any event - or indeed in sight of any event - to talk it over with her.

"Miss Betty told me it was to be a choice and select few,"said Miss Pole, as she and Miss Matty compared notes.

"Yes, so she said. Not even Mrs Fitz-Adam."

Now Mrs Fitz-Adam was the widowed sister of the Cranford surgeon, whom I have named before. Their parents were respectable farmers, content with their station. The name of these good people was Hoggins. Mr Hoggins was the Cranford doctor now; we disliked the name and considered it coarse; but, as Miss Jenkyns said, if he changed it to Piggins it would not be much better. We had hoped to discover a relationship between him and that Marchioness of Exeter whose name was Molly Hoggins; but the man, careless of his own interests, utterly ignored and denied any such relationship, although, as dear Miss Jenkyns had said, he had a sister called Mary, and the same Christian names were very apt to run in families.

Soon after Miss Mary Hoggins married Mr Fitz-Adam, she disappeared from the neighbourhood for many years. She did not move in a sphere in Cranford society sufficiently high to make any of us care to know what Mr Fitz-Adam was. He died and was gathered to his fathers without our ever having thought about him at all. And then Mrs Fitz-Adam reappeared in Cranford ("as bold as a lion," Miss Pole said), a well-to-do widow, dressed in rustling black silk, so soon after her husband's death that poor Miss Jenkyns was justified in the remark she made, that "bombazine would have shown a deeper sense of her loss."

I remember the convocation of ladies who assembled to decide whether or not Mrs Fitz-Adam should be called upon by the old blue-blooded inhabitants of Cranford. She had taken a large rambling house, which had been usually considered to confer a patent of gentility upon its tenant, because, once upon a time, seventy or eighty years before, the spinster daughter of an earl had resided in it. I am not sure if the inhabiting this house was not also believed to convey some unusual power of intellect; for the earl's daughter, Lady Jane, had a sister, Lady Anne, who had married a general officer in the time of the American war, and this general officer had written one or two comedies, which were still acted on the London boards, and which, when we saw them advertised, made us all draw up, and feel that Drury Lane was paying a very pretty compliment to Cranford. Still, it was not at all a settled thing that Mrs Fitz-Adam was to be visited, when dear Miss Jenkyns died; and, with her, something of the clear knowledge of the strict code of gentility went out too. As Miss Pole observed, "As most of the ladies of good family in Cranford were elderly spinsters, or widows without children, if we did not relax a little, and become less exclusive, by-and-by we should have no society at all."

Mrs Forrester continued on the same side.

"She had always understood that Fitz meant something aristocratic; there was Fitz-Roy - she thought that some of the

King's children had been called Fitz-Roy; and there was Fitz-Clarence, now - they were the children of dear good King William the Fourth. Fitz-Adam! - it was a pretty name, and she thought it very probably meant 'Child of Adam.' No one, who had not some good blood in their veins, would dare to be called Fitz; there was a deal in a name - she had had a cousin who spelt his name with two little ffs - ffoulkes - and he always looked down upon capital letters and said they belonged to lately-invented families. She had been afraid he would die a bachelor, he was so very choice. When he met with a Mrs ffarringdon, at a watering-place, he took to her immediately; and a very pretty genteel woman she was - a widow, with a very good fortune; and 'my cousin,' Mr ffoulkes, married her; and it was all owing to her two little ffs."

Mrs Fitz-Adam did not stand a chance of meeting with a Mr Fitz-anything in Cranford, so that could not have been her motive for settling there. Miss Matty thought it might have been the hope of being admitted into the society of the place, which would certainly be a very agreeable rise for *ci-devant* Miss Hoggins; and if this had been her hope it would be cruel to disappoint her.

So everybody called upon Mrs Fitz-Adam - everybody but Mrs Jamieson, who used to show how honourable she was by never seeing Mrs Fitz-Adam when they met at the Cranford parties. There would be only eight or ten ladies in the room, and Mrs Fitz-Adam was the largest of all, and she invariably used to stand up when Mrs Jamieson came in, and curtsey very low to her whenever she turned in her direction - so low, in fact, that I think Mrs Jamieson must have looked at the wall above her, for she never moved a muscle of her face, no more than if she had not seen her. Still Mrs Fitz-Adam persevered.

The spring evenings were getting bright and long when three or four ladies in calashes met at Miss Barker's door. Do you know what a calash is? It is a covering worn over caps, not unlike the heads fastened on old-fashioned gigs; but sometimes it is not quite so large. This kind of head-gear always made an awful impression on the children in Cranford; and now two or three left off their play in the quiet sunny little street, and gathered in wondering silence round Miss Pole, Miss Matty, and myself. We were silent too, so that we could hear loud, suppressed whispers inside Miss Barker's house: "Wait, Peggy! wait till I've run upstairs and washed my hands. When I cough, open the door; I'll not be a minute."

And, true enough it was not a minute before we heard a noise, between a sneeze and a crow; on which the door flew open. Behind it stood a round-eyed maiden, all aghast at the honourable company of calashes, who marched in without a word. She recovered presence of mind enough to usher us into a small room, which had been the shop, but was now converted into a temporary dressing-room. There we unpinned and shook ourselves, and arranged our features before the glass into a sweet and gracious company-face; and then, bowing backwards with "After you, ma'am," we allowed Mrs Forrester to take precedence up the narrow staircase that led to Miss Barker's drawing-room. There she sat, as stately and composed as though we had never heard that odd-sounding cough, from which her throat must have been even then sore and rough. Kind, gentle, shabbily-dressed Mrs Forrester was immediately conducted to the second place of honour - a seat arranged something like Prince Albert's near the Queen's - good, but not so good. The place of pre-eminence was, of course, reserved for the Honourable Mrs Jamieson, who presently came panting up the stairs - Carlo rushing round her on her progress, as if he meant to trip her up.

And now Miss Betty Barker was a proud and happy woman! She stirred the fire, and shut the door, and sat as near to it as she could, quite on the edge of her chair. When Peggy came in, tottering under the weight of the tea-tray, I noticed that Miss Barker was sadly afraid lest Peggy should not keep her distance sufficiently. She and her mistress were on very familiar terms in their every-day intercourse, and Peggy wanted now to make several little confidences to her, which Miss Barker was on thorns to hear, but which she thought it her duty, as a lady, to repress. So she turned away from all Peggy's asides and signs; but she made one or two very malapropos answers to what was said; and at last, seized with a bright idea, she exclaimed,"Poor, sweet Carlo! I'm forgetting him. Come downstairs with me, poor ittie doggie, and it shall have its tea, it shall!"

In a few minutes she returned, bland and benignant as before; but I thought she had forgotten to give the "poor ittie doggie"anything to eat, judging by the avidity with which he swallowed down chance pieces of cake. The tea-tray was abundantly loaded - I was pleased to see it, I was so hungry; but I was afraid the ladies present might think it vulgarly heaped up. I know they would have done at their own houses; but somehow the heaps disappeared here. I saw Mrs Jamieson eating seed-cake, slowly and considerately, as she did everything; and I was rather surprised, for I knew she had told us, on the occasion of her last party, that she never had it in her house, it reminded her so much of scented soap. She always gave us Savoy biscuits. However, Mrs Jamieson was kindly indulgent to Miss Barker's want of knowledge of the customs of high life; and, to spare her feelings, ate three large pieces of seed-cake, with a placid, ruminating expression of countenance, not unlike a cow's.

After tea there was some little demur and difficulty. We were six in number; four could play at Preference, and for the other two there was Cribbage. But all, except myself (I was rather afraid of the Cranford ladies at cards, for it was the most earnest and serious business they ever engaged in), were anxious to be of the "pool." Even Miss Barker, while declaring she did not know Spadille from Manille, was evidently hankering to take a hand. The dilemma was soon put an end to by a singular kind of noise. If a baron's daughter-in-law could ever be supposed to snore, I should have said Mrs Jamieson did so then; for, overcome by the heat of the room, and inclined to doze by nature, the temptation of that very comfortable arm-chair had been too much for her, and Mrs Jamieson was nodding. Once or twice she opened her eyes with an effort, and calmly but unconsciously smiled upon us; but by-and-by, even her benevolence was not equal to this exertion, and she was sound asleep.

"It is very gratifying to me," whispered Miss Barker at the card-table to her three opponents, whom, notwithstanding her ignorance of the game, she was "basting" most unmercifully - "very gratifying indeed, to see how completely Mrs Jamieson feels at home in my poor little dwelling; she could not have paid me a greater compliment."

Miss Barker provided me with some literature in the shape of three or four handsomely-bound fashion-books ten or twelve years old, observing, as she put a little table and a candle for my especial benefit, that she knew young people liked to look at pictures. Carlo lay and snorted, and started at his mistress's feet. He, too, was quite at home.

The card-table was an animated scene to watch; four ladies' heads, with niddle-noddling caps, all nearly meeting over the middle of the table in their eagerness to whisper quick enough and loud enough: and every now and then came Miss

Barker's "Hush, ladies! if you please, hush! Mrs Jamieson is asleep."

It was very difficult to steer clear between Mrs Forrester's deafness and Mrs Jamieson's sleepiness. But Miss Barker managed her arduous task well. She repeated the whisper to Mrs Forrester, distorting her face considerably, in order to show, by the motions of her lips, what was said; and then she smiled kindly all round at us, and murmured to herself, "Very gratifying, indeed; I wish my poor sister had been alive to see this day."

Presently the door was thrown wide open; Carlo started to his feet, with a loud snapping bark, and Mrs Jamieson awoke: or, perhaps, she had not been asleep - as she said almost directly, the room had been so light she had been glad to keep her eyes shut, but had been listening with great interest to all our amusing and agreeable conversation. Peggy came in once more, red with importance. Another tray! "Oh, gentility!" thought I, "can yon endure this last shock?" For Miss Barker had ordered (nay, I doubt not, prepared, although she did say, "Why, Peggy, what have you brought us?"and looked pleasantly surprised at the unexpected pleasure) all sorts of good things for supper - scalloped oysters, potted lobsters, jelly, a dish called "little Cupids" (which was in great favour with the Cranford ladies, although too expensive to be given, except on solemn and state occasions - macaroons sopped in brandy, I should have called it, if I had not known its more refined and classical name). In short, we were evidently to be feasted with all that was sweetest and best; and we thought it better to submit graciously, even at the cost of our gentility - which never ate suppers in general, but which, like most non-supper-eaters, was particularly hungry on all special occasions.

Miss Barker, in her former sphere, had, I daresay, been made acquainted with the beverage they call cherry-brandy. We none of us had ever seen such a thing, and rather shrank back when she proffered it us -"just a little, leetle glass, ladies; after the oysters and lobsters, you know. Shell-fish are sometimes thought not very wholesome." We all shook our heads like female mandarins; but, at last, Mrs Jamieson suffered herself to be persuaded, and we followed her lead. It was not exactly unpalatable, though so hot and so strong that we thought ourselves bound to give evidence that we were not accustomed to such things by coughing terribly - almost as strangely as Miss Barker had done, before we were admitted by Peggy.

"It's very strong," said Miss Pole, as she put down her empty glass; "I do believe there's spirit in it."

"Only a little drop - just necessary to make it keep," said Miss Barker. "You know we put brandy-pepper over our preserves to make them keep. I often feel tipsy myself from eating damson tart."

I question whether damson tart would have opened Mrs Jamieson's heart as the cherry-brandy did; but she told us of a coming event, respecting which she had been quite silent till that moment.

"My sister-in-law, Lady Glenmire, is coming to stay with me."

There was a chorus of "Indeed!" and then a pause. Each one rapidly reviewed her wardrobe, as to its fitness to appear in the presence of a baron's widow; for, of course, a series of small festivals were always held in Cranford on the arrival of a visitor at any of our friends' houses. We felt very pleasantly excited on the present occasion.

Not long after this the maids and the lanterns were announced. Mrs Jamieson had the sedan-chair, which had squeezed itself into Miss Barker's narrow lobby with some difficulty, and most literally "stopped the way." It required some skilful manoeuvring on the part of the old chairmen (shoemakers by day, but when summoned to carry the sedan dressed up in a strange old livery - long great-coats, with small capes, coeval with the sedan, and similar to the dress of the class in Hogarth's pictures) to edge, and back, and try at it again, and finally to succeed in carrying their burden out of Miss Barker's front door. Then we heard their quick pit-a-pat along the quiet little street as we put on our calashes and pinned up our gowns; Miss Barker hovering about us with offers of help, which, if she had not remembered her former occupation, and wished us to forget it, would have been much more pressing.

CHAPTER VIII - "YOUR LADYSHIP"

Early the next morning - directly after twelve - Miss Pole made her appearance at Miss Matty's. Some very trifling piece of business was alleged as a reason for the call; but there was evidently something behind. At last out it came.

"By the way, you'll think I'm strangely ignorant; but, do you really know, I am puzzled how we ought to address Lady Glenmire. Do you say, 'Your Ladyship,' where you would say 'you' to a common person? I have been puzzling all morning; and are we to say 'My Lady,' instead of 'Ma'am?' Now you knew Lady Arley - will you kindly tell me the most correct way of speaking to the peerage?"

Poor Miss Matty! she took off her spectacles and she put them on again- but how Lady Arley was addressed, she could not remember.

"It is so long ago," she said. "Dear! dear! how stupid I am! I don't think I ever saw her more than twice. I know we used to call Sir Peter, 'Sir Peter'- but he came much oftener to see us than Lady Arley did. Deborah would have known in a minute. 'My lady' - 'your ladyship.' It sounds very strange, and as if it was not natural. I never thought of it before; but, now you have named it, I am all in a puzzle."

It was very certain Miss Pole would obtain no wise decision from Miss Matty, who got more bewildered every moment, and more perplexed as to etiquettes of address.

"Well, I really think," said Miss Pole, "I had better just go and tell Mrs Forrester about our little difficulty. One sometimes grows nervous; and yet one would not have Lady Glenmire think we were quite ignorant of the etiquettes of high life in Cranford."

"And will you just step in here, dear Miss Pole, as you come back, please, and tell me what you decide upon? Whatever you and Mrs Forrester fix upon, will be quite right, I'm sure. 'Lady Arley,' 'Sir Peter,'" said Miss Matty to herself, trying to recall the old forms of words.

"Who is Lady Glenmire?" asked I.

"Oh, she's the widow of Mr Jamieson - that's Mrs Jamieson's late husband, you know - widow of his eldest brother. Mrs Jamieson was a Miss Walker, daughter of Governor Walker. 'Your ladyship.' My dear, if they fix on that way of speaking, you must just let me practice a little on you first, for I shall feel so foolish and hot saying it the first time to Lady Glenmire."

It was really a relief to Miss Matty when Mrs Jamieson came on a very unpolite errand. I notice that apathetic people have more quiet impertinence than others; and Mrs Jamieson came now to insinuate pretty plainly that she did not particularly wish that the Cranford ladies should call upon her sister-in-law. I can hardly say how she made this clear; for I grew very indignant and warm, while with slow deliberation she was explaining her wishes to Miss Matty, who, a true lady herself, could hardly understand the feeling which made Mrs Jamieson wish to appear to her noble sister-in-law as if she only visited "county"families. Miss Matty remained puzzled and perplexed long after I had found out the object of Mrs Jamieson's visit.

When she did understand the drift of the honourable lady's call, it was pretty to see with what quiet dignity she received the intimation thus uncourteously given. She was not in the least hurt - she was of too gentle a spirit for that; nor was she exactly conscious of disapproving of Mrs Jamieson's conduct; but there was something of this feeling in her mind, I am sure, which made her pass from the subject to others in a less flurried and more composed manner than usual. Mrs Jamieson was, indeed, the more flurried of the two, and I could see she was glad to take her leave.

A little while afterwards Miss Pole returned, red and indignant. "Well! to be sure! You've had Mrs Jamieson here, I find from Martha; and we are not to call on Lady Glenmire. Yes! I met Mrs Jamieson, half-way between here and Mrs Forrester's, and she told me; she took me so by surprise, I had nothing to say. I wish I had thought of something very sharp and sarcastic; I dare say I shall to-night. And Lady Glenmire is but the widow of a Scotch baron after all! I went on to look at Mrs Forrester's Peerage, to see who this lady was, that is to be kept under a glass case: widow of a Scotch peer - never sat in the House of Lords - and as poor as job, I dare say; and she - fifth daughter of some Mr Campbell or other. You are the daughter of a rector, at any rate, and related to the Arleys; and Sir Peter might have been Viscount Arley, every one says."

Miss Matty tried to soothe Miss Pole, but in vain. That lady, usually so kind and good-humoured, was now in a full flow of anger.

"And I went and ordered a cap this morning, to be quite ready,"said she at last, letting out the secret which gave sting to

Mrs Jamieson's intimation. "Mrs Jamieson shall see if it is so easy to get me to make fourth at a pool when she has none of her fine Scotch relations with her!"

In coming out of church, the first Sunday on which Lady Glenmire appeared in Cranford, we sedulously talked together, and turned our backs on Mrs Jamieson and her guest. If we might not call on her, we would not even look at her, though we were dying with curiosity to know what she was like. We had the comfort of questioning Martha in the afternoon. Martha did not belong to a sphere of society whose observation could be an implied compliment to Lady Glenmire, and Martha had made good use of her eyes.

"Well, ma'am! is it the little lady with Mrs Jamieson, you mean? I thought you would like more to know how young Mrs Smith was dressed; her being a bride." (Mrs Smith was the butcher's wife).

Miss Pole said, "Good gracious me! as if we cared about a Mrs Smith;" but was silent as Martha resumed her speech.

"The little lady in Mrs Jamieson's pew had on, ma'am, rather an old black silk, and a shepherd's plaid cloak, ma'am, and very bright black eyes she had, ma'am, and a pleasant, sharp face; not over young, ma'am, but yet, I should guess, younger than Mrs Jamieson herself. She looked up and down the church, like a bird, and nipped up her petticoats, when she came out, as quick and sharp as ever I see. I'll tell you what, ma'am, she's more like Mrs Deacon, at the 'Coach and Horses,' nor any one."

"Hush, Martha!" said Miss Matty, "that's not respectful."

"Isn't it, ma'am? I beg pardon, I'm sure; but Jem Hearn said so as well. He said, she was just such a sharp, stirring sort of a body" -

"Lady," said Miss Pole.

"Lady - as Mrs Deacon."

Another Sunday passed away, and we still averted our eyes from Mrs Jamieson and her guest, and made remarks to ourselves that we thought were very severe - almost too much so. Miss Matty was evidently uneasy at our sarcastic manner of speaking.

Perhaps by this time Lady Glenmire had found out that Mrs Jamieson's was not the gayest, liveliest house in the world; perhaps Mrs Jamieson had found out that most of the county families were in London, and that those who remained in the country were not so alive as they might have been to the circumstance of Lady Glenmire being in their neighbourhood. Great events spring out of small causes; so I will not pretend to say what induced Mrs Jamieson to alter her determination of excluding the Cranford ladies, and send notes of invitation all round for a small party on the following Tuesday. Mr Mulliner himself brought them round. He *would* always ignore the fact of there being a back-door to any house, and gave a louder rat-tat than his mistress, Mrs Jamieson. He had three little notes, which he carried in a large basket, in order to impress his mistress with an idea of their great weight, though they might easily have gone into his waistcoat pocket.

Miss Matty and I quietly decided that we would have a previous engagement at home: it was the evening on which Miss Matty usually made candle-lighters of all the notes and letters of the week; for on Mondays her accounts were always made straight - not a penny owing from the week before; so, by a natural arrangement, making candle-lighters fell upon a Tuesday evening, and gave us a legitimate excuse for declining Mrs Jamieson's invitation. But before our answer was written, in came Miss Pole, with an open note in her hand.

"So!" she said. "Ah! I see you have got your note, too. Better late than never. I could have told my Lady Glenmire she would be glad enough of our society before a fortnight was over."

"Yes," said Miss Matty, "we're asked for Tuesday evening. And perhaps you would just kindly bring your work across and drink tea with us that night. It is my usual regular time for looking over the last week's bills, and notes, and letters, and making candle-lighters of them; but that does not seem quite reason enough for saying I have a previous engagement at home, though I meant to make it do. Now, if you would come, my conscience would be quite at ease, and luckily the note is not written yet."

I saw Miss Pole's countenance change while Miss Matty was speaking.

"Don't you mean to go then?" asked she.

"Oh, no!" said, Miss Matty quietly. "You don't either, I suppose?"

"I don't know," replied Miss Pole. "Yes, I think I do," said she, rather briskly; and on seeing Miss Matty look surprised, she added, "You see, one would not like Mrs Jamieson to think that anything she could do, or say, was of consequence enough to give offence; it would be a kind of letting down of ourselves, that I, for one, should not like. It would be too flattering to Mrs Jamieson if we allowed her to suppose that what she had said affected us a week, nay ten days afterwards."

"Well! I suppose it is wrong to be hurt and annoyed so long about anything; and, perhaps, after all, she did not mean to vex us. But I must say, I could not have brought myself to say the things Mrs Jamieson did about our not calling. I really don't think I shall go."

"Oh, come! Miss Matty, you must go; you know our friend Mrs Jamieson is much more phlegmatic than most people, and does not enter into the little delicacies of feeling which you possess in so remarkable a degree."

"I thought you possessed them, too, that day Mrs Jamieson called to tell us not to go," said Miss Matty innocently.

But Miss Pole, in addition to her delicacies of feeling, possessed a very smart cap, which she was anxious to show to an admiring world; and so she seemed to forget all her angry words uttered not a fortnight before, and to be ready to act on what she called the great Christian principle of "Forgive and forget"; and she lectured dear Miss Matty so long on this head that she absolutely ended by assuring her it was her duty, as a deceased rector's daughter, to buy a new cap and go to the party at Mrs Jamieson's. So "we were most happy to accept," instead of "regretting that we were obliged to decline."

The expenditure on dress in Cranford was principally in that one article referred to. If the heads were buried in smart new caps, the ladies were like ostriches, and cared not what became of their bodies. Old gowns, white and venerable collars, any number of brooches, up and down and everywhere (some with dogs' eyes painted in them; some that were like small picture-frames with mausoleums and weeping-willows neatly executed in hair inside; some, again, with miniatures of ladies and gentlemen sweetly smiling out of a nest of stiff muslin), old brooches for a permanent ornament, and new caps to suit the fashion of the day- the ladies of Cranford always dressed with chaste elegance and propriety, as Miss Barker once prettily expressed it.

And with three new caps, and a greater array of brooches than had ever been seen together at one time since Cranford was a town, did Mrs Forrester, and Miss Matty, and Miss Pole appear on that memorable Tuesday evening. I counted seven brooches myself on Miss Pole's dress. Two were fixed negligently in her cap (one was a butterfly made of Scotch pebbles, which a vivid imagination might believe to be the real insect); one fastened her net neckerchief; one her collar; one ornamented the front of her gown, midway between her throat and waist; and another adorned the point of her stomacher. Where the seventh was I have forgotten, but it was somewhere about her, I am sure.

But I am getting on too fast, in describing the dresses of the company. I should first relate the gathering on the way to Mrs Jamieson's. That lady lived in a large house just outside the town. A road which had known what it was to be a street ran right before the house, which opened out upon it without any intervening garden or court. Whatever the sun was about, he never shone on the front of that house. To be sure, the living-rooms were at the back, looking on to a pleasant garden; the front windows only belonged to kitchens and housekeepers'rooms, and pantries, and in one of them Mr Mulliner was reported to sit. Indeed, looking askance, we often saw the back of a head covered with hair powder, which also extended itself over his coat-collar down to his very waist; and this imposing back was always engaged in reading the *St James's Chronicle*, opened wide, which, in some degree, accounted for the length of time the said newspaper was in reaching us - equal subscribers with Mrs Jamieson, though, in right of her honourableness, she always had the reading of it first. This very Tuesday, the delay in forwarding the last number had been particularly aggravating; just when both Miss Pole and Miss Matty, the former more especially, had been wanting to see it, in order to coach up the Court news ready for the evening's interview with aristocracy. Miss Pole told us she had absolutely taken time by the forelock, and been dressed by five o'clock, in order to be ready if the *St James's Chronicle* should come in at the last moment - the very *St James's Chronicle* which the powdered head was tranquilly and composedly reading as we passed the accustomed window this evening.

"The impudence of the man!" said Miss Pole, in a low indignant whisper. "I should like to ask him whether his mistress pays her quarter-share for his exclusive use."

We looked at her in admiration of the courage of her thought; for Mr Mulliner was an object of great awe to all of us. He seemed never to have forgotten his condescension in coming to live at Cranford. Miss Jenkyns, at times, had stood forth as the undaunted champion of her sex, and spoken to him on terms of equality; but even Miss Jenkyns could get no higher. In his pleasantest and most gracious moods he looked like a sulky cockatoo. He did not speak except in gruff monosyllables. He would wait in the hall when we begged him not to wait, and then look deeply offended because we had kept him there, while, with trembling, hasty hands we prepared ourselves for appearing in company.

Miss Pole ventured on a small joke as we went upstairs, intended, though addressed to us, to afford Mr Mulliner some slight amusement. We all smiled, in order to seem as if we felt at our ease, and timidly looked for Mr Mulliner's sympathy. Not a muscle of that wooden face had relaxed; and we were grave in an instant.

Mrs Jamieson's drawing-room was cheerful; the evening sun came streaming into it, and the large square window was clustered round with flowers. The furniture was white and gold; not the later style, Louis Quatorze, I think they call it, all shells and twirls; no, Mrs Jamieson's chairs and tables had not a curve or bend about them. The chair and table legs diminished as they neared the ground, and were straight and square in all their corners. The chairs were all a-row against the walls, with the exception of four or five which stood in a circle round the fire. They were railed with white bars across the back and knobbed with gold; neither the railings nor the knobs invited to ease. There was a japanned table devoted to literature, on which lay a Bible, a Peerage, and a Prayer-Book. There was another square Pembroke table dedicated to the Fine Arts, on which were a kaleidoscope, conversation-cards, puzzle-cards (tied together to an interminable length with faded pink satin ribbon), and a box painted in fond imitation of the drawings which decorate tea-chests. Carlo lay on the worsted-worked rug, and ungraciously barked at us as we entered. Mrs Jamieson stood up, giving us each a torpid smile of welcome, and looking helplessly beyond us at Mr Mulliner, as if she hoped he would place us in chairs, for, if he did not, she never could. I suppose he thought we could find our way to the circle round the fire, which reminded me of Stonehenge, I don't know why. Lady Glenmire came to the rescue of our hostess, and, somehow or other, we found ourselves for the first time placed agreeably, and not formally, in Mrs Jamieson's house. Lady Glenmire, now we had time to look at her, proved to be a bright little woman of middle age, who had been very pretty in the days of her youth, and who was even yet very pleasant-looking. I saw Miss Pole appraising her dress in the first five minutes, and I take her word when she said the next day -

"My dear! ten pounds would have purchased every stitch she had on - lace and all."

It was pleasant to suspect that a peeress could be poor, and partly reconciled us to the fact that her husband had never sat in the House of Lords; which, when we first heard of it, seemed a kind of swindling us out of our prospects on false pretences; a sort of "A Lord and No Lord" business.

We were all very silent at first. We were thinking what we could talk about, that should be high enough to interest My Lady. There had been a rise in the price of sugar, which, as preserving-time was near, was a piece of intelligence to all our house-keeping hearts, and would have been the natural topic if Lady Glenmire had not been by. But we were not sure if the peerage ate preserves - much less knew how they were made. At last, Miss Pole, who had always a great deal of courage and *savoir faire*, spoke to Lady Glenmire, who on her part had seemed just as much puzzled to know how to break the silence as we were.

"Has your ladyship been to Court lately?" asked she; and then gave a little glance round at us, half timid and half triumphant, as much as to say, "See how judiciously I have chosen a subject befitting the rank of the stranger."

"I never was there in my life," said Lady Glenmire, with a broad Scotch accent, but in a very sweet voice. And then, as if she had been too abrupt, she added: "We very seldom went to London - only twice, in fact, during all my married life; and before I was married my father had far too large a family" (fifth daughter of Mr Campbell was in all our minds, I am sure) "to take us often from our home, even to Edinburgh. Ye'll have been in Edinburgh, maybe?" said she, suddenly brightening up with the hope of a common interest. We had none of us been there; but Miss Pole had an uncle who once had passed a night there, which was very pleasant.

Mrs Jamieson, meanwhile, was absorbed in wonder why Mr Mulliner did not bring the tea; and at length the wonder oozed out of her mouth.

"I had better ring the bell, my dear, had not I?" said Lady Glenmire briskly.

"No - I think not - Mulliner does not like to be hurried."

We should have liked our tea, for we dined at an earlier hour than Mrs Jamieson. I suspect Mr Mulliner had to finish the *St James's Chronicle* before he chose to trouble himself about tea. His mistress fidgeted and fidgeted, and kept saying, I can't think why Mulliner does not bring tea. I can't think what he can be about." And Lady Glenmire at last grew quite impatient, but it was a pretty kind of impatience after all; and she rang the bell rather sharply, on receiving a half-permission from her sister-in-law to do so. Mr Mulliner appeared in dignified surprise. "Oh!"said Mrs Jamieson, "Lady Glenmire rang the bell; I believe it was for tea."

In a few minutes tea was brought. Very delicate was the china, very old the plate, very thin the bread and butter, and very small the lumps of sugar. Sugar was evidently Mrs Jamieson's favourite economy. I question if the little filigree sugar-tongs, made something like scissors, could have opened themselves wide enough to take up an honest, vulgar good-sized piece; and when I tried to seize two little minnikin pieces at once, so as not to be detected in too many returns to the sugar-basin, they absolutely dropped one, with a little sharp clatter, quite in a malicious and unnatural manner. But before this happened we had had a slight disappointment. In the little silver jug was cream, in the larger one was milk. As soon as Mr Mulliner came in, Carlo began to beg, which was a thing our manners forebade us to do, though I am sure we were just as hungry; and Mrs Jamieson said she was certain we would excuse her if she gave her poor dumb Carlo his tea first. She accordingly mixed a saucerful for him, and put it down for him to lap; and then she told us how intelligent and sensible the dear little fellow was; he knew cream quite well, and constantly refused tea with only milk in it: so the milk was left for us; but we silently thought we were quite as intelligent and sensible as Carlo, and felt as if insult were added to injury when we were called upon to admire the gratitude evinced by his wagging his tail for the cream which should have been ours.

After tea we thawed down into common-life subjects. We were thankful to Lady Glenmire for having proposed some more bread and butter, and this mutual want made us better acquainted with her than we should ever have been with talking about the Court, though Miss Pole did say she had hoped to know how the dear Queen was from some one who had seen her.

The friendship begun over bread and butter extended on to cards. Lady Glenmire played Preference to admiration, and was a complete authority as to Ombre and Quadrille. Even Miss Pole quite forgot to say "my lady," and "your ladyship," and said "Basto! ma'am"; "you have Spadille, I believe," just as quietly as if we had never held the great Cranford Parliament on the subject of the proper mode of addressing a peeress.

As a proof of how thoroughly we had forgotten that we were in the presence of one who might have sat down to tea with a coronet, instead of a cap, on her head, Mrs Forrester related a curious little fact to Lady Glenmire - an anecdote known to the circle of her intimate friends, but of which even Mrs Jamieson was not aware. It related to some fine old lace, the sole relic of better days, which Lady Glenmire was admiring on Mrs Forrester's collar.

"Yes," said that lady, "such lace cannot be got now for either love or money; made by the nuns abroad, they tell me. They say that they can't make it now even there. But perhaps they can, now they've passed the Catholic Emancipation Bill. I should not wonder. But, in the meantime, I treasure up my lace very much. I daren't even trust the washing of it to my maid" (the little charity school-girl I have named before, but who sounded well as "my maid"). "I always wash it myself. And once it had a narrow escape. Of course, your ladyship knows that such lace must never be starched or ironed. Some people wash it in sugar and water, and some in coffee, to make it the right yellow colour; but I myself have a very good receipt for washing it in milk, which stiffens it enough, and gives it a very good creamy colour. Well, ma'am, I had tacked it together (and the beauty of this fine lace is that, when it is wet, it goes into a very little space), and put it to soak in milk, when, unfortunately, I left the room; on my return, I found pussy on the table, looking very like a thief, but gulping very uncomfortably, as if she was half-chocked with something she wanted to swallow and could not. And, would you believe it? At first I pitied her, and said 'Poor pussy! poor pussy!' till, all at once, I looked and saw the cup of milk empty - cleaned out! 'You naughty cat!' said I, and I believe I was provoked enough to give her a slap, which did no good, but only helped the lace down - just as one slaps a choking child on the back. I could have cried, I was so vexed; but I determined I would not give the lace up without a struggle for it. I hoped the lace might disagree with her, at any rate; but it would have been too much for Job, if he had seen, as I did, that cat come in, quite placid and purring, not a quarter of an hour after, and almost expecting to be stroked. 'No, pussy!' said I, 'if you have any conscience you ought not to expect that!' And then a thought struck me; and I rang the bell for my maid, and sent her to Mr Hoggins, with my compliments, and would he be kind enough to lend me one of his top-boots for an hour? I did not think there was anything odd in the message; but Jenny said the young men in the surgery laughed as if they would be ill at my wanting a top-boot. When it came, Jenny and I put pussy in, with her forefeet straight down, so that they were fastened, and could not scratch, and we gave her a teaspoonful of current-jelly in which (your ladyship must excuse me) I had mixed some tartar emetic. I shall never forget how anxious I was for the next half-hour. I took pussy to my own room, and spread a clean towel on the floor. I could have kissed her when she returned the lace to sight, very much as it had gone down. Jenny had boiling water ready, and we soaked it and soaked it, and spread it on a lavender-bush in the sun before I could touch it again, even to put it in milk. But now your ladyship would never guess that it had been in pussy's inside."

We found out, in the course of the evening, that Lady Glenmire was going to pay Mrs Jamieson a long visit, as she had given up her apartments in Edinburgh, and had no ties to take her back there in a hurry. On the whole, we were rather glad to hear this, for she had made a pleasant impression upon us; and it was also very comfortable to find, from things which dropped out in the course of conversation, that, in addition to many other genteel qualities, she was far removed from the "vulgarity of wealth."

"Don't you find it very unpleasant walking?" asked Mrs Jamieson, as our respective servants were announced. It was a pretty regular question from Mrs Jamieson, who had her own carriage in the coach-house, and always went out in a sedan-chair to the very shortest distances. The answers were nearly as much a matter of course.

"Oh dear, no! it is so pleasant and still at night!" "Such a refreshment after the excitement of a party!" "The stars are so beautiful!" This last was from Miss Matty.

"Are you fond of astronomy?" Lady Glenmire asked.

"Not very," replied Miss Matty, rather confused at the moment to remember which was astronomy and which was astrology - but the answer was true under either circumstance, for she read, and was slightly alarmed at Francis Moore's astrological predictions; and, as to astronomy, in a private and confidential conversation, she had told me she never could believe that the earth was moving constantly, and that she would not believe it if she could, it made her feel so tired and dizzy whenever she thought about it.

In our pattens we picked our way home with extra care that night, so refined and delicate were our perceptions after drinking tea with "my lady."

CHAPTER IX - SIGNOR BRUNONI

Soon after the events of which I gave an account in my last paper, I was summoned home by my father's illness; and for a time I forgot, in anxiety about him, to wonder how my dear friends at Cranford were getting on, or how Lady Glenmire could reconcile herself to the dulness of the long visit which she was still paying to her sister-in-law, Mrs Jamieson. When my father grew a little stronger I accompanied him to the seaside, so that altogether I seemed banished from Cranford, and was deprived of the opportunity of hearing any chance intelligence of the dear little town for the greater part of that year.

Late in November - when we had returned home again, and my father was once more in good health - I received a letter from Miss Matty; and a very mysterious letter it was. She began many sentences without ending them, running them one into another, in much the same confused sort of way in which written words run together on blotting-paper. All I could make out was that, if my father was better (which she hoped he was), and would take warning and wear a great-coat from Michaelmas to Lady-day, if turbans were in fashion, could I tell her? Such a piece of gaiety was going to happen as had not been seen or known of since Wombwell's lions came, when one of them ate a little child's arm; and she was, perhaps, too old to care about dress, but a new cap she must have; and, having heard that turbans were worn, and some of the county families likely to come, she would like to look tidy, if I would bring her a cap from the milliner I employed; and oh, dear! how careless of her to forget that she wrote to beg I would come and pay her a visit next Tuesday; when she hoped to have something to offer me in the way of amusement, which she would not now more particularly describe, only sea-green was her favourite colour. So she ended her letter; but in a P.S. she added, she thought she might as well tell me what was the peculiar attraction to Cranford just now; Signor Brunoni was going to exhibit his wonderful magic in the Cranford Assembly Rooms on Wednesday and Friday evening in the following week.

I was very glad to accept the invitation from my dear Miss Matty, independently of the conjuror, and most particularly anxious to prevent her from disfiguring her small, gentle, mousey face with a great Saracen's head turban; and accordingly, I bought her a pretty, neat, middle-aged cap, which, however, was rather a disappointment to her when, on my arrival, she followed me into my bedroom, ostensibly to poke the fire, but in reality, I do believe, to see if the sea-green turban was not inside the cap-box with which I had travelled. It was in vain that I twirled the cap round on my hand to exhibit back and side fronts: her heart had been set upon a turban, and all she could do was to say, with resignation in her look and voice -

"I am sure you did your best, my dear. It is just like the caps all the ladies in Cranford are wearing, and they have had theirs for a year, I dare say. I should have liked something newer, I confess - something more like the turbans Miss Betty Barker tells me Queen Adelaide wears; but it is very pretty, my dear. And I dare say lavender will wear better than sea-green. Well, after all, what is dress, that we should care anything about it? You'll tell me if you want anything, my dear. Here is the bell. I suppose turbans have not got down to Drumble yet?"

So saying, the dear old lady gently bemoaned herself out of the room, leaving me to dress for the evening, when, as she informed me, she expected Miss Pole and Mrs Forrester, and she hoped I should not feel myself too much tired to join the party. Of course I should not; and I made some haste to unpack and arrange my dress; but, with all my speed, I heard the arrivals and the buzz of conversation in the next room before I was ready. Just as I opened the door, I caught the words, "I was foolish to expect anything very genteel out of the Drumble shops; poor girl! she did her best, I've no doubt." But, for all that, I had rather that she blamed Drumble and me than disfigured herself with a turban.

Miss Pole was always the person, in the trio of Cranford ladies now assembled, to have had adventures. She was in the habit of spending the morning in rambling from shop to shop, not to purchase anything (except an occasional reel of cotton or a piece of tape), but to see the new articles and report upon them, and to collect all the stray pieces of intelligence in the town. She had a way, too, of demurely popping hither and thither into all sorts of places to gratify her curiosity on any point - a way which, if she had not looked so very genteel and prim, might have been considered impertinent. And now, by the expressive way in which she cleared her throat, and waited for all minor subjects (such as caps and turbans) to be cleared off the course, we knew she had something very particular to relate, when the due pause came - and I defy any people possessed of common modesty to keep up a conversation long, where one among them sits up aloft in silence, looking down upon all the things they chance to say as trivial and contemptible compared to what they could disclose, if properly entreated. Miss Pole began -

"As I was stepping out of Gordon's shop to-day, I chanced to go into the 'George' (my Betty has a second-cousin who is chambermaid there, and I thought Betty would like to hear how she was), and, not seeing anyone about, I strolled up the staircase, and found myself in the passage leading to the Assembly Room (you and I remember the Assembly Room, I am sure, Miss Matty! and the minuets de la cour!); so I went on, not thinking of what I was about, when, all at once, I perceived that I was in the middle of the preparations for to-morrow night - the room being divided with great clothes-maids, over which Crosby's men were tacking red flannel; very dark and odd it seemed; it quite bewildered me, and I was going on behind the screens, in my absence of mind, when a gentleman (quite the gentleman, I can assure you) stepped forwards and asked if I had any business he could arrange for me. He spoke such pretty broken English, I could not help thinking of Thaddeus of Warsaw, and the Hungarian Brothers, and Santo Sebastiani; and while I was busy picturing his past life to myself, he had bowed me out of the room. But wait a minute! You have not heard half my story yet! I was going downstairs, when who should I meet but Betty's second-cousin. So, of course, I stopped to speak to her for Betty's sake; and she told me that I had really seen the conjuror - the gentleman who spoke broken English was Signor Brunoni himself. Just at this moment he passed us on the stairs, making such a graceful bow! in reply to which I dropped a curtsey - all foreigners have such polite manners, one catches something of it. But when he had gone downstairs, I bethought me that I had dropped my glove in the Assembly Room (it was safe in my muff all the time, but I never found it till afterwards); so I went back, and, just as I was creeping up the passage left on one side of the great screen that goes nearly across the room, who should I see but the very same gentleman that had met me before, and passed me on the stairs, coming now forwards from the inner part of the room, to which there is no entrance - you remember, Miss Matty - and just repeating, in his pretty broken English, the inquiry if I had any business there - I don't mean that he put it quite so bluntly, but he seemed very determined that I should not pass the screen - so, of course, I explained about my glove, which, curiously enough, I found at that very moment."

Miss Pole, then, had seen the conjuror - the real, live conjuror! and numerous were the questions we all asked her. "Had he a beard?" "Was he young, or old?" "Fair, or dark?" "Did he look" - (unable to shape my question prudently, I put it in another form) - "How did he look?" In short, Miss Pole was the heroine of the evening, owing to her morning's encounter. If she was not the rose (that is to say the conjuror) she had been near it.

Conjuration, sleight of hand, magic, witchcraft, were the subjects of the evening. Miss Pole was slightly sceptical, and inclined to think there might be a scientific solution found for even the proceedings of the Witch of Endor. Mrs Forrester believed everything, from ghosts to death-watches. Miss Matty ranged between the two - always convinced by the last speaker. I think she was naturally more inclined to Mrs Forrester's side, but a desire of proving herself a worthy sister to

Miss Jenkyns kept her equally balanced - Miss Jenkyns, who would never allow a servant to call the little rolls of tallow that formed themselves round candles "winding-sheets," but insisted on their being spoken of as "roley-poleys!" A sister of hers to be superstitious! It would never do.

After tea, I was despatched downstairs into the dining-parlour for that volume of the old Encyclopaedia which contained the nouns beginning with C, in order that Miss Pole might prime herself with scientific explanations for the tricks of the following evening. It spoilt the pool at Preference which Miss Matty and Mrs Forrester had been looking forward to, for Miss Pole became so much absorbed in her subject, and the plates by which it was illustrated, that we felt it would be cruel to disturb her otherwise than by one or two well-timed yawns, which I threw in now and then, for I was really touched by the meek way in which the two ladies were bearing their disappointment. But Miss Pole only read the more zealously, imparting to us no more information than this -

"Ah! I see; I comprehend perfectly. A represents the ball. Put A between B and D - no! between C and F, and turn the second joint of the third finger of your left hand over the wrist of your right H. Very clear indeed! My dear Mrs Forrester, conjuring and witchcraft is a mere affair of the alphabet. Do let me read you this one passage?"

Mrs Forrester implored Miss Pole to spare her, saying, from a child upwards, she never could understand being read aloud to; and I dropped the pack of cards, which I had been shuffling very audibly, and by this discreet movement I obliged Miss Pole to perceive that Preference was to have been the order of the evening, and to propose, rather unwillingly, that the pool should commence. The pleasant brightness that stole over the other two ladies' faces on this! Miss Matty had one or two twinges of self-reproach for having interrupted Miss Pole in her studies: and did not remember her cards well, or give her full attention to the game, until she had soothed her conscience by offering to lend the volume of the Encyclopaedia to Miss Pole, who accepted it thankfully, and said Betty should take it home when she came with the lantern.

The next evening we were all in a little gentle flutter at the idea of the gaiety before us. Miss Matty went up to dress betimes, and hurried me until I was ready, when we found we had an hour-and-a-half to wait before the "doors opened at seven precisely." And we had only twenty yards to go! However, as Miss Matty said, it would not do to get too much absorbed in anything, and forget the time; so she thought we had better sit quietly, without lighting the candles, till five minutes to seven. So Miss Matty dozed, and I knitted.

At length we set off; and at the door under the carriage-way at the"George," we met Mrs Forrester and Miss Pole: the latter was discussing the subject of the evening with more vehemence than ever, and throwing X's and B's at our heads like hailstones. She had even copied one or two of the "receipts" - as she called them - for the different tricks, on backs of letters, ready to explain and to detect Signor Brunoni's arts.

We went into the cloak-room adjoining the Assembly Room; Miss Matty gave a sigh or two to her departed youth, and the remembrance of the last time she had been there, as she adjusted her pretty new cap before the strange, quaint old mirror in the cloak-room. The Assembly Room had been added to the inn, about a hundred years before, by the different county families, who met together there once a month during the winter to dance and play at cards. Many a county beauty had first swung through the minuet that she afterwards danced before Queen Charlotte in this very room. It was said that one of the Gunnings had graced the apartment with her beauty; it was certain that a rich and beautiful widow, Lady Williams, had here been smitten with the noble figure of a young artist, who was staying with some family in the neighbourhood for professional purposes, and accompanied his patrons to the Cranford Assembly. And a pretty bargain poor Lady Williams had of her handsome husband, if all tales were true. Now, no beauty blushed and dimpled along the sides of the Cranford Assembly Room; no handsome artist won hearts by his bow, *chapeau bras* in hand; the old room was dingy; the salmon-coloured paint had faded into a drab; great pieces of plaster had chipped off from the fine wreaths and festoons on its walls; but still a mouldy odour of aristocracy lingered about the place, and a dusty recollection of the days that were gone made Miss Matty and Mrs Forrester bridle up as they entered, and walk mincingly up the room, as if there were a number of genteel observers, instead of two little boys with a stick of toffee between them with which to beguile the time.

We stopped short at the second front row; I could hardly understand why, until I heard Miss Pole ask a stray waiter if any of the county families were expected; and when he shook his head, and believed not, Mrs Forrester and Miss Matty moved forwards, and our party represented a conversational square. The front row was soon augmented and enriched by Lady Glenmire and Mrs Jamieson. We six occupied the two front rows, and our aristocratic seclusion was respected by the groups of shop-keepers who strayed in from time to time and huddled together on the back benches. At least I conjectured so, from the noise they made, and the sonorous bumps they gave in sitting down; but when, in weariness of the obstinate green curtain that would not draw up, but would stare at me with two odd eyes, seen through holes, as in the old tapestry story, I would fain have looked round at the merry chattering people behind me, Miss Pole clutched my arm, and begged me not to turn, for "it was not the thing." What "the thing" was, I never could find out, but it must have been something eminently dull and tiresome. However, we all sat eyes right, square front, gazing at the tantalising curtain, and hardly speaking intelligibly, we were so afraid of being caught in the vulgarity of making any noise in a place of public amusement. Mrs Jamieson was the most fortunate, for she fell asleep.

At length the eyes disappeared - the curtain quivered - one side went up before the other, which stuck fast; it was dropped again, and, with a fresh effort, and a vigorous pull from some unseen hand, it flew up, revealing to our sight a magnificent gentleman in the Turkish costume, seated before a little table, gazing at us (I should have said with the same eyes that I had last seen through the hole in the curtain) with calm and condescending dignity, "like a being of another sphere," as I heard a sentimental voice ejaculate behind me.

"That's not Signor Brunoni!" said Miss Pole decidedly; and so audibly that I am sure he heard, for he glanced down over his flowing beard at our party with an air of mute reproach. "Signor Brunoni had no beard - but perhaps he'll come soon." So she lulled herself into patience. Meanwhile, Miss Matty had reconnoitred through her eye-glass, wiped it, and looked again. Then she turned round, and said to me, in a kind, mild, sorrowful tone -

"You see, my dear, turbans *are* worn."

But we had no time for more conversation. The Grand Turk, as Miss Pole chose to call him, arose and announced himself as Signor Brunoni.

"I don't believe him!" exclaimed Miss Pole, in a defiant manner. He looked at her again, with the same dignified upbraiding in his countenance. "I don't!" she repeated more positively than ever. "Signor Brunoni had not got that muffy sort of thing about his chin, but looked like a close-shaved Christian gentleman."

Miss Pole's energetic speeches had the good effect of wakening up Mrs Jamieson, who opened her eyes wide, in sign of the deepest attention- a proceeding which silenced Miss Pole and encouraged the Grand Turk to proceed, which he did in very broken English - so broken that there was no cohesion between the parts of his sentences; a fact which he himself perceived at last, and so left off speaking and proceeded to action.

Now we *were* astonished. How he did his tricks I could not imagine; no, not even when Miss Pole pulled out her pieces of paper and began reading aloud - or at least in a very audible whisper - the separate "receipts" for the most common of his tricks. If ever I saw a man frown and look enraged, I saw the Grand Turk frown at Miss Pole; but, as she said, what could be expected but unchristian looks from a Mussulman? If Miss Pole were sceptical, and more engrossed with her receipts and diagrams than with his tricks, Miss Matty and Mrs Forrester were mystified and perplexed to the highest degree. Mrs Jamieson kept taking her spectacles off and wiping them, as if she thought it was something defective in them which made the legerdemain; and Lady Glenmire, who had seen many curious sights in Edinburgh, was very much struck with the tricks, and would not at all agree with Miss Pole, who declared that anybody could do them with a little practice, and that she would, herself, undertake to do all he did, with two hours given to study the Encyclopaedia and make her third finger flexible.

At last Miss Matty and Mrs Forrester became perfectly awestricken. They whispered together. I sat just behind them, so I could not help hearing what they were saying. Miss Matty asked Mrs Forrester"if she thought it was quite right to have come to see such things? She could not help fearing they were lending encouragement to something that was not quite" - A little shake of the head filled up the blank. Mrs Forrester replied, that the same thought had crossed her mind; she too was feeling very uncomfortable, it was so very strange. She was quite certain that it was her pocket-handkerchief which was in that loaf just now; and it had been in her own hand not five minutes before. She wondered who had furnished the bread? She was sure it could not be Dakin, because he was the churchwarden. Suddenly Miss Matty half-turned towards me -

"Will you look, my dear - you are a stranger in the town, and it won't give rise to unpleasant reports - will you just look round and see if the rector is here? If he is, I think we may conclude that this wonderful man is sanctioned by the Church, and that will be a great relief to my mind.

I looked, and I saw the tall, thin, dry, dusty rector, sitting surrounded by National School boys, guarded by troops of his own sex from any approach of the many Cranford spinsters. His kind face was all agape with broad smiles, and the boys around him were in chinks of laughing. I told Miss Matty that the Church was smiling approval, which set her mind at ease.

I have never named Mr Hayter, the rector, because I, as a well-to-do and happy young woman, never came in contact with him. He was an old bachelor, but as afraid of matrimonial reports getting abroad about him as any girl of eighteen: and he would rush into a shop or dive down an entry, sooner than encounter any of the Cranford ladies in the street; and, as for the Preference parties, I did not wonder at his not accepting invitations to them. To tell the truth, I always suspected Miss Pole of having given very vigorous chase to Mr Hayter when he first came to Cranford; and not the less, because now she appeared to share so vividly in his dread lest her name should ever be coupled with his. He found all his interests among the poor and helpless; he had treated the National School boys this very night to the performance; and virtue was for once its own reward, for they guarded him right and left, and clung round him as if he had been the queen-bee and they the swarm. He felt so safe in their environment that he could even afford to give our party a bow as we filed out. Miss Pole ignored his presence, and pretended to be absorbed in convincing us that we had been cheated, and had not seen Signor Brunoni after all.

CHAPTER X - THE PANIC

I think a series of circumstances dated from Signor Brunoni's visit to Cranford, which seemed at the time connected in our minds with him, though I don't know that he had anything really to do with them. All at once all sorts of uncomfortable rumours got afloat in the town. There were one or two robberies - real *bonâ fide* robberies; men had up before the magistrates and committed for trial - and that seemed to make us all afraid of being robbed; and for a long time, at Miss Matty's, I know, we used to make a regular expedition all round the kitchens and cellars every night, Miss Matty leading the way, armed with the poker, I following with the hearth-brush, and Martha carrying the shovel and fire-irons with which to sound the alarm; and by the accidental hitting together of them she often frightened us so much that we bolted ourselves up, all three together, in the back-kitchen, or store-room, or wherever we happened to be, till, when our affright was over, we recollected ourselves and set out afresh with double valiance. By day we heard strange stories from the shopkeepers and cottagers, of carts that went about in the dead of night, drawn by horses shod with felt, and guarded by men in dark clothes, going round the town, no doubt in search of some unwatched house or some unfastened door.

Miss Pole, who affected great bravery herself, was the principal person to collect and arrange these reports so as to make them assume their most fearful aspect. But we discovered that she had begged one of Mr Hoggins's worn-out hats to hang up in her lobby, and we (at least I) had doubts as to whether she really would enjoy the little adventure of having her house broken into, as she protested she should. Miss Matty made no secret of being an arrant coward, but she went regularly through her housekeeper's duty of inspection - only the hour for this became earlier and earlier, till at last we went the rounds at half-past six, and Miss Matty adjourned to bed soon after seven, "in order to get the night over the sooner."

Cranford had so long piqued itself on being an honest and moral town that it had grown to fancy itself too genteel and well-bred to be otherwise, and felt the stain upon its character at this time doubly. But we comforted ourselves with the assurance which we gave to each other that the robberies could never have been committed by any Cranford person; it must have been a stranger or strangers who brought this disgrace upon the town, and occasioned as many precautions as if we were living among the Red Indians or the French.

This last comparison of our nightly state of defence and fortification was made by Mrs Forrester, whose father had served under General Burgoyne in the American war, and whose husband had fought the French in Spain. She indeed inclined to the idea that, in some way, the French were connected with the small thefts, which were ascertained facts, and the burglaries and highway robberies, which were rumours. She had been deeply impressed with the idea of French spies at some time in her life; and the notion could never be fairly eradicated, but sprang up again from time to time. And now her theory was this:- The Cranford people respected themselves too much, and were too grateful to the aristocracy who were so kind as to live near the town, ever to disgrace their bringing up by being dishonest or immoral; therefore, we must believe that the robbers were strangers - if strangers, why not foreigners? - if foreigners, who so likely as the French? Signor Brunoni spoke broken English like a Frenchman; and, though he wore a turban like a Turk, Mrs Forrester had seen a print of Madame de Staël with a turban on, and another of Mr Denon in just such a dress as that in which the conjuror had made his appearance, showing clearly that the French, as well as the Turks, wore turbans. There could be no doubt Signor Brunoni was a Frenchman - a French spy come to discover the weak and undefended places of England, and doubtless he had his accomplices. For her part, she, Mrs Forrester, had always had her own opinion of Miss Pole's adventure at the "George Inn" - seeing two men where only one was believed to be. French people had ways and means which, she was thankful to say, the English knew nothing about; and she had never felt quite easy in her mind about going to see that conjuror - it was rather too much like a forbidden thing, though the rector was there. In short, Mrs Forrester grew more excited than we had ever known her before, and, being an officer's daughter and widow, we looked up to her opinion, of course.

Really I do not know how much was true or false in the reports which flew about like wildfire just at this time; but it seemed to me then that there was every reason to believe that at Mardon (a small town about eight miles from Cranford) houses and shops were entered by holes made in the walls, the bricks being silently carried away in the dead of the night, and all done so quietly that no sound was heard either in or out of the house. Miss Matty gave it up in despair when she heard of this. "What was the use," said she, "of locks and bolts, and bells to the windows, and going round the house every night? That last trick was fit for a conjuror. Now she did believe that Signor Brunoni was at the bottom of it."

One afternoon, about five o'clock, we were startled by a hasty knock at the door. Miss Matty bade me run and tell Martha on no account to open the door till she (Miss Matty) had reconnoitred through the window; and she armed herself with a footstool to drop down on the head of the visitor, in case he should show a face covered with black crape, as he looked up in answer to her inquiry of who was there. But it was nobody but Miss Pole and Betty. The former came upstairs, carrying a little hand-basket, and she was evidently in a state of great agitation.

"Take care of that!" said she to me, as I offered to relieve her of her basket. "It's my plate. I am sure there is a plan to rob my house to-night. I am come to throw myself on your hospitality, Miss Matty. Betty is going to sleep with her cousin at the 'George.' I can sit up here all night if you will allow me; but my house is so far from any neighbours, and I don't believe we could be heard if we screamed ever so!"

"But," said Miss Matty, "what has alarmed you so much? Have you seen any men lurking about the house?"

"Oh, yes!" answered Miss Pole. "Two very bad-looking men have gone three times past the house, very slowly; and an Irish beggar-woman came not half-an-hour ago, and all but forced herself in past Betty, saying her children were starving, and she must speak to the mistress. You see, she said 'mistress,' though there was a hat hanging up in the hall, and it would have been more natural to have said 'master.' But Betty shut the door in her face, and came up to me, and we got the spoons together, and sat in the parlour-window watching till we saw Thomas Jones going from his work, when we called to him and asked him to take care of us into the town."

We might have triumphed over Miss Pole, who had professed such bravery until she was frightened; but we were too glad to perceive that she shared in the weaknesses of humanity to exult over her; and I gave up my room to her very willingly, and shared Miss Matty's bed for the night. But before we retired, the two ladies rummaged up, out of the recesses of their memory, such horrid stories of robbery and murder that I quite quaked in my shoes. Miss Pole was evidently anxious to prove that such terrible events had occurred within her experience that she was justified in her sudden panic; and Miss Matty did not like to be outdone, and capped every story with one yet more horrible, till it reminded me oddly enough, of an old story I had read somewhere, of a nightingale and a musician, who strove one against the other which could produce the most admirable music, till poor Philomel dropped down dead.

One of the stories that haunted me for a long time afterwards was of a girl who was left in charge of a great house in Cumberland on some particular fair-day, when the other servants all went off to the gaieties. The family were away in London, and a pedlar came by, and asked to leave his large and heavy pack in the kitchen, saying he would call for it again at night; and the girl (a gamekeeper's daughter), roaming about in search of amusement, chanced to hit upon a gun hanging up in the hall, and took it down to look at the chasing; and it went off through the open kitchen door, hit the pack, and a slow dark thread of blood came oozing out. (How Miss Pole enjoyed this part of the story, dwelling on each word as if she loved it!) She rather hurried over the further account of the girl's bravery, and I have but a confused idea that, somehow, she baffled the robbers with Italian irons, heated red-hot, and then restored to blackness by being dipped in grease.

We parted for the night with an awe-stricken wonder as to what we should hear of in the morning - and, on my part, with a vehement desire for the night to be over and gone: I was so afraid lest the robbers should have seen, from some dark lurking-place, that Miss Pole had carried off her plate, and thus have a double motive for attacking our house.

But until Lady Glenmire came to call next day we heard of nothing unusual. The kitchen fire-irons were in exactly the same position against the back door as when Martha and I had skilfully piled them up, like spillikins, ready to fall with an awful clatter if only a cat had touched the outside panels. I had wondered what we should all do if thus awakened and alarmed, and had proposed to Miss Matty that we should cover up our faces under the bedclothes so that there should be no danger of the robbers thinking that we could identify them; but Miss Matty, who was trembling very much, scouted this idea, and said we owed it to society to apprehend them, and that she should certainly do her best to lay hold of them and lock them up in the garret till morning.

When Lady Glenmire came, we almost felt jealous of her. Mrs Jamieson's house had really been attacked; at least there were men's footsteps to be seen on the flower borders, underneath the kitchen windows, "where nae men should be;" and Carlo had barked all through the night as if strangers were abroad. Mrs Jamieson had been awakened by Lady Glenmire, and they had rung the bell which communicated with Mr Mulliner's room in the third storey, and when his night-capped head had appeared over the bannisters, in answer to the summons, they had told him of their alarm, and the reasons for it; whereupon he retreated into his bedroom, and locked the door (for fear of draughts, as he informed them in the morning), and opened the window, and called out valiantly to say, if the supposed robbers would come to him he would fight them; but, as Lady Glenmire observed, that was but poor comfort, since they would have to pass by Mrs Jamieson's room and her own before they could reach him, and must be of a very pugnacious disposition indeed if they neglected the opportunities of robbery presented by the unguarded lower storeys, to go up to a garret, and there force a door in order to get at the champion of the house. Lady Glenmire, after waiting and listening for some time in the drawing-room, had proposed to Mrs Jamieson that they should go to bed; but that lady said she should not feel comfortable unless she sat up and watched; and, accordingly, she packed herself warmly up on the sofa, where she was found by the housemaid, when she came into the room at six o'clock, fast asleep; but Lady Glenmire went to bed, and kept awake all night.

When Miss Pole heard of this, she nodded her head in great satisfaction. She had been sure we should hear of something happening in Cranford that night; and we had heard. It was clear enough they had first proposed to attack her house; but when they saw that she and Betty were on their guard, and had carried off the plate, they had changed their tactics and gone to Mrs Jamieson's, and no one knew what might have happened if Carlo had not barked, like a good dog as he was!

Poor Carlo! his barking days were nearly over. Whether the gang who infested the neighbourhood were afraid of him, or whether they were revengeful enough, for the way in which he had baffled them on the night in question, to poison him; or whether, as some among the more uneducated people thought, he died of apoplexy, brought on by too much feeding and too little exercise; at any rate, it is certain that, two days after this eventful night, Carlo was found dead, with his poor legs stretched out stiff in the attitude of running, as if by such unusual exertion he could escape the sure pursuer, Death.

We were all sorry for Carlo, the old familiar friend who had snapped at us for so many years; and the mysterious mode of his death made us very uncomfortable. Could Signor Brunoni be at the bottom of this? He had apparently killed a canary with only a word of command; his will seemed of deadly force; who knew but what he might yet be lingering in the neighbourhood willing all sorts of awful things!

We whispered these fancies among ourselves in the evenings; but in the mornings our courage came back with the daylight, and in a week's time we had got over the shock of Carlo's death; all but Mrs Jamieson. She, poor thing, felt it as she had felt no event since her husband's death; indeed, Miss Pole said, that as the Honourable Mr Jamieson drank a good deal, and occasioned her much uneasiness, it was possible that Carlo's death might be the greater affliction. But there was always a tinge of cynicism in Miss Pole's remarks. However, one thing was clear and certain - it was necessary for Mrs Jamieson to have some change of scene; and Mr Mulliner was very impressive on this point, shaking his head whenever we inquired after his mistress, and speaking of her loss of appetite and bad nights very ominously; and with justice too, for if she had two characteristics in her natural state of health they were a facility of eating and sleeping. If she could neither eat nor sleep, she must be indeed out of spirits and out of health.

Lady Glenmire (who had evidently taken very kindly to Cranford) did not like the idea of Mrs Jamieson's going to Cheltenham, and more than once insinuated pretty plainly that it was Mr Mulliner's doing, who had been much alarmed on the occasion of the house being attacked, and since had said, more than once, that he felt it a very responsible charge to have to defend so many women. Be that as it might, Mrs Jamieson went to Cheltenham, escorted by Mr Mulliner; and Lady Glenmire remained in possession of the house, her ostensible office being to take care that the maid-servants did not pick up followers. She made a very pleasant-looking dragon; and, as soon as it was arranged for her stay in Cranford, she found out that Mrs Jamieson's visit to Cheltenham was just the best thing in the world. She had let her house in Edinburgh, and was for the time house-less, so the charge of her sister-in-law's comfortable abode was very convenient and acceptable.

Miss Pole was very much inclined to instal herself as a heroine, because of the decided steps she had taken in flying from the two men and one woman, whom she entitled "that murderous gang." She described their appearance in glowing colours, and I noticed that every time she went over the story some fresh trait of villainy was added to their appearance. One was tall - he grew to be gigantic in height before we had done with him; he of course had black hair - and by-and-by it hung in elf-locks over his forehead and down his back. The other was short and broad - and a hump sprouted out on his shoulder before we heard the last of him; he had red hair - which deepened into carroty; and she was almost sure he had a cast in the eye - a decided squint. As for the woman, her eyes glared, and she was masculine-looking - a perfect virago; most probably a man dressed in woman's clothes; afterwards, we heard of a beard on her chin, and a manly voice and a stride.

If Miss Pole was delighted to recount the events of that afternoon to all inquirers, others were not so proud of their adventures in the robbery line. Mr Hoggins, the surgeon, had been attacked at his own door by two ruffians, who were concealed in the shadow of the porch, and so effectually silenced him that he was robbed in the interval between ringing his bell and the servant's answering it. Miss Pole was sure it would turn out that this robbery had been commited by "her men," and went the very day she heard the report to have her teeth examined, and to question Mr Hoggins. She came to us afterwards; so we heard what she had heard, straight and direct from the source, while we were yet in the excitement and flutter of the agitation caused by the first intelligence; for the event had only occurred the night before.

"Well!" said Miss Pole, sitting down with the decision of a person who has made up her mind as to the nature of life and the world (and such people never tread lightly, or seat themselves without a bump),"well, Miss Matty! men will be men. Every mother's son of them wishes to be considered Samson and Solomon rolled into one- too strong ever to be beaten or discomfited - too wise ever to be outwitted. If you will notice, they have always foreseen events, though they never tell one for one's warning before the events happen. My father was a man, and I know the sex pretty well."

She had talked herself out of breath, and we should have been very glad to fill up the necessary pause as chorus, but we did not exactly know what to say, or which man had suggested this diatribe against the sex; so we only joined in generally, with a grave shake of the head, and a soft murmur of "They are very incomprehensible, certainly!"

"Now, only think," said she. "There, I have undergone the risk of having one of my remaining teeth drawn (for one is terribly at the mercy of any surgeon-dentist; and I, for one, always speak them fair till I have got my mouth out of their clutches), and, after all, Mr Hoggins is too much of a man to own that he was robbed last night."

"Not robbed!" exclaimed the chorus.

"Don't tell me!" Miss Pole exclaimed, angry that we could be for a moment imposed upon. "I believe he was robbed, just as Betty told me, and he is ashamed to own it; and, to be sure, it was very silly of him to be robbed just at his own door; I daresay he feels that such a thing won't raise him in the eyes of Cranford society, and is anxious to conceal it - but he need not have tried to impose upon me, by saying I must have heard an exaggerated account of some petty theft of a neck of mutton, which, it seems, was stolen out of the safe in his yard last week; he had the impertinence to add, he believed that that was taken by the cat. I have no doubt, if I could get at the bottom of it, it was that Irishman dressed up in woman's clothes, who came spying about my house, with the story about the starving children."

After we had duly condemned the want of candour which Mr Hoggins had evinced, and abused men in general, taking him for the representative and type, we got round to the subject about which we had been talking when Miss Pole came in; namely, how far, in the present disturbed state of the country, we could venture to accept an invitation which Miss Matty had just received from Mrs Forrester, to come as usual and keep the anniversary of her wedding-day by drinking tea with her at five o'clock, and playing a quiet pool afterwards. Mrs Forrester had said that she asked us with some diffidence, because the roads were, she feared, very unsafe. But she suggested that perhaps one of us would not object to take the sedan, and that the others, by walking briskly, might keep up with the long trot of the chairmen, and so we might all arrive safely at Over Place, a suburb of the town. (No; that is too large an expression: a small cluster of houses separated from Cranford by about two hundred yards of a dark and lonely lane.) There was no doubt but that a similar note was awaiting Miss Pole at home; so her call was a very fortunate affair, as it enabled us to consult together. We would all much rather have declined this invitation; but we felt that it would not be quite kind to Mrs Forrester, who would otherwise be left to a solitary retrospect of her not very happy or fortunate life. Miss Matty and Miss Pole had been visitors on this occasion for many years, and now they gallantly determined to nail their colours to the mast, and to go through Darkness Lane rather than fail in loyalty to their friend.

But when the evening came, Miss Matty (for it was she who was voted into the chair, as she had a cold), before being shut down in the sedan, like jack-in-a-box, implored the chairmen, whatever might befall, not to run away and leave her fastened up there, to be murdered; and even after they had promised, I saw her tighten her features into the stern determination of a martyr, and she gave me a melancholy and ominous shake of the head through the glass. However, we got there safely, only rather out of breath, for it was who could trot hardest through Darkness Lane, and I am afraid poor

Miss Matty was sadly jolted.

Mrs Forrester had made extra preparations, in acknowledgment of our exertion in coming to see her through such dangers. The usual forms of genteel ignorance as to what her servants might send up were all gone through; and harmony and Preference seemed likely to be the order of the evening, but for an interesting conversation that began I don't know how, but which had relation, of course, to the robbers who infested the neighbourhood of Cranford.

Having braved the dangers of Darkness Lane, and thus having a little stock of reputation for courage to fall back upon; and also, I daresay, desirous of proving ourselves superior to men (*videlicet* Mr Hoggins) in the article of candour, we began to relate our individual fears, and the private precautions we each of us took. I owned that my pet apprehension was eyes - eyes looking at me, and watching me, glittering out from some dull, flat, wooden surface; and that if I dared to go up to my looking-glass when I was panic-stricken, I should certainly turn it round, with its back towards me, for fear of seeing eyes behind me looking out of the darkness. I saw Miss Matty nerving herself up for a confession; and at last out it came. She owned that, ever since she had been a girl, she had dreaded being caught by her last leg, just as she was getting into bed, by some one concealed under it. She said, when she was younger and more active, she used to take a flying leap from a distance, and so bring both her legs up safely into bed at once; but that this had always annoyed Deborah, who piqued herself upon getting into bed gracefully, and she had given it up in consequence. But now the old terror would often come over her, especially since Miss Pole's house had been attacked (we had got quite to believe in the fact of the attack having taken place), and yet it was very unpleasant to think of looking under a bed, and seeing a man concealed, with a great, fierce face staring out at you; so she had bethought herself of something - perhaps I had noticed that she had told Martha to buy her a penny ball, such as children play with- and now she rolled this ball under the bed every night: if it came out on the other side, well and good; if not she always took care to have her hand on the bell-rope, and meant to call out John and Harry, just as if she expected men-servants to answer her ring.

We all applauded this ingenious contrivance, and Miss Matty sank back into satisfied silence, with a look at Mrs Forrester as if to ask for*her* private weakness.

Mrs Forrester looked askance at Miss Pole, and tried to change the subject a little by telling us that she had borrowed a boy from one of the neighbouring cottages and promised his parents a hundredweight of coals at Christmas, and his supper every evening, for the loan of him at nights. She had instructed him in his possible duties when he first came; and, finding him sensible, she had given him the Major's sword (the Major was her late husband), and desired him to put it very carefully behind his pillow at night, turning the edge towards the head of the pillow. He was a sharp lad, she was sure; for, spying out the Major's cocked hat, he had said, if he might have that to wear, he was sure he could frighten two Englishmen, or four Frenchmen any day. But she had impressed upon him anew that he was to lose no time in putting on hats or anything else; but, if he heard any noise, he was to run at it with his drawn sword. On my suggesting that some accident might occur from such slaughterous and indiscriminate directions, and that he might rush on Jenny getting up to wash, and have spitted her before he had discovered that she was not a Frenchman, Mrs Forrester said she did not think that that was likely, for he was a very sound sleeper, and generally had to be well shaken or cold-pigged in a morning before they could rouse him. She sometimes thought such dead sleep must be owing to the hearty suppers the poor lad ate, for he was half-starved at home, and she told Jenny to see that he got a good meal at night.

Still this was no confession of Mrs Forrester's peculiar timidity, and we urged her to tell us what she thought would frighten her more than anything. She paused, and stirred the fire, and snuffed the candles, and then she said, in a sounding whisper -

"Ghosts!"

She looked at Miss Pole, as much as to say, she had declared it, and would stand by it. Such a look was a challenge in itself. Miss Pole came down upon her with indigestion, spectral illusions, optical delusions, and a great deal out of Dr Ferrier and Dr Hibbert besides. Miss Matty had rather a leaning to ghosts, as I have mentioned before, and what little she did say was all on Mrs Forrester's side, who, emboldened by sympathy, protested that ghosts were a part of her religion; that surely she, the widow of a major in the army, knew what to be frightened at, and what not; in short, I never saw Mrs Forrester so warm either before or since, for she was a gentle, meek, enduring old lady in most things. Not all the elder-wine that ever was mulled could this night wash out the remembrance of this difference between Miss Pole and her hostess. Indeed, when the elder-wine was brought in, it gave rise to a new burst of discussion; for Jenny, the little maiden who staggered under the tray, had to give evidence of having seen a ghost with her own eyes, not so many nights ago, in Darkness Lane, the very lane we were to go through on our way home.

In spite of the uncomfortable feeling which this last consideration gave me, I could not help being amused at Jenny's position, which was exceedingly like that of a witness being examined and cross-examined by two counsel who are not at all scrupulous about asking leading questions. The conclusion I arrived at was, that Jenny had certainly seen something beyond what a fit of indigestion would have caused. A lady all in white, and without her head, was what she deposed and adhered to, supported by a consciousness of the secret sympathy of her mistress under the withering scorn with which Miss Pole regarded her. And not only she, but many others, had seen this headless lady, who sat by the roadside wringing her hands as in deep grief. Mrs Forrester looked at us from time to time with an air of conscious triumph; but then she had not to pass through Darkness Lane before she could bury herself beneath her own familiar bed-clothes.

We preserved a discreet silence as to the headless lady while we were putting on our things to go home, for there was no knowing how near the ghostly head and ears might be, or what spiritual connection they might be keeping up with the unhappy body in Darkness Lane; and, therefore, even Miss Pole felt that it was as well not to speak lightly on such subjects, for fear of vexing or insulting that woebegone trunk. At least, so I conjecture; for, instead of the busy clatter usual in the operation, we tied on our cloaks as sadly as mutes at a funeral. Miss Matty drew the curtains round the windows of the chair to shut out disagreeable sights, and the men (either because they were in spirits that their labours were so nearly ended, or because they were going down hill), set off at such a round and merry pace, that it was all Miss Pole and I could do to keep up with them. She had breath for nothing beyond an imploring "Don't leave me!"uttered as she clutched my arm so tightly that I could not have quitted her, ghost or no ghost. What a relief it was when the men, weary of their burden and their quick trot, stopped just where Headingley Causeway branches off from Darkness Lane! Miss Pole unloosed me and caught at one of the men -

"Could not you - could not you take Miss Matty round by Headingley Causeway? - the pavement in Darkness Lane jolts so, and she is not very strong."

A smothered voice was heard from the inside of the chair -

"Oh! pray go on! What is the matter? What is the matter? I will give you sixpence more to go on very fast; pray don't stop here."

"And I'll give you a shilling," said Miss Pole, with tremulous dignity, "if you'll go by Headingley Causeway."

The two men grunted acquiescence and took up the chair, and went along the causeway, which certainly answered Miss Pole's kind purpose of saving Miss Matty's bones; for it was covered with soft, thick mud, and even a fall there would have been easy till the getting-up came, when there might have been some difficulty in extrication.

CHAPTER XI - SAMUEL BROWN

The next morning I met Lady Glenmire and Miss Pole setting out on a long walk to find some old woman who was famous in the neighbourhood for her skill in knitting woollen stockings. Miss Pole said to me, with a smile half-kindly and half-contemptuous upon her countenance,"I have been just telling Lady Glenmire of our poor friend Mrs Forrester, and her terror of ghosts. It comes from living so much alone, and listening to the bug-a-boo stories of that Jenny of hers." She was so calm and so much above superstitious fears herself that I was almost ashamed to say how glad I had been of her Headingley Causeway proposition the night before, and turned off the conversation to something else.

In the afternoon Miss Pole called on Miss Matty to tell her of the adventure - the real adventure they had met with on their morning's walk. They had been perplexed about the exact path which they were to take across the fields in order to find the knitting old woman, and had stopped to inquire at a little wayside public-house, standing on the high road to London, about three miles from Cranford. The good woman had asked them to sit down and rest themselves while she fetched her husband, who could direct them better than she could; and, while they were sitting in the sanded parlour, a little girl came in. They thought that she belonged to the landlady, and began some trifling conversation with her; but, on Mrs Roberts's return, she told them that the little thing was the only child of a couple who were staying in the house. And then she began a long story, out of which Lady Glenmire and Miss Pole could only gather one or two decided facts, which were that, about six weeks ago, a light spring-cart had broken down just before their door, in which there were two men, one woman, and this child. One of the men was seriously hurt - no bones broken, only "shaken,"the landlady called it; but he had probably sustained some severe internal injury, for he had languished in their house ever since, attended by his wife, the mother of this little girl. Miss Pole had asked what he was, what he looked like. And Mrs Roberts had made answer that he was not like a gentleman, nor yet like a common person; if it had not been that he and his wife were such decent, quiet people, she could almost have thought he was a mountebank, or something of that kind, for they had a great box in the cart, full of she did not know what. She had helped to unpack it, and take out their linen and clothes, when the other man - his twin-brother, she believed he was - had gone off with the horse and cart.

Miss Pole had begun to have her suspicions at this point, and expressed her idea that it was rather strange that the box and cart and horse and all should have disappeared; but good Mrs Roberts seemed to have become quite indignant at Miss Pole's implied suggestion; in fact, Miss Pole said she was as angry as if Miss Pole had told her that she herself was a swindler. As the best way of convincing the ladies, she bethought her of begging them to see the wife; and, as Miss Pole said, there was no doubting the honest, worn, bronzed face of the woman, who at the first tender word from Lady Glenmire, burst into tears, which she was too weak to check until some word from the landlady made her swallow down her sobs, in order that she might testify to the Christian kindness shown by Mr and Mrs Roberts. Miss Pole came round with a swing to as vehement a belief in the sorrowful tale as she had been sceptical before; and, as a proof of this, her energy in the poor sufferer's behalf was nothing daunted when she found out that he, and no other, was our Signor Brunoni, to whom all Cranford had been attributing all manner of evil this six weeks past! Yes! his wife said his proper name was Samuel Brown - "Sam," she called him - but to the last we preferred calling him "the Signor"; it sounded so much better.

The end of their conversation with the Signora Brunoni was that it was agreed that he should be placed under medical advice, and for any expense incurred in procuring this Lady Glenmire promised to hold herself responsible, and had accordingly gone to Mr Hoggins to beg him to ride over to the "Rising Sun" that very afternoon, and examine into the signor's real state; and, as Miss Pole said, if it was desirable to remove him to Cranford to be more immediately under Mr Hoggins's eye, she would undertake to see for lodgings and arrange about the rent. Mrs Roberts had been as kind as could be all throughout, but it was evident that their long residence there had been a slight inconvenience.

Before Miss Pole left us, Miss Matty and I were as full of the morning's adventure as she was. We talked about it all the evening, turning it in every possible light, and we went to bed anxious for the morning, when we should surely hear from someone what Mr Hoggins thought and recommended; for, as Miss Matty observed, though Mr Hoggins did say "Jack's up," "a fig for his heels," and called Preference "Pref." she believed he was a very worthy man and a very clever surgeon. Indeed, we were rather proud of our doctor at Cranford, as a doctor. We often wished, when we heard of Queen Adelaide or the Duke of Wellington being ill, that they would send for Mr Hoggins; but, on consideration, we were rather glad they did not, for, if we were ailing, what should we do if Mr Hoggins had been appointed physician-in-ordinary to the Royal Family? As a surgeon we were proud of him; but as a man - or rather, I should say, as a gentleman - we could only shake our heads over his name and himself, and wished that he had read Lord Chesterfield's Letters in the days when his manners were susceptible of improvement. Nevertheless, we all regarded his dictum in the signor's case as infallible, and when he said that with care and attention he might rally, we had no more fear for him.

But, although we had no more fear, everybody did as much as if there was great cause for anxiety - as indeed there was until Mr Hoggins took charge of him. Miss Pole looked out clean and comfortable, if homely, lodgings; Miss Matty sent the sedan-chair for him, and Martha and I aired it well before it left Cranford by holding a warming-pan full of red-hot coals in it, and then shutting it up close, smoke and all, until the time when he should get into it at the "Rising Sun." Lady Glenmire undertook the medical department under Mr Hoggins's directions, and rummaged up all Mrs Jamieson's medicine glasses, and spoons, and bed-tables, in a free-and-easy way, that made Miss Matty feel a little anxious as to what that lady and Mr Mulliner might say, if they knew. Mrs Forrester made some of the bread-jelly, for which she was so famous, to have ready as a refreshment in the lodgings when he should arrive. A present of this bread-jelly was the highest mark of favour dear Mrs Forrester could confer. Miss Pole had once asked her for the receipt, but she had met with a very decided rebuff; that lady told her that she could not part with it to any one during her life, and that after her death it was bequeathed, as her executors would find, to Miss Matty. What Miss Matty, or, as Mrs Forrester called her (remembering the clause in her will and the dignity of the occasion), Miss Matilda Jenkyns - might choose to do with the receipt when it came into her possession - whether to make it public, or to hand it down as an heirloom - she did not know, nor would she dictate. And a mould of this admirable, digestible, unique bread-jelly was sent by Mrs Forrester to our poor sick conjuror. Who says that the aristocracy are proud? Here was a lady by birth a Tyrrell, and descended from the great Sir Walter that shot King Rufus, and in whose veins ran the blood of him who murdered the little princes in the Tower, going every day to see what dainty dishes she could prepare for Samuel Brown, a mountebank! But, indeed, it was wonderful to see what kind feelings were called out by this poor man's coming amongst us. And also wonderful to see how the great Cranford panic, which had been occasioned by his first coming in his Turkish dress, melted away into thin air on his second coming - pale and feeble, and with his heavy, filmy eyes, that only brightened a very little when they fell upon the countenance of his faithful wife, or their pale and sorrowful little girl.

Somehow we all forgot to be afraid. I daresay it was that finding out that he, who had first excited our love of the marvellous by his unprecedented arts, had not sufficient every-day gifts to manage a shying horse, made us feel as if we were ourselves again. Miss Pole came with her little basket at all hours of the evening, as if her lonely house and the unfrequented road to it had never been infested by that "murderous gang"; Mrs Forrester said she thought that neither Jenny nor she need mind the headless lady who wept and wailed in Darkness Lane, for surely the power was never given to such beings to harm those who went about to try to do what little good was in their power, to which Jenny tremblingly assented; but the mistress's theory had little effect on the maid's practice until she had sewn two pieces of red flannel in the shape of a cross on her inner garment.

I found Miss Matty covering her penny ball - the ball that she used to roll under her bed - with gay-coloured worsted in rainbow stripes.

"My dear," said she, "my heart is sad for that little careworn child. Although her father is a conjuror, she looks as if she had never had a good game of play in her life. I used to make very pretty balls in this way when I was a girl, and I thought I would try if I could not make this one smart and take it to Phoebe this afternoon. I think 'the gang' must have left the neighbourhood, for one does not hear any more of their violence and robbery now."

We were all of us far too full of the signor's precarious state to talk either about robbers or ghosts. Indeed, Lady Glenmire said she never had heard of any actual robberies, except that two little boys had stolen some apples from Farmer Benson's orchard, and that some eggs had been missed on a market-day off Widow Hayward's stall. But that was expecting too much of us; we could not acknowledge that we had only had this small foundation for all our panic. Miss Pole drew herself up at this remark of Lady Glenmire's, and said "that she wished she could agree with her as to the very small reason we had had for alarm, but with the recollection of a man disguised as a woman who had endeavoured to force himself into her house while his confederates waited outside; with the knowledge gained from Lady Glenmire herself, of the footprints seen on Mrs Jamieson's flower borders; with the fact before her of the audacious robbery committed on Mr Hoggins at his own door" - But here Lady Glenmire broke in with a very strong expression of doubt as to whether this last story was not an entire fabrication founded upon the theft of a cat; she grew so red while she was saying all this that I was not surprised at Miss Pole's manner of bridling up, and I am certain, if Lady Glenmire had not been "her ladyship," we should have had a more emphatic contradiction than the "Well, to be sure!" and similar fragmentary ejaculations, which were all that she ventured upon in my lady's presence. But when she was gone Miss Pole began a long congratulation to Miss Matty that so far they had escaped marriage, which she noticed always made people credulous to the last degree; indeed, she thought it argued great natural credulity in a woman if she could not keep herself from being married; and in what Lady Glenmire had said about Mr Hoggins's robbery we had a specimen of what people came to if they gave way to such a weakness; evidently Lady Glenmire would swallow anything if she could believe the poor vamped-up story about a neck of mutton and a pussy with which he had tried to impose on Miss Pole, only she had always been on her guard against believing too much of what men said.

We were thankful, as Miss Pole desired us to be, that we had never been married; but I think, of the two, we were even more thankful that the robbers had left Cranford; at least I judge so from a speech of Miss Matty's that evening, as we sat over the fire, in which she evidently looked upon a husband as a great protector against thieves, burglars, and ghosts; and said that she did not think that she should dare to be always warning young people against matrimony, as Miss Pole did continually; to be sure, marriage was a risk, as she saw, now she had had some experience; but she remembered the time when she had looked forward to being married as much as any one.

"Not to any particular person, my dear," said she, hastily checking herself up, as if she were afraid of having admitted too much;"only the old story, you know, of ladies always saying, '*When*I marry,' and gentlemen, '*If*I marry.'" It was a joke spoken in rather a sad tone, and I doubt if either of us smiled; but I could not see Miss Matty's face by the flickering fire-light. In a little while she continued -

"But, after all, I have not told you the truth. It is so long ago, and no one ever knew how much I thought of it at the time, unless, indeed, my dear mother guessed; but I may say that there was a time when I did not think I should have been only Miss Matty Jenkyns all my life; for even if I did meet with any one who wished to marry me now (and, as Miss Pole says, one is never too safe), I could not take him - I hope he would not take it too much to heart, but I could*not* take him - or any one but the person I once thought I should be married to; and he is dead and gone, and he never knew how it all came about that I said 'No,' when I had thought many and many a time - Well, it's no matter what I thought. God ordains it all, and I am very happy, my dear. No one has such kind friends as I," continued she, taking my hand and holding it in hers.

If I had never known of Mr Holbrook, I could have said something in this pause, but as I had, I could not think of anything that would come in naturally, and so we both kept silence for a little time.

"My father once made us," she began, "keep a diary, in two columns; on one side we were to put down in the morning what we thought would be the course and events of the coming day, and at night we were to put down on the other side what really had happened. It would be to some people rather a sad way of telling their lives,"(a tear dropped upon my hand at these words) - "I don't mean that mine has been sad, only so very different to what I expected. I remember, one winter's evening, sitting over our bedroom fire with Deborah - I remember it as if it were yesterday - and we were planning our future lives, both of us were planning, though only she talked about it. She said she should like to marry an archdeacon, and write his charges; and you know, my dear, she never was married, and, for aught I know, she never spoke to an unmarried archdeacon in her life. I never was ambitious, nor could I have written charges, but I thought I could manage a house (my mother used to call me her right hand), and I was always so fond of little children - the shyest babies would stretch out their little arms to come to me; when I was a girl, I was half my leisure time nursing in the neighbouring cottages; but I don't know how it was, when I grew sad and grave - which I did a year or two after this time - the little things drew back from me, and I am afraid I lost the knack, though I am just as fond of children as ever, and have a strange yearning at my heart whenever I see a mother with her baby in her arms. Nay, my dear" (and by a sudden blaze which sprang up from a fall of the unstirred coals, I saw that her eyes were full of tears - gazing intently on some vision of what might have been),"do you know I dream sometimes that I have a little child - always the same - a little girl of about two years old; she never grows older, though I have dreamt about her for many years. I don't think I ever dream of any words or sound she makes; she is very noiseless and still, but she comes to me when she is very sorry or very glad, and I have wakened with the clasp of her dear little arms round my neck. Only last night - perhaps because I had gone to sleep thinking of this ball for Phoebe - my little darling came in my dream, and put up her mouth to be kissed, just as I have seen real babies do to real mothers before going to bed. But all this is nonsense, dear! only don't be frightened by Miss Pole from being married. I can fancy it may be a very happy state, and a little credulity helps one on through life very smoothly - better than always doubting and doubting and seeing difficulties and disagreeables in everything."

If I had been inclined to be daunted from matrimony, it would not have been Miss Pole to do it; it would have been the lot of poor Signor Brunoni and his wife. And yet again, it was an encouragement to see how, through all their cares and sorrows, they thought of each other and not of themselves; and how keen were their joys, if they only passed through each other, or through the little Phoebe.

The signora told me, one day, a good deal about their lives up to this period. It began by my asking her whether Miss Pole's story of the twin-brothers were true; it sounded so wonderful a likeness, that I should have had my doubts, if Miss Pole had not been unmarried. But the signora, or (as we found out she preferred to be called) Mrs Brown, said it was quite true; that her brother-in-law was by many taken for her husband, which was of great assistance to them in their profession;"though," she continued, "how people can mistake Thomas for the real Signor Brunoni, I can't conceive; but he says they do; so I suppose I must believe him. Not but what he is a very good man; I am sure I don't know how we should have paid our bill at the 'Rising Sun' but for the money he sends; but people must know very little about art if they can take him for my husband. Why, Miss, in the ball trick, where my husband spreads his fingers wide, and throws out his little finger with quite an air and a grace, Thomas just clumps up his hand like a fist, and might have ever so many balls hidden in it. Besides, he has never been in India, and knows nothing of the proper sit of a turban."

"Have you been in India?" said I, rather astonished.

"Oh, yes! many a year, ma'am. Sam was a sergeant in the 31st; and when the regiment was ordered to India, I drew a lot to go, and I was more thankful than I can tell; for it seemed as if it would only be a slow death to me to part from my husband. But, indeed, ma'am, if I had known all, I don't know whether I would not rather have died there and then than gone through what I have done since. To be sure, I've been able to comfort Sam, and to be with him; but, ma'am, I've lost six children,"said she, looking up at me with those strange eyes that I've never noticed but in mothers of dead children - with a kind of wild look in them, as if seeking for what they never more might find. "Yes! Six children died off, like little buds nipped untimely, in that cruel India. I thought, as each died, I never could - I never would - love a child again; and when the next came, it had not only its own love, but the deeper love that came from the thoughts of its little dead brothers and sisters. And when Phoebe was coming, I said to my husband, 'Sam, when the child is born, and I am strong, I shall leave you; it will cut my heart cruel; but if this baby dies too, I shall go mad; the madness is in me now; but if you let me go down to Calcutta, carrying my baby step by step, it will, maybe, work itself off; and I will save, and I will hoard, and I will beg - and I will die, to get a passage home to England, where our baby may live?' God bless him! he said I might go; and he saved up his pay, and I saved every pice I could get for washing or any way; and when Phoebe came, and I grew strong again, I set off. It was very lonely; through the thick forests, dark again with their heavy trees - along by the river's side (but I had been brought up near the Avon in Warwickshire, so that flowing noise sounded like home) - from station to station, from Indian village to village, I went along, carrying my child. I had seen one of the officer's ladies with a little picture, ma'am - done by a Catholic foreigner, ma'am - of the Virgin and the little Saviour, ma'am. She had him on her arm, and her form was softly curled round him, and their cheeks touched. Well, when I went to bid good-bye to this lady, for whom I had washed, she cried sadly; for she, too, had lost her children, but she had not another to save, like me; and I was bold enough to ask her would she give me that print. And she cried the more, and said her children were with that little blessed Jesus; and gave it me, and told me that she had heard it had been painted on the bottom of a cask, which made it have that round shape. And when my body was very weary, and my heart was sick (for there were times when I misdoubted if I could ever reach my home, and there were times when I thought of my husband, and one time when I thought my baby was dying), I took out that picture and looked at it, till I could have thought the mother spoke to me, and comforted me. And the natives were very kind. We could not understand one another; but they saw my baby on my breast, and they came out to me, and brought me rice and milk, and sometimes flowers - I have got some of the flowers dried. Then, the next morning, I was so tired; and they wanted me to stay with them - I could tell that - and tried to frighten me from going into the deep woods, which, indeed, looked very strange and dark; but it seemed to me as if Death was following me to take my baby away from me; and as if I must go on, and on - and I thought how God had cared for mothers ever since the world was made, and would care for me; so I bade them good-bye, and set off afresh. And once when my baby was ill, and both she and I needed rest, He led me to a place where I found a kind Englishman lived, right in the midst of the natives."

"And you reached Calcutta safely at last?"

"Yes, safely! Oh! when I knew I had only two days'journey more before me, I could not help it, ma'am - it might be idolatry, I cannot tell - but I was near one of the native temples, and I went into it with my baby to thank God for His great mercy; for it seemed to me that where others had prayed before to their God, in their joy or in their agony, was of itself a sacred place. And I got as servant to an invalid lady, who grew quite fond of my baby aboard-ship; and, in two years' time, Sam earned his discharge, and came home to me, and to our child. Then he had to fix on a trade; but he knew of none; and once, once upon a time, he had learnt some tricks from an Indian juggler; so he set up conjuring, and it answered so well that he took Thomas to help him - as his man, you know, not as another conjuror, though Thomas has set it up now on his own hook. But it has been a great help to us that likeness between the twins, and made a good many tricks go off well that they made up together. And Thomas is a good brother, only he has not the fine carriage of my husband, so that I can't think how he can be taken for Signor Brunoni himself, as he says he is."

"Poor little Phoebe!" said I, my thoughts going back to the baby she carried all those hundred miles.

"Ah! you may say so! I never thought I should have reared her, though, when she fell ill at Chunderabaddad; but that good, kind Aga Jenkyns took us in, which I believe was the very saving of her."

"Jenkyns!" said I.

"Yes, Jenkyns. I shall think all people of that name are kind; for here is that nice old lady who comes every day to take Phoebe a walk!"

But an idea had flashed through my head; could the Aga Jenkyns be the lost Peter? True he was reported by many to be dead. But, equally true, some had said that he had arrived at the dignity of Great Lama of Thibet. Miss Matty thought he was alive. I would make further inquiry.

CHAPTER XII - ENGAGED TO BE MARRIED

Was the "poor Peter" of Cranford the Aga Jenkyns of Chunderabaddad, or was he not? As somebody says, that was the question.

In my own home, whenever people had nothing else to do, they blamed me for want of discretion. Indiscretion was my bug-bear fault. Everybody has a bug-bear fault, a sort of standing characteristic - a *pièce de résistance* for their friends to cut at; and in general they cut and come again. I was tired of being called indiscreet and incautious; and I determined for once to prove myself a model of prudence and wisdom. I would not even hint my suspicions respecting the Aga. I would collect evidence and carry it home to lay before my father, as the family friend of the two Miss Jenkynses.

In my search after facts, I was often reminded of a description my father had once given of a ladies' committee that he had had to preside over. He said he could not help thinking of a passage in Dickens, which spoke of a chorus in which every man took the tune he knew best, and sang it to his own satisfaction. So, at this charitable committee, every lady took the subject uppermost in her mind, and talked about it to her own great contentment, but not much to the advancement of the subject they had met to discuss. But even that committee could have been nothing to the Cranford ladies when I attempted to gain some clear and definite information as to poor Peter's height, appearance, and when and where he was seen and heard of last. For instance, I remember asking Miss Pole (and I thought the question was very opportune, for I put it when I met her at a call at Mrs Forrester's, and both the ladies had known Peter, and I imagined that they might refresh each other's memories) - I asked Miss Pole what was the very last thing they had ever heard about him; and then she named the absurd report to which I have alluded, about his having been elected Great Lama of Thibet; and this was a signal for each lady to go off on her separate idea. Mrs Forrester's start was made on the veiled prophet in Lalla Rookh - whether I thought he was meant for the Great Lama, though Peter was not so ugly, indeed rather handsome, if he had not been freckled. I was thankful to see her double upon Peter; but, in a moment, the delusive lady was off upon Rowland's Kalydor, and the merits of cosmetics and hair oils in general, and holding forth so fluently that I turned to listen to Miss Pole, who (through the llamas, the beasts of burden) had got to Peruvian bonds, and the share market, and her poor opinion of joint-stock banks in general, and of that one in particular in which Miss Matty's money was invested. In vain I put in "When was it - in what year was it that you heard that Mr Peter was the Great Lama?" They only joined issue to dispute whether llamas were carnivorous animals or not; in which dispute they were not quite on fair grounds, as Mrs Forrester (after they had grown warm and cool again) acknowledged that she always confused carnivorous and graminivorous together, just as she did horizontal and perpendicular; but then she apologised for it very prettily, by saying that in her day the only use people made of four-syllabled words was to teach how they should be spelt.

The only fact I gained from this conversation was that certainly Peter had last been heard of in India, "or that neighbourhood";and that this scanty intelligence of his whereabouts had reached Cranford in the year when Miss Pole had brought her Indian muslin gown, long since worn out (we washed it and mended it, and traced its decline and fall into a window-blind before we could go on); and in a year when Wombwell came to Cranford, because Miss Matty had wanted to see an elephant in order that she might the better imagine Peter riding on one; and had seen a boa-constrictor too, which was more than she wished to imagine in her fancy-pictures of Peter's locality; and in a year when Miss Jenkyns had learnt some piece of poetry off by heart, and used to say, at all the Cranford parties, how Peter was "surveying mankind from China to Peru," which everybody had thought very grand, and rather appropriate, because India was between China and Peru, if you took care to turn the globe to the left instead of the right.

I suppose all these inquiries of mine, and the consequent curiosity excited in the minds of my friends, made us blind and deaf to what was going on around us. It seemed to me as if the sun rose and shone, and as if the rain rained on Cranford, just as usual, and I did not notice any sign of the times that could be considered as a prognostic of any uncommon event; and, to the best of my belief, not only Miss Matty and Mrs Forrester, but even Miss Pole herself, whom we looked upon as a kind of prophetess, from the knack she had of foreseeing things before they came to pass - although she did not like to disturb her friends by telling them her foreknowledge - even Miss Pole herself was breathless with astonishment when she came to tell us of the astounding piece of news. But I must recover myself; the contemplation of it, even at this distance of time, has taken away my breath and my grammar, and unless I subdue my emotion, my spelling will go too.

We were sitting - Miss Matty and I - much as usual, she in the blue chintz easy-chair, with her back to the light, and her knitting in her hand, I reading aloud the *St James's Chronicle*. A few minutes more, and we should have gone to make the little alterations in dress usual before calling-time (twelve o'clock) in Cranford. I remember the scene and the date well. We had been talking of the signor's rapid recovery since the warmer weather had set in, and praising Mr Hoggins's skill, and lamenting his want of refinement and manner (it seems a curious coincidence that this should have been our subject, but so it was), when a knock was heard - a caller's knock - three distinct taps - and we were flying (that is to say, Miss Matty could not walk very fast, having had a touch of rheumatism) to our rooms, to change cap and collars, when Miss Pole arrested us by calling out, as she came up the stairs, "Don't go - I can't wait - it is not twelve, I know - but never mind your dress - I must speak to you." We did our best to look as if it was not we who had made the hurried movement, the sound of which she had heard; for, of course, we did not like to have it supposed that we had any old clothes that it was convenient to wear out in the "sanctuary of home," as Miss Jenkyns once prettily called the back parlour, where she was tying up preserves. So we threw our gentility with double force into our manners, and very genteel we were for two minutes while Miss Pole recovered breath, and excited our curiosity strongly by lifting up her hands in amazement, and bringing them down in silence, as if what she had to say was too big for words, and could only be expressed by pantomime.

"What do you think, Miss Matty? What *do* you think? Lady Glenmire is to marry - is to be married, I mean - Lady Glenmire - Mr Hoggins - Mr Hoggins is going to marry Lady Glenmire!"

"Marry!" said we. "Marry! Madness!"

"Marry!" said Miss Pole, with the decision that belonged to her character. "*I* said marry! as you do; and I also said, 'What a fool my lady is going to make of herself!' I could have said 'Madness!' but I controlled myself, for it was in a public shop that I heard of it. Where feminine delicacy is gone to, I don't know! You and I, Miss Matty, would have been ashamed to have known that our marriage was spoken of in a grocer's shop, in the hearing of shopmen!"

"But," said Miss Matty, sighing as one recovering from a blow, "perhaps it is not true. Perhaps we are doing her injustice."

"No," said Miss Pole. "I have taken care to ascertain that. I went straight to Mrs Fitz-Adam, to borrow a cookery-book which I knew she had; and I introduced my congratulations *à propos* of the difficulty gentlemen must have in house-keeping; and Mrs Fitz-Adam bridled up, and said that she believed it was true, though how and where I could have heard it she did not know. She said her brother and Lady Glenmire had come to an understanding at last. 'Understanding!' such a coarse word! But my lady will have to come down to many a want of refinement. I have reason to believe Mr Hoggins sups on bread-and-cheese and beer every night.

"Marry!" said Miss Matty once again. "Well! I never thought of it. Two people that we know going to be married. It's coming very near!"

"So near that my heart stopped beating when I heard of it, while you might have counted twelve," said Miss Pole.

"One does not know whose turn may come next. Here, in Cranford, poor Lady Glenmire might have thought herself safe," said Miss Matty, with a gentle pity in her tones.

"Bah!" said Miss Pole, with a toss of her head. "Don't you remember poor dear Captain Brown's song 'Tibbie Fowler,' and the line -

'Set her on the Tintock tap,
The wind will blaw a man till her.'"

"That was because 'Tibbie Fowler' was rich, I think."

"Well! there was a kind of attraction about Lady Glenmire that I, for one, should be ashamed to have."

I put in my wonder. "But how can she have fancied Mr Hoggins? I am not surprised that Mr Hoggins has liked her."

"Oh! I don't know. Mr Hoggins is rich, and very pleasant-looking," said Miss Matty, "and very good-tempered and kind-hearted."

"She has married for an establishment, that's it. I suppose she takes the surgery with it," said Miss Pole, with a little dry laugh at her own joke. But, like many people who think they have made a severe and sarcastic speech, which yet is clever of its kind, she began to relax in her grimness from the moment when she made this allusion to the surgery; and we turned to speculate on the way in which Mrs Jamieson would receive the news. The person whom she had left in charge of her house to keep off followers from her maids to set up a follower of her own! And that follower a man whom Mrs Jamieson had tabooed as vulgar, and inadmissible to Cranford society, not merely on account of his name, but because of his voice, his complexion, his boots, smelling of the stable, and himself, smelling of drugs. Had he ever been to see Lady Glenmire at Mrs Jamieson's? Chloride of lime would not purify the house in its owner's estimation if he had. Or had their interviews been confined to the occasional meetings in the chamber of the poor sick conjuror, to whom, with all our sense of the *mésalliance*, we could not help allowing that they had both been exceedingly kind? And now it turned out that a servant of Mrs Jamieson's had been ill, and Mr Hoggins had been attending her for some weeks. So the wolf had got into the fold, and now he was carrying off the shepherdess. What would Mrs Jamieson say? We looked into the darkness of futurity as a child gazes after a rocket up in the cloudy sky, full of wondering expectation of the rattle, the discharge, and the brilliant shower of sparks and light. Then we brought ourselves down to earth and the present time by questioning each other (being all equally ignorant, and all equally without the slightest data to build any conclusions upon) as to when IT would take place? Where? How much a year Mr Hoggins had? Whether she would drop her title? And how Martha and the other correct servants in Cranford would ever be brought to announce a married couple as Lady Glenmire and Mr Hoggins? But would they be visited? Would Mrs Jamieson let us? Or must we choose between the Honourable Mrs Jamieson and the degraded Lady Glenmire? We all liked Lady Glenmire the best. She was bright, and kind, and sociable, and agreeable; and Mrs Jamieson was dull, and inert, and pompous, and tiresome. But we had acknowledged the sway of the latter so long, that it seemed like a kind of disloyalty now even to meditate disobedience to the prohibition we anticipated.

Mrs Forrester surprised us in our darned caps and patched collars; and we forgot all about them in our eagerness to see how she would bear the information, which we honourably left to Miss Pole, to impart, although, if we had been inclined to take unfair advantage, we might have rushed in ourselves, for she had a most out-of-place fit of coughing for five minutes after Mrs Forrester entered the room. I shall never forget the imploring expression of her eyes, as she looked at us over her pocket-handkerchief. They said, as plain as words could speak, "Don't let Nature deprive me of the treasure which is mine, although for a time I can make no use of it." And we did not.

Mrs Forrester's surprise was equal to ours; and her sense of injury rather greater, because she had to feel for her Order, and saw more fully than we could do how such conduct brought stains on the aristocracy.

When she and Miss Pole left us we endeavoured to subside into calmness; but Miss Matty was really upset by the intelligence she had heard. She reckoned it up, and it was more than fifteen years since she had heard of any of her acquaintance going to be married, with the one exception of Miss Jessie Brown; and, as she said, it gave her quite a shock, and made her feel as if she could not think what would happen next.

I don't know whether it is a fancy of mine, or a real fact, but I have noticed that, just after the announcement of an engagement in any set, the unmarried ladies in that set flutter out in an unusual gaiety and newness of dress, as much as to say, in a tacit and unconscious manner, "We also are spinsters." Miss Matty and Miss Pole talked and thought more about bonnets, gowns, caps, and shawls, during the fortnight that succeeded this call, than I had known them do for years before. But it might be the spring weather, for it was a warm and pleasant March; and merinoes and beavers, and woollen materials of all sorts were but ungracious receptacles of the bright sun's glancing rays. It had not been Lady Glenmire's dress that had won Mr Hoggins's heart, for she went about on her errands of kindness more shabby than ever. Although in the hurried glimpses I caught of her at church or elsewhere she appeared rather to shun meeting any of her friends, her face seemed to have almost something of the flush of youth in it; her lips looked redder and more trembling full than in their old compressed state, and her eyes dwelt on all things with a lingering light, as if she was learning to love Cranford and its belongings. Mr Hoggins looked broad and radiant, and creaked up the middle aisle at church in a brand-new pair of top-boots - an audible, as well as visible, sign of his purposed change of state; for the tradition went, that the boots he had worn till now were the identical pair in which he first set out on his rounds in Cranford twenty-five years ago; only they had been new-pieced, high and low, top and bottom, heel and sole, black leather and brown leather, more times than any one could tell.

None of the ladies in Cranford chose to sanction the marriage by congratulating either of the parties. We wished to ignore the whole affair until our liege lady, Mrs Jamieson, returned. Till she came back to give us our cue, we felt that it would be better to consider the engagement in the same light as the Queen of Spain's legs - facts which certainly existed, but the less said about the better. This restraint upon our tongues - for you see if we did not speak about it to any of the parties concerned, how could we get answers to the questions that we longed to ask? - was beginning to be irksome, and our idea of the dignity of silence was paling before our curiosity, when another direction was given to our thoughts, by an announcement on the part of the principal shopkeeper of Cranford, who ranged the trades from grocer and cheesemonger to man-milliner, as occasion required, that the spring fashions were arrived, and would be exhibited on the following Tuesday at his rooms in High Street. Now Miss Matty had been only waiting for this before buying herself a new silk gown. I had offered, it is true, to send to Drumble for patterns, but she had rejected my proposal, gently implying that she had not forgotten her disappointment about the sea-green turban. I was thankful that I was on the spot now, to counteract the dazzling fascination of any yellow or scarlet silk.

I must say a word or two here about myself. I have spoken of my father's old friendship for the Jenkyns family; indeed, I am not sure if there was not some distant relationship. He had willingly allowed me to remain all the winter at Cranford, in consideration of a letter which Miss Matty had written to him about the time of the panic, in which I suspect she had exaggerated my powers and my bravery as a defender of the house. But now that the days were longer and more cheerful, he was beginning to urge the necessity of my return; and I only delayed in a sort of odd forlorn hope that if I could obtain any clear information, I might make the account given by the signora of the Aga Jenkyns tally with that of "poor Peter," his appearance and disappearance, which I had winnowed out of the conversation of Miss Pole and Mrs Forrester.

CHAPTER XIII - STOPPED PAYMENT

The very Tuesday morning on which Mr Johnson was going to show the fashions, the post-woman brought two letters to the house. I say the post-woman, but I should say the postman's wife. He was a lame shoemaker, a very clean, honest man, much respected in the town; but he never brought the letters round except on unusual occasions, such as Christmas Day or Good Friday; and on those days the letters, which should have been delivered at eight in the morning, did not make their appearance until two or three in the afternoon, for every one liked poor Thomas, and gave him a welcome on these festive occasions. He used to say, "He was welly stawed wi' eating, for there were three or four houses where nowt would serve 'em but he must share in their breakfast;" and by the time he had done his last breakfast, he came to some other friend who was beginning dinner; but come what might in the way of temptation, Tom was always sober, civil, and smiling; and, as Miss Jenkyns used to say, it was a lesson in patience, that she doubted not would call out that precious quality in some minds, where, but for Thomas, it might have lain dormant and undiscovered. Patience was certainly very dormant in Miss Jenkyns's mind. She was always expecting letters, and always drumming on the table till the post-woman had called or gone past. On Christmas Day and Good Friday she drummed from breakfast till church, from church-time till two o'clock - unless when the fire wanted stirring, when she invariably knocked down the fire-irons, and scolded Miss Matty for it. But equally certain was the hearty welcome and the good dinner for Thomas; Miss Jenkyns standing over him like a bold dragoon, questioning him as to his children - what they were doing - what school they went to; upbraiding him if another was likely to make its appearance, but sending even the little babies the shilling and the mince-pie which was her gift to all the children, with half-a-crown in addition for both father and mother. The post was not half of so much consequence to dear Miss Matty; but not for the world would she have diminished Thomas's welcome and his dole, though I could see that she felt rather shy over the ceremony, which had been regarded by Miss Jenkyns as a glorious opportunity for giving advice and benefiting her fellow-creatures. Miss Matty would steal the money all in a lump into his hand, as if she were ashamed of herself. Miss Jenkyns gave him each individual coin separate, with a "There! that's for yourself; that's for Jenny," etc. Miss Matty would even beckon Martha out of the kitchen while he ate his food: and once, to my knowledge, winked at its rapid disappearance into a blue cotton pocket-handkerchief. Miss Jenkyns almost scolded him if he did not leave a clean plate, however heaped it might have been, and gave an injunction with every mouthful.

I have wandered a long way from the two letters that awaited us on the breakfast-table that Tuesday morning. Mine was from my father. Miss Matty's was printed. My father's was just a man's letter; I mean it was very dull, and gave no information beyond that he was well, that they had had a good deal of rain, that trade was very stagnant, and there were many disagreeable rumours afloat. He then asked me if I knew whether Miss Matty still retained her shares in the Town and County Bank, as there were very unpleasant reports about it; though nothing more than he had always foreseen, and had prophesied to Miss Jenkyns years ago, when she would invest their little property in it - the only unwise step that clever woman had ever taken, to his knowledge (the only time she ever acted against his advice, I knew). However, if anything had gone wrong, of course I was not to think of leaving Miss Matty while I could be of any use, etc.

"Who is your letter from, my dear? Mine is a very civil invitation, signed 'Edwin Wilson,' asking me to attend an important meeting of the shareholders of the Town and County Bank, to be held in Drumble, on Thursday the twenty-first. I am sure, it is very attentive of them to remember me."

I did not like to hear of this "important meeting," for, though I did not know much about business, I feared it confirmed what my father said: however, I thought, ill news always came fast enough, so I resolved to say nothing about my alarm, and merely told her that my father was well, and sent his kind regards to her. She kept turning over and admiring her letter. At last she spoke -

"I remember their sending one to Deborah just like this; but that I did not wonder at, for everybody knew she was so clear-headed. I am afraid I could not help them much; indeed, if they came to accounts, I should be quite in the way, for I never could do sums in my head. Deborah, I know, rather wished to go, and went so far as to order a new bonnet for the occasion: but when the time came she had a bad cold; so they sent her a very polite account of what they had done. Chosen a director, I think it was. Do you think they want me to help them to choose a director? I am sure I should choose your father at once!'

"My father has no shares in the bank," said I.

"Oh, no! I remember. He objected very much to Deborah's buying any, I believe. But she was quite the woman of business, and always judged for herself; and here, you see, they have paid eight per cent. all these years."

It was a very uncomfortable subject to me, with my half-knowledge; so I thought I would change the conversation, and I asked at what time she thought we had better go and see the fashions. "Well, my dear," she said, "the thing is this: it is not etiquette to go till after twelve; but then, you see, all Cranford will be there, and one does not like to be too curious about dress and trimmings and caps with all the world looking on. It is never genteel to be over-curious on these occasions. Deborah had the knack of always looking as if the latest fashion was nothing new to her; a manner she had caught from Lady Arley, who did see all the new modes in London, you know. So I thought we would just slip down - for I do want this morning, soon after breakfast half-a-pound of tea - and then we could go up and examine the things at our leisure, and see exactly how my new silk gown must be made; and then, after twelve, we could go with our minds disengaged, and free from thoughts of dress."

We began to talk of Miss Matty's new silk gown. I discovered that it would be really the first time in her life that she had had to choose anything of consequence for herself: for Miss Jenkyns had always been the more decided character, whatever her taste might have been; and it is astonishing how such people carry the world before them by the mere force of will. Miss Matty anticipated the sight of the glossy folds with as much delight as if the five sovereigns, set apart for the purchase, could buy all the silks in the shop; and (remembering my own loss of two hours in a toyshop before I could tell on what wonder to spend a silver threepence) I was very glad that we were going early, that dear Miss Matty might have leisure for the delights of perplexity.

If a happy sea-green could be met with, the gown was to be sea-green: if not, she inclined to maize, and I to silver gray; and we discussed the requisite number of breadths until we arrived at the shop-door. We were to buy the tea, select the silk, and then clamber up the iron corkscrew stairs that led into what was once a loft, though now a fashion show-room.

The young men at Mr Johnson's had on their best looks; and their best cravats, and pivoted themselves over the counter with surprising activity. They wanted to show us upstairs at once; but on the principle of business first and pleasure afterwards, we stayed to purchase the tea. Here Miss Matty's absence of mind betrayed itself. If she was made aware that she had been drinking green tea at any time, she always thought it her duty to lie awake half through the night afterward (I have known her take it in ignorance many a time without such effects), and consequently green tea was prohibited the house; yet to-day she herself asked for the obnoxious article, under the impression that she was talking about the silk. However, the mistake was soon rectified; and then the silks were unrolled in good truth. By this time the shop was pretty well filled, for it was Cranford market-day, and many of the farmers and country people from the neighbourhood round came in, sleeking down their hair, and glancing shyly about, from under their eyelids, as anxious to take back some notion of the unusual gaiety to the mistress or the lasses at home, and yet feeling that they were out of place among the smart shopmen and gay shawls and summer prints. One honest-looking man, however, made his way up to the counter at which we stood, and boldly asked to look at a shawl or two. The other country folk confined themselves to the grocery side; but our neighbour was evidently too full of some kind intention towards mistress, wife or daughter, to be shy; and it soon became a question with me, whether he or Miss Matty would keep their shopmen the longest time. He thought each shawl more beautiful than the last; and, as for Miss Matty, she smiled and sighed over each fresh bale that was brought out; one colour set off another, and the heap together would, as she said, make even the rainbow look poor.

"I am afraid," said she, hesitating, "Whichever I choose I shall wish I had taken another. Look at this lovely crimson! it would be so warm in winter. But spring is coming on, you know. I wish I could have a gown for every season," said she, dropping her voice - as we all did in Cranford whenever we talked of anything we wished for but could not afford. "However," she continued in a louder and more cheerful tone, "it would give me a great deal of trouble to take care of them if I had them; so, I think, I'll only take one. But which must it be, my dear?"

And now she hovered over a lilac with yellow spots, while I pulled out a quiet sage-green that had faded into insignificance under the more brilliant colours, but which was nevertheless a good silk in its humble way. Our attention was called off to our neighbour. He had chosen a shawl of about thirty shillings' value; and his face looked broadly happy, under the anticipation, no doubt, of the pleasant surprise he would give to some Molly or Jenny at home; he had tugged a leathern purse out of his breeches-pocket, and had offered a five-pound note in payment for the shawl, and for some parcels which had been brought round to him from the grocery counter; and it was just at this point that he attracted our notice. The shopman was examining the note with a puzzled, doubtful air.

"Town and County Bank! I am not sure, sir, but I believe we have received a warning against notes issued by this bank only this morning. I will just step and ask Mr Johnson, sir; but I'm afraid I must trouble you for payment in cash, or in a note of a different bank."

I never saw a man's countenance fall so suddenly into dismay and bewilderment. It was almost piteous to see the rapid change.

"Dang it!" said he, striking his fist down on the table, as if to try which was the harder, "the chap talks as if notes and gold were to be had for the picking up."

Miss Matty had forgotten her silk gown in her interest for the man. I don't think she had caught the name of the bank, and in my nervous cowardice I was anxious that she should not; and so I began admiring the yellow-spotted lilac gown that I had been utterly condemning only a minute before. But it was of no use.

"What bank was it? I mean, what bank did your note belong to?"

"Town and County Bank."

"Let me see it," said she quietly to the shopman, gently taking it out of his hand, as he brought it back to return it to the farmer.

Mr Johnson was very sorry, but, from information he had received, the notes issued by that bank were little better than waste paper.

"I don't understand it," said Miss Matty to me in a low voice. "That is our bank, is it not? - the Town and County Bank?"

"Yes," said I. "This lilac silk will just match the ribbons in your new cap, I believe," I continued, holding up the folds so as to catch the light, and wishing that the man would make haste and be gone, and yet having a new wonder, that had only just sprung up, how far it was wise or right in me to allow Miss Matty to make this expensive purchase, if the affairs of the bank were really so bad as the refusal of the note implied.

But Miss Matty put on the soft dignified manner, peculiar to her, rarely used, and yet which became her so well, and laying her hand gently on mine, she said -

"Never mind the silks for a few minutes, dear. I don't understand you, sir," turning now to the shopman, who had been attending to the farmer. "Is this a forged note?"

"Oh, no, ma'am. It is a true note of its kind; but you see, ma'am, it is a joint-stock bank, and there are reports out that it is likely to break. Mr Johnson is only doing his duty, ma'am, as I am sure Mr Dobson knows."

But Mr Dobson could not respond to the appealing bow by any answering smile. He was turning the note absently over in his fingers, looking gloomily enough at the parcel containing the lately-chosen shawl.

"It's hard upon a poor man," said he, "as earns every farthing with the sweat of his brow. However, there's no help for it. You must take back your shawl, my man; Lizzle must go on with her cloak for a while. And yon figs for the little ones - I promised them to 'em - I'll take them; but the'bacco, and the other things" -

"I will give you five sovereigns for your note, my good man," said Miss Matty. "I think there is some great mistake about it, for I am one of the shareholders, and I'm sure they would have told me if things had not been going on right."

The shopman whispered a word or two across the table to Miss Matty. She looked at him with a dubious air.

"Perhaps so," said she. "But I don't pretend to understand business; I only know that if it is going to fail, and if honest people are to lose their money because they have taken our notes - I can't explain myself," said she, suddenly becoming aware that she had got into a long sentence with four people for audience;"only I would rather exchange my gold for the note, if you please,"turning to the farmer, "and then you can take your wife the shawl. It is only going without my gown a few days longer," she continued, speaking to me. "Then, I have no doubt, everything will be cleared up."

"But if it is cleared up the wrong way?" said I.

"Why, then it will only have been common honesty in me, as a shareholder, to have given this good man the money. I am quite clear about it in my own mind; but, you know, I can never speak quite as comprehensibly as others can, only you must give me your note, Mr Dobson, if you please, and go on with your purchases with these sovereigns."

The man looked at her with silent gratitude - too awkward to put his thanks into words; but he hung back for a minute or two, fumbling with his note.

"I'm loth to make another one lose instead of me, if it is a loss; but, you see, five pounds is a deal of money to a man with a family; and, as you say, ten to one in a day or two the note will be as good as gold again."

"No hope of that, my friend," said the shopman.

"The more reason why I should take it," said Miss Matty quietly. She pushed her sovereigns towards the man, who slowly laid his note down in exchange. "Thank you. I will wait a day or two before I purchase any of these silks; perhaps you will then have a greater choice. My dear, will you come upstairs?"

We inspected the fashions with as minute and curious an interest as if the gown to be made after them had been bought. I could not see that the little event in the shop below had in the least damped Miss Matty's curiosity as to the make of sleeves or the sit of skirts. She once or twice exchanged congratulations with me on our private and leisurely view of the bonnets and shawls; but I was, all the time, not so sure that our examination was so utterly private, for I caught glimpses of a figure dodging behind the cloaks and mantles; and, by a dexterous move, I came face to face with Miss Pole, also in morning costume (the principal feature of which was her being without teeth, and wearing a veil to conceal the deficiency), come on the same errand as ourselves. But she quickly took her departure, because, as she said, she had a bad headache, and did not feel herself up to conversation.

As we came down through the shop, the civil Mr Johnson was awaiting us; he had been informed of the exchange of the note for gold, and with much good feeling and real kindness, but with a little want of tact, he wished to condole with Miss Matty, and impress upon her the true state of the case. I could only hope that he had heard an exaggerated rumour for he said that her shares were worse than nothing, and that the bank could not pay a shilling in the pound. I was glad that Miss Matty seemed still a little incredulous; but I could not tell how much of this was real or assumed, with that self-control which seemed habitual to ladies of Miss Matty's standing in Cranford, who would have thought their dignity compromised by the slightest expression of surprise, dismay, or any similar feeling to an inferior in station, or in a public shop. However, we walked home very silently. I am ashamed to say, I believe I was rather vexed and annoyed at Miss Matty's conduct in taking the note to herself so decidedly. I had so set my heart upon her having a new silk gown, which she wanted sadly; in general she was so undecided anybody might turn her round; in this case I had felt that it was no use attempting it, but I was not the less put out at the result.

Somehow, after twelve o'clock, we both acknowledged to a sated curiosity about the fashions, and to a certain fatigue of body (which was, in fact, depression of mind) that indisposed us to go out again. But still we never spoke of the note; till, all at once, something possessed me to ask Miss Matty if she would think it her duty to offer sovereigns for all the notes of the Town and County Bank she met with? I could have bitten my tongue out the minute I had said it. She looked up rather sadly, and as if I had thrown a new perplexity into her already distressed mind; and for a minute or two she did not speak. Then she said - my own dear Miss Matty - without a shade of reproach in her voice -

"My dear, I never feel as if my mind was what people call very strong; and it's often hard enough work for me to settle what I ought to do with the case right before me. I was very thankful to - I was very thankful, that I saw my duty this morning, with the poor man standing by me; but its rather a strain upon me to keep thinking and thinking what I should do if such and such a thing happened; and, I believe, I had rather wait and see what really does come; and I don't doubt I shall be helped then if I don't fidget myself, and get too anxious beforehand. You know, love, I'm not like Deborah. If Deborah had lived, I've no doubt she would have seen after them, before they had got themselves into this state."

We had neither of us much appetite for dinner, though we tried to talk cheerfully about indifferent things. When we returned into the drawing-room, Miss Matty unlocked her desk and began to look over her account-books. I was so penitent for what I had said in the morning, that I did not choose to take upon myself the presumption to suppose that I could assist her; I rather left her alone, as, with puzzled brow, her eye followed her pen up and down the ruled page. By-and-by she shut the book, locked the desk, and came and drew a chair to mine, where I sat in moody sorrow over the fire. I stole my hand into hers; she clasped it, but did not speak a word. At last she said, with forced composure in her voice, "If that bank goes wrong, I shall lose one hundred and forty-nine pounds thirteen shillings and fourpence a year; I shall only have thirteen pounds a year left." I squeezed her hand hard and tight. I did not know what to say. Presently (it was too dark to see her face) I felt her fingers work convulsively in my grasp; and I knew she was going to speak again. I heard the sobs in her voice as she said, "I hope it's not wrong - not wicked - but, oh! I am so glad poor Deborah is spared this. She could not have borne to come down in the world - she had such a noble, lofty spirit."

This was all she said about the sister who had insisted upon investing their little property in that unlucky bank. We were later in lighting the candle than usual that night, and until that light shamed us into speaking, we sat together very silently and sadly.

However, we took to our work after tea with a kind of forced cheerfulness (which soon became real as far as it went), talking of that never-ending wonder, Lady Glenmire's engagement. Miss Matty was almost coming round to think it a good thing.

"I don't mean to deny that men are troublesome in a house. I don't judge from my own experience, for my father was neatness itself, and wiped his shoes on coming in as carefully as any woman; but still a man has a sort of knowledge of what should be done in difficulties, that it is very pleasant to have one at hand ready to lean upon. Now, Lady Glenmire, instead of being tossed about, and wondering where she is to settle, will be certain of a home among pleasant and kind people, such as our good Miss Pole and Mrs Forrester. And Mr Hoggins is really a very personable man; and as for his manners, why, if they are not very polished, I have known people with very good hearts and very clever minds too, who were not what some people reckoned refined, but who were both true and tender."

She fell off into a soft reverie about Mr Holbrook, and I did not interrupt her, I was so busy maturing a plan I had had in my mind for some days, but which this threatened failure of the bank had brought to a crisis. That night, after Miss Matty went to bed, I treacherously lighted the candle again, and sat down in the drawing-room to compose a letter to the Aga Jenkyns, a letter which should affect him if he were Peter, and yet seem a mere statement of dry facts if he were a stranger. The church clock pealed out two before I had done.

The next morning news came, both official and otherwise, that the Town and County Bank had stopped payment. Miss Matty was ruined.

She tried to speak quietly to me; but when she came to the actual fact that she would have but about five shillings a week to live upon, she could not restrain a few tears.

"I am not crying for myself, dear," said she, wiping them away; "I believe I am crying for the very silly thought of how my mother would grieve if she could know; she always cared for us so much more than for herself. But many a poor person has less, and I am not very extravagant, and, thank God, when the neck of mutton, and Martha's wages, and the rent are paid, I have not a farthing owing. Poor Martha! I think she'll be sorry to leave me."

Miss Matty smiled at me through her tears, and she would fain have had me see only the smile, not the tears.

CHAPTER XIV - FRIENDS IN NEED

It was an example to me, and I fancy it might be to many others, to see how immediately Miss Matty set about the retrenchment which she knew to be right under her altered circumstances. While she went down to speak to Martha, and break the intelligence to her, I stole out with my letter to the Aga Jenkyns, and went to the signor's lodgings to obtain the exact address. I bound the signora to secrecy; and indeed her military manners had a degree of shortness and reserve in them which made her always say as little as possible, except when under the pressure of strong excitement. Moreover (which made my secret doubly sure), the signor was now so far recovered as to be looking forward to travelling and conjuring again in the space of a few days, when he, his wife, and little Phoebe would leave Cranford. Indeed, I found him looking over a great black and red placard, in which the Signor Brunoni's accomplishments were set forth, and to which only the name of the town where he would next display them was wanting. He and his wife were so much absorbed in deciding where the red letters would come in with most effect (it might have been the Rubric for that matter), that it was some time before I could get my question asked privately, and not before I had given several decisions, the which I questioned afterwards with equal wisdom of sincerity as soon as the signor threw in his doubts and reasons on the important subject. At last I got the address, spelt by sound, and very queer it looked. I dropped it in the post on my way home, and then for a minute I stood looking at the wooden pane with a gaping slit which divided me from the letter but a moment ago in my hand. It was gone from me like life, never to be recalled. It would get tossed about on the sea, and stained with sea-waves perhaps, and be carried among palm-trees, and scented with all tropical fragrance; the little piece of paper, but an hour ago so familiar and commonplace, had set out on its race to the strange wild countries beyond the Ganges! But I could not afford to lose much time on this speculation. I hastened home, that Miss Matty might not miss me. Martha opened the door to me, her face swollen with crying. As soon as she saw me she burst out afresh, and taking hold of my arm she pulled me in, and banged the door to, in order to ask me if indeed it was all true that Miss Matty had been saying.

"I'll never leave her! No; I won't. I told her so, and said I could not think how she could find in her heart to give me warning. I could not have had the face to do it, if I'd been her. I might ha' been just as good for nothing as Mrs Fitz-Adam's Rosy, who struck for wages after living seven years and a half in one place. I said I was not one to go and serve Mammon at that rate; that I knew when I'd got a good missus, if she didn't know when she'd got a good servant" -

"But, Martha," said I, cutting in while she wiped her eyes.

"Don't, 'but Martha' me," she replied to my deprecatory tone.

"Listen to reason" -

"I'll not listen to reason," she said, now in full possession of her voice, which had been rather choked with sobbing. "Reason always means what someone else has got to say. Now I think what I've got to say is good enough reason; but reason or not, I'll say it, and I'll stick to it. I've money in the Savings Bank, and I've a good stock of clothes, and I'm not going to leave Miss Matty. No, not if she gives me warning every hour in the day!"

She put her arms akimbo, as much as to say she defied me; and, indeed, I could hardly tell how to begin to remonstrate with her, so much did I feel that Miss Matty, in her increasing infirmity, needed the attendance of this kind and faithful woman.

"Well" - said I at last.

"I'm thankful you begin with 'well!' If you'd have begun with 'but,' as you did afore, I'd not ha' listened to you. Now you may go on."

"I know you would be a great loss to Miss Matty, Martha"-

"I telled her so. A loss she'd never cease to be sorry for," broke in Martha triumphantly.

"Still, she will have so little - so very little - to live upon, that I don't see just now how she could find you food - she will even be pressed for her own. I tell you this, Martha, because I feel you are like a friend to dear Miss Matty, but you know she might not like to have it spoken about."

Apparently this was even a blacker view of the subject than Miss Matty had presented to her, for Martha just sat down on the first chair that came to hand, and cried out loud (we had been standing in the kitchen).

At last she put her apron down, and looking me earnestly in the face, asked, "Was that the reason Miss Matty wouldn't order a pudding to-day? She said she had no great fancy for sweet things, and you and she would just have a mutton chop. But I'll be up to her. Never you tell, but I'll make her a pudding, and a pudding she'll like, too, and I'll pay for it myself; so mind you see she eats it. Many a one has been comforted in their sorrow by seeing a good dish come upon the table."

I was rather glad that Martha's energy had taken the immediate and practical direction of pudding-making, for it staved off the quarrelsome discussion as to whether she should or should not leave Miss Matty's service. She began to tie on a clean apron, and otherwise prepare herself for going to the shop for the butter, eggs, and what else she might require. She would not use a scrap of the articles already in the house for her cookery, but went to an old tea-pot in which her private store of money was deposited, and took out what she wanted.

I found Miss Matty very quiet, and not a little sad; but by-and-by she tried to smile for my sake. It was settled that I was to write to my father, and ask him to come over and hold a consultation, and as soon as this letter was despatched we began to talk over future plans. Miss Matty's idea was to take a single room, and retain as much of her furniture as would be necessary to fit up this, and sell the rest, and there to quietly exist upon what would remain after paying the rent. For my part, I was more ambitious and less contented. I thought of all the things by which a woman, past middle age, and with the education common to ladies fifty years ago, could earn or add to a living without materially losing caste; but at length I put even this last clause on one side, and wondered what in the world Miss Matty could do.

Teaching was, of course, the first thing that suggested itself. If Miss Matty could teach children anything, it would throw her among the little elves in whom her soul delighted. I ran over her accomplishments. Once upon a time I had heard her say she could play "Ah! vous dirai-je, maman?" on the piano, but that was long, long ago; that faint shadow of musical acquirement had died out years before. She had also once been able to trace out patterns very nicely for muslin embroidery, by dint of placing a piece of silver paper over the design to be copied, and holding both against the window-pane while she marked the scollop and eyelet-holes. But that was her nearest approach to the accomplishment of drawing, and I did not think it would go very far. Then again, as to the branches of a solid English education - fancy work and the use of the globes - such as the mistress of the Ladies' Seminary, to which all the tradespeople in Cranford sent their daughters, professed to teach. Miss Matty's eyes were failing her, and I doubted if she could discover the number of threads in a worsted-work pattern, or rightly appreciate the different shades required for Queen Adelaide's face in the loyal wool-work now fashionable in Cranford. As for the use of the globes, I had never been able to find it out myself, so perhaps I was not a good judge of Miss Matty's capability of instructing in this branch of education; but it struck me that equators and tropics, and such mystical circles, were very imaginary lines indeed to her, and that she looked upon the signs of the Zodiac as so many remnants of the Black Art.

What she piqued herself upon, as arts in which she excelled, was making candle-lighters, or "spills" (as she preferred calling them), of coloured paper, cut so as to resemble feathers, and knitting garters in a variety of dainty stitches. I had once said, on receiving a present of an elaborate pair, that I should feel quite tempted to drop one of them in the street, in order to have it admired; but I found this little joke (and it was a very little one) was such a distress to her sense of propriety, and was taken with such anxious, earnest alarm, lest the temptation might some day prove too strong for me, that I quite regretted having ventured upon it. A present of these delicately-wrought garters, a bunch of gay "spills," or a set of cards on which sewing-silk was wound in a mystical manner, were the well-known tokens of Miss Matty's favour. But would any one pay to have their children taught these arts? or, indeed, would Miss Matty sell, for filthy lucre, the knack and the skill with which she made trifles of value to those who loved her?

I had to come down to reading, writing, and arithmetic; and, in reading the chapter every morning, she always coughed before coming to long words. I doubted her power of getting through a genealogical chapter, with any number of coughs. Writing she did well and delicately - but spelling! She seemed to think that the more out-of-the-way this was, and the more trouble it cost her, the greater the compliment she paid to her correspondent; and words that she would spell quite correctly in her letters to me became perfect enigmas when she wrote to my father.

No! there was nothing she could teach to the rising generation of Cranford, unless they had been quick learners and ready imitators of her patience, her humility, her sweetness, her quiet contentment with all that she could not do. I pondered and pondered until dinner was announced by Martha, with a face all blubbered and swollen with crying.

Miss Matty had a few little peculiarities which Martha was apt to regard as whims below her attention, and appeared to consider as childish fancies of which an old lady of fifty-eight should try and cure herself. But to-day everything was attended to with the most careful regard. The bread was cut to the imaginary pattern of excellence that existed in Miss Matty's mind, as being the way which her mother had preferred, the curtain was drawn so as to exclude the dead brick wall of a neighbour's stable, and yet left so as to show every tender leaf of the poplar which was bursting into spring beauty. Martha's tone to Miss Matty was just such as that good, rough-spoken servant usually kept sacred for little children, and which I had never heard her use to any grown-up person.

I had forgotten to tell Miss Matty about the pudding, and I was afraid she might not do justice to it, for she had evidently very little appetite this day; so I seized the opportunity of letting her into the secret while Martha took away the meat. Miss Matty's eyes filled with tears, and she could not speak, either to express surprise or delight, when Martha returned bearing it aloft, made in the most wonderful representation of a lion *couchant* that ever was moulded. Martha's face gleamed with triumph as she set it down before Miss Matty with an exultant "There!" Miss Matty wanted to speak her thanks, but could not; so she took Martha's hand and shook it warmly, which set Martha off crying, and I myself could hardly keep up the necessary composure. Martha burst out of the room, and Miss Matty had to clear her voice once or twice before she could speak. At last she said, "I should like to keep this pudding under a glass shade, my dear!" and the notion of the lion *couchant*, with his currant eyes, being hoisted up to the place of honour on a mantelpiece, tickled my hysterical fancy, and I began to laugh, which rather surprised Miss Matty.

"I am sure, dear, I have seen uglier things under a glass shade before now," said she.

So had I, many a time and oft, and I accordingly composed my countenance (and now I could hardly keep from crying), and we both fell to upon the pudding, which was indeed excellent - only every morsel seemed to choke us, our hearts were so full.

We had too much to think about to talk much that afternoon. It passed over very tranquilly. But when the tea-urn was brought in a new thought came into my head. Why should not Miss Matty sell tea - be an agent to the East India Tea Company which then existed? I could see no objections to this plan, while the advantages were many - always supposing that Miss Matty could get over the degradation of condescending to anything like trade. Tea was neither greasy nor sticky - grease and stickiness being two of the qualities which Miss Matty could not endure. No shop-window would be required. A small, genteel notification of her being licensed to sell tea would, it is true, be necessary, but I hoped that it could be placed where no one would see it. Neither was tea a heavy article, so as to tax Miss Matty's fragile strength. The only thing against my plan was the buying and selling involved.

While I was giving but absent answers to the questions Miss Matty was putting - almost as absently - we heard a clumping sound on the stairs, and a whispering outside the door, which indeed once opened and shut as if by some invisible agency. After a little while Martha came in, dragging after her a great tall young man, all crimson with shyness, and finding his only relief in perpetually sleeking down his hair.

"Please, ma'am, he's only Jem Hearn," said Martha, by way of an introduction; and so out of breath was she that I imagine she had had some bodily struggle before she could overcome his reluctance to be presented on the courtly scene of Miss Matilda Jenkyns's drawing-room.

"And please, ma'am, he wants to marry me off-hand. And please, ma'am, we want to take a lodger - just one quiet lodger, to make our two ends meet; and we'd take any house conformable; and, oh dear Miss Matty, if I may be so bold, would you have any objections to lodging with us? Jem wants it as much as I do." [To Jem] - "You great oaf! why can't you back me! - But he does want it all the same, very bad - don't you, Jem? - only, you see, he's dazed at being called on to speak before quality."

"It's not that," broke in Jem. "It's that you've taken me all on a sudden, and I didn't think for to get married so soon - and such quick words does flabbergast a man. It's not that I'm against it, ma'am"(addressing Miss Matty), "only Martha has such quick ways with her when once she takes a thing into her head; and marriage, ma'am- marriage nails a man, as one may say. I dare say I shan't mind it after it's once over."

"Please, ma'am," said Martha - who had plucked at his sleeve, and nudged him with her elbow, and otherwise tried to interrupt him all the time he had been speaking - "don't mind him, he'll come to; 'twas only last night he was an-axing me, and an-axing me, and all the more because I said I could not think of it for years to come, and now he's only taken aback with the suddenness of the joy; but you know, Jem, you are just as full as me about wanting a lodger." (Another great nudge.)

"Ay! if Miss Matty would lodge with us - otherwise I've no mind to be cumbered with strange folk in the house," said Jem, with a want of tact which I could see enraged Martha, who was trying to represent a lodger as the great object they wished to obtain, and that, in fact, Miss Matty would be smoothing their path and conferring a favour, if she would only come and live with them.

Miss Matty herself was bewildered by the pair; their, or rather Martha's sudden resolution in favour of matrimony staggered her, and stood between her and the contemplation of the plan which Martha had at heart. Miss Matty began -

"Marriage is a very solemn thing, Martha."

"It is indeed, ma'am," quoth Jem. "Not that I've no objections to Martha."

"You've never let me a-be for asking me for to fix when I would be married," said Martha - her face all a-fire, and ready to cry with vexation - "and now you're shaming me before my missus and all."

"Nay, now! Martha don't ee! don't ee! only a man likes to have breathing-time," said Jem, trying to possess himself of her hand, but in vain. Then seeing that she was more seriously hurt than he had imagined, he seemed to try to rally his scattered faculties, and with more straightforward dignity than, ten minutes before, I should have thought it possible for him to assume, he turned to Miss Matty, and said, "I hope, ma'am, you know that I am bound to respect every one who has been kind to Martha. I always looked on her as to be my wife - some time; and she has often and often spoken of you as the kindest lady that ever was; and though the plain truth is, I would not like to be troubled with lodgers of the common run, yet if, ma'am, you'd honour us by living with us, I'm sure Martha would do her best to make you comfortable; and I'd keep out of your way as much as I could, which I reckon would be the best kindness such an awkward chap as me could do."

Miss Matty had been very busy with taking off her spectacles, wiping them, and replacing them; but all she could say was, "Don't let any thought of me hurry you into marriage: pray don't. Marriage is such a very solemn thing!"

"But Miss Matilda will think of your plan, Martha," said I, struck with the advantages that it offered, and unwilling to lose the opportunity of considering about it. "And I'm sure neither she nor I can ever forget your kindness; nor your's either, Jem."

"Why, yes, ma'am! I'm sure I mean kindly, though I'm a bit fluttered by being pushed straight ahead into matrimony, as it were, and mayn't express myself conformable. But I'm sure I'm willing enough, and give me time to get accustomed; so, Martha, wench, what's the use of crying so, and slapping me if I come near?"

This last was *sotto voce*, and had the effect of making Martha bounce out of the room, to be followed and soothed by her lover. Whereupon Miss Matty sat down and cried very heartily, and accounted for it by saying that the thought of Martha being married so soon gave her quite a shock, and that she should never forgive herself if she thought she was hurrying the poor creature. I think my pity was more for Jem, of the two; but both Miss Matty and I appreciated to the full the kindness of the honest couple, although we said little about this, and a good deal about the chances and dangers of matrimony.

The next morning, very early, I received a note from Miss Pole, so mysteriously wrapped up, and with so many seals on it to secure secrecy, that I had to tear the paper before I could unfold it. And when I came to the writing I could hardly understand the meaning, it was so involved and oracular. I made out, however, that I was to go to Miss Pole's at eleven o'clock; the number *eleven* being written in full length as well as in numerals, and A.M. twice dashed under, as if I were very likely to come at eleven at night, when all Cranford was usually a-bed and asleep by ten. There was no signature except Miss Pole's initials reversed, P.E.; but as Martha had given me the note, "with Miss Pole's kind regards," it needed no wizard to find out who sent it; and if the writer's name was to be kept secret, it was very well that I was alone when Martha delivered it.

I went as requested to Miss Pole's. The door was opened to me by her little maid Lizzy in Sunday trim, as if some grand event was impending over this work-day. And the drawing-room upstairs was arranged in accordance with this idea. The table was set out with the best green card-cloth, and writing materials upon it. On the little chiffonier was a tray with a newly-decanted bottle of cowslip wine, and some ladies'-finger biscuits. Miss Pole herself was in solemn array, as if to receive visitors, although it was only eleven o'clock. Mrs Forrester was there, crying quietly and sadly, and my arrival seemed only to call forth fresh tears. Before we had finished our greetings, performed with lugubrious mystery of demeanour, there was another rat-tat-tat, and Mrs Fitz-Adam appeared, crimson with walking and excitement. It seemed as if this was all the company expected; for now Miss Pole made several demonstrations of being about to open the business of the meeting, by stirring the fire, opening and shutting the door, and coughing and blowing her nose. Then she arranged us all round the table, taking care to place me opposite to her; and last of all, she inquired of me if the sad report was true, as she feared it was, that Miss Matty had lost all her fortune?

Of course, I had but one answer to make; and I never saw more unaffected sorrow depicted on any countenance than I did there on the three before me.

I wish Mrs Jamieson was here!" said Mrs Forrester at last; but to judge from Mrs Fitz-Adam's face, she could not second the wish.

"But without Mrs Jamieson," said Miss Pole, with just a sound of offended merit in her voice, "we, the ladies of Cranford, in my drawing-room assembled, can resolve upon something. I imagine we are none of us what may be called rich, though we all possess a genteel competency, sufficient for tastes that are elegant and refined, and would not, if they could, be vulgarly ostentatious." (Here I observed Miss Pole refer to a small card concealed in her hand, on which I imagine she had put down a few notes.)

"Miss Smith," she continued, addressing me (familiarly known as "Mary" to all the company assembled, but this was a state occasion), "I have conversed in private - I made it my business to do so yesterday afternoon - with these ladies on the misfortune which has happened to our friend, and one and all of us have agreed that while we have a superfluity, it is not only a duty, but a pleasure - a true pleasure, Mary!" - her voice was rather choked just here, and she had to wipe her spectacles before she could go on - "to give what we can to assist her - Miss Matilda Jenkyns. Only in consideration of the feelings of delicate independence existing in the mind of every refined female" - I was sure she had got back to the card now- "we wish to contribute our mites in a secret and concealed manner, so as not to hurt the feelings I have referred to. And our object in requesting you to meet us this morning is that, believing you are the daughter - that your father is, in fact, her confidential adviser, in all pecuniary matters, we imagined that, by consulting with him, you might devise some mode in which our contribution could be made to appear the legal due which Miss Matilda Jenkyns ought to receive from - Probably your father, knowing her investments, can fill up the blank."

Miss Pole concluded her address, and looked round for approval and agreement.

"I have expressed your meaning, ladies, have I not? And while Miss Smith considers what reply to make, allow me to offer you some little refreshment."

I had no great reply to make: I had more thankfulness at my heart for their kind thoughts than I cared to put into words; and so I only mumbled out something to the effect "that I would name what Miss Pole had said to my father, and that if anything could be arranged for dear Miss Matty," - and here I broke down utterly, and had to be refreshed with a glass of cowslip wine before I could check the crying which had been repressed for the last two or three days. The worst was, all the ladies cried in concert. Even Miss Pole cried, who had said a hundred times that to betray emotion before any one was a sign of weakness and want of self-control. She recovered herself into a slight degree of impatient anger, directed against me, as having set them all off; and, moreover, I think she was vexed that I could not make a speech back in return for hers; and if I had known beforehand what was to be said, and had a card on which to express the probable feelings that would rise in my heart, I would have tried to gratify her. As it was, Mrs Forrester was the person to speak when we had recovered our composure.

"I don't mind, among friends, stating that I - no! I'm not poor exactly, but I don't think I'm what you may call rich; I wish I were, for dear Miss Matty's sake - but, if you please, I'll write down in a sealed paper what I can give. I only wish it was more; my dear Mary, I do indeed."

Now I saw why paper, pens, and ink were provided. Every lady wrote down the sum she could give annually, signed the paper, and sealed it mysteriously. If their proposal was acceded to, my father was to be allowed to open the papers, under pledge of secrecy. If not, they were to be returned to their writers.

When the ceremony had been gone through, I rose to depart; but each lady seemed to wish to have a private conference with me. Miss Pole kept me in the drawing-room to explain why, in Mrs Jamieson's absence, she had taken the lead in this "movement," as she was pleased to call it, and also to inform me that she had heard from good sources that Mrs Jamieson was coming home directly in a state of high displeasure against her sister-in-law, who was forthwith to leave her house, and was, she believed, to return to Edinburgh that very afternoon. Of course this piece of intelligence could not be communicated before Mrs Fitz-Adam, more especially as Miss Pole was inclined to think that Lady Glenmire's engagement to Mr Hoggins could not possibly hold against the blaze of Mrs Jamieson's displeasure. A few hearty inquiries after Miss Matty's health concluded my interview with Miss Pole.

On coming downstairs I found Mrs Forrester waiting for me at the entrance to the dining-parlour; she drew me in, and when the door was shut, she tried two or three times to begin on some subject, which was so unapproachable apparently, that I began to despair of our ever getting to a clear understanding. At last out it came; the poor old lady trembling all the time as if it were a great crime which she was exposing to daylight, in telling me how very, very little she had to live upon; a confession which she was brought to make from a dread lest we should think that the small contribution named in her paper bore any proportion to her love and regard for Miss Matty. And yet that sum which she so eagerly relinquished was, in truth, more than a twentieth part of what she had to live upon, and keep house, and a little serving-maid, all as became one born a Tyrrell. And when the whole income does not nearly amount to a hundred pounds, to give up a twentieth of it will necessitate many careful economies, and many pieces of self-denial, small and insignificant in the world's account, but bearing a different value in another account-book that I have heard of. She did so wish she was rich, she said, and this wish she kept repeating, with no thought of herself in it, only with a longing, yearning desire to be able to heap up Miss Matty's measure of comforts.

It was some time before I could console her enough to leave her; and then, on quitting the house, I was waylaid by Mrs Fitz-Adam, who had also her confidence to make of pretty nearly the opposite description. She had not liked to put down all that she could afford and was ready to give. She told me she thought she never could look Miss Matty in the face again if she presumed to be giving her so much as she should like to do. "Miss Matty!" continued she, "that I thought was such a fine young lady when I was nothing but a country girl, coming to market with eggs and butter and such like things. For my father, though well-to-do, would always make me go on as my mother had done before me, and I had to come into Cranford every Saturday, and see after sales, and prices, and what not. And one day, I remember, I met Miss Matty in the lane that leads to Combehurst; she was walking on the footpath, which, you know, is raised a good way above the road, and a gentleman rode beside her, and was talking to her, and she was looking down at some primroses she had gathered, and pulling them all to pieces, and I do believe she was crying. But after she had passed, she turned round and ran after me to ask - oh, so kindly - about my poor mother, who lay on her death-bed; and when I cried she took hold of my hand to comfort me - and the gentleman waiting for her all the time - and her poor heart very full of something, I am sure; and I thought it such an honour to be spoken to in that pretty way by the rector's daughter, who visited at Arley Hall. I have loved her ever since, though perhaps I'd no right to do it; but if you can think of any way in which I might be allowed to give a little more without any one knowing it, I should be so much obliged to you, my dear. And my brother would be delighted to doctor her for nothing - medicines, leeches, and all. I know that he and her ladyship (my dear, I little thought in the days I was telling you of that I should ever come to be sister-in-law to a ladyship!) would do anything for her. We all would."

I told her I was quite sure of it, and promised all sorts of things in my anxiety to get home to Miss Matty, who might well be wondering what had become of me - absent from her two hours without being able to account for it. She had taken very little note of time, however, as she had been occupied in numberless little arrangements preparatory to the great step of giving up her house. It was evidently a relief to her to be doing something in the way of retrenchment, for, as she said, whenever she paused to think, the recollection of the poor fellow with his bad five-pound note came over her, and she felt quite dishonest; only if it made her so uncomfortable, what must it not be doing to the directors of the bank, who must know so much more of the misery consequent upon this failure? She almost made me angry by dividing her sympathy between these directors (whom she imagined overwhelmed by self-reproach for the mismanagement of other people's affairs) and those who were suffering like her. Indeed, of the two, she seemed to think poverty a lighter burden than self-reproach; but I privately doubted if the directors would agree with her.

Old hoards were taken out and examined as to their money value which luckily was small, or else I don't know how Miss Matty would have prevailed upon herself to part with such things as her mother's wedding-ring, the strange, uncouth brooch with which her father had disfigured his shirt-frill, &c. However, we arranged things a little in order as to their pecuniary estimation, and were all ready for my father when he came the next morning.

I am not going to weary you with the details of all the business we went through; and one reason for not telling about them is, that I did not understand what we were doing at the time, and cannot recollect it now. Miss Matty and I sat assenting to accounts, and schemes, and reports, and documents, of which I do not believe we either of us understood a word; for my father was clear-headed and decisive, and a capital man of business, and if we made the slightest inquiry, or expressed the slightest want of comprehension, he had a sharp way of saying, "Eh? eh? it's as dear as daylight. What's your objection?" And as we had not comprehended anything of what he had proposed, we found it rather difficult to shape our objections; in fact, we never were sure if we had any. So presently Miss Matty got into a nervously acquiescent state, and said "Yes," and "Certainly," at every pause, whether required or not; but when I once joined in as chorus to a "Decidedly," pronounced by Miss Matty in a tremblingly dubious tone, my father fired round at me and asked me "What there was to decide?" And I am sure to this day I have never known. But, in justice to him, I must say he had come over from Drumble to help Miss Matty when he could ill spare the time, and when his own affairs were in a very anxious state.

While Miss Matty was out of the room giving orders for luncheon - and sadly perplexed between her desire of honouring my father by a delicate, dainty meal, and her conviction that she had no right, now that all her money was gone, to indulge this desire - I told him of the meeting of the Cranford ladies at Miss Pole's the day before. He kept brushing his hand before his eyes as I spoke - and when I went back to Martha's offer the evening before, of receiving Miss Matty as a lodger, he fairly walked away from me to the window, and began drumming with his fingers upon it. Then he turned abruptly round, and said, "See, Mary, how a good, innocent life makes friends all around. Confound it! I could make a good lesson out of it if I were a parson; but, as it is, I can't get a tail to my sentences - only I'm sure you feel what I want to say. You and I will have a walk after lunch and talk a bit more about these plans."

The lunch - a hot savoury mutton-chop, and a little of the cold loin sliced and fried - was now brought in. Every morsel of this last dish was finished, to Martha's great gratification. Then my father bluntly told Miss Matty he wanted to talk to me alone, and that he would stroll out and see some of the old places, and then I could tell her what plan we thought desirable. Just before we went out, she called me back and said, "Remember, dear, I'm the only one left - I mean, there's no one to be hurt by what I do. I'm willing to do anything that's right and honest; and I don't think, if Deborah knows where she is, she'll care so very much if I'm not genteel; because, you see, she'll know all, dear. Only let me see what I can do, and pay the poor people as far as I'm able."

I gave her a hearty kiss, and ran after my father. The result of our conversation was this. If all parties were agreeable, Martha and Jem were to be married with as little delay as possible, and they were to live on in Miss Matty's present abode; the sum which the Cranford ladies had agreed to contribute annually being sufficient to meet the greater part of the rent, and leaving Martha free to appropriate what Miss Matty should pay for her lodgings to any little extra comforts required. About the sale, my father was dubious at first. He said the old rectory furniture, however carefully used and reverently treated, would fetch very little; and that little would be but as a drop in the sea of the debts of the Town and County Bank. But when I represented how Miss Matty's tender conscience would be soothed by feeling that she had done what she could, he gave way; especially after I had told him the five-pound note adventure, and he had scolded me well for allowing it. I then alluded to my idea that she might add to her small income by selling tea; and, to my surprise (for I had nearly given up the plan), my father grasped at it with all the energy of a tradesman. I think he reckoned his chickens before they were hatched, for he immediately ran up the profits of the sales that she could effect in Cranford to more than twenty pounds a year. The small dining-parlour was to be converted into a shop, without any of its degrading characteristics; a table was to be the counter; one window was to be retained unaltered, and the other changed into a glass door. I evidently rose in his estimation for having made this bright suggestion. I only hoped we should not both fall in Miss Matty's.

But she was patient and content with all our arrangements. She knew, she said, that we should do the best we could for her; and she only hoped, only stipulated, that she should pay every farthing that she could be said to owe, for her father's sake, who had been so respected in Cranford. My father and I had agreed to say as little as possible about the bank, indeed never to mention it again, if it could be helped. Some of the plans were evidently a little perplexing to her; but she had seen me sufficiently snubbed in the morning for want of comprehension to venture on too many inquiries now; and all passed over well with a hope on her part that no one would be hurried into marriage on her account. When we came to the proposal that she should sell tea, I could see it was rather a shock to her; not on account of any personal loss of gentility involved, but only because she distrusted her own powers of action in a new line of life, and would timidly have preferred a little more privation to any exertion for which she feared she was unfitted. However, when she saw my father was bent upon it, she sighed, and said she would try; and if she did not do well, of course she might give it up. One good thing about it was, she did not think men ever bought tea; and it was of men particularly she was afraid. They had such sharp loud ways with them; and did up accounts, and counted their change so quickly! Now, if she might only sell comfits to children, she was sure she could please them!

CHAPTER XV - A HAPPY RETURN

Before I left Miss Matty at Cranford everything had been comfortably arranged for her. Even Mrs Jamieson's approval of her selling tea had been gained. That oracle had taken a few days to consider whether by so doing Miss Matty would forfeit her right to the privileges of society in Cranford. I think she had some little idea of mortifying Lady Glenmire by the decision she gave at last; which was to this effect: that whereas a married woman takes her husband's rank by the strict laws of precedence, an unmarried woman retains the station her father occupied. So Cranford was allowed to visit Miss Matty; and, whether allowed or not, it intended to visit Lady Glenmire.

But what was our surprise - our dismay - when we learnt that Mr and *Mrs Hoggins* were returning on the following Tuesday! Mrs Hoggins! Had she absolutely dropped her title, and so, in a spirit of bravado, cut the aristocracy to become a Hoggins! She, who might have been called Lady Glenmire to her dying day! Mrs Jamieson was pleased. She said it only convinced her of what she had known from the first, that the creature had a low taste. But "the creature" looked very happy on Sunday at church; nor did we see it necessary to keep our veils down on that side of our bonnets on which Mr and Mrs Hoggins sat, as Mrs Jamieson did; thereby missing all the smiling glory of his face, and all the becoming blushes of hers. I am not sure if Martha and Jem looked more radiant in the afternoon, when they, too, made their first appearance. Mrs Jamieson soothed the turbulence of her soul by having the blinds of her windows drawn down, as if for a funeral, on the day when Mr and Mrs Hoggins received callers; and it was with some difficulty that she was prevailed upon to continue the *St James's Chronicle*, so indignant was she with its having inserted the announcement of the marriage.

Miss Matty's sale went off famously. She retained the furniture of her sitting-room and bedroom; the former of which she was to occupy till Martha could meet with a lodger who might wish to take it; and into this sitting-room and bedroom she had to cram all sorts of things, which were (the auctioneer assured her) bought in for her at the sale by an unknown friend. I always suspected Mrs Fitz-Adam of this; but she must have had an accessory, who knew what articles were particularly regarded by Miss Matty on account of their associations with her early days. The rest of the house looked rather bare, to be sure; all except one tiny bedroom, of which my father allowed me to purchase the furniture for my occasional use in case of Miss Matty's illness.

I had expended my own small store in buying all manner of comfits and lozenges, in order to tempt the little people whom Miss Matty loved so much to come about her. Tea in bright green canisters, and comfits in tumblers - Miss Matty and I felt quite proud as we looked round us on the evening before the shop was to be opened. Martha had scoured the boarded floor to a white cleanness, and it was adorned with a brilliant piece of oil-cloth, on which customers were to stand before the table-counter. The wholesome smell of plaster and whitewash pervaded the apartment. A very small "Matilda Jenkyns, licensed to sell tea," was hidden under the lintel of the new door, and two boxes of tea, with cabalistic inscriptions all over them, stood ready to disgorge their contents into the canisters.

Miss Matty, as I ought to have mentioned before, had had some scruples of conscience at selling tea when there was already Mr Johnson in the town, who included it among his numerous commodities; and, before she could quite reconcile herself to the adoption of her new business, she had trotted down to his shop, unknown to me, to tell him of the project that was entertained, and to inquire if it was likely to injure his business. My father called this idea of hers "great nonsense,"and "wondered how tradespeople were to get on if there was to be a continual consulting of each other's interests, which would put a stop to all competition directly." And, perhaps, it would not have done in Drumble, but in Cranford it answered very well; for not only did Mr Johnson kindly put at rest all Miss Matty's scruples and fear of injuring his business, but I have reason to know he repeatedly sent customers to her, saying that the teas he kept were of a common kind, but that Miss Jenkyns had all the choice sorts. And expensive tea is a very favourite luxury with well-to-do tradespeople and rich farmers' wives, who turn up their noses at the Congou and Souchong prevalent at many tables of gentility, and will have nothing else than Gunpowder and Pekoe for themselves.

But to return to Miss Matty. It was really very pleasant to see how her unselfishness and simple sense of justice called out the same good qualities in others. She never seemed to think any one would impose upon her, because she should be so grieved to do it to them. I have heard her put a stop to the asseverations of the man who brought her coals by quietly saying, "I am sure you would be sorry to bring me wrong weight;" and if the coals were short measure that time, I don't believe they ever were again. People would have felt as much ashamed of presuming on her good faith as they would have done on that of a child. But my father says "such simplicity might be very well in Cranford, but would never do in the world." And I fancy the world must be very bad, for with all my father's suspicion of every one with whom he has dealings, and in spite of all his many precautions, he lost upwards of a thousand pounds by roguery only last year.

I just stayed long enough to establish Miss Matty in her new mode of life, and to pack up the library, which the rector had purchased. He had written a very kind letter to Miss Matty, saying "how glad he should be to take a library, so well selected as he knew that the late Mr Jenkyns's must have been, at any valuation put upon them." And when she agreed to this, with a touch of sorrowful gladness that they would go back to the rectory and be arranged on the accustomed walls once more, he sent word that he feared that he had not room for them all, and perhaps Miss Matty would kindly allow him to leave some volumes on her shelves. But Miss Matty said that she had her Bible and "Johnson's Dictionary," and should not have much time for reading, she was afraid; still, I retained a few books out of consideration for the rector's kindness.

The money which he had paid, and that produced by the sale, was partly expended in the stock of tea, and part of it was invested against a rainy day - *i.e.* old age or illness. It was but a small sum, it is true; and it occasioned a few evasions of truth and white lies (all of which I think very wrong indeed - in theory - and would rather not put them in practice), for we knew Miss Matty would be perplexed as to her duty if she were aware of any little reserve - fund being made for her while the debts of the bank remained unpaid. Moreover, she had never been told of the way in which her friends were contributing to pay the rent. I should have liked to tell her this, but the mystery of the affair gave a piquancy to their deed of kindness which the ladies were unwilling to give up; and at first Martha had to shirk many a perplexed question as to her ways and means of living in such a house, but by-and-by Miss Matty's prudent uneasiness sank down into acquiescence with the existing arrangement.

I left Miss Matty with a good heart. Her sales of tea during the first two days had surpassed my most sanguine expectations. The whole country round seemed to be all out of tea at once. The only alteration I could have desired in Miss Matty's way of doing business was, that she should not have so plaintively entreated some of her customers not to buy green tea - running it down as a slow poison, sure to destroy the nerves, and produce all manner of evil. Their pertinacity in taking it, in spite of all her warnings, distressed her so much that I really thought she would relinquish the sale of it, and so lose half her custom; and I was driven to my wits' end for instances of longevity entirely attributable to a persevering use of green tea. But the final argument, which settled the question, was a happy reference of mine to the train-oil and tallow candles which the Esquimaux not only enjoy but digest. After that she acknowledged that "one man's meat might be another man's poison," and contented herself thence-forward with an occasional remonstrance when she thought the purchaser was too young and innocent to be acquainted with the evil effects green tea produced on some constitutions, and an habitual sigh when people old enough to choose more wisely would prefer it.

I went over from Drumble once a quarter at least to settle the accounts, and see after the necessary business letters. And, speaking of letters, I began to be very much ashamed of remembering my letter to the Aga Jenkyns, and very glad I had never named my writing to any one. I only hoped the letter was lost. No answer came. No sign was made.

About a year after Miss Matty set up shop, I received one of Martha's hieroglyphics, begging me to come to Cranford very soon. I was afraid that Miss Matty was ill, and went off that very afternoon, and took Martha by surprise when she saw me on opening the door. We went into the kitchen as usual, to have our confidential conference, and then Martha told me she was expecting her confinement very soon - in a week or two; and she did not think Miss Matty was aware of it, and she wanted me to break the news to her, "for indeed, miss,"continued Martha, crying hysterically, "I'm afraid she won't approve of it, and I'm sure I don't know who is to take care of her as she should be taken care of when I am laid up."

I comforted Martha by telling her I would remain till she was about again, and only wished she had told me her reason for this sudden summons, as then I would have brought the requisite stock of clothes. But Martha was so tearful and tender-spirited, and unlike her usual self, that I said as little as possible about myself, and endeavoured rather to comfort Martha under all the probable and possible misfortunes which came crowding upon her imagination.

I then stole out of the house-door, and made my appearance as if I were a customer in the shop, just to take Miss Matty by surprise, and gain an idea of how she looked in her new situation. It was warm May weather, so only the little half-door was closed; and Miss Matty sat behind the counter, knitting an elaborate pair of garters; elaborate they seemed to me, but the difficult stitch was no weight upon her mind, for she was singing in a low voice to herself as her needles went rapidly in and out. I call it singing, but I dare say a musician would not use that word to the tuneless yet sweet humming of the low worn voice. I found out from the words, far more than from the attempt at the tune, that it was the Old Hundredth she was crooning to herself; but the quiet continuous sound told of content, and gave me a pleasant feeling, as I stood in the street just outside the door, quite in harmony with that soft May morning. I went in. At first she did not catch who it was, and stood up as if to serve me; but in another minute watchful pussy had clutched her knitting, which was dropped in eager joy at seeing me. I found, after we had had a little conversation, that it was as Martha said, and that Miss Matty had no idea of the approaching household event. So I thought I would let things take their course, secure that when I went to her with the baby in my arms, I should obtain that forgiveness for Martha which she was needlessly frightening herself into believing that Miss Matty would withhold, under some notion that the new claimant would require attentions from its mother that it would be faithless treason to Miss Matty to render.

But I was right. I think that must be an hereditary quality, for my father says he is scarcely ever wrong. One morning, within a week after I arrived, I went to call Miss Matty, with a little bundle of flannel in my arms. She was very much awe-struck when I showed her what it was, and asked for her spectacles off the dressing-table, and looked at it curiously, with a sort of tender wonder at its small perfection of parts. She could not banish the thought of the surprise all day, but went about on tiptoe, and was very silent. But she stole up to see Martha and they both cried with joy, and she got into a complimentary speech to Jem, and did not know how to get out of it again, and was only extricated from her dilemma by the sound of the shop-bell, which was an equal relief to the shy, proud, honest Jem, who shook my hand so vigorously when I congratulated him, that I think I feel the pain of it yet.

I had a busy life while Martha was laid up. I attended on Miss Matty, and prepared her meals; I cast up her accounts, and examined into the state of her canisters and tumblers. I helped her, too, occasionally, in the shop; and it gave me no small amusement, and sometimes a little uneasiness, to watch her ways there. If a little child came in to ask for an ounce of almond-comfits (and four of the large kind which Miss Matty sold weighed that much), she always added one more by "way of make-weight," as she called it, although the scale was handsomely turned before; and when I remonstrated against this, her reply was, "The little things like it so much!" There was no use in telling her that the fifth comfit weighed a quarter of an ounce, and made every sale into a loss to her pocket. So I remembered the green tea, and winged my shaft with a feather out of her own plumage. I told her how unwholesome almond-comfits were, and how ill excess in them might make the little children. This argument produced some effect; for, henceforward, instead of the fifth comfit, she always told them to hold out their tiny palms, into which she shook either peppermint or ginger lozenges, as a preventive to the dangers that might arise from the previous sale. Altogether the lozenge trade, conducted on these principles, did not promise to be remunerative; but I was happy to find she had made more than twenty pounds during the last year by her sales of tea; and, moreover, that now she was accustomed to it, she did not dislike the employment, which brought her into kindly intercourse with many of the people round about. If she gave them good weight, they, in their turn, brought many a little country present to the "old rector's daughter"; a cream cheese, a few new-laid eggs, a little fresh ripe fruit, a bunch of flowers. The counter was quite loaded with these offerings sometimes, as she told me.

As for Cranford in general, it was going on much as usual. The Jamieson and Hoggins feud still raged, if a feud it could be called, when only one side cared much about it. Mr and Mrs Hoggins were very happy together, and, like most very happy people, quite ready to be friendly; indeed, Mrs Hoggins was really desirous to be restored to Mrs Jamieson's good graces, because of the former intimacy. But Mrs Jamieson considered their very happiness an insult to the Glenmire family, to which she had still the honour to belong, and she doggedly refused and rejected every advance. Mr Mulliner, like a faithful clansman, espoused his mistress' side with ardour. If he saw either Mr or Mrs Hoggins, he would cross the street, and appear absorbed in the contemplation of life in general, and his own path in particular, until he had passed them by. Miss Pole used to amuse herself with wondering what in the world Mrs Jamieson would do, if either she, or Mr Mulliner, or any other member of her household was taken ill; she could hardly have the face to call in Mr Hoggins after the way she had behaved to them. Miss Pole grew quite impatient for some indisposition or accident to befall Mrs Jamieson or her dependents, in order that Cranford might see how she would act under the perplexing circumstances.

Martha was beginning to go about again, and I had already fixed a limit, not very far distant, to my visit, when one afternoon, as I was sitting in the shop-parlour with Miss Matty - I remember the weather was colder now than it had been in May, three weeks before, and we had a fire and kept the door fully closed - we saw a gentleman go slowly past the window, and then stand opposite to the door, as if looking out for the name which we had so carefully hidden. He took out a double eyeglass and peered about for some time before he could discover it. Then he came in. And, all on a sudden, it flashed across me that it was the Aga himself! For his clothes had an out-of-the-way foreign cut about them, and his face was deep brown, as if tanned and re-tanned by the sun. His complexion contrasted oddly with his plentiful snow-white hair, his eyes were dark and piercing, and he had an odd way of contracting them and puckering up his cheeks into innumerable wrinkles when he looked earnestly at objects. He did so to Miss Matty when he first came in. His glance had first caught and lingered a little upon me, but then turned, with the peculiar searching look I have described, to Miss Matty. She was a little fluttered and nervous, but no more so than she always was when any man came into her shop. She thought that he would probably have a note, or a sovereign at least, for which she would have to give change, which was an operation she very much disliked to perform. But the present customer stood opposite to her, without asking for anything, only looking fixedly at her as he drummed upon the table with his fingers, just for all the world as Miss Jenkyns used to do. Miss Matty was on the point of asking him what he wanted (as she told me afterwards), when he turned sharp to me: "Is your name Mary Smith?"

"Yes!" said I.

All my doubts as to his identity were set at rest, and I only wondered what he would say or do next, and how Miss Matty would stand the joyful shock of what he had to reveal. Apparently he was at a loss how to announce himself, for he looked round at last in search of something to buy, so as to gain time, and, as it happened, his eye caught on the almond-comfits, and he boldly asked for a pound of "those things." I doubt if Miss Matty had a whole pound in the shop, and, besides the unusual magnitude of the order, she was distressed with the idea of the indigestion they would produce, taken in such unlimited quantities. She looked up to remonstrate. Something of tender relaxation in his face struck home to her heart. She said, "It is - oh, sir! can you be Peter?" and trembled from head to foot. In a moment he was round the table and had her in his arms, sobbing the tearless cries of old age. I brought her a glass of wine, for indeed her colour had changed so as to alarm me and Mr Peter too. He kept saying, "I have been too sudden for you, Matty - I have, my little girl."

I proposed that she should go at once up into the drawing-room and lie down on the sofa there. She looked wistfully at her brother, whose hand she had held tight, even when nearly fainting; but on his assuring her that he would not leave her, she allowed him to carry her upstairs.

I thought that the best I could do was to run and put the kettle on the fire for early tea, and then to attend to the shop, leaving the brother and sister to exchange some of the many thousand things they must have to say. I had also to break the news to Martha, who received it with a burst of tears which nearly infected me. She kept recovering herself to ask if I was sure it was indeed Miss Matty's brother, for I had mentioned that he had grey hair, and she had always heard that he was a very handsome young man. Something of the same kind perplexed Miss Matty at tea-time, when she was installed in the great easy-chair opposite to Mr Jenkyns in order to gaze her fill. She could hardly drink for looking at him, and as for eating, that was out of the question.

"I suppose hot climates age people very quickly," said she, almost to herself. "When you left Cranford you had not a grey hair in your head."

"But how many years ago is that?" said Mr Peter, smiling.

"Ah, true! yes, I suppose you and I are getting old. But still I did not think we were so very old! But white hair is very becoming to you, Peter," she continued - a little afraid lest she had hurt him by revealing how his appearance had impressed her.

"I suppose I forgot dates too, Matty, for what do you think I have brought for you from India? I have an Indian muslin gown and a pearl necklace for you somewhere in my chest at Portsmouth." He smiled as if amused at the idea of the incongruity of his presents with the appearance of his sister; but this did not strike her all at once, while the elegance of the articles did. I could see that for a moment her imagination dwelt complacently on the idea of herself thus attired; and instinctively she put her hand up to her throat - that little delicate throat which (as Miss Pole had told me) had been one of her youthful charms; but the hand met the touch of folds of soft muslin in which she was always swathed up to her chin, and the sensation recalled a sense of the unsuitableness of a pearl necklace to her age. She said, "I'm afraid I'm too old; but it was very kind of you to think of it. They are just what I should have liked years ago - when I was young."

"So I thought, my little Matty. I remembered your tastes; they were so like my dear mother's." At the mention of that name the brother and sister clasped each other's hands yet more fondly, and, although they were perfectly silent, I fancied they might have something to say if they were unchecked by my presence, and I got up to arrange my room for Mr Peter's occupation that night, intending myself to share Miss Matty's bed. But at my movement, he started up. "I must go and settle about a room at the 'George.' My carpet-bag is there too."

"No!" said Miss Matty, in great distress - "you must not go; please, dear Peter - pray, Mary - oh! you must not go!"

She was so much agitated that we both promised everything she wished. Peter sat down again and gave her his hand, which for better security she held in both of hers, and I left the room to accomplish my arrangements.

Long, long into the night, far, far into the morning, did Miss Matty and I talk. She had much to tell me of her brother's life and adventures, which he had communicated to her as they had sat alone. She said all was thoroughly clear to her; but I never quite understood the whole story; and when in after days I lost my awe of Mr Peter enough to question him myself, he laughed at my curiosity, and told me stories that sounded so very much like Baron Munchausen's, that I was sure he was making fun of me. What I heard from Miss Matty was that he had been a volunteer at the siege of Rangoon; had been taken prisoner by the Burmese; and somehow obtained favour and eventual freedom from knowing how to bleed the chief of the small tribe in some case of dangerous illness; that on his release from years of captivity he had had his letters returned from England with the ominous word "Dead"marked upon them; and, believing himself to be the last of his race, he had settled down as an indigo planter, and had proposed to spend the remainder of his life in the country to whose inhabitants and modes of life he had become habituated, when my letter had reached him; and, with the odd vehemence which characterised him in age as it had done in youth, he had sold his land and all his possessions to the first purchaser, and come home to the poor old sister, who was more glad and rich than any princess when she looked at him. She talked me to sleep at last, and then I was awakened by a slight sound at the door, for which she begged my pardon as she crept penitently into bed; but it seems that when I could no longer confirm her belief that the long-lost was really here - under the same roof - she had begun to fear lest it was only a waking dream of hers; that there never had been a Peter sitting by her all that blessed evening - but that the real Peter lay dead far away beneath some wild sea-wave, or under some strange eastern tree. And so strong had this nervous feeling of hers become, that she was fain to get up and go and convince herself that he was really there by listening through the door to his even, regular breathing - I don't like to call it snoring, but I heard it myself through two closed doors- and by-and-by it soothed Miss Matty to sleep.

I don't believe Mr Peter came home from India as rich as a nabob; he even considered himself poor, but neither he nor Miss Matty cared much about that. At any rate, he had enough to live upon "very genteelly" at Cranford; he and Miss Matty together. And a day or two after his arrival, the shop was closed, while troops of little urchins gleefully awaited the shower of comfits and lozenges that came from time to time down upon their faces as they stood up-gazing at Miss Matty's drawing-room windows. Occasionally Miss Matty would say to them (half-hidden behind the curtains), "My dear children, don't make yourselves ill;" but a strong arm pulled her back, and a more rattling shower than ever succeeded. A part of the tea was sent in presents to the Cranford ladies; and some of it was distributed among the old people who remembered Mr Peter in the days of his frolicsome youth. The Indian muslin gown was reserved for darling Flora Gordon (Miss Jessie Brown's daughter). The Gordons had been on the Continent for the last few years, but were now expected to return very soon; and Miss Matty, in her sisterly pride, anticipated great delight in the joy of showing them Mr Peter. The pearl necklace disappeared; and about that time many handsome and useful presents made their appearance in the households of Miss Pole and Mrs Forrester; and some rare and delicate Indian ornaments graced the drawing-rooms of Mrs Jamieson and Mrs Fitz-Adam. I myself was not forgotten. Among other things, I had the handsomest-bound and best edition of Dr Johnson's works that could be procured; and dear Miss Matty, with tears in her eyes, begged me to consider it as a present from her sister as well as herself. In short, no one was forgotten; and, what was more, every one, however insignificant, who had shown kindness to Miss Matty at any time, was sure of Mr Peter's cordial regard.

CHAPTER XVI - PEACE TO CRANFORD

It was not surprising that Mr Peter became such a favourite at Cranford. The ladies vied with each other who should admire him most; and no wonder, for their quiet lives were astonishingly stirred up by the arrival from India - especially as the person arrived told more wonderful stories than Sindbad the Sailor; and, as Miss Pole said, was quite as good as an Arabian Night any evening. For my own part, I had vibrated all my life between Drumble and Cranford, and I thought it was quite possible that all Mr Peter's stories might be true, although wonderful; but when I found that, if we swallowed an anecdote of tolerable magnitude one week, we had the dose considerably increased the next, I began to have my doubts; especially as I noticed that when his sister was present the accounts of Indian life were comparatively tame; not that she knew more than we did, perhaps less. I noticed also that when the rector came to call, Mr Peter talked in a different way about the countries he had been in. But I don't think the ladies in Cranford would have considered him such a wonderful traveller if they had only heard him talk in the quiet way he did to him. They liked him the better, indeed, for being what they called "so very Oriental."

One day, at a select party in his honour, which Miss Pole gave, and from which, as Mrs Jamieson honoured it with her presence, and had even offered to send Mr Mulliner to wait, Mr and Mrs Hoggins and Mrs Fitz-Adam were necessarily - excluded one day at Miss Pole's, Mr Peter said he was tired of sitting upright against the hard-backed uneasy chairs, and asked if he might not indulge himself in sitting cross-legged. Miss Pole's consent was eagerly given, and down he went with the utmost gravity. But when Miss Pole asked me, in an audible whisper, "if he did not remind me of the Father of the Faithful?" I could not help thinking of poor Simon Jones, the lame tailor, and while Mrs Jamieson slowly commented on the elegance and convenience of the attitude, I remembered how we had all followed that lady's lead in condemning Mr Hoggins for vulgarity because he simply crossed his legs as he sat still on his chair. Many of Mr Peter's ways of eating were a little strange amongst such ladies as Miss Pole, and Miss Matty, and Mrs Jamieson, especially when I recollected the untasted green peas and two-pronged forks at poor Mr Holbrook's dinner.

The mention of that gentleman's name recalls to my mind a conversation between Mr Peter and Miss Matty one evening in the summer after he returned to Cranford. The day had been very hot, and Miss Matty had been much oppressed by the weather, in the heat of which her brother revelled. I remember that she had been unable to nurse Martha's baby, which had become her favourite employment of late, and which was as much at home in her arms as in its mother's, as long as it remained a light-weight, portable by one so fragile as Miss Matty. This day to which I refer, Miss Matty had seemed more than usually feeble and languid, and only revived when the sun went down, and her sofa was wheeled to the open window, through which, although it looked into the principal street of Cranford, the fragrant smell of the neighbouring hayfields came in every now and then, borne by the soft breezes that stirred the dull air of the summer twilight, and then died away. The silence of the sultry atmosphere was lost in the murmuring noises which came in from many an open window and door; even the children were abroad in the street, late as it was (between ten and eleven), enjoying the game of play for which they had not had spirits during the heat of the day. It was a source of satisfaction to Miss Matty to see how few candles were lighted, even in the apartments of those houses from which issued the greatest signs of life. Mr Peter, Miss Matty, and I had all been quiet, each with a separate reverie, for some little time, when Mr Peter broke in -

"Do you know, little Matty, I could have sworn you were on the high road to matrimony when I left England that last time! If anybody had told me you would have lived and died an old maid then, I should have laughed in their faces."

Miss Matty made no reply, and I tried in vain to think of some subject which should effectually turn the conversation; but I was very stupid; and before I spoke he went on -

"It was Holbrook, that fine manly fellow who lived at Woodley, that I used to think would carry off my little Matty. You would not think it now, I dare say, Mary; but this sister of mine was once a very pretty girl - at least, I thought so, and so I've a notion did poor Holbrook. What business had he to die before I came home to thank him for all his kindness to a good-for-nothing cub as I was? It was that that made me first think he cared for you; for in all our fishing expeditions it was Matty, Matty, we talked about. Poor Deborah! What a lecture she read me on having asked him home to lunch one day, when she had seen the Arley carriage in the town, and thought that my lady might call. Well, that's long years ago; more than half a life-time, and yet it seems like yesterday! I don't know a fellow I should have liked better as a brother-in-law. You must have played your cards badly, my little Matty, somehow or another - wanted your brother to be a good go-between, eh, little one?"said he, putting out his hand to take hold of hers as she lay on the sofa. "Why, what's this? you're shivering and shaking, Matty, with that confounded open window. Shut it, Mary, this minute!"

I did so, and then stooped down to kiss Miss Matty, and see if she really were chilled. She caught at my hand, and gave it a hard squeeze - but unconsciously, I think - for in a minute or two she spoke to us quite in her usual voice, and smiled our uneasiness away, although she patiently submitted to the prescriptions we enforced of a warm bed and a glass of weak negus. I was to leave Cranford the next day, and before I went I saw that all the effects of the open window had quite vanished. I had superintended most of the alterations necessary in the house and household during the latter weeks of my stay. The shop was once more a parlour: the empty resounding rooms again furnished up to the very garrets.

There had been some talk of establishing Martha and Jem in another house, but Miss Matty would not hear of this. Indeed, I never saw her so much roused as when Miss Pole had assumed it to be the most desirable arrangement. As long as Martha would remain with Miss Matty, Miss Matty was only too thankful to have her about her; yes, and Jem too, who was a very pleasant man to have in the house, for she never saw him from week's end to week's end. And as for the probable children, if they would all turn out such little darlings as her god-daughter, Matilda, she should not mind the number, if Martha didn't. Besides, the next was to be called Deborah - a point which Miss Matty had reluctantly yielded to Martha's stubborn determination that her first-born was to be Matilda. So Miss Pole had to lower her colours, and even her voice, as she said to me that, as Mr and Mrs Hearn were still to go on living in the same house with Miss Matty, we had certainly done a wise thing in hiring Martha's niece as an auxiliary.

I left Miss Matty and Mr Peter most comfortable and contented; the only subject for regret to the tender heart of the one, and the social friendly nature of the other, being the unfortunate quarrel between Mrs Jamieson and the plebeian

Hogginses and their following. In joke, I prophesied one day that this would only last until Mrs Jamieson or Mr Mulliner were ill, in which case they would only be too glad to be friends with Mr Hoggins; but Miss Matty did not like my looking forward to anything like illness in so light a manner, and before the year was out all had come round in a far more satisfactory way.

I received two Cranford letters on one auspicious October morning. Both Miss Pole and Miss Matty wrote to ask me to come over and meet the Gordons, who had returned to England alive and well with their two children, now almost grown up. Dear Jessie Brown had kept her old kind nature, although she had changed her name and station; and she wrote to say that she and Major Gordon expected to be in Cranford on the fourteenth, and she hoped and begged to be remembered to Mrs Jamieson (named first, as became her honourable station), Miss Pole and Miss Matty - could she ever forget their kindness to her poor father and sister? - Mrs Forrester, Mr Hoggins (and here again came in an allusion to kindness shown to the dead long ago), his new wife, who as such must allow Mrs Gordon to desire to make her acquaintance, and who was, moreover, an old Scotch friend of her husband's. In short, every one was named, from the rector - who had been appointed to Cranford in the interim between Captain Brown's death and Miss Jessie's marriage, and was now associated with the latter event - down to Miss Betty Barker. All were asked to the luncheon; all except Mrs Fitz-Adam, who had come to live in Cranford since Miss Jessie Brown's days, and whom I found rather moping on account of the omission. People wondered at Miss Betty Barker's being included in the honourable list; but, then, as Miss Pole said, we must remember the disregard of the genteel proprieties of life in which the poor captain had educated his girls, and for his sake we swallowed our pride. Indeed, Mrs Jamieson rather took it as a compliment, as putting Miss Betty (formerly *her* maid) on a level with "those Hogginses."

But when I arrived in Cranford, nothing was as yet ascertained of Mrs Jamieson's own intentions; would the honourable lady go, or would she not? Mr Peter declared that she should and she would; Miss Pole shook her head and desponded. But Mr Peter was a man of resources. In the first place, he persuaded Miss Matty to write to Mrs Gordon, and to tell her of Mrs Fitz-Adam's existence, and to beg that one so kind, and cordial, and generous, might be included in the pleasant invitation. An answer came back by return of post, with a pretty little note for Mrs Fitz-Adam, and a request that Miss Matty would deliver it herself and explain the previous omission. Mrs Fitz-Adam was as pleased as could be, and thanked Miss Matty over and over again. Mr Peter had said, "Leave Mrs Jamieson to me;" so we did; especially as we knew nothing that we could do to alter her determination if once formed.

I did not know, nor did Miss Matty, how things were going on, until Miss Pole asked me, just the day before Mrs Gordon came, if I thought there was anything between Mr Peter and Mrs Jamieson in the matrimonial line, for that Mrs Jamieson was really going to the lunch at the "George." She had sent Mr Mulliner down to desire that there might be a footstool put to the warmest seat in the room, as she meant to come, and knew that their chairs were very high. Miss Pole had picked this piece of news up, and from it she conjectured all sorts of things, and bemoaned yet more. "If Peter should marry, what would become of poor dear Miss Matty? And Mrs Jamieson, of all people!" Miss Pole seemed to think there were other ladies in Cranford who would have done more credit to his choice, and I think she must have had someone who was unmarried in her head, for she kept saying, "It was so wanting in delicacy in a widow to think of such a thing."

When I got back to Miss Matty's I really did begin to think that Mr Peter might be thinking of Mrs Jamieson for a wife, and I was as unhappy as Miss Pole about it. He had the proof sheet of a great placard in his hand. "Signor Brunoni, Magician to the King of Delhi, the Rajah of Oude, and the great Lama of Thibet," &c.& c., was going to "perform in Cranford for one night only,"the very next night; and Miss Matty, exultant, showed me a letter from the Gordons, promising to remain over this gaiety, which Miss Matty said was entirely Peter's doing. He had written to ask the signor to come, and was to be at all the expenses of the affair. Tickets were to be sent gratis to as many as the room would hold. In short, Miss Matty was charmed with the plan, and said that to-morrow Cranford would remind her of the Preston Guild, to which she had been in her youth - a luncheon at the "George," with the dear Gordons, and the signor in the Assembly Room in the evening. But I - I looked only at the fatal words:-

"*Under the Patronage of the* HONOURABLE MRS JAMIESON."

She, then, was chosen to preside over this entertainment of Mr Peter's; she was perhaps going to displace my dear Miss Matty in his heart, and make her life lonely once more! I could not look forward to the morrow with any pleasure; and every innocent anticipation of Miss Matty's only served to add to my annoyance.

So, angry and irritated, and exaggerating every little incident which could add to my irritation, I went on till we were all assembled in the great parlour at the "George." Major and Mrs Gordon and pretty Flora and Mr Ludovic were all as bright and handsome and friendly as could be; but I could hardly attend to them for watching Mr Peter, and I saw that Miss Pole was equally busy. I had never seen Mrs Jamieson so roused and animated before; her face looked full of interest in what Mr Peter was saying. I drew near to listen. My relief was great when I caught that his words were not words of love, but that, for all his grave face, he was at his old tricks. He was telling her of his travels in India, and describing the wonderful height of the Himalaya mountains: one touch after another added to their size, and each exceeded the former in absurdity; but Mrs Jamieson really enjoyed all in perfect good faith. I suppose she required strong stimulants to excite her to come out of her apathy. Mr Peter wound up his account by saying that, of course, at that altitude there were none of the animals to be found that existed in the lower regions; the game, - everything was different. Firing one day at some flying creature, he was very much dismayed when it fell, to find that he had shot a cherubim! Mr Peter caught my eye at this moment, and gave me such a funny twinkle, that I felt sure he had no thoughts of Mrs Jamieson as a wife from that time. She looked uncomfortably amazed -

"But, Mr Peter, shooting a cherubim - don't you think -I am afraid that was sacrilege!"

Mr Peter composed his countenance in a moment, and appeared shocked at the idea, which, as he said truly enough, was now presented to him for the first time; but then Mrs Jamieson must remember that he had been living for a long time among savages - all of whom were heathens- some of them, he was afraid, were downright Dissenters. Then, seeing Miss Matty draw near, he hastily changed the conversation, and after a little while, turning to me, he said, "Don't be shocked, prim little Mary, at all my wonderful stories. I consider Mrs Jamieson fair game, and besides I am bent on propitiating her, and the first step towards it is keeping her well awake. I bribed her here by asking her to let me have her name as patroness for my poor conjuror this evening; and I don't want to give her time enough to get up her rancour against the Hogginses, who are just coming in. I want everybody to be friends, for it harasses Matty so much to hear of these quarrels. I shall go at it again by-and-by, so you need not look shocked. I intend to enter the Assembly Room to-night with Mrs Jamieson on one side, and my lady, Mrs Hoggins, on the other. You see if I don't."

Somehow or another he did; and fairly got them into conversation together. Major and Mrs Gordon helped at the good work with their perfect ignorance of any existing coolness between any of the inhabitants of Cranford.

Ever since that day there has been the old friendly sociability in Cranford society; which I am thankful for, because of my dear Miss Matty's love of peace and kindliness. We all love Miss Matty, and I somehow think we are all of us better when she is near us.

Naomi entreating Ruth and Orpah to return to the land of Moab by William Blake, 1795

RUTH

by

ELIZABETH GASKELL

First published in book form by Chapman and Hall in 1853

> Drop, drop, slow tears!
> And bathe those beauteous feet,
> Which brought from heaven
> The news and Prince of peace.
> Cease not, wet eyes,
> For mercy to entreat:
> To cry for vengeance
> Sin doth never cease.
> In your deep floods
> Drown all my faults and fears;

Nor let His eye
See sin, but through my tears.

Phineas Fletcher

CHAPTER I

The Dressmaker's Apprentice at Work

There is an assize-town in one of the eastern counties which was much distinguished by the Tudor sovereigns, and, in consequence of their favour and protection, attained a degree of importance that surprises the modern traveller.

A hundred years ago its appearance was that of picturesque grandeur. The old houses, which were the temporary residences of such of the county-families as contented themselves with the gaieties of a provincial town, crowded the streets and gave them the irregular but noble appearance yet to be seen in the cities of Belgium. The sides of the streets had a quaint richness, from the effect of the gables, and the stacks of chimneys which cut against the blue sky above; while, if the eye fell lower down, the attention was arrested by all kinds of projections in the shape of balcony and oriel; and it was amusing to see the infinite variety of windows that had been crammed into the walls long before Mr Pitt's days of taxation. The streets below suffered from all these projections and advanced stories above; they were dark, and ill-paved with large, round, jolting pebbles, and with no side-path protected by kerb-stones; there were no lamp-posts for long winter nights; and no regard was paid to the wants of the middle class, who neither drove about in coaches of their own, nor were carried by their own men in their own sedans into the very halls of their friends. The professional men and their wives, the shopkeepers and their spouses, and all such people, walked about at considerable peril both night and day. The broad unwieldy carriages hemmed them up against the houses in the narrow streets. The inhospitable houses projected their flights of steps almost into the carriage-way, forcing pedestrians again into the danger they had avoided for twenty or thirty paces. Then, at night, the only light was derived from the glaring, flaring oil-lamps hung above the doors of the more aristocratic mansions; just allowing space for the passers-by to become visible, before they again disappeared into the darkness, where it was no uncommon thing for robbers to be in waiting for their prey.

The traditions of those bygone times, even to the smallest social particular, enable one to understand more clearly the circumstances which contributed to the formation of character. The daily life into which people are born, and into which they are absorbed before they are well aware, forms chains which only one in a hundred has moral strength enough to despise, and to break when the right time comes—when an inward necessity for independent individual action arises, which is superior to all outward conventionalities. Therefore it is well to know what were the chains of daily domestic habit which were the natural leading-strings of our forefathers before they learnt to go alone.

The picturesqueness of those ancient streets has departed now. The Astleys, the Dunstans, the Waverhams—names of power in that district—go up duly to London in the season, and have sold their residences in the county-town fifty years ago, or more. And when the county-town lost its attraction for the Astleys, the Dunstans, the Waverhams, how could it be supposed that the Domvilles, the Bextons, and the Wildes would continue to go and winter there in their second-rate houses, and with their increased expenditure? So the grand old houses stood empty awhile; and then speculators ventured to purchase, and to turn the deserted mansions into many smaller dwellings, fitted for professional men, or even (bend your ear lower, lest the shade of Marmaduke, first Baron Waverham, hear) into shops!

Even that was not so very bad, compared with the next innovation on the old glories. The shopkeepers found out that the once fashionable street was dark, and that the dingy light did not show off their goods to advantage; the surgeon could not see to draw his patient's teeth; the lawyer had to ring for candles an hour earlier than he was accustomed to do when living in a more plebeian street. In short, by mutual consent, the whole front of one side of the street was pulled down, and rebuilt in the flat, mean, unrelieved style of George the Third. The body of the houses was too solidly grand to submit to alteration; so people were occasionally surprised, after passing through a commonplace-looking shop, to find themselves at the foot of a grand carved oaken staircase, lighted by a window of stained glass, storied all over with armorial bearings.

Up such a stair—past such a window (through which the moonlight fell on her with a glory of many colours)—Ruth Hilton passed wearily one January night, now many years ago. I call it night; but, strictly speaking, it was morning. Two o'clock in the morning chimed forth the old bells of St Saviour's. And yet more than a dozen girls still sat in the room into which Ruth entered, stitching away as if for very life, not daring to gape, or show any outward manifestation of sleepiness. They only sighed a little when Ruth told Mrs Mason the hour of the night, as the result of her errand; for they knew that, stay up as late as they might, the work-hours of the next day must begin at eight, and their young limbs were very weary.

Mrs Mason worked away as hard as any of them; but she was older and tougher; and, besides, the gains were hers. But even she perceived that some rest was needed. "Young ladies! there will be an interval allowed of half an hour. Ring the bell, Miss Sutton. Martha shall bring you up some bread and cheese and beer. You will be so good as to eat it standing—away from the dresses—and to have your hands washed ready for work when I return. In half an hour," said she once more, very distinctly; and then she left the room.

It was curious to watch the young girls as they instantaneously availed themselves of Mrs Mason's absence. One fat, particularly heavy-looking damsel laid her head on her folded arms and was asleep in a moment; refusing to be wakened for her share in the frugal supper, but springing up with a frightened look at the sound of Mrs Mason's returning footstep, even while it was still far off on the echoing stairs. Two or three others huddled over the scanty fireplace, which, with every possible economy of space, and no attempt whatever at anything of grace or ornament, was inserted in the slight, flat-looking wall, that had been run up by the present owner of the property to portion off this division of the grand old drawing-room of the mansion. Some employed the time in eating their bread and cheese, with as measured and incessant a motion of the jaws (and almost as stupidly placid an expression of countenance), as you may see in cows ruminating in the first meadow you happen to pass.

Some held up admiringly the beautiful ball-dress in progress, while others examined the effect, backing from the object to be criticised in the true artistic manner. Others stretched themselves into all sorts of postures to relieve the weary muscles; one or two gave vent to all the yawns, coughs, and sneezes that had been pent up so long in the presence of Mrs Mason. But Ruth Hilton sprang to the large old window, and pressed against it as a bird presses against the bars of its cage. She put back the blind, and gazed into the quiet moonlight night. It was doubly light—almost as much so as day—for everything was covered with the deep snow which had been falling silently ever since the evening before. The window was in a square recess; the old strange little panes of glass had been replaced by those which gave more light. A little distance off, the feathery branches of a larch waved softly to and fro in the scarcely perceptible night-breeze. Poor old larch! the time had been when it had stood in a pleasant lawn, with the tender grass creeping caressingly up to its very trunk; but now the lawn was divided into yards and squalid back premises, and the larch was pent up and girded about with flag-stones. The snow lay thick on its boughs, and now and then fell noiselessly down. The old stables had been added to, and altered into a dismal street of mean-looking houses, back to back with the ancient mansions. And over all these changes from grandeur to squalor, bent down the purple heavens with their unchanging splendour!

Ruth pressed her hot forehead against the cold glass, and strained her aching eyes in gazing out on the lovely sky of a winter's night. The impulse was strong upon her to snatch up a shawl, and wrapping it round her head, to sally forth and enjoy the glory; and time was when that impulse would have been instantly followed; but now, Ruth's eyes filled with tears, and she stood quite still, dreaming of the days that were gone. Some one touched her shoulder while her thoughts were far away, remembering past January nights, which had resembled this, and were yet so different.

"Ruth, love," whispered a girl who had unwillingly distinguished herself by a long hard fit of coughing, "come and have some supper. You don't know yet how it helps one through the night."

"One run—one blow of the fresh air would do me more good," said Ruth.

"Not such a night as this," replied the other, shivering at the very thought.

"And why not such a night as this, Jenny?" answered Ruth. "Oh! at home I have many a time run up the lane all the way to the mill, just to see the icicles hang on the great wheel; and when I was once out, I could hardly find in my heart to come in, even to mother, sitting by the fire;—even to mother," she added, in a low, melancholy tone, which had something of inexpressible sadness in it. "Why, Jenny!" said she, rousing herself, but not before her eyes were swimming with tears, "own, now, that you never saw those dismal, hateful, tumble-down old houses there look half so—what shall I call them? almost beautiful—as they do now, with that soft, pure, exquisite covering; and if they are so improved, think of what trees, and grass, and ivy must be on such a night as this."

Jenny could not be persuaded into admiring the winter's night, which to her came only as a cold and dismal time, when her cough was more troublesome, and the pain in her side worse than usual. But she put her arm round Ruth's neck, and stood by her, glad that the orphan apprentice, who was not yet inured to the hardship of a dressmaker's workroom, should find so much to give her pleasure in such a common occurrence as a frosty night.

They remained deep in separate trains of thought till Mrs Mason's step was heard, when each returned, supperless but refreshed, to her seat.

Ruth's place was the coldest and the darkest in the room, although she liked it the best; she had instinctively chosen it for the sake of the wall opposite to her, on which was a remnant of the beauty of the old drawing-room, which must once have been magnificent, to judge from the faded specimen left. It was divided into panels of pale sea-green, picked out with white and gold; and on these panels were painted—were thrown with the careless, triumphant hand of a master—the most lovely wreaths of flowers, profuse and luxuriant beyond description, and so real-looking, that you could almost fancy you smelt their fragrance, and heard the south wind go softly rustling in and out among the crimson roses—the branches of purple and white lilac—the floating golden-tressed laburnum boughs. Besides these, there were stately white lilies, sacred to the Virgin—hollyhocks, fraxinella, monk's-hood, pansies, primroses; every flower which blooms profusely in charming old-fashioned country gardens was there, depicted among its graceful foliage, but not in the wild disorder in which I have enumerated them. At the bottom of the panel lay a holly-branch, whose stiff straightness was ornamented by a twining drapery of English ivy and mistletoe and winter aconite; while down either side hung pendant garlands of spring and autumn flowers; and, crowning all, came gorgeous summer with the sweet musk-roses, and the rich-coloured flowers of June and July.

Surely Monnoyer, or whoever the dead and gone artist might be, would have been gratified to know the pleasure his handiwork, even in its wane, had power to give to the heavy heart of a young girl; for they conjured up visions of other sister-flowers that grew, and blossomed, and withered away in her early home.

Mrs Mason was particularly desirous that her workwomen should exert themselves to-night, for, on the next, the annual hunt-ball was to take place. It was the one gaiety of the town since the assize-balls had been discontinued. Many were the dresses she had promised should be sent home "without fail" the next morning; she had not let one slip through her fingers, for fear, if it did, it might fall into the hands of the rival dressmaker, who had just established herself in the very same street.

She determined to administer a gentle stimulant to the flagging spirits, and with a little preliminary cough to attract attention, she began:

"I may as well inform you, young ladies, that I have been requested this year, as on previous occasions, to allow some of my young people to attend in the ante-chamber of the assembly-room with sandal ribbon, pins, and such little matters, and to be ready to repair any accidental injury to the ladies' dresses. I shall send four—of the most diligent." She laid a marked emphasis on the last words, but without much effect; they were too sleepy to care for any of the pomps and vanities, or, indeed, for any of the comforts of this world, excepting one sole thing—their beds.

Mrs Mason was a very worthy woman, but, like many other worthy women, she had her foibles; and one (very natural to her calling) was to pay an extreme regard to appearances. Accordingly, she had already selected in her own mind the four girls who were most likely to do credit to the "establishment;" and these were secretly determined upon, although it was very well to promise the reward to the most diligent. She was really not aware of the falseness of this conduct; being an adept in that species of sophistry with which people persuade themselves that what they wish to do is right.

At last there was no resisting the evidence of weariness. They were told to go to bed; but even that welcome command was languidly obeyed. Slowly they folded up their work, heavily they moved about, until at length all was put away, and they trooped up the wide, dark staircase.

"Oh! how shall I get through five years of these terrible nights! in that close room! and in that oppressive stillness! which lets every sound of the thread be heard as it goes eternally backwards and forwards," sobbed out Ruth, as she threw herself on her bed, without even undressing herself.

"Nay, Ruth, you know it won't be always as it has been to-night. We often get to bed by ten o'clock; and by-and-by you won't mind the closeness of the room. You're worn out to-night, or you would not have minded the sound of the needle; I never hear it. Come, let me unfasten you," said Jenny.

"What is the use of undressing? We must be up again and at work in three hours."

"And in those three hours you may get a great deal of rest, if you will but undress yourself and fairly go to bed. Come, love."

Jenny's advice was not resisted; but before Ruth went to sleep, she said:

"Oh! I wish I was not so cross and impatient. I don't think I used to be."

"No, I am sure not. Most new girls get impatient at first; but it goes off, and they don't care much for anything after awhile. Poor child! she's asleep already," said Jenny to herself.

She could not sleep or rest. The tightness at her side was worse than usual. She almost thought she ought to mention it in her letters home; but then she remembered the premium her father had struggled hard to pay, and the large family, younger than herself, that had to be cared for, and she determined to bear on, and trust that when the warm weather came both the pain and the cough would go away. She would be prudent about herself.

What was the matter with Ruth? She was crying in her sleep as if her heart would break. Such agitated slumber could be no rest; so Jenny wakened her.

"Ruth! Ruth!"

"Oh, Jenny!" said Ruth, sitting up in bed, and pushing back the masses of hair that were heating her forehead, "I thought I saw mamma by the side of the bed, coming, as she used to do, to see if I were asleep and comfortable; and when I tried to take hold of her, she went away and left me alone—I don't know where; so strange!"

"It was only a dream; you know you'd been talking about her to me, and you're feverish with sitting up late. Go to sleep again, and I'll watch, and waken you if you seem uneasy."

"But you'll be so tired. Oh, dear! dear!" Ruth was asleep again, even while she sighed.

Morning came, and though their rest had been short, the girls arose refreshed.

"Miss Sutton, Miss Jennings, Miss Booth, and Miss Hilton, you will see that you are ready to accompany me to the shire-hall by eight o'clock."

One or two of the girls looked astonished, but the majority, having anticipated the selection, and knowing from experience the unexpressed rule by which it was made, received it with the sullen indifference which had become their feeling with regard to most events—a deadened sense of life, consequent upon their unnatural mode of existence, their sedentary days, and their frequent nights of late watching.

But to Ruth it was inexplicable. She had yawned, and loitered, and looked off at the beautiful panel, and lost herself in thoughts of home, until she fully expected the reprimand which at any other time she would have been sure to receive, and now, to her surprise, she was singled out as one of the most diligent!

Much as she longed for the delight of seeing the noble shire-hall—the boast of the county—and of catching glimpses of the dancers, and hearing the band; much as she longed for some variety to the dull, monotonous life she was leading, she could not feel happy to accept a privilege, granted, as she believed, in ignorance of the real state of the case; so she startled her companions by rising abruptly and going up to Mrs Mason, who was finishing a dress which ought to have been sent home two hours before:

"If you please, Mrs Mason, I was not one of the most diligent; I am afraid—I believe—I was not diligent at all. I was very tired; and I could not help thinking, and when I think, I can't attend to my work." She stopped, believing she had sufficiently explained her meaning; but Mrs Mason would not understand, and did not wish for any further elucidation.

"Well, my dear, you must learn to think and work too; or, if you can't do both, you must leave off thinking. Your guardian, you know, expects you to make great progress in your business, and I am sure you won't disappoint him."

But that was not to the point. Ruth stood still an instant, although Mrs Mason resumed her employment in a manner which any one but a "new girl" would have known to be intelligible enough, that she did not wish for any more conversation just then.

"But as I was not diligent I ought not to go, ma'am. Miss Wood was far more industrious than I, and many of the others."

"Tiresome girl!" muttered Mrs Mason; "I've half a mind to keep her at home for plaguing me so." But, looking up, she was struck afresh with the remarkable beauty which Ruth possessed; such a credit to the house, with her waving outline of figure, her striking face, with dark eyebrows and dark lashes, combined with auburn hair and a fair complexion. No! diligent or idle, Ruth Hilton must appear to-night.

"Miss Hilton," said Mrs Mason, with stiff dignity, "I am not accustomed (as these young ladies can tell you) to have my decisions questioned. What I say, I mean; and I have my reasons. So sit down, if you please, and take care and be ready by eight. Not a word more," as she fancied she saw Ruth again about to speak.

"Jenny! you ought to have gone, not me," said Ruth, in no low voice to Miss Wood, as she sat down by her.

"Hush! Ruth. I could not go if I might, because of my cough. I would rather give it up to you than any one, if it were mine to give. And suppose it is, and take the pleasure as my present, and tell me every bit about it when you come home to-night."

"Well! I shall take it in that way, and not as if I'd earned it, which I haven't. So thank you. You can't think how I shall enjoy it now. I did work diligently for five minutes last night, after I heard of it, I wanted to go so much. But I could not keep it up. Oh, dear! and I shall really hear a band! and see the inside of that beautiful shire-hall!"

CHAPTER II

Ruth Goes to the Shire-Hall

In due time that evening, Mrs Mason collected "her young ladies" for an inspection of their appearance before proceeding to the shire-hall. Her eager, important, hurried manner of summoning them was not unlike that of a hen clucking her chickens together; and to judge from the close investigation they had to undergo, it might have been thought that their part in the evening's performance was to be far more important than that of temporary ladies'-maids.

"Is that your best frock, Miss Hilton?" asked Mrs Mason, in a half-dissatisfied tone, turning Ruth about; for it was only her Sunday black silk, and was somewhat worn and shabby.

"Yes, ma'am," answered Ruth, quietly.

"Oh! indeed. Then it will do" (still the half-satisfied tone). "Dress, young ladies, you know, is a very secondary consideration. Conduct is everything. Still, Miss Hilton, I think you should write and ask your guardian to send you money for another gown. I am sorry I did not think of it before."

"I do not think he would send any if I wrote," answered Ruth, in a low voice. "He was angry when I wanted a shawl, when the cold weather set in."

Mrs Mason gave her a little push of dismissal, and Ruth fell into the ranks by her friend, Miss Wood.

"Never mind, Ruthie; you're prettier than any of them," said a merry, good-natured girl, whose plainness excluded her from any of the envy of rivalry.

"Yes! I know I am pretty," said Ruth, sadly, "but I am sorry I have no better gown, for this is very shabby. I am ashamed of it myself, and I can see Mrs Mason is twice as much ashamed. I wish I need not go. I did not know we should have to think about our own dress at all, or I should not have wished to go."

"Never mind, Ruth," said Jenny, "you've been looked at now, and Mrs Mason will soon be too busy to think about you and your gown."

"Did you hear Ruth Hilton say she knew she was pretty?" whispered one girl to another, so loudly that Ruth caught the words.

"I could not help knowing," answered she, simply, "for many people have told me so."

At length these preliminaries were over, and they were walking briskly through the frosty air; the free motion was so inspiriting that Ruth almost danced along, and quite forgot all about shabby gowns and grumbling guardians. The shire-hall was even more striking than she had expected. The sides of the staircase were painted with figures that showed ghostly in the dim light, for only their faces looked out of the dark, dingy canvas, with a strange fixed stare of expression.

The young milliners had to arrange their wares on tables in the ante-room, and make all ready before they could venture to peep into the ball-room, where the musicians were already tuning their instruments, and where one or two char-women (strange contrast! with their dirty, loose attire, and their incessant chatter, to the grand echoes of the vaulted room) were completing the dusting of benches and chairs.

They quitted the place as Ruth and her companions entered. They had talked lightly and merrily in the ante-room, but now their voices were hushed, awed by the old magnificence of the vast apartment. It was so large, that objects showed dim at the further end, as through a mist. Full-length figures of county worthies hung around, in all varieties of costume, from the days of Holbein to the present time. The lofty roof was indistinct, for the lamps were not fully lighted yet; while through the richly-painted Gothic window at one end the moonbeams fell, many-tinted, on the floor, and mocked with their vividness the struggles of the artificial light to illuminate its little sphere.

High above sounded the musicians, fitfully trying some strain of which they were not certain. Then they stopped playing and talked, and their voices sounded goblin-like in their dark recess, where candles were carried about in an uncertain wavering manner, reminding Ruth of the flickering zigzag motion of the will-o'-the-wisp.

Suddenly the room sprang into the full blaze of light, and Ruth felt less impressed with its appearance, and more willing to obey Mrs Mason's sharp summons to her wandering flock, than she had been when it was dim and mysterious. They had presently enough to do in rendering offices of assistance to the ladies who thronged in, and whose voices drowned all the muffled sound of the band Ruth had longed so much to hear. Still, if one pleasure was less, another was greater than she had anticipated.

"On condition" of such a number of little observances that Ruth thought Mrs Mason would never have ended enumerating them, they were allowed during the dances to stand at a side-door and watch. And what a beautiful sight it was! Floating away to that bounding music—now far away, like garlands of fairies, now near, and showing as lovely women, with every ornament of graceful dress—the elite of the county danced on, little caring whose eyes gazed and were dazzled. Outside all was cold, and colourless, and uniform, one coating of snow over all. But inside it was warm, and glowing, and vivid; flowers scented the air, and wreathed the head, and rested on the bosom, as if it were midsummer. Bright colours flashed on the eye and were gone, and succeeded by others as lovely in the rapid movement of the dance. Smiles dimpled every face, and low tones of happiness murmured indistinctly through the room in every pause of the music.

Ruth did not care to separate the figures that formed a joyous and brilliant whole; it was enough to gaze, and dream of the happy smoothness of the lives in which such music, and such profusion of flowers, of jewels, elegance of every description, and beauty of all shapes and hues, were everyday things. She did not want to know who the people were; although to hear a catalogue of names seemed to be the great delight of most of her companions.

In fact, the enumeration rather disturbed her; and to avoid the shock of too rapid a descent into the commonplace world of Miss Smiths and Mr Thomsons, she returned to her post in the ante-room. There she stood thinking, or dreaming. She was startled back to actual life by a voice close to her. One of the dancing young ladies had met with a misfortune. Her dress, of some gossamer material, had been looped up by nosegays of flowers, and one of these had fallen off in the dance, leaving her gown to trail. To repair this, she had begged her partner to bring her to the room where the assistants should have been. None were there but Ruth.

"Shall I leave you?" asked the gentleman. "Is my absence necessary?"

"Oh, no!" replied the lady. "A few stitches will set all to rights. Besides, I dare not enter that room by myself." So far she spoke sweetly and prettily. But now she addressed Ruth. "Make haste. Don't keep me an hour." And her voice became cold and authoritative.

She was very pretty, with long dark ringlets and sparkling black eyes. These had struck Ruth in the hasty glance she had taken, before she knelt down to her task. She also saw that the gentleman was young and elegant.

"Oh, that lovely galop! How I long to dance to it! Will it never be done? What a frightful time you are taking; and I'm dying to return in time for this galop!"

By way of showing a pretty, childlike impatience, she began to beat time with her feet to the spirited air the band was playing. Ruth could not darn the rent in her dress with this continual motion, and she looked up to remonstrate. As she threw her head back for this purpose, she caught the eye of the gentleman who was standing by; it was so expressive of amusement at the airs and graces of his pretty partner, that Ruth was infected by the feeling, and had to bend her face down to conceal the smile that mantled there. But not before he had seen it, and not before his attention had been thereby drawn to consider the kneeling figure, that, habited in black up to the throat, with the noble head bent down to the occupation in which she was engaged, formed such a contrast to the flippant, bright, artificial girl who sat to be served with an air as haughty as a queen on her throne.

"Oh, Mr Bellingham! I'm ashamed to detain you so long. I had no idea any one could have spent so much time over a little tear. No wonder Mrs Mason charges so much for dress-making, if her work-women are so slow."

It was meant to be witty, but Mr Bellingham looked grave. He saw the scarlet colour of annoyance flush to that beautiful cheek which was partially presented to him. He took a candle from the table, and held it so that Ruth had more light. She did not look up to thank him, for she felt ashamed that he should have seen the smile which she had caught from him.

"I am sorry I have been so long, ma'am," said she, gently, as she finished her work. "I was afraid it might tear out again if I did not do it carefully." She rose.

"I would rather have had it torn than have missed that charming galop," said the young lady, shaking out her dress as a bird shakes its plumage. "Shall we go, Mr Bellingham?" looking up at him.

He was surprised that she gave no word or sign of thanks to the assistant. He took up a camellia that some one had left on the table.

"Allow me, Miss Duncombe, to give this in your name to this young lady, as thanks for her dexterous help."

"Oh—of course," said she.

Ruth received the flower silently, but with a grave, modest motion of her head. They had gone, and she was once more alone. Presently, her companions returned.

"What was the matter with Miss Duncombe? Did she come here?" asked they.

"Only her lace dress was torn, and I mended it," answered Ruth, quietly.

"Did Mr Bellingham come with her? They say he's going to be married to her; did he come, Ruth?"

"Yes," said Ruth, and relapsed into silence.

Mr Bellingham danced on gaily and merrily through the night, and flirted with Miss Duncombe, as he thought good. But he looked often to the side-door where the milliner's apprentices stood; and once he recognised the tall, slight figure, and the rich auburn hair of the girl in black; and then his eye sought for the camellia. It was there, snowy white in her bosom. And he danced on more gaily than ever.

The cold grey dawn was drearily lighting up the streets when Mrs Mason and her company returned home. The lamps were extinguished, yet the shutters of the shops and dwelling-houses were not opened. All sounds had an echo unheard by day. One or two houseless beggars sat on doorsteps, and, shivering, slept, with heads bowed on their knees, or resting against the cold hard support afforded by the wall.

Ruth felt as if a dream had melted away, and she were once more in the actual world. How long it would be, even in the most favourable chance, before she should again enter the shire-hall! or hear a band of music! or even see again those bright, happy people—as much without any semblance of care or woe as if they belonged to another race of beings. Had they ever to deny themselves a wish, much less a want? Literally and figuratively, their lives seemed to wander through flowery pleasure-paths. Here was cold, biting mid-winter for her, and such as her—for those poor beggars almost a season of death; but to Miss Duncombe and her companions, a happy, merry time, when flowers still bloomed, and fires crackled, and comforts and luxuries were piled around them like fairy gifts. What did they know of the meaning of the word, so terrific to the poor? What was winter to them? But Ruth fancied that Mr Bellingham looked as if he could understand the feelings of those removed from him by circumstance and station. He had drawn up the windows of his carriage, it is true, with a shudder.

Ruth, then, had been watching him.

Yet she had no idea that any association made her camellia precious to her. She believed it was solely on account of its exquisite beauty that she tended it so carefully. She told Jenny every particular of its presentation, with open, straight-looking eye, and without the deepening of a shade of colour.

"Was it not kind of him? You can't think how nicely he did it, just when I was a little bit mortified by her ungracious ways."

"It was very nice, indeed," replied Jenny. "Such a beautiful flower! I wish it had some scent."

"I wish it to be exactly as it is; it is perfect. So pure!" said Ruth, almost clasping her treasure as she placed it in water. "Who is Mr Bellingham?"

"He is son to that Mrs Bellingham of the Priory, for whom we made the grey satin pelisse," answered Jenny, sleepily.

"That was before my time," said Ruth. But there was no answer. Jenny was asleep.

It was long before Ruth followed her example. Even on a winter day, it was clear morning light that fell upon her face as she smiled in her slumber. Jenny would not waken her, but watched her face with admiration; it was so lovely in its happiness.

"She is dreaming of last night," thought Jenny.

It was true she was; but one figure flitted more than all the rest through her visions. He presented flower after flower to her in that baseless morning dream, which was all too quickly ended. The night before, she had seen her dead mother in her sleep, and she wakened, weeping. And now she dreamed of Mr Bellingham, and smiled.

And yet, was this a more evil dream than the other?

The realities of life seemed to cut more sharply against her heart than usual that morning. The late hours of the preceding nights, and perhaps the excitement of the evening before, had indisposed her to bear calmly the rubs and crosses which beset all Mrs Mason's young ladies at times.

For Mrs Mason, though the first dressmaker in the county, was human after all; and suffered, like her apprentices, from the same causes that affected them. This morning she was disposed to find fault with everything, and everybody. She seemed to have risen with the determination of putting the world and all that it contained (her world, at least) to rights before night; and abuses and negligences, which had long passed unreproved, or winked at, were to-day to be dragged to light, and sharply reprimanded. Nothing less than perfection would satisfy Mrs Mason at such times.

She had her ideas of justice, too; but they were not divinely beautiful and true ideas; they were something more resembling a grocer's, or tea-dealer's ideas of equal right. A little over-indulgence last night was to be balanced by a good deal of over-severity to-day; and this manner of rectifying previous errors fully satisfied her conscience.

Ruth was not inclined for, or capable of, much extra exertion; and it would have tasked all her powers to have pleased her superior. The work-room seemed filled with sharp calls. "Miss Hilton! where have you put the blue Persian? Whenever things are mislaid, I know it has been Miss Hilton's evening for siding away!"

"Miss Hilton was going out last night, so I offered to clear the workroom for her. I will find it directly, ma'am," answered one of the girls.

"Oh, I am well aware of Miss Hilton's custom of shuffling off her duties upon any one who can be induced to relieve her," replied Mrs Mason.

Ruth reddened, and tears sprang to her eyes; but she was so conscious of the falsity of the accusation, that she rebuked herself for being moved by it, and, raising her head, gave a proud look round, as if in appeal to her companions.

"Where is the skirt of Lady Farnham's dress? The flounces not put on! I am surprised. May I ask to whom this work was entrusted yesterday?" inquired Mrs Mason, fixing her eyes on Ruth.

"I was to have done it, but I made a mistake, and had to undo it. I am very sorry."

"I might have guessed, certainly. There is little difficulty, to be sure, in discovering, when work has been neglected or spoilt, into whose hands it has fallen."

Such were the speeches which fell to Ruth's share on this day of all days, when she was least fitted to bear them with equanimity.

In the afternoon it was necessary for Mrs Mason to go a few miles into the country. She left injunctions, and orders, and directions, and prohibitions without end; but at last she was gone, and in the relief of her absence, Ruth laid her arms on the table, and, burying her head, began to cry aloud, with weak, unchecked sobs.

"Don't cry, Miss Hilton,"—"Ruthie, never mind the old dragon,"—"How will you bear on for five years, if you don't spirit yourself up not to care a straw for what she says?"—were some of the modes of comfort and sympathy administered by the young workwomen.

Jenny, with a wiser insight into the grievance and its remedy, said:

"Suppose Ruth goes out instead of you, Fanny Barton, to do the errands. The fresh air will do her good; and you know you dislike the cold east winds, while Ruth says she enjoys frost and snow, and all kinds of shivery weather."

Fanny Barton was a great sleepy-looking girl, huddling over the fire. No one so willing as she to relinquish the walk on this bleak afternoon, when the east wind blew keenly down the street, drying up the very snow itself. There was no temptation to come abroad, for those who were not absolutely obliged to leave their warm rooms; indeed, the dusk hour showed that it was the usual tea-time for the humble inhabitants of that part of the town through which Ruth had to pass on her shopping expedition. As she came to the high ground just above the river, where the street sloped rapidly down to the bridge, she saw the flat country beyond all covered with snow, making the black dome of the cloud-laden sky appear yet blacker; as if the winter's night had never fairly gone away, but had hovered on the edge of the world all through the short bleak day. Down by the bridge (where there was a little shelving bank, used as a landing-place for any pleasure-boats that could float on that shallow stream) some children were playing, and defying the cold; one of them had got a large washing-tub, and with the use of a broken oar kept steering and pushing himself hither and thither in the little creek, much to the admiration of his companions, who stood gravely looking on, immovable in their attentive observation of the hero, although their faces were blue with cold, and their hands crammed deep into their pockets with some faint hope of finding warmth there. Perhaps they feared that, if they unpacked themselves from their lumpy attitudes and began to move about, the cruel wind would find its way into every cranny of their tattered dress. They were all huddled up, and still; with eyes intent on the embryo sailor. At last, one little man, envious of the reputation that his playfellow was acquiring by his daring, called out:

"I'll set thee a craddy, Tom! Thou dar'n't go over yon black line in the water, out into the real river."

Of course the challenge was not to be refused, and Tom paddled away towards the dark line, beyond which the river swept with smooth, steady current. Ruth (a child in years herself) stood at the top of the declivity watching the adventurer, but as unconscious of any danger as the group of children below. At their playfellow's success, they broke through the calm gravity of observation into boisterous marks of applause, clapping their hands, and stamping their impatient little feet, and shouting, "Well done, Tom; thou hast done it rarely!"

Tom stood in childish dignity for a moment, facing his admirers; then, in an instant, his washing-tub boat was whirled round, and he lost his balance, and fell out; and both he and his boat were carried away slowly, but surely, by the strong full river which eternally moved onwards to the sea.

The children shrieked aloud with terror; and Ruth flew down to the little bay, and far into its shallow waters, before she felt how useless such an action was, and that the sensible plan would have been to seek for efficient help. Hardly had this thought struck her, when, louder and sharper than the sullen roar of the stream that was ceaselessly and unrelentingly flowing on, came the splash of a horse galloping through the water in which she was standing. Past her like lightning—down in the stream, swimming along with the current—a stooping rider—an outstretched, grasping arm—a little life redeemed, and a child saved to those who loved it! Ruth stood dizzy and sick with emotion while all this took place; and when the rider turned his swimming horse, and slowly breasted up the river to the landing-place, she recognised him as the Mr Bellingham of the night before. He carried the unconscious child across his horse; the body hung in so lifeless a manner that Ruth believed it was dead, and her eyes were suddenly blinded with tears. She waded back to the beach, to the point towards which Mr Bellingham was directing his horse.

"Is he dead?" asked she, stretching out her arms to receive the little fellow; for she instinctively felt that the position in which he hung was not the most conducive to returning consciousness, if, indeed, it would ever return.

"I think not," answered Mr Bellingham, as he gave the child to her, before springing off his horse. "Is he your brother? Do you know who he is?"

"Look!" said Ruth, who had sat down upon the ground, the better to prop the poor lad, "his hand twitches! he lives! oh, sir, he lives! Whose boy is he?" (to the people, who came hurrying and gathering to the spot at the rumour of an accident).

"He's old Nelly Brownson's," said they. "Her grandson."

"We must take him into a house directly," said she. "Is his home far off?"

"No, no; it's just close by."

"One of you go for a doctor at once," said Mr Bellingham, authoritatively, "and bring him to the old woman's without delay. You must not hold him any longer," he continued, speaking to Ruth, and remembering her face now for the first time; "your dress is dripping wet already. Here! you fellow, take him up, d'ye see!"

But the child's hand had nervously clenched Ruth's dress, and she would not have him disturbed. She carried her heavy burden very tenderly towards a mean little cottage indicated by the neighbours; an old crippled woman was coming out of the door, shaking all over with agitation.

"Dear heart!" said she, "he's the last of 'em all, and he's gone afore me."

"Nonsense," said Mr Bellingham, "the boy is alive, and likely to live."

But the old woman was helpless and hopeless, and insisted on believing that her grandson was dead; and dead he would have been if it had not been for Ruth, and one or two of the more sensible neighbours, who, under Mr Bellingham's directions, bustled about, and did all that was necessary until animation was restored.

"What a confounded time these people are in fetching the doctor," said Mr Bellingham to Ruth, between whom and himself a sort of silent understanding had sprung up from the circumstance of their having been the only two (besides mere children) who had witnessed the accident, and also the only two to whom a certain degree of cultivation had given the power of understanding each other's thoughts and even each other's words.

"It takes so much to knock an idea into such stupid people's heads. They stood gaping and asking which doctor they were to go for, as if it signified whether it was Brown or Smith, so long as he had his wits about him. I have no more time to waste here, either; I was on the gallop when I caught sight of the lad; and, now he has fairly sobbed and opened his eyes, I see no use in my staying in this stifling atmosphere. May I trouble you with one thing? Will you be so good as to see that the little fellow has all that he wants? If you'll allow me, I'll leave you my purse," continued he, giving it to Ruth, who was only too glad to have this power entrusted to her of procuring one or two requisites which she had perceived to be wanted. But she saw some gold between the net-work; she did not like the charge of such riches.

"I shall not want so much, really, sir. One sovereign will be plenty—more than enough. May I take that out, and I will give you back what is left of it when I see you again? or, perhaps I had better send it to you, sir?"

"I think you had better keep it all at present. Oh! what a horrid dirty place this is; insufferable two minutes longer. You must not stay here; you'll be poisoned with this abominable air. Come towards the door, I beg. Well, if you think one sovereign will be enough, I will take my purse; only, remember you apply to me if you think they want more."

They were standing at the door, where some one was holding Mr Bellingham's horse. Ruth was looking at him with her earnest eyes (Mrs Mason and her errands quite forgotten in the interest of the afternoon's event), her whole thoughts bent upon rightly understanding and following out his wishes for the little boy's welfare; and until now this had been the first object in his own mind. But at this moment the strong perception of Ruth's exceeding beauty came again upon him. He almost lost the sense of what he was saying, he was so startled into admiration. The night before, he had not seen her eyes; and now they looked straight and innocently full at him, grave, earnest, and deep. But when she instinctively read the change in the expression of his countenance, she dropped her large white veiling lids; and he thought her face was lovelier still.

The irresistible impulse seized him to arrange matters so that he might see her again before long.

"No!" said he. "I see it would be better that you should keep the purse. Many things may be wanted for the lad which we cannot calculate upon now. If I remember rightly, there are three sovereigns and some loose change; I shall, perhaps, see you again in a few days, when, if there be any money left in the purse, you can restore it to me."

"Oh, yes, sir," said Ruth, alive to the magnitude of the wants to which she might have to administer, and yet rather afraid of the responsibility implied in the possession of so much money.

"Is there any chance of my meeting you again in this house?" asked he.

"I hope to come whenever I can, sir; but I must run in errand-times, and I don't know when my turn may be."

"Oh"—he did not fully understand this answer—"I should like to know how you think the boy is going on, if it is not giving you too much trouble; do you ever take walks?"

"Not for walking's sake, sir."

"Well!" said he, "you go to church, I suppose? Mrs Mason does not keep you at work on Sundays, I trust?"

"Oh, no, sir. I go to church regularly."

"Then, perhaps, you will be so good as to tell me what church you go to, and I will meet you there next Sunday afternoon?"

"I go to St Nicholas', sir. I will take care and bring you word how the boy is, and what doctor they get; and I will keep an account of the money I spend."

"Very well; thank you. Remember, I trust to you."

He meant that he relied on her promise to meet him; but Ruth thought that he was referring to the responsibility of doing the best she could for the child. He was going away, when a fresh thought struck him, and he turned back into the cottage once more, and addressed Ruth, with a half smile on his countenance:

"It seems rather strange, but we have no one to introduce us; my name is Bellingham—yours is—?"

"Ruth Hilton, sir," she answered, in a low voice, for, now that the conversation no longer related to the boy, she felt shy and restrained.

He held out his hand to shake hers, and just as she gave it to him, the old grandmother came tottering up to ask some question. The interruption jarred upon him, and made him once more keenly alive to the closeness of the air, and the squalor and dirt by which he was surrounded.

"My good woman," said he to Nelly Brownson, "could you not keep your place a little neater and cleaner? It is more fit for pigs than human beings. The air in this room is quite offensive, and the dirt and filth is really disgraceful."

By this time he was mounted, and, bowing to Ruth, he rode away.

Then the old woman's wrath broke out.

"Who may you be, that knows no better manners than to come into a poor woman's house to abuse it?—fit for pigs, indeed! What d'ye call yon fellow?"

"He is Mr Bellingham," said Ruth, shocked at the old woman's apparent ingratitude. "It was he that rode into the water to save your grandson. He would have been drowned but for Mr Bellingham. I thought once they would both have been swept away by the current, it was so strong."

"The river is none so deep, either," the old woman said, anxious to diminish as much as possible the obligation she was under to one who had offended her. "Some one else would have saved him, if this fine young spark had never been near. He's an orphan, and God watches over orphans, they say. I'd rather it had been any one else as had picked him out, than one who comes into a poor body's house only to abuse it."

"He did not come in only to abuse it," said Ruth, gently. "He came with little Tom; he only said it was not quite so clean as it might be."

"What! you're taking up the cry, are you? Wait till you are an old woman like me, crippled with rheumatiz, and a lad to see after like Tom, who is always in mud when he isn't in water; and his food and mine to scrape together (God knows we're often short, and do the best I can), and water to fetch up that steep brow."

She stopped to cough; and Ruth judiciously changed the subject, and began to consult the old woman as to the wants of her grandson, in which consultation they were soon assisted by the medical man.

When Ruth had made one or two arrangements with a neighbour, whom she asked to procure the most necessary things, and had heard from the doctor that all would be right in a day or two, she began to quake at the recollection of the length of time she had spent at Nelly Brownson's, and to remember, with some affright, the strict watch kept by Mrs Mason over her apprentices' out-goings and in-comings on working days. She hurried off to the shops, and tried to recall her wandering thoughts to the respective merits of pink and blue as a match to lilac, found she had lost her patterns, and went home with ill-chosen things, and in a fit of despair at her own stupidity.

The truth was, that the afternoon's adventure filled her mind; only, the figure of Tom (who was now safe, and likely to do well) was receding into the background, and that of Mr Bellingham becoming more prominent than it had been. His spirited and natural action of galloping into the water to save the child, was magnified by Ruth into the most heroic deed of daring; his interest about the boy was tender, thoughtful benevolence in her eyes, and his careless liberality of money was fine generosity; for she forgot that generosity implies some degree of self-denial. She was gratified, too, by the power of dispensing comfort he had entrusted to her, and was busy with Alnaschar visions of wise expenditure, when the necessity of opening Mrs Mason's house-door summoned her back into actual present life, and the dread of an immediate scolding.

For this time, however, she was spared; but spared for such a reason that she would have been thankful for some blame in preference to her impunity. During her absence, Jenny's difficulty of breathing had suddenly become worse, and the girls had, on their own responsibility, put her to bed, and were standing round her in dismay, when Mrs Mason's return home (only a few minutes before Ruth arrived) fluttered them back into the workroom.

And now, all was confusion and hurry; a doctor to be sent for; a mind to be unburdened of directions for a dress to a forewoman, who was too ill to understand; scoldings to be scattered with no illiberal hand amongst a group of frightened girls, hardly sparing the poor invalid herself for her inopportune illness. In the middle of all this turmoil, Ruth crept quietly to her place, with a heavy saddened heart at the indisposition of the gentle forewoman. She would gladly have nursed Jenny herself, and often longed to do it, but she could not be spared. Hands, unskilful in fine and delicate work, would be well enough qualified to tend the sick, until the mother arrived from home. Meanwhile, extra diligence was required in the workroom; and Ruth found no opportunity of going to see little Tom, or to fulfil the plans for making him and his grandmother more comfortable, which she had proposed to herself. She regretted her rash promise to Mr Bellingham, of attending to the little boy's welfare; all that she could do was done by means of Mrs Mason's servant, through whom she made inquiries, and sent the necessary help.

The subject of Jenny's illness was the prominent one in the house. Ruth told of her own adventure, to be sure; but when she was at the very crisis of the boy's fall into the river, the more fresh and vivid interest of some tidings of Jenny was brought into the room, and Ruth ceased, almost blaming herself for caring for anything besides the question of life or death to be decided in that very house.

Then a pale, gentle-looking woman was seen moving softly about; and it was whispered that this was the mother come to nurse her child. Everybody liked her, she was so sweet-looking, and gave so little trouble, and seemed so patient, and so thankful for any inquiries about her daughter, whose illness, it was understood, although its severity was mitigated, was likely to be long and tedious. While all the feelings and thoughts relating to Jenny were predominant, Sunday arrived. Mrs Mason went the accustomed visit to her father's, making some little show of apology to Mrs Wood for leaving her and her daughter; the apprentices dispersed to the various friends with whom they were in the habit of spending the day; and Ruth went to St Nicholas', with a sorrowful heart, depressed on account of Jenny, and self-reproachful at having rashly undertaken what she had been unable to perform.

As she came out of church, she was joined by Mr Bellingham. She had half hoped that he might have forgotten the arrangement, and yet she wished to relieve herself of her responsibility. She knew his step behind her, and the contending feelings made her heart beat hard, and she longed to run away.

"Miss Hilton, I believe," said he, overtaking her, and bowing forward, so as to catch a sight of her rose-red face. "How is our little sailor going on? Well, I trust, from the symptoms the other day."

"I believe, sir, he is quite well now. I am very sorry, but I have not been able to go and see him. I am so sorry—I could not help it. But I have got one or two things through another person. I have put them down on this slip of paper; and here is your purse, sir, for I am afraid I can do nothing more for him. We have illness in the house, and it makes us very busy."

Ruth had been so much accustomed to blame of late, that she almost anticipated some remonstrance or reproach now, for not having fulfilled her promise better. She little guessed that Mr Bellingham was far more busy trying to devise some excuse for meeting her again, during the silence that succeeded her speech, than displeased with her for not bringing a more particular account of the little boy, in whom he had ceased to feel any interest.

She repeated, after a minute's pause:

"I am very sorry I have done so little, sir."

"Oh, yes, I am sure you have done all you could. It was thoughtless in me to add to your engagements."

"He is displeased with me," thought Ruth, "for what he believes to have been neglect of the boy, whose life he risked his own to save. If I told all, he would see that I could not do more; but I cannot tell him all the sorrows and worries that have taken up my time."

"And yet I am tempted to give you another little commission, if it is not taking up too much of your time, and presuming too much on your good-nature," said he, a bright idea having just struck him. "Mrs Mason lives in Heneage Place, does not she? My mother's ancestors lived there; and once, when the house was being repaired, she took me in to show me the old place. There was an old hunting-piece painted on a panel over one of the chimney-pieces; the figures were portraits of my ancestors. I have often thought I should like to purchase it, if it still remained there. Can you ascertain this for me, and bring me word next Sunday?"

"Oh, yes, sir," said Ruth, glad that this commission was completely within her power to execute, and anxious to make up for her previous seeming neglect. "I'll look directly I get home, and ask Mrs Mason to write and let you know."

"Thank you," said he, only half satisfied; "I think perhaps, however, it might be as well not to trouble Mrs Mason about it; you see, it would compromise me, and I am not quite determined to purchase the picture; if you would ascertain whether the painting is there, and tell me, I would take a little time to reflect, and afterwards I could apply to Mrs Mason myself."

"Very well, sir; I will see about it." So they parted.

Before the next Sunday, Mrs Wood had taken her daughter to her distant home, to recruit in that quiet place. Ruth watched her down the street from an upper window, and, sighing deep and long, returned to the workroom, whence the warning voice and the gentle wisdom had departed.

CHAPTER III

Sunday at Mrs Mason's

Mr Bellingham attended afternoon service at St Nicholas' church the next Sunday. His thoughts had been far more occupied by Ruth than hers by him, although his appearance upon the scene of her life was more an event to her than it was to him. He was puzzled by the impression she had produced on him, though he did not in general analyse the nature of his feelings, but simply enjoyed them with the delight which youth takes in experiencing new and strong emotion.

He was old compared to Ruth, but young as a man; hardly three-and-twenty. The fact of his being an only child had given him, as it does to many, a sort of inequality in those parts of the character which are usually formed by the number of years that a person has lived.

The unevenness of discipline to which only children are subjected; the thwarting, resulting from over-anxiety; the indiscreet indulgence, arising from a love centred all in one object; had been exaggerated in his education, probably from the circumstance that his mother (his only surviving parent) had been similarly situated to himself.

He was already in possession of the comparatively small property he inherited from his father. The estate on which his mother lived was her own; and her income gave her the means of indulging or controlling him, after he had grown to man's estate, as her wayward disposition and her love of power prompted her.

Had he been double-dealing in his conduct towards her, had he condescended to humour her in the least, her passionate love for him would have induced her to strip herself of all her possessions to add to his dignity or happiness. But although he felt the warmest affection for her, the regardlessness which she had taught him (by example, perhaps, more than by precept) of the feelings of others, was continually prompting him to do things that she, for the time being, resented as mortal affronts. He would mimic the clergyman she specially esteemed, even to his very face; he would refuse to visit her schools for months and months; and, when wearied into going at last, revenge himself by puzzling the children with the most ridiculous questions (gravely put) that he could imagine.

All these boyish tricks annoyed and irritated her far more than the accounts which reached her of more serious misdoings at college and in town. Of these grave offences she never spoke; of the smaller misdeeds she hardly ever ceased speaking.

Still, at times, she had great influence over him, and nothing delighted her more than to exercise it. The submission of his will to hers was sure to be liberally rewarded; for it gave her great happiness to extort, from his indifference or his affection, the concessions which she never sought by force of reason, or by appeals to principle—concessions which he frequently withheld, solely for the sake of asserting his independence of her control.

She was anxious for him to marry Miss Duncombe. He cared little or nothing about it—it was time enough to be married ten years hence; and so he was dawdling through some months of his life—sometimes flirting with the nothing-loath Miss Duncombe, sometimes plaguing, and sometimes delighting his mother, at all times taking care to please himself—when he first saw Ruth Hilton, and a new, passionate, hearty feeling shot through his whole being. He did not know why he was so fascinated by her. She was very beautiful, but he had seen others equally beautiful, and with many more *agaceries* calculated to set off the effect of their charms.

There was, perhaps, something bewitching in the union of the grace and loveliness of womanhood with the *naïveté*, simplicity, and innocence of an intelligent child. There was a spell in the shyness, which made her avoid and shun all admiring approaches to acquaintance. It would be an exquisite delight to attract and tame her wildness, just as he had often allured and tamed the timid fawns in his mother's park.

By no over-bold admiration, or rash, passionate word, would he startle her; and, surely, in time she might be induced to look upon him as a friend, if not something nearer and dearer still.

In accordance with this determination, he resisted the strong temptation of walking by her side the whole distance home after church. He only received the intelligence she brought respecting the panel with thanks, spoke a few words about the weather, bowed, and was gone. Ruth believed she should never see him again; and, in spite of sundry self-upbraidings for her folly, she could not help feeling as if a shadow were drawn over her existence for several days to come.

Mrs Mason was a widow, and had to struggle for the sake of the six or seven children left dependent on her exertions; thus there was some reason, and great excuse, for the pinching economy which regulated her household affairs.

On Sundays she chose to conclude that all her apprentices had friends who would be glad to see them to dinner, and give them a welcome reception for the remainder of the day; while she, and those of her children who were not at school, went to spend the day at her father's house, several miles out of the town. Accordingly, no dinner was cooked on Sundays for the young workwomen; no fires were lighted in any rooms to which they had access. On this morning they breakfasted in Mrs Mason's own parlour, after which the room was closed against them through the day by some understood, though unspoken prohibition.

What became of such as Ruth, who had no home and no friends in that large, populous, desolate town? She had hitherto commissioned the servant, who went to market on Saturdays for the family, to buy her a bun or biscuit, whereon she made her fasting dinner in the deserted workroom, sitting in her walking-dress to keep off the cold, which clung to her in spite of shawl and bonnet. Then she would sit at the window, looking out on the dreary prospect till her eyes were often blinded by tears; and, partly to shake off thoughts and recollections, the indulgence in which she felt to be productive of no good, and partly to have some ideas to dwell upon during the coming week beyond those suggested by the constant view of the same room, she would carry her Bible, and place herself in the window-seat on the wide landing, which commanded the street in front of the house. From thence she could see the irregular grandeur of the place; she caught a view of the grey church-tower, rising hoary and massive into mid-air; she saw one or two figures loiter along on the sunny side of the street, in all the enjoyment of their fine clothes and Sunday leisure; and she imagined histories for them, and tried to picture to herself their homes and their daily doings.

And before long, the bells swung heavily in the church-tower, and struck out with musical clang the first summons to afternoon church.

After church was over, she used to return home to the same window-seat, and watch till the winter twilight was over and gone, and the stars came out over the black masses of houses. And then she would steal down to ask for a candle, as a companion to her in the deserted workroom. Occasionally the servant would bring her up some tea; but of late Ruth had declined taking any, as she had discovered she was robbing the kind-hearted creature of part of the small provision left out for her by Mrs Mason. She sat on, hungry and cold, trying to read her Bible, and to think the old holy thoughts which had been her childish meditations at her mother's knee, until one after another the apprentices returned, weary with their day's enjoyment, and their week's late watching; too weary to make her in any way a partaker of their pleasure by entering into details of the manner in which they had spent their day.

And last of all, Mrs Mason returned; and, summoning her "young people" once more into the parlour, she read a prayer before dismissing them to bed. She always expected to find them all in the house when she came home, but asked no questions as to their proceedings through the day; perhaps because she dreaded to hear that one or two had occasionally nowhere to go, and that it would be sometimes necessary to order a Sunday's dinner, and leave a lighted fire on that day.

For five months Ruth had been an inmate at Mrs Mason's, and such had been the regular order of the Sundays. While the forewoman stayed there, it is true, she was ever ready to give Ruth the little variety of hearing of recreations in which she was no partaker; and however tired Jenny might be at night, she had ever some sympathy to bestow on Ruth for the dull length of day she had passed. After her departure, the monotonous idleness of the Sunday seemed worse to bear than the incessant labour of the work-days; until the time came when it seemed to be a recognised hope in her mind, that on

Sunday afternoons she should see Mr Bellingham, and hear a few words from him, as from a friend who took an interest in her thoughts and proceedings during the past week.

Ruth's mother had been the daughter of a poor curate in Norfolk, and, early left without parents or home, she was thankful to marry a respectable farmer a good deal older than herself. After their marriage, however, everything seemed to go wrong. Mrs Hilton fell into a delicate state of health, and was unable to bestow the ever-watchful attention to domestic affairs so requisite in a farmer's wife. Her husband had a series of misfortunes—of a more important kind than the death of a whole brood of turkeys from getting among the nettles, or the year of bad cheeses spoilt by a careless dairymaid—which were the consequences (so the neighbours said) of Mr Hilton's mistake in marrying a delicate, fine lady. His crops failed; his horses died; his barn took fire; in short, if he had been in any way a remarkable character, one might have supposed him to be the object of an avenging fate, so successive were the evils which pursued him; but as he was only a somewhat commonplace farmer, I believe we must attribute his calamities to some want in his character of the one quality required to act as keystone to many excellences. While his wife lived, all worldly misfortunes seemed as nothing to him; her strong sense and lively faculty of hope upheld him from despair; her sympathy was always ready, and the invalid's room had an atmosphere of peace and encouragement, which affected all who entered it. But when Ruth was about twelve, one morning in the busy hay-time, Mrs Hilton was left alone for some hours. This had often happened before, nor had she seemed weaker than usual when they had gone forth to the field; but on their return, with merry voices, to fetch the dinner prepared for the haymakers, they found an unusual silence brooding over the house; no low voice called out gently to welcome them, and ask after the day's progress; and, on entering the little parlour, which was called Mrs Hilton's, and was sacred to her, they found her lying dead on her accustomed sofa. Quite calm and peaceful she lay; there had been no struggle at last; the struggle was for the survivors, and one sank under it. Her husband did not make much ado at first—at least, not in outward show; her memory seemed to keep in check all external violence of grief; but, day by day, dating from his wife's death, his mental powers decreased. He was still a hale-looking elderly man, and his bodily health appeared as good as ever; but he sat for hours in his easy-chair, looking into the fire, not moving, nor speaking, unless when it was absolutely necessary to answer repeated questions. If Ruth, with coaxings and draggings, induced him to come out with her, he went with measured steps around his fields, his head bent to the ground with the same abstracted, unseeing look; never smiling—never changing the expression of his face, not even to one of deeper sadness, when anything occurred which might be supposed to remind him of his dead wife. But in this abstraction from all outward things, his worldly affairs went ever lower down. He paid money away, or received it, as if it had been so much water; the gold mines of Potosi could not have touched the deep grief of his soul; but God in His mercy knew the sure balm, and sent the Beautiful Messenger to take the weary one home.

After his death, the creditors were the chief people who appeared to take any interest in the affairs; and it seemed strange to Ruth to see people, whom she scarcely knew, examining and touching all that she had been accustomed to consider as precious and sacred. Her father had made his will at her birth. With the pride of newly and late-acquired paternity, he had considered the office of guardian to his little darling as one which would have been an additional honour to the lord-lieutenant of the county; but as he had not the pleasure of his lordship's acquaintance, he selected the person of most consequence amongst those whom he did know; not any very ambitious appointment, in those days of comparative prosperity; but certainly the flourishing maltster of Skelton was a little surprised, when, fifteen years later, he learnt that he was executor to a will bequeathing many vanished hundreds of pounds, and guardian to a young girl whom he could not remember ever to have seen.

He was a sensible, hard-headed man of the world; having a very fair proportion of conscience as consciences go; indeed, perhaps more than many people; for he had some ideas of duty extending to the circle beyond his own family; and did not, as some would have done, decline acting altogether, but speedily summoned the creditors, examined into the accounts, sold up the farming-stock, and discharged all the debts; paid about £80 into the Skelton bank for a week, while he inquired for a situation or apprenticeship of some kind for poor heart-broken Ruth; heard of Mrs Mason's; arranged all with her in two short conversations; drove over for Ruth in his gig; waited while she and the old servant packed up her clothes; and grew very impatient while she ran, with her eyes streaming with tears, round the garden, tearing off in a passion of love whole boughs of favourite China and damask roses, late flowering against the casement-window of what had been her mother's room. When she took her seat in the gig, she was little able, even if she had been inclined, to profit by her guardian's lectures on economy and self-reliance; but she was quiet and silent, looking forward with longing to the night-time, when, in her bedroom, she might give way to all her passionate sorrow at being wrenched from the home where she had lived with her parents, in that utter absence of any anticipation of change, which is either the blessing or the curse of childhood. But at night there were four other girls in her room, and she could not cry before them. She watched and waited till, one by one, they dropped off to sleep, and then she buried her face in the pillow, and shook with sobbing grief; and then she paused to conjure up, with fond luxuriance, every recollection of the happy days, so little valued in their uneventful peace while they lasted, so passionately regretted when once gone for ever; to remember every look and word of the dear mother, and to moan afresh over the change caused by her death;—the first clouding in of Ruth's day of life. It was Jenny's sympathy on this first night, when awakened by Ruth's irrepressible agony, that had made the bond between them. But Ruth's loving disposition, continually sending forth fibres in search of nutriment, found no other object for regard among those of her daily life to compensate for the want of natural ties.

But, almost insensibly, Jenny's place in Ruth's heart was filled up; there was some one who listened with tender interest to all her little revelations; who questioned her about her early days of happiness, and, in return, spoke of his own childhood—not so golden in reality as Ruth's, but more dazzling, when recounted with stories of the beautiful cream-coloured Arabian pony, and the old picture-gallery in the house, and avenues, and terraces, and fountains in the garden, for Ruth to paint, with all the vividness of imagination, as scenery and background for the figure which was growing by slow degrees most prominent in her thoughts.

It must not be supposed that this was effected all at once, though the intermediate stages have been passed over. On Sunday, Mr Bellingham only spoke to her to receive the information about the panel; nor did he come to St Nicholas' the next, nor yet the following Sunday. But the third he walked by her side a little way, and, seeing her annoyance, he left her; and then she wished for him back again, and found the day very dreary, and wondered why a strange undefined feeling had made her imagine she was doing wrong in walking alongside of one so kind and good as Mr Bellingham; it had been very foolish of her to be self-conscious all the time, and if ever he spoke to her again she would not think of what people might say, but enjoy the pleasure which his kind words and evident interest in her might give. Then she thought it was very likely he never would notice her again, for she knew she had been very rude with her short answers; it was very provoking that she had behaved so rudely. She should be sixteen in another month, and she was still childish and awkward. Thus she lectured herself, after parting with Mr Bellingham; and the consequence was, that on the following Sunday she was ten times as blushing and conscious, and (Mr Bellingham thought) ten times more beautiful than ever. He suggested, that instead of going straight home through High-street, she should take the round by the Leasowes; at first she declined, but then, suddenly wondering and questioning herself why she refused a thing which was, as far as reason and knowledge (*her* knowledge) went, so innocent, and which was certainly so tempting and pleasant, she agreed to go the round; and when she was once in the meadows that skirted the town, she forgot all doubt and awkwardness—nay, almost forgot the presence of Mr Bellingham—in her delight at the new tender beauty of an early spring day in February. Among the last year's brown ruins, heaped together by the wind in the hedgerows, she found the fresh green crinkled leaves and pale star-like flowers of the primroses. Here and there a golden celandine made brilliant the sides of the little brook that (full of water in "February fill-dyke") bubbled along by the side of the path; the sun was low in the horizon, and once, when they came to a higher part of the Leasowes, Ruth burst into an exclamation of delight at the evening glory of mellow light which was in the sky behind the purple distance, while the brown leafless woods in the foreground derived an almost metallic lustre from the golden mist and haze of the sunset. It was but three-quarters of a mile round by the meadows, but somehow it took them an hour to walk it. Ruth turned to thank Mr Bellingham for his kindness in taking her home by this beautiful way, but his look of admiration at her glowing, animated face, made her suddenly silent; and, hardly wishing him good-bye, she quickly entered the house with a beating, happy, agitated heart.

"How strange it is," she thought that evening, "that I should feel as if this charming afternoon's walk were, somehow, not exactly wrong, but yet as if it were not right. Why can it be? I am not defrauding Mrs Mason of any of her time; that I know would be wrong; I am left to go where I like on Sundays. I have been to church, so it can't be because I have missed doing my duty. If I had gone this walk with Jenny, I wonder whether I should have felt as I do now. There must be something wrong in me, myself, to feel so guilty when I have done nothing which is not right; and yet I can thank God for the happiness I have had in this charming spring walk, which dear mamma used to say was a sign when pleasures were innocent and good for us."

She was not conscious, as yet, that Mr Bellingham's presence had added any charm to the ramble; and when she might have become aware of this, as, week after week, Sunday after Sunday, loitering ramble after loitering ramble succeeded each other, she was too much absorbed with one set of thoughts to have much inclination for self-questioning.

"Tell me everything, Ruth, as you would to a brother; let me help you, if I can, in your difficulties," he said to her one afternoon. And he really did try to understand, and to realise, how an insignificant and paltry person like Mason the dressmaker could be an object of dread, and regarded as a person having authority, by Ruth. He flamed up with indignation when, by way of impressing him with Mrs Mason's power and consequence, Ruth spoke of some instance of the effects of her employer's displeasure. He declared his mother should never have a gown made again by such a tyrant— such a Mrs Brownrigg; that he would prevent all his acquaintances from going to such a cruel dressmaker; till Ruth was alarmed at the threatened consequences of her one-sided account, and pleaded for Mrs Mason as earnestly as if a young man's menace of this description were likely to be literally fulfilled.

"Indeed, sir, I have been very wrong; if you please, sir, don't be so angry. She is often very good to us; it is only sometimes she goes into a passion; and we are very provoking, I dare say. I know I am for one. I have often to undo my work, and you can't think how it spoils anything (particularly silk) to be unpicked; and Mrs Mason has to bear all the blame. Oh! I am sorry I said anything about it. Don't speak to your mother about it, pray, sir. Mrs Mason thinks so much of Mrs Bellingham's custom."

"Well, I won't this time"—recollecting that there might be some awkwardness in accounting to his mother for the means by which he had obtained his very correct information as to what passed in Mrs Mason's workroom—"but if ever she does so again, I'll not answer for myself."

"I will take care and not tell again, sir," said Ruth, in a low voice.

"Nay, Ruth, you are not going to have secrets from me, are you? Don't you remember your promise to consider me as a brother? Go on telling me everything that happens to you, pray; you cannot think how much interest I take in all your interests. I can quite fancy that charming home at Milham you told me about last Sunday. I can almost fancy Mrs Mason's workroom; and that, surely, is a proof either of the strength of my imagination, or of your powers of description."

Ruth smiled. "It is, indeed, sir. Our workroom must be so different to anything you ever saw. I think you must have passed through Milham often on your way to Lowford."

"Then you don't think it is any stretch of fancy to have so clear an idea as I have of Milham Grange? On the left hand of the road, is it, Ruth?"

"Yes, sir, just over the bridge, and up the hill where the elm-trees meet overhead and make a green shade; and then comes the dear old Grange, that I shall never see again."

"Never! Nonsense, Ruthie; it is only six miles off; you may see it any day. It is not an hour's ride."

"Perhaps I may see it again when I am grown old; I did not think exactly what 'never' meant; it is so very long since I was there, and I don't see any chance of my going for years and years, at any rate."

"Why, Ruth, you—we may go next Sunday afternoon, if you like."

She looked up at him with a lovely light of pleasure in her face at the idea. "How, sir? Can I walk it between afternoon service and the time Mrs Mason comes home? I would go for only one glimpse; but if I could get into the house—oh, sir! if I could just see mamma's room again!"

He was revolving plans in his head for giving her this pleasure, and he had also his own in view. If they went in any of his carriages, the loitering charm of the walk would be lost; and they must, to a certain degree, be encumbered by, and exposed to, the notice of servants.

"Are you a good walker, Ruth? Do you think you can manage six miles? If we set off at two o'clock, we shall be there by four, without hurrying; or say half-past four. Then we might stay two hours, and you could show me all the old walks and old places you love, and we could still come leisurely home. Oh, it's all arranged directly!"

"But do you think it would be right, sir? It seems as if it would be such a great pleasure, that it must be in some way wrong."

"Why, you little goose, what can be wrong in it?"

"In the first place, I miss going to church by setting out at two," said Ruth, a little gravely.

"Only for once. Surely you don't see any harm in missing church for once? You will go in the morning, you know."

"I wonder if Mrs Mason would think it right—if she would allow it?"

"No, I dare say not. But you don't mean to be governed by Mrs Mason's notions of right and wrong. She thought it right to treat that poor girl Palmer in the way you told me about. You would think that wrong, you know, and so would every one of sense and feeling. Come, Ruth, don't pin your faith on any one, but judge for yourself. The pleasure is perfectly innocent; it is not a selfish pleasure either, for I shall enjoy it to the full as much as you will. I shall like to see the places where you spent your childhood; I shall almost love them as much as you do." He had dropped his voice; and spoke in low, persuasive tones. Ruth hung down her head, and blushed with exceeding happiness; but she could not speak, even to urge her doubts afresh. Thus it was in a manner settled.

How delightfully happy the plan made her through the coming week! She was too young when her mother died to have received any cautions or words of advice respecting *the* subject of a woman's life—if, indeed, wise parents ever directly speak of what, in its depth and power, cannot be put into words—which is a brooding spirit with no definite form or shape that men should know it, but which is there, and present before we have recognised and realised its existence. Ruth was innocent and snow-pure. She had heard of falling in love, but did not know the signs and symptoms thereof; nor, indeed, had she troubled her head much about them. Sorrow had filled up her days, to the exclusion of all lighter thoughts than the consideration of present duties, and the remembrance of the happy time which had been. But the interval of blank, after the loss of her mother and during her father's life-in-death, had made her all the more ready to value and cling to sympathy—first from Jenny, and now from Mr Bellingham. To see her home again, and to see it with him; to show him (secure of his interest) the haunts of former times, each with its little tale of the past—of dead and gone events!—No coming shadow threw its gloom over this week's dream of happiness—a dream which was too bright to be spoken about to common and indifferent ears.

CHAPTER IV

Treading in Perilous Places

Sunday came, as brilliant as if there were no sorrow, or death, or guilt in the world; a day or two of rain had made the earth fresh and brave as the blue heavens above. Ruth thought it was too strong a realisation of her hopes, and looked for an over-clouding at noon; but the glory endured, and at two o'clock she was in the Leasowes, with a beating heart full of joy, longing to stop the hours, which would pass too quickly through the afternoon.

They sauntered through the fragrant lanes, as if their loitering would prolong the time, and check the fiery-footed steeds galloping apace towards the close of the happy day. It was past five o'clock before they came to the great mill-wheel, which stood in Sabbath idleness, motionless in a brown mass of shade, and still wet with yesterday's immersion in the deep transparent water beneath. They clambered the little hill, not yet fully shaded by the overarching elms; and then Ruth checked Mr Bellingham, by a slight motion of the hand which lay within his arm, and glanced up into his face to see what that face should express as it looked on Milham Grange, now lying still and peaceful in its afternoon shadows. It was a house of after-thoughts; building materials were plentiful in the neighbourhood, and every successive owner had found a necessity for some addition or projection, till it was a picturesque mass of irregularity—of broken light and shadow— which, as a whole, gave a full and complete idea of a "Home." All its gables and nooks were blended and held together by the tender green of the climbing roses and young creepers. An old couple were living in the house until it should be let, but they dwelt in the back part, and never used the front door; so the little birds had grown tame and familiar, and perched upon the window-sills and porch, and on the old stone cistern which caught the water from the roof.

They went silently through the untrimmed garden, full of the pale-coloured flowers of spring. A spider had spread her web over the front door. The sight of this conveyed a sense of desolation to Ruth's heart; she thought it was possible the state entrance had never been used since her father's dead body had been borne forth, and, without speaking a word, she turned abruptly away, and went round the house to another door. Mr Bellingham followed without questioning, little understanding her feelings, but full of admiration for the varying expression called out upon her face.

The old woman had not yet returned from church, or from the weekly gossip or neighbourly tea which succeeded. The husband sat in the kitchen, spelling the psalms for the day in his Prayer-book, and reading the words out aloud—a habit he had acquired from the double solitude of his life, for he was deaf. He did not hear the quiet entrance of the pair, and they were struck with the sort of ghostly echo which seems to haunt half-furnished and uninhabited houses. The verses he was reading were the following:

Why art thou so vexed, O my soul: and why art thou so disquieted within me?

O put thy trust in God: for I will yet thank him, which is the help of my countenance, and my God.

And when he had finished he shut the book, and sighed with the satisfaction of having done his duty. The words of holy trust, though perhaps they were not fully understood, carried a faithful peace down into the depths of his soul. As he looked up, he saw the young couple standing on the middle of the floor. He pushed his iron-rimmed spectacles on to his forehead, and rose to greet the daughter of his old master and ever-honoured mistress.

"God bless thee, lass; God bless thee! My old eyes are glad to see thee again."

Ruth sprang forward to shake the horny hand stretched forward in the action of blessing. She pressed it between both of hers, as she rapidly poured out questions. Mr Bellingham was not altogether comfortable at seeing one whom he had already begun to appropriate as his own, so tenderly familiar with a hard-featured, meanly-dressed day-labourer. He sauntered to the window, and looked out into the grass-grown farm-yard; but he could not help overhearing some of the conversation, which seemed to him carried on too much in the tone of equality. "And who's yon?" asked the old labourer at last. "Is he your sweetheart? Your missis's son, I reckon. He's a spruce young chap, anyhow."

Mr Bellingham's "blood of all the Howards" rose and tingled about his ears, so that he could not hear Ruth's answer. It began by "Hush, Thomas; pray hush!" but how it went on he did not catch. The idea of his being Mrs Mason's son! It was really too ridiculous; but, like most things which are "too ridiculous," it made him very angry. He was hardly himself again when Ruth shyly came to the window-recess and asked him if he would like to see the house-place, into which the front door entered; many people thought it very pretty, she said, half timidly, for his face had unconsciously assumed a hard and haughty expression, which he could not instantly soften down. He followed her, however; but before he left the kitchen he saw the old man standing, looking at Ruth's companion with a strange, grave air of dissatisfaction.

They went along one or two zigzag, damp-smelling stone passages, and then entered the house-place, or common sitting-room for a farmer's family in that part of the country. The front door opened into it, and several other apartments issued out of it, such as the dairy, the state bedroom (which was half-parlour as well), and a small room which had been appropriated to the late Mrs Hilton, where she sat, or more frequently lay, commanding through the open door the comings and goings of her household. In those days the house-place had been a cheerful room, full of life, with the passing to and fro of husband, child, and servants; with a great merry wood fire crackling and blazing away every evening, and hardly let out in the very heat of summer; for with the thick stone walls, and the deep window-seats, and the drapery of vine-leaves and ivy, that room, with its flag-floor, seemed always to want the sparkle and cheery warmth of a fire. But now the green shadows from without seemed to have become black in the uninhabited desolation. The oaken shovel-board, the heavy dresser, and the carved cupboards, were now dull and damp, which were formerly polished up to the brightness of a looking-glass where the fire-blaze was for ever glinting; they only added to the oppressive gloom; the flag-floor was wet with heavy moisture. Ruth stood gazing into the room, seeing nothing of what was present. She saw a vision of former days—an evening in the days of her childhood; her father sitting in the "master's corner" near the fire, sedately smoking his pipe, while he dreamily watched his wife and child; her mother reading to her, as she sat on a little stool at her feet. It was gone—all gone into the land of shadows; but for the moment it seemed so present in the old room, that Ruth believed her actual life to be the dream. Then, still silent, she went on into her mother's parlour. But there, the bleak look of what had once been full of peace and mother's love, struck cold on her heart. She uttered a cry, and threw herself down by the sofa, hiding her face in her hands, while her frame quivered with her repressed sobs.

"Dearest Ruth, don't give way so. It can do no good; it cannot bring back the dead," said Mr Bellingham, distressed at witnessing her distress.

"I know it cannot," murmured Ruth; "and that is why I cry. I cry because nothing will ever bring them back again." She sobbed afresh, but more gently, for his kind words soothed her, and softened, if they could not take away, her sense of desolation.

"Come away; I cannot have you stay here, full of painful associations as these rooms must be. Come"—raising her with gentle violence—"show me your little garden you have often told me about. Near the window of this very room, is it not? See how well I remember everything you tell me."

He led her round through the back part of the house into the pretty old-fashioned garden. There was a sunny border just under the windows, and clipped box and yew-trees by the grass-plat, further away from the house; and she prattled again of her childish adventures and solitary plays. When they turned round they saw the old man, who had hobbled out with the help of his stick, and was looking at them with the same grave, sad look of anxiety.

Mr Bellingham spoke rather sharply:

"Why does that old man follow us about in that way? It is excessively impertinent of him, I think."

"Oh, don't call old Thomas impertinent. He is so good and kind, he is like a father to me. I remember sitting on his knee many and many a time when I was a child, whilst he told me stories out of the 'Pilgrim's Progress.' He taught me to suck up milk through a straw. Mamma was very fond of him too. He used to sit with us always in the evenings when papa was away at market, for mamma was rather afraid of having no man in the house, and used to beg old Thomas to stay; and he would take me on his knee, and listen just as attentively as I did while mamma read aloud."

"You don't mean to say you have sat upon that old fellow's knee?"

"Oh, yes! many and many a time."

Mr Bellingham looked graver than he had done while witnessing Ruth's passionate emotion in her mother's room. But he lost his sense of indignity in admiration of his companion as she wandered among the flowers, seeking for favourite bushes or plants, to which some history or remembrance was attached. She wound in and out in natural, graceful, wavy lines between the luxuriant and overgrown shrubs, which were fragrant with a leafy smell of spring growth; she went on, careless of watching eyes, indeed unconscious, for the time, of their existence. Once she stopped to take hold of a spray of jessamine, and softly kiss it; it had been her mother's favourite flower.

Old Thomas was standing by the horse-mount, and was also an observer of all her goings-on. But, while Mr Bellingham's feeling was that of passionate admiration mingled with a selfish kind of love, the old man gazed with tender anxiety, and his lips moved in words of blessing:

"She's a pretty creature, with a glint of her mother about her; and she's the same kind lass as ever. Not a bit set up with yon fine manty-maker's shop she's in. I misdoubt that young fellow though, for all she called him a real gentleman, and checked me when I asked if he was her sweetheart. If his are not sweetheart's looks, I've forgotten all my young days. Here! they're going, I suppose. Look! he wants her to go without a word to the old man; but she is none so changed as that, I reckon."

Not Ruth, indeed! She never perceived the dissatisfied expression of Mr Bellingham's countenance, visible to the old man's keen eye; but came running up to Thomas to send her love to his wife, and to shake him many times by the hand.

"Tell Mary I'll make her such a fine gown, as soon as ever I set up for myself; it shall be all in the fashion, big gigot sleeves, that she shall not know herself in them! Mind you tell her that, Thomas, will you?"

"Aye, that I will, lass; and I reckon she'll be pleased to hear thou hast not forgotten thy old merry ways. The Lord bless thee—the Lord lift up the light of His countenance upon thee."

Ruth was half-way towards the impatient Mr Bellingham when her old friend called her back. He longed to give her a warning of the danger that he thought she was in, and yet he did not know how. When she came up, all he could think of to say was a text; indeed, the language of the Bible was the language in which he thought, whenever his ideas went beyond practical everyday life into expressions of emotion or feeling. "My dear, remember the devil goeth about as a roaring lion, seeking whom he may devour; remember that, Ruth."

The words fell on her ear, but gave no definite idea. The utmost they suggested was the remembrance of the dread she felt as a child when this verse came into her mind, and how she used to imagine a lion's head with glaring eyes peering out of the bushes in a dark shady part of the wood, which, for this reason, she had always avoided, and even now could hardly think of without a shudder. She never imagined that the grim warning related to the handsome young man who awaited her with a countenance beaming with love, and tenderly drew her hand within his arm.

The old man sighed as he watched them away. "The Lord may help her to guide her steps aright. He may. But I'm afeard she's treading in perilous places. I'll put my missis up to going to the town and getting speech of her, and telling her a bit of her danger. An old motherly woman like our Mary will set about it better nor a stupid fellow like me."

The poor old labourer prayed long and earnestly that night for Ruth. He called it "wrestling for her soul;" and I think his prayers were heard, for "God judgeth not as man judgeth."

Ruth went on her way, all unconscious of the dark phantoms of the future that were gathering around her; her melancholy turned, with the pliancy of childish years, at sixteen not yet lost, into a softened manner which was infinitely charming. By-and-by she cleared up into sunny happiness. The evening was still and full of mellow light, and the new-born summer was so delicious that, in common with all young creatures, she shared its influence and was glad.

They stood together at the top of a steep ascent, "the hill" of the hundred. At the summit there was a level space, sixty or seventy yards square, of unenclosed and broken ground, over which the golden bloom of the gorse cast a rich hue, while its delicious scent perfumed the fresh and nimble air. On one side of this common, the ground sloped down to a clear bright pond, in which were mirrored the rough sand-cliffs that rose abrupt on the opposite bank; hundreds of martens found a home there, and were now wheeling over the transparent water, and dipping in their wings in their evening sport. Indeed, all sorts of birds seemed to haunt the lonely pool; the water-wagtails were scattered around its margin, the linnets perched on the topmost sprays of the gorse-bushes, and other hidden warblers sang their vespers on the uneven ground beyond. On the far side of the green waste, close by the road, and well placed for the requirements of horses or their riders who might be weary with the ascent of the hill, there was a public-house, which was more of a farm than an inn. It was a long, low building, rich in dormer-windows on the weather side, which were necessary in such an exposed situation, and with odd projections and unlooked-for gables on every side; there was a deep porch in front, on whose hospitable benches a dozen persons might sit and enjoy the balmy air. A noble sycamore grew right before the house, with seats all round it ("such tents the patriarchs loved"); and a nondescript sign hung from a branch on the side next to the road, which, being wisely furnished with an interpretation, was found to mean King Charles in the oak.

Near this comfortable, quiet, unfrequented inn, there was another pond, for household and farm-yard purposes, from which the cattle were drinking, before returning to the fields after they had been milked. Their very motions were so lazy and slow, that they served to fill up the mind with the sensation of dreamy rest. Ruth and Mr Bellingham plunged through the broken ground to regain the road near the wayside inn. Hand-in-hand, now pricked by the far-spreading gorse, now ankle-deep in sand; now pressing the soft, thick heath, which should make so brave an autumn show; and now over wild thyme and other fragrant herbs, they made their way, with many a merry laugh. Once on the road, at the summit, Ruth stood silent, in breathless delight at the view before her. The hill fell suddenly down into the plain, extending for a dozen miles or more. There was a clump of dark Scotch firs close to them, which cut clear against the western sky, and threw back the nearest levels into distance. The plain below them was richly wooded, and was tinted by the young tender hues of the earliest summer, for all the trees of the wood had donned their leaves except the cautious ash, which here and there gave a soft, pleasant greyness to the landscape. Far away in the champaign were spires, and towers, and stacks of chimneys belonging to some distant hidden farm-house, which were traced downwards through the golden air by the thin columns of blue smoke sent up from the evening fires. The view was bounded by some rising ground in deep purple shadow against the sunset sky.

When first they stopped, silent with sighing pleasure, the air seemed full of pleasant noises; distant church-bells made harmonious music with the little singing-birds near at hand; nor were the lowings of the cattle, nor the calls of the farm-servants discordant, for the voices seemed to be hushed by the brooding consciousness of the Sabbath. They stood loitering before the house, quietly enjoying the view. The clock in the little inn struck eight, and it sounded clear and sharp in the stillness.

"Can it be so late?" asked Ruth.

"I should not have thought it possible," answered Mr Bellingham. "But, never mind, you will be at home long before nine. Stay, there is a shorter road, I know, through the fields; just wait a moment, while I go in and ask the exact way." He dropped Ruth's arm, and went into the public-house.

A gig had been slowly toiling up the sandy hill behind, unperceived by the young couple, and now it reached the table-land, and was close upon them as they separated. Ruth turned round, when the sound of the horse's footsteps came distinctly as he reached the level. She faced Mrs Mason!

They were not ten—no, not five yards apart. At the same moment they recognised each other, and, what was worse, Mrs Mason had clearly seen, with her sharp, needle-like eyes, the attitude in which Ruth had stood with the young man who had just quitted her. Ruth's hand had been lying in his arm, and fondly held there by his other hand.

Mrs Mason was careless about the circumstances of temptation into which the girls entrusted to her as apprentices were thrown, but severely intolerant if their conduct was in any degree influenced by the force of these temptations. She called this intolerance "keeping up the character of her establishment." It would have been a better and more Christian thing, if she had kept up the character of her girls by tender vigilance and maternal care.

This evening, too, she was in an irritated state of temper. Her brother had undertaken to drive her round by Henbury, in order to give her the unpleasant information of the misbehaviour of her eldest son, who was an assistant in a draper's shop in a neighbouring town. She was full of indignation against want of steadiness, though not willing to direct her indignation against the right object—her ne'er-do-well darling. While she was thus charged with anger (for her brother justly defended her son's master and companions from her attacks), she saw Ruth standing with a lover, far away from home, at such a time in the evening, and she boiled over with intemperate displeasure.

"Come here directly, Miss Hilton," she exclaimed, sharply. Then, dropping her voice to low, bitter tones of concentrated wrath, she said to the trembling, guilty Ruth:

"Don't attempt to show your face at my house again after this conduct. I saw you, and your spark, too. I'll have no slurs on the character of my apprentices. Don't say a word. I saw enough. I shall write and tell your guardian to-morrow."

The horse started away, for he was impatient to be off, and Ruth was left standing there, stony, sick, and pale, as if the lightning had torn up the ground beneath her feet. She could not go on standing, she was so sick and faint; she staggered back to the broken sand-bank, and sank down, and covered her face with her hands.

"My dearest Ruth! are you ill? Speak, darling! My love, my love, do speak to me!"

What tender words after such harsh ones! They loosened the fountain of Ruth's tears, and she cried bitterly.

"Oh! did you see her—did you hear what she said?"

"She! Who, my darling? Don't sob so, Ruth; tell me what it is. Who has been near you?—who has been speaking to you to make you cry so?"

"Oh, Mrs Mason." And there was a fresh burst of sorrow.

"You don't say so! are you sure? I was not away five minutes."

"Oh, yes, sir, I'm quite sure. She was so angry; she said I must never show my face there again. Oh, dear! what shall I do?"

It seemed to the poor child as if Mrs Mason's words were irrevocable, and, that being so, she was shut out from every house. She saw how much she had done that was deserving of blame, now when it was too late to undo it. She knew with what severity and taunts Mrs Mason had often treated her for involuntary failings, of which she had been quite unconscious; and now she had really done wrong, and shrank with terror from the consequences. Her eyes were so blinded by the fast-falling tears, she did not see (nor had she seen would she have been able to interpret) the change in Mr Bellingham's countenance, as he stood silently watching her. He was silent so long, that even in her sorrow she began to wonder that he did not speak, and to wish to hear his soothing words once more.

"It is very unfortunate," he began, at last; and then he stopped; then he began again: "It is very unfortunate; for, you see, I did not like to name it to you before, but, I believe—I have business, in fact, which obliges me to go to town to-morrow—to London, I mean; and I don't know when I shall be able to return."

"To London!" cried Ruth; "are you going away? Oh, Mr Bellingham!" She wept afresh, giving herself up to the desolate feeling of sorrow, which absorbed all the terror she had been experiencing at the idea of Mrs Mason's anger. It seemed to her at this moment as though she could have borne everything but his departure; but she did not speak again; and after two or three minutes had elapsed, he spoke—not in his natural careless voice, but in a sort of constrained, agitated tone.

"I can hardly bear the idea of leaving you, my own Ruth. In such distress, too; for where you can go I do not know at all. From all you have told me of Mrs Mason, I don't think she is likely to mitigate her severity in your case."

No answer, but tears quietly, incessantly flowing. Mrs Mason's displeasure seemed a distant thing; his going away was the present distress. He went on:

"Ruth, would you go with me to London? My darling, I cannot leave you here without a home; the thought of leaving you at all is pain enough, but in these circumstances—so friendless, so homeless—it is impossible. You must come with me, love, and trust to me."

Still she did not speak. Remember how young, and innocent, and motherless she was! It seemed to her as if it would be happiness enough to be with him; and as for the future, he would arrange and decide for that. The future lay wrapped in a golden mist, which she did not care to penetrate; but if he, her sun, was out of sight and gone, the golden mist became dark heavy gloom, through which no hope could come. He took her hand.

"Will you not come with me? Do you not love me enough to trust me? Oh, Ruth," (reproachfully), "can you not trust me?"

She had stopped crying, but was sobbing sadly.

"I cannot bear this, love. Your sorrow is absolute pain to me; but it is worse to feel how indifferent you are—how little you care about our separation."

He dropped her hand. She burst into a fresh fit of crying.

"I may have to join my mother in Paris; I don't know when I shall see you again. Oh, Ruth!" said he, vehemently, "do you love me at all?"

She said something in a very low voice; he could not hear it, though he bent down his head—but he took her hand again.

"What was it you said, love? Was it not that you did love me? My darling, you do! I can tell it by the trembling of this little hand; then you will not suffer me to go away alone and unhappy, most anxious about you? There is no other course open to you; my poor girl has no friends to receive her. I will go home directly, and return in an hour with a carriage. You make me too happy by your silence, Ruth."

"Oh, what can I do!" exclaimed Ruth. "Mr Bellingham, you should help me, and instead of that you only bewilder me."

"How, my dearest Ruth? Bewilder you! It seems so clear to me. Look at the case fairly! Here you are, an orphan, with only one person to love you, poor child!—thrown off, for no fault of yours, by the only creature on whom you have a claim, that creature a tyrannical, inflexible woman; what is more natural (and, being natural, more right) than that you should throw yourself upon the care of the one who loves you dearly—who would go through fire and water for you—who would shelter you from all harm? Unless, indeed, as I suspect, you do not care for him. If so, Ruth! if you do not care for me, we had better part—I will leave you at once; it will be better for me to go, if you do not care for me."

He said this very sadly (it seemed so to Ruth, at least), and made as though he would have drawn his hand from hers, but now she held it with soft force.

"Don't leave me, please, sir. It is very true I have no friend but you. Don't leave me, please. But, oh! do tell me what I must do!"

"Will you do it if I tell you? If you will trust me, I will do my very best for you. I will give you my best advice. You see your position. Mrs Mason writes and gives her own exaggerated account to your guardian; he is bound by no great love to you, from what I have heard you say, and throws you off; I, who might be able to befriend you—through my mother, perhaps—I, who could at least comfort you a little (could not I, Ruth?), am away, far away, for an indefinite time; that is your position at present. Now, what I advise is this. Come with me into this little inn; I will order tea for you—(I am sure you require it sadly)—and I will leave you there, and go home for the carriage. I will return in an hour at the latest. Then we are together, come what may; that is enough for me; is it not for you, Ruth? Say, yes—say it ever so low, but give me the delight of hearing it. Ruth, say yes."

Low and soft, with much hesitation, came the "Yes;" the fatal word of which she so little imagined the infinite consequences. The thought of being with him was all and everything.

"How you tremble, my darling! You are cold, love! Come into the house, and I'll order tea directly and be off."

She rose, and, leaning on his arm, went into the house. She was shaking and dizzy with the agitation of the last hour. He spoke to the civil farmer-landlord, who conducted them into a neat parlour, with windows opening into the garden at the back of the house. They had admitted much of the evening's fragrance through their open casements, before they were hastily closed by the attentive host.

"Tea, directly, for this lady!" The landlord vanished.

"Dearest Ruth, I must go; there is not an instant to be lost; promise me to take some tea, for you are shivering all over, and deadly pale with the fright that abominable woman has given you. I must go; I shall be back in half an hour—and then no more partings, darling."

He kissed her pale cold face, and went away. The room whirled round before Ruth; it was a dream—a strange, varying, shifting dream—with the old home of her childhood for one scene, with the terror of Mrs Mason's unexpected appearance for another; and then, strangest, dizziest, happiest of all, there was the consciousness of his love, who was all the world to her; and the remembrance of the tender words, which still kept up their low soft echo in her heart.

Her head ached so much that she could hardly see; even the dusky twilight was a dazzling glare to her poor eyes; and when the daughter of the house brought in the sharp light of the candles, preparatory for tea, Ruth hid her face in the sofa pillows with a low exclamation of pain.

"Does your head ache, miss?" asked the girl, in a gentle, sympathising voice. "Let me make you some tea, miss, it will do you good. Many's the time poor mother's headaches were cured by good strong tea."

Ruth murmured acquiescence; the young girl (about Ruth's own age, but who was the mistress of the little establishment, owing to her mother's death) made tea, and brought Ruth a cup to the sofa where she lay. Ruth was feverish and thirsty, and eagerly drank it off, although she could not touch the bread and butter which the girl offered her. She felt better and fresher, though she was still faint and weak.

"Thank you," said Ruth. "Don't let me keep you; perhaps you are busy. You have been very kind, and the tea has done me a great deal of good."

The girl left the room. Ruth became as hot as she had previously been cold, and went and opened the window, and leant out into the still, sweet, evening air. The bush of sweetbrier, underneath the window, scented the place, and the delicious fragrance reminded her of her old home. I think scents affect and quicken the memory more than either sights or sounds; for Ruth had instantly before her eyes the little garden beneath the window of her mother's room, with the old man leaning on his stick, watching her, just as he had done, not three hours before, on that very afternoon.

"Dear old Thomas! He and Mary would take me in, I think; they would love me all the more if I were cast off. And Mr Bellingham would, perhaps, not be so very long away; and he would know where to find me if I stayed at Milham Grange. Oh, would it not be better to go to them? I wonder if he would be very sorry! I could not bear to make him sorry, so kind as he has been to me; but I do believe it would be better to go to them, and ask their advice, at any rate. He would follow me there; and I could talk over what I had better do, with the three best friends I have in the world—the only friends I have."

She put on her bonnet, and opened the parlour-door; but then she saw the square figure of the landlord standing at the open house-door, smoking his evening pipe, and looming large and distinct against the dark air and landscape beyond. Ruth remembered the cup of tea that she had drank; it must be paid for, and she had no money with her. She feared that he would not let her quit the house without paying. She thought that she would leave a note for Mr Bellingham, saying where she was gone, and how she had left the house in debt, for (like a child) all dilemmas appeared of equal magnitude to her; and the difficulty of passing the landlord while he stood there, and of giving him an explanation of the circumstances (as far as such explanation was due to him), appeared insuperable, and as awkward, and fraught with inconvenience, as far more serious situations. She kept peeping out of her room, after she had written her little pencil-note, to see if the outer door was still obstructed. There he stood, motionless, enjoying his pipe, and looking out into the darkness which gathered thick with the coming night. The fumes of the tobacco were carried by the air into the house, and brought back Ruth's sick headache. Her energy left her; she became stupid and languid, and incapable of spirited exertion; she modified her plan of action, to the determination of asking Mr Bellingham to take her to Milham Grange, to the care of her humble friends, instead of to London. And she thought, in her simplicity, that he would instantly consent when he had heard her reasons.

She started up. A carriage dashed up to the door. She hushed her beating heart, and tried to stop her throbbing head to listen. She heard him speaking to the landlord, though she could not distinguish what he said; heard the jingling of money, and, in another moment, he was in the room, and had taken her arm to lead her to the carriage.

"Oh, sir! I want you to take me to Milham Grange," said she, holding back. "Old Thomas would give me a home."

"Well, dearest, we'll talk of all that in the carriage; I am sure you will listen to reason. Nay, if you will go to Milham you must go in the carriage," said he, hurriedly. She was little accustomed to oppose the wishes of any one—obedient and docile by nature, and unsuspicious and innocent of any harmful consequences. She entered the carriage, and drove towards London.

CHAPTER V

In North Wales

The June of 18— had been glorious and sunny, and full of flowers; but July came in with pouring rain, and it was a gloomy time for travellers and for weather-bound tourists, who lounged away the days in touching up sketches, dressing flies, and reading over again for the twentieth time the few volumes they had brought with them. A number of the *Times*, five days old, had been in constant demand in all the sitting-rooms of a certain inn in a little mountain village of North Wales, through a long July morning. The valleys around were filled with thick cold mist, which had crept up the hillsides till the hamlet itself was folded in its white dense curtain, and from the inn-windows nothing was seen of the beautiful scenery around. The tourists who thronged the rooms might as well have been "wi' their dear little bairnies at hame;" and so some of them seemed to think, as they stood, with their faces flattened against the window-panes, looking abroad in search of an event to fill up the dreary time. How many dinners were hastened that day, by way of getting through the morning, let the poor Welsh kitchen-maid say! The very village children kept indoors; or if one or two more adventurous stole out into the land of temptation and puddles, they were soon clutched back by angry and busy mothers.

It was only four o'clock, but most of the inmates of the inn thought it must be between six and seven, the morning had seemed so long—so many hours had passed since dinner—when a Welsh car, drawn by two horses, rattled briskly up to the door. Every window of the ark was crowded with faces at the sound; the leathern curtains were undrawn to their curious eyes, and out sprang a gentleman, who carefully assisted a well-cloaked-up lady into the little inn, despite the landlady's assurances of not having a room to spare.

The gentleman (it was Mr Bellingham) paid no attention to the speeches of the hostess, but quietly superintended the unpacking of the carriage, and paid the postillion; then, turning round with his face to the light, he spoke to the landlady, whose voice had been rising during the last five minutes:

"Nay, Jenny, you're strangely altered, if you can turn out an old friend on such an evening as this. If I remember right, Pen trê Voelas is twenty miles across the bleakest mountain road I ever saw."

"Indeed, sir, and I did not know you; Mr Bellingham, I believe. Indeed, sir, Pen trê Voelas is not above eighteen miles—we only charge for eighteen; it may not be much above seventeen; and we're quite full, indeed, more's the pity."

"Well, but Jenny, to oblige me, an old friend, you can find lodgings out for some of your people—the house across, for instance."

"Indeed, sir, and it's at liberty; perhaps you would not mind lodging there yourself; I could get you the best rooms, and send over a trifle or so of furniture, if they weren't as you'd wish them to be."

"No, Jenny! here I stay. You'll not induce me to venture over into those rooms, whose dirt I know of old. Can't you persuade some one who is not an old friend to move across? Say, if you like, that I had written beforehand to bespeak the rooms. Oh! I know you can manage it—I know your good-natured ways."

"Indeed, sir—well! I'll see, if you and the lady will just step into the back parlour, sir—there's no one there just now; the lady is keeping her bed to-day for a cold, and the gentleman is having a rubber at whist in number three. I'll see what I can do."

"Thank you, thank you. Is there a fire? if not, one must be lighted. Come, Ruthie, come."

He led the way into a large, bow-windowed room, which looked gloomy enough that afternoon, but which I have seen bright and buoyant with youth and hope within, and sunny lights creeping down the purple mountain slope, and stealing over the green, soft meadows, till they reached the little garden, full of roses and lavender-bushes, lying close under the window. I have seen—but I shall see no more.

"I did not know you had been here before," said Ruth, as Mr Bellingham helped her off with her cloak.

"Oh, yes; three years ago I was here on a reading party. We were here above two months, attracted by Jenny's kind heart and oddities; but driven away finally by the insufferable dirt. However, for a week or two it won't much signify."

"But can she take us in, sir? I thought I heard her saying her house was full."

"Oh, yes—I dare say it is; but I shall pay her well; she can easily make excuses to some poor devil, and send him over to the other side; and, for a day or two, so that we have shelter, it does not much signify."

"Could not we go to the house on the other side, sir?"

"And have our meals carried across to us in a half-warm state, to say nothing of having no one to scold for bad cooking! You don't know these out-of-the-way Welsh inns yet, Ruthie."

"No! I only thought it seemed rather unfair—" said Ruth, gently; but she did not end her sentence, for Mr Bellingham formed his lips into a whistle, and walked to the window to survey the rain.

The remembrance of his former good payment prompted many little lies of which Mrs Morgan was guilty that afternoon, before she succeeded in turning out a gentleman and lady, who were only planning to remain till the ensuing Saturday at the outside, so, if they did fulfil their threat, and leave on the next day, she would be no very great loser.

These household arrangements complete, she solaced herself with tea in her own little parlour, and shrewdly reviewed the circumstances of Mr Bellingham's arrival.

"Indeed! and she's not his wife," thought Jenny, "that's clear as day. His wife would have brought her maid, and given herself twice as many airs about the sitting-rooms; while this poor miss never spoke, but kept as still as a mouse. Indeed, and young men will be young men; and, as long as their fathers and mothers shut their eyes, it's none of my business to go about asking questions."

In this manner they settled down to a week's enjoyment of that Alpine country. It was most true enjoyment to Ruth. It was opening a new sense; vast ideas of beauty and grandeur filled her mind at the sight of the mountains now first beheld in full majesty. She was almost overpowered by the vague and solemn delight; but by-and-by her love for them equalled her awe, and in the night-time she would softly rise, and steal to the window to see the white moonlight, which gave a new aspect to the everlasting hills that girdle the mountain village.

Their breakfast-hour was late, in accordance with Mr Bellingham's tastes and habits; but Ruth was up betimes, and out and away, brushing the dew-drops from the short crisp grass; the lark sung high above her head, and she knew not if she moved or stood still, for the grandeur of this beautiful earth absorbed all idea of separate and individual existence. Even rain was a pleasure to her. She sat in the window-seat of their parlour (she would have gone out gladly, but that such a proceeding annoyed Mr Bellingham, who usually at such times lounged away the listless hours on a sofa, and relieved himself by abusing the weather); she saw the swift-fleeting showers come athwart the sunlight like a rush of silver arrows; she watched the purple darkness on the heathery mountain-side, and then the pale golden gleam which succeeded. There was no change or alteration of nature that had not its own peculiar beauty in the eyes of Ruth; but if she had complained of the changeable climate, she would have pleased Mr Bellingham more; her admiration and her content made him angry, until her pretty motions and loving eyes soothed down his impatience.

"Really, Ruth," he exclaimed one day, when they had been imprisoned by rain a whole morning, "one would think you had never seen a shower of rain before; it quite wearies me to see you sitting there watching this detestable weather with such a placid countenance; and for the last two hours you have said nothing more amusing or interesting than—'Oh, how beautiful!' or, 'There's another cloud coming across Moel Wynn.'"

Ruth left her seat very gently, and took up her work. She wished she had the gift of being amusing; it must be dull for a man accustomed to all kinds of active employments to be shut up in the house. She was recalled from her absolute self-forgetfulness. What could she say to interest Mr Bellingham? While she thought, he spoke again:

"I remember when we were reading here three years ago, we had a week of just such weather as this; but Howard and Johnson were capital whist players, and Wilbraham not bad, so we got through the days famously. Can you play écarté, Ruth, or picquet?"

"No, sir; I have sometimes played at beggar-my-neighbour," answered Ruth, humbly, regretting her own deficiencies.

He murmured impatiently, and there was silence for another half-hour. Then he sprang up, and rung the bell violently. "Ask Mrs Morgan for a pack of cards. Ruthie, I'll teach you écarté," said he.

But Ruth was stupid, not so good as a dummy, he said; and it was no fun betting against himself. So the cards were flung across the table—on the floor—anywhere. Ruth picked them up. As she rose, she sighed a little with the depression of spirits consequent upon her own want of power to amuse and occupy him she loved.

"You're pale, love!" said he, half repenting of his anger at her blunders over the cards. "Go out before dinner; you know you don't mind this cursed weather; and see that you come home full of adventures to relate. Come, little blockhead! give me a kiss, and begone."

She left the room with a feeling of relief; for if he were dull without her, she should not feel responsible, and unhappy at her own stupidity. The open air, that kind soothing balm which gentle mother Nature offers to us all in our seasons of depression, relieved her. The rain had ceased, though every leaf and blade was loaded with trembling glittering drops. Ruth went down to the circular dale, into which the brown-foaming mountain river fell and made a deep pool, and, after resting there for a while, ran on between broken rocks down to the valley below. The waterfall was magnificent, as she had anticipated; she longed to extend her walk to the other side of the stream, so she sought the stepping-stones, the usual crossing-place, which were over-shadowed by trees, a few yards from the pool. The waters ran high and rapidly, as busy as life, between the pieces of grey rock; but Ruth had no fear, and went lightly and steadily on. About the middle, however, there was a great gap; either one of the stones was so covered with water as to be invisible, or it had been washed lower down; at any rate, the spring from stone to stone was long, and Ruth hesitated for a moment before taking it. The sound of rushing waters was in her ears to the exclusion of every other noise; her eyes were on the current running swiftly below her feet; and thus she was startled to see a figure close before her on one of the stones, and to hear a voice offering help.

She looked up and saw a man, who was apparently long past middle life, and of the stature of a dwarf; a second glance accounted for the low height of the speaker, for then she saw he was deformed. As the consciousness of this infirmity came into her mind, it must have told itself in her softened eyes, for a faint flush of colour came into the pale face of the deformed gentleman, as he repeated his words:

"The water is very rapid; will you take my hand? Perhaps I can help you."

Ruth accepted the offer, and with this assistance she was across in a moment. He made way for her to precede him in the narrow wood path, and then silently followed her up the glen.

When they had passed out of the wood into the pasture-land beyond, Ruth once more turned to mark him. She was struck afresh with the mild beauty of the face, though there was something in the countenance which told of the body's deformity, something more and beyond the pallor of habitual ill-health, something of a quick spiritual light in the deep set-eyes, a sensibility about the mouth; but altogether, though a peculiar, it was a most attractive face.

"Will you allow me to accompany you if you are going the round by Cwm Dhu, as I imagine you are? The hand-rail is blown away from the little wooden bridge by the storm last night, and the rush of waters below may make you dizzy; and it is really dangerous to fall there, the stream is so deep."

They walked on without much speech. She wondered who her companion might be. She should have known him, if she had seen him among the strangers at the inn; and yet he spoke English too well to be a Welshman; he knew the country and the paths so perfectly, he must be a resident; and so she tossed him from England to Wales and back again in her imagination.

"I only came here yesterday," said he, as a widening in the path permitted them to walk abreast. "Last night I went to the higher waterfalls; they are most splendid."

"Did you go out in all that rain?" asked Ruth, timidly.

"Oh, yes. Rain never hinders me from walking. Indeed, it gives a new beauty to such a country as this. Besides, my time for my excursion is so short, I cannot afford to waste a day."

"Then, you do not live here?" asked Ruth.

"No! my home is in a very different place. I live in a busy town, where at times it is difficult to feel the truth that

There are in this loud stunning tide
Of human care and crime,
With whom the melodies abide
Of th' everlasting chime;
Who carry music in their heart
Through dusky lane and crowded mart,
Plying their task with busier feet,
Because their secret souls a holy strain repeat.

I have an annual holiday, which I generally spend in Wales; and often in this immediate neighbourhood."

"I do not wonder at your choice," replied Ruth. "It is a beautiful country."

"It is, indeed; and I have been inoculated by an old innkeeper at Conway with a love for its people, and history, and traditions. I have picked up enough of the language to understand many of their legends; and some are very fine and awe-inspiring, others very poetic and fanciful."

Ruth was too shy to keep up the conversation by any remark of her own, although his gentle, pensive manner was very winning.

"For instance," said he, touching a long bud-laden stem of fox-glove in the hedge-side, at the bottom of which one or two crimson-speckled flowers were bursting from their green sheaths, "I dare say, you don't know what makes this fox-glove bend and sway so gracefully. You think it is blown by the wind, don't you?" He looked at her with a grave smile, which did not enliven his thoughtful eyes, but gave an inexpressible sweetness to his face.

"I always thought it was the wind. What is it?" asked Ruth, innocently.

"Oh, the Welsh tell you that this flower is sacred to the fairies, and that it has the power of recognising them, and all spiritual beings who pass by, and that it bows in deference to them as they waft along. Its Welsh name is Maneg Ellyllyn—the good people's glove; and hence, I imagine, our folk's-glove or fox-glove."

"It's a very pretty fancy," said Ruth, much interested, and wishing that he would go on, without expecting her to reply.

But they were already at the wooden bridge; he led her across, and then, bowing his adieu, he had taken a different path even before Ruth had thanked him for his attention.

It was an adventure to tell Mr Bellingham, however; and it roused and amused him till dinner-time came, after which he sauntered forth with a cigar.

"Ruth," said he, when he returned, "I've seen your little hunchback. He looks like Riquet-with-the-Tuft. He's not a gentleman, though. If it had not been for his deformity, I should not have made him out from your description; you called him a gentleman."

"And don't you, sir?" asked Ruth, surprised.

"Oh, no! he's regularly shabby and seedy in his appearance; lodging, too, the ostler told me, over that horrible candle and cheese shop, the smell of which is insufferable twenty yards off—no gentleman could endure it; he must be a traveller or artist, or something of that kind."

"Did you see his face, sir?" asked Ruth.

"No; but a man's back—his *tout ensemble* has character enough in it to decide his rank."

"His face was very singular; quite beautiful!" said she, softly; but the subject did not interest Mr Bellingham, and he let it drop.

CHAPTER VI

Troubles Gather About Ruth

The next day the weather was brave and glorious; a perfect "bridal of the earth and sky;" and every one turned out of the inn to enjoy the fresh beauty of nature. Ruth was quite unconscious of being the object of remark, and, in her light, rapid passings to and fro, had never looked at the doors and windows, where many watchers stood observing her, and commenting upon her situation or her appearance.

"She's a very lovely creature," said one gentleman, rising from the breakfast-table to catch a glimpse of her as she entered from her morning's ramble. "Not above sixteen, I should think. Very modest and innocent-looking in her white gown!"

His wife, busy administering to the wants of a fine little boy, could only say (without seeing the young girl's modest ways, and gentle, downcast countenance):

"Well! I do think it's a shame such people should be allowed to come here. To think of such wickedness under the same roof! Do come away, my dear, and don't flatter her by such notice."

The husband returned to the breakfast-table; he smelt the broiled ham and eggs, and he heard his wife's commands. Whether smelling or hearing had most to do in causing his obedience, I cannot tell; perhaps you can.

"Now, Harry, go and see if nurse and baby are ready to go out with you. You must lose no time this beautiful morning."

Ruth found Mr Bellingham was not yet come down; so she sallied out for an additional half-hour's ramble. Flitting about through the village, trying to catch all the beautiful sunny peeps at the scenery between the cold stone houses, which threw the radiant distance into aërial perspective far away, she passed by the little shop; and, just issuing from it, came the nurse and baby, and little boy. The baby sat in placid dignity in her nurse's arms, with a face of queenly calm. Her fresh, soft, peachy complexion was really tempting; and Ruth, who was always fond of children, went up to coo and to smile at the little thing, and, after some "peep-boing," she was about to snatch a kiss, when Harry, whose face had been reddening ever since the play began, lifted up his sturdy little right arm and hit Ruth a great blow on the face.

"Oh, for shame, sir!" said the nurse, snatching back his hand; "how dare you do that to the lady who is so kind as to speak to Sissy."

"She's not a lady!" said he, indignantly. "She's a bad naughty girl—mamma said so, she did; and she shan't kiss our baby."

The nurse reddened in her turn. She knew what he must have heard; but it was awkward to bring it out, standing face to face with the elegant young lady.

"Children pick up such notions, ma'am," said she at last, apologetically, to Ruth, who stood, white and still, with a new idea running through her mind.

"It's no notion; it's true, nurse; and I heard you say it yourself. Go away, naughty woman!" said the boy, in infantile vehemence of passion to Ruth.

To the nurse's infinite relief, Ruth turned away, humbly and meekly, with bent head, and slow, uncertain steps. But as she turned, she saw the mild sad face of the deformed gentleman, who was sitting at the open window above the shop; he looked sadder and graver than ever; and his eyes met her glance with an expression of deep sorrow. And so, condemned alike by youth and age, she stole with timid step into the house. Mr Bellingham was awaiting her coming in the sitting-room. The glorious day restored all his buoyancy of spirits. He talked gaily away, without pausing for a reply; while Ruth made tea, and tried to calm her heart, which was yet beating with the agitation of the new ideas she had received from the occurrence of the morning. Luckily for her, the only answers required for some time were mono-syllables; but those few words were uttered in so depressed and mournful a tone, that at last they struck Mr Bellingham with surprise and displeasure, as the condition of mind they unconsciously implied did not harmonise with his own.

"Ruth, what is the matter this morning? You really are very provoking. Yesterday, when everything was gloomy, and you might have been aware that I was out of spirits, I heard nothing but expressions of delight; to-day, when every creature under heaven is rejoicing, you look most deplorable and woe-begone. You really should learn to have a little sympathy."

The tears fell quickly down Ruth's cheeks, but she did not speak. She could not put into words the sense she was just beginning to entertain of the estimation in which she was henceforward to be held. She thought he would be as much grieved as she was at what had taken place that morning; she fancied she should sink in his opinion if she told him how others regarded her; besides, it seemed ungenerous to dilate upon the suffering of which he was the cause.

"I will not," thought she, "embitter his life; I will try and be cheerful. I must not think of myself so much. If I can but make him happy, what need I care for chance speeches?"

Accordingly, she made every effort possible to be as light-hearted as he was; but, somehow, the moment she relaxed, thoughts would intrude, and wonders would force themselves upon her mind; so that altogether she was not the gay and bewitching companion Mr Bellingham had previously found her.

They sauntered out for a walk. The path they chose led to a wood on the side of a hill, and they entered, glad of the shade of the trees. At first, it appeared like any common grove, but they soon came to a deep descent, on the summit of which they stood, looking down on the tree-tops, which were softly waving far beneath their feet. There was a path leading sharp down, and they followed it; the ledge of rock made it almost like going down steps, and their walk grew into a bounding, and their bounding into a run, before they reached the lowest plane. A green gloom reigned there; it was the still hour of noon; the little birds were quiet in some leafy shade. They went on a few yards, and then they came to a circular pool overshadowed by the trees, whose highest boughs had been beneath their feet a few minutes before. The pond was hardly below the surface of the ground, and there was nothing like a bank on any side. A heron was standing there motionless, but when he saw them he flapped his wings and slowly rose, and soared above the green heights of the wood up into the very sky itself, for at that depth the trees appeared to touch the round white clouds which brooded over the earth. The speed-well grew in the shallowest water of the pool, and all around its margin, but the flowers were hardly seen at first, so deep was the green shadow cast by the trees. In the very middle of the pond the sky was mirrored clear and dark, a blue which looked as if a black void lay behind.

"Oh, there are water-lilies," said Ruth, her eye catching on the farther side. "I must go and get some."

"No; I will get them for you. The ground is spongy all round there. Sit still, Ruth; this heap of grass will make a capital seat."

He went round, and she waited quietly for his return. When he came back he took off her bonnet, without speaking, and began to place his flowers in her hair. She was quite still while he arranged her coronet, looking up in his face with loving eyes, with a peaceful composure. She knew that he was pleased from his manner, which had the joyousness of a child playing with a new toy, and she did not think twice of his occupation. It was pleasant to forget everything except his pleasure. When he had decked her out, he said:

"There, Ruth! now you'll do. Come and look at yourself in the pond. Here, where there are no weeds. Come."

She obeyed, and could not help seeing her own loveliness; it gave her a sense of satisfaction for an instant, as the sight of any other beautiful object would have done, but she never thought of associating it with herself. She knew that she was beautiful; but that seemed abstract, and removed from herself. Her existence was in feeling, and thinking, and loving.

Down in that green hollow they were quite in harmony. Her beauty was all that Mr Bellingham cared for, and it was supreme. It was all he recognised of her, and he was proud of it. She stood in her white dress against the trees which grew around; her face was flushed into a brilliancy of colour which resembled that of a rose in June; the great heavy white flowers drooped on either side of her beautiful head, and if her brown hair was a little disordered, the very disorder only seemed to add a grace. She pleased him more by looking so lovely than by all her tender endeavours to fall in with his varying humour.

But when they left the wood, and Ruth had taken out her flowers, and resumed her bonnet, as they came near the inn, the simple thought of giving him pleasure was not enough to secure Ruth's peace. She became pensive and sad, and could not rally into gaiety.

"Really, Ruth," said he, that evening, "you must not encourage yourself in this habit of falling into melancholy reveries without any cause. You have been sighing twenty times during the last half-hour. Do be a little cheerful. Remember, I have no companion but you in this out-of-the-way place."

"I am very sorry, sir," said Ruth, her eyes filling with tears; and then she remembered that it was very dull for him to be alone with her, heavy-hearted as she had been all day. She said in a sweet, penitent tone:

"Would you be so kind as to teach me one of those games at cards you were speaking about yesterday, sir? I would do my best to learn."

Her soft, murmuring voice won its way. They rang for the cards, and he soon forgot that there was such a thing as depression or gloom in the world, in the pleasure of teaching such a beautiful ignoramus the mysteries of card-playing.

"There!" said he, at last, "that's enough for one lesson. Do you know, little goose, your blunders have made me laugh myself into one of the worst headaches I have had for years."

He threw himself on the sofa, and in an instant she was by his side.

"Let me put my cool hands on your forehead," she begged; "that used to do mamma good."

He lay still, his face away from the light, and not speaking. Presently he fell asleep. Ruth put out the candles, and sat patiently by him for a long time, fancying he would awaken refreshed. The room grew cool in the night air; but Ruth dared not rouse him from what appeared to be sound, restoring slumber. She covered him with her shawl, which she had thrown over a chair on coming in from their twilight ramble. She had ample time to think; but she tried to banish thought. At last, his breathing became quick and oppressed, and, after listening to it for some minutes with increasing affright, Ruth ventured to waken him. He seemed stupified and shivery. Ruth became more and more terrified; all the household were asleep except one servant-girl, who was wearied out of what little English she had knowledge of in more waking hours, and she could only answer, "Iss, indeed, ma'am," to any question put to her by Ruth.

She sat by the bedside all night long. He moaned and tossed, but never spoke sensibly. It was a new form of illness to the miserable Ruth. Her yesterday's suffering went into the black distance of long-past years. The present was all-in-all. When she heard people stirring, she went in search of Mrs Morgan, whose shrewd, sharp manners, unsoftened by inward respect for the poor girl, had awed Ruth even when Mr Bellingham was by to protect her.

"Mrs Morgan," said she, sitting down in the little parlour appropriated to the landlady, for she felt her strength suddenly desert her—"Mrs Morgan, I'm afraid Mr Bellingham is very ill;"—here she burst into tears, but instantly checking herself, "Oh, what must I do?" continued she; "I don't think he has known anything all through the night, and he looks so strange and wild this morning."

She gazed up into Mrs Morgan's face, as if reading an oracle.

"Indeed, miss, ma'am, and it's a very awkward thing. But don't cry, that can do no good, 'deed it can't. I'll go and see the poor young man myself, and then I can judge if a doctor is wanting."

Ruth followed Mrs Morgan upstairs. When they entered the sick-room Mr Bellingham was sitting up in bed, looking wildly about him, and as he saw them, he exclaimed:

"Ruth! Ruth! come here; I won't be left alone!" and then he fell down exhausted on the pillow. Mrs Morgan went up and spoke to him, but he did not answer or take any notice.

"I'll send for Mr Jones, my dear, 'deed and I will; we'll have him here in a couple of hours, please God."

"Oh, can't he come sooner?" asked Ruth, wild with terror.

"'Deed no; he lives at Llanglâs when he's at home, and that's seven mile away, and he may be gone a round eight or nine mile on the other side Llanglâs; but I'll send a boy on the pony directly."

Saying this, Mrs Morgan left Ruth alone. There was nothing to be done, for Mr Bellingham had again fallen into a heavy sleep. Sounds of daily life began, bells rang, breakfast-services clattered up and down the passages, and Ruth sat on shivering by the bedside in that darkened room. Mrs Morgan sent her breakfast upstairs by a chambermaid, but Ruth motioned it away in her sick agony, and the girl had no right to urge her to partake of it. That alone broke the monotony of the long morning. She heard the sound of merry parties setting out on excursions, on horseback or in carriages; and once, stiff and wearied, she stole to the window, and looked out on one side of the blind; but the day looked bright and discordant to her aching, anxious heart. The gloom of the darkened room was better and more befitting.

It was some hours after he was summoned before the doctor made his appearance. He questioned his patient, and, receiving no coherent answers, he asked Ruth concerning the symptoms; but when she questioned him in turn he only shook his head and looked grave. He made a sign to Mrs Morgan to follow him out of the room, and they went down to her parlour, leaving Ruth in a depth of despair, lower than she could have thought it possible there remained for her to experience, an hour before.

"I am afraid this is a bad case," said Mr Jones to Mrs Morgan in Welsh. "A brain-fever has evidently set in."

"Poor young gentleman! poor young man! He looked the very picture of health!"

"That very appearance of robustness will, in all probability, make his disorder more violent. However, we must hope for the best, Mrs Morgan. Who is to attend upon him? He will require careful nursing. Is that young lady his sister? She looks too young to be his wife?"

"No, indeed! Gentlemen like you must know, Mr Jones, that we can't always look too closely into the ways of young men who come to our houses. Not but what I'm sorry for her, for she's an innocent, inoffensive young creature. I always think it right, for my own morals, to put a little scorn into my manners when such as her come to stay here; but, indeed, she's so gentle, I've found it hard work to show the proper contempt."

She would have gone on to her inattentive listener if she had not heard a low tap at the door, which recalled her from her morality, and Mr Jones from his consideration of the necessary prescriptions.

"Come in!" said Mrs Morgan, sharply. And Ruth came in. She was white and trembling; but she stood in that dignity which strong feeling, kept down by self-command, always imparts.

"I wish you, sir, to be so kind as to tell me, clearly and distinctly, what I must do for Mr Bellingham. Every direction you give me shall be most carefully attended to. You spoke about leeches—I can put them on, and see about them. Tell me everything, sir, that you wish to have done!"

Her manner was calm and serious, and her countenance and deportment showed that the occasion was calling out strength sufficient to meet it. Mr Jones spoke with a deference which he had not thought of using upstairs, even while he supposed her to be the sister of the invalid. Ruth listened gravely; she repeated some of the injunctions, in order that she might be sure that she fully comprehended them, and then, bowing, left the room.

"She is no common person," said Mr Jones. "Still she is too young to have the responsibility of such a serious case. Have you any idea where his friends live, Mrs Morgan?"

"Indeed and I have. His mother, as haughty a lady as you would wish to see, came travelling through Wales last year; she stopped here, and, I warrant you, nothing was good enough for her; she was real quality. She left some clothes and books behind her (for the maid was almost as fine as the mistress, and little thought of seeing after her lady's clothes, having a taste for going to see scenery along with the man-servant), and we had several letters from her. I have them locked in the drawers in the bar, where I keep such things."

"Well! I should recommend your writing to the lady, and telling her her son's state."

"It would be a favour, Mr Jones, if you would just write it yourself. English writing comes so strange to my pen."

The letter was written, and, in order to save time, Mr Jones took it to the Llanglâs post-office.

CHAPTER VII

The Crisis—Watching and Waiting

Ruth put away every thought of the past or future; everything that could unfit her for the duties of the present. Exceeding love supplied the place of experience. She never left the room after the first day; she forced herself to eat, because his service needed her strength. She did not indulge in any tears, because the weeping she longed for would make her less able to attend upon him. She watched, and waited, and prayed: prayed with an utter forgetfulness of self, only with a consciousness that God was all-powerful, and that he, whom she loved so much, needed the aid of the Mighty One.

Day and night, the summer night, seemed merged into one. She lost count of time in the hushed and darkened room. One morning Mrs Morgan beckoned her out; and she stole on tiptoe into the dazzling gallery, on one side of which the bedrooms opened.

"She's come," whispered Mrs Morgan, looking very much excited, and forgetting that Ruth had never heard that Mrs Bellingham had been summoned.

"Who is come?" asked Ruth. The idea of Mrs Mason flashed through her mind—but with a more terrible, because a more vague dread, she heard that it was his mother; the mother of whom he had always spoken as a person whose opinion was to be regarded more than that of any other individual.

"What must I do? Will she be angry with me?" said she, relapsing into her child-like dependence on others; and feeling that even Mrs Morgan was some one to stand between her and Mrs Bellingham.

Mrs Morgan herself was a little perplexed. Her morality was rather shocked at the idea of a proper real lady like Mrs Bellingham discovering that she had winked at the connexion between her son and Ruth. She was quite inclined to encourage Ruth in her inclination to shrink out of Mrs Bellingham's observation, an inclination which arose from no definite consciousness of having done wrong, but principally from the representations she had always heard of the lady's awfulness. Mrs Bellingham swept into her son's room as if she were unconscious what poor young creature had lately haunted it; while Ruth hurried into some unoccupied bedroom, and, alone there, she felt her self-restraint suddenly give way, and burst into the saddest, most utterly wretched weeping she had ever known. She was worn out with watching, and exhausted by passionate crying, and she lay down on the bed and fell asleep. The day passed on; she slumbered unnoticed and unregarded; she awoke late in the evening with a sense of having done wrong in sleeping so long; the strain upon her responsibility had not yet left her. Twilight was closing fast around; she waited until it had become night, and then she stole down to Mrs Morgan's parlour.

"If you please, may I come in?" asked she.

Jenny Morgan was doing up the hieroglyphics which she called her accounts; she answered sharply enough, but it was a permission to enter, and Ruth was thankful for it.

"Will you tell me how he is? Do you think I may go back to him?"

"No, indeed, that you may not. Nest, who has made his room tidy these many days, is not fit to go in now. Mrs Bellingham has brought her own maid, and the family nurse, and Mr Bellingham's man; such a tribe of servants and no end to packages; water-beds coming by the carrier, and a doctor from London coming down to-morrow, as if feather-beds and Mr Jones was not good enough. Why, she won't let a soul of us into the room; there's no chance for you!"

Ruth sighed. "How is he?" she inquired, after a pause.

"How can I tell indeed, when I'm not allowed to go near him? Mr Jones said to-night was a turning point; but I doubt it, for it is four days since he was taken ill, and who ever heard of a sick person taking a turn on an even number of days; it's always on the third, or the fifth, or seventh, or so on. He'll not turn till to-morrow night, take my word for it, and their fine London doctor will get all the credit, and honest Mr Jones will be thrown aside. I don't think he will get better myself, though—Gelert does not howl for nothing. My patience! what's the matter with the girl?—lord, child, you're never going to faint, and be ill on my hands?" Her sharp voice recalled Ruth from the sick unconsciousness that had been creeping over her as she listened to the latter part of this speech. She sat down and could not speak—the room whirled round and round—her white feebleness touched Mrs Morgan's heart.

"You've had no tea, I guess. Indeed, and the girls are very careless." She rang the bell with energy, and seconded her pull by going to the door and shouting out sharp directions, in Welsh, to Nest and Gwen, and three or four other rough, kind, slatternly servants.

They brought her tea, which was comfortable, according to the idea of comfort prevalent in that rude, hospitable place; there was plenty to eat, too much, indeed, for it revolted the appetite it was intended to provoke. But the heartiness with which the kind, rosy waiter pressed her to eat, and the scolding Mrs Morgan gave her when she found the buttered toast untouched (toast on which she had herself desired that the butter might not be spared), did Ruth more good than the tea. She began to hope, and to long for the morning when hope might have become certainty. It was all in vain that she was told that the room she had been in all day was at her service; she did not say a word, but she was not going to bed that night, of all nights in the year, when life or death hung trembling in the balance. She went into the bedroom till the bustling house was still, and heard busy feet passing to and fro in the room she might not enter; and voices, imperious, though hushed down to a whisper, ask for innumerable things. Then there was silence; and when she thought that all were dead asleep, except the watchers, she stole out into the gallery. On the other side were two windows, cut into the thick stone wall, and flower pots were placed on the shelves thus formed, where great, untrimmed, straggling geraniums grew, and strove to reach the light. The window near Mr Bellingham's door was open; the soft, warm-scented night air came sighing in in faint gusts, and then was still. It was summer; there was no black darkness in the twenty-four hours; only the light grew dusky, and colour disappeared from objects, of which the shape and form remained distinct. A soft grey oblong of barred light fell on the flat wall opposite to the windows, and deeper grey shadows marked out the tracery of the plants, more graceful thus than in reality. Ruth crouched where no light fell. She sat on the ground close by the door; her whole existence was absorbed in listening; all was still; it was only her heart beating with the strong, heavy, regular sound of a hammer. She wished she could stop its rushing, incessant clang. She heard a rustle of a silken gown, and knew it ought not to have been worn in a sick-room; for her senses seemed to have passed into the keeping of the invalid, and to feel only as he felt. The noise was probably occasioned by some change of posture in the watcher inside, for it was once more dead-still. The soft wind outside sank with a low, long, distant moan among the windings of the hills, and lost itself there, and came no more again. But Ruth's heart beat loud. She rose with as little noise as if she were a vision, and crept to the open window to try and lose the nervous listening for the ever-recurring sound. Out beyond, under the calm sky, veiled with a mist rather than with a cloud, rose the high, dark outlines of the mountains, shutting in that village as if it lay in a nest. They stood, like giants, solemnly watching for the end of Earth and Time. Here and there a black round shadow reminded Ruth of some "Cwm," or hollow, where she and her lover had rambled in sun and in gladness. She then thought the land enchanted into everlasting brightness and happiness; she fancied, then, that into a region so lovely no bale or woe could enter, but would be charmed away and disappear before the sight of the glorious guardian mountains. Now she knew the truth, that earth has no barrier which avails against agony. It comes lightning-like down from heaven, into the mountain house and the town garret; into the palace and into the cottage. The garden lay close under the house; a bright spot enough by day; for in that soil, whatever was planted grew and blossomed in spite of neglect. The white roses glimmered out in the dusk all the night through; the red were lost in shadow. Between the low boundary of the garden and the hills swept one or two green meadows; Ruth looked into the grey darkness till she traced each separate wave of outline. Then she heard a little restless bird chirp out its wakefulness from a nest in the ivy round the walls of the house. But the mother-bird spread her soft feathers, and hushed it into silence. Presently, however, many little birds began to scent the coming dawn, and rustled among the leaves, and chirruped loud and clear. Just above the horizon, too, the mist became a silvery grey cloud hanging on the edge of the world; presently it turned shimmering white; and then, in an instant, it flushed into rose, and the mountain-tops sprang into heaven, and bathed in the presence of the shadow of God. With a bound, the sun of a molten fiery red came above the horizon, and immediately thousands of little birds sang out for joy, and a soft chorus of mysterious, glad murmurs came forth from the earth; the low whispering wind left its hiding-place among the clefts and hollows of the hills, and wandered among the rustling herbs and trees, waking the flower-buds to the life of another day. Ruth gave a sigh of relief that the night was over and gone; for she knew that soon suspense would be ended, and the verdict known, whether for life or for death. She grew faint and sick with anxiety; it almost seemed as if she must go into the room and learn the truth. Then she heard movements, but they were not sharp or rapid, as if prompted by any emergency; then, again, it was still. She sat curled up upon the floor, with her head thrown back against the wall, and her hands clasped round her knees. She had yet to wait. Meanwhile, the invalid was slowly rousing himself from a long, deep, sound, health-giving sleep. His mother had sat by him the night through, and was now daring to change her position for the first time; she was even venturing to give directions in a low voice to the old nurse, who had dozed away in an arm-chair, ready to obey any summons of her mistress. Mrs Bellingham went on tiptoe towards the door, and chiding herself because her stiff, weary limbs made some slight noise. She had an irrepressible longing for a few minutes' change of scene after her night of watching. She felt that the crisis was over; and the relief to her mind made her conscious of every bodily feeling and irritation, which had passed unheeded as long as she had been in suspense.

She slowly opened the door. Ruth sprang upright at the first sound of the creaking handle. Her very lips were stiff and unpliable with the force of the blood which rushed to her head. It seemed as if she could not form words. She stood right before Mrs Bellingham. "How is he, madam?"

Mrs Bellingham was for a moment surprised at the white apparition which seemed to rise out of the ground. But her quick, proud mind understood it all in an instant. This was the girl, then, whose profligacy had led her son astray; had raised up barriers in the way of her favourite scheme of his marriage with Miss Duncombe; nay, this was the real cause of his illness, his mortal danger at this present time, and of her bitter, keen anxiety. If, under any circumstances, Mrs Bellingham could have been guilty of the ill-breeding of not answering a question, it was now; and for a moment she was tempted to pass on in silence. Ruth could not wait; she spoke again:

"For the love of God, madam, speak! How is he? Will he live?"

If she did not answer her, she thought the creature was desperate enough to force her way into his room. So she spoke.

"He has slept well: he is better."

"Oh! my God, I thank Thee," murmured Ruth, sinking back against the wall.

It was too much to hear this wretched girl thanking God for her son's life; as if, in fact, she had any lot or part in him, and to dare to speak to the Almighty on her son's behalf! Mrs Bellingham looked at her with cold, contemptuous eyes, whose glances were like ice-bolts, and made Ruth shiver up away from them.

"Young woman, if you have any propriety or decency left, I trust that you will not dare to force yourself into his room."

She stood for a moment as if awaiting an answer, and half expecting it to be a defiance. But she did not understand Ruth. She did not imagine the faithful trustfulness of her heart. Ruth believed that if Mr Bellingham was alive and likely to live, all was well. When he wanted her, he would send for her, ask for her, yearn for her, till every one would yield before his steadfast will. At present she imagined that he was probably too weak to care or know who was about him; and though it would have been an infinite delight to her to hover and brood around him, yet it was of him she thought and not of herself. She gently drew herself on one side to make way for Mrs Bellingham to pass.

By-and-by Mrs Morgan came up. Ruth was still near the door, from which it seemed as if she could not tear herself away.

"Indeed, miss, and you must not hang about the door in this way; it is not pretty manners. Mrs Bellingham has been speaking very sharp and cross about it, and I shall lose the character of my inn if people take to talking as she does. Did not I give you a room last night to keep in, and never be seen or heard of; and did I not tell you what a particular lady Mrs Bellingham was, but you must come out here right in her way? Indeed, it was not pretty, nor grateful to me, Jenny Morgan, and that I must say."

Ruth turned away like a chidden child. Mrs Morgan followed her to her room, scolding as she went; and then, having cleared her heart after her wont by uttering hasty words, her real kindness made her add, in a softened tone:

"You stop up here like a good girl. I'll send you your breakfast by-and-by, and let you know from time to time how he is; and you can go out for a walk, you know; but if you do, I'll take it as a favour if you'll go out by the side door. It will, maybe, save scandal."

All that day long, Ruth kept herself close prisoner in the room to which Mrs Morgan accorded her; all that day, and many succeeding days. But at nights, when the house was still, and even the little brown mice had gathered up the crumbs, and darted again to their holes, Ruth stole out, and crept to his door to catch, if she could, the sound of his beloved voice. She could tell by its tones how he felt, and how he was getting on, as well as any of the watchers in the room. She yearned and pined to see him once more; but she had reasoned herself down into something like patience. When he was well enough to leave his room, when he had not always one of the nurses with him, then he would send for her, and she would tell him how very patient she had been for his dear sake. But it was long to wait even with this thought of the manner in which the waiting would end. Poor Ruth! her faith was only building up vain castles in the air; they towered up into heaven, it is true, but, after all, they were but visions.

CHAPTER VIII

Mrs Bellingham "Does the Thing Handsomely"

If Mr Bellingham did not get rapidly well, it was more owing to the morbid querulous fancy attendant on great weakness than from any unfavourable medical symptom. But he turned away with peevish loathing from the very sight of food, prepared in the slovenly manner which had almost disgusted him when he was well. It was of no use telling him that Simpson, his mother's maid, had superintended the preparation at every point. He offended her by detecting something offensive and to be avoided in her daintiest messes, and made Mrs Morgan mutter many a hasty speech, which, however, Mrs Bellingham thought it better not to hear until her son should be strong enough to travel.

"I think you are better to-day," said she, as his man wheeled his sofa to the bedroom window. "We shall get you downstairs to-morrow."

"If it were to get away from this abominable place, I could go down to-day; but I believe I'm to be kept prisoner here for ever. I shall never get well here, I'm sure."

He sank back on his sofa in impatient despair. The surgeon was announced, and eagerly questioned by Mrs Bellingham as to the possibility of her son's removal; and he, having heard the same anxiety for the same end expressed by Mrs Morgan in the regions below, threw no great obstacles in the way. After the doctor had taken his departure, Mrs Bellingham cleared her throat several times. Mr Bellingham knew the prelude of old, and winced with nervous annoyance.

"Henry, there is something I must speak to you about; an unpleasant subject, certainly, but one which has been forced upon me by the very girl herself; you must be aware to what I refer without giving me the pain of explaining myself."

Mr Bellingham turned himself sharply round to the wall, and prepared himself for a lecture by concealing his face from her notice; but she herself was in too nervous a state to be capable of observation.

"Of course," she continued, "it was my wish to be as blind to the whole affair as possible, though you can't imagine how Mrs Mason has blazoned it abroad; all Fordham rings with it; but of course it could not be pleasant, or, indeed, I may say correct, for me to be aware that a person of such improper character was under the same—I beg your pardon, dear Henry, what do you say?"

"Ruth is no improper character, mother; you do her injustice!"

"My dear boy, you don't mean to uphold her as a paragon of virtue!"

"No, mother, but I led her wrong; I—"

"We will let all discussions into the cause or duration of her present character drop, if you please," said Mrs Bellingham, with the sort of dignified authority which retained a certain power over her son—a power which originated in childhood, and which he only defied when he was roused into passion. He was too weak in body to oppose himself to her, and fight the ground inch by inch. "As I have implied, I do not wish to ascertain your share of blame; from what I saw of her one morning, I am convinced of her forward, intrusive manners, utterly without shame, or even common modesty."

"What are you referring to?" asked Mr Bellingham, sharply.

"Why, when you were at the worst, and I had been watching you all night, and had just gone out in the morning for a breath of fresh air, this girl pushed herself before me, and insisted upon speaking to me. I really had to send Mrs Morgan to her before I could return to your room. A more impudent, hardened manner, I never saw."

"Ruth was neither impudent nor hardened; she was ignorant enough, and might offend from knowing no better."

He was getting weary of the discussion, and wished it had never been begun. From the time he had become conscious of his mother's presence, he had felt the dilemma he was in in regard to Ruth, and various plans had directly crossed his brain; but it had been so troublesome to weigh and consider them all properly, that they had been put aside to be settled when he grew stronger. But this difficulty in which he was placed by his connexion with Ruth, associated the idea of her in his mind with annoyance and angry regret at the whole affair. He wished, in the languid way in which he wished and felt everything not immediately relating to his daily comfort, that he had never seen her. It was a most awkward, a most unfortunate affair. Notwithstanding this annoyance connected with and arising out of Ruth, he would not submit to hear her abused; and something in his manner impressed this on his mother, for she immediately changed her mode of attack.

"We may as well drop all dispute as to the young woman's manners; but I suppose you do not mean to defend your connexion with her; I suppose you are not so lost to all sense of propriety as to imagine it fit or desirable that your mother and this degraded girl should remain under the same roof, liable to meet at any hour of the day?" She waited for an answer, but no answer came.

"I ask you a simple question; is it, or is it not desirable?"

"I suppose it is not," he replied, gloomily.

"And *I* suppose, from your manner, that you think the difficulty would be best solved by my taking my departure, and leaving you with your vicious companion?"

Again no answer, but inward and increasing annoyance, of which Mr Bellingham considered Ruth the cause. At length he spoke.

"Mother, you are not helping me in my difficulty. I have no desire to banish you, nor to hurt you, after all your care for me. Ruth has not been so much to blame as you imagine, that I must say; but I do not wish to see her again, if you can tell me how to arrange it otherwise, without behaving unhandsomely. Only spare me all this worry while I am so weak. I put myself in your hands. Dismiss her, as you wish it; but let it be done handsomely, and let me hear no more about it; I cannot bear it; let me have a quiet life, without being lectured while I am pent up here, and unable to shake off unpleasant thoughts."

"My dear Henry, rely upon me."

"No more, mother; it's a bad business, and I can hardly avoid blaming myself in the matter; I don't want to dwell upon it."

"Don't be too severe in your self-reproaches while you are so feeble, dear Henry; it is right to repent, but I have no doubt in my own mind she led you wrong with her artifices. But, as you say, everything should be done handsomely. I confess I was deeply grieved when I first heard of the affair, but since I have seen the girl— Well! I'll say no more about her, since I see it displeases you; but I am thankful to God that you see the error of your ways."

She sat silent, thinking for a little while, and then sent for her writing-case, and began to write. Her son became restless, and nervously irritated.

"Mother," he said, "this affair worries me to death. I cannot shake off the thoughts of it."

"Leave it to me, I'll arrange it satisfactorily."

"Could we not leave to-night? I should not be so haunted by this annoyance in another place. I dread seeing her again, because I fear a scene; and yet I believe I ought to see her, in order to explain."

"You must not think of such a thing, Henry," said she, alarmed at the very idea. "Sooner than that, we will leave in half an hour, and try to get to Pen trê Voelas to-night. It is not yet three, and the evenings are very long. Simpson should stay and finish the packing; she could go straight to London and meet us there. Macdonald and nurse could go with us. Could you bear twenty miles, do you think?"

Anything to get rid of his uneasiness. He felt that he was not behaving as he should do, to Ruth, though the really right never entered his head. But it would extricate him from his present dilemma, and save him many lectures; he knew that his mother, always liberal where money was concerned, would "do the thing handsomely," and it would always be easy to write and give Ruth what explanation he felt inclined, in a day or two; so he consented, and soon lost some of his uneasiness in watching the bustle of the preparation for their departure.

All this time Ruth was quietly spending in her room, beguiling the waiting, weary hours, with pictures of the meeting at the end. Her room looked to the back, and was in a side-wing away from the principal state apartments, consequently she was not roused to suspicion by any of the commotion; but, indeed, if she had heard the banging of doors, the sharp directions, the carriage-wheels, she would still not have suspected the truth; her own love was too faithful.

It was four o'clock and past, when some one knocked at her door, and, on entering, gave her a note, which Mrs Bellingham had left. That lady had found some difficulty in wording it, so as to satisfy herself, but it was as follows:

My son, on recovering from his illness, is, I thank God, happily conscious of the sinful way in which he has been living with you. By his earnest desire, and in order to avoid seeing you again, we are on the point of leaving this place; but before I go, I wish to exhort you to repentance, and to remind you that you will not have your own guilt alone upon your head, but that of any young man whom you may succeed in entrapping into vice. I shall pray that you may turn to an honest life, and I strongly recommend you, if indeed you are not 'dead in trespasses and sins,' to enter some penitentiary. In accordance with my son's wishes, I forward you in this envelope a bank-note of fifty pounds.

Margaret Bellingham.

Was this the end of all? Had he, indeed, gone? She started up, and asked this last question of the servant, who, half guessing at the purport of the note, had lingered about the room, curious to see the effect produced.

"Iss, indeed, miss; the carriage drove from the door as I came upstairs. You'll see it now on the Yspytty road, if you'll please to come to the window of No. 24."

Ruth started up, and followed the chambermaid. Aye, there it was, slowly winding up the steep white road, on which it seemed to move at a snail's pace.

She might overtake him—she might—she might speak one farewell word to him, print his face on her heart with a last look—nay, when he saw her he might retract, and not utterly, for ever, leave her. Thus she thought; and she flew back to her room, and snatching up her bonnet, ran, tying the strings with her trembling hands as she went down the stairs, out at the nearest door, little heeding the angry words of Mrs Morgan; for the hostess, more irritated at Mrs Bellingham's severe upbraiding at parting, than mollified by her ample payment, was offended by the circumstance of Ruth, in her wild haste, passing through the prohibited front door.

But Ruth was away before Mrs Morgan had finished her speech, out and away, scudding along the road, thought-lost in the breathless rapidity of her motion. Though her heart and head beat almost to bursting, what did it signify if she could but overtake the carriage? It was a nightmare, constantly evading the most passionate wishes and endeavours, and constantly gaining ground. Every time it was visible it was in fact more distant, but Ruth would not believe it. If she could but gain the summit of that weary, everlasting hill, she believed that she could run again, and would soon be nigh upon the carriage. As she ran, she prayed with wild eagerness; she prayed that she might see his face once more, even if she died on the spot before him. It was one of those prayers which God is too merciful to grant; but despairing and wild as it was, Ruth put her soul into it, and prayed it again, and yet again.

Wave above wave of the ever-rising hills were gained, were crossed, and at last Ruth struggled up to the very top and stood on the bare table of moor, brown and purple, stretching far away till it was lost in the haze of the summer afternoon; and the white road was all flat before her, but the carriage she sought and the figure she sought had disappeared. There was no human being there; a few wild, black-faced mountain sheep quietly grazing near the road, as if it were long since they had been disturbed by the passing of any vehicle, was all the life she saw on the bleak moorland.

She threw herself down on the ling by the side of the road in despair. Her only hope was to die, and she believed she was dying. She could not think; she could believe anything. Surely life was a horrible dream, and God would mercifully awaken her from it. She had no penitence, no consciousness of error or offence; no knowledge of any one circumstance but that he was gone. Yet afterwards, long afterwards, she remembered the exact motion of a bright green beetle busily meandering among the wild thyme near her, and she recalled the musical, balanced, wavering drop of a skylark into her nest near the heather-bed where she lay. The sun was sinking low, the hot air had ceased to quiver near the hotter earth, when she bethought her once more of the note which she had impatiently thrown down before half mastering its contents. "Oh, perhaps," she thought, "I have been too hasty. There may be some words of explanation from him on the other side of the page, to which, in my blind anguish, I never turned. I will go and find it."

She lifted herself heavily and stiffly from the crushed heather. She stood dizzy and confused with her change of posture; and was so unable to move at first, that her walk was but slow and tottering; but, by-and-by, she was tasked and goaded by thoughts which forced her into rapid motion, as if, by it, she could escape from her agony. She came down on the level ground, just as many gay or peaceful groups were sauntering leisurely home with hearts at ease; with low laughs and quiet smiles, and many an exclamation at the beauty of the summer evening.

Ever since her adventure with the little boy and his sister, Ruth had habitually avoided encountering these happy—innocents, may I call them?—these happy fellow-mortals! And even now, the habit grounded on sorrowful humiliation had power over her; she paused, and then, on looking back, she saw more people who had come into the main road from a side path. She opened a gate into a pasture-field, and crept up to the hedge-bank until all should have passed by, and she could steal into the inn unseen. She sat down on the sloping turf by the roots of an old hawthorn-tree which grew in the hedge; she was still tearless with hot burning eyes; she heard the merry walkers pass by; she heard the footsteps of the village children as they ran along to their evening play; she saw the small black cows come into the fields after being milked; and life seemed yet abroad. When would the world be still and dark, and fit for such a deserted, desolate creature as she was? Even in her hiding-place she was not long at peace. The little children, with their curious eyes peering here and there, had peeped through the hedge, and through the gate, and now they gathered from all the four corners of the hamlet, and crowded round the gate; and one more adventurous than the rest had run into the field to cry, "Gi' me a halfpenny," which set the example to every little one, emulous of his boldness; and there, where she sat, low on the ground, and longing for the sure hiding-place earth gives to the weary, the children kept running in, and pushing one another forwards, and laughing. Poor things; their time had not come for understanding what sorrow is. Ruth would have begged them to leave her alone, and not madden her utterly; but they knew no English save the one eternal "Gi' me a halfpenny." She felt in her heart that there was no pity anywhere. Suddenly, while she thus doubted God, a shadow fell across her garments, on which her miserable eyes were bent. She looked up. The deformed gentleman she had twice before seen, stood there. He had been attracted by the noisy little crowd, and had questioned them in Welsh, but not understanding enough of the language to comprehend their answers, he had obeyed their signs, and entered the gate to which they pointed. There he saw the young girl whom he had noticed at first for her innocent beauty, and the second time for the idea he had gained respecting her situation; there he saw her, crouched up like some hunted creature, with a wild, scared look of despair, which almost made her lovely face seem fierce; he saw her dress soiled and dim, her bonnet crushed and battered with her tossings to and fro on the moorland bed; he saw the poor, lost wanderer, and when he saw her, he had compassion on her.

There was some look of heavenly pity in his eyes, as gravely and sadly they met her upturned gaze, which touched her stony heart. Still looking at him, as if drawing some good influence from him, she said low and mournfully, "He has left me, sir!—sir, he has indeed—he has gone and left me!"

Before he could speak a word to comfort her, she had burst into the wildest, dreariest crying ever mortal cried. The settled form of the event, when put into words, went sharp to her heart; her moans and sobs wrung his soul; but as no speech of his could be heard, if he had been able to decide what best to say, he stood by her in apparent calmness, while she, wretched, wailed and uttered her woe. But when she lay worn out, and stupefied into silence, she heard him say to himself, in a low voice:

"Oh, my God! for Christ's sake, pity her!"

Ruth lifted up her eyes, and looked at him with a dim perception of the meaning of his words. She regarded him fixedly in a dreamy way, as if they struck some chord in her heart, and she were listening to its echo; and so it was. His pitiful look, or his words, reminded her of the childish days when she knelt at her mother's knee, and she was only conscious of a straining, longing desire to recall it all.

He let her take her time, partly because he was powerfully affected himself by all the circumstances, and by the sad pale face upturned to his; and partly by an instinctive consciousness that the softest patience was required. But suddenly she startled him, as she herself was startled into a keen sense of the suffering agony of the present; she sprang up and pushed him aside, and went rapidly towards the gate of the field. He could not move as quickly as most men, but he put forth his utmost speed. He followed across the road, on to the rocky common; but as he went along, with his uncertain gait, in the dusk gloaming, he stumbled, and fell over some sharp projecting stone. The acute pain which shot up his back forced a short cry from him; and, when bird and beast are hushed into rest and the stillness of the night is over all, a high-pitched sound, like the voice of pain, is carried far in the quiet air. Ruth, speeding on in her despair, heard the sharp utterance, and stopped suddenly short. It did what no remonstrance could have done; it called her out of herself. The tender nature was in her still, in that hour when all good angels seemed to have abandoned her. In the old days she could never bear to hear or see bodily suffering in any of God's meanest creatures, without trying to succour them; and now, in her rush to the awful death of the suicide, she stayed her wild steps, and turned to find from whom that sharp sound of anguish had issued.

He lay among the white stones, too faint with pain to move, but with an agony in his mind far keener than any bodily pain, as he thought that by his unfortunate fall he had lost all chance of saving her. He was almost overpowered by his intense thankfulness when he saw her white figure pause, and stand listening, and turn again with slow footsteps, as if searching for some lost thing. He could hardly speak, but he made a sound which, though his heart was inexpressibly glad, was like a groan. She came quickly towards him.

"I am hurt," said he; "do not leave me;" his disabled and tender frame was overcome by the accident and the previous emotions, and he fainted away. Ruth flew to the little mountain stream, the dashing sound of whose waters had been tempting her, but a moment before, to seek forgetfulness in the deep pool into which they fell. She made a basin of her joined hands, and carried enough of the cold fresh water back to dash into his face and restore him to consciousness. While he still kept silence, uncertain what to say best fitted to induce her to listen to him, she said softly:

"Are you better, sir?—are you very much hurt?"

"Not very much; I am better. Any quick movement is apt to cause me a sudden loss of power in my back, and I believe I stumbled over some of these projecting stones. It will soon go off, and you will help me to go home, I am sure."

"Oh, yes! Can you go now? I am afraid of your lying too long on this heather; there is a heavy dew."

He was so anxious to comply with her wish, and not weary out her thought for him, and so turn her back upon herself, that he tried to rise. The pain was acute, and this she saw.

"Don't hurry yourself, sir; I can wait."

Then came across her mind the recollection of the business that was thus deferred; but the few homely words which had been exchanged between them seemed to have awakened her from her madness. She sat down by him, and, covering her face with her hands, cried mournfully and unceasingly. She forgot his presence, and yet she had a consciousness that some one looked for her kind offices, that she was wanted in the world, and must not rush hastily out of it. The consciousness did not take this definite form, it did not become a thought, but it kept her still, and it was gradually soothing her.

"Can you help me to rise now?" said he, after a while. She did not speak, but she helped him up, and then he took her arm, and she led him tenderly through all the little velvet paths, where the turf grew short and soft between the rugged stones. Once more on the highway, they slowly passed along in the moonlight. He guided her by a slight motion of the arm, through the more unfrequented lanes, to his lodgings at the shop; for he thought for her, and conceived the pain she would have in seeing the lighted windows of the inn. He leant more heavily on her arm, as they awaited the opening of the door.

"Come in," said he, not relaxing his hold, and yet dreading to tighten it, lest she should defy restraint, and once more rush away.

They went slowly into the little parlour behind the shop. The bonny-looking hostess, Mrs Hughes by name, made haste to light the candle, and then they saw each other, face to face. The deformed gentleman looked very pale, but Ruth looked as if the shadow of death was upon her.

CHAPTER IX

The Storm-Spirit Subdued

Mrs Hughes bustled about with many a sympathetic exclamation, now in pretty broken English, now in more fluent Welsh, which sounded as soft as Russian or Italian, in her musical voice. Mr Benson, for that was the name of the hunchback, lay on the sofa, thinking; while the tender Mrs Hughes made every arrangement for his relief from pain. He had lodged with her for three successive years, and she knew and loved him.

Ruth stood in the little bow-window, looking out. Across the moon, and over the deep blue heavens, large, torn, irregular-shaped clouds went hurrying, as if summoned by some storm-spirit. The work they were commanded to do was not here; the mighty gathering-place lay eastward, immeasurable leagues, and on they went, chasing each other over the silent earth, now black, now silver-white at one transparent edge, now with the moon shining like Hope through their darkest centre, now again with a silver lining; and now, utterly black, they sailed lower in the lift, and disappeared behind the immovable mountains; they were rushing in the very direction in which Ruth had striven and struggled to go that afternoon; they, in their wild career, would soon pass over the very spot where he (her world's he) was lying sleeping, or perhaps not sleeping, perhaps thinking of her. The storm was in her mind, and rent and tore her purposes into forms as wild and irregular as the heavenly shapes she was looking at. If, like them, she could pass the barrier horizon in the night, she might overtake him.

Mr Benson saw her look, and read it partially. He saw her longing gaze outwards upon the free, broad world, and thought that the syren waters, whose deadly music yet rang in her ears, were again tempting her. He called her to him, praying that his feeble voice might have power.

"My dear young lady, I have much to say to you; and God has taken my strength from me now when I most need it.—Oh, I sin to speak so—but, for His sake, I implore you to be patient here, if only till to-morrow morning." He looked at her, but her face was immovable, and she did not speak. She could not give up her hope, her chance, her liberty till to-morrow.

"God help me," said he, mournfully, "my words do not touch her;" and, still holding her hand, he sank back on the pillows. Indeed, it was true that his words did not vibrate in her atmosphere. The storm-spirit raged there, and filled her heart with the thought that she was an outcast; and the holy words, "for His sake," were answered by the demon, who held possession, with a blasphemous defiance of the merciful God:

"What have I to do with Thee?"

He thought of every softening influence of religion which over his own disciplined heart had power, but put them aside as useless. Then the still small voice whispered, and he spake:

"In your mother's name, whether she be dead or alive, I command you to stay here until I am able to speak to you."

She knelt down at the foot of the sofa, and shook it with her sobs. Her heart was touched, and he hardly dared to speak again. At length he said:

"I know you will not go—you could not—for her sake. You will not, will you?"

"No," whispered Ruth; and then there was a great blank in her heart. She had given up her chance. She was calm, in the utter absence of all hope.

"And now you will do what I tell you," said he, gently, but, unconsciously to himself, in the tone of one who has found the hidden spell by which to rule spirits.

She slowly said, "Yes." But she was subdued.

He called Mrs Hughes. She came from her adjoining shop.

"You have a bedroom within yours, where your daughter used to sleep, I think? I am sure you will oblige me, and I shall consider it as a great favour, if you will allow this young lady to sleep there to-night. Will you take her there now? Go, my dear. I have full trust in your promise not to leave until I can speak to you." His voice died away to silence; but as Ruth rose from her knees at his bidding, she looked at his face through her tears. His lips were moving in earnest, unspoken prayer, and she knew it was for her.

That night, although his pain was relieved by rest, he could not sleep; and, as in fever, the coming events kept unrolling themselves before him in every changing and fantastic form. He met Ruth in all possible places and ways, and addressed her in every manner he could imagine most calculated to move and affect her to penitence and virtue. Towards morning he fell asleep, but the same thoughts haunted his dreams; he spoke, but his voice refused to utter aloud; and she fled, relentless, to the deep, black pool.

But God works in His own way.

The visions melted into deep, unconscious sleep. He was awakened by a knock at the door, which seemed a repetition of what he had heard in his last sleeping moments.

It was Mrs Hughes. She stood at the first word of permission within the room.

"Please, sir, I think the young lady is very ill indeed, sir; perhaps you would please to come to her."

"How is she ill?" said he, much alarmed.

"Quite quiet-like, sir; but I think she is dying, that's all, indeed, sir!"

"Go away, I will be with you directly!" he replied, his heart sinking within him.

In a very short time he was standing with Mrs Hughes by Ruth's bedside. She lay as still as if she were dead, her eyes shut, her wan face numbed into a fixed anguish of expression. She did not speak when they spoke, though after a while they thought she strove to do so. But all power of motion and utterance had left her. She was dressed in everything, except her bonnet, as she had been the day before; although sweet, thoughtful Mrs Hughes had provided her with nightgear, which lay on the little chest of drawers that served as a dressing-table. Mr Benson lifted up her arm to feel her feeble, fluttering pulse; and when he let go her hand, it fell upon the bed in a dull, heavy way, as if she were already dead.

"You gave her some food?" said he, anxiously, to Mrs Hughes.

"Indeed, and I offered her the best in the house, but she shook her poor pretty head, and only asked if I would please to get her a cup of water. I brought her some milk though, and 'deed, I think she'd rather have had the water; but not to seem sour and cross, she took some milk." By this time Mrs Hughes was fairly crying.

"When does the doctor come up here?"

"Indeed, sir, and he's up nearly every day now, the inn is so full."

"I'll go for him. And can you manage to undress her and lay her in bed? Open the window too, and let in the air; if her feet are cold, put bottles of hot water to them."

It was a proof of the true love, which was the nature of both, that it never crossed their minds to regret that this poor young creature had been thus thrown upon their hands. On the contrary, Mrs Hughes called it "a blessing."

"It blesseth him that gives, and him that takes."

CHAPTER X

A Note and the Answer

At the inn everything was life and bustle. Mr Benson had to wait long in Mrs Morgan's little parlour before she could come to him, and he kept growing more and more impatient. At last she made her appearance and heard his story.

People may talk as they will about the little respect that is paid to virtue, unaccompanied by the outward accidents of wealth or station; but I rather think it will be found that, in the long run, true and simple virtue always has its proportionate reward in the respect and reverence of every one whose esteem is worth having. To be sure, it is not rewarded after the way of the world as mere worldly possessions are, with low obeisance and lip-service; but all the better and more noble qualities in the hearts of others make ready and go forth to meet it on its approach, provided only it be pure, simple, and unconscious of its own existence.

Mr Benson had little thought for outward tokens of respect just then, nor had Mrs Morgan much time to spare; but she smoothed her ruffled brow, and calmed her bustling manner, as soon as ever she saw who it was that awaited her; for Mr Benson was well known in the village where he had taken up his summer holiday among the mountains year after year, always a resident at the shop, and seldom spending a shilling at the inn.

Mrs Morgan listened patiently—for her.

"Mr Jones will come this afternoon. But it is a shame you should be troubled with such as her. I had but little time yesterday, but I guessed there was something wrong, and Gwen has just been telling me her bed has not been slept in. They were in a pretty hurry to be gone yesterday, for all that the gentleman was not fit to travel, to my way of thinking; indeed, William Wynn, the post-boy, said he was weary enough before he got to the end of that Yspytty road; and he thought they would have to rest there a day or two before they could go further than Pen trê Voelas. Indeed, and anyhow, the servant is to follow them with the baggage this very morning; and now I remember, William Wynn said they would wait for her. You'd better write a note, Mr Benson, and tell them her state."

It was good, though unpalatable advice. It came from one accustomed to bring excellent, if unrefined sense, to bear quickly upon any emergency, and to decide rapidly. She was, in truth, so little accustomed to have her authority questioned, that before Mr Benson had made up his mind, she had produced paper, pens, and ink from the drawer in her bureau, placed them before him, and was going to leave the room.

"Leave the note on this shelf, and trust me that it goes by the maid. The boy that drives her there in the car shall bring you an answer back."

She was gone before he could rally his scattered senses enough to remember that he had not the least idea of the name of the party to whom he was to write. The quiet leisure and peace of his little study at home favoured his habit of reverie and long deliberation, just as her position as mistress of an inn obliged her to quick, decisive ways.

Her advice, though good in some points, was unpalatable in others. It was true that Ruth's condition ought to be known by those who were her friends; but were these people to whom he was now going to write, friends? He knew there was a rich mother, and a handsome, elegant son; and he had also some idea of the circumstances which might a little extenuate their mode of quitting Ruth. He had wide enough sympathy to understand that it must have been a most painful position in which the mother had been placed, on finding herself under the same roof with a girl who was living with her son, as Ruth was. And yet he did not like to apply to her; to write to the son was still more out of the question, as it seemed like asking him to return. But through one or the other lay the only clue to her friends, who certainly ought to be made acquainted with her position. At length he wrote:

MADAM,—I write to tell you of the condition of the poor young woman—[here came a long pause of deliberation]—who accompanied your son on his arrival here, and who was left behind on your departure yesterday. She is lying (as it appears to me) in a very dangerous state at my lodgings; and, if I may suggest, it would be kind to allow your maid to return and attend upon her until she is sufficiently recovered to be restored to her friends, if, indeed, they could not come to take charge of her themselves.

I remain, madam,
Your obedient servant,

THURSTAN BENSON.

The note was very unsatisfactory after all his consideration, but it was the best he could do. He made inquiry of a passing servant as to the lady's name, directed the note, and placed it on the indicated shelf. He then returned to his lodgings, to await the doctor's coming and the post-boy's return. There was no alteration in Ruth; she was as one stunned into unconsciousness; she did not move her posture, she hardly breathed. From time to time Mrs Hughes wetted her mouth with some liquid, and there was a little mechanical motion of the lips; that was the only sign of life she gave. The doctor came and shook his head,—"a thorough prostration of strength, occasioned by some great shock on the nerves,"—and prescribed care and quiet, and mysterious medicines, but acknowledged that the result was doubtful, very doubtful. After his departure, Mr Benson took his Welsh grammar and tried again to master the ever-puzzling rules for the mutations of letters; but it was of no use, for his thoughts were absorbed by the life-in-death condition of the young creature, who was lately bounding and joyous.

The maid and the luggage, the car and the driver, had arrived before noon at their journey's end, and the note had been delivered. It annoyed Mrs Bellingham exceedingly. It was the worst of these kind of connexions, there was no calculating the consequences; they were never-ending. All sorts of claims seemed to be established, and all sorts of people to step in to their settlement. The idea of sending her maid! Why, Simpson would not go if she asked her. She soliloquised thus while reading the letter; and then, suddenly turning round to the favourite attendant, who had been listening to her mistress's remarks with no inattentive ear, she asked:

"Simpson, would you go and nurse this creature, as this—" she looked at the signature—"Mr Benson, whoever he is, proposes?"

"Me! no, indeed, ma'am," said the maid, drawing herself up, stiff in her virtue. "I'm sure, ma'am, you would not expect it of me; I could never have the face to dress a lady of character again."

"Well, well! don't be alarmed; I cannot spare you; by the way, just attend to the strings on my dress; the chambermaid here pulled them into knots, and broke them terribly, last night. It is awkward though, very," said she, relapsing into a musing fit over the condition of Ruth.

"If you'll allow me, ma'am, I think I might say something that would alter the case. I believe, ma'am, you put a bank-note into the letter to the young woman yesterday?"

Mrs Bellingham bowed acquiescence, and the maid went on:

"Because, ma'am, when the little deformed man wrote that note (he's Mr Benson, ma'am), I have reason to believe neither he nor Mrs Morgan knew of any provision being made for the young woman. Me and the chambermaid found your letter and the bank-note lying quite promiscuous, like waste paper, on the floor of her room; for I believe she rushed out like mad after you left."

"That, as you say, alters the case. This letter, then, is principally a sort of delicate hint that some provision ought to have been made, which is true enough, only it has been attended to already; what became of the money?"

"Law, ma'am! do you ask? Of course, as soon as I saw it, I picked it up and took it to Mrs Morgan, in trust for the young person."

"Oh, that's right. What friends has she? Did you ever hear from Mason?—perhaps they ought to know where she is."

"Mrs Mason did tell me, ma'am, she was an orphan; with a guardian who was no-ways akin, and who washed his hands of her when she ran off; but Mrs Mason was sadly put out, and went into hysterics, for fear you would think she had not seen after her enough, and that she might lose your custom; she said it was no fault of hers, for the girl was always a forward creature, boasting of her beauty, and saying how pretty she was, and striving to get where her good looks could be seen and admired,—one night in particular, ma'am, at a county ball; and how Mrs Mason had found out she used to meet Mr Bellingham at an old woman's house, who was a regular old witch, ma'am, and lives in the lowest part of the town, where all the bad characters haunt."

"There! that's enough," said Mrs Bellingham, sharply, for the maid's chattering had outrun her tact; and in her anxiety to vindicate the character of her friend Mrs Mason by blackening that of Ruth, she had forgotten that she a little implicated her mistress's son, whom his proud mother did not like to imagine as ever passing through a low and degraded part of the town.

"If she has no friends, and is the creature you describe (which is confirmed by my own observation), the best place for her is, as I said before, the Penitentiary. Her fifty pounds will keep her for a week or so, if she is really unable to travel, and pay for her journey; and if on her return to Fordham she will let me know, I will undertake to obtain her admission immediately."

"I'm sure it's well for her she has to do with a lady who will take any interest in her, after what has happened."

Mrs Bellingham called for her writing-desk, and wrote a few hasty lines to be sent back by the post-boy, who was on the point of starting:

Mrs Bellingham presents her compliments to her unknown correspondent, Mr Benson, and begs to inform him of a circumstance of which she believes he was ignorant when he wrote the letter with which she has been favoured; namely, that provision to the amount of £50 was left for the unfortunate young person who is the subject of Mr Benson's letter. This sum is in the hands of Mrs Morgan, as well as a note from Mrs Bellingham to the miserable girl, in which she proposes to procure her admission into the Fordham Penitentiary, the best place for such a character, as by this profligate action she has forfeited the only friend remaining to her in the world. This proposition, Mrs Bellingham repeats; and they are the young woman's best friends who most urge her to comply with the course now pointed out.

"Take care Mr Bellingham hears nothing of this Mr Benson's note," said Mrs Bellingham, as she delivered the answer to her maid; "he is so sensitive just now that it would annoy him sadly, I am sure."

CHAPTER XI

Thurstan and Faith Benson

You have now seen the note which was delivered into Mr Benson's hands, as the cool shades of evening stole over the glowing summer sky. When he had read it, he again prepared to write a few hasty lines before the post went out. The post-boy was even now sounding his horn through the village as a signal for letters to be ready; and it was well that Mr Benson, in his long morning's meditation, had decided upon the course to be pursued, in case of such an answer as that which he had received from Mrs Bellingham. His present note was as follows:

DEAR FAITH,—You must come to this place directly, where I earnestly desire you and your advice. I am well myself, so do not be alarmed. I have no time for explanation, but I am sure you will not refuse me; let me trust that I shall see you on Saturday at the latest. You know the mode by which I came; it is the best for expedition and cheapness. Dear Faith, do not fail me.

Your affectionate brother,

THURSTAN BENSON.

P.S.—I am afraid the money I left may be running short. Do not let this stop you. Take my Facciolati to Johnson's, he will advance upon it; it is the third row, bottom shelf. Only come.

When this letter was despatched he had done all he could; and the next two days passed like a long monotonous dream of watching, thought, and care, undisturbed by any event, hardly by the change from day to night, which, now the harvest moon was at her full, was scarcely perceptible. On Saturday morning the answer came.

DEAREST THURSTAN,—Your incomprehensible summons has just reached me, and I obey, thereby proving my right to my name of Faith. I shall be with you almost as soon as this letter. I cannot help feeling anxious, as well as curious. I have money enough, and it is well I have; for Sally, who guards your room like a dragon, would rather see me walk the whole way, than have any of your things disturbed.

Your affectionate sister,

FAITH BENSON.

It was a great relief to Mr Benson to think that his sister would so soon be with him. He had been accustomed from childhood to rely on her prompt judgment and excellent sense; and to her care he felt that Ruth ought to be consigned, as it was too much to go on taxing good Mrs Hughes with night watching and sick nursing, with all her other claims on her time. He asked her once more to sit by Ruth, while he went to meet his sister.

The coach passed by the foot of the steep ascent which led up to Llan-dhu. He took a boy to carry his sister's luggage when she arrived; they were too soon at the bottom of the hill, and the boy began to make ducks and drakes in the shallowest part of the stream, which there flowed glassy and smooth, while Mr Benson sat down on a great stone, under the shadow of an alder bush which grew where the green, flat meadow skirted the water. It was delightful to be once more in the open air, and away from the scenes and thoughts which had been pressing on him for the last three days. There was new beauty in everything: from the blue mountains which glimmered in the distant sunlight, down to the flat, rich, peaceful vale, with its calm round shadows, where he sat. The very margin of white pebbles which lay on the banks of the stream had a sort of cleanly beauty about it. He felt calmer and more at ease than he had done for some days; and yet, when he began to think, it was rather a strange story which he had to tell his sister, in order to account for his urgent summons. Here was he, sole friend and guardian of a poor sick girl, whose very name he did not know; about whom all that he did know was, that she had been the mistress of a man who had deserted her, and that he feared—he believed— she had contemplated suicide. The offence, too, was one for which his sister, good and kind as she was, had little compassion. Well, he must appeal to her love for him, which was a very unsatisfactory mode of proceeding, as he would far rather have had her interest in the girl founded on reason, or some less personal basis than showing it merely because her brother wished it.

The coach came slowly rumbling over the stony road. His sister was outside, but got down in a brisk active way, and greeted her brother heartily and affectionately. She was considerably taller than he was, and must have been very handsome; her black hair was parted plainly over her forehead, and her dark, expressive eyes and straight nose still retained the beauty of her youth. I do not know whether she was older than her brother, but, probably owing to his infirmity requiring her care, she had something of a mother's manner towards him.

"Thurstan, you are looking pale! I do not believe you are well, whatever you may say. Have you had the old pain in your back?"

"No—a little—never mind that, dearest Faith. Sit down here, while I send the boy up with your box." And then, with some little desire to show his sister how well he was acquainted with the language, he blundered out his directions in very grammatical Welsh; so grammatical, in fact, and so badly pronounced, that the boy, scratching his head, made answer,

"Dim Saesoneg."

So he had to repeat it in English.

"Well now, Thurstan, here I sit as you bid me. But don't try me too long; tell me why you sent for me."

Now came the difficulty, and oh! for a seraph's tongue, and a seraph's powers of representation! but there was no seraph at hand, only the soft running waters singing a quiet tune, and predisposing Miss Benson to listen with a soothed spirit to any tale, not immediately involving her brother's welfare, which had been the cause of her seeing that lovely vale.

"It is an awkward story to tell, Faith, but there is a young woman lying ill at my lodgings whom I wanted you to nurse."

He thought he saw a shadow on his sister's face, and detected a slight change in her voice as she spoke.

"Nothing very romantic, I hope, Thurstan. Remember, I cannot stand much romance; I always distrust it."

"I don't know what you mean by romance. The story is real enough, and not out of the common way, I'm afraid."

He paused; he did not get over the difficulty.

"Well, tell it me at once, Thurstan. I am afraid you have let some one, or perhaps only your own imagination, impose upon you; but don't try my patience too much; you know I've no great stock."

"Then I'll tell you. The young girl was brought to the inn here by a gentleman, who has left her; she is very ill, and has no one to see after her."

Miss Benson had some masculine tricks, and one was whistling a long, low whistle when surprised or displeased. She had often found it a useful vent for feelings, and she whistled now. Her brother would rather she had spoken.

"Have you sent for her friends?" she asked at last.

"She has none."

Another pause and another whistle, but rather softer and more wavering than the last.

"How is she ill?"

"Pretty nearly as quiet as if she were dead. She does not speak, or move, or even sigh."

"It would be better for her to die at once, I think."

"Faith!"

That one word put them right. It was spoken in the tone which had authority over her; it was so full of grieved surprise and mournful upbraiding. She was accustomed to exercise a sway over him, owing to her greater decision of character, and, probably, if everything were traced to its cause, to her superior vigour of constitution; but at times she was humbled before his pure, childlike nature, and felt where she was inferior. She was too good and true to conceal this feeling, or to resent its being forced upon her. After a time she said,

"Thurstan, dear, let us go to her."

She helped him with tender care, and gave him her arm up the long and tedious hill; but when they approached the village, without speaking a word on the subject, they changed their position, and she leant (apparently) on him. He stretched himself up into as vigorous a gait as he could, when they drew near to the abodes of men.

On the way they had spoken but little. He had asked after various members of his congregation, for he was a Dissenting minister in a country town, and she had answered; but they neither of them spoke of Ruth, though their minds were full of her.

Mrs Hughes had tea ready for the traveller on her arrival. Mr Benson chafed a little internally at the leisurely way in which his sister sipped and sipped, and paused to tell him some trifling particular respecting home affairs, which she had forgotten before.

"Mr Bradshaw has refused to let the children associate with the Dixons any longer, because one evening they played at acting charades."

"Indeed;—a little more bread and butter, Faith?"

"Thank you. This Welsh air does make one hungry. Mrs Bradshaw is paying poor old Maggie's rent, to save her from being sent into the workhouse."

"That's right. Won't you have another cup of tea?"

"I have had two. However, I think I'll take another."

Mr Benson could not refrain from a little sigh as he poured it out. He thought he had never seen his sister so deliberately hungry and thirsty before. He did not guess that she was feeling the meal rather a respite from a distasteful interview, which she was aware was awaiting her at its conclusion. But all things come to an end, and so did Miss Benson's tea.

"Now, will you go and see her?"

"Yes."

And so they went. Mrs Hughes had pinned up a piece of green calico, by way of a Venetian blind, to shut out the afternoon sun; and in the light thus shaded lay Ruth, still, and wan, and white. Even with her brother's account of Ruth's state, such death-like quietness startled Miss Benson—startled her into pity for the poor lovely creature who lay thus stricken and felled. When she saw her, she could no longer imagine her to be an impostor, or a hardened sinner; such prostration of woe belonged to neither. Mr Benson looked more at his sister's face than at Ruth's; he read her countenance as a book.

Mrs Hughes stood by, crying.

Mr Benson touched his sister, and they left the room together.

"Do you think she will live?" asked he.

"I cannot tell," said Miss Benson, in a softened voice. "But how young she looks! Quite a child, poor creature! When will the doctor come, Thurstan? Tell me all about her; you have never told me the particulars."

Mr Benson might have said, she had never cared to hear them before, and had rather avoided the subject; but he was too happy to see this awakening of interest in his sister's warm heart to say anything in the least reproachful. He told her the story as well as he could; and, as he felt it deeply, he told it with heart's eloquence; and, as he ended and looked at her, there were tears in the eyes of both.

"And what does the doctor say?" asked she, after a pause.

"He insists upon quiet; he orders medicines and strong broth. I cannot tell you all; Mrs Hughes can. She has been so truly good. 'Doing good, hoping for nothing again.'"

"She looks very sweet and gentle. I shall sit up to-night and watch her myself; and I shall send you and Mrs Hughes early to bed, for you have both a worn look about you I don't like. Are you sure the effect of that fall has gone off? Do you feel anything of it in your back still? After all, I owe her something for turning back to your help. Are you sure she was going to drown herself?"

"I cannot be sure, for I have not questioned her. She has not been in a state to be questioned; but I have no doubt whatever about it. But you must not think of sitting up after your journey, Faith."

"Answer me, Thurstan. Do you feel any bad effect from that fall?"

"No, hardly any. Don't sit up, Faith, to-night!"

"Thurstan, it's no use talking, for I shall; and, if you go on opposing me, I dare say I shall attack your back, and put a blister on it. Do tell me what that 'hardly any' means. Besides, to set you quite at ease, you know I have never seen mountains before, and they fill me and oppress me so much that I could not sleep; I must keep awake this first night, and see that they don't fall on the earth and overwhelm it. And now answer my questions about yourself."

Miss Benson had the power, which some people have, of carrying her wishes through to their fulfilment; her will was strong, her sense was excellent, and people yielded to her—they did not know why. Before ten o'clock she reigned sole power and potentate in Ruth's little chamber. Nothing could have been better devised for giving her an interest in the invalid. The very dependence of one so helpless upon her care inclined her heart towards her. She thought she perceived a slight improvement in the symptoms during the night, and she was a little pleased that this progress should have been made while she reigned monarch of the sick-room. Yes, certainly there was an improvement. There was more consciousness in the look of the eyes, although the whole countenance still retained its painful traces of acute suffering, manifested in an anxious, startled, uneasy aspect. It was broad morning light, though barely five o'clock, when Miss Benson caught the sight of Ruth's lips moving, as if in speech. Miss Benson stooped down to listen.

"Who are you?" asked Ruth, in the faintest of whispers.

"Miss Benson—Mr Benson's sister," she replied.

The words conveyed no knowledge to Ruth; on the contrary, weak as a babe in mind and body as she was, her lips began to quiver, and her eyes to show a terror similar to that of any little child who wakens in the presence of a stranger, and sees no dear, familiar face of mother or nurse to reassure its trembling heart.

Miss Benson took her hand in hers, and began to stroke it caressingly.

"Don't be afraid, dear; I'm a friend come to take care of you. Would you like some tea now, my love?"

The very utterance of these gentle words was unlocking Miss Benson's heart. Her brother was surprised to see her so full of interest, when he came to inquire later on in the morning. It required Mrs Hughes's persuasions, as well as his own, to induce her to go to bed for an hour or two after breakfast; and, before she went, she made them promise that she should be called when the doctor came. He did not come until late in the afternoon. The invalid was rallying fast, though rallying to a consciousness of sorrow, as was evinced by the tears which came slowly rolling down her pale sad cheeks—tears which she had not the power to wipe away.

Mr Benson had remained in the house all day to hear the doctor's opinion; and now that he was relieved from the charge of Ruth by his sister's presence, he had the more time to dwell upon the circumstances of her case—so far as they were known to him. He remembered his first sight of her; her little figure swaying to and fro as she balanced herself on the slippery stones, half smiling at her own dilemma, with a bright, happy light in the eyes that seemed like a reflection from the glancing waters sparkling below. Then he recalled the changed, affrighted look of those eyes as they met his, after the child's rebuff of her advances;—how that little incident filled up the tale at which Mrs Hughes had hinted, in a kind of sorrowful way, as if loath (as a Christian should be) to believe evil. Then that fearful evening, when he had only just saved her from committing suicide, and that nightmare sleep! And now, lost, forsaken, and but just delivered from the jaws of death, she lay dependent for everything on his sister and him,—utter strangers a few weeks ago. Where was her lover? Could he be easy and happy? Could he grow into perfect health, with these great sins pressing on his conscience with a strong and hard pain? Or had he a conscience?

Into whole labyrinths of social ethics Mr Benson's thoughts wandered, when his sister entered suddenly and abruptly.

"What does the doctor say? Is she better?"

"Oh, yes! she's better," answered Miss Benson, sharp and short. Her brother looked at her in dismay. She bumped down into a chair in a cross, disconcerted manner. They were both silent for a few minutes; only Miss Benson whistled and clucked alternately.

"What is the matter, Faith? You say she is better."

"Why, Thurstan, there is something so shocking the matter, that I cannot tell you."

Mr Benson changed colour with affright. All things possible and impossible crossed his mind but the right one. I said, "all things possible;" I made a mistake. He never believed Ruth to be more guilty than she seemed.

"Faith, I wish you would tell me, and not bewilder me with those noises of yours," said he, nervously.

"I beg your pardon; but something so shocking has just been discovered—I don't know how to word it—She will have a child. The doctor says so."

She was allowed to make noises unnoticed for a few minutes. Her brother did not speak. At last she wanted his sympathy.

"Isn't it shocking, Thurstan? You might have knocked me down with a straw when he told me."

"Does she know?"

"Yes; and I am not sure that that isn't the worst part of all."

"How?—what do you mean?"

"Oh! I was just beginning to have a good opinion of her, but I'm afraid she is very depraved. After the doctor was gone, she pulled the bed-curtain aside, and looked as if she wanted to speak to me. (I can't think how she heard, for we were close to the window, and spoke very low.) Well, I went to her, though I really had taken quite a turn against her. And she whispered, quite eagerly, 'Did he say I should have a baby?' Of course, I could not keep it from her; but I thought it my duty to look as cold and severe as I could. She did not seem to understand how it ought to be viewed, but took it just as if she had a right to have a baby. She said, 'Oh, my God, I thank Thee! Oh! I will be so good!' I had no patience with her then, so I left the room."

"Who is with her?"

"Mrs Hughes. She is not seeing the thing in a moral light, as I should have expected."

Mr Benson was silent again. After some time he began:

"Faith, I don't see this affair quite as you do. I believe I am right."

"You surprise me, brother! I don't understand you."

"Wait awhile! I want to make my feelings very clear to you, but I don't know where to begin, or how to express myself."

"It is, indeed, an extraordinary subject for us to have to talk about; but if once I get clear of this girl, I'll wash my hands of all such cases again."

Her brother was not attending to her; he was reducing his own ideas to form.

"Faith, do you know I rejoice in this child's advent?"

"May God forgive you, Thurstan!—if you know what you are saying. But, surely, it is a temptation, dear Thurstan."

"I do not think it is a delusion. The sin appears to me to be quite distinct from its consequences."

"Sophistry—and a temptation," said Miss Benson, decidedly.

"No, it is not," said her brother, with equal decision. "In the eye of God, she is exactly the same as if the life she has led had left no trace behind. We knew her errors before, Faith."

"Yes, but not this disgrace—this badge of her shame!"

"Faith, Faith! let me beg of you not to speak so of the little innocent babe, who may be God's messenger to lead her back to Him. Think again of her first words—the burst of nature from her heart! Did she not turn to God, and enter into a covenant with Him—'I will be so good?' Why, it draws her out of herself! If her life has hitherto been self-seeking, and wickedly thoughtless, here is the very instrument to make her forget herself, and be thoughtful for another. Teach her (and God will teach her, if man does not come between) to reverence her child; and this reverence will shut out sin,—will be purification."

He was very much excited; he was even surprised at his own excitement; but his thoughts and meditations through the long afternoon had prepared his mind for this manner of viewing the subject.

"These are quite new ideas to me," said Miss Benson, coldly. "I think you, Thurstan, are the first person I ever heard rejoicing over the birth of an illegitimate child. It appears to me, I must own, rather questionable morality."

"I do not rejoice. I have been all this afternoon mourning over the sin which has blighted this young creature; I have been dreading lest, as she recovered consciousness, there should be a return of her despair. I have been thinking of every holy word, every promise to the penitent—of the tenderness which led the Magdalen aright. I have been feeling, severely and reproachfully, the timidity which has hitherto made me blink all encounter with evils of this particular kind. Oh, Faith! once for all, do not accuse me of questionable morality, when I am trying more than ever I did in my life to act as my blessed Lord would have done."

He was very much agitated. His sister hesitated, and then she spoke more softly than before.

"But, Thurstan, everything might have been done to 'lead her right' (as you call it), without this child, this miserable offspring of sin."

"The world has, indeed, made such children miserable, innocent as they are; but I doubt if this be according to the will of God, unless it be His punishment for the parents' guilt; and even then the world's way of treatment is too apt to harden the mother's natural love into something like hatred. Shame, and the terror of friends' displeasure, turn her mad—defile her holiest instincts; and, as for the fathers—God forgive them! I cannot—at least, not just now."

Miss Benson thought on what her brother said. At length she asked, "Thurstan (remember I'm not convinced), how would you have this girl treated according to your theory?"

"It will require some time, and much Christian love, to find out the best way. I know I'm not very wise; but the way I think it would be right to act in, would be this—" He thought for some time before he spoke, and then said:

"She has incurred a responsibility—that we both acknowledge. She is about to become a mother, and have the direction and guidance of a little tender life. I fancy such a responsibility must be serious and solemn enough, without making it into a heavy and oppressive burden, so that human nature recoils from bearing it. While we do all we can to strengthen her sense of responsibility, I would likewise do all we can to make her feel that it is responsibility for what may become a blessing."

"Whether the children are legitimate or illegitimate?" asked Miss Benson, drily.

"Yes!" said her brother, firmly. "The more I think, the more I believe I am right. No one," said he, blushing faintly as he spoke, "can have a greater recoil from profligacy than I have. You yourself have not greater sorrow over this young creature's sin than I have: the difference is this, you confuse the consequences with the sin."

"I don't understand metaphysics."

"I am not aware that I am talking metaphysics. I can imagine that if the present occasion be taken rightly, and used well, all that is good in her may be raised to a height unmeasured but by God; while all that is evil and dark may, by His blessing, fade and disappear in the pure light of her child's presence. Oh, Father! listen to my prayer, that her redemption may date from this time. Help us to speak to her in the loving spirit of thy Holy Son!"

The tears were full in his eyes; he almost trembled in his earnestness. He was faint with the strong power of his own conviction, and with his inability to move his sister. But she was shaken. She sat very still for a quarter of an hour or more, while he leaned back, exhausted by his own feelings.

"The poor child!" said she, at length—"the poor, poor child! what it will have to struggle through and endure! Do you remember Thomas Wilkins, and the way he threw the registry of his birth and baptism back in your face? Why, he would not have the situation; he went to sea and was drowned, rather than present the record of his shame."

"I do remember it all. It has often haunted me. She must strengthen her child to look to God, rather than to man's opinion. It will be the discipline, the penance, she has incurred. She must teach it to be (humanly speaking) self-dependent."

"But after all," said Miss Benson (for she had known and esteemed poor Thomas Wilkins, and had mourned over his untimely death, and the recollection thereof softened her)—"after all, it might be concealed. The very child need never know its illegitimacy."

"How?" asked her brother.

"Why—we know so little about her yet; but in that letter, it said she had no friends;—now, could she not go into quite a fresh place, and be passed off as a widow?"

Ah, tempter! unconscious tempter! Here was a way of evading the trials for the poor little unborn child, of which Mr Benson had never thought. It was the decision—the pivot, on which the fate of years moved; and he turned it the wrong way. But it was not for his own sake. For himself, he was brave enough to tell the truth; for the little helpless baby, about to enter a cruel, biting world, he was tempted to evade the difficulty. He forgot what he had just said, of the discipline and penance to the mother consisting in strengthening her child to meet, trustfully and bravely, the consequences of her own weakness. He remembered more clearly the wild fierceness, the Cain-like look, of Thomas Wilkins, as the obnoxious word in the baptismal registry told him that he must go forth branded into the world, with his hand against every man's, and every man's against him.

"How could it be managed, Faith?"

"Nay, I must know much more, which she alone can tell us, before I can see how it is to be managed. It is certainly the best plan."

"Perhaps it is," said her brother, thoughtfully, but no longer clearly or decidedly; and so the conversation dropped.

Ruth moved the bed-curtain aside, in her soft manner, when Miss Benson re-entered the room; she did not speak, but she looked at her as if she wished her to come near. Miss Benson went and stood by her. Ruth took her hand in hers and kissed it; then, as if fatigued even by this slight movement, she fell asleep.

Miss Benson took up her work, and thought over her brother's speeches. She was not convinced, but she was softened and bewildered.

CHAPTER XII

Losing Sight of the Welsh Mountains

Miss Benson continued in an undecided state of mind for the two next days; but on the third, as they sat at breakfast, she began to speak to her brother.

"That young creature's name is Ruth Hilton."

"Indeed! how did you find it out?"

"From herself, of course. She is much stronger. I slept with her last night, and I was aware she was awake long before I liked to speak, but at last I began. I don't know what I said, or how it went on, but I think it was a little relief to her to tell me something about herself. She sobbed and cried herself to sleep; I think she is asleep now."

"Tell me what she said about herself."

"Oh, it was really very little; it was evidently a most painful subject. She is an orphan, without brother or sister, and with a guardian, whom, I think she said, she never saw but once. He apprenticed her (after her father's death) to a dressmaker. This Mr Bellingham got acquainted with her, and they used to meet on Sunday afternoons. One day they were late, lingering on the road, when the dressmaker came up by accident. She seems to have been very angry, and not unnaturally so. The girl took fright at her threats, and the lover persuaded her to go off with him to London, there and then. Last May, I think it was. That's all."

"Did she express any sorrow for her error?"

188

"No, not in words, but her voice was broken with sobs, though she tried to make it steady. After a while she began to talk about her baby, but shyly, and with much hesitation. She asked me how much I thought she could earn as a dressmaker, by working very, very hard; and that brought us round to her child. I thought of what you had said, Thurstan, and I tried to speak to her as you wished me. I am not sure if it was right; I am doubtful in my own mind still."

"Don't be doubtful, Faith! Dear Faith, I thank you for your kindness."

"There is really nothing to thank me for. It is almost impossible to help being kind to her; there is something so meek and gentle about her, so patient, and so grateful!"

"What does she think of doing?"

"Poor child! she thinks of taking lodgings—very cheap ones, she says; there she means to work night and day to earn enough for her child. For, she said to me, with such pretty earnestness, 'It must never know want, whatever I do. I have deserved suffering, but it will be such a little innocent darling!' Her utmost earnings would not be more than seven or eight shillings a week, I'm afraid; and then she is so young and so pretty!"

"There is that fifty pounds Mrs Morgan brought me, and those two letters. Does she know about them yet?"

"No; I did not like to tell her till she is a little stronger. Oh, Thurstan! I wish there was not this prospect of a child. I cannot help it. I do—I could see a way in which we might help her, if it were not for that."

"How do you mean?"

"Oh, it's no use thinking of it, as it is! Or else we might have taken her home with us, and kept her till she had got a little dress-making in the congregation, but for this meddlesome child; that spoils everything. You must let me grumble to you, Thurstan. I was very good to her, and spoke as tenderly and respectfully of the little thing as if it were the Queen's, and born in lawful matrimony."

"That's right, my dear Faith! Grumble away to me, if you like. I'll forgive you, for the kind thought of taking her home with us. But do you think her situation is an insuperable objection?"

"Why, Thurstan!—it's so insuperable, it puts it quite out of the question."

"How?—that's only repeating your objection. Why is it out of the question?"

"If there had been no child coming, we might have called her by her right name—Miss Hilton; that's one thing. Then, another is, the baby in our house. Why, Sally would go distraught!"

"Never mind Sally. If she were an orphan relation of our own, left widowed," said he, pausing, as if in doubt. "You yourself suggested she should be considered as a widow, for the child's sake. I'm only taking up your ideas, dear Faith. I respect you for thinking of taking her home; it is just what we ought to do. Thank you for reminding me of my duty."

"Nay, it was only a passing thought. Think of Mr Bradshaw. Oh! I tremble at the thought of his grim displeasure."

"We must think of a higher than Mr Bradshaw. I own I should be a very coward, if he knew. He is so severe, so inflexible. But after all he sees so little of us; he never comes to tea, you know, but is always engaged when Mrs Bradshaw comes. I don't think he knows of what our household consists."

"Not know Sally? Oh yes, but he does. He asked Mrs Bradshaw one day, if she knew what wages we gave her, and said we might get a far more efficient and younger servant for the money. And, speaking about money, think what our expenses would be if we took her home for the next six months."

That consideration was a puzzling one; and both sat silent and perplexed for a time. Miss Benson was as sorrowful as her brother, for she was becoming as anxious as he was to find it possible that her plan could be carried out.

"There's the fifty pounds," said he, with a sigh of reluctance at the idea.

"Yes, there's the fifty pounds," echoed his sister, with the same sadness in her tone. "I suppose it is hers."

"I suppose it is; and being so, we must not think who gave it to her. It will defray her expenses. I am very sorry, but I think we must take it."

"It would never do to apply to him under the present circumstances," said Miss Benson, in a hesitating manner.

"No, that we won't," said her brother, decisively. "If she consents to let us take care of her, we will never let her stoop to request anything from him, even for his child. She can live on bread and water. We can all live on bread and water rather than that."

"Then I will speak to her and propose the plan. Oh, Thurstan! from a child you could persuade me to anything! I hope I am doing right. However much I oppose you at first, I am sure to yield soon; almost in proportion to my violence at first. I think I am very weak."

"No, not in this instance. We are both right: I, in the way in which the child ought to be viewed; you, dear good Faith, for thinking of taking her home with us. God bless you, dear, for it!"

When Ruth began to sit up (and the strange, new, delicious prospect of becoming a mother seemed to give her some mysterious source of strength, so that her recovery was rapid and swift from that time), Miss Benson brought her the letters and the bank-note.

"Do you recollect receiving this letter, Ruth?" asked she, with grave gentleness. Ruth changed colour, and took it and read it again without making any reply to Miss Benson. Then she sighed, and thought a while; and then took up and read the second note—the note which Mrs Bellingham had sent to Mr Benson in answer to his. After that she took up the bank-note and turned it round and round, but not as if she saw it. Miss Benson noticed that her fingers trembled sadly, and that her lips were quivering for some time before she spoke.

"If you please, Miss Benson, I should like to return this money."

"Why, my dear?"

"I have a strong feeling against taking it. While he," said she, deeply blushing, and letting her large white lids drop down and veil her eyes, "loved me, he gave me many things—my watch—oh, many things; and I took them from him gladly and thankfully because he loved me—for I would have given him anything—and I thought of them as signs of love. But this money pains my heart. He has left off loving me, and has gone away. This money seems—oh, Miss Benson—it seems as if he could comfort me, for being forsaken, by money." And at that word the tears, so long kept back and repressed, forced their way like rain.

She checked herself, however, in the violence of her emotion, for she thought of her child.

"So, will you take the trouble of sending it back to Mrs Bellingham?"

"That I will, my dear. I am glad of it, that I am! They don't deserve to have the power of giving: they don't deserve that you should take it."

Miss Benson went and enclosed it up, there and then; simply writing these words in the envelope, "From Ruth Hilton."

"And now we wash our hands of these Bellinghams," said she, triumphantly. But Ruth looked tearful and sad; not about returning the note, but from the conviction that the reason she had given for the ground of her determination was true—he no longer loved her.

To cheer her, Miss Benson began to speak of the future. Miss Benson was one of those people who, the more she spoke of a plan in its details, and the more she realised it in her own mind, the more firmly she became a partisan of the project. Thus she grew warm and happy in the idea of taking Ruth home; but Ruth remained depressed and languid under the conviction that he no longer loved her. No home, no future, but the thought of her child, could wean her from this sorrow. Miss Benson was a little piqued; and this pique showed itself afterwards in talking to her brother of the morning's proceedings in the sick-chamber.

"I admired her at the time for sending away her fifty pounds so proudly; but I think she has a cold heart: she hardly thanked me at all for my proposal of taking her home with us."

"Her thoughts are full of other things just now; and people have such different ways of showing feeling: some by silence, some by words. At any rate, it is unwise to expect gratitude."

"What do you expect—not indifference or ingratitude?"

"It is better not to expect or calculate consequences. The longer I live, the more fully I see that. Let us try simply to do right actions, without thinking of the feelings they are to call out in others. We know that no holy or self-denying effort can fall to the ground vain and useless; but the sweep of eternity is large, and God alone knows when the effect is to be produced. We are trying to do right now, and to feel right; don't let us perplex ourselves with endeavouring to map out how she should feel, or how she should show her feelings."

"That's all very fine, and I dare say very true," said Miss Benson, a little chagrined. "But 'a bird in the hand is worth two in the bush;' and I would rather have had one good, hearty 'Thank you,' now, for all I have been planning to do for her, than the grand effects you promise me in the 'sweep of eternity.' Don't be grave and sorrowful, Thurstan, or I'll go out of the room. I can stand Sally's scoldings, but I can't bear your look of quiet depression whenever I am a little hasty or impatient. I had rather you would give me a good box on the ear."

"And I would often rather you would speak, if ever so hastily, instead of whistling. So, if I box your ears when I am vexed with you, will you promise to scold me when you are put out of the way, instead of whistling?"

"Very well! that's a bargain. You box, and I scold. But, seriously, I began to calculate our money when she so cavalierly sent off the fifty-pound note (I can't help admiring her for it), and I am very much afraid we shall not have enough to pay the doctor's bill, and take her home with us."

"She must go inside the coach whatever we do," said Mr Benson, decidedly. "Who's there? Come in! Oh! Mrs Hughes! Sit down."

"Indeed, sir, and I cannot stay; but the young lady has just made me find up her watch for her, and asked me to get it sold to pay the doctor, and the little things she has had since she came; and please, sir, indeed, I don't know where to sell it nearer than Carnarvon."

"That is good of her," said Miss Benson, her sense of justice satisfied; and, remembering the way in which Ruth had spoken of the watch, she felt what a sacrifice it must have been to resolve to part with it.

"And her goodness just helps us out of our dilemma," said her brother, who was unaware of the feelings with which Ruth regarded her watch, or, perhaps, he might have parted with his Facciolati.

Mrs Hughes patiently awaited their leisure for answering her practical question. Where could the watch be sold? Suddenly her face brightened.

"Mr Jones, the doctor, is going to be married, perhaps he would like nothing better than to give this pretty watch to his bride; indeed, and I think it's very likely; and he'll pay money for it as well as letting alone his bill. I'll ask him, sir, at any rate."

Mr Jones was only too glad to obtain possession of so elegant a present at so cheap a rate. He even, as Mrs Hughes had foretold, "paid money for it;" more than was required to defray the expenses of Ruth's accommodation; as the most of the articles of food she had were paid for at the time by Mr or Miss Benson, but they strictly forbade Mrs Hughes to tell Ruth of this.

"Would you object to my buying you a black gown?" said Miss Benson to her the day after the sale of the watch. She hesitated a little, and then went on:

"My brother and I think it would be better to call you—as if in fact you were—a widow. It will save much awkwardness, and it will spare your child much—" Mortification she was going to have added, but that word did not exactly do. But, at the mention of her child, Ruth started and turned ruby-red; as she always did when allusion was made to it.

"Oh, yes! certainly. Thank you much for thinking of it. Indeed," said she, very low, as if to herself, "I don't know how to thank you for all you are doing; but I do love you, and will pray for you, if I may."

"If you may, Ruth!" repeated Miss Benson, in a tone of surprise.

"Yes, if I may. If you will let me pray for you."

"Certainly, my dear. My dear Ruth, you don't know how often I sin; I do so wrong, with my few temptations. We are both of us great sinners in the eyes of the Most Holy; let us pray for each other. Don't speak so again, my dear; at least, not to me!"

Miss Benson was actually crying. She had always looked upon herself as so inferior to her brother in real goodness; had seen such heights above her, that she was distressed by Ruth's humility. After a short time she resumed the subject.

"Then I may get you a black gown?—and we may call you Mrs Hilton?"

"No; not Mrs Hilton!" said Ruth, hastily.

Miss Benson, who had hitherto kept her eyes averted from Ruth's face from a motive of kindly delicacy, now looked at her with surprise.

"Why not?" asked she.

"It was my mother's name," said Ruth, in a low voice. "I had better not be called by it."

"Then, let us call you by my mother's name," said Miss Benson, tenderly. "She would have— But I'll talk to you about my mother some other time. Let me call you Mrs Denbigh. It will do very well, too. People will think you are a distant relation."

When she told Mr Benson this choice of name, he was rather sorry; it was like his sister's impulsive kindness—impulsive in everything—and he could imagine how Ruth's humility had touched her. He was sorry, but he said nothing.

And now the letter was written home, announcing the probable arrival of the brother and sister on a certain day, "with a distant relation, early left a widow," as Miss Benson expressed it. She desired the spare room might be prepared, and made every provision she could think of for Ruth's comfort; for Ruth still remained feeble and weak.

When the black gown, at which she had stitched away incessantly, was finished—when nothing remained but to rest for the next day's journey—Ruth could not sit still. She wandered from window to window, learning off each rock and tree by heart. Each had its tale, which it was agony to remember; but which it would have been worse agony to forget. The sound of running waters she heard that quiet evening, was in her ears as she lay on her death-bed; so well had she learnt their tune.

And now all was over. She had driven in to Llan-dhu, sitting by her lover's side, living in the bright present, and strangely forgetful of the past or the future; she had dreamed out her dream, and she had awakened from the vision of love. She walked slowly and sadly down the long hill, her tears fast falling, but as quickly wiped away; while she strove to make steady the low quivering voice which was often called upon to answer some remark of Miss Benson's.

They had to wait for the coach. Ruth buried her face in some flowers which Mrs Hughes had given her on parting; and was startled when the mail drew up with a sudden pull, which almost threw the horses on their haunches. She was placed inside, and the coach had set off again, before she was fully aware that Mr and Miss Benson were travelling on the outside; but it was a relief to feel she might now cry without exciting their notice. The shadow of a heavy thunder-cloud was on the valley, but the little upland village church (that showed the spot in which so much of her life had passed) stood out clear in the sunshine. She grudged the tears that blinded her as she gazed. There was one passenger, who tried after a while to comfort her.

"Don't cry, miss," said the kind-hearted woman. "You're parting from friends, maybe? Well, that's bad enough, but when you come to my age, you'll think none of it. Why, I've three sons, and they're soldiers and sailors, all of them—here, there, and everywhere. One is in America, beyond seas; another is in China, making tea; and another is at Gibraltar, three miles from Spain; and yet, you see, I can laugh and eat and enjoy myself. I sometimes think I'll try and fret a bit, just to make myself a better figure; but, Lord! it's no use, it's against my nature; so I laugh and grow fat again. I'd be quite thankful for a fit of anxiety as would make me feel easy in my clothes, which them manty-makers will make so tight I'm fairly throttled."

Ruth durst cry no more; it was no relief, now she was watched and noticed, and plied with a sandwich or a gingerbread each time she looked sad. She lay back with her eyes shut, as if asleep, and went on, and on, the sun never seeming to move from his high place in the sky, nor the bright hot day to show the least sign of waning. Every now and then, Miss Benson scrambled down, and made kind inquiries of the pale, weary Ruth; and once they changed coaches, and the fat old lady left her with a hearty shake of the hand.

"It is not much further now," said Miss Benson, apologetically, to Ruth. "See! we are losing sight of the Welsh mountains. We have about eighteen miles of plain, and then we come to the moors and the rising ground, amidst which Eccleston lies. I wish we were there, for my brother is sadly tired."

The first wonder in Ruth's mind was, why then, if Mr Benson were so tired, did they not stop where they were for the night; for she knew little of the expenses of a night at an inn. The next thought was, to beg that Mr Benson would take her place inside the coach, and allow her to mount up by Miss Benson. She proposed this, and Miss Benson was evidently pleased.

"Well, if you're not tired, it would make a rest and a change for him, to be sure; and if you were by me I could show you the first sight of Eccleston, if we reach there before it is quite dark."

So Mr Benson got down, and changed places with Ruth.

She hardly yet understood the numerous small economies which he and his sister had to practise—the little daily self-denials,—all endured so cheerfully, and simply, that they had almost ceased to require an effort, and it had become natural to them to think of others before themselves. Ruth had not understood that it was for economy that their places had been taken on the outside of the coach, while hers, as an invalid requiring rest, was to be the inside; and that the biscuits which supplied the place of a dinner were, in fact, chosen because the difference in price between the two would go a little way towards fulfilling their plan for receiving her as an inmate. Her thought about money had been hitherto a child's thought; the subject had never touched her; but afterwards, when she had lived a little with the Bensons, her eyes were opened, and she remembered their simple kindness on the journey, and treasured the remembrance of it in her heart.

A low grey cloud was the first sign of Eccleston; it was the smoke of the town hanging over the plain. Beyond the place where she was expected to believe it existed, arose round, waving uplands; nothing to the fine outlines of the Welsh mountains, but still going up nearer to heaven than the rest of the flat world into which she had now entered. Rumbling stones, lamp-posts, a sudden stop, and they were in the town of Eccleston; and a strange, uncouth voice, on the dark side of the coach, was heard to say,

"Be ye there, measter?"

"Yes, yes!" said Miss Benson, quickly. "Did Sally send you, Ben? Get the ostler's lantern, and look out the luggage."

CHAPTER XIII

The Dissenting Minister's Household

Miss Benson had resumed every morsel of the briskness which she had rather lost in the middle of the day; her foot was on her native stones, and a very rough set they were, and she was near her home and among known people. Even Mr Benson spoke very cheerfully to Ben, and made many inquiries of him respecting people whose names were strange to Ruth. She was cold, and utterly weary. She took Miss Benson's offered arm, and could hardly drag herself as far as the little quiet street in which Mr Benson's house was situated. The street was so quiet that their footsteps sounded like a loud disturbance, and announced their approach as effectually as the "trumpet's lordly blare" did the coming of Abdallah. A door flew open, and a lighted passage stood before them. As soon as they had entered, a stout, elderly servant emerged from behind the door, her face radiant with welcome.

"Eh, bless ye! are ye back again? I thought I should ha' been lost without ye."

She gave Mr Benson a hearty shake of the hand, and kissed Miss Benson warmly; then, turning to Ruth, she said, in a loud whisper,

"Who's yon?"

Mr Benson was silent, and walked a step onwards. Miss Benson said boldly out,

"The lady I named in my note, Sally—Mrs Denbigh, a distant relation."

"Aye, but you said hoo was a widow. Is this chit a widow?"

"Yes, this is Mrs Denbigh," answered Miss Benson.

"If I'd been her mother, I'd ha' given her a lollypop instead of a husband. Hoo looks fitter for it."

"Hush! Sally, Sally! Look, there's your master trying to move that heavy box." Miss Benson calculated well when she called Sally's attention to her master; for it was well believed by every one, and by Sally herself, that his deformity was owing to a fall he had had when he was scarcely more than a baby, and entrusted to her care—a little nurse-girl, as she then was, not many years older than himself. For years the poor girl had cried herself to sleep on her pallet-bed, moaning over the blight her carelessness had brought upon her darling; nor was this self-reproach diminished by the forgiveness of the gentle mother, from whom Thurstan Benson derived so much of his character. The way in which comfort stole into Sally's heart was in the gradually-formed resolution that she would never leave him nor forsake him, but serve him faithfully all her life long; and she had kept to her word. She loved Miss Benson, but she almost worshipped the brother. The reverence for him was in her heart, however, and did not always show itself in her manners. But if she scolded him herself, she allowed no one else that privilege. If Miss Benson differed from her brother, and ventured to think his sayings or doings might have been improved, Sally came down upon her like a thunder-clap.

"My goodness gracious, Master Thurstan, when will you learn to leave off meddling with other folks' business! Here, Ben! help me up with these trunks."

The little narrow passage was cleared, and Miss Benson took Ruth into the sitting-room. There were only two sitting-rooms on the ground-floor, one behind the other. Out of the back room the kitchen opened, and for this reason the back parlour was used as the family sitting-room; or else, being, with its garden aspect, so much the pleasanter of the two, both Sally and Miss Benson would have appropriated it for Mr Benson's study. As it was, the front room, which looked to the street, was his room; and many a person coming for help—help of which giving money was the lowest kind—was admitted, and let forth by Mr Benson, unknown to any one else in the house. To make amends for his having the least cheerful room on the ground-floor, he had the garden bedroom, while his sister slept over his study. There were two more rooms again over these, with sloping ceilings, though otherwise large and airy. The attic looking into the garden was the spare bedroom; while the front belonged to Sally. There was no room over the kitchen, which was, in fact, a supplement to the house. The sitting-room was called by the pretty, old-fashioned name of the parlour, while Mr Benson's room was styled the study.

The curtains were drawn in the parlour; there was a bright fire and a clean hearth; indeed, exquisite cleanliness seemed the very spirit of the household, for the door which was open to the kitchen showed a delicately-white and spotless floor, and bright glittering tins, on which the ruddy firelight danced.

From the place in which Ruth sat she could see all Sally's movements; and though she was not conscious of close or minute observation at the time (her body being weary, and her mind full of other thoughts), yet it was curious how faithfully that scene remained depicted on her memory in after years. The warm light filled every corner of the kitchen, in strong distinction to the faint illumination of the one candle in the parlour, whose radiance was confined, and was lost in the dead folds of window-curtains, carpet, and furniture. The square, stout, bustling figure, neat and clean in every respect, but dressed in the peculiar, old-fashioned costume of the county, namely, a dark-striped linsey-woolsey petticoat, made very short, displaying sturdy legs in woollen stockings beneath; a loose kind of jacket called there a "bedgown," made of pink print; a snow-white apron and cap, both of linen, and the latter made in the shape of a "mutch;"—these articles completed Sally's costume, and were painted on Ruth's memory. Whilst Sally was busied in preparing tea, Miss Benson took off Ruth's things; and the latter instinctively felt that Sally, in the midst of her movements, was watching their proceedings. Occasionally she also put in a word in the conversation, and these little sentences were uttered quite in the tone of an equal, if not of a superior. She had dropped the more formal "you," with which at first she had addressed Miss Benson, and thou'd her quietly and habitually.

All these particulars sank unconsciously into Ruth's mind; but they did not rise to the surface, and become perceptible, for a length of time. She was weary, and much depressed. Even the very kindness that ministered to her was overpowering. But over the dark, misty moor a little light shone,—a beacon; and on that she fixed her eyes, and struggled out of her present deep dejection—the little child that was coming to her!

Mr Benson was as languid and weary as Ruth, and was silent during all this bustle and preparation. His silence was more grateful to Ruth than Miss Benson's many words, although she felt their kindness. After tea, Miss Benson took her upstairs to her room. The white dimity bed, and the walls, stained green, had something of the colouring and purity of effect of a snowdrop; while the floor, rubbed with a mixture that turned it into a rich dark brown, suggested the idea of the garden-mould out of which the snowdrop grows. As Miss Benson helped the pale Ruth to undress, her voice became less full-toned and hurried; the hush of approaching night subdued her into a softened, solemn kind of tenderness, and the murmured blessing sounded like granted prayer.

When Miss Benson came downstairs, she found her brother reading some letters which had been received during his absence. She went and softly shut the door of communication between the parlour and the kitchen; and then, fetching a grey worsted stocking which she was knitting, sat down near him, her eyes not looking at her work but fixed on the fire; while the eternal rapid click of the knitting-needles broke the silence of the room, with a sound as monotonous and incessant as the noise of a hand-loom. She expected him to speak, but he did not. She enjoyed an examination into, and discussion of, her feelings; it was an interest and amusement to her, while he dreaded and avoided all such conversation. There were times when his feelings, which were always earnest, and sometimes morbid, burst forth, and defied control, and overwhelmed him; when a force was upon him compelling him to speak. But he, in general, strove to preserve his composure, from a fear of the compelling pain of such times, and the consequent exhaustion. His heart had been very full of Ruth all day long, and he was afraid of his sister beginning the subject; so he read on, or seemed to do so, though he hardly saw the letter he held before him. It was a great relief to him when Sally threw open the middle door with a bang, which did not indicate either calmness of mind or sweetness of temper.

"Is yon young woman going to stay any length o' time with us?" asked she of Miss Benson.

Mr Benson put his hand gently on his sister's arm, to check her from making any reply, while he said,

"We cannot exactly tell, Sally. She will remain until after her confinement."

"Lord bless us and save us!—a baby in the house! Nay, then my time's come, and I'll pack up and begone. I never could abide them things. I'd sooner have rats in the house."

Sally really did look alarmed.

"Why, Sally!" said Mr Benson, smiling, "I was not much more than a baby when you came to take care of me."

"Yes, you were, Master Thurstan; you were a fine bouncing lad of three year old and better."

Then she remembered the change she had wrought in the "fine bouncing lad," and her eyes filled with tears, which she was too proud to wipe away with her apron; for, as she sometimes said to herself, "she could not abide crying before folk."

"Well, it's no use talking, Sally," said Miss Benson, too anxious to speak to be any longer repressed. "We've promised to keep her, and we must do it; you'll have none of the trouble, Sally, so don't be afraid."

"Well, I never! as if I minded trouble! You might ha' known me better nor that. I've scoured master's room twice over, just to make the boards look white, though the carpet is to cover them, and now you go and cast up about me minding my trouble. If them's the fashions you've learnt in Wales, I'm thankful I've never been there."

Sally looked red, indignant, and really hurt. Mr Benson came in with his musical voice and soft words of healing.

"Faith knows you don't care for trouble, Sally; she is only anxious about this poor young woman, who has no friends but ourselves. We know there will be more trouble in consequence of her coming to stay with us; and I think, though we never spoke about it, that in making our plans we reckoned on your kind help, Sally, which has never failed us yet when we needed it."

"You've twice the sense of your sister, Master Thurstan, that you have. Boys always has. It's truth there will be more trouble, and I shall have my share on't, I reckon. I can face it if I'm told out and out, but I cannot abide the way some folk has of denying there's trouble or pain to be met; just as if their saying there was none, would do away with it. Some folk treats one like a babby, and I don't like it. I'm not meaning *you*, Master Thurstan."

"No, Sally, you need not say that. I know well enough who you mean when you say 'some folk.' However, I admit I was wrong in speaking as if you minded trouble, for there never was a creature minded it less. But I want you to like Mrs Denbigh," said Miss Benson.

"I dare say I should, if you'd let me alone. I did na like her sitting down in master's chair. Set her up, indeed, in an arm-chair wi' cushions! Wenches in my day were glad enough of stools."

"She was tired to-night," said Mr Benson. "We are all tired; so if you have done your work, Sally, come in to reading."

The three quiet people knelt down side by side, and two of them prayed earnestly for "them that had gone astray." Before ten o'clock, the household were in bed.

Ruth, sleepless, weary, restless with the oppression of a sorrow which she dared not face and contemplate bravely, kept awake all the early part of the night. Many a time did she rise, and go to the long casement window, and look abroad over the still and quiet town—over the grey stone walls, and chimneys, and old high-pointed roofs—on to the far-away hilly line of the horizon, lying calm under the bright moonshine. It was late in the morning when she woke from her long-deferred slumbers; and when she went downstairs, she found Mr and Miss Benson awaiting her in the parlour. That homely, pretty, old-fashioned little room! How bright and still and clean it looked! The window (all the windows at the back of the house were casements) was open, to let in the sweet morning air, and streaming eastern sunshine. The long jessamine sprays, with their white-scented stars, forced themselves almost into the room. The little square garden beyond, with grey stone walls all round, was rich and mellow in its autumnal colouring, running from deep crimson hollyhocks up to amber and gold nasturtiums, and all toned down by the clear and delicate air. It was so still, that the gossamer-webs, laden with dew, did not tremble or quiver in the least; but the sun was drawing to himself the sweet incense of many flowers, and the parlour was scented with the odours of mignonette and stocks. Miss Benson was arranging a bunch of China and damask roses in an old-fashioned jar; they lay, all dewy and fresh, on the white breakfast-cloth when Ruth entered. Mr Benson was reading in some large folio. With gentle morning speech they greeted her; but the quiet repose of the scene was instantly broken by Sally popping in from the kitchen, and glancing at Ruth with sharp reproach. She said:

"I reckon I may bring in breakfast, now?" with a strong emphasis on the last word.

"I am afraid I am very late," said Ruth.

"Oh, never mind," said Mr Benson, gently. "It was our fault for not telling you our breakfast hour. We always have prayers at half-past seven; and, for Sally's sake, we never vary from that time; for she can so arrange her work, if she knows the hour of prayers, as to have her mind calm and untroubled."

"Ahem!" said Miss Benson, rather inclined to "testify" against the invariable calmness of Sally's mind at any hour of the day; but her brother went on as if he did not hear her.

"But the breakfast does not signify being delayed a little; and I am sure you were sadly tired with your long day yesterday."

Sally came slapping in, and put down some withered, tough, dry toast,with—

"It's not my doing if it is like leather;" but as no one appeared to hear her, she withdrew to her kitchen, leaving Ruth's cheeks like crimson at the annoyance she had caused.

All day long, she had that feeling common to those who go to stay at a fresh house among comparative strangers: a feeling of the necessity that she should become accustomed to the new atmosphere in which she was placed, before she could move and act freely; it was, indeed, a purer ether, a diviner air, which she was breathing in now, than what she had been accustomed to for long months. The gentle, blessed mother, who had made her childhood's home holy ground, was in her very nature so far removed from any of earth's stains and temptations, that she seemed truly one of those

Who ask not if Thine eye
Be on them; who, in love and truth,
Where no misgiving is, rely
Upon the genial sense of youth.

In the Bensons' house there was the same unconsciousness of individual merit, the same absence of introspection and analysis of motive, as there had been in her mother; but it seemed that their lives were pure and good, not merely from a lovely and beautiful nature, but from some law, the obedience to which was, of itself, harmonious peace, and which governed them almost implicitly, and with as little questioning on their part, as the glorious stars which haste not, rest not, in their eternal obedience. This household had many failings: they were but human, and, with all their loving desire to bring their lives into harmony with the will of God, they often erred and fell short; but, somehow, the very errors and faults of one individual served to call out higher excellences in another, and so they reacted upon each other, and the result of short discords was exceeding harmony and peace. But they had themselves no idea of the real state of things; they did not trouble themselves with marking their progress by self-examination; if Mr Benson did sometimes, in hours of sick incapacity for exertion, turn inwards, it was to cry aloud with almost morbid despair, "God be merciful to me a sinner!" But he strove to leave his life in the hands of God, and to forget himself.

Ruth sat still and quiet through the long first day. She was languid and weary from her journey; she was uncertain what help she might offer to give in the household duties, and what she might not. And, in her languor and in her uncertainty, it was pleasant to watch the new ways of the people among whom she was placed. After breakfast, Mr Benson withdrew to his study, Miss Benson took away the cups and saucers, and, leaving the kitchen door open, talked sometimes to Ruth, sometimes to Sally, while she washed them up. Sally had upstairs duties to perform, for which Ruth was thankful, as she kept receiving rather angry glances for her unpunctuality as long as Sally remained downstairs. Miss Benson assisted in the preparation for the early dinner, and brought some kidney-beans to shred into a basin of bright, pure spring-water, which caught and danced in the sunbeams as she sat near the open casement of the parlour, talking to Ruth of things and people which as yet the latter did not understand, and could not arrange and comprehend. She was like a child who gets a few pieces of a dissected map, and is confused until a glimpse of the whole unity is shown him. Mr and Mrs Bradshaw were the centre pieces in Ruth's map; their children, their servants, were the accessories; and one or two other names were occasionally mentioned. Ruth wondered and almost wearied at Miss Benson's perseverance in talking to her about people whom she did not know; but, in truth, Miss Benson heard the long-drawn, quivering sighs which came from the poor heavy heart, when it was left to silence, and had leisure to review the past; and her quick accustomed ear caught also the low mutterings of the thunder in the distance, in the shape of Sally's soliloquies, which, like the asides at a theatre, were intended to be heard. Suddenly, Miss Benson called Ruth out of the room, upstairs into her own bed-chamber, and then began rummaging in little old-fashioned boxes, drawn out of an equally old-fashioned bureau, half desk, half table, and wholly drawers.

"My dear, I've been very stupid and thoughtless. Oh! I'm so glad I thought of it before Mrs Bradshaw came to call. Here it is!" and she pulled out an old wedding-ring, and hurried it on Ruth's finger. Ruth hung down her head, and reddened deep with shame; her eyes smarted with the hot tears that filled them. Miss Benson talked on, in a nervous hurried way:

"It was my grandmother's; it's very broad; they made them so then, to hold a posy inside: there's one in that;

Thine own sweetheart
Till death doth part,

I think it is. There, there! Run away, and look as if you'd always worn it."

Ruth went up to her room, and threw herself down on her knees by the bedside, and cried as if her heart would break; and then, as if a light had come down into her soul, she calmed herself and prayed—no words can tell how humbly, and with what earnest feeling. When she came down, she was tear-stained and wretchedly pale; but even Sally looked at her with new eyes, because of the dignity with which she was invested by an earnestness of purpose which had her child for its object. She sat and thought, but she no longer heaved those bitter sighs which had wrung Miss Benson's heart in the morning. In this way the day wore on; early dinner, early tea, seemed to make it preternaturally long to Ruth; the only event was some unexplained absence of Sally's, who had disappeared out of the house in the evening, much to Miss Benson's surprise, and somewhat to her indignation.

At night, after Ruth had gone up to her room, this absence was explained to her at least. She had let down her long waving glossy hair, and was standing absorbed in thought in the middle of the room, when she heard a round clumping knock at her door, different from that given by the small knuckles of delicate fingers, and in walked Sally, with a judge-like severity of demeanour, holding in her hand two widow's caps of commonest make and coarsest texture. Queen Eleanor herself, when she presented the bowl to Fair Rosamond, had not a more relentless purpose stamped on her demeanour than had Sally at this moment. She walked up to the beautiful, astonished Ruth, where she stood in her long, soft, white dressing-gown, with all her luxuriant brown hair hanging dishevelled down her figure, and thus Sally spoke:

"Missus—or miss, as the case may be—I've my doubts as to you. I'm not going to have my master and Miss Faith put upon, or shame come near them. Widows wears these sort o' caps, and has their hair cut off; and whether widows wears wedding-rings or not, they shall have their hair cut off—they shall. I'll have no half work in this house. I've lived with the family forty-nine year come Michaelmas, and I'll not see it disgraced by any one's fine long curls. Sit down and let me snip off your hair, and let me see you sham decently in a widow's cap to-morrow, or I'll leave the house. Whatten's come over Miss Faith, as used to be as mim a lady as ever was, to be taken by such as you, I dunnot know. Here! sit down with ye, and let me crop you."

She laid no light hand on Ruth's shoulder; and the latter, partly intimidated by the old servant, who had hitherto only turned her vixen lining to observation, and partly because she was broken-spirited enough to be indifferent to the measure proposed, quietly sat down. Sally produced the formidable pair of scissors that always hung at her side, and began to cut in a merciless manner. She expected some remonstrance or some opposition, and had a torrent of words ready to flow forth at the least sign of rebellion; but Ruth was still and silent, with meekly-bowed head, under the strange hands that were shearing her beautiful hair into the clipped shortness of a boy's. Long before she had finished, Sally had some slight misgivings as to the fancied necessity of her task; but it was too late, for half the curls were gone, and the rest must now come off. When she had done, she lifted up Ruth's face by placing her hand under the round white chin. She gazed into the countenance, expecting to read some anger there, though it had not come out in words; but she only met the large, quiet eyes, that looked at her with sad gentleness out of their finely-hollowed orbits. Ruth's soft, yet dignified submission, touched Sally with compunction, though she did not choose to show the change in her feelings. She tried to hide it, indeed, by stooping to pick up the long bright tresses; and, holding them up admiringly, and letting them drop down and float on the air (like the pendant branches of the weeping birch), she said: "I thought we should ha' had some crying—I did. They're pretty curls enough; you've not been so bad to let them be cut off neither. You see, Master Thurstan is no wiser than a babby in some things; and Miss Faith just lets him have his own way; so it's all left to me to keep him out of scrapes. I'll wish you a very good night. I've heard many a one say as long hair was not wholesome. Good night."

But in a minute she popped her head into Ruth's room once more:

"You'll put on them caps to-morrow morning. I'll make you a present on them."

Sally had carried away the beautiful curls, and she could not find it in her heart to throw such lovely chestnut tresses away, so she folded them up carefully in paper, and placed them in a safe corner of her drawer.

CHAPTER XIV

Ruth's First Sunday at Eccleston

Ruth felt very shy when she came down (at half-past seven) the next morning, in her widow's cap. Her smooth, pale face, with its oval untouched by time, looked more young and childlike than ever, when contrasted with the head-gear usually associated with ideas of age. She blushed very deeply as Mr and Miss Benson showed the astonishment, which they could not conceal, in their looks. She said in a low voice to Miss Benson,

"Sally thought I had better wear it."

Miss Benson made no reply; but was startled at the intelligence, which she thought was conveyed in this speech, of Sally's acquaintance with Ruth's real situation. She noticed Sally's looks particularly this morning. The manner in which the old servant treated Ruth had in it far more of respect than there had been the day before; but there was a kind of satisfied way of braving out Miss Benson's glances which made the latter uncertain and uncomfortable.

She followed her brother into his study.

"Do you know, Thurstan, I am almost certain Sally suspects."

Mr Benson sighed. The deception grieved him, and yet he thought he saw its necessity.

"What makes you think so?" asked he.

"Oh! many little things. It was her odd way of ducking her head about, as if to catch a good view of Ruth's left hand, that made me think of the wedding-ring; and once, yesterday, when I thought I had made up quite a natural speech, and was saying how sad it was for so young a creature to be left a widow, she broke in with 'widow be farred!' in a very strange, contemptuous kind of manner."

"If she suspects, we had far better tell her the truth at once. She will never rest till she finds it out, so we must make a virtue of necessity."

"Well, brother, you shall tell her then, for I am sure I daren't. I don't mind doing the thing, since you talked to me that day, and since I've got to know Ruth; but I do mind all the clatter people will make about it."

"But Sally is not 'people.'"

"Oh, I see it must be done; she'll talk as much as all the other persons put together, so that's the reason I call her 'people.' Shall I call her?" (For the house was too homely and primitive to have bells.)

Sally came, fully aware of what was now going to be told her, and determined not to help them out in telling their awkward secret, by understanding the nature of it before it was put into the plainest language. In every pause, when they hoped she had caught the meaning they were hinting at, she persisted in looking stupid and perplexed, and in saying, "Well," as if quite unenlightened as to the end of the story. When it was all complete and plain before her, she said, honestly enough,

"It's just as I thought it was; and I think you may thank me for having had the sense to put her into widow's caps, and clip off that bonny brown hair that was fitter for a bride in lawful matrimony than for such as her. She took it very well, though. She was as quiet as a lamb, and I clipped her pretty roughly at first. I must say, though, if I'd ha' known who your visitor was, I'd ha' packed up my things and cleared myself out of the house before such as her came into it. As it's done, I suppose I must stand by you, and help you through with it; I only hope I shan't lose my character,—and me a parish clerk's daughter."

"Oh, Sally! people know you too well to think any ill of you," said Miss Benson, who was pleased to find the difficulty so easily got over; for, in truth, Sally had been much softened by the unresisting gentleness with which Ruth had submitted to the "clipping" of the night before.

"If I'd been with you, Master Thurstan, I'd ha' seen sharp after you, for you're always picking up some one or another as nobody else would touch with a pair of tongs. Why, there was that Nelly Brandon's child as was left at our door, if I hadn't gone to th' overseer we should have had that Irish tramp's babby saddled on us for life; but I went off and told th' overseer, and th' mother was caught."

"Yes," said Mr Benson, sadly, "and I often lie awake and wonder what is the fate of that poor little thing, forced back on the mother who tried to get quit of it. I often doubt whether I did right; but it's no use thinking about it now."

"I'm thankful it isn't," said Sally; "and now, if we've talked doctrine long enough, I'll go make th' beds. Yon girl's secret is safe enough for me."

Saying this she left the room, and Miss Benson followed. She found Ruth busy washing the breakfast things; and they were done in so quiet and orderly a manner, that neither Miss Benson nor Sally, both particular enough, had any of their little fancies or prejudices annoyed. She seemed to have an instinctive knowledge of the exact period when her help was likely to become a hindrance, and withdrew from the busy kitchen just at the right time.

That afternoon, as Miss Benson and Ruth sat at their work, Mrs and Miss Bradshaw called. Miss Benson was so nervous as to surprise Ruth, who did not understand the probable and possible questions which might be asked respecting any visitor at the minister's house. Ruth went on sewing, absorbed in her own thoughts, and glad that the conversation between the two elder ladies and the silence of the younger one, who sat at some distance from her, gave her an opportunity of retreating into the haunts of memory; and soon the work fell from her hands, and her eyes were fixed on the little garden beyond, but she did not see its flowers or its walls; she saw the mountains which girdled Llan-dhu, and saw the sun rise from behind their iron outline, just as it had done—how long ago? was it months or was it years?—since she had watched the night through, crouched up at *his* door. Which was the dream and which the reality? that distant life, or this? His moans rang more clearly in her ears than the buzzing of the conversation between Mrs Bradshaw and Miss Benson.

At length the subdued, scared-looking little lady and her bright-eyed silent daughter rose to take leave; Ruth started into the present, and stood up and curtseyed, and turned sick at heart with sudden recollection.

Miss Benson accompanied Mrs Bradshaw to the door; and in the passage gave her a long explanation of Ruth's (fictitious) history. Mrs Bradshaw looked so much interested and pleased, that Miss Benson enlarged a little more than was necessary, and rounded off her invention with one or two imaginary details, which, she was quite unconscious, were overheard by her brother through the half-open study door.

She was rather dismayed when he called her into his room after Mrs Bradshaw's departure, and asked her what she had been saying about Ruth?

"Oh! I thought it was better to explain it thoroughly—I mean, to tell the story we wished to have believed once for all—you know we agreed about that, Thurstan?" deprecatingly.

"Yes; but I heard you saying you believed her husband had been a young surgeon, did I not?"

"Well, Thurstan, you know he must have been something; and young surgeons are so in the way of dying, it seemed very natural. Besides," said she, with sudden boldness, "I do think I've a talent for fiction, it is so pleasant to invent, and make the incidents dovetail together; and after all, if we are to tell a lie, we may as well do it thoroughly, or else it's of no use. A bungling lie would be worse than useless. And, Thurstan—it may be very wrong—but I believe—I am afraid I enjoy not being fettered by truth. Don't look so grave. You know it is necessary, if ever it was, to tell falsehoods now; and don't be angry with me because I do it well."

He was shading his eyes with his hand, and did not speak for some time. At last he said:

"If it were not for the child, I would tell all; but the world is so cruel. You don't know how this apparent necessity for falsehood pains me, Faith, or you would not invent all these details, which are so many additional lies."

"Well, well! I will restrain myself if I have to talk about Ruth again. But Mrs Bradshaw will tell every one who need to know. You don't wish me to contradict it, Thurstan, surely—it was such a pretty, probable story."

"Faith! I hope God will forgive us if we are doing wrong; and pray, dear, don't add one unnecessary word that is not true."

Another day elapsed, and then it was Sunday; and the house seemed filled with a deep peace. Even Sally's movements were less hasty and abrupt. Mr Benson seemed invested with a new dignity, which made his bodily deformity be forgotten in his calm, grave composure of spirit. Every trace of week-day occupation was put away; the night before, a bright new handsome tablecloth had been smoothed down over the table, and the jars had been freshly filled with flowers. Sunday was a festival and a holy day in the house. After the very early breakfast, little feet pattered into Mr Benson's study, for he had a class for boys—a sort of domestic Sunday-school, only that there was more talking between teacher and pupils, than dry, absolute lessons going on. Miss Benson, too, had her little, neat-tippeted maidens sitting with her in the parlour; and she was far more particular in keeping them to their reading and spelling, than her brother was with his boys. Sally, too, put in her word of instruction from the kitchen, helping, as she fancied, though her assistance was often rather *malapropos*; for instance, she called out, to a little fat, stupid, roly-poly girl, to whom Miss Benson was busy explaining the meaning of the word quadruped,

"Quadruped, a thing wi' four legs, Jenny; a chair is a quadruped, child!"

But Miss Benson had a deaf manner sometimes when her patience was not too severely tried, and she put it on now. Ruth sat on a low hassock, and coaxed the least of the little creatures to her, and showed it pictures till it fell asleep in her arms, and sent a thrill through her, at the thought of the tiny darling who would lie on her breast before long, and whom she would have to cherish and to shelter from the storms of the world.

And then she remembered, that she was once white and sinless as the wee lassie who lay in her arms; and she knew that she had gone astray. By-and-by the children trooped away, and Miss Benson summoned her to put on her things for chapel.

The chapel was up a narrow street, or rather *cul-de-sac*, close by. It stood on the outskirts of the town, almost in fields. It was built about the time of Matthew and Philip Henry, when the Dissenters were afraid of attracting attention or observation, and hid their places of worship in obscure and out-of-the-way parts of the towns in which they were built. Accordingly, it often happened, as in the present case, that the buildings immediately surrounding, as well as the chapels themselves, looked as if they carried you back to a period a hundred and fifty years ago. The chapel had a picturesque and old-world look, for luckily the congregation had been too poor to rebuild it, or new-face it, in George the Third's time. The staircases which led to the galleries were outside, at each end of the building, and the irregular roof and worn stone steps looked grey and stained by time and weather. The grassy hillocks, each with a little upright headstone, were shaded by a grand old wych-elm. A lilac-bush or two, a white rose-tree, and a few laburnums, all old and gnarled enough, were planted round the chapel yard; and the casement windows of the chapel were made of heavy-leaded, diamond-shaped panes, almost covered with ivy, producing a green gloom, not without its solemnity, within. This ivy was the home of an infinite number of little birds, which twittered and warbled, till it might have been thought that they were emulous of the power of praise possessed by the human creatures within, with such earnest, long-drawn strains did this crowd of winged songsters rejoice and be glad in their beautiful gift of life. The interior of the building was plain and simple as plain and simple could be. When it was fitted up, oak-timber was much cheaper than it is now, so the wood-work was all of that description; but roughly hewed, for the early builders had not much wealth to spare. The walls were whitewashed, and were recipients of the shadows of the beauty without; on their "white plains" the tracery of the ivy might be seen, now still, now stirred by the sudden flight of some little bird. The congregation consisted of here and there a farmer with his labourers, who came down from the uplands beyond the town to worship where their fathers worshipped, and who loved the place because they knew how much those fathers had suffered for it, although they never troubled themselves with the reason why they left the parish church; of a few shopkeepers, far more thoughtful and reasoning, who were Dissenters from conviction, unmixed with old ancestral association; and of one or two families of still higher worldly station. With many poor, who were drawn there by love for Mr Benson's character, and by a feeling that the faith which made him what he was could not be far wrong, for the base of the pyramid, and with Mr Bradshaw for its apex, the congregation stood complete.

The country people came in sleeking down their hair, and treading with earnest attempts at noiseless lightness of step over the floor of the aisle; and by-and-by, when all were assembled, Mr Benson followed, unmarshalled and unattended. When he had closed the pulpit-door, and knelt in prayer for an instant or two, he gave out a psalm from the dear old Scottish paraphrase, with its primitive inversion of the simple perfect Bible words; and a kind of precentor stood up, and, having sounded the note on a pitch-pipe, sang a couple of lines by way of indicating the tune; then all the congregation stood up, and sang aloud, Mr Bradshaw's great bass voice being half a note in advance of the others, in accordance with his place of precedence as principal member of the congregation. His powerful voice was like an organ very badly played, and very much out of tune; but as he had no ear, and no diffidence, it pleased him very much to hear the fine loud sound. He was a tall, large-boned, iron man; stern, powerful, and authoritative in appearance; dressed in clothes of the finest broadcloth, and scrupulously ill-made, as if to show that he was indifferent to all outward things. His wife was sweet and gentle-looking, but as if she was thoroughly broken into submission.

Ruth did not see this, or hear aught but the words which were reverently—oh, how reverently!—spoken by Mr Benson. He had had Ruth present in his thoughts all the time he had been preparing for his Sunday duty; and he had tried carefully to eschew everything which she might feel as an allusion to her own case. He remembered how the Good Shepherd, in Poussin's beautiful picture, tenderly carried the lambs which had wearied themselves by going astray, and felt how like tenderness was required towards poor Ruth. But where is the chapter which does not contain something which a broken and contrite spirit may not apply to itself? And so it fell out that, as he read, Ruth's heart was smitten, and she sank down, and down, till she was kneeling on the floor of the pew, and speaking to God in the spirit, if not in the words, of the Prodigal Son: "Father! I have sinned against Heaven and before Thee, and am no more worthy to be called Thy child!" Miss Benson was thankful (although she loved Ruth the better for this self-abandonment) that the minister's seat was far in the shade of the gallery. She tried to look most attentive to her brother, in order that Mr Bradshaw might not suspect anything unusual, while she stealthily took hold of Ruth's passive hand, as it lay helpless on the cushion, and pressed it softly and tenderly. But Ruth sat on the ground, bowed down and crushed in her sorrow, till all was ended.

Miss Benson loitered in her seat, divided between the consciousness that she, as *locum tenens* for the minister's wife, was expected to be at the door to receive the kind greetings of many after her absence from home, and her unwillingness to disturb Ruth, who was evidently praying, and, by her quiet breathing, receiving grave and solemn influences into her soul. At length she rose up, calm and composed even to dignity. The chapel was still and empty; but Miss Benson heard the buzz of voices in the chapel-yard without. They were probably those of people waiting for her; and she summoned courage, and taking Ruth's arm in hers, and holding her hand affectionately, they went out into the broad daylight. As they issued forth, Miss Benson heard Mr Bradshaw's strong bass voice speaking to her brother, and winced, as she knew he would be wincing, under the broad praise, which is impertinence, however little it may be intended or esteemed as such.

"Oh, yes!—my wife told me yesterday about her—her husband was a surgeon; my father was a surgeon too, as I think you have heard. Very much to your credit, I must say, Mr Benson, with your limited means, to burden yourself with a poor relation. Very creditable indeed."

Miss Benson glanced at Ruth; she either did not hear or did not understand, but passed on into the awful sphere of Mr Bradshaw's observation unmoved. He was in a bland and condescending humour of universal approval, and when he saw Ruth, he nodded his head in token of satisfaction. That ordeal was over, Miss Benson thought, and in the thought rejoiced.

"After dinner, you must go and lie down, my dear," said she, untying Ruth's bonnet-strings, and kissing her. "Sally goes to church again, but you won't mind staying alone in the house. I am sorry we have so many people to dinner, but my brother will always have enough on Sundays for any old or weak people, who may have come from a distance, to stay and dine with us; and to-day they all seem to have come, because it is his first Sabbath at home."

In this way Ruth's first Sabbath passed over.

CHAPTER XV

Mother and Child

"Here is a parcel for you, Ruth!" said Miss Benson on the Tuesday morning.

"For me!" said Ruth, all sorts of rushing thoughts and hopes filling her mind, and turning her dizzy with expectation. If it had been from "him," the new-born resolutions would have had a hard struggle for existence.

"It is directed 'Mrs Denbigh,'" said Miss Benson, before giving it up. "It is in Mrs Bradshaw's handwriting;" and, far more curious than Ruth, she awaited the untying of the close-knotted string. When the paper was opened, it displayed a whole piece of delicate cambric-muslin; and there was a short note from Mrs Bradshaw to Ruth, saying her husband had wished her to send this muslin in aid of any preparations Mrs Denbigh might have to make. Ruth said nothing, but coloured up, and sat down again to her employment.

"Very fine muslin indeed," said Miss Benson, feeling it, and holding it up against the light, with the air of a connoisseur; yet all the time she was glancing at Ruth's grave face. The latter kept silence, and showed no wish to inspect her present further. At last she said, in a low voice,

"I suppose I may send it back again?"

"My dear child! send it back to Mr Bradshaw! You'd offend him for life. You may depend upon it, he means it as a mark of high favour!"

"What right had he to send it me?" asked Ruth, still in her quiet voice.

"What right? Mr Bradshaw thinks— I don't know exactly what you mean by 'right.'"

Ruth was silent for a moment, and then said:

"There are people to whom I love to feel that I owe gratitude—gratitude which I cannot express, and had better not talk about—but I cannot see why a person whom I do not know should lay me under an obligation. Oh! don't say I must take this muslin, please, Miss Benson!"

What Miss Benson might have said if her brother had not just then entered the room, neither he nor any other person could tell; but she felt his presence was most opportune, and called him in as umpire. He had come hastily, for he had much to do; but he no sooner heard the case than he sat down, and tried to draw some more explicit declaration of her feeling from Ruth, who had remained silent during Miss Benson's explanation.

"You would rather send this present back?" said he.

"Yes," she answered, softly. "Is it wrong?"

"Why do you want to return it?"

"Because I feel as if Mr Bradshaw had no right to offer it me."

Mr Benson was silent.

"It's beautifully fine," said Miss Benson, still examining the piece.

"You think that it is a right which must be earned?"

"Yes," said she, after a minute's pause. "Don't you?"

"I understand what you mean. It is a delight to have gifts made to you by those whom you esteem and love, because then such gifts are merely to be considered as fringes to the garment—as inconsiderable additions to the mighty treasure of their affection, adding a grace, but no additional value, to what before was precious, and proceeding as naturally out of that as leaves burgeon out upon the trees; but you feel it to be different when there is no regard for the giver to idealise the gift—when it simply takes its stand among your property as so much money's value. Is this it, Ruth?"

"I think it is. I never reasoned why I felt as I did; I only knew that Mr Bradshaw's giving me a present hurt me, instead of making me glad."

"Well, but there is another side of the case we have not looked at yet—we must think of that, too. You know who said, 'Do unto others as ye would that they should do unto you'? Mr Bradshaw may not have had that in his mind when he desired his wife to send you this; he may have been self-seeking, and only anxious to gratify his love of patronising—that is the worst motive we can give him; and that would be no excuse for your thinking only of yourself, and returning his present."

"But you would not have me pretend to be obliged?" asked Ruth.

"No, I would not. I have often been similarly situated to you, Ruth; Mr Bradshaw has frequently opposed me on the points on which I feel the warmest—am the most earnestly convinced. He, no doubt, thinks me Quixotic, and often speaks of me, and to me, with great contempt when he is angry. I suppose he has a little fit of penitence afterwards, or perhaps he thinks he can pay for ungracious speeches by a present; so, formerly, he invariably sent me something after these occasions. It was a time, of all others, to feel as you are doing now; but I became convinced it would be right to accept them, giving only the very cool thanks which I felt. This omission of all show of much gratitude had the best effect—the presents have much diminished; but if the gifts have lessened, the unjustifiable speeches have decreased in still greater proportion, and I am sure we respect each other more. Take this muslin, Ruth, for the reason I named; and thank him as your feelings prompt you. Overstrained expressions of gratitude always seem like an endeavour to place the receiver of these expressions in the position of debtor for future favours. But you won't fall into this error."

Ruth listened to Mr Benson; but she had not yet fallen sufficiently into the tone of his mind to understand him fully. She only felt that he comprehended her better than Miss Benson, who once more tried to reconcile her to her present, by calling her attention to the length and breadth thereof.

"I will do what you wish me," she said, after a little pause of thoughtfulness. "May we talk of something else?"

Mr Benson saw that his sister's frame of mind was not particularly congenial with Ruth's, any more than Ruth's was with Miss Benson's; and, putting aside all thought of returning to the business which had appeared to him so important when he came into the room (but which principally related to himself), he remained above an hour in the parlour, interesting them on subjects far removed from the present, and left them at the end of that time soothed and calm.

But the present gave a new current to Ruth's ideas. Her heart was as yet too sore to speak, but her mind was crowded with plans. She asked Sally to buy her (with the money produced by the sale of a ring or two) the coarsest linen, the homeliest dark blue print, and similar materials; on which she set busily to work to make clothes for herself; and as they were made, she put them on; and as she put them on, she gave a grace to each, which such homely material and simple shaping had never had before. Then the fine linen and delicate soft white muslin, which she had chosen in preference to more expensive articles of dress when Mr Bellingham had given her *carte blanche* in London, were cut into small garments, most daintily stitched and made ready for the little creature, for whom in its white purity of soul nothing could be too precious.

The love which dictated this extreme simplicity and coarseness of attire, was taken for stiff, hard economy by Mr Bradshaw, when he deigned to observe it. And economy by itself, without any soul or spirit in it to make it living and holy, was a great merit in his eyes. Indeed, Ruth altogether found favour with him. Her quiet manner, subdued by an internal consciousness of a deeper cause for sorrow than he was aware of, he interpreted into a very proper and becoming awe of him. He looked off from his own prayers to observe how well she attended to hers at chapel; when he came to any verse in the hymn relating to immortality or a future life, he sang it unusually loud, thinking he should thus comfort her in her sorrow for her deceased husband. He desired Mrs Bradshaw to pay her every attention she could; and even once remarked, that he thought her so respectable a young person that he should not object to her being asked to tea the next time Mr and Miss Benson came. He added, that he thought, indeed, Benson had looked last Sunday as if he rather hoped to get an invitation; and it was right to encourage the ministers, and to show them respect, even though their salaries were small. The only thing against this Mrs Denbigh was the circumstance of her having married too early, and without any provision for a family. Though Ruth pleaded delicacy of health, and declined accompanying Mr and Miss Benson on their visit to Mr Bradshaw, she still preserved her place in his esteem; and Miss Benson had to call a little upon her "talent for fiction" to spare Ruth from the infliction of further presents, in making which his love of patronising delighted.

The yellow and crimson leaves came floating down on the still October air; November followed, bleak and dreary; it was more cheerful when the earth put on her beautiful robe of white, which covered up all the grey naked stems, and loaded the leaves of the hollies and evergreens each with its burden of feathery snow. When Ruth sank down to languor and sadness, Miss Benson trotted upstairs, and rummaged up every article of spare or worn-out clothing, and bringing down a variety of strange materials, she tried to interest Ruth in making them up into garments for the poor. But though Ruth's fingers flew through the work, she still sighed with thought and remembrance. Miss Benson was at first disappointed, and then she was angry. When she heard the low, long sigh, and saw the dreamy eyes filling with glittering tears, she would say, "What is the matter, Ruth?" in a half-reproachful tone, for the sight of suffering was painful to her; she had done all in her power to remedy it; and, though she acknowledged a cause beyond her reach for Ruth's deep sorrow, and, in fact, loved and respected her all the more for these manifestations of grief, yet at the time they irritated her. Then Ruth would snatch up the dropped work, and stitch away with drooping eyes, from which the hot tears fell fast; and Miss Benson was then angry with herself, yet not at all inclined to agree with Sally when she asked her mistress "why she kept 'mithering' the poor lass with asking her for ever what was the matter, as if she did not know well enough." Some element of harmony was wanting—some little angel of peace, in loving whom all hearts and natures should be drawn together, and their discords hushed.

The earth was still "hiding her guilty front with innocent snow," when a little baby was laid by the side of the pale white mother. It was a boy; beforehand she had wished for a girl, as being less likely to feel the want of a father—as being what a mother, worse than widowed, could most effectually shelter. But now she did not think or remember this. What it was, she would not have exchanged for a wilderness of girls. It was her own, her darling, her individual baby, already, though not an hour old, separate and sole in her heart, strangely filling up its measure with love and peace, and even hope. For here was a new, pure, beautiful, innocent life, which she fondly imagined, in that early passion of maternal love, she could guard from every touch of corrupting sin by ever watchful and most tender care. And *her* mother had thought the same, most probably; and thousands of others think the same, and pray to God to purify and cleanse their souls, that they may be fit guardians for their little children. Oh, how Ruth prayed, even while she was yet too weak to speak; and how she felt the beauty and significance of the words, "Our Father!"

She was roused from this holy abstraction by the sound of Miss Benson's voice. It was very much as if she had been crying.

"Look, Ruth!" it said, softly, "my brother sends you these. They are the first snowdrops in the garden." And she put them on the pillow by Ruth; the baby lay on the opposite side.

"Won't you look at him?" said Ruth; "he is so pretty!"

Miss Benson had a strange reluctance to see him. To Ruth, in spite of all that had come and gone, she was reconciled—nay, more, she was deeply attached; but over the baby there hung a cloud of shame and disgrace. Poor little creature! her heart was closed against it—firmly, as she thought. But she could not resist Ruth's low faint voice, nor her pleading eyes, and she went round to peep at him as he lay in his mother's arm, as yet his shield and guard.

"Sally says he will have black hair, she thinks," said Ruth. "His little hand is quite a man's, already. Just feel how firmly he closes it;" and with her own weak fingers she opened his little red fist, and taking Miss Benson's reluctant hand, placed one of her fingers in his grasp. That baby-touch called out her love; the doors of her heart were thrown open wide for the little infant to go in and take possession.

"Ah, my darling!" said Ruth, falling back weak and weary. "If God will but spare you to me, never mother did more than I will. I have done you a grievous wrong—but, if I may but live, I will spend my life in serving you!"

"And in serving God!" said Miss Benson, with tears in her eyes. "You must not make him into an idol, or God will, perhaps, punish you through him."

A pang of affright shot through Ruth's heart at these words; had she already sinned and made her child into an idol, and was there punishment already in store for her through him? But then the internal voice whispered that God was "Our Father," and that He knew our frame, and knew how natural was the first outburst of a mother's love; so, although she treasured up the warning, she ceased to affright herself for what had already gushed forth.

"Now go to sleep, Ruth," said Miss Benson, kissing her, and darkening the room. But Ruth could not sleep; if her heavy eyes closed, she opened them again with a start, for sleep seemed to be an enemy stealing from her the consciousness of being a mother. That one thought excluded all remembrance and all anticipation, in those first hours of delight.

But soon remembrance and anticipation came. There was the natural want of the person, who alone could take an interest similar in kind, though not in amount, to the mother's. And sadness grew like a giant in the still watches of the night, when she remembered that there would be no father to guide and strengthen the child, and place him in a favourable position for fighting the hard "Battle of Life." She hoped and believed that no one would know the sin of his parents, and that that struggle might be spared to him. But a father's powerful care and mighty guidance would never be his; and then, in those hours of spiritual purification, came the wonder and the doubt of how far the real father would be the one to whom, with her desire of heaven for her child, whatever might become of herself, she would wish to entrust him. Slight speeches, telling of a selfish, worldly nature, unnoticed at the time, came back upon her ear, having a new significance. They told of a low standard, of impatient self-indulgence, of no acknowledgment of things spiritual and heavenly. Even while this examination was forced upon her, by the new spirit of maternity that had entered into her, and made her child's welfare supreme, she hated and reproached herself for the necessity there seemed upon her of examining and judging the absent father of her child. And so the compelling presence that had taken possession of her wearied her into a kind of feverish slumber; in which she dreamt that the innocent babe that lay by her side in soft ruddy slumber had started up into man's growth, and, instead of the pure and noble being whom she had prayed to present as her child to "Our Father in heaven," he was a repetition of his father; and, like him, lured some maiden (who in her dream seemed strangely like herself, only more utterly sad and desolate even than she) into sin, and left her there to even a worse fate than that of suicide. For Ruth believed there was a worse. She dreamt she saw the girl, wandering, lost; and that she saw her son in high places, prosperous—but with more than blood on his soul. She saw her son dragged down by the clinging girl into some pit of horrors into which she dared not look, but from whence his father's voice was heard, crying aloud, that in his day and generation he had not remembered the words of God, and that now he was "tormented in this flame." Then she started in sick terror, and saw, by the dim rushlight, Sally, nodding in an arm-chair by the fire; and felt her little soft warm babe, nestled up against her breast, rocked by her heart, which yet beat hard from the effects of the evil dream. She dared not go to sleep again, but prayed. And every time she prayed, she asked with a more complete wisdom, and a more utter and self-forgetting faith. Little child! thy angel was with God, and drew her nearer and nearer to Him, whose face is continually beheld by the angels of little children.

CHAPTER XVI

Sally Tells of Her Sweethearts,
and Discourses on the Duties of Life

Sally and Miss Benson took it in turns to sit up, or rather, they took it in turns to nod by the fire; for if Ruth was awake she lay very still in the moonlight calm of her sick bed. That time resembled a beautiful August evening, such as I have seen. The white, snowy rolling mist covers up under its great sheet all trees and meadows, and tokens of earth; but it cannot rise high enough to shut out the heavens, which on such nights seem bending very near, and to be the only real and present objects; and so near, so real and present, did heaven, and eternity, and God seem to Ruth, as she lay encircling her mysterious holy child.

One night Sally found out she was not asleep.

"I'm a rare hand at talking folks to sleep," said she. "I'll try on thee, for thou must get strength by sleeping and eating. What must I talk to thee about, I wonder. Shall I tell thee a love story or a fairy story, such as I've telled Master Thurstan many a time and many a time, for all his father set his face again fairies, and called it vain talking; or shall I tell you the dinner I once cooked, when Mr Harding, as was Miss Faith's sweetheart, came unlooked for, and we'd nought in the house but a neck of mutton, out of which I made seven dishes, all with a different name?"

"Who was Mr Harding?" asked Ruth.

"Oh, he was a grand gentleman from Lunnon, as had seen Miss Faith, and been struck by her pretty looks when she was out on a visit, and came here to ask her to marry him. She said, 'No, she would never leave Master Thurstan, as could never marry;' but she pined a deal at after he went away. She kept up afore Master Thurstan, but I seed her fretting, though I never let on that I did, for I thought she'd soonest get over it and be thankful at after she'd the strength to do right. However, I've no business to be talking of Miss Benson's concerns. I'll tell you of my own sweethearts and welcome, or I'll tell you of the dinner, which was the grandest thing I ever did in my life, but I thought a Lunnoner should never think country folks knew nothing; and, my word! I puzzled him with his dinner. I'm doubting whether to this day he knows whether what he was eating was fish, flesh, or fowl. Shall I tell you how I managed?"

But Ruth said she would rather hear about Sally's sweethearts, much to the disappointment of the latter, who considered the dinner by far the greatest achievement.

"Well, you see, I don't know as I should call them sweethearts; for excepting John Rawson, who was shut up in the mad-house the next week, I never had what you may call a downright offer of marriage but once. But I had once; and so I may say I had a sweetheart. I was beginning to be afeard though, for one likes to be axed; that's but civility; and I remember, after I had turned forty, and afore Jeremiah Dixon had spoken, I began to think John Rawson had perhaps not been so very mad, and that I'd done ill to lightly his offer, as a madman's, if it was to be the only one I was ever to have; I don't mean as I'd have had him, but I thought, if it was to come o'er again, I'd speak respectful of him to folk, and say it were only his way to go about on all fours, but that he was a sensible man in most things. However, I'd had my laugh, and so had others, at my crazy lover, and it was late now to set him up as a Solomon. However, I thought it would be no bad thing to be tried again; but I little thought the trial would come when it did. You see, Saturday night is a leisure night in counting-houses and such-like places, while it's the busiest of all for servants. Well! it was a Saturday night, and I'd my baize apron on, and the tails of my bed-gown pinned together behind, down on my knees, pipeclaying the kitchen, when a knock comes to the back door. 'Come in!' says I; but it knocked again, as if it were too stately to open the door for itself; so I got up, rather cross, and opened the door; and there stood Jerry Dixon, Mr Holt's head clerk; only he was not head clerk then. So I stood, stopping up the door, fancying he wanted to speak to master; but he kind of pushed past me, and telling me summut about the weather (as if I could not see it for myself), he took a chair, and sat down by the oven. 'Cool and easy!' thought I; meaning hisself, not his place, which I knew must be pretty hot. Well! it seemed no use standing waiting for my gentleman to go; not that he had much to say either; but he kept twirling his hat round and round, and smoothing the nap on't with the back of his hand. So at last I squatted down to my work, and thinks I, I shall be on my knees all ready if he puts up a prayer, for I knew he was a Methodee by bringing-up, and had only lately turned to master's way of thinking; and them Methodees are terrible hands at unexpected prayers when one least looks for 'em. I can't say I like their way of taking one by surprise, as it were; but then I'm a parish clerk's daughter, and could never demean myself to dissenting fashions, always save and except Master Thurstan's, bless him. However, I'd been caught once or twice unawares, so this time I thought I'd be up to it, and I moved a dry duster wherever I went, to kneel upon in case he began when I were in a wet place. By-and-by I thought, if the man would pray it would be a blessing, for it would prevent his sending his eyes after me wherever I went; for when they takes to praying they shuts their eyes, and quivers th' lids in a queer kind o' way—them Dissenters does. I can speak pretty plain to you, for you're bred in the Church like mysel', and must find it as out o' the way as I do to be among dissenting folk. God forbid I should speak disrespectful of Master Thurstan and Miss Faith, though; I never think on them as Church or Dissenters, but just as Christians. But to come back to Jerry. First, I tried always to be cleaning at his back; but when he wheeled round, so as always to face me, I thought I'd try a different game. So, says I, 'Master Dixon, I ax your pardon, but I must pipeclay under your chair. Will you please to move?' Well, he moved; and by-and-by I was at him again with the same words; and at after that, again and again, till he were always moving about wi' his chair behind him, like a snail as carries its house on its back. And the great gaupus never seed that I were pipeclaying the same places twice over. At last I got desperate cross, he were so in my way; so I made two big crosses on the tails of his brown coat; for you see, whenever he went, up or down, he drew out the tails of his coat from under him, and stuck them through the bars of the chair; and flesh and blood could not resist pipeclaying them for him; and a pretty brushing he'd have, I reckon, to get it off again. Well! at length he clears his throat uncommon loud; so I spreads my duster, and shuts my eyes all ready; but when nought comed of it, I opened my eyes a little bit to see what he were about. My word! if there he wasn't down on his knees right facing me, staring as hard as he could. Well! I thought it would be hard work to stand that, if he made a long ado; so I shut my eyes again, and tried to think serious, as became what I fancied were coming; but, forgive me! but I thought why couldn't the fellow go in and pray wi' Master Thurstan, as had always a calm spirit ready for prayer, instead o' me, who had my dresser to scour, let alone an apron to iron. At last he says, says he, 'Sally! will you oblige me with your hand?' So I thought it were, maybe, Methodee fashion to pray hand in hand; and I'll not deny but I wished I'd washed it better after black-leading the kitchen fire. I thought I'd better tell him it were not so clean as I could wish, so says I, 'Master Dixon, you shall have it, and welcome, if I may just go and wash 'em first.' But, says he, 'My dear Sally, dirty or clean it's all the same to me, seeing I'm only speaking in a figuring way. What I'm asking on my bended knees is, that you'd please to be so kind as to be my wedded wife; week after next will suit me, if it's agreeable to you!' My word! I were up on my feet in an instant! It were odd now, weren't it? I never thought of taking the fellow, and getting married; for all, I'll not deny, I had been thinking it would be agreeable to be axed. But all at once, I couldn't abide the chap. 'Sir,' says I, trying to look shame-faced as became the occasion, but for all that, feeling a twittering round my mouth that I were afeard might end in a laugh—'Master Dixon, I'm obleeged to you for the compliment, and thank ye all the same, but I think I'd prefer a single life.' He looked mighty taken aback; but in a minute he cleared up, and was as sweet as ever. He still kept on his knees, and I wished he'd take himself up; but, I reckon, he thought it would give force to his words; says he, 'Think again, my dear Sally. I've a four-roomed house, and furniture conformable; and eighty pound a year. You may never have such a chance again.' There were truth enough in that, but it was not pretty in the man to say it; and it put me up a bit. 'As for that, neither you nor I can tell, Master Dixon. You're not the first chap as I've had down on his knees afore me, axing me to marry him (you see I were thinking of John Rawson, only I thought there were no need to say he were on all fours—it were truth he were on his knees, you know), and maybe you'll not be the last. Anyhow, I've no wish to change my condition just now.' 'I'll wait till Christmas,' says he. 'I've a pig as will be ready for killing then, so I must get married before that.' Well now! would you believe it? the pig were a temptation. I'd a receipt for curing hams, as Miss Faith would never let me try, saying the old way were good enough. However, I resisted. Says I, very stern, because I felt I'd been wavering, 'Master Dixon, once for all, pig or no pig, I'll not marry you. And if you'll take my advice, you'll get up off your knees. The flags is but damp yet, and it would be an awkward thing to have rheumatiz just before winter.' With that he got up, stiff enough. He looked as sulky a chap as ever I clapped eyes on. And as he were so black and cross, I thought I'd done well (whatever came of the pig) to say 'No' to him. 'You may live to repent this,' says he, very red. 'But I'll not be too hard upon ye, I'll give you another chance. I'll let you have the night to think about it, and I'll just call in to hear your second thoughts, after chapel to-morrow.' Well now! did ever you hear the like? But that is the way with all of them men, thinking so much of theirselves, and that it's but ask and have. They've never had me, though; and I shall be sixty-one next Martinmas, so there's not much time left for them to try me, I reckon. Well! when Jeremiah said that, he put me up more than ever, and I says, 'My first thoughts, second thoughts, and third thoughts is all one and the same; you've but tempted me once, and that was when you spoke of your pig. But of yoursel' you're nothing to boast on, and so I'll bid you good night, and I'll keep my manners, or else, if I told the truth, I should say it had been a great loss of time listening to you. But I'll be civil—so good night.' He never said a word, but went off as black as thunder, slamming the door after him. The master called me in to prayers, but I can't say I could put my mind to them, for my heart was beating so. However, it was a comfort to have had an offer of holy matrimony; and though it flustered me, it made me think more of myself. In the night, I began to wonder if I'd not been cruel and hard to him. You see, I were feverish-like; and the old song of Barbary Allen would keep running in my head, and I thought I were Barbary, and he were young Jemmy Gray, and that maybe he'd die for love of me; and I pictured him to mysel', lying on his death-bed, with his face turned to the wall, 'wi' deadly sorrow sighing,' and I could ha' pinched mysel' for having been so like cruel Barbary Allen. And when I got up next day, I found it hard to think on the real Jerry Dixon I had seen the night before, apart from the sad and sorrowful Jerry I thought on a-dying, when I were between sleeping and waking. And for many a day I turned sick, when I heard the passing bell, for I thought it were the bell loud-knelling which were to break my heart wi' a sense of what I'd missed in saying 'No' to Jerry, and so killing him with cruelty. But in less than a three week, I heard parish bells a-ringing merrily for a wedding; and in the course of a morning, some one says to me, 'Hark! how the bells is ringing for Jerry Dixon's wedding!' And, all on a sudden, he changed back again from a heart-broken young fellow, like Jemmy Gray, into a stout, middle-aged man, ruddy-complexioned, with a wart on his left cheek like life!"

Sally waited for some exclamation at the conclusion of her tale; but receiving none, she stepped softly to the bedside, and there lay Ruth, peaceful as death, with her baby on her breast.

"I thought I'd lost some of my gifts if I could not talk a body to sleep," said Sally, in a satisfied and self-complacent tone.

Youth is strong and powerful, and makes a hard battle against sorrow. So Ruth strove and strengthened, and her baby flourished accordingly; and before the little celandines were out on the hedge-banks, or the white violets had sent forth their fragrance from the border under the south wall of Miss Benson's small garden, Ruth was able to carry her baby into that sheltered place on sunny days.

She often wished to thank Mr Benson and his sister, but she did not know how to tell the deep gratitude she felt, and therefore she was silent. But they understood her silence well. One day, as she watched her sleeping child, she spoke to Miss Benson, with whom she happened to be alone.

"Do you know of any cottage where the people are clean, and where they would not mind taking me in?" asked she.

"Taking you in! What do you mean?" said Miss Benson, dropping her knitting, in order to observe Ruth more closely.

"I mean," said Ruth, "where I might lodge with my baby—any very poor place would do, only it must be clean, or he might be ill."

"And what in the world do you want to go and lodge in a cottage for?" said Miss Benson, indignantly.

Ruth did not lift up her eyes, but she spoke with a firmness which showed that she had considered the subject.

"I think I could make dresses. I know I did not learn as much as I might, but perhaps I might do for servants, and people who are not particular."

"Servants are as particular as any one," said Miss Benson, glad to lay hold of the first objection that she could.

"Well! somebody who would be patient with me," said Ruth.

"Nobody is patient over an ill-fitting gown," put in Miss Benson. "There's the stuff spoilt, and what not!"

"Perhaps I could find plain work to do," said Ruth, very meekly. "That I can do very well; mamma taught me, and I liked to learn from her. If you would be so good, Miss Benson, you might tell people I could do plain work very neatly, and punctually, and cheaply."

"You'd get sixpence a day, perhaps," said Miss Benson, "and who would take care of baby, I should like to know? Prettily he'd be neglected, would not he? Why, he'd have the croup and the typhus fever in no time, and be burnt to ashes after."

"I have thought of all. Look how he sleeps! Hush, darling;" for just at this point he began to cry, and to show his determination to be awake, as if in contradiction to his mother's words. Ruth took him up, and carried him about the room while she went on speaking.

"Yes, just now I know he will not sleep; but very often he will, and in the night he always does."

"And so you'd work in the night and kill yourself, and leave your poor baby an orphan. Ruth! I'm ashamed of you. Now, brother" (Mr Benson had just come in), "is not this too bad of Ruth; here she is planning to go away and leave us, just as we—as I, at least, have grown so fond of baby, and he's beginning to know me."

"Where were you thinking of going to, Ruth?" interrupted Mr Benson, with mild surprise.

"Anywhere to be near you and Miss Benson; in any poor cottage where I might lodge very cheaply, and earn my livelihood by taking in plain sewing, and perhaps a little dressmaking; and where I could come and see you and dear Miss Benson sometimes and bring baby."

"If he was not dead before then of some fever, or burn, or scald, poor neglected child; or you had not worked yourself to death with never sleeping," said Miss Benson.

Mr Benson thought a minute or two, and then he spoke to Ruth.

"Whatever you may do when this little fellow is a year old, and able to dispense with some of a mother's care, let me beg you, Ruth, as a favour to me—as a still greater favour to my sister, is it not, Faith?"

"Yes; you may put it so if you like."

"To stay with us," continued he, "till then. When baby is twelve months old, we'll talk about it again, and very likely before then some opening may be shown us. Never fear leading an idle life, Ruth. We'll treat you as a daughter, and set you all the household tasks; and it is not for your sake that we ask you to stay, but for this little dumb helpless child's; and it is not for our sake that you must stay, but for his."

Ruth was sobbing.

"I do not deserve your kindness," said she, in a broken voice; "I do not deserve it."

Her tears fell fast and soft like summer rain, but no further word was spoken. Mr Benson quietly passed on to make the inquiry for which he had entered the room.

But when there was nothing to decide upon, and no necessity for entering upon any new course of action, Ruth's mind relaxed from its strung-up state. She fell into trains of reverie, and mournful regretful recollections which rendered her languid and tearful. This was noticed both by Miss Benson and Sally, and as each had keen sympathies, and felt depressed when they saw any one near them depressed, and as each, without much reasoning on the cause or reason for such depression, felt irritated at the uncomfortable state into which they themselves were thrown, they both resolved to speak to Ruth on the next fitting occasion.

Accordingly, one afternoon—the morning of that day had been spent by Ruth in housework, for she had insisted on Mr Benson's words, and had taken Miss Benson's share of the more active and fatiguing household duties, but she went through them heavily, and as if her heart was far away—in the afternoon when she was nursing her child, Sally, on coming into the back parlour, found her there alone, and easily detected the fact that she had been crying.

"Where's Miss Benson?" said Sally, gruffly.

"Gone out with Mr Benson," answered Ruth, with an absent sadness in her voice and manner. Her tears, scarce checked while she spoke, began to fall afresh; and as Sally stood and gazed she saw the babe look back in his mother's face, and his little lip begin to quiver, and his open blue eye to grow over-clouded, as with some mysterious sympathy with the sorrowful face bent over him. Sally took him briskly from his mother's arms; Ruth looked up in grave surprise, for in truth she had forgotten Sally's presence, and the suddenness of the motion startled her.

"My bonny boy! are they letting the salt tears drop on thy sweet face before thou'rt weaned! Little somebody knows how to be a mother—I could make a better myself. 'Dance, thumbkin, dance—dance, ye merry men every one.' Aye, that's it! smile, my pretty. Any one but a child like thee," continued she, turning to Ruth, "would have known better than to bring ill-luck on thy babby by letting tears fall on its face before it was weaned. But thou'rt not fit to have a babby, and so I've said many a time. I've a great mind to buy thee a doll, and take thy babby mysel'."

Sally did not look at Ruth, for she was too much engaged in amusing the baby with the tassel of the string to the window-blind, or else she would have seen the dignity which the mother's soul put into Ruth at that moment. Sally was quelled into silence by the gentle composure, the self-command over her passionate sorrow, which gave to Ruth an unconscious grandeur of demeanour as she came up to the old servant.

"Give him back to me, please. I did not know it brought ill-luck, or if my heart broke I would not have let a tear drop on his face—I never will again. Thank you, Sally," as the servant relinquished him to her who came in the name of a mother. Sally watched Ruth's grave, sweet smile, as she followed up Sally's play with the tassel, and imitated, with all the docility inspired by love, every movement and sound which had amused her babe.

"Thou'lt be a mother, after all," said Sally, with a kind of admiration of the control which Ruth was exercising over herself. "But why talk of thy heart breaking? I don't question thee about what's past and gone; but now thou'rt wanting for nothing, nor thy child either; the time to come is the Lord's, and in His hands; and yet thou goest about a-sighing and a-moaning in a way that I can't stand or thole."

"What do I do wrong?" said Ruth; "I try to do all I can."

"Yes, in a way," said Sally, puzzled to know how to describe her meaning. "Thou dost it—but there's a right and a wrong way of setting about everything—and to my thinking, the right way is to take a thing up heartily, if it is only making a bed. Why! dear ah me, making a bed may be done after a Christian fashion, I take it, or else what's to come of such as me in heaven, who've had little enough time on earth for clapping ourselves down on our knees for set prayers? When I was a girl, and wretched enough about Master Thurstan, and the crook on his back which came of the fall I gave him, I took to praying and sighing, and giving up the world; and I thought it were wicked to care for the flesh, so I made heavy puddings, and was careless about dinner and the rooms, and thought I was doing my duty, though I did call myself a miserable sinner. But one night, the old missus (Master Thurstan's mother) came in, and sat down by me, as I was a-scolding myself, without thinking of what I was saying; and, says she, 'Sally! what are you blaming yourself about, and groaning over? We hear you in the parlour every night, and it makes my heart ache.' 'Oh, ma'am,' says I, 'I'm a miserable sinner, and I'm travailing in the new birth.' 'Was that the reason,' says she, 'why the pudding was so heavy to-day?' 'Oh, ma'am, ma'am,' said I, 'if you would not think of the things of the flesh, but trouble yourself about your immortal soul.' And I sat a-shaking my head to think about her soul. 'But,' says she, in her sweet-dropping voice, 'I do try to think of my soul every hour of the day, if by that you mean trying to do the will of God, but we'll talk now about the pudding; Master Thurstan could not eat it, and I know you'll be sorry for that.' Well! I was sorry, but I didn't choose to say so, as she seemed to expect me; so says I, 'It's a pity to see children brought up to care for things of the flesh;' and then I could have bitten my tongue out, for the missus looked so grave, and I thought of my darling little lad pining for want of his food. At last, says she, 'Sally, do you think God has put us into the world just to be selfish, and do nothing but see after our own souls? or to help one another with heart and hand, as Christ did to all who wanted help?' I was silent, for, you see, she puzzled me. So she went on, 'What is that beautiful answer in your Church catechism, Sally?' I were pleased to hear a Dissenter, as I did not think would have done it, speak so knowledgeably about the catechism, and she went on: '"to do my duty in that station of life unto which it shall please God to call me;" well, your station is a servant, and it is as honourable as a king's, if you look at it right; you are to help and serve others in one way, just as a king is to help others in another. Now what way are you to help and serve, or to do your duty, in that station of life unto which it has pleased God to call you? Did it answer God's purpose, and serve Him, when the food was unfit for a child to eat, and unwholesome for any one?' Well! I would not give it up, I was so pig-headed about my soul; so says I, 'I wish folks would be content with locusts and wild honey, and leave other folks in peace to workout their salvation;' and I groaned out pretty loud to think of missus's soul. I often think since she smiled a bit at me; but she said, 'Well, Sally, to-morrow, you shall have time to work out your salvation; but as we have no locusts in England, and I don't think they'd agree with Master Thurstan if we had, I will come and make the pudding; but I shall try and do it well, not only for him to like it, but because everything may be done in a right way or a wrong; the right way is to do it as well as we can, as in God's sight; the wrong is to do it in a self-seeking spirit, which either leads us to neglect it to follow out some device of our own for our own ends, or to give up too much time and thought to it both before and after the doing.' Well! I thought of all old missus's words this morning, when I saw you making the beds. You sighed so, you could not half shake the pillows; your heart was not in your work; and yet it was the duty God had set you, I reckon; I know it's not the work parsons preach about; though I don't think they go so far off the mark when they read, 'whatsoever thy hand findeth to do, that do with all thy might.' Just try for a day to think of all the odd jobs as has to be done well and truly as in God's sight, not just slurred over anyhow, and you'll go through them twice as cheerfully, and have no thought to spare for sighing or crying."

Sally bustled off to set on the kettle for tea, and felt half ashamed, in the quiet of the kitchen, to think of the oration she had made in the parlour. But she saw with much satisfaction, that henceforward Ruth nursed her boy with a vigour and cheerfulness that were reflected back from him; and the household work was no longer performed with a languid indifference, as if life and duty were distasteful. Miss Benson had her share in this improvement, though Sally placidly took all the credit to herself. One day as she and Ruth sat together, Miss Benson spoke of the child, and thence went on to talk about her own childhood. By degrees they spoke of education, and the book-learning that forms one part of it; and the result was that Ruth determined to get up early all through the bright summer mornings, to acquire the knowledge hereafter to be given to her child. Her mind was uncultivated, her reading scant; beyond the mere mechanical arts of education she knew nothing; but she had a refined taste, and excellent sense and judgment to separate the true from the false. With these qualities, she set to work under Mr Benson's directions. She read in the early morning the books that he marked out; she trained herself with strict perseverance to do all thoroughly; she did not attempt to acquire any foreign language, although her ambition was to learn Latin, in order to teach it to her boy. Those summer mornings were happy, for she was learning neither to look backwards nor forwards, but to live faithfully and earnestly in the present. She rose while the hedge-sparrow was yet singing his *réveillé* to his mate; she dressed and opened her window, shading the soft-blowing air and the sunny eastern light from her baby. If she grew tired, she went and looked at him, and all her thoughts were holy prayers for him. Then she would gaze awhile out of the high upper window on to the moorlands, that swelled in waves one behind the other, in the grey, cool morning light. These were her occasional relaxations, and after them she returned with strength to her work.

CHAPTER XVII

Leonard's Christening

In that body of Dissenters to which Mr Benson belonged, it is not considered necessary to baptize infants as early as the ceremony can be performed; and many circumstances concurred to cause the solemn thanksgiving and dedication of the child (for so these Dissenters look upon christenings) to be deferred until it was probably somewhere about six months old. There had been many conversations in the little sitting-room between the brother and sister and their *protegée*, which had consisted more of questions betraying a thoughtful wondering kind of ignorance on the part of Ruth, and answers more suggestive than explanatory from Mr Benson; while Miss Benson kept up a kind of running commentary, always simple and often quaint, but with that intuition into the very heart of all things truly religious which is often the gift of those who seem, at first sight, to be only affectionate and sensible. When Mr Benson had explained his own views of what a christening ought to be considered, and, by calling out Ruth's latent feelings into pious earnestness, brought her into a right frame of mind, he felt that he had done what he could to make the ceremony more than a mere form, and to invest it, quiet, humble, and obscure as it must necessarily be in outward shape—mournful and anxious as much of its antecedents had rendered it—with the severe grandeur of an act done in faith and truth.

It was not far to carry the little one, for, as I said, the chapel almost adjoined the minister's house. The whole procession was to have consisted of Mr and Miss Benson, Ruth carrying her baby, and Sally, who felt herself, as a Church-of-England woman, to be condescending and kind in requesting leave to attend a baptism among "them Dissenters;" but unless she had asked permission, she would not have been desired to attend, so careful was the habit of her master and mistress that she should be allowed that freedom which they claimed for themselves. But they were glad she wished to go; they liked the feeling that all were of one household, and that the interests of one were the interests of all. It produced a consequence, however, which they did not anticipate. Sally was full of the event which her presence was to sanction, and, as it were, to redeem from the character of being utterly schismatic; she spoke about it with an air of patronage to three or four, and among them to some of the servants at Mr Bradshaw's.

Miss Benson was rather surprised to receive a call from Jemima Bradshaw, on the very morning of the day on which little Leonard was to be baptized; Miss Bradshaw was rosy and breathless with eagerness. Although the second in the family, she had been at school when her younger sisters had been christened, and she was now come, in the full warmth of a girl's fancy, to ask if she might be present at the afternoon's service. She had been struck with Mrs Denbigh's grace and beauty at the very first sight, when she had accompanied her mother to call upon the Bensons on their return from Wales; and had kept up an enthusiastic interest in the widow only a little older than herself, whose very reserve and retirement but added to her unconscious power of enchantment.

"Oh, Miss Benson! I never saw a christening; papa says I may go, if you think Mr Benson and Mrs Denbigh would not dislike it; and I will be quite quiet, and sit up behind the door, or anywhere; and that sweet little baby! I should so like to see him christened; is he to be called Leonard, did you say? After Mr Denbigh, is it?"

"No—not exactly," said Miss Benson, rather discomfited.

"Was not Mr Denbigh's name Leonard, then? Mamma thought it would be sure to be called after him, and so did I. But I may come to the christening, may I not, dear Miss Benson?"

Miss Benson gave her consent with a little inward reluctance. Both her brother and Ruth shared in this feeling, although no one expressed it; and it was presently forgotten.

Jemima stood grave and quiet in the old-fashioned vestry adjoining the chapel, as they entered with steps subdued to slowness. She thought Ruth looked so pale and awed because she was left a solitary parent; but Ruth came to the presence of God, as one who had gone astray, and doubted her own worthiness to be called His child; she came as a mother who had incurred a heavy responsibility, and who entreated His almighty aid to enable her to discharge it; full of passionate, yearning love which craved for more faith in God, to still her distrust and fear of the future that might hang over her darling. When she thought of her boy, she sickened and trembled; but when she heard of God's loving-kindness, far beyond all tender mother's love, she was hushed into peace and prayer. There she stood, her fair pale cheek resting on her baby's head, as he slumbered on her bosom; her eyes went slanting down under their half-closed white lids; but their gaze was not on the primitive cottage-like room, it was earnestly fixed on a dim mist, through which she fain would have seen the life that lay before her child; but the mist was still and dense, too thick a veil for anxious human love to penetrate. The future was hid with God.

Mr Benson stood right under the casement window that was placed high up in the room; he was almost in shade, except for one or two marked lights which fell on hair already silvery white; his voice was always low and musical when he spoke to few; it was too weak to speak so as to be heard by many without becoming harsh and strange; but now it filled the little room with a loving sound, like the stock-dove's brooding murmur over her young. He and Ruth forgot all in their earnestness of thought; and when he said "Let us pray," and the little congregation knelt down, you might have heard the baby's faint breathing, scarcely sighing out upon the stillness, so absorbed were all in the solemnity. But the prayer was long; thought followed thought, and fear crowded upon fear, and all were to be laid bare before God, and His aid and counsel asked. Before the end Sally had shuffled quietly out of the vestry into the green chapel-yard, upon which the door opened. Miss Benson was alive to this movement, and so full of curiosity as to what it might mean that she could no longer attend to her brother, and felt inclined to rush off and question Sally the moment all was ended. Miss Bradshaw hung about the babe and Ruth, and begged to be allowed to carry the child home, but Ruth pressed him to her, as if there was no safe harbour for him but in his mother's breast. Mr Benson saw her feeling, and caught Miss Bradshaw's look of disappointment.

"Come home with us," said he, "and stay to tea. You have never drank tea with us since you went to school."

"I wish I might," said Miss Bradshaw, colouring with pleasure. "But I must ask papa. May I run home and ask?"

"To be sure, my dear!"

Jemima flew off; and fortunately her father was at home; for her mother's permission would have been deemed insufficient. She received many directions about her behaviour.

"Take no sugar in your tea, Jemima. I am sure the Bensons ought not to be able to afford sugar, with their means. And do not eat much; you can have plenty at home on your return; remember Mrs Denbigh's keep must cost them a great deal."

So Jemima returned considerably sobered, and very much afraid of her hunger leading her to forget Mr Benson's poverty. Meanwhile Miss Benson and Sally, acquainted with Mr Benson's invitation to Jemima, set about making some capital tea-cakes on which they piqued themselves. They both enjoyed the offices of hospitality; and were glad to place some home-made tempting dainty before their guests.

"What made ye leave the chapel-vestry before my brother had ended?" inquired Miss Benson.

"Indeed, ma'am, I thought master had prayed so long he'd be drouthy. So I just slipped out to put on the kettle for tea."

Miss Benson was on the point of reprimanding her for thinking of anything besides the object of the prayer, when she remembered how she herself had been unable to attend after Sally's departure for wondering what had become of her; so she was silent.

It was a disappointment to Miss Benson's kind and hospitable expectation when Jemima, as hungry as a hound, confined herself to one piece of the cake which her hostess had had such pleasure in making. And Jemima wished she had not a prophetic feeling all tea-time of the manner in which her father would inquire into the particulars of the meal, elevating his eyebrows at every viand named beyond plain bread-and-butter, and winding up with some such sentence as this: "Well, I marvel how, with Benson's salary, he can afford to keep such a table." Sally could have told of self-denial when no one was by, when the left hand did not know what the right hand did, on the part of both her master and mistress, practised without thinking even to themselves that it was either a sacrifice or a virtue, in order to enable them to help those who were in need, or even to gratify Miss Benson's kind, old-fashioned feelings on such occasions as the present, when a stranger came to the house. Her homely, affectionate pleasure in making others comfortable, might have shown that such little occasional extravagances were not waste, but a good work; and were not to be gauged by the standard of money-spending. This evening her spirits were damped by Jemima's refusal to eat. Poor Jemima! the cakes were so good, and she was so hungry; but still she refused.

While Sally was clearing away the tea-things, Miss Benson and Jemima accompanied Ruth upstairs, when she went to put little Leonard to bed.

"A christening is a very solemn service," said Miss Bradshaw; "I had no idea it was so solemn. Mr Benson seemed to speak as if he had a weight of care on his heart that God alone could relieve or lighten."

"My brother feels these things very much," said Miss Benson, rather wishing to cut short the conversation, for she had been aware of several parts in the prayer which she knew were suggested by the peculiarity and sadness of the case before him.

"I could not quite follow him all through," continued Jemima; "what did he mean by saying, 'This child, rebuked by the world and bidden to stand apart, Thou wilt not rebuke, but wilt suffer it to come to Thee and be blessed with Thine almighty blessing'? Why is this little darling to be rebuked? I do not think I remember the exact words, but he said something like that."

"My dear! your gown is dripping wet! it must have dipped into the tub; let me wring it out."

"Oh, thank you! Never mind my gown!" said Jemima, hastily, and wanting to return to her question; but just then she caught the sight of tears falling fast down the cheeks of the silent Ruth as she bent over her child, crowing and splashing away in his tub. With a sudden consciousness that unwittingly she had touched on some painful chord, Jemima rushed into another subject, and was eagerly seconded by Miss Benson. The circumstance seemed to die away, and leave no trace; but in after-years it rose, vivid and significant, before Jemima's memory. At present it was enough for her, if Mrs Denbigh would let her serve her in every possible way. Her admiration for beauty was keen, and little indulged at home; and Ruth was very beautiful in her quiet mournfulness; her mean and homely dress left herself only the more open to admiration, for she gave it a charm by her unconscious wearing of it that made it seem like the drapery of an old Greek statue— subordinate to the figure it covered, yet imbued by it with an unspeakable grace. Then the pretended circumstances of her life were such as to catch the imagination of a young romantic girl. Altogether, Jemima could have kissed her hand and professed herself Ruth's slave. She moved away all the articles used at this little *coucher*; she folded up Leonard's day-clothes; she felt only too much honoured when Ruth trusted him to her for a few minutes—only too amply rewarded when Ruth thanked her with a grave, sweet smile, and a grateful look of her loving eyes.

When Jemima had gone away with the servant who was sent to fetch her, there was a little chorus of praise.

"She's a warm-hearted girl," said Miss Benson. "She remembers all the old days before she went to school. She is worth two of Mr Richard. They're each of them just the same as they were when they were children, when they broke that window in the chapel, and he ran away home, and she came knocking at our door, with a single knock, just like a beggar's, and I went to see who it was, and was quite startled to see her round, brown, honest face looking up at me, half-frightened, and telling me what she had done, and offering me the money in her savings bank to pay for it. We never should have heard of Master Richard's share in the business if it had not been for Sally."

"But remember," said Mr Benson, "how strict Mr Bradshaw has always been with his children. It is no wonder if poor Richard was a coward in those days."

"He is now, or I'm much mistaken," answered Miss Benson. "And Mr Bradshaw was just as strict with Jemima, and she's no coward. But I've no faith in Richard. He has a look about him that I don't like. And when Mr Bradshaw was away on business in Holland last year, for those months my young gentleman did not come half as regularly to chapel, and I always believe that story of his being seen out with the hounds at Smithiles."

"Those are neither of them great offences in a young man of twenty," said Mr Benson, smiling.

"No! I don't mind them in themselves; but when he could change back so easily to being regular and mim when his father came home, I don't like that."

"Leonard shall never be afraid of me," said Ruth, following her own train of thought. "I will be his friend from the very first; and I will try and learn how to be a wise friend, and you will teach me, won't you, sir?"

"What made you wish to call him Leonard, Ruth?" asked Miss Benson.

"It was my mother's father's name; and she used to tell me about him and his goodness, and I thought if Leonard could be likehim—"

"Do you remember the discussion there was about Miss Bradshaw's name, Thurstan? Her father wanting her to be called Hepzibah, but insisting that she was to have a Scripture name at any rate; and Mrs Bradshaw wanting her to be Juliana, after some novel she had read not long before; and at last Jemima was fixed upon, because it would do either for a Scripture name or a name for a heroine out of a book."

"I did not know Jemima was a Scripture name," said Ruth.

"Oh yes, it is. One of Job's daughters; Jemima, Kezia, and Keren-Happuch. There are a good many Jemimas in the world, and some Kezias, but I never heard of a Keren-Happuch; and yet we know just as much of one as of another. People really like a pretty name, whether in Scripture or out of it."

"When there is no particular association with the name," said Mr Benson.

"Now, I was called Faith after the cardinal virtue; and I like my name, though many people would think it too Puritan; that was according to our gentle mother's pious desire. And Thurstan was called by his name because my father wished it; for, although he was what people called a radical and a democrat in his ways of talking and thinking, he was very proud in his heart of being descended from some old Sir Thurstan, who figured away in the French wars."

"The difference between theory and practice, thinking and being," put in Mr Benson, who was in a mood for allowing himself a little social enjoyment. He leant back in his chair, with his eyes looking at, but not seeing the ceiling. Miss Benson was clicking away with her eternal knitting-needles, looking at her brother, and seeing him, too. Ruth was arranging her child's clothes against the morrow. It was but their usual way of spending an evening; the variety was given by the different tone which the conversation assumed on the different nights. Yet, somehow, the peacefulness of the time, the window open into the little garden, the scents that came stealing in, and the clear summer heaven above, made the time be remembered as a happy festival by Ruth. Even Sally seemed more placid than usual when she came in to prayers; and she and Miss Benson followed Ruth to her bedroom, to look at the beautiful sleeping Leonard.

"God bless him!" said Miss Benson, stooping down to kiss his little dimpled hand, which lay outside the coverlet, tossed abroad in the heat of the evening.

"Now, don't get up too early, Ruth! Injuring your health will be short-sighted wisdom and poor economy. Good night!"

"Good night, dear Miss Benson. Good night, Sally." When Ruth had shut her door, she went again to the bed, and looked at her boy till her eyes filled with tears.

"God bless thee, darling! I only ask to be one of His instruments, and not thrown aside as useless—or worse than useless."

So ended the day of Leonard's christening.

Mr Benson had sometimes taught the children of different people as an especial favour, when requested by them. But then his pupils were only children, and by their progress he was little prepared for Ruth's. She had had early teaching, of that kind which need never be unlearnt, from her mother; enough to unfold many of her powers; they had remained inactive now for several years, but had grown strong in the dark and quiet time. Her tutor was surprised at the bounds by which she surmounted obstacles, the quick perception and ready adaptation of truths and first principles, and her immediate sense of the fitness of things. Her delight in what was strong and beautiful called out her master's sympathy; but, most of all, he admired the complete unconsciousness of uncommon power, or unusual progress. It was less of a wonder than he considered it to be, it is true, for she never thought of comparing what she was now with her former self, much less with another. Indeed, she did not think of herself at all, but of her boy, and what she must learn in order to teach him to be and to do as suited her hope and her prayer. If any one's devotion could have flattered her into self-consciousness, it was Jemima's. Mr Bradshaw never dreamed that his daughter could feel herself inferior to the minister's *protegée*, but so it was; and no knight-errant of old could consider himself more honoured by his ladye's commands than did Jemima, if Ruth allowed her to do anything for her or for her boy. Ruth loved her heartily, even while she was rather annoyed at the open expressions Jemima used of admiration.

"Please, I really would rather not be told if people do think me pretty."

"But it was not merely beautiful; it was sweet-looking and good, Mrs Postlethwaite called you," replied Jemima.

"All the more I would rather not hear it. I may be pretty, but I know I am not good. Besides, I don't think we ought to hear what is said of us behind our backs."

Ruth spoke so gravely, that Jemima feared lest she was displeased.

"Dear Mrs Denbigh, I never will admire or praise you again. Only let me love you."

"And let me love you!" said Ruth, with a tender kiss.

Jemima would not have been allowed to come so frequently if Mr Bradshaw had not been possessed with the idea of patronising Ruth. If the latter had chosen, she might have gone dressed from head to foot in the presents which he wished to make her, but she refused them constantly; occasionally to Miss Benson's great annoyance. But if he could not load her with gifts, he could show his approbation by asking her to his house; and after some deliberation, she consented to accompany Mr and Miss Benson there. The house was square and massy-looking, with a great deal of drab-colour about the furniture. Mrs Bradshaw, in her lackadaisical, sweet-tempered way, seconded her husband in his desire of being kind to Ruth; and as she cherished privately a great taste for what was beautiful or interesting, as opposed to her husband's love of the purely useful, this taste of hers had rarely had so healthy and true a mode of gratification as when she watched Ruth's movements about the room, which seemed in its unobtrusiveness and poverty of colour to receive the requisite ornament of light and splendour from Ruth's presence. Mrs Bradshaw sighed, and wished she had a daughter as lovely, about whom to weave a romance; for castle-building, after the manner of the Minerva press, was the outlet by which she escaped from the pressure of her prosaic life, as Mr Bradshaw's wife. Her perception was only of external beauty, and she was not always alive to that, or she might have seen how a warm, affectionate, ardent nature, free from all envy or carking care of self, gave an unspeakable charm to her plain, bright-faced daughter Jemima, whose dark eyes kept challenging admiration for her friend. The first evening spent at Mr Bradshaw's passed like many succeeding visits there. There was tea, the equipage for which was as handsome and as ugly as money could purchase. Then the ladies produced their sewing, while Mr Bradshaw stood before the fire, and gave the assembled party the benefit of his opinions on many subjects. The opinions were as good and excellent as the opinions of any man can be who sees one side of a case very strongly, and almost ignores the other. They coincided in many points with those held by Mr Benson, but he once or twice interposed with a plea for those who might differ; and then he was heard by Mr Bradshaw with a kind of evident and indulgent pity, such as one feels for a child who unwittingly talks nonsense. By-and-by, Mrs Bradshaw and Miss Benson fell into one *tête à tête*, and Ruth and Jemima into another. Two well-behaved but unnaturally quiet children were sent to bed early in the evening, in an authoritative voice, by their father, because one of them had spoken too loud while he was enlarging on an alteration in the tariff. Just before the supper-tray was brought in, a gentleman was announced whom Ruth had never previously seen, but who appeared well known to the rest of the party. It was Mr Farquhar, Mr Bradshaw's partner; he had been on the Continent for the last year, and had only recently returned. He seemed perfectly at home, but spoke little. He leaned back in his chair, screwed up his eyes, and watched everybody; yet there was nothing unpleasant or impertinent in his keenness of observation. Ruth wondered to hear him contradict Mr Bradshaw, and almost expected some rebuff; but Mr Bradshaw, if he did not yield the point, admitted, for the first time that evening, that it was possible something might be said on the other side. Mr Farquhar differed also from Mr Benson, but it was in a more respectful manner than Mr Bradshaw had done. For these reasons, although Mr Farquhar had never spoken to Ruth, she came away with the impression that he was a man to be respected, and perhaps liked.

Sally would have thought herself mightily aggrieved if, on their return, she had not heard some account of the evening. As soon as Miss Benson came in, the old servant began:

"Well, and who was there? and what did they give you for supper?"

"Only Mr Farquhar besides ourselves; and sandwiches, sponge-cake, and wine; there was no occasion for anything more," replied Miss Benson, who was tired and preparing to go upstairs.

"Mr Farquhar! Why they do say he's thinking of Miss Jemima!"

"Nonsense, Sally! why he's old enough to be her father!" said Miss Benson, half way up the first flight.

"There's no need for it to be called nonsense, though he may be ten year older," muttered Sally, retreating towards the kitchen. "Bradshaw's Betsy knows what she's about, and wouldn't have said it for nothing."

Ruth wondered a little about it. She loved Jemima well enough to be interested in what related to her; but, after thinking for a few minutes, she decided that such a marriage was, and would ever be, very unlikely.

CHAPTER XVIII

Ruth Becomes a Governess in Mr Bradshaw's Family

One afternoon, not long after this, Mr and Miss Benson set off to call upon a farmer, who attended the chapel, but lived at some distance from the town. They intended to stay to tea if they were invited, and Ruth and Sally were left to spend a long afternoon together. At first, Sally was busy in her kitchen, and Ruth employed herself in carrying her baby out into the garden. It was now nearly a year since she came to the Bensons'; it seemed like yesterday, and yet as if a lifetime had gone between. The flowers were budding now, that were all in bloom when she came down, on the first autumnal morning, into the sunny parlour. The yellow jessamine, that was then a tender plant, had now taken firm root in the soil, and was sending out strong shoots; the wall-flowers, which Miss Benson had sown on the wall a day or two after her arrival, were scenting the air with their fragrant flowers. Ruth knew every plant now; it seemed as though she had always lived here, and always known the inhabitants of the house. She heard Sally singing her accustomed song in the kitchen, a song she never varied over her afternoon's work. It began,

As I was going to Derby, sir,
Upon a market-day.

And if music is a necessary element in a song, perhaps I had better call it by some other name.

But the strange change was in Ruth herself. She was conscious of it though she could not define it, and did not dwell upon it. Life had become significant and full of duty to her. She delighted in the exercise of her intellectual powers, and liked the idea of the infinite amount of which she was ignorant; for it was a grand pleasure to learn—to crave, and be satisfied. She strove to forget what had gone before this last twelve months. She shuddered up from contemplating it; it was like a bad, unholy dream. And yet, there was a strange yearning kind of love for the father of the child whom she pressed to her heart, which came, and she could not bid it begone as sinful, it was so pure and natural, even when thinking of it, as in the sight of God. Little Leonard cooed to the flowers, and stretched after their bright colours; and Ruth laid him on the dry turf, and pelted him with the gay petals. He chinked and crowed with laughing delight, and clutched at her cap, and pulled it off. Her short rich curls were golden-brown in the slanting sunlight, and by their very shortness made her look more child-like. She hardly seemed as if she could be the mother of the noble babe over whom she knelt, now snatching kisses, now matching his cheek with rose-leaves. All at once, the bells of the old church struck the hour; and far away, high up in the air, began slowly to play the old tune of "Life let us cherish;" they had played it for years—for the life of man—and it always sounded fresh and strange and aërial. Ruth was still in a moment, she knew not why; and the tears came into her eyes as she listened. When it was ended, she kissed her baby, and bade God bless him.

Just then Sally came out, dressed for the evening, with a leisurely look about her. She had done her work, and she and Ruth were to drink tea together in the exquisitely clean kitchen; but while the kettle was boiling, she came out to enjoy the flowers. She gathered a piece of southern-wood, and stuffed it up her nose, by way of smelling it.

"Whatten you call this in your country?" asked she.

"Old-man," replied Ruth.

"We call it here lad's-love. It and peppermint-drops always remind me of going to church in the country. Here! I'll get you a black-currant leaf to put in the teapot. It gives it a flavour. We had bees once against this wall; but when missus died, we forgot to tell 'em, and put 'em in mourning, and, in course, they swarmed away without our knowing, and the next winter came a hard frost, and they died. Now, I dare say, the water will be boiling; and it's time for little master there to come in, for the dew is falling. See, all the daisies is shutting themselves up."

Sally was most gracious as a hostess. She quite put on her company manners to receive Ruth in the kitchen. They laid Leonard to sleep on the sofa in the parlour, that they might hear him the more easily, and then they sat quietly down to their sewing by the bright kitchen fire. Sally was, as usual, the talker; and, as usual, the subject was the family of whom for so many years she had formed a part.

"Aye! things was different when I was a girl," quoth she. "Eggs was thirty for a shilling, and butter only sixpence a pound. My wage when I came here was but three pound, and I did on it, and was always clean and tidy, which is more than many a lass can say now who gets her seven and eight pound a year; and tea was kept for an afternoon drink, and pudding was eaten afore meat in them days, and the upshot was, people paid their debts better; aye, aye! we'n gone backwards, and we thinken we'n gone forrards."

After shaking her head a little over the degeneracy of the times, Sally returned to a part of the subject on which she thought she had given Ruth a wrong idea.

"You'll not go for to think now that I've not more than three pound a year. I've a deal above that now. First of all, old missus gave me four pound, for she said I were worth it, and I thought in my heart that I were; so I took it without more ado; but after her death, Master Thurstan and Miss Faith took a fit of spending, and says they to me, one day as I carried tea in, 'Sally, we think your wages ought to be raised.' 'What matter what you think!' said I, pretty sharp, for I thought they'd ha' shown more respect to missus if they'd let things stand as they were in her time; and they'd gone and moved the sofa away from the wall to where it stands now, already that very day. So I speaks up sharp, and, says I, 'As long as I'm content, I think it's no business of yours to be meddling wi' me and my money matters.' 'But,' says Miss Faith (she's always the one to speak first if you'll notice, though it's master that comes in and clinches the matter with some reason she'd never ha' thought of—he were always a sensible lad), 'Sally, all the servants in the town have six pound and better, and you have as hard a place as any of 'em.' 'Did you ever hear me grumble about my work that you talk about it in that way? wait till I grumble,' says I, 'but don't meddle wi' me till then.' So I flung off in a huff; but in the course of the evening, Master Thurstan came in and sat down in the kitchen, and he's such winning ways he wiles one over to anything; and besides, a notion had come into my head—now, you'll not tell," said she, glancing round the room, and hitching her chair nearer to Ruth in a confidential manner; Ruth promised, and Sally went on:

"I thought I should like to be an heiress wi' money, and leave it all to Master and Miss Faith; and I thought if I'd six pound a year I could, maybe, get to be an heiress; all I was feared on was that some chap or other might marry me for my money, but I've managed to keep the fellows off; so I looks mim and grateful, and I thanks Master Thurstan for his offer, and I takes the wages; and what do you think I've done?" asked Sally, with an exultant air.

"What have you done?" asked Ruth.

"Why," replied Sally, slowly and emphatically, "I've saved thirty pound! but that's not it. I've getten a lawyer to make me a will; that's it, wench!" said she, slapping Ruth on the back.

"How did you manage it?" asked Ruth.

"Aye, that was it," said Sally; "I thowt about it many a night before I hit on the right way. I was afeard the money might be thrown into Chancery, if I didn't make it all safe, and yet I could na' ask Master Thurstan. At last and at length, John Jackson, the grocer, had a nephew come to stay a week with him, as was 'prentice to a lawyer in Liverpool; so now was my time, and here was my lawyer. Wait a minute! I could tell you my story better if I had my will in my hand; and I'll scomfish you if ever you go for to tell."

She held up her hand, and threatened Ruth as she left the kitchen to fetch the will.

When she came back, she brought a parcel tied up in a blue pocket-handkerchief; she sat down, squared her knees, untied the handkerchief, and displayed a small piece of parchment.

"Now, do you know what this is?" said she, holding it up. "It's parchment, and it's the right stuff to make wills on. People gets into Chancery if they don't make them o' this stuff, and I reckon Tom Jackson thowt he'd have a fresh job on it if he could get it into Chancery; for the rascal went and wrote it on a piece of paper at first, and came and read it me out loud off a piece of paper no better than what one writes letters upon. I were up to him; and, thinks I, Come, come, my lad, I'm not a fool, though you may think so; I know a paper will won't stand, but I'll let you run your rig. So I sits and I listens. And would you belie' me, he read it out as if it were as clear a business as your giving me that thimble—no more ado, though it were thirty pound! I could understand it mysel'—that were no law for me. I wanted summat to consider about, and for th' meaning to be wrapped up as I wrap up my best gown. So says I, 'Tom! it's not on parchment. I mun have it on parchment.' 'This 'ill do as well,' says he. 'We'll get it witnessed, and it will stand good.' Well! I liked the notion of having it witnessed, and for a while that soothed me; but after a bit, I felt I should like it done according to law, and not plain out as anybody might ha' done it; I mysel', if I could have written. So says I, 'Tom! I mun have it on parchment.' 'Parchment costs money,' says he, very grave. 'Oh, oh, my lad! are ye there?' thinks I. 'That's the reason I'm clipped of law.' So says I, 'Tom! I mun have it on parchment. I'll pay the money and welcome. It's thirty pound, and what I can lay to it. I'll make it safe. It shall be on parchment, and I'll tell thee what, lad! I'll gie ye sixpence for every good law-word you put in it, sounding like, and not to be caught up as a person runs. Your master had need to be ashamed of you as a 'prentice if you can't do a thing more tradesman-like than this!' Well! he laughed above a bit, but I were firm, and stood to it. So he made it out on parchment. Now, woman, try and read it!" said she, giving it to Ruth.

Ruth smiled, and began to read; Sally listening with rapt attention. When Ruth came to the word "testatrix," Sally stopped her.

"That was the first sixpence," said she. "I thowt he was going to fob me off again wi' plain language; but when that word came, I out wi' my sixpence, and gave it to him on the spot. Now go on."

Presently Ruth read, "accruing."

"That was the second sixpence. Four sixpences it were in all, besides six-and-eightpence as we bargained at first, and three-and-fourpence parchment. There! that's what I call a will; witnessed according to law, and all. Master Thurstan will be prettily taken in when I die, and he finds all his extra wage left back to him. But it will teach him it's not so easy as he thinks for, to make a woman give up her way."

The time was now drawing near when little Leonard might be weaned—the time appointed by all three for Ruth to endeavour to support herself in some way more or less independent of Mr and Miss Benson. This prospect dwelt much in all of their minds, and was in each shaded with some degree of perplexity; but they none of them spoke of it for fear of accelerating the event. If they had felt clear and determined as to the best course to be pursued, they were none of them deficient in courage to commence upon that course at once. Miss Benson would, perhaps, have objected the most to any alteration in their present daily mode of life; but that was because she had the habit of speaking out her thoughts as they arose, and she particularly disliked and dreaded change. Besides this, she had felt her heart open out, and warm towards the little helpless child, in a strong and powerful manner. Nature had intended her warm instincts to find vent in a mother's duties; her heart had yearned after children, and made her restless in her childless state, without her well knowing why; but now, the delight she experienced in tending, nursing, and contriving for the little boy—even contriving to the point of sacrificing many of her cherished whims—made her happy and satisfied and peaceful. It was more difficult to sacrifice her whims than her comforts; but all had been given up when and where required by the sweet lordly baby, who reigned paramount in his very helplessness.

From some cause or other, an exchange of ministers for one Sunday was to be effected with a neighbouring congregation, and Mr Benson went on a short absence from home. When he returned on Monday, he was met at the house-door by his sister, who had evidently been looking out for him for some time. She stepped out to greet him.

"Don't hurry yourself, Thurstan! all's well; only I wanted to tell you something. Don't fidget yourself—baby is quite well, bless him! It's only good news. Come into your room, and let me talk a little quietly with you."

She drew him into his study, which was near the outer door, and then she took off his coat, and put his carpet-bag in a corner, and wheeled a chair to the fire, before she would begin.

"Well, now! to think how often things fall out just as we want them, Thurstan! Have not you often wondered what was to be done with Ruth when the time came at which we promised her she should earn her living? I am sure you have, because I have so often thought about it myself. And yet I never dared to speak out my fear, because that seemed giving it a shape.

And now Mr Bradshaw has put all to rights. He invited Mr Jackson to dinner yesterday, just as we were going into chapel; and then he turned to me and asked me if I would come to tea—straight from afternoon chapel, because Mrs Bradshaw wanted to speak to me. He made it very clear I was not to bring Ruth; and, indeed, she was only too happy to stay at home with baby. And so I went; and Mrs Bradshaw took me into her bedroom, and shut the doors, and said Mr Bradshaw had told her, that he did not like Jemima being so much confined with the younger ones while they were at their lessons, and that he wanted some one above a nursemaid to sit with them while their masters were there—some one who would see about their learning their lessons, and who would walk out with them; a sort of nursery governess, I think she meant, though she did not say so; and Mr Bradshaw (for, of course, I saw his thoughts and words constantly peeping out, though he had told her to speak to me) believed that our Ruth would be the very person. Now, Thurstan, don't look so surprised, as if she had never come into your head! I am sure I saw what Mrs Bradshaw was driving at, long before she came to the point; and I could scarcely keep from smiling, and saying, 'We'd jump at the proposal'—long before I ought to have known anything about it."

"Oh, I wonder what we ought to do!" said Mr Benson. "Or rather, I believe I see what we ought to do, if I durst but do it."

"Why, what ought we to do?" asked his sister, in surprise.

"I ought to go and tell Mr Bradshaw the whole story—"

"And get Ruth turned out of our house," said Miss Benson, indignantly.

"They can't make us do that," said her brother. "I do not think they would try."

"Yes, Mr Bradshaw would try; and he would blazon out poor Ruth's sin, and there would not be a chance for her left. I know him well, Thurstan; and why should he be told now, more than a year ago?"

"A year ago he did not want to put her in a situation of trust about his children."

"And you think she'll abuse that trust, do you? You've lived a twelvemonth in the house with Ruth, and the end of it is, you think she will do his children harm! Besides, who encouraged Jemima to come to the house so much to see Ruth? Did you not say it would do them both good to see something of each other?"

Mr Benson sat thinking.

"If you had not known Ruth as well as you do—if during her stay with us you had marked anything wrong, or forward, or deceitful, or immodest, I would say at once, 'Don't allow Mr Bradshaw to take her into his house;' but still I would say, 'Don't tell of her sin and her sorrow to so severe a man—so unpitiful a judge.' But here I ask you, Thurstan, can you, or I, or Sally (quick-eyed as she is), say, that in any one thing we have had true, just occasion to find fault with Ruth? I don't mean that she is perfect—she acts without thinking, her temper is sometimes warm and hasty; but have we any right to go and injure her prospects for life, by telling Mr Bradshaw all we know of her errors—only sixteen when she did so wrong, and never to escape from it all her many years to come—to have the despair which would arise from its being known, clutching her back into worse sin? What harm do you think she can do? What is the risk to which you think you are exposing Mr Bradshaw's children?" She paused, out of breath, her eyes glittering with tears of indignation, and impatient for an answer, that she might knock it to pieces.

"I do not see any danger that can arise," said he at length, and with slow difficulty, as if not fully convinced. "I have watched Ruth, and I believe she is pure and truthful; and the very sorrow and penitence she has felt—the very suffering she has gone through—has given her a thoughtful conscientiousness beyond her age."

"That and the care of her baby," said Miss Benson, secretly delighted at the tone of her brother's thoughts.

"Ah, Faith! that baby you so much dreaded once, is turning out a blessing, you see," said Thurstan, with a faint, quiet smile.

"Yes! any one might be thankful, and better too, for Leonard; but how could I tell that it would be like him?"

"But to return to Ruth and Mr Bradshaw. What did you say?"

"Oh! with my feelings, of course, I was only too glad to accept the proposal, and so I told Mrs Bradshaw then; and I afterwards repeated it to Mr Bradshaw, when he asked me if his wife had mentioned their plans. They would understand that I must consult you and Ruth, before it could be considered as finally settled."

"And have you named it to her?"

"Yes," answered Miss Benson, half afraid lest he should think she had been too precipitate.

"And what did she say?" asked he, after a little pause of grave silence.

"At first she seemed very glad, and fell into my mood of planning how it should all be managed; how Sally and I should take care of the baby the hours that she was away at Mr Bradshaw's; but by-and-by she became silent and thoughtful, and knelt down by me and hid her face in my lap, and shook a little as if she was crying; and then I heard her speak in a very low smothered voice, for her head was still bent down—quite hanging down, indeed, so that I could not see her face, so I stooped to listen, and I heard her say, 'Do you think I should be good enough to teach little girls, Miss Benson?' She said it so humbly and fearfully that all I thought of was how to cheer her, and I answered and asked her if she did not hope to be good enough to bring up her own darling to be a brave Christian man? And she lifted up her head, and I saw her eyes looking wild and wet and earnest, and she said, 'With God's help, that will I try to make my child.' And I said then, 'Ruth, as you strive and as you pray for your own child, so you must strive and pray to make Mary and Elizabeth good, if you are trusted with them.' And she said out quite clear, though her face was hidden from me once more, 'I will strive, and I will pray.' You would not have had any fears, Thurstan, if you could have heard and seen her last night."

"I have no fear," said he, decidedly. "Let the plan go on." After a minute, he added, "But I am glad it was so far arranged before I heard of it. My indecision about right and wrong—my perplexity as to how far we are to calculate consequences—grows upon me, I fear."

"You look tired and weary, dear. You should blame your body rather than your conscience at these times."

"A very dangerous doctrine."

The scroll of Fate was closed, and they could not foresee the Future; and yet, if they could have seen it, though they might have shrunk fearfully at first, they would have smiled and thanked God when all was done and said.

CHAPTER XIX

After Five Years

The quiet days grew into weeks and months, and even years, without any event to startle the little circle into the consciousness of the lapse of time. One who had known them at the date of Ruth's becoming a governess in Mr Bradshaw's family, and had been absent until the time of which I am now going to tell you, would have noted some changes which had imperceptibly come over all; but he, too, would have thought, that the life which had brought so little of turmoil and vicissitude must have been calm and tranquil, and in accordance with the bygone activity of the town in which their existence passed away.

The alterations that he would have perceived were those caused by the natural progress of time. The Benson home was brightened into vividness by the presence of the little Leonard, now a noble boy of six, large and grand in limb and stature, and with a face of marked beauty and intelligence. Indeed, he might have been considered by many as too intelligent for his years; and often the living with old and thoughtful people gave him, beyond most children, the appearance of pondering over the mysteries which meet the young on the threshold of life, but which fade away as advancing years bring us more into contact with the practical and tangible—fade away and vanish, until it seems to require the agitation of some great storm of the soul before we can again realise spiritual things.

But, at times, Leonard seemed oppressed and bewildered, after listening intent, with grave and wondering eyes, to the conversation around him; at others, the bright animal life shone forth radiant, and no three-months' kitten—no foal, suddenly tossing up its heels by the side of its sedate dam, and careering around the pasture in pure mad enjoyment—no young creature of any kind, could show more merriment and gladness of heart.

"For ever in mischief," was Sally's account of him at such times; but it was not intentional mischief; and Sally herself would have been the first to scold any one else who had used the same words in reference to her darling. Indeed, she was once nearly giving warning, because she thought the boy was being ill-used. The occasion was this: Leonard had for some time shown a strange, odd disregard of truth; he invented stories, and told them with so grave a face, that unless there was some internal evidence of their incorrectness (such as describing a cow with a bonnet on), he was generally believed, and his statements, which were given with the full appearance of relating a real occurrence, had once or twice led to awkward results. All the three, whose hearts were pained by this apparent unconsciousness of the difference between truth and falsehood, were unaccustomed to children, or they would have recognised this as a stage through which most infants, who have lively imaginations, pass; and, accordingly, there was a consultation in Mr Benson's study one morning. Ruth was there, quiet, very pale, and with compressed lips, sick at heart as she heard Miss Benson's arguments for the necessity of whipping, in order to cure Leonard of his story-telling. Mr Benson looked unhappy and uncomfortable. Education was but a series of experiments to them all, and they all had a secret dread of spoiling the noble boy, who was the darling of their hearts. And, perhaps, this very intensity of love begot an impatient, unnecessary anxiety, and made them resolve on sterner measures than the parent of a large family (where love was more spread abroad) would have dared to use. At any rate, the vote for whipping carried the day; and even Ruth, trembling and cold, agreed that it must be done; only she asked, in a meek, sad voice, if she need be present (Mr Benson was to be the executioner—the scene, the study); and being instantly told that she had better not, she went slowly and languidly up to her room, and kneeling down, she closed her ears, and prayed.

Miss Benson, having carried her point, was very sorry for the child, and would have begged him off; but Mr Benson had listened more to her arguments than now to her pleadings, and only answered, "If it is right, it shall be done!" He went into the garden, and deliberately, almost as if he wished to gain time, chose and cut off a little switch from the laburnum-tree. Then he returned through the kitchen, and gravely taking the awed and wondering little fellow by the hand, he led him silently into the study, and placing him before him, began an admonition on the importance of truthfulness, meaning to conclude with what he believed to be the moral of all punishment: "As you cannot remember this of yourself, I must give you a little pain to make you remember it. I am very sorry it is necessary, and that you cannot recollect without my doing so."

But before he had reached this very proper and desirable conclusion, and while he was yet working his way, his heart aching with the terrified look of the child at the solemnly sad face and words of upbraiding, Sally burst in:

"And what may ye be going to do with that fine switch I saw ye gathering, Master Thurstan?" asked she, her eyes gleaming with anger at the answer she knew must come, if answer she had at all.

"Go away, Sally," said Mr Benson, annoyed at the fresh difficulty in his path.

"I'll not stir never a step till you give me that switch, as you've got for some mischief, I'll be bound."

"Sally! remember where it is said, 'He that spareth the rod, spoileth the child,'" said Mr Benson, austerely.

"Aye, I remember; and I remember a bit more than you want me to remember, I reckon. It were King Solomon as spoke them words, and it were King Solomon's son that were King Rehoboam, and no great shakes either. I can remember what is said on him, 2 Chronicles, xii. chapter, 14th verse: 'And he,' that's King Rehoboam, the lad that tasted the rod, 'did evil, because he prepared not his heart to seek the Lord.' I've not been reading my chapters every night for fifty year to be caught napping by a Dissenter, neither!" said she, triumphantly. "Come along, Leonard." She stretched out her hand to the child, thinking that she had conquered.

But Leonard did not stir. He looked wistfully at Mr Benson. "Come!" said she, impatiently. The boy's mouth quivered.

"If you want to whip me, uncle, you may do it. I don't much mind."

Put in this form, it was impossible to carry out his intentions; and so Mr Benson told the lad he might go—that he would speak to him another time. Leonard went away, more subdued in spirit than if he had been whipped. Sally lingered a moment. She stopped to add: "I think it's for them without sin to throw stones at a poor child, and cut up good laburnum-branches to whip him. I only do as my betters do, when I call Leonard's mother Mrs Denbigh." The moment she had said this she was sorry; it was an ungenerous advantage after the enemy had acknowledged himself defeated. Mr Benson dropped his head upon his hands, and hid his face, and sighed deeply.

Leonard flew in search of his mother, as in search of a refuge. If he had found her calm, he would have burst into a passion of crying after his agitation; as it was, he came upon her kneeling and sobbing, and he stood quite still. Then he threw his arms round her neck, and said: "Mamma! mamma! I will be good—I make a promise; I will speak true—I make a promise." And he kept his word.

Miss Benson piqued herself upon being less carried away by her love for this child than any one else in the house; she talked severely, and had capital theories; but her severity ended in talk, and her theories would not work. However, she read several books on education, knitting socks for Leonard all the while; and, upon the whole, I think, the hands were more usefully employed than the head, and the good honest heart better than either. She looked older than when we first knew her, but it was a ripe, kindly age that was coming over her. Her excellent practical sense, perhaps, made her a more masculine character than her brother. He was often so much perplexed by the problems of life, that he let the time for action go by; but she kept him in check by her clear, pithy talk, which brought back his wandering thoughts to the duty that lay straight before him, waiting for action; and then he remembered that it was the faithful part to "wait patiently upon God," and leave the ends in His hands, who alone knows why Evil exists in this world, and why it ever hovers on either side of Good. In this respect, Miss Benson had more faith than her brother—or so it seemed; for quick, resolute action in the next step of Life was all she required, while he deliberated and trembled, and often did wrong from his very deliberation, when his first instinct would have led him right.

But although decided and prompt as ever, Miss Benson was grown older since the summer afternoon when she dismounted from the coach at the foot of the long Welsh hill that led to Llan-dhu, where her brother awaited her to consult her about Ruth. Though her eye was as bright and straight-looking as ever, quick and brave in its glances, her hair had become almost snowy white; and it was on this point she consulted Sally, soon after the date of Leonard's last untruth. The two were arranging Miss Benson's room one morning, when, after dusting the looking-glass, she suddenly stopped in her operation, and after a close inspection of herself, startled Sally by this speech:

"Sally! I'm looking a great deal older than I used to do!"

Sally, who was busy dilating on the increased price of flour, considered this remark of Miss Benson's as strangely irrelevant to the matter in hand, and only noticed it by a

"To be sure! I suppose we all on us do. But two-and-fourpence a dozen is too much to make us pay for it."

Miss Benson went on with her inspection of herself, and Sally with her economical projects.

"Sally!" said Miss Benson, "my hair is nearly white. The last time I looked it was only pepper-and-salt. What must I do?"

"Do—why, what would the wench do?" asked Sally, contemptuously. "Ye're never going to be taken in, at your time of life, by hair-dyes and such gimcracks, as can only take in young girls whose wisdom-teeth are not cut."

"And who are not very likely to want them," said Miss Benson, quietly. "No! but you see, Sally, it's very awkward having such grey hair, and feeling so young. Do you know, Sally, I've as great a mind for dancing, when I hear a lively tune on the street-organs, as ever; and as great a mind to sing when I'm happy—to sing in my old way, Sally, you know."

"Aye, you had it from a girl," said Sally; "and many a time, when the door's been shut, I did not know if it was you in the parlour, or a big bumble-bee in the kitchen, as was making that drumbling noise. I heard you at it yesterday."

"But an old woman with grey hair ought not to have a fancy for dancing or singing," continued Miss Benson.

"Whatten nonsense are ye talking?" said Sally, roused to indignation. "Calling yoursel' an old woman when you're better than ten years younger than me! and many a girl has grey hair at five-and-twenty."

"But I'm more than five-and-twenty, Sally. I'm fifty-seven next May!"

"More shame for ye, then, not to know better than to talk of dyeing your hair. I cannot abide such vanities!"

"Oh, dear! Sally, when will you understand what I mean? I want to know how I am to keep remembering how old I am, so as to prevent myself from feeling so young? I was quite startled just now to see my hair in the glass, for I can generally tell if my cap is straight by feeling. I'll tell you what I'll do—I'll cut off a piece of my grey hair, and plait it together for a marker in my Bible!" Miss Benson expected applause for this bright idea, but Sally only made answer:

"You'll be taking to painting your cheeks next, now you've once thought of dyeing your hair." So Miss Benson plaited her grey hair in silence and quietness, Leonard holding one end of it while she wove it, and admiring the colour and texture all the time, with a sort of implied dissatisfaction at the auburn colour of his own curls, which was only half-comforted away by Miss Benson's information, that, if he lived long enough, his hair would be like hers.

Mr Benson, who had looked old and frail while he was yet but young, was now stationary as to the date of his appearance. But there was something more of nervous restlessness in his voice and ways than formerly; that was the only change six years had brought to him. And as for Sally, she chose to forget age and the passage of years altogether, and had as much work in her, to use her own expression, as she had at sixteen; nor was her appearance very explicit as to the flight of time. Fifty, sixty, or seventy, she might be—not more than the last, not less than the first—though her usual answer to any circuitous inquiry as to her age was now (what it had been for many years past), "I'm feared I shall never see thirty again."

Then as to the house. It was not one where the sitting-rooms are refurnished every two or three years; not now, even (since Ruth came to share their living) a place where, as an article grew shabby or worn, a new one was purchased. The furniture looked poor, and the carpets almost threadbare; but there was such a dainty spirit of cleanliness abroad, such exquisite neatness of repair, and altogether so bright and cheerful a look about the rooms—everything so above-board—no shifts to conceal poverty under flimsy ornament—that many a splendid drawing-room would give less pleasure to those who could see evidences of character in inanimate things. But whatever poverty there might be in the house, there was full luxuriance in the little square wall-encircled garden, on two sides of which the parlour and kitchen looked. The laburnum-tree, which when Ruth came was like a twig stuck into the ground, was now a golden glory in spring, and a pleasant shade in summer. The wild hop, that Mr Benson had brought home from one of his country rambles, and planted by the parlour-window, while Leonard was yet a baby in his mother's arms, was now a garland over the casement, hanging down long tendrils, that waved in the breezes, and threw pleasant shadows and traceries, like some Bacchanalian carving, on the parlour-walls, at "morn or dusky eve." The yellow rose had clambered up to the window of Mr Benson's bedroom, and its blossom-laden branches were supported by a jargonelle pear-tree rich in autumnal fruit.

But, perhaps, in Ruth herself there was the greatest external change; for of the change which had gone on in her heart, and mind, and soul, or if there had been any, neither she nor any one around her was conscious; but sometimes Miss Benson did say to Sally, "How very handsome Ruth is grown!" To which Sally made ungracious answer, "Yes! she's well enough. Beauty is deceitful, and favour a snare, and I'm thankful the Lord has spared me from such man-traps and spring-guns." But even Sally could not help secretly admiring Ruth. If her early brilliancy of colour was gone, a clear ivory skin, as smooth as satin, told of complete and perfect health, and was as lovely, if not so striking in effect, as the banished lilies and roses. Her hair had grown darker and deeper, in the shadow that lingered in its masses; her eyes, even if you could have guessed that they had shed bitter tears in their day, had a thoughtful, spiritual look about them, that made you wonder at their depth, and look—and look again. The increase of dignity in her face had been imparted to her form. I do not know if she had grown taller since the birth of her child, but she looked as if she had. And although she had lived in a very humble home, yet there was something about either it or her, or the people amongst whom she had been thrown during the last few years, which had so changed her, that whereas, six or seven years ago, you would have perceived that she was not altogether a lady by birth and education, yet now she might have been placed among the highest in the land, and would have been taken by the most critical judge for their equal, although ignorant of their conventional etiquette—an ignorance which she would have acknowledged in a simple child-like way, being unconscious of any false shame.

Her whole heart was in her boy. She often feared that she loved him too much—more than God Himself—yet she could not bear to pray to have her love for her child lessened. But she would kneel down by his little bed at night—at the deep, still midnight—with the stars that kept watch over Rizpah shining down upon her, and tell God what I have now told you, that she feared she loved her child too much, yet could not, would not, love him less; and speak to Him of her one treasure as she could speak to no earthly friend. And so, unconsciously, her love for her child led her up to love to God, to the All-knowing, who read her heart.

It might be superstition—I dare say it was—but, somehow, she never lay down to rest without saying, as she looked her last on her boy, "Thy will, not mine, be done;" and even while she trembled and shrank with infinite dread from sounding the depths of what that will might be, she felt as if her treasure were more secure to waken up rosy and bright in the morning, as one over whose slumbers God's holy angels had watched, for the very words which she had turned away in sick terror from realising the night before.

Her daily absence at her duties to the Bradshaw children only ministered to her love for Leonard. Everything does minister to love when its foundation lies deep in a true heart, and it was with an exquisite pang of delight that, after a moment of vague fear,

(Oh, mercy! to myself I said,
If Lucy should be dead!),

she saw her child's bright face of welcome as he threw open the door every afternoon on her return home. For it was his silently-appointed work to listen for her knock, and rush breathless to let her in. If he were in the garden, or upstairs among the treasures of the lumber-room, either Miss Benson, or her brother, or Sally, would fetch him to his happy little task; no one so sacred as he to the allotted duty. And the joyous meeting was not deadened by custom, to either mother or child.

Ruth gave the Bradshaws the highest satisfaction, as Mr Bradshaw often said both to her and to the Bensons; indeed, she rather winced under his pompous approbation. But his favourite recreation was patronising; and when Ruth saw how quietly and meekly Mr Benson submitted to gifts and praise, when an honest word of affection, or a tacit, implied acknowledgment of equality, would have been worth everything said and done, she tried to be more meek in spirit, and to recognise the good that undoubtedly existed in Mr Bradshaw. He was richer and more prosperous than ever;—a keen, far-seeing man of business, with an undisguised contempt for all who failed in the success which he had achieved. But it was not alone those who were less fortunate in obtaining wealth than himself that he visited with severity of judgment; every moral error or delinquency came under his unsparing comment. Stained by no vice himself, either in his own eyes or in that of any human being who cared to judge him, having nicely and wisely proportioned and adapted his means to his ends, he could afford to speak and act with a severity which was almost sanctimonious in its ostentation of thankfulness as to himself. Not a misfortune or a sin was brought to light but Mr Bradshaw could trace it to its cause in some former mode of action, which he had long ago foretold would lead to shame. If another's son turned out wild or bad, Mr Bradshaw had little sympathy; it might have been prevented by a stricter rule, or more religious life at home; young Richard Bradshaw was quiet and steady, and other fathers might have had sonslike him if they had taken the same pains to enforce obedience. Richard was an only son, and yet Mr Bradshaw might venture to say, he had never had his own way in his life. Mrs Bradshaw was, he confessed (Mr Bradshaw did not dislike confessing his wife's errors), rather less firm than he should have liked with the girls; and with some people, he believed, Jemima was rather headstrong; but to his wishes she had always shown herself obedient. All children were obedient, if their parents were decided and authoritative; and every one would turn out well, if properly managed. If they did not prove good, they must take the consequences of their errors.

Mrs Bradshaw murmured faintly at her husband when his back was turned; but if his voice was heard, or his footsteps sounded in the distance, she was mute, and hurried her children into the attitude or action most pleasing to their father. Jemima, it is true, rebelled against this manner of proceeding, which savoured to her a little of deceit; but even she had not, as yet, overcome her awe of her father sufficiently to act independently of him, and according to her own sense of right—or rather, I should say, according to her own warm, passionate impulses. Before him the wilfulness which made her dark eyes blaze out at times was hushed and still; he had no idea of her self-tormenting, no notion of the almost southern jealousy which seemed to belong to her brunette complexion. Jemima was not pretty; the flatness and shortness of her face made her almost plain; yet most people looked twice at her expressive countenance, at the eyes which flamed or melted at every trifle, at the rich colour which came at every expressed emotion into her usually sallow face, at the faultless teeth which made her smile like a sunbeam. But then, again, when she thought she was not kindly treated, when a suspicion crossed her mind, or when she was angry with herself, her lips were tight-pressed together, her colour was wan and almost livid, and a stormy gloom clouded her eyes as with a film. But before her father her words were few, and he did not notice looks or tones.

Her brother Richard had been equally silent before his father in boyhood and early youth; but since he had gone to be clerk in a London house, preparatory to assuming his place as junior partner in Mr Bradshaw's business, he spoke more on his occasional visits at home. And very proper and highly moral was his conversation; set sentences of goodness, which were like the flowers that children stick in the ground, and that have not sprung upwards from roots—deep down in the hidden life and experience of the heart. He was as severe a judge as his father of other people's conduct, but you felt that Mr Bradshaw was sincere in his condemnation of all outward error and vice, and that he would try himself by the same laws as he tried others; somehow, Richard's words were frequently heard with a lurking distrust, and many shook their heads over the pattern son; but then it was those whose sons had gone astray, and been condemned, in no private or tender manner, by Mr Bradshaw, so it might be revenge in them. Still, Jemima felt that all was not right; her heart sympathised in the rebellion against his father's commands, which her brother had confessed to her in an unusual moment of confidence, but her uneasy conscience condemned the deceit which he had practised.

The brother and sister were sitting alone over a blazing Christmas fire, and Jemima held an old newspaper in her hand to shield her face from the hot light. They were talking of family events, when, during a pause, Jemima's eye caught the name of a great actor, who had lately given prominence and life to a character in one of Shakspeare's plays. The criticism in the paper was fine, and warmed Jemima's heart.

"How I should like to see a play!" exclaimed she.

"Should you?" said her brother, listlessly.

"Yes, to be sure! Just hear this!" and she began to read a fine passage of criticism.

"Those newspaper people can make an article out of anything," said he, yawning. "I've seen the man myself, and it was all very well, but nothing to make such a fuss about."

"You! you seen ——! Have you seen a play, Richard? Oh, why did you never tell me before? Tell me all about it! Why did you never name seeing —— in your letters?"

He half smiled, contemptuously enough. "Oh! at first it strikes one rather, but after a while one cares no more for the theatre than one does for mince-pies."

"Oh, I wish I might go to London!" said Jemima, impatiently. "I've a great mind to ask papa to let me go to the George Smiths', and then I could see ——. I would not think him like mince-pies."

"You must not do any such thing!" said Richard, now neither yawning nor contemptuous. "My father would never allow you to go to the theatre; and the George Smiths are such old fogeys—they would be sure to tell."

"How do you go, then? Does my father give you leave?"

"Oh! many things are right for men which are not for girls."

Jemima sat and pondered. Richard wished he had not been so confidential.

"You need not name it," said he, rather anxiously.

"Name what?" said she, startled, for her thoughts had gone far afield.

"Oh, name my going once or twice to the theatre!"

"No, I shan't name it!" said she. "No one here would care to hear it."

But it was with some little surprise, and almost with a feeling of disgust, that she heard Richard join with her father in condemning some one, and add to Mr Bradshaw's list of offences, by alleging that the young man was a playgoer. He did not think his sister heard his words.

Mary and Elizabeth were the two girls whom Ruth had in charge; they resembled Jemima more than their brother in character. The household rules were occasionally a little relaxed in their favour, for Mary, the elder, was nearly eight years younger than Jemima, and three intermediate children had died. They loved Ruth dearly, made a great pet of Leonard, and had many profound secrets together, most of which related to their wonders if Jemima and Mr Farquhar would ever be married. They watched their sister closely; and every day had some fresh confidence to make to each other, confirming or discouraging to their hopes.

Ruth rose early, and shared the household work with Sally and Miss Benson till seven; and then she helped Leonard to dress, and had a quiet time alone with him till prayers and breakfast. At nine she was to be at Mr Bradshaw's house. She sat in the room with Mary and Elizabeth during the Latin, the writing, and arithmetic lessons, which they received from masters; then she read, and walked with them, they clinging to her as to an elder sister; she dined with her pupils at the family lunch, and reached home by four. That happy home—those quiet days!

And so the peaceful days passed on into weeks, and months, and years, and Ruth and Leonard grew and strengthened into the riper beauty of their respective ages; while as yet no touch of decay had come on the quaint, primitive elders of the household.

CHAPTER XX

Jemima Refuses to Be Managed

It was no wonder that the lookers-on were perplexed as to the state of affairs between Jemima and Mr Farquhar, for they too were sorely puzzled themselves at the sort of relationship between them. Was it love, or was it not? that was the question in Mr Farquhar's mind. He hoped it was not; he believed it was not; and yet he felt as if it were. There was something preposterous, he thought, in a man nearly forty years of age being in love with a girl of twenty. He had gone on reasoning through all the days of his manhood on the idea of a staid, noble-minded wife, grave and sedate, the fit companion in experience of her husband. He had spoken with admiration of reticent characters, full of self-control and dignity; and he hoped—he trusted, that all this time he had not been allowing himself unconsciously to fall in love with a wild-hearted, impetuous girl, who knew nothing of life beyond her father's house, and who chafed under the strict discipline enforced there. For it was rather a suspicious symptom of the state of Mr Farquhar's affections, that he had discovered the silent rebellion which continued in Jemima's heart, unperceived by any of her own family, against the severe laws and opinions of her father. Mr Farquhar shared in these opinions; but in him they were modified, and took a milder form. Still, he approved of much that Mr Bradshaw did and said; and this made it all the more strange that he should wince so for Jemima, whenever anything took place which he instinctively knew that she would dislike. After an evening at Mr Bradshaw's, when Jemima had gone to the very verge of questioning or disputing some of her father's severe judgments, Mr Farquhar went home in a dissatisfied, restless state of mind, which he was almost afraid to analyse. He admired the inflexible integrity—and almost the pomp of principle—evinced by Mr Bradshaw on every occasion; he wondered how it was that Jemima could not see how grand a life might be, whose every action was shaped in obedience to some eternal law; instead of which, he was afraid she rebelled against every law, and was only guided by impulse. Mr Farquhar had been taught to dread impulses as promptings of the devil. Sometimes, if he tried to present her father's opinions before her in another form, so as to bring himself and her rather more into that state of agreement he longed for, she flashed out upon him with the indignation of difference that she dared not show to, or before, her father, as if she had some diviner instinct which taught her more truly than they knew, with all their experience; at least, in her first expressions there seemed something good and fine; but opposition made her angry and irritable, and the arguments which he was constantly provoking (whenever he was with her in her father's absence) frequently ended in some vehemence of expression on her part that offended Mr Farquhar, who did not see how she expiated her anger in tears and self-reproaches when alone in her chamber. Then he would lecture himself severely on the interest he could not help feeling in a wilful girl; he would determine not to interfere with her opinions in future, and yet, the very next time they differed, he strove to argue her into harmony with himself, in spite of all resolutions to the contrary.

Mr Bradshaw saw just enough of this interest which Jemima had excited in his partner's mind, to determine him in considering their future marriage as a settled affair. The fitness of the thing had long ago struck him; her father's partner—so the fortune he meant to give her might continue in the business; a man of such steadiness of character, and such a capital eye for a desirable speculation as Mr Farquhar—just the right age to unite the paternal with the conjugal affection, and consequently the very man for Jemima, who had something unruly in her, which might break out under a *régime* less wisely adjusted to the circumstances than was Mr Bradshaw's (in his own opinion)—a house ready-furnished, at a convenient distance from her home—no near relations on Mr Farquhar's side, who might be inclined to consider his residence as their own for an indefinite time, and so add to the household expenses—in short, what could be more suitable in every way? Mr Bradshaw respected the very self-restraint he thought he saw in Mr Farquhar's demeanour, attributing it to a wise desire to wait until trade should be rather more slack, and the man of business more at leisure to become the lover.

As for Jemima, at times she thought she almost hated Mr Farquhar.

"What business has he," she would think, "to lecture me? Often I can hardly bear it from papa, and I will not bear it from him. He treats me just like a child, and as if I should lose all my present opinions when I know more of the world. I am sure I should like never to know the world, if it was to make me think as he does, hard man that he is! I wonder what made him take Jem Brown on as gardener again, if he does not believe that above one criminal in a thousand is restored to goodness. I'll ask him, some day, if that was not acting on impulse rather than principle. Poor impulse! how you do get abused. But I will tell Mr Farquhar I will not let him interfere with me. If I do what papa bids me, no one has a right to notice whether I do it willingly or not."

So then she tried to defy Mr Farquhar, by doing and saying things that she knew he would disapprove. She went so far that he was seriously grieved, and did not even remonstrate and "lecture," and then she was disappointed and irritated; for, somehow, with all her indignation at interference, she liked to be lectured by him; not that she was aware of this liking of hers, but still it would have been more pleasant to be scolded than so quietly passed over. Her two little sisters, with their wide-awake eyes, had long ago put things together, and conjectured. Every day they had some fresh mystery together, to be imparted in garden walks and whispered talks.

"Lizzie, did you see how the tears came into Mimie's eyes when Mr Farquhar looked so displeased when she said good people were always dull? I think she's in love." Mary said the last words with grave emphasis, and felt like an oracle of twelve years of age.

"I don't," said Lizzie. "I know I cry often enough when papa is cross, and I'm not in love with him."

"Yes! but you don't look as Mimie did."

"Don't call her Mimie—you know papa does not like it."

"Yes; but there are so many things papa does not like I can never remember them all. Never mind about that; but listen to something I've got to tell you, if you'll never, never tell."

"No, indeed I won't, Mary. What is it?"

"Not to Mrs Denbigh?"

"No, not even to Mrs Denbigh."

"Well, then, the other day—last Friday, Mimie—"

"Jemima!" interrupted the more conscientious Elizabeth.

"Jemima, if it must be so," jerked out Mary, "sent me to her desk for an envelope, and what do you think I saw?"

"What?" asked Elizabeth, expecting nothing less than a red-hot Valentine, signed Walter Farquhar, *pro* Bradshaw, Farquhar, and Co., in full.

"Why, a piece of paper, with dull-looking lines upon it, just like the scientific dialogues; and I remembered all about it. It was once when Mr Farquhar had been telling us that a bullet does not go in a straight line, but in a something curve, and he drew some lines on a piece of paper; and Mimie—"

"Jemima," put in Elizabeth.

"Well, well! she had treasured it up, and written in a corner, 'W. F., April 3rd.' Now, that's rather like love, is not it? For Jemima hates useful information just as much as I do, and that's saying a great deal; and yet she had kept this paper, and dated it."

"If that's all, I know Dick keeps a paper with Miss Benson's name written on it, and yet he's not in love with her; and perhaps Jemima may like Mr Farquhar, and he may not like her. It seems such a little while since her hair was turned up, and he has always been a grave middle-aged man ever since I can recollect; and then, have you never noticed how often he finds fault with her—almost lectures her?"

"To be sure," said Mary; "but he may be in love, for all that. Just think how often papa lectures mamma; and yet, of course, they're in love with each other."

"Well! we shall see," said Elizabeth.

Poor Jemima little thought of the four sharp eyes that watched her daily course while she sat alone, as she fancied, with her secret in her own room. For, in a passionate fit of grieving, at the impatient, hasty temper which had made her so seriously displease Mr Farquhar that he had gone away without remonstrance, without more leave-taking than a distant bow, she had begun to suspect that rather than not be noticed at all by him, rather than be an object of indifference to him—oh! far rather would she be an object of anger and upbraiding; and the thoughts that followed this confession to herself, stunned and bewildered her; and for once that they made her dizzy with hope, ten times they made her sick with fear. For an instant she planned to become and to be all he could wish her; to change her very nature for him. And then a great gush of pride came over her, and she set her teeth tight together, and determined that he should either love her as she was, or not at all. Unless he could take her with all her faults, she would not care for his regard; "love" was too noble a word to call such cold, calculating feeling as his must be, who went about with a pattern idea in his mind, trying to find a wife to match. Besides, there was something degrading, Jemima thought, in trying to alter herself to gain the love of any human creature. And yet, if he did not care for her, if this late indifference were to last, what a great shroud was drawn over life! Could she bear it?

From the agony she dared not look at, but which she was going to risk encountering, she was aroused by the presence of her mother.

"Jemima! your father wants to speak to you in the dining-room."

"What for?" asked the girl.

"Oh! he is fidgeted by something Mr Farquhar said to me, and which I repeated. I am sure I thought there was no harm in it, and your father always likes me to tell him what everybody says in his absence."

Jemima went with a heavy heart into her father's presence.

He was walking up and down the room, and did not see her at first.

"Oh, Jemima! is that you? Has your mother told you what I want to speak to you about?"

"No!" said Jemima. "Not exactly."

"She has been telling me what proves to me how very seriously you must have displeased and offended Mr Farquhar, before he could have expressed himself to her as he did, when he left the house. You know what he said?"

"No!" said Jemima, her heart swelling within her. "He has no right to say anything about me." She was desperate, or she durst not have said this before her father.

"No right!—what do you mean, Jemima?" said Mr Bradshaw, turning sharp round. "Surely you must know that I hope he may one day be your husband; that is to say, if you prove yourself worthy of the excellent training I have given you. I cannot suppose Mr Farquhar would take any undisciplined girl as a wife."

Jemima held tight by a chair near which she was standing. She did not speak; her father was pleased by her silence—it was the way in which he liked his projects to be received.

"But you cannot suppose," he continued, "that Mr Farquhar will consent to marry you—"

"Consent to marry me!" repeated Jemima, in a low tone of brooding indignation; were those the terms upon which her rich woman's heart was to be given, with a calm consent of acquiescent acceptance, but a little above resignation on the part of the receiver?

—"if you give way to a temper which, although you have never dared to show it to me, I am well aware exists, although I hoped the habits of self-examination I had instilled had done much to cure you of manifesting it. At one time, Richard promised to be the more headstrong of the two; now, I must desire you to take pattern by him. Yes," he continued, falling into his old train of thought, "it would be a most fortunate connexion for you in every way. I should have you under my own eye, and could still assist you in the formation of your character, and I should be at hand to strengthen and confirm your principles. Mr Farquhar's connexion with the firm would be convenient and agreeable to me in a pecuniary point of view. He—" Mr Bradshaw was going on in his enumeration of the advantages which he in particular, and Jemima in the second place, would derive from this marriage, when his daughter spoke, at first so low that he could not hear her, as he walked up and down the room with his creaking boots, and he had to stop to listen.

"Has Mr Farquhar ever spoken to you about it?" Jemima's cheek was flushed as she asked the question; she wished that she might have been the person to whom he had first addressed himself.

Mr Bradshaw answered,

"No, not spoken. It has been implied between us for some time. At least, I have been so aware of his intentions that I have made several allusions, in the course of business, to it, as a thing that might take place. He can hardly have misunderstood; he must have seen that I perceived his design, and approved of it," said Mr Bradshaw, rather doubtfully; as he remembered how very little, in fact, passed between him and his partner which could have reference to the subject, to any but a mind prepared to receive it. Perhaps Mr Farquhar had not really thought of it; but then again, that would imply that his own penetration had been mistaken, a thing not impossible certainly, but quite beyond the range of probability. So he reassured himself, and (as he thought) his daughter, by saying,

"The whole thing is so suitable—the advantages arising from the connexion are so obvious; besides which, I am quite aware, from many little speeches of Mr Farquhar's, that he contemplates marriage at no very distant time; and he seldom leaves Eccleston, and visits few families besides our own—certainly, none that can compare with ours in the advantages you have all received in moral and religious training." But then Mr Bradshaw was checked in his implied praises of himself (and only himself could be his martingale when he once set out on such a career) by a recollection that Jemima must not feel too secure, as she might become if he dwelt too much on the advantages of her being her father's daughter. Accordingly, he said: "But you must be aware, Jemima, that you do very little credit to the education I have given you, when you make such an impression as you must have done to-day, before Mr Farquhar could have said what he did of you!"

"What did he say?" asked Jemima, still in the low, husky tone of suppressed anger.

"Your mother says he remarked to her, 'What a pity it is, that Jemima cannot maintain her opinions without going into a passion; and what a pity it is, that her opinions are such as to sanction, rather than curb, these fits of rudeness and anger!'"

"Did he say that?" said Jemima, in a still lower tone, not questioning her father, but speaking rather to herself.

"I have no doubt he did," replied her father, gravely. "Your mother is in the habit of repeating accurately to me what takes place in my absence; besides which, the whole speech is not one of hers; she has not altered a word in the repetition, I am convinced. I have trained her to habits of accuracy very unusual in a woman."

At another time, Jemima might have been inclined to rebel against this system of carrying constant intelligence to headquarters, which she had long ago felt as an insurmountable obstacle to any free communication with her mother; but now, her father's means of acquiring knowledge faded into insignificance before the nature of the information he imparted. She stood quite still, grasping the chair-back, longing to be dismissed.

"I have said enough now, I hope, to make you behave in a becoming manner to Mr Farquhar; if your temper is too unruly to be always under your own control, at least have respect to my injunctions, and take some pains to curb it before him."

"May I go?" asked Jemima, chafing more and more.

"You may," said her father. When she left the room he gently rubbed his hands together, satisfied with the effect he had produced, and wondering how it was, that one so well brought up as his daughter could ever say or do anything to provoke such a remark from Mr Farquhar as that which he had heard repeated.

"Nothing can be more gentle and docile than she is when spoken to in the proper manner. I must give Farquhar a hint," said Mr Bradshaw to himself.

Jemima rushed upstairs, and locked herself into her room. She began pacing up and down at first, without shedding a tear; but then she suddenly stopped, and burst out crying with passionate indignation.

"So! I am to behave well, not because it is right—not because it is right—but to show off before Mr Farquhar. Oh, Mr Farquhar!" said she, suddenly changing to a sort of upbraiding tone of voice, "I did not think so of you an hour ago. I did not think you could choose a wife in that cold-hearted way, though you did profess to act by rule and line; but you think to have me, do you? because it is fitting and suitable, and you want to be married, and can't spare time for wooing" (she was lashing herself up by an exaggeration of all her father had said). "And how often I have thought you were too grand for me! but now I know better. Now I can believe that all you do is done from calculation; you are good because it adds to your business credit—you talk in that high strain about principle because it sounds well, and is respectable—and even these things are better than your cold way of looking out for a wife, just as you would do for a carpet, to add to your comforts, and settle you respectably. But I won't be that wife. You shall see something of me which shall make you not acquiesce so quietly in the arrangements of the firm." She cried too vehemently to go on thinking or speaking. Then she stopped, and said:

"Only an hour ago I was hoping—I don't know what I was hoping—but I thought—oh! how I was deceived!—I thought he had a true, deep, loving, manly heart, which God might let me win; but now I know he has only a calm, calculating head—"

If Jemima had been vehement and passionate before this conversation with her father, it was better than the sullen reserve she assumed now whenever Mr Farquhar came to the house. He felt it deeply; no reasoning with himself took off the pain he experienced. He tried to speak on the subjects she liked, in the manner she liked, until he despised himself for the unsuccessful efforts.

He stood between her and her father once or twice, in obvious inconsistency with his own previously expressed opinions; and Mr Bradshaw piqued himself upon his admirable management, in making Jemima feel that she owed his indulgence or forbearance to Mr Farquhar's interference; but Jemima—perverse, miserable Jemima—thought that she hated Mr Farquhar all the more. She respected her father inflexible, much more than her father pompously giving up to Mr Farquhar's subdued remonstrances on her behalf. Even Mr Bradshaw was perplexed, and shut himself up to consider how Jemima was to be made more fully to understand his wishes and her own interests. But there was nothing to take hold of as a ground for any further conversation with her. Her actions were so submissive that they were spiritless; she did all her father desired; she did it with a nervous quickness and haste, if she thought that otherwise Mr Farquhar would interfere in any way. She wished evidently to owe nothing to him. She had begun by leaving the room when he came in, after the conversation she had had with her father; but at Mr Bradshaw's first expression of his wish that she should remain, she remained—silent, indifferent, inattentive to all that was going on; at least there was this appearance of inattention. She would work away at her sewing as if she were to earn her livelihood by it; the light was gone out of her eyes as she lifted them up heavily before replying to any question, and the eyelids were often swollen with crying.

But in all this there was no positive fault. Mr Bradshaw could not have told her not to do this, or to do that, without her doing it; for she had become much more docile of late.

It was a wonderful proof of the influence Ruth had gained in the family, that Mr Bradshaw, after much deliberation, congratulated himself on the wise determination he had made of requesting her to speak to Jemima, and find out what feeling was at the bottom of all this change in her ways of going on.

He rang the bell.

"Is Mrs Denbigh here?" he inquired of the servant who answered it.

"Yes, sir; she is just come."

"Beg her to come to me in this room as soon as she can leave the young ladies."

Ruth came.

"Sit down, Mrs Denbigh; sit down. I want to have a little conversation with you; not about your pupils, they are going on well under your care, I am sure; and I often congratulate myself on the choice I made—I assure you I do. But now I want to speak to you about Jemima. She is very fond of you, and perhaps you could take some opportunity of observing to her—in short, of saying to her, that she is behaving very foolishly—in fact, disgusting Mr Farquhar (who was, I know, inclined to like her) by the sullen, sulky way she behaves in, when he is by."

He paused for the ready acquiescence he expected. But Ruth did not quite comprehend what was required of her, and disliked the glimpse she had gained of the task very much.

"I hardly understand, sir. You are displeased with Miss Bradshaw's manners to Mr Farquhar."

"Well, well! not quite that; I am displeased with her manners—they are sulky and abrupt, particularly when he is by—and I want you (of whom she is so fond) to speak to her about it."

"But I have never had the opportunity of noticing them. Whenever I have seen her, she has been most gentle and affectionate."

"But I think you do not hesitate to believe me, when I say that I have noticed the reverse," said Mr Bradshaw, drawing himself up.

"No, sir. I beg your pardon if I have expressed myself so badly as to seem to doubt. But am I to tell Miss Bradshaw that you have spoken of her faults to me?" asked Ruth, a little astonished, and shrinking more than ever from the proposed task.

"If you would allow me to finish what I have got to say, without interruption, I could then tell you what I do wish."

"I beg your pardon, sir," said Ruth, gently.

"I wish you to join our circle occasionally in an evening; Mrs Bradshaw shall send you an invitation when Mr Farquhar is likely to be here. Warned by me, and, consequently, with your observation quickened, you can hardly fail to notice instances of what I have pointed out; and then I will trust to your own good sense" (Mr Bradshaw bowed to her at this part of his sentence) "to find an opportunity to remonstrate with her."

Ruth was beginning to speak, but he waved his hand for another minute of silence.

"Only a minute, Mrs Denbigh. I am quite aware that, in requesting your presence occasionally in the evening, I shall be trespassing upon the time which is, in fact, your money; you may be assured that I shall not forget this little circumstance, and you can explain what I have said on this head to Benson and his sister."

"I am afraid I cannot do it," Ruth began; but while she was choosing words delicate enough to express her reluctance to act as he wished, he had almost bowed her out of the room; and thinking that she was modest in her estimate of her qualifications for remonstrating with his daughter, he added, blandly,

"No one so able, Mrs Denbigh. I have observed many qualities in you—observed when, perhaps, you have little thought it."

If he had observed Ruth that morning, he would have seen an absence of mind, and depression of spirits, not much to her credit as a teacher; for she could not bring herself to feel that she had any right to go into the family purposely to watch over and find fault with any one member of it. If she had seen anything wrong in Jemima, Ruth loved her so much that she would have told her of it in private; and with many doubts, how far she was the one to pull out the mote from any one's eye, even in the most tender manner;—she would have had to conquer reluctance before she could have done even this; but there was something undefinably repugnant to her in the manner of acting which Mr Bradshaw had proposed, and she determined not to accept the invitations which were to place her in so false a position.

But as she was leaving the house, after the end of the lessons, while she stood in the hall tying on her bonnet, and listening to the last small confidences of her two pupils, she saw Jemima coming in through the garden-door, and was struck by the change in her looks. The large eyes, so brilliant once, were dim and clouded; the complexion sallow and colourless; a lowering expression was on the dark brow, and the corners of her mouth drooped as with sorrowful thoughts. She looked up, and her eyes met Ruth's.

"Oh! you beautiful creature!" thought Jemima, "with your still, calm, heavenly face, what are you to know of earth's trials! You have lost your beloved by death—but that is a blessed sorrow; the sorrow I have pulls me down and down, and makes me despise and hate every one—not you, though." And, her face changing to a soft, tender look, she went up to Ruth, and kissed her fondly; as if it were a relief to be near some one on whose true, pure heart she relied. Ruth returned the caress; and even while she did so, she suddenly rescinded her resolution to keep clear of what Mr Bradshaw had desired her to do. On her way home she resolved, if she could, to find out what were Jemima's secret feelings; and if (as, from some previous knowledge, she suspected) they were morbid and exaggerated in any way, to try and help her right with all the wisdom which true love gives. It was time that some one should come to still the storm in Jemima's turbulent heart, which was daily and hourly knowing less and less of peace. The irritating difficulty was to separate the two characters, which at two different times she had attributed to Mr Farquhar—the old one, which she had formerly believed to be true, that he was a man acting up to a high standard of lofty principle, and acting up without a struggle (and this last had been the circumstance which had made her rebellious and irritable once); the new one, which her father had excited in her suspicious mind, that Mr Farquhar was cold and calculating in all he did, and that she was to be transferred by the former, and accepted by the latter, as a sort of stock-in-trade—these were the two Mr Farquhars who clashed together in her mind. And in this state of irritation and prejudice, she could not bear the way in which he gave up his opinions to please her; that was not the way to win her; she liked him far better when he inflexibly and rigidly adhered to his idea of right and wrong, not even allowing any force to temptation, and hardly any grace to repentance, compared with that beauty of holiness which had never yielded to sin. He had been her idol in those days, as she found out now, however much at the time she had opposed him with violence.

As for Mr Farquhar, he was almost weary of himself; no reasoning, even no principle, seemed to have influence over him, for he saw that Jemima was not at all what he approved of in woman. He saw her uncurbed and passionate, affecting to despise the rules of life he held most sacred, and indifferent to, if not positively disliking him; and yet he loved her dearly. But he resolved to make a great effort of will, and break loose from these trammels of sense. And while he resolved, some old recollection would bring her up, hanging on his arm, in all the confidence of early girlhood, looking up in his face with her soft, dark eyes, and questioning him upon the mysterious subjects which had so much interest for both of them at that time, although they had become only matter for dissension in these later days.

It was also true, as Mr Bradshaw had said, Mr Farquhar wished to marry, and had not much choice in the small town of Eccleston. He never put this so plainly before himself, as a reason for choosing Jemima, as her father had done to her; but it was an unconscious motive all the same. However, now he had lectured himself into the resolution to make a pretty long absence from Eccleston, and see if, amongst his distant friends, there was no woman more in accordance with his ideal, who could put the naughty, wilful, plaguing Jemima Bradshaw out of his head, if he did not soon perceive some change in her for the better.

A few days after Ruth's conversation with Mr Bradshaw, the invitation she had been expecting, yet dreading, came. It was to her alone. Mr and Miss Benson were pleased at the compliment to her, and urged her acceptance of it. She wished that they had been included; she had not thought it right, or kind to Jemima, to tell them why she was going, and she feared now lest they should feel a little hurt that they were not asked too. But she need not have been afraid. They were glad and proud of the attention to her, and never thought of themselves.

"Ruthie, what gown shall you wear to-night? your dark grey one, I suppose?" asked Miss Benson.

"Yes, I suppose so. I never thought of it; but that is my best."

"Well; then, I shall quill up a ruff for you. You know I am a famous quiller of net."

Ruth came downstairs with a little flush on her cheeks when she was ready to go. She held her bonnet and shawl in her hand, for she knew Miss Benson and Sally would want to see her dressed.

"Is not mamma pretty?" asked Leonard, with a child's pride.

"She looks very nice and tidy," said Miss Benson, who had an idea that children should not talk or think about beauty.

"I think my ruff looks so nice," said Ruth, with gentle pleasure. And indeed it did look nice, and set off the pretty round throat most becomingly. Her hair, now grown long and thick, was smoothed as close to her head as its waving nature would allow, and plaited up in a great rich knot low down behind. The grey gown was as plain as plain could be.

"You should have light gloves, Ruth," said Miss Benson. She went upstairs, and brought down a delicate pair of Limerick ones, which had been long treasured up in a walnut-shell.

"They say them gloves is made of chickens'-skins," said Sally, examining them curiously. "I wonder how they set about skinning 'em."

"Here, Ruth," said Mr Benson, coming in from the garden, "here's a rose or two for you. I am sorry there are no more; I hoped I should have had my yellow rose out by this time, but the damask and the white are in a warmer corner, and have got the start."

Miss Benson and Leonard stood at the door, and watched her down the little passage-street till she was out of sight.

She had hardly touched the bell at Mr Bradshaw's door, when Mary and Elizabeth opened it with boisterous glee.

"We saw you coming—we've been watching for you—we want you to come round the garden before tea; papa is not come in yet. Do come!"

She went round the garden with a little girl clinging to each arm. It was full of sunshine and flowers, and this made the contrast between it and the usual large family room (which fronted the north-east, and therefore had no evening sun to light up its cold, drab furniture) more striking than usual. It looked very gloomy. There was the great dining-table, heavy and square; the range of chairs, straight and square; the work-boxes, useful and square; the colouring of walls, and carpet, and curtains, all of the coldest description; everything was handsome, and everything was ugly. Mrs Bradshaw was asleep in her easy-chair when they came in. Jemima had just put down her work, and, lost in thought, she leant her cheek on her hand. When she saw Ruth she brightened a little, and went to her and kissed her. Mrs Bradshaw jumped up at the sound of their entrance, and was wide awake in a moment.

"Oh! I thought your father was here," said she, evidently relieved to find that he had not come in and caught her sleeping.

"Thank you, Mrs Denbigh, for coming to us to-night," said she, in the quiet tone in which she generally spoke in her husband's absence. When he was there, a sort of constant terror of displeasing him made her voice sharp and nervous; the children knew that many a thing passed over by their mother when their father was away, was sure to be noticed by her when he was present; and noticed, too, in a cross and querulous manner, for she was so much afraid of the blame which on any occasion of their misbehaviour fell upon her. And yet she looked up to her husband with a reverence and regard, and a faithfulness of love, which his decision of character was likely to produce on a weak and anxious mind. He was a rest and a support to her, on whom she cast all her responsibilities; she was an obedient, unremonstrating wife to him; no stronger affection had ever brought her duty to him into conflict with any desire of her heart. She loved her children dearly, though they all perplexed her very frequently. Her son was her especial darling, because he very seldom brought her into any scrapes with his father; he was so cautious and prudent, and had the art of "keeping a calm sough" about any difficulty he might be in. With all her dutiful sense of the obligation, which her husband enforced upon her, to notice and tell him everything that was going wrong in the household, and especially among his children, Mrs Bradshaw, somehow, contrived to be honestly blind to a good deal that was not praiseworthy in Master Richard.

Mr Bradshaw came in before long, bringing with him Mr Farquhar. Jemima had been talking to Ruth with some interest before then; but, on seeing Mr Farquhar, she bent her head down over her work, went a little paler, and turned obstinately silent. Mr Bradshaw longed to command her to speak; but even he had a suspicion that what she might say, when so commanded, might be rather worse in its effect than her gloomy silence; so he held his peace, and a discontented, angry kind of peace it was. Mrs Bradshaw saw that something was wrong, but could not tell what; only she became every moment more trembling, and nervous, and irritable, and sent Mary and Elizabeth off on all sorts of contradictory errands to the servants, and made the tea twice as strong, and sweetened it twice as much as usual, in hopes of pacifying her husband with good things.

Mr Farquhar had gone for the last time, or so he thought. He had resolved (for the fifth time) that he would go and watch Jemima once more, and if her temper got the better of her, and she showed the old sullenness again, and gave the old proofs of indifference to his good opinion, he would give her up altogether, and seek a wife elsewhere. He sat watching her with folded arms, and in silence. Altogether they were a pleasant family party!

Jemima wanted to wind a skein of wool. Mr Farquhar saw it, and came to her, anxious to do her this little service. She turned away pettishly, and asked Ruth to hold it for her.

Ruth was hurt for Mr Farquhar, and looked sorrowfully at Jemima; but Jemima would not see her glance of upbraiding, as Ruth, hoping that she would relent, delayed a little to comply with her request. Mr Farquhar did; and went back to his seat to watch them both. He saw Jemima turbulent and stormy in look; he saw Ruth, to all appearance heavenly calm as the angels, or with only that little tinge of sorrow which her friend's behaviour had called forth. He saw the unusual beauty of her face and form, which he had never noticed before; and he saw Jemima, with all the brilliancy she once possessed in eyes and complexion, dimmed and faded. He watched Ruth, speaking low and soft to the little girls, who seemed to come to her in every difficulty; and he remarked her gentle firmness when their bedtime came, and they pleaded to stay up longer (their father was absent in his counting-house, or they would not have dared to do so). He liked Ruth's soft, distinct, unwavering "No! you must go. You must keep to what is right," far better than the good-natured yielding to entreaty he had formerly admired in Jemima. He was wandering off into this comparison, while Ruth, with delicate and unconscious tact, was trying to lead Jemima into some subject which should take her away from the thoughts, whatever they were, that made her so ungracious and rude.

Jemima was ashamed of herself before Ruth, in a way which she had never been before any one else. She valued Ruth's good opinion so highly, that she dreaded lest her friend should perceive her faults. She put a check upon herself—a check at first; but after a little time she had forgotten something of her trouble, and listened to Ruth, and questioned her about Leonard, and smiled at his little witticisms; and only the sighs, that would come up from the very force of habit, brought back the consciousness of her unhappiness. Before the end of the evening, Jemima had allowed herself to speak to Mr Farquhar in the old way—questioning, differing, disputing. She was recalled to the remembrance of that miserable conversation by the entrance of her father. After that she was silent. But he had seen her face more animated, and bright with a smile, as she spoke to Mr Farquhar; and although he regretted the loss of her complexion (for she was still very pale), he was highly pleased with the success of his project. He never doubted but that Ruth had given her some sort of private exhortation to behave better. He could not have understood the pretty art with which, by simply banishing unpleasant subjects, and throwing a wholesome natural sunlit tone over others, Ruth had insensibly drawn Jemima out of her gloom. He resolved to buy Mrs Denbigh a handsome silk gown the very next day. He did not believe she had a silk gown, poor creature! He had noticed that dark grey stuff, this long, long time, as her Sunday dress. He liked the colour; the silk one should be just the same tinge. Then he thought that it would, perhaps, be better to choose a lighter shade, one which might be noticed as different to the old gown. For he had no doubt she would like to have it remarked, and, perhaps, would not object to tell people, that it was a present from Mr Bradshaw—a token of his approbation. He smiled a little to himself as he thought of this additional source of pleasure to Ruth. She, in the meantime, was getting up to go home. While Jemima was lighting the bed-candle at the lamp, Ruth came round to bid good night. Mr Bradshaw could not allow her to remain till the morrow, uncertain whether he was satisfied or not.

"Good night, Mrs Denbigh," said he. "Good night. Thank you. I am obliged to you—I am exceedingly obliged to you."

He laid emphasis on these words, for he was pleased to see Mr Farquhar step forward to help Jemima in her little office.

Mr Farquhar offered to accompany Ruth home; but the streets that intervened between Mr Bradshaw's and the Chapel-house were so quiet that he desisted, when he learnt from Ruth's manner how much she disliked his proposal. Mr Bradshaw, too, instantly observed:

"Oh! Mrs Denbigh need not trouble you, Farquhar. I have servants at liberty at any moment to attend on her, if she wishes it."

In fact, he wanted to make hay while the sun shone, and to detain Mr Farquhar a little longer, now that Jemima was so gracious. She went upstairs with Ruth to help her to put on her things.

"Dear Jemima!" said Ruth, "I am so glad to see you looking better to-night! You quite frightened me this morning, you looked so ill."

"Did I?" replied Jemima. "Oh, Ruth! I have been so unhappy lately. I want you to come and put me to rights," she continued, half smiling. "You know I'm a sort of out-pupil of yours, though we are so nearly of an age. You ought to lecture me, and make me good."

"Should I, dear?" said Ruth. "I don't think I'm the one to do it."

"Oh, yes! you are—you've done me good to-night."

"Well, if I can do anything for you, tell me what it is?" asked Ruth, tenderly.

"Oh, not now—not now," replied Jemima. "I could not tell you here. It's a long story, and I don't know that I can tell you at all. Mamma might come up at any moment, and papa would be sure to ask what we had been talking about so long."

"Take your own time, love," said Ruth; "only remember, as far as I can, how glad I am to help you."

"You're too good, my darling!" said Jemima, fondly.

"Don't say so," replied Ruth, earnestly, almost as if she were afraid. "God knows I am not."

"Well! we're none of us too good," answered Jemima; "I know that. But you *are* very good. Nay, I won't call you so, if it makes you look so miserable. But come away downstairs."

With the fragrance of Ruth's sweetness lingering about her, Jemima was her best self during the next half-hour. Mr Bradshaw was more and more pleased, and raised the price of the silk, which he was going to give Ruth, sixpence a yard during the time. Mr Farquhar went home through the garden-way, happier than he had been this long time. He even caught himself humming the old refrain:

On revient, on revient toujours,
A ses premiers amours.

But as soon as he was aware of what he was doing, he cleared away the remnants of the song into a cough, which was sonorous, if not perfectly real.

CHAPTER XXI

Mr Farquhar's Attentions Transferred

The next morning, as Jemima and her mother sat at their work, it came into the head of the former to remember her father's very marked way of thanking Ruth the evening before.

"What a favourite Mrs Denbigh is with papa," said she. "I am sure I don't wonder at it. Did you notice, mamma, how he thanked her for coming here last night?"

"Yes, dear; but I don't think it was all—" Mrs Bradshaw stopped short. She was never certain if it was right or wrong to say anything.

"Not all what?" asked Jemima, when she saw her mother was not going to finish the sentence.

"Not all because Mrs Denbigh came to tea here," replied Mrs Bradshaw.

"Why, what else could he be thanking her for? What has she done?" asked Jemima, stimulated to curiosity by her mother's hesitating manner.

"I don't know if I ought to tell you," said Mrs Bradshaw.

"Oh, very well!" said Jemima, rather annoyed.

"Nay, dear! your papa never said I was not to tell; perhaps I may."

"Never mind! I don't want to hear," in a piqued tone.

There was silence for a little while. Jemima was trying to think of something else, but her thoughts would revert to the wonder what Mrs Denbigh could have done for her father.

"I think I may tell you, though," said Mrs Bradshaw, half questioning.

Jemima had the honour not to urge any confidence, but she was too curious to take any active step towards repressing it.

Mrs Bradshaw went on. "I think you deserve to know. It is partly your doing that papa is so pleased with Mrs Denbigh. He is going to buy her a silk gown this morning, and I think you ought to know why."

"Why?" asked Jemima.

"Because papa is so pleased to find that you mind what she says."

"I mind what she says! To be sure I do, and always did. But why should papa give her a gown for that? I think he ought to give it me rather," said Jemima, half laughing.

"I am sure he would, dear; he will give you one, I am certain, if you want one. He was so pleased to see you like your old self to Mr Farquhar last night. We neither of us could think what had come over you this last month; but now all seems right."

A dark cloud came over Jemima's face. She did not like this close observation and constant comment upon her manners; and what had Ruth to do with it?

"I am glad you were pleased," said she, very coldly. Then, after a pause, she added, "But you have not told me what Mrs Denbigh had to do with my good behaviour."

"Did not she speak to you about it?" asked Mrs Bradshaw, looking up.

"No; why should she? She has no right to criticise what I do. She would not be so impertinent," said Jemima, feeling very uncomfortable and suspicious.

"Yes, love! she would have had a right, for papa had desired her to do it."

"Papa desired her! What do you mean, mamma?"

"Oh, dear! I dare say I should not have told you," said Mrs Bradshaw, perceiving, from Jemima's tone of voice, that something had gone wrong. "Only you spoke as if it would be impertinent in Mrs Denbigh, and I am sure she would not do anything that was impertinent. You know, it would be but right for her to do what papa told her; and he said a great deal to her, the other day, about finding out why you were so cross, and bringing you right. And you are right now, dear!" said Mrs Bradshaw, soothingly, thinking that Jemima was annoyed (like a good child) at the recollection of how naughty she had been.

"Then papa is going to give Mrs Denbigh a gown because I was civil to Mr Farquhar last night?"

"Yes, dear!" said Mrs Bradshaw, more and more frightened at Jemima's angry manner of speaking—low-toned, but very indignant.

Jemima remembered, with smouldered anger, Ruth's pleading way of wiling her from her sullenness the night before. Management everywhere! but in this case it was peculiarly revolting; so much so, that she could hardly bear to believe that the seemingly-transparent Ruth had lent herself to it.

"Are you sure, mamma, that papa asked Mrs Denbigh to make me behave differently? It seems so strange."

"I am quite sure. He spoke to her last Friday morning in the study. I remember it was Friday, because Mrs Dean was working here."

Jemima remembered now that she had gone into the school-room on the Friday, and found her sisters lounging about, and wondering what papa could possibly want with Mrs Denbigh.

After this conversation, Jemima repulsed all Ruth's timid efforts to ascertain the cause of her disturbance, and to help her if she could. Ruth's tender, sympathising manner, as she saw Jemima daily looking more wretched, was distasteful to the latter in the highest degree. She could not say that Mrs Denbigh's conduct was positively wrong—it might even be quite right; but it was inexpressibly repugnant to her to think of her father consulting with a stranger (a week ago she almost considered Ruth as a sister) how to manage his daughter, so as to obtain the end he wished for; yes, even if that end was for her own good.

She was thankful and glad to see a brown paper parcel lying on the hall-table, with a note in Ruth's handwriting, addressed to her father. She *knew* what it was, the grey silk dress. That she was sure Ruth would never accept.

No one henceforward could induce Jemima to enter into conversation with Mr Farquhar. She suspected manœuvring in the simplest actions, and was miserable in this constant state of suspicion. She would not allow herself to like Mr Farquhar, even when he said things the most after her own heart. She heard him, one evening, talking with her father about the principles of trade. Her father stood out for the keenest, sharpest work, consistent with honesty; if he had not been her father she would, perhaps, have thought some of his sayings inconsistent with true Christian honesty. He was for driving hard bargains, exacting interest and payment of just bills to a day. That was (he said) the only way in which trade could be conducted. Once allow a margin of uncertainty, or where feelings, instead of maxims, were to be the guide, and all hope of there ever being any good men of business was ended.

"Suppose a delay of a month in requiring payment might save a man's credit—prevent his becoming a bankrupt?" put in Mr Farquhar.

"I would not give it him. I would let him have money to set up again as soon as he had passed the Bankruptcy Court; if he never passed, I might, in some cases, make him an allowance; but I would always keep my justice and my charity separate."

"And yet charity (in your sense of the word) degrades; justice, tempered with mercy and consideration, elevates."

"That is not justice—justice is certain and inflexible. No! Mr Farquhar, you must not allow any Quixotic notions to mingle with your conduct as a tradesman."

And so they went on; Jemima's face glowing with sympathy in all Mr Farquhar said; till once, on looking up suddenly with sparkling eyes, she saw a glance of her father's which told her, as plain as words could say, that he was watching the effect of Mr Farquhar's speeches upon his daughter. She was chilled thenceforward; she thought her father prolonged the argument, in order to call out those sentiments which he knew would most recommend his partner to his daughter. She would so fain have let herself love Mr Farquhar; but this constant manœuvring, in which she did not feel clear that he did not take a passive part, made her sick at heart. She even wished that they might not go through the form of pretending to try to gain her consent to the marriage, if it involved all this premeditated action and speech-making—such moving about of every one into their right places, like pieces at chess. She felt as if she would rather be bought openly, like an Oriental daughter, where no one is degraded in their own eyes by being parties to such a contract. The consequences of all this "admirable management" of Mr Bradshaw's would have been very unfortunate to Mr Farquhar (who was innocent of all connivance in any of the plots—indeed, would have been as much annoyed at them as Jemima, had he been aware of them), but that the impression made upon him by Ruth on the evening I have so lately described, was deepened by the contrast which her behaviour made to Miss Bradshaw's on one or two more recent occasions.

There was no use, he thought, in continuing attentions so evidently distasteful to Jemima. To her, a young girl hardly out of the schoolroom, he probably appeared like an old man; and he might even lose the friendship with which she used to regard him, and which was, and ever would be, very dear to him, if he persevered in trying to be considered as a lover. He should always feel affectionately towards her; her very faults gave her an interest in his eyes, for which he had blamed himself most conscientiously and most uselessly when he was looking upon her as his future wife, but which the said conscience would learn to approve of when she sank down to the place of a young friend, over whom he might exercise a good and salutary interest. Mrs Denbigh, if not many months older in years, had known sorrow and cares so early that she was much older in character. Besides, her shy reserve, and her quiet daily walk within the lines of duty, were much in accordance with Mr Farquhar's notion of what a wife should be. Still, it was a wrench to take his affections away from Jemima. If she had not helped him to do so by every means in her power, he could never have accomplished it.

Yes! by every means in her power had Jemima alienated her lover, her beloved—for so he was in fact. And now her quick-sighted eyes saw he was gone for ever—past recall; for did not her jealous, sore heart feel, even before he himself was conscious of the fact, that he was drawn towards sweet, lovely, composed, and dignified Ruth—one who always thought before she spoke (as Mr Farquhar used to bid Jemima do)—who never was tempted by sudden impulse, but walked the world calm and self-governed. What now availed Jemima's reproaches, as she remembered the days when he had watched her with earnest, attentive eyes, as he now watched Ruth; and the times since, when, led astray by her morbid fancy, she had turned away from all his advances!

"It was only in March—last March, he called me 'dear Jemima.' Ah, don't I remember it well? The pretty nosegay of green-house flowers that he gave me in exchange for the wild daffodils—and how he seemed to care for the flowers I gave him—and how he looked at me, and thanked me—that is all gone and over now."

Her sisters came in bright and glowing.

"Oh, Jemima, how nice and cool you are, sitting in this shady room!" (She had felt it even chilly.) "We have been such a long walk! We are so tired. It is so hot."

"Why did you go, then?" said she.

"Oh! we wanted to go. We would not have stayed at home on any account. It has been so pleasant," said Mary.

"We've been to Scaurside Wood, to gather wild strawberries," said Elizabeth. "Such a quantity! We've left a whole basketful in the dairy. Mr Farquhar says he'll teach us how to dress them in the way he learnt in Germany, if we can get him some hock. Do you think papa will let us have some?"

"Was Mr Farquhar with you?" asked Jemima, a dull light coming into her eyes.

"Yes; we told him this morning that mamma wanted us to take some old linen to the lame man at Scaurside Farm, and that we meant to coax Mrs Denbigh to let us go into the wood and gather strawberries," said Elizabeth.

"I thought he would make some excuse and come," said the quick-witted Mary, as eager and thoughtless an observer of one love-affair as of another, and quite forgetting that, not many weeks ago, she had fancied an attachment between him and Jemima.

"Did you? I did not," replied Elizabeth. "At least I never thought about it. I was quite startled when I heard his horse's feet behind us on the road."

"He said he was going to the farm, and could take our basket. Was not it kind of him?" Jemima did not answer, so Mary continued:

"You know it's a great pull up to the farm, and we were so hot already. The road was quite white and baked; it hurt my eyes terribly. I was so glad when Mrs Denbigh said we might turn into the wood. The light was quite green there, the branches are so thick overhead."

"And there are whole beds of wild strawberries," said Elizabeth, taking up the tale now Mary was out of breath. Mary fanned herself with her bonnet, while Elizabeth went on:

"You know where the grey rock crops out, don't you, Jemima? Well, there was a complete carpet of strawberry runners. So pretty! And we could hardly step without treading the little bright scarlet berries under foot."

"We did so wish for Leonard," put in Mary.

"Yes! but Mrs Denbigh gathered a great many for him. And Mr Farquhar gave her all his."

"I thought you said he had gone on to Dawson's farm," said Jemima.

"Oh, yes! he just went up there; and then he left his horse there, like a wise man, and came to us in the pretty, cool, green wood. Oh, Jemima, it was so pretty—little flecks of light coming down here and there through the leaves, and quivering on the ground. You must go with us to-morrow."

"Yes," said Mary, "we're going again to-morrow. We could not gather nearly all the strawberries."

"And Leonard is to go too, to-morrow."

"Yes! we thought of such a capital plan. That's to say, Mr Farquhar thought of it—we wanted to carry Leonard up the hill in a king's cushion, but Mrs Denbigh would not hear of it."

"She said it would tire us so; and yet she wanted him to gather strawberries!"

"And so," interrupted Mary, for by this time the two girls were almost speaking together, "Mr Farquhar is to bring him up before him on his horse."

"You'll go with us, won't you, dear Jemima?" asked Elizabeth; "it will be at—"

"No! I can't go!" said Jemima, abruptly. "Don't ask me—I can't."

The little girls were hushed into silence by her manner; for whatever she might be to those above her in age and position, to those below her Jemima was almost invariably gentle. She felt that they were wondering at her.

"Go upstairs and take off your things. You know papa does not like you to come into this room in the shoes in which you have been out."

She was glad to cut her sisters short in the details which they were so mercilessly inflicting—details which she must harden herself to, before she could hear them quietly and unmoved. She saw that she had lost her place as the first object in Mr Farquhar's eyes—a position she had hardly cared for while she was secure in the enjoyment of it; but the charm of it now was redoubled, in her acute sense of how she had forfeited it by her own doing, and her own fault. For if he were the cold, calculating man her father had believed him to be, and had represented him as being to her, would he care for a portionless widow in humble circumstances like Mrs Denbigh; no money, no connexion, encumbered with her boy? The very action which proved Mr Farquhar to be lost to Jemima reinstated him on his throne in her fancy. And she must go on in hushed quietness, quivering with every fresh token of his preference for another! That other, too, one so infinitely more worthy of him than herself; so that she could not have even the poor comfort of thinking that he had no discrimination, and was throwing himself away on a common or worthless person. Ruth was beautiful, gentle, good, and conscientious. The hot colour flushed up into Jemima's sallow face as she became aware that, even while she acknowledged these excellences on Mrs Denbigh's part, she hated her. The recollection of her marble face wearied her even to sickness; the tones of her low voice were irritating from their very softness. Her goodness, undoubted as it was, was more distasteful than many faults which had more savour of human struggle in them.

"What was this terrible demon in her heart?" asked Jemima's better angel. "Was she, indeed, given up to possession? Was not this the old stinging hatred which had prompted so many crimes? The hatred of all sweet virtues which might win the love denied to us? The old anger that wrought in the elder brother's heart, till it ended in the murder of the gentle Abel, while yet the world was young?"

"Oh, God! help me! I did not know I was so wicked," cried Jemima aloud in her agony. It had been a terrible glimpse into the dark, lurid gulf—the capability for evil, in her heart. She wrestled with the demon, but he would not depart; it was to be a struggle whether or not she was to be given up to him, in this her time of sore temptation.

All the next day long she sat and pictured the happy strawberry gathering going on, even then, in pleasant Scaurside Wood. Every touch of fancy which could heighten her idea of their enjoyment, and of Mr Farquhar's attention to the blushing, conscious Ruth—every such touch which would add a pang to her self-reproach and keen jealousy, was added by her imagination. She got up and walked about, to try and stop her over-busy fancy by bodily exercise. But she had eaten little all day, and was weak and faint in the intense heat of the sunny garden. Even the long grass-walk under the filbert-hedge, was parched and dry in the glowing August sun. Yet her sisters found her there when they returned, walking quickly up and down, as if to warm herself on some winter's day. They were very weary; and not half so communicative as on the day before, now that Jemima was craving for every detail to add to her agony.

"Yes! Leonard came up before Mr Farquhar. Oh! how hot it is, Jemima; do sit down, and I'll tell you about it, but I can't if you keep walking so!"

"I can't sit still to-day," said Jemima, springing up from the turf as soon as she had sat down. "Tell me! I can hear you while I walk about."

"Oh! but I can't shout; I can hardly speak I am so tired. Mr Farquhar brought Leonard—"

"You've told me that before," said Jemima, sharply.

"Well! I don't know what else to tell. Somebody had been since yesterday, and gathered nearly all the strawberries off the grey rock. Jemima! Jemima!" said Elizabeth, faintly, "I am so dizzy—I think I am ill."

The next minute the tired girl lay swooning on the grass. It was an outlet for Jemima's fierce energy. With a strength she had never again, and never had known before, she lifted up her fainting sister, and bidding Mary run and clear the way, she carried her in through the open garden-door, up the wide old-fashioned stairs, and laid her on the bed in her own room, where the breeze from the window came softly and pleasantly through the green shade of the vine-leaves and jessamine.

"Give me the water. Run for mamma, Mary," said Jemima, as she saw that the fainting-fit did not yield to the usual remedy of a horizontal position and the water sprinkling.

"Dear! dear Lizzie!" said Jemima, kissing the pale, unconscious face. "I think you loved me, darling."

The long walk on the hot day had been too much for the delicate Elizabeth, who was fast outgrowing her strength. It was many days before she regained any portion of her spirit and vigour. After that fainting-fit, she lay listless and weary, without appetite or interest, through the long sunny autumn weather, on the bed or on the couch in Jemima's room, whither she had been carried at first. It was a comfort to Mrs Bradshaw to be able at once to discover what it was that had knocked up Elizabeth; she did not rest easily until she had settled upon a cause for every ailment or illness in the family. It was a stern consolation to Mr Bradshaw, during his time of anxiety respecting his daughter, to be able to blame somebody. He could not, like his wife, have taken comfort from an inanimate fact; he wanted the satisfaction of feeling that some one had been in fault, or else this never could have happened. Poor Ruth did not need his implied reproaches. When she saw her gentle Elizabeth lying feeble and languid, her heart blamed her for thoughtlessness so severely as to make her take all Mr Bradshaw's words and hints as too light censure for the careless way in which, to please her own child, she had allowed her two pupils to fatigue themselves with such long walks. She begged hard to take her share of nursing. Every spare moment she went to Mr Bradshaw's, and asked, with earnest humility, to be allowed to pass them with Elizabeth; and, as it was often a relief to have her assistance, Mrs Bradshaw received these entreaties very kindly, and desired her to go upstairs, where Elizabeth's pale countenance brightened when she saw her, but where Jemima sat in silent annoyance that her own room was now become open ground for one, whom her heart rose up against, to enter in and be welcomed. Whether it was that Ruth, who was not an inmate of the house, brought with her a fresher air, more change of thought to the invalid, I do not know, but Elizabeth always gave her a peculiarly tender greeting; and if she had sunk down into languid fatigue, in spite of all Jemima's endeavours to interest her, she roused up into animation when Ruth came in with a flower, a book, or a brown and ruddy pear, sending out the warm fragrance it retained from the sunny garden-wall at Chapel-house.

The jealous dislike which Jemima was allowing to grow up in her heart against Ruth was, as she thought, never shown in word or deed. She was cold in manner, because she could not be hypocritical; but her words were polite and kind in purport; and she took pains to make her actions the same as formerly. But rule and line may measure out the figure of a man; it is the soul that gives it life; and there was no soul, no inner meaning, breathing out in Jemima's actions. Ruth felt the change acutely. She suffered from it some time before she ventured to ask what had occasioned it. But, one day, she took Miss Bradshaw by surprise, when they were alone together for a few minutes, by asking her if she had vexed her in any way, she was so changed? It is sad when friendship has cooled so far as to render such a question necessary. Jemima went rather paler than usual, and then made answer:

"Changed! How do you mean? How am I changed? What do I say or do different from what I used to do?"

But the tone was so constrained and cold, that Ruth's heart sank within her. She knew now, as well as words could have told her, that not only had the old feeling of love passed away from Jemima, but that it had gone unregretted, and no attempt had been made to recall it. Love was very precious to Ruth now, as of old time. It was one of the faults of her nature to be ready to make any sacrifices for those who loved her, and to value affection almost above its price. She had yet to learn the lesson, that it is more blessed to love than to be beloved; and lonely as the impressible years of her youth had been—without parents, without brother or sister—it was, perhaps, no wonder that she clung tenaciously to every symptom of regard, and could not relinquish the love of any one without a pang.

The doctor who was called in to Elizabeth prescribed sea-air as the best means of recruiting her strength. Mr Bradshaw, who liked to spend money ostentatiously, went down straight to Abermouth, and engaged a house for the remainder of the autumn; for, as he told the medical man, money was no object to him in comparison with his children's health; and the doctor cared too little about the mode in which his remedy was administered, to tell Mr Bradshaw that lodgings would have done as well, or better, than the complete house he had seen fit to take. For it was now necessary to engage servants, and take much trouble, which might have been obviated, and Elizabeth's removal effected more quietly and speedily, if she had gone into lodgings. As it was, she was weary of hearing all the planning and talking, and deciding and un-deciding, and re-deciding, before it was possible for her to go. Her only comfort was in the thought that dear Mrs Denbigh was to go with her.

It had not been entirely by way of pompously spending his money that Mr Bradshaw had engaged this seaside house. He was glad to get his little girls and their governess out of the way; for a busy time was impending, when he should want his head clear for electioneering purposes, and his house clear for electioneering hospitality. He was the mover of a project for bringing forward a man on the Liberal and Dissenting interest, to contest the election with the old Tory member, who had on several successive occasions walked over the course, as he and his family owned half the town, and votes and rent were paid alike to the landlord.

Kings of Eccleston had Mr Cranworth and his ancestors been this many a long year; their right was so little disputed that they never thought of acknowledging the allegiance so readily paid to them. The old feudal feeling between land-owner and tenant did not quake prophetically at the introduction of manufactures; the Cranworth family ignored the growing power of the manufacturers, more especially as the principal person engaged in the trade was a Dissenter. But notwithstanding this lack of patronage from the one great family in the neighbourhood, the business flourished, increased, and spread wide; and the Dissenting head thereof looked around, about the time of which I speak, and felt himself powerful enough to defy the great Cranworth interest even in their hereditary stronghold, and, by so doing, avenge the slights of many years—slights which rankled in Mr Bradshaw's mind as much as if he did not go to chapel twice every Sunday, and pay the largest pew-rent of any member of Mr Benson's congregation.

Accordingly, Mr Bradshaw had applied to one of the Liberal parliamentary agents in London—a man whose only principle was to do wrong on the Liberal side; he would not act, right or wrong, for a Tory, but for a Whig the latitude of his conscience had never yet been discovered. It was possible Mr Bradshaw was not aware of the character of this agent; at any rate, he knew he was the man for his purpose, which was to hear of some one who would come forward as a candidate for the representation of Eccleston on the Dissenting interest.

"There are in round numbers about six hundred voters," said he; "two hundred are decidedly in the Cranworth interest—dare not offend Mr Cranworth, poor souls! Two hundred more we may calculate upon as pretty certain—factory hands, or people connected with our trade in some way or another—who are indignant at the stubborn way in which Cranworth has contested the right of water; two hundred are doubtful."

"Don't much care either way," said the parliamentary agent. "Of course, we must make them care."

Mr Bradshaw rather shrunk from the knowing look with which this was said. He hoped that Mr Pilson did not mean to allude to bribery; but he did not express this hope, because he thought it would deter the agent from using this means, and it was possible it might prove to be the only way. And if he (Mr Bradshaw) once embarked on such an enterprise, there must be no failure. By some expedient or another, success must be certain, or he could have nothing to do with it.

The parliamentary agent was well accustomed to deal with all kinds and shades of scruples. He was most at home with men who had none; but still he could allow for human weakness; and he perfectly understood Mr Bradshaw.

"I have a notion I know of a man who will just suit your purpose. Plenty of money—does not know what to do with it, in fact—tired of yachting, travelling; wants something new. I heard, through some of the means of intelligence I employ, that not very long ago he was wishing for a seat in Parliament."

"A Liberal?" said Mr Bradshaw.

"Decidedly. Belongs to a family who were in the Long Parliament in their day."

Mr Bradshaw rubbed his hands.

"Dissenter?" asked he.

"No, no! Not so far as that. But very lax Church."

"What is his name?" asked Mr Bradshaw, eagerly.

"Excuse me. Until I am certain that he would like to come forward for Eccleston, I think I had better not mention his name."

The anonymous gentleman did like to come forward, and his name proved to be Donne. He and Mr Bradshaw had been in correspondence during all the time of Mr Ralph Cranworth's illness; and when he died, everything was arranged ready for a start, even before the Cranworths had determined who should keep the seat warm till the eldest son came of age, for the father was already member for the county. Mr Donne was to come down to canvass in person, and was to take up his abode at Mr Bradshaw's; and therefore it was that the seaside house, within twenty miles' distance of Eccleston, was found to be so convenient as an infirmary and nursery for those members of his family who were likely to be useless, if not positive encumbrances, during the forthcoming election.

CHAPTER XXII

The Liberal Candidate and His Precursor

Jemima did not know whether she wished to go to Abermouth or not. She longed for change. She wearied of the sights and sounds of home. But yet she could not bear to leave the neighbourhood of Mr Farquhar; especially as, if she went to Abermouth, Ruth would in all probability be left to take her holiday at home.

When Mr Bradshaw decided that she was to go, Ruth tried to feel glad that he gave her the means of repairing her fault towards Elizabeth; and she resolved to watch over the two girls most faithfully and carefully, and to do all in her power to restore the invalid to health. But a tremor came over her whenever she thought of leaving Leonard; she had never quitted him for a day, and it seemed to her as if her brooding, constant care was his natural and necessary shelter from all evils— from very death itself. She would not go to sleep at nights, in order to enjoy the blessed consciousness of having him near her; when she was away from him teaching her pupils, she kept trying to remember his face, and print it deep on her heart, against the time when days and days would elapse without her seeing that little darling countenance. Miss Benson would wonder to her brother that Mr Bradshaw did not propose that Leonard should accompany his mother; he only begged her not to put such an idea into Ruth's head, as he was sure Mr Bradshaw had no thoughts of doing any such thing, yet to Ruth it might be a hope, and then a disappointment. His sister scolded him for being so cold-hearted; but he was full of sympathy, although he did not express it, and made some quiet little sacrifices in order to set himself at liberty to take Leonard a long walking expedition on the day when his mother left Eccleston.

Ruth cried until she could cry no longer, and felt very much ashamed of herself as she saw the grave and wondering looks of her pupils, whose only feeling on leaving home was delight at the idea of Abermouth, and into whose minds the possibility of death to any of their beloved ones never entered. Ruth dried her eyes, and spoke cheerfully as soon as she caught the perplexed expression of their faces; and by the time they arrived at Abermouth, she was as much delighted with all the new scenery as they were, and found it hard work to resist their entreaties to go rambling out on the seashore at once; but Elizabeth had undergone more fatigue that day than she had had before for many weeks, and Ruth was determined to be prudent.

Meanwhile, the Bradshaws' house at Eccleston was being rapidly adapted for electioneering hospitality. The partition-wall between the unused drawing-room and the school-room was broken down, in order to admit of folding doors; the "ingenious" upholsterer of the town (and what town does not boast of the upholsterer full of contrivances and resources, in opposition to the upholsterer of steady capital and no imagination, who looks down with uneasy contempt on ingenuity?) had come in to give his opinion, that "nothing could be easier than to convert a bathroom into a bedroom, by the assistance of a little drapery to conceal the shower-bath," the string of which was to be carefully concealed, for fear that the unconscious occupier of the bath-bed might innocently take it for a bell-rope. The professional cook of the town had been already engaged to take up her abode for a month at Mr Bradshaw's, much to the indignation of Betsy, who became a vehement partisan of Mr Cranworth, as soon as ever she heard of the plan of her deposition from sovereign authority in the kitchen, in which she had reigned supreme for fourteen years. Mrs Bradshaw sighed and bemoaned herself in all her leisure moments, which were not many, and wondered why their house was to be turned into an inn for this Mr Donne, when everybody knew that the George was good enough for the Cranworths, who never thought of asking the electors to the Hall;—and they had lived at Cranworth ever since Julius Caesar's time, and if that was not being an old family, she did not know what was. The excitement soothed Jemima. There was something to do. It was she who planned with the upholsterer; it was she who soothed Betsy into angry silence; it was she who persuaded her mother to lie down and rest, while she herself went out to buy the heterogeneous things required to make the family and house presentable to Mr Donne and his precursor—the friend of the parliamentary agent. This latter gentleman never appeared himself on the scene of action, but pulled all the strings notwithstanding. The friend was a Mr Hickson, a lawyer—a briefless barrister, some people called him; but he himself professed a great disgust to the law, as a "great sham," which involved an immensity of underhand action, and truckling, and time-serving, and was perfectly encumbered by useless forms and ceremonies, and dead obsolete words. So, instead of putting his shoulder to the wheel to reform the law, he talked eloquently against it, in such a high-priest style, that it was occasionally a matter of surprise how he could ever have made a friend of the parliamentary agent before mentioned. But, as Mr Hickson himself said, it was the very corruptness of the law which he was fighting against, in doing all he could to effect the return of certain members to Parliament; these certain members being pledged to effect a reform in the law, according to Mr Hickson. And, as he once observed confidentially, "If you had to destroy a hydra-headed monster, would you measure swords with the demon as if he were a gentleman? Would you not rather seize the first weapon that came to hand? And so do I. My great object in life, sir, is to reform the law of England, sir. Once get a majority of Liberal members into the House, and the thing is done. And I consider myself justified, for so high—for, I may say, so holy—an end, in using men's weaknesses to work out my purpose. Of course, if men were angels, or even immaculate—men invulnerable to bribes, we would not bribe."

"Could you?" asked Jemima, for the conversation took place at Mr Bradshaw's dinner-table, where a few friends were gathered together to meet Mr Hickson; and among them was Mr Benson.

"We neither would nor could," said the ardent barrister, disregarding in his vehemence the point of the question, and floating on over the bar of argument into the wide ocean of his own eloquence: "As it is—as the world stands, they who would succeed even in good deeds must come down to the level of expediency; and therefore, I say once more, if Mr Donne is the man for your purpose, and your purpose is a good one, a lofty one, a holy one" (for Mr Hickson remembered the Dissenting character of his little audience, and privately considered the introduction of the word "holy" a most happy hit), "then, I say, we must put all the squeamish scruples which might befit Utopia, or some such place, on one side, and treat men as they are. If they are avaricious, it is not we who have made them so; but as we have to do with them, we must consider their failings in dealing with them; if they have been careless or extravagant, or have had their little peccadillos, we must administer the screw. The glorious reform of the law will justify, in my idea, all means to obtain the end—that law, from the profession of which I have withdrawn myself from perhaps a too scrupulous conscience!" he concluded softly to himself.

"We are not to do evil that good may come," said Mr Benson. He was startled at the deep sound of his own voice as he uttered these words; but he had not been speaking for some time, and his voice came forth strong and unmodulated.

"True, sir; most true," said Mr Hickson, bowing. "I honour you for the observation." And he profited by it, insomuch that he confined his further remarks on elections to the end of the table, where he sat near Mr Bradshaw, and one or two equally eager, though not equally influential partisans of Mr Donne's. Meanwhile, Mr Farquhar took up Mr Benson's quotation, at the end where he and Jemima sat near to Mrs Bradshaw and him.

"But in the present state of the world, as Mr Hickson says, it is rather difficult to act upon that precept."

"Oh, Mr Farquhar!" said Jemima, indignantly, the tears springing to her eyes with a feeling of disappointment. For she had been chafing under all that Mr Hickson had been saying, perhaps the more for one or two attempts on his part at a flirtation with the daughter of his wealthy host, which she resented with all the loathing of a pre-occupied heart; and she had longed to be a man, to speak out her wrath at this paltering with right and wrong. She had felt grateful to Mr Benson for his one clear, short precept, coming down with a divine force against which there was no appeal; and now to have Mr Farquhar taking the side of expediency! It was too bad.

"Nay, Jemima!" said Mr Farquhar, touched, and secretly flattered by the visible pain his speech had given. "Don't be indignant with me till I have explained myself a little more. I don't understand myself yet; and it is a very intricate question, or so it appears to me, which I was going to put, really, earnestly, and humbly, for Mr Benson's opinion. Now, Mr Benson, may I ask, if you always find it practicable to act strictly in accordance with that principle? For if you do not, I am sure no man living can! Are there not occasions when it is absolutely necessary to wade through evil to good? I am not speaking in the careless, presumptuous way of that man yonder," said he, lowering his voice, and addressing himself to

Jemima more exclusively; "I am really anxious to hear what Mr Benson will say on the subject, for I know no one to whose candid opinion I should attach more weight."

But Mr Benson was silent. He did not see Mrs Bradshaw and Jemima leave the room. He was really, as Mr Farquhar supposed him, completely absent, questioning himself as to how far his practice tallied with his principle. By degrees he came to himself; he found the conversation still turned on the election; and Mr Hickson, who felt that he had jarred against the little minister's principles, and yet knew, from the *carte du pays* which the scouts of the parliamentary agent had given him, that Mr Benson was a person to be conciliated, on account of his influence over many of the working people, began to ask him questions with an air of deferring to superior knowledge, that almost surprised Mr Bradshaw, who had been accustomed to treat "Benson" in a very different fashion, of civil condescending indulgence, just as one listens to a child who can have had no opportunities of knowing better.

At the end of a conversation that Mr Hickson held with Mr Benson, on a subject in which the latter was really interested, and on which he had expressed himself at some length, the young barrister turned to Mr Bradshaw, and said very audibly,

"I wish Donne had been here. This conversation during the last half-hour would have interested him almost as much as it has done me."

Mr Bradshaw little guessed the truth, that Mr Donne was, at that very moment, coaching up the various subjects of public interest in Eccleston, and privately cursing the particular subject on which Mr Benson had been holding forth, as being an unintelligible piece of Quixotism; or the leading Dissenter of the town need not have experienced a pang of jealousy at the possible future admiration his minister might excite in the possible future member for Eccleston. And if Mr Benson had been clairvoyant, he need not have made an especial subject of gratitude out of the likelihood that he might have an opportunity of so far interesting Mr Donne in the condition of the people of Eccleston as to induce him to set his face against any attempts at bribery.

Mr Benson thought of this half the night through; and ended by determining to write a sermon on the Christian view of political duties, which might be good for all, both electors and member, to hear on the eve of an election. For Mr Donne was expected at Mr Bradshaw's before the next Sunday; and, of course, as Mr and Miss Benson had settled it, he would appear at the chapel with them on that day. But the stinging conscience refused to be quieted. No present plan of usefulness allayed the aching remembrance of the evil he had done that good might come. Not even the look of Leonard, as the early dawn fell on him, and Mr Benson's sleepless eyes saw the rosy glow on his firm round cheeks; his open mouth, through which the soft, long-drawn breath came gently quivering; and his eyes not fully shut, but closed to outward sight—not even the aspect of the quiet, innocent child could soothe the troubled spirit.

Leonard and his mother dreamt of each other that night. Her dream of him was one of undefined terror—terror so great that it wakened her up, and she strove not to sleep again, for fear that ominous ghastly dream should return. He, on the contrary, dreamt of her sitting watching and smiling by his bedside, as her gentle self had been many a morning; and when she saw him awake (so it fell out in the dream), she smiled still more sweetly, and bending down she kissed him, and then spread out large, soft, white-feathered wings (which in no way surprised her child—he seemed to have known they were there all along), and sailed away through the open window far into the blue sky of a summer's day. Leonard wakened up then, and remembered how far away she really was—far more distant and inaccessible than the beautiful blue sky to which she had betaken herself in his dream—and cried himself to sleep again.

In spite of her absence from her child, which made one great and abiding sorrow, Ruth enjoyed her seaside visit exceedingly. In the first place, there was the delight of seeing Elizabeth's daily and almost hourly improvement. Then, at the doctor's express orders, there were so few lessons to be done, that there was time for the long exploring rambles, which all three delighted in. And when the rain came and the storms blew, the house, with its wild sea-views, was equally delightful.

It was a large house, built on the summit of a rock, which nearly overhung the shore below; there were, to be sure, a series of zigzag tacking paths down the face of this rock, but from the house they could not be seen. Old or delicate people would have considered the situation bleak and exposed; indeed, the present proprietor wanted to dispose of it on this very account; but by its present inhabitants, this exposure and bleakness were called by other names, and considered as charms. From every part of the rooms they saw the grey storms gather on the sea-horizon, and put themselves in marching array; and soon the march became a sweep, and the great dome of the heavens was covered with the lurid clouds, between which and the vivid green earth below there seemed to come a purple atmosphere, making the very threatening beautiful; and by-and-by the house was wrapped in sheets of rain shutting out sky, and sea, and inland view; till, of a sudden, the storm was gone by, and the heavy rain-drops glistened in the sun as they hung on leaf and grass, and the "little birds sang east, and the little birds sang west," and there was a pleasant sound of running waters all abroad.

"Oh! if papa would but buy this house!" exclaimed Elizabeth, after one such storm, which she had watched silently from the very beginning of the "little cloud no bigger than a man's hand."

"Mamma would never like it, I am afraid," said Mary. "She would call our delicious gushes of air, draughts, and think we should catch cold."

"Jemima would be on our side. But how long Mrs Denbigh is! I hope she was near enough the post-office when the rain came on!"

Ruth had gone to "the shop" in the little village, about half-a-mile distant, where all letters were left till fetched. She only expected one, but that one was to tell her of Leonard. She, however, received two; the unexpected one was from Mr Bradshaw, and the news it contained was, if possible, a greater surprise than the letter itself. Mr Bradshaw informed her, that he planned arriving by dinner-time the following Saturday at Eagle's Crag; and more, that he intended bringing Mr Donne and one or two other gentlemen with him, to spend the Sunday there! The letter went on to give every possible direction regarding the household preparations. The dinner-hour was fixed to be at six; but, of course, Ruth and the girls would have dined long before. The (professional) cook would arrive the day before, laden with all the provisions that could not be obtained on the spot. Ruth was to engage a waiter from the inn, and this it was that detained her so long. While she sat in the little parlour, awaiting the coming of the landlady, she could not help wondering why Mr Bradshaw was bringing this strange gentleman to spend two days at Abermouth, and thus giving himself so much trouble and fuss of preparation.

There were so many small reasons that went to make up the large one which had convinced Mr Bradshaw of the desirableness of this step, that it was not likely that Ruth should guess at one half of them. In the first place, Miss Benson, in the pride and fulness of her heart, had told Mrs Bradshaw what her brother had told her; how he meant to preach upon the Christian view of the duties involved in political rights; and as, of course, Mrs Bradshaw had told Mr Bradshaw, he began to dislike the idea of attending chapel on that Sunday at all; for he had an uncomfortable idea that by the Christian standard—that divine test of the true and pure—bribery would not be altogether approved of; and yet he was tacitly coming round to the understanding that "packets" would be required, for what purpose both he and Mr Donne were to be supposed to remain ignorant. But it would be very awkward, so near to the time, if he were to be clearly convinced that bribery, however disguised by names and words, was in plain terms a sin. And yet he knew Mr Benson had once or twice convinced him against his will of certain things, which he had thenceforward found it impossible to do, without such great uneasiness of mind, that he had left off doing them, which was sadly against his interest. And if Mr Donne (whom he had intended to take with him to chapel, as fair Dissenting prey) should also become convinced, why, the Cranworths would win the day, and he should be the laughing-stock of Eccleston. No! in this one case bribery must be allowed—was allowable; but it was a great pity human nature was so corrupt, and if his member succeeded, he would double his subscription to the schools, in order that the next generation might be taught better. There were various other reasons, which strengthened Mr Bradshaw in the bright idea of going down to Abermouth for the Sunday; some connected with the out-of-door politics, and some with the domestic. For instance, it had been the plan of the house to have a cold dinner on the Sundays—Mr Bradshaw had piqued himself on this strictness—and yet he had an instinctive feeling that Mr Donne was not quite the man to partake of cold meat for conscience' sake with cheerful indifference to his fare.

Mr Donne had, in fact, taken the Bradshaw household a little by surprise. Before he came, Mr Bradshaw had pleased himself with thinking, that more unlikely things had happened than the espousal of his daughter with the member of a small borough. But this pretty airy bubble burst as soon as he saw Mr Donne; and its very existence was forgotten in less than half an hour, when he felt the quiet but incontestible difference of rank and standard that there was, in every respect, between his guest and his own family. It was not through any circumstance so palpable, and possibly accidental, as the bringing down a servant, whom Mr Donne seemed to consider as much a matter of course as a carpet-bag (though the smart gentleman's arrival "fluttered the Volscians in Corioli" considerably more than his gentle-spoken master's). It was nothing like this; it was something indescribable—a quiet being at ease, and expecting every one else to be so—an attention to women, which was so habitual as to be unconsciously exercised to those subordinate persons in Mr Bradshaw's family—a happy choice of simple and expressive words, some of which it must be confessed were slang, but fashionable slang, and that makes all the difference—a measured, graceful way of utterance, with a style of pronunciation quite different to that of Eccleston. All these put together make but a part of the indescribable whole which unconsciously affected Mr Bradshaw, and established Mr Donne in his estimation as a creature quite different to any he had seen before, and as most unfit to mate with Jemima. Mr Hickson, who had appeared as a model of gentlemanly ease before Mr Donne's arrival, now became vulgar and coarse in Mr Bradshaw's eyes. And yet, such was the charm of that languid, high-bred manner, that Mr Bradshaw "cottoned" (as he expressed it to Mr Farquhar) to his new candidate at once. He was only afraid lest Mr Donne was too indifferent to all things under the sun to care whether he gained or lost the election; but he was reassured after the first conversation they had together on the subject. Mr Donne's eye lightened with an eagerness that was almost fierce, though his tones were as musical, and nearly as slow, as ever; and when Mr Bradshaw alluded distantly to "probable expenses" and "packets," Mr Donne replied,

"Oh, of course! disagreeable necessity! Better speak as little about such things as possible; other people can be found to arrange all the dirty work. Neither you nor I would like to soil our fingers by it, I am sure. Four thousand pounds are in Mr Pilson's hands, and I shall never inquire what becomes of them; they may, very probably, be absorbed in the law expenses, you know. I shall let it be clearly understood from the hustings, that I most decidedly disapprove of bribery, and leave the rest to Hickson's management. He is accustomed to these sort of things. I am not."

Mr Bradshaw was rather perplexed by this want of bustling energy on the part of the new candidate; and if it had not been for the four thousand pounds aforesaid, would have doubted whether Mr Donne cared sufficiently for the result of the election. Jemima thought differently. She watched her father's visitor attentively, with something like the curious observation which a naturalist bestows on a new species of animal.

"Do you know what Mr Donne reminds me of, mamma?" said she, one day, as the two sat at work, while the gentlemen were absent canvassing.

"No! he is not like anybody I ever saw. He quite frightens me, by being so ready to open the door for me if I am going out of the room, and by giving me a chair when I come in. I never saw any one like him. Who is it, Jemima?"

"Not any person—not any human being, mamma," said Jemima, half smiling. "Do you remember our stopping at Wakefield once, on our way to Scarborough, and there were horse-races going on somewhere, and some of the racers were in the stables at the inn where we dined?"

"Yes! I remember it; but what about that?"

"Why, Richard, somehow, knew one of the jockeys, and, as we were coming in from our ramble through the town, this man, or boy, asked us to look at one of the racers he had the charge of."

"Well, my dear!"

"Well, mamma! Mr Donne is like that horse!"

"Nonsense, Jemima; you must not say so. I don't know what your father would say, if he heard you likening Mr Donne to a brute."

"Brutes are sometimes very beautiful, mamma. I am sure I should think it a compliment to be likened to a race-horse, such as the one we saw. But the thing in which they are alike, is the sort of repressed eagerness in both."

"Eager! Why, I should say there never was any one cooler than Mr Donne. Think of the trouble your papa has had this month past, and then remember the slow way in which Mr Donne moves when he is going out to canvass, and the low, drawling voice in which he questions the people who bring him intelligence. I can see your papa standing by, ready to shake them to get out their news."

"But Mr Donne's questions are always to the point, and force out the grain without the chaff. And look at him, if any one tells him ill news about the election! Have you never seen a dull red light come into his eyes? That is like my race-horse. Her flesh quivered all over, at certain sounds and noises which had some meaning to her; but she stood quite still, pretty creature! Now, Mr Donne is just as eager as she was, though he may be too proud to show it. Though he seems so gentle, I almost think he is very headstrong in following out his own will."

"Well! don't call him like a horse again, for I am sure papa would not like it. Do you know, I thought you were going to say he was like little Leonard, when you asked me who he was like."

"Leonard! Oh, mamma, he is not in the least like Leonard. He is twenty times more like my race-horse."

"Now, my dear Jemima, do be quiet. Your father thinks racing so wrong, that I am sure he would be very seriously displeased if he were to hear you."

To return to Mr Bradshaw, and to give one more of his various reasons for wishing to take Mr Donne to Abermouth. The wealthy Eccleston manufacturer was uncomfortably impressed with an indefinable sense of inferiority to his visitor. It was not in education, for Mr Bradshaw was a well-educated man; it was not in power, for, if he chose, the present object of Mr Donne's life might be utterly defeated; it did not arise from anything overbearing in manner, for Mr Donne was habitually polite and courteous, and was just now anxious to propitiate his host, whom he looked upon as a very useful man. Whatever this sense of inferiority arose from, Mr Bradshaw was anxious to relieve himself of it, and imagined that if he could make more display of his wealth his object would be obtained. Now his house in Eccleston was old-fashioned, and ill-calculated to exhibit money's worth. His mode of living, though strained to a high pitch just at this time, he became aware was no more than Mr Donne was accustomed to every day of his life. The first day at dessert, some remark (some opportune remark, as Mr Bradshaw in his innocence had thought) was made regarding the price of pine-apples, which was rather exorbitant that year, and Mr Donne asked Mrs Bradshaw, with quiet surprise, if they had no pinery, as if to be without a pinery were indeed a depth of pitiable destitution. In fact, Mr Donne had been born and cradled in all that wealth could purchase, and so had his ancestors before him for so many generations, that refinement and luxury seemed the natural condition of man, and they that dwelt without were in the position of monsters. The absence was noticed; but not the presence.

Now, Mr Bradshaw knew that the house and grounds of Eagle's Crag were exorbitantly dear, and yet he really thought of purchasing them. And as one means of exhibiting his wealth, and so raising himself up to the level of Mr Donne, he thought that if he could take the latter down to Abermouth, and show him the place for which, "because his little girls had taken a fancy to it," he was willing to give the fancy-price of fourteen thousand pounds, he should at last make those half-shut dreamy eyes open wide, and their owner confess that, in wealth at least, the Eccleston manufacturer stood on a par with him.

All these mingled motives caused the determination which made Ruth sit in the little inn-parlour at Abermouth during the wild storm's passage.

She wondered if she had fulfilled all Mr Bradshaw's directions. She looked at the letter. Yes! everything was done. And now home with her news, through the wet lane, where the little pools by the roadside reflected the deep blue sky and the round white clouds with even deeper blue and clearer white; and the rain-drops hung so thick on the trees, that even a little bird's flight was enough to shake them down in a bright shower as of rain. When she told the news, Mary exclaimed,

"Oh, how charming! Then we shall see this new member after all!" while Elizabeth added,

"Yes! I shall like to do that. But where must we be? Papa will want the dining-room and this room, and where must we sit?"

"Oh!" said Ruth, "in the dressing-room next to my room. All that your papa wants always, is that you are quiet and out of the way."

CHAPTER XXIII

Recognition

Saturday came. Torn, ragged clouds were driven across the sky. It was not a becoming day for the scenery, and the little girls regretted it much. First they hoped for a change at twelve o'clock, and then at the afternoon tide-turning. But at neither time did the sun show his face.

"Papa will never buy this dear place," said Elizabeth, sadly, as she watched the weather. "The sun is everything to it. The sea looks quite leaden to-day, and there is no sparkle on it. And the sands, that were so yellow and sun-speckled on Thursday, are all one dull brown now."

"Never mind! to-morrow may be better," said Ruth, cheerily.

"I wonder what time they will come at?" inquired Mary.

"Your papa said they would be at the station at five o'clock. And the landlady at the Swan said it would take them half an hour to get here."

"And they are to dine at six?" asked Elizabeth.

"Yes," answered Ruth. "And I think if we had our tea half an hour earlier, at half-past four, and then went out for a walk, we should be nicely out of the way just during the bustle of the arrival and dinner; and we could be in the drawing-room ready against your papa came in after dinner."

"Oh! that would be nice," said they; and tea was ordered accordingly.

The south-westerly wind had dropped, and the clouds were stationary, when they went out on the sands. They dug little holes near the in-coming tide, and made canals to them from the water, and blew the light sea-foam against each other; and then stole on tiptoe near to the groups of grey and white sea-gulls, which despised their caution, flying softly and slowly away to a little distance as soon as they drew near. And in all this Ruth was as great a child as any. Only she longed for Leonard with a mother's longing, as indeed she did every day, and all hours of the day. By-and-by the clouds thickened yet more, and one or two drops of rain were felt. It was very little, but Ruth feared a shower for her delicate Elizabeth, and besides, the September evening was fast closing in the dark and sunless day. As they turned homewards in the rapidly increasing dusk, they saw three figures on the sand near the rocks, coming in their direction.

"Papa and Mr Donne!" exclaimed Mary. "Now we shall see him!"

"Which do you make out is him?" asked Elizabeth.

"Oh! the tall one, to be sure. Don't you see how papa always turns to him, as if he was speaking to him and not to the other?"

"Who is the other?" asked Elizabeth.

"Mr Bradshaw said that Mr Farquhar and Mr Hickson would come with him. But that is not Mr Farquhar, I am sure," said Ruth.

The girls looked at each other, as they always did, when Ruth mentioned Mr Farquhar's name; but she was perfectly unconscious both of the look and of the conjectures which gave rise to it.

As soon as the two parties drew near, Mr Bradshaw called out in his strong voice,

"Well, my dears! we found there was an hour before dinner, so we came down upon the sands, and here you are."

The tone of his voice assured them that he was in a bland and indulgent mood, and the two little girls ran towards him. He kissed them, and shook hands with Ruth; told his companions that these were the little girls who were tempting him to this extravagance of purchasing Eagle's Crag; and then, rather doubtfully, and because he saw that Mr Donne expected it, he introduced "My daughters' governess, Mrs Denbigh."

It was growing darker every moment, and it was time they should hasten back to the rocks, which were even now indistinct in the grey haze. Mr Bradshaw held a hand of each of his daughters, and Ruth walked alongside, the two strange gentlemen being on the outskirts of the party.

Mr Bradshaw began to give his little girls some home news. He told them that Mr Farquhar was ill, and could not accompany them; but Jemima and their mamma were quite well.

The gentleman nearest to Ruth spoke to her.

"Are you fond of the sea?" asked he. There was no answer, so he repeated his question in a different form.

"Do you enjoy staying by the seaside? I should rather ask."

The reply was "Yes," rather breathed out in a deep inspiration than spoken in a sound. The sands heaved and trembled beneath Ruth. The figures near her vanished into strange nothingness; the sounds of their voices were as distant sounds in a dream, while the echo of one voice thrilled through and through. She could have caught at his arm for support, in the awful dizziness which wrapped her up, body and soul. That voice! No! if name, and face, and figure were all changed, that voice was the same which had touched her girlish heart, which had spoken most tender words of love, which had won, and wrecked her, and which she had last heard in the low mutterings of fever. She dared not look round to see the figure of him who spoke, dark as it was. She knew he was there—she heard him speak in the manner in which he used to address strangers years ago; perhaps she answered him, perhaps she did not—God knew. It seemed as if weights were tied to her feet—as if the steadfast rocks receded—as if time stood still;—it was so long, so terrible, that path across the reeling sand.

At the foot of the rocks they separated. Mr Bradshaw, afraid lest dinner should cool, preferred the shorter way for himself and his friends. On Elizabeth's account, the girls were to take the longer and easier path, which wound upwards through a rocky field, where larks' nests abounded, and where wild thyme and heather were now throwing out their sweets to the soft night air.

The little girls spoke in eager discussion of the strangers. They appealed to Ruth, but Ruth did not answer, and they were too impatient to convince each other to repeat the question. The first little ascent from the sands to the field surmounted, Ruth sat down suddenly and covered her face with her hands. This was so unusual—their wishes, their good, was so invariably the rule of motion or of rest in their walks—that the girls, suddenly checked, stood silent and affrighted in surprise. They were still more startled when Ruth wailed aloud some inarticulate words.

"Are you not well, dear Mrs Denbigh?" asked Elizabeth, gently, kneeling down on the grass by Ruth.

She sat facing the west. The low watery twilight was on her face as she took her hands away. So pale, so haggard, so wild and wandering a look the girls had never seen on human countenance before.

"Well! what are you doing here with me? You should not be with me," said she, shaking her head slowly.

They looked at each other.

"You are sadly tired," said Elizabeth, soothingly. "Come home, and let me help you to bed. I will tell papa you are ill, and ask him to send for a doctor."

Ruth looked at her as if she did not understand the meaning of her words. No more she did at first. But by-and-by the dulled brain began to think most vividly and rapidly, and she spoke in a sharp way which deceived the girls into a belief that nothing had been the matter.

"Yes! I was tired. I am tired. Those sands—oh! those sands, those weary, dreadful sands! But that is all over now. Only my heart aches still. Feel how it flutters and beats," said she, taking Elizabeth's hand, and holding it to her side. "I am quite well, though," she continued, reading pity in the child's looks, as she felt the trembling, quivering beat. "We will go straight to the dressing-room, and read a chapter; that will still my heart; and then I'll go to bed, and Mr Bradshaw will excuse me, I know, this one night. I only ask for one night. Put on your right frocks, dears, and do all you ought to do. But I know you will," said she, bending down to kiss Elizabeth, and then, before she had done so, raising her head abruptly. "You are good and dear girls—God keep you so!"

By a strong effort at self-command, she went onwards at an even pace, neither rushing nor pausing to sob and think. The very regularity of motion calmed her. The front and back doors of the house were on two sides, at right angles with each other. They all shrunk a little from the idea of going in at the front door, now that the strange gentlemen were about, and, accordingly, they went through the quiet farm-yard right into the bright, ruddy kitchen, where the servants were dashing about with the dinner things. It was a contrast in more than colour to the lonely, dusky field, which even the little girls perceived; and the noise, the warmth, the very bustle of the servants, were a positive relief to Ruth, and for the time lifted off the heavy press of pent-up passion. A silent house, with moonlit rooms, or with a faint gloom brooding over the apartments, would have been more to be dreaded. Then, she must have given way, and cried out. As it was, she went up the old awkward back stairs, and into the room they were to sit in. There was no candle. Mary volunteered to go down for one; and when she returned she was full of the wonders of preparation in the drawing-room, and ready and eager to dress, so as to take her place there before the gentlemen had finished dinner. But she was struck by the strange paleness of Ruth's face, now that the light fell upon it.

"Stay up here, dear Mrs Denbigh! We'll tell papa you are tired, and are gone to bed."

Another time Ruth would have dreaded Mr Bradshaw's displeasure; for it was an understood thing that no one was to be ill or tired in his household without leave asked, and cause given and assigned. But she never thought of that now. Her great desire was to hold quiet till she was alone. Quietness it was not—it was rigidity; but she succeeded in being rigid in look and movement, and went through her duties to Elizabeth (who preferred remaining with her upstairs) with wooden precision. But her heart felt at times like ice, at times like burning fire; always a heavy, heavy weight within her. At last Elizabeth went to bed. Still Ruth dared not think. Mary would come upstairs soon; and with a strange, sick, shrinking yearning, Ruth awaited her—and the crumbs of intelligence she might drop out about *him*. Ruth's sense of hearing was quickened to miserable intensity as she stood before the chimney-piece, grasping it tight with both hands—gazing into the dying fire, but seeing—not the dead grey embers, or the little sparks of vivid light that ran hither and thither among the wood-ashes—but an old farm-house, and climbing, winding road, and a little golden breezy common, with a rural inn on the hill-top, far, far away. And through the thoughts of the past came the sharp sounds of the present—of three voices, one of which was almost silence, it was so hushed. Indifferent people would only have guessed that Mr Donne was speaking by the quietness in which the others listened; but Ruth heard the voice and many of the words, though they conveyed no idea to her mind. She was too much stunned even to feel curious to know to what they related. *He* spoke. That was her one fact.

Presently up came Mary, bounding, exultant. Papa had let her stay up one quarter of an hour longer, because Mr Hickson had asked. Mr Hickson was so clever! She did not know what to make of Mr Donne, he seemed such a dawdle. But he was very handsome. Had Ruth seen him? Oh, no! She could not, it was so dark on those stupid sands. Well, never mind, she would see him to-morrow. She *must* be well to-morrow. Papa seemed a good deal put out that neither she nor Elizabeth were in the drawing-room to-night; and his last words were, "Tell Mrs Denbigh I hope" (and papa's "hopes" always meant "expect") "she will be able to make breakfast at nine o'clock;" and then she would see Mr Donne.

That was all Ruth heard about him. She went with Mary into her bedroom, helped her to undress, and put the candle out. At length she was alone in her own room! At length!

But the tension did not give way immediately. She fastened her door, and threw open the window, cold and threatening as was the night. She tore off her gown; she put her hair back from her heated face. It seemed now as if she could not think—as if thought and emotion had been repressed so sternly that they would not come to relieve her stupified brain.

Till all at once, like a flash of lightning, her life, past and present, was revealed to her in its minutest detail. And when she saw her very present "Now," the strange confusion of agony was too great to be borne, and she cried aloud. Then she was quite dead, and listened as to the sound of galloping armies.

"If I might see him! If I might see him! If I might just ask him why he left me; if I had vexed him in any way; it was so strange—so cruel! It was not him; it was his mother," said she, almost fiercely, as if answering herself. "Oh, God! but he might have found me out before this," she continued, sadly. "He did not care for me, as I did for him. He did not care for me at all," she went on wildly and sharply. "He did me cruel harm. I can never again lift up my face in innocence. They think I have forgotten all, because I do not speak. Oh, darling love! am I talking against you?" asked she, tenderly. "I am so torn and perplexed! You, who are the father of my child!"

But that very circumstance, full of such tender meaning in many cases, threw a new light into her mind. It changed her from the woman into the mother—the stern guardian of her child. She was still for a time, thinking. Then she began again, but in a low, deep voice,

"He left me. He might have been hurried off, but he might have inquired—he might have learnt, and explained. He left me to bear the burden and the shame; and never cared to learn, as he might have done, of Leonard's birth. He has no love for his child, and I will have no love for him."

She raised her voice while uttering this determination, and then, feeling her own weakness, she moaned out, "Alas! alas!"

And then she started up, for all this time she had been rocking herself backwards and forwards as she sat on the ground, and began to pace the room with hurried steps.

"What am I thinking of? Where am I? I who have been praying these years and years to be worthy to be Leonard's mother. My God! what a depth of sin is in my heart! Why, the old time would be as white as snow to what it would be now, if I sought him out, and prayed for the explanation, which should re-establish him in my heart. I who have striven (or made a mock of trying) to learn God's holy will, in order to bring up Leonard into the full strength of a Christian—I who have taught his sweet innocent lips to pray, 'Lead us not into temptation, but deliver us from evil;' and yet, somehow, I've been longing to give him to his father, who is—who is—" she almost choked, till at last she cried sharp out, "Oh, my God! I do believe Leonard's father is a bad man, and yet, oh! pitiful God, I love him; I cannot forget—I cannot!"

She threw her body half out of the window into the cold night air. The wind was rising, and came in great gusts. The rain beat down on her. It did her good. A still, calm night would not have soothed her as this did. The wild tattered clouds, hurrying past the moon, gave her a foolish kind of pleasure that almost made her smile a vacant smile. The blast-driven rain came on her again, and drenched her hair through and through. The words "stormy wind fulfilling His word" came into her mind.

She sat down on the floor. This time her hands were clasped round her knees. The uneasy rocking motion was stilled.

"I wonder if my darling is frightened with this blustering, noisy wind. I wonder if he is awake."

And then her thoughts went back to the various times of old, when, affrighted by the weather—sounds so mysterious in the night—he had crept into her bed and clung to her, and she had soothed him, and sweetly awed him into stillness and childlike faith, by telling him of the goodness and power of God.

Of a sudden she crept to a chair, and there knelt as in the very presence of God, hiding her face, at first not speaking a word (for did He not know her heart), but by-and-by moaning out, amid her sobs and tears (and now for the first time she wept),

"Oh, my God, help me, for I am very weak. My God! I pray Thee be my rock and my strong fortress, for I of myself am nothing. If I ask in His name, Thou wilt give it me. In the name of Jesus Christ I pray for strength to do Thy will!"

She could not think, or, indeed, remember anything but that she was weak, and God was strong, and "a very present help in time of trouble;" and the wind rose yet higher, and the house shook and vibrated as, in measured time, the great and terrible gusts came from the four quarters of the heavens and blew around it, dying away in the distance with loud and unearthly wails, which were not utterly still before the sound of the coming blast was heard like the trumpets of the vanguard of the Prince of Air.

There was a knock at the bedroom door—a little, gentle knock, and a soft child's voice.

"Mrs Denbigh, may I come in, please? I am so frightened!"

It was Elizabeth. Ruth calmed her passionate breathing by one hasty draught of water, and opened the door to the timid girl.

"Oh, Mrs Denbigh! did you ever hear such a night? I am so frightened! and Mary sleeps so sound."

Ruth was too much shaken to be able to speak all at once; but she took Elizabeth in her arms to reassure her. Elizabeth stood back.

"Why, how wet you are, Mrs Denbigh! and there's the window open, I do believe! Oh, how cold it is!" said she, shivering.

"Get into my bed, dear!" said Ruth.

"But do come too! The candle gives such a strange light with that long wick, and, somehow, your face does not look like you. Please, put the candle out, and come to bed. I am so frightened, and it seems as if I should be safer if you were by me."

Ruth shut the window, and went to bed. Elizabeth was all shivering and quaking. To soothe her, Ruth made a great effort; and spoke of Leonard and his fears, and, in a low hesitating voice, she spoke of God's tender mercy, but very humbly, for she feared lest Elizabeth should think her better and holier than she was. The little girl was soon asleep, her fears forgotten; and Ruth, worn out by passionate emotion, and obliged to be still for fear of awaking her bedfellow, went off into a short slumber, through the depths of which the echoes of her waking sobs quivered up.

When she awoke the grey light of autumnal dawn was in the room. Elizabeth slept on; but Ruth heard the servants about, and the early farmyard sounds. After she had recovered from the shock of consciousness and recollection, she collected her thoughts with a stern calmness. He was here. In a few hours she must meet him. There was no escape, except through subterfuges and contrivances that were both false and cowardly. How it would all turn out she could not say, or even guess. But of one thing she was clear, and to one thing she would hold fast: that was, that, come what might, she would obey God's law, and, be the end of all what it might, she would say, "Thy will be done!" She only asked for strength enough to do this when the time came. How the time would come—what speech or action would be requisite on her part, she did not know—she did not even try to conjecture. She left that in His hands.

She was icy cold, but very calm, when the breakfast-bell rang. She went down immediately; because she felt that there was less chance of a recognition if she were already at her place beside the tea-urn, and busied with the cups, than if she came in after all were settled. Her heart seemed to stand still, but she felt almost a strange exultant sense of power over herself. She felt, rather than saw, that he was not there. Mr Bradshaw and Mr Hickson were, and so busy talking election-politics that they did not interrupt their conversation even when they bowed to her. Her pupils sat one on each side of her. Before they were quite settled, and while the other two gentlemen yet hung over the fire, Mr Donne came in. Ruth felt as if that moment was like death. She had a kind of desire to make some sharp sound, to relieve a choking sensation, but it was over in an instant, and she sat on very composed and silent—to all outward appearance the very model of a governess who knew her place. And by-and-by she felt strangely at ease in her sense of power. She could even listen to what was being said. She had never dared as yet to look at Mr Donne, though her heart burnt to see him once again. He sounded changed. The voice had lost its fresh and youthful eagerness of tone, though in peculiarity of modulation it was the same. It could never be mistaken for the voice of another person. There was a good deal said at that breakfast, for none seemed inclined to hurry, although it was Sunday morning. Ruth was compelled to sit there, and it was good for her that she did. That half-hour seemed to separate the present Mr Donne very effectively from her imagination of what Mr Bellingham had been. She was no analyser; she hardly even had learnt to notice character; but she felt there was some strange difference between the people she had lived with lately and the man who now leant back in his chair, listening in a careless manner to the conversation, but never joining in, or expressing any interest in it, unless it somewhere, or somehow, touched himself. Now, Mr Bradshaw always threw himself into a subject; it might be in a pompous, dogmatic sort of way, but he did do it, whether it related to himself or not; and it was part of Mr Hickson's trade to assume an interest if he felt it not. But Mr Donne did neither the one nor the other. When the other two were talking of many of the topics of the day, he put his glass in his eye, the better to examine into the exact nature of a cold game-pie at the other side of the table. Suddenly Ruth felt that his attention was caught by her. Until now, seeing his short-sightedness, she had believed herself safe; now her face flushed with a painful, miserable blush. But in an instant she was strong and quiet. She looked up straight at his face; and, as if this action took him aback, he dropped his glass, and began eating away with great diligence. She had seen him. He was changed, she knew not how. In fact, the expression, which had been only occasional formerly, when his worse self predominated, had become permanent. He looked restless and dissatisfied. But he was very handsome still; and her quick eye had recognised, with a sort of strange pride, that the eyes and mouth were like Leonard's. Although perplexed by the straightforward, brave look she had sent right at him, he was not entirely baffled. He thought this Mrs Denbigh was certainly like poor Ruth; but this woman was far handsomer. Her face was positively Greek; and then such a proud, superb turn of her head; quite queenly! A governess in Mr Bradshaw's family! Why, she might be a Percy or a

Howard for the grandeur of her grace! Poor Ruth! This woman's hair was darker, though; and she had less colour; altogether a more refined-looking person. Poor Ruth! and, for the first time for several years, he wondered what had become of her; though, of course, there was but one thing that could have happened, and perhaps it was as well he did not know her end, for most likely it would have made him very uncomfortable. He leant back in his chair, and, unobserved (for he would not have thought it gentlemanly to look so fixedly at her if she or any one noticed him), he put up his glass again. She was speaking to one of her pupils, and did not see him.

By Jove! it must be she, though! There were little dimples came out about the mouth as she spoke, just like those he used to admire so much in Ruth, and which he had never seen in any one else—the sunshine without the positive movement of a smile. The longer he looked the more he was convinced; and it was with a jerk that he recovered himself enough to answer Mr Bradshaw's question, whether he wished to go to church or not.

"Church? how far—a mile? No; I think I shall perform my devotions at home to-day."

He absolutely felt jealous when Mr Hickson sprang up to open the door as Ruth and her pupils left the room. He was pleased to feel jealous again. He had been really afraid he was too much "used-up" for such sensations. But Hickson must keep his place. What he was paid for was doing the talking to the electors, not paying attention to the ladies in their families. Mr Donne had noticed that Mr Hickson had tried to be gallant to Miss Bradshaw; let him, if he liked; but let him beware how he behaved to this fair creature, Ruth or no Ruth. It certainly was Ruth; only how the devil had she played her cards so well as to be the governess—the respected governess, in such a family as Mr Bradshaw's?

Mr Donne's movements were evidently to be the guide of Mr Hickson's. Mr Bradshaw always disliked going to church, partly from principle, partly because he never could find the places in the Prayer-book. Mr Donne was in the drawing-room as Mary came down ready equipped; he was turning over the leaves of the large and handsome Bible. Seeing Mary, he was struck with a new idea.

"How singular it is," said he, "that the name of Ruth is so seldom chosen by those good people who go to the Bible before they christen their children. It is a pretty name, I think."

Mr Bradshaw looked up. "Why, Mary!" said he, "is not that Mrs Denbigh's name?"

"Yes, papa," replied Mary, eagerly; "and I know two other Ruths; there's Ruth Brown here, and Ruth Macartney at Eccleston."

"And I have an aunt called Ruth, Mr Donne! I don't think your observation holds good. Besides my daughters' governess, I know three other Ruths."

"Oh! I have no doubt I was wrong. It was just a speech of which one perceives the folly the moment it is made."

But, secretly, he rejoiced with a fierce joy over the success of his device.

Elizabeth came to summon Mary.

Ruth was glad when she got into the open air, and away from the house. Two hours were gone and over. Two out of a day, a day and a half—for it might be late on Monday morning before the Eccleston party returned.

She felt weak and trembling in body, but strong in power over herself. They had left the house in good time for church, so they needed not to hurry; and they went leisurely along the road, now and then passing some country person whom they knew, and with whom they exchanged a kindly, placid greeting. But presently, to Ruth's dismay, she heard a step behind, coming at a rapid pace, a peculiar clank of rather high-heeled boots, which gave a springy sound to the walk, that she had known well long ago. It was like a nightmare, where the Evil dreaded is never avoided, never completely shunned, but is by one's side at the very moment of triumph in escape. There he was by her side; and there was a quarter of a mile intervening between her and the church; but even yet she trusted that he had not recognised her.

"I have changed my mind, you see," said he, quietly. "I have some curiosity to see the architecture of the church; some of these old country churches have singular bits about them. Mr Bradshaw kindly directed me part of the way, but I was so much puzzled by 'turns to the right,' and 'turns to the left,' that I was quite glad to espy your party."

That speech required no positive answer of any kind; and no answer did it receive. He had not expected a reply. He knew, if she were Ruth, she could not answer any indifferent words of his; and her silence made him more certain of her identity with the lady by his side.

"The scenery here is of a kind new to me; neither grand, wild, nor yet marked by high cultivation; and yet it has great charms. It reminds me of some parts of Wales." He breathed deeply, and then added, "You have been in Wales, I believe?"

He spoke low; almost in a whisper. The little church-bell began to call the lagging people with its quick, sharp summons. Ruth writhed in body and spirit, but struggled on. The church-door would be gained at last; and in that holy place she would find peace.

He repeated in a louder tone, so as to compel an answer in order to conceal her agitation from the girls:

"Have you never been in Wales?" He used "never" instead of "ever," and laid the emphasis on that word, in order to mark his meaning to Ruth, and Ruth only. But he drove her to bay.

"I have been in Wales, sir," she replied, in a calm, grave tone. "I was there many years ago. Events took place there, which contribute to make the recollection of that time most miserable to me. I shall be obliged to you, sir, if you will make no further reference to it."

The little girls wondered how Mrs Denbigh could speak in such a tone of quiet authority to Mr Donne, who was almost a member of Parliament. But they settled that her husband must have died in Wales, and, of course, that would make the recollection of the country "most miserable," as she said.

Mr Donne did not dislike the answer, and he positively admired the dignity with which she spoke. His leaving her as he did must have made her very miserable; and he liked the pride that made her retain her indignation, until he could speak to her in private, and explain away a good deal of what she might complain of with some justice.

The church was reached. They all went up the middle aisle into the Eagle's Crag pew. He followed them in, entered himself, and shut the door. Ruth's heart sank as she saw him there; just opposite to her; coming between her and the clergyman who was to read out the Word of God. It was merciless—it was cruel to haunt her there. She durst not lift her eyes to the bright eastern light—she could not see how peacefully the marble images of the dead lay on their tombs, for he was between her and all Light and Peace. She knew that his look was on her; that he never turned his glance away. She could not join in the prayer for the remission of sins while he was there, for his very presence seemed as a sign that their stain would never be washed out of her life. But, although goaded and chafed by her thoughts and recollections, she kept very still. No sign of emotion, no flush of colour was on her face as he looked at her. Elizabeth could not find her place, and then Ruth breathed once, long and deeply, as she moved up the pew, and out of the straight, burning glance of those eyes of evil meaning. When they sat down for the reading of the first lesson, Ruth turned the corner of the seat so as no longer to be opposite to him. She could not listen. The words seemed to be uttered in some world far away, from which she was exiled and cast out; their sound, and yet more their meaning, was dim and distant. But in this extreme tension of mind to hold in her bewildered agony, it so happened that one of her senses was preternaturally acute. While all the church and the people swam in misty haze, one point in a dark corner grew clearer and clearer till she saw (what at another time she could not have discerned at all) a face—a gargoyle I think they call it—at the end of the arch next to the narrowing of the nave into the chancel, and in the shadow of that contraction. The face was beautiful in feature (the next to it was a grinning monkey), but it was not the features that were the most striking part. There was a half-open mouth, not in any way distorted out of its exquisite beauty by the intense expression of suffering it conveyed. Any distortion of the face by mental agony implies that a struggle with circumstance is going on. But in this face, if such struggle had been, it was over now. Circumstance had conquered; and there was no hope from mortal endeavour, or help from mortal creature to be had. But the eyes looked onward and upward to the "Hills from whence cometh our help." And though the parted lips seemed ready to quiver with agony, yet the expression of the whole face, owing to these strange, stony, and yet spiritual eyes, was high and consoling. If mortal gaze had never sought its meaning before, in the deep shadow where it had been placed long centuries ago, yet Ruth's did now. Who could have imagined such a look? Who could have witnessed—perhaps felt—such infinite sorrow, and yet dared to lift it up by Faith into a peace so pure? Or was it a mere conception? If so, what a soul the unknown carver must have had! for creator and handicraftsman must have been one; no two minds could have been in such perfect harmony. Whatever it was—however it came there—imaginer, carver, sufferer, all were long passed away. Human art was ended—human life done—human suffering over; but this remained; it stilled Ruth's beating heart to look on it. She grew still enough to hear words which have come to many in their time of need, and awed them in the presence of the extremest suffering that the hushed world has ever heard of.

The second lesson for the morning of the 25th of September is the 26th chapter of St Matthew's Gospel.

And when they prayed again, Ruth's tongue was unloosed, and she also could pray, in His name, who underwent the agony in the garden.

As they came out of church, there was a little pause and gathering at the door. It had begun to rain; those who had umbrellas were putting them up; those who had not were regretting, and wondering how long it would last. Standing for a moment, impeded by the people who were thus collected under the porch, Ruth heard a voice close to her say, very low, but very distinctly,

"I have much to say to you—much to explain. I entreat you to give me the opportunity."

Ruth did not reply. She would not acknowledge that she heard; but she trembled nevertheless, for the well-remembered voice was low and soft, and had yet its power to thrill. She earnestly desired to know why and how he had left her. It appeared to her as if that knowledge could alone give her a relief from the restless wondering that distracted her mind, and that one explanation could do no harm.

"*No!*" the higher spirit made answer; "*it must not be.*"

Ruth and the girls had each an umbrella. She turned to Mary, and said,

"Mary, give your umbrella to Mr Donne, and come under mine." Her way of speaking was short and decided; she was compressing her meaning into as few words as possible. The little girl obeyed in silence. As they went first through the churchyard stile, Mr Donne spoke again.

"You are unforgiving," said he. "I only ask you to hear me. I have a right to be heard, Ruth! I won't believe you are so much changed, as not to listen to me when I entreat."

He spoke in a tone of soft complaint. But he himself had done much to destroy the illusion which had hung about his memory for years, whenever Ruth had allowed herself to think of it. Besides which, during the time of her residence in the Benson family, her feeling of what people ought to be had been unconsciously raised and refined; and Mr Donne, even while she had to struggle against the force of past recollections, repelled her so much by what he was at present, that every speech of his, every minute they were together, served to make her path more and more easy to follow. His voice retained something of its former influence. When he spoke, without her seeing him, she could not help remembering former days.

She did not answer this last speech any more than the first. She saw clearly, that, putting aside all thought as to the character of their former relationship, it had been dissolved by his will—his act and deed; and that, therefore, the power to refuse any further intercourse whatsoever remained with her.

It sometimes seems a little strange how, after having earnestly prayed to be delivered from temptation, and having given ourselves with shut eyes into God's hand, from that time every thought, every outward influence, every acknowledged law of life, seems to lead us on from strength to strength. It seems strange sometimes, because we notice the coincidence; but it is the natural, unavoidable consequence of all truth and goodness being one and the same, and therefore carried out in every circumstance, external and internal, of God's creation.

When Mr Donne saw that Ruth would not answer him, he became only the more determined that she should hear what he had to say. What that was he did not exactly know. The whole affair was most mysterious and piquant.

The umbrella protected Ruth from more than the rain on that walk homewards, for under its shelter she could not be spoken to unheard. She had not rightly understood at what time she and the girls were to dine. From the gathering at meal-times she must not shrink. She must show no sign of weakness. But, oh! the relief, after that walk, to sit in her own room, locked up, so that neither Mary nor Elizabeth could come by surprise, and to let her weary frame (weary with being so long braced up to rigidity and stiff quiet) fall into a chair anyhow—all helpless, nerveless, motionless, as if the very bones had melted out of her!

The peaceful rest which her mind took was in thinking of Leonard. She dared not look before or behind, but she could see him well at present. She brooded over the thought of him, till she dreaded his father more and more. By the light of her child's purity and innocence, she saw evil clearly, and yet more clearly. She thought that, if Leonard ever came to know the nature of his birth, she had nothing for it but to die out of his sight. He could never know—human heart could never know, her ignorant innocence, and all the small circumstances which had impelled her onwards. But God knew. And if Leonard heard of his mother's error, why, nothing remained but death; for she felt, then, as if she had it in her power to die innocently out of such future agony; but that escape is not so easy. Suddenly a fresh thought came, and she prayed that, through whatever suffering, she might be purified. Whatever trials, woes, measureless pangs, God might see fit to chastise her with, she would not shrink, if only at last she might come into His presence in Heaven. Alas! the shrinking from suffering we cannot help. That part of her prayer was vain. And as for the rest, was not the sure justice of His law finding her out even now? His laws once broken, His justice and the very nature of those laws bring the immutable retribution; but if we turn penitently to Him, He enables us to bear our punishment with a meek and docile heart, "for His mercy endureth for ever."

Mr Bradshaw had felt himself rather wanting in proper attention to his guest, inasmuch as he had been unable, all in a minute, to comprehend Mr Donne's rapid change of purpose; and, before it had entered into his mind that, notwithstanding the distance of the church, Mr Donne was going thither, that gentleman was out of the sight, and far out of the reach, of his burly host. But though the latter had so far neglected the duties of hospitality as to allow his visitor to sit in the Eagle's Crag pew with no other guard of honour than the children and the governess, Mr Bradshaw determined to make up for it by extra attention during the remainder of the day. Accordingly he never left Mr Donne. Whatever wish that gentleman expressed, it was the study of his host to gratify. Did he hint at the pleasure which a walk in such beautiful scenery would give him, Mr Bradshaw was willing to accompany him, although at Eccleston it was a principle with him not to take any walks for pleasure on a Sunday. When Mr Donne turned round, and recollected letters which must be written, and which would compel him to stay at home, Mr Bradshaw instantly gave up the walk, and remained at hand, ready to furnish him with any writing-materials which could be wanted, and which were not laid out in the half-furnished house. Nobody knew where Mr Hickson was all this time. He had sauntered out after Mr Donne, when the latter set off for church, and he had never returned. Mr Donne kept wondering if he could have met Ruth—if, in fact, she had gone out with her pupils, now that the afternoon had cleared up. This uneasy wonder, and a few mental imprecations on his host's polite attention, together with the letter-writing pretence, passed away the afternoon—the longest afternoon he had ever spent; and of weariness he had had his share. Lunch was lingering in the dining-room, left there for the truant Mr Hickson; but of the children or Ruth there was no sign. He ventured on a distant inquiry as to their whereabouts.

"They dine early; they are gone to church again. Mrs Denbigh was a member of the Establishment once; and, though she attends chapel at home, she seems glad to have an opportunity of going to church."

Mr Donne was on the point of asking some further questions about "Mrs Denbigh," when Mr Hickson came in, loud-spoken, cheerful, hungry, and as ready to talk about his ramble, and the way in which he had lost and found himself, as he was about everything else. He knew how to dress up the commonest occurrence with a little exaggeration, a few puns, and a happy quotation or two, so as to make it sound very agreeable. He could read faces, and saw that he had been missed; both host and visitor looked moped to death. He determined to devote himself to their amusement during the remainder of the day, for he had really lost himself, and felt that he had been away too long on a dull Sunday, when people were apt to get hypped if not well amused.

"It is really a shame to be indoors in such a place. Rain? yes, it rained some hours ago, but now it is splendid weather. I feel myself quite qualified for guide, I assure you. I can show you all the beauties of the neighbourhood, and throw in a bog and a nest of vipers to boot."

Mr Donne languidly assented to this proposal of going out; and then he became restless until Mr Hickson had eaten a hasty lunch, for he hoped to meet Ruth on the way from church, to be near her, and watch her, though he might not be able to speak to her. To have the slow hours roll away—to know he must leave the next day—and yet, so close to her, not to be seeing her—was more than he could bear. In an impetuous kind of way, he disregarded all Mr Hickson's offers of guidance to lovely views, and turned a deaf ear to Mr Bradshaw's expressed wish of showing him the land belonging to the house ("very little for fourteen thousand pounds"), and set off wilfully on the road leading to the church, from which, he averred, he had seen a view which nothing else about the place could equal.

They met the country people dropping homewards. No Ruth was there. She and her pupils had returned by the field-way, as Mr Bradshaw informed his guests at dinner-time. Mr Donne was very captious all through dinner. He thought it would never be over, and cursed Hickson's interminable stories, which were told on purpose to amuse him. His heart gave a fierce bound when he saw her in the drawing-room with the little girls.

She was reading to them—with how sick and trembling a heart, no words can tell. But she could master and keep down outward signs of her emotion. An hour more to-night (part of which was to be spent in family prayer, and all in the safety of company), another hour in the morning (when all would be engaged in the bustle of departure)—if, during this short space of time, she could not avoid speaking to him, she could at least keep him at such a distance as to make him feel that henceforward her world and his belonged to separate systems, wide as the heavens apart.

By degrees she felt that he was drawing near to where she stood. He was by the table examining the books that lay upon it. Mary and Elizabeth drew off a little space, awe-stricken by the future member for Eccleston. As he bent his head over a book, he said, "I implore you; five minutes alone."

The little girls could not hear; but Ruth, hemmed in so that no escape was possible, did hear.

She took sudden courage, and said, in a clear voice,

"Will you read the whole passage aloud? I do not remember it."

Mr Hickson, hovering at no great distance, heard these words, and drew near to second Mrs Denbigh's request. Mr Bradshaw, who was very sleepy after his unusually late dinner, and longing for bedtime, joined in the request, for it would save the necessity for making talk, and he might, perhaps, get in a nap, undisturbed and unnoticed, before the servants came in to prayers.

Mr Donne was caught; he was obliged to read aloud, although he did not know what he was reading. In the middle of some sentence the door opened, a rush of servants came in, and Mr Bradshaw became particularly wide awake in an instant, and read them a long sermon with great emphasis and unction, winding up with a prayer almost as long.

Ruth sat with her head drooping, more from exhaustion after a season of effort than because she shunned Mr Donne's looks. He had so lost his power over her—his power, which had stirred her so deeply the night before—that, except as one knowing her error and her shame, and making a cruel use of such knowledge, she had quite separated him from the idol of her youth. And yet, for the sake of that first and only love, she would gladly have known what explanation he could offer to account for leaving her. It would have been something gained to her own self-respect, if she had learnt that he was not then, as she felt him to be now, cold and egotistical, caring for no one and nothing but what related to himself.

Home, and Leonard—how strangely peaceful the two seemed! Oh, for the rest that a dream about Leonard would bring!

Mary and Elizabeth went to bed immediately after prayers, and Ruth accompanied them. It was planned that the gentlemen should leave early the next morning. They were to breakfast half an hour sooner, to catch the railway train; and this by Mr Donne's own arrangement, who had been as eager about his canvassing, the week before, as it was possible for him to be, but who now wished Eccleston and the Dissenting interest therein very fervently at the devil.

Just as the carriage came round, Mr Bradshaw turned to Ruth: "Any message for Leonard beyond love, which is a matter of course?"

Ruth gasped—for she saw Mr Donne catch at the name; she did not guess the sudden sharp jealousy called out by the idea that Leonard was a grown-up man.

"Who is Leonard?" said he to the little girl standing by him; he did not know which she was.

"Mrs Denbigh's little boy," answered Mary.

Under some pretence or other, he drew near to Ruth; and in that low voice, which she had learnt to loathe, he said,

"Our child!"

By the white misery that turned her face to stone—by the wild terror in her imploring eyes—by the gasping breath which came out as the carriage drove away—he knew that he had seized the spell to make her listen at last.

282

CHAPTER XXIV

The Meeting on the Sands

"He will take him away from me! He will take the child from me!"

These words rang like a tolling bell through Ruth's head. It seemed to her that her doom was certain. Leonard would be taken from her! She had a firm conviction—not the less firm because she knew not on what it was based—that a child, whether legitimate or not, belonged of legal right to the father. And Leonard, of all children, was the prince and monarch. Every man's heart would long to call Leonard "Child!" She had been too strongly taxed to have much power left her to reason coolly and dispassionately, just then, even if she had been with any one who could furnish her with information from which to draw correct conclusions. The one thought haunted her night and day—"He will take my child away from me!" In her dreams she saw Leonard borne away into some dim land, to which she could not follow. Sometimes he sat in a swiftly-moving carriage, at his father's side, and smiled on her as he passed by, as if going to promised pleasure. At another time he was struggling to return to her; stretching out his little arms, and crying to her for the help she could not give. How she got through the days, she did not know; her body moved about and habitually acted, but her spirit was with her child. She thought often of writing and warning Mr Benson of Leonard's danger; but then she shrank from recurring to circumstances, all mention of which had ceased years ago; the very recollection of which seemed buried deep for ever. Besides, she feared occasioning discord or commotion in the quiet circle in which she lived. Mr Benson's deep anger against her betrayer had been shown too clearly in the old time to allow her to think that he would keep it down without expression now. He would cease to do anything to forward his election; he would oppose him as much as he could; and Mr Bradshaw would be angry, and a storm would arise, from the bare thought of which Ruth shrank with the cowardliness of a person thoroughly worn out with late contest. She was bodily wearied with her spiritual buffeting.

One morning, three or four days after their departure, she received a letter from Miss Benson. She could not open it at first, and put it on one side, clenching her hand over it all the time. At last she tore it open. Leonard was safe as yet. There were a few lines in his great round hand, speaking of events no larger than the loss of a beautiful "alley." There was a sheet from Miss Benson. She always wrote letters in the manner of a diary. "Monday we did so-and-so; Tuesday, so-and-so, &c." Ruth glanced rapidly down the page. Yes, here it was! Sick, fluttering heart, be still!

"In the middle of the damsons, when they were just on the fire, there was a knock at the door. My brother was out, and Sally was washing up, and I was stirring the preserve with my great apron and bib on; so I bade Leonard come in from the garden and open the door. But I would have washed his face first, if I had known who it was! It was Mr Bradshaw and the Mr Donne that they hope to send up to the House of Commons, as member of Parliament for Eccleston, and another gentleman, whose name I never heard. They had come canvassing; and when they found my brother was out, they asked Leonard if they could see me. The child said, 'Yes! if I could leave the damsons;' and straightway came to call me, leaving them standing in the passage. I whipped off my apron, and took Leonard by the hand, for I fancied I should feel less awkward if he was with me; and then I went and asked them all into the study, for I thought I should like them to see how many books Thurstan had got. Then they began talking politics at me in a very polite manner, only I could not make head or tail of what they meant; and Mr Donne took a deal of notice of Leonard, and called him to him; and I am sure he noticed what a noble, handsome boy he was, though his face was very brown and red, and hot with digging, and his curls all tangled. Leonard talked back as if he had known him all his life, till, I think, Mr Bradshaw thought he was making too much noise, and bid him remember he ought to be seen, not heard. So he stood as still and stiff as a soldier, close to Mr Donne; and as I could not help looking at the two, and thinking how handsome they both were in their different ways, I could not tell Thurstan half the messages the gentlemen left for him. But there was one thing more I must tell you, though I said I would not. When Mr Donne was talking to Leonard, he took off his watch and chain and put it round the boy's neck, who was pleased enough, you may be sure. I bade him give it back to the gentleman, when they were all going away; and I was quite surprised, and very uncomfortable, when Mr Donne said he had given it to Leonard, and that he was to keep it for his own. I could see Mr Bradshaw was annoyed, and he and the other gentleman spoke to Mr Donne, and I heard them say, 'too barefaced;' and I shall never forget Mr Donne's proud, stubborn look back at them, nor his way of saying, 'I allow no one to interfere with what I choose to do with my own.' And he looked so haughty and displeased, I durst say nothing at the time. But when I told Thurstan, he was very grieved and angry; and said he had heard that our party were bribing, but that he never could have thought they would have tried to do it at his house. Thurstan is very much out of spirits about this election altogether; and, indeed, it does make sad work up and down the town. However, he sent back the watch with a letter to Mr Bradshaw; and Leonard was very good about it, so I gave him a taste of the new damson-preserve on his bread for supper."

Although a stranger might have considered this letter wearisome from the multiplicity of the details, Ruth craved greedily after more. What had Mr Donne said to Leonard? Had Leonard liked his new acquaintance? Were they likely to meet again? After wondering and wondering over these points, Ruth composed herself by the hope that in a day or two she should hear again; and to secure this end, she answered the letters by return of post. That was on Thursday. On Friday she had another letter, in a strange hand. It was from Mr Donne. No name, no initials were given. If it had fallen into another person's hands, they could not have recognised the writer, nor guessed to whom it was sent. It contained simply these words:

"For our child's sake, and in his name, I summon you to appoint a place where I can speak, and you can listen, undisturbed. The time must be on Sunday; the limit of distance may be the circumference of your power of walking. My words may be commands, but my fond heart entreats. More I shall not say now, but, remember! your boy's welfare depends on your acceding to this request. Address B. D., Post-Office, Eccleston."

Ruth did not attempt to answer this letter till the last five minutes before the post went out. She could not decide until forced to it. Either way she dreaded. She was very nearly leaving the letter altogether unanswered. But suddenly she resolved she would know all, the best, the worst. No cowardly dread of herself, or of others, should make her neglect aught that came to her in her child's name. She took up a pen and wrote:

"The sands below the rocks, where we met you the other night. Time, afternoon church."

Sunday came.

"I shall not go to church this afternoon. You know the way, of course; and I can trust you to go steadily by yourselves."

When they came to kiss her before leaving her, according to their fond wont, they were struck by the coldness of her face and lips.

"Are you not well, dear Mrs Denbigh? How cold you are!"

"Yes, darling! I am well;" and tears sprang into her eyes as she looked at their anxious little faces. "Go now, dears. Five o'clock will soon be here, and then we will have tea."

"And that will warm you!" said they, leaving the room.

"And then it will be over," she murmured—"over."

It never came into her head to watch the girls as they disappeared down the lane on their way to church. She knew them too well to distrust their doing what they were told. She sat still, her head bowed on her arms for a few minutes, and then rose up and went to put on her walking things. Some thoughts impelled her to sudden haste. She crossed the field by the side of the house, ran down the steep and rocky path, and was carried by the impetus of her descent far out on the level sands—but not far enough for her intent. Without looking to the right hand or to the left, where comers might be seen, she went forwards to the black posts, which, rising above the heaving waters, marked where the fishermen's nets were laid. She went straight towards this place, and hardly stinted her pace even where the wet sands were glittering with the receding waves. Once there, she turned round, and in a darting glance, saw that as yet no one was near. She was perhaps half-a-mile or more from the grey, silvery rocks, which sloped away into brown moorland, interspersed with a field here and there of golden, waving corn. Behind were purple hills, with sharp, clear outlines, touching the sky. A little on one side from where she stood, she saw the white cottages and houses which formed the village of Abermouth, scattered up and down, and, on a windy hill, about a mile inland, she saw the little grey church, where even now many were worshipping in peace.

"Pray for me!" she sighed out, as this object caught her eye.

And now, close under the heathery fields, where they fell softly down and touched the sands, she saw a figure moving in the direction of the great shadow made by the rocks—going towards the very point where the path from Eagle's Crag came down to the shore.

"It is he!" said she to herself. And she turned round and looked seaward. The tide had turned; the waves were slowly receding, as if loath to lose the hold they had, so lately, and with such swift bounds, gained on the yellow sands. The eternal moan they have made since the world began filled the ear, broken only by the skirl of the grey sea-birds as they alighted in groups on the edge of the waters, or as they rose up with their measured, balancing motion, and the sunlight caught their white breasts. There was no sign of human life to be seen; no boat, or distant sail, or near shrimper. The black posts there were all that spoke of men's work or labour. Beyond a stretch of the waters, a few pale grey hills showed like films; their summits clear, though faint, their bases lost in a vapoury mist.

On the hard, echoing sands, and distinct from the ceaseless murmur of the salt sea waves, came footsteps—nearer—nearer. Very near they were when Ruth, unwilling to show the fear that rioted in her heart, turned round, and faced Mr Donne.

He came forward, with both hands extended.

"This is kind! my own Ruth," said he. Ruth's arms hung down motionless at her sides.

"What! Ruth, have you no word for me?"

"I have nothing to say," said Ruth.

"Why, you little revengeful creature! And so I am to explain all before you will even treat me with decent civility."

"I do not want explanations," said Ruth, in a trembling tone. "We must not speak of the past. You asked me to come in Leonard's—in my child's name, and to hear what you had to say about him."

"But what I have to say about him relates to you even more. And how can we talk about him without recurring to the past? That past, which you try to ignore—I know you cannot do it in your heart—is full of happy recollections to me. Were you not happy in Wales?" he said, in his tenderest tone.

But there was no answer; not even one faint sigh, though he listened intently.

"You dare not speak; you dare not answer me. Your heart will not allow you to prevaricate, and you know you were happy."

Suddenly Ruth's beautiful eyes were raised to him, full of lucid splendour, but grave and serious in their expression; and her cheeks, heretofore so faintly tinged with the tenderest blush, flashed into a ruddy glow.

"I was happy. I do not deny it. Whatever comes, I will not blench from the truth. I have answered you."

"And yet," replied he, secretly exulting in her admission, and not perceiving the inner strength of which she must have been conscious before she would have dared to make it—"and yet, Ruth, we are not to recur to the past! Why not? If it was happy at the time, is the recollection of it so miserable to you?"

He tried once more to take her hand, but she quietly stepped back.

"I came to hear what you had to say about my child," said she, beginning to feel very weary.

"*Our* child, Ruth."

She drew herself up, and her face went very pale.

"What have you to say about him?" asked she, coldly.

"Much," exclaimed he—"much that may affect his whole life. But it all depends upon whether you will hear me or not."

"I listen."

"Good Heavens! Ruth, you will drive me mad. Oh! what a changed person you are from the sweet, loving creature you were! I wish you were not so beautiful." She did not reply, but he caught a deep, involuntary sigh.

"Will you hear me if I speak, though I may not begin all at once to talk of this boy—a boy of whom any mother—any parent, might be proud? I could see that, Ruth. I have seen him; he looked like a prince in that cramped, miserable house, and with no earthly advantages. It is a shame he should not have every kind of opportunity laid open before him."

There was no sign of maternal ambition on the motionless face, though there might be some little spring in her heart, as it beat quick and strong at the idea of the proposal she imagined he was going to make of taking her boy away to give him the careful education she had often craved for him. She should refuse it, as she would everything else which seemed to imply that she acknowledged a claim over Leonard; but yet sometimes, for her boy's sake, she had longed for a larger opening—a more extended sphere.

"Ruth! you acknowledge we were happy once;—there were circumstances which, if I could tell you them all in detail, would show you how in my weak, convalescent state I was almost passive in the hands of others. Ah, Ruth! I have not forgotten the tender nurse who soothed me in my delirium. When I am feverish, I dream that I am again at Llan-dhu, in the little old bed-chamber, and you, in white—which you always wore then, you know—flitting about me."

The tears dropped, large and round, from Ruth's eyes—she could not help it—how could she?

"We were happy then," continued he, gaining confidence from the sight of her melted mood, and recurring once more to the admission which he considered so much in his favour. "Can such happiness never return?" Thus he went on, quickly, anxious to lay before her all he had to offer, before she should fully understand his meaning.

"If you would consent, Leonard should be always with you—educated where and how you liked—money to any amount you might choose to name should be secured to you and him—if only, Ruth—if only those happy days might return."

Ruth spoke.

"I said that I was happy, because I had asked God to protect and help me—and I dared not tell a lie. I was happy. Oh! what is happiness or misery that we should talk about them now?"

Mr Donne looked at her, as she uttered these words, to see if she was wandering in her mind, they seemed to him so utterly strange and incoherent.

"I dare not think of happiness—I must not look forward to sorrow. God did not put me here to consider either of these things."

"My dear Ruth, compose yourself! There is no hurry in answering the question I asked."

"What was it?" said Ruth.

"I love you so, I cannot live without you. I offer you my heart, my life—I offer to place Leonard wherever you would have him placed. I have the power and the means to advance him in any path of life you choose. All who have shown kindness to you shall be rewarded by me, with a gratitude even surpassing your own. If there is anything else I can do that you can suggest, I will do it."

"Listen to me!" said Ruth, now that the idea of what he proposed had entered her mind. "When I said that I was happy with you long ago, I was choked with shame as I said it. And yet it may be a vain, false excuse that I make for myself. I was very young; I did not know how such a life was against God's pure and holy will—at least, not as I know it now; and I tell you truth—all the days of my years since I have gone about with a stain on my hidden soul—a stain which made me loathe myself, and envy those who stood spotless and undefiled; which made me shrink from my child—from Mr Benson, from his sister, from the innocent girls whom I teach—nay, even I have cowered away from God Himself; and what I did wrong then, I did blindly to what I should do now if I listened to you."

She was so strongly agitated that she put her hands over her face, and sobbed without restraint. Then, taking them away, she looked at him with a glowing face, and beautiful, honest, wet eyes, and tried to speak calmly, as she asked if she needed to stay longer (she would have gone away at once but that she thought of Leonard, and wished to hear all that his father might have to say). He was so struck anew by her beauty, and understood her so little, that he believed that she only required a little more urging to consent to what he wished; for in all she had said there was no trace of the anger and resentment for his desertion of her, which he had expected would be a prominent feature—the greatest obstacle he had to encounter. The deep sense of penitence she expressed, he mistook for earthly shame; which he imagined he could soon soothe away.

"Yes, I have much more to say. I have not said half. I cannot tell you how fondly I will—how fondly I do love you—how my life shall be spent in ministering to your wishes. Money, I see—I know, youdespise—"

"Mr Bellingham! I will not stay to hear you speak to me so again. I have been sinful, but it is not you who should—" She could not speak, she was so choking with passionate sorrow.

He wanted to calm her, as he saw her shaken with repressed sobs. He put his hand on her arm. She shook it off impatiently, and moved away in an instant.

"Ruth!" said he, nettled by her action of repugnance, "I begin to think you never loved me."

"I!—I never loved you! Do you dare to say so?"

Her eyes flamed on him as she spoke. Her red, round lip curled into beautiful contempt.

"Why do you shrink so from me?" said he, in his turn getting impatient.

"I did not come here to be spoken to in this way," said she. "I came, if by any chance I could do Leonard good. I would submit to many humiliations for his sake—but to no more from you."

"Are not you afraid to brave me so?" said he. "Don't you know how much you are in my power?"

She was silent. She longed to go away, but dreaded lest he should follow her, where she might be less subject to interruption than she was here—near the fisherman's nets, which the receding tide was leaving every moment barer and more bare, and the posts they were fastened to more blackly uprising above the waters.

Mr Donne put his hands on her arms as they hung down before her—her hands tightly clasped together.

"Ask me to let you go," said he. "I will, if you will ask me." He looked very fierce and passionate and determined. The vehemence of his action took Ruth by surprise, and the painful tightness of the grasp almost made her exclaim. But she was quite still and mute.

"Ask me," said he, giving her a little shake. She did not speak. Her eyes, fixed on the distant shore, were slowly filling with tears. Suddenly a light came through the mist that obscured them, and the shut lips parted. She saw some distant object that gave her hope.

"It is Stephen Bromley," said she. "He is coming to his nets. They say he is a very desperate, violent man, but he will protect me."

"You obstinate, wilful creature!" said Mr Donne, releasing his grasp. "You forget that one word of mine could undeceive all these good people at Eccleston; and that if I spoke out ever so little, they would throw you off in an instant. Now!" he continued, "do you understand how much you are in my power?"

"Mr and Miss Benson know all—they have not thrown me off," Ruth gasped out. "Oh! for Leonard's sake! you would not be so cruel."

"Then do not you be cruel to him—to me. Think once more!"

"I think once more;" she spoke solemnly. "To save Leonard from the shame and agony of knowing my disgrace, I would lie down and die. Oh! perhaps it would be best for him—for me, if I might; my death would be a stingless grief—but to go back into sin would be the real cruelty to him. The errors of my youth may be washed away by my tears—it was so once when the gentle, blessed Christ was upon earth; but now, if I went into wilful guilt, as you would have me, how could I teach Leonard God's holy will? I should not mind his knowing my past sin, compared to the awful corruption it would be if he knew me living now, as you would have me, lost to all fear of God—" Her speech was broken by sobs. "Whatever may be my doom—God is just—I leave myself in His hands. I will save Leonard from evil. Evil would it be for him if I lived with you. I will let him die first!" She lifted her eyes to heaven, and clasped and wreathed her hands together tight. Then she said: "You have humbled me enough, sir. I shall leave you now."

She turned away resolutely. The dark, grey fisherman was at hand. Mr Donne folded his arms, and set his teeth, and looked after her.

"What a stately step she has! How majestic and graceful all her attitudes were! She thinks she has baffled me now. We will try something more, and bid a higher price." He unfolded his arms, and began to follow her. He gained upon her, for her beautiful walk was now wavering and unsteady. The works which had kept her in motion were running down fast.

"Ruth!" said he, overtaking her. "You shall hear me once more. Aye, look round! Your fisherman is near. He may hear me, if he chooses—hear your triumph. I am come to offer to marry you, Ruth; come what may, I will have you. Nay—I will make you hear me. I will hold this hand till you have heard me. To-morrow I will speak to any one in Eccleston you like—to Mr Bradshaw; Mr ——, the little minister, I mean. We can make it worth while for him to keep our secret, and no one else need know but what you are really Mrs Denbigh. Leonard shall still bear this name, but in all things else he shall be treated as my son. He and you would grace any situation. I will take care the highest paths are open to him!"

He looked to see the lovely face brighten into sudden joy; on the contrary, the head was still hung down with a heavy droop.

"I cannot," said she; her voice was very faint and low.

"It is sudden for you, my dearest. But be calm. It will all be easily managed. Leave it to me."

"I cannot," repeated she, more distinct and clear, though still very low.

"Why! what on earth makes you say that?" asked he, in a mood to be irritated by any repetition of such words.

"I do not love you. I did once. Don't say I did not love you then; but I do not now. I could never love you again. All you have said and done since you came with Mr Bradshaw to Abermouth first, has only made me wonder how I ever could have loved you. We are very far apart. The time that has pressed down my life like brands of hot iron, and scarred me for ever, has been nothing to you. You have talked of it with no sound of moaning in your voice—no shadow over the brightness of your face; it has left no sense of sin on your conscience, while me it haunts and haunts; and yet I might plead that I was an ignorant child—only I will not plead anything, for God knows all— But this is only one piece of our greatdifference—"

"You mean that I am no saint," he said, impatient at her speech. "Granted. But people who are no saints have made very good husbands before now. Come, don't let any morbid, overstrained conscientiousness interfere with substantial happiness—happiness both to you and to me—for I am sure I can make you happy—aye! and make you love me, too, in spite of your pretty defiance. I love you so dearly I must win love back. And here are advantages for Leonard, to be gained by you quite in a holy and legitimate way."

She stood very erect.

"If there was one thing needed to confirm me, you have named it. You shall have nothing to do with my boy, by my consent, much less by my agency. I would rather see him working on the roadside than leading such a life—being such a one as you are. You have heard my mind now, Mr Bellingham. You have humbled me—you have baited me; and if at last I have spoken out too harshly, and too much in a spirit of judgment, the fault is yours. If there were no other reason to prevent our marriage but the one fact that it would bring Leonard into contact with you, that would be enough."

"It is enough!" said he, making her a low bow. "Neither you nor your child shall ever more be annoyed by me. I wish you a good evening."

They walked apart—he back to the inn, to set off instantly, while the blood was hot within him, from the place where he had been so mortified—she to steady herself along till she reached the little path, more like a rude staircase than anything else, by which she had to climb to the house.

She did not turn round for some time after she was fairly lost to the sight of any one on the shore; she clambered on, almost stunned by the rapid beating of her heart. Her eyes were hot and dry; and at last became as if she were suddenly blind. Unable to go on, she tottered into the tangled underwood which grew among the stones, filling every niche and crevice, and little shelving space, with green and delicate tracery. She sank down behind a great overhanging rock, which hid her from any one coming up the path. An ash-tree was rooted in this rock, slanting away from the sea-breezes that were prevalent in most weathers; but this was a still, autumnal Sabbath evening. As Ruth's limbs fell, so they lay. She had no strength, no power of volition to move a finger. She could not think or remember. She was literally stunned. The first sharp sensation which roused her from her torpor was a quick desire to see him once more; up she sprang, and climbed to an out-jutting dizzy point of rock, but a little above her sheltered nook, yet commanding a wide view over the bare, naked sands;—far away below, touching the rippling water-line, was Stephen Bromley, busily gathering in his nets; besides him there was no living creature visible. Ruth shaded her eyes, as if she thought they might have deceived her; but no, there was no one there. She went slowly down to her old place, crying sadly as she went.

"Oh! if I had not spoken so angrily to him—the last things I said were so bitter—so reproachful!—and I shall never, never see him again!"

She could not take in the general view and scope of their conversation—the event was too near her for that; but her heart felt sore at the echo of her last words, just and true as their severity was. Her struggle, her constant flowing tears, which fell from very weakness, made her experience a sensation of intense bodily fatigue; and her soul had lost the power of throwing itself forward, or contemplating anything beyond the dreary present, when the expanse of grey, wild, bleak moors, stretching wide away below a sunless sky, seemed only an outward sign of the waste world within her heart, for which she could claim no sympathy;—for she could not even define what its woes were; and if she could, no one would understand how the present time was haunted by the terrible ghost of the former love.

"I am so weary! I am so weary!" she moaned aloud at last. "I wonder if I might stop here, and just die away."

She shut her eyes, until through the closed lids came a ruddy blaze of light. The clouds had parted away, and the sun was going down in a crimson glory behind the distant purple hills. The whole western sky was one flame of fire. Ruth forgot herself in looking at the gorgeous sight. She sat up gazing, and, as she gazed, the tears dried on her cheeks; and, somehow, all human care and sorrow were swallowed up in the unconscious sense of God's infinity. The sunset calmed her more than any words, however wise and tender, could have done. It even seemed to give her strength and courage; she did not know how or why, but so it was.

She rose, and went slowly towards home. Her limbs were very stiff, and every now and then she had to choke down an unbidden sob. Her pupils had been long returned from church, and had busied themselves in preparing tea—an occupation which had probably made them feel the time less long.

If they had ever seen a sleep-walker, they might have likened Ruth to one for the next few days, so slow and measured did her movements seem—so far away was her intelligence from all that was passing around her—so hushed and strange were the tones of her voice. They had letters from home announcing the triumphant return of Mr Donne as M.P. for Eccleston. Mrs Denbigh heard the news without a word, and was too languid to join in the search after purple and yellow flowers with which to deck the sitting-room at Eagle's Crag.

A letter from Jemima came the next day, summoning them home. Mr Donne and his friends had left the place, and quiet was restored in the Bradshaw household; so it was time that Mary's and Elizabeth's holiday should cease. Mrs Denbigh had also a letter—a letter from Miss Benson, saying that Leonard was not quite well. There was so much pains taken to disguise anxiety, that it was very evident much anxiety was felt; and the girls were almost alarmed by Ruth's sudden change from taciturn langour to eager, vehement energy. Body and mind seemed strained to exertion. Every plan that could facilitate packing and winding-up affairs at Abermouth, every errand and arrangement that could expedite their departure by one minute, was done by Ruth with stern promptitude. She spared herself in nothing. She made them rest, made them lie down, while she herself lifted weights and transacted business with feverish power, never resting, and trying never to have time to think.

For in remembrance of the Past there was Remorse,—how had she forgotten Leonard these last few days!—how had she repined and been dull of heart to her blessing! And in anticipation of the Future there was one sharp point of red light in the darkness which pierced her brain with agony, and which she would not see or recognise—and saw and recognised all the more for such mad determination—which is not the true shield against the bitterness of the arrows of Death.

When the seaside party arrived in Eccleston, they were met by Mrs and Miss Bradshaw and Mr Benson. By a firm resolution, Ruth kept from shaping the question, "Is he alive?" as if by giving shape to her fears she made their realisation more imminent. She said merely, "How is he?" but she said it with drawn, tight, bloodless lips, and in her eyes Mr Benson read her anguish of anxiety.

"He is very ill, but we hope he will soon be better. It is what every child has to go through."

CHAPTER XXV

Jemima Makes a Discovery

Mr Bradshaw had been successful in carrying his point. His member had been returned; his proud opponents mortified. So the public thought he ought to be well pleased; but the public were disappointed to see that he did not show any of the gratification they supposed him to feel.

The truth was, that he had met with so many small mortifications during the progress of the election, that the pleasure which he would otherwise have felt in the final success of his scheme was much diminished.

He had more than tacitly sanctioned bribery; and now that the excitement was over, he regretted it; not entirely from conscientious motives, though he was uneasy from a slight sense of wrong-doing; but he was more pained, after all, to think that, in the eyes of some of his townsmen, his hitherto spotless character had received a blemish. He, who had been so stern and severe a censor on the undue influence exercised by the opposite party in all preceding elections, could not expect to be spared by their adherents now, when there were rumours that the hands of the scrupulous Dissenters were not clean. Before, it had been his boast that neither friend nor enemy could say one word against him; now, he was constantly afraid of an indictment for bribery, and of being compelled to appear before a Committee to swear to his own share in the business.

His uneasy, fearful consciousness made him stricter and sterner than ever; as if he would quench all wondering, slanderous talk about him in the town by a renewed austerity of uprightness; that the slack-principled Mr Bradshaw of one month of ferment and excitement might not be confounded with the highly-conscientious and deeply-religious Mr Bradshaw, who went to chapel twice a day, and gave a hundred pounds a-piece to every charity in the town, as a sort of thank-offering that his end was gained.

But he was secretly dissatisfied with Mr Donne. In general, that gentleman had been rather too willing to act in accordance with any one's advice, no matter whose; as if he had thought it too much trouble to weigh the wisdom of his friends, in which case Mr Bradshaw's would have, doubtless, proved the most valuable. But now and then he unexpectedly, and utterly without reason, took the conduct of affairs into his own hands, as when he had been absent without leave only just before the day of nomination. No one guessed whither he had gone; but the fact of his being gone was enough to chagrin Mr Bradshaw, who was quite ready to pick a quarrel on this very head, if the election had not terminated favourably. As it was, he had a feeling of proprietorship in Mr Donne which was not disagreeable. He had given the new M.P. his seat; his resolution, his promptitude, his energy, had made Mr Donne "our member;" and Mr Bradshaw began to feel proud of him accordingly. But there had been no one circumstance during this period to bind Jemima and Mr Farquhar together. They were still misunderstanding each other with all their power. The difference in the result was this: Jemima loved him all the more, in spite of quarrels and coolness. He was growing utterly weary of the petulant temper of which he was never certain; of the reception which varied day after day, according to the mood she was in and the thoughts that were uppermost; and he was almost startled to find how very glad he was that the little girls and Mrs Denbigh were coming home. His was a character to bask in peace; and lovely, quiet Ruth, with her low tones and quiet replies, her delicate waving movements, appeared to him the very type of what a woman should be—a calm, serene soul, fashioning the body to angelic grace.

It was, therefore, with no slight interest that Mr Farquhar inquired daily after the health of little Leonard. He asked at the Bensons' house; and Sally answered him, with swollen and tearful eyes, that the child was very bad—very bad indeed. He asked at the doctor's; and the doctor told him, in a few short words, that "it was only a bad kind of measles, and that the lad might have a struggle for it, but he thought he would get through. Vigorous children carried their force into everything; never did things by halves; if they were ill, they were sure to be in a high fever directly; if they were well, there was no peace in the house for their rioting. For his part," continued the doctor, "he thought he was glad he had had no children; as far as he could judge, they were pretty much all plague and no profit." But as he ended his speech he sighed; and Mr Farquhar was none the less convinced that common report was true, which represented the clever, prosperous surgeon of Eccleston as bitterly disappointed at his failure of offspring.

While these various interests and feelings had their course outside the Chapel-house, within there was but one thought which possessed all the inmates. When Sally was not cooking for the little invalid, she was crying; for she had had a dream about green rushes, not three months ago, which, by some queer process of oneiromancy she interpreted to mean the death of a child; and all Miss Benson's endeavours were directed to making her keep silence to Ruth about this dream. Sally thought that the mother ought to be told; what were dreams sent for but for warnings? But it was just like a pack of Dissenters, who would not believe anything like other folks. Miss Benson was too much accustomed to Sally's contempt for Dissenters, as viewed from the pinnacle of the Establishment, to pay much attention to all this grumbling; especially as Sally was willing to take as much trouble about Leonard as if she believed he was going to live, and that his recovery depended upon her care. Miss Benson's great object was to keep her from having any confidential talks with Ruth; as if any repetition of the dream could have deepened the conviction in Ruth's mind that the child would die.

It seemed to her that his death would only be the fitting punishment for the state of indifference towards him—towards life and death—towards all things earthly or divine, into which she had suffered herself to fall since her last interview with Mr Donne. She did not understand that such exhaustion is but the natural consequence of violent agitation and severe tension of feeling. The only relief she experienced was in constantly serving Leonard; she had almost an animal's jealousy lest any one should come between her and her young. Mr Benson saw this jealous suspicion, although he could hardly understand it; but he calmed his sister's wonder and officious kindness, so that the two patiently and quietly provided all that Ruth might want, but did not interfere with her right to nurse Leonard. But when he was recovering, Mr Benson, with the slight tone of authority he knew how to assume when need was, bade Ruth lie down and take some rest, while his sister watched. Ruth did not answer, but obeyed in a dull, weary kind of surprise at being so commanded. She lay down by her child, gazing her fill at his calm slumber; and as she gazed, her large white eyelids were softly pressed down as with a gentle irresistible weight, and she fell asleep.

She dreamed that she was once more on the lonely shore, striving to carry Leonard away from some pursuer—some human pursuer—she knew he was human, and she knew who he was, although she dared not say his name even to herself, he seemed so close and present, gaining on her flying footsteps, rushing after her as with the sound of the roaring tide. Her feet seemed heavy weights fixed to the ground; they would not move. All at once, just near the shore, a great black whirlwind of waves clutched her back to her pursuer; she threw Leonard on to land, which was safety; but whether he reached it or no, or was swept back like her into a mysterious something too dreadful to be borne, she did not know, for the terror awakened her. At first the dream seemed yet a reality, and she thought that the pursuer was couched even there, in that very room, and the great boom of the sea was still in her ears. But as full consciousness returned, she saw herself safe in the dear old room—the haven of rest—the shelter from storms. A bright fire was glowing in the little old-fashioned, cup-shaped grate, niched into a corner of the wall, and guarded on either side by whitewashed bricks, which rested on hobs. On one of these the kettle hummed and buzzed, within two points of boiling whenever she or Leonard required tea. In her dream that home-like sound had been the roaring of the relentless sea, creeping swiftly on to seize its prey. Miss Benson sat by the fire, motionless and still; it was too dark to read any longer without a candle; but yet on the ceiling and upper part of the walls the golden light of the setting sun was slowly moving—so slow, and yet a motion gives the feeling of rest to the weary yet more than perfect stillness. The old clock on the staircase told its monotonous click-clack, in that soothing way which more marked the quiet of the house than disturbed with any sense of sound. Leonard still slept that renovating slumber, almost in her arms, far from that fatal pursuing sea, with its human form of cruelty. The dream was a vision; the reality which prompted the dream was over and past—Leonard was safe—she was safe; all this loosened the frozen springs, and they gushed forth in her heart, and her lips moved in accordance with her thoughts.

"What were you saying, my darling?" said Miss Benson, who caught sight of the motion, and fancied she was asking for something. Miss Benson bent over the side of the bed on which Ruth lay, to catch the low tones of her voice.

"I only said," replied Ruth, timidly, "thank God! I have so much to thank Him for, you don't know."

"My dear, I am sure we have all of us cause to be thankful that our boy is spared. See! he is wakening up; and we will have a cup of tea together."

Leonard strode on to perfect health; but he was made older in character and looks by his severe illness. He grew tall and thin, and the lovely child was lost in the handsome boy. He began to wonder, and to question. Ruth mourned a little over the vanished babyhood, when she was all in all, and over the childhood, whose petals had fallen away; it seemed as though two of her children were gone—the one an infant, the other a bright, thoughtless darling; and she wished that they could have remained quick in her memory for ever, instead of being absorbed in loving pride for the present boy. But these were only fanciful regrets, flitting like shadows across a mirror. Peace and thankfulness were once more the atmosphere of her mind; nor was her unconsciousness disturbed by any suspicion of Mr Farquhar's increasing approbation and admiration, which he was diligently nursing up into love for her. She knew that he had sent—she did not know how often he had brought—fruit for the convalescent Leonard. She heard, on her return from her daily employment, that Mr Farquhar had brought a little gentle pony on which Leonard, weak as he was, might ride. To confess the truth, her maternal pride was such that she thought that all kindness shown to such a boy as Leonard was but natural; she believed him to be

A child whom all that looked on, loved.

As in truth he was; and the proof of this was daily shown in many kind inquiries, and many thoughtful little offerings, besides Mr Farquhar's. The poor (warm and kind of heart to all sorrow common to humanity) were touched with pity for the young widow, whose only child lay ill, and nigh unto death. They brought what they could—a fresh egg, when eggs were scarce—a few ripe pears that grew on the sunniest side of the humblest cottage, where the fruit was regarded as a source of income—a call of inquiry, and a prayer that God would spare the child, from an old crippled woman, who could scarcely drag herself so far as the Chapel-house, yet felt her worn and weary heart stirred with a sharp pang of sympathy, and a very present remembrance of the time when she too was young, and saw the life-breath quiver out of her child, now an angel in that heaven which felt more like home to the desolate old creature than this empty earth. To all such, when Leonard was better, Ruth went, and thanked them from her heart. She and the old cripple sat hand in hand over the scanty fire on the hearth of the latter, while she told in solemn, broken, homely words, how her child sickened and died. Tears fell like rain down Ruth's cheeks; but those of the old woman were dry. All tears had been wept out of her long ago, and now she sat patient and quiet, waiting for death. But after this, Ruth "clave unto her," and the two were henceforward a pair of friends. Mr Farquhar was only included in the general gratitude which she felt towards all who had been kind to her boy.

The winter passed away in deep peace after the storms of the autumn, yet every now and then a feeling of insecurity made Ruth shake for an instant. Those wild autumnal storms had torn aside the quiet flowers and herbage that had gathered over the wreck of her early life, and shown her that all deeds, however hidden and long passed by, have their eternal consequences. She turned sick and faint whenever Mr Donne's name was casually mentioned. No one saw it; but she felt the miserable stop in her heart's beating, and wished that she could prevent it by any exercise of self-command. She had never named his identity with Mr Bellingham, nor had she spoken about the seaside interview. Deep shame made her silent and reserved on all her life before Leonard's birth; from that time she rose again in her self-respect, and spoke as openly as a child (when need was) of all occurrences which had taken place since then; except that she could not, and would not, tell of this mocking echo, this haunting phantom, this past, that would not rest in its grave. The very circumstance that it was stalking abroad in the world, and might reappear at any moment, made her a coward: she trembled away from contemplating what the reality had been; only she clung more faithfully than before to the thought of the great God, who was a rock in the dreary land, where no shadow was.

Autumn and winter, with their lowering skies, were less dreary than the woeful, desolate feelings that shed a gloom on Jemima. She found too late that she had considered Mr Farquhar so securely her own for so long a time, that her heart refused to recognise him as lost to her, unless her reason went through the same weary, convincing, miserable evidence day after day, and hour after hour. He never spoke to her now, except from common civility. He never cared for her contradictions; he never tried, with patient perseverance, to bring her over to his opinions; he never used the wonted wiles (so tenderly remembered now they had no existence but in memory) to bring her round out of some wilful mood—and such moods were common enough now! Frequently she was sullenly indifferent to the feelings of others—not from any unkindness, but because her heart seemed numb and stony, and incapable of sympathy. Then afterwards her self-reproach was terrible—in the dead of night, when no one saw it. With a strange perversity, the only intelligence she cared to hear, the only sights she cared to see, were the circumstances which gave confirmation to the idea that Mr Farquhar was thinking of Ruth for a wife. She craved with stinging curiosity to hear something of their affairs every day; partly because the torture which such intelligence gave was almost a relief from the deadness of her heart to all other interests.

And so spring (*gioventu dell'anno*) came back to her, bringing all the contrasts which spring alone can bring to add to the heaviness of the soul. The little winged creatures filled the air with bursts of joy; the vegetation came bright and hopefully onwards, without any check of nipping frost. The ash-trees in the Bradshaws' garden were out in leaf by the middle of May, which that year wore more the aspect of summer than most Junes do. The sunny weather mocked Jemima, and the unusual warmth oppressed her physical powers. She felt very weak and languid; she was acutely sensible that no one else noticed her want of strength; father, mother, all seemed too full of other things to care if, as she believed, her life was waning. She herself felt glad that it was so. But her delicacy was not unnoticed by all. Her mother often anxiously asked her husband if he did not think Jemima was looking ill; nor did his affirmation to the contrary satisfy her, as most of his affirmations did. She thought every morning, before she got up, how she could tempt Jemima to eat, by ordering some favourite dainty for dinner; in many other little ways she tried to minister to her child; but the poor girl's own abrupt irritability of temper had made her mother afraid of openly speaking to her about her health.

Ruth, too, saw that Jemima was not looking well. How she had become an object of dislike to her former friend she did not know; but she was sensible that Miss Bradshaw disliked her now. She was not aware that this feeling was growing and strengthening almost into repugnance, for she seldom saw Jemima out of school-hours, and then only for a minute or two. But the evil element of a fellow-creature's dislike oppressed the atmosphere of her life. That fellow-creature was one who had once loved her so fondly, and whom she still loved, although she had learnt to fear her, as we fear those whose faces cloud over when we come in sight—who cast unloving glances at us, of which we, though not seeing, are conscious, as of some occult influence; and the cause of whose dislike is unknown to us, though every word and action seems to increase it. I believe that this sort of dislike is only shown by the jealous, and that it renders the disliker even more miserable, because more continually conscious than the object; but the growing evidence of Jemima's feeling made Ruth very unhappy at times. This very May, too, an idea had come into her mind, which she had tried to repress—namely, that Mr Farquhar was in love with her. It annoyed her extremely; it made her reproach herself that she ever should think such a thing possible. She tried to strangle the notion, to drown it, to starve it out by neglect—its existence caused her such pain and distress.

The worst was, he had won Leonard's heart, who was constantly seeking him out; or, when absent, talking about him. The best was some journey connected with business, which would take him to the Continent for several weeks; and, during that time, surely this disagreeable fancy of his would die away, if untrue; and if true, some way would be opened by which she might put a stop to all increase of predilection on his part, and yet retain him as a friend for Leonard—that darling for whom she was far-seeing and covetous, and miserly of every scrap of love and kindly regard.

Mr Farquhar would not have been flattered if he had known how much his departure contributed to Ruth's rest of mind on the Saturday afternoon on which he set out on his journey. It was a beautiful day; the sky of that intense quivering blue which seemed as though you could look through it for ever, yet not reach the black, infinite space which is suggested as lying beyond. Now and then a thin, torn, vaporous cloud floated slowly within the vaulted depth; but the soft air that gently wafted it was not perceptible among the leaves on the trees, which did not even tremble. Ruth sat at her work in the shadow formed by the old grey garden wall; Miss Benson and Sally—the one in the parlour window-seat mending stockings, the other hard at work in her kitchen—were both within talking distance, for it was weather for open doors and windows; but none of the three kept up any continued conversation; and in the intervals Ruth sang low a brooding song, such as she remembered her mother singing long ago. Now and then she stopped to look at Leonard, who was labouring away with vehement energy at digging over a small plot of ground, where he meant to prick out some celery plants that had been given to him. Ruth's heart warmed at the earnest, spirited way in which he thrust his large spade deep down into the brown soil, his ruddy face glowing, his curly hair wet with the exertion; and yet she sighed to think that the days were over when her deeds of skill could give him pleasure. Now, his delight was in acting himself; last year, not fourteen months ago, he had watched her making a daisy-chain for him, as if he could not admire her cleverness enough; this year—this week, when she had been devoting every spare hour to the simple tailoring which she performed for her boy (she had always made every article he wore, and felt almost jealous of the employment), he had come to her with a wistful look, and asked when he might begin to have clothes made by a man?

Ever since the Wednesday when she had accompanied Mary and Elizabeth, at Mrs Bradshaw's desire, to be measured for spring clothes by the new Eccleston dressmaker, she had been looking forward to this Saturday afternoon's pleasure of making summer trousers for Leonard; but the satisfaction of the employment was a little taken away by Leonard's speech. It was a sign, however, that her life was very quiet and peaceful, that she had leisure to think upon the thing at all; and often she forgot it entirely in her low, chanting song, or in listening to the thrush warbling out his afternoon ditty to his patient mate in the holly-bush below.

The distant rumble of carts through the busy streets (it was market-day) not only formed a low rolling bass to the nearer and pleasanter sounds, but enhanced the sense of peace by the suggestion of the contrast afforded to the repose of the garden by the bustle not far off.

But besides physical din and bustle, there is mental strife and turmoil.

That afternoon, as Jemima was restlessly wandering about the house, her mother desired her to go on an errand to Mrs Pearson's, the new dressmaker, in order to give some directions about her sisters' new frocks. Jemima went, rather than have the trouble of resisting; or else she would have preferred staying at home, moving or being outwardly quiet according to her own fitful will. Mrs Bradshaw, who, as I have said, had been aware for some time that something was wrong with her daughter, and was very anxious to set it to rights if she only knew how, had rather planned this errand with a view to dispel Jemima's melancholy.

"And, Mimie, dear," said her mother, "when you are there, look out for a new bonnet for yourself; she has got some very pretty ones, and your old one is so shabby."

"It does for me, mother," said Jemima, heavily. "I don't want a new bonnet."

"But I want you to have one, my lassie. I want my girl to look well and nice."

There was something of homely tenderness in Mrs Bradshaw's tone that touched Jemima's heart. She went to her mother, and kissed her with more of affection than she had shown to any one for weeks before; and the kiss was returned with warm fondness.

"I think you love me, mother," said Jemima.

"We all love you, dear, if you would but think so. And if you want anything, or wish for anything, only tell me, and with a little patience I can get your father to give it you, I know. Only be happy, there's a good girl."

"Be happy! as if one could by an effort of will!" thought Jemima, as she went along the street, too absorbed in herself to notice the bows of acquaintances and friends, but instinctively guiding herself right among the throng and press of carts, and gigs, and market people in High Street.

But her mother's tones and looks, with their comforting power, remained longer in her recollection than the inconsistency of any words spoken. When she had completed her errand about the frocks, she asked to look at some bonnets, in order to show her recognition of her mother's kind thought.

Mrs Pearson was a smart, clever-looking woman of five or six and thirty. She had all the variety of small-talk at her finger-ends that was formerly needed by barbers to amuse the people who came to be shaved. She had admired the town till Jemima was weary of its praises, sick and oppressed by its sameness, as she had been these many weeks.

"Here are some bonnets, ma'am, that will be just the thing for you—elegant and tasty, yet quite of the simple style, suitable to young ladies. Oblige me by trying on this white silk!"

Jemima looked at herself in the glass; she was obliged to own it was very becoming, and perhaps not the less so for the flush of modest shame which came into her cheeks as she heard Mrs Pearson's open praises of the "rich, beautiful hair," and the "Oriental eyes" of the wearer.

"I induced the young lady who accompanied your sisters the other day—the governess, is she, ma'am?"

"Yes—Mrs Denbigh is her name," said Jemima, clouding over.

"Thank you, ma'am. Well, I persuaded Mrs Denbigh to try on that bonnet, and you can't think how charming she looked in it; and yet I don't think it became her as much as it does you."

"Mrs Denbigh is very beautiful," said Jemima, taking off the bonnet, and not much inclined to try on any other.

"Very, ma'am. Quite a peculiar style of beauty. If I might be allowed, I should say that hers was a Grecian style of loveliness, while yours was Oriental. She reminded me of a young person I once knew in Fordham." Mrs Pearson sighed an audible sigh.

"In Fordham!" said Jemima, remembering that Ruth had once spoken of the place as one in which she had spent some time, while the county in which it was situated was the same in which Ruth was born. "In Fordham! Why, I think Mrs Denbigh comes from that neighbourhood."

"Oh, ma'am! she cannot be the young person I mean—I am sure, ma'am—holding the position she does in your establishment. I should hardly say I knew her myself; for I only saw her two or three times at my sister's house; but she was so remarked for her beauty, that I remember her face quite well—the more so, on account of her vicious conduct afterwards."

"Her vicious conduct!" repeated Jemima, convinced by these words that there could be no identity between Ruth and the "young person" alluded to. "Then it could not have been our Mrs Denbigh."

"Oh, no, ma'am! I am sure I should be sorry to be understood to have suggested anything of the kind. I beg your pardon if I did so. All I meant to say—and perhaps that was a liberty I ought not to have taken, considering what Ruth Hilton was—"

"Ruth Hilton!" said Jemima, turning suddenly round, and facing Mrs Pearson.

"Yes, ma'am, that was the name of the young person I allude to."

"Tell me about her—what did she do?" asked Jemima, subduing her eagerness of tone and look as best she might, but trembling as on the verge of some strange discovery.

"I don't know whether I ought to tell you, ma'am—it is hardly a fit story for a young lady; but this Ruth Hilton was an apprentice to my sister-in-law, who had a first-rate business in Fordham, which brought her a good deal of patronage from the county families; and this young creature was very artful and bold, and thought sadly too much of her beauty; and, somehow, she beguiled a young gentleman, who took her into keeping (I am sure, ma'am, I ought to apologise for polluting your ears—)"

"Go on," said Jemima, breathlessly.

"I don't know much more. His mother followed him into Wales. She was a lady of a great deal of religion, and of a very old family, and was much shocked at her son's misfortune in being captivated by such a person; but she led him to repentance, and took him to Paris, where, I think, she died; but I am not sure, for, owing to family differences, I have not been on terms for some years with my sister-in-law, who was my informant."

"Who died?" interrupted Jemima—"the young man's mother, or—or Ruth Hilton?"

"Oh dear, ma'am! pray don't confuse the two. It was the mother, Mrs—I forget the name—something like Billington. It was the lady who died."

"And what became of the other?" asked Jemima, unable, as her dark suspicion seemed thickening, to speak the name.

"The girl? Why, ma'am, what could become of her? Not that I know exactly—only one knows they can but go from bad to worse, poor creatures! God forgive me, if I am speaking too transiently of such degraded women, who, after all, are a disgrace to our sex."

"Then you know nothing more about her?" asked Jemima.

"I did hear that she had gone off with another gentleman that she met with in Wales, but I'm sure I can't tell who told me."

There was a little pause. Jemima was pondering on all she had heard. Suddenly she felt that Mrs Pearson's eyes were upon her, watching her; not with curiosity, but with a newly-awakened intelligence;—and yet she must ask one more question; but she tried to ask it in an indifferent, careless tone, handling the bonnet while she spoke.

"How long is it since all this—all you have been telling me about—happened?" (Leonard was eight years old.)

"Why—let me see. It was before I was married, and I was married three years, and poor dear Pearson has been deceased five—I should say going on for nine years this summer. Blush roses would become your complexion, perhaps, better than these lilacs," said she, as with superficial observation she watched Jemima turning the bonnet round and round on her hand—the bonnet that her dizzy eyes did not see.

"Thank you. It is very pretty. But I don't want a bonnet. I beg your pardon for taking up your time." And with an abrupt bow to the discomfited Mrs Pearson, she was out and away in the open air, threading her way with instinctive energy along the crowded street. Suddenly she turned round, and went back to Mrs Pearson's with even more rapidity than she had been walking away from the house.

"I have changed my mind," said she, as she came, breathless, up into the show-room. "I will take the bonnet. How much is it?"

"Allow me to change the flowers; it can be done in an instant, and then you can see if you would not prefer the roses; but with either foliage it is a lovely little bonnet," said Mrs Pearson, holding it up admiringly on her hand.

"Oh! never mind the flowers—yes! change them to roses." And she stood by, agitated (Mrs Pearson thought with impatience), all the time the milliner was making the alteration with skilful, busy haste.

"By the way," said Jemima, when she saw the last touches were being given, and that she must not delay executing the purpose which was the real cause of her return—"Papa, I am sure, would not like your connecting Mrs Denbigh's name with such a—story as you have been telling me."

"Oh dear! ma'am, I have too much respect for you all to think of doing such a thing! Of course I know, ma'am, that it is not to be cast up to any lady that she is like anybody disreputable."

"But I would rather you did not name the likeness to any one," said Jemima; "not to any one. Don't tell any one the story you have told me this morning."

"Indeed, ma'am, I should never think of such a thing! My poor husband could have borne witness that I am as close as the grave where there is anything to conceal."

"Oh dear!" said Jemima, "Mrs Pearson, there is nothing to conceal; only you must not speak about it."

"I certainly shall not do it, ma'am; you may rest assured of me."

This time Jemima did not go towards home, but in the direction of the outskirts of the town, on the hilly side. She had some dim recollection of hearing her sisters ask if they might not go and invite Leonard and his mother to tea; and how could she face Ruth, after the conviction had taken possession of her heart that she, and the sinful creature she had just heard of, were one and the same?

It was yet only the middle of the afternoon; the hours were early in the old-fashioned town of Eccleston. Soft white clouds had come slowly sailing up out of the west; the plain was flecked with thin floating shadows, gently borne along by the westerly wind that was waving the long grass in the hay-fields into alternate light and shade. Jemima went into one of these fields, lying by the side of the upland road. She was stunned by the shock she had received. The diver, leaving the green sward, smooth and known, where his friends stand with their familiar smiling faces, admiring his glad bravery—the diver, down in an instant in the horrid depths of the sea, close to some strange, ghastly, lidless-eyed monster, can hardly more feel his blood curdle at the near terror than did Jemima now. Two hours ago—but a point of time on her mind's dial—she had never imagined that she should ever come in contact with any one who had committed open sin; she had never shaped her conviction into words and sentences, but still it was *there*, that all the respectable, all the family and religious circumstances of her life, would hedge her in, and guard her from ever encountering the great shock of coming face to face with vice. Without being pharisaical in her estimation of herself, she had all a Pharisee's dread of publicans and sinners, and all a child's cowardliness—that cowardliness which prompts it to shut its eyes against the object of terror, rather than acknowledge its existence with brave faith. Her father's often reiterated speeches had not been without their effect. He drew a clear line of partition, which separated mankind into two great groups, to one of which, by the grace of God, he and his belonged; while the other was composed of those whom it was his duty to try and reform, and bring the whole force of his morality to bear upon, with lectures, admonitions, and exhortations—a duty to be performed, because it was a duty—but with very little of that Hope and Faith which is the Spirit that maketh alive. Jemima had rebelled against these hard doctrines of her father's, but their frequent repetition had had its effect, and led her to look upon those who had gone astray with shrinking, shuddering recoil, instead of with a pity so Christ-like as to have both wisdom and tenderness in it.

And now she saw among her own familiar associates one, almost her housefellow, who had been stained with that evil most repugnant to her womanly modesty, that would fain have ignored its existence altogether. She loathed the thought of meeting Ruth again. She wished that she could take her up, and put her down at a distance somewhere—anywhere—

where she might never see or hear of her more; never be reminded, as she must be whenever she saw her, that such things were in this sunny, bright, lark-singing earth, over which the blue dome of heaven bent softly down as Jemima sat in the hayfield that June afternoon; her cheeks flushed and red, but her lips pale and compressed, and her eyes full of a heavy, angry sorrow. It was Saturday, and the people in that part of the country left their work an hour earlier on that day. By this, Jemima knew it must be growing time for her to be at home. She had had so much of conflict in her own mind of late, that she had grown to dislike struggle, or speech, or explanation; and so strove to conform to times and hours much more than she had done in happier days. But oh! how full of hate her heart was growing against the world! And oh! how she sickened at the thought of seeing Ruth! Who was to be trusted more, if Ruth—calm, modest, delicate, dignified Ruth—had a memory blackened by sin?

As she went heavily along, the thought of Mr Farquhar came into her mind. It showed how terrible had been the stun, that he had been forgotten until now. With the thought of him came in her first merciful feeling towards Ruth. This would never have been, had there been the least latent suspicion in Jemima's jealous mind that Ruth had purposely done aught— looked a look—uttered a word—modulated a tone—for the sake of attracting. As Jemima recalled all the passages of their intercourse, she slowly confessed to herself how pure and simple had been all Ruth's ways in relation to Mr Farquhar. It was not merely that there had been no coquetting, but there had been simple unconsciousness on Ruth's part, for so long a time after Jemima had discovered Mr Farquhar's inclination for her; and when at length she had slowly awakened to some perception of the state of his feelings, there had been a modest, shrinking dignity of manner, not startled, or emotional, or even timid, but pure, grave, and quiet; and this conduct of Ruth's, Jemima instinctively acknowledged to be of necessity transparent and sincere. Now, and here, there was no hypocrisy; but some time, somewhere, on the part of somebody, what hypocrisy, what lies must have been acted, if not absolutely spoken, before Ruth could have been received by them all as the sweet, gentle, girlish widow, which she remembered they had all believed Mrs Denbigh to be when first she came among them! Could Mr and Miss Benson know? Could they be a party to the deceit? Not sufficiently acquainted with the world to understand how strong had been the temptation to play the part they did, if they wished to give Ruth a chance, Jemima could not believe them guilty of such deceit as the knowledge of Mrs Denbigh's previous conduct would imply; and yet how it darkened the latter into a treacherous hypocrite, with a black secret shut up in her soul for years— living in apparent confidence, and daily household familiarity with the Bensons for years, yet never telling the remorse that ought to be corroding her heart! Who was true? Who was not? Who was good and pure? Who was not? The very foundations of Jemima's belief in her mind were shaken.

Could it be false? Could there be two Ruth Hiltons? She went over every morsel of evidence. It could not be. She knew that Mrs Denbigh's former name had been Hilton. She had heard her speak casually, but charily, of having lived in Fordham. She knew she had been in Wales but a short time before she made her appearance in Eccleston. There was no doubt of the identity. Into the middle of Jemima's pain and horror at the afternoon's discovery, there came a sense of the power which the knowledge of this secret gave her over Ruth; but this was no relief, only an aggravation of the regret with which Jemima looked back on her state of ignorance. It was no wonder that when she arrived at home, she was so oppressed with headache that she had to go to bed directly.

"Quiet, mother! quiet, dear, dear mother" (for she clung to the known and tried goodness of her mother more than ever now), "that is all I want." And she was left to the stillness of her darkened room, the blinds idly flapping to and fro in the soft evening breeze, and letting in the rustling sound of the branches which waved close to her window, and the thrush's gurgling warble, and the distant hum of the busy town.

Her jealousy was gone—she knew not how or where. She might shun and recoil from Ruth, but she now thought that she could never more be jealous of her. In her pride of innocence, she felt almost ashamed that such a feeling could have had existence. Could Mr Farquhar hesitate between her own self and one who— No! she could not name what Ruth had been, even in thought. And yet he might never know, so fair a seeming did her rival wear. Oh! for one ray of God's holy light to know what was seeming, and what was truth, in this traitorous hollow earth! It might be—she used to think such things possible, before sorrow had embittered her—that Ruth had worked her way through the deep purgatory of repentance up to something like purity again; God only knew! If her present goodness was real—if, after having striven back thus far on the heights, a fellow-woman was to throw her down into some terrible depth with her unkind, incontinent tongue, that would be too cruel! And yet, if—there was such woeful uncertainty and deceit somewhere—if Ruth— No! that Jemima, with noble candour, admitted was impossible. Whatever Ruth had been, she was good, and to be respected as such, now. It did not follow that Jemima was to preserve the secret always; she doubted her own power to do so, if Mr Farquhar came home again, and were still constant in his admiration of Mrs Denbigh, and if Mrs Denbigh gave him any—the least encouragement. But this last she thought, from what she knew of Ruth's character, was impossible. Only, what was impossible after this afternoon's discovery? At any rate, she would watch and wait. Come what might, Ruth was in her power. And, strange to say, this last certainty gave Jemima a kind of protecting, almost pitying, feeling for Ruth. Her horror at the wrong was not diminished; but the more she thought of the struggles that the wrong-doer must have made to extricate herself, the more she felt how cruel it would be to baffle all by revealing what had been. But for her sisters' sake she had a duty to perform; she must watch Ruth. For her love's sake she could not have helped watching; but she was too much stunned to recognise the force of her love, while duty seemed the only stable thing to cling to. For the present she would neither meddle nor mar in Ruth's course of life.

CHAPTER XXVI

Mr Bradshaw's Virtuous Indignation

So it was that Jemima no longer avoided Ruth, nor manifested by word or look the dislike which for a long time she had been scarce concealing. Ruth could not help noticing that Jemima always sought to be in her presence while she was at Mr Bradshaw's house; either when daily teaching Mary and Elizabeth, or when she came as an occasional visitor with Mr and Miss Benson, or by herself. Up to this time Jemima had used no gentle skill to conceal the abruptness with which she would leave the room rather than that Ruth and she should be brought into contact—rather than that it should fall to her lot to entertain Ruth during any part of the evening. It was months since Jemima had left off sitting in the schoolroom, as had been her wont during the first few years of Ruth's governess-ship. Now, each morning Miss Bradshaw seated herself at a little round table in the window, at her work, or at her writing; but whether she sewed, or wrote, or read, Ruth felt that she was always watching—watching. At first Ruth had welcomed all these changes in habit and behaviour, as giving her a chance, she thought, by some patient waiting or some opportune show of enduring, constant love, to regain her lost friend's regard; but by-and-by the icy chillness, immovable and grey, struck more to her heart than many sudden words of unkindness could have done. They might be attributed to the hot impulses of a hasty temper—to the vehement anger of an accuser; but this measured manner was the conscious result of some deep-seated feeling; this cold sternness befitted the calm implacability of some severe judge. The watching, which Ruth felt was ever upon her, made her unconsciously shiver, as you would if you saw that the passionless eyes of the dead were visibly gazing upon you. Her very being shrivelled and parched up in Jemima's presence, as if blown upon by a bitter, keen, east wind.

Jemima bent every power she possessed upon the one object of ascertaining what Ruth really was. Sometimes the strain was very painful; the constant tension made her soul weary; and she moaned aloud, and upbraided circumstance (she dared not go higher—to the Maker of circumstance) for having deprived her of her unsuspicious happy ignorance.

Things were in this state when Mr Richard Bradshaw came on his annual home visit. He was to remain another year in London, and then to return and be admitted into the firm. After he had been a week at home, he grew tired of the monotonous regularity of his father's household, and began to complain of it to Jemima.

"I wish Farquhar were at home. Though he is such a stiff, quiet old fellow, his coming in in the evenings makes a change. What has become of the Millses? They used to drink tea with us sometimes, formerly."

"Oh! papa and Mr Mills took opposite sides at the election, and we have never visited since. I don't think they are any great loss."

"Anybody is a loss—the stupidest bore that ever was would be a blessing, if he only would come in sometimes."

"Mr and Miss Benson have drank tea here twice since you came."

"Come, that's capital! Apropos of stupid bores, you talk of the Bensons. I did not think you had so much discrimination, my little sister."

Jemima looked up in surprise; and then reddened angrily.

"I never meant to say a word against Mr or Miss Benson, and that you know quite well, Dick."

"Never mind! I won't tell tales. They are stupid old fogeys, but they are better than nobody, especially as that handsome governess of the girls always comes with them to be looked at."

There was a little pause; Richard broke it by saying:

"Do you know, Mimie, I've a notion, if she plays her cards well, she may hook Farquhar!"

"Who?" asked Jemima, shortly, though she knew quite well.

"Mrs Denbigh, to be sure. We were talking of her, you know. Farquhar asked me to dine with him at his hotel as he passed through town, and—I'd my own reasons for going and trying to creep up his sleeve—I wanted him to tip me, as he used to do."

"For shame! Dick," burst in Jemima.

"Well! well! not tip me exactly, but lend me some money. The governor keeps me so deucedly short."

"Why! it was only yesterday, when my father was speaking about your expenses, and your allowance, I heard you say that you'd more than you knew how to spend."

"Don't you see that was the perfection of art? If my father had thought me extravagant, he would have kept me in with a tight rein; as it is, I'm in great hopes of a handsome addition, and I can tell you it's needed. If my father had given me what I ought to have had at first, I should not have been driven to the speculations and messes I've got into."

"What speculations? What messes?" asked Jemima, with anxious eagerness.

"Oh! messes was not the right word. Speculations hardly was; for they are sure to turn out well, and then I shall surprise my father with my riches." He saw that he had gone a little too far in his confidence, and was trying to draw in.

"But, what do you mean? Do explain it to me."

"Never you trouble your head about my business, my dear. Women can't understand the share-market, and such things. Don't think I've forgotten the awful blunders you made when you tried to read the state of the money-market aloud to my father, that night when he had lost his spectacles. What were we talking of? Oh! of Farquhar and pretty Mrs Denbigh. Yes! I soon found out that was the subject my gentleman liked me to dwell on. He did not talk about her much himself, but his eyes sparkled when I told him what enthusiastic letters Polly and Elizabeth wrote about her. How old d'ye think she is?"

"I know!" said Jemima. "At least, I heard her age spoken about, amongst other things, when first she came. She will be five-and-twenty this autumn."

"And Farquhar is forty, if he is a day. She's young, too, to have such a boy as Leonard; younger-looking, or full as young-looking as she is! I tell you what, Mimie, she looks younger than you. How old are you? Three-and-twenty, ain't it?"

"Last March," replied Jemima.

"You'll have to make haste and pick up somebody, if you're losing your good looks at this rate. Why, Jemima, I thought you had a good chance of Farquhar a year or two ago. How come you to have lost him? I'd far rather you'd had him than that proud, haughty Mrs Denbigh, who flashes her great grey eyes upon me if ever I dare to pay her a compliment. She ought to think it an honour that I take that much notice of her. Besides, Farquhar is rich, and it's keeping the business of the firm in one's own family; and if he marries Mrs Denbigh she will be sure to be wanting Leonard in when he's of age, and I won't have that. Have a try for Farquhar, Mimie! Ten to one it's not too late. I wish I'd brought you a pink bonnet down. You go about so dowdy—so careless of how you look."

"If Mr Farquhar has not liked me as I am," said Jemima, choking, "I don't want to owe him to a pink bonnet."

"Nonsense! I don't like to have my sisters' governess stealing a march on my sister. I tell you Farquhar is worth trying for. If you'll wear the pink bonnet I'll give it you, and I'll back you against Mrs Denbigh. I think you might have done something with 'our member,' as my father calls him, when you had him so long in the house. But, altogether, I should like Farquhar best for a brother-in-law. By the way, have you heard down here that Donne is going to be married? I heard of it in town, just before I left, from a man that was good authority. Some Sir Thomas Campbell's seventh daughter: a girl without a penny; father ruined himself by gambling, and obliged to live abroad. But Donne is not a man to care for any obstacle, from all accounts, when once he has taken a fancy. It was love at first sight, they say. I believe he did not know of her existence a month ago."

"No! we have not heard of it," replied Jemima. "My father will like to know; tell it him;" continued she, as she was leaving the room, to be alone, in order to still her habitual agitation whenever she heard Mr Farquhar and Ruth coupled together.

Mr Farquhar came home the day before Richard Bradshaw left for town. He dropped in after tea at the Bradshaws'; he was evidently disappointed to see none but the family there, and looked round whenever the door opened.

"Look! look!" said Dick to his sister. "I wanted to make sure of his coming in to-night, to save me my father's parting exhortations against the temptations of the world (as if I did not know much more of the world than he does!), so I used a spell I thought would prove efficacious; I told him that we should be by ourselves, with the exception of Mrs Denbigh, and look how he is expecting her to come in!"

Jemima did see; did understand. She understood, too, why certain packets were put carefully on one side, apart from the rest of the purchases of Swiss toys and jewellery, by which Mr Farquhar proved that none of Mr Bradshaw's family had been forgotten by him during his absence. Before the end of the evening, she was very conscious that her sore heart had not forgotten how to be jealous. Her brother did not allow a word, a look, or an incident, which might be supposed on Mr Farquhar's side to refer to Ruth, to pass unnoticed; he pointed out all to his sister, never dreaming of the torture he was inflicting, only anxious to prove his own extreme penetration. At length Jemima could stand it no longer, and left the room. She went into the schoolroom, where the shutters were not closed, as it only looked into the garden. She opened the window, to let the cool night air blow in on her hot cheeks. The clouds were hurrying over the moon's face in a tempestuous and unstable manner, making all things seem unreal; now clear out in its bright light, now trembling and quivering in shadow. The pain at her heart seemed to make Jemima's brain grow dull; she laid her head on her arms, which rested on the window-sill, and grew dizzy with the sick weary notion that the earth was wandering lawless and aimless through the heavens, where all seemed one tossed and whirling wrack of clouds. It was a waking nightmare, from the uneasy heaviness of which she was thankful to be roused by Dick's entrance.

"What, you are here, are you? I have been looking everywhere for you. I wanted to ask you if you have any spare money you could lend me for a few weeks?"

"How much do you want?" asked Jemima, in a dull, hopeless voice.

"Oh! the more the better. But I should be glad of any trifle, I am kept so confoundedly short."

When Jemima returned with her little store, even her careless, selfish brother was struck by the wanness of her face, lighted by the bed-candle she carried.

"Come, Mimie, don't give it up. If I were you, I would have a good try against Mrs Denbigh. I'll send you the bonnet as soon as ever I get back to town, and you pluck up a spirit, and I'll back you against her even yet."

It seemed to Jemima strange—and yet only a fitting part of this strange, chaotic world—to find that her brother, who was the last person to whom she could have given her confidence in her own family, and almost the last person of her acquaintance to whom she could look for real help and sympathy, should have been the only one to hit upon the secret of her love. And the idea passed away from his mind as quickly as all ideas not bearing upon his own self-interests did.

The night, the sleepless night, was so crowded and haunted by miserable images, that she longed for day; and when day came, with its stinging realities, she wearied and grew sick for the solitude of night. For the next week, she seemed to see and hear nothing but what confirmed the idea of Mr Farquhar's decided attachment to Ruth. Even her mother spoke of it as a thing which was impending, and which she wondered how Mr Bradshaw would like; for his approval or disapproval was the standard by which she measured all things.

"Oh! merciful God," prayed Jemima, in the dead silence of the night, "the strain is too great—I cannot bear it longer—my life—my love—the very essence of me, which is myself through time and eternity; and on the other side there is all-pitying Charity. If she had not been what she is—if she had shown any sign of triumph—any knowledge of her prize—if she had made any effort to gain his dear heart, I must have given way long ago, and taunted her, even if I did not tell others—taunted her, even though I sank down to the pit the next moment.

"The temptation is too strong for me. Oh Lord! where is Thy peace that I believed in, in my childhood?—that I hear people speaking of now, as if it hushed up the troubles of life, and had not to be sought for—sought for, as with tears of blood!"

There was no sound nor sight in answer to this wild imploring cry, which Jemima half thought must force out a sign from Heaven. But there was a dawn stealing on through the darkness of her night.

It was glorious weather for the end of August. The nights were as full of light as the days—everywhere, save in the low dusky meadows by the river-side, where the mists rose and blended the pale sky with the lands below. Unknowing of the care and trouble around them, Mary and Elizabeth exulted in the weather, and saw some new glory in every touch of the year's decay. They were clamorous for an expedition to the hills, before the calm stillness of the autumn should be disturbed by storms. They gained permission to go on the next Wednesday—the next half-holiday. They had won their mother over to consent to a full holiday, but their father would not hear of it. Mrs Bradshaw had proposed an early dinner, but the idea was scouted at by the girls. What would the expedition be worth if they did not carry their dinners with them in baskets? Anything out of a basket, and eaten in the open air, was worth twenty times as much as the most sumptuous meal in the house. So the baskets were packed up, while Mrs Bradshaw wailed over probable colds to be caught from sitting on the damp ground. Ruth and Leonard were to go; they four. Jemima had refused all invitations to make one of the party; and yet she had a half-sympathy with her sisters' joy—a sort of longing, lingering look back to the time when she too would have revelled in the prospect that lay before them. They, too, would grow up, and suffer; though now they played, regardless of their doom.

The morning was bright and glorious; just cloud enough, as some one said, to make the distant plain look beautiful from the hills, with its floating shadows passing over the golden corn-fields. Leonard was to join them at twelve, when his lessons with Mr Benson, and the girls' with their masters, should be over. Ruth took off her bonnet, and folded her shawl with her usual dainty, careful neatness, and laid them aside in a corner of the room to be in readiness. She tried to forget the pleasure she always anticipated from a long walk towards the hills, while the morning's work went on; but she showed enough of sympathy to make the girls cling round her with many a caress of joyous love. Everything was beautiful in their eyes; from the shadows of the quivering leaves on the wall to the glittering beads of dew, not yet absorbed by the sun, which decked the gossamer web in the vine outside the window. Eleven o'clock struck. The Latin master went away, wondering much at the radiant faces of his pupils, and thinking that it was only very young people who could take such pleasure in the "Delectus." Ruth said, "Now, do let us try to be very steady this next hour," and Mary pulled back Ruth's head, and gave the pretty budding mouth a kiss. They sat down to work, while Mrs Denbigh read aloud. A fresh sun-gleam burst into the room, and they looked at each other with glad, anticipating eyes.

Jemima came in, ostensibly to seek for a book, but really from that sort of restless weariness of any one place or employment, which had taken possession of her since Mr Farquhar's return. She stood before the bookcase in the recess, languidly passing over the titles in search of the one she wanted. Ruth's voice lost a tone or two of its peacefulness, and her eyes looked more dim and anxious at Jemima's presence. She wondered in her heart if she dared to ask Miss Bradshaw to accompany them in their expedition. Eighteen months ago she would have urged it on her friend with soft, loving entreaty; now she was afraid even to propose it as a hard possibility; everything she did or said was taken so wrongly—seemed to add to the old dislike, or the later stony contempt with which Miss Bradshaw had regarded her. While they were in this way Mr Bradshaw came into the room. His entrance—his being at home at all at this time—was so unusual a thing, that the reading was instantly stopped; and all four involuntarily looked at him, as if expecting some explanation of his unusual proceeding.

His face was almost purple with suppressed agitation.

"Mary and Elizabeth, leave the room. Don't stay to pack up your books. Leave the room, I say!" He spoke with trembling anger, and the frightened girls obeyed without a word. A cloud passing over the sun cast a cold gloom into the room which was late so bright and beaming; but, by equalising the light, it took away the dark shadow from the place where Jemima had been standing, and her figure caught her father's eye.

"Leave the room, Jemima," said he.

"Why, father?" replied she, in an opposition that was strange even to herself, but which was prompted by the sullen passion which seethed below the stagnant surface of her life, and which sought a vent in defiance. She maintained her ground, facing round upon her father, and Ruth—Ruth, who had risen, and stood trembling, shaking, a lightning-fear having shown her the precipice on which she stood. It was of no use; no quiet, innocent life—no profound silence, even to her own heart, as to the Past; the old offence could never be drowned in the Deep; but thus, when all was calm on the great, broad, sunny sea, it rose to the surface, and faced her with its unclosed eyes and its ghastly countenance. The blood bubbled up to her brain, and made such a sound there, as of boiling waters, that she did not hear the words which Mr Bradshaw first spoke; indeed, his speech was broken and disjointed by intense passion. But she needed not to hear; she knew. As she rose up at first, so she stood now—numb and helpless. When her ears heard again (as if the sounds were drawing nearer, and becoming more distinct, from some faint, vague distance of space), Mr Bradshaw was saying, "If there be one sin I hate—I utterly loathe—more than all others, it is wantonness. It includes all other sins. It is but of a piece that you should have come with your sickly, hypocritical face, imposing upon us all. I trust Benson did not know of it—for his own sake, I trust not. Before God, if he got you into my house on false pretences, he shall find his charity at other men's expense shall cost him dear—you—the common talk of Eccleston for your profligacy—" He was absolutely choked by his boiling indignation. Ruth stood speechless, motionless. Her head drooped a little forward, her eyes were more than half veiled by the large quivering lids, her arms hung down straight and heavy. At last she heaved the weight off her heart enough to say, in a faint, moaning voice, speaking with infinite difficulty:

"I was so young."

"The more depraved, the more disgusting you," Mr Bradshaw exclaimed, almost glad that the woman, unresisting so long, should now begin to resist. But to his surprise (for in his anger he had forgotten her presence) Jemima moved forwards, and said, "Father!"

"You hold your tongue, Jemima. You have grown more and more insolent—more and more disobedient every day. I now know who to thank for it. When such a woman came into my family there is no wonder at any corruption—any evil—anydefilement—"

"Father!"

"Not a word! If, in your disobedience, you choose to stay and hear what no modest young woman would put herself in the way of hearing, you shall be silent when I bid you. The only good you can gain is in the way of warning. Look at that woman" (indicating Ruth, who moved her drooping head a little on one side, as if by such motion she could avert the pitiless pointing—her face growing whiter and whiter still every instant)—"look at that woman, I say—corrupt long before she was your age—hypocrite for years! If ever you, or any child of mine, cared for her, shake her off from you, as St Paul shook off the viper—even into the fire." He stopped for very want of breath. Jemima, all flushed and panting, went up and stood side by side with wan Ruth. She took the cold, dead hand which hung next to her in her warm convulsive grasp, and holding it so tight that it was blue and discoloured for days, she spoke out beyond all power of restraint from her father.

"Father, I will speak. I will not keep silence. I will bear witness to Ruth. I have hated her—so keenly, may God forgive me! but you may know, from that, that my witness is true. I have hated her, and my hatred was only quenched into contempt—not contempt now, dear Ruth—dear Ruth"—(this was spoken with infinite softness and tenderness, and in spite of her father's fierce eyes and passionate gesture)—"I heard what you have learnt now, father, weeks and weeks ago—a year it may be, all time of late has been so long; and I shuddered up from her and from her sin; and I might have spoken of it, and told it there and then, if I had not been afraid that it was from no good motive I should act in so doing, but to gain a way to the desire of my own jealous heart. Yes, father, to show you what a witness I am for Ruth, I will own that I was stabbed to the heart with jealousy; some one—some one cared for Ruth that—oh, father! spare me saying all." Her face was double-dyed with crimson blushes, and she paused for one moment—no more.

"I watched her, and I watched her with my wild-beast eyes. If I had seen one paltering with duty—if I had witnessed one flickering shadow of untruth in word or action—if, more than all things, my woman's instinct had ever been conscious of the faintest speck of impurity in thought, or word, or look, my old hate would have flamed out with the flame of hell! my contempt would have turned to loathing disgust, instead of my being full of pity, and the stirrings of new-awakened love, and most true respect. Father, I have borne my witness!"

"And I will tell you how much your witness is worth," said her father, beginning low, that his pent-up wrath might have room to swell out. "It only convinces me more and more how deep is the corruption this wanton has spread in my family. She has come amongst us with her innocent seeming, and spread her nets well and skilfully. She has turned right into wrong, and wrong into right, and taught you all to be uncertain whether there be any such thing as Vice in the world, or whether it ought not to be looked upon as Virtue. She has led you to the brink of the deep pit, ready for the first chance circumstance to push you in. And I trusted her—I trusted her—I welcomed her."

"I have done very wrong," murmured Ruth, but so low, that perhaps he did not hear her, for he went on, lashing himself up.

"I welcomed her. I was duped into allowing her bastard—(I sicken at the thought of it)—"

At the mention of Leonard, Ruth lifted up her eyes for the first time since the conversation began, the pupils dilating, as if she were just becoming aware of some new agony in store for her. I have seen such a look of terror on a poor dumb animal's countenance, and once or twice on human faces. I pray I may never see it again on either! Jemima felt the hand she held in her strong grasp writhe itself free. Ruth spread her arms before her, clasping and lacing her fingers together, her head thrown a little back, as if in intensest suffering.

Mr Bradshaw went on:

"That very child and heir of shame to associate with my own innocent children! I trust they are not contaminated."

"I cannot bear it—I cannot bear it!" were the words wrung out of Ruth.

"Cannot bear it! cannot bear it!" he repeated. "You must bear it, madam. Do you suppose your child is to be exempt from the penalties of his birth? Do you suppose that he alone is to be saved from the upbraiding scoff? Do you suppose that he is ever to rank with other boys, who are not stained and marked with sin from their birth? Every creature in Eccleston may know what he is; do you think they will spare him their scorn? 'Cannot bear it,' indeed! Before you went into your sin, you should have thought whether you could bear the consequences or not—have had some idea how far your offspring would be degraded and scouted, till the best thing that could happen to him would be for him to be lost to all sense of shame, dead to all knowledge of guilt, for his mother's sake."

Ruth spoke out. She stood like a wild creature at bay, past fear now. "I appeal to God against such a doom for my child. I appeal to God to help me. I am a mother, and as such I cry to God for help—for help to keep my boy in His pitying sight, and to bring him up in His holy fear. Let the shame fall on me! I have deserved it, but he—he is so innocent and good."

Ruth had caught up her shawl, and was tying on her bonnet with her trembling hands. What if Leonard was hearing of her shame from common report? What would be the mysterious shock of the intelligence? She must face him, and see the look in his eyes, before she knew whether he recoiled from her; he might have his heart turned to hate her, by their cruel jeers.

Jemima stood by, dumb and pitying. Her sorrow was past her power. She helped in arranging the dress, with one or two gentle touches, which were hardly felt by Ruth, but which called out all Mr Bradshaw's ire afresh; he absolutely took her by the shoulders and turned her by force out of the room. In the hall, and along the stairs, her passionate woeful crying was heard. The sound only concentrated Mr Bradshaw's anger on Ruth. He held the street-door open wide, and said, between his teeth, "If ever you, or your bastard, darken this door again, I will have you both turned out by the police!"

He need not have added this, if he had seen Ruth's face.

CHAPTER XXVII

Preparing to Stand on the Truth

As Ruth went along the accustomed streets, every sight and every sound seemed to bear a new meaning, and each and all to have some reference to her boy's disgrace. She held her head down, and scudded along dizzy with fear, lest some word should have told him what she had been, and what he was, before she could reach him. It was a wild, unreasoning fear, but it took hold of her as strongly as if it had been well founded. And, indeed, the secret whispered by Mrs Pearson, whose curiosity and suspicion had been excited by Jemima's manner, and confirmed since by many a little corroborating circumstance, had spread abroad, and was known to most of the gossips in Eccleston before it reached Mr Bradshaw's ears.

As Ruth came up to the door of the Chapel-house, it was opened, and Leonard came out, bright and hopeful as the morning, his face radiant at the prospect of the happy day before him. He was dressed in the clothes it had been such a pleasant pride to her to make for him. He had the dark blue ribbon tied round his neck that she had left out for him that very morning, with a smiling thought of how it would set off his brown, handsome face. She caught him by the hand as they met, and turned him, with his face homewards, without a word. Her looks, her rushing movement, her silence, awed him; and although he wondered, he did not stay to ask why she did so. The door was on the latch; she opened it, and only said, "Upstairs," in a hoarse whisper. Up they went into her own room. She drew him in, and bolted the door; and then, sitting down, she placed him (she had never let go of him) before her, holding him with her hands on each of his shoulders, and gazing into his face with a woeful look of the agony that could not find vent in words. At last she tried to speak; she tried with strong bodily effort, almost amounting to convulsion. But the words would not come; it was not till she saw the absolute terror depicted on his face that she found utterance; and then the sight of that terror changed the words from what she meant them to have been. She drew him to her, and laid her head upon his shoulder; hiding her face even there.

"My poor, poor boy! my poor, poor darling! Oh! would that I had died—I had died, in my innocent girlhood!"

"Mother! mother!" sobbed Leonard. "What is the matter? Why do you look so wild and ill? Why do you call me your 'poor boy'? Are we not going to Scaurside-hill? I don't much mind it, mother; only please don't gasp and quiver so. Dearest mother, are you ill? Let me call Aunt Faith!"

Ruth lifted herself up, and put away the hair that had fallen over and was blinding her eyes. She looked at him with intense wistfulness.

"Kiss me, Leonard!" said she—"kiss me, my darling, once more in the old way!" Leonard threw himself into her arms and hugged her with all his force, and their lips clung together as in the kiss given to the dying.

"Leonard!" said she at length, holding him away from her, and nerving herself up to tell him all by one spasmodic effort—"listen to me." The boy stood breathless and still, gazing at her. On her impetuous transit from Mr Bradshaw's to the Chapel-house, her wild, desperate thought had been that she would call herself by every violent, coarse name which the world might give her—that Leonard should hear those words applied to his mother first from her own lips; but the influence of his presence—for he was a holy and sacred creature in her eyes, and this point remained steadfast, though all the rest were upheaved—subdued her; and now it seemed as if she could not find words fine enough, and pure enough, to convey the truth that he must learn, and should learn from no tongue but hers.

"Leonard—when I was very young I did very wrong. I think God, who knows all, will judge me more tenderly than men—but I did wrong in a way which you cannot understand yet" (she saw the red flush come into his cheek, and it stung her as the first token of that shame which was to be his portion through life)—"in a way people never forget, never forgive. You will hear me called the hardest names that ever can be thrown at women—I have been, to-day; and, my child, you must bear it patiently, because they will be partly true. Never get confused, by your love for me, into thinking that what I did was right.—Where was I?" said she, suddenly faltering, and forgetting all she had said and all she had got to say; and then, seeing Leonard's face of wonder, and burning shame and indignation, she went on more rapidly, as fearing lest her strength should fail before she had ended.

"And, Leonard," continued she, in a trembling, sad voice, "this is not all. The punishment of punishments lies awaiting me still. It is to see you suffer for my wrongdoing. Yes, darling! they will speak shameful things of you, poor innocent child! as well as of me, who am guilty. They will throw it in your teeth through life, that your mother was never married—was not married when you wereborn—"

"Were not you married? Are not you a widow?" asked he abruptly, for the first time getting anything like a clear idea of the real state of the case.

"No! May God forgive me, and help me!" exclaimed she, as she saw a strange look of repugnance cloud over the boy's face, and felt a slight motion on his part to extricate himself from her hold. It was as slight, as transient as it could be—over in an instant. But she had taken her hands away, and covered up her face with them as quickly—covered up her face in shame before her child; and in the bitterness of her heart she was wailing out, "Oh, would to God I had died—that I had died as a baby—that I had died as a little baby hanging at my mother's breast!"

"Mother," said Leonard, timidly putting his hand on her arm; but she shrunk from him, and continued her low, passionate wailing. "Mother," said he, after a pause, coming nearer, though she saw it not—"mammy darling," said he, using the caressing name, which he had been trying to drop as not sufficiently manly, "mammy, my own, own dear, dear, darling mother, I don't believe them—I don't, I don't, I don't, I don't!" He broke out into a wild burst of crying as he said this. In a moment her arms were round the poor boy, and she was hushing him up like a baby on her bosom. "Hush, Leonard! Leonard, be still, my child! I have been too sudden with you!—I have done you harm—oh! I have done you nothing but harm," cried she, in a tone of bitter self-reproach.

"No, mother," said he, stopping his tears, and his eyes blazing out with earnestness; "there never was such a mother as you have been to me, and I won't believe any one who says it. I won't; and I'll knock them down if they say it again, I will!" He clenched his fist, with a fierce, defiant look on his face.

"You forget, my child," said Ruth, in the sweetest, saddest tone that ever was heard, "I said it of myself; I said it because it was true." Leonard threw his arms tight round her, and hid his face against her bosom. She felt him pant there like some hunted creature. She had no soothing comfort to give him. "Oh, that she and he lay dead!"

At last, exhausted, he lay so still and motionless, that she feared to look. She wanted him to speak, yet dreaded his first words. She kissed his hair, his head, his very clothes, murmuring low, inarticulate, moaning sounds.

"Leonard," said she, "Leonard, look up at me! Leonard, look up!" But he only clung the closer, and hid his face the more.

"My boy!" said she, "what can I do or say? If I tell you never to mind it—that it is nothing—I tell you false. It is a bitter shame and a sorrow that I have drawn down upon you. A shame, Leonard, because of me, your mother; but, Leonard, it is no disgrace or lowering of you in the eyes of God." She spoke now as if she had found the clue which might lead him to rest and strength at last. "Remember that, always. Remember that, when the time of trial comes—and it seems a hard and cruel thing that you should be called reproachful names by men, and all for what was no fault of yours—remember God's pity and God's justice; and though my sin shall have made you an outcast in the world—oh, my child, my child!"—(she felt him kiss her, as if mutely trying to comfort her—it gave her strength to go on)—"remember, darling of my heart, it is only your own sin that can make you an outcast from God."

She grew so faint that her hold of him relaxed. He looked up affrighted. He brought her water—he threw it over her; in his terror at the notion that she was going to die and leave him, he called her by every fond name, imploring her to open her eyes.

When she partially recovered, he helped her to the bed, on which she lay still, wan and death-like. She almost hoped the swoon that hung around her might be Death, and in that imagination she opened her eyes to take a last look at her boy. She saw him pale and terror-stricken; and pity for his affright roused her, and made her forget herself in the wish that he should not see her death, if she were indeed dying.

"Go to Aunt Faith!" whispered she; "I am weary, and want sleep."

Leonard arose slowly and reluctantly. She tried to smile upon him, that what she thought would be her last look might dwell in his remembrance as tender and strong; she watched him to the door; she saw him hesitate, and return to her. He came back to her, and said in a timid, apprehensive tone:

"Mother—will *they* speak to me about—it?"

Ruth closed her eyes, that they might not express the agony she felt, like a sharp knife, at this question. Leonard had asked it with a child's desire of avoiding painful and mysterious topics,—from no personal sense of shame as she understood it, shame beginning thus early, thus instantaneously.

"No," she replied. "You may be sure they will not."

So he went. But now she would have been thankful for the unconsciousness of fainting; that one little speech bore so much meaning to her hot, irritable brain. Mr and Miss Benson, all in their house, would never speak to the boy—but in his home alone would he be safe from what he had already learnt to dread. Every form in which shame and opprobrium could overwhelm her darling, haunted her. She had been exercising strong self-control for his sake ever since she had met him at the house-door; there was now a reaction. His presence had kept her mind on its perfect balance. When that was withdrawn, the effect of the strain of power was felt. And athwart the fever-mists that arose to obscure her judgment, all sorts of will-o'-the-wisp plans flittered before her; tempting her to this and that course of action—to anything rather than patient endurance—to relieve her present state of misery by some sudden spasmodic effort, that took the semblance of being wise and right. Gradually all her desires, all her longing, settled themselves on one point. What had she done—what could she do, to Leonard, but evil? If she were away, and gone no one knew where—lost in mystery, as if she were dead— perhaps the cruel hearts might relent, and show pity on Leonard; while her perpetual presence would but call up the remembrance of his birth. Thus she reasoned in her hot, dull brain; and shaped her plans in accordance.

Leonard stole downstairs noiselessly. He listened to find some quiet place where he could hide himself. The house was very still. Miss Benson thought the purposed expedition had taken place, and never dreamed but that Ruth and Leonard were on distant, sunny Scaurside-hill; and after a very early dinner, she had set out to drink tea with a farmer's wife who lived in the country two or three miles off. Mr Benson meant to have gone with her; but while they were at dinner, he had received an unusually authoritative note from Mr Bradshaw desiring to speak with him, so he went to that gentleman's house instead. Sally was busy in her kitchen, making a great noise (not unlike a groom rubbing down a horse) over her cleaning. Leonard stole into the sitting-room, and crouched behind the large old-fashioned sofa to ease his sore, aching heart, by crying with all the prodigal waste and abandonment of childhood.

Mr Benson was shown into Mr Bradshaw's own particular room. The latter gentleman was walking up and down, and it was easy to perceive that something had occurred to chafe him to great anger.

"Sit down, sir!" said he to Mr Benson, nodding to a chair.

Mr Benson sat down. But Mr Bradshaw continued his walk for a few minutes longer without speaking. Then he stopped abruptly, right in front of Mr Benson; and in a voice which he tried to render calm, but which trembled with passion— with a face glowing purple as he thought of his wrongs (and real wrongs they were), he began:

"Mr Benson, I have sent for you to ask—I am almost too indignant at the bare suspicion to speak as becomes me—but did you—I really shall be obliged to beg your pardon, if you are as much in the dark as I was yesterday as to the character of that woman who lives under your roof?"

There was no answer from Mr Benson. Mr Bradshaw looked at him very earnestly. His eyes were fixed on the ground—he made no inquiry—he uttered no expression of wonder or dismay. Mr Bradshaw ground his foot on the floor with gathering rage; but just as he was about to speak, Mr Benson rose up—a poor deformed old man—before the stern and portly figure that was swelling and panting with passion.

"Hear me, sir!" (stretching out his hand as if to avert the words which were impending). "Nothing you can say, can upbraid me like my own conscience; no degradation you can inflict, by word or deed, can come up to the degradation I have suffered for years, at being a party to a deceit, even for a goodend—"

"For a good end!—Nay! what next?"

The taunting contempt with which Mr Bradshaw spoke these words almost surprised himself by what he imagined must be its successful power of withering; but in spite of it, Mr Benson lifted his grave eyes to Mr Bradshaw's countenance, and repeated:

"For a good end. The end was not, as perhaps you consider it to have been, to obtain her admission into your family—nor yet to put her in the way of gaining her livelihood; my sister and I would willingly have shared what we have with her; it was our intention to do so at first, if not for any length of time, at least as long as her health might require it. Why I advised (perhaps I only yielded to advice) a change of name—an assumption of a false state of widowhood—was because I earnestly desired to place her in circumstances in which she might work out her self-redemption; and you, sir, know how terribly the world goes against all such as have sinned as Ruth did. She was so young, too."

"You mistake, sir; my acquaintance has not lain so much among that class of sinners as to give me much experience of the way in which they are treated. But, judging from what I have seen, I should say they meet with full as much leniency as they deserve; and supposing they do not—I know there are plenty of sickly sentimentalists just now who reserve all their interest and regard for criminals—why not pick out one of these to help you in your task of washing the blackamoor white? Why choose me to be imposed upon—my household into which to intrude your protégée? Why were my innocent children to be exposed to corruption? I say," said Mr Bradshaw, stamping his foot, "how dared you come into this house, where you were looked upon as a minister of religion, with a lie in your mouth? How dared you single me out, of all people, to be gulled and deceived, and pointed at through the town as the person who had taken an abandoned woman into his house to teach his daughters?"

"I own my deceit was wrong and faithless."

"Yes! you can own it, now it is found out! There is small merit in that, I think!"

"Sir! I claim no merit. I take shame to myself. I did not single you out. You applied to me with your proposal that Ruth should be your children's governess."

"Pah!"

"And the temptation was too great— No! I will not say that—but the temptation was greater than I could stand—it seemed to open out a path of usefulness."

"Now, don't let me hear you speak so," said Mr Bradshaw, blazing up. "I can't stand it. It is too much to talk in that way when the usefulness was to consist in contaminating my innocent girls."

"God knows that if I had believed there had been any danger of such contamination—God knows how I would have died sooner than have allowed her to enter your family. Mr Bradshaw, you believe me, don't you?" asked Mr Benson, earnestly.

"I really must be allowed the privilege of doubting what you say in future," said Mr Bradshaw, in a cold, contemptuous manner.

"I have deserved this," Mr Benson replied. "But," continued he, after a moment's pause, "I will not speak of myself, but of Ruth. Surely, sir, the end I aimed at (the means I took to obtain it were wrong; you cannot feel that more than I do) was a right one; and you will not—you cannot say, that your children have suffered from associating with her. I had her in my family, under the watchful eyes of three anxious persons for a year or more; we saw faults—no human being is without them—and poor Ruth's were but slight venial errors; but we saw no sign of a corrupt mind—no glimpse of boldness or forwardness—no token of want of conscientiousness; she seemed, and was, a young and gentle girl, who had been led astray before she fairly knew what life was."

"I suppose most depraved women have been innocent in their time," said Mr Bradshaw, with bitter contempt.

"Oh, Mr Bradshaw! Ruth was not depraved, and you know it. You cannot have seen her—have known her daily, all these years, without acknowledging that!" Mr Benson was almost breathless, awaiting Mr Bradshaw's answer. The quiet self-control which he had maintained so long, was gone now.

"I saw her daily—I did *not* know her. If I had known her, I should have known she was fallen and depraved, and consequently not fit to come into my house, nor to associate with my pure children."

"Now I wish God would give me power to speak out convincingly what I believe to be His truth, that not every woman who has fallen is depraved; that many—how many the Great Judgment Day will reveal to those who have shaken off the poor, sore, penitent hearts on earth—many, many crave and hunger after a chance for virtue—the help which no man gives to them—help—that gentle, tender help which Jesus gave once to Mary Magdalen." Mr Benson was almost choked by his own feelings.

"Come, come, Mr Benson, let us have no more of this morbid way of talking. The world has decided how such women are to be treated; and, you may depend upon it, there is so much practical wisdom in the world that its way of acting is right in the long run, and that no one can fly in its face with impunity, unless, indeed, they stoop to deceit and imposition."

"I take my stand with Christ against the world," said Mr Benson, solemnly, disregarding the covert allusion to himself. "What have the world's ways ended in? Can we be much worse than we are?"

"Speak for yourself, if you please."

"Is it not time to change some of our ways of thinking and acting? I declare before God, that if I believe in any one human truth, it is this—that to every woman who, like Ruth, has sinned, should be given a chance of self-redemption—and that such a chance should be given in no supercilious or contemptuous manner, but in the spirit of the holy Christ."

"Such as getting her into a friend's house under false colours."

"I do not argue on Ruth's case. In that I have acknowledged my error. I do not argue on any case. I state my firm belief, that it is God's will that we should not dare to trample any of His creatures down to the hopeless dust; that it is God's will that the women who have fallen should be numbered among those who have broken hearts to be bound up, not cast aside as lost beyond recall. If this be God's will, as a thing of God it will stand; and He will open a way."

"I should have attached much more importance to all your exhortation on this point if I could have respected your conduct in other matters. As it is, when I see a man who has deluded himself into considering falsehood right, I am disinclined to take his opinion on subjects connected with morality; and I can no longer regard him as a fitting exponent of the will of God. You perhaps understand what I mean, Mr Benson. I can no longer attend your chapel."

If Mr Benson had felt any hope of making Mr Bradshaw's obstinate mind receive the truth, that he acknowledged and repented of his connivance at the falsehood by means of which Ruth had been received into the Bradshaw family, this last sentence prevented his making the attempt. He simply bowed and took his leave—Mr Bradshaw attending him to the door with formal ceremony.

He felt acutely the severance of the tie which Mr Bradshaw had just announced to him. He had experienced many mortifications in his intercourse with that gentleman, but they had fallen off from his meek spirit like drops of water from a bird's plumage; and now he only remembered the acts of substantial kindness rendered (the ostentation all forgotten)— many happy hours and pleasant evenings—the children whom he had loved dearer than he thought till now—the young people about whom he had cared, and whom he had striven to lead aright. He was but a young man when Mr Bradshaw first came to his chapel; they had grown old together; he had never recognised Mr Bradshaw as an old familiar friend so completely as now when they were severed.

It was with a heavy heart that he opened his own door. He went to his study immediately; he sat down to steady himself into his position.

How long he was there—silent and alone—reviewing his life—confessing his sins—he did not know; but he heard some unusual sound in the house that disturbed him—roused him to present life. A slow, languid step came along the passage to the front door—the breathing was broken by many sighs.

Ruth's hand was on the latch when Mr Benson came out. Her face was very white, except two red spots on each cheek— her eyes were deep-sunk and hollow, but glittered with feverish lustre. "Ruth!" exclaimed he. She moved her lips, but her throat and mouth were too dry for her to speak.

"Where are you going?" asked he; for she had all her walking things on, yet trembled so, even as she stood, that it was evident she could not walk far without falling.

She hesitated—she looked up at him, still with the same dry glittering eyes. At last she whispered (for she could only speak in a whisper), "To Helmsby—I am going to Helmsby."

"Helmsby! my poor girl—may God have mercy upon you!" for he saw she hardly knew what she was saying. "Where is Helmsby?"

"I don't know. In Lincolnshire, I think."

"But why are you going there?"

"Hush! he's asleep," said she, as Mr Benson had unconsciously raised his voice.

"Who is asleep?" asked Mr Benson.

"That poor little boy," said she, beginning to quiver and cry.

"Come here!" said he, authoritatively, drawing her into the study.

"Sit down in that chair. I will come back directly."

He went in search of his sister, but she had not returned. Then he had recourse to Sally, who was as busy as ever about her cleaning.

"How long has Ruth been at home?" asked he.

"Ruth! She has never been at home sin' morning. She and Leonard were to be off for the day somewhere or other with them Bradshaw girls."

"Then she has had no dinner?"

"Not here, at any rate. I can't answer for what she may have done at other places."

"And Leonard—where is he?"

"How should I know? With his mother, I suppose. Leastways, that was what was fixed on. I've enough to do of my own, without routing after other folks."

She went on scouring in no very good temper. Mr Benson stood silent for a moment.

"Sally," he said, "I want a cup of tea. Will you make it as soon as you can; and some dry toast too? I'll come for it in ten minutes."

Struck by something in his voice, she looked up at him for the first time.

"What ha' ye been doing to yourself, to look so grim and grey? Tiring yourself all to tatters, looking after some naught, I'll be bound! Well! well! I mun make ye your tea, I reckon; but I did hope as you grew older you'd ha' grown wiser!"

Mr Benson made no reply, but went to look for Leonard, hoping that the child's presence might bring back to his mother the power of self-control. He opened the parlour-door, and looked in, but saw no one. Just as he was shutting it, however, he heard a deep, broken, sobbing sigh; and, guided by the sound, he found the boy lying on the floor, fast asleep, but with his features all swollen and disfigured by passionate crying.

"Poor child! This was what she meant, then," thought Mr Benson. "He has begun his share of the sorrows too," he continued, pitifully. "No! I will not waken him back to consciousness." So he returned alone into the study. Ruth sat where he had placed her, her head bent back, and her eyes shut. But when he came in she started up.

"I must be going," she said, in a hurried way.

"Nay, Ruth, you must not go. You must not leave us. We cannot do without you. We love you too much."

"Love me!" said she, looking at him wistfully. As she looked, her eyes filled slowly with tears. It was a good sign, and Mr Benson took heart to go on.

"Yes! Ruth. You know we do. You may have other things to fill up your mind just now, but you know we love you; and nothing can alter our love for you. You ought not to have thought of leaving us. You would not, if you had been quite well."

"Do you know what has happened?" she asked, in a low, hoarse voice.

"Yes. I know all," he answered. "It makes no difference to us. Why should it?"

"Oh! Mr Benson, don't you know that my shame is discovered?" she replied, bursting into tears—"and I must leave you, and leave Leonard, that you may not share in my disgrace."

"You must do no such thing. Leave Leonard! You have no right to leave Leonard. Where could you go to?"

"To Helmsby," she said, humbly. "It would break my heart to go, but I think I ought, for Leonard's sake. I know I ought." She was crying sadly by this time, but Mr Benson knew the flow of tears would ease her brain. "It will break my heart to go, but I know I must."

"Sit still here at present," said he, in a decided tone of command. He went for the cup of tea. He brought it to her without Sally's being aware for whom it was intended.

"Drink this!" He spoke as you would do to a child, if desiring it to take medicine. "Eat some toast." She took the tea, and drank it feverishly; but when she tried to eat, the food seemed to choke her. Still she was docile, and she tried.

"I cannot," said she at last, putting down the piece of toast. There was a return to something of her usual tone in the words. She spoke gently and softly; no longer in the shrill, hoarse voice she had used at first. Mr Benson sat down by her.

"Now, Ruth, we must talk a little together. I want to understand what your plan was. Where is Helmsby? Why did you fix to go there?"

"It is where my mother lived," she answered. "Before she was married she lived there; and wherever she lived, the people all loved her dearly; and I thought—I think, that for her sake some one would give me work. I meant to tell them the truth," said she, dropping her eyes; "but still they would, perhaps, give me some employment—I don't care what—for her sake. I could do many things," said she, suddenly looking up. "I am sure I could weed—I could in gardens—if they did not like to have me in their houses. But perhaps some one, for my mother's sake—oh! my dear, dear mother!—do you know where and what I am?" she cried out, sobbing afresh.

Mr Benson's heart was very sore, though he spoke authoritatively, and almost sternly.

"Ruth! you must be still and quiet. I cannot have this. I want you to listen to me. Your thought of Helmsby would be a good one, if it was right for you to leave Eccleston; but I do not think it is. I am certain of this, that it would be a great sin in you to separate yourself from Leonard. You have no right to sever the tie by which God has bound you together."

"But if I am here they will all know and remember the shame of his birth; and if I go away they may forget—"

"And they may not. And if you go away, he may be unhappy or ill; and you, who above all others have—and have from God—remember *that*, Ruth!—the power to comfort him, the tender patience to nurse him, have left him to the care of strangers. Yes; I know! But we ourselves are as strangers, dearly as we love him, compared to a mother. He may turn to sin, and want the long forbearance, the serene authority of a parent; and where are you? No dread of shame, either for yourself, or even for him, can ever make it right for you to shake off your responsibility." All this time he was watching her narrowly, and saw her slowly yield herself up to the force of what he was saying.

"Besides, Ruth," he continued, "we have gone on falsely hitherto. It has been my doing, my mistake, my sin. I ought to have known better. Now, let us stand firm on the truth. You have no new fault to repent of. Be brave and faithful. It is to God you answer, not to men. The shame of having your sin known to the world, should be as nothing to the shame you felt at having sinned. We have dreaded men too much, and God too little, in the course we have taken. But now be of good cheer. Perhaps you will have to find your work in the world very low—not quite working in the fields," said he, with a gentle smile, to which she, downcast and miserable, could give no response. "Nay, perhaps, Ruth," he went on, "you may have to stand and wait for some time; no one may be willing to use the services you would gladly render; all may turn aside from you, and may speak very harshly of you. Can you accept all this treatment meekly, as but the reasonable and just penance God has laid upon you—feeling no anger against those who slight you, no impatience for the time to come (and come it surely will—I speak as having the word of God for what I say) when He, having purified you, even as by fire, will make a straight path for your feet? My child, it is Christ the Lord who has told us of this infinite mercy of God. Have you faith enough in it to be brave, and bear on, and do rightly in patience and in tribulation?"

Ruth had been hushed and very still until now, when the pleading earnestness of his question urged her to answer:

"Yes!" said she. "I hope—I believe I can be faithful for myself, for I have sinned and done wrong. But Leonard—" She looked up at him.

"But Leonard," he echoed. "Ah! there it is hard, Ruth. I own the world is hard and persecuting to such as he." He paused to think of the true comfort for this sting. He went on. "The world is not everything, Ruth; nor is the want of men's good opinion and esteem the highest need which man has. Teach Leonard this. You would not wish his life to be one summer's day. You dared not make it so, if you had the power. Teach him to bid a noble, Christian welcome to the trials which God sends—and this is one of them. Teach him not to look on a life of struggle, and perhaps of disappointment and incompleteness, as a sad and mournful end, but as the means permitted to the heroes and warriors in the army of Christ, by which to show their faithful following. Tell him of the hard and thorny path which was trodden once by the bleeding feet of One. Ruth! think of the Saviour's life and cruel death, and of His divine faithfulness. Oh, Ruth!" exclaimed he, "when I look and see what you may be—what you *must* be to that boy, I cannot think how you could be coward enough, for a moment, to shrink from your work! But we have all been cowards hitherto," he added, in bitter self-accusation. "God help us to be so no longer!"

Ruth sat very quiet. Her eyes were fixed on the ground, and she seemed lost in thought. At length she rose up.

"Mr Benson!" said she, standing before him, and propping herself by the table, as she was trembling sadly from weakness, "I mean to try very, very hard, to do my duty to Leonard—and to God," she added, reverently. "I am only afraid my faith may sometimes fail about Leonard—"

"Ask, and it shall be given unto you. That is no vain or untried promise, Ruth!"

She sat down again, unable longer to stand. There was another long silence.

"I must never go to Mr Bradshaw's again," she said at last, as if thinking aloud.

"No, Ruth, you shall not," he answered.

"But I shall earn no money!" added she, quickly, for she thought that he did not perceive the difficulty that was troubling her.

"You surely know, Ruth, that while Faith and I have a roof to shelter us, or bread to eat, you and Leonard share it with us."

"I know—I know your most tender goodness," said she, "but it ought not to be."

"It must be at present," he said, in a decided manner. "Perhaps before long you may have some employment; perhaps it may be some time before an opportunity occurs."

"Hush," said Ruth; "Leonard is moving about in the parlour. I must go to him."

But when she stood up, she turned so dizzy, and tottered so much, that she was glad to sit down again immediately.

"You must rest here. I will go to him," said Mr Benson. He left her; and when he was gone, she leaned her head on the back of the chair, and cried quietly and incessantly; but there was a more patient, hopeful, resolved feeling in her heart, which all along, through all the tears she shed, bore her onwards to higher thoughts, until at last she rose to prayers.

Mr Benson caught the new look of shrinking shame in Leonard's eye, as it first sought, then shunned, meeting his. He was pained, too, by the sight of the little sorrowful, anxious face, on which, until now, hope and joy had been predominant. The constrained voice, the few words the boy spoke, when formerly there would have been a glad and free utterance—all this grieved Mr Benson inexpressibly, as but the beginning of an unwonted mortification, which must last for years. He himself made no allusion to any unusual occurrence; he spoke of Ruth as sitting, overcome by headache, in the study for quietness: he hurried on the preparations for tea, while Leonard sat by in the great arm-chair, and looked on with sad, dreamy eyes. He strove to lessen the shock which he knew Leonard had received, by every mixture of tenderness and cheerfulness that Mr Benson's gentle heart prompted; and now and then a languid smile stole over the boy's face. When his bedtime came, Mr Benson told him of the hour, although he feared that Leonard would have but another sorrowful crying of himself to sleep; but he was anxious to accustom the boy to cheerful movement within the limits of domestic law, and by no disobedience to it to weaken the power of glad submission to the Supreme; to begin the new life that lay before him, where strength to look up to God as the Law-giver and Ruler of events would be pre-eminently required. When Leonard had gone upstairs, Mr Benson went immediately to Ruth, and said,

"Ruth! Leonard is just gone up to bed," secure in the instinct which made her silently rise, and go up to the boy—certain, too, that they would each be the other's best comforter, and that God would strengthen each through the other.

Now, for the first time, he had leisure to think of himself; and to go over all the events of the day. The half-hour of solitude in his study, that he had before his sister's return, was of inestimable value; he had leisure to put events in their true places, as to importance and eternal significance.

Miss Faith came in laden with farm produce. Her kind entertainers had brought her in their shandry to the opening of the court in which the Chapel-house stood; but she was so heavily burdened with eggs, mushrooms, and plums, that when her brother opened the door she was almost breathless.

"Oh, Thurstan! take this basket—it is such a weight! Oh, Sally, is that you? Here are some magnum-bonums which we must preserve to-morrow. There are guinea-fowl eggs in that basket."

Mr Benson let her unburden her body, and her mind too, by giving charges to Sally respecting her housekeeping treasures, before he said a word; but when she returned into the study, to tell him the small pieces of intelligence respecting her day at the farm, she stood aghast.

"Why, Thurstan, dear! What's the matter? Is your back hurting you?"

He smiled to reassure her; but it was a sickly and forced smile.

"No, Faith! I am quite well, only rather out of spirits, and wanting to talk to you to cheer me."

Miss Faith sat down, straight, sitting bolt-upright to listen the better.

"I don't know how, but the real story about Ruth is found out."

"Oh, Thurstan!" exclaimed Miss Benson, turning quite white.

For a moment, neither of them said another word. Then she went on.

"Does Mr Bradshaw know?"

"Yes! He sent for me, and told me."

"Does Ruth know that it has all come out?"

"Yes. And Leonard knows."

"How? Who told him?"

"I do not know. I have asked no questions. But of course it was his mother."

"She was very foolish and cruel, then," said Miss Benson, her eyes blazing, and her lips trembling, at the thought of the suffering her darling boy must have gone through.

"I think she was wise. I am sure it was not cruel. He must have soon known that there was some mystery, and it was better that it should be told him openly and quietly by his mother than by a stranger."

"How could she tell him quietly?" asked Miss Benson, still indignant.

"Well! perhaps I used the wrong word—of course no one was by—and I don't suppose even they themselves could now tell how it was told, or in what spirit it was borne."

Miss Benson was silent again.

"Was Mr Bradshaw very angry?"

"Yes, very; and justly so. I did very wrong in making that false statement at first."

"No! I am sure you did not," said Miss Faith. "Ruth has had some years of peace, in which to grow stronger and wiser, so that she can bear her shame now in a way she never could have done at first."

"All the same it was wrong in me to do what I did."

"I did it too, as much or more than you. And I don't think it wrong. I'm certain it was quite right, and I would do just the same again."

"Perhaps it has not done you the harm it has done me."

"Nonsense! Thurstan. Don't be morbid. I'm sure you are as good—and better than ever you were."

"No, I am not. I have got what you call morbid just in consequence of the sophistry by which I persuaded myself that wrong could be right. I torment myself. I have lost my clear instincts of conscience. Formerly, if I believed that such or such an action was according to the will of God, I went and did it, or at least I tried to do it, without thinking of consequences. Now, I reason and weigh what will happen if I do so and so—I grope where formerly I saw. Oh, Faith! it is such a relief to me to have the truth known, that I am afraid I have not been sufficiently sympathising with Ruth."

"Poor Ruth!" said Miss Benson. "But at any rate our telling a lie has been the saving of her. There is no fear of her going wrong now."

"God's omnipotence did not need our sin."

They did not speak for some time.

"You have not told me what Mr Bradshaw said."

"One can't remember the exact words that are spoken on either side in moments of such strong excitement. He was very angry, and said some things about me that were very just, and some about Ruth that were very hard. His last words were that he should give up coming to chapel."

"Oh, Thurstan! did it come to that?"

"Yes."

"Does Ruth know all he said?"

"No! Why should she? I don't know if she knows he has spoken to me at all. Poor creature! she had enough to craze her almost without that! She was for going away and leaving us, that we might not share in her disgrace. I was afraid of her being quite delirious. I did so want you, Faith! However, I did the best I could; I spoke to her very coldly, and almost sternly, all the while my heart was bleeding for her. I dared not give her sympathy; I tried to give her strength. But I did so want you, Faith."

"And I was so full of enjoyment, I am ashamed to think of it. But the Dawsons are so kind—and the day was so fine— Where is Ruth now?"

"With Leonard. He is her great earthly motive—I thought that being with him would be best. But he must be in bed and asleep now."

"I will go up to her," said Miss Faith.

She found Ruth keeping watch by Leonard's troubled sleep; but when she saw Miss Faith she rose up, and threw herself on her neck and clung to her, without speaking. After a while Miss Benson said:

"You must go to bed, Ruth!" So, after she had kissed the sleeping boy, Miss Benson led her away, and helped to undress her, and brought her up a cup of soothing violet tea—not so soothing as tender actions and soft loving tones.

CHAPTER XXVIII

An Understanding Between Lovers

It was well they had so early and so truly strengthened the spirit to bear, for the events which had to be endured soon came thick and threefold.

Every evening Mr and Miss Benson thought the worst must be over; and every day brought some fresh occurrence to touch upon the raw place. They could not be certain, until they had seen all their acquaintances, what difference it would make in the cordiality of their reception: in some cases it made much; and Miss Benson was proportionably indignant. She felt this change in behaviour more than her brother. His great pain arose from the coolness of the Bradshaws. With all the faults which had at times grated on his sensitive nature (but which he now forgot, and remembered only their kindness), they were his old familiar friends—his kind, if ostentatious, patrons—his great personal interest, out of his own family; and he could not get over the suffering he experienced from seeing their large square pew empty on Sundays—from perceiving how Mr Bradshaw, though he bowed in a distant manner when he and Mr Benson met face to face, shunned him as often as he possibly could. All that happened in the household, which once was as patent to him as his own, was now a sealed book; he heard of its doings by chance, if he heard at all. Just at the time when he was feeling the most depressed from this cause, he met Jemima at a sudden turn of the street. He was uncertain for a moment how to accost her, but she saved him all doubt; in an instant she had his hand in both of hers, her face flushed with honest delight.

"Oh, Mr Benson, I am so glad to see you! I have so wanted to know all about you! How is poor Ruth? dear Ruth! I wonder if she has forgiven me my cruelty to her? And I may not go to her now, when I should be so glad and thankful to make up for it."

"I never heard you had been cruel to her. I am sure she does not think so."

"She ought; she must. What is she doing? Oh! I have so much to ask, I can never hear enough; and papa says"—she hesitated a moment, afraid of giving pain, and then, believing that they would understand the state of affairs, and the reason for her behaviour better if she told the truth, she went on: "Papa says I must not go to your house—I suppose it's right to obey him?"

"Certainly, my dear. It is your clear duty. We know how you feel towards us."

"Oh! but if I could do any good—if I could be of any use or comfort to any of you—especially to Ruth, I should come, duty or not. I believe it would be my duty," said she, hurrying on to try and stop any decided prohibition from Mr Benson. "No! don't be afraid; I won't come till I know I can do some good. I hear bits about you through Sally every now and then, or I could not have waited so long. Mr Benson," continued she, reddening very much, "I think you did quite right about poor Ruth."

"Not in the falsehood, my dear."

"No! not perhaps in that. I was not thinking of that. But I have been thinking a great deal about poor Ruth's—you know I could not help it when everybody was talking about it—and it made me think of myself, and what I am. With a father and mother, and home and careful friends, I am not likely to be tempted like Ruth; but oh! Mr Benson," said she, lifting her eyes, which were full of tears, to his face, for the first time since she began to speak, "if you knew all I have been thinking and feeling this last year, you would see how I have yielded to every temptation that was able to come to me; and, seeing how I have no goodness or strength in me, and how I might just have been like Ruth, or rather, worse than she ever was, because I am more headstrong and passionate by nature, I do so thank you and love you for what you did for her! And will you tell me really and truly now if I can ever do anything for Ruth? If you'll promise me that, I won't rebel unnecessarily against papa; but if you don't, I will, and come and see you all this very afternoon. Remember! I trust you!" said she, breaking away. Then turning back, she came to ask after Leonard.

"He must know something of it," said she. "Does he feel it much?"

"Very much," said Mr Benson. Jemima shook her head sadly.

"It is hard upon him," said she.

"It is," Mr Benson replied.

For in truth, Leonard was their greatest anxiety indoors. His health seemed shaken, he spoke half sentences in his sleep, which showed that in his dreams he was battling on his mother's behalf against an unkind and angry world. And then he would wail to himself, and utter sad words of shame, which they never thought had reached his ears. By day, he was in general grave and quiet; but his appetite varied, and he was evidently afraid of going into the streets, dreading to be pointed at as an object of remark. Each separately in their hearts longed to give him change of scene, but they were all silent, for where was the requisite money to come from?

His temper became fitful and variable. At times he would be most sullen against his mother; and then give way to a passionate remorse. When Mr Benson caught Ruth's look of agony at her child's rebuffs, his patience failed; or rather, I should say, he believed that a stronger, severer hand than hers was required for the management of the lad. But, when she heard Mr Benson say so, she pleaded with him.

"Have patience with Leonard," she said. "I have deserved the anger that is fretting in his heart. It is only I who can reinstate myself in his love and respect. I have no fear. When he sees me really striving hard and long to do what is right, he must love me. I am not afraid."

Even while she spoke, her lips quivered, and her colour went and came with eager anxiety. So Mr Benson held his peace, and let her take her course. It was beautiful to see the intuition by which she divined what was passing in every fold of her child's heart, so as to be always ready with the right words to soothe or to strengthen him. Her watchfulness was unwearied, and with no thought of self-tainting in it, or else she might have often paused to turn aside and weep at the clouds of shame which came over Leonard's love for her, and hid it from all but her faithful heart; she believed and knew that he was yet her own affectionate boy, although he might be gloomily silent, or apparently hard and cold. And in all this, Mr Benson could not choose but admire the way in which she was insensibly teaching Leonard to conform to the law of right, to recognise Duty in the mode in which every action was performed. When Mr Benson saw this, he knew that all goodness would follow, and that the claims which his mother's infinite love had on the boy's heart would be acknowledged at last, and all the more fully because she herself never urged them, but silently admitted the force of the reason that caused them to be for a time forgotten. By-and-by Leonard's remorse at his ungracious and sullen ways to his mother— ways that alternated with passionate, fitful bursts of clinging love—assumed more the character of repentance; he tried to do so no more. But still his health was delicate; he was averse to going out-of-doors; he was much graver and sadder than became his age. It was what must be, an inevitable consequence of what had been; and Ruth had to be patient, and pray in secret, and with many tears, for the strength she needed.

She knew what it was to dread the going out into the streets after her story had become known. For days and days she had silently shrunk from this effort. But one evening towards dusk, Miss Benson was busy, and asked her to go an errand for her; and Ruth got up and silently obeyed her. That silence as to inward suffering was only one part of her peculiar and exquisite sweetness of nature; part of the patience with which she "accepted her penance." Her true instincts told her that it was not right to disturb others with many expressions of her remorse; that the holiest repentance consisted in a quiet and daily sacrifice. Still there were times when she wearied pitifully of her inaction. She was so willing to serve and work, and every one despised her services. Her mind, as I have said before, had been well cultivated during these last few years; so now she used all the knowledge she had gained in teaching Leonard, which was an employment that Mr Benson relinquished willingly, because he felt that it would give her some of the occupation that she needed. She endeavoured to make herself useful in the house in every way she could; but the waters of housekeeping had closed over her place during the time of her absence at Mr Bradshaw's—and, besides, now that they were trying to restrict every unnecessary expense, it was sometimes difficult to find work for three women. Many and many a time Ruth turned over in her mind every possible chance of obtaining employment for her leisure hours, and nowhere could she find it. Now and then Sally, who was her confidante in this wish, procured her some needlework, but it was of a coarse and common kind, soon done, lightly paid for. But whatever it was, Ruth took it, and was thankful, although it added but a few pence to the household purse. I do not mean that there was any great need of money; but a new adjustment of expenditure was required—a reduction of wants which had never been very extravagant.

Ruth's salary of forty pounds was gone, while more of her "keep," as Sally called it, was thrown upon the Bensons. Mr Benson received about eighty pounds a year for his salary as minister. Of this, he knew that twenty pounds came from Mr Bradshaw; and when the old man appointed to collect the pew-rents brought him the quarterly amount, and he found no diminution in them, he inquired how it was, and learnt that, although Mr Bradshaw had expressed to the collector his determination never to come to chapel again, he had added, that of course his pew-rent should be paid all the same. But this Mr Benson could not suffer; and the old man was commissioned to return the money to Mr Bradshaw, as being what his deserted minister could not receive.

Mr and Miss Benson had about thirty or forty pounds coming in annually from a sum which, in happier days, Mr Bradshaw had invested in Canal shares for them. Altogether their income did not fall much short of a hundred a year, and they lived in the Chapel-house free of rent. So Ruth's small earnings were but very little in actual hard commercial account, though in another sense they were much; and Miss Benson always received them with quiet simplicity. By degrees, Mr Benson absorbed some of Ruth's time in a gracious and natural way. He employed her mind in all the kind offices he was accustomed to render to the poor around him. And as much of the peace and ornament of life as they gained now, was gained on a firm basis of truth. If Ruth began low down to find her place in the world, at any rate there was no flaw in the foundation.

Leonard was still their great anxiety. At times the question seemed to be, could he live through all this trial of the elasticity of childhood? And then they knew how precious a blessing—how true a pillar of fire, he was to his mother; and how black the night, and how dreary the wilderness would be, when he was not. The child and the mother were each messengers of God—angels to each other.

They had long gaps between the pieces of intelligence respecting the Bradshaws. Mr Bradshaw had at length purchased the house at Abermouth, and they were much there. The way in which the Bensons heard most frequently of the family of their former friends, was through Mr Farquhar. He called on Mr Benson about a month after the latter had met Jemima in the street. Mr Farquhar was not in the habit of paying calls on any one; and though he had always entertained and evinced the most kind and friendly feeling towards Mr Benson, he had rarely been in the Chapel-house. Mr Benson received him courteously, but he rather expected that there would be some especial reason alleged, before the conclusion of the visit, for its occurrence; more particularly as Mr Farquhar sat talking on the topics of the day in a somewhat absent manner, as if they were not the subjects most present to his mind. The truth was, he could not help recurring to the last time when he was in that room, waiting to take Leonard a ride, and his heart beating rather more quickly than usual at the idea that Ruth might bring the boy in when he was equipped. He was very full now of the remembrance of Ruth; and yet he was also most thankful, most self-gratulatory, that he had gone no further in his admiration of her—that he had never expressed his regard in words—that no one, as he believed, was cognisant of the incipient love which had grown partly out of his admiration, and partly out of his reason. He was thankful to be spared any implication in the nine-days' wonder which her story had made in Eccleston. And yet his feeling for her had been of so strong a character, that he winced, as with extreme pain, at every application of censure to her name. These censures were often exaggerated, it is true; but when they were just in their judgment of the outward circumstances of the case, they were not the less painful and distressing to him. His first rebound to Jemima was occasioned by Mrs Bradshaw's account of how severely her husband was displeased at her daughter's having taken part with Ruth; and he could have thanked and almost blessed Jemima when she dropped in (she dared do no more) her pleading excuses and charitable explanations on Ruth's behalf. Jemima had learnt some humility from the discovery which had been to her so great a shock; standing, she had learnt to take heed lest she fell; and when she had once been aroused to a perception of the violence of the hatred which she had indulged against Ruth, she was more reticent and measured in the expression of all her opinions. It showed how much her character had been purified from pride, that now she felt aware that what in her was again attracting Mr Farquhar was her faithful advocacy of her rival, wherever such advocacy was wise or practicable. He was quite unaware that Jemima had been conscious of his great admiration for Ruth; he did not know that she had ever cared enough for him to be jealous. But the unacknowledged bond between them now was their grief, and sympathy, and pity for Ruth; only in Jemima these feelings were ardent, and would fain have become active; while in Mr Farquhar they were strongly mingled with thankfulness that he had escaped a disagreeable position, and a painful notoriety. His natural caution induced him to make a resolution never to think of any woman as a wife until he had ascertained all her antecedents, from her birth upwards; and the same spirit of caution, directed inwardly, made him afraid of giving too much pity to Ruth, for fear of the conclusions to which such a feeling might lead him. But still his old regard for her, for Leonard, and his esteem and respect for the Bensons, induced him to lend a willing ear to Jemima's earnest entreaty that he would go and call on Mr Benson, in order that she might learn something about the family in general, and Ruth in particular. It was thus that he came to sit by Mr Benson's study fire, and to talk, in an absent way, to that gentleman. How they got on the subject he did not know, more than one-half of his attention being distracted; but they were speaking about politics, when Mr Farquhar learned that Mr Benson took in no newspaper.

"Will you allow me to send you over my *Times*? I have generally done with it before twelve o'clock, and after that it is really waste-paper in my house. You will oblige me by making use of it."

"I am sure I am very much obliged to you for thinking of it. But do not trouble yourself to send it; Leonard can fetch it."

"How is Leonard now?" asked Mr Farquhar, and he tried to speak indifferently; but a grave look of intelligence clouded his eyes as he looked for Mr Benson's answer. "I have not met him lately."

"No!" said Mr Benson, with an expression of pain in his countenance, though he, too, strove to speak in his usual tone.

"Leonard is not strong, and we find it difficult to induce him to go much out-of-doors."

There was a little silence for a minute or two, during which Mr Farquhar had to check an unbidden sigh. But, suddenly rousing himself into a determination to change the subject, he said:

"You will find rather a lengthened account of the exposure of Sir Thomas Campbell's conduct at Baden. He seems to be a complete blackleg, in spite of his baronetcy. I fancy the papers are glad to get hold of anything just now."

"Who is Sir Thomas Campbell?" asked Mr Benson.

"Oh, I thought you might have heard the report—a true one, I believe—of Mr Donne's engagement to his daughter. He must be glad she jilted him now, I fancy, after this public exposure of her father's conduct." (That was an awkward speech, as Mr Farquhar felt; and he hastened to cover it, by going on without much connexion:)

"Dick Bradshaw is my informant about all these projected marriages in high life—they are not much in my way; but since he has come down from London to take his share in the business, I think I have heard more of the news and the scandal of what, I suppose, would be considered high life, than ever I did before; and Mr Donne's proceedings seem to be an especial object of interest to him."

"And Mr Donne is engaged to a Miss Campbell, is he?"

"Was engaged; if I understood right, she broke off the engagement to marry some Russian prince or other—a better match, Dick Bradshaw told me. I assure you," continued Mr Farquhar, smiling, "I am a very passive recipient of all such intelligence, and might very probably have forgotten all about it, if the *Times* of this morning had not been so full of the disgrace of the young lady's father."

"Richard Bradshaw has quite left London, has he?" asked Mr Benson, who felt far more interest in his old patron's family than in all the Campbells that ever were or ever would be.

"Yes. He has come to settle down here. I hope he may do well, and not disappoint his father, who has formed very high expectations from him; I am not sure if they are not too high for any young man to realise." Mr Farquhar could have said more, but Dick Bradshaw was Jemima's brother, and an object of anxiety to her.

"I am sure, I trust such a mortification—such a grief as any disappointment in Richard, may not befall his father," replied Mr Benson.

"Jemima—Miss Bradshaw," said Mr Farquhar, hesitating, "was most anxious to hear of you all. I hope I may tell her you are all well" (with an emphasis on *all*);"that—"

"Thank you. Thank her for us. We are all well; all except Leonard, who is not strong, as I said before. But we must be patient. Time, and such devoted, tender love as he has from his mother, must do much."

Mr Farquhar was silent.

"Send him to my house for the papers. It will be a little necessity for him to have some regular exercise, and to face the world. He must do it, sooner or later."

The two gentlemen shook hands with each other on parting; but no further allusion was made to either Ruth or Leonard.

So Leonard went for the papers. Stealing along by back streets—running with his head bent down—his little heart panting with dread of being pointed out as his mother's child—so he used to come back, and run trembling to Sally, who would hush him up to her breast with many a rough-spoken word of pity and sympathy.

Mr Farquhar tried to catch him to speak to him, and tame him as it were; and, by-and-by, he contrived to interest him sufficiently to induce the boy to stay a little while in the house, or stables, or garden. But the race through the streets was always to be dreaded as the end of ever so pleasant a visit.

Mr Farquhar kept up the intercourse with the Bensons which he had thus begun. He persevered in paying calls—quiet visits, where not much was said, political or local news talked about, and the same inquiries always made and answered as to the welfare of the two families, who were estranged from each other. Mr Farquhar's reports were so little varied that Jemima grew anxious to know more particulars.

"Oh, Mr Farquhar!" said she; "do you think they tell you the truth? I wonder what Ruth can be doing to support herself and Leonard? Nothing that you can hear of, you say; and, of course, one must not ask the downright question. And yet I am sure they must be pinched in some way. Do you think Leonard is stronger?"

"I am not sure. He is growing fast; and such a blow as he has had will be certain to make him more thoughtful and full of care than most boys of his age; both these circumstances may make him thin and pale, which he certainly is."

"Oh! how I wish I might go and see them all! I could tell in a twinkling the real state of things." She spoke with a tinge of her old impatience.

"I will go again, and pay particular attention to anything you wish me to observe. You see, of course, I feel a delicacy about asking any direct questions, or even alluding in any way to these late occurrences."

"And you never see Ruth by any chance?"

"Never!"

They did not look at each other while this last question was asked and answered.

"I will take the paper to-morrow myself; it will be an excuse for calling again, and I will try to be very penetrating; but I have not much hope of success."

"Oh, thank you. It is giving you a great deal of trouble; but you are very kind."

"Kind, Jemima!" he repeated, in a tone which made her go very red and hot; "must I tell you how you can reward me?—Will you call me Walter?—say, thank you, Walter—just for once."

Jemima felt herself yielding to the voice and tone in which this was spoken; but her very consciousness of the depth of her love made her afraid of giving way, and anxious to be wooed, that she might be reinstated in her self-esteem.

"No!" said she, "I don't think I can call you so. You are too old. It would not be respectful." She meant it half in joke, and had no idea he would take the allusion to his age so seriously as he did. He rose up, and coldly, as a matter of form, in a changed voice, wished her "Good-bye." Her heart sank; yet the old pride was there. But as he was at the very door, some sudden impulse made her speak:

"I have not vexed you, have I, Walter?"

He turned round, glowing with a thrill of delight. She was as red as any rose; her looks dropped down to the ground.

They were not raised when, half an hour afterwards, she said, "You won't forbid my going to see Ruth, will you? because if you do, I give you notice I shall disobey you." The arm around her waist clasped her yet more fondly at the idea, suggested by this speech, of the control which he should have a right to exercise over her actions at some future day.

"Tell me," said he, "how much of your goodness to me, this last happy hour, has been owing to the desire of having more freedom as a wife than as a daughter?"

She was almost glad that he should think she needed any additional motive to her love for him before she could have accepted him. She was afraid that she had betrayed the deep, passionate regard with which she had long looked upon him. She was lost in delight at her own happiness. She was silent for a time. At length she said:

"I don't think you know how faithful I have been to you ever since the days when you first brought me pistachio-candy from London—when I was quite a little girl."

"Not more faithful than I have been to you," for in truth, the recollection of his love for Ruth had utterly faded away, and he thought himself a model of constancy; "and you have tried me pretty well. What a vixen you have been!"

Jemima sighed; smitten with the consciousness of how little she had deserved her present happiness; humble with the recollection of the evil thoughts that had raged in her heart during the time (which she remembered well, though he might have forgotten it) when Ruth had had the affection which her jealous rival coveted.

"I may speak to your father, may not I, Jemima?"

No! for some reason or fancy which she could not define, and could not be persuaded out of, she wished to keep their mutual understanding a secret. She had a natural desire to avoid the congratulations she expected from her family. She dreaded her father's consideration of the whole affair as a satisfactory disposal of his daughter to a worthy man, who, being his partner, would not require any abstraction of capital from the concern, and Richard's more noisy delight at his sister's having "hooked" so good a match. It was only her simple-hearted mother that she longed to tell. She knew that her mother's congratulations would not jar upon her, though they might not sound the full organ-peal of her love. But all that her mother knew passed onwards to her father; so for the present, at any rate, she determined to realise her secret position alone. Somehow, the sympathy of all others that she most longed for was Ruth's; but the first communication of such an event was due to her parents. She imposed very strict regulations on Mr Farquhar's behaviour; and quarrelled and differed from him more than ever, but with a secret joyful understanding with him in her heart, even while they disagreed with each other—for similarity of opinion is not always—I think not often—needed for fulness and perfection of love.

After Ruth's "detection," as Mr Bradshaw used to call it, he said he could never trust another governess again; so Mary and Elizabeth had been sent to school the following Christmas, and their place in the family was but poorly supplied by the return of Mr Richard Bradshaw, who had left London, and been received as a partner.

CHAPTER XXIX

Sally Takes Her Money Out of the Bank

The conversation narrated in the last chapter as taking place between Mr Farquhar and Jemima, occurred about a year after Ruth's dismissal from her situation. That year, full of small events, and change of place to the Bradshaws, had been monotonous and long in its course to the other household. There had been no want of peace and tranquillity; there had, perhaps, been more of them than in the preceding years, when, though unacknowledged by any, all must have occasionally felt the oppression of the falsehood—and a slight glancing dread must have flashed across their most prosperous state, lest, somehow or another, the mystery should be disclosed. But now, as the shepherd-boy in John Bunyan sweetly sang, "He that is low need fear no fall."

Still, their peace was as the stillness of a grey autumnal day, when no sun is to be seen above, and when a quiet film seems drawn before both sky and earth, as if to rest the wearied eyes after the summer's glare. Few events broke the monotony of their lives, and those events were of a depressing kind. They consisted in Ruth's futile endeavours to obtain some employment, however humble; in Leonard's fluctuations of spirits and health; in Sally's increasing deafness; in the final and unmendable wearing-out of the parlour carpet, which there was no spare money to replace, and so they cheerfully supplied its want by a large hearth-rug that Ruth made out of ends of list; and, what was more a subject of unceasing regret to Mr Benson than all, the defection of some of the members of his congregation, who followed Mr Bradshaw's lead. Their places, to be sure, were more than filled up by the poor, who thronged to his chapel; but still it was a disappointment to find that people about whom he had been earnestly thinking—to whom he had laboured to do good— should dissolve the connexion without a word of farewell or explanation. Mr Benson did not wonder that they should go; nay, he even felt it right that they should seek that spiritual help from another, which he, by his error, had forfeited his power to offer; he only wished they had spoken of their intention to him in an open and manly way. But not the less did he labour on among those to whom God permitted him to be of use. He felt age stealing upon him apace, although he said nothing about it, and no one seemed to be aware of it; and he worked the more diligently while "it was yet day." It was not the number of his years that made him feel old, for he was only sixty, and many men are hale and strong at that time of life; in all probability, it was that early injury to his spine which affected the constitution of his mind as well as his body, and predisposed him, in the opinion of some at least, to a feminine morbidness of conscience. He had shaken off somewhat of this since the affair with Mr Bradshaw; he was simpler and more dignified than he had been for several years before, during which time he had been anxious and uncertain in his manner, and more given to thought than to action.

The one happy bright spot in this grey year was owing to Sally. As she said of herself, she believed she grew more "nattered" as she grew older; but that she was conscious of her "natteredness" was a new thing, and a great gain to the comfort of the house, for it made her very grateful for forbearance, and more aware of kindness than she had ever been before. She had become very deaf; yet she was uneasy and jealous if she were not informed of all the family thoughts, plans, and proceedings, which often had (however private in their details) to be shouted to her at the full pitch of the voice. But she always heard Leonard perfectly. His clear and bell-like voice, which was similar to his mother's, till sorrow had taken the ring out of it, was sure to be heard by the old servant, though every one else had failed. Sometimes, however, she "got her hearing sudden," as she phrased it, and was alive to every word and noise, more particularly when they did not want her to hear; and at such times she resented their continuance of the habit of speaking loud as a mortal offence. One day, her indignation at being thought deaf called out one of the rare smiles on Leonard's face; she saw it, and said, "Bless thee, lad! if it but amuses thee, they may shout through a ram's horn to me, and I'll never let on I'm not deaf. It's as good a use as I can be of," she continued to herself, "if I can make that poor lad smile a bit."

If she expected to be everybody's confidante, she made Leonard hers. "There!" said she, when she came home from her marketing one Saturday night, "look here, lad! Here's forty-two pound, seven shillings, and twopence! It's a mint of money, isn't it? I took it all in sovereigns for fear of fire."

"What is it all for, Sally?" said he.

"Aye, lad! that's asking. It's Mr Benson's money," said she, mysteriously, "that I've been keeping for him. Is he in the study, think ye?"

"Yes! I think so. Where have you been keeping it?"

"Never you mind!" She went towards the study, but thinking she might have been hard on her darling in refusing to gratify his curiosity, she turned back, and said:

"I say—if thou wilt, thou mayst do me a job of work some day. I'm wanting a frame made for a piece of writing."

And then she returned to go into the study, carrying her sovereigns in her apron.

"Here, Master Thurstan," said she, pouring them out on the table before her astonished master. "Take it, it's all yours."

"All mine! What can you mean?" asked he, bewildered.

She did not hear him, and went on:

"Lock it up safe, out o' the way. Dunnot go and leave it about to tempt folks. I'll not answer for myself if money's left about. I may be cribbing a sovereign."

"But where does it come from?" said he.

"Come from!" she replied. "Where does all money come from, but the bank, to be sure? I thought any one could tell that."

"I have no money in the bank!" said he, more and more perplexed.

"No! I knowed that; but I had. Dunnot ye remember how you would raise my wage, last Martinmas eighteen year? You and Faith were very headstrong, but I was too deep for you. See thee! I went and put it i' th' bank. I was never going to touch it; and if I had died it would have been all right, for I'd a will made, all regular and tight—made by a lawyer (leastways he would have been a lawyer, if he hadn't got transported first). And now, thinks I, I think I'll just go and get it out and give it 'em. Banks is not always safe."

"I'll take care of it for you with the greatest pleasure. Still, you know, banks allow interest."

"D'ye suppose I don't know all about interest, and compound interest too, by this time? I tell ye I want ye to spend it. It's your own. It's not mine. It always was yours. Now you're not going to fret me by saying you think it mine."

Mr Benson held out his hand to her, for he could not speak. She bent forward to him as he sat there, and kissed him.

"Eh, bless ye, lad! It's the first kiss I've had of ye sin' ye were a little lad, and it's a great refreshment. Now don't you and Faith go and bother me with talking about it. It's just yours, and make no more ado."

She went back into the kitchen, and brought out her will, and gave Leonard directions how to make a frame for it; for the boy was a very tolerable joiner, and had a box of tools which Mr Bradshaw had given him some years ago.

"It's a pity to lose such fine writing," said she; "though I can't say as I can read it. Perhaps you'd just read it for me, Leonard." She sat open-mouthed with admiration at all the long words.

The frame was made, and the will hung up opposite to her bed, unknown to any one but Leonard; and, by dint of his repeated reading it over to her, she learnt all the words, except "testatrix," which she would always call "testy tricks." Mr Benson had been too much gratified and touched, by her unconditional gift of all she had in the world, to reject it; but he only held it in his hands as a deposit until he could find a safe investment befitting so small a sum. The little rearrangements of the household expenditure had not touched him as they had done the women. He was aware that meat dinners were not now every-day occurrences; but he preferred puddings and vegetables, and was glad of the exchange. He observed, too, that they all sat together in the kitchen in the evenings; but the kitchen, with the well-scoured dresser, the shining saucepans, the well-blacked grate and whitened hearth, and the warmth which seemed to rise up from the very flags, and ruddily cheer the most distant corners, appeared a very cozy and charming sitting-room; and, besides, it appeared but right that Sally, in her old age, should have the companionship of those with whom she had lived in love and faithfulness for so many years. He only wished he could more frequently leave the solitary comfort of his study, and join the kitchen party, where Sally sat as mistress in the chimney-corner, knitting by fire-light, and Miss Benson and Ruth, with the candle between them, stitched away at their work; while Leonard strewed the ample dresser with his slate and books. He did not mope and pine over his lessons; they were the one thing that took him out of himself. As yet his mother could teach him, though in some respects it was becoming a strain upon her acquirements and powers. Mr Benson saw this, but reserved his offers of help as long as he could, hoping that before his assistance became absolutely necessary, some mode of employment beyond that of occasional plain-work might be laid open to Ruth.

In spite of the communication they occasionally had with Mr Farquhar, when he gave them the intelligence of his engagement to Jemima, it seemed like a glimpse into a world from which they were shut out. They wondered—Miss

Benson and Ruth did at least—much about the details. Ruth sat over her sewing, fancying how all had taken place; and as soon as she had arranged the events which were going on among people and places once so familiar to her, she found some discrepancy, and set-to afresh to picture the declaration of love, and the yielding, blushing acceptance; for Mr Farquhar had told little beyond the mere fact that there was an engagement between himself and Jemima which had existed for some time, but which had been kept secret until now, when it was acknowledged, sanctioned, and to be fulfilled as soon as he returned from an arrangement of family affairs in Scotland. This intelligence had been enough for Mr Benson, who was the only person Mr Farquhar saw; as Ruth always shrank from the post of opening the door, and Mr Benson was apt at recognising individual knocks, and always prompt to welcome Mr Farquhar.

Miss Benson occasionally thought—and what she thought she was in the habit of saying—that Jemima might have come herself to announce such an event to old friends; but Mr Benson decidedly vindicated her from any charge of neglect, by expressing his strong conviction that to her they owed Mr Farquhar's calls—his all but outspoken offers of service—his quiet, steady interest in Leonard; and, moreover (repeating the conversation he had had with her in the street, the first time they met after the disclosure), Mr Benson told his sister how glad he was to find that, with all the warmth of her impetuous disposition hurrying her on to rebellion against her father, she was now attaining to that just self-control which can distinguish between mere wishes and true reasons—that she could abstain from coming to see Ruth while she could do but little good, reserving herself for some great occasion or strong emergency.

Ruth said nothing, but she yearned all the more in silence to see Jemima. In her recollection of that fearful interview with Mr Bradshaw, which haunted her yet, sleeping or waking, she was painfully conscious that she had not thanked Jemima for her generous, loving advocacy; it had passed unregarded at the time in intensity of agony—but now she recollected that by no word, or tone, or touch, had she given any sign of gratitude. Mr Benson had never told her of his meeting with Jemima; so it seemed as if there were no hope of any future opportunity: for it is strange how two households, rent apart by some dissension, can go through life, their parallel existences running side by side, yet never touching each other, near neighbours as they are, habitual and familiar guests as they may have been.

Ruth's only point of hope was Leonard. She was weary of looking for work and employment, which everywhere seemed held above her reach. She was not impatient of this, but she was very, very sorry. She felt within her such capability, and all ignored her, and passed her by on the other side. But she saw some progress in Leonard. Not that he could continue to have the happy development, and genial ripening, which other boys have; leaping from childhood to boyhood, and thence to youth, with glad bounds, and unconsciously enjoying every age. At present there was no harmony in Leonard's character; he was as full of thought and self-consciousness as many men, planning his actions long beforehand, so as to avoid what he dreaded, and what she could not yet give him strength to face, coward as she was herself, and shrinking from hard remarks. Yet Leonard was regaining some of his lost tenderness towards his mother; when they were alone he would throw himself on her neck and smother her with kisses, without any apparent cause for such a passionate impulse. If any one was by, his manner was cold and reserved. The hopeful parts of his character were the determination evident in him to be a "law unto himself," and the serious thought which he gave to the formation of this law. There was an inclination in him to reason, especially and principally with Mr Benson, on the great questions of ethics which the majority of the world have settled long ago. But I do not think he ever so argued with his mother. Her lovely patience, and her humility, was earning its reward; and from her quiet piety, bearing sweetly the denial of her wishes—the refusal of her begging—the disgrace in which she lay, while others, less worthy, were employed—this, which perplexed him, and almost angered him at first, called out his reverence at last, and what she said he took for his law with proud humility; and thus softly, she was leading him up to God. His health was not strong; it was not likely to be. He moaned and talked in his sleep, and his appetite was still variable, part of which might be owing to his preference of the hardest lessons to any outdoor exercise. But this last unnatural symptom was vanishing before the assiduous kindness of Mr Farquhar, and the quiet but firm desire of his mother. Next to Ruth, Sally had perhaps the most influence over him; but he dearly loved both Mr and Miss Benson; although he was reserved on this, as on every point not purely intellectual. His was a hard childhood, and his mother felt that it was so. Children bear any moderate degree of poverty and privation cheerfully; but, in addition to a good deal of this, Leonard had to bear a sense of disgrace attaching to him and to the creature he loved best; this it was that took out of him the buoyancy and natural gladness of youth, in a way which no scantiness of food or clothing, or want of any outward comfort, could ever have done.

Two years had passed away—two long, eventless years. Something was now going to happen, which touched their hearts very nearly, though out of their sight and hearing. Jemima was going to be married this August, and by-and-by the very day was fixed. It was to be on the 14th. On the evening of the 13th, Ruth was sitting alone in the parlour, idly gazing out on the darkening shadows in the little garden; her eyes kept filling with quiet tears, that rose, not for her own isolation from all that was going on of bustle and preparation for the morrow's event, but because she had seen how Miss Benson had felt that she and her brother were left out from the gathering of old friends in the Bradshaw family. As Ruth sat, suddenly she was aware of a figure by her; she started up, and in the gloom of the apartment she recognised Jemima. In an instant they were in each other's arms—a long, fast embrace.

"Can you forgive me?" whispered Jemima in Ruth's ear.

"Forgive you! What do you mean? What have I to forgive? The question is, can I ever thank you as I long to do, if I could find words?"

"Oh, Ruth, how I hated you once!"

"It was all the more noble in you to stand by me as you did. You must have hated me when you knew how I was deceiving you all!"

"No, that was not it that made me hate you. It was before that. Oh, Ruth, I did hate you!"

They were silent for some time, still holding each other's hands. Ruth spoke first.

"And you are going to be married to-morrow!"

"Yes," said Jemima. "To-morrow, at nine o'clock. But I don't think I could have been married without coming to wish Mr Benson and Miss Faith good-bye."

"I will go for them," said Ruth.

"No, not just yet. I want to ask you one or two questions first. Nothing very particular; only it seems as if there had been such a strange, long separation between us. Ruth," said she, dropping her voice, "is Leonard stronger than he was? I was so sorry to hear about him from Walter. But he is better?" asked she, anxiously.

"Yes, he is better. Not what a boy of his age should be," replied his mother, in a tone of quiet but deep mournfulness. "Oh, Jemima!" continued she, "my sharpest punishment comes through him. To think what he might have been, and what he is!"

"But Walter says he is both stronger in health, and not so—nervous and shy." Jemima added the last words in a hesitating and doubtful manner, as if she did not know how to express her full meaning without hurting Ruth.

"He does not show that he feels his disgrace so much. I cannot talk about it, Jemima, my heart aches so about him. But he is better," she continued, feeling that Jemima's kind anxiety required an answer at any cost of pain to herself. "He is only studying too closely now; he takes to his lessons evidently as a relief from thought. He is very clever, and I hope and trust, yet I tremble to say it, I believe he is very good."

"You must let him come and see us very often when we come back. We shall be two months away. We are going to Germany, partly on Walter's business. Ruth, I have been talking to papa to-night, very seriously and quietly, and it has made me love him so much more, and understand him so much better."

"Does he know of your coming here? I hope he does," said Ruth.

"Yes. Not that he liked my doing it at all. But, somehow, I can always do things against a person's wishes more easily when I am on good terms with them—that's not exactly what I meant; but now to-night, after papa had been showing me that he really loved me more than I ever thought he had done (for I always fancied he was so absorbed in Dick, he did not care much for us girls), I felt brave enough to say that I intended to come here and bid you all good-bye. He was silent for a minute, and then said I might do it, but I must remember he did not approve of it, and was not to be compromised by my coming; still I can tell that, at the bottom of his heart, there is some of the old kindly feeling to Mr and Miss Benson, and I don't despair of its all being made up, though, perhaps, I ought to say that mamma does."

"Mr and Miss Benson won't hear of my going away," said Ruth, sadly.

"They are quite right."

"But I am earning nothing. I cannot get any employment. I am only a burden and an expense."

"Are you not also a pleasure? And Leonard, is he not a dear object of love? It is easy for me to talk, I know, who am so impatient. Oh, I never deserved to be so happy as I am! You don't know how good Walter is. I used to think him so cold and cautious. But now, Ruth, will you tell Mr and Miss Benson that I am here? There is signing of papers, and I don't know what to be done at home. And when I come back, I hope to see you often, if you'll let me."

Mr and Miss Benson gave her a warm greeting. Sally was called in, and would bring a candle with her, to have a close inspection of her, in order to see if she was changed—she had not seen her for so long a time, she said; and Jemima stood laughing and blushing in the middle of the room, while Sally studied her all over, and would not be convinced that the old gown which she was wearing for the last time was not one of the new wedding ones. The consequence of which misunderstanding was, that Sally, in her short petticoats and bedgown, turned up her nose at the old-fashioned way in which Miss Bradshaw's gown was made. But Jemima knew the old woman, and rather enjoyed the contempt for her dress. At last she kissed them all, and ran away to her impatient Mr Farquhar, who was awaiting her.

Not many weeks after this, the poor old woman whom I have named as having become a friend of Ruth's, during Leonard's illness three years ago, fell down and broke her hip-bone. It was a serious—probably a fatal injury, for one so old; and as soon as Ruth heard of it she devoted all her leisure time to old Ann Fleming. Leonard had now outstript his mother's powers of teaching, and Mr Benson gave him his lessons; so Ruth was a great deal at the cottage both night and day.

There Jemima found her one November evening, the second after their return from their prolonged stay on the Continent. She and Mr Farquhar had been to the Bensons, and had sat there some time; and now Jemima had come on just to see Ruth for five minutes, before the evening was too dark for her to return alone. She found Ruth sitting on a stool before the fire, which was composed of a few sticks on the hearth. The blaze they gave was, however, enough to enable her to read; and she was deep in study of the Bible, in which she had read aloud to the poor old woman, until the latter had fallen asleep. Jemima beckoned her out, and they stood on the green just before the open door, so that Ruth could see if Ann awoke.

"I have not many minutes to stay, only I felt as if I must see you. And we want Leonard to come to us to see all our German purchases, and hear all our German adventures. May he come to-morrow?"

"Yes; thank you. Oh! Jemima, I have heard something—I have got a plan that makes me so happy! I have not told any one yet. But Mr Wynne (the parish doctor, you know) has asked me if I would go out as a sick nurse—he thinks he could find me employment."

"You, a sick nurse!" said Jemima, involuntarily glancing over the beautiful lithe figure, and the lovely refinement of Ruth's face as the light of the rising moon fell upon it. "My dear Ruth, I don't think you are fitted for it!"

"Don't you?" said Ruth, a little disappointed. "I think I am; at least, that I should be very soon. I like being about sick and helpless people; I always feel so sorry for them; and then I think I have the gift of a very delicate touch, which is such a comfort in many cases. And I should try to be very watchful and patient. Mr Wynne proposed it himself."

"It was not in that way I meant you were not fitted for it. I meant that you were fitted for something better. Why, Ruth, you are better educated than I am!"

"But if nobody will allow me to teach?—for that is what I suppose you mean. Besides, I feel as if all my education would be needed to make me a good sick nurse."

"Your knowledge of Latin, for instance," said Jemima, hitting, in her vexation at the plan, on the first acquirement of Ruth she could think of.

"Well!" said Ruth, "that won't come amiss; I can read the prescriptions."

"Which the doctors would rather you did not do."

"Still, you can't say that any knowledge of any kind will be in my way, or will unfit me for my work."

"Perhaps not. But all your taste and refinement will be in your way, and will unfit you."

"You have not thought about this so much as I have, or you would not say so. Any fastidiousness I shall have to get rid of, and I shall be better without; but any true refinement I am sure I shall find of use; for don't you think that every power we have may be made to help us in any right work, whatever that is? Would you not rather be nursed by a person who spoke gently and moved quietly about than by a loud bustling woman?"

"Yes, to be sure; but a person unfit for anything else may move quietly, and speak gently, and give medicine when the doctor orders it, and keep awake at night; and those are the best qualities I ever heard of in a sick nurse."

Ruth was quite silent for some time. At last she said: "At any rate it is work, and as such I am thankful for it. You cannot discourage me—and perhaps you know too little of what my life has been—how set apart in idleness I have been—to sympathise with me fully."

"And I wanted you to come to see us—me in my new home. Walter and I had planned that we would persuade you to come to us very often" (she had planned, and Mr Farquhar had consented); "and now you will have to be fastened up in a sick-room."

"I could not have come," said Ruth quickly. "Dear Jemima! it is like you to have thought of it—but I could not come to your house. It is not a thing to reason about. It is just feeling. But I do feel as if I could not go. Dear Jemima! if you are ill or sorrowful, and want me, I will come—"

"So you would and must to any one, if you take up that calling."

"But I should come to you, love, in quite a different way; I should go to you with my heart full of love—so full that I am afraid I should be too anxious."

"I almost wish I were ill, that I might make you come at once."

"And I am almost ashamed to think how I should like you to be in some position in which I could show you how well I remember that day—that terrible day in the school-room. God bless you for it, Jemima!"

CHAPTER XXX

The Forged Deed

Mr Wynne, the parish surgeon, was right. He could and did obtain employment for Ruth as a sick nurse. Her home was with the Bensons; every spare moment was given to Leonard and to them; but she was at the call of all the invalids in the town. At first her work lay exclusively among the paupers. At first, too, there was a recoil from many circumstances, which impressed upon her the most fully the physical sufferings of those whom she tended. But she tried to lose the sense of these—or rather to lessen them, and make them take their appointed places—in thinking of the individuals themselves, as separate from their decaying frames; and all along she had enough self-command to control herself from expressing any sign of repugnance. She allowed herself no nervous haste of movement or touch that should hurt the feelings of the poorest, most friendless creature, who ever lay a victim to disease. There was no rough getting over of all the disagreeable and painful work of her employment. When it was a lessening of pain to have the touch careful and delicate, and the ministration performed with gradual skill, Ruth thought of her charge, and not of herself. As she had foretold, she found a use for all her powers. The poor patients themselves were unconsciously gratified and soothed by her harmony and refinement of manner, voice, and gesture. If this harmony and refinement had been merely superficial, it would not have had this balmy effect. That arose from its being the true expression of a kind, modest, and humble spirit. By degrees her reputation as a nurse spread upwards, and many sought her good offices who could well afford to pay for them. Whatever remuneration was offered to her, she took it simply and without comment; for she felt that it was not hers to refuse; that it was, in fact, owing to the Bensons for her and her child's subsistence. She went wherever her services were first called for. If the poor bricklayer, who broke both his legs in a fall from the scaffolding, sent for her when she was disengaged, she went and remained with him until he could spare her, let who would be the next claimant. From the happy and prosperous in all but health, she would occasionally beg off, when some one less happy and more friendless wished for her; and sometimes she would ask for a little money from Mr Benson to give to such in their time of need. But it was astonishing how much she was able to do without money.

Her ways were very quiet; she never spoke much. Any one who has been oppressed with the weight of a vital secret for years, and much more any one the character of whose life has been stamped by one event, and that producing sorrow and shame, is naturally reserved. And yet Ruth's silence was not like reserve; it was too gentle and tender for that. It had more the effect of a hush of all loud or disturbing emotions, and out of the deep calm the words that came forth had a beautiful power. She did not talk much about religion; but those who noticed her knew that it was the unseen banner which she was following. The low-breathed sentences which she spoke into the ear of the sufferer and the dying carried them upwards to God.

She gradually became known and respected among the roughest boys of the rough populace of the town. They would make way for her when she passed along the streets with more deference than they used to most; for all knew something of the tender care with which she had attended this or that sick person, and, besides, she was so often in connexion with Death that something of the superstitious awe with which the dead were regarded by those rough boys in the midst of their strong life, surrounded her.

She herself did not feel changed. She felt just as faulty—as far from being what she wanted to be, as ever. She best knew how many of her good actions were incomplete, and marred with evil. She did not feel much changed from the earliest Ruth she could remember. Everything seemed to change but herself. Mr and Miss Benson grew old, and Sally grew deaf, and Leonard was shooting up, and Jemima was a mother. She and the distant hills that she saw from her chamber window, seemed the only things which were the same as when she first came to Eccleston. As she sat looking out, and taking her fill of solitude, which sometimes was her most thorough rest—as she sat at the attic window looking abroad—she saw their next-door neighbour carried out to sun himself in his garden. When she first came to Eccleston, this neighbour and his daughter were often seen taking long and regular walks; by-and-by his walks became shorter, and the attentive daughter would convoy him home, and set out afresh to finish her own. Of late years he had only gone out in the garden behind his house; but at first he had walked pretty briskly there by his daughter's help—now he was carried, and placed in a large, cushioned easy-chair, his head remaining where it was placed against the pillow, and hardly moving when his kind daughter, who was now middle-aged, brought him the first roses of the summer. This told Ruth of the lapse of life and time.

Mr and Mrs Farquhar were constant in their attentions; but there was no sign of Mr Bradshaw ever forgiving the imposition which had been practised upon him, and Mr Benson ceased to hope for any renewal of their intercourse. Still, he thought that he must know of all the kind attentions which Jemima paid to them, and of the fond regard which both she and her husband bestowed on Leonard. This latter feeling even went so far that Mr Farquhar called one day, and with much diffidence begged Mr Benson to urge Ruth to let him be sent to school at his (Mr Farquhar's) expense.

Mr Benson was taken by surprise, and hesitated. "I do not know. It would be a great advantage in some respects; and yet I doubt whether it would in others. His mother's influence over him is thoroughly good, and I should fear that any thoughtless allusions to his peculiar position might touch the raw spot in his mind."

"But he is so unusually clever, it seems a shame not to give him all the advantages he can have. Besides, does he see much of his mother now?"

"Hardly a day passes without her coming home to be an hour or so with him, even at her busiest times; she says it is her best refreshment. And often, you know, she is disengaged for a week or two, except the occasional services which she is always rendering to those who need her. Your offer is very tempting, but there is so decidedly another view of the question to be considered, that I believe we must refer it to her."

"With all my heart. Don't hurry her to a decision. Let her weigh it well. I think she will find the advantages preponderate."

"I wonder if I might trouble you with a little business, Mr Farquhar, as you are here?"

"Certainly; I am only too glad to be of any use to you."

"Why, I see from the report of the Star Life Assurance Company in the *Times*, which you are so good as to send me, that they have declared a bonus on the shares; now it seems strange that I have received no notification of it, and I thought that perhaps it might be lying at your office, as Mr Bradshaw was the purchaser of the shares, and I have always received the dividends through your firm."

Mr Farquhar took the newspaper, and ran his eye over the report.

"I've no doubt that's the way of it," said he. "Some of our clerks have been careless about it; or it may be Richard himself. He is not always the most punctual and exact of mortals; but I'll see about it. Perhaps after all it mayn't come for a day or two; they have always such numbers of these circulars to send out."

"Oh! I'm in no hurry about it. I only want to receive it some time before I incur any expenses, which the promise of this bonus may tempt me to indulge in."

Mr Farquhar took his leave. That evening there was a long conference, for, as it happened, Ruth was at home. She was strenuously against the school plan. She could see no advantages that would counterbalance the evil which she dreaded from any school for Leonard; namely, that the good opinion and regard of the world would assume too high an importance in his eyes. The very idea seemed to produce in her so much shrinking affright, that by mutual consent the subject was dropped; to be taken up again, or not, according to circumstances.

Mr Farquhar wrote the next morning, on Mr Benson's behalf, to the Insurance Company, to inquire about the bonus. Although he wrote in the usual formal way, he did not think it necessary to tell Mr Bradshaw what he had done; for Mr Benson's name was rarely mentioned between the partners; each had been made fully aware of the views which the other entertained on the subject that had caused the estrangement; and Mr Farquhar felt that no external argument could affect Mr Bradshaw's resolved disapproval and avoidance of his former minister.

As it happened, the answer from the Insurance Company (directed to the firm) was given to Mr Bradshaw along with the other business letters. It was to the effect that Mr Benson's shares had been sold and transferred above a twelvemonth ago, which sufficiently accounted for the circumstance that no notification of the bonus had been sent to him.

Mr Bradshaw tossed the letter on one side, not displeased to have a good reason for feeling a little contempt at the unbusiness-like forgetfulness of Mr Benson, at whose instance some one had evidently been writing to the Insurance Company. On Mr Farquhar's entrance he expressed this feeling to him.

"Really," he said, "these Dissenting ministers have no more notion of exactitude in their affairs than a child! The idea of forgetting that he has sold his shares, and applying for the bonus, when it seems he has transferred them only a year ago!"

Mr Farquhar was reading the letter while Mr Bradshaw spoke.

"I don't quite understand it," said he. "Mr Benson was quite clear about it. He could not have received his half-yearly dividends unless he had been possessed of these shares; and I don't suppose Dissenting ministers, with all their ignorance of business, are unlike other men in knowing whether or not they receive the money that they believe to be owing to them."

"I should not wonder if they were—if Benson was, at any rate. Why, I never knew his watch to be right in all my life—it was always too fast or too slow; it must have been a daily discomfort to him. It ought to have been. Depend upon it, his money matters are just in the same irregular state; no accounts kept, I'll be bound."

"I don't see that that follows," said Mr Farquhar, half amused. "That watch of his is a very curious one—belonged to his father and grandfather, I don't know how far back."

"And the sentimental feelings which he is guided by prompt him to keep it, to the inconvenience of himself and every one else."

Mr Farquhar gave up the subject of the watch as hopeless.

"But about this letter. I wrote, at Mr Benson's desire, to the Insurance Office, and I am not satisfied with this answer. All the transaction has passed through our hands. I do not think it is likely Mr Benson would write and sell the shares without, at any rate, informing us at the time, even though he forgot all about it afterwards."

"Probably he told Richard, or Mr Watson."

"We can ask Mr Watson at once. I am afraid we must wait till Richard comes home, for I don't know where a letter would catch him."

Mr Bradshaw pulled the bell that rang into the head-clerk's room, saying as he did so,

"You may depend upon it, Farquhar, the blunder lies with Benson himself. He is just the man to muddle away his money in indiscriminate charity, and then to wonder what has become of it."

Mr Farquhar was discreet enough to hold his tongue.

"Mr Watson," said Mr Bradshaw, as the old clerk made his appearance, "here is some mistake about those Insurance shares we purchased for Benson ten or a dozen years ago. He spoke to Mr Farquhar about some bonus they are paying to the shareholders, it seems; and, in reply to Mr Farquhar's letter, the Insurance Company say the shares were sold twelve months since. Have you any knowledge of the transaction? Has the transfer passed through your hands? By the way" (turning to Mr Farquhar), "who kept the certificates? Did Benson or we?"

"I really don't know," said Mr Farquhar. "Perhaps Mr Watson can tell us."

Mr Watson meanwhile was studying the letter. When he had ended it, he took off his spectacles, wiped them, and replacing them, he read it again.

"It seems very strange, sir," he said at length, with his trembling, aged voice, "for I paid Mr Benson the account of the dividends myself last June, and got a receipt in form, and that is since the date of the alleged transfer."

"Pretty nearly twelve months after it took place," said Mr Farquhar.

"How did you receive the dividends? An order on the Bank, along with old Mrs Cranmer's?" asked Mr Bradshaw, sharply.

"I don't know how they came. Mr Richard gave me the money, and desired me to get the receipt."

"It's unlucky Richard is from home," said Mr Bradshaw. "He could have cleared up this mystery for us."

Mr Farquhar was silent.

"Do you know where the certificates were kept, Mr Watson?" said he.

"I'll not be sure, but I think they were with Mrs Cranmer's papers and deeds in box A, 24."

"I wish old Cranmer would have made any other man his executor. She, too, is always coming with some unreasonable request or other."

"Mr Benson's inquiry about his bonus is perfectly reasonable, at any rate."

Mr Watson, who was dwelling in the slow fashion of age on what had been said before, now spoke:

"I'll not be sure, but I am almost certain, Mr Benson said, when I paid him last June, that he thought he ought to give the receipt on a stamp, and had spoken about it to Mr Richard the time before, but that Mr Richard said it was of no consequence. Yes," continued he, gathering up his memory as he went on, "he did—I remember now—and I thought to myself that Mr Richard was but a young man. Mr Richard will know all about it."

"Yes," said Mr Farquhar, gravely.

"I shan't wait till Richard's return," said Mr Bradshaw. "We can soon see if the certificates are in the box Watson points out; if they are there, the Insurance people are no more fit to manage their concern than that cat, and I shall tell them so. If they are not there (as I suspect will prove to be the case), it is just forgetfulness on Benson's part, as I have said from the first."

"You forget the payment of the dividends," said Mr Farquhar, in a low voice.

"Well, sir! what then?" said Mr Bradshaw, abruptly. While he spoke—while his eye met Mr Farquhar's—the hinted meaning of the latter flashed through his mind; but he was only made angry to find that such a suspicion could pass through any one's imagination.

"I suppose I may go, sir," said Watson, respectfully, an uneasy consciousness of what was in Mr Farquhar's thoughts troubling the faithful old clerk.

"Yes. Go. What do you mean about the dividends?" asked Mr Bradshaw, impetuously of Mr Farquhar.

"Simply, that I think there can have been no forgetfulness—no mistake on Mr Benson's part," said Mr Farquhar, unwilling to put his dim suspicion into words.

"Then of course it is some blunder of that confounded Insurance Company. I will write to them to-day, and make them a little brisker and more correct in their statements."

"Don't you think it would be better to wait till Richard's return? He may be able to explain it."

"No, sir!" said Mr Bradshaw, sharply. "I do not think it would be better. It has not been my way of doing business to spare any one, or any company, the consequences of their own carelessness; nor to obtain information second-hand when I could have it direct from the source. I shall write to the Insurance Office by the next post."

Mr Farquhar saw that any further remonstrance on his part would only aggravate his partner's obstinacy; and, besides, it was but a suspicion—an uncomfortable suspicion. It was possible that some of the clerks at the Insurance Office might have made a mistake. Watson was not sure, after all, that the certificates had been deposited in box A, 24; and when he and Mr Farquhar could not find them there, the old man drew more and yet more back from his first assertion of belief that they had been placed there.

Mr Bradshaw wrote an angry and indignant reproach of carelessness to the Insurance Company. By the next mail one of their clerks came down to Eccleston; and having leisurely refreshed himself at the inn, and ordered his dinner with care, he walked up to the great warehouse of Bradshaw and Co., and sent in his card, with a pencil notification, "On the part of the Star Insurance Company," to Mr Bradshaw himself.

Mr Bradshaw held the card in his hand for a minute or two without raising his eyes. Then he spoke out loud and firm:

"Desire the gentleman to walk up. Stay! I will ring my bell in a minute or two, and then show him upstairs."

When the errand-boy had closed the door, Mr Bradshaw went to a cupboard where he usually kept a glass and a bottle of wine (of which he very seldom partook, for he was an abstemious man). He intended now to take a glass, but the bottle was empty; and though there was plenty more to be had for ringing, or even simply going into another room, he would not allow himself to do this. He stood and lectured himself in thought.

"After all, I am a fool for once in my life. If the certificates are in no box which I have yet examined, that does not imply they may not be in some one which I have not had time to search. Farquhar would stay so late last night! And even if they are in none of the boxes here, that does not prove—" He gave the bell a jerking ring, and it was yet sounding when Mr Smith, the insurance clerk, entered.

The manager of the Insurance Company had been considerably nettled at the tone of Mr Bradshaw's letter; and had instructed the clerk to assume some dignity at first in vindicating (as it was well in his power to do) the character of the proceedings of the Company, but at the same time he was not to go too far, for the firm of Bradshaw and Co. was daily looming larger in the commercial world, and if any reasonable explanation could be given it was to be received, and bygones be bygones.

"Sit down, sir!" said Mr Bradshaw.

"You are aware, sir, I presume, that I come on the part of Mr Dennison, the manager of the Star Insurance Company, to reply in person to a letter of yours, of the 29th, addressed to him?"

Mr Bradshaw bowed. "A very careless piece of business," he said, stiffly.

"Mr Dennison does not think you will consider it as such when you have seen the deed of transfer, which I am commissioned to show you."

Mr Bradshaw took the deed with a steady hand. He wiped his spectacles quietly, without delay, and without hurry, and adjusted them on his nose. It is possible that he was rather long in looking over the document—at least, the clerk had just begun to wonder if he was reading through the whole of it, instead of merely looking at the signature, when Mr Bradshaw said: "It is possible that it may be—of

course, you will allow me to take this paper to Mr Benson, to—to inquire if this be his signature?"

"There can be no doubt of it, I think, sir," said the clerk, calmly smiling, for he knew Mr Benson's signature well.

"I don't know, sir—I don't know." (He was speaking as if the pronunciation of every word required a separate effort of will, like a man who has received a slight paralytic stroke.)

"You have heard, sir, of such a thing as forgery—forgery, sir?" said he, repeating the last word very distinctly; for he feared that the first time he had said it, it was rather slurred over.

"Oh, sir! there is no room for imagining such a thing, I assure you. In our affairs we become aware of curious forgetfulness on the part of those who are not of business habits."

"Still I should like to show it Mr Benson, to prove to him his forgetfulness, you know. I believe, on my soul, it is some of his careless forgetfulness—I do, sir," said he. Now he spoke very quickly. "It must have been. Allow me to convince myself. You shall have it back to-night, or the first thing in the morning."

The clerk did not quite like to relinquish the deed, nor yet did he like to refuse Mr Bradshaw. If that very uncomfortable idea of forgery should have any foundation in truth—and he had given up the writing! There were a thousand chances to one against its being anything but a stupid blunder; the risk was more imminent of offending one of the directors.

As he hesitated, Mr Bradshaw spoke, very calmly, and almost with a smile on his face. He had regained his self-command. "You are afraid, I see. I assure you, you may trust me. If there has been any fraud—if I have the slightest suspicion of the truth of the surmise I threw out just now,"—he could not quite speak the bare naked word that was chilling his heart—"I will not fail to aid the ends of justice, even though the culprit should be my own son."

He ended, as he began, with a smile—such a smile!—the stiff lips refused to relax and cover the teeth. But all the time he kept saying to himself:

"I don't believe it—I don't believe it. I'm convinced it's a blunder of that old fool Benson."

But when he had dismissed the clerk, and secured the piece of paper, he went and locked the door, and laid his head on his desk, and moaned aloud.

He had lingered in the office for the two previous nights; at first, occupying himself in searching for the certificates of the Insurance shares; but, when all the boxes and other repositories for papers had been ransacked, the thought took hold of him that they might be in Richard's private desk; and, with the determination which overlooks the means to get at the end, he had first tried all his own keys on the complicated lock, and then broken it open with two decided blows of a poker, the instrument nearest at hand. He did not find the certificates. Richard had always considered himself careful in destroying any dangerous or tell-tale papers; but the stern father found enough, in what remained, to convince him that his pattern son—more even than his pattern son, his beloved pride—was far other than what he seemed.

Mr Bradshaw did not skip or miss a word. He did not shrink while he read. He folded up letter by letter; he snuffed the candle just when its light began to wane, and no sooner; but he did not miss or omit one paper—he read every word.

Then, leaving the letters in a heap upon the table, and the broken desk to tell its own tale, he locked the door of the room which was appropriated to his son as junior partner, and carried the key away with him.

There was a faint hope, even after this discovery of many circumstances of Richard's life which shocked and dismayed his father—there was still a faint hope that he might not be guilty of forgery—that it might be no forgery after all—only a blunder—an omission—a stupendous piece of forgetfulness. That hope was the one straw that Mr Bradshaw clung to.

Late that night Mr Benson sat in his study. Every one else in the house had gone to bed; but he was expecting a summons to someone who was dangerously ill. He was not startled, therefore, at the knock which came to the front door about twelve; but he was rather surprised at the character of the knock, so slow and loud, with a pause between each rap. His study-door was but a step from that which led into the street. He opened it, and there stood—Mr Bradshaw; his large, portly figure not to be mistaken even in the dusky night.

He said, "That is right. It was you I wanted to see." And he walked straight into the study. Mr Benson followed, and shut the door. Mr Bradshaw was standing by the table, fumbling in his pocket. He pulled out the deed; and opening it, after a pause, in which you might have counted five, he held it out to Mr Benson.

"Read it!" said he. He spoke not another word until time had been allowed for its perusal. Then he added:

"That is your signature?" The words were an assertion, but the tone was that of question.

"No, it is not," said Mr Benson, decidedly. "It is very like my writing. I could almost say it was mine, but I know it is not."

"Recollect yourself a little. The date is August the third of last year, fourteen months ago. You may have forgotten it." The tone of the voice had a kind of eager entreaty in it, which Mr Benson did not notice,—he was so startled at the fetch of his own writing.

"It is most singularly like mine; but I could not have signed away these shares—all the property I have—without the slightest remembrance of it."

"Stranger things have happened. For the love of Heaven, think if you did not sign it. It's a deed of transfer for those Insurance shares, you see. You don't remember it? You did not write this name—these words?" He looked at Mr Benson with craving wistfulness for one particular answer. Mr Benson was struck at last by the whole proceeding, and glanced anxiously at Mr Bradshaw, whose manner, gait, and voice were so different from usual that he might well excite attention. But as soon as the latter was aware of this momentary inspection, he changed his tone all at once.

"Don't imagine, sir, I wish to force any invention upon you as a remembrance. If you did not write this name, I know who did. Once more I ask you,—does no glimmering recollection of—having needed money, we'll say—I never wanted you to refuse my subscription to the chapel, God knows!—of having sold these accursed shares?—Oh! I see by your face you did not write it; you need not speak to me—I know."

He sank down into a chair near him. His whole figure drooped. In a moment he was up, and standing straight as an arrow, confronting Mr Benson, who could find no clue to this stern man's agitation.

"You say you did not write these words?" pointing to the signature, with an untrembling finger. "I believe you; Richard Bradshaw did write them."

"My dear sir—my dear old friend!" exclaimed Mr Benson, "you are rushing to a conclusion for which, I am convinced, there is no foundation; there is no reason to suppose thatbecause—"

"There is reason, sir. Do not distress yourself—I am perfectly calm." His stony eyes and immovable face did indeed look rigid. "What we have now to do is to punish the offence. I have not one standard for myself and those I love—(and, Mr Benson, I did love him)—and another for the rest of the world. If a stranger had forged my name, I should have known it was my duty to prosecute him. You must prosecute Richard."

"I will not," said Mr Benson.

"You think, perhaps, that I shall feel it acutely. You are mistaken. He is no longer as my son to me. I have always resolved to disown any child of mine who was guilty of sin. I disown Richard. He is as a stranger to me. I shall feel no more at his exposure—his punishment—" He could not go on, for his voice was choking. "Of course, you understand that I must feel shame at our connexion; it is that that is troubling me; that is but consistent with a man who has always prided himself on the integrity of his name; but as for that boy, who has been brought up all his life as I have brought up my children, it must be some innate wickedness! Sir, I can cut him off, though he has been as my right hand—beloved. Let me be no hindrance to the course of justice, I beg. He has forged your name—he has defrauded you of money—of your all, I think you said."

"Someone has forged my name. I am not convinced that it was your son. Until I know all the circumstances, I decline to prosecute."

"What circumstances?" asked Mr Bradshaw, in an authoritative manner, which would have shown irritation but for his self-command.

"The force of the temptation—the previous habits of theperson—"

"Of Richard. He is the person," Mr Bradshaw put in.

Mr Benson went on, without taking any notice. "I should think it right to prosecute, if I found out that this offence against me was only one of a series committed, with premeditation, against society. I should then feel, as a protector of others more helpless thanmyself—"

"It was your all," said Mr Bradshaw.

"It was all my money; it was not my all," replied Mr Benson; and then he went on as if the interruption had never been: "Against an habitual offender. I shall not prosecute Richard. Not because he is your son—do not imagine that! I should decline taking such a step against any young man without first ascertaining the particulars about him, which I know already about Richard, and which determine me against doing what would blast his character for life—would destroy every good quality he has."

"What good quality remains to him?" asked Mr Bradshaw. "He has deceived me—he has offended God."

"Have we not all offended Him?" Mr Benson said, in a low tone.

"Not consciously. I never do wrong consciously. But Richard—Richard." The remembrance of the undeceiving letters—the forgery—filled up his heart so completely that he could not speak for a minute or two. Yet when he saw Mr Benson on the point of saying something, he broke in:

"It is no use talking, sir. You and I cannot agree on these subjects. Once more, I desire you to prosecute that boy, who is no longer a child of mine."

"Mr Bradshaw, I shall not prosecute him. I have said it once for all. To-morrow you will be glad that I do not listen to you. I should only do harm by saying more at present."

There is always something aggravating in being told, that the mood in which we are now viewing things strongly will not be our mood at some other time. It implies that our present feelings are blinding us, and that some more clear-sighted spectator is able to distinguish our future better than we do ourselves. The most shallow person dislikes to be told that any one can gauge his depth. Mr Bradshaw was not soothed by this last remark of Mr Benson's. He stooped down to take up his hat and be gone. Mr Benson saw his dizzy way of groping, and gave him what he sought for; but he received no word of thanks. Mr Bradshaw went silently towards the door, but, just as he got there, he turned round, and said:

"If there were more people like me, and fewer like you, there would be less evil in the world, sir. It's your sentimentalists that nurse up sin."

Although Mr Benson had been very calm during this interview, he had been much shocked by what had been let out respecting Richard's forgery; not by the fact itself so much as by what it was a sign of. Still, he had known the young man from childhood, and had seen, and often regretted, that his want of moral courage had rendered him peculiarly liable to all the bad effects arising from his father's severe and arbitrary mode of treatment. Dick would never have had "pluck" enough to be a hardened villain, under any circumstances; but, unless some good influence, some strength, was brought to bear upon him, he might easily sink into the sneaking scoundrel. Mr Benson determined to go to Mr Farquhar's the first thing in the morning, and consult him as a calm, clear-headed family friend—partner in the business, as well as son and brother-in-law to the people concerned.

CHAPTER XXXI

An Accident to the Dover Coach

While Mr Benson lay awake for fear of oversleeping himself, and so being late at Mr Farquhar's (it was somewhere about six o'clock—dark as an October morning is at that time), Sally came to his door and knocked. She was always an early riser; and if she had not been gone to bed long before Mr Bradshaw's visit last night, Mr Benson might safely have trusted to her calling him.

"Here's a woman down below as must see you directly. She'll be upstairs after me if you're not down quick."

"Is it any one from Clarke's?"

"No, no! not it, master," said she, through the keyhole; "I reckon it's Mrs Bradshaw, for all she's muffled up."

He needed no other word. When he went down, Mrs Bradshaw sat in his easy-chair, swaying her body to and fro, and crying without restraint. Mr Benson came up to her, before she was aware that he was there.

"Oh! sir," said she, getting up and taking hold of both his hands, "you won't be so cruel, will you? I have got some money somewhere—some money my father settled on me, sir; I don't know how much, but I think it's more than two thousand pounds, and you shall have it all. If I can't give it you now, I'll make a will, sir. Only be merciful to poor Dick—don't go and prosecute him, sir."

"My dear Mrs Bradshaw, don't agitate yourself in this way. I never meant to prosecute him."

"But Mr Bradshaw says that you must."

"I shall not, indeed. I have told Mr Bradshaw so."

"Has he been here? Oh! is not he cruel? I don't care. I've been a good wife till now. I know I have. I have done all he bid me, ever since we were married. But now I will speak my mind, and say to everybody how cruel he is—how hard to his own flesh and blood! If he puts poor Dick in prison, I will go too. If I'm to choose between my husband and my son, I choose my son; for he will have no friends, unless I am with him."

"Mr Bradshaw will think better of it. You will see that, when his first anger and disappointment are over, he will not be hard or cruel."

"You don't know Mr Bradshaw," said she, mournfully, "if you think he'll change. I might beg and beg—I have done many a time, when we had little children, and I wanted to save them a whipping—but no begging ever did any good. At last I left it off. He'll not change."

"Perhaps not for human entreaty. Mrs Bradshaw, is there nothing more powerful?"

The tone of his voice suggested what he did not say.

"If you mean that God may soften his heart," replied she, humbly, "I'm not going to deny God's power—I have need to think of Him," she continued, bursting into fresh tears, "for I am a very miserable woman. Only think! he cast it up against me last night, and said, if I had not spoilt Dick this never would have happened."

"He hardly knew what he was saying last night. I will go to Mr Farquhar's directly, and see him; and you had better go home, my dear Mrs Bradshaw; you may rely upon our doing all that we can."

With some difficulty he persuaded her not to accompany him to Mr Farquhar's; but he had, indeed, to take her to her own door before he could convince her that, at present, she could do nothing but wait the result of the consultation of others.

It was before breakfast, and Mr Farquhar was alone; so Mr Benson had a quiet opportunity of telling the whole story to the husband before the wife came down. Mr Farquhar was not much surprised, though greatly distressed. The general opinion he had always entertained of Richard's character had predisposed him to fear, even before the inquiry respecting the Insurance shares. But it was still a shock when it came, however much it might have been anticipated.

"What can we do?" said Mr Benson, as Mr Farquhar sat gloomily silent.

"That is just what I was asking myself. I think I must see Mr Bradshaw, and try and bring him a little out of this unmerciful frame of mind. That must be the first thing. Will you object to accompany me at once? It seems of particular consequence that we should subdue his obduracy before the affair gets wind."

"I will go with you willingly. But I believe I rather serve to irritate Mr Bradshaw; he is reminded of things he has said to me formerly, and which he thinks he is bound to act up to. However, I can walk with you to the door, and wait for you (if you'll allow me) in the street. I want to know how he is to-day, both bodily and mentally; for indeed, Mr Farquhar, I should not have been surprised last night if he had dropped down dead, so terrible was his strain upon himself."

Mr Benson was left at the door as he had desired, while Mr Farquhar went in.

"Oh, Mr Farquhar, what is the matter?" exclaimed the girls, running to him. "Mamma sits crying in the old nursery. We believe she has been there all night. She will not tell us what it is, nor let us be with her; and papa is locked up in his room, and won't even answer us when we speak, though we know he is up and awake, for we heard him tramping about all night."

"Let me go up to him," said Mr Farquhar.

"He won't let you in. It will be of no use." But in spite of what they said, he went up; and to their surprise, after hearing who it was, their father opened the door, and admitted their brother-in-law. He remained with Mr Bradshaw about half an hour, and then came into the dining-room, where the two girls stood huddled over the fire, regardless of the untasted breakfast behind them; and, writing a few lines, he desired them to take his note up to their mother, saying it would comfort her a little, and that he should send Jemima, in two or three hours, with the baby—perhaps to remain some days with them. He had no time to tell them more; Jemima would.

He left them, and rejoined Mr Benson. "Come home and breakfast with me. I am off to London in an hour or two, and must speak with you first."

On reaching his house, he ran upstairs to ask Jemima to breakfast alone in her dressing-room, and returned in five minutes or less.

"Now I can tell you about it," said he. "I see my way clearly to a certain point. We must prevent Dick and his father meeting just now, or all hope of Dick's reformation is gone for ever. His father is as hard as the nether mill-stone. He has forbidden me his house."

"Forbidden you!"

"Yes; because I would not give up Dick as utterly lost and bad; and because I said I should return to London with the clerk, and fairly tell Dennison (he's a Scotchman, and a man of sense and feeling) the real state of the case. By the way, we must not say a word to the clerk; otherwise he will expect an answer, and make out all sorts of inferences for himself, from the unsatisfactory reply he must have. Dennison will be upon honour—will see every side of the case—will know you refuse to prosecute; the Company of which he is manager are no losers. Well! when I said what I thought wise, of all this—when I spoke as if my course were a settled and decided thing, the grim old man asked me if he was to be an automaton in his own house. He assured me he had no feeling for Dick—all the time he was shaking like an aspen; in short, repeated much the same things he must have said to you last night. However, I defied him; and the consequence is, I'm forbidden the house, and, what is more, he says he will not come to the office while I remain a partner."

"What shall you do?"

"Send Jemima and the baby. There's nothing like a young child for bringing people round to a healthy state of feeling; and you don't know what Jemima is, Mr Benson! No! though you've known her from her birth. If she can't comfort her mother, and if the baby can't steal into her grandfather's heart, why—I don't know what you may do to me. I shall tell Jemima all, and trust to her wit and wisdom to work at this end, while I do my best at the other."

"Richard is abroad, is not he?"

"He will be in England to-morrow. I must catch him somewhere; but that I can easily do. The difficult point will be, what to do with him—what to say to him, when I find him. He must give up his partnership, that's clear. I did not tell his father so, but I am resolved upon it. There shall be no tampering with the honour of the firm to which I belong."

"But what will become of him?" asked Mr Benson, anxiously.

"I do not yet know. But, for Jemima's sake—for his dear old father's sake—I will not leave him adrift. I will find him some occupation as clear from temptation as I can. I will do all in my power. And he will do much better, if he has any good in him, as a freer agent, not cowed by his father into a want of individuality and self-respect. I believe I must dismiss you, Mr Benson," said he, looking at his watch; "I have to explain all to my wife, and to go to that clerk. You shall hear from me in a day or two."

Mr Benson half envied the younger man's elasticity of mind, and power of acting promptly. He himself felt as if he wanted to sit down in his quiet study, and think over the revelations and events of the last twenty-four hours. It made him dizzy even to follow Mr Farquhar's plans, as he had briefly detailed them; and some solitude and consideration would be required before Mr Benson could decide upon their justice and wisdom. He had been much shocked by the discovery of the overt act of guilt which Richard had perpetrated, low as his opinion of that young man had been for some time; and the consequence was, that he felt depressed, and unable to rally for the next few days. He had not even the comfort of his sister's sympathy, as he felt bound in honour not to tell her anything; and she was luckily so much absorbed in some household contest with Sally that she did not notice her brother's quiet languor.

Mr Benson felt that he had no right at this time to intrude into the house which he had been once tacitly forbidden. If he went now to Mr Bradshaw's without being asked, or sent for, he thought it would seem like presuming on his knowledge of the hidden disgrace of one of the family. Yet he longed to go: he knew that Mr Farquhar must be writing almost daily to Jemima, and he wanted to hear what he was doing. The fourth day after her husband's departure she came, within half an hour of the post-delivery, and asked to speak to Mr Benson alone.

She was in a state of great agitation, and had evidently been crying very much.

"Oh, Mr Benson!" said she, "will you come with me, and tell papa this sad news about Dick? Walter has written me a letter at last to say he has found him—he could not at first; but now it seems that, the day before yesterday, he heard of an accident which had happened to the Dover coach; it was overturned—two passengers killed, and several badly hurt. Walter says we ought to be thankful, as he is, that Dick was not killed. He says it was such a relief to him on going to the place— the little inn nearest to where the coach was overturned—to find that Dick was only severely injured; not one of those who was killed. But it is a terrible shock to us all. We had had no more dreadful fear to lessen the shock; mamma is quite unfit for anything, and we none of us dare to tell papa." Jemima had hard work to keep down her sobs thus far, and now they overmastered her.

"How is your father? I have wanted to hear every day," asked Mr Benson, tenderly.

"It was careless of me not to come and tell you; but, indeed, I have had so much to do. Mamma would not go near him. He has said something which she seems as if she could not forgive. Because he came to meals, she would not. She has almost lived in the nursery; taking out all Dick's old playthings, and what clothes of his were left, and turning them over, and crying over them."

"Then Mr Bradshaw has joined you again; I was afraid, from what Mr Farquhar said, he was going to isolate himself from you all?"

"I wish he had," said Jemima, crying afresh. "It would have been more natural than the way he has gone on; the only difference from his usual habits is, that he has never gone near the office, or else he has come to meals just as usual, and talked just as usual; and even done what I never knew him do before, tried to make jokes—all in order to show us how little he cares."

"Does he not go out at all?"

"Only in the garden. I am sure he does care after all; he must care; he cannot shake off a child in this way, though he thinks he can; and that makes me so afraid of telling him of this accident. Will you come, Mr Benson?"

He needed no other word. He went with her, as she rapidly threaded her way through the by-streets. When they reached the house, she went in without knocking, and putting her husband's letter into Mr Benson's hand, she opened the door of her father's room, and saying—"Papa, here is Mr Benson," left them alone.

Mr Benson felt nervously incapable of knowing what to do, or to say. He had surprised Mr Bradshaw sitting idly over the fire—gazing dreamily into the embers. But he had started up, and drawn his chair to the table, on seeing his visitor; and, after the first necessary words of politeness were over, he seemed to expect him to open the conversation.

"Mrs Farquhar has asked me," said Mr Benson, plunging into the subject with a trembling heart, "to tell you about a letter she has received from her husband;" he stopped for an instant, for he felt that he did not get nearer the real difficulty, and yet could not tell the best way of approaching it.

"She need not have given you that trouble. I am aware of the reason of Mr Farquhar's absence. I entirely disapprove of his conduct. He is regardless of my wishes; and disobedient to the commands which, as my son-in-law, I thought he would have felt bound to respect. If there is any more agreeable subject that you can introduce, I shall be glad to hear you, sir."

"Neither you, nor I, must think of what we like to hear or to say. You must hear what concerns your son."

"I have disowned the young man who was my son," replied he, coldly.

"The Dover coach has been overturned," said Mr Benson, stimulated into abruptness by the icy sternness of the father. But, in a flash, he saw what lay below that terrible assumption of indifference. Mr Bradshaw glanced up in his face one look of agony—and then went grey-pale; so livid that Mr Benson got up to ring the bell in affright, but Mr Bradshaw motioned to him to sit still.

"Oh! I have been too sudden, sir—he is alive, he is alive!" he exclaimed, as he saw the ashy face working in a vain attempt to speak; but the poor lips (so wooden, not a minute ago) went working on and on, as if Mr Benson's words did not sink down into the mind, or reach the understanding. Mr Benson went hastily for Mrs Farquhar.

"Oh, Jemima!" said he, "I have done it so badly—I have been so cruel—he is very ill, I fear—bring water, brandy—" and he returned with all speed into the room. Mr Bradshaw—the great, strong, iron man—lay back in his chair in a swoon, a fit.

"Fetch my mother, Mary. Send for the doctor, Elizabeth," said Jemima, rushing to her father. She and Mr Benson did all in their power to restore him. Mrs Bradshaw forgot all her vows of estrangement from the dead-like husband, who might never speak to her, or hear her again, and bitterly accused herself for every angry word she had spoken against him during these last few miserable days.

Before the doctor came, Mr Bradshaw had opened his eyes and partially rallied, although he either did not, or could not speak. He looked struck down into old age. His eyes were sensible in their expression, but had the dim glaze of many years of life upon them. His lower jaw fell from his upper one, giving a look of melancholy depression to the face, although the lips hid the unclosed teeth. But he answered correctly (in monosyllables, it is true) all the questions which the doctor chose to ask. And the medical man was not so much impressed with the serious character of the seizure as the family, who knew all the hidden mystery behind, and had seen their father lie for the first time with the precursor aspect of death upon his face. Rest, watching, and a little medicine were what the doctor prescribed; it was so slight a prescription, for what had appeared to Mr Benson so serious an attack, that he wished to follow the medical man out of the room to make further inquiries, and learn the real opinion which he thought must lurk behind. But as he was following the doctor, he—they all—were aware of the effort Mr Bradshaw was making to rise, in order to arrest Mr Benson's departure. He did stand up, supporting himself with one hand on the table, for his legs shook under him. Mr

Benson came back instantly to the spot where he was. For a moment it seemed as if he had not the right command of his voice: but at last he said, with a tone of humble, wistful entreaty, which was very touching:

"He is alive, sir; is he not?"

"Yes, sir—indeed he is; he is only hurt. He is sure to do well. Mr Farquhar is with him," said Mr Benson, almost unable to speak for tears.

Mr Bradshaw did not remove his eyes from Mr Benson's face for more than a minute after his question had been answered. He seemed as though he would read his very soul, and there see if he spoke the truth. Satisfied at last, he sank slowly into his chair; and they were silent for a little space, waiting to perceive if he would wish for any further information just then. At length he put his hands slowly together in the clasped attitude of prayer, and said—"Thank God!"

CHAPTER XXXII

The Bradshaw Pew Again Occupied

If Jemima allowed herself now and then to imagine that one good would result from the discovery of Richard's delinquency, in the return of her father and Mr Benson to something of their old understanding and their old intercourse—if this hope fluttered through her mind, it was doomed to disappointment. Mr Benson would have been most happy to go, if Mr Bradshaw had sent for him; he was on the watch for what might be even the shadow of such an invitation—but none came. Mr Bradshaw, on his part, would have been thoroughly glad if the wilful seclusion of his present life could have been broken by the occasional visits of the old friend whom he had once forbidden the house; but this prohibition having passed his lips, he stubbornly refused to do anything which might be construed into unsaying it. Jemima was for some time in despair of his ever returning to the office, or resuming his old habits of business. He had evidently threatened as much to her husband. All that Jemima could do was to turn a deaf ear to every allusion to this menace, which he threw out from time to time, evidently with a view to see if it had struck deep enough into her husband's mind for him to have repeated it to his wife. If Mr Farquhar had named it—if it was known only to two or three to have been, but for one half-hour even, his resolution—Mr Bradshaw could have adhered to it, without any other reason than the maintenance of what he called consistency, but which was in fact doggedness. Jemima was often thankful that her mother was absent, and gone to nurse her son. If she had been at home, she would have entreated and implored her husband to fall back into his usual habits, and would have shown such a dread of his being as good as his word, that he would have been compelled to adhere to it by the very consequence affixed to it. Mr Farquhar had hard work, as it was, in passing rapidly enough between the two places—attending to his business at Eccleston; and deciding, comforting, and earnestly talking, in Richard's sick-room. During an absence of his, it was necessary to apply to one of the partners on some matter of importance; and accordingly, to Jemima's secret joy, Mr Watson came up and asked if her father was well enough to see him on business? Jemima carried in this inquiry literally; and the hesitating answer which her father gave was in the affirmative. It was not long before she saw him leave the house, accompanied by the faithful old clerk; and when he met her at dinner, he made no allusion to his morning visitor, or to his subsequent going out. But from that time forwards he went regularly to the office. He received all the information about Dick's accident, and his progress towards recovery, in perfect silence, and in as indifferent a manner as he could assume; but yet he lingered about the family sitting-room every morning until the post had come in which brought all letters from the south.

When Mr Farquhar at last returned to bring the news of Dick's perfect convalescence, he resolved to tell Mr Bradshaw all that he had done and arranged for his son's future career; but, as Mr Farquhar told Mr Benson afterwards, he could not really say if Mr Bradshaw had attended to one word that he said.

"Rely upon it," said Mr Benson, "he has not only attended to it, but treasured up every expression you have used."

"Well, I tried to get some opinion, or sign of emotion, out of him. I had not much hope of the latter, I must own; but I thought he would have said whether I had done wisely or not in procuring that Glasgow situation for Dick—that he would, perhaps, have been indignant at my ousting him from the partnership so entirely on my own responsibility."

"How did Richard take it?"

"Oh, nothing could exceed his penitence. If one had never heard of the proverb, 'When the devil was sick, the devil a monk would be,' I should have had greater faith in him; or if he had had more strength of character to begin with, or more reality and less outward appearance of good principle instilled into him. However, this Glasgow situation is the very thing; clear, defined duties, no great trust reposed in him, a kind and watchful head, and introductions to a better class of associates than I fancy he has ever been thrown amongst before. For, you know, Mr Bradshaw dreaded all intimacies for his son, and wanted him to eschew all society beyond his own family—would never allow him to ask a friend home. Really, when I think of the unnatural life Mr Bradshaw expected him to lead, I get into charity with him, and have hopes. By the way, have you ever succeeded in persuading his mother to send Leonard to school? He may run the same risk from isolation as Dick: not be able to choose his companions wisely when he grows up, but be too much overcome by the excitement of society to be very discreet as to who are his associates. Have you spoken to her about my plan?"

"Yes! but to no purpose. I cannot say that she would even admit an argument on the subject. She seemed to have an invincible repugnance to the idea of exposing him to the remarks of other boys on his peculiar position."

"They need never know of it. Besides, sooner or later, he must step out of his narrow circle, and encounter remark and scorn."

"True," said Mr Benson, mournfully. "And you may depend upon it, if it really is the best for Leonard, she will come round to it by-and-by. It is almost extraordinary to see the way in which her earnest and most unselfish devotion to this boy's real welfare leads her to right and wise conclusions."

"I wish I could tame her so as to let me meet her as a friend. Since the baby was born, she comes to see Jemima. My wife tells me, that she sits and holds it soft in her arms, and talks to it as if her whole soul went out to the little infant. But if she hears a strange footstep on the stair, what Jemima calls the 'wild-animal look' comes back into her eyes, and she steals away like some frightened creature. With all that she has done to redeem her character, she should not be so timid of observation."

"You may well say 'with all that she has done!' We of her own household hear little or nothing of what she does. If she wants help, she simply tells us how and why; but if not—perhaps because it is some relief to her to forget for a time the scenes of suffering in which she has been acting the part of comforter, and perhaps because there always was a shy, sweet reticence about her—we never should know what she is and what she does, except from the poor people themselves, who would bless her in words if the very thought of her did not choke them with tears. Yet, I do assure you, she passes out of all this gloom, and makes sunlight in our house. We are never so cheerful as when she is at home. She always had the art of diffusing peace, but now it is positive cheerfulness. And about Leonard; I doubt if the wisest and most thoughtful schoolmaster could teach half as much directly, as his mother does unconsciously and indirectly every hour that he is with her. Her noble, humble, pious endurance of the consequences of what was wrong in her early life, seems expressly fitted to act upon him, whose position is (unjustly, for he has done no harm) so similar to hers."

"Well! I suppose we must leave it alone for the present. You will think me a hard practical man when I own to you, that all I expect from Leonard's remaining a home-bird is that, with such a mother, it will do him no harm. At any rate, remember my offer is the same for a year—two years hence, as now. What does she look forward to making him into, finally?"

"I don't know. The wonder comes into my mind sometimes; but never into hers, I think. It is part of her character—part perhaps of that which made her what she was—that she never looks forward, and seldom back. The present is enough for her."

And so the conversation ended. When Mr Benson repeated the substance of it to his sister, she mused awhile, breaking out into an occasional whistle (although she had cured herself of this habit in a great measure), and at last she said:

"Now, do you know, I never liked poor Dick; and yet I'm angry with Mr Farquhar for getting him out of the partnership in such a summary way. I can't get over it, even though he has offered to send Leonard to school. And here he's reigning lord-paramount at the office! As if you, Thurstan, weren't as well able to teach him as any schoolmaster in England! But I should not mind that affront, if I were not sorry to think of Dick (though I never could abide him) labouring away in Glasgow for a petty salary of nobody knows how little, while Mr Farquhar is taking halves, instead of thirds, of the profits here!"

But her brother could not tell her—and even Jemima did not know, till long afterwards—that the portion of income which would have been Dick's as a junior partner, if he had remained in the business, was carefully laid aside for him by Mr Farquhar; to be delivered up, with all its accumulated interest, when the prodigal should have proved his penitence by his conduct.

When Ruth had no call upon her time, it was indeed a holiday at Chapel-house. She threw off as much as she could of the care and the sadness in which she had been sharing; and returned fresh and helpful, ready to go about in her soft, quiet way, and fill up every measure of service, and heap it with the fragrance of her own sweet nature. The delicate mending, that the elder women could no longer see to do, was put by for Ruth's swift and nimble fingers. The occasional copying, or patient writing to dictation, that gave rest to Mr Benson's weary spine, was done by her with sunny alacrity. But, most of all, Leonard's heart rejoiced when his mother came home. Then came the quiet confidences, the tender exchange of love, the happy walks from which he returned stronger and stronger—going from strength to strength as his mother led the way. It was well, as they saw now, that the great shock of the disclosure had taken place when it did. She, for her part, wondered at her own cowardliness in having even striven to keep back the truth from her child—the truth that was so certain to be made clear, sooner or later, and which it was only owing to God's mercy that she was alive to encounter with him, and, by so encountering, shield and give him good courage. Moreover, in her secret heart, she was thankful that all occurred while he was yet too young to have much curiosity as to his father. If an unsatisfied feeling of this kind occasionally stole into his mind, at any rate she never heard any expression of it; for the past was a sealed book between them. And so, in the bright strength of good endeavour, the days went on, and grew again to months and years.

Perhaps one little circumstance which occurred during this time had scarcely external importance enough to be called an event; but in Mr Benson's mind it took rank as such. One day, about a year after Richard Bradshaw had ceased to be a partner in his father's house, Mr Benson encountered Mr Farquhar in the street, and heard from him of the creditable and respectable manner in which Richard was conducting himself in Glasgow, where Mr Farquhar had lately been on business.

"I am determined to tell his father of this," said he; "I think his family are far too obedient to his tacit prohibition of all mention of Richard's name."

"Tacit prohibition?" inquired Mr Benson.

"Oh! I dare say I use the words in a wrong sense for the correctness of a scholar; but what I mean is, that he made a point of immediately leaving the room if Richard's name was mentioned; and did it in so marked a manner, that by degrees they understood that it was their father's desire that he should never be alluded to; which was all very well as long as there was nothing pleasant to be said about him; but to-night I am going there, and shall take good care he does not escape me before I have told him all I have heard and observed about Richard. He will never be a hero of virtue, for his education has drained him of all moral courage; but with care, and the absence of all strong temptation for a time, he will do very well; nothing to gratify paternal pride, but certainly nothing to be ashamed of."

It was on the Sunday after this that the little circumstance to which I have alluded took place.

During the afternoon service, Mr Benson became aware that the large Bradshaw pew was no longer unoccupied. In a dark corner Mr Bradshaw's white head was to be seen, bowed down low in prayer. When last he had worshipped there, the hair on that head was iron-grey, and even in prayer he had stood erect, with an air of conscious righteousness sufficient for all his wants, and even some to spare with which to judge others. Now, that white and hoary head was never uplifted; part of his unobtrusiveness might, it is true, be attributed to the uncomfortable feeling which was sure to attend any open withdrawal of the declaration he had once made, never to enter the chapel in which Mr Benson was minister again; and as such a feeling was natural to all men, and especially to such a one as Mr Bradshaw, Mr Benson instinctively respected it, and passed out of the chapel with his household, without ever directing his regards to the obscure place where Mr Bradshaw still remained immovable.

From this day Mr Benson felt sure that the old friendly feeling existed once more between them, although some time might elapse before any circumstance gave the signal for a renewal of their intercourse.

CHAPTER XXXIII

A Mother to Be Proud Of

Old people tell of certain years when typhus fever swept over the country like a pestilence; years that bring back the remembrance of deep sorrow—refusing to be comforted—to many a household; and which those whose beloved passed through the fiery time unscathed, shrink from recalling: for great and tremulous was the anxiety—miserable the constant watching for evil symptoms; and beyond the threshold of home a dense cloud of depression hung over society at large. It seemed as if the alarm was proportionate to the previous light-heartedness of fancied security—and indeed it was so; for, since the days of King Belshazzar, the solemn decrees of Doom have ever seemed most terrible when they awe into silence the merry revellers of life. So it was this year to which I come in the progress of my story.

The summer had been unusually gorgeous. Some had complained of the steaming heat, but others had pointed to the lush vegetation, which was profuse and luxuriant. The early autumn was wet and cold, but people did not regard it, in contemplation of some proud rejoicing of the nation, which filled every newspaper and gave food to every tongue. In Eccleston these rejoicings were greater than in most places; for, by the national triumph of arms, it was supposed that a new market for the staple manufacture of the place would be opened; and so the trade, which had for a year or two been languishing, would now revive with redoubled vigour. Besides these legitimate causes of good spirits, there was the rank excitement of a coming election, in consequence of Mr Donne having accepted a Government office, procured for him by one of his influential relations. This time, the Cranworths roused themselves from their magnificent torpor of security in good season, and were going through a series of pompous and ponderous hospitalities, in order to bring back the Eccleston voters to their allegiance.

While the town was full of these subjects by turns—now thinking and speaking of the great revival of trade—now of the chances of the election, as yet some weeks distant—now of the balls at Cranworth Court, in which Mr Cranworth had danced with all the belles of the shopocracy of Eccleston—there came creeping, creeping, in hidden, slimy courses, the terrible fever—that fever which is never utterly banished from the sad haunts of vice and misery, but lives in such darkness, like a wild beast in the recesses of his den. It had begun in the low Irish lodging-houses; but there it was so common it excited little attention. The poor creatures died almost without the attendance of the unwarned medical men, who received their first notice of the spreading plague from the Roman Catholic priests.

Before the medical men of Eccleston had had time to meet together and consult, and compare the knowledge of the fever which they had severally gained, it had, like the blaze of a fire which had long smouldered, burst forth in many places at once—not merely among the loose-living and vicious, but among the decently poor—nay, even among the well-to-do and respectable. And to add to the horror, like all similar pestilences, its course was most rapid at first, and was fatal in the great majority of cases—hopeless from the beginning. There was a cry, and then a deep silence, and then rose the long wail of the survivors.

A portion of the Infirmary of the town was added to that already set apart for a fever-ward; the smitten were carried thither at once, whenever it was possible, in order to prevent the spread of infection; and on that lazar-house was concentrated all the medical skill and force of the place.

But when one of the physicians had died, in consequence of his attendance—when the customary staff of matrons and nurses had been swept off in two days—and the nurses belonging to the Infirmary had shrunk from being drafted into the pestilential fever-ward—when high wages had failed to tempt any to what, in their panic, they considered as certain death—when the doctors stood aghast at the swift mortality among the untended sufferers, who were dependent only on the care of the most ignorant hirelings, too brutal to recognise the solemnity of Death (all this had happened within a week from the first acknowledgment of the presence of the plague)—Ruth came one day, with a quieter step than usual, into Mr Benson's study, and told him she wanted to speak to him for a few minutes.

"To be sure, my dear! Sit down," said he; for she was standing and leaning her head against the chimney-piece, idly gazing into the fire. She went on standing there, as if she had not heard his words; and it was a few moments before she began to speak. Then she said:

"I want to tell you, that I have been this morning and offered myself as matron to the fever-ward while it is so full. They have accepted me; and I am going this evening."

"Oh, Ruth! I feared this; I saw your look this morning as we spoke of this terrible illness."

"Why do you say 'fear,' Mr Benson? You yourself have been with John Harrison, and old Betty, and many others, I dare say, of whom we have not heard."

"But this is so different! in such poisoned air! among such malignant cases! Have you thought and weighed it enough, Ruth?"

She was quite still for a moment, but her eyes grew full of tears. At last she said, very softly, with a kind of still solemnity:

"Yes! I have thought, and I have weighed. But through the very midst of all my fears and thoughts I have felt that I must go."

The remembrance of Leonard was present in both their minds; but for a few moments longer they neither of them spoke. Then Ruth said:

"I believe I have no fear. That is a great preservative, they say. At any rate, if I have a little natural shrinking, it is quite gone when I remember that I am in God's hands! Oh, Mr Benson," continued she, breaking out into the irrepressible tears—"Leonard, Leonard!"

And now it was his turn to speak out the brave words of faith.

"Poor, poor mother!" said he. "Be of good heart. He, too, is in God's hands. Think what a flash of time only will separate you from him, if you should die in this work!"

"But he—but he—it will be long to him, Mr Benson! He will be alone!"

"No, Ruth, he will not. God and all good men will watch over him. But if you cannot still this agony of fear as to what will become of him, you ought not to go. Such tremulous passion will predispose you to take the fever."

"I will not be afraid," she replied, lifting up her face, over which a bright light shone, as of God's radiance. "I am not afraid for myself. I will not be so for my darling."

After a little pause, they began to arrange the manner of her going, and to speak of the length of time that she might be absent on her temporary duties. In talking of her return, they assumed it to be certain, although the exact time when was to them unknown, and would be dependent entirely on the duration of the fever; but not the less, in their secret hearts, did they feel where alone the issue lay. Ruth was to communicate with Leonard and Miss Faith through Mr Benson alone, who insisted on his determination to go every evening to the Hospital to learn the proceedings of the day, and the state of Ruth's health.

"It is not alone on your account, my dear! There may be many sick people of whom, if I can give no other comfort, I can take intelligence to their friends."

All was settled with grave composure; yet still Ruth lingered, as if nerving herself up for some effort. At length she said, with a faint smile upon her pale face:

"I believe I am a great coward. I stand here talking because I dread to tell Leonard."

"You must not think of it," exclaimed he. "Leave it to me. It is sure to unnerve you."

"I must think of it. I shall have self-control enough in a minute to do it calmly—to speak hopefully. For only think," continued she, smiling through the tears that would gather in her eyes, "what a comfort the remembrance of the last few words may be to the poor fellow, if—" The words were choked, but she smiled bravely on. "No!" said she, "that must be done; but perhaps you will spare me one thing—will you tell Aunt Faith? I suppose I am very weak, but, knowing that I must go, and not knowing what may be the end, I feel as if I could not bear to resist her entreaties just at last. Will you tell her, sir, while I go to Leonard?"

Silently he consented, and the two rose up and came forth, calm and serene. And calmly and gently did Ruth tell her boy of her purpose; not daring even to use any unaccustomed tenderness of voice or gesture, lest, by so doing, she should alarm him unnecessarily as to the result. She spoke hopefully, and bade him be of good courage; and he caught her bravery, though his, poor boy, had root rather in his ignorance of the actual imminent danger than in her deep faith.

When he had gone down, Ruth began to arrange her dress. When she came downstairs she went into the old familiar garden and gathered a nosegay of the last lingering autumn flowers—a few roses and the like.

Mr Benson had tutored his sister well; and although Miss Faith's face was swollen with crying, she spoke with almost exaggerated cheerfulness to Ruth. Indeed, as they all stood at the front door, making-believe to have careless nothings to say, just as at an ordinary leave-taking, you would not have guessed the strained chords of feeling there were in each heart. They lingered on, the last rays of the setting sun falling on the group. Ruth once or twice had roused herself to the pitch of saying "Good-bye," but when her eye fell on Leonard she was forced to hide the quivering of her lips, and conceal her trembling mouth amid the bunch of roses.

"They won't let you have your flowers, I'm afraid," said Miss Benson. "Doctors so often object to the smell."

"No; perhaps not," said Ruth, hurriedly. "I did not think of it. I will only keep this one rose. Here, Leonard, darling!" She gave the rest to him. It was her farewell; for having now no veil to hide her emotion, she summoned all her bravery for one parting smile, and, smiling, turned away. But she gave one look back from the street, just from the last point at which the door could be seen, and catching a glimpse of Leonard standing foremost on the step, she ran back, and he met her half-way, and mother and child spoke never a word in that close embrace.

"Now, Leonard," said Miss Faith, "be a brave boy. I feel sure she will come back to us before very long."

But she was very near crying herself; and she would have given way, I believe, if she had not found the wholesome outlet of scolding Sally, for expressing just the same opinion respecting Ruth's proceedings as she herself had done not two hours before. Taking what her brother had said to her as a text, she delivered such a lecture to Sally on want of faith that she was astonished at herself, and so much affected by what she had said that she had to shut the door of communication between the kitchen and the parlour pretty hastily, in order to prevent Sally's threatened reply from weakening her belief in the righteousness of what Ruth had done. Her words had gone beyond her conviction.

Evening after evening Mr Benson went forth to gain news of Ruth; and night after night he returned with good tidings. The fever, it is true, raged; but no plague came nigh her. He said her face was ever calm and bright, except when clouded by sorrow as she gave the accounts of the deaths which occurred in spite of every care. He said he had never seen her face so fair and gentle as it was now, when she was living in the midst of disease and woe.

One evening Leonard (for they had grown bolder as to the infection) accompanied him to the street on which the hospital abutted. Mr Benson left him there, and told him to return home; but the boy lingered, attracted by the crowd that had gathered, and were gazing up intently towards the lighted windows of the hospital. There was nothing beyond to be seen; but the greater part of these poor people had friends or relations in that palace of Death.

Leonard stood and listened. At first their talk consisted of vague and exaggerated accounts (if such could be exaggerated) of the horrors of the fever. Then they spoke of Ruth—of his mother; and Leonard held his breath to hear.

"They say she has been a great sinner, and that this is her penance," quoth one. And as Leonard gasped, before rushing forward to give the speaker straight the lie, an old man spoke:

"Such a one as her has never been a great sinner; nor does she do her work as a penance, but for the love of God, and of the blessed Jesus. She will be in the light of God's countenance when you and I will be standing afar off. I tell you, man, when my poor wench died, as no one would come near, her head lay at that hour on this woman's sweet breast. I could fell you," the old man went on, lifting his shaking arm, "for calling that woman a great sinner. The blessing of them who were ready to perish is upon her."

Immediately there arose a clamour of tongues, each with some tale of his mother's gentle doings, till Leonard grew dizzy with the beatings of his glad, proud heart. Few were aware how much Ruth had done; she never spoke of it, shrinking with sweet shyness from over-much allusion to her own work at all times. Her left hand truly knew not what her right hand did; and Leonard was overwhelmed now to hear of the love and the reverence with which the poor and outcast had surrounded her. It was irrepressible. He stepped forward with a proud bearing, and touching the old man's arm who had first spoken, Leonard tried to speak; but for an instant he could not, his heart was too full: tears came before words, but at length he managed to say:

"Sir, I am her son!"

"Thou! thou her bairn! God bless you, lad," said an old woman, pushing through the crowd. "It was but last night she kept my child quiet with singing psalms the night through. Low and sweet, low and sweet, they tell me—till many poor things were hushed, though they were out of their minds, and had not heard psalms this many a year. God in heaven bless you, lad!"

Many other wild, woe-begone creatures pressed forward with blessings on Ruth's son, while he could only repeat:

"She is my mother."

From that day forward Leonard walked erect in the streets of Eccleston, where "many arose and called her blessed."

After some weeks the virulence of the fever abated; and the general panic subsided—indeed, a kind of fool-hardiness succeeded. To be sure, in some instances the panic still held possession of individuals to an exaggerated extent. But the number of patients in the hospital was rapidly diminishing, and, for money, those were to be found who could supply Ruth's place. But to her it was owing that the overwrought fear of the town was subdued; it was she who had gone voluntarily, and, with no thought of greed or gain, right into the very jaws of the fierce disease. She bade the inmates of the hospital farewell, and after carefully submitting herself to the purification recommended by Mr Davis, the principal surgeon of the place, who had always attended Leonard, she returned to Mr Benson's just at gloaming time.

They each vied with the other in the tenderest cares. They hastened tea; they wheeled the sofa to the fire; they made her lie down; and to all she submitted with the docility of a child; and when the candles came, even Mr Benson's anxious eye could see no change in her looks, but that she seemed a little paler. The eyes were as full of spiritual light, the gently parted lips as rosy, and the smile, if more rare, yet as sweet as ever.

CHAPTER XXXIV

"I Must Go and Nurse Mr Bellingham"

The next morning, Miss Benson would insist upon making Ruth lie down on the sofa. Ruth longed to do many things; to be much more active; but she submitted, when she found that it would gratify Miss Faith if she remained as quiet as if she were really an invalid.

Leonard sat by her holding her hand. Every now and then he looked up from his book, as if to make sure that she indeed was restored to him. He had brought her down the flowers which she had given him the day of her departure, and which he had kept in water as long as they had any greenness or fragrance, and then had carefully dried and put by. She too, smiling, had produced the one rose which she had carried away to the hospital. Never had the bond between her and her boy been drawn so firm and strong.

Many visitors came this day to the quiet Chapel-house. First of all Mrs Farquhar appeared. She looked very different from the Jemima Bradshaw of three years ago. Happiness had called out beauty; the colouring of her face was lovely, and vivid as that of an autumn day; her berry-red lips scarce closed over the short white teeth for her smiles; and her large dark eyes glowed and sparkled with daily happiness. They were softened by a mist of tears as she looked upon Ruth.

"Lie still! Don't move! You must be content to-day to be waited upon, and nursed! I have just seen Miss Benson in the lobby, and had charge upon charge not to fatigue you. Oh, Ruth! how we all love you, now we have you back again! Do you know, I taught Rosa to say her prayers as soon as ever you were gone to that horrid place, just on purpose that her little innocent lips might pray for you—I wish you could hear her say it—'Please, dear God, keep Ruth safe.' Oh, Leonard! are not you proud of your mother?"

Leonard said "Yes," rather shortly, as if he were annoyed that any one else should know, or even have a right to imagine, how proud he was. Jemima went on:

"Now, Ruth! I have got a plan for you. Walter and I have partly made it; and partly it's papa's doing. Yes, dear! papa has been quite anxious to show his respect for you. We all want you to go to the dear Eagle's Crag for this next month, and get strong, and have some change in that fine air at Abermouth. I am going to take little Rosa there. Papa has lent it to us. And the weather is often very beautiful in November."

"Thank you very much. It is very tempting; for I have been almost longing for some such change. I cannot tell all at once whether I can go; but I will see about it, if you will let me leave it open a little."

"Oh! as long as you like, so that you will but go at last. And, Master Leonard! you are to come too. Now, I know I have you on my side."

Ruth thought of the place. Her only reluctance arose from the remembrance of that one interview on the sands. That walk she could never go again; but how much remained! How much that would be a charming balm and refreshment to her!

"What happy evenings we shall have together! Do you know, I think Mary and Elizabeth may perhaps come."

A bright gleam of sunshine came into the room. "Look! how bright and propitious for our plans. Dear Ruth, it seems like an omen for the future!"

Almost while she spoke, Miss Benson entered, bringing with her Mr Grey, the rector of Eccleston. He was an elderly man, short and stoutly-built, with something very formal in his manner; but any one might feel sure of his steady benevolence who noticed the expression of his face, and especially of the kindly black eyes that gleamed beneath his grey and shaggy eyebrows. Ruth had seen him at the hospital once or twice, and Mrs Farquhar had met him pretty frequently in general society.

"Go and tell your uncle," said Miss Benson to Leonard.

"Stop, my boy! I have just met Mr Benson in the street, and my errand now is to your mother. I should like you to remain and hear what it is; and I am sure that my business will give these ladies"—bowing to Miss Benson and Jemima—"so much pleasure, that I need not apologise for entering upon it in their presence."

He pulled out his double eye-glass, saying, with a grave smile:

"You ran away from us yesterday so quietly and cunningly, Mrs Denbigh, that you were, perhaps, not aware that the Board was sitting at that very time, and trying to form a vote sufficiently expressive of our gratitude to you. As Chairman, they requested me to present you with this letter, which I shall have the pleasure of reading."

With all due emphasis he read aloud a formal letter from the Secretary to the Infirmary, conveying a vote of thanks to Ruth.

The good rector did not spare her one word, from date to signature; and then, folding the letter up, he gave it to Leonard, saying:

"There, sir! when you are an old man, you may read that testimony to your mother's noble conduct with pride and pleasure. For, indeed," continued he, turning to Jemima, "no words can express the relief it was to us. I speak of the gentlemen composing the Board of the Infirmary. When Mrs Denbigh came forward, the panic was at its height, and the alarm of course aggravated the disorder. The poor creatures died rapidly; there was hardly time to remove the dead bodies before others were brought in to occupy the beds, so little help was to be procured on account of the universal terror; and the morning when Mrs Denbigh offered us her services, we seemed at the very worst. I shall never forget the sensation of relief in my mind when she told us what she proposed to do; but we thought it right to warn her to the full extent—"

"Nay, madam," said he, catching a glimpse of Ruth's changing colour, "I will spare you any more praises. I will only say, if I can be a friend to you, or a friend to your child, you may command my poor powers to the utmost."

He got up, and bowing formally, he took his leave. Jemima came and kissed Ruth. Leonard went upstairs to put the precious letter away. Miss Benson sat crying heartily in a corner of the room. Ruth went to her and threw her arms round her neck, and said:

"I could not tell him just then. I durst not speak for fear of breaking down; but if I have done right, it was all owing to you and Mr Benson. Oh! I wish I had said how the thought first came into my head from seeing the things Mr Benson has done so quietly ever since the fever first came amongst us. I could not speak; and it seemed as if I was taking those praises to myself, when all the time I was feeling how little I deserved them—how it was all owing to you."

"Under God, Ruth," said Miss Benson, speaking through her tears.

"Oh! I think there is nothing humbles one so much as undue praise. While he was reading that letter, I could not help feeling how many things I have done wrong! Could he know of—of what I have been?" asked she, dropping her voice very low.

"Yes!" said Jemima, "he knew—everybody in Eccleston did know—but the remembrance of those days is swept away. Miss Benson," she continued, for she was anxious to turn the subject, "you must be on my side, and persuade Ruth to come to Abermouth for a few weeks. I want her and Leonard both to come."

"I'm afraid my brother will think that Leonard is missing his lessons sadly. Just of late we could not wonder that the poor child's heart was so full; but he must make haste, and get on all the more for his idleness." Miss Benson piqued herself on being a disciplinarian.

"Oh, as for lessons, Walter is so very anxious that you should give way to his superior wisdom, Ruth, and let Leonard go to school. He will send him to any school you fix upon, according to the mode of life you plan for him."

"I have no plan," said Ruth. "I have no means of planning. All I can do is to try and make him ready for anything."

"Well," said Jemima, "we must talk it over at Abermouth; for I am sure you won't refuse to come, dearest, dear Ruth! Think of the quiet, sunny days, and the still evenings, that we shall have together, with little Rosa to tumble about among the fallen leaves; and there's Leonard to have his first sight of the sea."

"I do think of it," said Ruth, smiling at the happy picture Jemima drew. And both smiling at the hopeful prospect before them, they parted—never to meet again in life.

No sooner had Mrs Farquhar gone than Sally burst in.

"Oh! dear, dear!" said she, looking around her. "If I had but known that the rector was coming to call, I'd ha' put on the best covers, and the Sunday tablecloth! You're well enough," continued she, surveying Ruth from head to foot; "you're always trim and dainty in your gowns, though I reckon they cost but tuppence a yard, and you've a face to set 'em off; but as for you" (as she turned to Miss Benson), "I think you might ha' had something better on than that old stuff, if it had only been to do credit to a parishioner like me, whom he has known ever sin' my father was his clerk."

"You forget, Sally, I have been making jelly all the morning. How could I tell it was Mr Grey when there was a knock at the door?" Miss Benson replied.

"You might ha' letten me do the jelly; I'se warrant I could ha' pleased Ruth as well as you. If I had but known he was coming, I'd ha' slipped round the corner and bought ye a neck-ribbon, or summut to lighten ye up. I'se loath he should think I'm living with Dissenters, that don't know how to keep themselves trig and smart."

"Never mind, Sally; he never thought of me. What he came for, was to see Ruth; and, as you say, she's always neat and dainty."

"Well! I reckon it cannot be helped now; but if I buy ye a ribbon, will you promise to wear it when church-folks come? for I cannot abide the way they have of scoffing at the Dissenters about their dress."

"Very well! we'll make that bargain," said Miss Benson; "and now, Ruth, I'll go and fetch you a cup of warm jelly."

"Oh! indeed, Aunt Faith," said Ruth, "I am very sorry to balk you; but if you're going to treat me as an invalid, I am afraid I shall rebel."

But when she found that Aunt Faith's heart was set upon it, she submitted very graciously, only dimpling up a little, as she found that she must consent to lie on the sofa, and be fed, when, in truth, she felt full of health, with a luxurious sensation of languor stealing over her now and then, just enough to make it very pleasant to think of the salt breezes, and the sea beauty which awaited her at Abermouth.

Mr Davis called in the afternoon, and his visit was also to Ruth. Mr and Miss Benson were sitting with her in the parlour, and watching her with contented love, as she employed herself in household sewing, and hopefully spoke about the Abermouth plan.

"Well! so you had our worthy rector here to-day; I am come on something of the same kind of errand; only I shall spare you the reading of my letter, which, I'll answer for it, he did not. Please to take notice," said he, putting down a sealed letter, "that I have delivered you a vote of thanks from my medical brothers; and open and read it at your leisure; only not just now, for I want to have a little talk with you on my own behoof. I want to ask you a favour, Mrs Denbigh."

"A favour!" exclaimed Ruth; "what can I do for you? I think I may say I will do it, without hearing what it is."

"Then you're a very imprudent woman," replied he; "however, I'll take you at your word. I want you to give me your boy."

"Leonard!"

"Aye! there it is, you see, Mr Benson. One minute she is as ready as can be, and the next, she looks at me as if I was an ogre!"

"Perhaps we don't understand what you mean," said Mr Benson.

"The thing is this. You know I've no children; and I can't say I've ever fretted over it much; but my wife has; and whether it is that she has infected me, or that I grieve over my good practice going to a stranger, when I ought to have had a son to take it after me, I don't know; but, of late, I've got to look with covetous eyes on all healthy boys, and at last I've settled down my wishes on this Leonard of yours, Mrs Denbigh."

Ruth could not speak; for, even yet, she did not understand what he meant. He went on:

"Now, how old is the lad?" He asked Ruth, but Miss Benson replied:

"He'll be twelve next February."

"Umph! only twelve! He's tall and old-looking for his age. You look young enough, it is true." He said this last sentence as if to himself, but seeing Ruth crimson up, he abruptly changed his tone.

"Twelve, is he! Well, I take him from now. I don't mean that I really take him away from you," said he, softening all at once, and becoming grave and considerate. "His being your son—the son of one whom I have seen—as I have seen you, Mrs Denbigh (out and out the best nurse I ever met with, Miss Benson; and good nurses are things we doctors know how to value)—his being your son is his great recommendation to me; not but what the lad himself is a noble boy. I shall be glad to leave him with you as long and as much as we can; he could not be tied to your apron-strings all his life, you know. Only I provide for his education, subject to your consent and good pleasure, and he is bound apprentice to me. I, his guardian, bind him to myself, the first surgeon in Eccleston, be the other who he may; and in process of time he becomes partner, and some day or other succeeds me. Now, Mrs Denbigh, what have you got to say against this plan? My wife is just as full of it as me. Come! begin with your objections. You're not a woman if you have not a whole bag-full of them ready to turn out against any reasonable proposal."

"I don't know," faltered Ruth. "It is so sudden—"

"It is very, very kind of you, Mr Davis," said Miss Benson, a little scandalised at Ruth's non-expression of gratitude.

"Pooh! pooh! I'll answer for it, in the long run, I am taking good care of my own interests. Come, Mrs Denbigh, is it a bargain?"

Now Mr Benson spoke.

"Mr Davis, it is rather sudden, as she says. As far as I can see, it is the best as well as the kindest proposal that could have been made; but I think we must give her a little time to think about it."

"Well, twenty-four hours! Will that do?"

Ruth lifted up her head. "Mr Davis, I am not ungrateful because I can't thank you" (she was crying while she spoke); "let me have a fortnight to consider about it. In a fortnight I will make up my mind. Oh, how good you all are!"

"Very well. Then this day fortnight—Thursday the 28th—you will let me know your decision. Mind! if it's against me, I shan't consider it a decision, for I'm determined to carry my point. I'm not going to make Mrs Denbigh blush, Mr Benson, by telling you, in her presence, of all I have observed about her this last three weeks, that has made me sure of the good qualities I shall find in this boy of hers. I was watching her when she little thought it. Do you remember that night when Hector O'Brien was so furiously delirious, Mrs Denbigh?"

Ruth went very white at the remembrance.

"Why now, look there! how pale she is at the very thought of it. And yet, I assure you, she was the one to go up and take the piece of glass from him which he had broken out of the window for the sole purpose of cutting his throat, or the throat of any one else, for that matter. I wish we had some others as brave as she is."

"I thought the great panic was passed away!" said Mr Benson.

"Aye! the general feeling of alarm is much weaker; but, here and there, there are as great fools as ever. Why, when I leave here, I am going to see our precious member, MrDonne—"

"Mr Donne?" said Ruth.

"Mr Donne, who lies ill at the Queen's—came last week, with the intention of canvassing, but was too much alarmed by what he heard of the fever to set to work; and, in spite of all his precautions, he has taken it; and you should see the terror they are in at the hotel; landlord, landlady, waiters, servants—all; there's not a creature will go near him, if they can help it; and there's only his groom—a lad he saved from drowning, I'm told—to do anything for him. I must get him a proper nurse, somehow or somewhere, for all my being a Cranworth man. Ah, Mr Benson! you don't know the temptations we medical men have. Think, if I allowed your member to die now, as he might very well, if he had no nurse—how famously Mr Cranworth would walk over the course!—Where's Mrs Denbigh gone to? I hope I've not frightened her away by reminding her of Hector O'Brien, and that awful night, when I do assure you she behaved like a heroine!"

As Mr Benson was showing Mr Davis out, Ruth opened the study-door, and said, in a very calm, low voice:

"Mr Benson! will you allow me to speak to Mr Davis alone?"

Mr Benson immediately consented, thinking that, in all probability, she wished to ask some further questions about Leonard; but as Mr Davis came into the room, and shut the door, he was struck by her pale, stern face of determination, and awaited her speaking first.

"Mr Davis! I must go and nurse Mr Bellingham," said she at last, clenching her hands tight together, but no other part of her body moving from its intense stillness.

"Mr Bellingham?" asked he, astonished at the name.

"Mr Donne, I mean," said she, hurriedly. "His name was Bellingham."

"Oh! I remember hearing he had changed his name for some property. But you must not think of any more such work just now. You are not fit for it. You are looking as white as ashes."

"I must go," she repeated.

"Nonsense! Here's a man who can pay for the care of the first hospital nurses in London—and I doubt if his life is worth the risk of one of theirs even, much more of yours."

"We have no right to weigh human lives against each other."

"No! I know we have not. But it's a way we doctors are apt to get into; and, at any rate, it's ridiculous of you to think of such a thing. Just listen to reason."

"I can't! I can't!" cried she, with sharp pain in her voice. "You must let me go, dear Mr Davis!" said she, now speaking with soft entreaty.

"No!" said he, shaking his head authoritatively. "I'll do no such thing."

"Listen," said she, dropping her voice, and going all over the deepest scarlet; "he is Leonard's father! Now! you will let me go!"

Mr Davis was indeed staggered by what she said, and for a moment he did not speak. So she went on:

"You will not tell! You must not tell! No one knows, not even Mr Benson, who it was. And now—it might do him so much harm to have it known. You will not tell!"

"No! I will not tell," replied he. "But, Mrs Denbigh, you must answer me this one question, which I ask you in all true respect, but which I must ask, in order to guide both myself and you aright—of course I knew Leonard was illegitimate— in fact, I will give you secret for secret: it was being so myself that first made me sympathise with him, and desire to adopt him. I knew that much of your history; but tell me, do you now care for this man? Answer me truly—do you love him?"

For a moment or two she did not speak; her head was bent down; then she raised it up, and looked with clear and honest eyes into his face.

"I have been thinking—but I do not know—I cannot tell—I don't think I should love him, if he were well and happy— but you said he was ill—and alone—how can I help caring for him?—how can I help caring for him?" repeated she, covering her face with her hands, and the quick hot tears stealing through her fingers. "He is Leonard's father," continued she, looking up at Mr Davis suddenly. "He need not know—he shall not—that I have ever been near him. If he is like the others, he must be delirious—I will leave him before he comes to himself—but now let me go—I must go."

"I wish my tongue had been bitten out before I had named him to you. He would do well enough without you; and, I dare say, if he recognises you, he will only be annoyed."

"It is very likely," said Ruth, heavily.

"Annoyed,—why! he may curse you for your unasked-for care of him. I have heard my poor mother—and she was as pretty and delicate a creature as you are—cursed for showing tenderness when it was not wanted. Now, be persuaded by an old man like me, who has seen enough of life to make his heart ache—leave this fine gentleman to his fate. I'll promise you to get him as good a nurse as can be had for money."

"No!" said Ruth, with dull persistency—as if she had not attended to his dissuasions; "I must go. I will leave him before he recognises me."

"Why, then," said the old surgeon, "if you're so bent upon it, I suppose I must let you. It is but what my mother would have done—poor, heart-broken thing! However, come along, and let us make the best of it. It saves me a deal of trouble, I know; for, if I have you for a right hand, I need not worry myself continually with wondering how he is taken care of. Go! get your bonnet, you tender-hearted fool of a woman! Let us get you out of the house without any more scenes or explanations; I'll make all straight with the Bensons."

"You will not tell my secret, Mr Davis," she said, abruptly.

"No! not I! Does the woman think I had never to keep a secret of the kind before? I only hope he'll lose his election, and never come near the place again. After all," continued he, sighing, "I suppose it is but human nature!" He began recalling the circumstances of his own early life, and dreamily picturing scenes in the grey dying embers of the fire; and he was almost startled when she stood before him, ready equipped, grave, pale, and quiet.

"Come along!" said he. "If you're to do any good at all, it must be in these next three days. After that, I'll ensure his life for this bout; and mind! I shall send you home then; for he might know you, and I'll have no excitement to throw him back again, and no sobbing and crying from you. But now every moment your care is precious to him. I shall tell my own story to the Bensons, as soon as I have installed you."

Mr Donne lay in the best room of the Queen's Hotel—no one with him but his faithful, ignorant servant, who was as much afraid of the fever as any one else could be, but who, nevertheless, would not leave his master—his master who had saved his life as a child, and afterwards put him in the stables at Bellingham Hall, where he learnt all that he knew. He stood in a farther corner of the room, watching his delirious master with affrighted eyes, not daring to come near him, nor yet willing to leave him.

"Oh! if that doctor would but come! He'll kill himself or me—and them stupid servants won't stir a step over the threshold; how shall I get over the night? Blessings on him—here's the old doctor back again! I hear him creaking and scolding up the stairs!"

The door opened, and Mr Davis entered, followed by Ruth.

"Here's the nurse, my good man—such a nurse as there is not in the three counties. Now, all you'll have to do is to mind what she says."

"Oh, sir! he's mortal bad! won't you stay with us through the night, sir?"

"Look there!" whispered Mr Davis to the man, "see how she knows how to manage him! Why, I could not do it better myself!"

She had gone up to the wild, raging figure, and with soft authority had made him lie down: and then, placing a basin of cold water by the bedside, she had dipped in it her pretty hands, and was laying their cool dampness on his hot brow, speaking in a low soothing voice all the time, in a way that acted like a charm in hushing his mad talk.

"But I will stay," said the doctor, after he had examined his patient; "as much on her account as his! and partly to quieten the fears of this poor, faithful fellow."

CHAPTER XXXV

Out of Darkness into Light

The third night after this was to be the crisis—the turning-point between Life and Death. Mr Davis came again to pass it by the bedside of the sufferer. Ruth was there, constant and still, intent upon watching the symptoms, and acting according to them, in obedience to Mr Davis's directions. She had never left the room. Every sense had been strained in watching—every power of thought or judgment had been kept on the full stretch. Now that Mr Davis came and took her place, and that the room was quiet for the night, she became oppressed with heaviness, which yet did not tend to sleep.

She could not remember the present time, or where she was. All times of her earliest youth—the days of her childhood—were in her memory with a minuteness and fulness of detail which was miserable; for all along she felt that she had no real grasp on the scenes that were passing through her mind—that, somehow, they were long gone by, and gone by for ever—and yet she could not remember who she was now, nor where she was, and whether she had now any interests in life to take the place of those which she was conscious had passed away, although their remembrance filled her mind with painful acuteness. Her head lay on her arms, and they rested on the table. Every now and then she opened her eyes, and saw the large room, handsomely furnished with articles that were each one incongruous with the other, as if bought at sales. She saw the flickering night-light—she heard the ticking of the watch, and the two breathings, each going on at a separate rate—one hurried, abruptly stopping, and then panting violently, as if to make up for lost time; and the other slow, steady, and regular, as if the breather was asleep; but this supposition was contradicted by an occasional repressed sound of yawning. The sky through the uncurtained window looked dark and black—would this night never have an end? Had the sun gone down for ever, and would the world at last awaken to a general sense of everlasting night?

Then she felt as if she ought to get up, and go and see how the troubled sleeper in yonder bed was struggling through his illness; but she could not remember who the sleeper was, and she shrunk from seeing some phantom-face on the pillow, such as now began to haunt the dark corners of the room, and look at her, jibbering and mowing as they looked. So she covered her face again, and sank into a whirling stupor of sense and feeling. By-and-by she heard her fellow-watcher stirring, and a dull wonder stole over her as to what he was doing; but the heavy languor pressed her down, and kept her still. At last she heard the words, "Come here," and listlessly obeyed the command. She had to steady herself in the rocking chamber before she could walk to the bed by which Mr Davis stood; but the effort to do so roused her, and, although conscious of an oppressive headache, she viewed with sudden and clear vision all the circumstances of her present position. Mr Davis was near the head of the bed, holding the night-lamp high, and shading it with his hand, that it might not disturb the sick person, who lay with his face towards them, in feeble exhaustion, but with every sign that the violence of the fever had left him. It so happened that the rays of the lamp fell bright and full upon Ruth's countenance, as she stood with her crimson lips parted with the hurrying breath, and the fever-flush brilliant on her cheeks. Her eyes were wide open, and their pupils distended. She looked on the invalid in silence, and hardly understood why Mr Davis had summoned her there.

"Don't you see the change? He is better!—the crisis is past!"

But she did not speak; her looks were riveted on his softly-unclosing eyes, which met hers as they opened languidly. She could not stir or speak. She was held fast by that gaze of his, in which a faint recognition dawned, and grew to strength.

He murmured some words. They strained their sense to hear. He repeated them even lower than before; but this time they caught what he was saying.

"Where are the water-lilies? Where are the lilies in her hair?"

Mr Davis drew Ruth away.

"He is still rambling," said he, "but the fever has left him."

The grey dawn was now filling the room with its cold light; was it that made Ruth's cheek so deadly pale? Could that call out the wild entreaty of her look, as if imploring help against some cruel foe that held her fast, and was wrestling with her Spirit of Life? She held Mr Davis's arm. If she had let it go, she would have fallen.

"Take me home," she said, and fainted dead away.

Mr Davis carried her out of the chamber, and sent the groom to keep watch by his master. He ordered a fly to convey her to Mr Benson's, and lifted her in when it came, for she was still half unconscious. It was he who carried her upstairs to her room, where Miss Benson and Sally undressed and laid her in her bed.

He awaited their proceedings in Mr Benson's study. When Mr Benson came in, Mr Davis said:

"Don't blame me. Don't add to my self-reproach. I have killed her. I was a cruel fool to let her go. Don't speak to me."

"It may not be so bad," said Mr Benson, himself needing comfort in that shock. "She may recover. She surely will recover. I believe she will."

"No, no! she won't. But by —— she shall, if I can save her." Mr Davis looked defiantly at Mr Benson, as if he were Fate. "I tell you she shall recover, or else I am a murderer. What business had I to take her to nurse him—"

He was cut short by Sally's entrance and announcement that Ruth was now prepared to see him.

From that time forward Mr Davis devoted all his leisure, his skill, his energy, to save her. He called on the rival surgeon to beg him to undertake the management of Mr Donne's recovery, saying, with his usual self-mockery, "I could not answer it to Mr Cranworth if I had brought his opponent round, you know, when I had had such a fine opportunity in my power. Now, with your patients, and general Radical interest, it will be rather a feather in your cap; for he may want a good deal of care yet, though he is getting on famously—so rapidly, in fact, that it's a strong temptation to me to throw him back—a relapse, you know."

The other surgeon bowed gravely, apparently taking Mr Davis in earnest, but certainly very glad of the job thus opportunely thrown in his way. In spite of Mr Davis's real and deep anxiety about Ruth, he could not help chuckling over his rival's literal interpretation of all he had said.

"To be sure, what fools men are! I don't know why one should watch and strive to keep them in the world. I have given this fellow something to talk about confidentially to all his patients; I wonder how much stronger a dose the man would have swallowed! I must begin to take care of my practice for that lad yonder. Well-a-day! well-a-day! What was this sick fine gentleman sent here for, that she should run a chance of her life for him? or why was he sent into the world at all, for that matter?"

Indeed, however much Mr Davis might labour with all his professional skill—however much they might all watch—and pray—and weep—it was but too evident that Ruth "home must go, and take her wages." Poor, poor Ruth!

It might be that, utterly exhausted by watching and nursing, first in the hospital, and then by the bedside of her former lover, the power of her constitution was worn out; or, it might be, her gentle, pliant sweetness, but she displayed no outrage or discord even in her delirium. There she lay in the attic-room in which her baby had been born, her watch over him kept, her confession to him made; and now she was stretched on the bed in utter helplessness, softly gazing at vacancy with her open, unconscious eyes, from which all the depth of their meaning had fled, and all they told was of a sweet, child-like insanity within. The watchers could not touch her with their sympathy, or come near her in her dim world;—so, mutely, but looking at each other from time to time with tearful eyes, they took a poor comfort from the one evident fact that, though lost and gone astray, she was happy and at peace. They had never heard her sing; indeed, the simple art which her mother had taught her, had died, with her early joyousness, at that dear mother's death. But now she sang continually, very soft and low. She went from one childish ditty to another without let or pause, keeping a strange sort of time with her pretty fingers, as they closed and unclosed themselves upon the counterpane. She never looked at any one with the slightest glimpse of memory or intelligence in her face; no, not even at Leonard.

Her strength faded day by day; but she knew it not. Her sweet lips were parted to sing, even after the breath and the power to do so had left her, and her fingers fell idly on the bed. Two days she lingered thus—all but gone from them, and yet still there.

They stood around her bedside, not speaking, or sighing, or moaning; they were too much awed by the exquisite peacefulness of her look for that. Suddenly she opened wide her eyes, and gazed intently forwards, as if she saw some happy vision, which called out a lovely, rapturous, breathless smile. They held their very breaths.

"I see the Light coming," said she. "The Light is coming," she said. And, raising herself slowly, she stretched out her arms, and then fell back, very still for evermore.

They did not speak. Mr Davis was the first to utter a word.

"It is over!" said he. "She is dead!"

Out rang through the room the cry of Leonard:

"Mother! mother! mother! You have not left me alone! You will not leave me alone! You are not dead! Mother! Mother!"

They had pent in his agony of apprehension till then, that no wail of her child might disturb her ineffable calm. But now there was a cry heard through the house, of one refusing to be comforted: "Mother! Mother!"

But Ruth lay dead.

CHAPTER XXXVI

The End

A stupor of grief succeeded to Leonard's passionate cries. He became so much depressed, physically as well as mentally, before the end of the day, that Mr Davis was seriously alarmed for the consequences. He hailed with gladness a proposal made by the Farquhars, that the boy should be removed to their house, and placed under the fond care of his mother's friend, who sent her own child to Abermouth the better to devote herself to Leonard.

When they told him of this arrangement, he at first refused to go and leave *her*; but when Mr Benson said:

"*She* would have wished it, Leonard! Do it for her sake!" he went away very quietly; not speaking a word, after Mr Benson had made the voluntary promise that he should see her once again. He neither spoke nor cried for many hours; and all Jemima's delicate wiles were called forth, before his heavy heart could find the relief of tears. And then he was so weak, and his pulse so low, that all who loved him feared for his life.

Anxiety about him made a sad distraction from the sorrow for the dead. The three old people, who now formed the household in the Chapel-house, went about slowly and dreamily, each with a dull wonder at their hearts why they, the infirm and worn-out, were left, while she was taken in her lovely prime.

The third day after Ruth's death, a gentleman came to the door and asked to speak to Mr Benson. He was very much wrapped up in furs and cloaks, and the upper, exposed part of his face was sunk and hollow, like that of one but partially recovered from illness. Mr and Miss Benson were at Mr Farquhar's, gone to see Leonard, and poor old Sally had been having a hearty cry over the kitchen fire before answering the door-knock. Her heart was tenderly inclined just then towards any one who had the aspect of suffering; so, although her master was out, and she was usually chary of admitting strangers, she proposed to Mr Donne (for it was he) that he should come in and await Mr Benson's return in the study. He was glad enough to avail himself of her offer; for he was feeble and nervous, and come on a piece of business which he exceedingly disliked, and about which he felt very awkward. The fire was nearly, if not quite, out; nor did Sally's vigorous blows do much good, although she left the room with an assurance that it would soon burn up. He leant against the chimney-piece, thinking over events, and with a sensation of discomfort, both external and internal, growing and gathering upon him. He almost wondered whether the proposal he meant to make with regard to Leonard could not be better arranged by letter than by an interview. He became very shivery, and impatient of the state of indecision to which his bodily weakness had reduced him.

Sally opened the door and came in. "Would you like to walk upstairs, sir?" asked she, in a trembling voice, for she had learnt who the visitor was from the driver of the fly, who had run up to the house to inquire what was detaining the gentleman that he had brought from the Queen's Hotel; and, knowing that Ruth had caught the fatal fever from her attendance on Mr Donne, Sally imagined that it was but a piece of sad civility to invite him upstairs to see the poor dead body, which she had laid out and decked for the grave, with such fond care that she had grown strangely proud of its marble beauty.

Mr Donne was glad enough of any proposal of a change from the cold and comfortless room where he had thought uneasy, remorseful thoughts. He fancied that a change of place would banish the train of reflection that was troubling him; but the change he anticipated was to a well-warmed, cheerful sitting-room, with signs of life, and a bright fire therein; and he was on the last flight of stairs,—at the door of the room where Ruth lay—before he understood whither Sally was conducting him. He shrank back for an instant, and then a strange sting of curiosity impelled him on. He stood in the humble low-roofed attic, the window open, and the tops of the distant snow-covered hills filling up the whiteness of the general aspect. He muffled himself up in his cloak, and shuddered, while Sally reverently drew down the sheet, and showed the beautiful, calm, still face, on which the last rapturous smile still lingered, giving an ineffable look of bright serenity. Her arms were crossed over her breast; the wimple-like cap marked the perfect oval of her face, while two braids of the waving auburn hair peeped out of the narrow border, and lay on the delicate cheeks.

He was awed into admiration by the wonderful beauty of that dead woman.

"How beautiful she is!" said he, beneath his breath. "Do all dead people look so peaceful—so happy?"

"Not all," replied Sally, crying. "Few has been as good and as gentle as she was in their lives." She quite shook with her sobbing.

Mr Donne was disturbed by her distress.

"Come, my good woman! we must all die—" he did not know what to say, and was becoming infected by her sorrow. "I am sure you loved her very much, and were very kind to her in her lifetime; you must take this from me to buy yourself some remembrance of her." He had pulled out a sovereign, and really had a kindly desire to console her, and reward her, in offering it to her.

But she took her apron from her eyes, as soon as she became aware of what he was doing, and, still holding it midway in her hands, she looked at him indignantly, before she burst out:

"And who are you, that think to pay for my kindness to her by money? And I was not kind to you, my darling," said she, passionately addressing the motionless, serene body—"I was not kind to you. I frabbed you, and plagued you from the first, my lamb! I came and cut off your pretty locks in this very room—I did—and you said never an angry word to me;—no! not then, nor many a time after, when I was very sharp and cross to you.—No! I never was kind to you, and I dunnot think the world was kind to you, my darling,—but you are gone where the angels are very tender to such as you—you are, my poor wench!" She bent down and kissed the lips, from whose marble, unyielding touch Mr Donne recoiled, even in thought.

Just then, Mr Benson entered the room. He had returned home before his sister, and come upstairs in search of Sally, to whom he wanted to speak on some subject relating to the funeral. He bowed in recognition of Mr Donne, whom he knew as the member for the town, and whose presence impressed him painfully, as his illness had been the proximate cause of Ruth's death. But he tried to check this feeling, as it was no fault of Mr Donne's. Sally stole out of the room, to cry at leisure in her kitchen.

"I must apologise for being here," said Mr Donne. "I was hardly conscious where your servant was leading me to, when she expressed her wish that I should walk upstairs."

"It is a very common idea in this town, that it is a gratification to be asked to take a last look at the dead," replied Mr Benson.

"And in this case I am glad to have seen her once more," said Mr Donne. "Poor Ruth!"

Mr Benson glanced up at him at the last word. How did he know her name? To him she had only been Mrs Denbigh. But Mr Donne had no idea that he was talking to one unaware of the connexion that had formerly existed between them; and, though he would have preferred carrying on the conversation in a warmer room, yet, as Mr Benson was still gazing at her with sad, lingering love, he went on:

"I did not recognise her when she came to nurse me; I believe I was delirious. My servant, who had known her long ago, in Fordham, told me who she was. I cannot tell how I regret that she should have died in consequence of her love of me."

Mr Benson looked up at him again, a stern light filling his eyes as he did so. He waited impatiently to hear more, either to quench or confirm his suspicions. If she had not been lying there, very still and calm, he would have forced the words out of Mr Donne, by some abrupt question. As it was, he listened silently, his heart quick-beating.

"I know that money is but a poor compensation,—is no remedy for this event, or for my youthful folly."

Mr Benson set his teeth hard together, to keep in words little short of a curse.

"Indeed, I offered her money to almost any amount before;—do me justice, sir," catching the gleam of indignation on Mr Benson's face; "I offered to marry her, and provide for the boy as if he had been legitimate. It's of no use recurring to that time," said he, his voice faltering; "what is done cannot be undone. But I came now to say, that I should be glad to leave the boy still under your charge, and that every expense you think it right to incur in his education I will defray;—and place a sum of money in trust for him—say, two thousand pounds—or more: fix what you will. Of course, if you decline retaining him, I must find some one else; but the provision for him shall be the same, for my poor Ruth's sake."

Mr Benson did not speak. He could not, till he had gathered some peace from looking at the ineffable repose of the Dead.

Then, before he answered, he covered up her face; and in his voice there was the stillness of ice.

"Leonard is not unprovided for. Those that honoured his mother will take care of him. He shall never touch a penny of your money. Every offer of service you have made, I reject in his name,—and in her presence," said he, bending towards the Dead. "Men may call such actions as yours, youthful follies! There is another name for them with God. Sir! I will follow you downstairs."

All the way down, Mr Benson heard Mr Donne's voice urging and entreating, but the words he could not recognise for the thoughts that filled his brain—the rapid putting together of events that was going on there. And when Mr Donne turned at the door, to speak again, and repeat his offers of service to Leonard, Mr Benson made answer, without well knowing whether the answer fitted the question or not:

"I thank God, you have no right, legal or otherwise, over the child. And for her sake, I will spare him the shame of ever hearing your name as his father."

He shut the door in Mr Donne's face.

"An ill-bred, puritanical old fellow! He may have the boy, I am sure, for aught I care. I have done my duty, and will get out of this abominable place as soon as I can. I wish my last remembrance of my beautiful Ruth was not mixed up with all these people."

Mr Benson was bitterly oppressed with this interview; it disturbed the peace with which he was beginning to contemplate events. His anger ruffled him, although such anger had been just, and such indignation well deserved; and both had been unconsciously present in his heart for years against the unknown seducer, whom he met face to face by the death-bed of Ruth.

It gave him a shock which he did not recover from for many days. He was nervously afraid lest Mr Donne should appear at the funeral; and not all the reasons he alleged to himself against this apprehension, put it utterly away from him. Before then, however, he heard casually (for he would allow himself no inquiries) that he had left the town. No! Ruth's funeral passed over in calm and simple solemnity. Her child, her own household, her friend, and Mr Farquhar, quietly walked after the bier, which was borne by some of the poor to whom she had been very kind in her lifetime. And many others stood aloof in the little burying-ground, sadly watching that last ceremony.

They slowly dispersed; Mr Benson leading Leonard by the hand, and secretly wondering at his self-restraint. Almost as soon as they had let themselves into the Chapel-house, a messenger brought a note from Mrs Bradshaw, with a pot of quince marmalade, which, she said to Miss Benson, she thought that Leonard might fancy, and if he did, they were to be sure and let her know, as she had plenty more; or, was there anything else that he would like? She would gladly make him whatever he fancied.

Poor Leonard! he lay stretched on the sofa, white and tearless, beyond the power of any such comfort, however kindly offered; but this was only one of the many homely, simple attentions, which all came round him to offer, from Mr Grey, the rector, down to the nameless poor who called at the back door to inquire how it fared with *her* child.

Mr Benson was anxious, according to Dissenting custom, to preach an appropriate funeral sermon. It was the last office he could render to her; it should be done well and carefully. Moreover, it was possible that the circumstances of her life, which were known to all, might be made effective in this manner to work conviction of many truths. Accordingly, he made great preparation of thought and paper; he laboured hard, destroying sheet after sheet—his eyes filling with tears between-whiles, as he remembered some fresh proof of the humility and sweetness of her life. Oh, that he could do her justice! but words seemed hard and inflexible, and refused to fit themselves to his ideas. He sat late on Saturday, writing; he watched through the night till Sunday morning was far advanced. He had never taken such pains with any sermon, and he was only half satisfied with it after all.

Mrs Farquhar had comforted the bitterness of Sally's grief by giving her very handsome mourning. At any rate, she felt oddly proud and exulting when she thought of her new black gown; but when she remembered why she wore it, she scolded herself pretty sharply for her satisfaction, and took to crying afresh with redoubled vigour. She spent the Sunday morning in alternately smoothing down her skirts and adjusting her broad hemmed collar, or bemoaning the occasion with tearful earnestness. But the sorrow overcame the little quaint vanity of her heart, as she saw troop after troop of humbly-dressed mourners pass by into the old chapel. They were very poor—but each had mounted some rusty piece of crape, or some faded black ribbon. The old came halting and slow—the mothers carried their quiet, awe-struck babes.

And not only these were there—but others—equally unaccustomed to nonconformist worship: Mr Davis, for instance, to whom Sally acted as chaperone; for he sat in the minister's pew, as a stranger; and, as she afterwards said, she had a fellow-feeling with him, being a Church-woman herself, and Dissenters had such awkward ways; however, she had been there before, so she could set him to rights about their fashions.

From the pulpit, Mr Benson saw one and all—the well-filled Bradshaw pew—all in deep mourning, Mr Bradshaw conspicuously so (he would have attended the funeral gladly if they would have asked him)—the Farquhars—the many strangers—the still more numerous poor—one or two wild-looking outcasts, who stood afar off, but wept silently and continually. Mr Benson's heart grew very full.

His voice trembled as he read and prayed. But he steadied it as he opened his sermon—his great, last effort in her honour—the labour that he had prayed God to bless to the hearts of many. For an instant the old man looked on all the upturned faces, listening, with wet eyes, to hear what he could say to interpret that which was in their hearts, dumb and unshaped, of God's doings as shown in her life. He looked, and, as he gazed, a mist came before him, and he could not see his sermon, nor his hearers, but only Ruth, as she had been—stricken low, and crouching from sight, in the upland field by Llan-dhu—like a woeful, hunted creature. And now her life was over! her struggle ended! Sermon and all was forgotten. He sat down, and hid his face in his hands for a minute or so. Then he arose, pale and serene. He put the sermon away, and opened the Bible, and read the seventh chapter of Revelations, beginning at the ninth verse.

Before it was finished, most of his hearers were in tears. It came home to them as more appropriate than any sermon could have been. Even Sally, though full of anxiety as to what her fellow-Churchman would think of such proceedings, let the sobs come freely as she heard the words:

And he said to me, These are they which came out of great tribulation, and have washed their robes, and made them white in the blood of the Lamb.

Therefore are they before the throne of God, and serve him day and night in his temple; and he that sitteth on the throne shall dwell among them.

They shall hunger no more, neither thirst any more; neither shall the sun light on them, nor any heat.

For the Lamb which is in the midst of the throne shall feed them, and shall lead them unto living fountains of waters, and God shall wipe away all tears from their eyes.

"He preaches sermons sometimes," said Sally, nudging Mr Davis, as they rose from their knees at last. "I make no doubt there was as grand a sermon in yon paper-book as ever we hear in church. I've heard him pray uncommon fine—quite beyond any but learned folk."

Mr Bradshaw had been anxious to do something to testify his respect for the woman, who, if all had entertained his opinions, would have been driven into hopeless sin. Accordingly, he ordered the first stonemason of the town to meet him in the chapel-yard on Monday morning, to take measurement and receive directions for a tombstone. They threaded their way among the grassy heaps to where Ruth was buried, in the south corner, beneath the great Wych-elm. When they got there, Leonard raised himself up from the new-stirred turf. His face was swollen with weeping; but when he saw Mr Bradshaw he calmed himself, and checked his sobs, and, as an explanation of being where he was when thus surprised, he could find nothing to say but the simple words:

"My mother is dead, sir."

His eyes sought those of Mr Bradshaw with a wild look of agony, as if to find comfort for that great loss in human sympathy; and at the first word—the first touch of Mr Bradshaw's hand on his shoulder—he burst out afresh.

"Come, come! my boy!—Mr Francis, I will see you about this to-morrow—I will call at your house.—Let me take you home, my poor fellow. Come, my lad, come!"

The first time, for years, that he had entered Mr Benson's house, he came leading and comforting her son—and, for a moment, he could not speak to his old friend, for the sympathy which choked up his voice, and filled his eyes with tears.

The Grey Woman

By Mrs. (Elizabeth) Gaskell

THE GREY WOMAN.

PORTION I.

There is a mill by the Neckar-side, to which many people resort for coffee, according to the fashion which is almost national in Germany. There is nothing particularly attractive in the situation of this mill; it is on the Mannheim (the flat and unromantic) side of Heidelberg. The river turns the mill-wheel with a plenteous gushing sound; the out-buildings and the dwelling-house of the miller form a well-kept dusty quadrangle. Again, further from the river, there is a garden full of willows, and arbours, and flower-beds not well kept, but very profuse in flowers and luxuriant creepers, knotting and looping the arbours together. In each of these arbours is a stationary table of white painted wood, and light moveable chairs of the same colour and material.

I went to drink coffee there with some friends in 184—. The stately old miller came out to greet us, as some of the party were known to him of old. He was of a grand build of a man, and his loud musical voice, with its tone friendly and familiar, his rolling laugh of welcome, went well with the keen bright eye, the fine cloth of his coat, and the general look of substance about the place. Poultry of all kinds abounded in the mill-yard, where there were ample means of livelihood for them strewed on the ground; but not content with this, the miller took out handfuls of corn from the sacks, and threw liberally to the cocks and hens that ran almost under his feet in their eagerness. And all the time he was doing this, as it were habitually, he was talking to us, and ever and anon calling to his daughter and the serving-maids, to bid them hasten the coffee we had ordered. He followed us to an arbour, and saw us served to his satisfaction with the best of everything we could ask for; and then left us to go round to the different arbours and see that each party was properly attended to; and, as he went, this great, prosperous, happy-looking man whistled softly one of the most plaintive airs I ever heard.

"His family have held this mill ever since the old Palatinate days; or rather, I should say, have possessed the ground ever since then, for two successive mills of theirs have been burnt down by the French. If you want to see Scherer in a passion, just talk to him of the possibility of a French invasion."

But at this moment, still whistling that mournful air, we saw the miller going down the steps that led from the somewhat raised garden into the mill-yard; and so I seemed to have lost my chance of putting him in a passion.

We had nearly finished our coffee, and our "kucken," and our cinnamon cake, when heavy splashes fell on our thick leafy covering; quicker and quicker they came, coming through the tender leaves as if they were tearing them asunder; all the people in the garden were hurrying under shelter, or seeking for their carriages standing outside. Up the steps the miller came hastening, with a crimson umbrella, fit to cover every one left in the garden, and followed by his daughter, and one or two maidens, each bearing an umbrella.

"Come into the house—come in, I say. It is a summer-storm, and will flood the place for an hour or two, till the river carries it away. Here, here."

And we followed him back into his own house. We went into the kitchen first. Such an array of bright copper and tin vessels I never saw; and all the wooden things were as thoroughly scoured. The red tile floor was spotless when we went in, but in two minutes it was all over slop and dirt with the tread of many feet; for the kitchen was filled, and still the worthy miller kept bringing in more people under his great crimson umbrella. He even called the dogs in, and made them lie down under the tables.

His daughter said something to him in German, and he shook his head merrily at her. Everybody laughed.

"What did she say?" I asked.

"She told him to bring the ducks in next; but indeed if more people come we shall be suffocated. What with the thundery weather, and the stove, and all these steaming clothes, I really think we must ask leave to pass on. Perhaps we might go in and see Frau Scherer."

My friend asked the daughter of the house for permission to go into an inner chamber and see her mother. It was granted, and we went into a sort of saloon, overlooking the Neckar; very small, very bright, and very close. The floor was slippery with polish; long narrow pieces of looking-glass against the walls reflected the perpetual motion of the river opposite; a white porcelain stove, with some old-fashioned ornaments of brass about it; a sofa, covered with Utrecht velvet, a table before it, and a piece of worsted-worked carpet under it; a vase of artificial flowers; and, lastly, an alcove with a bed in it, on which lay the paralysed wife of the good miller, knitting busily, formed the furniture. I spoke as if this was all that was to be seen in the room; but, sitting quietly, while my friend kept up a brisk conversation in a language which I but half understood, my eye was caught by a picture in a dark corner of the room, and I got up to examine it more nearly.

It was that of a young girl of extreme beauty; evidently of middle rank. There was a sensitive refinement in her face, as if she almost shrank from the gaze which, of necessity, the painter must have fixed upon her. It was not over-well painted, but I felt that it must have been a good likeness, from this strong impress of peculiar character which I have tried to describe. From the dress, I should guess it to have been painted in the latter half of the last century. And I afterwards heard that I was right.

There was a little pause in the conversation.

"Will you ask Frau Scherer who this is?"

My friend repeated my question, and received a long reply in German. Then she turned round and translated it to me.

"It is the likeness of a great-aunt of her husband's." (My friend was standing by me, and looking at the picture with sympathetic curiosity.) "See! here is the name on the open page of this Bible, 'Anna Scherer, 1778.' Frau Scherer says there is a tradition in the family that this pretty girl, with her complexion of lilies and roses, lost her colour so entirely through fright, that she was known by the name of the Grey Woman. She speaks as if this Anna Scherer lived in some state of life-long terror. But she does not know details; refers me to her husband for them. She thinks he has some papers which were written by the original of that picture for her daughter, who died in this very house not long after our friend there was married. We can ask Herr Scherer for the whole story if you like."

"Oh yes, pray do!" said I. And, as our host came in at this moment to ask how we were faring, and to tell us that he had sent to Heidelberg for carriages to convey us home, seeing no chance of the heavy rain abating, my friend, after thanking him, passed on to my request.

"Ah!" said he, his face changing, "the aunt Anna had a sad history. It was all owing to one of those hellish Frenchmen; and her daughter suffered for it—the cousin Ursula, as we all called her when I was a child. To be sure, the good cousin Ursula was his child as well. The sins of the fathers are visited on their children. The lady would like to know all about it, would she? Well, there are papers—a kind of apology the aunt Anna wrote for putting an end to her daughter's engagement—or rather facts which she revealed, that prevented cousin Ursula from marrying the man she loved; and so she would never have any other good fellow, else I have heard say my father would have been thankful to have made her his wife." All this time he was rummaging in the drawer of an old-fashioned bureau, and now he turned round, with a bundle of yellow MSS. in his hand, which he gave to my friend, saying, "Take it home, take it home, and if you care to make out our crabbed German writing, you may keep it as long as you like, and read it at your leisure. Only I must have it back again when you have done with it, that's all."

And so we became possessed of the manuscript of the following letter, which it was our employment, during many a long evening that ensuing winter, to translate, and in some parts to abbreviate. The letter began with some reference to the pain which she had already inflicted upon her daughter by some unexplained opposition to a project of marriage; but I doubt if, without the clue with which the good miller had furnished us, we could have made out even this much from the passionate, broken sentences that made us fancy that some scene between the mother and daughter—and possibly a third person—had occurred just before the mother had begun to write.

"Thou dost not love thy child, mother! Thou dost not care if her heart is broken!" Ah, God! and these words of my heart-beloved Ursula ring in my ears as if the sound of them would fill them when I lie a-dying. And her poor tear-stained face comes between me and everything else. Child! hearts do not break; life is very tough as well as very terrible. But I will not decide for thee. I will tell thee all; and thou shalt bear the burden of choice. I may be wrong; I have little wit left, and never had much, I think; but an instinct serves me in place of judgment, and that instinct tells me that thou and thy Henri must never be married. Yet I may be in error. I would fain make my child happy. Lay this paper before the good priest Schriesheim; if, after reading it, thou hast doubts which make thee uncertain. Only I will tell thee all now, on condition that no spoken word ever passes between us on the subject. It would kill me to be questioned. I should have to see all present again.

My father held, as thou knowest, the mill on the Neckar, where thy new-found uncle, Scherer, now lives. Thou rememberest the surprise with which we were received there last vintage twelvemonth. How thy uncle disbelieved me when I said that I was his sister Anna, whom he had long believed to be dead, and how I had to lead thee underneath the picture, painted of me long ago, and point out, feature by feature, the likeness between it and thee; and how, as I spoke, I recalled first to my own mind, and then by speech to his, the details of the time when it was painted; the merry words that passed between us then, a happy boy and girl; the position of the articles of furniture in the room; our father's habits; the cherry-tree, now cut down, that shaded the window of my bedroom, through which my brother was wont to squeeze himself, in order to spring on to the topmost bough that would bear his weight; and thence would pass me back his cap laden with fruit to where I sat on the window-sill, too sick with fright for him to care much for eating the cherries.

And at length Fritz gave way, and believed me to be his sister Anna, even as though I were risen from the dead. And thou rememberest how he fetched in his wife, and told her that I was not dead, but was come back to the old home once more, changed as I was. And she would scarce believe him, and scanned me with a cold, distrustful eye, till at length—for I knew her of old as Babette Müller—I said that I was well-to-do, and needed not to seek out friends for what they had to give. And then she asked—not me, but her husband—why I had kept silent so long, leading all—father, brother, every one that loved me in my own dear home—to esteem me dead. And then thine uncle (thou rememberest?) said he cared not to know more than I cared to tell; that I was his Anna, found again, to be a blessing to him in his old age, as I had been in his boyhood. I thanked him in my heart for his trust; for were the need for telling all less than it seems to me now I could not speak of my past life. But she, who was my sister-in-law still, held back her welcome, and, for want of that, I did not go to live in Heidelberg as I had planned beforehand, in order to be near my brother Fritz, but contented myself with his promise to be a father to my Ursula when I should die and leave this weary world.

That Babette Müller was, as I may say, the cause of all my life's suffering. She was a baker's daughter in Heidelberg—a great beauty, as people said, and, indeed, as I could see for myself. I, too—thou sawest my picture—was reckoned a beauty, and I believe I was so. Babette Müller looked upon me as a rival. She liked to be admired, and had no one much to love her. I had several people to love me—thy grandfather, Fritz, the old servant Kätchen, Karl, the head apprentice at the mill—and I feared admiration and notice, and the being stared at as the "Schöne Müllerin," whenever I went to make my purchases in Heidelberg.

Those were happy, peaceful days. I had Kätchen to help me in the housework, and whatever we did pleased my brave old father, who was always gentle and indulgent towards us women, though he was stern enough with the apprentices in the mill. Karl, the oldest of these, was his favourite; and I can see now that my father wished him to marry me, and that Karl himself was desirous to do so. But Karl was rough-spoken, and passionate—not with me, but with the others—and I shrank from him in a way which, I fear, gave him pain. And then came thy uncle Fritz's marriage; and Babette was brought to the mill to be its mistress. Not that I cared much for giving up my post, for, in spite of my father's great kindness, I always feared that I did not manage well for so large a family (with the men, and a girl under Kätchen, we sat down eleven each night to supper). But when Babette began to find fault with Kätchen, I was unhappy at the blame that fell on faithful servants; and by-and-by I began to see that Babette was egging on Karl to make more open love to me, and, as she once said, to get done with it, and take me off to a home of my own. My father was growing old, and did not perceive all my daily discomfort. The more Karl advanced, the more I disliked him. He was good in the main, but I had no notion of being married, and could not bear any one who talked to me about it.

Things were in this way when I had an invitation to go to Carlsruhe to visit a schoolfellow, of whom I had been very fond. Babette was all for my going; I don't think I wanted to leave home, and yet I had been very fond of Sophie Rupprecht. But I was always shy among strangers. Somehow the affair was settled for me, but not until both Fritz and my father had made inquiries as to the character and position of the Rupprechts. They learned that the father had held some kind of inferior position about the Grand-duke's court, and was now dead, leaving a widow, a noble lady, and two daughters, the elder of whom was Sophie, my friend. Madame Rupprecht was not rich, but more than respectable—genteel. When this was ascertained, my father made no opposition to my going; Babette forwarded it by all the means in her power, and even my dear Fritz had his word to say in its favour. Only Kätchen was against it—Kätchen and Karl. The opposition of Karl did more to send me to Carlsruhe than anything. For I could have objected to go; but when he took upon himself to ask what was the good of going a-gadding, visiting strangers of whom no one knew anything, I yielded to circumstances—to the pulling of Sophie and the pushing of Babette. I was silently vexed, I remember, at Babette's inspection of my clothes; at the way in which she settled that this gown was too old-fashioned, or that too common, to go with me on my visit to a noble lady; and at the way in which she took upon herself to spend the money my father had given me to buy what was requisite for the occasion. And yet I blamed myself, for every one else thought her so kind for doing all this; and she herself meant kindly, too.

At last I quitted the mill by the Neckar-side. It was a long day's journey, and Fritz went with me to Carlsruhe. The Rupprechts lived on the third floor of a house a little behind one of the principal streets, in a cramped-up court, to which we gained admittance through a doorway in the street. I remember how pinched their rooms looked after the large space we had at the mill, and yet they had an air of grandeur about them which was new to me, and which gave me pleasure, faded as some of it was. Madame Rupprecht was too formal a lady for me; I was never at my ease with her; but Sophie was all that I had recollected her at school: kind, affectionate, and only rather too ready with her expressions of admiration and regard. The little sister kept out of our way; and that was all we needed, in the first enthusiastic renewal of our early friendship. The one great object of Madame Rupprecht's life was to retain her position in society; and as her means were much diminished since her husband's death, there was not much comfort, though there was a great deal of show, in their way of living; just the opposite of what it was at my father's house. I believe that my coming was not too much desired by

Madame Rupprecht, as I brought with me another mouth to be fed; but Sophie had spent a year or more in entreating for permission to invite me, and her mother, having once consented, was too well bred not to give me a stately welcome.

The life in Carlsruhe was very different from what it was at home. The hours were later, the coffee was weaker in the morning, the pottage was weaker, the boiled beef less relieved by other diet, the dresses finer, the evening engagements constant. I did not find these visits pleasant. We might not knit, which would have relieved the tedium a little; but we sat in a circle, talking together, only interrupted occasionally by a gentleman, who, breaking out of the knot of men who stood near the door, talking eagerly together, stole across the room on tiptoe, his hat under his arm, and, bringing his feet together in the position we called the first at the dancing-school, made a low bow to the lady he was going to address. The first time I saw these manners I could not help smiling; but Madame Rupprecht saw me, and spoke to me next morning rather severely, telling me that, of course, in my country breeding I could have seen nothing of court manners, or French fashions, but that that was no reason for my laughing at them. Of course I tried never to smile again in company. This visit to Carlsruhe took place in '89, just when every one was full of the events taking place at Paris; and yet at Carlsruhe French fashions were more talked of than French politics. Madame Rupprecht, especially, thought a great deal of all French people. And this again was quite different to us at home. Fritz could hardly bear the name of a Frenchman; and it had nearly been an obstacle to my visit to Sophie that her mother preferred being called Madame to her proper title of Frau.

Monsieur de la Tourelle

One night I was sitting next to Sophie, and longing for the time when we might have supper and go home, so as to be able to speak together, a thing forbidden by Madame Rupprecht's rules of etiquette, which strictly prohibited any but the most necessary conversation passing between members of the same family when in society. I was sitting, I say, scarcely keeping back my inclination to yawn, when two gentlemen came in, one of whom was evidently a stranger to the whole party, from the formal manner in which the host led him up, and presented him to the hostess. I thought I had never seen any one so handsome or so elegant. His hair was powdered, of course, but one could see from his complexion that it was fair in its natural state. His features were as delicate as a girl's, and set off by two little "mouches," as we called patches in those days, one at the left corner of his mouth, the other prolonging, as it were, the right eye. His dress was blue and silver. I was so lost in admiration of this beautiful young man, that I was as much surprised as if the angel Gabriel had spoken to me, when the lady of the house brought him forward to present him to me. She called him Monsieur de la Tourelle, and he began to speak to me in French; but though I understood him perfectly, I dared not trust myself to reply to him in that language. Then he tried German, speaking it with a kind of soft lisp that I thought charming. But, before the end of the evening, I became a little tired of the affected softness and effeminacy of his manners, and the exaggerated compliments he paid me, which had the effect of making all the company turn round and look at me. Madame Rupprecht was, however, pleased with the precise thing that displeased me. She liked either Sophie or me to create a sensation; of course she would have preferred that it should have been her daughter, but her daughter's friend was next best. As we went away, I heard Madame Rupprecht and Monsieur de la Tourelle reciprocating civil speeches with might and main, from which I found out that the French gentleman was coming to call on us the next day. I do not know whether I was more glad or frightened, for I had been kept upon stilts of good manners all the evening. But still I was flattered when Madame Rupprecht spoke as if she had invited him, because he had shown pleasure in my society, and even more gratified by Sophie's ungrudging delight at the evident interest I had excited in so fine and agreeable a gentleman. Yet, with all this, they had hard work to keep me from running out of the salon the next day, when we heard his voice inquiring at the gate on the stairs for Madame Rupprecht. They had made me put on my Sunday gown, and they themselves were dressed as for a reception.

When he was gone away, Madame Rupprecht congratulated me on the conquest I had made; for, indeed, he had scarcely spoken to any one else, beyond what mere civility required, and had almost invited himself to come in the evening to bring some new song, which was all the fashion in Paris, he said. Madame Rupprecht had been out all morning, as she told me, to glean information about Monsieur de la Tourelle. He was a propriétaire, had a small château on the Vosges mountains; he owned land there, but had a large income from some sources quite independent of this property. Altogether, he was a good match, as she emphatically observed. She never seemed to think that I could refuse him after this account of his wealth, nor do I believe she would have allowed Sophie a choice, even had he been as old and ugly as he was young and handsome. I do not quite know—so many events have come to pass since then, and blurred the clearness of my recollections—if I loved him or not. He was very much devoted to me; he almost frightened me by the excess of his demonstrations of love. And he was very charming to everybody around me, who all spoke of him as the most fascinating of men, and of me as the most fortunate of girls. And yet I never felt quite at my ease with him. I was always relieved when his visits were over, although I missed his presence when he did not come. He prolonged his visit to the friend with whom he was staying at Carlsruhe, on purpose to woo me. He loaded me with presents, which I was unwilling to take, only Madame Rupprecht seemed to consider me an affected prude if I refused them. Many of these presents consisted of articles of valuable old jewellery, evidently belonging to his family; by accepting these I doubled the ties which were formed around me by circumstances even more than by my own consent. In those days we did not write letters to absent friends as frequently as is done now, and I had been unwilling to name him in the few letters that I wrote home. At length, however, I learned from Madame Rupprecht that she had written to my father to announce the splendid conquest I had made, and to request his presence at my betrothal. I started with astonishment. I had not realized that affairs had gone so far as this. But when she asked me, in a stern, offended manner, what I had meant by my conduct if I did not intend to marry Monsieur de la Tourelle—I had received his visits, his presents, all his various advances without showing any unwillingness or repugnance—(and it was all true; I had shown no repugnance, though I did not wish to be married to him,—at least, not so soon)—what could I do but hang my head, and silently consent to the rapid enunciation of the only course which now remained for me if I would not be esteemed a heartless coquette all the rest of my days?

There was some difficulty, which I afterwards learnt that my sister-in-law had obviated, about my betrothal taking place from home. My father, and Fritz especially, were for having me return to the mill, and there be betrothed, and from thence be married. But the Rupprechts and Monsieur de la Tourelle were equally urgent on the other side; and Babette was unwilling to have the trouble of the commotion at the mill; and also, I think, a little disliked the idea of the contrast of my grander marriage with her own.

So my father and Fritz came over to the betrothal. They were to stay at an inn in Carlsruhe for a fortnight, at the end of which time the marriage was to take place. Monsieur de la Tourelle told me he had business at home, which would oblige him to be absent during the interval between the two events; and I was very glad of it, for I did not think that he valued my father and my brother as I could have wished him to do. He was very polite to them; put on all the soft, grand manner, which he had rather dropped with me; and complimented us all round, beginning with my father and Madame Rupprecht, and ending with little Alwina. But he a little scoffed at the old-fashioned church ceremonies which my father insisted on; and I fancy Fritz must have taken some of his compliments as satire, for I saw certain signs of manner by which I knew that my future husband, for all his civil words, had irritated and annoyed my brother. But all the money arrangements were liberal in the extreme, and more than satisfied, almost surprised, my father. Even Fritz lifted up his eyebrows and whistled. I alone did not care about anything. I was bewitched,—in a dream,—a kind of despair. I had got into a net through my own timidity and weakness, and I did not see how to get out of it. I clung to my own home-people that fortnight as I had never done before. Their voices, their ways were all so pleasant and familiar to me, after the constraint in which I had been living. I might speak and do as I liked without being corrected by Madame Rupprecht, or reproved in a delicate, complimentary way by Monsieur de la Tourelle. One day I said to my father that I did not want to be married, that I would rather go back to the dear old mill; but he seemed to feel this speech of mine as a dereliction of duty as great as if I had committed perjury; as if, after the ceremony of betrothal, no one had any right over me but my future husband. And yet he asked me some solemn questions; but my answers were not such as to do me any good.

"Dost thou know any fault or crime in this man that should prevent God's blessing from resting on thy marriage with him? Dost thou feel aversion or repugnance to him in any way?"

And to all this what could I say? I could only stammer out that I did not think I loved him enough; and my poor old father saw in this reluctance only the fancy of a silly girl who did not know her own mind, but who had now gone too far to recede.

So we were married, in the Court chapel, a privilege which Madame Rupprecht had used no end of efforts to obtain for us, and which she must have thought was to secure us all possible happiness, both at the time and in recollection afterwards.

We were married; and after two days spent in festivity at Carlsruhe, among all our new fashionable friends there, I bade good-by for ever to my dear old father. I had begged my husband to take me by way of Heidelberg to his old castle in the Vosges; but I found an amount of determination, under that effeminate appearance and manner, for which I was not prepared, and he refused my first request so decidedly that I dared not urge it. "Henceforth, Anna," said he, "you will move in a different sphere of life; and though it is possible that you may have the power of showing favour to your relations from time to time, yet much or familiar intercourse will be undesirable, and is what I cannot allow." I felt almost afraid, after this formal speech, of asking my father and Fritz to come and see me; but, when the agony of bidding them farewell overcame all my prudence, I did beg them to pay me a visit ere long. But they shook their heads, and spoke of business at home, of different kinds of life, of my being a Frenchwoman now. Only my father broke out at last with a blessing, and said, "If my child is unhappy—which God forbid—let her remember that her father's house is ever open to her." I was on the point of crying out, "Oh! take me back then now, my father! oh, my father!" when I felt, rather than saw, my husband present near me. He looked on with a slightly contemptuous air; and, taking my hand in his, he led me weeping away, saying that short farewells were always the best when they were inevitable.

It took us two days to reach his château in the Vosges, for the roads were bad and the way difficult to ascertain. Nothing could be more devoted than he was all the time of the journey. It seemed as if he were trying in every way to make up for the separation which every hour made me feel the more complete between my present and my former life. I seemed as if I were only now wakening up to a full sense of what marriage was, and I dare say I was not a cheerful companion on the tedious journey. At length, jealousy of my regret for my father and brother got the better of M. de la Tourelle, and he became so much displeased with me that I thought my heart would break with the sense of desolation. So it was in no cheerful frame of mind that we approached Les Rochers, and I thought that perhaps it was because I was so unhappy that the place looked so dreary. On one side, the château looked like a raw new building, hastily run up for some immediate purpose, without any growth of trees or underwood near it, only the remains of the stone used for building, not yet cleared away from the immediate neighbourhood, although weeds and lichens had been suffered to grow near and over the heaps of rubbish; on the other, were the great rocks from which the place took its name, and rising close against them, as if almost a natural formation, was the old castle, whose building dated many centuries back.

It was not large nor grand, but it was strong and picturesque, and I used to wish that we lived in it rather than in the smart, half-furnished apartment in the new edifice, which had been hastily got ready for my reception. Incongruous as the two parts were, they were joined into a whole by means of intricate passages and unexpected doors, the exact positions of which I never fully understood. M. de la Tourelle led me to a suite of rooms set apart for me, and formally installed me in them, as in a domain of which I was sovereign. He apologised for the hasty preparation which was all he had been able to make for me, but promised, before I asked, or even thought of complaining, that they should be made as luxurious as heart could wish before many weeks had elapsed. But when, in the gloom of an autumnal evening, I caught my own face and figure reflected in all the mirrors, which showed only a mysterious background in the dim light of the many candles which failed to illuminate the great proportions of the half-furnished salon, I clung to M. de la Tourelle, and begged to be taken to the rooms he had occupied before his marriage, he seemed angry with me, although he affected to laugh, and so decidedly put aside the notion of my having any other rooms but these, that I trembled in silence at the fantastic figures and shapes which my imagination called up as peopling the background of those gloomy mirrors. There was my boudoir, a little less dreary—my bedroom, with its grand and tarnished furniture, which I commonly made into my sitting-room, locking up the various doors which led into the boudoir, the salon, the passages—all but one, through which M. de la Tourelle always entered from his own apartments in the older part of the castle. But this preference of mine for occupying my bedroom annoyed M. de la Tourelle, I am sure, though he did not care to express his displeasure. He would always allure me back into the salon, which I disliked more and more from its complete separation from the rest of the building by the long passage into which all the doors of my apartment opened. This passage was closed by heavy doors and portières, through which I could not hear a sound from the other parts of the house, and, of course, the servants could not hear any movement or cry of mine unless expressly summoned. To a girl brought up as I had been in a household where every individual lived all day in the sight of every other member of the family, never wanted either cheerful words or the sense of silent companionship, this grand isolation of mine was very formidable; and the more so, because M. de la Tourelle, as landed proprietor, sportsman, and what not, was generally out of doors the greater part of every day, and sometimes for two or three days at a time. I had no pride to keep me from associating with the domestics; it would have been natural to me in many ways to have sought them out for a word of sympathy in those dreary days when I was left so entirely to myself, had they been like our kindly German servants. But I disliked them, one and all; I could not tell why. Some were civil, but there was a familiarity in their civility which repelled me; others were rude, and treated me more as if I were an intruder than their master's chosen wife; and yet of the two sets I liked these last the best.

The principal male servant belonged to this latter class. I was very much afraid of him, he had such an air of suspicious surliness about him in all he did for me; and yet M. de la Tourelle spoke of him as most valuable and faithful. Indeed, it sometimes struck me that Lefebvre ruled his master in some things; and this I could not make out. For, while M. de la Tourelle behaved towards me as if I were some precious toy or idol, to be cherished, and fostered, and petted, and indulged, I soon found out how little I, or, apparently, any one else, could bend the terrible will of the man who had on first acquaintance appeared to me too effeminate and languid to exert his will in the slightest particular. I had learnt to know his face better now; and to see that some vehement depth of feeling, the cause of which I could not fathom, made his grey eye glitter with pale light, and his lips contract, and his delicate cheek whiten on certain occasions. But all had been so open and above board at home, that I had no experience to help me to unravel any mysteries among those who lived under the same roof. I understood that I had made what Madame Rupprecht and her set would have called a great marriage, because I lived in a château with many servants, bound ostensibly to obey me as a mistress. I understood that M. de la Tourelle was fond enough of me in his way—proud of my beauty, I dare say (for he often enough spoke about it to me)—but he was also jealous, and suspicious, and uninfluenced by my wishes, unless they tallied with his own. I felt at this time as if I could have been fond of him too, if he would have let me; but I was timid from my childhood, and before long my dread of his displeasure (coming down like thunder into the midst of his love, for such slight causes as a hesitation in reply, a wrong word, or a sigh for my father), conquered my humorous inclination to love one who was so handsome, so accomplished, so indulgent and devoted. But if I could not please him when indeed I loved him, you may imagine how often I did wrong when I was so much afraid of him as to quietly avoid his company for fear of his outbursts of passion. One thing I remember noticing, that the more M. de la Tourelle was displeased with me, the more Lefebvre seemed to chuckle; and when I was restored to favour, sometimes on as sudden an impulse as that which occasioned my disgrace, Lefebvre would look askance at me with his cold, malicious eyes, and once or twice at such times he spoke most disrespectfully to M. de la Tourelle.

I have almost forgotten to say that, in the early days of my life at Les Rochers, M. de la Tourelle, in contemptuous indulgent pity at my weakness in disliking the dreary grandeur of the salon, wrote up to the milliner in Paris from whom my corbeille de mariage had come, to desire her to look out for me a maid of middle age, experienced in the toilette, and with so much refinement that she might on occasion serve as companion to me.

PORTION II.

A Norman woman, Amante by name, was sent to Les Rochers by the Paris milliner, to become my maid. She was tall and handsome, though upwards of forty, and somewhat gaunt. But, on first seeing her, I liked her; she was neither rude nor familiar in her manners, and had a pleasant look of straightforwardness about her that I had missed in all the inhabitants of the château, and had foolishly set down in my own mind as a national want. Amante was directed by M. de la Tourelle to sit in my boudoir, and to be always within call. He also gave her many instructions as to her duties in matters which, perhaps, strictly belonged to my department of management. But I was young and inexperienced, and thankful to be spared any responsibility.

I daresay it was true what M. de la Tourelle said—before many weeks had elapsed—that, for a great lady, a lady of a castle, I became sadly too familiar with my Norman waiting-maid. But you know that by birth we were not very far apart in rank: Amante was the daughter of a Norman farmer, I of a German miller; and besides that, my life was so lonely! It almost seemed as if I could not please my husband. He had written for some one capable of being my companion at times, and now he was jealous of my free regard for her—angry because I could sometimes laugh at her original tunes and amusing proverbs, while when with him I was too much frightened to smile.

From time to time families from a distance of some leagues drove through the bad roads in their heavy carriages to pay us a visit, and there was an occasional talk of our going to Paris when public affairs should be a little more settled. These little events and plans were the only variations in my life for the first twelve months, if I except the alternations in M. de la Tourelle's temper, his unreasonable anger, and his passionate fondness.

Perhaps one of the reasons that made me take pleasure and comfort in Amante's society was, that whereas I was afraid of everybody (I do not think I was half as much afraid of things as of persons), Amante feared no one. She would quietly beard Lefebvre, and he respected her all the more for it; she had a knack of putting questions to M. de la Tourelle, which respectfully informed him that she had detected the weak point, but forebore to press him too closely upon it out of deference to his position as her master. And with all her shrewdness to others, she had quite tender ways with me; all the more so at this time because she knew, what I had not yet ventured to tell M. de la Tourelle, that by-and-by I might become a mother—that wonderful object of mysterious interest to single women, who no longer hope to enjoy such blessedness themselves.

It was once more autumn; late in October. But I was reconciled to my habitation; the walls of the new part of the building no longer looked bare and desolate; the *débris* had been so far cleared away by M. de la Tourelle's desire as to make me a little flower-garden, in which I tried to cultivate those plants that I remembered as growing at home. Amante and I had moved the furniture in the rooms, and adjusted it to our liking; my husband had ordered many an article from time to time that he thought would give me pleasure, and I was becoming tame to my apparent imprisonment in a certain part of the great building, the whole of which I had never yet explored. It was October, as I say, once more. The days were lovely, though short in duration, and M. de la Tourelle had occasion, so he said, to go to that distant estate the superintendence of which so frequently took him away from home. He took Lefebvre with him, and possibly some more of the lacqueys; he often did. And my spirits rose a little at the thought of his absence; and then the new sensation that he was the father of my unborn babe came over me, and I tried to invest him with this fresh character. I tried to believe that it was his passionate love for me that made him so jealous and tyrannical, imposing, as he did, restrictions on my very intercourse with my dear father, from whom I was so entirely separated, as far as personal intercourse was concerned.

I had, it is true, let myself go into a sorrowful review of all the troubles which lay hidden beneath the seeming luxury of my life. I knew that no one cared for me except my husband and Amante; for it was clear enough to see that I, as his wife, and also as a *parvenue*, was not popular among the few neighbours who surrounded us; and as for the servants, the women were all hard and impudent-looking, treating me with a semblance of respect that had more of mockery than reality in it; while the men had a lurking kind of fierceness about them, sometimes displayed even to M. de la Tourelle, who on his part, it must be confessed, was often severe even to cruelty in his management of them. My husband loved me, I said to myself, but I said it almost in the form of a question. His love was shown fitfully, and more in ways calculated to please himself than to please me. I felt that for no wish of mine would he deviate one tittle from any predetermined course of action. I had learnt the inflexibility of those thin, delicate lips; I knew how anger would turn his fair complexion to deadly white, and bring the cruel light into his pale blue eyes. The love I bore to any one seemed to be a reason for his hating them, and so I went on pitying myself one long dreary afternoon during that absence of his of which I have spoken, only sometimes remembering to check myself in my murmurings by thinking of the new unseen link between us, and then crying afresh to think how wicked I was. Oh, how well I remember that long October evening! Amante came in from time to time, talking away to cheer me—talking about dress and Paris, and I hardly know what, but from time to time looking at me keenly with her friendly dark eyes, and with serious interest, too, though all her words were about frivolity. At length she heaped the fire with wood, drew the heavy silken curtains close; for I had been anxious hitherto to keep them open, so that I might see the pale moon mounting the skies, as I used to see her—the same moon—rise from behind the Kaiser Stuhl at Heidelberg; but the sight made me cry, so Amante shut it out. She dictated to me as a nurse does to a child.

"Now, madame must have the little kitten to keep her company," she said, "while I go and ask Marthon for a cup of coffee." I remember that speech, and the way it roused me, for I did not like Amante to think I wanted amusing by a kitten. It might be my petulance, but this speech—such as she might have made to a child—annoyed me, and I said that I had reason for my lowness of spirits—meaning that they were not of so imaginary a nature that I could be diverted from them by the gambols of a kitten. So, though I did not choose to tell her all, I told her a part; and as I spoke, I began to suspect that the good creature knew much of what I withheld, and that the little speech about the kitten was more thoughtfully kind than it had seemed at first. I said that it was so long since I had heard from my father; that he was an old man, and so many things might happen—I might never see him again—and I so seldom heard from him or my brother. It was a more complete and total separation than I had ever anticipated when I married, and something of my home and of my life previous to my marriage I told the good Amante; for I had not been brought up as a great lady, and the sympathy of any human being was precious to me.

Amante listened with interest, and in return told me some of the events and sorrows of her own life. Then, remembering her purpose, she set out in search of the coffee, which ought to have been brought to me an hour before; but, in my husband's absence, my wishes were but seldom attended to, and I never dared to give orders.

Presently she returned, bringing the coffee and a great large cake.

"See!" said she, setting it down. "Look at my plunder. Madame must eat. Those who eat always laugh. And, besides, I have a little news that will please madame." Then she told me that, lying on a table in the great kitchen, was a bundle of letters, come by the courier from Strasburg that very afternoon: then, fresh from her conversation with me, she had hastily untied the string that bound them, but had only just traced out one that she thought was from Germany, when a servant-man came in, and, with the start he gave her, she dropped the letters, which he picked up, swearing at her for having untied and disarranged them. She told him that she believed there was a letter there for her mistress; but he only swore the more, saying, that if there was it was no business of hers, or of his either, for that he had the strictest orders always to take all letters that arrived during his master's absence into the private sitting-room of the latter—a room into which I had never entered, although it opened out of my husband's dressing-room.

I asked Amante if she had not conquered and brought me this letter. No, indeed, she replied, it was almost as much as her life was worth to live among such a set of servants: it was only a month ago that Jacques had stabbed Valentin for some jesting talk. Had I never missed Valentin—that handsome young lad who carried up the wood into my salon? Poor fellow! he lies dead and cold now, and they said in the village he had put an end to himself, but those of the household knew better. Oh! I need not be afraid; Jacques was gone, no one knew where; but with such people it was not safe to upbraid or insist. Monsieur would be at home the next day, and it would not be long to wait.

But I felt as if I could not exist till the next day, without the letter. It might be to say that my father was ill, dying—he might cry for his daughter from his death-bed! In short, there was no end to the thoughts and fancies that haunted me. It was of no use for Amante to say that, after all, she might be mistaken—that she did not read writing well—that she had but a glimpse of the address; I let my coffee cool, my food all became distasteful, and I wrung my hands with impatience to get at the letter, and have some news of my dear ones at home. All the time, Amante kept her imperturbable good temper, first reasoning, then scolding. At last she said, as if wearied out, that if I would consent to make a good supper, she would see what could be done as to our going to monsieur's room in search of the letter, after the servants were all gone to bed. We agreed to go together when all was still, and look over the letters; there could be no harm in that; and yet, somehow, we were such cowards we dared not do it openly and in the face of the household.

Presently my supper came up—partridges, bread, fruits, and cream. How well I remember that supper! We put the untouched cake away in a sort of buffet, and poured the cold coffee out of the window, in order that the servants might not take offence at the apparent fancifulness of sending down for food I could not eat. I was so anxious for all to be in bed, that I told the footman who served that he need not wait to take away the plates and dishes, but might go to bed. Long after I thought the house was quiet, Amante, in her caution, made me wait. It was past eleven before we set out, with cat-like steps and veiled light, along the passages, to go to my husband's room and steal my own letter, if it was indeed there; a fact about which Amante had become very uncertain in the progress of our discussion.

To make you understand my story, I must now try to explain to you the plan of the château. It had been at one time a fortified place of some strength, perched on the summit of a rock, which projected from the side of the mountain. But additions had been made to the old building (which must have borne a strong resemblance to the castles overhanging the Rhine), and these new buildings were placed so as to command a magnificent view, being on the steepest side of the rock, from which the mountain fell away, as it were, leaving the great plain of France in full survey. The ground-plan was something of the shape of three sides of an oblong; my apartments in the modern edifice occupied the narrow end, and had this grand prospect. The front of the castle was old, and ran parallel to the road far below. In this were contained the offices and public rooms of various descriptions, into which I never penetrated. The back wing (considering the new building, in which my apartments were, as the centre) consisted of many rooms, of a dark and gloomy character, as the mountain-side shut out much of the sun, and heavy pine woods came down within a few yards of the windows. Yet on this side—on a projecting plateau of the rock—my husband had formed the flower-garden of which I have spoken; for he was a great cultivator of flowers in his leisure moments.

Now my bedroom was the corner room of the new buildings on the part next to the mountain. Hence I could have let myself down into the flower-garden by my hands on the window-sill on one side, without danger of hurting myself; while the windows at right angles with these looked sheer down a descent of a hundred feet at least. Going still farther along this wing, you came to the old building; in fact, these two fragments of the ancient castle had formerly been attached by some such connecting apartments as my husband had rebuilt. These rooms belonged to M. de la Tourelle. His bedroom opened into mine, his dressing-room lay beyond; and that was pretty nearly all I knew, for the servants, as well as he himself, had a knack of turning me back, under some pretence, if ever they found me walking about alone, as I was inclined to do, when first I came, from a sort of curiosity to see the whole of the place of which I found myself mistress. M. de la Tourelle never encouraged me to go out alone, either in a carriage or for a walk, saying always that the roads were unsafe in those disturbed times; indeed, I have sometimes fancied since that the flower-garden, to which the only access from the castle was through his rooms, was designed in order to give me exercise and employment under his own eye.

But to return to that night. I knew, as I have said, that M. de la Tourelle's private room opened out of his dressing-room, and this out of his bedroom, which again opened into mine, the corner-room. But there were other doors into all these rooms, and these doors led into a long gallery, lighted by windows, looking into the inner court. I do not remember our consulting much about it; we went through my room into my husband's apartment through the dressing-room, but the door of communication into his study was locked, so there was nothing for it but to turn back and go by the gallery to the other door. I recollect noticing one or two things in these rooms, then seen by me for the first time. I remember the sweet perfume that hung in the air, the scent bottles of silver that decked his toilet-table, and the whole apparatus for bathing and dressing, more luxurious even than those which he had provided for me. But the room itself was less splendid in its proportions than mine. In truth, the new buildings ended at the entrance to my husband's dressing-room. There were deep window recesses in walls eight or nine feet thick, and even the partitions between the chambers were three feet deep; but over all these doors or windows there fell thick, heavy draperies, so that I should think no one could have heard in one room what passed in another. We went back into my room, and out into the gallery. We had to shade our candle, from a fear that possessed us, I don't know why, lest some of the servants in the opposite wing might trace our progress towards the part of the castle unused by any one except my husband. Somehow, I had always the feeling that all the domestics, except Amante, were spies upon me, and that I was trammelled in a web of observation and unspoken limitation extending over all my actions.

There was a light in the upper room; we paused, and Amante would have again retreated, but I was chafing under the delays. What was the harm of my seeking my father's unopened letter to me in my husband's study? I, generally the coward, now blamed Amante for her unusual timidity. But the truth was, she had far more reason for suspicion as to the proceedings of that terrible household than I had ever known of. I urged her on, I pressed on myself; we came to the door, locked, but with the key in it; we turned it, we entered; the letters lay on the table, their white oblongs catching the light in an instant, and revealing themselves to my eager eyes, hungering after the words of love from my peaceful, distant home. But just as I pressed forward to examine the letters, the candle which Amante held, caught in some draught, went out, and we were in darkness. Amante proposed that we should carry the letters back to my salon, collecting them as well as we could in the dark, and returning all but the expected one for me; but I begged her to return to my room, where I kept tinder and flint, and to strike a fresh light; and so she went, and I remained alone in the room, of which I could only just distinguish the size, and the principal articles of furniture: a large table, with a deep, overhanging cloth, in the middle, escritoires and other heavy articles against the walls; all this I could see as I stood there, my hand on the table close by the letters, my face towards the window, which, both from the darkness of the wood growing high up the mountain-side and the faint light of the declining moon, seemed only like an oblong of paler purpler black than the shadowy room. How much I remembered from my one instantaneous glance before the candle went out, how much I saw as my eyes became accustomed to the darkness, I do not know, but even now, in my dreams, comes up that room of horror, distinct in its profound shadow. Amante could hardly have been gone a minute before I felt an additional gloom before the window, and heard soft movements outside—soft, but resolute, and continued until the end was accomplished, and the window raised.

In mortal terror of people forcing an entrance at such an hour, and in such a manner as to leave no doubt of their purpose, I would have turned to fly when first I heard the noise, only that I feared by any quick motion to catch their attention, as I also ran the danger of doing by opening the door, which was all but closed, and to whose handlings I was unaccustomed. Again, quick as lightning, I bethought me of the hiding-place between the locked door to my husband's dressing-room and the portière which covered it; but I gave that up, I felt as if I could not reach it without screaming or fainting. So I sank down softly, and crept under the table, hidden, as I hoped, by the great, deep table-cover, with its heavy fringe. I had not recovered my swooning senses fully, and was trying to reassure myself as to my being in a place of comparative safety, for, above all things, I dreaded the betrayal of fainting, and struggled hard for such courage as I might attain by deadening myself to the danger I was in by inflicting intense pain on myself. You have often asked me the reason of that mark on my hand; it was where, in my agony, I bit out a piece of flesh with my relentless teeth, thankful for the pain, which helped to numb my terror. I say, I was but just concealed when I heard the window lifted, and one after another stepped over the sill, and stood by me so close that I could have touched their feet. Then they laughed and whispered; my brain swam so that I could not tell the meaning of their words, but I heard my husband's laughter among the rest—low, hissing, scornful—as he kicked something heavy that they had dragged in over the floor, and which lay near me; so near, that my husband's kick, in touching it, touched me too. I don't know why—I can't tell how—but some feeling, and not curiosity, prompted me to put out my hand, ever so softly, ever so little, and feel in the darkness for what lay spurned beside me. I stole my groping palm upon the clenched and chilly hand of a corpse!

Strange to say, this roused me to instant vividness of thought. Till this moment I had almost forgotten Amante; now I planned with feverish rapidity how I could give her a warning not to return; or rather, I should say, I tried to plan, for all my projects were utterly futile, as I might have seen from the first. I could only hope she would hear the voices of those who were now busy in trying to kindle a light, swearing awful oaths at the mislaid articles which would have enabled them to strike fire. I heard her step outside coming nearer and nearer; I saw from my hiding-place the line of light beneath the door more and more distinctly; close to it her footstep paused; the men inside—at the time I thought they had been only two, but I found out afterwards there were three—paused in their endeavours, and were quite still, as breathless as myself, I suppose. Then she slowly pushed the door open with gentle motion, to save her flickering candle from being again extinguished. For a moment all was still. Then I heard my husband say, as he advanced towards her (he wore riding-boots, the shape of which I knew well, as I could see them in the light),—

"Amante, may I ask what brings you here into my private room?"

He stood between her and the dead body of a man, from which ghastly heap I shrank away as it almost touched me, so close were we all together. I could not tell whether she saw it or not; I could give her no warning, nor make any dumb utterance of signs to bid her what to say—if, indeed, I knew myself what would be best for her to say.

Her voice was quite changed when she spoke; quite hoarse, and very low; yet it was steady enough as she said, what was the truth, that she had come to look for a letter which she believed had arrived for me from Germany. Good, brave Amante! Not a word about me. M. de la Tourelle answered with a grim blasphemy and a fearful threat. He would have no one prying into his premises; madame should have her letters, if there were any, when he chose to give them to her, if, indeed, he thought it well to give them to her at all. As for Amante, this was her first warning, but it was also her last; and, taking the candle out of her hand, he turned her out of the room, his companions discreetly making a screen, so as to throw the corpse into deep shadow. I heard the key turn in the door after her—if I had ever had any thought of escape it was gone now. I only hoped that whatever was to befal me might soon be over, for the tension of nerve was growing more than I could bear. The instant she could be supposed to be out of hearing, two voices began speaking in the most angry terms to my husband, upbraiding him for not having detained her, gagged her—nay, one was for killing her, saying he had seen her eye fall on the face of the dead man, whom he now kicked in his passion. Though the form of their speech was as if they were speaking to equals, yet in their tone there was something of fear. I am sure my husband was their superior, or captain, or somewhat. He replied to them almost as if he were scoffing at them, saying it was such an expenditure of labour having to do with fools; that, ten to one, the woman was only telling the simple truth, and that she was frightened enough by discovering her master in his room to be thankful to escape and return to her mistress, to whom he could easily explain on the morrow how he happened to return in the dead of night. But his companions fell to cursing me, and saying that since M. de la Tourelle had been married he was fit for nothing but to dress himself fine and scent himself with perfume; that, as for me, they could have got him twenty girls prettier, and with far more spirit in them. He quietly answered that I suited him, and that was enough. All this time they were doing something—I could not see what—to the corpse; sometimes they were too busy rifling the dead body, I believe, to talk; again they let it fall with a heavy, resistless thud, and took to quarrelling. They taunted my husband with angry vehemence, enraged at his scoffing and scornful replies, his mocking laughter. Yes, holding up his poor dead victim, the better to strip him of whatever he wore that was valuable, I heard my husband laugh just as he had done when exchanging repartees in the little salon of the Rupprechts at Carlsruhe. I hated and dreaded him from that moment. At length, as if to make an end of the subject, he said, with cool determination in his voice,—

"Now, my good friends, what is the use of all this talking, when you know in your hearts that, if I suspected my wife of knowing more than I chose of my affairs, she would not outlive the day? Remember Victorine. Because she merely joked about my affairs in an imprudent manner, and rejected my advice to keep a prudent tongue—to see what she liked, but ask nothing and say nothing—she has gone a long journey—longer than to Paris."

"But this one is different to her; we knew all that Madame Victorine knew, she was such a chatterbox; but this one may find out a vast deal, and never breathe a word about it, she is so sly. Some fine day we may have the country raised, and the gendarmes down upon us from Strasburg, and all owing to your pretty doll, with her cunning ways of coming over you."

I think this roused M. de la Tourelle a little from his contemptuous indifference, for he ground an oath through his teeth, and said, "Feel! this dagger is sharp, Henri. If my wife breathes a word, and I am such a fool as not to have stopped her mouth effectually before she can bring down gendarmes upon us, just let that good steel find its way to my heart. Let her guess but one tittle, let her have but one slight suspicion that I am not a 'grand propriétaire,' much less imagine that I am a chief of Chauffeurs, and she follows Victorine on the long journey beyond Paris that very day."

"She'll outwit you yet; or I never judged women well. Those still silent ones are the devil. She'll be off during some of your absences, having picked out some secret that will break us all on the wheel."

"Bah!" said his voice; and then in a minute he added, "Let her go if she will. But, where she goes, I will follow; so don't cry before you're hurt."

By this time, they had nearly stripped the body; and the conversation turned on what they should do with it. I learnt that the dead man was the Sieur de Poissy, a neighbouring gentleman, whom I had often heard of as hunting with my husband. I had never seen him, but they spoke as if he had come upon them while they were robbing some Cologne merchant, torturing him after the cruel practice of the Chauffeurs, by roasting the feet of their victims in order to compel them to reveal any hidden circumstances connected with their wealth, of which the Chauffeurs afterwards made use; and this Sieur de Poissy coming down upon them, and recognising M. de la Tourelle, they had killed him, and brought him thither after nightfall. I heard him whom I called my husband, laugh his little light laugh as he spoke of the way in which the dead body had been strapped before one of the riders, in such a way that it appeared to any passer-by as if, in truth, the murderer were tenderly supporting some sick person. He repeated some mocking reply of double meaning, which he himself had given to some one who made inquiry. He enjoyed the play upon words, softly applauding his own wit. And all the time the poor helpless outstretched arms of the dead lay close to his dainty boot! Then another stooped (my heart stopped beating), and picked up a letter lying on the ground—a letter that had dropped out of M. de Poissy's pocket—a letter from his wife, full of tender words of endearment and pretty babblings of love. This was read aloud, with coarse ribald comments on every sentence, each trying to outdo the previous speaker. When they came to some pretty words about a sweet Maurice, their little child away with its mother on some visit, they laughed at M. de la Tourelle, and told him that he would be hearing such woman's drivelling some day. Up to that moment, I think, I had only feared him, but his unnatural, half-ferocious reply made me hate even more than I dreaded him. But now they grew weary of their savage merriment; the jewels and watch had been apprised, the money and papers examined; and apparently there was some necessity for the body being interred quietly and before daybreak. They had not dared to leave him where he was slain for fear lest people should come and recognise him, and raise the hue and cry upon them. For they all along spoke as if it was their constant endeavour to keep the immediate neighbourhood of Les Rochers in the most orderly and tranquil condition, so as never to give cause for visits from the gendarmes. They disputed a little as to whether they should make their way into the castle larder through the gallery, and satisfy their hunger before the hasty interment, or afterwards. I listened with eager feverish interest as soon as this meaning of their speeches reached my hot and troubled brain, for at the time the words they uttered seemed only to stamp themselves with terrible force on my memory, so that I could hardly keep from repeating them aloud like a dull, miserable, unconscious echo; but my brain was numb to the sense of what they said, unless I myself were named, and then, I suppose, some instinct of self-preservation stirred within me, and quickened my sense. And how I strained my ears, and nerved my hands and limbs, beginning to twitch with convulsive movements, which I feared might betray me! I gathered every word they spoke, not knowing which proposal to wish for, but feeling that whatever was finally decided upon, my only chance of escape was drawing near. I once feared lest my husband should go to his bedroom before I had had that one chance, in which case he would most likely have perceived my absence. He said that his hands were soiled (I shuddered, for it might be with life-blood), and he would go and cleanse them; but some bitter jest turned his purpose, and he left the room with the other two—left it by the gallery door. Left me alone in the dark with the stiffening corpse!

Now, now was my time, if ever; and yet I could not move. It was not my cramped and stiffened joints that crippled me, it was the sensation of that dead man's close presence. I almost fancied—I almost fancy still—I heard the arm nearest to me move; lift itself up, as if once more imploring, and fall in dead despair. At that fancy—if fancy it were—I screamed aloud in mad terror, and the sound of my own strange voice broke the spell. I drew myself to the side of the table farthest from the corpse, with as much slow caution as if I really could have feared the clutch of that poor dead arm, powerless for evermore. I softly raised myself up, and stood sick and trembling, holding by the table, too dizzy to know what to do next. I nearly fainted, when a low voice spoke—when Amante, from the outside of the door, whispered, "Madame!" The faithful creature had been on the watch, had heard my scream, and having seen the three ruffians troop along the gallery down the stairs, and across the court to the offices in the other wing of the castle, she had stolen to the door of the room in which I was. The sound of her voice gave me strength; I walked straight towards it, as one benighted on a dreary moor, suddenly perceiving the small steady light which tells of human dwellings, takes heart, and steers straight onward. Where I was, where that voice was, I knew not; but go to it I must, or die. The door once opened—I know not by which of us—I fell upon her neck, grasping her tight, till my hands ached with the tension of their hold. Yet she never uttered a word. Only she took me up in her vigorous arms, and bore me to my room, and laid me on my bed. I do not know more; as soon as I was placed there I lost sense; I came to myself with a horrible dread lest my husband was by me, with a belief that he was in the room, in hiding, waiting to hear my first words, watching for the least sign of the terrible knowledge I possessed to murder me. I dared not breathe quicker, I measured and timed each heavy inspiration; I did not speak, nor move, nor even open my eyes, for long after I was in my full, my miserable senses. I heard some one treading softly about the room, as if with a purpose, not as if for curiosity, or merely to beguile the time; some one passed in and out of the salon; and I still lay quiet, feeling as if death were inevitable, but wishing that the agony of death were past. Again faintness stole over me; but just as I was sinking into the horrible feeling of nothingness, I heard Amante's voice close to me, saying,—

"Drink this, madame, and let us begone. All is ready."

I let her put her arm under my head and raise me, and pour something down my throat. All the time she kept talking in a quiet, measured voice, unlike her own, so dry and authoritative; she told me that a suit of her clothes lay ready for me, that she herself was as much disguised as the circumstances permitted her to be, that what provisions I had left from my supper were stowed away in her pockets, and so she went on, dwelling on little details of the most commonplace description, but never alluding for an instant to the fearful cause why flight was necessary. I made no inquiry as to how she knew, or what she knew. I never asked her either then or afterwards, I could not bear it—we kept our dreadful secret close. But I suppose she must have been in the dressing-room adjoining, and heard all.

In fact, I dared not speak even to her, as if there were anything beyond the most common event in life in our preparing thus to leave the house of blood by stealth in the dead of night. She gave me directions—short condensed directions, without reasons—just as you do to a child; and like a child I obeyed her. She went often to the door and listened; and often, too, she went to the window, and looked anxiously out. For me, I saw nothing but her, and I dared not let my eyes wander from her for a minute; and I heard nothing in the deep midnight silence but her soft movements, and the heavy beating of my own heart. At last she took my hand, and led me in the dark, through the salon, once more into the terrible gallery, where across the black darkness the windows admitted pale sheeted ghosts of light upon the floor. Clinging to her I went; unquestioning—for she was human sympathy to me after the isolation of my unspeakable terror. On we went, turning to the left instead of to the right, past my suite of sitting-rooms where the gilding was red with blood, into that unknown wing of the castle that fronted the main road lying parallel far below. She guided me along the basement passages to which we had now descended, until we came to a little open door, through which the air blew chill and cold, bringing for the first time a sensation of life to me. The door led into a kind of cellar, through which we groped our way to an opening like a window, but which, instead of being glazed, was only fenced with iron bars, two of which were loose, as Amante evidently knew, for she took them out with the ease of one who had performed the action often before, and then helped me to follow her out into the free, open air.

We stole round the end of the building, and on turning the corner—she first—I felt her hold on me tighten for an instant, and the next step I, too, heard distant voices, and the blows of a spade upon the heavy soil, for the night was very warm and still.

We had not spoken a word; we did not speak now. Touch was safer and as expressive. She turned down towards the high road; I followed. I did not know the path; we stumbled again and again, and I was much bruised; so doubtless was she; but bodily pain did me good. At last, we were on the plainer path of the high road.

I had such faith in her that I did not venture to speak, even when she paused, as wondering to which hand she should turn. But now, for the first time, she spoke:—

"Which way did you come when he brought you here first?"

I pointed, I could not speak.

We turned in the opposite direction; still going along the high road. In about an hour, we struck up to the mountain-side, scrambling far up before we even dared to rest; far up and away again before day had fully dawned. Then we looked about for some place of rest and concealment: and now we dared to speak in whispers. Amante told me that she had locked the door of communication between his bedroom and mine, and, as in a dream, I was aware that she had also locked and brought away the key of the door between the latter and the salon.

"He will have been too busy this night to think much about you—he will suppose you are asleep—I shall be the first to be missed; but they will only just now be discovering our loss."

I remember those last words of hers made me pray to go on; I felt as if we were losing precious time in thinking either of rest or concealment; but she hardly replied to me, so busy was she in seeking out some hiding-place. At length, giving it up in despair, we proceeded onwards a little way; the mountain-side sloped downwards rapidly, and in the full morning light we saw ourselves in a narrow valley, made by a stream which forced its way along it. About a mile lower down there rose the pale blue smoke of a village, a mill-wheel was lashing up the water close at hand, though out of sight. Keeping under the cover of every sheltering tree or bush, we worked our way down past the mill, down to a one-arched bridge, which doubtless formed part of the road between the village and the mill.

"This will do," said she; and we crept under the space, and climbing a little way up the rough stone-work, we seated ourselves on a projecting ledge, and crouched in the deep damp shadow. Amante sat a little above me, and made me lay my head on her lap. Then she fed me, and took some food herself; and opening out her great dark cloak, she covered up every light-coloured speck about us; and thus we sat, shivering and shuddering, yet feeling a kind of rest through it all, simply from the fact that motion was no longer imperative, and that during the daylight our only chance of safety was to be still. But the damp shadow in which we were sitting was blighting, from the circumstance of the sunlight never penetrating there; and I dreaded lest, before night and the time for exertion again came on, I should feel illness creeping all over me. To add to our discomfort, it had rained the whole day long, and the stream, fed by a thousand little mountain brooklets, began to swell into a torrent, rushing over the stones with a perpetual and dizzying noise.

Every now and then I was wakened from the painful doze into which I continually fell, by a sound of horses' feet over our head: sometimes lumbering heavily as if dragging a burden, sometimes rattling and galloping, and with the sharper cry of men's voices coming cutting through the roar of the waters. At length, day fell. We had to drop into the stream, which came above our knees as we waded to the bank. There we stood, stiff and shivering. Even Amante's courage seemed to fail.

"We must pass this night in shelter, somehow," said she. For indeed the rain was coming down pitilessly. I said nothing. I thought that surely the end must be death in some shape; and I only hoped that to death might not be added the terror of the cruelty of men. In a minute or so she had resolved on her course of action. We went up the stream to the mill. The familiar sounds, the scent of the wheat, the flour whitening the walls—all reminded me of home, and it seemed to me as if I must struggle out of this nightmare and waken, and find myself once more a happy girl by the Neckar-side. They were long in unbarring the door at which Amante had knocked: at length, an old feeble voice inquired who was there, and what was sought? Amante answered shelter from the storm for two women; but the old woman replied, with suspicious hesitation, that she was sure it was a man who was asking for shelter, and that she could not let us in. But at length she satisfied herself, and unbarred the heavy door, and admitted us. She was not an unkindly woman; but her thoughts all travelled in one circle, and that was, that her master, the miller, had told her on no account to let any man into the place during his absence, and that she did not know if he would not think two women as bad; and yet that as we were not men, no one could say she had disobeyed him, for it was a shame to let a dog be out such a night as this. Amante, with ready wit, told her to let no one know that we had taken shelter there that night, and that then her master could not blame her; and while she was thus enjoining secrecy as the wisest course, with a view to far other people than the miller, she was hastily helping me to take off my wet clothes, and spreading them, as well as the brown mantle that had covered us both, before the great stove which warmed the room with the effectual heat that the old woman's failing vitality required. All this time the poor creature was discussing with herself as to whether she had disobeyed orders, in a kind of garrulous way that made me fear much for her capability of retaining anything secret if she was questioned. By-and-by, she wandered away to an unnecessary revelation of her master's whereabouts: gone to help in the search for his landlord, the Sieur de Poissy, who lived at the château just above, and who had not returned from his chase the day before; so the intendant imagined he might have met with some accident, and had summoned the neighbours to beat the forest and the hill-side. She told us much besides, giving us to understand that she would fain meet with a place as housekeeper where there were more servants and less to do, as her life here was very lonely and dull, especially since her master's son had gone away— gone to the wars. She then took her supper, which was evidently apportioned out to her with a sparing hand, as, even if the idea had come into her head, she had not enough to offer us any. Fortunately, warmth was all that we required, and that, thanks to Amante's cares, was returning to our chilled bodies. After supper, the old woman grew drowsy; but she seemed uncomfortable at the idea of going to sleep and leaving us still in the house. Indeed, she gave us pretty broad hints as to the propriety of our going once more out into the bleak and stormy night; but we begged to be allowed to stay under shelter of some kind; and, at last, a bright idea came over her, and she bade us mount by a ladder to a kind of loft, which went half over the lofty mill-kitchen in which we were sitting. We obeyed her—what else could we do?—and found ourselves in a spacious floor, without any safeguard or wall, boarding, or railing, to keep us from falling over into the kitchen in case we went too near the edge. It was, in fact, the store-room or garret for the household. There was bedding piled up, boxes and chests, mill sacks, the winter store of apples and nuts, bundles of old clothes, broken furniture, and many other things. No sooner were we up there, than the old woman dragged the ladder, by which we had ascended, away with a chuckle, as if she was now secure that we could do no mischief, and sat herself down again once more, to doze and await her master's return. We pulled out some bedding, and gladly laid ourselves down in our dried clothes and in some warmth, hoping to have the sleep we so much needed to refresh us and prepare us for the next day. But I could not sleep, and I was aware, from her breathing, that Amante was equally wakeful. We could both see through the crevices between the boards that formed the flooring into the kitchen below, very partially lighted by the common lamp that hung against the wall near the stove on the opposite side to that on which we were.

PORTION III.

Far on in the night there were voices outside reached us in our hiding-place; an angry knocking at the door, and we saw through the chinks the old woman rouse herself up to go and open it for her master, who came in, evidently half drunk. To my sick horror, he was followed by Lefebvre, apparently as sober and wily as ever. They were talking together as they came in, disputing about something; but the miller stopped the conversation to swear at the old woman for having fallen asleep, and, with tipsy anger, and even with blows, drove the poor old creature out of the kitchen to bed. Then he and Lefebvre went on talking—about the Sieur de Poissy's disappearance. It seemed that Lefebvre had been out all day, along with other of my husband's men, ostensibly assisting in the search; in all probability trying to blind the Sieur de Poissy's followers by putting them on a wrong scent, and also, I fancied, from one or two of Lefebvre's sly questions, combining the hidden purpose of discovering us.

Although the miller was tenant and vassal to the Sieur de Poissy, he seemed to me to be much more in league with the people of M. de la Tourelle. He was evidently aware, in part, of the life which Lefebvre and the others led; although, again, I do not suppose he knew or imagined one-half of their crimes; and also, I think, he was seriously interested in discovering the fate of his master, little suspecting Lefebvre of murder or violence. He kept talking himself, and letting out all sorts of thoughts and opinions; watched by the keen eyes of Lefebvre gleaming out below his shaggy eyebrows. It was evidently not the cue of the latter to let out that his master's wife had escaped from that vile and terrible den; but though he never breathed a word relating to us, not the less was I certain he was thirsting for our blood, and lying in wait for us at every turn of events. Presently he got up and took his leave; and the miller bolted him out, and stumbled off to bed. Then we fell asleep, and slept sound and long.

The next morning, when I awoke, I saw Amante, half raised, resting on one hand, and eagerly gazing, with straining eyes, into the kitchen below. I looked too, and both heard and saw the miller and two of his men eagerly and loudly talking about the old woman, who had not appeared as usual to make the fire in the stove, and prepare her master's breakfast, and who now, late on in the morning, had been found dead in her bed; whether from the effect of her master's blows the night before, or from natural causes, who can tell? The miller's conscience upbraided him a little, I should say, for he was eagerly declaring his value for his housekeeper, and repeating how often she had spoken of the happy life she led with him. The men might have their doubts, but they did not wish to offend the miller, and all agreed that the necessary steps should be taken for a speedy funeral. And so they went out, leaving us in our loft, but so much alone, that, for the first time almost, we ventured to speak freely, though still in a hushed voice, pausing to listen continually. Amante took a more cheerful view of the whole occurrence than I did. She said that, had the old woman lived, we should have had to depart that morning, and that this quiet departure would have been the best thing we could have had to hope for, as, in all probability, the housekeeper would have told her master of us and of our resting-place, and this fact would, sooner or later, have been brought to the knowledge of those from whom we most desired to keep it concealed; but that now we had time to rest, and a shelter to rest in, during the first hot pursuit, which we knew to a fatal certainty was being carried on. The remnants of our food, and the stored-up fruit, would supply us with provision; the only thing to be feared was, that something might be required from the loft, and the miller or some one else mount up in search of it. But even then, with a little arrangement of boxes and chests, one part might be so kept in shadow that we might yet escape observation. All this comforted me a little; but, I asked, how were we ever to escape? The ladder was taken away, which was our only means of descent. But Amante replied that she could make a sufficient ladder of the rope lying coiled among other things, to drop us down the ten feet or so—with the advantage of its being portable, so that we might carry it away, and thus avoid all betrayal of the fact that any one had ever been hidden in the loft.

During the two days that intervened before we did escape, Amante made good use of her time. She looked into every box and chest during the man's absence at his mill; and finding in one box an old suit of man's clothes, which had probably belonged to the miller's absent son, she put them on to see if they would fit her; and, when she found that they did, she cut her own hair to the shortness of a man's, made me clip her black eyebrows as close as though they had been shaved, and by cutting up old corks into pieces such as would go into her cheeks, she altered both the shape of her face and her voice to a degree which I should not have believed possible.

All this time I lay like one stunned; my body resting, and renewing its strength, but I myself in an almost idiotic state—else surely I could not have taken the stupid interest which I remember I did in all Amante's energetic preparations for disguise. I absolutely recollect once the feeling of a smile coming over my stiff face as some new exercise of her cleverness proved a success.

But towards the second day, she required me, too, to exert myself; and then all my heavy despair returned. I let her dye my fair hair and complexion with the decaying shells of the stored-up walnuts, I let her blacken my teeth, and even voluntarily broke a front tooth the better to effect my disguise. But through it all I had no hope of evading my terrible husband. The third night the funeral was over, the drinking ended, the guests gone; the miller put to bed by his men, being too drunk to help himself. They stopped a little while in the kitchen, talking and laughing about the new housekeeper likely to come; and they, too, went off, shutting, but not locking the door. Everything favoured us. Amante had tried her ladder on one of the two previous nights, and could, by a dexterous throw from beneath, unfasten it from the hook to which it was fixed, when it had served its office; she made up a bundle of worthless old clothes in order that we might the better preserve our characters of a travelling pedlar and his wife; she stuffed a hump on her back, she thickened my figure, she left her own clothes deep down beneath a heap of others in the chest from which she had taken the man's dress which she wore; and with a few francs in her pocket—the sole money we had either of us had about us when we escaped—we let ourselves down the ladder, unhooked it, and passed into the cold darkness of night again.

We had discussed the route which it would be well for us to take while we lay perdues in our loft. Amante had told me then that her reason for inquiring, when we first left Les Rochers, by which way I had first been brought to it, was to avoid the pursuit which she was sure would first be made in the direction of Germany; but that now she thought we might return to that district of country where my German fashion of speaking French would excite least observation. I thought that Amante herself had something peculiar in her accent, which I had heard M. de la Tourelle sneer at as Norman patois; but I said not a word beyond agreeing to her proposal that we should bend our steps towards Germany. Once there, we should, I thought, be safe. Alas! I forgot the unruly time that was overspreading all Europe, overturning all law, and all the protection which law gives.

How we wandered—not daring to ask our way—how we lived, how we struggled through many a danger and still more terrors of danger, I shall not tell you now. I will only relate two of our adventures before we reached Frankfort. The first, although fatal to an innocent lady, was yet, I believe, the cause of my safety; the second I shall tell you, that you may understand why I did not return to my former home, as I had hoped to do when we lay in the miller's loft, and I first became capable of groping after an idea of what my future life might be. I cannot tell you how much in these doubtings and wanderings I became attached to Amante. I have sometimes feared since, lest I cared for her only because she was so necessary to my own safety; but, no! it was not so; or not so only, or principally. She said once that she was flying for her own life as well as for mine; but we dared not speak much on our danger, or on the horrors that had gone before. We planned a little what was to be our future course; but even for that we did not look forward long; how could we, when every day we scarcely knew if we should see the sun go down? For Amante knew or conjectured far more than I did of the atrocity of the gang to which M. de la Tourelle belonged; and every now and then, just as we seemed to be sinking into the calm of security, we fell upon traces of a pursuit after us in all directions. Once I remember—we must have been nearly three weeks wearily walking through unfrequented ways, day after day, not daring to make inquiry as to our whereabouts, nor yet to seem purposeless in our wanderings—we came to a kind of lonely roadside farrier's and blacksmith's. I was so tired, that Amante declared that, come what might, we would stay there all night; and accordingly she entered the house, and boldly announced herself as a travelling tailor, ready to do any odd jobs of work that might be required, for a night's lodging and food for herself and wife. She had adopted this plan once or twice before, and with good success; for her father had been a tailor in Rouen, and as a girl she had often helped him with his work, and knew the tailors' slang and habits, down to the particular whistle and cry which in France tells so much to those of a trade. At this blacksmith's, as at most other solitary houses far away from a town, there was not only a store of men's clothes laid by as wanting mending when the housewife could afford time, but there was a natural craving after news from a distance, such news as a wandering tailor is bound to furnish. The early November afternoon was closing into evening, as we sat down, she cross-legged on the great table in the blacksmith's kitchen, drawn close to the window, I close behind her, sewing at another part of the same garment, and from time to time well scolded by my seeming husband. All at once she turned round to speak to me. It was only one word, "Courage!" I had seen nothing; I sat out of the light; but I turned sick for an instant, and then I braced myself up into a strange strength of endurance to go through I knew not what.

The blacksmith's forge was in a shed beside the house, and fronting the road. I heard the hammers stop plying their continual rhythmical beat. She had seen why they ceased. A rider had come up to the forge and dismounted, leading his horse in to be re-shod. The broad red light of the forge-fire had revealed the face of the rider to Amante, and she apprehended the consequence that really ensued.

The rider, after some words with the blacksmith, was ushered in by him into the house-place where we sat.

"Here, good wife, a cup of wine and some galette for this gentleman."

"Anything, anything, madame, that I can eat and drink in my hand while my horse is being shod. I am in haste, and must get on to Forbach to-night."

The blacksmith's wife lighted her lamp; Amante had asked her for it five minutes before. How thankful we were that she had not more speedily complied with our request! As it was, we sat in dusk shadow, pretending to stitch away, but scarcely able to see. The lamp was placed on the stove, near which my husband, for it was he, stood and warmed himself. By-and-by he turned round, and looked all over the room, taking us in with about the same degree of interest as the inanimate furniture. Amante, cross-legged, fronting him, stooped over her work, whistling softly all the while. He turned again to the stove, impatiently rubbing his hands. He had finished his wine and galette, and wanted to be off.

"I am in haste, my good woman. Ask thy husband to get on more quickly. I will pay him double if he makes haste."

The woman went out to do his bidding; and he once more turned round to face us. Amante went on to the second part of the tune. He took it up, whistled a second for an instant or so, and then the blacksmith's wife re-entering, he moved towards her, as if to receive her answer the more speedily.

"One moment, monsieur—only one moment. There was a nail out of the off-foreshoe which my husband is replacing; it would delay monsieur again if that shoe also came off."

"Madame is right," said he, "but my haste is urgent. If madame knew my reasons, she would pardon my impatience. Once a happy husband, now a deserted and betrayed man, I pursue a wife on whom I lavished all my love, but who has abused my confidence, and fled from my house, doubtless to some paramour; carrying off with her all the jewels and money on which she could lay her hands. It is possible madame may have heard or seen something of her; she was accompanied in her flight by a base, profligate woman from Paris, whom I, unhappy man, had myself engaged for my wife's waiting-maid, little dreaming what corruption I was bringing into my house!"

"Is it possible?" said the good woman, throwing up her hands.

Amante went on whistling a little lower, out of respect to the conversation.

"However, I am tracing the wicked fugitives; I am on their track" (and the handsome, effeminate face looked as ferocious as any demon's). "They will not escape me; but every minute is a minute of misery to me, till I meet my wife. Madame has sympathy, has she not?"

He drew his face into a hard, unnatural smile, and then both went out to the forge, as if once more to hasten the blacksmith over his work.

Amante stopped her whistling for one instant.

"Go on as you are, without change of an eyelid even; in a few minutes he will be gone, and it will be over!"

It was a necessary caution, for I was on the point of giving way, and throwing myself weakly upon her neck. We went on; she whistling and stitching, I making semblance to sew. And it was well we did so; for almost directly he came back for his whip, which he had laid down and forgotten; and again I felt one of those sharp, quick-scanning glances, sent all round the room, and taking in all.

Then we heard him ride away; and then, it had been long too dark to see well, I dropped my work, and gave way to my trembling and shuddering. The blacksmith's wife returned. She was a good creature. Amante told her I was cold and weary, and she insisted on my stopping my work, and going to sit near the stove; hastening, at the same time, her preparations for supper, which, in honour of us, and of monsieur's liberal payment, was to be a little less frugal than ordinary. It was well for me that she made me taste a little of the cider-soup she was preparing, or I could not have held up, in spite of Amante's warning look, and the remembrance of her frequent exhortations to act resolutely up to the characters we had assumed, whatever befel. To cover my agitation, Amante stopped her whistling, and began to talk; and, by the time the blacksmith came in, she and the good woman of the house were in full flow. He began at once upon the handsome gentleman, who had paid him so well; all his sympathy was with him, and both he and his wife only wished he might overtake his wicked wife, and punish her as she deserved. And then the conversation took a turn, not uncommon to those whose lives are quiet and monotonous; every one seemed to vie with each other in telling about some horror; and the savage and mysterious band of robbers called the Chauffeurs, who infested all the roads leading to the Rhine, with Schinderhannes at their head, furnished many a tale which made the very marrow of my bones run cold, and quenched even Amante's power of talking. Her eyes grew large and wild, her cheeks blanched, and for once she sought by her looks help from me. The new call upon me roused me. I rose and said, with their permission my husband and I would seek our bed, for that we had travelled far and were early risers. I added that we would get up betimes, and finish our piece of work. The blacksmith said we should be early birds if we rose before him; and the good wife seconded my proposal with kindly bustle. One other such story as those they had been relating, and I do believe Amante would have fainted.

As it was, a night's rest set her up; we arose and finished our work betimes, and shared the plentiful breakfast of the family. Then we had to set forth again; only knowing that to Forbach we must not go, yet believing, as was indeed the case, that Forbach lay between us and that Germany to which we were directing our course. Two days more we wandered on, making a round, I suspect, and returning upon the road to Forbach, a league or two nearer to that town than the blacksmith's house. But as we never made inquiries I hardly knew where we were, when we came one night to a small town, with a good large rambling inn in the very centre of the principal street. We had begun to feel as if there were more safety in towns than in the loneliness of the country. As we had parted with a ring of mine not many days before to a travelling jeweller, who was too glad to purchase it far below its real value to make many inquiries as to how it came into the possession of a poor working tailor, such as Amante seemed to be, we resolved to stay at this inn all night, and gather such particulars and information as we could by which to direct our onward course.

We took our supper in the darkest corner of the *salle-à-manger*, having previously bargained for a small bedroom across the court, and over the stables. We needed food sorely; but we hurried on our meal from dread of any one entering that public room who might recognize us. Just in the middle of our meal, the public diligence drove lumbering up under the *porte-cochère*, and disgorged its passengers. Most of them turned into the room where we sat, cowering and fearful, for the door was opposite to the porter's lodge, and both opened on to the wide-covered entrance from the street. Among the passengers came in a young, fair-haired lady, attended by an elderly French maid. The poor young creature tossed her head, and shrank away from the common room, full of evil smells and promiscuous company, and demanded, in German French, to be taken to some private apartment. We heard that she and her maid had come in the coupé, and, probably from pride, poor young lady! she had avoided all association with her fellow-passengers, thereby exciting their dislike and ridicule. All these little pieces of hearsay had a significance to us afterwards, though, at the time, the only remark made that bore upon the future was Amante's whisper to me that the young lady's hair was exactly the colour of mine, which she had cut off and burnt in the stove in the miller's kitchen in one of her descents from our hiding-place in the loft.

As soon as we could, we struck round in the shadow, leaving the boisterous and merry fellow-passengers to their supper. We crossed the court, borrowed a lantern from the ostler, and scrambled up the rude steps to our chamber above the stable. There was no door into it; the entrance was the hole into which the ladder fitted. The window looked into the court. We were tired and soon fell asleep. I was wakened by a noise in the stable below. One instant of listening, and I wakened Amante, placing my hand on her mouth, to prevent any exclamation in her half-roused state. We heard my husband speaking about his horse to the ostler. It was his voice. I am sure of it. Amante said so too. We durst not move to rise and satisfy ourselves. For five minutes or so he went on giving directions. Then he left the stable, and, softly stealing to our window, we saw him cross the court and re-enter the inn. We consulted as to what we should do. We feared to excite remark or suspicion by descending and leaving our chamber, or else immediate escape was our strongest idea. Then the ostler left the stable, locking the door on the outside.

"We must try and drop through the window—if, indeed, it is well to go at all," said Amante.

With reflection came wisdom. We should excite suspicion by leaving without paying our bill. We were on foot, and might easily be pursued. So we sat on our bed's edge, talking and shivering, while from across the court the laughter rang merrily, and the company slowly dispersed one by one, their lights flitting past the windows as they went upstairs and settled each one to his rest.

We crept into our bed, holding each other tight, and listening to every sound, as if we thought we were tracked, and might meet our death at any moment. In the dead of night, just at the profound stillness preceding the turn into another day, we heard a soft, cautious step crossing the yard. The key into the stable was turned—some one came into the stable—we felt rather than heard him there. A horse started a little, and made a restless movement with his feet, then whinnied recognition. He who had entered made two or three low sounds to the animal, and then led him into the court. Amante sprang to the window with the noiseless activity of a cat. She looked out, but dared not speak a word. We heard the great door into the street open—a pause for mounting, and the horse's footsteps were lost in distance.

Then Amante came back to me. "It was he! he is gone!" said she, and once more we lay down, trembling and shaking.

This time we fell sound asleep. We slept long and late. We were wakened by many hurrying feet, and many confused voices; all the world seemed awake and astir. We rose and dressed ourselves, and coming down we looked around among the crowd collected in the court-yard, in order to assure ourselves *he* was not there before we left the shelter of the stable.

The instant we were seen, two or three people rushed to us.

"Have you heard?—Do you know?—That poor young lady—oh, come and see!" and so we were hurried, almost in spite of ourselves, across the court, and up the great open stairs of the main building of the inn, into a bed-chamber, where lay the beautiful young German lady, so full of graceful pride the night before, now white and still in death. By her stood the French maid, crying and gesticulating.

"Oh, madame! if you had but suffered me to stay with you! Oh! the baron, what will he say?" and so she went on. Her state had but just been discovered; it had been supposed that she was fatigued, and was sleeping late, until a few minutes before. The surgeon of the town had been sent for, and the landlord of the inn was trying vainly to enforce order until he came, and, from time to time, drinking little cups of brandy, and offering them to the guests, who were all assembled there, pretty much as the servants were doing in the court-yard.

At last the surgeon came. All fell back, and hung on the words that were to fall from his lips.

"See!" said the landlord. "This lady came last night by the diligence with her maid. Doubtless a great lady, for she must have a private sitting-room——"

"She was Madame the Baroness de Rœder," said the French maid.

—"And was difficult to please in the matter of supper, and a sleeping-room. She went to bed well, though fatigued. Her maid left her——"

"I begged to be allowed to sleep in her room, as we were in a strange inn, of the character of which we knew nothing; but she would not let me, my mistress was such a great lady."

—"And slept with my servants," continued the landlord. "This morning we thought madame was still slumbering; but when eight, nine, ten, and near eleven o'clock came, I bade her maid use my pass-key, and enter her room——"

"The door was not locked, only closed. And here she was found—dead is she not, monsieur?—with her face down on her pillow, and her beautiful hair all scattered wild; she never would let me tie it up, saying it made her head ache. Such hair!" said the waiting-maid, lifting up a long golden tress, and letting it fall again.

I remembered Amante's words the night before, and crept close up to her.

Meanwhile, the doctor was examining the body underneath the bed-clothes, which the landlord, until now, had not allowed to be disarranged. The surgeon drew out his hand, all bathed and stained with blood; and holding up a short, sharp knife, with a piece of paper fastened round it.

"Here has been foul play," he said. "The deceased lady has been murdered. This dagger was aimed straight at her heart." Then, putting on his spectacles, he read the writing on the bloody paper, dimmed and horribly obscured as it was:—

NUMÉRO UN.
Ainsi les Chauffeurs se vengent.

"Let us go!" said I to Amante. "Oh, let us leave this horrible place!"

"Wait a little," said she. "Only a few minutes more. It will be better."

Immediately the voices of all proclaimed their suspicions of the cavalier who had arrived last the night before. He had, they said, made so many inquiries about the young lady, whose supercilious conduct all in the *salle-à-manger* had been discussing on his entrance. They were talking about her as we left the room; he must have come in directly afterwards, and not until he had learnt all about her, had he spoken of the business which necessitated his departure at dawn of day, and made his arrangements with both landlord and ostler for the possession of the keys of the stable and *porte-cochère*. In short, there was no doubt as to the murderer, even before the arrival of the legal functionary who had been sent for by the surgeon; but the word on the paper chilled every one with terror. Les Chauffeurs, who were they? No one knew, some of the gang might even then be in the room overhearing, and noting down fresh objects for vengeance. In Germany, I had heard little of this terrible gang, and I had paid no greater heed to the stories related once or twice about them in Carlsruhe than one does to tales about ogres. But here in their very haunts, I learnt the full amount of the terror they inspired. No one would be legally responsible for any evidence criminating the murderer. The public prosecutor shrank from the duties of his office. What do I say? Neither Amante nor I, knowing far more of the actual guilt of the man who had killed that poor sleeping young lady, durst breathe a word. We appeared to be wholly ignorant of everything: we, who might have told so much. But how could we? we were broken down with terrific anxiety and fatigue, with the knowledge that we, above all, were doomed victims; and that the blood, heavily dripping from the bed-clothes on to the floor, was dripping thus out of the poor dead body, because, when living, she had been mistaken for me.

At length Amante went up to the landlord, and asked permission to leave his inn, doing all openly and humbly, so as to excite neither ill-will nor suspicion. Indeed, suspicion was otherwise directed, and he willingly gave us leave to depart. A few days afterwards we were across the Rhine, in Germany, making our way towards Frankfort, but still keeping our disguises, and Amante still working at her trade.

On the way, we met a young man, a wandering journeyman from Heidelberg. I knew him, although I did not choose that he should know me. I asked him, as carelessly as I could, how the old miller was now? He told me he was dead. This realization of the worst apprehensions caused by his long silence shocked me inexpressibly. It seemed as though every prop gave way from under me. I had been talking to Amante only that very day of the safety and comfort of the home that awaited her in my father's house; of the gratitude which the old man would feel towards her; and how there, in that peaceful dwelling, far away from the terrible land of France, she should find ease and security for all the rest of her life. All this I thought I had to promise, and even yet more had I looked for, for myself. I looked to the unburdening of my heart and conscience by telling all I knew to my best and wisest friend. I looked to his love as a sure guidance as well as a comforting stay, and, behold, he was gone away from me for ever!

I had left the room hastily on hearing of this sad news from the Heidelberger. Presently, Amante followed:

"Poor madame," said she, consoling me to the best of her ability. And then she told me by degrees what more she had learned respecting my home, about which she knew almost as much as I did, from my frequent talks on the subject both at Les Rochers and on the dreary, doleful road we had come along. She had continued the conversation after I left, by asking about my brother and his wife. Of course, they lived on at the mill, but the man said (with what truth I know not, but I believed it firmly at the time) that Babette had completely got the upper hand of my brother, who only saw through her eyes and heard with her ears. That there had been much Heidelberg gossip of late days about her sudden intimacy with a grand French gentleman who had appeared at the mill—a relation, by marriage—married, in fact, to the miller's sister, who, by all accounts, had behaved abominably and ungratefully. But that was no reason for Babette's extreme and sudden intimacy with him, going about everywhere with the French gentleman; and since he left (as the Heidelberger said he knew for a fact) corresponding with him constantly. Yet her husband saw no harm in it all, seemingly; though, to be sure, he was so out of spirits, what with his father's death and the news of his sister's infamy, that he hardly knew how to hold up his head.

"Now," said Amante, "all this proves that M. de la Tourelle has suspected that you would go back to the nest in which you were reared, and that he has been there, and found that you have not yet returned; but probably he still imagines that you will do so, and has accordingly engaged your sister-in-law as a kind of informant. Madame has said that her sister-in-law bore her no extreme good-will; and the defamatory story he has got the start of us in spreading, will not tend to increase the favour in which your sister-in-law holds you. No doubt the assassin was retracing his steps when we met him near Forbach, and having heard of the poor German lady, with her French maid, and her pretty blonde complexion, he followed her. If madame will still be guided by me—and, my child, I beg of you still to trust me," said Amante, breaking out of her respectful formality into the way of talking more natural to those who had shared and escaped from common dangers—more natural, too, where the speaker was conscious of a power of protection which the other did not possess— "we will go on to Frankfort, and lose ourselves, for a time, at least, in the numbers of people who throng a great town; and you have told me that Frankfort is a great town. We will still be husband and wife; we will take a small lodging, and you shall housekeep and live in-doors. I, as the rougher and the more alert, will continue my father's trade, and seek work at the tailors' shops."

I could think of no better plan, so we followed this out. In a back street at Frankfort we found two furnished rooms to let on a sixth story. The one we entered had no light from day; a dingy lamp swung perpetually from the ceiling, and from that, or from the open door leading into the bedroom beyond, came our only light. The bedroom was more cheerful, but very small. Such as it was, it almost exceeded our possible means. The money from the sale of my ring was almost exhausted, and Amante was a stranger in the place, speaking only French, moreover, and the good Germans were hating the French people right heartily. However, we succeeded better than our hopes, and even laid by a little against the time of my confinement. I never stirred abroad, and saw no one, and Amante's want of knowledge of German kept her in a state of comparative isolation.

At length my child was born—my poor worse than fatherless child. It was a girl, as I had prayed for. I had feared lest a boy might have something of the tiger nature of its father, but a girl seemed all my own. And yet not all my own, for the faithful Amante's delight and glory in the babe almost exceeded mine; in outward show it certainly did.

We had not been able to afford any attendance beyond what a neighbouring sage-femme could give, and she came frequently, bringing in with her a little store of gossip, and wonderful tales culled out of her own experience, every time. One day she began to tell me about a great lady in whose service her daughter had lived as scullion, or some such thing. Such a beautiful lady! with such a handsome husband. But grief comes to the palace as well as to the garret, and why or wherefore no one knew, but somehow the Baron de Rœder must have incurred the vengeance of the terrible Chauffeurs; for not many months ago, as madame was going to see her relations in Alsace, she was stabbed dead as she lay in bed at some hotel on the road. Had I not seen it in the *Gazette*? Had I not heard? Why, she had been told that as far off as Lyons there were placards offering a heavy reward on the part of the Baron de Rœder for information respecting the murderer of his wife. But no one could help him, for all who could bear evidence were in such terror of the Chauffeurs; there were hundreds of them she had been told, rich and poor, great gentlemen and peasants, all leagued together by most frightful oaths to hunt to the death any one who bore witness against them; so that even they who survived the tortures to which the Chauffeurs subjected many of the people whom they plundered, dared not to recognise them again, would not dare, even did they see them at the bar of a court of justice; for, if one were condemned, were there not hundreds sworn to avenge his death?

I told all this to Amante, and we began to fear that if M. de la Tourelle, or Lefebvre, or any of the gang at Les Rochers, had seen these placards, they would know that the poor lady stabbed by the former was the Baroness de Rœder, and that they would set forth again in search of me.

This fresh apprehension told on my health and impeded my recovery. We had so little money we could not call in a physician, at least, not one in established practice. But Amante found out a young doctor for whom, indeed, she had sometimes worked; and offering to pay him in kind, she brought him to see me, her sick wife. He was very gentle and thoughtful, though, like ourselves, very poor. But he gave much time and consideration to the case, saying once to Amante that he saw my constitution had experienced some severe shock from which it was probable that my nerves would never entirely recover. By-and-by I shall name this doctor, and then you will know, better than I can describe, his character.

I grew strong in time—stronger, at least. I was able to work a little at home, and to sun myself and my baby at the garret-window in the roof. It was all the air I dared to take. I constantly wore the disguise I had first set out with; as constantly had I renewed the disfiguring dye which changed my hair and complexion. But the perpetual state of terror in which I had been during the whole months succeeding my escape from Les Rochers made me loathe the idea of ever again walking in the open daylight, exposed to the sight and recognition of every passer-by. In vain Amante reasoned—in vain the doctor urged. Docile in every other thing, in this I was obstinate. I would not stir out. One day Amante returned from her work, full of news—some of it good, some such as to cause us apprehension. The good news was this; the master for whom she worked as journeyman was going to send her with some others to a great house at the other side of Frankfort, where there were to be private theatricals, and where many new dresses and much alteration of old ones would be required. The tailors employed were all to stay at this house until the day of representation was over, as it was at some distance from the town, and no one could tell when their work would be ended. But the pay was to be proportionately good.

The other thing she had to say was this: she had that day met the travelling jeweller to whom she and I had sold my ring. It was rather a peculiar one, given to me by my husband; we had felt at the time that it might be the means of tracing us, but we were penniless and starving, and what else could we do? She had seen that this Frenchman had recognised her at the same instant that she did him, and she thought at the same time that there was a gleam of more than common intelligence on his face as he did so. This idea had been confirmed by his following her for some way on the other side of the street; but she had evaded him with her better knowledge of the town, and the increasing darkness of the night. Still it was well that she was going to such a distance from our dwelling on the next day; and she had brought me in a stock of provisions, begging me to keep within doors, with a strange kind of fearful oblivion of the fact that I had never set foot beyond the threshold of the house since I had first entered it—scarce ever ventured down the stairs. But, although my poor, my dear, very faithful Amante was like one possessed that last night, she spoke continually of the dead, which is a bad sign for the living. She kissed you—yes! it was you, my daughter, my darling, whom I bore beneath my bosom away from the fearful castle of your father—I call him so for the first time, I must call him so once again before I have done—Amante kissed you, sweet baby, blessed little comforter, as if she never could leave off. And then she went away, alive.

Two days, three days passed away. That third evening I was sitting within my bolted doors—you asleep on your pillow by my side—when a step came up the stair, and I knew it must be for me; for ours were the topmost rooms. Some one knocked; I held my very breath. But some one spoke, and I knew it was the good Doctor Voss. Then I crept to the door, and answered.

"Are you alone?" asked I.

"Yes," said he, in a still lower voice. "Let me in." I let him in, and he was as alert as I in bolting and barring the door. Then he came and whispered to me his doleful tale. He had come from the hospital in the opposite quarter of the town, the hospital which he visited; he should have been with me sooner, but he had feared lest he should be watched. He had come from Amante's death-bed. Her fears of the jeweller were too well founded. She had left the house where she was employed that morning, to transact some errand connected with her work in the town; she must have been followed, and dogged on her way back through solitary wood-paths, for some of the wood-rangers belonging to the great house had found her lying there, stabbed to death, but not dead; with the poniard again plunged through the fatal writing, once more; but this time with the word "un" underlined, so as to show that the assassin was aware of his previous mistake.

Numéro *Un*.

Ainsi les Chauffeurs se vengent.

They had carried her to the house, and given her restoratives till she had recovered the feeble use of her speech. But, oh, faithful, dear friend and sister! even then she remembered me, and refused to tell (what no one else among her fellow workmen knew), where she lived or with whom. Life was ebbing away fast, and they had no resource but to carry her to the nearest hospital, where, of course, the fact of her sex was made known. Fortunately both for her and for me, the doctor in attendance was the very Doctor Voss whom we already knew. To him, while awaiting her confessor, she told enough to enable him to understand the position in which I was left; before the priest had heard half her tale Amante was dead.

Doctor Voss told me he had made all sorts of *détours*, and waited thus, late at night, for fear of being watched and followed. But I do not think he was. At any rate, as I afterwards learnt from him, the Baron Rœder, on hearing of the similitude of this murder with that of his wife in every particular, made such a search after the assassins, that, although they were not discovered, they were compelled to take to flight for the time.

I can hardly tell you now by what arguments Dr. Voss, at first merely my benefactor, sparing me a portion of his small modicum, at length persuaded me to become his wife. His wife he called it, I called it; for we went through the religious ceremony too much slighted at the time, and as we were both Lutherans, and M. de la Tourelle had pretended to be of the reformed religion, a divorce from the latter would have been easily procurable by German law both ecclesiastical and legal, could we have summoned so fearful a man into any court.

The good doctor took me and my child by stealth to his modest dwelling; and there I lived in the same deep retirement, never seeing the full light of day, although when the dye had once passed away from my face my husband did not wish me to renew it. There was no need; my yellow hair was grey, my complexion was ashen-coloured, no creature could have recognized the fresh-coloured, bright-haired young woman of eighteen months before. The few people whom I saw knew me only as Madame Voss; a widow much older than himself, whom Dr. Voss had secretly married. They called me the Grey Woman.

He made me give you his surname. Till now you have known no other father—while he lived you needed no father's love. Once only, only once more, did the old terror come upon me. For some reason which I forget, I broke through my usual custom, and went to the window of my room for some purpose, either to shut or to open it. Looking out into the street for an instant, I was fascinated by the sight of M. de la Tourelle, gay, young, elegant as ever, walking along on the opposite side of the street. The noise I had made with the window caused him to look up; he saw me, an old grey woman, and he did not recognize me! Yet it was not three years since we had parted, and his eyes were keen and dreadful like those of the lynx.

I told M. Voss, on his return home, and he tried to cheer me, but the shock of seeing M. de la Tourelle had been too terrible for me. I was ill for long months afterwards.

Once again I saw him. Dead. He and Lefebvre were at last caught; hunted down by the Baron de Rœder in some of their crimes. Dr. Voss had heard of their arrest; their condemnation, their death; but he never said a word to me, until one day he bade me show him that I loved him by my obedience and my trust. He took me a long carriage journey, where to I know not, for we never spoke of that day again; I was led through a prison, into a closed court-yard, where, decently draped in the last robes of death, concealing the marks of decapitation, lay M. de la Tourelle, and two or three others, whom I had known at Les Rochers.

After that conviction Dr. Voss tried to persuade me to return to a more natural mode of life, and to go out more. But although I sometimes complied with his wish, yet the old terror was ever strong upon me, and he, seeing what an effort it was, gave up urging me at last.

You know all the rest. How we both mourned bitterly the loss of that dear husband and father—for such I will call him ever—and as such you must consider him, my child, after this one revelation is over.

Why has it been made, you ask. For this reason, my child. The lover, whom you have only known as M. Lebrun, a French artist, told me but yesterday his real name, dropped because the blood-thirsty republicans might consider it as too aristocratic. It is Maurice de Poissy.

CURIOUS IF TRUE.

(EXTRACT FROM A LETTER FROM RICHARD WHITTINGHAM, ESQ.)

You were formerly so much amused at my pride in my descent from that sister of Calvin's, who married a Whittingham, Dean of Durham, that I doubt if you will be able to enter into the regard for my distinguished relation that has led me to France, in order to examine registers and archives, which, I thought, might enable me to discover collateral descendants of the great reformer, with whom I might call cousins. I shall not tell you of my troubles and adventures in this research; you are not worthy to hear of them; but something so curious befel me one evening last August, that if I had not been perfectly certain I was wide awake, I might have taken it for a dream.

For the purpose I have named, it was necessary that I should make Tours my head-quarters for a time. I had traced descendants of the Calvin family out of Normandy into the centre of France; but I found it was necessary to have a kind of permission from the bishop of the diocese before I could see certain family papers, which had fallen into the possession of the Church; and, as I had several English friends at Tours, I awaited the answer to my request to Monseigneur de ——, at that town. I was ready to accept any invitation; but I received very few; and was sometimes a little at a loss what to do with my evenings. The *table d'hôte* was at five o'clock; I did not wish to go to the expense of a private sitting-room, disliked the dinnery atmosphere of the *salle à manger*, could not play either at pool or billiards, and the aspect of my fellow guests was unprepossessing enough to make me unwilling to enter into any *tête-à-tête* gamblings with them. So I usually rose from table early, and tried to make the most of the remaining light of the August evenings in walking briskly off to explore the surrounding country; the middle of the day was too hot for this purpose, and better employed in lounging on a bench in the Boulevards, lazily listening to the distant band, and noticing with equal laziness the faces and figures of the women who passed by.

One Thursday evening, the 18th of August it was, I think, I had gone further than usual in my walk, and I found that it was later than I had imagined when I paused to turn back. I fancied I could make a round; I had enough notion of the direction in which I was, to see that by turning up a narrow straight lane to my left I should shorten my way back to Tours. And so I believe I should have done, could I have found an outlet at the right place, but field-paths are almost unknown in that part of France, and my lane, stiff and straight as any street, and marked into terribly vanishing perspective by the regular row of poplars on each side, seemed interminable. Of course night came on, and I was in darkness. In England I might have had a chance of seeing a light in some cottage only a field or two off, and asking my way from the inhabitants; but here I could see no such welcome sight; indeed, I believe French peasants go to bed with the summer daylight, so if there were any habitations in the neighbourhood I never saw them. At last—I believe I must have walked two hours in the darkness,—I saw the dusky outline of a wood on one side of the weariful lane, and, impatiently careless of all forest laws and penalties for trespassers, I made my way to it, thinking that if the worst came to the worst, I could find some covert—some shelter where I could lie down and rest, until the morning light gave me a chance of finding my way back to Tours. But the plantation, on the outskirts of what appeared to me a dense wood, was of young trees, too closely planted to be more than slender stems growing up to a good height, with scanty foliage on their summits. On I went towards the thicker forest, and once there I slackened my pace, and began to look about me for a good lair. I was as dainty as Lochiel's grandchild, who made his grandsire indignant at the luxury of his pillow of snow: this brake was too full of brambles, that felt damp with dew; there was no hurry, since I had given up all hope of passing the night between four walls; and I went leisurely groping about, and trusting that there were no wolves to be poked up out of their summer drowsiness by my stick, when all at once I saw a château before me, not a quarter of a mile off, at the end of what seemed to be an ancient avenue (now overgrown and irregular), which I happened to be crossing, when I looked to my right, and saw the welcome sight. Large, stately, and dark was its outline against the dusky night-sky; there were pepper-boxes and tourelles and what-not fantastically going up into the dim starlight. And more to the purpose still, though I could not see the details of the building that I was now facing, it was plain enough that there were lights in many windows, as if some great entertainment was going on.

"They are hospitable people, at any rate," thought I. "Perhaps they will give me a bed. I don't suppose French propriétaires have traps and horses quite as plentiful as English gentlemen; but they are evidently having a large party, and some of their guests may be from Tours, and will give me a cast back to the Lion d'Or. I am not proud, and I am dog-tired. I am not above hanging on behind, if need be."

So, putting a little briskness and spirit into my walk, I went up to the door, which was standing open, most hospitably, and showing a large lighted hall, all hung round with spoils of the chase, armour, &c., the details of which I had not time to notice, for the instant I stood on the threshold a huge porter appeared, in a strange, old-fashioned dress, a kind of livery which well befitted the general appearance of the house. He asked me, in French (so curiously pronounced that I thought I had hit upon a new kind of *patois*), my name, and whence I came. I thought he would not be much the wiser, still it was but civil to give it before I made my request for assistance; so, in reply, I said—

"My name is Whittingham—Richard Whittingham, an English gentleman, staying at ——." To my infinite surprise, a light of pleased intelligence came over the giant's face; he made me a low bow, and said (still in the same curious dialect) that I was welcome, that I was long expected.

"Long expected!" What could the fellow mean? Had I stumbled on a nest of relations by John Calvin's side, who had heard of my genealogical inquiries, and were gratified and interested by them? But I was too much pleased to be under shelter for the night to think it necessary to account for my agreeable reception before I enjoyed it. Just as he was opening the great heavy*battants* of the door that led from the hall to the interior, he turned round and said,—

"Apparently Monsieur le Géanquilleur is not come with you."

"No! I am all alone; I have lost my way,"—and I was going on with my explanation, when he, as if quite indifferent to it, led the way up a great stone staircase, as wide as many rooms, and having on each landing-place massive iron wickets, in a heavy framework; these the porter unlocked with the solemn slowness of age. Indeed, a strange, mysterious awe of the centuries that had passed away since this château was built, came over me as I waited for the turning of the ponderous keys in the ancient locks. I could almost have fancied that I heard a mighty rushing murmur (like the ceaseless sound of a distant sea, ebbing and flowing for ever and for ever), coming forth from the great vacant galleries that opened out on each side of the broad staircase, and were to be dimly perceived in the darkness above us. It was as if the voices of generations of men yet echoed and eddied in the silent air. It was strange, too, that my friend the porter going before me, ponderously infirm, with his feeble old hands striving in vain to keep the tall flambeau he held steadily before him,—strange, I say, that he was the only domestic I saw in the vast halls and passages, or met with on the grand staircase. At length we stood before the gilded doors that led into the saloon where the family—or it might be the company, so great was the buzz of voices—was assembled. I would have remonstrated when I found he was going to introduce me, dusty and travel-smeared, in a morning costume that was not even my best, into this grand *salon*, with nobody knew how many ladies and gentlemen assembled; but the obstinate old man was evidently bent upon taking me straight to his master, and paid no heed to my words.

The doors flew open, and I was ushered into a saloon curiously full of pale light, which did not culminate on any spot, nor proceed from any centre, nor flicker with any motion of the air, but filled every nook and corner, making all things deliciously distinct; different from our light of gas or candle, as is the difference between a clear southern atmosphere and that of our misty England.

At the first moment, my arrival excited no attention, the apartment was so full of people, all intent on their own conversation. But my friend the porter went up to a handsome lady of middle age, richly attired in that antique manner which fashion has brought round again of late years, and, waiting first in an attitude of deep respect till her attention fell upon him, told her my name and something about me, as far as I could guess from the gestures of the one and the sudden glance of the eye of the other.

She immediately came towards me with the most friendly actions of greeting, even before she had advanced near enough to speak. Then,—and was it not strange?—her words and accent were that of the commonest peasant of the country. Yet she herself looked high-bred, and would have been dignified had she been a shade less restless, had her countenance worn a little less lively and inquisitive expression. I had been poking a good deal about the old parts of Tours, and had had to understand the dialect of the people who dwelt in the Marché au Vendredi and similar places, or I really should not have understood my handsome hostess, as she offered to present me to her husband, a henpecked, gentlemanly man, who was more quaintly attired than she in the very extreme of that style of dress. I thought to myself that in France, as in England, it is the provincials who carry fashion to such an excess as to become ridiculous.

However, he spoke (still in the *patois*) of his pleasure in making my acquaintance, and led me to a strange uneasy easy-chair, much of a piece with the rest of the furniture, which might have taken its place without any anachronism by the side of that in the Hôtel Cluny. Then again began the clatter of French voices, which my arrival had for an instant interrupted, and I had leisure to look about me. Opposite to me sat a very sweet-looking lady, who must have been a great beauty in her youth, I should think, and would be charming in old age, from the sweetness of her countenance. She was, however, extremely fat, and on seeing her feet laid up before her on a cushion, I at once perceived that they were so swollen as to render her incapable of walking, which probably brought on her excessive *embonpoint*. Her hands were plump and small, but rather coarse-grained in texture, not quite so clean as they might have been, and altogether not so aristocratic-looking as the charming face. Her dress was of superb black velvet, ermine-trimmed, with diamonds thrown all abroad over it.

Not far from her stood the least little man I had ever seen; of such admirable proportions no one could call him a dwarf, because with that word we usually associate something of deformity; but yet with an elfin look of shrewd, hard, worldly wisdom in his face that marred the impression which his delicate regular little features would otherwise have conveyed. Indeed, I do not think he was quite of equal rank with the rest of the company, for his dress was inappropriate to the occasion (and he apparently was an invited, while I was an involuntary guest); and one or two of his gestures and actions were more like the tricks of an uneducated rustic than anything else. To explain what I mean: his boots had evidently seen much service, and had been re-topped, re-heeled, re-soled to the extent of cobbler's powers. Why should he have come in them if they were not his best—his only pair? And what can be more ungenteel than poverty? Then again he had an uneasy trick of putting his hand up to his throat, as if he expected to find something the matter with it; and he had the awkward habit—which I do not think he could have copied from Dr. Johnson, because most probably he had never heard of him—of trying always to retrace his steps on the exact boards on which he had trodden to arrive at any particular part of the room. Besides, to settle the question, I once heard him addressed as Monsieur Poucet, without any aristocratic "de" for a prefix; and nearly every one else in the room was a marquis, at any rate.

I say, "nearly every one;" for some strange people had the entrée; unless, indeed, they were, like me, benighted. One of the guests I should have taken for a servant, but for the extraordinary influence he seemed to have over the man I took for his master, and who never did anything without, apparently, being urged thereto by this follower. The master, magnificently dressed, but ill at ease in his clothes, as if they had been made for some one else, was a weak-looking, handsome man, continually sauntering about, and I almost guessed an object of suspicion to some of the gentlemen present, which, perhaps, drove him on the companionship of his follower, who was dressed something in the style of an ambassador's chasseur; yet it was not a chasseur's dress after all; it was something more thoroughly old-world; boots half way up his ridiculously small legs, which clattered as he walked along, as if they were too large for his little feet; and a great quantity of grey fur, as trimming to coat, court-mantle, boots, cap—everything. You know the way in which certain countenances remind you perpetually of some animal, be it bird or beast! Well, this chasseur (as I will call him for want of a better name) was exceedingly like the great Tom-cat that you have seen so often in my chambers, and laughed at almost as often for his uncanny gravity of demeanour. Grey whiskers has my Tom—grey whiskers had the chasseur: grey hair overshadows the upper lip of my Tom—grey mustachios hid that of the chasseur. The pupils of Tom's eyes dilate and contract as I had thought cats' pupils only could do, until I saw those of the chasseur. To be sure, canny as Tom is, the chasseur had the advantage in the more intelligent expression. He seemed to have obtained most complete sway over his master or patron, whose looks he watched, and whose steps he followed, with a kind of distrustful interest that puzzled me greatly.

There were several other groups in the more distant part of the saloon, all of the stately old school, all grand and noble, I conjectured from their bearing. They seemed perfectly well acquainted with each other, as if they were in the habit of meeting. But I was interrupted in my observations by the tiny little gentleman on the opposite side of the room coming across to take a place beside me. It is no difficult matter to a Frenchman to slide into conversation, and so gracefully did my pigmy friend keep up the character of the nation, that we were almost confidential before ten minutes had elapsed.

Now I was quite aware that the welcome which all had extended to me, from the porter up to the vivacious lady and meek lord of the castle, was intended for some other person. But it required either a degree of moral courage, of which I cannot boast, or the self-reliance and conversational powers of a bolder and cleverer man than I, to undeceive people who had fallen into so fortunate a mistake for me. Yet the little man by my side insinuated himself so much into my confidence, that I had half a mind to tell him of my exact situation, and to turn him into a friend and an ally.

"Madame is perceptibly growing older," said he, in the midst of my perplexity, glancing at our hostess.

"Madame is still a very fine woman," replied I.

"Now, is it not strange," continued he, lowering his voice, "how women almost invariably praise the absent, or departed, as if they were angels of light, while as for the present, or the living"—here he shrugged up his little shoulders, and made an expressive pause. "Would you believe it! Madame is always praising her late husband to monsieur's face; till, in fact, we guests are quite perplexed how to look: for, you know, the late M. de Retz's character was quite notorious,—everybody has heard of him." All the world of Touraine, thought I, but I made an assenting noise.

At this instant, monsieur our host came up to me, and with a civil look of tender interest (such as some people put on when they inquire after your mother, about whom they do not care one straw), asked if I had heard lately how my cat was? "How my cat was!" What could the man mean? My cat! Could he mean the tailless Tom, born in the Isle of Man, and now supposed to be keeping guard against the incursions of rats and mice into my chambers in London? Tom is, as you know, on pretty good terms with some of my friends, using their legs for rubbing-posts without scruple, and highly esteemed by them for his gravity of demeanour, and wise manner of winking his eyes. But could his fame have reached across the Channel? However, an answer must be returned to the inquiry, as monsieur's face was bent down to mine with a look of polite anxiety; so I, in my turn, assumed an expression of gratitude, and assured him that, to the best of my belief, my cat was in remarkably good health.

"And the climate agrees with her?"

"Perfectly," said I, in a maze of wonder at this deep solicitude in a tailless cat who had lost one foot and half an ear in some cruel trap. My host smiled a sweet smile, and, addressing a few words to my little neighbour, passed on.

"How wearisome those aristocrats are!" quoth my neighbour, with a slight sneer. "Monsieur's conversation rarely extends to more than two sentences to any one. By that time his faculties are exhausted, and he needs the refreshment of silence. You and I, monsieur, are, at any rate, indebted to our own wits for our rise in the world!"

Here again I was bewildered! As you know, I am rather proud of my descent from families which, if not noble themselves, are allied to nobility,—and as to my "rise in the world"—if I had risen, it would have been rather for balloon-like qualities than for mother-wit, to being unencumbered with heavy ballast either in my head or my pockets. However, it was my cue to agree: so I smiled again.

"For my part," said he, "if a man does not stick at trifles, if he knows how to judiciously add to, or withhold facts, and is not sentimental in his parade of humanity, he is sure to do well; sure to affix a *de* or *von* to his name, and end his days in comfort. There is an example of what I am saying"—and he glanced furtively at the weak-looking master of the sharp, intelligent servant, whom I have called the chasseur.

"Monsieur le Marquis would never have been anything but a miller's son, if it had not been for the talents of his servant. Of course you know his antecedents?"

I was going to make some remarks on the changes in the order of the peerage since the days of Louis XVI.—going, in fact, to be very sensible and historical—when there was a slight commotion among the people at the other end of the room. Lacqueys in quaint liveries must have come in from behind the tapestry, I suppose (for I never saw them enter, though I sate right opposite to the doors), and were handing about the slight beverages and slighter viands which are considered sufficient refreshments, but which looked rather meagre to my hungry appetite. These footmen were standing solemnly opposite to a lady,—beautiful, splendid as the dawn, but—sound asleep in a magnificent settee. A gentleman who showed so much irritation at her ill-timed slumbers, that I think he must have been her husband, was trying to awaken her with actions not far removed from shakings. All in vain; she was quite unconscious of his annoyance, or the smiles of the company, or the automatic solemnity of the waiting footman, or the perplexed anxiety of monsieur and madame.

My little friend sat down with a sneer, as if his curiosity was quenched in contempt.

"Moralists would make an infinity of wise remarks on that scene," said he. "In the first place, note the ridiculous position into which their superstitious reverence for rank and title puts all these people. Because monsieur is a reigning prince over some minute principality, the exact situation of which no one has as yet discovered, no one must venture to take their glass of eau sucré till Madame la Princesse awakens; and, judging from past experience, those poor lacqueys may have to stand for a century before that happens. Next—always speaking as a moralist, you will observe—note how difficult it is to break off bad habits acquired in youth!"

Just then the prince succeeded, by what means I did not see, in awaking the beautiful sleeper. But at first she did not remember where she was, and looking up at her husband with loving eyes, she smiled and said:

"Is it you, my prince?"

But he was too conscious of the suppressed amusement of the spectators and his own consequent annoyance, to be reciprocally tender, and turned away with some little French expression, best rendered into English by "Pooh, pooh, my dear!"

After I had had a glass of delicious wine of some unknown quality, my courage was in rather better plight than before, and I told my cynical little neighbour—whom I must say I was beginning to dislike—that I had lost my way in the wood, and had arrived at the château quite by mistake.

He seemed mightily amused at my story; said that the same thing had happened to himself more than once; and told me that I had better luck than he had on one of these occasions, when, from his account, he must have been in considerable danger of his life. He ended his story by making me admire his boots, which he said he still wore, patched though they were, and all their excellent quality lost by patching, because they were of such a first-rate make for long pedestrian excursions. "Though, indeed," he wound up by saying, "the new fashion of railroads would seem to supersede the necessity for this description of boots."

When I consulted him as to whether I ought to make myself known to my host and hostess as a benighted traveller, instead of the guest whom they had taken me for, he exclaimed, "By no means! I hate such squeamish morality." And he seemed much offended by my innocent question, as if it seemed by implication to condemn something in himself. He was offended and silent; and just at this moment I caught the sweet, attractive eyes of the lady opposite—that lady whom I named at first as being no longer in the bloom of youth, but as being somewhat infirm about the feet, which were supported on a raised cushion before her. Her looks seemed to say, "Come here, and let us have some conversation together;" and, with a bow of silent excuse to my little companion, I went across to the lame old lady. She acknowledged my coming with the prettiest gesture of thanks possible; and, half apologetically, said, "It is a little dull to be unable to move about on such evenings as this; but it is a just punishment to me for my early vanities. My poor feet, that were by nature so small, are now taking their revenge for my cruelty in forcing them into such little slippers....Besides, monsieur," with a pleasant smile, "I thought it was possible you might be weary of the malicious sayings of your little neighbour. He has not borne the best character in his youth, and such men are sure to be cynical in their old age."

"Who is he?" asked I, with English abruptness.

"His name is Poucet, and his father was, I believe, a wood-cutter, or charcoal burner, or something of the sort. They do tell sad stories of connivance at murder, ingratitude, and obtaining money on false pretences—but you will think me as bad as he if I go on with my slanders. Rather let us admire the lovely lady coming up towards us, with the roses in her hand—I never see her without roses, they are so closely connected with her past history, as you are doubtless aware. Ah, beauty!" said my companion to the lady drawing near to us, "it is like you to come to me, now that I can no longer go to you." Then turning to me, and gracefully drawing me into the conversation, she said, "You must know that, although we never met until we were both married, we have been almost like sisters ever since. There have been so many points of resemblance in our circumstances, and I think I may say in our characters. We had each two elder sisters—mine were but half-sisters, though—who were not so kind to us as they might have been."

"But have been sorry for it since," put in the other lady.

"Since we have married princes," continued the same lady, with an arch smile that had nothing of unkindness in it, "for we both have married far above our original stations in life; we are both unpunctual in our habits, and, in consequence of this failing of ours, we have both had to suffer mortification and pain."

"And both are charming," said a whisper close behind me. "My lord the marquis, say it—say, 'And both are charming.'"

"And both are charming," was spoken aloud by another voice. I turned, and saw the wily cat-like chasseur, prompting his master to make civil speeches.

The ladies bowed with that kind of haughty acknowledgment which shows that compliments from such a source are distasteful. But our trio of conversation was broken up, and I was sorry for it. The marquis looked as if he had been stirred up to make that one speech, and hoped that he would not be expected to say more; while behind him stood the chasseur, half impertinent and half servile in his ways and attitudes. The ladies, who were real ladies, seemed to be sorry for the awkwardness of the marquis, and addressed some trifling questions to him, adapting themselves to the subjects on which he could have no trouble in answering. The chasseur, meanwhile, was talking to himself in a growling tone of voice. I had fallen a little into the background at this interruption in a conversation which promised to be so pleasant, and I could not help hearing his words.

"Really, De Carabas grows more stupid every day. I have a great mind to throw off his boots, and leave him to his fate. I was intended for a court, and to a court I will go, and make my own fortune as I have made his. The emperor will appreciate my talents."

And such are the habits of the French, or such his forgetfulness of good manners in his anger, that he spat right and left on the parquetted floor.

Just then a very ugly, very pleasant-looking man, came towards the two ladies to whom I had lately been speaking, leading up to them a delicate, fair woman, dressed all in the softest white, as if she were *vouée au blanc*. I do not think there was a bit of colour about her. I thought I heard her making, as she came along, a little noise of pleasure, not exactly like the singing of a tea-kettle, nor yet like the cooing of a dove, but reminding me of each sound.

"Madame de Mioumiou was anxious to see you," said he, addressing the lady with the roses, "so I have brought her across to give you a pleasure!" What an honest, good face! but oh! how ugly! And yet I liked his ugliness better than most persons' beauty. There was a look of pathetic acknowledgment of his ugliness, and a deprecation of your too hasty judgment, in his countenance that was positively winning. The soft, white lady kept glancing at my neighbour the chasseur, as if they had had some former acquaintance, which puzzled me very much, as they were of such different rank. However, their nerves were evidently strung to the same tune, for at a sound behind the tapestry, which was more like the scuttering of rats and mice than anything else, both Madame de Mioumiou and the chasseur started with the most eager look of anxiety on their countenances, and by their restless movements—madame's panting, and the fiery dilation of his eyes—one might see that commonplace sounds affected them both in a manner very different to the rest of the company. The ugly husband of the lovely lady with the roses now addressed himself to me.

"We are much disappointed," he said, "in finding that monsieur is not accompanied by his countryman—le grand Jean d'Angleterre; I cannot pronounce his name rightly"—and he looked at me to help him out.

"Le grand Jean d'Angleterre!" now who was le grand Jean d'Angleterre? John Bull? John Russell? John Bright?

"Jean—Jean"—continued the gentleman, seeing my embarrassment. "Ah, these terrible English names—'Jean de Géanquilleur!'"

I was as wise as ever. And yet the name struck me as familiar, but slightly disguised. I repeated it to myself. It was mighty like John the Giant-killer, only his friends always call that worthy "Jack." I said the name aloud.

"Ah, that is it!" said he. "But why has he not accompanied you to our little reunion to-night?"

I had been rather puzzled once or twice before, but this serious question added considerably to my perplexity. Jack the Giant-killer had once, it is true, been rather an intimate friend of mine, as far as (printer's) ink and paper can keep up a friendship, but I had not heard his name mentioned for years; and for aught I knew he lay enchanted with King Arthur's knights, who lie entranced until the blast of the trumpets of four mighty kings shall call them to help at England's need. But the question had been asked in serious earnest by that gentleman, whom I more wished to think well of me than I did any other person in the room. So I answered respectfully that it was long since I had heard anything of my countryman; but that I was sure it would have given him as much pleasure as it was doing myself to have been present at such an agreeable gathering of friends. He bowed, and then the lame lady took up the word.

"To-night is the night when, of all the year, this great old forest surrounding the castle is said to be haunted by the phantom of a little peasant girl who once lived hereabouts; the tradition is that she was devoured by a wolf. In former days I have seen her on this night out of yonder window at the end of the gallery. Will you, ma belle, take monsieur to see the view outside by the moonlight (you may possibly see the phantom-child); and leave me to a little *tête-à-tête* with your husband?"

With a gentle movement the lady with the roses complied with the other's request, and we went to a great window, looking down on the forest, in which I had lost my way. The tops of the far-spreading and leafy trees lay motionless beneath us in that pale, wan light, which shows objects almost as distinct in form, though not in colour, as by day. We looked down on the countless avenues, which seemed to converge from all quarters to the great old castle; and suddenly across one, quite near to us, there passed the figure of a little girl, with the "capuchon" on, that takes the place of a peasant girl's bonnet in France. She had a basket on one arm, and by her, on the side to which her head was turned, there went a wolf. I could almost have said it was licking her hand, as if in penitent love, if either penitence or love had ever been a quality of wolves,—but though not of living, perhaps it may be of phantom wolves.

"There, we have seen her!" exclaimed my beautiful companion. "Though so long dead, her simple story of household goodness and trustful simplicity still lingers in the hearts of all who have ever heard of her; and the country-people about here say that seeing that phantom-child on this anniversary brings good luck for the year. Let us hope that we shall share in the traditionary good fortune. Ah! here is Madame de Retz—she retains the name of her first husband, you know, as he was of higher rank than the present." We were joined by our hostess.

"If monsieur is fond of the beauties of nature and art," said she, perceiving that I had been looking at the view from the great window, "he will perhaps take pleasure in seeing the picture." Here she sighed, with a little affectation of grief. "You know the picture I allude to," addressing my companion, who bowed assent, and smiled a little maliciously, as I followed the lead of madame.

I went after her to the other end of the saloon, noting by the way with what keen curiosity she caught up what was passing either in word or action on each side of her. When we stood opposite to the end wall, I perceived a full-length picture of a handsome, peculiar-looking man, with—in spite of his good looks—a very fierce and scowling expression. My hostess clasped her hands together as her arms hung down in front, and sighed once more. Then, half in soliloquy, she said—

"He was the love of my youth; his stern yet manly character first touched this heart of mine. When—when shall I cease to deplore his loss!"

Not being acquainted with her enough to answer this question (if, indeed, it were not sufficiently answered by the fact of her second marriage), I felt awkward; and, by way of saying something, I remarked,—

"The countenance strikes me as resembling something I have seen before—in an engraving from an historical picture, I think; only, it is there the principal figure in a group: he is holding a lady by her hair, and threatening her with his scimitar, while two cavaliers are rushing up the stairs, apparently only just in time to save her life."

"Alas, alas!" said she, "you too accurately describe a miserable passage in my life, which has often been represented in a false light. The best of husbands"—here she sobbed, and became slightly inarticulate with her grief—"will sometimes be displeased. I was young and curious, he was justly angry with my disobedience—my brothers were too hasty—the consequence is, I became a widow!"

After due respect for her tears, I ventured to suggest some commonplace consolation. She turned round sharply:—

"No, monsieur: my only comfort is that I have never forgiven the brothers who interfered so cruelly, in such an uncalled-for manner, between my dear husband and myself. To quote my friend Monsieur Sganarelle—'Ce sont petites choses qui sont de temps en temps necessaires dans l'amitié; et cinq ou six coups d'épée entre gens qui s'aiment ne font que ragaillardir l'affection.' You observe the colouring is not quite what it should be?"

"In this light the beard is of rather a peculiar tint," said I.

"Yes: the painter did not do it justice. It was most lovely, and gave him such a distinguished air, quite different from the common herd. Stay, I will show you the exact colour, if you will come near this flambeau!" And going near the light, she took off a bracelet of hair, with a magnificent clasp of pearls. It was peculiar, certainly. I did not know what to say. "His precious lovely beard!" said she. "And the pearls go so well with the delicate blue!"

Her husband, who had come up to us, and waited till her eye fell upon him before venturing to speak, now said, "It is strange Monsieur Ogre is not yet arrived!"

"Not at all strange," said she, tartly. "He was always very stupid, and constantly falls into mistakes, in which he comes worse off; and it is very well he does, for he is a credulous and cowardly fellow. Not at all strange! If you will"—turning to her husband, so that I hardly heard her words, until I caught—"Then everybody would have their rights, and we should have no more trouble. Is it not, monsieur?" addressing me.

"If I were in England, I should imagine madame was speaking of the reform bill, or the millennium,—but I am in ignorance."

And just as I spoke, the great folding-doors were thrown open wide, and every one started to their feet to greet a little old lady, leaning on a thin black wand—and—

"Madame la Féemarraine," was announced by a chorus of sweet shrill voices.

And in a moment I was lying in the grass close by a hollow oak-tree, with the slanting glory of the dawning day shining full in my face, and thousands of little birds and delicate insects piping and warbling out their welcome to the ruddy splendour.

SIX WEEKS AT HEPPENHEIM.

After I left Oxford, I determined to spend some months in travel before settling down in life. My father had left me a few thousands, the income arising from which would be enough to provide for all the necessary requirements of a lawyer's education; such as lodgings in a quiet part of London, fees and payment to the distinguished barrister with whom I was to read; but there would be small surplus left over for luxuries or amusements; and as I was rather in debt on leaving college, since I had forestalled my income, and the expenses of my travelling would have to be defrayed out of my capital, I determined that they should not exceed fifty pounds. As long as that sum would last me I would remain abroad; when it was spent my holiday should be over, and I would return and settle down somewhere in the neighbourhood of Russell Square, in order to be near Mr. ——'s chambers in Lincoln's-inn. I had to wait in London for one day while my passport was being made out, and I went to examine the streets in which I purposed to live; I had picked them out, from studying a map, as desirable; and so they were, if judged entirely by my reason; but their aspect was very depressing to one country-bred, and just fresh from the beautiful street-architecture of Oxford. The thought of living in such a monotonous gray district for years made me all the more anxious to prolong my holiday by all the economy which could eke out my fifty pounds. I thought I could make it last for one hundred days at least. I was a good walker, and had no very luxurious tastes in the matter of accommodation or food; I had as fair a knowledge of German and French as any untravelled Englishman can have; and I resolved to avoid expensive hotels such as my own countrymen frequented.

I have stated this much about myself to explain how I fell in with the little story that I am going to record, but with which I had not much to do,—my part in it being little more than that of a sympathizing spectator. I had been through France into Switzerland, where I had gone beyond my strength in the way of walking, and I was on my way home, when one evening I came to the village of Heppenheim, on the Berg-Strasse. I had strolled about the dirty town of Worms all morning, and dined in a filthy hotel; and after that I had crossed the Rhine, and walked through Lorsch to Heppenheim. I was unnaturally tired and languid as I dragged myself up the rough-paved and irregular village street to the inn recommended to me. It was a large building, with a green court before it. A cross-looking but scrupulously clean hostess received me, and showed me into a large room with a dinner-table in it, which, though it might have accommodated thirty or forty guests, only stretched down half the length of the eating-room. There were windows at each end of the room; two looked to the front of the house, on which the evening shadows had already fallen; the opposite two were partly doors, opening into a large garden full of trained fruit-trees and beds of vegetables, amongst which rose-bushes and other flowers seemed to grow by permission, not by original intention. There was a stove at each end of the room, which, I suspect, had originally been divided into two. The door by which I had entered was exactly in the middle, and opposite to it was another, leading to a great bed-chamber, which my hostess showed me as my sleeping quarters for the night.

If the place had been much less clean and inviting, I should have remained there; I was almost surprised myself at my vis inertiæ; once seated in the last warm rays of the slanting sun by the garden window, I was disinclined to move, or even to speak. My hostess had taken my orders as to my evening meal, and had left me. The sun went down, and I grew shivery. The vast room looked cold and bare; the darkness brought out shadows that perplexed me, because I could not fully make out the objects that produced them after dazzling my eyes by gazing out into the crimson light.

Some one came in; it was the maiden to prepare for my supper. She began to lay the cloth at one end of the large table. There was a smaller one close by me. I mustered up my voice, which seemed a little as if it was getting beyond my control, and called to her,—

"Will you let me have my supper here on this table?"

She came near; the light fell on her while I was in shadow. She was a tall young woman, with a fine strong figure, a pleasant face, expressive of goodness and sense, and with a good deal of comeliness about it, too, although the fair complexion was bronzed and reddened by weather, so as to have lost much of its delicacy, and the features, as I had afterwards opportunity enough of observing, were anything but regular. She had white teeth, however, and well-opened blue eyes—grave-looking eyes which had shed tears for past sorrow—plenty of light-brown hair, rather elaborately plaited, and fastened up by two great silver pins. That was all—perhaps more than all—I noticed that first night. She began to lay the cloth where I had directed. A shiver passed over me: she looked at me, and then said,—

"The gentleman is cold: shall I light the stove?"

Something vexed me—I am not usually so impatient: it was the coming-on of serious illness—I did not like to be noticed so closely; I believed that food would restore me, and I did not want to have my meal delayed, as I feared it might be by the lighting of the stove; and most of all I was feverishly annoyed by movement. I answered sharply and abruptly,—

"No; bring supper quickly; that is all I want."

Her quiet, sad eyes met mine for a moment; but I saw no change in their expression, as if I had vexed her by my rudeness: her countenance did not for an instant lose its look of patient sense, and that is pretty nearly all I can remember of Thekla that first evening at Heppenheim.

I suppose I ate my supper, or tried to do so, at any rate; and I must have gone to bed, for days after I became conscious of lying there, weak as a new-born babe, and with a sense of past pain in all my weary limbs. As is the case in recovering from fever, one does not care to connect facts, much less to reason upon them; so how I came to be lying in that strange bed, in that large, half-furnished room; in what house that room was; in what town, in what country, I did not take the trouble to recal. It was of much more consequence to me then to discover what was the well-known herb that gave the scent to the clean, coarse sheets in which I lay. Gradually I extended my observations, always confining myself to the present. I must have been well cared-for by some one, and that lately, too, for the window was shaded, so as to prevent the morning sun from coming in upon the bed; there was the crackling of fresh wood in the great white china stove, which must have been newly replenished within a short time.

By-and-by the door opened slowly. I cannot tell why, but my impulse was to shut my eyes as if I were still asleep. But I could see through my apparently closed eyelids. In came, walking on tip-toe, with a slow care that defeated its object, two men. The first was aged from thirty to forty, in the dress of a Black Forest peasant,—old-fashioned coat and knee-breeches of strong blue cloth, but of a thoroughly good quality; he was followed by an older man, whose dress, of more pretension as to cut and colour (it was all black), was, nevertheless, as I had often the opportunity of observing afterwards, worn threadbare.

Their first sentences, in whispered German, told me who they were: the landlord of the inn where I was lying a helpless log, and the village doctor who had been called in. The latter felt my pulse, and nodded his head repeatedly in approbation. I had instinctively known that I was getting better, and hardly cared for this confirmation; but it seemed to give the truest pleasure to the landlord, who shook the hand of the doctor, in a pantomime expressive of as much thankfulness as if I had been his brother. Some low-spoken remarks were made, and then some question was asked, to which, apparently, my host was unable to reply. He left the room, and in a minute or two returned, followed by Thekla, who was questioned by the doctor, and replied with a quiet clearness, showing how carefully the details of my illness had been observed by her. Then she left the room, and, as if every minute had served to restore to my brain its power of combining facts, I was suddenly prompted to open my eyes, and ask in the best German I could muster what day of the month it was; not that I clearly remembered the date of my arrival at Heppenheim, but I knew it was about the beginning of September.

Again the doctor conveyed his sense of extreme satisfaction in a series of rapid pantomimic nods, and then replied in deliberate but tolerable English, to my great surprise,—

"It is the 29th of September, my dear sir. You must thank the dear God. Your fever has made its course of twenty-one days. Now patience and care must be practised. The good host and his household will have the care; you must have the patience. If you have relations in England, I will do my endeavours to tell them the state of your health."

"I have no near relations," said I, beginning in my weakness to cry, as I remembered, as if it had been a dream, the days when I had father, mother, sister.

"Chut, chut!" said he; then, turning to the landlord, he told him in German to make Thekla bring me one of her good bouillons; after which I was to have certain medicines, and to sleep as undisturbedly as possible. For days, he went on, I should require constant watching and careful feeding; every twenty minutes I was to have something, either wine or soup, in small quantities.

A dim notion came into my hazy mind that my previous husbandry of my fifty pounds, by taking long walks and scanty diet, would prove in the end very bad economy; but I sank into dozing unconsciousness before I could quite follow out my idea. I was roused by the touch of a spoon on my lips; it was Thekla feeding me. Her sweet, grave face had something approaching to a mother's look of tenderness upon it, as she gave me spoonful after spoonful with gentle patience and dainty care: and then I fell asleep once more. When next I wakened it was night; the stove was lighted, and the burning wood made a pleasant crackle, though I could only see the outlines and edges of red flame through the crevices of the small iron door. The uncurtained window on my left looked into the purple, solemn night. Turning a little, I saw Thekla sitting near a table, sewing diligently at some great white piece of household work. Every now and then she stopped to snuff the candle; sometimes she began to ply her needle again immediately; but once or twice she let her busy hands lie idly in her lap, and looked into the darkness, and thought deeply for a moment or two; these pauses always ended in a kind of sobbing sigh, the sound of which seemed to restore her to self-consciousness, and she took to her sewing even more diligently than before. Watching her had a sort of dreamy interest for me; this diligence of hers was a pleasant contrast to my repose; it seemed to enhance the flavour of my rest. I was too much of an animal just then to have my sympathy, or even my curiosity, strongly excited by her look of sad remembrance, or by her sighs.

After a while she gave a little start, looked at a watch lying by her on the table, and came, shading the candle by her hand, softly to my bedside. When she saw my open eyes she went to a porringer placed at the top of the stove, and fed me with soup. She did not speak while doing this. I was half aware that she had done it many times since the doctor's visit, although this seemed to be the first time that I was fully awake. She passed her arm under the pillow on which my head rested, and raised me a very little; her support was as firm as a man's could have been. Again back to her work, and I to my slumbers, without a word being exchanged.

It was broad daylight when I wakened again; I could see the sunny atmosphere of the garden outside stealing in through the nicks at the side of the shawl hung up to darken the room—a shawl which I was sure had not been there when I had observed the window in the night. How gently my nurse must have moved about while doing her thoughtful act!

My breakfast was brought me by the hostess; she who had received me on my first arrival at this hospitable inn. She meant to do everything kindly, I am sure; but a sick room was not her place; by a thousand little mal-adroitnesses she fidgeted me past bearing; her shoes creaked, her dress rustled; she asked me questions about myself which it irritated me to answer; she congratulated me on being so much better, while I was faint for want of the food which she delayed giving me in order to talk. My host had more sense in him when he came in, although his shoes creaked as well as hers. By this time I was somewhat revived, and could talk a little; besides, it seemed churlish to be longer without acknowledging so much kindness received.

"I am afraid I have been a great trouble," said I. "I can only say that I am truly grateful."

His good broad face reddened, and he moved a little uneasily.

"I don't see how I could have done otherwise than I——than we, did," replied he, in the soft German of the district. "We were all glad enough to do what we could; I don't say it was a pleasure, because it is our busiest time of year,—but then," said he, laughing a little awkwardly, as if he feared his expression might have been misunderstood, "I don't suppose it has been a pleasure to you either, sir, to be laid up so far from home."

"No, indeed."

"I may as well tell you now, sir, that we had to look over your papers and clothes. In the first place, when you were so ill I would fain have let your kinsfolk know, if I could have found a clue; and besides, you needed linen."

"I am wearing a shirt of yours though," said I, touching my sleeve.

"Yes, sir!" said he again, reddening a little. "I told Thekla to take the finest out of the chest; but I am afraid you find it coarser than your own."

For all answer I could only lay my weak hand on the great brown paw resting on the bed-side. He gave me a sudden squeeze in return that I thought would have crushed my bones.

"I beg your pardon, sir," said he, misinterpreting the sudden look of pain which I could not repress; "but watching a man come out of the shadow of death into life makes one feel very friendly towards him."

"No old or true friend that I have had could have done more for me than you, and your wife, and Thekla, and the good doctor."

"I am a widower," said he, turning round the great wedding-ring that decked his third finger. "My sister keeps house for me, and takes care of the children,—that is to say, she does it with the help of Thekla, the house-maiden. But I have other servants," he continued. "I am well to do, the good God be thanked! I have land, and cattle, and vineyards. It will soon be our vintage-time, and then you must go and see my grapes as they come into the village. I have a *'chasse'*, too, in the Odenwald; perhaps one day you will be strong enough to go and shoot the *'chevreuil'* with me."

His good, true heart was trying to make me feel like a welcome guest. Some time afterwards I learnt from the doctor that—my poor fifty pounds being nearly all expended—my host and he had been brought to believe in my poverty, as the necessary examination of my clothes and papers showed so little evidence of wealth. But I myself have but little to do with my story; I only name these things, and repeat these conversations, to show what a true, kind, honest man my host was. By the way, I may as well call him by his name henceforward, Fritz Müller. The doctor's name, Wiedermann.

I was tired enough with this interview with Fritz Müller; but when Dr. Wiedermann came he pronounced me to be much better; and through the day much the same course was pursued as on the previous one: being fed, lying still, and sleeping, were my passive and active occupations. It was a hot, sunshiny day, and I craved for air. Fresh air does not enter into the pharmacopœia of a German doctor; but somehow I obtained my wish. During the morning hours the window through which the sun streamed—the window looking on to the front court—was opened a little; and through it I heard the sounds of active life, which gave me pleasure and interest enough. The hen's cackle, the cock's exultant call when he had found the treasure of a grain of corn,—the movements of a tethered donkey, and the cooing and whirring of the pigeons which lighted on the window-sill, gave me just subjects enough for interest. Now and then a cart or carriage drove up,—I could hear them ascending the rough village street long before they stopped at the "Halbmond," the village inn. Then there came a sound of running and haste in the house; and Thekla was always called for in sharp, imperative tones. I heard little children's footsteps, too, from time to time; and once there must have been some childish accident or hurt, for a shrill, plaintive little voice kept calling out, "Thekla, Thekla, liebe Thekla." Yet, after the first early morning hours, when my hostess attended on my wants, it was always Thekla who came to give me my food or my medicine; who redded up my room; who arranged the degree of light, shifting the temporary curtain with the shifting sun; and always as quietly and deliberately as though her attendance upon me were her sole work. Once or twice my hostess came into the large eating-room (out of which my room opened), and called Thekla away from whatever was her occupation in my room at the time, in a sharp, injured, imperative whisper. Once I remember it was to say that sheets were wanted for some stranger's bed, and to ask where she, the speaker, could have put the keys, in a tone of irritation, as though Thekla were responsible for Fräulein Müller's own forgetfulness.

Night came on; the sounds of daily life died away into silence; the children's voices were no more heard; the poultry were all gone to roost; the beasts of burden to their stables; and travellers were housed. Then Thekla came in softly and quietly, and took up her appointed place, after she had done all in her power for my comfort. I felt that I was in no state to be left all those weary hours which intervened between sunset and sunrise; but I did feel ashamed that this young woman, who had watched by me all the previous night, and for aught I knew, for many before, and had worked hard, been run off her legs, as English servants would say, all day long, should come and take up her care of me again; and it was with a feeling of relief that I saw her head bend forwards, and finally rest on her arms, which had fallen on the white piece of sewing spread before her on the table. She slept; and I slept. When I wakened dawn was stealing into the room, and making pale the lamplight. Thekla was standing by the stove, where she had been preparing the bouillon I should require on wakening. But she did not notice my half-open eyes, although her face was turned towards the bed. She was reading a letter slowly, as if its words were familiar to her, yet as though she were trying afresh to extract some fuller or some different meaning from their construction. She folded it up softly and slowly, and replaced it in her pocket with the quiet movement habitual to her. Then she looked before her, not at me, but at vacancy filled up by memories; and as the enchanter brought up the scenes and people which she saw, but I could not, her eyes filled with tears—tears that gathered almost imperceptibly to herself as it would seem—for when one large drop fell on her hands (held slightly together before her as she stood) she started a little, and brushed her eyes with the back of her hand, and then came towards the bed to see if I was awake. If I had not witnessed her previous emotion, I could never have guessed that she had any hidden sorrow or pain from her manner; tranquil, self-restrained as usual. The thought of this letter haunted me, especially as more than once I, wakeful or watchful during the ensuing nights, either saw it in her hands, or suspected that she had been recurring to it from noticing the same sorrowful, dreamy look upon her face when she thought herself unobserved. Most likely every one has noticed how inconsistently out of proportion some ideas become when one is shut up in any place without change of scene or thought. I really grew quite irritated about this letter. If I did not see it, I suspected it lay *perdu* in her pocket. What was in it? Of course it was a love-letter; but if so, what was going wrong in the course of her love? I became like a spoilt child in my recovery; every one whom I saw for the time being was thinking only of me, so it was perhaps no wonder that I became my sole object of thought; and at last the gratification of my curiosity about this letter seemed to me a duty that I owed to myself. As long as my fidgety inquisitiveness remained ungratified, I felt as if I could not get well. But to do myself justice, it was more than inquisitiveness. Thekla had tended me with the gentle, thoughtful care of a sister, in the midst of her busy life. I could often hear the Fräulein's sharp voice outside blaming her for something that had gone wrong; but I never heard much from Thekla in reply. Her name was called in various tones by different people, more frequently than I could count, as if her services were in perpetual requisition, yet I was never neglected, or even long uncared-for. The doctor was kind and attentive; my host friendly and really generous; his sister subdued her acerbity of manner when in my room, but Thekla was the one of all to whom I owed my comforts, if not my life. If I could do anything to smooth her path (and a little money goes a great way in these primitive parts of Germany), how willingly would I give it? So one night I began—she was no longer needed to watch by my bedside, but she was arranging my room before leaving me for the night—

"Thekla," said I, "you don't belong to Heppenheim, do you?"

She looked at me, and reddened a little.

"No. Why do you ask?"

"You have been so good to me that I cannot help wanting to know more about you. I must needs feel interested in one who has been by my side through my illness as you have. Where do your friends live? Are your parents alive?"

All this time I was driving at the letter.

"I was born at Altenahr. My father is an innkeeper there. He owns the 'Golden Stag.' My mother is dead, and he has married again, and has many children."

"And your stepmother is unkind to you," said I, jumping to a conclusion.

"Who said so?" asked she, with a shade of indignation in her tone. "She is a right good woman, and makes my father a good wife."

"Then why are you here living so far from home?"

Now the look came back to her face which I had seen upon it during the night hours when I had watched her by stealth; a dimming of the grave frankness of her eyes, a light quiver at the corners of her mouth. But all she said was, "It was better."

Somehow, I persisted with the wilfulness of an invalid. I am half ashamed of it now.

"But why better, Thekla? Was there——" How should I put it? I stopped a little, and then rushed blindfold at my object: "Has not that letter which you read so often something to do with your being here?"

She fixed me with her serious eyes till I believe I reddened far more than she; and I hastened to pour out, incoherently enough, my conviction that she had some secret care, and my desire to help her if she was in any trouble.

"You cannot help me," said she, a little softened by my explanation, though some shade of resentment at having been thus surreptitiously watched yet lingered in her manner. "It is an old story; a sorrow gone by, past, at least it ought to be, only sometimes I am foolish"—her tones were softening now—"and it is punishment enough that you have seen my folly."

"If you had a brother here, Thekla, you would let him give you his sympathy if he could not give you his help, and you would not blame yourself if you had shown him your sorrow, should you? I tell you again, let me be as a brother to you."

"In the first place, sir"—this "sir" was to mark the distinction between me and the imaginary brother—"I should have been ashamed to have shown even a brother my sorrow, which is also my reproach and my disgrace." These were strong words; and I suppose my face showed that I attributed to them a still stronger meaning than they warranted; but *honi soit qui mal y pense*—for she went on dropping her eyes and speaking hurriedly.

"My shame and my reproach is this: I have loved a man who has not loved me"—she grasped her hands together till the fingers made deep white dents in the rosy flesh—"and I can't make out whether he ever did, or whether he did once and is changed now; if only he did once love me, I could forgive myself."

With hasty, trembling hands she began to rearrange the tisane and medicines for the night on the little table at my bed-side. But, having got thus far, I was determined to persevere.

"Thekla," said I, "tell me all about it, as you would to your mother, if she were alive. There are often misunderstandings which, never set to rights, make the misery and desolation of a life-time."

She did not speak at first. Then she pulled out the letter, and said, in a quiet, hopeless tone of voice:—

"You can read German writing? Read that, and see if I have any reason for misunderstanding."

The letter was signed "Franz Weber," and dated from some small town in Switzerland—I forget what—about a month previous to the time when I read it. It began with acknowledging the receipt of some money which had evidently been requested by the writer, and for which the thanks were almost fulsome; and then, by the quietest transition in the world, he went on to consult her as to the desirability of his marrying some girl in the place from which he wrote, saying that this Anna Somebody was only eighteen and very pretty, and her father a well-to-do shopkeeper, and adding, with coarse coxcombry, his belief that he was not indifferent to the maiden herself. He wound up by saying that, if this marriage did take place, he should certainly repay the various sums of money which Thekla had lent him at different times.

I was some time in making out all this. Thekla held the candle for me to read it; held it patiently and steadily, not speaking a word till I had folded up the letter again, and given it back to her. Then our eyes met.

"There is no misunderstanding possible, is there, sir?" asked she, with a faint smile.

"No," I replied; "but you are well rid of such a fellow."

She shook her head a little. "It shows his bad side, sir. We have all our bad sides. You must not judge him harshly; at least, I cannot. But then we were brought up together."

"At Altenahr?"

"Yes; his father kept the other inn, and our parents, instead of being rivals, were great friends. Franz is a little younger than I, and was a delicate child. I had to take him to school, and I used to be so proud of it and of my charge. Then he grew strong, and was the handsomest lad in the village. Our fathers used to sit and smoke together, and talk of our marriage, and Franz must have heard as much as I. Whenever he was in trouble, he would come to me for what advice I could give him; and he danced twice as often with me as with any other girl at all the dances, and always brought his nosegay to me. Then his father wished him to travel, and learn the ways at the great hotels on the Rhine before he settled down in Altenahr. You know that is the custom in Germany, sir. They go from town to town as journeymen, learning something fresh everywhere, they say."

"I knew that was done in trades," I replied.

"Oh, yes; and among inn-keepers, too," she said. "Most of the waiters at the great hotels in Frankfort, and Heidelberg, and Mayence, and, I daresay, at all the other places, are the sons of innkeepers in small towns, who go out into the world to learn new ways, and perhaps to pick up a little English and French; otherwise, they say, they should never get on. Franz went off from Altenahr on his journeyings four years ago next May-day; and before he went, he brought me back a ring from Bonn, where he bought his new clothes. I don't wear it now; but I have got it upstairs, and it comforts me to see something that shows me it was not all my silly fancy. I suppose he fell among bad people, for he soon began to play for money,—and then he lost more than he could always pay—and sometimes I could help him a little, for we wrote to each other from time to time, as we knew each other's addresses; for the little ones grew around my father's hearth, and I thought that I, too, would go forth into the world and earn my own living, so that——well, I will tell the truth—I thought that by going into service, I could lay by enough for buying a handsome stock of household linen, and plenty of pans and kettles against—against what will never come to pass now."

"Do the German women buy the pots and kettles, as you call them, when they are married?" asked I, awkwardly, laying hold of a trivial question to conceal the indignant sympathy with her wrongs which I did not like to express.

"Oh, yes; the bride furnishes all that is wanted in the kitchen, and all the store of house-linen. If my mother had lived, it would have been laid by for me, as she could have afforded to buy it, but my stepmother will have hard enough work to provide for her own four little girls. However," she continued, brightening up, "I can help her, for now I shall never marry; and my master here is just and liberal, and pays me sixty florins a year, which is high wages." (Sixty florins are about five pounds sterling.) "And now, good-night, sir. This cup to the left holds the tisane, that to the right the acorn-tea." She shaded the candle, and was leaving the room. I raised myself on my elbow, and called her back.

"Don't go on thinking about this man," said I. "He was not good enough for you. You are much better unmarried."

"Perhaps so," she answered gravely. "But you cannot do him justice; you do not know him."

A few minutes after, I heard her soft and cautious return; she had taken her shoes off, and came in her stockinged feet up to my bedside, shading the light with her hand. When she saw that my eyes were open, she laid down two letters on the table, close by my night-lamp.

"Perhaps, some time, sir, you would take the trouble to read these letters; you would then see how noble and clever Franz really is. It is I who ought to be blamed, not he."

No more was said that night.

Some time the next morning I read the letters. They were filled with vague, inflated, sentimental descriptions of his inner life and feelings; entirely egotistical, and intermixed with quotations from second-rate philosophers and poets. There was, it must be said, nothing in them offensive to good principle or good feeling, however much they might be opposed to good taste. I was to go into the next room that afternoon for the first time of leaving my sick chamber. All morning I lay and ruminated. From time to time I thought of Thekla and Franz Weber. She was the strong, good, helpful character, he the weak and vain; how strange it seemed that she should have cared for one so dissimilar; and then I remembered the various happy marriages when[**where?] to an outsider it seemed as if one was so inferior to the other that their union would have appeared a subject for despair if it had been looked at prospectively. My host came in, in the midst of these meditations, bringing a great flowered dressing-gown, lined with flannel, and the embroidered smoking-cap which he evidently considered as belonging to this Indian-looking robe. They had been his father's, he told me; and as he helped me to dress, he went on with his communications on small family matters. His inn was flourishing; the numbers increased every year of those who came to see the church at Heppenheim: the church which was the pride of the place, but which I had never yet seen. It was built by the great Kaiser Karl. And there was the Castle of Starkenburg, too, which the Abbots of Lorsch had often defended, stalwart churchmen as they were, against the temporal power of the emperors. And Melibocus was not beyond a walk either. In fact, it was the work of one person to superintend the inn alone; but he had his farm and his vineyards beyond, which of themselves gave him enough to do. And his sister was oppressed with the perpetual calls made upon her patience and her nerves in an inn; and would rather go back and live at Worms. And his children wanted so much looking after. By the time he had placed himself in a condition for requiring my full sympathy, I had finished my slow toilette; and I had to interrupt his confidences, and accept the help of his good strong arm to lead me into the great eating-room, out of which my chamber opened. I had a dreamy recollection of the vast apartment. But how pleasantly it was changed! There was the bare half of the room, it is true, looking as it had done on that first afternoon, sunless and cheerless, with the long, unoccupied table, and the necessary chairs for the possible visitors; but round the windows that opened on the garden a part of the room was enclosed by the household clothes'-horses hung with great pieces of the blue homespun cloth of which the dress of the Black Forest peasant is made. This shut-in space was warmed by the lighted stove, as well as by the lowering rays of the October sun. There was a little round walnut table with some flowers upon it, and a great cushioned armchair placed so as to look out upon the garden and the hills beyond. I felt sure that this was all Thekla's arrangement; I had rather wondered that I had seen so little of her this day. She had come once or twice on necessary errands into my room in the morning, but had appeared to be in great haste, and had avoided meeting my eye. Even when I had returned the letters, which she had entrusted to me with so evident a purpose of placing the writer in my good opinion, she had never inquired as to how far they had answered her design; she had merely taken them with some low word of thanks, and put them hurriedly into her pocket. I suppose she shrank from remembering how fully she had given me her confidence the night before, now that daylight and actual life pressed close around her. Besides, there surely never was anyone in such constant request as Thekla. I did not like this estrangement, though it was the natural consequence of my improved health, which would daily make me less and less require services which seemed so urgently claimed by others. And, moreover, after my host left me—I fear I had cut him a little short in the recapitulation of his domestic difficulties, but he was too thorough and good-hearted a man to bear malice—I wanted to be amused or interested. So I rang my little hand-bell, hoping that Thekla would answer it, when I could have fallen into conversation with her, without specifying any decided want. Instead of Thekla the Fräulein came, and I had to invent a wish; for I could not act as a baby, and say that I wanted my nurse. However, the Fräulein was better than no one, so I asked her if I could have some grapes, which had been provided for me on every day but this, and which were especially grateful to my feverish palate. She was a good, kind woman, although, perhaps, her temper was not the best in the world; and she expressed the sincerest regret as she told me that there were no more in the house. Like an invalid I fretted at my wish not being granted, and spoke out.

"But Thekla told me the vintage was not till the fourteenth; and you have a vineyard close beyond the garden on the slope of the hill out there, have you not?"

"Yes; and grapes for the gathering. But perhaps the gentleman does not know our laws. Until the vintage—(the day of beginning the vintage is fixed by the Grand Duke, and advertised in the public papers)—until the vintage, all owners of vineyards may only go on two appointed days in every week to gather their grapes; on those two days (Tuesdays and Fridays this year) they must gather enough for the wants of their families; and if they do not reckon rightly, and gather short measure, why they have to go without. And these two last days the Half-Moon has been besieged with visitors, all of whom have asked for grapes. But to-morrow the gentleman can have as many as he will; it is the day for gathering them."

"What a strange kind of paternal law," I grumbled out. "Why is it so ordained? Is it to secure the owners against pilfering from their unfenced vineyards?"

"I am sure I cannot tell," she replied. "Country people in these villages have strange customs in many ways, as I daresay the English gentleman has perceived. If he would come to Worms he would see a different kind of life."

"But not a view like this," I replied, caught by a sudden change of light—some cloud passing away from the sun, or something. Right outside of the windows was, as I have so often said, the garden. Trained plum-trees with golden leaves, great bushes of purple, Michaelmas daisy, late flowering roses, apple-trees partly stripped of their rosy fruit, but still with enough left on their boughs to require the props set to support the luxuriant burden; to the left an arbour covered over with honeysuckle and other sweet-smelling creepers—all bounded by a low gray stone wall which opened out upon the steep vineyard, that stretched up the hill beyond, one hill of a series rising higher and higher into the purple distance. "Why is there a rope with a bunch of straw tied in it stretched across the opening of the garden into the vineyard?" I inquired, as my eye suddenly caught upon the object.

"It is the country way of showing that no one must pass along that path. To-morrow the gentleman will see it removed; and then he shall have the grapes. Now I will go and prepare his coffee." With a curtsey, after the fashion of Worms gentility, she withdrew. But an under-servant brought me my coffee; and with her I could not exchange a word: she spoke in such an execrable patois. I went to bed early, weary, and depressed. I must have fallen asleep immediately, for I never heard any one come to arrange my bed-side table; yet in the morning I found that every usual want or wish of mine had been attended to.

I was wakened by a tap at my door, and a pretty piping child's voice asking, in broken German, to come in. On giving the usual permission, Thekla entered, carrying a great lovely boy of two years old, or thereabouts, who had only his little night-shirt on, and was all flushed with sleep. He held tight in his hands a great cluster of muscatel and noble grapes. He seemed like a little Bacchus, as she carried him towards me with an expression of pretty loving pride upon her face as she looked at him. But when he came close to me—the grim, wasted, unshorn—he turned quick away, and hid his face in her neck, still grasping tight his bunch of grapes. She spoke to him rapidly and softly, coaxing him as I could tell full well, although I could not follow her words; and in a minute or two the little fellow obeyed her, and turned and stretched himself almost to overbalancing out of her arms, and half-dropped the fruit on the bed by me. Then he clutched at her again, burying his face in her kerchief, and fastening his little fists in her luxuriant hair.

He seemed like a little Bacchus.

"It is my master's only boy," said she, disentangling his fingers with quiet patience, only to have them grasp her braids afresh. "He is my little Max, my heart's delight, only he must not pull so hard. Say his 'to-meet-again,' and kiss his hand lovingly, and we will go." The promise of a speedy departure from my dusky room proved irresistible; he babbled out his Aufwiedersehen, and kissing his chubby hand, he was borne away joyful and chattering fast in his infantile half-language. I did not see Thekla again until late afternoon, when she brought me in my coffee. She was not like the same creature as the blooming, cheerful maiden whom I had seen in the morning; she looked wan and careworn, older by several years.

"What is the matter, Thekla?" said I, with true anxiety as to what might have befallen my good, faithful nurse.

She looked round before answering. "I have seen him," she said. "He has been here, and the Fräulein has been so angry! She says she will tell my master. Oh, it has been such a day!" The poor young woman, who was usually so composed and self-restrained, was on the point of bursting into tears; but by a strong effort she checked herself, and tried to busy herself with rearranging the white china cup, so as to place it more conveniently to my hand.

"Come, Thekla," said I, "tell me all about it. I have heard loud voices talking, and I fancied something had put the Fräulein out; and Lottchen looked flurried when she brought me my dinner. Is Franz here? How has he found you out?"

"He is here. Yes, I am sure it is he; but four years makes such a difference in a man; his whole look and manner seemed so strange to me; but he knew me at once, and called me all the old names which we used to call each other when we were children; and he must needs tell me how it had come to pass that he had not married that Swiss Anna. He said he had never loved her; and that now he was going home to settle, and he hoped that I would come too, and——" There she stopped short.

"And marry him, and live at the inn at Altenahr," said I, smiling, to reassure her, though I felt rather disappointed about the whole affair.

"No," she replied. "Old Weber, his father, is dead; he died in debt, and Franz will have no money. And he was always one that needed money. Some are, you know; and while I was thinking, and he was standing near me, the Fräulein came in; and—and—I don't wonder—for poor Franz is not a pleasant-looking man now-a-days—she was very angry, and called me a bold, bad girl, and said she could have no such goings on at the 'Halbmond,' but would tell my master when he came home from the forest."

"But you could have told her that you were old friends." I hesitated, before saying the word lovers, but, after a pause, out it came.

"Franz might have said so," she replied, a little stiffly. "I could not; but he went off as soon as she bade him. He went to the 'Adler' over the way, only saying he would come for my answer to-morrow morning. I think it was he that should have told her what we were—neighbours' children and early friends—not have left it all to me. Oh," said she, clasping her hands tight together, "she will make such a story of it to my master."

"Never mind," said I, "tell the master I want to see him, as soon as he comes in from the forest, and trust me to set him right before the Fräulein has the chance to set him wrong."

She looked up at me gratefully, and went away without any more words. Presently the fine burly figure of my host stood at the opening to my enclosed sitting-room. He was there, three-cornered hat in hand, looking tired and heated as a man does after a hard day's work, but as kindly and genial as ever, which is not what every man is who is called to business after such a day, before he has had the necessary food and rest.

I had been reflecting a good deal on Thekla's story; I could not quite interpret her manner to-day to my full satisfaction; but yet the love which had grown with her growth, must assuredly have been called forth by her lover's sudden reappearance; and I was inclined to give him some credit for having broken off an engagement to Swiss Anna, which had promised so many worldly advantages; and, again, I had considered that if he was a little weak and sentimental, it was Thekla, who would marry him by her own free will, and perhaps she had sense and quiet resolution enough for both. So I gave the heads of the little history I have told you to my good friend and host, adding that I should like to have a man's opinion of this man; but that if he were not an absolute good-for-nothing, and if Thekla still loved him, as I believed, I would try and advance them the requisite money towards establishing themselves in the hereditary inn at Altenahr.

Such was the romantic ending to Thekla's sorrows, I had been planning and brooding over for the last hour. As I narrated my tale, and hinted at the possible happy conclusion that might be in store, my host's face changed. The ruddy colour faded, and his look became almost stern—certainly very grave in expression. It was so unsympathetic, that I instinctively cut my words short. When I had done, he paused a little, and then said: "You would wish me to learn all I can respecting this stranger now at the 'Adler,' and give you the impression I receive of the fellow."

"Exactly so," said I; "I want to learn all I can about him for Thekla's sake."

"For Thekla's sake I will do it," he gravely repeated.

"And come to me to-night, even if I am gone to bed?"

"Not so," he replied. "You must give me all the time you can in a matter like this."

"But he will come for Thekla's answer in the morning."

"Before he comes you shall know all I can learn."

I was resting during the fatigues of dressing the next day, when my host tapped at my door. He looked graver and sterner than I had ever seen him do before; he sat down almost before I had begged him to do so.

"He is not worthy of her," he said. "He drinks brandy right hard; he boasts of his success at play, and"—here he set his teeth hard—"he boasts of the women who have loved him. In a village like this, sir, there are always those who spend their evenings in the gardens of the inns; and this man, after he had drank his fill, made no secrets; it needed no spying to find out what he was, else I should not have been the one to do it."

"Thekla must be told of this," said I. "She is not the woman to love any one whom she cannot respect."

Herr Müller laughed a low bitter laugh, quite unlike himself. Then he replied,—

"As for that matter, sir, you are young; you have had no great experience of women. From what my sister tells me there can be little doubt of Thekla's feeling towards him. She found them standing together by the window; his arm round Thekla's waist, and whispering in her ear—and to do the maiden justice she is not the one to suffer such familiarities from every one. No"—continued he, still in the same contemptuous tone—"you'll find she will make excuses for his faults and vices; or else, which is perhaps more likely, she will not believe your story, though I who tell it you can vouch for the truth of every word I say." He turned short away and left the room. Presently I saw his stalwart figure in the hill-side vineyard, before my windows, scaling the steep ascent with long regular steps, going to the forest beyond. I was otherwise occupied than in watching his progress during the next hour; at the end of that time he re-entered my room, looking heated and slightly tired, as if he had been walking fast, or labouring hard; but with the cloud off his brows, and the kindly light shining once again out of his honest eyes.

"I ask your pardon, sir," he began, "for troubling you afresh. I believe I was possessed by the devil this morning. I have been thinking it over. One has perhaps no right to rule for another person's happiness. To have such a"—here the honest fellow choked a little—"such a woman as Thekla to love him ought to raise any man. Besides, I am no judge for him or for her. I have found out this morning that I love her myself, and so the end of it is, that if you, sir, who are so kind as to interest yourself in the matter, and if you think it is really her heart's desire to marry this man—which ought to be his salvation both for earth and heaven—I shall be very glad to go halves with you in any place for setting them up in the inn at Altenahr; only allow me to see that whatever money we advance is well and legally tied up, so that it is secured to her. And be so kind as to take no notice of what I have said about my having found out that I have loved her; I named it as a kind of apology for my hard words this morning, and as a reason why I was not a fit judge of what was best." He had hurried on, so that I could not have stopped his eager speaking even had I wished to do so; but I was too much interested in the revelation of what was passing in his brave tender heart to desire to stop him. Now, however, his rapid words tripped each other up, and his speech ended in an unconscious sigh.

"But," I said, "since you were here Thekla has come to me, and we have had a long talk. She speaks now as openly to me as she would if I were her brother; with sensible frankness, where frankness is wise, with modest reticence, where confidence would be unbecoming. She came to ask me, if I thought it her duty to marry this fellow, whose very appearance, changed for the worse, as she says it is, since she last saw him four years ago, seemed to have repelled her."

"She could let him put his arm round her waist yesterday," said Herr Müller, with a return of his morning's surliness.

"And she would marry him now if she could believe it to be her duty. For some reason of his own, this Franz Weber has tried to work upon this feeling of hers. He says it would be the saving of him."

"As if a man had not strength enough in him—a man who is good for aught—to save himself, but needed a woman to pull him through life!"

"Nay," I replied, hardly able to keep from smiling. "You yourself said, not five minutes ago, that her marrying him might be his salvation both for earth and heaven."

"That was when I thought she loved the fellow," he answered quick. "Now——but what did you say to her, sir?"

"I told her, what I believe to be as true as gospel, that as she owned she did not love him any longer now his real self had come to displace his remembrance, that she would be sinning in marrying him; doing evil that possible good might come. I was clear myself on this point, though I should have been perplexed how to advise, if her love had still continued."

"And what answer did she make?"

"She went over the history of their lives; she was pleading against her wishes to satisfy her conscience. She said that all along through their childhood she had been his strength; that while under her personal influence he had been negatively good; away from her, he had fallen into mischief—"

"Not to say vice," put in Herr Müller.

"And now he came to her penitent, in sorrow, desirous of amendment, asking her for the love she seems to have considered as tacitly plighted to him in years gone by—"

"And which he has slighted and insulted. I hope you told her of his words and conduct last night in the 'Adler' gardens?"

"No. I kept myself to the general principle, which, I am sure, is a true one. I repeated it in different forms; for the idea of the duty of self-sacrifice had taken strong possession of her fancy. Perhaps, if I had failed in setting her notion of her duty in the right aspect, I might have had recourse to the statement of facts, which would have pained her severely, but would have proved to her how little his words of penitence and promises of amendment were to be trusted to."

"And it ended?"

"Ended by her being quite convinced that she would be doing wrong instead of right if she married a man whom she had entirely ceased to love, and that no real good could come from a course of action based on wrong-doing."

"That is right and true," he replied, his face broadening into happiness again.

"But she says she must leave your service, and go elsewhere."

"Leave my service she shall; go elsewhere she shall not."

"I cannot tell what you may have the power of inducing her to do; but she seems to me very resolute."

"Why?" said he, firing round at me, as if I had made her resolute.

"She says your sister spoke to her before the maids of the household, and before some of the townspeople, in a way that she could not stand; and that you yourself by your manner to her last night showed how she had lost your respect. She added, with her face of pure maidenly truth, that he had come into such close contact with her only the instant before your sister had entered the room."

"With your leave, sir," said Herr Müller, turning towards the door, "I will go and set all that right at once."

It was easier said than done. When I next saw Thekla, her eyes were swollen up with crying, but she was silent, almost defiant towards me. A look of resolute determination had settled down upon her face. I learnt afterwards that parts of my conversation with Herr Müller had been injudiciously quoted by him in the talk he had had with her. I thought I would leave her to herself, and wait till she unburdened herself of the feeling of unjust resentment towards me. But it was days before she spoke to me with anything like her former frankness. I had heard all about it from my host long before.

He had gone to her straight on leaving me; and like a foolish, impetuous lover, had spoken out his mind and his wishes to her in the presence of his sister, who, it must be remembered, had heard no explanation of the conduct which had given her propriety so great a shock the day before. Herr Müller thought to re-instate Thekla in his sister's good opinion by giving her in the Fräulein's very presence the highest possible mark of his own love and esteem. And there in the kitchen, where the Fräulein was deeply engaged in the hot work of making some delicate preserve on the stove, and ordering Thekla about with short, sharp displeasure in her tones, the master had come in, and possessing himself of the maiden's hand, had, to her infinite surprise—to his sister's infinite indignation—made her the offer of his heart, his wealth, his life; had begged of her to marry him. I could gather from his account that she had been in a state of trembling discomfiture at first; she had not spoken, but had twisted her hand out of his, and had covered her face with her apron. And then the Fräulein had burst forth—"accursed words" he called her speech. Thekla uncovered her face to listen; to listen to the end; to listen to the passionate recrimination between the brother and the sister. And then she went up, close up to the angry Fräulein, and had said quite quietly, but with a manner of final determination which had evidently sunk deep into her suitor's heart, and depressed him into hopelessness, that the Fräulein had no need to disturb herself; that on this very day she had been thinking of marrying another man, and that her heart was not like a room to let, into which as one tenant went out another might enter. Nevertheless, she felt the master's goodness. He had always treated her well from the time when she had entered the house as his servant. And she should be sorry to leave him; sorry to leave the children; very sorry to leave little Max: yes, she should even be sorry to leave the Fräulein, who was a good woman, only a little too apt to be hard on other women. But she had already been that very day and deposited her warning at the police office; the busy time would be soon over, and she should be glad to leave their service on All Saints' Day. Then (he thought) she had felt inclined to cry, for she suddenly braced herself up, and said, yes, she should be very glad; for somehow, though they had been kind to her, she had been very unhappy at Heppenheim; and she would go back to her home for a time, and see her old father and kind stepmother, and her nursling half-sister Ida, and be among her own people again.

I could see it was this last part that most of all rankled in Herr Müller's mind. In all probability Franz Weber was making his way back to Heppenheim too; and the bad suspicion would keep welling up that some lingering feeling for her old lover and disgraced playmate was making her so resolute to leave and return to Altenahr.

For some days after this I was the confidant of the whole household, excepting Thekla. She, poor creature, looked miserable enough; but the hardy, defiant expression was always on her face. Lottchen spoke out freely enough; the place would not be worth having if Thekla left it; it was she who had the head for everything, the patience for everything; who stood between all the under-servants and the Fräulein's tempers. As for the children, poor motherless children! Lottchen was sure that the master did not know what he was doing when he allowed his sister to turn Thekla away—and all for what? for having a lover, as every girl had who could get one. Why, the little boy Max slept in the room which Lottchen shared with Thekla; and she heard him in the night as quickly as if she was his mother; when she had been sitting up with me, when I was so ill, Lottchen had had to attend to him; and it was weary work after a hard day to have to get up and soothe a teething child; she knew she had been cross enough sometimes; but Thekla was always good and gentle with him, however tired he was. And as Lottchen left the room I could hear her repeating that she thought she should leave when Thekla went, for that her place would not be worth having.

Even the Fräulein had her word of regret—regret mingled with self-justification. She thought she had been quite right in speaking to Thekla for allowing such familiarities; how was she to know that the man was an old friend and playmate? He looked like a right profligate good-for-nothing. And to have a servant take up her scolding as an unpardonable offence, and persist in quitting her place, just when she had learnt all her work, and was so useful in the household—so useful that the Fräulein could never put up with any fresh, stupid house-maiden, but, sooner than take the trouble of teaching the new servant where everything was, and how to give out the stores if she was busy, she would go back to Worms. For, after all, housekeeping for a brother was thankless work; there was no satisfying men; and Heppenheim was but a poor ignorant village compared to Worms.

She must have spoken to her brother about her intention of leaving him, and returning to her former home; indeed a feeling of coolness had evidently grown up between the brother and sister during these latter days. When one evening Herr Müller brought in his pipe, and, as his custom had sometimes been, sat down by my stove to smoke, he looked gloomy and annoyed. I let him puff away, and take his own time. At length he began,—

"I have rid the village of him at last. I could not bear to have him here disgracing Thekla with speaking to her whenever she went to the vineyard or the fountain. I don't believe she likes him a bit."

"No more do I," I said. He turned on me.

"Then why did she speak to him at all? Why cannot she like an honest man who likes her? Why is she so bent on going home to Altenahr?"

"She speaks to him because she has known him from a child, and has a faithful pity for one whom she has known so innocent, and who is now so lost in all good men's regard. As for not liking an honest man—(though I may have my own opinion about that)—liking goes by fancy, as we say in English; and Altenahr is her home; her father's house is at Altenahr, as you know."

"I wonder if he will go there," quoth Herr Müller, after two or three more puffs. "He was fast at the 'Adler;' he could not pay his score, so he kept on staying here, saying that he should receive a letter from a friend with money in a day or two; lying in wait, too, for Thekla, who is well-known and respected all through Heppenheim: so his being an old friend of hers made him have a kind of standing. I went in this morning and paid his score, on condition that he left the place this day; and he left the village as merrily as a cricket, caring no more for Thekla than for the Kaiser who built our church: for he never looked back at the 'Halbmond,' but went whistling down the road."

"That is a good riddance," said I.

"Yes. But my sister says she must return to Worms. And Lottchen has given notice; she says the place will not be worth having when Thekla leaves. I wish I could give notice too."

"Try Thekla again."

"Not I," said he, reddening. "It would seem now as if I only wanted her for a housekeeper. Besides, she avoids me at every turn, and will not even look at me. I am sure she bears me some ill-will about that ne'er-do-well."

There was silence between us for some time, which he at length broke.

"The pastor has a good and comely daughter. Her mother is a famous housewife. They often have asked me to come to the parsonage and smoke a pipe. When the vintage is over, and I am less busy, I think I will go there, and look about me."

"When is the vintage?" asked I. "I hope it will take place soon, for I am growing so well and strong I fear I must leave you shortly; but I should like to see the vintage first."

"Oh, never fear! you must not travel yet awhile; and Government has fixed the grape-gathering to begin on the fourteenth."

"What a paternal Government! How does it know when the grapes will be ripe? Why cannot every man fix his own time for gathering his own grapes?"

"That has never been our way in Germany. There are people employed by the Government to examine the vines, and report when the grapes are ripe. It is necessary to make laws about it; for, as you must have seen, there is nothing but the fear of the law to protect our vineyards and fruit-trees; there are no enclosures along the Berg-Strasse, as you tell me you have in England; but, as people are only allowed to go into the vineyards on stated days, no one, under pretence of gathering his own produce, can stray into his neighbour's grounds and help himself, without some of the duke's foresters seeing him."

"Well," said I, "to each country its own laws."

I think it was on that very evening that Thekla came in for something. She stopped arranging the tablecloth and the flowers, as if she had something to say, yet did not know how to begin. At length I found that her sore, hot heart, wanted some sympathy; her hand was against every one's, and she fancied every one had turned against her. She looked up at me, and said, a little abruptly,—

"Does the gentleman know that I go on the fifteenth?"

"So soon?" said I, with surprise. "I thought you were to remain here till All Saints' Day."

"So I should have done—so I must have done—if the Fräulein had not kindly given me leave to accept of a place—a very good place too—of housekeeper to a widow lady at Frankfort. It is just the sort of situation I have always wished for. I expect I shall be so happy and comfortable there."

"Methinks the lady doth profess too much," came into my mind. I saw she expected me to doubt the probability of her happiness, and was in a defiant mood.

"Of course," said I, "you would hardly have wished to leave Heppenheim if you had been happy here; and every new place always promises fair, whatever its performance may be. But wherever you go, remember you have always a friend in me."

"Yes," she replied, "I think you are to be trusted. Though, from my experience, I should say that of very few men."

"You have been unfortunate," I answered; "many men would say the same of women."

She thought a moment, and then said, in a changed tone of voice, "The Fräulein here has been much more friendly and helpful of these late days than her brother; yet I have served him faithfully, and have cared for his little Max as though he were my own brother. But this morning he spoke to me for the first time for many days,—he met me in the passage, and, suddenly stopping, he said he was glad I had met with so comfortable a place, and that I was at full liberty to go whenever I liked: and then he went quickly on, never waiting for my answer."

"And what was wrong in that? It seems to me he was trying to make you feel entirely at your ease, to do as you thought best, without regard to his own interests."

"Perhaps so. It is silly, I know," she continued, turning full on me her grave, innocent eyes; "but one's vanity suffers a little when every one is so willing to part with one."

"Thekla! I owe you a great debt—let me speak to you openly. I know that your master wanted to marry you, and that you refused him. Do not deceive yourself. You are sorry for that refusal now?"

She kept her serious look fixed upon me; but her face and throat reddened all over.

"No," said she, at length; "I am not sorry. What can you think I am made of; having loved one man ever since I was a little child until a fortnight ago, and now just as ready to love another? I know you do not rightly consider what you say, or I should take it as an insult."

"You loved an ideal man; he disappointed you, and you clung to your remembrance of him. He came, and the reality dispelled all illusions."

"I do not understand philosophy," said she. "I only know that I think that Herr Müller had lost all respect for me from what his sister had told him; and I know that I am going away; and I trust I shall be happier in Frankfort than I have been here of late days." So saying, she left the room.

I was wakened up on the morning of the fourteenth by the merry ringing of church bells, and the perpetual firing and popping off of guns and pistols. But all this was over by the time I was up and dressed, and seated at breakfast in my partitioned room. It was a perfect October day; the dew not yet off the blades of grass, glistening on the delicate gossamer webs, which stretched from flower to flower in the garden, lying in the morning shadow of the house. But beyond the garden, on the sunny hill-side, men, women, and children were clambering up the vineyards like ants,—busy, irregular in movement, clustering together, spreading wide apart,—I could hear the shrill merry voices as I sat,—and all along the valley, as far as I could see, it was much the same; for every one filled his house for the day of the vintage, that great annual festival. Lottchen, who had brought in my breakfast, was all in her Sunday best, having risen early to get her work done and go abroad to gather grapes. Bright colours seemed to abound; I could see dots of scarlet, and crimson, and orange through the fading leaves; it was not a day to languish in the house; and I was on the point of going out by myself, when Herr Müller came in to offer me his sturdy arm, and help me in walking to the vineyard. We crept through the garden scented with late flowers and sunny fruit,—we passed through the gate I had so often gazed at from the easy-chair, and were in the busy vineyard; great baskets lay on the grass already piled nearly full of purple and yellow grapes. The wine made from these was far from pleasant to my taste; for the best Rhine wine is made from a smaller grape, growing in closer, harder clusters; but the larger and less profitable grape is by far the most picturesque in its mode of growth, and far the best to eat into the bargain. Wherever we trod, it was on fragrant, crushed vine-leaves; every one we saw had his hands and face stained with the purple juice. Presently I sat down on a sunny bit of grass, and my host left me to go farther afield, to look after the more distant vineyards. I watched his progress. After he left me, he took off coat and waistcoat, displaying his snowy shirt and gaily-worked braces; and presently he was as busy as any one. I looked down on the village; the gray and orange and crimson roofs lay glowing in the noonday sun. I could see down into the streets; but they were all empty—even the old people came toiling up the hill-side to share in the general festivity. Lottchen had brought up cold dinners for a regiment of men; every one came and helped himself. Thekla was there, leading the little Karoline, and helping the toddling steps of Max; but she kept aloof from me; for I knew, or suspected, or had probed too much. She alone looked sad and grave, and spoke so little, even to her friends, that it was evident to see that she was trying to wean herself finally from the place. But I could see that she had lost her short, defiant manner. What she did say was kindly and gently spoken. The Fräulein came out late in the morning, dressed, I suppose, in the latest Worms fashion—quite different to anything I had ever seen before. She came up to me, and talked very graciously to me for some time.

"Here comes the proprietor (squire) and his lady, and their dear children. See, the vintagers have tied bunches of the finest grapes on to a stick, heavier than the children or even the lady can carry. Look! look! how he bows!—one can tell he has been an *attaché* at Vienna. That is the court way of bowing there—holding the hat right down before them, and bending the back at right angles. How graceful! And here is the doctor! I thought he would spare time to come up here. Well, doctor, you will go all the more cheerfully to your next patient for having been up into the vineyards. Nonsense, about grapes making other patients for you. Ah, here is the pastor and his wife, and the Fräulein Anna. Now, where is my brother, I wonder? Up in the far vineyard, I make no doubt. Mr. Pastor, the view up above is far finer than what it is here, and the best grapes grow there; shall I accompany you and madame, and the dear Fräulein? The gentleman will excuse me."

I was left alone. Presently I thought I would walk a little farther, or at any rate change my position. I rounded a corner in the pathway, and there I found Thekla, watching by little sleeping Max. He lay on her shawl; and over his head she had made an arching canopy of broken vine-branches, so that the great leaves threw their cool, flickering shadows on his face. He was smeared all over with grape-juice, his sturdy fingers grasped a half-eaten bunch even in his sleep. Thekla was keeping Lina quiet by teaching her how to weave a garland for her head out of field-flowers and autumn-tinted leaves. The maiden sat on the ground, with her back to the valley beyond, the child kneeling by her, watching the busy fingers with eager intentness. Both looked up as I drew near, and we exchanged a few words.

"Where is the master?" I asked. "I promised to await his return; he wished to give me his arm down the wooden steps; but I do not see him."

"He is in the higher vineyard," said Thekla, quietly, but not looking round in that direction. "He will be some time there, I should think. He went with the pastor and his wife; he will have to speak to his labourers and his friends. My arm is strong, and I can leave Max in Lina's care for five minutes. If you are tired, and want to go back, let me help you down the steps; they are steep and slippery."

I had turned to look up the valley. Three or four hundred yards off, in the higher vineyard, walked the dignified pastor, and his homely, decorous wife. Behind came the Fräulein Anna, in her short-sleeved Sunday gown, daintily holding a parasol over her luxuriant brown hair. Close behind her came Herr Müller, stopping now to speak to his men,—again, to cull out a bunch of grapes to tie on to the Fräulein's stick; and by my feet sate the proud serving-maid in her country dress, waiting for my answer, with serious, up-turned eyes, and sad, composed face.

"No, I am much obliged to you, Thekla; and if I did not feel so strong I would have thankfully taken your arm. But I only wanted to leave a message for the master, just to say that I have gone home."

"Lina will give it to the father when he comes down," said Thekla.

I went slowly down into the garden. The great labour of the day was over, and the younger part of the population had returned to the village, and were preparing the fireworks and pistol-shootings for the evening. Already one or two of those well-known German carts (in the shape of a V) were standing near the vineyard gates, the patient oxen meekly waiting while basketful after basketful of grapes were being emptied into the leaf-lined receptacle.

As I sat down in my easy-chair close to the open window through which I had entered, I could see the men and women on the hill-side drawing to a centre, and all stand round the pastor, bareheaded, for a minute or so. I guessed that some words of holy thanksgiving were being said, and I wished that I had stayed to hear them, and mark my especial gratitude for having been spared to see that day. Then I heard the distant voices, the deep tones of the men, the shriller pipes of women and children, join in the German harvest-hymn, which is generally sung on such occasions;[1] then silence, while I concluded that a blessing was spoken by the pastor, with outstretched arms; and then they once more dispersed, some to the village, some to finish their labours for the day among the vines. I saw Thekla coming through the garden with Max in her arms, and Lina clinging to her woollen skirts. Thekla made for my open window; it was rather a shorter passage into the house than round by the door. "I may come through, may I not?" she asked, softly. "I fear Max is not well; I cannot understand his look, and he wakened up so strange!" She paused to let me see the child's face; it was flushed almost to a crimson look of heat, and his breathing was laboured and uneasy, his eyes half-open and filmy.

"Something is wrong, I am sure," said I. "I don't know anything about children, but he is not in the least like himself."

She bent down and kissed the cheek so tenderly that she would not have bruised the petal of a rose. "Heart's darling," she murmured. He quivered all over at her touch, working his fingers in an unnatural kind of way, and ending with a convulsive twitching all over his body. Lina began to cry at the grave, anxious look on our faces.

"You had better call the Fräulein to look at him," said I. "I feel sure he ought to have a doctor; I should say he was going to have a fit."

"The Fräulein and the master are gone to the pastor's for coffee, and Lottchen is in the higher vineyard, taking the men their bread and beer. Could you find the kitchen girl, or old Karl? he will be in the stables, I think. I must lose no time." Almost without waiting for my reply, she had passed through the room, and in the empty house I could hear her firm, careful footsteps going up the stair; Lina's pattering beside her; and the one voice wailing, the other speaking low comfort.

I was tired enough, but this good family had treated me too much like one of their own for me not to do what I could in such a case as this. I made my way out into the street, for the first time since I had come to the house on that memorable evening six weeks ago. I bribed the first person I met to guide me to the doctor's, and send him straight down to the "Halbmond," not staying to listen to the thorough scolding he fell to giving me; then on to the parsonage, to tell the master and the Fräulein of the state of things at home.

I was sorry to be the bearer of bad news into such a festive chamber as the pastor's. There they sat, resting after heat and fatigue, each in their best gala dress, the table spread with "Dicker-milch," potato-salad, cakes of various shapes and kinds—all the dainty cates dear to the German palate. The pastor was talking to Herr Müller, who stood near the pretty young Fräulein Anna, in her fresh white chemisette, with her round white arms, and her youthful coquettish airs, as she prepared to pour out the coffee; our Fräulein was talking busily to the Frau Mama; the younger boys and girls of the family filling up the room. A ghost would have startled the assembled party less than I did, and would probably have been more welcome, considering the news I brought. As he listened, the master caught up his hat and went forth, without apology or farewell. Our Fräulein made up for both, and questioned me fully; but now she, I could see, was in haste to go, although restrained by her manners, and the kind-hearted Frau Pastorin soon set her at liberty to follow her inclination. As for me I was dead-beat, and only too glad to avail myself of the hospitable couple's pressing request that I would stop and share their meal. Other magnates of the village came in presently, and relieved me of the strain of keeping up a German conversation about nothing at all with entire strangers. The pretty Fräulein's face had clouded over a little at Herr Müller's sudden departure; but she was soon as bright as could be, giving private chase and sudden little scoldings to her brothers, as they made raids upon the dainties under her charge. After I was duly rested and refreshed, I took my leave; for I, too, had my quieter anxieties about the sorrow in the Müller family.

The only person I could see at the "Halbmond" was Lottchen; every one else was busy about the poor little Max, who was passing from one fit into another. I told Lottchen to ask the doctor to come in and see me before he took his leave for the night, and tired as I was, I kept up till after his visit, though it was very late before he came; I could see from his face how anxious he was. He would give me no opinion as to the child's chances of recovery, from which I guessed that he had not much hope. But when I expressed my fear he cut me very short.

"The truth is, you know nothing about it; no more do I, for that matter. It is enough to try any man, much less a father, to hear his perpetual moans—not that he is conscious of pain, poor little worm; but if she stops for a moment in her perpetual carrying him backwards and forwards, he plains so piteously it is enough to—enough to make a man bless the Lord who never led him into the pit of matrimony. To see the father up there, following her as she walks up and down the room, the child's head over her shoulder, and Müller trying to make the heavy eyes recognize the old familiar ways of play, and the chirruping sounds which he can scarce make for crying——I shall be here to-morrow early, though before that either life or death will have come without the old doctor's help."

All night long I dreamt my feverish dream—of the vineyard—the carts, which held little coffins instead of baskets of grapes—of the pastor's daughter, who would pull the dying child out of Thekla's arms; it was a bad, weary night! I slept long into the morning; the broad daylight filled my room, and yet no one had been near to waken me! Did that mean life or death? I got up and dressed as fast as I could; for I was aching all over with the fatigue of the day before. Out into the sitting-room; the table was laid for breakfast, but no one was there. I passed into the house beyond, up the stairs, blindly seeking for the room where I might know whether it was life or death. At the door of a room I found Lottchen crying; at the sight of me in that unwonted place she started, and began some kind of apology, broken both by tears and smiles, as she told me that the doctor said the danger was over—past, and that Max was sleeping a gentle peaceful slumber in Thekla's arms—arms that had held him all through the livelong night.

"Look at him, sir; only go in softly; it is a pleasure to see the child to-day; tread softly, sir."

She opened the chamber-door. I could see Thekla sitting, propped up by cushions and stools, holding her heavy burden, and bending over him with a look of tenderest love. Not far off stood the Fräulein, all disordered and tearful, stirring or seasoning some hot soup, while the master stood by her impatient. As soon as it was cooled or seasoned enough he took the basin and went to Thekla, and said something very low; she lifted up her head, and I could see her face; pale, weary with watching, but with a soft peaceful look upon it, which it had not worn for weeks. Fritz Müller began to feed her, for her hands were occupied in holding his child; I could not help remembering Mrs. Inchbald's pretty description of Dorriforth's anxiety in feeding Miss Milner; she compares it, if I remember rightly, to that of a tender-hearted boy, caring for his darling bird, the loss of which would embitter all the joys of his holidays. We closed the door without noise, so as not to waken the sleeping child. Lottchen brought me my coffee and bread; she was ready either to laugh or to weep on the slightest occasion. I could not tell if it was in innocence or mischief. She asked me the following question,—

"Do you think Thekla will leave to-day, sir?"

In the afternoon I heard Thekla's step behind my extemporary screen. I knew it quite well. She stopped for a moment before emerging into my view.

She was trying to look as composed as usual, but, perhaps because her steady nerves had been shaken by her night's watching, she could not help faint touches of dimples at the corners of her mouth, and her eyes were veiled from any inquisitive look by their drooping lids.

"I thought you would like to know that the doctor says Max is quite out of danger now. He will only require care."

"Thank you, Thekla; Doctor —— has been in already this afternoon to tell me so, and I am truly glad."

She went to the window, and looked out for a moment. Many people were in the vineyards again to-day; although we, in our household anxiety, had paid them but little heed. Suddenly she turned round into the room, and I saw that her face was crimson with blushes. In another instant Herr Müller entered by the window.

"Has she told you, sir?" said he, possessing himself of her hand, and looking all a-glow with happiness. "Hast thou told our good friend?" addressing her.

"No. I was going to tell him, but I did not know how to begin."

"Then I will prompt thee. Say after me—'I have been a wilful, foolish woman——'"

She wrenched her hand out of his, half-laughing—"I am a foolish woman, for I have promised to marry him. But he is a still more foolish man, for he wishes to marry me. That is what I say."

"And I have sent Babette to Frankfort with the pastor. He is going there, and will explain all to Frau v. Schmidt; and Babette will serve her for a time. When Max is well enough to have the change of air the doctor prescribes for him, thou shalt take him to Altenahr, and thither will I also go; and become known to thy people and thy father. And before Christmas the gentleman here shall dance at our wedding."

"I must go home to England, dear friends, before many days are over. Perhaps we may travel together as far as Remagen. Another year I will come back to Heppenheim and see you."

As I planned it, so it was. We left Heppenheim all together on a lovely All-Saints' Day. The day before—the day of All-Souls—I had watched Fritz and Thekla lead little Lina up to the Acre of God, the Field of Rest, to hang the wreath of immortelles on her mother's grave. Peace be with the dead and the living.

LIBBIE MARSH'S THREE ERAS.

ERA I.

VALENTINE'S DAY.

Last November but one, there was a flitting in our neighbourhood; hardly a flitting, after all, for it was only a single person changing her place of abode from one lodging to another; and instead of a cartload of drawers and baskets, dressers and beds, with old king clock at the top of all, it was only one large wooden chest to be carried after the girl, who moved slowly and heavily along the streets, listless and depressed, more from the state of her mind than of her body. It was Libbie Marsh, who had been obliged to quit her room in Dean Street, because the acquaintances whom she had been living with were leaving Manchester. She tried to think herself fortunate in having met with lodgings rather more out of the town, and with those who were known to be respectable; she did indeed try to be contented, but in spite of her reason, the old feeling of desolation came over her, as she was now about to be thrown again entirely among strangers.

No. 2, —— Court, Albemarle Street, was reached at last, and the pace, slow as it was, slackened as she drew near the spot where she was to be left by the man who carried her box, for, trivial as her acquaintance with him was, he was not quite a stranger, as every one else was, peering out of their open doors, and satisfying themselves it was only "Dixon's new lodger."

Dixon's house was the last on the left-hand side of the court. A high dead brick wall connected it with its opposite neighbour. All the dwellings were of the same monotonous pattern, and one side of the court looked at its exact likeness opposite, as if it were seeing itself in a looking-glass.

Dixon's house was shut up, and the key left next door; but the woman in whose charge it was left knew that Libbie was expected, and came forward to say a few explanatory words, to unlock the door, and stir the dull grey ashes that were lazily burning in the grate: and then she returned to her own house, leaving poor Libbie standing alone with the great big chest in the middle of the house-place floor, with no one to say a word to (even a common-place remark would have been better than this dull silence), that could help her to repel the fast-coming tears.

Dixon and his wife, and their eldest girl, worked in factories, and were absent all day from the house: the youngest child, also a little girl, was boarded out on the week-days at the neighbour's where the door-key was deposited, but although busy making dirt-pies, at the entrance to the court, when Libbie came in, she was too young to care much about her parents' new lodger. Libbie knew that she was to sleep with the elder girl in the front bedroom, but, as you may fancy, it seemed a liberty even to go upstairs to take off her things, when no one was at home to marshal the way up the ladder-like steps. So she could only take off her bonnet, and sit down, and gaze at the now blazing fire, and think sadly on the past, and on the lonely creature she was in this wide world—father and mother gone, her little brother long since dead—he would been more than nineteen had he been alive, but she only thought of him as the darling baby; her only friends (to call friends) living far away at their new house; her employers, kind enough people in their way, but too rapidly twirling round on this bustling earth to have leisure to think of the little work-woman, excepting when they wanted gowns turned, carpets mended, or household linen darned; and hardly even the natural though hidden hope of a young girl's heart, to cheer her on with the bright visions of a home of her own at some future day, where, loving and beloved, she might fulfil a woman's dearest duties.

For Libbie was very plain, as she had known so long that the consciousness of it had ceased to mortify her. You can hardly live in Manchester without having some idea of your personal appearance: the factory lads and lasses take good care of that; and if you meet them at the hours when they are pouring out of the mills, you are sure to hear a good number of truths, some of them combined with such a spirit of impudent fun, that you can scarcely keep from laughing, even at the joke against yourself. Libbie had often and often been greeted by such questions as—"How long is it since you were a beauty?"—"What would you take a day to stand in the fields to scare away the birds?"& c., for her to linger under any impression as to her looks.

While she was thus musing, and quietly crying, under the pictures her fancy had conjured up, the Dixons came dropping in, and surprised her with her wet cheeks and quivering lips.

She almost wished to have the stillness again that had so oppressed her an hour ago, they talked and laughed so loudly and so much, and bustled about so noisily over everything they did. Dixon took hold of one iron handle of her box, and helped her to bump it upstairs, while his daughter Anne followed to see the unpacking, and what sort of clothes "little sewing body had gotten." Mrs. Dixon rattled out her tea-things, and put the kettle on, fetched home her youngest child, which added to the commotion. Then she called Anne downstairs, and sent her for this thing and that: eggs to put to the cream, it was so thin; ham, to give a relish to the bread and butter; some new bread, hot, if she could get it. Libbie heard all these orders, given at full pitch of Mrs. Dixon's voice, and wondered at their extravagance, so different from the habits of the place where she had last lodged. But they were fine spinners, in the receipt of good wages; and confined all day in an atmosphere ranging from seventy-five to eighty degrees. They had lost all natural, healthy appetite for simple food, and, having no higher tastes, found their greatest enjoyment in their luxurious meals.

When tea was ready, Libbie was called downstairs, with a rough but hearty invitation, to share their meal; she sat mutely at the corner of the tea-table, while they went on with their own conversation about people and things she knew nothing about, till at length she ventured to ask for a candle, to go and finish her unpacking before bedtime, as she had to go out sewing for several succeeding days. But once in the comparative peace of her bedroom, her energy failed her, and she contented herself with locking her Noah's ark of a chest, and put out her candle, and went to sit by the window, and gaze out at the bright heavens; for ever and ever "the blue sky, that bends over all," sheds down a feeling of sympathy with the sorrowful at the solemn hours when the ceaseless stars are seen to pace its depths.

By-and-by her eye fell down to gazing at the corresponding window to her own, on the opposite side of the court. It was lighted, but the blind was drawn down: upon the blind she saw, first unconsciously, the constant weary motion of a little spectral shadow, a child's hand and arm—no more; long, thin fingers hanging down from the wrist, while the arm moved up and down, as if keeping time to the heavy pulses of dull pain. She could not help hoping that sleep would soon come to still that incessant, feeble motion: and now and then it did cease, as if the little creature had dropped into a slumber from very weariness; but presently the arm jerked up with the fingers clenched, as if with a sudden start of agony. When Anne came up to bed, Libbie was still sitting, watching the shadow, and she directly asked to whom it belonged.

"It will be Margaret Hall's lad. Last summer, when it was so hot, there was no biding with the window shut at night, and theirs was open too: and many's the time he has waked me with his moans; they say he's been better sin' cold weather came."

"Is he always in bed? Whatten ails him?" asked Libbie.

"Summat's amiss wi' his backbone, folks say; he's better and worse, like. He's a nice little chap enough, and his mother's not that bad either; only my mother and her had words, so now we don't speak."

Libbie went on watching, and when she next spoke, to ask who and what his mother was, Anne Dixon was fast asleep.

Time passed away, and as usual unveiled the hidden things. Libbie found out that Margaret Hall was a widow, who earned her living as a washerwoman; that the little suffering lad was her only child, her dearly beloved. That while she scolded, pretty nearly, everybody else, "till her name was up" in the neighbourhood for a termagant, to him she was evidently most tender and gentle. He lay alone on his little bed, near the window, through the day, while she was away toiling for a livelihood. But when Libbie had plain sewing to do at her lodgings, instead of going out to sew, she used to watch from her bedroom window for the time when the shadows opposite, by their mute gestures, told that the mother had returned to bend over her child, to smooth his pillow, to alter his position, to get him his nightly cup of tea. And often in the night Libbie could not help rising gently from bed, to see if the little arm was waving up and down, as was his accustomed habit when sleepless from pain.

Libbie had a good deal of sewing to do at home that winter, and whenever it was not so cold as to benumb her fingers, she took it upstairs, in order to watch the little lad in her few odd moments of pause. On his better days he could sit up enough to peep out of his window, and she found he liked to look at her. Presently she ventured to nod to him across the court; and his faint smile, and ready nod back again, showed that this gave him pleasure. I think she would have been encouraged by this smile to have proceeded to a speaking acquaintance, if it had not been for his terrible mother, to whom it seemed to be irritation enough to know that Libbie was a lodger at the Dixons' for her to talk at her whenever they encountered each other, and to live evidently in wait for some good opportunity of abuse.

With her constant interest in him, Libbie soon discovered his great want of an object on which to occupy his thoughts, and which might distract his attention, when alone through the long day, from the pain he endured. He was very fond of flowers. It was November when she had first removed to her lodgings, but it had been very mild weather, and a few flowers yet lingered in the gardens, which the country people gathered into nosegays, and brought on market-days into Manchester. His mother had brought him a bunch of Michaelmas daisies the very day Libbie had become a neighbour, and she watched their history. He put them first in an old teapot, of which the spout was broken off and the lid lost; and he daily replenished the teapot from the jug of water his mother left near him to quench his feverish thirst. By-and-by, one or two of the constellation of lilac stars faded, and then the time he had hitherto spent in admiring, almost caressing them, was devoted to cutting off those flowers whose decay marred the beauty of the nosegay. It took him half the morning, with his feeble, languid motions, and his cumbrous old scissors, to trim up his diminished darlings. Then at last he seemed to think he had better preserve the few that remained by drying them; so they were carefully put between the leaves of the old Bible; and then, whenever a better day came, when he had strength enough to lift the ponderous book, he used to open the pages to look at his flower friends. In winter he could have no more living flowers to tend.

Libbie thought and thought, till at last an idea flashed upon her mind, that often made a happy smile steal over her face as she stitched away, and that cheered her through the solitary winter—for solitary it continued to be, though the Dixons were very good sort of people, never pressed her for payment, if she had had but little work to do that week; never grudged her a share of their extravagant meals, which were far more luxurious than she could have met with anywhere else, for her previously agreed payment in case of working at home; and they would fain have taught her to drink rum in her tea, assuring her that she should have it for nothing and welcome. But they were too touchy, too prosperous, too much absorbed in themselves, to take off Libbie's feeling of solitariness; not half as much as the little face by day, and the shadow by night, of him with whom she had never yet exchanged a word.

Her idea was this: her mother came from the east of England, where, as perhaps you know, they have the pretty custom of sending presents on St. Valentine's day, with the donor's name unknown, and, of course, the mystery constitutes half the enjoyment. The fourteenth of February was Libbie's birthday too, and many a year, in the happy days of old, had her mother delighted to surprise her with some little gift, of which she more than half-guessed the giver, although each Valentine's day the manner of its arrival was varied. Since then the fourteenth of February had been the dreariest of all the year, because the most haunted by memory of departed happiness. But now, this year, if she could not have the old gladness of heart herself, she would try and brighten the life of another. She would save, and she would screw, but she would buy a canary and a cage for that poor little laddie opposite, who wore out his monotonous life with so few pleasures, and so much pain.

I doubt I may not tell you here of the anxieties and the fears, of the hopes and the self-sacrifices—all, perhaps small in the tangible effect as the widow's mite, yet not the less marked by the viewless angels who go about continually among us—which varied Libbie's life before she accomplished her purpose. It is enough to say it was accomplished. The very day before the fourteenth she found time to go with her half-guinea to a barber's who lived near Albemarle Street, and who was famous for his stock of singing-birds. There are enthusiasts about all sorts of things, both good and bad, and many of the weavers in Manchester know and care more about birds than any one would easily credit. Stubborn, silent, reserved men on many things, you have only to touch on the subject of birds to light up their faces with brightness. They will tell you who won the prizes at the last canary show, where the prize birds may be seen, and give you all the details of those funny, but pretty and interesting mimicries of great people's cattle shows. Among these amateurs, Emanuel Morris the barber was an oracle.

He took Libbie into his little back room, used for private shaving of modest men, who did not care to be exhibited in the front shop decked out in the full glories of lather; and which was hung round with birds in rude wicker cages, with the exception of those who had won prizes, and were consequently honoured with gilt-wire prisons. The longer and thinner the body of the bird was, the more admiration it received, as far as external beauty went; and when, in addition to this, the colour was deep and clear, and its notes strong and varied, the more did Emanuel dwell upon its perfections. But these were all prize birds; and, on inquiry, Libbie heard, with some little sinking at heart, that their price ran from one to two guineas.

"I'm not over-particular as to shape and colour," said she, "I should like a good singer, that's all!"

She dropped a little in Emanuel's estimation. However, he showed her his good singers, but all were above Libbie's means.

"After all, I don't think I care so much about the singing very loud; it's but a noise after all, and sometimes noise fidgets folks."

"They must be nesh folks as is put out with the singing o' birds," replied Emanuel, rather affronted.

"It's for one who is poorly," said Libbie, deprecatingly.

"Well," said he, as if considering the matter, "folk that are cranky, often take more to them as shows 'em love, than to them as is clever and gifted. Happen yo'd rather have this'n," opening a cage-door, and calling to a dull-coloured bird, sitting moped up in a corner, "Here—Jupiter, Jupiter!"

The bird smoothed its feathers in an instant, and, uttering a little note of delight, flew to Emanuel, putting his beak to his lips, as if kissing him, and then, perching on his head, it began a gurgling warble of pleasure, not by any means so varied or so clear as the song of the others, but which pleased Libbie more; for she was always one to find out she liked the gooseberries that were accessible, better than the grapes that were beyond her reach. The price too was just right, so she gladly took possession of the cage, and hid it under her cloak, preparatory to carrying it home. Emanuel meanwhile was giving her directions as to its food, with all the minuteness of one loving his subject.

"Will it soon get to know any one?" asked she.

"Give him two days only, and you and he'll be as thick as him and me are now. You've only to open his door, and call him, and he'll follow you round the room; but he'll first kiss you, and then perch on your head. He only wants larning, which I've no time to give him, to do many another accomplishment."

"What's his name? I did not rightly catch it."

"Jupiter,—it's not common; but the town's o'errun with Bobbies and Dickies, and as my birds are thought a bit out o' the way, I like to have better names for 'em, so I just picked a few out o' my lad's school books. It's just as ready, when you're used to it, to say Jupiter as Dicky."

"I could bring my tongue round to Peter better; would he answer to Peter?" asked Libbie, now on the point of departing.

"Happen he might; but I think he'd come readier to the three syllables."

On Valentine's day, Jupiter's cage was decked round with ivy leaves, making quite a pretty wreath on the wicker work; and to one of them was pinned a slip of paper, with these words, written in Libbie's best round hand:—

"From your faithful Valentine. Please take notice his name is Peter, and he'll come if you call him, after a bit."

But little work did Libbie do that afternoon, she was so engaged in watching for the messenger who was to bear her present to her little valentine, and run away as soon as he had delivered up the canary, and explained to whom it was sent.

At last he came; then there was a pause before the woman of the house was at liberty to take it upstairs. Then Libbie saw the little face flush up into a bright colour, the feeble hands tremble with delighted eagerness, the head bent down to try and make out the writing (beyond his power, poor lad, to read), the rapturous turning round of the cage in order to see the canary in every point of view, head, tail, wings, and feet; an intention in which Jupiter, in his uneasiness at being again among strangers, did not second, for he hopped round so, as continually to present a full front to the boy. It was a source of never wearying delight to the little fellow, till daylight closed in; he evidently forgot to wonder who had sent it him, in his gladness at his possession of such a treasure; and when the shadow of his mother darkened on the blind, and the bird had been exhibited, Libbie saw her do what, with all her tenderness, seemed rarely to have entered into her thoughts—she bent down and kissed her boy, in a mother's sympathy with the joy of her child.

The canary was placed for the night between the little bed and window; and when Libbie rose once, to take her accustomed peep, she saw the little arm put fondly round the cage, as if embracing his new treasure even in his sleep. How Jupiter slept this first night is quite another thing.

So ended the first day in Libbie's three eras in last year.

ERA II.

WHITSUNTIDE.

The brightest, fullest daylight poured down into No. 2,—— Court, Albemarle Street, and the heat, even at the early hour of five, as at the noontide on the June days of many years past.

The court seemed alive, and merry with voices and laughter. The bedroom windows were open wide, and had been so all night, on account of the heat; and every now and then you might see a head and a pair of shoulders, simply encased in shirt sleeves, popped out, and you might hear the inquiry passed from one to the other,—"Well, Jack, and where art thee bound for?"

"Dunham!"

"Why, what an old-fashioned chap thou be'st. Thy grandad afore thee went to Dunham: but thou wert always a slow coach. I'm off to Alderley,—me and my missis."

"Ay, that's because there's only thee and thy missis. Wait till thou hast gotten four childer, like me, and thou'lt be glad enough to take 'em to Dunham, oud-fashioned way, for fourpence apiece."

"I'd still go to Alderley; I'd not be bothered with my children; they should keep house at home."

A pair of hands, the person to whom they belonged invisible, boxed his ears on this last speech, in a very spirited, though playful, manner, and the neighbours all laughed at the surprised look of the speaker, at this assault from an unseen foe. The man who had been holding conversation with him cried out,—

"Sarved him right, Mrs. Slater: he knows nought about it yet; but when he gets them he'll be as loth to leave the babbies at home on a Whitsuntide as any on us. We shall live to see him in Dunham Park yet, wi' twins in his arms, and another pair on 'em clutching at daddy's coat-tails, let alone your share of youngsters, missis."

At this moment our friend Libbie appeared at her window, and Mrs. Slater, who had taken her discomfited husband's place, called out,—

"Elizabeth Marsh, where are Dixons and you bound to?"

"Dixons are not up yet; he said last night he'd take his holiday out in lying in bed. I'm going to the old-fashioned place, Dunham."

"Thou art never going by thyself, moping!"

"No. I'm going with Margaret Hall and her lad," replied Libbie, hastily withdrawing from the window, in order to avoid hearing any remarks on the associates she had chosen for her day of pleasure—the scold of the neighbourhood, and her sickly, ailing child!

But Jupiter might have been a dove, and his ivy leaves an olive branch, for the peace he had brought, the happiness he had caused, to three individuals at least. For of course it could not long be a mystery who had sent little Frank Hall his valentine; nor could his mother long entertain her hard manner towards one who had given her child a new pleasure. She was shy, and she was proud, and for some time she struggled against the natural desire of manifesting her gratitude; but one evening, when Libbie was returning home, with a bundle of work half as large as herself, as she dragged herself along through the heated streets, she was overtaken by Margaret Hall, her burden gently pulled from her, and her way home shortened, and her weary spirits soothed and cheered, by the outpourings of Margaret's heart; for the barrier of reserve once broken down, she had much to say, to thank her for days of amusement and happy employment for her lad, to speak of his gratitude, to tell of her hopes and fears,—the hopes and fears that made up the dates of her life. From that time, Libbie lost her awe of the termagant in interest for the mother, whose all was ventured in so frail a bark. From this time, Libbie was a fast friend with both mother and son, planning mitigations for the sorrowful days of the latter as eagerly as poor Margaret Hall, and with far more success. His life had flickered up under the charm and excitement of the last few months. He even seemed strong enough to undertake the journey to Dunham, which Libbie had arranged as a Whitsuntide treat, and for which she and his mother had been hoarding up for several weeks. The canal boat left Knott-mill at six, and it was now past five; so Libbie let herself out very gently, and went across to her friends. She knocked at the door of their lodging-room, and, without waiting for an answer, entered.

Franky's face was flushed, and he was trembling with excitement,—partly with pleasure, but partly with some eager wish not yet granted.

"He wants sore to take Peter with him," said his mother to Libbie, as if referring the matter to her. The boy looked imploringly at her.

"He would like it, I know; for one thing, he'd miss me sadly, and chirrup for me all day long, he'd be so lonely. I could not be half so happy a-thinking on him, left alone here by himself. Then, Libbie, he's just like a Christian, so fond of flowers and green leaves, and them sort of things. He chirrups to me so when mother brings me a pennyworth of wall-flowers to put round his cage. He would talk if he could, you know; but I can tell what he means quite as one as if he spoke. Do let Peter go, Libbie; I'll carry him in my own arms."

So Jupiter was allowed to be of the party. Now Libbie had overcome the great difficulty of conveying Franky to the boat, by offering to "slay" for a coach, and the shouts and exclamations of the neighbours told them that their conveyance awaited them at the bottom of the court. His mother carried Franky, light in weight, though heavy in helplessness, and he would hold the cage, believing that he was thus redeeming his pledge, that Peter should be a trouble to no one. Libbie proceeded to arrange the bundle containing their dinner, as a support in the corner of the coach. The neighbours came out with many blunt speeches, and more kindly wishes, and one or two of them would have relieved Margaret of her burden, if she would have allowed it. The presence of that little crippled fellow seemed to obliterate all the angry feelings which had existed between his mother and her neighbours, and which had formed the politics of that little court for many a day.

And now they were fairly off! Franky bit his lips in attempted endurance of the pain the motion caused him; he winced and shrank, until they were fairly on a Macadamized thoroughfare, when he closed his eyes, and seemed desirous of a few minutes' rest. Libbie felt very shy, and very much afraid of being seen by her employers, "set up in a coach!" and so she hid herself in a corner, and made herself as small as possible; while Mrs. Hall had exactly the opposite feeling, and was delighted to stand up, stretching out of the window, and nodding to pretty nearly every one they met or passed on the foot-paths; and they were not a few, for the streets were quite gay, even at that early hour, with parties going to this or that railway station, or to the boats which crowded the canals on this bright holiday week; and almost every one they met seemed to enter into Mrs. Hall's exhilaration of feeling, and had a smile or nod in return. At last she plumped down by Libbie, and exclaimed, "I never was in a coach but once afore, and that was when I was a-going to be married. It's like heaven; and all done over with such beautiful gimp, too!" continued she, admiring the lining of the vehicle. Jupiter did not enjoy it so much.

As if the holiday time, the lovely weather, and the "sweet hour of prime" had a genial influence, as no doubt they have, everybody's heart seemed softened towards poor Franky. The driver lifted him out with the tenderness of strength, and bore him carefully down to the boat; the people then made way, and gave him the best seat in their power,—or rather I should call it a couch, for they saw he was weary, and insisted on his lying down,—an attitude he would have been ashamed to assume without the protection of his mother and Libbie, who now appeared, bearing their baskets and carrying Peter.

Away the boat went, to make room for others, for every conveyance, both by land and water, is in requisition in Whitsun-week, to give the hard-worked crowds the opportunity of enjoying the charms of the country. Even every standing-place in the canal packets was occupied, and as they glided along, the banks were lined with people, who seemed to find it object enough to watch the boats go by, packed close and full with happy beings brimming with anticipations of a day's pleasure.

The country through which they passed is as uninteresting as can well be imagined; but still it is the country: and the screams of delight from the children, and the low laughs of pleasure from the parents, at every blossoming tree that trailed its wreath against some cottage wall, or at the tufts of late primroses which lingered in the cool depths of grass along the canal banks, the thorough relish of everything, as if dreading to let the least circumstance of this happy day pass over without its due appreciation, made the time seem all too short, although it took two hours to arrive at a place only eight miles from Manchester. Even Franky, with all his impatience to see Dunham woods (which I think he confused with London, believing both to be paved with gold), enjoyed the easy motion of the boat so much, floating along, while pictures moved before him, that he regretted when the time came for landing among the soft, green meadows, that came sloping down to the dancing water's brim. His fellow-passengers carried him to the park, and refused all payment, although his mother had laid by sixpence on purpose, as a recompense for this service.

"Oh, Libbie, how beautiful! Oh, mother, mother! is the whole world out of Manchester as beautiful as this? I did not know trees were like this! Such green homes for birds! Look, Peter! would not you like to be there, up among those boughs? But I can't let you go, you know, because you're my little bird brother, and I should be quite lost without you."

They spread a shawl upon the fine mossy turf, at the root of a beech-tree, which made a sort of natural couch, and there they laid him, and bade him rest, in spite of the delight which made him believe himself capable of any exertion. Where he lay,—always holding Jupiter's cage, and often talking to him as to a playfellow,—he was on the verge of a green area, shut in by magnificent trees, in all the glory of their early foliage, before the summer heats had deepened their verdure into one rich, monotonous tint. And hither came party after party; old men and maidens, young men and children,—whole families trooped along after the guiding fathers, who bore the youngest in their arms, or astride upon their backs, while they turned round occasionally to the wives, with whom they shared some fond local remembrance. For years has Dunham Park been the favourite resort of the Manchester work-people; for more years than I can tell; probably ever since "the Duke," by his canals, opened out the system of cheap travelling. Its scenery, too, which presents such a complete contrast to the whirl and turmoil of Manchester; so thoroughly woodland, with its ancestral trees (here and there lightning blanched); its "verdurous walls;" its grassy walks, leading far away into some glade, where you start at the rabbit rustling among the last year's fern, and where the wood-pigeon's call seems the only fitting and accordant sound. Depend upon it, this complete sylvan repose, this accessible quiet, this lapping the soul in green images of the country, forms the most complete contrast to a town's-person, and consequently has over such the greatest power to charm.

Presently Libbie found out she was very hungry. Now they were but provided with dinner, which was, of course, to be eaten as near twelve o'clock as might be; and Margaret Hall, in her prudence, asked a working-man near to tell her what o'clock it was.

"Nay," said he, "I'll ne'er look at clock or watch to-day. I'll not spoil my pleasure by finding out how fast it's going away. If thou'rt hungry, eat. I make my own dinner hour, and I have eaten mine an hour ago."

So they had their veal pies, and then found out it was only about half-past ten o'clock; by so many pleasurable events had that morning been marked. But such was their buoyancy of spirits, that they only enjoyed their mistake, and joined in the general laugh against the man who had eaten his dinner somewhere about nine. He laughed most heartily of all, till, suddenly stopping, he said,—

"I must not go on at this rate; laughing gives one such an appetite."

"Oh! if that's all," said a merry-looking man, lying at full length, and brushing the fresh scent out of the grass, while two or three little children tumbled over him, and crept about him, as kittens or puppies frolic with their parents, "if that's all, we'll have a subscription of eatables for them improvident folk as have eaten their dinner for their breakfast. Here's a sausage pasty and a handful of nuts for my share. Bring round a hat, Bob, and see what the company will give."

Bob carried out the joke, much to little Franky's amusement; and no one was so churlish as to refuse, although the contributions varied from a peppermint drop up to a veal pie and a sausage pasty.

"It's a thriving trade," said Bob, as he emptied his hatful of provisions on the grass by Libbie's side. "Besides, it's tiptop, too, to live on the public. Hark! what is that?"

The laughter and the chat were suddenly hushed, and mothers told their little ones to listen,—as, far away in the distance, now sinking and falling, now swelling and clear, came a ringing peal of children's voices, blended together in one of those psalm tunes which we are all of us familiar with, and which bring to mind the old, old days, when we, as wondering children, were first led to worship "Our Father," by those beloved ones who have since gone to the more perfect worship. Holy was that distant choral praise, even to the most thoughtless; and when it, in fact, was ended, in the instant's pause, during which the ear awaits the repetition of the air, they caught the noontide hum and buzz of the myriads of insects who danced away their lives in the glorious day; they heard the swaying of the mighty woods in the soft but resistless breeze, and then again once more burst forth the merry jests and the shouts of childhood; and again the elder ones resumed their happy talk, as they lay or sat "under the greenwood tree." Fresh parties came dropping in; some laden with wild flowers— almost with branches of hawthorn, indeed; while one or two had made prizes of the earliest dog-roses, and had cast away campion, stitchwort, ragged robin, all to keep the lady of the hedges from being obscured or hidden by the community.

One after another drew near to Franky, and looked on with interest as he lay sorting the flowers given to him. Happy parents stood by, with their household bands around them, in health and comeliness, and felt the sad prophecy of those shrivelled limbs, those wasted fingers, those lamp-like eyes, with their bright, dark lustre. His mother was too eagerly watching his happiness to read the meaning of those grave looks, but Libbie saw them and understood them; and a chill shudder went through her, even on that day, as she thought on the future.

"Ay! I thought we should give you a start!"

A start they did give, with their terrible slap on Libbie's back, as she sat idly grouping flowers, and following out her sorrowful thoughts. It was the Dixons. Instead of keeping their holiday by lying in bed, they and their children had roused themselves, and had come by the omnibus to the nearest point. For an instant the meeting was an awkward one, on account of the feud between Margaret Hall and Mrs. Dixon, but there was no long resisting of kindly mother Nature's soothings, at that holiday time, and in that lonely tranquil spot; or if they could have been unheeded, the sight of Franky would have awed every angry feeling into rest, so changed was he since the Dixons had last seen him; and since he had been the Puck or Robin Goodfellow of the neighbourhood, whose marbles were always rolling under other people's feet, and whose top-strings were always hanging in nooses to catch the unwary. Yes, he, the feeble, mild, almost girlish-looking lad, had once been a merry, happy rogue, and as such often cuffed by Mrs. Dixon, the very Mrs. Dixon who now stood gazing with the tears in her eyes. Could she, in sight of him, the changed, the fading, keep up a quarrel with his mother?

"How long hast thou been here?" asked Dixon.

"Welly on for all day," answered Libbie.

"Hast never been to see the deer, or the king and queen oaks? Lord, how stupid."

His wife pinched his arm, to remind him of Franky's helpless condition, which of course tethered the otherwise willing feet. But Dixon had a remedy. He called Bob, and one or two others, and each taking a corner of the strong plaid shawl, they slung Franky as in a hammock, and thus carried him merrily along, down the wood paths, over the smooth, grassy turf, while the glimmering shine and shadow fell on his upturned face. The women walked behind, talking, loitering along, always in sight of the hammock; now picking up some green treasure from the ground, now catching at the low hanging branches of the horse-chestnut. The soul grew much on this day, and in these woods, and all unconsciously, as souls do grow. They followed Franky's hammock-bearers up a grassy knoll, on the top of which stood a group of pine trees, whose stems looked like dark red gold in the sunbeams. They had taken Franky there to show him Manchester, far away in the blue plain, against which the woodland foreground cut with a soft clear line. Far, far away in the distance on that flat plain, you might see the motionless cloud of smoke hanging over a great town, and that was Manchester,—ugly, smoky Manchester, dear, busy, earnest, noble-working Manchester; where their children had been born, and where, perhaps, some lay buried; where their homes were, and where God had cast their lives, and told them to work out their destiny.

"Hurrah! for oud smoke-jack!" cried Bob, putting Franky softly down on the grass, before he whirled his hat round, preparatory to a shout. "Hurrah! hurrah!" from all the men. "There's the rim of my hat lying like a quoit yonder," observed Bob quietly, as he replaced his brimless hat on his head with the gravity of a judge.

"Here's the Sunday-school children a-coming to sit on this shady side, and have their buns and milk. Hark! they're singing the infant-school grace."

They sat close at hand, so that Franky could hear the words they sang, in rings of children, making, in their gay summer prints, newly donned for that week, garlands of little faces, all happy and bright upon that green hill-side. One little "Dot" of a girl came shily behind Franky, whom she had long been watching, and threw her half-bun at his side, and then ran away and hid herself, in very shame at the boldness of her own sweet impulse. She kept peeping from her screen at Franky all the time; and he meanwhile was almost too much pleased and happy to eat; the world was so beautiful, and men, women, and children all so tender and kind; so softened, in fact, by the beauty of this earth, so unconsciously touched by the spirit of love, which was the Creator of this lovely earth. But the day drew to an end; the heat declined; the birds once more began their warblings; the fresh scents again hung about plant, and tree, and grass, betokening the fragrant presence of the reviving dew, and—the boat time was near. As they trod the meadow-path once more, they were joined by many a party they had encountered during the day, all abounding in happiness, all full of the day's adventures. Long-cherished quarrels had been forgotten, new friendships formed. Fresh tastes and higher delights had been imparted that day. We have all of us our look, now and then, called up by some noble or loving thought (our highest on earth), which will be our likeness in heaven. I can catch the glance on many a face, the glancing light of the cloud of glory from heaven, "which is our home." That look was present on many a hard-worked, wrinkled countenance, as they turned backwards to catch a longing, lingering look at Dunham woods, fast deepening into blackness of night, but whose memory was to haunt, in greenness and freshness, many a loom, and workshop, and factory, with images of peace and beauty.

That night, as Libbie lay awake, revolving the incidents of the day, she caught Franky's voice through the open windows. Instead of the frequent moan of pain, he was trying to recall the burden of one of the children's hymns,—

Here we suffer grief and pain,
Here we meet to part again;
In Heaven we part no more.
Oh! that will be joyful, &c.

She recalled his question, the whispered question, to her, in the happiest part of the day. He asked Libbie, "Is Dunham like heaven? the people here are as kind as angels, and I don't want heaven to be more beautiful than this place. If you and mother would but die with me, I should like to die, and live always there!" She had checked him, for she feared he was impious; but now the young child's craving for some definite idea of the land to which his inner wisdom told him he was hastening, had nothing in it wrong, or even sorrowful, for—

In Heaven we part no more.

ERA III.

MICHAELMAS.

The church clocks had struck three; the crowds of gentlemen returning to business, after their early dinners, had disappeared within offices and warehouses; the streets were clear and quiet, and ladies were venturing to sally forth for their afternoon shoppings and their afternoon calls.

Slowly, slowly, along the streets, elbowed by life at every turn, a little funeral wound its quiet way. Four men bore along a child's coffin; two women with bowed heads followed meekly.

I need not tell you whose coffin it was, or who were those two mourners. All was now over with little Frank Hall: his romps, his games, his sickening, his suffering, his death. All was now over, but the Resurrection and the Life.

His mother walked as in a stupor. Could it be that he was dead! If he had been less of an object of her thoughts, less of a motive for her labours, she could sooner have realized it. As it was, she followed his poor, cast-off, worn-out body as if she were borne along by some oppressive dream. If he were really dead, how could she be still alive?

Libbie's mind was far less stunned, and consequently far more active, than Margaret Hall's. Visions, as in a phantasmagoria, came rapidly passing before her—recollections of the time (which seemed now so long ago) when the shadow of the feebly-waving arm first caught her attention; of the bright, strangely isolated day at Dunham Park, where the world had seemed so full of enjoyment, and beauty, and life; of the long-continued heat, through which poor Franky had panted away his strength in the little close room, where there was no escaping the hot rays of the afternoon sun; of the long nights when his mother and she had watched by his side, as he moaned continually, whether awake or asleep; of the fevered moaning slumber of exhaustion; of the pitiful little self-upbraidings for his own impatience of suffering, only impatient in his own eyes—most true and holy patience in the sight of others; and then the fading away of life, the loss of power, the increased unconsciousness, the lovely look of angelic peace, which followed the dark shadow on the countenance, where was he—what was he now?

And so they laid him in his grave, and heard the solemn funeral words; but far off in the distance, as if not addressed to them.

Margaret Hall bent over the grave to catch one last glance—she had not spoken, nor sobbed, nor done aught but shiver now and then, since the morning; but now her weight bore more heavily on Libbie's arm, and without sigh or sound she fell an unconscious heap on the piled-up gravel. They helped Libbie to bring her round; but long after her half-opened eyes and altered breathingshowed that her senses were restored, she lay, speechless and motionless, without attempting to rise from her strange bed, as if the earth contained nothing worth even that trifling exertion.

At last Libbie and she left that holy, consecrated spot, and bent their steps back to the only place more consecrated still; where he had rendered up his spirit; and where memories of him haunted each common, rude piece of furniture that their eyes fell upon. As the woman of the house opened the door, she pulled Libbie on one side, and said—

"Anne Dixon has been across to see you; she wants to have a word with you."

"I cannot go now," replied Libbie, as she pushed hastily along, in order to enter the room (*his* room), at the same time with the childless mother: for, as she had anticipated, the sight of that empty spot, the glance at the uncurtained open window, letting in the fresh air, and the broad, rejoicing light of day, where all had so long been darkened and subdued, unlocked the waters of the fountain, and long and shrill were the cries for her boy that the poor woman uttered.

"Oh! dear Mrs. Hall," said Libbie, herself drenched in tears, "do not take on so badly; I'm sure it would grieve *him* sore if he were alive, and you know he is—Bible tells us so; and may be he's here watching how we go on without him, and hoping we don't fret over much."

Mrs. Hall's sobs grew worse and more hysterical.

"Oh! listen," said Libbie, once more struggling against her own increasing agitation. "Listen! there's Peter chirping as he always does when he's put about, frightened like; and you know he that's gone could never abide to hear the canary chirp in that shrill way."

Margaret Hall did check herself, and curb her expressions of agony, in order not to frighten the little creature he had loved; and as her outward grief subsided, Libbie took up the large old Bible, which fell open at the never-failing comfort of the fourteenth chapter of St. John's Gospel.

How often these large family Bibles do open at that chapter! as if, unused in more joyous and prosperous times, the soul went home to its words of loving sympathy when weary and sorrowful, just as the little child seeks the tender comfort of its mother in all its griefs and cares.

And Margaret put back her wet, ruffled, grey hair from her heated, tear-stained, woeful face, and listened with such earnest eyes, trying to form some idea of the "Father's house," where her boy had gone to dwell.

They were interrupted by a low tap at the door. Libbie went. "Anne Dixon has watched you home, and wants to have a word with you," said the woman of the house, in a whisper. Libbie went back and closed the book, with a word of explanation to Margaret Hall, and then ran downstairs, to learn the reason of Anne's anxiety to see her.

"Oh, Libbie!" she burst out with, and then, checking herself with the remembrance of Libbie's last solemn duty, "how's Margaret Hall? But, of course, poor thing, she'll fret a bit at first; she'll be some time coming round, mother says, seeing it's as well that poor lad is taken; for he'd always ha' been a cripple, and a trouble to her—he was a fine lad once, too."

She had come full of another and a different subject; but the sight of Libbie's sad, weeping face, and the quiet, subdued tone of her manner, made her feel it awkward to begin on any other theme than the one which filled up her companion's mind. To her last speech Libbie answered sorrowfully—

"No doubt, Anne, it's ordered for the best; but oh! don't call him, don't think he could ever ha' been, a trouble to his mother, though he were a cripple. She loved him all the more for each thing she had to do for him—I am sure I did." Libbie cried a little behind her apron. Anne Dixon felt still more awkward in introducing the discordant subject.

"Well! 'flesh is grass,' Bible says," and having fulfilled the etiquette of quoting a text if possible, if not of making a moral observation on the fleeting nature of earthly things, she thought she was at liberty to pass on to her real errand.

"You must not go on moping yourself, Libbie Marsh. What I wanted special for to see you this afternoon, was to tell you, you must come to my wedding to-morrow. Nanny Dawson has fallen sick, and there's none as I should like to have bridesmaid in her place as well as you."

"To-morrow! Oh, I cannot!—indeed I cannot!"

"Why not?"

Libbie did not answer, and Anne Dixon grew impatient.

"Surely, in the name o' goodness, you're never going to baulk yourself of a day's pleasure for the sake of yon little cripple that's dead and gone!"

"No,—it's not baulking myself of—don't be angry, Anne Dixon, with him, please; but I don't think it would be a pleasure to me,—I don't feel as if I could enjoy it; thank you all the same. But I did love that little lad very dearly—I did," sobbing a little, "and I can't forget him and make merry so soon."

"Well—I never!" exclaimed Anne, almost angrily.

"Indeed, Anne, I feel your kindness, and you and Bob have my best wishes,—that's what you have; but even if I went, I should be thinking all day of him, and of his poor, poor mother, and they say it's bad to think very much on them that's dead, at a wedding."

"Nonsense," said Anne, "I'll take the risk of the ill-luck. After all, what is marrying? Just a spree, Bob says. He often says he does not think I shall make him a good wife, for I know nought about house matters, wi' working in a factory; but he says he'd rather be uneasy wi' me than easy wi' anybody else. There's love for you! And I tell him I'd rather have him tipsy than any one else sober."

"Oh! Anne Dixon, hush! you don't know yet what it is to have a drunken husband. I have seen something of it: father used to get fuddled, and, in the long run, it killed mother, let alone—oh! Anne, God above only knows what the wife of a drunken man has to bear. Don't tell," said she, lowering her voice, "but father killed our little baby in one of his bouts; mother never looked up again, nor father either, for that matter, only his was in a different way. Mother will have gotten to little Jemmie now, and they'll be so happy together,—and perhaps Franky too. Oh!" said she, recovering herself from her train of thought, "never say aught lightly of the wife's lot whose husband is given to drink!"

"Dear, what a preachment. I tell you what, Libbie, you're as born an old maid as ever I saw. You'll never be married to either drunken or sober."

Libbie's face went rather red, but without losing its meek expression.

"I know that as well as you can tell me; and more reason, therefore, as God has seen fit to keep me out of woman's natural work, I should try and find work for myself. I mean," seeing Anne Dixon's puzzled look, "that as I know I'm never likely to have a home of my own, or a husband that would look to me to make all straight, or children to watch over or care for, all which I take to be woman's natural work, I must not lose time in fretting and fidgetting after marriage, but just look about me for somewhat else to do. I can see many a one misses it in this. They will hanker after what is ne'er likely to be theirs, instead of facing it out, and settling down to be old maids; and, as old maids, just looking round for the odd jobs God leaves in the world for such as old maids to do. There's plenty of such work, and there's the blessing of God on them as does it." Libbie was almost out of breath at this outpouring of what had long been her inner thoughts.

"That's all very true, I make no doubt, for them as is to be old maids; but as I'm not, please God to-morrow comes, you might have spared your breath to cool your porridge. What I want to know is, whether you'll be bridesmaid to-morrow or not. Come, now do; it will do you good, after all your working, and watching, and slaving yourself for that poor Franky Hall."

"It was one of my odd jobs," said Libbie, smiling, though her eyes were brimming over with tears; "but, dear Anne," said she, recovering itself, "I could not do it to-morrow, indeed I could not."

"And I can't wait," said Anne Dixon, almost sulkily, "Bob and I put it off from to-day, because of the funeral, and Bob had set his heart on its being on Michaelmas-day; and mother says the goose won't keep beyond to-morrow. Do come: father finds eatables, and Bob finds drink, and we shall be so jolly! and after we've been to church, we're to walk round the town in pairs, white satin ribbon in our bonnets, and refreshments at any public-house we like, Bob says. And after dinner there's to be a dance. Don't be a fool; you can do no good by staying. Margaret Hall will have to go out washing, I'll be bound."

"Yes, she must go to Mrs. Wilkinson's, and, for that matter, I must go working too. Mrs. Williams has been after me to make her girl's winter things ready; only I could not leave Franky, he clung so to me."

"Then you won't be bridesmaid! is that your last word?"

"It is; you must not be angry with me, Anne Dixon," said Libbie, deprecatingly.

But Anne was gone without a reply.

With a heavy heart Libbie mounted the little staircase, for she felt how ungracious her refusal of Anne's kindness must appear, to one who understood so little the feelings which rendered her acceptance of it a moral impossibility.

On opening the door she saw Margaret Hall, with the Bible open on the table before her. For she had puzzled out the place where Libbie was reading, and, with her finger under the line, was spelling out the words of consolation, piecing the syllables together aloud, with the earnest anxiety of comprehension with which a child first learns to read. So Libbie took the stool by her side, before she was aware that any one had entered the room.

"What did she want you for?" asked Margaret. "But I can guess; she wanted you to be at th' wedding that is to come off this week, they say. Ay, they'll marry, and laugh, and dance, all as one as if my boy was alive," said she, bitterly. "Well, he was neither kith nor kin of yours, so I maun try and be thankful for what you've done for him, and not wonder at your forgetting him afore he's well settled in his grave."

"I never can forget him, and I'm not going to the wedding," said Libbie, quietly, for she understood the mother's jealousy of her dead child's claims.

"I must go work at Mrs. Williams' to-morrow," she said, in explanation, for she was unwilling to boast of her tender, fond regret, which had been her principal motive for declining Anne's invitation.

"And I mun go washing, just as if nothing had happened," sighed forth Mrs. Hall, "and I mun come home at night, and find his place empty, and all still where I used to be sure of hearing his voice ere ever I got up the stair: no one will ever call me mother again." She fell crying pitifully, and Libbie could not speak for her own emotion for some time. But during this silence she put the keystone in the arch of thoughts she had been building up for many days; and when Margaret was again calm in her sorrow, Libbie said, "Mrs. Hall, I should like—would you like me to come for to live here altogether?"

Margaret Hall looked up with a sudden light in her countenance, which encouraged Libbie to go on.

"I could sleep with you, and pay half, you know; and we should be together in the evenings; and her as was home first would watch for the other, and" (dropping her voice) "we could talk of him at nights, you know."

She was going on, but Mrs. Hall interrupted her.

"Oh, Libbie Marsh! and can you really think of coming to live wi' me. I should like it above—but no! it must not be; you've no notion on what a creature I am, at times; more like a mad one when I'm in a rage, and I cannot keep it down. I seem to get out of bed wrong side in the morning, and I must have my passion out with the first person I meet. Why, Libbie," said she, with a doleful look of agony on her face, "I even used to fly out on him, poor sick lad as he was, and you may judge how little you can keep it down frae that. No, you must not come. I must live alone now," sinking her voice into the low tones of despair.

But Libbie's resolution was brave and strong. "I'm not afraid," said she, smiling. "I know you better than you know yourself, Mrs. Hall. I've seen you try of late to keep it down, when you've been boiling over, and I think you'll go on a-doing so. And at any rate, when you've had your fit out, you're very kind, and I can forget if you've been a bit put out. But I'll try not to put you out. Do let me come: I think *he* would like us to keep together. I'll do my very best to make you comfortable."

"It's me! it's me as will be making your life miserable with my temper; or else, God knows, how my heart clings to you. You and me is folk alone in the world, for we both loved one who is dead, and who had none else to love him. If you will live with me, Libbie, I'll try as I never did afore to be gentle and quiet-tempered. Oh! will you try me, Libbie Marsh?" So out of the little grave there sprang a hope and a resolution, which made life an object to each of the two.

When Elizabeth Marsh returned home the next evening from her day's labours, Anne (Dixon no longer) crossed over, all in her bridal finery, to endeavour to induce her to join the dance going on in her father's house.

"Dear Anne, this is good of you, a-thinking of me to-night," said Libbie, kissing her, "and though I cannot come,—I've promised Mrs. Hall to be with her,—I shall think on you, and I trust you'll be happy. I have got a little needle-case I have looked out for you; stay, here it is,—I wish it were more—only——"

"Only, I know what. You've been a-spending all your money in nice things for poor Franky. Thou'rt a real good un, Libbie, and I'll keep your needle-book to my dying day, that I will." Seeing Anne in such a friendly mood, emboldened Libbie to tell her of her change of place; of her intention of lodging henceforward with Margaret Hall.

"Thou never will! Why father and mother are as fond of thee as can be; they'll lower thy rent if that's what it is—and thou knowst they never grudge thee bit or drop. And Margaret Hall, of all folk, to lodge wi'! She's such a Tartar! Sooner than not have a quarrel, she'd fight right hand against left. Thou'lt have no peace of thy life. What on earth can make you think of such a thing, Libbie Marsh?"

"She'll be so lonely without me," pleaded Libbie. "I'm sure I could make her happier, even if she did scold me a bit now and then, than she'd be a living alone, and I'm not afraid of her; and I mean to do my best not to vex her: and it will ease her heart, maybe, to talk to me at times about Franky. I shall often see your father and mother, and I shall always thank them for their kindness to me. But they have you and little Mary, and poor Mrs. Hall has no one."

Anne could only repeat, "Well, I never!" and hurry off to tell the news at home.

But Libbie was right. Margaret Hall is a different woman to the scold of the neighbourhood she once was; touched and softened by the two purifying angels, Sorrow and Love. And it is beautiful to see her affection, her reverence, for Libbie

Marsh. Her dead mother could hardly have cared for her more tenderly than does the hard-hearted washerwoman, not long ago so fierce and unwomanly. Libbie, herself, has such peace shining on her countenance, as almost makes it beautiful, as she tenders the services of a daughter to Franky's mother, no longer the desolate lonely orphan, a stranger on the earth.

Do you ever read the moral, concluding sentence of a story? I never do, but I once (in the year 1811, I think) heard of a deaf old lady, living by herself, who did; and as she may have left some descendants with the same amiable peculiarity, I will put in, for their benefit, what I believe to be the secret of Libbie's peace of mind, the real reason why she no longer feels oppressed at her own loneliness in the world,—

She has a purpose in life; and that purpose is a holy one.

CHRISTMAS STORMS AND SUNSHINE.

In the town of —— (no matter where) there circulated two local newspapers (no matter when). Now the *Flying Post* was long established and respectable—alias bigoted and Tory; the *Examiner* was spirited and intelligent—alias new-fangled and democratic. Every week these newspapers contained articles abusing each other; as cross and peppery as articles could be, and evidently the production of irritated minds, although they seemed to have one stereotyped commencement,—"Though the article appearing in last week's *Post* (or *Examiner*) is below contempt, yet we have been induced," &c., &c., and every Saturday the Radical shopkeepers shook hands together, and agreed that the *Post* was done for, by the slashing, clever *Examiner*, while the more dignified Tories began by regretting that Johnson should think that low paper, only read by a few of the vulgar, worth wasting his wit upon; however the *Examiner* was at its last gasp.

It was not though. It lived and flourished; at least it paid its way, as one of the heroes of my story could tell. He was chief compositor, or whatever title may be given to the head-man of the mechanical part of a newspaper. He hardly confined himself to that department. Once or twice, unknown to the editor, when the manuscript had fallen short, he had filled up the vacant space by compositions of his own; announcements of a forthcoming crop of green peas in December; a grey thrush having been seen, or a white hare, or such interesting phenomena; invented for the occasion, I must confess; but what of that? His wife always knew when to expect a little specimen of her husband's literary talent by a peculiar cough, which served as prelude; and, judging from this encouraging sign, and the high-pitched and emphatic voice in which he read them, she was inclined to think, that an "Ode to an early Rose-bud," in the corner devoted to original poetry, and a letter in the correspondence department, signed "Pro Bono Publico," were her husband's writing, and to hold up her head accordingly.

I never could find out what it was that occasioned the Hodgsons to lodge in the same house as the Jenkinses. Jenkins held the same office in the Tory paper as Hodgson did in the *Examiner*, and, as I said before, I leave you to give it a name. But Jenkins had a proper sense of his position, and a proper reverence for all in authority, from the king down to the editor and sub-editor. He would as soon have thought of borrowing the king's crown for a nightcap, or the king's sceptre for a walking-stick, as he would have thought of filling up any spare corner with any production of his own; and I think it would have even added to his contempt of Hodgson (if that were possible), had he known of the "productions of his brain," as the latter fondly alluded to the paragraphs he inserted, when speaking to his wife.

Jenkins had his wife too. Wives were wanting to finish the completeness of the quarrel, which existed one memorable Christmas week, some dozen years ago, between the two neighbours, the two compositors. And with wives, it was a very pretty, a very complete quarrel. To make the opposing parties still more equal, still more well-matched, if the Hodgsons had a baby ("such a baby!—a poor, puny little thing"), Mrs. Jenkins had a cat ("such a cat! a great, nasty, miowling tomcat, that was always stealing the milk put by for little Angel's supper"). And now, having matched Greek with Greek, I must proceed to the tug of war. It was the day before Christmas; such a cold east wind! such an inky sky! such a blue-black look in people's faces, as they were driven out more than usual, to complete their purchases for the next day's festival.

Before leaving home that morning, Jenkins had given some money to his wife to buy the next day's dinner.

"My dear, I wish for turkey and sausages. It may be a weakness, but I own I am partial to sausages. My deceased mother was. Such tastes are hereditary. As to the sweets—whether plum-pudding or mince-pies—I leave such considerations to you; I only beg you not to mind expense. Christmas comes but once a year."

And again he had called out from the bottom of the first flight of stairs, just close to the Hodgsons' door ("such ostentatiousness," as Mrs. Hodgson observed), "You will not forget the sausages, my dear?"

"I should have liked to have had something above common, Mary," said Hodgson, as they too made their plans for the next day, "but I think roast beef must do for us. You see, love, we've a family."

"Only one, Jem! I don't want more than roast beef, though, I'm sure. Before I went to service, mother and me would have thought roast beef a very fine dinner."

"Well, let's settle it then, roast beef and a plum-pudding; and now, good-by. Mind and take care of little Tom. I thought he was a bit hoarse this morning."

And off he went to his work.

Now, it was a good while since Mrs. Jenkins and Mrs. Hodgson had spoken to each other, although they were quite as much in possession of the knowledge of events and opinions as though they did. Mary knew that Mrs. Jenkins despised her for not having a real lace cap, which Mrs. Jenkins had; and for having been a servant, which Mrs. Jenkins had not; and the little occasional pinchings which the Hodgsons were obliged to resort to, to make both ends meet, would have been very patiently endured by Mary, if she had not winced under Mrs. Jenkins's knowledge of such economy. But she had her revenge. She had a child, and Mrs. Jenkins had none. To have had a child, even such a puny baby as little Tom, Mrs.

Jenkins would have worn commonest caps, and cleaned grates, and drudged her fingers to the bone. The great unspoken disappointment of her life soured her temper, and turned her thoughts inward, and made her morbid and selfish.

"Hang that cat! he's been stealing again! he's gnawed the cold mutton in his nasty mouth till it's not fit to set before a Christian; and I've nothing else for Jem's dinner. But I'll give it him now I've caught him, that I will!"

So saying, Mary Hodgson caught up her husband's Sunday cane, and despite pussy's cries and scratches, she gave him such a beating as she hoped might cure him of his thievish propensities; when lo! and behold, Mrs. Jenkins stood at the door with a face of bitter wrath.

"Aren't you ashamed of yourself, ma'am, to abuse a poor dumb animal, ma'am, as knows no better than to take food when he sees it, ma'am? He only follows the nature which God has given, ma'am; and it's a pity your nature, ma'am, which I've heard, is of the stingy saving species, does not make you shut your cupboard-door a little closer. There is such a thing as law for brute animals. I'll ask Mr. Jenkins, but I don't think them Radicals has done away with that law yet, for all their Reform Bill, ma'am. My poor precious love of a Tommy, is he hurt? and is his leg broke for taking a mouthful of scraps, as most people would give away to a beggar,—if he'd take 'em?" wound up Mrs. Jenkins, casting a contemptuous look on the remnant of a scrag end of mutton.

Mary felt very angry and very guilty. For she really pitied the poor limping animal as he crept up to his mistress, and there lay down to bemoan himself; she wished she had not beaten him so hard, for it certainly was her own careless way of never shutting the cupboard-door that had tempted him to his fault. But the sneer at her little bit of mutton turned her penitence to fresh wrath, and she shut the door in Mrs. Jenkins's face, as she stood caressing her cat in the lobby, with such a bang, that it wakened little Tom, and he began to cry.

Everything was to go wrong with Mary to-day. Now baby was awake, who was to take her husband's dinner to the office? She took the child in her arms, and tried to hush him off to sleep again, and as she sung she cried, she could hardly tell why,—a sort of reaction from her violent angry feelings. She wished she had never beaten the poor cat; she wondered if his leg was really broken. What would her mother say if she knew how cross and cruel her little Mary was getting? If she should live to beat her child in one of her angry fits?

It was of no use lullabying while she sobbed so; it must be given up, and she must just carry her baby in her arms, and take him with her to the office, for it was long past dinner-time. So she pared the mutton carefully, although by so doing she reduced the meat to an infinitesimal quantity, and taking the baked potatoes out of the oven, she popped them piping hot into her basket with the et-cæteras of plate, butter, salt, and knife and fork.

It was, indeed, a bitter wind. She bent against it as she ran, and the flakes of snow were sharp and cutting as ice. Baby cried all the way, though she cuddled him up in her shawl. Then her husband had made his appetite up for a potato pie, and (literary man as he was) his body got so much the better of his mind, that he looked rather black at the cold mutton. Mary had no appetite for her own dinner when she arrived at home again. So, after she had tried to feed baby, and he had fretfully refused to take his bread and milk, she laid him down as usual on his quilt, surrounded by playthings, while she sided away, and chopped suet for the next day's pudding. Early in the afternoon a parcel came, done up first in brown paper, then in such a white, grass-bleached, sweet-smelling towel, and a note from her dear, dear mother; in which quaint writing she endeavoured to tell her daughter that she was not forgotten at Christmas time; but that learning that Farmer Burton was killing his pig, she had made interest for some of his famous pork, out of which she had manufactured some sausages, and flavoured them just as Mary used to like when she lived at home.

"Dear, dear mother!" said Mary to herself. "There never was any one like her for remembering other folk. What rare sausages she used to make! Home things have a smack with 'em, no bought things can ever have. Set them up with their sausages! I've a notion if Mrs. Jenkins had ever tasted mother's she'd have no fancy for them town-made things Fanny took in just now."

And so she went on thinking about home, till the smiles and the dimples came out again at the remembrance of that pretty cottage, which would look green even now in the depth of winter, with its pyracanthus, and its holly-bushes, and the great Portugal laurel that was her mother's pride. And the back path through the orchard to Farmer Burton's; how well she remembered it. The bushels of unripe apples she had picked up there, and distributed among his pigs, till he had scolded her for giving them so much green trash.

She was interrupted—her baby (I call him a baby, because his father and mother did, and because he was so little of his age, but I rather think he was eighteen months old,) had fallen asleep some time before among his playthings; an uneasy, restless sleep; but of which Mary had been thankful, as his morning's nap had been too short, and as she was so busy. But now he began to make such a strange crowing noise, just like a chair drawn heavily and gratingly along a kitchen-floor! His eyes were open, but expressive of nothing but pain.

"Mother's darling!" said Mary, in terror, lifting him up. "Baby, try not to make that noise. Hush, hush, darling; what hurts him?" But the noise came worse and worse.

"Fanny! Fanny!" Mary called in mortal fright, for her baby was almost black with his gasping breath, and she had no one to ask for aid or sympathy but her landlady's daughter, a little girl of twelve or thirteen, who attended to the house in her mother's absence, as daily cook in gentlemen's families. Fanny was more especially considered the attendant of the upstairs lodgers (who paid for the use of the kitchen, "for Jenkins could not abide the smell of meat cooking"), but just now she was fortunately sitting at her afternoon's work of darning stockings, and hearing Mrs. Hodgson's cry of terror, she ran to her sitting-room, and understood the case at a glance.

"He's got the croup! Oh, Mrs. Hodgson, he'll die as sure as fate. Little brother had it, and he died in no time. The doctor said he could do nothing for him—it had gone too far. He said if we'd put him in a warm bath at first, it might have saved him; but, bless you! he was never half so bad as your baby." Unconsciously there mingled in her statement some of a child's love of producing an effect; but the increasing danger was clear enough.

"Oh, my baby! my baby! Oh, love, love! don't look so ill; I cannot bear it. And my fire so low! There, I was thinking of home, and picking currants, and never minding the fire. Oh, Fanny! what is the fire like in the kitchen? Speak."

"Mother told me to screw it up, and throw some slack on as soon as Mrs. Jenkins had done with it, and so I did. It's very low and black. But, oh, Mrs. Hodgson! let me run for the doctor—I cannot abear to hear him, it's so like little brother."

Through her streaming tears Mary motioned her to go; and trembling, sinking, sick at heart, she laid her boy in his cradle, and ran to fill her kettle.

Mrs. Jenkins, having cooked her husband's snug little dinner, to which he came home; having told him her story of pussy's beating, at which he was justly and dignifiedly indignant, saying it was all of a piece with that abusive *Examiner*; having received the sausages, and turkey, and mince pies, which her husband had ordered; and cleaned up the room, and prepared everything for tea, and coaxed and duly bemoaned her cat (who had pretty nearly forgotten his beating, but very much enjoyed the petting), having done all these and many other things, Mrs. Jenkins sate down to get up the real lace cap. Every thread was pulled out separately, and carefully stretched: when, what was that? Outside, in the street, a chorus of piping children's voices sang the old carol she had heard a hundred times in the days of her youth:—

"As Joseph was a walking he heard an angel sing,
'This night shall be born our heavenly King.
He neither shall be born in housen nor in hall,
Nor in the place of Paradise, but in an ox's stall.
He neither shall be clothed in purple nor in pall,
But all in fair linen, as were babies all:
He neither shall be rocked in silver nor in gold,
But in a wooden cradle that rocks on the mould,'" &c.

She got up and went to the window. There, below, stood the group of grey black little figures, relieved against the snow, which now enveloped everything. "For old sake's sake," as she phrased it, she counted out a halfpenny apiece for the singers, out of the copper bag, and threw them down below.

The room had become chilly while she had been counting out and throwing down her money, so she stirred her already glowing fire, and sat down right before it—but not to stretch her lace; like Mary Hodgson, she began to think over long-past days, on softening remembrances of the dead and gone, on words long forgotten, on holy stories heard at her mother's knee.

"I cannot think what's come over me to-night," said she, half aloud, recovering herself by the sound of her own voice from her train of thought—"My head goes wandering on them old times. I'm sure more texts have come into my head with thinking on my mother within this last half hour, than I've thought on for years and years. I hope I'm not going to die. Folks say, thinking too much on the dead betokens we're going to join 'em; I should be loth to go just yet—such a fine turkey as we've got for dinner to-morrow, too!"

Knock, knock, knock, at the door, as fast as knuckles could go. And then, as if the comer could not wait, the door was opened, and Mary Hodgson stood there as white as death.

"Mrs. Jenkins!—oh, your kettle is boiling, thank God! Let me have the water for my baby, for the love of God! He's got croup, and is dying!"

Mrs. Jenkins turned on her chair with a wooden inflexible look on her face, that (between ourselves) her husband knew and dreaded for all his pompous dignity.

"I'm sorry I can't oblige you, ma'am; my kettle is wanted for my husband's tea. Don't be afeared, Tommy, Mrs. Hodgson won't venture to intrude herself where she's not desired. You'd better send for the doctor, ma'am, instead of wasting your time in wringing your hands, ma'am—my kettle is engaged."

Mary clasped her hands together with passionate force, but spoke no word of entreaty to that wooden face—that sharp, determined voice; but, as she turned away, she prayed for strength to bear the coming trial, and strength to forgive Mrs. Jenkins.

Mrs. Jenkins watched her go away meekly, as one who has no hope, and then she turned upon herself as sharply as she ever did on any one else.

"What a brute I am, Lord forgive me! What's my husband's tea to a baby's life? In croup, too, where time is everything. You crabbed old vixen, you!—any one may know you never had a child!"

She was down stairs (kettle in hand) before she had finished her self-upbraiding; and when in Mrs. Hodgson's room, she rejected all thanks (Mary had not the voice for many words), saying, stiffly, "I do it for the poor babby's sake, ma'am, hoping he may live to have mercy to poor dumb beasts, if he does forget to lock his cupboards."

But she did everything, and more than Mary, with her young inexperience, could have thought of. She prepared the warm bath, and tried it with her husband's own thermometer (Mr. Jenkins was as punctual as clockwork in noting down the temperature of every day). She let his mother place her baby in the tub, still preserving the same rigid, affronted aspect, and then she went upstairs without a word. Mary longed to ask her to stay, but dared not; though, when she left the room, the tears chased each other down her cheeks faster than ever. Poor young mother! how she counted the minutes till the doctor should come. But, before he came, down again stalked Mrs. Jenkins, with something in her hand.

"I've seen many of these croup-fits, which, I take it, you've not, ma'am. Mustard plaisters is very sovereign, put on the throat; I've been up and made one, ma'am, and, by your leave, I'll put it on the poor little fellow."

Mary could not speak, but she signed her grateful assent.

It began to smart while they still kept silence; and he looked up to his mother as if seeking courage from her looks to bear the stinging pain; but she was softly crying, to see him suffer, and her want of courage reacted upon him, and he began to sob aloud. Instantly Mrs. Jenkins's apron was up, hiding her face: "Peep-bo, baby," said she, as merrily as she could. His little face brightened, and his mother having once got the cue, the two women kept the little fellow amused, until his plaister had taken effect.

"He's better,—oh, Mrs. Jenkins, look at his eyes! how different! And he breathes quite softly——"

As Mary spoke thus, the doctor entered. He examined his patient. Baby was really better.

"It has been a sharp attack, but the remedies you have applied have been worth all the Pharmacopœia an hour later.—I shall send a powder," &c. &c.

Mrs. Jenkins stayed to hear this opinion; and (her heart wonderfully more easy) was going to leave the room, when Mary seized her hand and kissed it; she could not speak her gratitude.

Mrs. Jenkins looked affronted and awkward, and as if she must go upstairs and wash her hand directly.

But, in spite of these sour looks, she came softly down an hour or so afterwards to see how baby was.

The little gentleman slept well after the fright he had given his friends; and on Christmas morning, when Mary awoke and looked at the sweet little pale face lying on her arm, she could hardly realize the danger he had been in.

When she came down (later than usual), she found the household in a commotion. What do you think had happened? Why, pussy had been a traitor to his best friend, and eaten up some of Mr. Jenkins's own especial sausages; and gnawed and tumbled the rest so, that they were not fit to be eaten! There were no bounds to that cat's appetite! he would have eaten his own father if he had been tender enough. And now Mrs. Jenkins stormed and cried—"Hang the cat!"

Christmas Day, too! and all the shops shut! "What was turkey without sausages?" gruffly asked Mr. Jenkins.

"Oh, Jem!" whispered Mary, "hearken what a piece of work he's making about sausages,—I should like to take Mrs. Jenkins up some of mother's; they're twice as good as bought sausages."

"I see no objection, my dear. Sausages do not involve intimacies, else his politics are what I can no ways respect."

"But, oh, Jem, if you had seen her last night about baby! I'm sure she may scold me for ever, and I'll not answer. I'd even make her cat welcome to the sausages." The tears gathered to Mary's eyes as she kissed her boy.

"Better take 'em upstairs, my dear, and give them to the cat's mistress." And Jem chuckled at his saying.

Mary put them on a plate, but still she loitered.

"What must I say, Jem? I never know."

"Say—I hope you'll accept of these sausages, as my mother—no, that's not grammar;—say what comes uppermost, Mary, it will be sure to be right."

So Mary carried them upstairs and knocked at the door; and when told to "come in," she looked very red, but went up to Mrs. Jenkins, saying, "Please take these. Mother made them." And was away before an answer could be given.

Just as Hodgson was ready to go to church, Mrs. Jenkins came downstairs, and called Fanny. In a minute, the latter entered the Hodgsons' room, and delivered Mr. and Mrs. Jenkins's compliments, and they would be particular glad if Mr. and Mrs. Hodgson would eat their dinner with them.

"And carry baby upstairs in a shawl, be sure," added Mrs. Jenkins's voice in the passage, close to the door, whither she had followed her messenger. There was no discussing the matter, with the certainty of every word being overheard.

Mary looked anxiously at her husband. She remembered his saying he did not approve of Mr. Jenkins's politics.

"Do you think it would do for baby?" asked he.

"Oh, yes," answered she, eagerly; "I would wrap him up so warm."

"And I've got our room up to sixty-five already, for all it's so frosty," added the voice outside.

Now, how do you think they settled the matter? The very best way in the world. Mr. and Mrs. Jenkins came down into the Hodgsons' room, and dined there. Turkey at the top, roast beef at the bottom, sausages at one side, potatoes at the other. Second course, plum-pudding at the top, and mince pies at the bottom.

And after dinner, Mrs. Jenkins would have baby on her knee; and he seemed quite to take to her; she declared he was admiring the real lace on her cap, but Mary thought (though she did not say so) that he was pleased by her kind looks and coaxing words. Then he was wrapped up and carried carefully upstairs to tea, in Mrs. Jenkins's room. And after tea, Mrs. Jenkins, and Mary, and her husband, found out each other's mutual liking for music, and sat singing old glees and catches, till I don't know what o'clock, without one word of politics or newspapers.

Before they parted, Mary had coaxed pussy on to her knee; for Mrs. Jenkins would not part with baby, who was sleeping on her lap.

"When you're busy, bring him to me. Do, now, it will be a real favour. I know you must have a deal to do, with another coming; let him come up to me. I'll take the greatest of cares of him; pretty darling, how sweet he looks when he's asleep!"

When the couples were once more alone, the husbands unburdened their minds to their wives.

Mr. Jenkins said to his—"Do you know, Burgess tried to make me believe Hodgson was such a fool as to put paragraphs into the *Examiner* now and then; but I see he knows his place, and has got too much sense to do any such thing."

Hodgson said—"Mary, love, I almost fancy from Jenkins's way of speaking (so much civiler than I expected), he guesses I wrote that 'Pro Bono' and the 'Rose-bud,'—at any rate, I've no objection to your naming it, if the subject should come uppermost; I should like him to know I'm a literary man."

Well! I've ended my tale; I hope you don't think it too long; but, before I go, just let me say one thing.

If any of you have any quarrels, or misunderstandings, or coolnesses, or cold shoulders, or shynesses, or tiffs, or miffs, or huffs, with any one else, just make friends before Christmas,—you will be so much merrier if you do.

I ask it of you for the sake of that old angelic song, heard so many years ago by the shepherds, keeping watch by night, on Bethlehem Heights.

HAND AND HEART.

"Mother, I should so like to have a great deal of money," said little Tom Fletcher one evening, as he sat on a low stool by his mother's knee. His mother was knitting busily by the firelight, and they had both been silent for some time.

"What would you do with a great deal of money if you had it?"

"Oh! I don't know—I would do a great many things. But should not you like to have a great deal of money, mother?" persisted he.

"Perhaps I should," answered Mrs. Fletcher. "I am like you sometimes, dear, and think that I should be very glad of a little more money. But then I don't think I am like you in one thing, for I have always some little plan in my mind, for which I should want the money. I never wish for it just for its own sake."

"Why, mother! there are so many things we could do if we had but money;—real good, wise things I mean."

"And if we have real good, wise things in our head to do, which cannot be done without money, I can quite enter into the wish for money. But you know, my little boy, you did not tell me of any good or wise thing."

"No! I believe I was not thinking of good or wise things just then, but only how much I should like money to do what I liked," answered little Tom ingenuously, looking up in his mother's face. She smiled down upon him, and stroked his head. He knew she was pleased with him for having told her openly what was passing in his mind. Presently he began again.

"Mother, if you wanted to do something very good and wise, and if you could not do it without money, what should you do?"

"There are two ways of obtaining money for such wants; one is by earning; and the other is by saving. Now both are good, because both imply self-denial. Do you understand me, Tom? If you have to earn money, you must steadily go on doing what you do not like perhaps; such as working when you would like to be playing, or in bed, or sitting talking with me over the fire. You deny yourself these little pleasures; and that is a good habit in itself, to say nothing of the industry and energy you have to exert in working. If you save money, you can easily see how you exercise self-denial. You do without something you wish for in order to possess the money it would have cost. Inasmuch as self-denial, energy, and industry are all good things, you do well either to earn or to save. But you see the purpose for which you want the money must be taken into consideration. You say, for 'something wise and good.' Either earning or saving becomes holy in this case. I must then think which will be most consistent with my other duties, before I decide whether I will earn or save money."

"I don't quite know what you mean, mother."

"I will try and explain myself. You know I have to keep a little shop, and to try and get employment in knitting stockings, and to clean my house, and to mend our clothes, and many other things. Now, do you think I should be doing my duty if I left you in the evenings, when you come home from school, to go out as a waiter at ladies' parties? I could earn a good deal of money by it, and I could spend it well among those who are poorer than I am (such as lame Harry), but then I should be leaving you alone in the little time that we have to be together; I do not think I should be doing right even for our 'good and wise purpose' to earn money, if it took me away from you at nights: do you, Tom?"

"No, indeed; you never mean to do it, do you, mother?"

"No," said she, smiling; "at any rate not till you are older. You see at present then, I cannot *earn* money, if I want a little more than usual to help a sick neighbour. I must then try and *save* money. Nearly every one can do that."

"Can *we*, mother? We are so careful of everything. Ned Dixon calls us stingy: what could *we* save?"

"Oh, many and many a little thing. We use many things which are luxuries; which we do not want, but only use them for pleasure. Tea and sugar—butter—our Sunday's dinner of bacon or meat—the grey ribbon I bought for my bonnet, because you thought it prettier than the black, which was cheaper; all these are luxuries. We use very little tea or sugar, it is true; but we might do without any."

"You did do without any, mother, for a long, long time, you know, to help widow Black; it was only for your bad head-aches."

"Well! but you see we can save money; a penny, a halfpenny a day, or even a penny a week, would in time make a little store ready to be applied to the 'good and wise' purpose, when the time comes. But do you know, my little boy, I think we may be considering money too much as the only thing required if we want to do a kindness."

"If it is not the only thing, it is the chief thing, at any rate."

"No, love, it is not the chief thing. I should think very poorly of that beggar who liked sixpence given with a curse (as I have sometimes heard it), better than the kind and gentle words some people use in refusing to give. The curse sinks deep into the heart; or if it does not, it is a proof that the poor creature has been made hard before by harsh treatment. And mere money can do little to cheer a sore heart. It is kindness only that can do this. Now we have all of us kindness in our power. The little child of two years old, who can only just totter about, can show kindness."

"Can I, mother?"

"To be sure, dear; and you often do, only perhaps not quite so often as you might do. Neither do I. But instead of wishing for money (of which I don't think either you or I are ever likely to have much), suppose you try to-morrow how you can make people happier, by thinking of little loving actions of help. Let us try and take for our text, 'Silver and gold I have none, but such as I have give I unto thee.'"

"Ay, mother, we will."

Must I tell you about little Tom's "to-morrow."

I do not know if little Tom dreamed of what his mother and he had been talking about, but I do know that the first thing he thought about, when he awoke in the morning, was his mother's saying that he might try how many kind actions he could do that day without money; and he was so impatient to begin, that he jumped up and dressed himself, although it was more than an hour before his usual time of getting up. All the time he kept wondering what a little boy like him, only eight years old, could do for other people; till at last he grew so puzzled with inventing occasions for showing kindness, that he very wisely determined to think no more about it, but learn his lessons very perfectly; that was the first thing he had to do; and then he would try, without too much planning beforehand, to keep himself ready to lend a helping hand, or to give a kind word, when the right time came. So he screwed himself into a corner, out of the way of his mother's sweeping and dusting, and tucked his feet up on the rail of the chair, turned his face to the wall, and in about half an hour's time, he could turn round with a light heart, feeling he had learnt his lesson well, and might employ his time as he liked till breakfast was ready. He looked round the room; his mother had arranged all neatly, and was now gone to the bedroom; but the coal-scuttle and the can for water were empty, and Tom ran away to fill them; and as he came back with the latter from the pump, he saw Ann Jones (the scold of the neighbourhood) hanging out her clothes on a line stretched across from side to side of the little court, and speaking very angrily and loudly to her little girl, who was getting into some mischief in the house-place, as her mother perceived through the open door.

"There never were such plagues as my children are, to be sure," said Ann Jones, as she went into her house, looking very red and passionate. Directly after, Tom heard the sound of a slap, and then a little child's cry of pain.

"I wonder," thought he, "if I durst go and offer to nurse and play with little Hester. Ann Jones is fearful cross, and just as likely to take me wrong as right; but she won't box me for mother's sake; mother nursed Jemmy many a day through the fever, so she won't slap me, I think. Any rate, I'll try." But it was with a beating heart he said to the fierce-looking Mrs. Jones, "Please, may I go and play with Hester. May be I could keep her quiet while you're busy hanging out clothes."

"What! and let you go slopping about, I suppose, just when I'd made all ready for my master's breakfast. Thank you, but my own children's mischief is as much as I reckon on; I'll have none of strange lads in my house."

"I did not mean to do mischief or slop," said Tom, a little sadly at being misunderstood in his good intentions. "I only wanted to help."

"If you want to help, lift me up those clothes' pegs, and save me stooping; my back's broken with it."

Tom would much rather have gone to play with and amuse little Hester; but it was true enough that giving Mrs. Jones the clothes' pegs as she wanted them would help her as much; and perhaps keep her from being so cross with her children if they did anything to hinder her. Besides, little Hester's cry had died away, and she was evidently occupied in some new pursuit (Tom could only hope that it was not in mischief this time); so he began to give Ann the pegs as she wanted them, and she, soothed by his kind help, opened her heart a little to him.

"I wonder how it is your mother has trained you up to be so handy, Tom; you're as good as a girl—better than many a girl. I don't think Hester in three years' time will be as thoughtful as you. There!" (as a fresh scream reached them from the little ones inside the house), "they are at some mischief again; but I'll teach 'em," said she, getting down from her stool in a fresh access of passion.

"Let me go," said Tom, in a begging voice, for he dreaded the cruel sound of another slap. "I'll lift the basket of pegs on to a stool, so that you need not stoop; and I'll keep the little ones safe out of mischief till you're done. Do let me go, missus."

With some grumblings at losing his help, she let him go into the house-place. He found Hester, a little girl of five, and two younger ones. They had been fighting for a knife, and in the struggle, the second, Johnnie, had cut his finger—not very badly, but he was frightened at the sight of the blood; and Hester, who might have helped, and who was really sorry, stood sullenly aloof, dreading the scolding her mother always gave her if either of the little ones hurt themselves while under her care.

"Hester," said Tom, "will you get me some cold water, please? it will stop the bleeding better than anything. I daresay you can find me a basin to hold it."

Hester trotted off, pleased at Tom's confidence in her power. When the bleeding was partly stopped, he asked her to find him a bit of rag, and she scrambled under the dresser for a little piece she had hidden there the day before. Meanwhile, Johnny ceased crying, he was so interested in all the preparation for dressing his little wound, and so much pleased to find himself an object of so much attention and consequence. The baby, too, sat on the floor, gravely wondering at the commotion; and thus busily occupied, they were quiet and out of mischief till Ann Jones came in, and, having hung out her clothes, and finished that morning's piece of work, she was ready to attend to her children in her rough, hasty kind of way.

The Cut Finger.

"Well! I'm sure, Tom, you've tied it up as neatly as I could have done. I wish I'd always such an one as you to see after the children; but you must run off now, lad, your mother was calling you as I came in, and I said I'd send you—good-by, and thank you."

As Tom was going away, the baby, sitting in square gravity on the floor, but somehow conscious of Tom's gentle helpful ways, put up her mouth to be kissed; and he stooped down in answer to the little gesture, feeling very happy, and very full of love and kindliness.

After breakfast, his mother told him it was school time, and he must set off, as she did not like him to run in out of breath and flurried, just when the schoolmaster was going to begin; but she wished him to come in decently and in order, with quiet decorum, and thoughtfulness as to what he was going to do. So Tom got his cap and his bag, and went off with a light heart, which I suppose made his footsteps light, for he found himself above half way to school while it wanted yet a quarter to the time. So he slackened his pace, and looked about him a little more than he had been doing. There was a little girl on the other side of the street carrying a great big basket, and lugging along a little child just able to walk; but who, I suppose, was tired, for he was crying pitifully, and sitting down every two or three steps. Tom ran across the street, for, as perhaps you have found out, he was very fond of babies, and could not bear to hear them cry.

"Little girl, what is he crying about? Does he want to be carried? I'll take him up, and carry him as far as I go alongside of you."

So saying, Tom was going to suit the action to the word; but the baby did not choose that any one should carry him but his sister, and refused Tom's kindness. Still he could carry the heavy basket of potatoes for the little girl, which he did as far as their road lay together, when she thanked him, and bade him good-by, and said she could manage very well now, her home was so near. So Tom went into school very happy and peaceful; and had a good character to take home to his mother for that morning's lesson.

It happened that this very day was the weekly half-holiday, so that Tom had many hours unoccupied that afternoon. Of course, his first employment after dinner was to learn his lessons for the next day; and then, when he had put his books away, he began to wonder what he should do next.

He stood lounging against the door wishing all manner of idle wishes; a habit he was apt to fall into. He wished he were the little boy who lived opposite, who had three brothers ready to play with him on half-holidays; he wished he were Sam Harrison, whose father had taken him one day a trip by the railroad; he wished he were the little boy who always went with the omnibuses,—it must be so pleasant to go riding about on the step, and to see so many people; he wished he were a sailor, to sail away to the countries where grapes grew wild, and monkeys and parrots were to be had for the catching. Just as he was wishing himself the little Prince of Wales, to drive about in a goat-carriage, and wondering if he should not feel very shy with the three great ostrich-feathers always niddle-noddling on his head, for people to know him by, his mother came from washing up the dishes, and saw him deep in the reveries little boys and girls are apt to fall into when they are the only children in a house.

"My dear Tom," said she, "why don't you go out, and make the most of this fine afternoon?"

"Oh, mother," answered he (suddenly recalled to the fact that he was little Tom Fletcher, instead of the Prince of Wales, and consequently feeling a little bit flat), "it is so dull going out by myself. I have no one to play with. Can't you go with me, mother—just this once, into the fields?"

Poor Mrs. Fletcher heartily wished she could gratify this very natural desire of her little boy; but she had the shop to mind, and many a little thing besides to do; it was impossible. But however much she might regret a thing, she was too faithful to repine. So, after a moment's thought, she said, cheerfully, "Go into the fields for a walk, and see how many wild flowers you can bring me home, and I'll get down father's jug for you to put them in when you come back."

"But, mother, there are so few pretty flowers near a town," said Tom, a little unwillingly, for it was a coming down from being Prince of Wales, and he was not yet quite reconciled to it.

"Oh dear! there are a great many if you'll only look for them. I dare say you'll make me up as many as twenty different kinds."

"Will you reckon daisies, mother?"

"To be sure; they are just as pretty as any."

"Oh, if you'll reckon such as them, I dare say I can bring you more than twenty."

So off he ran; his mother watching him till he was out of sight, and then she returned to her work. In about two hours he came back, his pale cheeks looking quite rosy, and his eyes quite bright. His country walk, taken with cheerful spirits, had done him all the good his mother desired, and had restored his usually even, happy temper.

"Look, mother! here are three-and-twenty different kinds; you said I might count all, so I have even counted this thing like a nettle with lilac flowers, and this little common blue thing."

"Robin-run-in-the-hedge is its name," said his mother. "It's very pretty if you look at it close. One, two, three"—she counted them all over, and there really were three-and-twenty. She went to reach down the best jug.

"Mother," said little Tom, "do you like them very much?"

"Yes, very much," said she, not understanding his meaning. He was silent, and gave a little sigh. "Why, my dear?"

"Oh, only—it does not signify if you like them very much; but I thought how nice it would be to take them to lame Harry, who can never walk so far as the fields, and can hardly know what summer is like, I think."

"Oh, that will be very nice; I am glad you thought of it."

Lame Harry was sitting by himself, very patiently, in a neighbouring cellar. He was supported by his daughter's earnings; but as she worked in a factory, he was much alone.

If the bunch of flowers had looked pretty in the fields, they looked ten times as pretty in the cellar to which they were now carried. Lame Harry's eyes brightened up with pleasure at the sight; and he began to talk of the times long ago, when he was a little boy in the country, and had a corner of his father's garden to call his own, and grow lad's-love and wall-flower in. Little Tom put them in water for him, and put the jug on the table by him; on which his daughter had placed the old Bible, worn with much reading, although treated with careful reverence. It was lying open, with Harry's horn spectacles put in to mark the place.

"I reckon my spectacles are getting worn out; they are not so clear as they used to be; they are dim-like before my eyes, and it hurts me to read long together," said Harry. "It's a sad miss to me. I never thought the time long when I could read; but now I keep wearying for the day to be over, though the nights, when I cannot sleep for my legs paining me, are almost as bad. However, it's the Lord's will."

"Would you like me—I cannot read very well aloud, but I'd do my best, if you'd like me to read a bit to you. I'll just run home and get my tea, and be back directly." And off Tom ran.

He found it very pleasant reading aloud to lame Harry, for the old man had so much to say that was worth listening to, and was so glad of a listener, that I think there was as much talking as reading done that evening. But the Bible served as a text-book to their conversation; for in a long life old Harry had seen and heard so much, which he had connected with events, or promises, or precepts contained in the Scriptures, that it was quite curious to find how everything was brought in and dove-tailed, as an illustration of what they were reading.

When Tom got up to go away, lame Harry gave him many thanks, and told him he would not sleep the worse for having made an old man's evening so pleasant. Tom came home in high self-satisfaction. "Mother," said he, "it's all very true what you said about the good that may be done without money: I've done many pieces of good to-day without a farthing. First," said he, taking hold of his little finger, "I helped Ann Jones with hanging out her clothes when she was"—

His mother had been listening while she turned over the pages of the New Testament which lay by her, and now having found what she wanted, she put her arm gently round his waist, and drew him fondly towards her. He saw her finger put under one passage, and read,—

"Let not thy left hand know what thy right hand doeth."

He was silent in a moment.

Then his mother spoke in her soft low voice:—"Dearest Tom, though I don't want us to talk about it, as if you had been doing more than just what you ought, I am glad you have seen the truth of what I said; how far more may be done by the loving heart than by mere money-giving; and every one may have the loving heart."

I have told you of one day of little Tom's life, when he was eight years old, and lived with his mother. I must now pass over a year, and tell you of a very different kind of life he had then to lead. His mother had never been very strong, and had had a good deal of anxiety; at last she was taken ill, and soon felt that there was no hope for her recovery. For a long time the thought of leaving her little boy was a great distress to her, and a great trial to her faith. But God strengthened her, and sent his peace into her soul, and before her death she was content to leave her precious child in his hands, who is a Father to the fatherless, and defendeth the cause of the widow.

When she felt that she had not many more days to live, she sent for her husband's brother, who lived in a town not many miles off; and gave her little Tom in charge to him to bring up.

"There are a few pounds in the savings-bank—I don't know how many exactly—and the furniture and bit of stock in the shop; perhaps they would be enough to bring him up to be a joiner, like his father before him."

She spoke feebly, and with many pauses. Her brother-in-law, though a rough kind of man, wished to do all he could to make her feel easy in her last moments, and touched with the reference to his dead brother, promised all she required.

"I'll take him back with me after"—the funeral, he was going to say, but he stopped. She smiled gently, fully understanding his meaning.

"We shall, may be, not be so tender with him as you've been; but I'll see he comes to no harm. It will be a good thing for him to rough it a bit with other children,—he's too nesh for a boy; but I'll pay them if they aren't kind to him in the long run, never fear."

Though this speech was not exactly what she liked, there was quite enough of good feeling in it to make her thankful for such a protector and friend for her boy. And so, thankful for the joys she had had, and thankful for the sorrows which had taught her meekness, thankful for life, and thankful for death, she died.

Her brother-in-law arranged all as she had wished. After the quiet simple funeral was over, he took Tom by the hand, and set off on the six-mile walk to his home. Tom had cried till he could cry no more, but sobs came quivering up from his heart every now and then, as he passed some well-remembered cottage, or thorn-bush, or tree on the road. His uncle was very sorry for him, but did not know what to say, or how to comfort him.

"Now mind, lad, thou com'st to me if thy cousins are o'er hard upon thee. Let me hear if they misuse thee, and I'll give it them."

Tom shrunk from the idea that this gave him of the cousins, whose companionship he had, until then, been looking forward to as a pleasure. He was not reassured when, after threading several streets and by-ways, they came into a court of dingy-looking houses, and his uncle opened the door of one, from which the noise of loud, if not angry voices was heard.

A tall large woman was whirling one child out of her way with a rough movement of her arm; while she was scolding a boy a little older than Tom, who stood listening sullenly to her angry words.

"I'll tell father of thee, I will," said she; and turning to uncle John, she began to pour out her complaints against Jack, without taking any notice of little Tom, who clung to his uncle's hand as to a protector in the scene of violence into which he had entered.

"Well, well, wife!—I'll leather Jack the next time I catch him letting the water out of the pipe; but now get this lad and me some tea, for we're weary and tired."

His aunt seemed to wish Jack might be leathered now, and to be angry with her husband for not revenging her injuries; for an injury it was that the boy had done her in letting the water all run off, and that on the very eve of the washing day. The mother grumbled as she left off mopping the wet floor, and went to the fire to stir it up ready for the kettle, without a word of greeting to her little nephew, or of welcome to her husband. On the contrary, she complained of the trouble of getting tea ready afresh, just when she had put slack on the fire, and had no water in the house to fill the kettle with. Her husband grew angry, and Tom was frightened to hear his uncle speaking sharply.

"If I can't have a cup of tea in my own house without all this ado, I'll go to the Spread Eagle, and take Tom with me. They've a bright fire there at all times, choose how they manage it; and no scolding wives. Come, Tom, let's be off."

Jack had been trying to scrape acquaintance with his cousin by winks and grimaces behind his mother's back, and now made a sign of drinking out of an imaginary glass. But Tom clung to his uncle, and softly pulled him down again on his chair, from which he had risen to go to the public-house.

"If you please, ma'am," said he, sadly frightened of his aunt, "I think I could find the pump, if you'd let me try."

She muttered something like an acquiescence; so Tom took up the kettle, and, tired as he was, went out to the pump. Jack, who had done nothing but mischief all day, stood amazed, but at last settled that his cousin was a "softy."

When Tom came back, he tried to blow the fire with the broken bellows, and at last the water boiled, and the tea was made. "Thou'rt a rare lad, Tom," said his uncle. "I wonder when our Jack will be of as much use."

This comparison did not please either Jack or his mother, who liked to keep to herself the privilege of directing their father's dissatisfaction with his children. Tom felt their want of kindliness towards him; and now that he had nothing to do but rest and eat, he began to feel very sad, and his eyes kept filling with tears, which he brushed away with the back of his hand, not wishing to have them seen. But his uncle noticed him.

"Thou had'st better have had a glass at the Spread Eagle," said he, compassionately.

"No; I only am rather tired. May I go to bed?" said he, longing for a good cry unobserved under the bed-clothes.

"Where's he to sleep?" asked the husband of the wife.

"Nay," said she, still offended on Jack's account, "that's thy look-out. He's thy flesh and blood, not mine."

"Come, wife," said uncle John, "he's an orphan, poor chap. An orphan is kin to every one."

She was softened directly, for she had much kindness in her, although this evening she had been so much put out.

"There's no place for him but with Jack and Dick. We've the baby, and the other three are packed close enough."

She took Tom up to the little back room, and stopped to talk with him for a minute or two, for her husband's words had smitten her heart, and she was sorry for the ungracious reception she had given Tom at first.

"Jack and Dick are never in bed till we come, and it's work enough to catch them then on fine evenings," said she, as she took the candle away.

Tom tried to speak to God as his mother had taught him, out of the fulness of his little heart, which was heavy enough that night. He tried to think how she would have wished him to speak and to do, and when he felt puzzled with the remembrance of the scene of disorder and anger which he had seen, he earnestly prayed God would make and keep clear his path before him. And then he fell asleep.

He had had a long dream of other and happier days, and had thought he was once more taking a Sunday evening walk with his mother, when he was roughly wakened up by his cousins.

"I say, lad, you're lying right across the bed. You must get up, and let Dick and me come in, and then creep into the space that's left."

Tom got up dizzy and half awake. His cousins got into bed, and then squabbled about the largest share. It ended in a kicking match, during which Tom stood shivering by the bedside.

"I'm sure we're pinched enough as it is," said Dick at last. "And why they've put Tom in with us I can't think. But I'll not stand it. Tom shan't sleep with us. He may lie on the floor, if he likes. I'll not hinder him."

He expected an opposition from Tom, and was rather surprised when he heard the little fellow quietly lie down, and cover himself as well as he could with his clothes. After some more quarrelling, Jack and Dick fell asleep. But in the middle of the night Dick awoke, and heard by Tom's breathing that he was still awake, and was crying gently.

"What! molly-coddle, crying for a softer bed?" asked Dick.

"Oh, no—I don't care for that—if—oh! if mother were but alive," little Tom sobbed aloud.

"I say," said Dick, after a pause. "There's room at my back, if you'll creep in. There! don't be afraid—why, how cold you are, lad."

Dick was sorry for his cousin's loss, but could not speak about it. However, his kind tone sank into Tom's heart, and he fell asleep once more.

The three boys all got up at the same time in the morning, but were not inclined to talk. Jack and Dick put on their clothes as fast as possible, and ran downstairs; but this was quite a different way of going on to what Tom had been accustomed. He looked about for some kind of basin or mug to wash in; there was none—not even a jug of water in the room. He slipped on a few necessary clothes, and went downstairs, found a pitcher, and went off to the pump. His cousins, who were playing in the court, laughed at him, and would not tell him where the soap was kept: he had to look some minutes before he could find it. Then he went back to the bedroom; but on entering it from the fresh air, the smell was so oppressive that he could not endure it. Three people had been breathing the air all night, and had used up every particle many times over and over again; and each time that it had been sent out from the lungs, it was less fit than before to be breathed again. They had not felt how poisonous it was while they stayed in it; they had only felt tired and unrefreshed, with a dull headache; but now that Tom came back again into it, he could not mistake its oppressive nature. He went to the window to try and open it. It was what people call a "Yorkshire light," where you know one-half has to be pushed on one side. It was very stiff, for it had not been opened for a long time. Tom pushed against it with all his might; at length it gave way with a jerk; and the shake sent out a cracked pane, which fell on the floor in a hundred little bits. Tom was sadly frightened when he saw what he had done. He would have been sorry to have done mischief at any time, but he had seen enough of his aunt the evening before to find out that she was sharp, and hasty, and cross; and it was hard to have to begin the first day in his new home by getting into a scrape. He sat down on the bedside, and began to cry. But the morning air blowing in upon him, refreshed him, and made him feel stronger. He grew braver as he washed himself in the pure, cold water. "She can't be cross with me longer than a day; by to-night it will be all over; I can bear it for a day."

Dick came running upstairs for something he had forgotten.

"My word, Tom! but you'll catch it!" exclaimed he, when he saw the broken window. He was half pleased at the event, and half sorry for Tom. "Mother did so beat Jack last week for throwing a stone right through the window downstairs. He kept out of the way till night, but she was on the look-out for him, and as soon as she saw him, she caught hold of him and gave it him. Eh! Tom, I would not be you for a deal!"

Tom began to cry again at this account of his aunt's anger; Dick became more and more sorry for him.

"I'll tell thee what; we'll go down and say it was a lad in yon back-yard throwing stones, and that one went smack through the window. I've got one in my pocket that will just do to show."

"No," said Tom, suddenly stopping crying. "I dare not do that."

"Daren't! Why you'll have to dare much more if you go down and face mother without some such story."

"No! I shan't. I shan't have to dare God's anger. Mother taught me to fear that; she said I need never be really afraid of aught else. Just be quiet, Dick, while I say my prayers."

Dick watched his little cousin kneel down by the bed, and bury his face in the clothes; he did not say any set prayer (which Dick was accustomed to think was the only way of praying), but Tom seemed, by the low murmuring which Dick heard, to be talking to a dear friend; and though at first he sobbed and cried, as he asked for help and strength, yet when he got up, his face looked calm and bright, and he spoke quietly as he said to Dick, "Now I'm ready to go and tell aunt."

"Aunt" meanwhile had missed her pitcher and her soap, and was in no good-tempered mood when Tom came to make his confession. She had been hindered in her morning's work by his taking her things away; and now he was come to tell her of the pane being broken and that it must be mended, and money must go all for a child's nonsense.

She gave him (as he had been led to expect) one or two very sharp blows. Jack and Dick looked on with curiosity, to see how he would take it; Jack, at any rate, expecting a hearty crying from "softy" (Jack himself had cried loudly at his last beating), but Tom never shed a tear, though his face did go very red, and his mouth did grow set with the pain. But what struck the boys more even than his being "hard" in bearing such blows, was his quietness afterwards. He did not grumble loudly, as Jack would have done, nor did he turn sullen, as was Dick's custom; but the minute afterwards he was ready to run an errand for his aunt; nor did he make any mention of the hard blows, when his uncle came in to breakfast, as his aunt had rather expected he would. She was glad he did not, for she knew her husband would have been displeased to know how early she had begun to beat his orphan nephew. So she almost felt grateful to Tom for his silence, and certainly began to be sorry she had struck him so hard.

Poor Tom! he did not know that his cousins were beginning to respect him, nor that his aunt was learning to like him; and he felt very lonely and desolate that first morning. He had nothing to do. Jack went to work at the factory; and Dick went grumbling to school. Tom wondered if he was to go to school again, but he did not like to ask. He sat on a little stool, as much out of his terrible aunt's way as he could. She had her youngest child, a little girl of about a year and a half old, crawling about on the floor. Tom longed to play with her; but he was not sure how far his aunt would like it. But he kept smiling at her, and doing every little thing he could to attract her attention and make her come to him. At last she was coaxed to come upon his knee. His aunt saw it, and though she did not speak, she did not look displeased. He did everything he could think of to amuse little Annie; and her mother was very glad to have her attended to. When Annie grew sleepy, she still kept fast hold of one of Tom's fingers in her little, round, soft hand, and he began to know the happy feeling of loving somebody again. Only the night before, when his cousins had made him get out of bed, he had wondered if he should live to be an old man, and never have anybody to love all that long time; but now his heart felt quite warm to the little thing that lay on his lap.

"She'll tire you, Tom," said her mother, "you'd better let me put her down in the cot."

"Oh, no!" said he, "please don't! I like so much to have her here." He never moved, though she lay very heavy on his arm, for fear of wakening her.

When she did rouse up, his aunt said, "Thank you, Tom. I've got my work done rarely with you for a nurse. Now take a run in the yard, and play yourself a bit."

His aunt was learning something, and Tom was teaching, though they would both have been very much surprised to hear it. Whenever, in a family, every one is selfish, and (as it is called) "stands up for his own rights," there are no feelings of gratitude; the gracefulness of "thanks" is never called for; nor can there be any occasion for thoughtfulness for others when those others are sure to get the start in thinking for themselves, and taking care of number one. Tom's aunt had never had to remind Jack or Dick to go out to play. They were ready enough to see after their own pleasures.

Well! dinner-time came, and all the family gathered to the meal. It seemed to be a scramble who should be helped first, and cry out for the best pieces. Tom looked very red. His aunt in her new-born liking for him, helped him early to what she thought he would like. But he did not begin to eat. It had been his mother's custom to teach her little son to say a simple "grace" with her before they began their dinner. He expected his uncle to follow the same observance; and waited. Then he felt very hot and shy; but, thinking that it was right to say it, he put away his shyness, and very quietly, but very solemnly said the old accustomed sentence of thanksgiving. Jack burst out laughing when he had done; for which Jack's father gave him a sharp rap and a sharp word, which made him silent through the rest of the dinner. But, excepting Jack, who was angry, I think all the family were the happier for having listened reverently (if with some surprise) to Tom's thanksgiving. They were not an ill-disposed set of people, but wanted thoughtfulness in their every-day life; that sort of thoughtfulness which gives order to a home, and makes a wise and holy spirit of love the groundwork of order.

From that first day Tom never went back in the regard he began then to win. He was useful to his aunt, and patiently bore her hasty ways, until for very shame she left off being hasty with one who was always so meek and mild. His uncle sometimes said he was more like a girl than a boy, as was to be looked for from being brought up for so many years by a woman; but that was the greatest fault he ever had to find with him; and in spite of it, he really respected him for the very qualities which are most truly "manly;" for the courage with which he dared to do what was right, and the quiet firmness with which he bore many kinds of pain. As for little Annie, her friendship and favour and love were the delight of Tom's heart. He did not know how much the others were growing to like him, but Annie showed it in every way, and he loved her in return most dearly. Dick soon found out how useful Tom could be to him in his lessons; for though older than his cousin, Master Dick was a regular dunce, and had never even wished to learn till Tom came; and long before Jack could be brought to acknowledge it, Dick maintained that "Tom had a great deal of pluck in him, though it was not of Jack's kind."

Now I shall jump another year, and tell you a very little about the household twelve months after Tom had entered it. I said above that his aunt had learned to speak less crossly to one who was always gentle after her scoldings. By-and-by her ways to all became less hasty and passionate, for she grew ashamed of speaking to any one in an angry way before Tom; he always looked so sad and sorry to hear her. She has also spoken to him sometimes about his mother; at first because she thought he would like it; but latterly because she became really interested to hear of her ways; and Tom being an only child, and his mother's friend and companion, has been able to tell her of many household arts of comfort, which coming quite unconscious of any purpose, from the lips of a child, have taught her many things which she would have been too proud to learn from an older person. Her husband is softened by the additional cleanliness and peace of his home. He does not now occasionally take refuge in a public-house, to get out of the way of noisy children, an unswept hearth, and a scolding wife. Once when Tom was ill for a day or two, his uncle missed the accustomed grace, and began to say it himself. He is now the person to say "Silence, boys;" and then to ask the blessing on the meal. It makes them gather round the table, instead of sitting down here and there in the comfortless, unsociable way they used to do. Tom and Dick go to school together now, and Dick is getting on famously, and will soon be able to help his next brother over his lessons, as Tom has helped him.

Even Jack has been heard to acknowledge that Tom has "pluck" in him; and as "pluck" in Jack's mind is a short way of summing up all the virtues, he has lately become very fond of his cousin. Tom does not think about happiness, but is happy; and I think we may hope that he, and the household among whom he is adopted, will go "from strength to strength."

Now do you not see how much happier this family are from the one circumstance of a little child's coming among them? Could money have made one-tenth part of this real and increasing happiness? I think you will all say no. And yet Tom was no powerful person; he was not clever; he was very friendless at first; but he was loving and good; and on those two qualities, which any of us may have if we try, the blessing of God lies in rich abundance.

BESSY'S TROUBLES AT HOME.

"Well, mother, I've got you a Southport ticket," said Bessy Lee, as she burst into a room where a pale, sick woman lay dressed on the outside of a bed. "Aren't you glad?" asked she, as her mother moved uneasily, but did not speak.

"Yes, dear, I'm very thankful to you; but your sudden coming in has made my heart flutter so, I'm ready to choke."

Poor Bessy's eyes filled with tears: but, it must be owned, they were tears half of anger. She had taken such pains, ever since the doctor said that Southport was the only thing for her mother, to get her an order from some subscriber to the charity; and she had rushed to her, in the full glow of success, and now her mother seemed more put out by the noise she had made on coming in, than glad to receive the news she had brought.

Mrs. Lee took her hand and tried to speak, but, as she said, she was almost choked with the palpitation at her heart.

"You think it very silly in me, dear, to be so easily startled; but it is not altogether silliness; it is I am so weak that every little noise gives me quite a fright. I shall be better, love, please God, when I come back from Southport. I am so glad you've got the order, for you've taken a deal of pains about it." Mrs. Lee sighed.

"Don't you want to go?" asked Bessy, rather sadly. "You always seem so sorrowful and anxious when we talk about it."

"It's partly my being ailing that makes me anxious, I know," said Mrs. Lee. "But it seems as if so many things might happen while I was away."

Bessy felt a little impatient. Young people in strong health can hardly understand the fears that beset invalids. Bessy was a kind-hearted girl, but rather headstrong, and just now a little disappointed. She forgot that her mother had had to struggle hard with many cares ever since she had been left a widow, and that her illness now had made her nervous.

"What nonsense, mother! What can happen? I can take care of the house and the little ones, and Tom and Jem can take care of themselves. What is to happen?"

"Jenny may fall into the fire," murmured Mrs. Lee, who found little comfort in being talked to in this way. "Or your father's watch may be stolen while you are in, talking with the neighbours, or——"

"Now come, mother, you know I've had the charge of Jenny ever since father died, and you began to go out washing—and I'll lock father's watch up in the box in our room."

"Then Tom and Jem won't know at what time to go to the factory. Besides, Bessy," said she, raising herself up, "they're are but young lads, and there's a deal of temptation to take them away from their homes, if their homes are not comfortable and pleasant to them. It's that, more than anything, I've been fretting about all the time I've been ill,—that I've lost the power of making this house the cleanest and brightest place they know. But it's no use fretting," said she, falling back weakly upon the bed and sighing. "I must leave it in God's hands. He raiseth up and He bringeth low."

Bessy stood silent for a minute or two. Then she said, "Well, mother, I will try to make home comfortable for the lads, if you'll but keep your mind easy, and go off to Southport quiet and cheerful."

"I'll try," said Mrs. Lee, taking hold of Bessy's hand, and looking up thankfully in her face.

The next Wednesday she set off, leaving home with a heavy heart, which, however, she struggled against, and tried to make more faithful. But she wished her three weeks at Southport were over.

Tom and Jem were both older than Bessy, and she was fifteen. Then came Bill and Mary and little Jenny. They were all good children, and all had faults. Tom and Jem helped to support the family by their earnings at the factory, and gave up their wages very cheerfully for this purpose, to their mother, who, however, insisted on a little being put by every week in the savings' bank. It was one of her griefs now that, when the doctor ordered her some expensive delicacy in the way of diet during her illness (a thing which she persisted in thinking she could have done without), her boys had gone and taken their money out in order to procure it for her. The article in question did not cost one quarter of the amount of their savings, but they had put off returning the remainder into the bank, saying the doctor's bill had yet to be paid, and that it seemed so silly to be always taking money in and out. But meanwhile Mrs. Lee feared lest it should be spent, and begged them to restore it to the savings' bank. This had not been done when she left for Southport. Bill and Mary went to school. Little Jenny was the darling of all, and toddled about at home, having been her sister Bessy's especial charge when all went on well, and the mother used to go out to wash.

Mrs. Lee, however, had always made a point of giving all her children who were at home a comfortable breakfast at seven, before she set out to her day's work; and she prepared the boys' dinner ready for Bessy to warm for them. At night, too, she was anxious to be at home as soon after her boys as she could; and many of her employers respected her wish, and, finding her hard-working and conscientious, took care to set her at liberty early in the evening.

Bessy felt very proud and womanly when she returned home from seeing her mother off by the railway. She looked round the house with a new feeling of proprietorship, and then went to claim little Jenny from the neighbour's where she had been left while Bessy had gone to the station. They asked her to stay and have a bit of chat; but she replied that she could not, for that it was near dinner-time, and she refused the invitation that was then given her to go in some evening. She was full of good plans and resolutions.

That afternoon she took Jenny and went to her teacher's to borrow a book, which she meant to ask one of her brothers to read to her in the evenings while she worked. She knew that it was a book which Jem would like, for though she had never read it, one of her school-fellows had told her it was all about the sea, and desert islands, and cocoanut-trees, just the things that Jem liked to hear about. How happy they would all be this evening.

She hurried Jenny off to bed before her brothers came home; Jenny did not like to go so early, and had to be bribed and coaxed to give up the pleasure of sitting on brother Tom's knee; and when she was in bed, she could not go to sleep, and kept up a little whimper of distress. Bessy kept calling out to her, now in gentle, now in sharp tones, as she made the hearth clean and bright against her brothers' return, as she settled Bill and Mary to their next day's lessons, and got her work ready for a happy evening.

Presently the elder boys came in.

"Where's Jenny?" asked Tom, the first thing.

"I've put her to bed," said Bessy. "I've borrowed a book for you to read to me while I darn the stockings; and it was time for Jenny to go."

"Mother never puts her to bed so soon," said Tom, dissatisfied.

"But she'd be so in the way of any quietness over our reading," said Bessy.

"I don't want to read," said Tom; "I want Jenny to sit on my knee, as she always does, while I eat my supper."

"Tom, Tom, dear Tom!" called out little Jenny, who had heard his voice, and, perhaps, a little of the conversation.

Tom made but two steps upstairs, and re-appeared with Jenny in his arms, in her night-clothes. The little girl looked at Bessy half triumphant and half afraid. Bessy did not speak, but she was evidently very much displeased. Tom began to eat his porridge with Jenny on his knee. Bessy sat in sullen silence; she was vexed with Tom, vexed with Jenny, and vexed with Jem, to gratify whose taste for reading travels she had especially borrowed this book, which he seemed to care so little about. She brooded over her fancied wrongs, ready to fall upon the first person who might give the slightest occasion for anger. It happened to be poor little Jenny, who, by some awkward movement, knocked over the jug of milk, and made a great splash on Bessy's clean white floor.

"Never mind!" said Tom, as Jenny began to cry. "I like my porridge as well without milk as with it."

"Oh, never mind!" said Bessy, her colour rising, and her breath growing shorter. "Never mind dirtying anything, Jenny; it's only giving trouble to Bessy! But I'll make you mind," continued she, as she caught a glance of intelligence peep from Jem's eyes to Tom; and she slapped Jenny's head. The moment she had done it she was sorry for it; she could have beaten herself now with the greatest pleasure for having given way to passion; for she loved little Jenny dearly, and she saw that she really had hurt her. But Jem, with his loud, deep, "For shame, Bessy!" and Tom, with his excess of sympathy with his little sister's wrongs, checked back any expression which Bessy might have uttered of sorrow and regret. She sat there ten times more unhappy than she had been before the accident, hardening her heart to the reproaches of her conscience, yet feeling most keenly that she had been acting wrongly. No one seemed to notice her; this was the evening she had planned and arranged for so busily; and the others, who never thought about it at all, were all quiet and happy, at least in outward appearance, while she was so wretched. By-and-by, she felt the touch of a little soft hand stealing into her own. She looked to see who it was; it was Mary, who till now had been busy learning her lessons, but uncomfortably conscious of the discordant spirit prevailing in the room; and who had at last ventured up to Bessy, as the one who looked the most unhappy, to express, in her own little gentle way, her sympathy in sorrow. Mary was not a quick child; she was plain and awkward in her ways, and did not seem to have many words in which to tell her feelings, but she was very tender and loving, and submitted meekly and humbly to the little slights and rebuffs she often met with for her stupidity.

"Dear Bessy! good night!" said she, kissing her sister; and, at the soft kiss, Bessy's eyes filled with tears, and her heart began to melt.

"Jenny," continued Mary, going to the little spoilt, wilful girl, "will you come to bed with me, and I'll tell you stories about school, and sing you my songs as I undress? Come, little one!" said she, holding out her arms. Jenny was tempted by this speech, and went off to bed in a more reasonable frame of mind than any one had dared to hope.

And now all seemed clear and open for the reading, but each was too proud to propose it. Jem, indeed, seemed to have forgotten the book altogether, he was so busy whittling away at a piece of wood. At last Tom, by a strong effort, said, "Bessy, mayn't we have the book now?"

"No!" said Jem, "don't begin reading, for I must go out and try and make Ned Bates give me a piece of ash-wood—deal is just good for nothing."

"Oh!" said Bessy, "I don't want any one to read this book who does not like it. But I know mother would be better pleased if you were stopping at home quiet, rather than rambling to Ned Bates's at this time of night."

"I know what mother would like as well as you, and I'm not going to be preached to by a girl," said Jem, taking up his cap and going out. Tom yawned and went up to bed. Bessy sat brooding over the evening.

"So much as I thought and I planned! I'm sure I tried to do what was right, and make the boys happy at home. And yet nothing has happened as I wanted it to do. Every one has been so cross and contrary. Tom would take Jenny up when she ought to have been in bed. Jem did not care a straw for this book that I borrowed on purpose for him, but sat laughing. I saw, though he did not think I did, when all was going provoking and vexatious. Mary—no! Mary was a help and a comfort, as she always is, I think, though she is so stupid over her book. Mary always contrives to get people right, and to have her own way somehow; and yet I'm sure she does not take half the trouble I do to please people."

Jem came back soon, disappointed because Ned Bates was out, and could not give him any ash-wood. Bessy said it served him right for going at that time of night, and the brother and sister spoke angrily to each other all the way upstairs, and parted without even saying good-night. Jenny was asleep when Bessy entered the bedroom which she shared with her sisters and her mother; but she saw Mary's wakeful eyes looking at her as she came in.

"Oh, Mary," said she, "I wish mother was back. The lads would mind her, and now I see they'll just go and get into mischief to spite and plague me."

"I don't think it's for that," said Mary, softly. "Jem did want that ash-wood, I know, for he told me in the morning he didn't think that deal would do. He wants to make a wedge to keep the window from rattling so on windy nights; you know how that fidgets mother."

The next day, little Mary, on her way to school, went round by Ned Bates's to beg a piece of wood for her brother Jem; she brought it home to him at dinner-time, and asked him to be so good as to have everything ready for a quiet whittling at night, while Tom or Bessy read aloud. She told Jenny she would make haste with her lessons, so as to be ready to come to bed early, and talk to her about school (a grand, wonderful place, in Jenny's eyes), and thus Mary quietly and gently prepared for a happy evening, by attending to the kind of happiness for which every one wished.

While Mary had thus been busy preparing for a happy evening, Bessy had been spending part of the afternoon at a Mrs. Foster's, a neighbour of her mother's, and a very tidy, industrious old widow. Mrs. Foster earned part of her livelihood by working for the shops where knitted work of all kinds is to be sold; and Bessy's attention was caught, almost as soon as she went in, by a very gay piece of wool-knitting, in a new stitch, that was to be used as a warm covering for the feet. After admiring its pretty looks, Bessy thought how useful it might be to her mother; and when Mrs. Foster heard this, she offered to teach Bessy how to do it. But where were the wools to come from? Those which Mrs. Foster used were provided her by the shop; and she was a very poor woman—too poor to make presents, though rich enough (as we all are) to give help of many other kinds, and willing too to do what she could (which some of us are not).

The two sat perplexed. "How much did you say it would cost?" said Bessy at last; as if the article was likely to have become cheaper, since she asked the question before.

"Well! it's sure to be more than two shillings if it's German wool. You might get it for eighteenpence if you could be content with English."

"But I've not got eighteenpence," said Bessy, gloomily.

"I could lend it you," said Mrs. Foster, "if I was sure of having it back before Monday. But it's part of my rent-money. Could you make sure, do you think?"

"Oh, yes!" said Bessy, eagerly. "At least I'd try. But perhaps I had better not take it, for after all I don't know where I could get it. What Tom and Jem earn is little enough for the house, now that mother's washing is cut off."

"They are good, dutiful lads, to give it to their mother," said Mrs. Foster, sighing: for she thought of her own boys, that had left her in her old age to toil on, with faded eyesight and weakened strength.

"Oh! but mother makes them each keep a shilling out of it for themselves," said Bessy, in a complaining tone, for she wanted money, and was inclined to envy any one who possessed it.

"That's right enough," said Mrs. Foster. "They that earn it should have some of the power over it."

"But about this wool; this eighteenpence! I wish I was a boy and could earn money. I wish mother would have let me go to work in the factory."

"Come now, Bessy, I can have none of that nonsense. Thy mother knows what's best for thee; and I'm not going to hear thee complain of what she has thought right. But may be, I can help you to a way of gaining eighteenpence. Mrs. Scott at the worsted shop told me that she should want some one to clean on Saturday; now you're a good strong girl, and can do a woman's work if you've a mind. Shall I say you will go? and then I don't mind if I lend you my eighteenpence. You'll pay me before I want my rent on Monday."

"Oh! thank you, dear Mrs. Foster," said Bessy. "I can scour as well as any woman, mother often says so; and I'll do my best on Saturday; they shan't blame you for having spoken up for me."

"No, Bessy, they won't, I'm sure, if you do your best. You're a good sharp girl for your years."

Bessy lingered for some time, hoping that Mrs. Foster would remember her offer of lending her the money; but finding that she had quite forgotten it, she ventured to remind the kind old woman. That it was nothing but forgetfulness, was evident from the haste with which Mrs. Foster bustled up to her tea-pot and took from it the money required.

"You're as welcome to it as can be, Bessy, as long as I'm sure of its being repaid by Monday. But you're in a mighty hurry about this coverlet," continued she, as she saw Bessy put on her bonnet and prepare to go out. "Stay, you must take patterns, and go to the right shop in St. Mary's Gate. Why, your mother won't be back this three weeks, child."

"No. But I can't abide waiting, and I want to set to it before it is dark; and you'll teach me the stitch, won't you, when I come back with the wools? I won't be half an hour away."

But Mary and Bill had to "abide waiting" that afternoon; for though the neighbour at whose house the key was left could let them into the house, there was no supper ready for them on their return from school; even Jenny was away spending the afternoon with a playfellow; the fire was nearly out, the milk had been left at a neighbour's; altogether home was very comfortless to the poor tired children, and Bill grumbled terribly; Mary's head ached, and the very tones of her brother's voice, as he complained, gave her pain; and for a minute she felt inclined to sit down and cry. But then she thought of many little sayings which she had heard from her teacher—such as "Never complain of what you can cure," "Bear and forbear," and several other short sentences of a similar description. So she began to make up the fire, and asked Bill to fetch some chips; and when he gave her the gruff answer, that he did not see any use in making a fire when there was nothing to cook by it, she went herself and brought the wood without a word of complaint.

Presently Bill said, "Here! you lend me those bellows; you're not blowing it in the right way; girls never do!" He found out that Mary was wise in making a bright fire ready; for before the blowing was ended, the neighbour with whom the milk had been left brought it in, and little handy Mary prepared the porridge as well as the mother herself could have done. They had just ended when Bessy came in almost breathless; for she had suddenly remembered, in the middle of her knitting-lesson, that Bill and Mary must be at home from school.

"Oh!" she said, "that's right. I have so hurried myself! I was afraid the fire would be out. Where's Jenny? You were to have called for her, you know, as you came from school. Dear! how stupid you are, Mary. I am sure I told you over and over again. Now don't cry, silly child. The best thing you can do is to run off back again for her."

"But my lessons, Bessy. They are so bad to learn. It's tables day to-morrow," pleaded Mary.

"Nonsense; tables are as easy as can be. I can say up to sixteen times sixteen in no time."

"But you know, Bessy, I'm very stupid, and my head aches so to-night!"

"Well! the air will do it good. Really, Mary, I would go myself, only I'm so busy; and you know Bill is too careless, mother says, to fetch Jenny through the streets; and besides they would quarrel, and you can always manage Jenny."

Mary sighed, and went away to bring her sister home. Bessy sat down to her knitting. Presently Bill came up to her with some question about his lesson. She told him the answer without looking at the book; it was all wrong, and made nonsense; but Bill did not care to understand what he learnt, and went on saying, "Twelve inches make one shilling," as contentedly as if it were right.

Mary brought Jenny home quite safely. Indeed, Mary always did succeed in everything, except learning her lessons well; and sometimes, if the teacher could have known how many tasks fell upon the willing, gentle girl at home, she would not have thought that poor Mary was slow or a dunce; and such thoughts would come into the teacher's mind sometimes, although she fully appreciated Mary's sweetness and humility of disposition.

To-night she tried hard at her tables, and all to no use. Her head ached so, she could not remember them, do what she would. She longed to go to her mother, whose cool hands around her forehead always seemed to do her so much good, and whose soft, loving words were such a help to her when she had to bear pain. She had arranged so many plans for to-night, and now all were deranged by Bessy's new fancy for knitting. But Mary did not see this in the plain, clear light in which I have put it before you. She only was sorry that she could not make haste with her lessons, as she had promised Jenny, who was now upbraiding her with the non-fulfilment of her words. Jenny was still up when Tom and Jem came in. They spoke sharply to Bessy for not having their porridge ready; and while she was defending herself, Mary, even at the risk of imperfect lessons, began to prepare the supper for her brothers. She did it all so quietly, that, almost before they were aware, it was ready for them; and Bessy, suddenly ashamed of herself, and touched by Mary's quiet helpfulness, bent down and kissed her, as once more she settled to the never-ending difficulty of her lesson.

Mary threw her arms round Bessy's neck, and began to cry, for this little mark of affection went to her heart; she had been so longing for a word or a sign of love in her suffering.

"Come, Molly," said Jem, "don't cry like a baby;" but he spoke very kindly. "What's the matter? the old headache come back? Never mind. Go to bed, and it will be better in the morning."

"But I can't go to bed. I don't know my lesson!" Mary looked happier, though the tears were in her eyes.

"I know mine," said Bill, triumphantly.

"Come here," said Jem. "There! I've time enough to whittle away at this before mother comes back. Now let's see this difficult lesson."

Jem's help soon enabled Mary to conquer her lesson; but, meanwhile, Jenny and Bill had taken to quarrelling in spite of Bessy's scolding, administered in small sharp doses, as she looked up from her all-absorbing knitting.

"Well," said Tom, "with this riot on one side, and this dull lesson on the other, and Bessy as cross as can be in the midst, I can understand what makes a man go out to spend his evenings from home."

Bessy looked up, suddenly wakened up to a sense of the danger which her mother had dreaded.

Bessy thought it was very fortunate that it fell on a Saturday, of all days in the week, that Mrs. Scott wanted her; for Mary would be at home, who could attend to the household wants of everybody; and so she satisfied her conscience at leaving the post of duty that her mother had assigned to her, and that she had promised to fulfil. She was so eager about her own plans that she did not consider this; she did not consider at all, or else I think she would have seen many things to which she seemed to be blind now. When were Mary's lessons for Monday to be learnt? Bessy knew as well as we do, that lesson-learning was hard work to Mary. If Mary worked as hard as she could after morning school she could hardly get the house cleaned up bright and comfortable before her brothers came home from the factory, which "loosed" early on the Saturday afternoon; and if pails of water, chairs heaped up one on the other, and tables put topsy-turvy on the dresser, were the most prominent objects in the house-place, there would be no temptation for the lads to stay at home; besides which, Mary, tired and weary (however gentle she might be), would not be able to give the life to the evening that Bessy, a clever, spirited girl, near their own age, could easily do, if she chose to be interested and sympathising in what they had to tell. But Bessy did not think of all this. What she did think about was the pleasant surprise she should give her mother by the warm and pretty covering for her feet, which she hoped to present her with on her return home. And if she had done the duties she was pledged to on her mother's departure first, if they had been compatible with her plan of being a whole day absent from home, in order to earn the money for the wools, the project of the surprise would have been innocent and praiseworthy.

Bessy prepared everything for dinner before she left home that Saturday morning. She made a potato-pie all ready for putting in the oven; she was very particular in telling Mary what was to be cleaned, and how it was all to be cleaned; and then she kissed the children, and ran off to Mrs. Scott's. Mary was rather afraid of the responsibility thrust upon her; but still she was pleased that Bessy could trust her to do so much. She took Jenny to the ever-useful neighbour, as she and Bill went to school; but she was rather frightened when Mrs. Jones began to grumble about these frequent visits of the child.

"I was ready enough to take care of the wench when thy mother was ill; there was reason for that. And the child is a nice child enough, when she is not cross; but still there are some folks, it seems, who, if you give them an inch, will take an ell. Where's Bessy, that she can't mind her own sister?"

"Gone out charing," said Mary, clasping the little hand in hers tighter, for she was afraid of Mrs. Jones's anger.

"I could go out charing every day in the week if I'd the face to trouble other folks with my children," said Mrs. Jones, in a surly tone.

"Shall I take her back, ma'am?" said Mary, timidly, though she knew this would involve her staying away from school, and being blamed by the dear teacher. But Mrs. Jones growled worse than she bit, this time at least.

"No," said she, "you may leave her with me. I suppose she's had her breakfast?"

"Yes; and I'll fetch her away as soon as ever I can after twelve."

If Mary had been one to consider the hardships of her little lot, she might have felt this morning's occurrence as one;—that she, who dreaded giving trouble to anybody, and was painfully averse from asking any little favour for herself, should be the very one on whom it fell to presume upon another person's kindness. But Mary never did think of any hardships; they seemed the natural events of life, and as if it was fitting and proper that she, who managed things badly, and was such a dunce, should be blamed. Still she was rather flurried by Mrs. Jones's scolding; and almost wished that she had taken Jenny home again. Her lessons were not well said, owing to the distraction of her mind.

When she went for Jenny she found that Mrs. Jones, repenting of her sharp words, had given the little girl bread and treacle, and made her very comfortable; so much so that Jenny was not all at once ready to leave her little playmates, and when once she had set out on the road, she was in no humour to make haste. Mary thought of the potato-pie and her brothers, and could almost have cried, as Jenny, heedless of her sister's entreaties, would linger at the picture-shops.

"I shall be obliged to go and leave you, Jenny! I must get dinner ready."

"I don't care," said Jenny. "I don't want any dinner, and I can come home quite well by myself."

Mary half longed to give her a fright, it was so provoking. But she thought of her mother, who was so anxious always about Jenny, and she did not do it. She kept patiently trying to attract her onwards, and at last they were at home. Mary stirred up the fire, which was to all appearance quite black; it blazed up, but the oven was cold. She put the pie in, and blew the fire; but the paste was quite white and soft when her brothers came home, eager and hungry.

"Oh! Mary, what a manager you are!" said Tom. "Any one else would have remembered and put the pie in in time."

Mary's eyes filled full of tears; but she did not try to justify herself. She went on blowing, till Jem took the bellows, and kindly told her to take off her bonnet, and lay the cloth. Jem was always kind. He gave Tom the best baked side of the pie, and quietly took the side himself where the paste was little better than dough, and the potatoes quite hard; and when he caught Mary's little anxious face watching him, as he had to leave part of his dinner untasted, he said, "Mary, I should like this pie warmed up for supper; there is nothing so good as potato-pie made hot the second time."

Tom went off saying, "Mary, I would not have you for a wife on any account. Why, my dinner would never be ready, and your sad face would take away my appetite if it were."

But Jem kissed her and said, "Never mind, Mary! you and I will live together, old maid and old bachelor."

So she could set to with spirit to her cleaning, thinking there never was such a good brother as Jem; and as she dwelt upon his perfections, she thought who it was who had given her such a good, kind brother, and felt her heart full of gratitude to Him. She scoured and cleaned in right-down earnest. Jenny helped her for some time, delighted to be allowed to touch and lift things. But then she grew tired; and Bill was out of doors; so Mary had to do all by herself, and grew very nervous and frightened, lest all should not be finished and tidy against Tom came home. And the more frightened she grew, the worse she got on. Her hands trembled, and things slipped out of them; and she shook so, she could not lift heavy pieces of furniture quickly and sharply; and in the middle the clock struck the hour for her brothers' return, when all ought to have been tidy and ready for tea. She gave it up in despair, and began to cry.

"Oh, Bessy, Bessy! why did you go away? I have tried hard, and I cannot do it," said she aloud, as if Bessy could hear.

"Dear Mary, don't cry," said Jenny, suddenly coming away from her play. "I'll help you. I am very strong. I can do anything. I can lift that pan off the fire."

The pan was full of boiling water, ready for Mary. Jenny took hold of the handle, and dragged it along the bar over the fire. Mary sprung forwards in terror to stop the little girl. She never knew how it was, but the next moment her arm and side were full of burning pain, which turned her sick and dizzy, and Jenny was crying passionately beside her.

"Oh, Mary! Mary! Mary! my hand is so scalded. What shall I do? I cannot bear it. It's all about my feet on the ground." She kept shaking her hand to cool it by the action of the air. Mary thought that she herself was dying, so acute and terrible was the pain; she could hardly keep from screaming out aloud; but she felt that if she once began she could not stop herself, so she sat still, moaning, and the tears running down her face like rain. "Go, Jenny," said she, "and tell some one to come."

"I can't, I can't, my hand hurts so," said Jenny. But she flew wildly out of the house the next minute, crying out, "Mary is dead. Come, come, come!" For Mary could bear it no longer; but had fainted away, and looked, indeed, like one that was dead. Neighbours flocked in; and one ran for a doctor. In five minutes Tom and Jem came home. What a home it seems! People they hardly knew standing in the house-place, which looked as if it had never been cleaned—all was so wet, and in such disorder, and dirty with the trampling of many feet; Jenny still crying passionately, but half comforted at being at present the only authority as to how the affair happened; and faint moans from the room upstairs, where some women were cutting the clothes off poor Mary, preparatory for the doctor's inspection. Jem said directly, "Some one go straight to Mrs. Scott's, and fetch our Bessy. Her place is here, with Mary."

And then he civilly, but quietly, dismissed all the unnecessary and useless people, feeling sure that in case of any kind of illness, quiet was the best thing. Then he went upstairs.

Mary's face was scarlet now with violent pain; but she smiled a little through her tears at seeing Jem. As for him, he cried outright.

"I don't think it was anybody's fault, Jem," said she, softly. "It was very heavy to lift."

"Are you in great pain, dear?" asked Jem, in a whisper.

"I think I'm killed, Jem. I do think I am. And I did so want to see mother again."

"Nonsense!" said the woman who had been helping Mary. For, as she said afterwards, whether Mary died or lived, crying was a bad thing for her; and she saw the girl was ready to cry when she thought of her mother, though she had borne up bravely all the time the clothes were cut off.

Bessy's face, which had been red with hard running, faded to a dead white when she saw Mary; she looked so shocked and ill that Jem had not the heart to blame her, although the minute before she came in, he had been feeling very angry with her. Bessy stood quite still at the foot of Mary's bed, never speaking a word, while the doctor examined her side and felt her pulse; only great round tears gathered in her eyes, and rolled down her cheeks, as she saw Mary quiver with pain. Jem followed the doctor downstairs. Then Bessy went and knelt beside Mary, and wiped away the tears that were trickling down the little face.

"Is it very bad, Mary?" asked Bessy.

"Oh yes! yes! if I speak, I shall scream."

Then Bessy covered her head in the bed-clothes and cried outright.

"I was not cross, was I? I did not mean to be—but I hardly know what I am saying," moaned out little Mary. "Please forgive me, Bessy, if I was cross."

"God forgive me!" said Bessy, very low. They were the first words she had spoken since she came home. But there could be no more talking between the sisters, for now the woman returned who had at first been assisting Mary. Presently Jem came to the door, and beckoned. Bessy rose up, and went with, him below. Jem looked very grave, yet not so sad as he had done before the doctor came. "He says she must go into the infirmary. He will see about getting her in."

"Oh, Jem! I did so want to nurse her myself!" said Bessy, imploringly. "It was all my own fault," (she choked with crying); "and I thought I might do that for her, to make up."

"My dear Bessy,"—before he had seen Bessy, he had thought he could never call her "dear" again, but now he began— "My dear Bessy, we both want Mary to get better, don't we? I am sure we do. And we want to take the best way of making her so, whatever that is; well, then, I think we must not be considering what we should like best just for ourselves, but what people, who know as well as doctors do, say is the right way. I can't remember all that he said; but I'm clear that he told me, all wounds on the skin required more and better air to heal in than Mary could have here: and there the doctor will see her twice a day, if need be."

Bessy shook her head, but could not speak at first. At last she said, "Jem, I did so want to do something for her. No one could nurse her as I should."

Jem was silent. At last he took Bessy's hand, for he wanted to say something to her that he was afraid might vex her, and yet that he thought he ought to say.

"Bessy!" said he, "when mother went away, you planned to do all things right at home, and to make us all happy. I know you did. Now may I tell you how I think you went wrong? Don't be angry, Bessy."

"I think I shall never have spirit enough in me to be angry again," said Bessy, humbly and sadly.

"So much the better, dear. But don't over-fret about Mary. The doctor has good hopes of her, if he can get her into the infirmary. Now, I'm going on to tell you how I think you got wrong after mother left. You see, Bessy, you wanted to make us all happy your way—as you liked; just as you are wanting now to nurse Mary in your way, and as you like. Now, as far as I can make out, those folks who make home the happiest, are people who try and find out how others think they could be happy, and then, if it's not wrong, help them on with their wishes as far as they can. You know, you wanted us all to listen to your book; and very kind it was in you to think of it; only, you see, one wanted to whittle, and another wanted to do this or that, and then you were vexed with us all. I don't say but what I should have been if I had been in your place, and planned such a deal for others; only lookers-on always see a deal; and I saw that if you'd done what poor little Mary did next day, we should all have been far happier. She thought how she could forward us in our plans, instead of trying to force a plan of her own on us. She got me my right sort of wood for whittling, and arranged all nicely to get the little ones off to bed, so as to get the house quiet, if you wanted some reading, as she thought you did. And that's the way, I notice, some folks have of making a happy home. Others may mean just as well, but they don't hit the thing."

"I dare say it's true," said Bessy. "But sometimes you all hang about as if you did not know what to do. And I thought reading travels would just please you all."

Jem was touched by Bessy's humble way of speaking, so different from her usual cheerful, self-confident manner. He answered, "I know you did, dear. And many a time we should have been glad enough of it, when we had nothing to do, as you say."

"I had promised mother to try and make you all happy, and this is the end of it!" said Bessy, beginning to cry afresh.

"But, Bessy! I think you were not thinking of your promise, when you fixed to go out and char."

"I thought of earning money."

"Earning money would not make us happy. We have enough, with care and management. If you were to have made us happy, you should have been at home, with a bright face, ready to welcome us; don't you think so, dear Bessy?"

"I did not want the money for home. I wanted to make mother a present of such a pretty thing!"

"Poor mother! I am afraid we must send for her home now. And she has only been three days at Southport!"

"Oh!" said Bessy, startled by this notion of Jem's; "don't, don't send for mother. The doctor did say so much about her going to Southport being the only thing for her, and I did so try to get her an order! It will kill her, Jem! indeed it will; you don't know how weak and frightened she is,—oh, Jem, Jem!"

Jem felt the truth of what his sister was saying. At last, he resolved to leave the matter for the doctor to decide, as he had attended his mother, and now knew exactly how much danger there was about Mary. He proposed to Bessy that they should go and relieve the kind neighbour who had charge of Mary.

"But you won't send for mother," pleaded Bessy; "if it's the best thing for Mary, I'll wash up her things to-night, all ready for her to go into the infirmary. I won't think of myself, Jem."

"Well! I must speak to the doctor," said Jem. "I must not try and fix any way just because we wish it, but because it is right."

All night long, Bessy washed and ironed, and yet was always ready to attend to Mary when Jem called her. She took Jenny's scalded hand in charge as well, and bathed it with the lotion the doctor sent; and all was done so meekly and patiently that even Tom was struck with it, and admired the change. The doctor came very early. He had prepared everything for Mary's admission into the infirmary. And Jem consulted him about sending for his mother home. Bessy sat trembling, awaiting his answer.

"I am very unwilling to sanction any concealment. And yet, as you say, your mother is in a very delicate state. It might do her serious harm if she had any shock. Well! suppose for this once, I take it on myself. If Mary goes on as I hope, why— well! well! we'll see. Mind that your mother is told all when she comes home. And if our poor Mary grows worse—but I'm not afraid of that, with infirmary care and nursing—but if she does, I'll write to your mother myself, and arrange with a kind friend I have at Southport all about sending her home. And now," said he, turning suddenly to Bessy, "tell me what you were doing from home when this happened. Did not your mother leave you in charge of all at home?"

"Yes, sir!" said Bessy, trembling. "But, sir, I thought I could earn money to make mother a present!"

"Thought! fiddle-de-dee. I'll tell you what; never you neglect the work clearly laid out for you by either God or man, to go making work for yourself, according to your own fancies. God knows what you are most fit for. Do that. And then wait; if you don't see your next duty clearly. You will not long be idle in this world, if you are ready for a summons. Now let me see that you send Mary all clean and tidy to the infirmary."

Jem was holding Bessy's hand. "She has washed everything and made it fit for a queen. Our Bessy worked all night long, and was content to let me be with Mary (where she wished sore to be), because I could lift her better, being the stronger."

"That's right. Even when you want to be of service to others, don't think how to please yourself."

I have not much more to tell you about Bessy. This sad accident of Mary's did her a great deal of good, although it cost her so much sorrow at first. It taught her several lessons, which it is good for every woman to learn, whether she is called upon, as daughter, sister, wife, or mother, to contribute to the happiness of a home. And Mary herself was hardly more thoughtful and careful to make others happy in their own way, provided that way was innocent, than was Bessy hereafter. It was a struggle between her and Mary which could be the least selfish, and do the duties nearest to them with the most faithfulness and zeal. The mother stayed at Southport her full time, and came home well and strong. Then Bessy put her arms round her mother's neck, and told her all—and far more severely against herself than either the doctor or Jem did, when they related the same story afterwards.

DISAPPEARANCES.

I am not in the habit of seeing the *Household Words* regularly; but a friend, who lately sent me some of the back numbers, recommended me to read "all the papers relating to the Detective and Protective Police," which I accordingly did—not as the generality of readers have done, as they appeared week by week, or with pauses between, but consecutively, as a popular history of the Metropolitan Police; and, as I suppose it may also be considered, a history of the police force in every large town in England. When I had ended these papers, I did not feel disposed to read any others at that time, but preferred falling into a train of reverie and recollection.

First of all I remembered, with a smile, the unexpected manner in which a relation of mine was discovered by an acquaintance, who had mislaid or forgotten Mr. B.'s address. Now my dear cousin, Mr. B., charming as he is in many points, has the little peculiarity of liking to change his lodgings once every three months on an average, which occasions some bewilderment to his country friends, who have no sooner learnt the 19, Belle Vue Road, Hampstead, than they have to take pains to forget that address, and to remember the 27½, Upper Brown Street, Camberwell; and so on, till I would rather learn a page of *Walker's Pronouncing Dictionary*, than try to remember the variety of directions which I have had to put on my letters to Mr. B. during the last three years. Last summer it pleased him to remove to a beautiful village not ten miles out of London, where there is a railway station. Thither his friend sought him. (I do not now speak of the following scent there had been through three or four different lodgings, where Mr. B. had been residing, before his country friend ascertained that he was now lodging at R——.) He spent the morning in making inquiries as to Mr. B.'s whereabouts in the village; but many gentlemen were lodging there for the summer, and neither butcher nor baker could inform him where Mr. B. was staying; his letters were unknown at the post-office, which was accounted for by the circumstance of their always being directed to his office in town. At last the country friend sauntered back to the railway-office, and while he waited for the train he made inquiry, as a last resource, of the book-keeper at the station. "No, sir, I cannot tell you where Mr. B. lodges—so many gentlemen go by the trains; but I have no doubt but that the person standing by that pillar can inform you." The individual to whom he directed the inquirer's attention had the appearance of a tradesman—respectable enough, yet with no pretensions to "gentility," and had, apparently, no more urgent employment than lazily watching the passengers who came dropping in to the station. However, when he was spoken to, he answered civilly and promptly. "Mr. B.? tall gentleman, with light hair? Yes, sir, I know Mr. B. He lodges at No. 8, Morton Villas—has done these three weeks or more; but you'll not find him there, sir, now. He went to town by the eleven o'clock train, and does not usually return until the half-past four train."

The country friend had no time to lose in returning to the village, to ascertain the truth of this statement. He thanked his informant, and said he would call on Mr. B. at his office in town; but before he left R——station, he asked the book-keeper who the person was to whom he had referred him for information as to his friend's place of residence. "One of the Detective Police, sir," was the answer. I need hardly say that Mr. B., not without a little surprise, confirmed the accuracy of the policeman's report in every particular.

When I heard this anecdote of my cousin and his friend, I thought that there could be no more romances written on the same kind of plot as Caleb Williams; the principal interest of which, to the superficial reader, consists in the alternation of hope and fear, that the hero may, or may not, escape his pursuer. It is long since I have read the story, and I forget the name of the offended and injured gentleman, whose privacy Caleb has invaded; but I know that his pursuit of Caleb—his detection of the various hiding-places of the latter—his following up of slight clues—all, in fact, depended upon his own energy, sagacity, and perseverance. The interest was caused by the struggle of man against man; and the uncertainty as to which would ultimately be successful in his object; the unrelenting pursuer, or the ingenious Caleb, who seeks by every device to conceal himself. Now, in 1851, the offended master would set the Detective Police to work; there would be no doubt as to their success; the only question would be as to the time that would elapse before the hiding-place could be detected, and that could not be a question long. It is no longer a struggle between man and man, but between a vast organized machinery, and a weak, solitary individual; we have no hopes, no fears—only certainty. But if the materials of pursuit and evasion, as long as the chase is confined to England, are taken away from the store-house of the romancer, at any rate we can no more be haunted by the idea of the possibility of mysterious disappearances; and any one who has associated much with those who were alive at the end of the last century, can testify that there was some reason for such fears.

When I was a child, I was sometimes permitted to accompany a relation to drink tea with a very clever old lady, of one hundred and twenty—or, so I thought then; I now think she, perhaps, was only about seventy. She was lively, and intelligent, and had seen and known much that was worth narrating. She was a cousin of the Sneyds, the family whence Mr. Edgeworth took two of his wives; had known Major André; had mixed in the Old Whig Society that the beautiful Duchess of Devonshire and "Buff and Blue Mrs. Crewe" gathered round them; her father had been one of the early patrons of the lovely Miss Linley. I name these facts to show that she was too intelligent and cultivated by association, as well as by natural powers, to lend an over-easy credence to the marvellous; and yet I have heard her relate stories of disappearances which haunted my imagination longer than any tale of wonder. One of her stories was this:—Her father's estate lay in Shropshire, and his park-gates opened right on to a scattered village of which he was landlord. The houses formed a straggling irregular street—here a garden, next a gable-end of a farm, there a row of cottages, and so on. Now, at the end house or cottage lived a very respectable man and his wife. They were well known in the village, and were esteemed for the patient attention which they paid to the husband's father, a paralytic old man. In winter, his chair was near the fire; in summer, they carried him out into the open space in front of the house to bask in the sunshine, and to receive what placid amusement he could from watching the little passings to and fro of the villagers. He could not move from his bed to his chair without help. One hot and sultry June day, all the village turned out to the hay-fields. Only the very old and the very young remained.

The old father of whom I have spoken was carried out to bask in the sunshine that afternoon as usual, and his son and daughter-in-law went to the hay-making. But when they came home in the early evening, their paralysed father had disappeared—was gone! and from that day forwards, nothing more was ever heard of him. The old lady, who told this story, said with the quietness that always marked the simplicity of her narration, that every inquiry which her father could make was made, and that it could never be accounted for. No one had observed any stranger in the village; no small household robbery, to which the old man might have been supposed an obstacle, had been committed in his son's dwelling that afternoon. The son and daughter-in-law (noted too for their attention to the helpless father) had been a-field among all the neighbours the whole of the time. In short, it never was accounted for; and left a painful impression on many minds.

I will answer for it, the Detective Police would have ascertained every fact relating to it in a week.

This story from its mystery was painful, but had no consequences to make it tragical. The next which I shall tell (and although traditionary, these anecdotes of disappearances which I relate in this paper are correctly repeated, and were believed by my informants to be strictly true), had consequences, and melancholy ones too. The scene of it is in a little country-town, surrounded by the estates of several gentlemen of large property. About a hundred years ago there lived in this small town an attorney, with his mother and sister. He was agent for one of the squires near, and received rents for him on stated days, which of course were well known. He went at these times to a small public-house, perhaps five miles from ——, where the tenants met him, paid their rents, and were entertained at dinner afterwards. One night he did not return from this festivity. He never returned. The gentleman whose agent he was, employed the Dogberrys of the time to find him, and the missing cash; the mother, whose support and comfort he was, sought him with all the perseverance of faithful love. But he never returned; and by-and-by the rumour spread that he must have gone abroad with the money; his mother heard the whispers all around her, and could not disprove it; and so her heart broke, and she died. Years after, I think as many as fifty, the well-to-do butcher and grazier of —— died; but, before his death, he confessed that he had waylaid Mr. ——on the heath close to the town, almost within call of his own house, intending only to rob him, but meeting with more resistance than he anticipated, had been provoked to stab him; and had buried him that very night deep under the loose sand of the heath. There his skeleton was found; but too late for his poor mother to know that his fame was cleared. His sister, too, was dead, unmarried, for no one liked the possibilities which might arise from being connected with the family. None cared if he was guilty or innocent now.

If our Detective Police had only been in existence!

This last is hardly a story of unaccounted-for disappearance. It is only unaccounted for in one generation. But disappearances never to be accounted for on any supposition are not uncommon, among the traditions of the last century. I have heard (and I think I have read it in one of the earlier numbers of *Chambers's Journal*), of a marriage which took place in Lincolnshire about the year 1750. It was not then *de rigueur* that the happy couple should set out on a wedding journey; but instead, they and their friends had a merry jovial dinner at the house of either bride or groom; and in this instance the whole party adjourned to the bridegroom's residence, and dispersed, some to ramble in the garden, some to rest in the house until the dinner-hour. The bridegroom, it is to be supposed, was with his bride, when he was suddenly summoned away by a domestic, who said that a stranger wished to speak to him; and henceforward he was never seen more. The same tradition hangs about an old deserted Welsh Hall standing in a wood near Festiniog; there, too, the bridegroom was sent for to give audience to a stranger on his wedding-day, and disappeared from the face of the earth from that time; but there, they tell in addition, that the bride lived long,—that she passed her three-score years and ten, but that daily during all those years, while there was light of sun or moon to lighten the earth, she sat watching,—watching at one particular window which commanded a view of the approach to the house. Her whole faculties, her whole mental powers, became absorbed in that weary watching; long before she died, she was childish, and only conscious of one wish—to sit in that long high window, and watch the road, along which he might come. She was as faithful as Evangeline, if pensive and inglorious.

That these two similar stories of disappearance on a wedding-day "obtained," as the French say, shows us that anything which adds to our facility of communication, and organization of means, adds to our security of life. Only let a bridegroom try to disappear from an untamed *Katherine* of a bride, and he will soon be brought home, like a recreant coward, overtaken by the electric telegraph, and clutched back to his fate by a detective policeman.

Two more stories of disappearance, and I have done. I will give you the last in date first, because it is the most melancholy; and we will wind up cheerfully (after a fashion). Some time between 1820 and 1830, there lived in North Shields a respectable old woman, and her son, who was trying to struggle into sufficient knowledge of medicine, to go out as ship-surgeon in a Baltic vessel, and perhaps in this manner to earn money enough to spend a session in Edinburgh. He was furthered in all his plans by the late benevolent Dr. G——, of that town. I believe the usual premium was not required in his case; the young man did many useful errands and offices which a finer young gentleman would have considered beneath him; and he resided with his mother in one of the alleys (or "chares,") which lead down from the main street of North Shields to the river. Dr. G——had been with a patient all night, and left her very early on a winter's morning to return home to bed; but first he stepped down to his apprentice's home, and bade him get up, and follow him to his own house, where some medicine was to be mixed, and then taken to the lady. Accordingly the poor lad came, prepared the dose, and set off with it some time between five and six on a winter's morning. He was never seen again. Dr. G——waited, thinking he was at his mother's house; she waited, considering that he had gone to his day's work. And meanwhile, as people remembered afterwards, the small vessel bound to Edinburgh sailed out of port. The mother expected him back her whole life long; but some years afterwards occurred the discoveries of the Hare and Burke horrors, and people seemed to gain a dark glimpse at his fate; but I never heard that it was fully ascertained, or indeed more than surmised. I ought to add that all who knew him spoke emphatically as to his steadiness of purpose, and conduct, so as to render it improbable in the highest degree that he had run off to sea, or suddenly changed his plan of life in any way.

My last story is one of a disappearance which was accounted for after many years. There is a considerable street in Manchester leading from the centre of the town to some of the suburbs. This street is called at one part Garratt, and afterwards, where it emerges into gentility and, comparatively, country, Brook Street. It derives its former name from an old black-and-white hall of the time of Richard the Third, or thereabouts, to judge from the style of building; they have closed in what is left of the old hall now; but a few years since this old house was visible from the main road; it stood low on some vacant ground, and appeared to be half in ruins. I believe it was occupied by several poor families who rented tenements in the tumble-down dwelling. But formerly it was Gerard Hall, (what a difference between Gerard and Garratt!) and was surrounded by a park with a clear brook running through it, with pleasant fish-ponds, (the name of these was preserved until very lately, on a street near,) orchards, dovecotes, and similar appurtenances to the manor-houses of former days. I am almost sure that the family to whom it belonged were Mosleys, probably a branch of the tree of the lord of the Manor of Manchester. Any topographical work of the last century relating to their district would give the name of the last proprietor of the old stock, and it is to him that my story refers.

Many years ago there lived in Manchester two old maiden ladies, of high respectability. All their lives had been spent in the town, and they were fond of relating the changes which had taken place within their recollection, which extended back to seventy or eighty years from the present time. They knew much of its traditionary history from their father, as well; who, with his father before him, had been respectable attorneys in Manchester, during the greater part of the last century: they were, also, agents for several of the county families, who, driven from their old possessions by the enlargement of the town, found some compensation in the increased value of any land which they might choose to sell. Consequently the Messrs. S——, father and son, were conveyancers in good repute, and acquainted with several secret pieces of family history, one of which related to Garratt Hall.

The owner of this estate, some time in the first half of the last century, married young; he and his wife had several children, and lived together in a quiet state of happiness for many years. At last, business of some kind took the husband up to London; a week's journey in those days. He wrote and announced his arrival; I do not think he ever wrote again. He seemed to be swallowed up in the abyss of the metropolis, for no friend (and the lady had many and powerful friends) could ever ascertain for her what had become of him; the prevalent idea was that he had been attacked by some of the street-robbers who prowled about in those days, that he had resisted, and had been murdered. His wife gradually gave up all hopes of seeing him again, and devoted herself to the care of her children; and so they went on, tranquilly enough, until the heir came of age, when certain deeds were necessary before he could legally take possession of the property. These deeds Mr. S—— (the family lawyer) stated had been given up by him into the missing gentleman's keeping just before the last mysterious journey to London, with which I think they were in some way concerned. It was possible that they were still in existence; some one in London might have them in possession, and be either conscious or unconscious of their importance. At any rate, Mr. S——'s advice to his client was that he should put an advertisement in the London papers, worded so skilfully that any one who might hold the important documents should understand to what it referred, and no one else. This was accordingly done; and although repeated at intervals for some time, it met with no success. But at last a mysterious answer was sent; to the effect that the deeds were in existence, and should be given up; but only on certain conditions, and to the heir himself. The young man, in consequence, went up to London, and adjourned, according to directions, to an old house in Barbican, where he was told by a man, apparently awaiting him, that he must submit to be blindfolded, and must follow his guidance. He was taken through several long passages before he left the house; at the termination of one of these he was put into a sedan-chair, and carried about for an hour or more; he always reported that there were many turnings, and that he imagined he was set down finally not very far from his starting point.

When his eyes were unbandaged, he was in a decent sitting-room, with tokens of family occupation lying about. A middle-aged gentleman entered, and told him that, until a certain time had elapsed (which should be indicated to him in a particular way, but of which the length was not then named), he must swear to secrecy as to the means by which he obtained possession of the deeds. This oath was taken; and then the gentleman, not without some emotion, acknowledged himself to be the missing father of the heir. It seems that he had fallen in love with a damsel, a friend of the person with whom he lodged. To this young woman he had represented himself as unmarried; she listened willingly to his wooing, and her father, who was a shopkeeper in the City, was not averse to the match, as the Lancashire squire had a goodly presence, and many similar qualities, which the shopkeeper thought might be acceptable to his customers. The bargain was struck; the descendant of a knightly race married the only daughter of the City shopkeeper, and became a junior partner in the business. He told his son that he had never repented the step he had taken; that his lowly-born wife was sweet, docile, and affectionate; that his family by her was large; and that he and they were thriving and happy. He inquired after his first (or rather, I should say, his true) wife with friendly affection; approved of what she had done with regard to his estate, and the education of his children; but said that he considered he was dead to her, as she was to him. When he really died he promised that a particular message, the nature of which he specified, should be sent to his son at Garrett; until then they would not hear more of each other; for it was of no use attempting to trace him under his incognito, even if the oath did not render such an attempt forbidden. I dare say the youth had no great desire to trace out the father, who had been one in name only. He returned to Lancashire; took possession of the property at Manchester; and many years elapsed before he received the mysterious intimation of his father's real death. After that, he named the particulars connected with the recovery of the title-deeds to Mr. S., and one or two intimate friends. When the family became extinct, or removed from Garratt, it became no longer any very closely kept secret, and I was told the tale of the disappearance by Miss S., the aged daughter of the family agent.

Once more, let me say I am thankful I live in the days of the Detective Police; if I am murdered, or commit bigamy, at any rate my friends will have the comfort of knowing all about it.

A correspondent has favoured us with the sequel of the disappearance of the pupil of Dr. G., who vanished from North Shields, in charge of certain potions he was entrusted with, very early one morning, to convey to a patient:—"Dr. G.'s son married my sister, and the young man who disappeared was a pupil in the house. When he went out with the medicine, he was hardly dressed, having merely thrown on some clothes; and he went in slippers—which incidents induced the belief that he was made away with. After some months his family put on mourning; and the G.'s (*very* timid people) were so sure that he was murdered, that they wrote verses to his memory, and became sadly worn by terror. But, after a long time (I fancy, but am not sure, about a year and a half), came a letter from the young man, who was doing well in America. His explanation was, that a vessel was lying at the wharf about to sail in the morning, and the youth, who had long meditated evasion, thought it a good opportunity, and stepped on board, after leaving the medicine at the proper door. I spent some weeks at Dr. G.'s after the occurrence; and very doleful we used to be about it. But the next time I went they were, naturally, very angry with the inconsiderate young man."

FOOTNOTES

1.

Wir pflügen und wir streuen
Den Saamen auf das Land;

Das Wachsen und Gedeihen

Steht in des höchsten Hand.

Er sendet Thau und Regen,

Und Sonn und Mondeschein;

Von Ihm kommt aller Segen,

Von unserm Gott allein:

Alle gute Gabe kommt her

Von Gott dem Herrn,

Drum dankt und hofft auf.

SYLVIA'S LOVERS.

BY

ELIZABETH GASKELL

Oh for thy voice to soothe and bless!

What hope of answer, or redress?

Behind the veil! Behind the veil!—Tennyson

IN THREE VOLUMES.

VOL. III.

LONDON:

M.DCCC.LXIII.

CHAPTER XXX

HAPPY DAYS

And now Philip seemed as prosperous as his heart could desire. The business flourished, and money beyond his moderate wants came in. As for himself he required very little; but he had always looked forward to placing his idol in a befitting shrine; and means for this were now furnished to him. The dress, the comforts, the position he had desired for Sylvia were all hers. She did not need to do a stroke of household work if she preferred to 'sit in her parlour and sew up a seam'. Indeed Phoebe resented any interference in the domestic labour, which she had performed so long, that she looked upon the kitchen as a private empire of her own. 'Mrs Hepburn' (as Sylvia was now termed) had a good dark silk gown-piece in her drawers, as well as the poor dove-coloured, against the day when she chose to leave off mourning; and stuff for either gray or scarlet cloaks was hers at her bidding.

What she cared for far more were the comforts with which it was in her power to surround her mother. In this Philip vied with her; for besides his old love, and new pity for his aunt Bell, he never forgot how she had welcomed him to Haytersbank, and favoured his love to Sylvia, in the yearning days when he little hoped he should ever win his cousin to be his wife. But even if he had not had these grateful and affectionate feelings towards the poor woman, he would have done much for her if only to gain the sweet, rare smiles which his wife never bestowed upon him so freely as when she saw him attending to 'mother,' for so both of them now called Bell. For her creature comforts, her silk gowns, and her humble luxury, Sylvia did not care; Philip was almost annoyed at the indifference she often manifested to all his efforts to surround her with such things. It was even a hardship to her to leave off her country dress, her uncovered hair, her linsey petticoat, and loose bed-gown, and to don a stiff and stately gown for her morning dress. Sitting in the dark parlour at the back of the shop, and doing 'white work,' was much more wearying to her than running out into the fields to bring up the cows, or spinning wool, or making up butter. She sometimes thought to herself that it was a strange kind of life where there were no out-door animals to look after; the 'ox and the ass' had hitherto come into all her ideas of humanity; and her care and gentleness had made the dumb creatures round her father's home into mute friends with loving eyes, looking at her as if wistful to speak in words the grateful regard that she could read without the poor expression of language.

She missed the free open air, the great dome of sky above the fields; she rebelled against the necessity of 'dressing' (as she called it) to go out, although she acknowledged that it was a necessity where the first step beyond the threshold must be into a populous street.

It is possible that Philip was right at one time when he had thought to win her by material advantages; but the old vanities had been burnt out of her by the hot iron of acute suffering. A great deal of passionate feeling still existed, concealed and latent; but at this period it appeared as though she were indifferent to most things, and had lost the power of either hoping or fearing much. She was stunned into a sort of temporary numbness on most points; those on which she was sensitive being such as referred to the injustice and oppression of her father's death, or anything that concerned her mother.

She was quiet even to passiveness in all her dealings with Philip; he would have given not a little for some of the old bursts of impatience, the old pettishness, which, naughty as they were, had gone to form his idea of the former Sylvia. Once or twice he was almost vexed with her for her docility; he wanted her so much to have a will of her own, if only that he might know how to rouse her to pleasure by gratifying it. Indeed he seldom fell asleep at nights without his last thoughts being devoted to some little plan for the morrow, that he fancied she would like; and when he wakened in the early dawn he looked to see if she were indeed sleeping by his side, or whether it was not all a dream that he called Sylvia 'wife.'

He was aware that her affection for him was not to be spoken of in the same way as his for her, but he found much happiness in only being allowed to love and cherish her; and with the patient perseverance that was one remarkable feature in his character, he went on striving to deepen and increase her love when most other men would have given up the endeavour, made themselves content with half a heart, and turned to some other object of attainment. All this time Philip was troubled by a dream that recurred whenever he was over-fatigued, or otherwise not in perfect health. Over and over again in this first year of married life he dreamt this dream; perhaps as many as eight or nine times, and it never varied. It was always of Kinraid's return; Kinraid was full of life in Philip's dream, though in his waking hours he could and did convince himself by all the laws of probability that his rival was dead. He never remembered the exact sequence of events in that terrible dream after he had roused himself, with a fight and a struggle, from his feverish slumbers. He was generally sitting up in bed when he found himself conscious, his heart beating wildly, with a conviction of Kinraid's living presence somewhere near him in the darkness. Occasionally Sylvia was disturbed by his agitation, and would question him about his dreams, having, like most of her class at that time, great faith in their prophetic interpretation; but Philip never gave her any truth in his reply.

After all, and though he did not acknowledge it even to himself, the long-desired happiness was not so delicious and perfect as he had anticipated. Many have felt the same in their first year of married life; but the faithful, patient nature that still works on, striving to gain love, and capable itself of steady love all the while, is a gift not given to all.

For many weeks after their wedding, Kester never came near them: a chance word or two from Sylvia showed Philip that she had noticed this and regretted it; and, accordingly, he made it his business at the next leisure opportunity to go to Haytersbank (never saying a word to his wife of his purpose), and seek out Kester.

All the whole place was altered! It was new white-washed, new thatched: the patches of colour in the surrounding ground were changed with altered tillage; the great geraniums were gone from the window, and instead, was a smart knitted blind. Children played before the house-door; a dog lying on the step flew at Philip; all was so strange, that it was even the strangest thing of all for Kester to appear where everything else was so altered!

Philip had to put up with a good deal of crabbed behaviour on the part of the latter before he could induce Kester to promise to come down into the town and see Sylvia in her new home.

Somehow, the visit when paid was but a failure; at least, it seemed so at the time, though probably it broke the ice of restraint which was forming over the familiar intercourse between Kester and Sylvia. The old servant was daunted by seeing Sylvia in a strange place, and stood, sleeking his hair down, and furtively looking about him, instead of seating himself on the chair Sylvia had so eagerly brought forward for him.

Then his sense of the estrangement caused by their new positions infected her, and she began to cry pitifully, saying,—

'Oh, Kester! Kester! tell me about Haytersbank! Is it just as it used to be in feyther's days?'

'Well, a cannot say as it is,' said Kester, thankful to have a subject started. 'They'n pleughed up t' oud pasture-field, and are settin' it for 'taters. They're not for much cattle, isn't Higginses. They'll be for corn in t' next year, a reckon, and they'll just ha' their pains for their payment. But they're allays so pig-headed, is folk fra' a distance.'

So they went on discoursing on Haytersbank and the old days, till Bell Robson, having finished her afternoon nap, came slowly down-stairs to join them; and after that the conversation became so broken up, from the desire of the other two to attend and reply as best they could to her fragmentary and disjointed talk, that Kester took his leave before long; falling, as he did so, into the formal and unnaturally respectful manner which he had adopted on first coming in.

But Sylvia ran after him, and brought him back from the door.

'To think of thy going away, Kester, without either bit or drink; nay, come back wi' thee, and taste wine and cake.'

Kester stood at the door, half shy, half pleased, while Sylvia, in all the glow and hurry of a young housekeeper's hospitality, sought for the decanter of wine, and a wine-glass in the corner cupboard, and hastily cut an immense wedge of cake, which she crammed into his hand in spite of his remonstrances; and then she poured him out an overflowing glass of wine, which Kester would far rather have gone without, as he knew manners too well to suppose that he might taste it without having gone through the preliminary ceremony of wishing the donor health and happiness. He stood red and half smiling, with his cake in one hand, his wine in the other, and then began,—

'Long may ye live,
Happy may ye he,
And blest with a num'rous
Pro-ge-ny.'

'Theere, that's po'try for yo' as I larnt i' my youth. But there's a deal to be said as cannot be put int' po'try, an' yet a cannot say it, somehow. It 'd tax a parson t' say a' as a've getten i' my mind. It's like a heap o' woo' just after shearin' time; it's worth a deal, but it tak's a vast o' combin', an' cardin', an' spinnin' afore it can be made use on. If a were up to t' use o' words, a could say a mighty deal; but somehow a'm tongue-teed when a come to want my words most, so a'll only just mak' bold t' say as a think yo've done pretty well for yo'rsel', getten a house-full o' furniture' (looking around him as he said this), 'an' vittle an' clothin' for t' axing, belike, an' a home for t' missus in her time o' need; an' mebbe not such a bad husband as a once thought yon man 'ud mak'; a'm not above sayin' as he's, mebbe, better nor a took him for;—so here's to ye both, and wishin' ye health and happiness, ay, and money to buy yo' another, as country folk say.'

Having ended his oration, much to his own satisfaction, Kester tossed off his glass of wine, smacked his lips, wiped his mouth with the back of his hand, pocketed his cake, and made off.

That night Sylvia spoke of his visit to her husband. Philip never said how he himself had brought it to pass, nor did he name the fact that he had heard the old man come in just as he himself had intended going into the parlour for tea, but had kept away, as he thought Sylvia and Kester would most enjoy their interview undisturbed. And Sylvia felt as if her husband's silence was unsympathizing, and shut up the feelings that were just beginning to expand towards him. She sank again into the listless state of indifference from which nothing but some reference to former days, or present consideration for her mother, could rouse her.

Hester was almost surprised at Sylvia's evident liking for her. By slow degrees Hester was learning to love the woman, whose position as Philip's wife she would have envied so keenly had she not been so truly good and pious. But Sylvia seemed as though she had given Hester her whole affection all at once. Hester could not understand this, while she was touched and melted by the trust it implied. For one thing Sylvia remembered and regretted—her harsh treatment of Hester the rainy, stormy night on which the latter had come to Haytersbank to seek her and her mother, and bring them into Monkshaven to see the imprisoned father and husband. Sylvia had been struck with Hester's patient endurance of her rudeness, a rudeness which she was conscious that she herself should have immediately and vehemently resented. Sylvia did not understand how a totally different character from hers might immediately forgive the anger she could not forget; and because Hester had been so meek at the time, Sylvia, who knew how passing and transitory was her own anger, thought that all was forgotten; while Hester believed that the words, which she herself could not have uttered except under deep provocation, meant much more than they did, and admired and wondered at Sylvia for having so entirely conquered her anger against her.

Again, the two different women were divergently affected by the extreme fondness which Bell had shown towards Hester ever since Sylvia's wedding-day. Sylvia, who had always received more love from others than she knew what to do with, had the most entire faith in her own supremacy in her mother's heart, though at times Hester would do certain things more to the poor old woman's satisfaction. Hester, who had craved for the affection which had been withheld from her, and had from that one circumstance become distrustful of her own power of inspiring regard, while she exaggerated the delight of being beloved, feared lest Sylvia should become jealous of her mother's open display of great attachment and occasional preference for Hester. But such a thought never entered Sylvia's mind. She was more thankful than she knew how to express towards any one who made her mother happy; as has been already said, the contributing to Bell Robson's pleasures earned Philip more of his wife's smiles than anything else. And Sylvia threw her whole heart into the words and caresses she lavished on Hester whenever poor Mrs. Robson spoke of the goodness and kindness of the latter. Hester attributed more virtue to these sweet words and deeds of gratitude than they deserved; they did not imply in Sylvia any victory over evil temptation, as they would have done in Hester.

It seemed to be Sylvia's fate to captivate more people than she cared to like back again. She turned the heads of John and Jeremiah Foster, who could hardly congratulate Philip enough on his choice of a wife.

They had been prepared to be critical on one who had interfered with their favourite project of a marriage between Philip and Hester; and, though full of compassion for the cruelty of Daniel Robson's fate, they were too completely men of business not to have some apprehension that the connection of Philip Hepburn with the daughter of a man who was hanged, might injure the shop over which both his and their name appeared. But all the possible proprieties demanded that they should pay attention to the bride of their former shopman and present successor; and the very first visitors whom Sylvia had received after her marriage had been John and Jeremiah Foster, in their sabbath-day clothes. They found her in the parlour (so familiar to both of them!) clear-starching her mother's caps, which had to be got up in some particular fashion that Sylvia was afraid of dictating to Phoebe.

She was a little disturbed at her visitors discovering her at this employment; but she was on her own ground, and that gave her self-possession; and she welcomed the two old men so sweetly and modestly, and looked so pretty and feminine, and, besides, so notable in her handiwork, that she conquered all their prejudices at one blow; and their first thought on leaving the shop was how to do her honour, by inviting her to a supper party at Jeremiah Foster's house.

Sylvia was dismayed when she was bidden to this wedding feast, and Philip had to use all his authority, though tenderly, to make her consent to go at all. She had been to merry country parties like the Corneys', and to bright haymaking romps in the open air; but never to a set stately party at a friend's house.

She would fain have made attendance on her mother an excuse; but Philip knew he must not listen to any such plea, and applied to Hester in the dilemma, asking her to remain with Mrs. Robson while he and Sylvia went out visiting; and Hester had willingly, nay, eagerly consented—it was much more to her taste than going out.

So Philip and Sylvia set out, arm-in-arm, down Bridge Street, across the bridge, and then clambered up the hill. On the way he gave her the directions she asked for about her behaviour as bride and most honoured guest; and altogether succeeded, against his intention and will, in frightening her so completely as to the grandeur and importance of the occasion, and the necessity of remembering certain set rules, and making certain set speeches and attending to them when the right time came, that, if any one so naturally graceful could have been awkward, Sylvia would have been so that night.

As it was, she sate, pale and weary-looking, on the very edge of her chair; she uttered the formal words which Philip had told her were appropriate to the occasion, and she heartily wished herself safe at home and in bed. Yet she left but one unanimous impression on the company when she went away, namely, that she was the prettiest and best-behaved woman they had ever seen, and that Philip Hepburn had done well in choosing her, felon's daughter though she might be.

Both the hosts had followed her into the lobby to help Philip in cloaking her, and putting on her pattens. They were full of old-fashioned compliments and good wishes; one speech of theirs came up to her memory in future years:—

'Now, Sylvia Hepburn,' said Jeremiah, 'I've known thy husband long, and I don't say but what thou hast done well in choosing him; but if he ever neglects or ill-uses thee, come to me, and I'll give him a sound lecture on his conduct. Mind, I'm thy friend from this day forrards, and ready to take thy part against him!'

Philip smiled as if the day would never come when he should neglect or ill-use his darling; Sylvia smiled a little, without much attending to, or caring for, the words that were detaining her, tired as she was; John and Jeremiah chuckled over the joke; but the words came up again in after days, as words idly spoken sometimes do.

Before the end of that first year, Philip had learnt to be jealous of his wife's new love for Hester. To the latter, Sylvia gave the free confidence on many things which Philip fancied she withheld from him. A suspicion crossed his mind, from time to time, that Sylvia might speak of her former lover to Hester. It would be not unnatural, he thought, if she did so, believing him to be dead; but the idea irritated him.

He was entirely mistaken, however; Sylvia, with all her apparent frankness, kept her deep sorrows to herself. She never mentioned her father's name, though he was continually present to her mind. Nor did she speak of Kinraid to human being, though, for his sake, her voice softened when, by chance, she spoke to a passing sailor; and for his sake her eyes lingered on such men longer than on others, trying to discover in them something of the old familiar gait; and partly for his dead sake, and partly because of the freedom of the outlook and the freshness of the air, she was glad occasionally to escape from the comfortable imprisonment of her 'parlour', and the close streets around the market-place, and to mount the cliffs and sit on the turf, gazing abroad over the wide still expanse of the open sea; for, at that height, even breaking waves only looked like broken lines of white foam on the blue watery plain.

She did not want any companion on these rambles, which had somewhat of the delight of stolen pleasures; for all the other respectable matrons and town-dwellers whom she knew were content to have always a business object for their walk, or else to stop at home in their own households; and Sylvia was rather ashamed of her own yearnings for solitude and open air, and the sight and sound of the mother-like sea. She used to take off her hat, and sit there, her hands clasping her knees, the salt air lifting her bright curls, gazing at the distant horizon over the sea, in a sad dreaminess of thought; if she had been asked on what she meditated, she could not have told you.

But, by-and-by, the time came when she was a prisoner in the house; a prisoner in her room, lying in bed with a little baby by her side—her child, Philip's child. His pride, his delight knew no bounds; this was a new fast tie between them; this would reconcile her to the kind of life that, with all its respectability and comfort, was so different from what she had lived before, and which Philip had often perceived that she felt to be dull and restraining. He already began to trace in the little girl, only a few days old, the lovely curves that he knew so well by heart in the mother's face. Sylvia, too, pale, still, and weak, was very happy; yes, really happy for the first time since her irrevocable marriage. For its irrevocableness had weighed much upon her with a sense of dull hopelessness; she felt all Philip's kindness, she was grateful to him for his tender regard towards her mother, she was learning to love him as well as to like and respect him. She did not know what else she could have done but marry so true a friend, and she and her mother so friendless; but, at the same time, it was like lead on her morning spirits when she awoke and remembered that the decision was made, the deed was done, the choice taken which comes to most people but once in their lives. Now the little baby came in upon this state of mind like a ray of sunlight into a gloomy room.

Even her mother was rejoiced and proud; even with her crazed brain and broken heart, the sight of sweet, peaceful infancy brought light to her. All the old ways of holding a baby, of hushing it to sleep, of tenderly guarding its little limbs from injury, came back, like the habits of her youth, to Bell; and she was never so happy or so easy in her mind, or so sensible and connected in her ideas, as when she had Sylvia's baby in her arms.

It was a pretty sight to see, however familiar to all of us such things may be—the pale, worn old woman, in her quaint, old-fashioned country dress, holding the little infant on her knees, looking at its open, unspeculative eyes, and talking the little language to it as though it could understand; the father on his knees, kept prisoner by a small, small finger curled round his strong and sinewy one, and gazing at the tiny creature with wondering idolatry; the young mother, fair, pale, and smiling, propped up on pillows in order that she, too, might see the wonderful babe; it was astonishing how the doctor could come and go without being drawn into the admiring vortex, and look at this baby just as if babies came into the world every day.

'Philip,' said Sylvia, one night, as he sate as still as a mouse in her room, imagining her to be asleep. He was by her bed-side in a moment.

'I've been thinking what she's to be called. Isabella, after mother; and what were yo'r mother's name?'

'Margaret,' said he.

'Margaret Isabella; Isabella Margaret. Mother's called Bell. She might be called Bella.'

'I could ha' wished her to be called after thee.'

She made a little impatient movement.

'Nay; Sylvia's not a lucky name. Best be called after thy mother and mine. And I want for to ask Hester to be godmother.'

'Anything thou likes, sweetheart. Shall we call her Rose, after Hester Rose?'

'No, no!' said Sylvia; 'she mun be called after my mother, or thine, or both. I should like her to be called Bella, after mother, because she's so fond of baby.'

'Anything to please thee, darling.'

'Don't say that as if it didn't signify; there's a deal in having a pretty name,' said Sylvia, a little annoyed. 'I ha' allays hated being called Sylvia. It were after father's mother, Sylvia Steele.'

'I niver thought any name in a' the world so sweet and pretty as Sylvia,' said Philip, fondly; but she was too much absorbed in her own thoughts to notice either his manner or his words.

'There, yo'll not mind if it is Bella, because yo' see my mother is alive to be pleased by its being named after her, and Hester may be godmother, and I'll ha' t' dove-coloured silk as yo' gave me afore we were married made up into a cloak for it to go to church in.'

'I got it for thee,' said Philip, a little disappointed. 'It'll be too good for the baby.'

'Eh! but I'm so careless, I should be spilling something on it? But if thou got it for me I cannot find i' my heart for t' wear it on baby, and I'll have it made into a christening gown for mysel'. But I'll niver feel at my ease in it, for fear of spoiling it.'

'Well! an' if thou does spoil it, love, I'll get thee another. I make account of riches only for thee; that I may be able to get thee whativer thou's a fancy for, for either thysel', or thy mother.'

She lifted her pale face from her pillow, and put up her lips to kiss him for these words.

Perhaps on that day Philip reached the zenith of his life's happiness.

CHAPTER XXXI

EVIL OMENS

The first step in Philip's declension happened in this way. Sylvia had made rapid progress in her recovery; but now she seemed at a stationary point of weakness; wakeful nights succeeding to languid days. Occasionally she caught a little sleep in the afternoons, but she usually awoke startled and feverish.

One afternoon Philip had stolen upstairs to look at her and his child; but the efforts he made at careful noiselessness made the door creak on its hinges as he opened it. The woman employed to nurse her had taken the baby into another room that no sound might rouse her from her slumber; and Philip would probably have been warned against entering the chamber where his wife lay sleeping had he been perceived by the nurse. As it was, he opened the door, made a noise, and Sylvia started up, her face all one flush, her eyes wild and uncertain; she looked about her as if she did not know where she was; pushed the hair off her hot forehead; all which actions Philip saw, dismayed and regretful. But he kept still, hoping that she would lie down and compose herself. Instead she stretched out her arms imploringly, and said, in a voice full of yearning and tears,—

'Oh! Charley! come to me—come to me!' and then as she more fully became aware of the place where she was, her actual situation, she sank back and feebly began to cry. Philip's heart boiled within him; any man's would under the circumstances, but he had the sense of guilty concealment to aggravate the intensity of his feelings. Her weak cry after another man, too, irritated him, partly through his anxious love, which made him wise to know how much physical harm she was doing herself. At this moment he stirred, or unintentionally made some sound: she started up afresh, and called out,—

'Oh, who's theere? Do, for God's sake, tell me who yo' are!'

'It's me,' said Philip, coming forwards, striving to keep down the miserable complication of love and jealousy, and remorse and anger, that made his heart beat so wildly, and almost took him out of himself. Indeed, he must have been quite beside himself for the time, or he could never have gone on to utter the unwise, cruel words he did. But she spoke first, in a distressed and plaintive tone of voice.

'Oh, Philip, I've been asleep, and yet I think I was awake! And I saw Charley Kinraid as plain as iver I see thee now, and he wasn't drowned at all. I'm sure he's alive somewheere; he were so clear and life-like. Oh! what shall I do? what shall I do?'

She wrung her hands in feverish distress. Urged by passionate feelings of various kinds, and also by his desire to quench the agitation which was doing her harm, Philip spoke, hardly knowing what he said.

'Kinraid's dead, I tell yo', Sylvie! And what kind of a woman are yo' to go dreaming of another man i' this way, and taking on so about him, when yo're a wedded wife, with a child as yo've borne to another man?'

In a moment he could have bitten out his tongue. She looked at him with the mute reproach which some of us see (God help us!) in the eyes of the dead, as they come before our sad memories in the night-season; looked at him with such a solemn, searching look, never saying a word of reply or defence. Then she lay down, motionless and silent. He had been instantly stung with remorse for his speech; the words were not beyond his lips when an agony had entered his heart; but her steady, dilated eyes had kept him dumb and motionless as if by a spell.

Now he rushed to the bed on which she lay, and half knelt, half threw himself upon it, imploring her to forgive him; regardless for the time of any evil consequences to her, it seemed as if he must have her pardon—her relenting—at any price, even if they both died in the act of reconciliation. But she lay speechless, and, as far as she could be, motionless, the bed trembling under her with the quivering she could not still.

Philip's wild tones caught the nurse's ears, and she entered full of the dignified indignation of wisdom.

'Are yo' for killing yo'r wife, measter?' she asked. 'She's noane so strong as she can bear flytin' and scoldin', nor will she be for many a week to come. Go down wi' ye, and leave her i' peace if yo're a man as can be called a man!'

Her anger was rising as she caught sight of Sylvia's averted face. It was flushed crimson, her eyes full of intense emotion of some kind, her lips compressed; but an involuntary twitching overmastering her resolute stillness from time to time. Philip, who did not see the averted face, nor understand the real danger in which he was placing his wife, felt as though he must have one word, one responsive touch of the hand which lay passive in his, which was not even drawn away from the kisses with which he covered it, any more than if it had been an impassive stone. The nurse had fairly to take him by the shoulders, and turn him out of the room.

In half an hour the doctor had to be summoned. Of course, the nurse gave him her version of the events of the afternoon, with much *animus* against Philip; and the doctor thought it his duty to have some very serious conversation with him.

'I do assure you, Mr. Hepburn, that, in the state your wife has been in for some days, it was little less than madness on your part to speak to her about anything that could give rise to strong emotion.'

'It was madness, sir!' replied Philip, in a low, miserable tone of voice. The doctor's heart was touched, in spite of the nurse's accusations against the scolding husband. Yet the danger was now too serious for him to mince matters.

'I must tell you that I cannot answer for her life, unless the greatest precautions are taken on your part, and unless the measures I shall use have the effect I wish for in the next twenty-four hours. She is on the verge of a brain fever. Any allusion to the subject which has been the final cause of the state in which she now is must be most cautiously avoided, even to a chance word which may bring it to her memory.'

And so on; but Philip seemed to hear only this: then he might not express contrition, or sue for pardon, he must go on unforgiven through all this stress of anxiety; and even if she recovered the doctor warned him of the undesirableness of recurring to what had passed!

Heavy miserable times of endurance and waiting have to be passed through by all during the course of their lives; and Philip had had his share of such seasons, when the heart, and the will, and the speech, and the limbs, must be bound down with strong resolution to patience.

For many days, nay, for weeks, he was forbidden to see Sylvia, as the very sound of his footstep brought on a recurrence of the fever and convulsive movement. Yet she seemed, from questions she feebly asked the nurse, to have forgotten all that had happened on the day of her attack from the time when she dropped off to sleep. But how much she remembered of after occurrences no one could ascertain. She was quiet enough when, at length, Philip was allowed to see her. But he was half jealous of his child, when he watched how she could smile at it, while she never changed a muscle of her face at all he could do or say.

And of a piece with this extreme quietude and reserve was her behaviour to him when at length she had fully recovered, and was able to go about the house again. Philip thought many a time of the words she had used long before—before their marriage. Ominous words they were.

'It's not in me to forgive; I sometimes think it's not in me to forget.'

Philip was tender even to humility in his conduct towards her. But nothing stirred her from her fortress of reserve. And he knew she was so different; he knew how loving, nay, passionate, was her nature—vehement, demonstrative—oh! how could he stir her once more into expression, even if the first show or speech she made was of anger? Then he tried being angry with her himself; he was sometimes unjust to her consciously and of a purpose, in order to provoke her into defending herself, and appealing against his unkindness. He only seemed to drive her love away still more.

If any one had known all that was passing in that household, while yet the story of it was not ended, nor, indeed, come to its crisis, their hearts would have been sorry for the man who lingered long at the door of the room in which his wife sate cooing and talking to her baby, and sometimes laughing back to it, or who was soothing the querulousness of failing age with every possible patience of love; sorry for the poor listener who was hungering for the profusion of tenderness thus scattered on the senseless air, yet only by stealth caught the echoes of what ought to have been his.

It was so difficult to complain, too; impossible, in fact. Everything that a wife could do from duty she did; but the love seemed to have fled, and, in such cases, no reproaches or complaints can avail to bring it back. So reason outsiders, and are convinced of the result before the experiment is made. But Philip could not reason, or could not yield to reason; and so he complained and reproached. She did not much answer him; but he thought that her eyes expressed the old words,—

'It's not in me to forgive; I sometimes think it's not in me to forget.'

However, it is an old story, an ascertained fact, that, even in the most tender and stable masculine natures, at the supremest season of their lives, there is room for other thoughts and passions than such as are connected with love. Even with the most domestic and affectionate men, their emotions seem to be kept in a cell distinct and away from their actual lives. Philip had other thoughts and other occupations than those connected with his wife during all this time.

An uncle of his mother's, a Cumberland 'statesman', of whose existence he was barely conscious, died about this time, leaving to his unknown great-nephew four or five hundred pounds, which put him at once in a different position with regard to his business. Henceforward his ambition was roused,—such humble ambition as befitted a shop-keeper in a country town sixty or seventy years ago. To be respected by the men around him had always been an object with him, and was, perhaps, becoming more so than ever now, as a sort of refuge from his deep, sorrowful mortification in other directions. He was greatly pleased at being made a sidesman; and, in preparation for the further honour of being churchwarden, he went regularly twice a day to church on Sundays. There was enough religious feeling in him to make him disguise the worldly reason for such conduct from himself. He believed that he went because he thought it right to attend public worship in the parish church whenever it was offered up; but it may be questioned of him, as of many others, how far he would have been as regular in attendance in a place where he was not known. With this, however, we have nothing to do. The fact was that he went regularly to church, and he wished his wife to accompany him to the pew, newly painted, with his name on the door, where he sate in full sight of the clergyman and congregation.

Sylvia had never been in the habit of such regular church-going, and she felt it as a hardship, and slipped out of the duty as often as ever she could. In her unmarried days, she and her parents had gone annually to the mother-church of the parish in which Haytersbank was situated: on the Monday succeeding the Sunday next after the Romish Saint's Day, to whom the church was dedicated, there was a great feast or wake held; and, on the Sunday, all the parishioners came to church from far and near. Frequently, too, in the course of the year, Sylvia would accompany one or other of her parents to Scarby Moorside afternoon service,—when the hay was got in, and the corn not ready for cutting, or the cows were dry and there was no afternoon milking. Many clergymen were languid in those days, and did not too curiously inquire into the reasons which gave them such small congregations in country parishes.

Now she was married, this weekly church-going which Philip seemed to expect from her, became a tie and a small hardship, which connected itself with her life of respectability and prosperity. 'A crust of bread and liberty' was much more accordant to Sylvia's nature than plenty of creature comforts and many restraints. Another wish of Philip's, against which she said no word, but constantly rebelled in thought and deed, was his desire that the servant he had engaged during the time of her illness to take charge of the baby, should always carry it whenever it was taken out for a walk. Sylvia often felt, now she was strong, as if she would far rather have been without the responsibility of having this nursemaid, of whom she was, in reality, rather afraid. The good side of it was that it set her at liberty to attend to her mother at times when she would have been otherwise occupied with her baby; but Bell required very little from any one: she was easily pleased, unexacting, and methodical even in her dotage; preserving the quiet, undemonstrative habits of her earlier life now that the faculty of reason, which had been at the basis of the formation of such habits, was gone. She took great delight in watching the baby, and was pleased to have it in her care for a short time; but she dozed so much that it prevented her having any strong wish on the subject.

So Sylvia contrived to get her baby as much as possible to herself, in spite of the nursemaid; and, above all, she would carry it out, softly cradled in her arms, warm pillowed on her breast, and bear it to the freedom and solitude of the sea-shore on the west side of the town where the cliffs were not so high, and there was a good space of sand and shingle at all low tides.

Once here, she was as happy as she ever expected to be in this world. The fresh sea-breeze restored something of the colour of former days to her cheeks, the old buoyancy to her spirits; here she might talk her heart-full of loving nonsense to her baby; here it was all her own; no father to share in it, no nursemaid to dispute the wisdom of anything she did with it. She sang to it, she tossed it; it crowed and it laughed back again, till both were weary; and then she would sit down on a broken piece of rock, and fall to gazing on the advancing waves catching the sunlight on their crests, advancing, receding, for ever and for ever, as they had done all her life long—as they did when she had walked with them that once by the side of Kinraid; those cruel waves that, forgetful of the happy lovers' talk by the side of their waters, had carried one away, and drowned him deep till he was dead. Every time she sate down to look at the sea, this process of thought was gone through up to this point; the next step would, she knew, bring her to the question she dared not, must not ask. He was dead; he must be dead; for was she not Philip's wife? Then came up the recollection of Philip's speech, never forgotten, only buried out of sight: 'What kind of a woman are yo' to go on dreaming of another man, and yo' a wedded wife?' She used to shudder as if cold steel had been plunged into her warm, living body as she remembered these words; cruel words, harmlessly provoked. They were too much associated with physical pains to be dwelt upon; only their memory was always there. She paid for these happy rambles with her baby by the depression which awaited her on her re-entrance into the dark, confined house that was her home; its very fulness of comfort was an oppression. Then, when her husband saw her pale and fatigued, he was annoyed, and sometimes upbraided her for doing what was so unnecessary as to load herself with her child. She knew full well it was not that that caused her weariness. By-and-by, when he inquired and discovered that all these walks were taken in one direction, out towards the sea, he grew jealous of her love for the inanimate ocean. Was it connected in her mind with the thought of Kinraid? Why did she so perseveringly, in wind or cold, go out to the sea-shore; the western side, too, where, if she went but far enough, she would come upon the mouth of the Haytersbank gully, the point at which she had last seen Kinraid? Such fancies haunted Philip's mind for hours after she had acknowledged the direction of her walks. But he never said a word that could distinctly tell her he disliked her going to the sea, otherwise she would have obeyed him in this, as in everything else; for absolute obedience to her husband seemed to be her rule of life at this period—obedience to him who would so gladly have obeyed her smallest wish had she but expressed it! She never knew that Philip had any painful association with the particular point on the sea-shore that she instinctively avoided, both from a consciousness of wifely duty, and also because the sight of it brought up so much sharp pain.

Philip used to wonder if the dream that preceded her illness was the suggestive cause that drew her so often to the shore. Her illness consequent upon that dream had filled his mind, so that for many months he himself had had no haunting vision of Kinraid to disturb his slumbers. But now the old dream of Kinraid's actual presence by Philip's bedside began to return with fearful vividness. Night after night it recurred; each time with some new touch of reality, and close approach; till it was as if the fate that overtakes all men were then, even then, knocking at his door.

In his business Philip prospered. Men praised him because he did well to himself. He had the perseverance, the capability for head-work and calculation, the steadiness and general forethought which might have made him a great merchant if he had lived in a large city. Without any effort of his own, almost, too, without Coulson's being aware of it, Philip was now in the position of superior partner; the one to suggest and arrange, while Coulson only carried out the plans that emanated from Philip. The whole work of life was suited to the man: he did not aspire to any different position, only to the full development of the capabilities of that which he already held. He had originated several fresh schemes with regard to the traffic of the shop; and his old masters, with all their love of tried ways, and distrust of everything new, had been candid enough to confess that their successors' plans had resulted in success. 'Their successors.' Philip was content with having the power when the exercise of it was required, and never named his own important share in the new improvements.

Possibly, if he had, Coulson's vanity might have taken the alarm, and he might not have been so acquiescent for the future. As it was, he forgot his own subordinate share, and always used the imperial 'we', 'we thought', 'it struck us,' &c.

CHAPTER XXXII

RESCUED FROM THE WAVES

Meanwhile Hester came and went as usual; in so quiet and methodical a way, with so even and undisturbed a temper, that she was almost forgotten when everything went well in the shop or household. She was a star, the brightness of which was only recognized in times of darkness. She herself was almost surprised at her own increasing regard for Sylvia. She had not thought she should ever be able to love the woman who had been such a laggard in acknowledging Philip's merits; and from all she had ever heard of Sylvia before she came to know her, from the angry words with which Sylvia had received her when she had first gone to Haytersbank Farm, Hester had intended to remain on friendly terms, but to avoid intimacy. But her kindness to Bell Robson had won both the mother's and daughter's hearts; and in spite of herself, certainly against her own mother's advice, she had become the familiar friend and welcome guest of the household.

Now the very change in Sylvia's whole manner and ways, which grieved and vexed Philip, made his wife the more attractive to Hester. Brought up among Quakers, although not one herself, she admired and respected the staidness and outward peacefulness common amongst the young women of that sect. Sylvia, whom she had expected to find volatile, talkative, vain, and wilful, was quiet and still, as if she had been born a Friend: she seemed to have no will of her own; she served her mother and child for love; she obeyed her husband in all things, and never appeared to pine after gaiety or pleasure. And yet at times Hester thought, or rather a flash came across her mind, as if all things were not as right as they seemed. Philip looked older, more care-worn; nay, even Hester was obliged to allow to herself that she had heard him speak to his wife in sharp, aggrieved tones. Innocent Hester! she could not understand how the very qualities she so admired in Sylvia were just what were so foreign to her nature that the husband, who had known her from a child, felt what an unnatural restraint she was putting upon herself, and would have hailed petulant words or wilful actions with an unspeakable thankfulness for relief.

One day—it was in the spring of 1798—Hester was engaged to stay to tea with the Hepburns, in order that after that early meal she might set to again in helping Philip and Coulson to pack away the winter cloths and flannels, for which there was no longer any use. The tea-time was half-past four; about four o'clock a heavy April shower came on, the hail pattering against the window-panes so as to awaken Mrs. Robson from her afternoon's nap. She came down the corkscrew stairs, and found Phoebe in the parlour arranging the tea-things.

Phoebe and Mrs. Robson were better friends than Phoebe and her young mistress; and so they began to talk a little together in a comfortable, familiar way. Once or twice Philip looked in, as if he would be glad to see the tea-table in readiness; and then Phoebe would put on a spurt of busy bustle, which ceased almost as soon as his back was turned, so eager was she to obtain Mrs. Robson's sympathy in some little dispute that had occurred between her and the nurse-maid. The latter had misappropriated some hot water, prepared and required by Phoebe, to the washing of the baby's clothes; it was a long story, and would have tired the patience of any one in full possession of their senses; but the details were just within poor Bell's comprehension, and she was listening with the greatest sympathy. Both the women were unaware of the lapse of time; but it was of consequence to Philip, as the extra labour was not to be begun until after tea, and the daylight hours were precious.

At a quarter to five Hester and he came in, and then Phoebe began to hurry. Hester went up to sit by Bell and talk to her. Philip spoke to Phoebe in the familiar words of country-folk. Indeed, until his marriage, Phoebe had always called him by his Christian name, and had found it very difficult to change it into 'master.'

'Where's Sylvie?' said he.

'Gone out wi' t' babby,' replied Phoebe.

'Why can't Nancy carry it out?' asked Philip.

It was touching on the old grievance: he was tired, and he spoke with sharp annoyance. Phoebe might easily have told him the real state of the case; Nancy was busy at her washing, which would have been reason enough. But the nursemaid had vexed her, and she did not like Philip's sharpness, so she only said,—

'It's noane o' my business; it's yo' t' look after yo'r own wife and child; but yo'r but a lad after a'.'

This was not conciliatory speech, and just put the last stroke to Philip's fit of ill-temper.

'I'm not for my tea to-night,' said he, to Hester, when all was ready. 'Sylvie's not here, and nothing is nice, or as it should be. I'll go and set to on t' stock-taking. Don't yo' hurry, Hester; stop and chat a bit with th' old lady.'

'Nay, Philip,' said Hester, 'thou's sadly tired; just take this cup o' tea; Sylvia 'll be grieved if yo' haven't something.'

'Sylvia doesn't care whether I'm full or fasting,' replied he, impatiently putting aside the cup. 'If she did she'd ha' taken care to be in, and ha' seen to things being as I like them.'

Now in general Philip was the least particular of men about meals; and to do Sylvia justice, she was scrupulously attentive to every household duty in which old Phoebe would allow her to meddle, and always careful to see after her husband's comforts. But Philip was too vexed at her absence to perceive the injustice of what he was saying, nor was he aware how Bell Robson had been attending to what he said. But she was sadly discomfited by it, understanding just enough of the grievance in hand to think that her daughter was neglectful of those duties which she herself had always regarded as paramount to all others; nor could Hester convince her that Philip had not meant what he said; neither could she turn the poor old woman's thoughts from the words which had caused her distress.

Presently Sylvia came in, bright and cheerful, although breathless with hurry.

'Oh,' said she, taking off her wet shawl, 'we've had to shelter from such a storm of rain, baby and me—but see! she's none the worse for it, as bonny as iver, bless her.'

Hester began some speech of admiration for the child in order to prevent Bell from delivering the lecture she felt sure was coming down on the unsuspecting Sylvia; but all in vain.

'Philip's been complaining on thee, Sylvie,' said Bell, in the way in which she had spoken to her daughter when she was a little child; grave and severe in tone and look, more than in words. 'I forget justly what about, but he spoke on thy neglecting him continual. It's not right, my lass, it's not right; a woman should—but my head's very tired, and all I can think on to say is, it's not right.'

'Philip been complaining of me, and to mother!' said Sylvia, ready to burst into tears, so grieved and angry was she.

'No!' said Hester, 'thy mother has taken it a little too strong; he were vexed like at his tea not being ready.'

Sylvia said no more, but the bright colour faded from her cheek, and the contraction of care returned to her brow. She occupied herself with taking off her baby's walking things. Hester lingered, anxious to soothe and make peace; she was looking sorrowfully at Sylvia, when she saw tears dropping on the baby's cloak, and then it seemed as if she must speak a word of comfort before going to the shop-work, where she knew she was expected by both Philip and Coulson. She poured out a cup of tea, and coming close up to Sylvia, and kneeling down by her, she whispered,—

'Just take him this into t' ware-room; it'll put all to rights if thou'll take it to him wi' thy own hands.'

Sylvia looked up, and Hester then more fully saw how she had been crying. She whispered in reply, for fear of disturbing her mother,—

'I don't mind anything but his speaking ill on me to mother. I know I'm for iver trying and trying to be a good wife to him, an' it's very dull work; harder than yo' think on, Hester,—an' I would ha' been home for tea to-night only I was afeared of baby getting wet wi' t' storm o' hail as we had down on t' shore; and we sheltered under a rock. It's a weary coming home to this dark place, and to find my own mother set against me.'

'Take him his tea, like a good lassie. I'll answer for it he'll be all right. A man takes it hardly when he comes in tired, a-thinking his wife '11 be there to cheer him up a bit, to find her off, and niver know nought of t' reason why.'

'I'm glad enough I've getten a baby,' said Sylvia, 'but for aught else I wish I'd niver been married, I do!'

'Hush thee, lass!' said Hester, rising up indignant; 'now that is a sin. Eh! if thou only knew the lot o' some folk. But let's talk no more on that, that cannot be helped; go, take him his tea, for it's a sad thing to think on him fasting all this time.'

Hester's voice was raised by the simple fact of her change of position; and the word fasting caught Mrs. Robson's ear, as she sate at her knitting by the chimney-corner.

'Fasting? he said thou didn't care if he were full or fasting. Lassie! it's not right in thee, I say; go, take him his tea at once.'

Sylvia rose, and gave up the baby, which she had been suckling, to Nancy, who having done her washing, had come for her charge, to put it to bed. Sylvia kissed it fondly, making a little moan of sad, passionate tenderness as she did so. Then she took the cup of tea; but she said, rather defiantly, to Hester,—

'I'll go to him with it, because mother bids me, and it'll ease her mind.'

Then louder to her mother, she added,—

'Mother, I'll take him his tea, though I couldn't help the being out.'

If the act itself was conciliatory, the spirit in which she was going to do it was the reverse. Hester followed her slowly into the ware-room, with intentional delay, thinking that her presence might be an obstacle to their mutually understanding one another. Sylvia held the cup and plate of bread and butter out to Philip, but avoided meeting his eye, and said not a word of explanation, or regret, or self-justification. If she had spoken, though ever so crossly, Philip would have been relieved, and would have preferred it to her silence. He wanted to provoke her to speech, but did not know how to begin.

'Thou's been out again wandering on that sea-shore!' said he. She did not answer him. 'I cannot think what's always taking thee there, when one would ha' thought a walk up to Esdale would be far more sheltered, both for thee and baby in such weather as this. Thou'll be having that baby ill some of these days.'

At this, she looked up at him, and her lips moved as though she were going to say something. Oh, how he wished she would, that they might come to a wholesome quarrel, and a making friends again, and a tender kissing, in which he might whisper penitence for all his hasty words, or unreasonable vexation. But she had come resolved not to speak, for fear of showing too much passion, too much emotion. Only as she was going away she turned and said,—

'Philip, mother hasn't many more years to live; dunnot grieve her, and set her again' me by finding fault wi' me afore her. Our being wed were a great mistake; but before t' poor old widow woman let us make as if we were happy.'

'Sylvie! Sylvie!' he called after her. She must have heard, but she did not turn. He went after her, and seized her by the arm rather roughly; she had stung him to the heart with her calm words, which seemed to reveal a long-formed conviction.

'Sylvie!' said he, almost fiercely, 'what do yo' mean by what you've said? Speak! I will have an answer.'

He almost shook her: she was half frightened by his vehemence of behaviour, which she took for pure anger, while it was the outburst of agonized and unrequited love.

'Let me go! Oh, Philip, yo' hurt me!'

Just at this moment Hester came up; Philip was ashamed of his passionate ways in her serene presence, and loosened his grasp of his wife, and she ran away; ran into her mother's empty room, as to a solitary place, and there burst into that sobbing, miserable crying which we instinctively know is too surely lessening the length of our days on earth to be indulged in often.

When she had exhausted that first burst and lay weak and quiet for a time, she listened in dreading expectation of the sound of his footstep coming in search of her to make friends. But he was detained below on business, and never came. Instead, her mother came clambering up the stairs; she was now in the habit of going to bed between seven and eight, and to-night she was retiring at even an earlier hour.

Sylvia sprang up and drew down the window-blind, and made her face and manner as composed as possible, in order to soothe and comfort her mother's last waking hours. She helped her to bed with gentle patience; the restraint imposed upon her by her tender filial love was good for her, though all the time she was longing to be alone to have another wild outburst. When her mother was going off to sleep, Sylvia went to look at her baby, also in a soft sleep. Then she gazed out at the evening sky, high above the tiled roofs of the opposite houses, and the longing to be out under the peaceful heavens took possession of her once more.

'It's my only comfort,' said she to herself; 'and there's no earthly harm in it. I would ha' been at home to his tea, if I could; but when he doesn't want me, and mother doesn't want me, and baby is either in my arms or asleep; why, I'll go any cry my fill out under yon great quiet sky. I cannot stay in t' house to be choked up wi' my tears, nor yet to have him coming about me either for scolding or peace-making.'

So she put on her things and went out again; this time along the High Street, and up the long flights of steps towards the parish church, and there she stood and thought that here she had first met Kinraid, at Darley's burying, and she tried to recall the very look of all the sad, earnest faces round the open grave—the whole scene, in fact; and let herself give way to the miserable regrets she had so often tried to control. Then she walked on, crying bitterly, almost unawares to herself; on through the high, bleak fields at the summit of the cliffs; fields bounded by loose stone fences, and far from all sight of the habitation of man. But, below, the sea rose and raged; it was high water at the highest tide, and the wind blew gustily from the land, vainly combating the great waves that came invincibly up with a roar and an impotent furious dash against the base of the cliffs below.

Sylvia heard the sound of the passionate rush and rebound of many waters, like the shock of mighty guns, whenever the other sound of the blustering gusty wind was lulled for an instant. She was more quieted by this tempest of the elements than she would have been had all nature seemed as still as she had imagined it to be while she was yet in-doors and only saw a part of the serene sky.

She fixed on a certain point, in her own mind, which she would reach, and then turn back again. It was where the outline of the land curved inwards, dipping into a little bay. Here the field-path she had hitherto followed descended somewhat abruptly to a cluster of fishermen's cottages, hardly large enough to be called a village; and then the narrow roadway wound up the rising ground till it again reached the summit of the cliffs that stretched along the coast for many and many a mile.

Sylvia said to herself that she would turn homewards when she came within sight of this cove,—Headlington Cove, they called it. All the way along she had met no one since she had left the town, but just as she had got over the last stile, or ladder of stepping-stones, into the field from which the path descended, she came upon a number of people—quite a crowd, in fact; men moving forward in a steady line, hauling at a rope, a chain, or something of that kind; boys, children, and women holding babies in their arms, as if all were fain to come out and partake in some general interest.

They kept within a certain distance from the edge of the cliff, and Sylvia, advancing a little, now saw the reason why. The great cable the men held was attached to some part of a smack, which could now be seen by her in the waters below, half dismantled, and all but a wreck, yet with her deck covered with living men, as far as the waning light would allow her to see. The vessel strained to get free of the strong guiding cable; the tide was turning, the wind was blowing off shore, and Sylvia knew without being told, that almost parallel to this was a line of sunken rocks that had been fatal to many a ship before now, if she had tried to take the inner channel instead of keeping out to sea for miles, and then steering in straight for Monkshaven port. And the ships that had been thus lost had been in good plight and order compared to this vessel, which seemed nothing but a hull without mast or sail.

By this time, the crowd—the fishermen from the hamlet down below, with their wives and children—all had come but the bedridden—had reached the place where Sylvia stood. The women, in a state of wild excitement, rushed on, encouraging their husbands and sons by words, even while they hindered them by actions; and, from time to time, one of them would run to the edge of the cliff and shout out some brave words of hope in her shrill voice to the crew on the deck below. Whether these latter heard it or not, no one could tell; but it seemed as if all human voice must be lost in the tempestuous stun and tumult of wind and wave. It was generally a woman with a child in her arms who so employed herself. As the strain upon the cable became greater, and the ground on which they strove more uneven, every hand was needed to hold and push, and all those women who were unencumbered held by the dear rope on which so many lives were depending. On they came, a long line of human beings, black against the ruddy sunset sky. As they came near Sylvia, a woman cried out,—

'Dunnot stand idle, lass, but houd on wi' us; there's many a bonny life at stake, and many a mother's heart a-hangin' on this bit o' hemp. Tak' houd, lass, and give a firm grip, and God remember thee i' thy need.'

Sylvia needed no second word; a place was made for her, and in an instant more the rope was pulling against her hands till it seemed as though she was holding fire in her bare palms. Never a one of them thought of letting go for an instant, though when all was over many of their hands were raw and bleeding. Some strong, experienced fishermen passed a word along the line from time to time, giving directions as to how it should be held according to varying occasions; but few among the rest had breath or strength enough to speak. The women and children that accompanied them ran on before, breaking down the loose stone fences, so as to obviate delay or hindrance; they talked continually, exhorting, encouraging, explaining. From their many words and fragmentary sentences, Sylvia learnt that the vessel was supposed to be a Newcastle smack sailing from London, that had taken the dangerous inner channel to save time, and had been caught in the storm, which she was too crazy to withstand; and that if by some daring contrivance of the fishermen who had first seen her the cable had not been got ashore, she would have been cast upon the rocks before this, and 'all on board perished'.

'It were dayleet then,' quoth one woman; 'a could see their faces, they were so near. They were as pale as dead men, an' one was prayin' down on his knees. There was a king's officer aboard, for I saw t' gowd about him.'

'He'd maybe come from these hom'ard parts, and be comin' to see his own folk; else it's no common for king's officers to sail in aught but king's ships.'

'Eh! but it's gettin' dark! See there's t' leeghts in t' houses in t' New Town! T' grass is crispin' wi' t' white frost under out feet. It'll be a hard tug round t' point, and then she'll be gettin' into still waters.'

One more great push and mighty strain, and the danger was past; the vessel—or what remained of her—was in the harbour, among the lights and cheerful sounds of safety. The fishermen sprang down the cliff to the quay-side, anxious to see the men whose lives they had saved; the women, weary and over-excited, began to cry. Not Sylvia, however; her fount of tears had been exhausted earlier in the day: her principal feeling was of gladness and high rejoicing that they were saved who had been so near to death not half an hour before.

She would have liked to have seen the men, and shaken hands with them all round. But instead she must go home, and well would it be with her if she was in time for her husband's supper, and escaped any notice of her absence. So she separated herself from the groups of women who sate on the grass in the churchyard, awaiting the return of such of their husbands as could resist the fascinations of the Monkshaven public houses. As Sylvia went down the church steps, she came upon one of the fishermen who had helped to tow the vessel into port.

'There was seventeen men and boys aboard her, and a navy-lieutenant as had comed as passenger. It were a good job as we could manage her. Good-neet to thee, thou'll sleep all t' sounder for havin' lent a hand.'

The street air felt hot and close after the sharp keen atmosphere of the heights above; the decent shops and houses had all their shutters put up, and were preparing for their early bed-time. Already lights shone here and there in the upper chambers, and Sylvia scarcely met any one.

She went round up the passage from the quay-side, and in by the private door. All was still; the basins of bread and milk that she and her husband were in the habit of having for supper stood in the fender before the fire, each with a plate upon them. Nancy had gone to bed, Phoebe dozed in the kitchen; Philip was still in the ware-room, arranging goods and taking stock along with Coulson, for Hester had gone home to her mother.

Sylvia was not willing to go and seek out Philip, after the manner in which they had parted. All the despondency of her life became present to her again as she sate down within her home. She had forgotten it in her interest and excitement, but now it came back again.

Still she was hungry, and youthful, and tired. She took her basin up, and was eating her supper when she heard a cry of her baby upstairs, and ran away to attend to it. When it had been fed and hushed away to sleep, she went in to see her mother, attracted by some unusual noise in her room.

She found Mrs. Robson awake, and restless, and ailing; dwelling much on what Philip had said in his anger against Sylvia. It was really necessary for her daughter to remain with her; so Sylvia stole out, and went quickly down-stairs to Philip—now sitting tired and worn out, and eating his supper with little or no appetite—and told him she meant to pass the night with her mother.

His answer of acquiescence was so short and careless, or so it seemed to her, that she did not tell him any more of what she had done or seen that evening, or even dwell upon any details of her mother's indisposition.

As soon as she had left the room, Philip set down his half-finished basin of bread and milk, and sate long, his face hidden in his folded arms. The wick of the candle grew long and black, and fell, and sputtered, and guttered; he sate on, unheeding either it or the pale gray fire that was dying out—dead at last.

CHAPTER XXXIII

AN APPARITION

Mrs. Robson was very poorly all night long. Uneasy thoughts seemed to haunt and perplex her brain, and she neither slept nor woke, but was restless and uneasy in her talk and movements.

Sylvia lay down by her, but got so little sleep, that at length she preferred sitting in the easy-chair by the bedside. Here she dropped off to slumber in spite of herself; the scene of the evening before seemed to be repeated; the cries of the many people, the heavy roar and dash of the threatening waves, were repeated in her ears; and something was said to her through all the conflicting noises,—what it was she could not catch, though she strained to hear the hoarse murmur that, in her dream, she believed to convey a meaning of the utmost importance to her.

This dream, that mysterious, only half-intelligible sound, recurred whenever she dozed, and her inability to hear the words uttered distressed her so much, that at length she sate bolt upright, resolved to sleep no more. Her mother was talking in a half-conscious way; Philip's speech of the evening before was evidently running in her mind.

'Sylvie, if thou're not a good wife to him, it'll just break my heart outright. A woman should obey her husband, and not go her own gait. I never leave the house wi'out telling father, and getting his leave.'

And then she began to cry pitifully, and to say unconnected things, till Sylvia, to soothe her, took her hand, and promised never to leave the house without asking her husband's permission, though in making this promise, she felt as if she were sacrificing her last pleasure to her mother's wish; for she knew well enough that Philip would always raise objections to the rambles which reminded her of her old free open-air life.

But to comfort and cherish her mother she would have done anything; yet this very morning that was dawning, she must go and ask his permission for a simple errand, or break her word.

She knew from experience that nothing quieted her mother so well as balm-tea; it might be that the herb really possessed some sedative power; it might be only early faith, and often repeated experience, but it had always had a tranquillizing effect; and more than once, during the restless hours of the night, Mrs. Robson had asked for it; but Sylvia's stock of last year's dead leaves was exhausted. Still she knew where a plant of balm grew in the sheltered corner of Haytersbank Farm garden; she knew that the tenants who had succeeded them in the occupation of the farm had had to leave it in consequence of a death, and that the place was unoccupied; and in the darkness she had planned that if she could leave her mother after the dawn came, and she had attended to her baby, she would walk quickly to the old garden, and gather the tender sprigs which she was sure to find there.

Now she must go and ask Philip; and till she held her baby to her breast, she bitterly wished that she were free from the duties and chains of matrimony. But the touch of its waxen fingers, the hold of its little mouth, made her relax into docility and gentleness. She gave it back to Nancy to be dressed, and softly opened the door of Philip's bed-room.

'Philip!' said she, gently. 'Philip!'

He started up from dreams of her; of her, angry. He saw her there, rather pale with her night's watch and anxiety, but looking meek, and a little beseeching.

'Mother has had such a bad night! she fancied once as some balm-tea would do her good—it allays used to: but my dried balm is all gone, and I thought there'd be sure to be some in t' old garden at Haytersbank. Feyther planted a bush just for mother, wheere it allays came up early, nigh t' old elder-tree; and if yo'd not mind, I could run theere while she sleeps, and be back again in an hour, and it's not seven now.'

'Thou's not wear thyself out with running, Sylvie,' said Philip, eagerly; 'I'll get up and go myself, or, perhaps,' continued he, catching the shadow that was coming over her face, 'thou'd rather go thyself: it's only that I'm so afraid of thy tiring thyself.'

'It'll not tire me,' said Sylvia. 'Afore I was married, I was out often far farther than that, afield to fetch up t' kine, before my breakfast.'

'Well, go if thou will,' said Philip. 'But get somewhat to eat first, and don't hurry; there's no need for that.'

She had got her hat and shawl, and was off before he had finished his last words.

The long High Street was almost empty of people at that early hour; one side was entirely covered by the cool morning shadow which lay on the pavement, and crept up the opposite houses till only the topmost story caught the rosy sunlight. Up the hill-road, through the gap in the stone wall, across the dewy fields, Sylvia went by the very shortest path she knew.

She had only once been at Haytersbank since her wedding-day. On that occasion the place had seemed strangely and dissonantly changed by the numerous children who were diverting themselves before the open door, and whose playthings and clothes strewed the house-place, and made it one busy scene of confusion and untidiness, more like the Corneys' kitchen in former times, than her mother's orderly and quiet abode. Those little children were fatherless now; and the house was shut up, awaiting the entry of some new tenant. There were no shutters to shut; the long low window was blinking in the rays of the morning sun; the house and cow-house doors were closed, and no poultry wandered about the field in search of stray grains of corn, or early worms. It was a strange and unfamiliar silence, and struck solemnly on Sylvia's mind. Only a thrush in the old orchard down in the hollow, out of sight, whistled and gurgled with continual shrill melody.

Sylvia went slowly past the house and down the path leading to the wild, deserted bit of garden. She saw that the last tenants had had a pump sunk for them, and resented the innovation, as though the well she was passing could feel the insult. Over it grew two hawthorn trees; on the bent trunk of one of them she used to sit, long ago: the charm of the position being enhanced by the possible danger of falling into the well and being drowned. The rusty unused chain was wound round the windlass; the bucket was falling to pieces from dryness. A lean cat came from some outhouse, and mewed pitifully with hunger; accompanying Sylvia to the garden, as if glad of some human companionship, yet refusing to allow itself to be touched. Primroses grew in the sheltered places, just as they formerly did; and made the uncultivated ground seem less deserted than the garden, where the last year's weeds were rotting away, and cumbering the ground.

Sylvia forced her way through the berry bushes to the herb-plot, and plucked the tender leaves she had come to seek; sighing a little all the time. Then she retraced her steps; paused softly before the house-door, and entered the porch and kissed the senseless wood.

She tried to tempt the poor gaunt cat into her arms, meaning to carry it home and befriend it; but it was scared by her endeavour and ran back to its home in the outhouse, making a green path across the white dew of the meadow. Then Sylvia began to hasten home, thinking, and remembering—at the stile that led into the road she was brought short up.

Some one stood in the lane just on the other side of the gap; his back was to the morning sun; all she saw at first was the uniform of a naval officer, so well known in Monkshaven in those days.

Sylvia went hurrying past him, not looking again, although her clothes almost brushed his, as he stood there still. She had not gone a yard—no, not half a yard—when her heart leaped up and fell again dead within her, as if she had been shot.

'Sylvia!' he said, in a voice tremulous with joy and passionate love. 'Sylvia!'

She looked round; he had turned a little, so that the light fell straight on his face. It was bronzed, and the lines were strengthened; but it was the same face she had last seen in Haytersbank Gully three long years ago, and had never thought to see in life again.

He was close to her and held out his fond arms; she went fluttering towards their embrace, as if drawn by the old fascination; but when she felt them close round her, she started away, and cried out with a great pitiful shriek, and put her hands up to her forehead as if trying to clear away some bewildering mist.

Then she looked at him once more, a terrible story in her eyes, if he could but have read it.

Twice she opened her stiff lips to speak, and twice the words were overwhelmed by the surges of her misery, which bore them back into the depths of her heart.

He thought that he had come upon her too suddenly, and he attempted to soothe her with soft murmurs of love, and to woo her to his outstretched hungry arms once more. But when she saw this motion of his, she made a gesture as though pushing him away; and with an inarticulate moan of agony she put her hands to her head once more, and turning away began to run blindly towards the town for protection.

For a minute or so he was stunned with surprise at her behaviour; and then he thought it accounted for by the shock of his accost, and that she needed time to understand the unexpected joy. So he followed her swiftly, ever keeping her in view, but not trying to overtake her too speedily.

'I have frightened my poor love,' he kept thinking. And by this thought he tried to repress his impatience and check the speed he longed to use; yet he was always so near behind that her quickened sense heard his well-known footsteps following, and a mad notion flashed across her brain that she would go to the wide full river, and end the hopeless misery she felt enshrouding her. There was a sure hiding-place from all human reproach and heavy mortal woe beneath the rushing waters borne landwards by the morning tide.

No one can tell what changed her course; perhaps the thought of her sucking child; perhaps her mother; perhaps an angel of God; no one on earth knows, but as she ran along the quay-side she all at once turned up an entry, and through an open door.

He, following all the time, came into a quiet dark parlour, with a cloth and tea-things on the table ready for breakfast; the change from the bright sunny air out of doors to the deep shadow of this room made him think for the first moment that she had passed on, and that no one was there, and he stood for an instant baffled, and hearing no sound but the beating of his own heart; but an irrepressible sobbing gasp made him look round, and there he saw her cowered behind the door, her face covered tight up, and sharp shudders going through her whole frame.

'My love, my darling!' said he, going up to her, and trying to raise her, and to loosen her hands away from her face. 'I've been too sudden for thee: it was thoughtless in me; but I have so looked forward to this time, and seeing thee come along the field, and go past me, but I should ha' been more tender and careful of thee. Nay! let me have another look of thy sweet face.'

All this he whispered in the old tones of manoeuvring love, in that voice she had yearned and hungered to hear in life, and had not heard, for all her longing, save in her dreams.

She tried to crouch more and more into the corner, into the hidden shadow—to sink into the ground out of sight.

Once more he spoke, beseeching her to lift up her face, to let him hear her speak.

But she only moaned.

'Sylvia!' said he, thinking he could change his tactics, and pique her into speaking, that he would make a pretence of suspicion and offence.

'Sylvia! one would think you weren't glad to see me back again at length. I only came in late last night, and my first thought on wakening was of you; it has been ever since I left you.'

Sylvia took her hands away from her face; it was gray as the face of death; her awful eyes were passionless in her despair.

'Where have yo' been?' she asked, in slow, hoarse tones, as if her voice were half strangled within her.

'Been!' said he, a red light coming into his eyes, as he bent his looks upon her; now, indeed, a true and not an assumed suspicion entering his mind.

'Been!' he repeated; then, coming a step nearer to her, and taking her hand, not tenderly this time, but with a resolution to be satisfied.

'Did not your cousin—Hepburn, I mean—did not he tell you?—he saw the press-gang seize me,—I gave him a message to you—I bade you keep true to me as I would be to you.'

Between every clause of this speech he paused and gasped for her answer; but none came. Her eyes dilated and held his steady gaze prisoner as with a magical charm—neither could look away from the other's wild, searching gaze. When he had ended, she was silent for a moment, then she cried out, shrill and fierce,—

'Philip!' No answer.

Wilder and shriller still, 'Philip!' she cried.

He was in the distant ware-room completing the last night's work before the regular shop hours began; before breakfast, also, that his wife might not find him waiting and impatient.

He heard her cry; it cut through doors, and still air, and great bales of woollen stuff; he thought that she had hurt herself, that her mother was worse, that her baby was ill, and he hastened to the spot whence the cry proceeded.

On opening the door that separated the shop from the sitting-room, he saw the back of a naval officer, and his wife on the ground, huddled up in a heap; when she perceived him come in, she dragged herself up by means of a chair, groping like a blind person, and came and stood facing him.

The officer turned fiercely round, and would have come towards Philip, who was so bewildered by the scene that even yet he did not understand who the stranger was, did not perceive for an instant that he saw the realization of his greatest dread.

But Sylvia laid her hand on Kinraid's arm, and assumed to herself the right of speech. Philip did not know her voice, it was so changed.

'Philip,' she said, 'this is Kinraid come back again to wed me. He is alive; he has niver been dead, only taken by t' press-gang. And he says yo' saw it, and knew it all t' time. Speak, was it so?'

Philip knew not what to say, whither to turn, under what refuge of words or acts to shelter.

Sylvia's influence was keeping Kinraid silent, but he was rapidly passing beyond it.

'Speak!' he cried, loosening himself from Sylvia's light grasp, and coming towards Philip, with a threatening gesture. 'Did I not bid you tell her how it was? Did I not bid you say how I would be faithful to her, and she was to be faithful to me? Oh! you damned scoundrel! have you kept it from her all that time, and let her think me dead, or false? Take that!'

His closed fist was up to strike the man, who hung his head with bitterest shame and miserable self-reproach; but Sylvia came swift between the blow and its victim.

'Charley, thou shan't strike him,' she said. 'He is a damned scoundrel' (this was said in the hardest, quietest tone) 'but he is my husband.'

'Oh! thou false heart!' exclaimed Kinraid, turning sharp on her. 'If ever I trusted woman, I trusted you, Sylvia Robson.'

He made as though throwing her from him, with a gesture of contempt that stung her to life.

'Oh, Charley!' she cried, springing to him, 'dunnot cut me to the quick; have pity on me, though he had none. I did so love thee; it was my very heart-strings as gave way when they told me thou was drowned—feyther, and th' Corneys, and all, iverybody. Thy hat and t' bit o' ribbon I gave thee were found drenched and dripping wi' sea-water; and I went mourning for thee all the day long—dunnot turn away from me; only hearken this once, and then kill me dead, and I'll bless yo',—and have niver been mysel' since; niver ceased to feel t' sun grow dark and th' air chill and dreary when I thought on t' time when thou was alive. I did, my Charley, my own love! And I thought thou was dead for iver, and I wished I were lying beside thee. Oh, Charley! Philip, theere, where he stands, could tell yo' this was true. Philip, wasn't it so?'

'Would God I were dead!' moaned forth the unhappy, guilty man. But she had turned to Kinraid, and was speaking again to him, and neither of them heard or heeded him—they were drawing closer and closer together—she, with her cheeks and eyes aflame, talking eagerly.

'And feyther was taken up, and all for setting some free as t' press-gang had gotten by a foul trick; and he were put i' York prison, and tried, and hung!—hung! Charley!—good kind feyther was hung on a gallows; and mother lost her sense and grew silly in grief, and we were like to be turned out on t' wide world, and poor mother dateless—and I thought yo' were dead—oh! I thought yo' were dead, I did—oh, Charley, Charley!'

By this time they were in each other's arms, she with her head on his shoulder, crying as if her heart would break.

Philip came forwards and took hold of her to pull her away; but Charley held her tight, mutely defying Philip. Unconsciously she was Philip's protection, in that hour of danger, from a blow which might have been his death if strong will could have aided it to kill.

'Sylvie!' said he, grasping her tight. 'Listen to me. He didn't love yo' as I did. He had loved other women. I, yo'—yo' alone. He loved other girls before yo', and had left off loving 'em. I—I wish God would free my heart from the pang; but it will go on till I die, whether yo' love me or not. And then—where was I? Oh! that very night that he was taken, I was a-thinking on yo' and on him; and I might ha' given yo' his message, but I heard them speaking of him as knew him well; talking of his false fickle ways. How was I to know he would keep true to thee? It might be a sin in me, I cannot say; my heart and my sense are gone dead within me. I know this, I've loved yo' as no man but me ever loved before. Have some pity and forgiveness on me, if it's only because I've been so tormented with my love.'

He looked at her with feverish eager wistfulness; it faded away into despair as she made no sign of having even heard his words. He let go his hold of her, and his arm fell loosely by his side.

'I may die,' he said, 'for my life is ended!'

'Sylvia!' spoke out Kinraid, bold and fervent, 'your marriage is no marriage. You were tricked into it. You are my wife, not his. I am your husband; we plighted each other our troth. See! here is my half of the sixpence.'

He pulled it out from his bosom, tied by a black ribbon round his neck.

'When they stripped me and searched me in th' French prison, I managed to keep this. No lies can break the oath we swore to each other. I can get your pretence of a marriage set aside. I'm in favour with my admiral, and he'll do a deal for me, and back me out. Come with me; your marriage shall be set aside, and we'll be married again, all square and above-board. Come away. Leave that damned fellow to repent of the trick he played an honest sailor; we'll be true, whatever has come and gone. Come, Sylvia.'

His arm was round her waist, and he was drawing her towards the door, his face all crimson with eagerness and hope. Just then the baby cried.

'Hark!' said she, starting away from Kinraid, 'baby's crying for me. His child—yes, it is his child—I'd forgotten that—forgotten all. I'll make my vow now, lest I lose mysel' again. I'll never forgive yon man, nor live with him as his wife again. All that's done and ended. He's spoilt my life,—he's spoilt it for as long as iver I live on this earth; but neither yo' nor him shall spoil my soul. It goes hard wi' me, Charley, it does indeed. I'll just give yo' one kiss—one little kiss—and then, so help me God, I'll niver see nor hear till—no, not that, not that is needed—I'll niver see—sure that's enough—I'll never see yo' again on this side heaven, so help me God! I'm bound and tied, but I've sworn my oath to him as well as yo': there's things I will do, and there's things I won't. Kiss me once more. God help me, he's gone!'

CHAPTER XXXIV

A RECKLESS RECRUIT

She lay across a chair, her arms helplessly stretched out, her face unseen. Every now and then a thrill ran through her body: she was talking to herself all the time with incessant low incontinence of words.

Philip stood near her, motionless: he did not know whether she was conscious of his presence; in fact, he knew nothing but that he and she were sundered for ever; he could only take in that one idea, and it numbed all other thought.

Once more her baby cried for the comfort she alone could give.

She rose to her feet, but staggered when she tried to walk; her glazed eyes fell upon Philip as he instinctively made a step to hold her steady. No light came into her eyes any more than if she had looked upon a perfect stranger; not even was there the contraction of dislike. Some other figure filled her mind, and she saw him no more than she saw the inanimate table. That way of looking at him withered him up more than any sign of aversion would have done.

He watched her laboriously climb the stairs, and vanish out of sight; and sat down with a sudden feeling of extreme bodily weakness.

The door of communication between the parlour and the shop was opened. That was the first event of which Philip took note; but Phoebe had come in unawares to him, with the intention of removing the breakfast things on her return from market, and seeing them unused, and knowing that Sylvia had sate up all night with her mother, she had gone back to the kitchen. Philip had neither seen nor heard her.

Now Coulson came in, amazed at Hepburn's non-appearance in the shop.

'Why! Philip, what's ado? How ill yo' look, man!' exclaimed he, thoroughly alarmed by Philip's ghastly appearance. 'What's the matter?'

'I!' said Philip, slowly gathering his thoughts. 'Why should there be anything the matter?'

His instinct, quicker to act than his reason, made him shrink from his misery being noticed, much more made any subject for explanation or sympathy.

'There may be nothing the matter wi' thee,' said Coulson, 'but thou's the look of a corpse on thy face. I was afeared something was wrong, for it's half-past nine, and thee so punctual!'

He almost guarded Philip into the shop, and kept furtively watching him, and perplexing himself with Philip's odd, strange ways.

Hester, too, observed the heavy broken-down expression on Philip's ashen face, and her heart ached for him; but after that first glance, which told her so much, she avoided all appearance of noticing or watching. Only a shadow brooded over her sweet, calm face, and once or twice she sighed to herself.

It was market-day, and people came in and out, bringing their store of gossip from the country, or the town—from the farm or the quay-side.

Among the pieces of news, the rescue of the smack the night before furnished a large topic; and by-and-by Philip heard a name that startled him into attention.

The landlady of a small public-house much frequented by sailors was talking to Coulson.

'There was a sailor aboard of her as knowed Kinraid by sight, in Shields, years ago; and he called him by his name afore they were well out o' t' river. And Kinraid was no ways set up, for all his lieutenant's uniform (and eh! but they say he looks handsome in it!); but he tells 'm all about it—how he was pressed aboard a man-o'-war, an' for his good conduct were made a warrant officer, boatswain, or something!'

All the people in the shop were listening now; Philip alone seemed engrossed in folding up a piece of cloth, so as to leave no possible chance of creases in it; yet he lost not a syllable of the good woman's narration.

She, pleased with the enlarged audience her tale had attracted, went on with fresh vigour.

'An' there's a gallant captain, one Sir Sidney Smith, and he'd a notion o' goin' smack into a French port, an' carryin' off a vessel from right under their very noses; an' says he, "Which of yo' British sailors 'll go along with me to death or glory?" So Kinraid stands up like a man, an' "I'll go with yo', captain," he says. So they, an' some others as brave, went off, an' did their work, an' choose whativer it was, they did it famously; but they got caught by them French, an' were clapped into prison i' France for iver so long; but at last one Philip—Philip somethin' (he were a Frenchman, I know)—helped 'em to escape, in a fishin'-boat. But they were welcomed by th' whole British squadron as was i' t' Channel for t' piece of daring they'd done i' cuttin' out t' ship from a French port; an' Captain Sir Sidney Smith was made an admiral, an' him as we used t' call Charley Kinraid, the specksioneer, is made a lieutenant, an' a commissioned officer i' t' King's service; and is come to great glory, and slep in my house this very blessed night as is just past!'

A murmur of applause and interest and rejoicing buzzed all around Philip. All this was publicly known about Kinraid,—and how much more? All Monkshaven might hear tomorrow—nay, to-day—of Philip's treachery to the hero of the hour; how he had concealed his fate, and supplanted him in his love.

Philip shrank from the burst of popular indignation which he knew must follow. Any wrong done to one who stands on the pinnacle of the people's favour is resented by each individual as a personal injury; and among a primitive set of country-folk, who recognize the wild passion in love, as it exists untamed by the trammels of reason and self-restraint, any story of baulked affections, or treachery in such matters, spreads like wildfire.

Philip knew this quite well; his doom of disgrace lay plain before him, if only Kinraid spoke the word. His head was bent down while he thus listened and reflected. He half resolved on doing something; he lifted up his head, caught the reflection of his face in the little strip of glass on the opposite side, in which the women might look at themselves in their contemplated purchases, and quite resolved.

The sight he saw in the mirror was his own long, sad, pale face, made plainer and grayer by the heavy pressure of the morning's events. He saw his stooping figure, his rounded shoulders, with something like a feeling of disgust at his personal appearance as he remembered the square, upright build of Kinraid; his fine uniform, with epaulette and sword-belt; his handsome brown face; his dark eyes, splendid with the fire of passion and indignation; his white teeth, gleaming out with the terrible smile of scorn.

The comparison drove Philip from passive hopelessness to active despair.

He went abruptly from the crowded shop into the empty parlour, and on into the kitchen, where he took up a piece of bread, and heedless of Phoebe's look and words, began to eat it before he even left the place; for he needed the strength that food would give; he needed it to carry him out of the sight and the knowledge of all who might hear what he had done, and point their fingers at him.

He paused a moment in the parlour, and then, setting his teeth tight together, he went upstairs.

First of all he went into the bit of a room opening out of theirs, in which his baby slept. He dearly loved the child, and many a time would run in and play a while with it; and in such gambols he and Sylvia had passed their happiest moments of wedded life.

The little Bella was having her morning slumber; Nancy used to tell long afterwards how he knelt down by the side of her cot, and was so strange she thought he must have prayed, for all it was nigh upon eleven o'clock, and folk in their senses only said their prayers when they got up, and when they went to bed.

Then he rose, and stooped over, and gave the child a long, lingering, soft, fond kiss. And on tip-toe he passed away into the room where his aunt lay; his aunt who had been so true a friend to him! He was thankful to know that in her present state she was safe from the knowledge of what was past, safe from the sound of the shame to come.

He had not meant to see Sylvia again; he dreaded the look of her hatred, her scorn, but there, outside her mother's bed, she lay, apparently asleep. Mrs. Robson, too, was sleeping, her face towards the wall. Philip could not help it; he went to have one last look at his wife. She was turned towards her mother, her face averted from him; he could see the tear-stains, the swollen eyelids, the lips yet quivering: he stooped down, and bent to kiss the little hand that lay listless by her side. As his hot breath neared that hand it was twitched away, and a shiver ran through the whole prostrate body. And then he knew that she was not asleep, only worn out by her misery,—misery that he had caused.

He sighed heavily; but he went away, down-stairs, and away for ever. Only as he entered the parlour his eyes caught on two silhouettes, one of himself, one of Sylvia, done in the first month of their marriage, by some wandering artist, if so he could be called. They were hanging against the wall in little oval wooden frames; black profiles, with the lights done in gold; about as poor semblances of humanity as could be conceived; but Philip went up, and after looking for a minute or so at Sylvia's, he took it down, and buttoned his waistcoat over it.

It was the only thing he took away from his home.

He went down the entry on to the quay. The river was there, and waters, they say, have a luring power, and a weird promise of rest in their perpetual monotony of sound. But many people were there, if such a temptation presented itself to Philip's mind; the sight of his fellow-townsmen, perhaps of his acquaintances, drove him up another entry—the town is burrowed with such—back into the High Street, which he straightway crossed into a well-known court, out of which rough steps led to the summit of the hill, and on to the fells and moors beyond.

He plunged and panted up this rough ascent. From the top he could look down on the whole town lying below, severed by the bright shining river into two parts. To the right lay the sea, shimmering and heaving; there were the cluster of masts rising out of the little port; the irregular roofs of the houses; which of them, thought he, as he carried his eye along the quay-side to the market-place, which of them was his? and he singled it out in its unfamiliar aspect, and saw the thin blue smoke rising from the kitchen chimney, where even now Phoebe was cooking the household meal that he never more must share.

Up at that thought and away, he knew not nor cared not whither. He went through the ploughed fields where the corn was newly springing; he came down upon the vast sunny sea, and turned his back upon it with loathing; he made his way inland to the high green pastures; the short upland turf above which the larks hung poised 'at heaven's gate'. He strode along, so straight and heedless of briar and bush, that the wild black cattle ceased from grazing, and looked after him with their great blank puzzled eyes.

He had passed all enclosures and stone fences now, and was fairly on the desolate brown moors; through the withered last year's ling and fern, through the prickly gorse, he tramped, crushing down the tender shoots of this year's growth, and heedless of the startled plover's cry, goaded by the furies. His only relief from thought, from the remembrance of Sylvia's looks and words, was in violent bodily action.

So he went on till evening shadows and ruddy evening lights came out upon the wild fells.

He had crossed roads and lanes, with a bitter avoidance of men's tracks; but now the strong instinct of self-preservation came out, and his aching limbs, his weary heart, giving great pants and beats for a time, and then ceasing altogether till a mist swam and quivered before his aching eyes, warned him that he must find some shelter and food, or lie down to die. He fell down now, often; stumbling over the slightest obstacle. He had passed the cattle pastures; he was among the black-faced sheep; and they, too, ceased nibbling, and looked after him, and somehow, in his poor wandering imagination, their silly faces turned to likenesses of Monkshaven people—people who ought to be far, far away.

'Thou'll be belated on these fells, if thou doesn't tak' heed,' shouted some one.

Philip looked abroad to see whence the voice proceeded.

An old stiff-legged shepherd, in a smock-frock, was within a couple of hundred yards. Philip did not answer, but staggered and stumbled towards him.

'Good lork!' said the man, 'wheere hast ta been? Thou's seen Oud Harry, I think, thou looks so scared.'

Philip rallied himself, and tried to speak up to the old standard of respectability; but the effort was pitiful to see, had any one been by, who could have understood the pain it caused to restrain cries of bodily and mental agony.

'I've lost my way, that's all.'

''Twould ha' been enough, too, I'm thinkin', if I hadn't come out after t' ewes. There's t' Three Griffins near at hand: a sup o' Hollands 'll set thee to reeghts.'

Philip followed faintly. He could not see before him, and was guided by the sound of footsteps rather than by the sight of the figure moving onwards. He kept stumbling; and he knew that the old shepherd swore at him; but he also knew such curses proceeded from no ill-will, only from annoyance at the delay in going and 'seem' after t' ewes.' But had the man's words conveyed the utmost expression of hatred, Philip would neither have wondered at them, nor resented them.

They came into a wild mountain road, unfenced from the fells. A hundred yards off, and there was a small public-house, with a broad ruddy oblong of firelight shining across the tract.

'Theere!' said the old man. 'Thee cannot well miss that. A dunno tho', thee bees sich a gawby.'

So he went on, and delivered Philip safely up to the landlord.

'Here's a felly as a fund on t' fell side, just as one as if he were drunk; but he's sober enough, a reckon, only summat's wrong i' his head, a'm thinkin'.'

'No!' said Philip, sitting down on the first chair he came to. 'I'm right enough; just fairly wearied out: lost my way,' and he fainted.

There was a recruiting sergeant of marines sitting in the house-place, drinking. He, too, like Philip, had lost his way; but was turning his blunder to account by telling all manner of wonderful stories to two or three rustics who had come in ready to drink on any pretence; especially if they could get good liquor without paying for it.

The sergeant rose as Philip fell back, and brought up his own mug of beer, into which a noggin of gin had been put (called in Yorkshire 'dog's-nose'). He partly poured and partly spilt some of this beverage on Philip's face; some drops went through the pale and parted lips, and with a start the worn-out man revived.

'Bring him some victual, landlord,' called out the recruiting sergeant. 'I'll stand shot.'

They brought some cold bacon and coarse oat-cake. The sergeant asked for pepper and salt; minced the food fine and made it savoury, and kept administering it by teaspoonfuls; urging Philip to drink from time to time from his own cup of dog's-nose.

A burning thirst, which needed no stimulant from either pepper or salt, took possession of Philip, and he drank freely, scarcely recognizing what he drank. It took effect on one so habitually sober; and he was soon in that state when the imagination works wildly and freely.

He saw the sergeant before him, handsome, and bright, and active, in his gay red uniform, without a care, as it seemed to Philip, taking life lightly; admired and respected everywhere because of his cloth.

If Philip were gay, and brisk, well-dressed like him, returning with martial glory to Monkshaven, would not Sylvia love him once more? Could not he win her heart? He was brave by nature, and the prospect of danger did not daunt him, if ever it presented itself to his imagination.

He thought he was cautious in entering on the subject of enlistment with his new friend, the sergeant; but the latter was twenty times as cunning as he, and knew by experience how to bait his hook.

Philip was older by some years than the regulation age; but, at that time of great demand for men, the question of age was lightly entertained. The sergeant was profuse in statements of the advantages presented to a man of education in his branch of the service; how such a one was sure to rise; in fact, it would have seemed from the sergeant's account, as though the difficulty consisted in remaining in the ranks.

Philip's dizzy head thought the subject over and over again, each time with failing power of reason.

At length, almost, as it would seem, by some sleight of hand, he found the fatal shilling in his palm, and had promised to go before the nearest magistrate to be sworn in as one of his Majesty's marines the next morning. And after that he remembered nothing more.

He wakened up in a little truckle-bed in the same room as the sergeant, who lay sleeping the sleep of full contentment; while gradually, drop by drop, the bitter recollections of the day before came, filling up Philip's cup of agony.

He knew that he had received the bounty-money; and though he was aware that he had been partly tricked into it, and had no hope, no care, indeed, for any of the advantages so liberally promised him the night before, yet he was resigned, with utterly despondent passiveness, to the fate to which he had pledged himself. Anything was welcome that severed him from his former life, that could make him forget it, if that were possible; and also welcome anything which increased the chances of death without the sinfulness of his own participation in the act. He found in the dark recess of his mind the dead body of his fancy of the previous night; that he might come home, handsome and glorious, to win the love that had never been his.

But he only sighed over it, and put it aside out of his sight—so full of despair was he. He could eat no breakfast, though the sergeant ordered of the best. The latter kept watching his new recruit out of the corner of his eye, expecting a remonstrance, or dreading a sudden bolt.

But Philip walked with him the two or three miles in the most submissive silence, never uttering a syllable of regret or repentance; and before Justice Cholmley, of Holm-Fell Hall, he was sworn into his Majesty's service, under the name of Stephen Freeman. With a new name, he began a new life. Alas! the old life lives for ever!

CHAPTER XXXV

THINGS UNUTTERABLE

After Philip had passed out of the room, Sylvia lay perfectly still, from very exhaustion. Her mother slept on, happily unconscious of all the turmoil that had taken place; yes, happily, though the heavy sleep was to end in death. But of this her daughter knew nothing, imagining that it was refreshing slumber, instead of an ebbing of life. Both mother and daughter lay motionless till Phoebe entered the room to tell Sylvia that dinner was on the table.

Then Sylvia sate up, and put back her hair, bewildered and uncertain as to what was to be done next; how she should meet the husband to whom she had discarded all allegiance, repudiated the solemn promise of love and obedience which she had vowed.

Phoebe came into the room, with natural interest in the invalid, scarcely older than herself.

'How is t' old lady?' asked she, in a low voice.

Sylvia turned her head round to look; her mother had never moved, but was breathing in a loud uncomfortable manner, that made her stoop over her to see the averted face more nearly.

'Phoebe!' she cried, 'come here! She looks strange and odd; her eyes are open, but don't see me. Phoebe! Phoebe!'

'Sure enough, she's in a bad way!' said Phoebe, climbing stiffly on to the bed to have a nearer view. 'Hold her head a little up t' ease her breathin' while I go for master; he'll be for sendin' for t' doctor, I'll be bound.'

Sylvia took her mother's head and laid it fondly on her breast, speaking to her and trying to rouse her; but it was of no avail: the hard, stertorous breathing grew worse and worse.

Sylvia cried out for help; Nancy came, the baby in her arms. They had been in several times before that morning; and the child came smiling and crowing at its mother, who was supporting her own dying parent.

'Oh, Nancy!' said Sylvia; 'what is the matter with mother? yo' can see her face; tell me quick!'

Nancy set the baby on the bed for all reply, and ran out of the room, crying out,

'Master! master! Come quick! T' old missus is a-dying!'

This appeared to be no news to Sylvia, and yet the words came on her with a great shock, but for all that she could not cry; she was surprised herself at her own deadness of feeling.

Her baby crawled to her, and she had to hold and guard both her mother and her child. It seemed a long, long time before any one came, and then she heard muffled voices, and a heavy tramp: it was Phoebe leading the doctor upstairs, and Nancy creeping in behind to hear his opinion.

He did not ask many questions, and Phoebe replied more frequently to his inquiries than did Sylvia, who looked into his face with a blank, tearless, speechless despair, that gave him more pain than the sight of her dying mother.

The long decay of Mrs. Robson's faculties and health, of which he was well aware, had in a certain manner prepared him for some such sudden termination of the life whose duration was hardly desirable, although he gave several directions as to her treatment; but the white, pinched face, the great dilated eye, the slow comprehension of the younger woman, struck him with alarm; and he went on asking for various particulars, more with a view of rousing Sylvia, if even it were to tears, than for any other purpose that the information thus obtained could answer.

'You had best have pillows propped up behind her—it will not be for long; she does not know that you are holding her, and it is only tiring you to no purpose!'

Sylvia's terrible stare continued: he put his advice into action, and gently tried to loosen her clasp, and tender hold. This she resisted; laying her cheek against her poor mother's unconscious face.

'Where is Hepburn?' said he. 'He ought to be here!'

Phoebe looked at Nancy, Nancy at Phoebe. It was the latter who replied,

'He's neither i' t' house nor i' t' shop. A seed him go past t' kitchen window better nor an hour ago; but neither William Coulson or Hester Rose knows where he's gone to.

Dr Morgan's lips were puckered up into a whistle, but he made no sound.

'Give me baby!' he said, suddenly. Nancy had taken her up off the bed where she had been sitting, encircled by her mother's arm. The nursemaid gave her to the doctor. He watched the mother's eye, it followed her child, and he was rejoiced. He gave a little pinch to the baby's soft flesh, and she cried out piteously; again the same action, the same result. Sylvia laid her mother down, and stretched out her arms for her child, hushing it, and moaning over it.

'So far so good!' said Dr Morgan to himself. 'But where is the husband? He ought to be here.' He went down-stairs to make inquiry for Philip; that poor young creature, about whose health he had never felt thoroughly satisfied since the fever after her confinement, was in an anxious condition, and with an inevitable shock awaiting her. Her husband ought to be with her, and supporting her to bear it.

Dr Morgan went into the shop. Hester alone was there. Coulson had gone to his comfortable dinner at his well-ordered house, with his common-place wife. If he had felt anxious about Philip's looks and strange disappearance, he had also managed to account for them in some indifferent way.

Hester was alone with the shop-boy; few people came in during the universal Monkshaven dinner-hour. She was resting her head on her hand, and puzzled and distressed about many things—all that was implied by the proceedings of the evening before between Philip and Sylvia; and that was confirmed by Philip's miserable looks and strange abstracted ways to-day. Oh! how easy Hester would have found it to make him happy! not merely how easy, but what happiness it would have been to her to merge her every wish into the one great object of fulfiling his will. To her, an on-looker, the course of married life, which should lead to perfect happiness, seemed to plain! Alas! it is often so! and the resisting forces which make all such harmony and delight impossible are not recognized by the bystanders, hardly by the actors. But if these resisting forces are only superficial, or constitutional, they are but the necessary discipline here, and do not radically affect the love which will make all things right in heaven.

Some glimmering of this latter comforting truth shed its light on Hester's troubled thoughts from time to time. But again, how easy would it have been to her to tread the maze that led to Philip's happiness; and how difficult it seemed to the wife he had chosen!

She was aroused by Dr Morgan's voice.

'So both Coulson and Hepburn have left the shop to your care, Hester. I want Hepburn, though; his wife is in a very anxious state. Where is he? can you tell me?'

'Sylvia in an anxious state! I've not seen her to-day, but last night she looked as well as could be.'

'Ay, ay; but many a thing happens in four-and-twenty hours. Her mother is dying, may be dead by this time; and her husband should be there with her. Can't you send for him?'

'I don't know where he is,' said Hester. 'He went off from here all on a sudden, when there was all the market-folks in t' shop; I thought he'd maybe gone to John Foster's about th' money, for they was paying a deal in. I'll send there and inquire.'

No! the messenger brought back word that he had not been seen at their bank all morning. Further inquiries were made by the anxious Hester, by the doctor, by Coulson; all they could learn was that Phoebe had seen him pass the kitchen window about eleven o'clock, when she was peeling the potatoes for dinner; and two lads playing on the quay-side thought they had seen him among a group of sailors; but these latter, as far as they could be identified, had no knowledge of his appearance among them.

Before night the whole town was excited about his disappearance. Before night Bell Robson had gone to her long home. And Sylvia still lay quiet and tearless, apparently more unmoved than any other creature by the events of the day, and the strange vanishing of her husband.

The only thing she seemed to care for was her baby; she held it tight in her arms, and Dr Morgan bade them leave it there, its touch might draw the desired tears into her weary, sleepless eyes, and charm the aching pain out of them.

They were afraid lest she should inquire for her husband, whose non-appearance at such a time of sorrow to his wife must (they thought) seem strange to her. And night drew on while they were all in this state. She had gone back to her own room without a word when they had desired her to do so; caressing her child in her arms, and sitting down on the first chair she came to, with a heavy sigh, as if even this slight bodily exertion had been too much for her. They saw her eyes turn towards the door every time it was opened, and they thought it was with anxious expectation of one who could not be found, though many were seeking for him in all probable places.

When night came some one had to tell her of her husband's disappearance; and Dr Morgan was the person who undertook this.

He came into her room about nine o'clock; her baby was sleeping in her arms; she herself pale as death, still silent and tearless, though strangely watchful of gestures and sounds, and probably cognizant of more than they imagined.

'Well, Mrs. Hepburn,' said he, as cheerfully as he could, 'I should advise your going to bed early; for I fancy your husband won't come home to-night. Some journey or other, that perhaps Coulson can explain better than I can, will most likely keep him away till to-morrow. It's very unfortunate that he should be away at such a sad time as this, as I'm sure he'll feel when he returns; but we must make the best of it.'

He watched her to see the effect of his words.

She sighed, that was all. He still remained a little while. She lifted her head up a little and asked,

'How long do yo' think she was unconscious, doctor? Could she hear things, think yo', afore she fell into that strange kind o' slumber?'

'I cannot tell,' said he, shaking his head. 'Was she breathing in that hard snoring kind of way when you left her this morning?'

'Yes, I think so; I cannot tell, so much has happened.'

'When you came back to her, after your breakfast, I think you said she was in much the same position?'

'Yes, and yet I may be telling yo' lies; if I could but think: but it's my head as is aching so; doctor, I wish yo'd go, for I need being alone, I'm so mazed.'

'Good-night, then, for you're a wise woman, I see, and mean to go to bed, and have a good night with baby there.'

But he went down to Phoebe, and told her to go in from time to time, and see how her mistress was.

He found Hester Rose and the old servant together; both had been crying, both were evidently in great trouble about the death and the mystery of the day.

Hester asked if she might go up and see Sylvia, and the doctor gave his leave, talking meanwhile with Phoebe over the kitchen fire. Hester came down again without seeing Sylvia. The door of the room was bolted, and everything quiet inside.

'Does she know where her husband is, think you?' asked the doctor at this account of Hester's. 'She's not anxious about him at any rate: or else the shock of her mother's death has been too much for her. We must hope for some change in the morning; a good fit of crying, or a fidget about her husband, would be more natural. Good-night to you both,' and off he went.

Phoebe and Hester avoided looking at each other at these words. Both were conscious of the probability of something having gone seriously wrong between the husband and wife. Hester had the recollection of the previous night, Phoebe the untasted breakfast of to-day to go upon.

She spoke first.

'A just wish he'd come home to still folks' tongues. It need niver ha' been known if t' old lady hadn't died this day of all others. It's such a thing for t' shop t' have one o' t' partners missin', an' no one for t' know what's comed on him. It niver happened i' Fosters' days, that's a' I know.'

'He'll maybe come back yet,' said Hester. 'It's not so very late.'

'It were market day, and a',' continued Phoebe, 'just as if iverything mun go wrong together; an' a' t' country customers'll go back wi' fine tale i' their mouths, as Measter Hepburn was strayed an' missin' just like a beast o' some kind.'

'Hark! isn't that a step?' said Hester suddenly, as a footfall sounded in the now quiet street; but it passed the door, and the hope that had arisen on its approach fell as the sound died away.

'He'll noane come to-night,' said Phoebe, who had been as eager a listener as Hester, however. 'Thou'd best go thy ways home; a shall stay up, for it's not seemly for us a' t' go to our beds, an' a corpse in t' house; an' Nancy, as might ha' watched, is gone to her bed this hour past, like a lazy boots as she is. A can hear, too, if t' measter does come home; tho' a'll be bound he wunnot; choose wheere he is, he'll be i' bed by now, for it's well on to eleven. I'll let thee out by t' shop-door, and stand by it till thou's close at home, for it's ill for a young woman to be i' t' street so late.'

So she held the door open, and shaded the candle from the flickering outer air, while Hester went to her home with a heavy heart.

Heavily and hopelessly did they all meet in the morning. No news of Philip, no change in Sylvia; an unceasing flow of angling and conjecture and gossip radiating from the shop into the town.

Hester could have entreated Coulson on her knees to cease from repeating the details of a story of which every word touched on a raw place in her sensitive heart; moreover, when they talked together so eagerly, she could not hear the coming footsteps on the pavement without.

Once some one hit very near the truth in a chance remark.

'It seems strange,' she said, 'how as one man turns up, another just disappears. Why, it were but upo' Tuesday as Kinraid come back, as all his own folk had thought to be dead; and next day here's Measter Hepburn as is gone no one knows wheere!'

'That's t' way i' this world,' replied Coulson, a little sententiously. 'This life is full o' changes o' one kind or another; them that's dead is alive; and as for poor Philip, though he was alive, he looked fitter to be dead when he came into t' shop o' Wednesday morning.'

'And how does she take it?' nodding to where Sylvia was supposed to be.

'Oh! she's not herself, so to say. She were just stunned by finding her mother was dying in her very arms when she thought as she were only sleeping; yet she's never been able to cry a drop; so that t' sorrow's gone inwards on her brain, and from all I can hear, she doesn't rightly understand as her husband is missing. T' doctor says if she could but cry, she'd come to a juster comprehension of things.'

'And what do John and Jeremiah Foster say to it all?'

'They're down here many a time in t' day to ask if he's come back, or how she is; for they made a deal on 'em both. They're going t' attend t' funeral to-morrow, and have given orders as t' shop is to be shut up in t' morning.'

To the surprise of every one, Sylvia, who had never left her room since the night of her mother's death, and was supposed to be almost unconscious of all that was going on in the house, declared her intention of following her mother to the grave. No one could do more than remonstrate: no one had sufficient authority to interfere with her. Dr Morgan even thought that she might possibly be roused to tears by the occasion; only he begged Hester to go with her, that she might have the solace of some woman's company.

She went through the greater part of the ceremony in the same hard, unmoved manner in which she had received everything for days past.

But on looking up once, as they formed round the open grave, she saw Kester, in his Sunday clothes, with a bit of new crape round his hat, crying as if his heart would break over the coffin of his good, kind mistress.

His evident distress, the unexpected sight, suddenly loosed the fountain of Sylvia's tears, and her sobs grew so terrible that Hester feared she would not be able to remain until the end of the funeral. But she struggled hard to stay till the last, and then she made an effort to go round by the place where Kester stood.

'Come and see me,' was all she could say for crying: and Kester only nodded his head—he could not speak a word.

CHAPTER XXXVI

MYSTERIOUS TIDINGS

That very evening Kester came, humbly knocking at the kitchen-door. Phoebe opened it. He asked to see Sylvia.

'A know not if she'll see thee,' said Phoebe. 'There's no makin' her out; sometimes she's for one thing, sometimes she's for another.'

'She bid me come and see her,' said Kester. 'Only this mornin', at missus' buryin', she told me to come.'

So Phoebe went off to inform Sylvia that Kester was there; and returned with the desire that he would walk into the parlour. An instant after he was gone, Phoebe heard him return, and carefully shut the two doors of communication between the kitchen and sitting-room.

Sylvia was in the latter when Kester came in, holding her baby close to her; indeed, she seldom let it go now-a-days to any one else, making Nancy's place quite a sinecure, much to Phoebe's indignation.

Sylvia's face was shrunk, and white, and thin; her lovely eyes alone retained the youthful, almost childlike, expression. She went up to Kester, and shook his horny hand, she herself trembling all over.

'Don't talk to me of her,' she said hastily. 'I cannot stand it. It's a blessing for her to be gone, but, oh——'

She began to cry, and then cheered herself up, and swallowed down her sobs.

'Kester,' she went on, hastily, 'Charley Kinraid isn't dead; dost ta know? He's alive, and he were here o' Tuesday—no, Monday, was it? I cannot tell—but he were here!'

'A knowed as he weren't dead. Every one is a-speaking on it. But a didn't know as thee'd ha' seen him. A took comfort i' thinkin' as thou'd ha' been wi' thy mother a' t' time as he were i' t' place.'

'Then he's gone?' said Sylvia.

'Gone; ay, days past. As far as a know, he but stopped a' neet. A thought to mysel' (but yo' may be sure a said nought to nobody), he's heerd as our Sylvia were married, and has put it in his pipe, and ta'en hissel' off to smoke it.'

'Kester!' said Sylvia, leaning forwards, and whispering. 'I saw him. He was here. Philip saw him. Philip had known as he wasn't dead a' this time!'

Kester stood up suddenly.

'By goom, that chap has a deal t' answer for.'

A bright red spot was on each of Sylvia's white cheeks; and for a minute or so neither of them spoke.

Then she went on, still whispering out her words.

'Kester, I'm more afeared than I dare tell any one: can they ha' met, think yo'? T' very thought turns me sick. I told Philip my mind, and took a vow again' him—but it would be awful to think on harm happening to him through Kinraid. Yet he went out that morning, and has niver been seen or heard on sin'; and Kinraid were just fell again' him, and as for that matter, so was I; but——'

The red spot vanished as she faced her own imagination.

Kester spoke.

'It's a thing as can be easy looked into. What day an' time were it when Philip left this house?'

'Tuesday—the day she died. I saw him in her room that morning between breakfast and dinner; I could a'most swear to it's being close after eleven. I mind counting t' clock. It was that very morn as Kinraid were here.'

'A'll go an' have a pint o' beer at t' King's Arms, down on t' quay-side; it were theere he put up at. An' a'm pretty sure as he only stopped one night, and left i' t' morning betimes. But a'll go see.'

'Do,' said Sylvia, 'and go out through t' shop; they're all watching and watching me to see how I take things; and daren't let on about t' fire as is burning up my heart. Coulson is i' t' shop, but he'll not notice thee like Phoebe.'

By-and-by Kester came back. It seemed as though Sylvia had never stirred; she looked eagerly at him, but did not speak.

'He went away i' Rob Mason's mail-cart, him as tak's t' letters to Hartlepool. T' lieutenant (as they ca' him down at t' King's Arms; they're as proud on his uniform as if it had been a new-painted sign to swing o'er their doors), t' lieutenant had reckoned upo' stayin' longer wi' 'em; but he went out betimes o' Tuesday morn', an' came back a' ruffled up, an paid his bill—paid for his breakfast, though he touched noane on it—an' went off i' Rob postman's mail-cart, as starts reg'lar at ten o'clock. Corneys has been theere askin' for him, an' makin' a piece o' work, as he niver went near em; and they bees cousins. Niver a one among 'em knows as he were here as far as a could mak' out.'

'Thank yo', Kester,' said Sylvia, falling back in her chair, as if all the energy that had kept her stiff and upright was gone now that her anxiety was relieved.

She was silent for a long time; her eyes shut, her cheek laid on her child's head. Kester spoke next.

'A think it's pretty clear as they'n niver met. But it's a' t' more wonder where thy husband's gone to. Thee and him had words about it, and thou told him thy mind, thou said?'

'Yes,' said Sylvia, not moving. 'I'm afeared lest mother knows what I said to him, there, where she's gone to—I am-' the tears filled her shut eyes, and came softly overflowing down her cheeks; 'and yet it were true, what I said, I cannot forgive him; he's just spoilt my life, and I'm not one-and-twenty yet, and he knowed how wretched, how very wretched, I were. A word fra' him would ha' mended it a'; and Charley had bid him speak the word, and give me his faithful love, and Philip saw my heart ache day after day, and niver let on as him I was mourning for was alive, and had sent me word as he'd keep true to me, as I were to do to him.'

'A wish a'd been theere; a'd ha' felled him to t' ground,' said Kester, clenching his stiff, hard hand with indignation.

Sylvia was silent again: pale and weary she sate, her eyes still shut.

Then she said,

'Yet he were so good to mother; and mother loved him so. Oh, Kester!' lifting herself up, opening her great wistful eyes, 'it's well for folks as can die; they're spared a deal o' misery.'

'Ay!' said he. 'But there's folk as one 'ud like to keep fra' shirkin' their misery. Think yo' now as Philip is livin'?'

Sylvia shivered all over, and hesitated before she replied.

'I dunnot know. I said such things; he deserved 'em all——'

'Well, well, lass!' said Kester, sorry that he had asked the question which was producing so much emotion of one kind or another. 'Neither thee nor me can tell; we can neither help nor hinder, seein' as he's ta'en hissel' off out on our sight, we'd best not think on him. A'll try an' tell thee some news, if a can think on it wi' my mind so full. Thou knows Haytersbank folk ha' flitted, and t' oud place is empty?'

'Yes!' said Sylvia, with the indifference of one wearied out with feeling.

'A only telled yo' t' account like for me bein' at a loose end i' Monkshaven. My sister, her as lived at Dale End an' is a widow, has comed int' town to live; an' a'm lodging wi' her, an' jobbin' about. A'm gettin' pretty well to do, an' a'm noane far t' seek, an' a'm going now: only first a just wanted for t' say as a'm thy oldest friend, a reckon, and if a can do a turn for thee, or go an errand, like as a've done to-day, or if it's any comfort to talk a bit to one who's known thy life from a babby, why yo've only t' send for me, an' a'd come if it were twenty mile. A'm lodgin' at Peggy Dawson's, t' lath and plaster cottage at t' right hand o' t' bridge, a' among t' new houses, as they're thinkin' o' buildin' near t' sea: no one can miss it.'

He stood up and shook hands with her. As he did so, he looked at her sleeping baby.

'She's liker yo' than him. A think a'll say, God bless her.'

With the heavy sound of his out-going footsteps, baby awoke. She ought before this time to have been asleep in her bed, and the disturbance made her cry fretfully.

'Hush thee, darling, hush thee!' murmured her mother; 'there's no one left to love me but thee, and I cannot stand thy weeping, my pretty one. Hush thee, my babe, hush thee!'

She whispered soft in the little one's ear as she took her upstairs to bed.

About three weeks after the miserable date of Bell Robson's death and Philip's disappearance, Hester Rose received a letter from him. She knew the writing on the address well; and it made her tremble so much that it was many minutes before she dared to open it, and make herself acquainted with the facts it might disclose.

But she need not have feared; there were no facts told, unless the vague date of 'London' might be something to learn. Even that much might have been found out by the post-mark, only she had been too much taken by surprise to examine it.

It ran as follows:—

'DEAR HESTER,—

'Tell those whom it may concern, that I have left Monkshaven for ever. No one need trouble themselves about me; I am provided for. Please to make my humble apologies to my kind friends, the Messrs Foster, and to my partner, William Coulson. Please to accept of my love, and to join the same to your mother. Please to give my particular and respectful duty and kind love to my aunt Isabella Robson. Her daughter Sylvia knows what I have always felt, and shall always feel, for her better than I can ever put into language, so I send her no message; God bless and keep my child. You must all look on me as one dead; as I am to you, and maybe shall soon be in reality.

'Your affectionate and obedient friend to command,

'PHILIP HEPBURN.

'P.S.—Oh, Hester! for God's sake and mine, look after ('my wife,' scratched out) Sylvia and my child. I think Jeremiah Foster will help you to be a friend to them. This is the last solemn request of P. H. She is but very young.'

Hester read this letter again and again, till her heart caught the echo of its hopelessness, and sank within her. She put it in her pocket, and reflected upon it all the day long as she served in the shop.

The customers found her as gentle, but far more inattentive than usual. She thought that in the evening she would go across the bridge, and consult with the two good old brothers Foster. But something occurred to put off the fulfilment of this plan.

That same morning Sylvia had preceded her, with no one to consult, because consultation would have required previous confidence, and confidence would have necessitated such a confession about Kinraid as it was most difficult for Sylvia to make. The poor young wife yet felt that some step must be taken by her; and what it was to be she could not imagine.

She had no home to go to; for as Philip was gone away, she remained where she was only on sufferance; she did not know what means of livelihood she had; she was willing to work, nay, would be thankful to take up her old life of country labour; but with her baby, what could she do?

In this dilemma, the recollection of the old man's kindly speech and offer of assistance, made, it is true, half in joke, at the end of her wedding visit, came into her mind; and she resolved to go and ask for some of the friendly counsel and assistance then offered.

It would be the first time of her going out since her mother's funeral, and she dreaded the effort on that account. More even than on that account did she shrink from going into the streets again. She could not get over the impression that Kinraid must be lingering near; and she distrusted herself so much that it was a positive terror to think of meeting him again. She felt as though, if she but caught a sight of him, the glitter of his uniform, or heard his well-known voice in only a distant syllable of talk, her heart would stop, and she should die from very fright of what would come next. Or rather so she felt, and so she thought before she took her baby in her arms, as Nancy gave it to her after putting on its out-of-door attire.

With it in her arms she was protected, and the whole current of her thoughts was changed. The infant was wailing and suffering with its teething, and the mother's heart was so occupied in soothing and consoling her moaning child, that the dangerous quay-side and the bridge were passed almost before she was aware; nor did she notice the eager curiosity and respectful attention of those she met who recognized her even through the heavy veil which formed part of the draping mourning provided for her by Hester and Coulson, in the first unconscious days after her mother's death.

Though public opinion as yet reserved its verdict upon Philip's disappearance—warned possibly by Kinraid's story against hasty decisions and judgments in such times as those of war and general disturbance—yet every one agreed that no more pitiful fate could have befallen Philip's wife.

Marked out by her striking beauty as an object of admiring interest even in those days when she sate in girlhood's smiling peace by her mother at the Market Cross—her father had lost his life in a popular cause, and ignominious as the manner of his death might be, he was looked upon as a martyr to his zeal in avenging the wrongs of his townsmen; Sylvia had married amongst them too, and her quiet daily life was well known to them; and now her husband had been carried off from her side just on the very day when she needed his comfort most.

For the general opinion was that Philip had been 'carried off'—in seaport towns such occurrences were not uncommon in those days—either by land-crimps or water-crimps.

So Sylvia was treated with silent reverence, as one sorely afflicted, by all the unheeded people she met in her faltering walk to Jeremiah Foster's.

She had calculated her time so as to fall in with him at his dinner hour, even though it obliged her to go to his own house rather than to the bank where he and his brother spent all the business hours of the day.

Sylvia was so nearly exhausted by the length of her walk and the weight of her baby, that all she could do when the door was opened was to totter into the nearest seat, sit down, and begin to cry.

In an instant kind hands were about her, loosening her heavy cloak, offering to relieve her of her child, who clung to her all the more firmly, and some one was pressing a glass of wine against her lips.

'No, sir, I cannot take it! wine allays gives me th' headache; if I might have just a drink o' water. Thank you, ma'am' (to the respectable-looking old servant), 'I'm well enough now; and perhaps, sir, I might speak a word with yo', for it's that I've come for.'

'It's a pity, Sylvia Hepburn, as thee didst not come to me at the bank, for it's been a long toil for thee all this way in the heat, with thy child. But if there's aught I can do or say for thee, thou hast but to name it, I am sure. Martha! wilt thou relieve her of her child while she comes with me into the parlour?'

But the wilful little Bella stoutly refused to go to any one, and Sylvia was not willing to part with her, tired though she was.

So the baby was carried into the parlour, and much of her after-life depended on this trivial fact.

Once installed in the easy-chair, and face to face with Jeremiah, Sylvia did not know how to begin.

Jeremiah saw this, and kindly gave her time to recover herself, by pulling out his great gold watch, and letting the seal dangle before the child's eyes, almost within reach of the child's eager little fingers.

'She favours you a deal,' said he, at last. 'More than her father,' he went on, purposely introducing Philip's name, so as to break the ice; for he rightly conjectured she had come to speak to him about something connected with her husband.

Still Sylvia said nothing; she was choking down tears and shyness, and unwillingness to take as confidant a man of whom she knew so little, on such slight ground (as she now felt it to be) as the little kindly speech with which she had been dismissed from that house the last time that she entered it.

'It's no use keeping yo', sir,' she broke out at last. 'It's about Philip as I comed to speak. Do yo' know any thing whatsomever about him? He niver had a chance o' saying anything, I know; but maybe he's written?'

'Not a line, my poor young woman!' said Jeremiah, hastily putting an end to that vain idea.

'Then he's either dead or gone away for iver,' she whispered. 'I mun be both feyther and mother to my child.'

'Oh! thee must not give it up,' replied he. 'Many a one is carried off to the wars, or to the tenders o' men-o'-war; and then they turn out to be unfit for service, and are sent home. Philip 'll come back before the year's out; thee'll see that.'

'No; he'll niver come back. And I'm not sure as I should iver wish him t' come back, if I could but know what was gone wi' him. Yo' see, sir, though I were sore set again' him, I shouldn't like harm to happen him.'

'There is something behind all this that I do not understand. Can thee tell me what it is?'

'I must, sir, if yo're to help me wi' your counsel; and I came up here to ask for it.'

Another long pause, during which Jeremiah made a feint of playing with the child, who danced and shouted with tantalized impatience at not being able to obtain possession of the seal, and at length stretched out her soft round little arms to go to the owner of the coveted possession. Surprise at this action roused Sylvia, and she made some comment upon it.

'I niver knew her t' go to any one afore. I hope she'll not be troublesome to yo', sir?'

The old man, who had often longed for a child of his own in days gone by, was highly pleased by this mark of baby's confidence, and almost forgot, in trying to strengthen her regard by all the winning wiles in his power, how her poor mother was still lingering over some painful story which she could not bring herself to tell.

'I'm afeared of speaking wrong again' any one, sir. And mother were so fond o' Philip; but he kept something from me as would ha' made me a different woman, and some one else, happen, a different man. I were troth-plighted wi' Kinraid the specksioneer, him as was cousin to th' Corneys o' Moss Brow, and comed back lieutenant i' t' navy last Tuesday three weeks, after ivery one had thought him dead and gone these three years.'

She paused.

'Well?' said Jeremiah, with interest; although his attention appeared to be divided between the mother's story and the eager playfulness of the baby on his knee.

'Philip knew he were alive; he'd seen him taken by t' press-gang, and Charley had sent a message to me by Philip.'

Her white face was reddening, her eyes flashing at this point of her story.

'And he niver told me a word on it, not when he saw me like to break my heart in thinking as Kinraid were dead; he kept it a' to hissel'; and watched me cry, and niver said a word to comfort me wi' t' truth. It would ha' been a great comfort, sir, only t' have had his message if I'd niver ha' been to see him again. But Philip niver let on to any one, as I iver heared on, that he'd seen Charley that morning as t' press-gang took him. Yo' know about feyther's death, and how friendless mother and me was left? and so I married him; for he were a good friend to us then, and I were dazed like wi' sorrow, and could see naught else to do for mother. He were allays very tender and good to her, for sure.'

Again a long pause of silent recollection, broken by one or two deep sighs.

'If I go on, sir, now, I mun ask yo' to promise as yo'll niver tell. I do so need some one to tell me what I ought to do, and I were led here, like, else I would ha' died wi' it all within my teeth. Yo'll promise, sir?'

Jeremiah Foster looked in her face, and seeing the wistful, eager look, he was touched almost against his judgment into giving the promise required; she went on.

'Upon a Tuesday morning, three weeks ago, I think, tho' for t' matter o' time it might ha' been three years, Kinraid come home; come back for t' claim me as his wife, and I were wed to Philip! I met him i' t' road at first; and I couldn't tell him theere. He followed me into t' house—Philip's house, sir, behind t' shop—and somehow I told him all, how I were a wedded wife to another. Then he up and said I'd a false heart—me false, sir, as had eaten my daily bread in bitterness, and had wept t' nights through, all for sorrow and mourning for his death! Then he said as Philip knowed all t' time he were alive and coming back for me; and I couldn't believe it, and I called Philip, and he come, and a' that Charley had said were true; and yet I were Philip's wife! So I took a mighty oath, and I said as I'd niver hold Philip to be my lawful husband again, nor iver forgive him for t' evil he'd wrought us, but hold him as a stranger and one as had done me a heavy wrong.'

She stopped speaking; her story seemed to her to end there. But her listener said, after a pause,

'It were a cruel wrong, I grant thee that; but thy oath were a sin, and thy words were evil, my poor lass. What happened next?'

'I don't justly remember,' she said, wearily. 'Kinraid went away, and mother cried out; and I went to her. She were asleep, I thought, so I lay down by her, to wish I were dead, and to think on what would come on my child if I died; and Philip came in softly, and I made as if I were asleep; and that's t' very last as I've iver seen or heared of him.'

Jeremiah Foster groaned as she ended her story. Then he pulled himself up, and said, in a cheerful tone of voice,

'He'll come back, Sylvia Hepburn. He'll think better of it: never fear!'

'I fear his coming back!' said she. 'That's what I'm feared on; I would wish as I knew on his well-doing i' some other place; but him and me can niver live together again.'

'Nay,' pleaded Jeremiah. 'Thee art sorry what thee said; thee were sore put about, or thee wouldn't have said it.'

He was trying to be a peace-maker, and to heal over conjugal differences; but he did not go deep enough.

'I'm not sorry,' said she, slowly. 'I were too deeply wronged to be "put about"; that would go off wi' a night's sleep. It's only the thought of mother (she's dead and happy, and knows nought of all this, I trust) that comes between me and hating Philip. I'm not sorry for what I said.'

Jeremiah had never met with any one so frank and undisguised in expressions of wrong feeling, and he scarcely knew what to say.

He looked extremely grieved, and not a little shocked. So pretty and delicate a young creature to use such strong relentless language!

She seemed to read his thoughts, for she made answer to them.

'I dare say you think I'm very wicked, sir, not to be sorry. Perhaps I am. I can't think o' that for remembering how I've suffered; and he knew how miserable I was, and might ha' cleared my misery away wi' a word; and he held his peace, and now it's too late! I'm sick o' men and their cruel, deceitful ways. I wish I were dead.'

She was crying before she had ended this speech, and seeing her tears, the child began to cry too, stretching out its little arms to go back to its mother. The hard stony look on her face melted away into the softest, tenderest love as she clasped the little one to her, and tried to soothe its frightened sobs.

A bright thought came into the old man's mind.

He had been taking a complete dislike to her till her pretty way with her baby showed him that she had a heart of flesh within her.

'Poor little one!' said he, 'thy mother had need love thee, for she's deprived thee of thy father's love. Thou'rt half-way to being an orphan; yet I cannot call thee one of the fatherless to whom God will be a father. Thou'rt a desolate babe, thou may'st well cry; thine earthly parents have forsaken thee, and I know not if the Lord will take thee up.'

Sylvia looked up at him affrighted; holding her baby tighter to her, she exclaimed.

'Don't speak so, sir! it's cursing, sir! I haven't forsaken her! Oh, sir! those are awful sayings.'

'Thee hast sworn never to forgive thy husband, nor to live with him again. Dost thee know that by the law of the land, he may claim his child; and then thou wilt have to forsake it, or to be forsworn? Poor little maiden!' continued he, once more luring the baby to him with the temptation of the watch and chain.

Sylvia thought for a while before speaking. Then she said,

'I cannot tell what ways to take. Whiles I think my head is crazed. It were a cruel turn he did me!'

'It was. I couldn't have thought him guilty of such baseness.'

This acquiescence, which was perfectly honest on Jeremiah's part, almost took Sylvia by surprise. Why might she not hate one who had been both cruel and base in his treatment of her? And yet she recoiled from the application of such hard terms by another to Philip, by a cool-judging and indifferent person, as she esteemed Jeremiah to be. From some inscrutable turn in her thoughts, she began to defend him, or at least to palliate the harsh judgment which she herself had been the first to pronounce.

'He were so tender to mother; she were dearly fond on him; he niver spared aught he could do for her, else I would niver ha' married him.'

'He was a good and kind-hearted lad from the time he was fifteen. And I never found him out in any falsehood, no more did my brother.'

'But it were all the same as a lie,' said Sylvia, swiftly changing her ground, 'to leave me to think as Charley were dead, when he knowed all t' time he were alive.'

'It was. It was a self-seeking lie; putting thee to pain to get his own ends. And the end of it has been that he is driven forth like Cain.'

'I niver told him to go, sir.'

'But thy words sent him forth, Sylvia.'

'I cannot unsay them, sir; and I believe as I should say them again.'

But she said this as one who rather hopes for a contradiction.

All Jeremiah replied, however, was, 'Poor wee child!' in a pitiful tone, addressed to the baby.

Sylvia's eyes filled with tears.

'Oh, sir, I'll do anything as iver yo' can tell me for her. That's what I came for t' ask yo'. I know I mun not stay theere, and Philip gone away; and I dunnot know what to do: and I'll do aught, only I must keep her wi' me. Whativer can I do, sir?'

Jeremiah thought it over for a minute or two. Then he replied,

'I must have time to think. I must talk it over with brother John.'

'But you've given me yo'r word, sir!' exclaimed she.

'I have given thee my word never to tell any one of what has passed between thee and thy husband, but I must take counsel with my brother as to what is to be done with thee and thy child, now that thy husband has left the shop.'

This was said so gravely as almost to be a reproach, and he got up, as a sign that the interview was ended.

He gave the baby back to its mother; but not without a solemn blessing, so solemn that, to Sylvia's superstitious and excited mind, it undid the terrors of what she had esteemed to be a curse.

'The Lord bless thee and keep thee! The Lord make His face to shine upon thee!'

All the way down the hill-side, Sylvia kept kissing the child, and whispering to its unconscious ears,—

'I'll love thee for both, my treasure, I will. I'll hap thee round wi' my love, so as thou shall niver need a feyther's.'

CHAPTER XXXVII

BEREAVEMENT

Hester had been prevented by her mother's indisposition from taking Philip's letter to the Fosters, to hold a consultation with them over its contents.

Alice Rose was slowly failing, and the long days which she had to spend alone told much upon her spirits, and consequently upon her health.

All this came out in the conversation which ensued after reading Hepburn's letter in the little parlour at the bank on the day after Sylvia had had her confidential interview with Jeremiah Foster.

He was a true man of honour, and never so much as alluded to her visit to him; but what she had then told him influenced him very much in the formation of the project which he proposed to his brother and Hester.

He recommended her remaining where she was, living still in the house behind the shop; for he thought within himself that she might have exaggerated the effect of her words upon Philip; that, after all, it might have been some cause totally disconnected with them, which had blotted out her husband's place among the men of Monkshaven; and that it would be so much easier for both to resume their natural relations, both towards each other and towards the world, if Sylvia remained where her husband had left her—in an expectant attitude, so to speak.

Jeremiah Foster questioned Hester straitly about her letter: whether she had made known its contents to any one. No, not to any one. Neither to her mother nor to William Coulson? No, to neither.

She looked at him as she replied to his inquiries, and he looked at her, each wondering if the other could be in the least aware that a conjugal quarrel might be at the root of the dilemma in which they were placed by Hepburn's disappearance.

But neither Hester, who had witnessed the misunderstanding between the husband and wife on the evening, before the morning on which Philip went away, nor Jeremiah Foster, who had learnt from Sylvia the true reason of her husband's disappearance, gave the slightest reason to the other to think that they each supposed they had a clue to the reason of Hepburn's sudden departure.

What Jeremiah Foster, after a night's consideration, had to propose was this; that Hester and her mother should come and occupy the house in the market-place, conjointly with Sylvia and her child. Hester's interest in the shop was by this time acknowledged. Jeremiah had made over to her so much of his share in the business, that she had a right to be considered as a kind of partner; and she had long been the superintendent of that department of goods which were exclusively devoted to women. So her daily presence was requisite for more reasons than one.

Yet her mother's health and spirits were such as to render it unadvisable that the old woman should be too much left alone; and Sylvia's devotion to her own mother seemed to point her out as the very person who could be a gentle and tender companion to Alice Rose during those hours when her own daughter would necessarily be engaged in the shop.

Many desirable objects seemed to be gained by this removal of Alice: an occupation was provided for Sylvia, which would detain her in the place where her husband had left her, and where (Jeremiah Foster fairly expected in spite of his letter) he was likely to come back to find her; and Alice Rose, the early love of one of the brothers, the old friend of the other, would be well cared for, and under her daughter's immediate supervision during the whole of the time that she was occupied in the shop.

Philip's share of the business, augmented by the money which he had put in from the legacy of his old Cumberland uncle, would bring in profits enough to support Sylvia and her child in ease and comfort until that time, which they all anticipated, when he should return from his mysterious wandering—mysterious, whether his going forth had been voluntary or involuntary.

Thus far was settled; and Jeremiah Foster went to tell Sylvia of the plan.

She was too much a child, too entirely unaccustomed to any independence of action, to do anything but leave herself in his hands. Her very confession, made to him the day before, when she sought his counsel, seemed to place her at his disposal. Otherwise, she had had notions of the possibility of a free country life once more—how provided for and arranged she hardly knew; but Haytersbank was to let, and Kester disengaged, and it had just seemed possible that she might have to return to her early home, and to her old life. She knew that it would take much money to stock the farm again, and that her hands were tied from much useful activity by the love and care she owed to her baby. But still, somehow, she hoped and she fancied, till Jeremiah Foster's measured words and carefully-arranged plan made her silently relinquish her green, breezy vision.

Hester, too, had her own private rebellion—hushed into submission by her gentle piety. If Sylvia had been able to make Philip happy, Hester could have felt lovingly and almost gratefully towards her; but Sylvia had failed in this.

Philip had been made unhappy, and was driven forth a wanderer into the wide world—never to come back! And his last words to Hester, the postscript of his letter, containing the very pith of it, was to ask her to take charge and care of the wife whose want of love towards him had uprooted him from the place where he was valued and honoured.

It cost Hester many a struggle and many a self-reproach before she could make herself feel what she saw all along—that in everything Philip treated her like a sister. But even a sister might well be indignant if she saw her brother's love disregarded and slighted, and his life embittered by the thoughtless conduct of a wife! Still Hester fought against herself, and for Philip's sake she sought to see the good in Sylvia, and she strove to love her as well as to take care of her.

With the baby, of course, the case was different. Without thought or struggle, or reason, every one loved the little girl. Coulson and his buxom wife, who were childless, were never weary of making much of her. Hester's happiest hours were spent with that little child. Jeremiah Foster almost looked upon her as his own from the day when she honoured him by yielding to the temptation of the chain and seal, and coming to his knee; not a customer to the shop but knew the smiling child's sad history, and many a country-woman would save a rosy-cheeked apple from out her store that autumn to bring it on next market-day for 'Philip Hepburn's baby, as had lost its father, bless it.'

Even stern Alice Rose was graciously inclined towards the little Bella; and though her idea of the number of the elect was growing narrower and narrower every day, she would have been loth to exclude the innocent little child, that stroked her wrinkled cheeks so softly every night in return for her blessing, from the few that should be saved. Nay, for the child's sake, she relented towards the mother; and strove to have Sylvia rescued from the many castaways with fervent prayer, or, as she phrased it, 'wrestling with the Lord'.

Alice had a sort of instinct that the little child, so tenderly loved by, so fondly loving, the mother whose ewe-lamb she was, could not be even in heaven without yearning for the creature she had loved best on earth; and the old woman believed that this was the principal reason for her prayers for Sylvia; but unconsciously to herself, Alice Rose was touched by the filial attentions she constantly received from the young mother, whom she believed to be foredoomed to condemnation.

Sylvia rarely went to church or chapel, nor did she read her Bible; for though she spoke little of her ignorance, and would fain, for her child's sake, have remedied it now it was too late, she had lost what little fluency of reading she had ever had, and could only make out her words with much spelling and difficulty. So the taking her Bible in hand would have been a mere form; though of this Alice Rose knew nothing.

No one knew much of what was passing in Sylvia; she did not know herself. Sometimes in the nights she would waken, crying, with a terrible sense of desolation; every one who loved her, or whom she had loved, had vanished out of her life; every one but her child, who lay in her arms, warm and soft.

But then Jeremiah Foster's words came upon her; words that she had taken for cursing at the time; and she would so gladly have had some clue by which to penetrate the darkness of the unknown region from whence both blessing and cursing came, and to know if she had indeed done something which should cause her sin to be visited on that soft, sweet, innocent darling.

If any one would teach her to read! If any one would explain to her the hard words she heard in church or chapel, so that she might find out the meaning of sin and godliness!—words that had only passed over the surface of her mind till now! For her child's sake she should like to do the will of God, if she only knew what that was, and how to be worked out in her daily life.

But there was no one she dared confess her ignorance to and ask information from. Jeremiah Foster had spoken as if her child, sweet little merry Bella, with a loving word and a kiss for every one, was to suffer heavily for the just and true words her wronged and indignant mother had spoken. Alice always spoke as if there were no hope for her; and blamed her, nevertheless, for not using the means of grace that it was not in her power to avail herself of.

And Hester, that Sylvia would fain have loved for her uniform gentleness and patience with all around her, seemed so cold in her unruffled and undemonstrative behaviour; and moreover, Sylvia felt that Hester blamed her perpetual silence regarding Philip's absence without knowing how bitter a cause Sylvia had for casting him off.

The only person who seemed to have pity upon her was Kester; and his pity was shown in looks rather than words; for when he came to see her, which he did from time to time, by a kind of mutual tacit consent, they spoke but little of former days.

He was still lodging with his sister, widow Dobson, working at odd jobs, some of which took him into the country for weeks at a time. But on his returns to Monkshaven he was sure to come and see her and the little Bella; indeed, when his employment was in the immediate neighbourhood of the town, he never allowed a week to pass away without a visit.

There was not much conversation between him and Sylvia at such times. They skimmed over the surface of the small events in which both took an interest; only now and then a sudden glance, a checked speech, told each that there were deeps not forgotten, although they were never mentioned.

Twice Sylvia—below her breath—had asked Kester, just as she was holding the door open for his departure, if anything had ever been heard of Kinraid since his one night's visit to Monkshaven: each time (and there was an interval of some months between the inquiries) the answer had been simply, no.

To no one else would Sylvia ever have named his name. But indeed she had not the chance, had she wished it ever so much, of asking any questions about him from any one likely to know. The Corneys had left Moss Brow at Martinmas, and gone many miles away towards Horncastle. Bessy Corney, it is true was married and left behind in the neighbourhood; but with her Sylvia had never been intimate; and what girlish friendship there might have been between them had cooled very much at the time of Kinraid's supposed death three years before.

One day before Christmas in this year, 1798, Sylvia was called into the shop by Coulson, who, with his assistant, was busy undoing the bales of winter goods supplied to them from the West Riding, and other places. He was looking at a fine Irish poplin dress-piece when Sylvia answered to his call.

'Here! do you know this again?' asked he, in the cheerful tone of one sure of giving pleasure.

'No! have I iver seen it afore?'

'Not this, but one for all t' world like it.'

She did not rouse up to much interest, but looked at it as if trying to recollect where she could have seen its like.

'My missus had one on at th' party at John Foster's last March, and yo' admired it a deal. And Philip, he thought o' nothing but how he could get yo' just such another, and he set a vast o' folk agait for to meet wi' its marrow; and what he did just the very day afore he went away so mysterious was to write through Dawson Brothers, o' Wakefield, to Dublin, and order that one should be woven for yo'. Jemima had to cut a bit off hers for to give him t' exact colour.'

Sylvia did not say anything but that it was very pretty, in a low voice, and then she quickly left the shop, much to Coulson's displeasure.

All the afternoon she was unusually quiet and depressed.

Alice Rose, sitting helpless in her chair, watched her with keen eyes.

At length, after one of Sylvia's deep, unconscious sighs, the old woman spoke:

'It's religion as must comfort thee, child, as it's done many a one afore thee.'

'How?' said Sylvia, looking up, startled to find herself an object of notice.

'How?' (The answer was not quite so ready as the precept had been.) 'Read thy Bible, and thou wilt learn.'

'But I cannot read,' said Sylvia, too desperate any longer to conceal her ignorance.

'Not read! and thee Philip's wife as was such a great scholar! Of a surety the ways o' this life are crooked! There was our Hester, as can read as well as any minister, and Philip passes over her to go and choose a young lass as cannot read her Bible.'

'Was Philip and Hester——'

Sylvia paused, for though a new curiosity had dawned upon her, she did not know how to word her question.

'Many a time and oft have I seen Hester take comfort in her Bible when Philip was following after thee. She knew where to go for consolation.'

'I'd fain read,' said Sylvia, humbly, 'if anybody would learn me; for perhaps it might do me good; I'm noane so happy.'

Her eyes, as she looked up at Alice's stern countenance, were full of tears.

The old woman saw it, and was touched, although she did not immediately show her sympathy. But she took her own time, and made no reply.

The next day, however, she bade Sylvia come to her, and then and there, as if her pupil had been a little child, she began to teach Sylvia to read the first chapter of Genesis; for all other reading but the Scriptures was as vanity to her, and she would not condescend to the weakness of other books. Sylvia was now, as ever, slow at book-learning; but she was meek and desirous to be taught, and her willingness in this respect pleased Alice, and drew her singularly towards one who, from being a pupil, might become a convert.

All this time Sylvia never lost the curiosity that had been excited by the few words Alice had let drop about Hester and Philip, and by degrees she approached the subject again, and had the idea then started confirmed by Alice, who had no scruple in using the past experience of her own, of her daughter's, or of any one's life, as an instrument to prove the vanity of setting the heart on anything earthly.

This knowledge, unsuspected before, sank deep into Sylvia's thoughts, and gave her a strange interest in Hester—poor Hester, whose life she had so crossed and blighted, even by the very blighting of her own. She gave Hester her own former passionate feelings for Kinraid, and wondered how she herself should have felt towards any one who had come between her and him, and wiled his love away. When she remembered Hester's unfailing sweetness and kindness towards herself from the very first, she could better bear the comparative coldness of her present behaviour.

She tried, indeed, hard to win back the favour she had lost; but the very means she took were blunders, and only made it seem to her as if she could never again do right in Hester's eyes.

For instance, she begged her to accept and wear the pretty poplin gown which had been Philip's especial choice; feeling within herself as if she should never wish to put it on, and as if the best thing she could do with it was to offer it to Hester. But Hester rejected the proffered gift with as much hardness of manner as she was capable of assuming; and Sylvia had to carry it upstairs and lay it by for the little daughter, who, Hester said, might perhaps learn to value things that her father had given especial thought to.

Yet Sylvia went on trying to win Hester to like her once more; it was one of her great labours, and learning to read from Hester's mother was another.

Alice, indeed, in her solemn way, was becoming quite fond of Sylvia; if she could not read or write, she had a deftness and gentleness of motion, a capacity for the household matters which fell into her department, that had a great effect on the old woman, and for her dear mother's sake Sylvia had a stock of patient love ready in her heart for all the aged and infirm that fell in her way. She never thought of seeking them out, as she knew that Hester did; but then she looked up to Hester as some one very remarkable for her goodness. If only she could have liked her!

Hester tried to do all she could for Sylvia; Philip had told her to take care of his wife and child; but she had the conviction that Sylvia had so materially failed in her duties as to have made her husband an exile from his home—a penniless wanderer, wifeless and childless, in some strange country, whose very aspect was friendless, while the cause of all lived on in the comfortable home where he had placed her, wanting for nothing—an object of interest and regard to many friends—with a lovely little child to give her joy for the present, and hope for the future; while he, the poor outcast, might even lie dead by the wayside. How could Hester love Sylvia?

Yet they were frequent companions that ensuing spring. Hester was not well; and the doctors said that the constant occupation in the shop was too much for her, and that she must, for a time at least, take daily walks into the country.

Sylvia used to beg to accompany her; she and the little girl often went with Hester up the valley of the river to some of the nestling farms that were hidden in the more sheltered nooks—for Hester was bidden to drink milk warm from the cow; and to go into the familiar haunts about a farm was one of the few things in which Sylvia seemed to take much pleasure. She would let little Bella toddle about while Hester sate and rested: and she herself would beg to milk the cow destined to give the invalid her draught.

One May evening the three had been out on some such expedition; the country side still looked gray and bare, though the leaves were showing on the willow and blackthorn and sloe, and by the tinkling runnels, making hidden music along the copse side, the pale delicate primrose buds were showing amid their fresh, green, crinkled leaves. The larks had been singing all the afternoon, but were now dropping down into their nests in the pasture fields; the air had just the sharpness in it which goes along with a cloudless evening sky at that time of the year.

But Hester walked homewards slowly and languidly, speaking no word. Sylvia noticed this at first without venturing to speak, for Hester was one who disliked having her ailments noticed. But after a while Hester stood still in a sort of weary dreamy abstraction; and Sylvia said to her,

'I'm afeared yo're sadly tired. Maybe we've been too far.'

Hester almost started.

'No!' said she, 'it's only my headache which is worse to-night. It has been bad all day; but since I came out it has felt just as if there were great guns booming, till I could almost pray 'em to be quiet. I am so weary o' th' sound.'

She stepped out quickly towards home after she had said this, as if she wished for neither pity nor comment on what she had said.

CHAPTER XXXVIII

THE RECOGNITION

Far away, over sea and land, over sunny sea again, great guns were booming on that 7th of May, 1799.

The Mediterranean came up with a long roar on a beach glittering white with snowy sand, and the fragments of innumerable sea-shells, delicate and shining as porcelain. Looking at that shore from the sea, a long ridge of upland ground, beginning from an inland depth, stretched far away into the ocean on the right, till it ended in a great mountainous bluff, crowned with the white buildings of a convent sloping rapidly down into the blue water at its base.

In the clear eastern air, the different characters of the foliage that clothed the sides of that sea-washed mountain might be discerned from a long distance by the naked eye; the silver gray of the olive-trees near its summit; the heavy green and bossy forms of the sycamores lower down; broken here and there by a solitary terebinth or ilex tree, of a deeper green and a wider spread; till the eye fell below on the maritime plain, edged with the white seaboard and the sandy hillocks; with here and there feathery palm-trees, either isolated or in groups—motionless and distinct against the hot purple air.

Look again; a little to the left on the sea-shore there are the white walls of a fortified town, glittering in sunlight, or black in shadow.

The fortifications themselves run out into the sea, forming a port and a haven against the wild Levantine storms; and a lighthouse rises out of the waves to guide mariners into safety.

Beyond this walled city, and far away to the left still, there is the same wide plain shut in by the distant rising ground, till the upland circuit comes closing in to the north, and the great white rocks meet the deep tideless ocean with its intensity of blue colour.

Above, the sky is literally purple with heat; and the pitiless light smites the gazer's weary eye as it comes back from the white shore. Nor does the plain country in that land offer the refuge and rest of our own soft green. The limestone rock underlies the vegetation, and gives a glittering, ashen hue to all the bare patches, and even to the cultivated parts which are burnt up early in the year. In spring-time alone does the country look rich and fruitful; then the corn-fields of the plain show their capability of bearing, 'some fifty, some an hundred fold'; down by the brook Kishon, flowing not far from the base of the mountainous promontory to the south, there grow the broad green fig-trees, cool and fresh to look upon; the orchards are full of glossy-leaved cherry-trees; the tall amaryllis puts forth crimson and yellow glories in the fields, rivalling the pomp of King Solomon; the daisies and the hyacinths spread their myriad flowers; the anemones, scarlet as blood, run hither and thither over the ground like dazzling flames of fire.

A spicy odour lingers in the heated air; it comes from the multitude of aromatic flowers that blossom in the early spring. Later on they will have withered and faded, and the corn will have been gathered, and the deep green of the eastern foliage will have assumed a kind of gray-bleached tint.

Even now in May, the hot sparkle of the everlasting sea, the terribly clear outline of all objects, whether near or distant, the fierce sun right overhead, the dazzling air around, were inexpressibly wearying to the English eyes that kept their skilled watch, day and night, on the strongly-fortified coast-town that lay out a little to the northward of where the British ships were anchored.

They had kept up a flanking fire for many days in aid of those besieged in St Jean d'Acre; and at intervals had listened, impatient, to the sound of the heavy siege guns, or the sharper rattle of the French musketry.

In the morning, on the 7th of May, a man at the masthead of the *Tigre* sang out that he saw ships in the offing; and in reply to the signal that was hastily run up, he saw the distant vessels hoist friendly flags. That May morning was a busy time. The besieged Turks took heart of grace; the French outside, under the command of their great general, made hasty preparations for a more vigorous assault than all many, both vigorous and bloody, that had gone before (for the siege was now at its fifty-first day), in hopes of carrying the town by storm before the reinforcement coming by sea could arrive; and Sir Sidney Smith, aware of Buonaparte's desperate intention, ordered all the men, both sailors and marines, that could be spared from the necessity of keeping up a continual flanking fire from the ships upon the French, to land, and assist the Turks and the British forces already there in the defence of the old historic city.

Lieutenant Kinraid, who had shared his captain's daring adventure off the coast of France three years before, who had been a prisoner with him and Westley Wright, in the Temple at Paris, and had escaped with them, and, through Sir Sidney's earnest recommendation, been promoted from being a warrant officer to the rank of lieutenant, received on this day the honour from his admiral of being appointed to an especial post of danger. His heart was like a war-horse, and said, Ha, ha! as the boat bounded over the waves that were to land him under the ancient machicolated walls where the Crusaders made their last stand in the Holy Land. Not that Kinraid knew or cared one jot about those gallant knights of old: all he knew was, that the French, under Boney, were trying to take the town from the Turks, and that his admiral said they must not, and so they should not.

He and his men landed on that sandy shore, and entered the town by the water-port gate; he was singing to himself his own country song,—

Weel may the keel row, the keel row, &C.

and his men, with sailors' aptitude for music, caught up the air, and joined in the burden with inarticulate sounds.

So, with merry hearts, they threaded the narrow streets of Acre, hemmed in on either side by the white walls of Turkish houses, with small grated openings high up, above all chance of peeping intrusion.

Here and there they met an ample-robed and turbaned Turk going along with as much haste as his stately self-possession would allow. But the majority of the male inhabitants were gathered together to defend the breach, where the French guns thundered out far above the heads of the sailors.

They went along none the less merrily for the sound to Djezzar Pacha's garden, where the old Turk sate on his carpet, beneath the shade of a great terebinth tree, listening to the interpreter, who made known to him the meaning of the eager speeches of Sir Sidney Smith and the colonel of the marines.

As soon as the admiral saw the gallant sailors of H.M.S. *Tigre*, he interrupted the council of war without much ceremony, and going to Kinraid, he despatched them, as before arranged, to the North Ravelin, showing them the way with rapid, clear directions.

Out of respect to him, they had kept silent while in the strange, desolate garden; but once more in the streets, the old Newcastle song rose up again till the men were, perforce, silenced by the haste with which they went to the post of danger.

It was three o'clock in the afternoon. For many a day these very men had been swearing at the terrific heat at this hour—even when at sea, fanned by the soft breeze; but now, in the midst of hot smoke, with former carnage tainting the air, and with the rush and whizz of death perpetually whistling in their ears, they were uncomplaining and light-hearted. Many an old joke, and some new ones, came brave and hearty, on their cheerful voices, even though the speaker was veiled from sight in great clouds of smoke, cloven only by the bright flames of death.

A sudden message came; as many of the crew of the *Tigre* as were under Lieutenant Kinraid's command were to go down to the Mole, to assist the new reinforcements (seen by the sailor from the masthead at day-dawn), under command of Hassan Bey, to land at the Mole, where Sir Sidney then was.

Off they went, almost as bright and thoughtless as before, though two of their number lay silent for ever at the North Ravelin—silenced in that one little half-hour. And one went along with the rest, swearing lustily at his ill-luck in having his right arm broken, but ready to do good business with his left.

They helped the Turkish troops to land more with good-will than tenderness; and then, led by Sir Sidney, they went under the shelter of English guns to the fatal breach, so often assailed, so gallantly defended, but never so fiercely contested as on this burning afternoon. The ruins of the massive wall that here had been broken down by the French, were used by them as stepping stones to get on a level with the besieged, and so to escape the heavy stones which the latter hurled down; nay, even the dead bodies of the morning's comrades were made into ghastly stairs.

When Djezzar Pacha heard that the British sailors were defending the breach, headed by Sir Sidney Smith, he left his station in the palace garden, gathered up his robes in haste, and hurried to the breach; where, with his own hands, and with right hearty good-will, he pulled the sailors down from the post of danger, saying that if he lost his English friends he lost all!

But little recked the crew of the *Tigre* of the one old man—Pacha or otherwise—who tried to hold them back from the fight; they were up and at the French assailants clambering over the breach in an instant; and so they went on, as if it were some game at play instead of a deadly combat, until Kinraid and his men were called off by Sir Sidney, as the reinforcement of Turkish troops under Hassan Bey were now sufficient for the defence of that old breach in the walls, which was no longer the principal object of the French attack; for the besiegers had made a new and more formidable breach by their incessant fire, knocking down whole streets of the city walls.

'Fight your best Kinraid!' said Sir Sidney; 'for there's Boney on yonder hill looking at you.'

And sure enough, on a rising ground, called Richard Coeur de Lion's Mount, there was a half-circle of French generals, on horseback, all deferentially attending to the motions, and apparently to the words, of a little man in their centre; at whose bidding the aide-de-camp galloped swift with messages to the more distant French camp.

The two ravelins which Kinraid and his men had to occupy, for the purpose of sending a flanking fire upon the enemy, were not ten yards from that enemy's van.

But at length there was a sudden rush of the French to that part of the wall where they imagined they could enter unopposed.

Surprised at this movement, Kinraid ventured out of the shelter of the ravelin to ascertain the cause; he, safe and untouched during that long afternoon of carnage, fell now, under a stray musket-shot, and lay helpless and exposed upon the ground undiscerned by his men, who were recalled to help in the hot reception which had been planned for the French; who, descending the city walls into the Pacha's garden, were attacked with sabre and dagger, and lay headless corpses under the flowering rose-bushes, and by the fountain side.

Kinraid lay beyond the ravelins, many yards outside the city walls.

He was utterly helpless, for the shot had broken his leg. Dead bodies of Frenchmen lay strewn around him; no Englishman had ventured out so far.

All the wounded men that he could see were French; and many of these, furious with pain, gnashed their teeth at him, and cursed him aloud, till he thought that his best course was to assume the semblance of death; for some among these men were still capable of dragging themselves up to him, and by concentrating all their failing energies into one blow, put him to a speedy end.

The outlying pickets of the French army were within easy rifle shot; and his uniform, although less conspicuous in colour than that of the marines, by whose sides he had been fighting, would make him a sure mark if he so much as moved his arm. Yet how he longed to turn, if ever so slightly, so that the cruel slanting sun might not beat full into his aching eyes. Fever, too, was coming upon him; the pain in his leg was every moment growing more severe; the terrible thirst of the wounded, added to the heat and fatigue of the day, made his lips and tongue feel baked and dry, and his whole throat seemed parched and wooden. Thoughts of other days, of cool Greenland seas, where ice abounded, of grassy English homes, began to make the past more real than the present.

With a great effort he brought his wandering senses back; he knew where he was now, and could weigh the chances of his life, which were but small; the unwonted tears came to his eyes as he thought of the newly-made wife in her English home, who might never know how he died thinking of her.

Suddenly he saw a party of English marines advance, under shelter of the ravelin, to pick up the wounded, and bear them within the walls for surgical help. They were so near he could see their faces, could hear them speak; yet he durst not make any sign to them when he lay within range of the French picket's fire.

For one moment he could not resist raising his head, to give himself a chance for life; before the unclean creatures that infest a camp came round in the darkness of the night to strip and insult the dead bodies, and to put to death such as had yet the breath of life within them. But the setting sun came full into his face, and he saw nothing of what he longed to see.

He fell back in despair; he lay there to die.

That strong clear sunbeam had wrought his salvation.

He had been recognized as men are recognized when they stand in the red glare of a house on fire; the same despair of help, of hopeless farewell to life, stamped on their faces in blood-red light.

One man left his fellows, and came running forwards, forwards in among the enemy's wounded, within range of their guns; he bent down over Kinraid; he seemed to understand without a word; he lifted him up, carrying him like a child; and with the vehement energy that is more from the force of will than the strength of body, he bore him back to within the shelter of the ravelin—not without many shots being aimed at them, one of which hit Kinraid in the fleshy part of his arm.

Kinraid was racked with agony from his dangling broken leg, and his very life seemed leaving him; yet he remembered afterwards how the marine recalled his fellows, and how, in the pause before they returned, his face became like one formerly known to the sick senses of Kinraid; yet it was too like a dream, too utterly improbable to be real.

Yet the few words this man said, as he stood breathless and alone by the fainting Kinraid, fitted in well with the belief conjured up by his personal appearance. He panted out,—

'I niver thought you'd ha' kept true to her!'

And then the others came up; and while they were making a sling of their belts, Kinraid fainted utterly away, and the next time that he was fully conscious, he was lying in his berth in the *Tigre*, with the ship surgeon setting his leg. After that he was too feverish for several days to collect his senses. When he could first remember, and form a judgment upon his recollections, he called the man especially charged to attend upon him, and bade him go and make inquiry in every possible manner for a marine named Philip Hepburn, and, when he was found, to entreat him to come and see Kinraid.

The sailor was away the greater part of the day, and returned unsuccessful in his search; he had been from ship to ship, hither and thither; he had questioned all the marines he had met with, no one knew anything of any Philip Hepburn.

Kinraid passed a miserably feverish night, and when the doctor exclaimed the next morning at his retrogression, he told him, with some irritation, of the ill-success of his servant; he accused the man of stupidity, and wished fervently that he were able to go himself.

Partly to soothe him, the doctor promised that he would undertake the search for Hepburn, and he engaged faithfully to follow all Kinraid's eager directions; not to be satisfied with men's careless words, but to look over muster-rolls and ships' books.

He, too, brought the same answer, however unwillingly given.

He had set out upon the search so confident of success, that he felt doubly discomfited by failure. However, he had persuaded himself that the lieutenant had been partially delirious from the effects of his wound, and the power of the sun shining down just where he lay. There had, indeed, been slight symptoms of Kinraid's having received a sun-stroke; and the doctor dwelt largely on these in his endeavour to persuade his patient that it was his imagination which had endued a stranger with the lineaments of some former friend.

Kinraid threw his arms out of bed with impatience at all this plausible talk, which was even more irritating than the fact that Hepburn was still undiscovered.

'The man was no friend of mine; I was like to have killed him when last I saw him. He was a shopkeeper in a country town in England. I had seen little enough of him; but enough to make me able to swear to him anywhere, even in a marine's uniform, and in this sweltering country.'

'Faces once seen, especially in excitement, are apt to return upon the memory in cases of fever,' quoth the doctor, sententiously.

The attendant sailor, reinstalled to some complacency by the failure of another in the search in which he himself had been unsuccessful, now put in his explanation.

'Maybe it was a spirit. It's not th' first time as I've heared of a spirit coming upon earth to save a man's life i' time o' need. My father had an uncle, a west-country grazier. He was a-coming over Dartmoor in Devonshire one moonlight night with a power o' money as he'd got for his sheep at t' fair. It were stowed i' leather bags under th' seat o' th' gig. It were a rough kind o' road, both as a road and in character, for there'd been many robberies there of late, and th' great rocks stood convenient for hiding-places. All at once father's uncle feels as if some one were sitting beside him on th' empty seat; and he turns his head and looks, and there he sees his brother sitting—his brother as had been dead twelve year and more. So he turns his head back again, eyes right, and never say a word, but wonders what it all means. All of a sudden two fellows come out upo' th' white road from some black shadow, and they looked, and they let th' gig go past, father's uncle driving hard, I'll warrant him. But for all that he heard one say to t' other, "By——, there's *two* on 'em!" Straight on he drove faster than ever, till he saw th' far lights of some town or other. I forget its name, though I've heared it many a time; and then he drew a long breath, and turned his head to look at his brother, and ask him how he'd managed to come out of his grave i' Barum churchyard, and th' seat was as empty as it had been when he set out; and then he knew that it were a spirit come to help him against th' men who thought to rob him, and would likely enough ha' murdered him.'

Kinraid had kept quiet through this story. But when the sailor began to draw the moral, and to say, 'And I think I may make bold to say, sir, as th' marine who carried you out o' th' Frenchy's gun-shot was just a spirit come to help you,' he exclaimed impatiently, swearing a great oath as he did so, 'It was no spirit, I tell you; and I was in my full senses. It was a man named Philip Hepburn. He said words to me, or over me, as none but himself would have said. Yet we hated each other like poison; and I can't make out why he should be there and putting himself in danger to save me. But so it was; and as you can't find him, let me hear no more of your nonsense. It was him, and not my fancy, doctor. It was flesh and blood, and not a spirit, Jack. So get along with you, and leave me quiet.'

All this time Stephen Freeman lay friendless, sick, and shattered, on board the *Thesus*.

He had been about his duty close to some shells that were placed on her deck; a gay young midshipman was thoughtlessly striving to get the fusee out of one of these by a mallet and spike-nail that lay close at hand; and a fearful explosion ensued, in which the poor marine, cleaning his bayonet near, was shockingly burnt and disfigured, the very skin of all the lower part of his face being utterly destroyed by gunpowder. They said it was a mercy that his eyes were spared; but he could hardly feel anything to be a mercy, as he lay tossing in agony, burnt by the explosion, wounded by splinters, and feeling that he was disabled for life, if life itself were preserved. Of all that suffered by that fearful accident (and they were many) none was so forsaken, so hopeless, so desolate, as the Philip Hepburn about whom such anxious inquiries were being made at that very time.

CHAPTER XXXIX

CONFIDENCES

It was a little later on in that same summer that Mrs. Brunton came to visit her sister Bessy.

Bessy was married to a tolerably well-to-do farmer who lived at an almost equal distance between Monkshaven and Hartswell; but from old habit and convenience the latter was regarded as the Dawsons' market-town; so Bessy seldom or never saw her old friends in Monkshaven.

But Mrs. Brunton was far too flourishing a person not to speak out her wishes, and have her own way. She had no notion, she said, of coming such a long journey only to see Bessy and her husband, and not to have a sight of her former acquaintances at Monkshaven. She might have added, that her new bonnet and cloak would be as good as lost if it was not displayed among those who, knowing her as Molly Corney, and being less fortunate in matrimony than she was, would look upon it with wondering admiration, if not with envy.

So one day farmer Dawson's market-cart deposited Mrs. Brunton in all her bravery at the shop in the market-place, over which Hepburn and Coulson's names still flourished in joint partnership.

After a few words of brisk recognition to Coulson and Hester, Mrs Brunton passed on into the parlour and greeted Sylvia with boisterous heartiness.

It was now four years and more since the friends had met; and each secretly wondered how they had ever come to be friends. Sylvia had a country, raw, spiritless look to Mrs. Brunton's eye; Molly was loud and talkative, and altogether distasteful to Sylvia, trained in daily companionship with Hester to appreciate soft slow speech, and grave thoughtful ways.

However, they kept up the forms of their old friendship, though their hearts had drifted far apart. They sat hand in hand while each looked at the other with eyes inquisitive as to the changes which time had made. Molly was the first to speak.

'Well, to be sure! how thin and pale yo've grown, Sylvia! Matrimony hasn't agreed wi' yo' as well as it's done wi me. Brunton is allays saying (yo' know what a man he is for his joke) that if he'd ha' known how many yards o' silk I should ha' ta'en for a gown, he'd ha' thought twice afore he'd ha' married me. Why, I've gained a matter o' thirty pound o' flesh sin' I were married!'

'Yo' do look brave and hearty!' said Sylvia, putting her sense of her companion's capacious size and high colour into the prettiest words she could.

'Eh! Sylvia! but I know what it is,' said Molly, shaking her head. 'It's just because o' that husband o' thine as has gone and left thee; thou's pining after him, and he's not worth it. Brunton said, when he heared on it—I mind he was smoking at t' time, and he took his pipe out of his mouth, and shook out t' ashes as grave as any judge—"The man," says he, "as can desert a wife like Sylvia Robson as was, deserves hanging!" That's what he says! Eh! Sylvia, but speakin' o' hanging I was so grieved for yo' when I heared of yo'r poor feyther! Such an end for a decent man to come to! Many a one come an' called on me o' purpose to hear all I could tell 'em about him!'

'Please don't speak on it!' said Sylvia, trembling all over.

'Well, poor creature, I wunnot. It is hard on thee, I grant. But to give t' devil his due, it were good i' Hepburn to marry thee, and so soon after there was a' that talk about thy feyther. Many a man would ha' drawn back, choose howiver far they'd gone. I'm noane so sure about Charley Kinraid. Eh, Sylvia! only think on his being alive after all. I doubt if our Bessy would ha' wed Frank Dawson if she'd known as he wasn't drowned. But it's as well she did, for Dawson's a man o' property, and has gotten twelve cows in his cow-house, beside three right down good horses; and Kinraid were allays a fellow wi' two strings to his bow. I've allays said and do maintain, that he went on pretty strong wi' yo', Sylvie; and I will say I think he cared more for yo' than for our Bessy, though it were only yesterday at e'en she were standing out that he liked her better than yo'. Yo'll ha' heared on his grand marriage?'

'No!' said Sylvia, with eager painful curiosity.

'No! It was in all t' papers! I wonder as yo' didn't see it. Wait a minute! I cut it out o' t' *Gentleman's Magazine*, as Brunton bought o' purpose, and put it i' my pocket-book when I were a-coming here: I know I've got it somewheere.'

She took out her smart crimson pocket-book, and rummaged in the pocket until she produced a little crumpled bit of printed paper, from which she read aloud,

'On January the third, at St Mary Redcliffe, Bristol, Charles Kinraid, Esq., lieutenant Royal Navy, to Miss Clarinda Jackson, with a fortune of 10,000*l.*'

'Theere!' said she, triumphantly, 'it's something as Brunton says, to be cousin to that.'

'Would yo' let me see it?' said Sylvia, timidly.

Mrs. Brunton graciously consented; and Sylvia brought her newly acquired reading-knowledge, hitherto principally exercised on the Old Testament, to bear on these words.

There was nothing wonderful in them, nothing that she might not have expected; and yet the surprise turned her giddy for a moment or two. She never thought of seeing him again, never. But to think of his caring for another woman as much as he had done for her, nay, perhaps more!

The idea was irresistibly forced upon her that Philip would not have acted so; it would have taken long years before he could have been induced to put another on the throne she had once occupied. For the first time in her life she seemed to recognize the real nature of Philip's love.

But she said nothing but 'Thank yo',' when she gave the scrap of paper back to Molly Brunton. And the latter continued giving her information about Kinraid's marriage.

'He were down in t' west, Plymouth or somewheere, when he met wi' her. She's no feyther; he'd been in t' sugar-baking business; but from what Kinraid wrote to old Turner, th' uncle as brought him up at Cullercoats, she's had t' best of edications: can play on t' instrument and dance t' shawl dance; and Kinraid had all her money settled on her, though she said she'd rayther give it all to him, which I must say, being his cousin, was very pretty on her. He's left her now, having to go off in t' *Tigre*, as is his ship, to t' Mediterranean seas; and she's written to offer to come and see old Turner, and make friends with his relations, and Brunton is going to gi'e me a crimson satin as soon as we know for certain when she's coming, for we're sure to be asked out to Cullercoats.'

'I wonder if she's very pretty?' asked Sylvia, faintly, in the first pause in this torrent of talk.

'Oh! she's a perfect beauty, as I understand. There was a traveller as come to our shop as had been at York, and knew some of her cousins theere that were in t' grocery line—her mother was a York lady—and they said she was just a picture of a woman, and iver so many gentlemen had been wantin' to marry her, but she just waited for Charley Kinraid, yo' see!'

'Well, I hope they'll be happy; I'm sure I do!' said Sylvia.

'That's just luck. Some folks is happy i' marriage, and some isn't. It's just luck, and there's no forecasting it. Men is such unaccountable animals, there's no prophesyin' upon 'em. Who'd ha' thought of yo'r husband, him as was so slow and sure—steady Philip, as we lasses used to ca' him—makin' a moonlight flittin', and leavin' yo' to be a widow bewitched?'

'He didn't go at night,' said Sylvia, taking the words 'moonlight flitting' in their literal sense.

'No! Well, I only said "moonlight flittin'" just because it come uppermost and I knowed no better. Tell me all about it, Sylvie, for I can't mak' it out from what Bessy says. Had he and yo' had words?—but in course yo' had.'

At this moment Hester came into the room; and Sylvia joyfully availed herself of the pretext for breaking off the conversation that had reached this painful and awkward point. She detained Hester in the room for fear lest Mrs. Brunton should repeat her inquiry as to how it all happened that Philip had gone away; but the presence of a third person seemed as though it would be but little restraint upon the inquisitive Molly, who repeatedly bore down upon the same questions till she nearly drove Sylvia distracted, between her astonishment at the news of Kinraid's marriage; her wish to be alone and quiet, so as to realize the full meaning of that piece of intelligence; her desire to retain Hester in the conversation; her efforts to prevent Molly's recurrence to the circumstances of Philip's disappearance, and the longing—more vehement every minute—for her visitor to go away and leave her in peace. She became so disturbed with all these thoughts and feelings that she hardly knew what she was saying, and assented or dissented to speeches without there being either any reason or truth in her words.

Mrs. Brunton had arranged to remain with Sylvia while the horse rested, and had no compunction about the length of her visit. She expected to be asked to tea, as Sylvia found out at last, and this she felt would be the worst of all, as Alice Rose was not one to tolerate the coarse, careless talk of such a woman as Mrs. Brunton without uplifting her voice in many a testimony against it. Sylvia sate holding Hester's gown tight in order to prevent her leaving the room, and trying to arrange her little plans so that too much discordance should not arise to the surface. Just then the door opened, and little Bella came in from the kitchen in all the pretty, sturdy dignity of two years old, Alice following her with careful steps, and protecting, outstretched arms, a slow smile softening the sternness of her grave face; for the child was the unconscious darling of the household, and all eyes softened into love as they looked on her. She made straight for her mother with something grasped in her little dimpled fist; but half-way across the room she seemed to have become suddenly aware of the presence of a stranger, and she stopped short, fixing her serious eyes full on Mrs. Brunton, as if to take in her appearance, nay, as if to penetrate down into her very real self, and then, stretching out her disengaged hand, the baby spoke out the words that had been hovering about her mother's lips for an hour past.

'Do away!' said Bella, decisively.

'What a perfect love!' said Mrs. Brunton, half in real admiration, half in patronage. As she spoke, she got up and went towards the child, as if to take her up.

'Do away! do away!' cried Bella, in shrill affright at this movement.

'Dunnot,' said Sylvia; 'she's shy; she doesn't know strangers.'

But Mrs. Brunton had grasped the struggling, kicking child by this time, and her reward for this was a vehement little slap in the face.

'Yo' naughty little spoilt thing!' said she, setting Bella down in a hurry. 'Yo' deserve a good whipping, yo' do, and if yo' were mine yo' should have it.'

Sylvia had no need to stand up for the baby who had run to her arms, and was soothing herself with sobbing on her mother's breast; for Alice took up the defence.

'The child said, as plain as words could say, "go away," and if thou wouldst follow thine own will instead of heeding her wish, thou mun put up with the wilfulness of the old Adam, of which it seems to me thee hast getten thy share at thirty as well as little Bella at two.'

'Thirty!' said Mrs. Brunton, now fairly affronted. 'Thirty! why, Sylvia, yo' know I'm but two years older than yo'; speak to that woman an' tell her as I'm only four-and-twenty. Thirty, indeed!'

'Molly's but four-and-twenty,' said Sylvia, in a pacificatory tone.

'Whether she be twenty, or thirty, or forty, is alike to me,' said Alice. 'I meant no harm. I meant but for t' say as her angry words to the child bespoke her to be one of the foolish. I know not who she is, nor what her age may be.'

'She's an old friend of mine,' said Sylvia. 'She's Mrs. Brunton now, but when I knowed her she was Molly Corney.'

'Ay! and yo' were Sylvia Robson, and as bonny and light-hearted a lass as any in a' t' Riding, though now yo're a poor widow bewitched, left wi' a child as I mustn't speak a word about, an' living wi' folk as talk about t' old Adam as if he wasn't dead and done wi' long ago! It's a change, Sylvia, as makes my heart ache for yo', to think on them old days when yo' were so thought on yo' might have had any man, as Brunton often says; it were a great mistake as yo' iver took up wi' yon man as has run away. But seven year '11 soon be past fro' t' time he went off, and yo'll only be six-and-twenty then; and there'll be a chance of a better husband for yo' after all, so keep up yo'r heart, Sylvia.'

Molly Brunton had put as much venom as she knew how into this speech, meaning it as a vengeful payment for the supposition of her being thirty, even more than for the reproof for her angry words about the child. She thought that Alice Rose must be either mother or aunt to Philip, from the serious cast of countenance that was remarkable in both; and she rather exulted in the allusion to a happier second marriage for Sylvia, with which she had concluded her speech. It roused Alice, however, as effectually as if she had been really a blood relation to Philip; but for a different reason. She was not slow to detect the intentional offensiveness to herself in what had been said; she was indignant at Sylvia for suffering the words spoken to pass unanswered; but in truth they were too much in keeping with Molly Brunton's character to make as much impression on Sylvia as they did on a stranger; and besides, she felt as if the less reply Molly received, the less likely would it be that she would go on in the same strain. So she coaxed and chattered to her child and behaved like a little coward in trying to draw out of the conversation, while at the same time listening attentively.

'As for Sylvia Hepburn as was Sylvia Robson, she knows my mind,' said Alice, in grim indignation. 'She's humbling herself now, I trust and pray, but she was light-minded and full of vanity when Philip married her, and it might ha' been a lift towards her salvation in one way; but it pleased the Lord to work in a different way, and she mun wear her sackcloth and ashes in patience. So I'll say naught more about her. But for him as is absent, as thee hast spoken on so lightly and reproachfully, I'd have thee to know he were one of a different kind to any thee ever knew, I reckon. If he were led away by a pretty face to slight one as was fitter for him, and who had loved him as the apple of her eye, it's him as is suffering for it, inasmuch as he's a wanderer from his home, and an outcast from wife and child.'

To the surprise of all, Molly's words of reply were cut short even when they were on her lips, by Sylvia. Pale, fire-eyed, and excited, with Philip's child on one arm, and the other stretched out, she said,—

'Noane can tell—noane know. No one shall speak a judgment 'twixt Philip and me. He acted cruel and wrong by me. But I've said my words to him hissel', and I'm noane going to make any plaint to others; only them as knows should judge. And it's not fitting, it's not' (almost sobbing), 'to go on wi' talk like this afore me.'

The two—for Hester, who was aware that her presence had only been desired by Sylvia as a check to an unpleasant *tete-a-tete* conversation, had slipped back to her business as soon as her mother came in—the two looked with surprise at Sylvia; her words, her whole manner, belonged to a phase of her character which seldom came uppermost, and which had not been perceived by either of them before.

Alice Rose, though astonished, rather approved of Sylvia's speech; it showed that she had more serious thought and feeling on the subject than the old woman had given her credit for; her general silence respecting her husband's disappearance had led Alice to think that she was too childish to have received any deep impression from the event. Molly Brunton gave vent to her opinion on Sylvia's speech in the following words:—

'Hoighty-toighty! That tells tales, lass. If yo' treated steady Philip to many such looks an' speeches as yo'n given us now, it's easy t' see why he took hisself off. Why, Sylvia, I niver saw it in yo' when yo' was a girl; yo're grown into a regular little vixen, theere wheere yo' stand!'

Indeed she did look defiant, with the swift colour flushing her cheeks to crimson on its return, and the fire in her eyes not yet died away. But at Molly's jesting words she sank back into her usual look and manner, only saying quietly,—

'It's for noane to say whether I'm vixen or not, as doesn't know th' past things as is buried in my heart. But I cannot hold them as my friends as go on talking on either my husband or me before my very face. What he was, I know; and what I am, I reckon he knows. And now I'll go hurry tea, for yo'll be needing it, Molly!'

The last clause of this speech was meant to make peace; but Molly was in twenty minds as to whether she should accept the olive-branch or not. Her temper, however, was of that obtuse kind which is not easily ruffled; her mind, stagnant in itself, enjoyed excitement from without; and her appetite was invariably good, so she stayed, in spite of the inevitable *tete-a-tete* with Alice. The latter, however, refused to be drawn into conversation again; replying to Mrs. Brunton's speeches with a curt yes or no, when, indeed, she replied at all.

When all were gathered at tea, Sylvia was quite calm again; rather paler than usual, and very attentive and subduced in her behaviour to Alice; she would evidently fain have been silent, but as Molly was her own especial guest, that could not be, so all her endeavours went towards steering the conversation away from any awkward points. But each of the four, let alone little Bella, was thankful when the market-cart drew up at the shop door, that was to take Mrs. Brunton back to her sister's house.

When she was fairly off, Alice Rose opened her mouth in strong condemnation; winding up with—

'And if aught in my words gave thee cause for offence, Sylvia, it was because my heart rose within me at the kind of talk thee and she had been having about Philip; and her evil and light-minded counsel to thee about waiting seven years, and then wedding another.'

Hard as these words may seem when repeated, there was something of a nearer approach to an apology in Mrs. Rose's manner than Sylvia had ever seen in it before. She was silent for a few moments, then she said,—

'I ha' often thought of telling yo' and Hester, special-like, when yo've been so kind to my little Bella, that Philip an' me could niver come together again; no, not if he came home this very night——'

She would have gone on speaking, but Hester interrupted her with a low cry of dismay.

Alice said,—

'Hush thee, Hester. It's no business o' thine. Sylvia Hepburn, thou'rt speaking like a silly child.'

'No. I'm speaking like a woman; like a woman as finds out she's been cheated by men as she trusted, and as has no help for it. I'm noane going to say any more about it. It's me as has been wronged, and as has to bear it: only I thought I'd tell yo' both this much, that yo' might know somewhat why he went away, and how I said my last word about it.'

So indeed it seemed. To all questions and remonstrances from Alice, Sylvia turned a deaf ear. She averted her face from Hester's sad, wistful looks; only when they were parting for the night, at the top of the little staircase, she turned, and putting her arms round Hester's neck she laid her head on her neck, and whispered,—

'Poor Hester—poor, poor Hester! if yo' an' he had but been married together, what a deal o' sorrow would ha' been spared to us all!'

Hester pushed her away as she finished these words; looked searchingly into her face, her eyes, and then followed Sylvia into her room, where Bella lay sleeping, shut the door, and almost knelt down at Sylvia's feet, clasping her, and hiding her face in the folds of the other's gown.

'Sylvia, Sylvia,' she murmured, 'some one has told you—I thought no one knew—it's no sin—it's done away with now—indeed it is—it was long ago—before yo' were married; but I cannot forget. It was a shame, perhaps, to have thought on it iver, when he niver thought o' me; but I niver believed as any one could ha' found it out. I'm just fit to sink into t' ground, what wi' my sorrow and my shame.'

Hester was stopped by her own rising sobs, immediately she was in Sylvia's arms. Sylvia was sitting on the ground holding her, and soothing her with caresses and broken words.

'I'm allays saying t' wrong things,' said she. 'It seems as if I were all upset to-day; and indeed I am;' she added, alluding to the news of Kinraid's marriage she had yet to think upon.

'But it wasn't yo', Hester: it were nothing yo' iver said, or did, or looked, for that matter. It were yo'r mother as let it out.'

'Oh, mother! mother!' wailed out Hester; 'I niver thought as any one but God would ha' known that I had iver for a day thought on his being more to me than a brother.'

Sylvia made no reply, only went on stroking Hester's smooth brown hair, off which her cap had fallen. Sylvia was thinking how strange life was, and how love seemed to go all at cross purposes; and was losing herself in bewilderment at the mystery of the world; she was almost startled when Hester rose up, and taking Sylvia's hands in both of hers, and looking solemnly at her, said,—

'Sylvia, yo' know what has been my trouble and my shame, and I'm sure yo're sorry for me—for I will humble myself to yo', and own that for many months before yo' were married, I felt my disappointment like a heavy burden laid on me by day and by night; but now I ask yo', if yo've any pity for me for what I went through, or if yo've any love for me because of yo'r dead mother's love for me, or because of any fellowship, or daily breadliness between us two,—put the hard thoughts of Philip away from out yo'r heart; he may ha' done yo' wrong, anyway yo' think that he has; I niver knew him aught but kind and good; but if he comes back from wheriver in th' wide world he's gone to (and there's not a night but I pray God to keep him, and send him safe back), yo' put away the memory of past injury, and forgive it all, and be, what yo' can be, Sylvia, if you've a mind to, just the kind, good wife he ought to have.'

'I cannot; yo' know nothing about it, Hester.'

'Tell me, then,' pleaded Hester.

'No!' said Sylvia, after a moment's hesitation; 'I'd do a deal for yo', I would, but I daren't forgive Philip, even if I could; I took a great oath again' him. Ay, yo' may look shocked at me, but it's him as yo' ought for to be shocked at if yo' knew all. I said I'd niver forgive him; I shall keep to my word.'

'I think I'd better pray for his death, then,' said Hester, hopelessly, and almost bitterly, loosing her hold of Sylvia's hands.

'If it weren't for baby theere, I could think as it were my death as 'ud be best. Them as one thinks t' most on, forgets one soonest.'

It was Kinraid to whom she was alluding; but Hester did not understand her; and after standing for a moment in silence, she kissed her, and left her for the night.

CHAPTER XL

AN UNEXPECTED MESSENGER

After this agitation, and these partial confidences, no more was said on the subject of Philip for many weeks. They avoided even the slightest allusion to him; and none of them knew how seldom or how often he might be present in the minds of the others.

One day the little Bella was unusually fractious with some slight childish indisposition, and Sylvia was obliged to have recourse to a never-failing piece of amusement; namely, to take the child into the shop, when the number of new, bright-coloured articles was sure to beguile the little girl out of her fretfulness. She was walking along the high terrace of the counter, kept steady by her mother's hand, when Mr. Dawson's market-cart once more stopped before the door. But it was not Mrs. Brunton who alighted now; it was a very smartly-dressed, very pretty young lady, who put one dainty foot before the other with care, as if descending from such a primitive vehicle were a new occurrence in her life. Then she looked up at the names above the shop-door, and after ascertaining that this was indeed the place she desired to find, she came in blushing.

'Is Mrs. Hepburn at home?' she asked of Hester, whose position in the shop brought her forwards to receive the customers, while Sylvia drew Bella out of sight behind some great bales of red flannel.

'Can I see her?' the sweet, south-country voice went on, still addressing Hester. Sylvia heard the inquiry, and came forwards, with a little rustic awkwardness, feeling both shy and curious.

'Will yo' please walk this way, ma'am?' said she, leading her visitor back into her own dominion of the parlour, and leaving Bella to Hester's willing care.

'You don't know me!' said the pretty young lady, joyously. 'But I think you knew my husband. I am Mrs. Kinraid!'

A sob of surprise rose to Sylvia's lips—she choked it down, however, and tried to conceal any emotion she might feel, in placing a chair for her visitor, and trying to make her feel welcome, although, if the truth must be told, Sylvia was wondering all the time why her visitor came, and how soon she would go.

'You knew Captain Kinraid, did you not?' said the young lady, with innocent inquiry; to which Sylvia's lips formed the answer, 'Yes,' but no clear sound issued therefrom.

'But I know your husband knew the captain; is he at home yet? Can I speak to him? I do so want to see him.'

Sylvia was utterly bewildered; Mrs. Kinraid, this pretty, joyous, prosperous little bird of a woman, Philip, Charley's wife, what could they have in common? what could they know of each other? All she could say in answer to Mrs. Kinraid's eager questions, and still more eager looks, was, that her husband was from home, had been long from home: she did not know where he was, she did not know when he would come back.

Mrs. Kinraid's face fell a little, partly from her own real disappointment, partly out of sympathy with the hopeless, indifferent tone of Sylvia's replies.

'Mrs. Dawson told me he had gone away rather suddenly a year ago, but I thought he might be come home by now. I am expecting the captain early next month. Oh! how I should have liked to see Mr. Hepburn, and to thank him for saving the captain's life!'

'What do yo' mean?' asked Sylvia, stirred out of all assumed indifference. 'The captain! is that' (not 'Charley', she could not use that familiar name to the pretty young wife before her) 'yo'r husband?'

'Yes, you knew him, didn't you? when he used to be staying with Mr Corney, his uncle?'

'Yes, I knew him; but I don't understand. Will yo' please to tell me all about it, ma'am?' said Sylvia, faintly.

'I thought your husband would have told you all about it; I hardly know where to begin. You know my husband is a sailor?'

Sylvia nodded assent, listening greedily, her heart beating thick all the time.

'And he's now a Commander in the Royal Navy, all earned by his own bravery! Oh! I am so proud of him!'

So could Sylvia have been if she had been his wife; as it was, she thought how often she had felt sure that he would be a great man some day.

'And he has been at the siege of Acre.'

Sylvia looked perplexed at these strange words, and Mrs. Kinraid caught the look.

'St Jean d'Acre, you know—though it's fine saying "you know", when I didn't know a bit about it myself till the captain's ship was ordered there, though I was the head girl at Miss Dobbin's in the geography class—Acre is a seaport town, not far from Jaffa, which is the modern name for Joppa, where St Paul went to long ago; you've read of that, I'm sure, and Mount Carmel, where the prophet Elijah was once, all in Palestine, you know, only the Turks have got it now?'

'But I don't understand yet,' said Sylvia, plaintively; 'I daresay it's all very true about St Paul, but please, ma'am, will yo' tell me about yo'r husband and mine—have they met again?'

'Yes, at Acre, I tell you,' said Mrs. Kinraid, with pretty petulance. 'The Turks held the town, and the French wanted to take it; and we, that is the British Fleet, wouldn't let them. So Sir Sidney Smith, a commodore and a great friend of the captain's, landed in order to fight the French; and the captain and many of the sailors landed with him; and it was burning hot; and the poor captain was wounded, and lay a-dying of pain and thirst within the enemy's—that is the French—fire; so that they were ready to shoot any one of his own side who came near him. They thought he was dead himself, you see, as he was very near; and would have been too, if your husband had not come out of shelter, and taken him up in his arms or on his back (I couldn't make out which), and carried him safe within the walls.'

'It couldn't have been Philip,' said Sylvia, dubiously.

'But it was. The captain says so; and he's not a man to be mistaken. I thought I'd got his letter with me; and I would have read you a part of it, but I left it at Mrs. Dawson's in my desk; and I can't send it to you,' blushing as she remembered certain passages in which 'the captain' wrote very much like a lover, 'or else I would. But you may be quite sure it was your husband that ventured into all that danger to save his old friend's life, or the captain would not have said so.'

'But they weren't—they weren't—not to call great friends.'

'I wish I'd got the letter here; I can't think how I could be so stupid; I think I can almost remember the very words, though—I've read them over so often. He says, "Just as I gave up all hope, I saw one Philip Hepburn, a man whom I had known at Monkshaven, and whom I had some reason to remember well"—(I'm sure he says so—"remember well"), "he saw me too, and came at the risk of his life to where I lay. I fully expected he would be shot down; and I shut my eyes not to see the end of my last chance. The shot rained about him, and I think he was hit; but he took me up and carried me under cover." I'm sure he says that, I've read it over so often; and he goes on and says how he hunted for Mr. Hepburn all through the ships, as soon as ever he could; but he could hear nothing of him, either alive or dead. Don't go so white, for pity's sake!' said she, suddenly startled by Sylvia's blanching colour. 'You see, because he couldn't find him alive is no reason for giving him up as dead; because his name wasn't to be found on any of the ships' books; so the captain thinks he must have been known by a different name to his real one. Only he says he should like to have seen him to have thanked him; and he says he would give a deal to know what has become of him; and as I was staying two days at Mrs. Dawson's, I told them I must come over to Monkshaven, if only for five minutes, just to hear if your good husband was come home, and to shake his hands, that helped to save my own dear captain.'

'I don't think it could have been Philip,' reiterated Sylvia.

'Why not?' asked her visitor; 'you say you don't know where he is; why mightn't he have been there where the captain says he was?'

'But he wasn't a sailor, nor yet a soldier.'

'Oh! but he was. I think somewhere the captain calls him a marine; that's neither one nor the other, but a little of both. He'll be coming home some day soon; and then you'll see!'

Alice Rose came in at this minute, and Mrs. Kinraid jumped to the conclusion that she was Sylvia's mother, and in her overflowing gratitude and friendliness to all the family of him who had 'saved the captain' she went forward, and shook the old woman's hand in that pleasant confiding way that wins all hearts.

'Here's your daughter, ma'am!' said she to the half-astonished, half-pleased Alice. 'I'm Mrs. Kinraid, the wife of the captain that used to be in these parts, and I'm come to bring her news of her husband, and she don't half believe me, though it's all to his credit, I'm sure.'

Alice looked so perplexed that Sylvia felt herself bound to explain.

'She says he's either a soldier or a sailor, and a long way off at some place named in t' Bible.'

'Philip Hepburn led away to be a soldier!' said she, 'who had once been a Quaker?'

'Yes, and a very brave one too, and one that it would do my heart good to look upon,' exclaimed Mrs. Kinraid. 'He's been saving my husband's life in the Holy Land, where Jerusalem is, you know.'

'Nay!' said Alice, a little scornfully. 'I can forgive Sylvia for not being over keen to credit thy news. Her man of peace becoming a man of war; and suffered to enter Jerusalem, which is a heavenly and a typical city at this time; while me, as is one of the elect, is obliged to go on dwelling in Monkshaven, just like any other body.'

'Nay, but,' said Mrs. Kinraid, gently, seeing she was touching on delicate ground, 'I did not say he had gone to Jerusalem, but my husband saw him in those parts, and he was doing his duty like a brave, good man; ay, and more than his duty; and, you may take my word for it, he'll be at home some day soon, and all I beg is that you'll let the captain and me know, for I'm sure if we can, we'll both come and pay our respects to him. And I'm very glad I've seen you,' said she, rising to go, and putting out her hand to shake that of Sylvia; 'for, besides being Hepburn's wife, I'm pretty sure I've heard the captain speak of you; and if ever you come to Bristol I hope you'll come and see us on Clifton Downs.'

She went away, leaving Sylvia almost stunned by the new ideas presented to her. Philip a soldier! Philip in a battle, risking his life. Most strange of all, Charley and Philip once more meeting together, not as rivals or as foes, but as saviour and saved! Add to all this the conviction, strengthened by every word that happy, loving wife had uttered, that Kinraid's old, passionate love for herself had faded away and vanished utterly: its very existence apparently blotted out of his memory. She had torn up her love for him by the roots, but she felt as if she could never forget that it had been.

Hester brought back Bella to her mother. She had not liked to interrupt the conversation with the strange lady before; and now she found her mother in an obvious state of excitement; Sylvia quieter than usual.

'That was Kinraid's wife, Hester! Him that was th' specksioneer as made such a noise about t' place at the time of Darley's death. He's now a captain—a navy captain, according to what she says. And she'd fain have us believe that Philip is abiding in all manner of Scripture places; places as has been long done away with, but the similitude whereof is in the heavens, where the elect shall one day see them. And she says Philip is there, and a soldier, and that he saved her husband's life, and is coming home soon. I wonder what John and Jeremiah 'll say to his soldiering then? It'll noane be to their taste, I'm thinking.'

This was all very unintelligible to Hester, and she would dearly have liked to question Sylvia; but Sylvia sate a little apart, with Bella on her knee, her cheek resting on her child's golden curls, and her eyes fixed and almost trance-like, as if she were seeing things not present.

So Hester had to be content with asking her mother as many elucidatory questions as she could; and after all did not gain a very clear idea of what had really been said by Mrs. Kinraid, as her mother was more full of the apparent injustice of Philip's being allowed the privilege of treading on holy ground—if, indeed, that holy ground existed on this side heaven, which she was inclined to dispute—than to confine herself to the repetition of words, or narration of facts.

Suddenly Sylvia roused herself to a sense of Hester's deep interest and balked inquiries, and she went over the ground rapidly.

'Yo'r mother says right—she is his wife. And he's away fighting; and got too near t' French as was shooting and firing all round him; and just then, according to her story, Philip saw him, and went straight into t' midst o' t' shots, and fetched him out o' danger. That's what she says, and upholds.'

'And why should it not be?' asked Hester, her cheek flushing.

But Sylvia only shook her head, and said,

'I cannot tell. It may be so. But they'd little cause to be friends, and it seems all so strange—Philip a soldier, and them meeting theere after all!'

Hester laid the story of Philip's bravery to her heart—she fully believed in it. Sylvia pondered it more deeply still; the causes for her disbelief, or, at any rate, for her wonder, were unknown to Hester! Many a time she sank to sleep with the picture of the event narrated by Mrs. Kinraid as present to her mind as her imagination or experience could make it: first one figure prominent, then another. Many a morning she wakened up, her heart beating wildly, why, she knew not, till she shuddered at the remembrance of the scenes that had passed in her dreams: scenes that might be acted in reality that very day; for Philip might come back, and then?

And where was Philip all this time, these many weeks, these heavily passing months?

CHAPTER XLI

THE BEDESMAN OF ST SEPULCHRE

Philip lay long ill on board the hospital ship. If his heart had been light, he might have rallied sooner; but he was so depressed he did not care to live. His shattered jaw-bone, his burnt and blackened face, his many injuries of body, were torture to both his physical frame, and his sick, weary heart. No more chance for him, if indeed there ever had been any, of returning gay and gallant, and thus regaining his wife's love. This had been his poor, foolish vision in the first hour of his enlistment; and the vain dream had recurred more than once in the feverish stage of excitement which the new scenes into which he had been hurried as a recruit had called forth. But that was all over now. He knew that it was the most unlikely thing in the world to have come to pass; and yet those were happy days when he could think of it as barely possible. Now all he could look forward to was disfigurement, feebleness, and the bare pittance that keeps pensioners from absolute want.

Those around him were kind enough to him in their fashion, and attended to his bodily requirements; but they had no notion of listening to any revelations of unhappiness, if Philip had been the man to make confidences of that kind. As it was, he lay very still in his berth, seldom asking for anything, and always saying he was better, when the ship-surgeon came round with his daily inquiries. But he did not care to rally, and was rather sorry to find that his case was considered so interesting in a surgical point of view, that he was likely to receive a good deal more than the average amount of attention. Perhaps it was owing to this that he recovered at all. The doctors said it was the heat that made him languid, for that his wounds and burns were all doing well at last; and by-and-by they told him they had ordered him 'home'. His pulse sank under the surgeon's finger at the mention of the word; but he did not say a word. He was too indifferent to life and the world to have a will; otherwise they might have kept their pet patient a little longer where he was.

Slowly passing from ship to ship as occasion served; resting here and there in garrison hospitals, Philip at length reached Portsmouth on the evening of a September day in 1799. The transport-ship in which he was, was loaded with wounded and invalided soldiers and sailors; all who could manage it in any way struggled on deck to catch the first view of the white coasts of England. One man lifted his arm, took off his cap, and feebly waved it aloft, crying, 'Old England for ever!' in a faint shrill voice, and then burst into tears and sobbed aloud. Others tried to pipe up 'Rule Britannia', while more sate, weak and motionless, looking towards the shores that once, not so long ago, they never thought to see again. Philip was one of these; his place a little apart from the other men. He was muffled up in a great military cloak that had been given him by one of his officers; he felt the September breeze chill after his sojourn in a warmer climate, and in his shattered state of health.

As the ship came in sight of Portsmouth harbour, the signal flags ran up the ropes; the beloved Union Jack floated triumphantly over all. Return signals were made from the harbour; on board all became bustle and preparation for landing; while on shore there was the evident movement of expectation, and men in uniform were seen pressing their way to the front, as if to them belonged the right of reception. They were the men from the barrack hospital, that had been signalled for, come down with ambulance litters and other marks of forethought for the sick and wounded, who were returning to the country for which they had fought and suffered.

With a dash and a great rocking swing the vessel came up to her appointed place, and was safely moored. Philip sat still, almost as if he had no part in the cries of welcome, the bustling care, the loud directions that cut the air around him, and pierced his nerves through and through. But one in authority gave the order; and Philip, disciplined to obedience, rose to find his knapsack and leave the ship. Passive as he seemed to be, he had his likings for particular comrades; there was one especially, a man as different from Philip as well could be, to whom the latter had always attached himself; a merry fellow from Somersetshire, who was almost always cheerful and bright, though Philip had overheard the doctors say he would never be the man he was before he had that shot through the side. This marine would often sit making his fellows laugh, and laughing himself at his own good-humoured jokes, till so terrible a fit of coughing came on that those around him feared he would die in the paroxysm. After one of these fits he had gasped out some words, which led Philip to question him a little; and it turned out that in the quiet little village of Potterne, far inland, nestled beneath the high stretches of Salisbury Plain, he had a wife and a child, a little girl, just the same age even to a week as Philip's own little Bella. It was this that drew Philip towards the man; and this that made Philip wait and go ashore along with the poor consumptive marine.

The litters had moved off towards the hospital, the sergeant in charge had given his words of command to the remaining invalids, who tried to obey them to the best of their power, falling into something like military order for their march; but soon, very soon, the weakest broke step, and lagged behind; and felt as if the rough welcomes and rude expressions of sympathy from the crowd around were almost too much for them. Philip and his companion were about midway, when suddenly a young woman with a child in her arms forced herself through the people, between the soldiers who kept pressing on either side, and threw herself on the neck of Philip's friend.

'Oh, Jem!' she sobbed, 'I've walked all the road from Potterne. I've never stopped but for food and rest for Nelly, and now I've got you once again, I've got you once again, bless God for it!'

She did not seem to see the deadly change that had come over her husband since she parted with him a ruddy young labourer; she had got him once again, as she phrased it, and that was enough for her; she kissed his face, his hands, his very coat, nor would she be repulsed from walking beside him and holding his hand, while her little girl ran along scared by the voices and the strange faces, and clinging to her mammy's gown.

Jem coughed, poor fellow! he coughed his churchyard cough; and Philip bitterly envied him—envied his life, envied his approaching death; for was he not wrapped round with that woman's tender love, and is not such love stronger than death? Philip had felt as if his own heart was grown numb, and as though it had changed to a cold heavy stone. But at the contrast of this man's lot to his own, he felt that he had yet the power of suffering left to him.

The road they had to go was full of people, kept off in some measure by the guard of soldiers. All sorts of kindly speeches, and many a curious question, were addressed to the poor invalids as they walked along. Philip's jaw, and the lower part of his face, were bandaged up; his cap was slouched down; he held his cloak about him, and shivered within its folds.

They came to a standstill from some slight obstacle at the corner of a street. Down the causeway of this street a naval officer with a lady on his arm was walking briskly, with a step that told of health and a light heart. He stayed his progress though, when he saw the convoy of maimed and wounded men; he said something, of which Philip only caught the words, 'same uniform,' 'for his sake,' to the young lady, whose cheek blanched a little, but whose eyes kindled. Then leaving her for an instant, he pressed forward; he was close to Philip,—poor sad Philip absorbed in his own thoughts,—so absorbed that he noticed nothing till he heard a voice at his ear, having the Northumbrian burr, the Newcastle inflections which he knew of old, and that were to him like the sick memory of a deadly illness; and then he turned his muffled face to the speaker, though he knew well enough who it was, and averted his eyes after one sight of the handsome, happy man,—the man whose life he had saved once, and would save again, at the risk of his own, but whom, for all that, he prayed that he might never meet more on earth.

'Here, my fine fellow, take this,' forcing a crown piece into Philip's hand. 'I wish it were more; I'd give you a pound if I had it with me.'

Philip muttered something, and held out the coin to Captain Kinraid, of course in vain; nor was there time to urge it back upon the giver, for the obstacle to their progress was suddenly removed, the crowd pressed upon the captain and his wife, the procession moved on, and Philip along with it, holding the piece in his hand, and longing to throw it far away. Indeed he was on the point of dropping it, hoping to do so unperceived, when he bethought him of giving it to Jem's wife, the footsore woman, limping happily along by her husband's side. They thanked him, and spoke in his praise more than he could well bear. It was no credit to him to give that away which burned his fingers as long as he kept it.

Philip knew that the injuries he had received in the explosion on board the *Theseus* would oblige him to leave the service. He also believed that they would entitle him to a pension. But he had little interest in his future life; he was without hope, and in a depressed state of health. He remained for some little time stationary, and then went through all the forms of dismissal on account of wounds received in service, and was turned out loose upon the world, uncertain where to go, indifferent as to what became of him.

It was fine, warm October weather as he turned his back upon the coast, and set off on his walk northwards. Green leaves were yet upon the trees; the hedges were one flush of foliage and the wild rough-flavoured fruits of different kinds; the fields were tawny with the uncleared-off stubble, or emerald green with the growth of the aftermath. The roadside cottage gardens were gay with hollyhocks and Michaelmas daisies and marigolds, and the bright panes of the windows glittered through a veil of China roses.

The war was a popular one, and, as a natural consequence, soldiers and sailors were heroes everywhere. Philip's long drooping form, his arm hung in a sling, his face scarred and blackened, his jaw bound up with a black silk handkerchief; these marks of active service were reverenced by the rustic cottagers as though they had been crowns and sceptres. Many a hard-handed labourer left his seat by the chimney corner, and came to his door to have a look at one who had been fighting the French, and pushed forward to have a grasp of the stranger's hand as he gave back the empty cup into the good wife's keeping, for the kind homely women were ever ready with milk or homebrewed to slake the feverish traveller's thirst when he stopped at their doors and asked for a drink of water.

At the village public-house he had had a welcome of a more interested character, for the landlord knew full well that his circle of customers would be large that night, if it was only known that he had within his doors a soldier or a sailor who had seen service. The rustic politicians would gather round Philip, and smoke and drink, and then question and discuss till they were drouthy again; and in their sturdy obtuse minds they set down the extra glass and the supernumerary pipe to the score of patriotism.

Altogether human nature turned its sunny side out to Philip just now; and not before he needed the warmth of brotherly kindness to cheer his shivering soul. Day after day he drifted northwards, making but the slow progress of a feeble man, and yet this short daily walk tired him so much that he longed for rest—for the morning to come when he needed not to feel that in the course of an hour or two he must be up and away.

He was toiling on with this longing at his heart when he saw that he was drawing near a stately city, with a great old cathedral in the centre keeping solemn guard. This place might be yet two or three miles distant; he was on a rising ground looking down upon it. A labouring man passing by, observed his pallid looks and his languid attitude, and told him for his comfort, that if he turned down a lane to the left a few steps farther on, he would find himself at the Hospital of St Sepulchre, where bread and beer were given to all comers, and where he might sit him down and rest awhile on the old stone benches within the shadow of the gateway. Obeying these directions, Philip came upon a building which dated from the time of Henry the Fifth. Some knight who had fought in the French wars of that time, and had survived his battles and come home to his old halls, had been stirred up by his conscience, or by what was equivalent in those days, his confessor, to build and endow a hospital for twelve decayed soldiers, and a chapel wherein they were to attend the daily masses he ordained to be said till the end of all time (which eternity lasted rather more than a century, pretty well for an eternity bespoken by a man), for his soul and the souls of those whom he had slain. There was a large division of the quadrangular building set apart for the priest who was to say these masses; and to watch over the well-being of the bedesmen. In process of years the origin and primary purpose of the hospital had been forgotten by all excepting the local antiquaries; and the place itself came to be regarded as a very pleasant quaint set of almshouses; and the warden's office (he who should have said or sung his daily masses was now called the warden, and read daily prayers and preached a sermon on Sundays) an agreeable sinecure.

Another legacy of old Sir Simon Bray was that of a small croft of land, the rent or profits of which were to go towards giving to all who asked for it a manchet of bread and a cup of good beer. This beer was, so Sir Simon ordained, to be made after a certain receipt which he left, in which ground ivy took the place of hops. But the receipt, as well as the masses, was modernized according to the progress of time.

Philip stood under a great broad stone archway; the back-door into the warden's house was on the right side; a kind of buttery-hatch was placed by the porter's door on the opposite side. After some consideration, Philip knocked at the closed shutter, and the signal seemed to be well understood. He heard a movement within; the hatch was drawn aside, and his bread and beer were handed to him by a pleasant-looking old man, who proved himself not at all disinclined for conversation.

'You may sit down on yonder bench,' said he. 'Nay, man! sit i' the sun, for it's a chilly place, this, and then you can look through the grate and watch th' old fellows toddling about in th' quad.'

Philip sat down where the warm October sun slanted upon him, and looked through the iron railing at the peaceful sight.

577

A great square of velvet lawn, intersected diagonally with broad flag-paved walks, the same kind of walk going all round the quadrangle; low two-storied brick houses, tinted gray and yellow by age, and in many places almost covered with vines, Virginian creepers, and monthly roses; before each house a little plot of garden ground, bright with flowers, and evidently tended with the utmost care; on the farther side the massive chapel; here and there an old or infirm man sunning himself, or leisurely doing a bit of gardening, or talking to one of his comrades—the place looked as if care and want, and even sorrow, were locked out and excluded by the ponderous gate through which Philip was gazing.

'It's a nice enough place, bean't it?' said the porter, interpreting Philip's looks pretty accurately. 'Leastways, for them as likes it. I've got a bit weary on it myself; it's so far from th' world, as a man may say; not a decent public within a mile and a half, where one can hear a bit o' news of an evening.'

'I think I could make myself very content here,' replied Philip. 'That's to say, if one were easy in one's mind.'

'Ay, ay, my man. That's it everywhere. Why, I don't think that I could enjoy myself—not even at th' White Hart, where they give you as good a glass of ale for twopence as anywhere i' th' four kingdoms—I couldn't, to say, flavour my ale even there, if my old woman lay a-dying; which is a sign as it's the heart, and not the ale, as makes the drink.'

Just then the warden's back-door opened, and out came the warden himself, dressed in full clerical costume.

He was going into the neighbouring city, but he stopped to speak to Philip, the wounded soldier; and all the more readily because his old faded uniform told the warden's experienced eye that he had belonged to the Marines.

'I hope you enjoy the victual provided for you by the founder of St Sepulchre,' said he, kindly. 'You look but poorly, my good fellow, and as if a slice of good cold meat would help your bread down.'

'Thank you, sir!' said Philip. 'I'm not hungry, only weary, and glad of a draught of beer.'

'You've been in the Marines, I see. Where have you been serving?'

'I was at the siege of Acre, last May, sir.'

'At Acre! Were you, indeed? Then perhaps you know my boy Harry? He was in the——th.'

'It was my company,' said Philip, warming up a little. Looking back upon his soldier's life, it seemed to him to have many charms, because it was so full of small daily interests.

'Then, did you know my son, Lieutenant Pennington?'

'It was he that gave me this cloak, sir, when they were sending me back to England. I had been his servant for a short time before I was wounded by the explosion on board the *Theseus*, and he said I should feel the cold of the voyage. He's very kind; and I've heard say he promises to be a first-rate officer.'

'You shall have a slice of roast beef, whether you want it or not,' said the warden, ringing the bell at his own back-door. 'I recognize the cloak now—the young scamp! How soon he has made it shabby, though,' he continued, taking up a corner where there was an immense tear not too well botched up. 'And so you were on board the *Theseus* at the time of the explosion? Bring some cold meat here for the good man—or stay! Come in with me, and then you can tell Mrs. Pennington and the young ladies all you know about Harry,—and the siege,—and the explosion.'

So Philip was ushered into the warden's house and made to eat roast beef almost against his will; and he was questioned and cross-questioned by three eager ladies, all at the same time, as it seemed to him. He had given all possible details on the subjects about which they were curious; and was beginning to consider how he could best make his retreat, when the younger Miss Pennington went up to her father—who had all this time stood, with his hat on, holding his coat-tails over his arms, with his back to the fire. He bent his ear down a very little to hear some whispered suggestion of his daughter's, nodded his head, and then went on questioning Philip, with kindly inquisitiveness and patronage, as the rich do question the poor.

'And where are you going to now?'

Philip did not answer directly. He wondered in his own mind where he was going. At length he said,

'Northwards, I believe. But perhaps I shall never reach there.'

'Haven't you friends? Aren't you going to them?'

There was again a pause; a cloud came over Philip's countenance. He said,

'No! I'm not going to my friends. I don't know that I've got any left.'

They interpreted his looks and this speech to mean that he had either lost his friends by death, or offended them by enlisting.

The warden went on,

'I ask, because we've got a cottage vacant in the mead. Old Dobson, who was with General Wolfe at the taking of Quebec, died a fortnight ago. With such injuries as yours, I fear you'll never be able to work again. But we require strict testimonials as to character,' he added, with as penetrating a look as he could summon up at Philip.

Philip looked unmoved, either by the offer of the cottage, or the illusion to the possibility of his character not being satisfactory. He was grateful enough in reality, but too heavy at heart to care very much what became of him.

The warden and his family, who were accustomed to consider a settlement at St Sepulchre's as the sum of all good to a worn-out soldier, were a little annoyed at Philip's cool way of receiving the proposition. The warden went on to name the contingent advantages.

'Besides the cottage, you would have a load of wood for firing on All Saints', on Christmas, and on Candlemas days—a blue gown and suit of clothes to match every Michaelmas, and a shilling a day to keep yourself in all other things. Your dinner you would have with the other men, in hall.'

'The warden himself goes into hall every day, and sees that everything is comfortable, and says grace,' added the warden's lady.

'I know I seem stupid,' said Philip, almost humbly, 'not to be more grateful, for it's far beyond what I iver expected or thought for again, and it's a great temptation, for I'm just worn out with fatigue. Several times I've thought I must lie down under a hedge, and just die for very weariness. But once I had a wife and a child up in the north,' he stopped.

'And are they dead?' asked one of the young ladies in a soft sympathizing tone. Her eyes met Philip's, full of dumb woe. He tried to speak; he wanted to explain more fully, yet not to reveal the truth.

'Well!' said the warden, thinking he perceived the real state of things, 'what I propose is this. You shall go into old Dobson's house at once, as a kind of probationary bedesman. I'll write to Harry, and get your character from him. Stephen Freeman I think you said your name was? Before I can receive his reply you'll have been able to tell how you'd like the kind of life; and at any rate you'll have the rest you seem to require in the meantime. You see, I take Harry's having given you that cloak as a kind of character,' added he, smiling kindly. 'Of course you'll have to conform to rules just like all the rest,—chapel at eight, dinner at twelve, lights out at nine; but I'll tell you the remainder of our regulations as we walk across quad to your new quarters.'

And thus Philip, almost in spite of himself, became installed in a bedesman's house at St Sepulchre.

CHAPTER XLII

A FABLE AT FAULT

Philip took possession of the two rooms which had belonged to the dead Sergeant Dobson. They were furnished sufficiently for every comfort by the trustees of the hospital. Some little fragments of ornament, some small articles picked up in distant countries, a few tattered books, remained in the rooms as legacies from their former occupant.

At first the repose of the life and the place was inexpressibly grateful to Philip. He had always shrunk from encountering strangers, and displaying his blackened and scarred countenance to them, even where such disfigurement was most regarded as a mark of honour. In St Sepulchre's he met none but the same set day after day, and when he had once told the tale of how it happened and submitted to their gaze, it was over for ever, if he so minded. The slight employment his garden gave him—there was a kitchen-garden behind each house, as well as the flower-plot in front—and the daily arrangement of his parlour and chamber were, at the beginning of his time of occupation, as much bodily labour as he could manage. There was something stately and utterly removed from all Philip's previous existence in the forms observed at every day's dinner, when the twelve bedesmen met in the large quaint hall, and the warden came in his college-cap and gown to say the long Latin grace which wound up with something very like a prayer for the soul of Sir Simon Bray. It took some time to get a reply to ship letters in those times when no one could exactly say where the fleet might be found.

And before Dr Pennington had received the excellent character of Stephen Freeman, which his son gladly sent in answer to his father's inquiries, Philip had become restless and uneasy in the midst of all this peace and comfort.

Sitting alone over his fire in the long winter evenings, the scenes of his past life rose before him; his childhood; his aunt Robson's care of him; his first going to Foster's shop in Monkshaven; Haytersbank Farm, and the spelling lessons in the bright warm kitchen there; Kinraid's appearance; the miserable night of the Corneys' party; the farewell he had witnessed on Monkshaven sands; the press-gang, and all the long consequences of that act of concealment; poor Daniel Robson's trial and execution; his own marriage; his child's birth; and then he came to that last day at Monkshaven: and he went over and over again the torturing details, the looks of contempt and anger, the words of loathing indignation, till he almost brought himself, out of his extreme sympathy with Sylvia, to believe that he was indeed the wretch she had considered him to be.

He forgot his own excuses for having acted as he had done; though these excuses had at one time seemed to him to wear the garb of reasons. After long thought and bitter memory came some wonder. What was Sylvia doing now? Where was she? What was his child like—his child as well as hers? And then he remembered the poor footsore wife and the little girl she carried in her arms, that was just the age of Bella; he wished he had noticed that child more, that a clear vision of it might rise up when he wanted to picture Bella.

One night he had gone round this mill-wheel circle of ideas till he was weary to the very marrow of his bones. To shake off the monotonous impression he rose to look for a book amongst the old tattered volumes, hoping that he might find something that would sufficiently lay hold of him to change the current of his thoughts. There was an old volume of *Peregrine Pickle*; a book of sermons; half an army list of 1774, and the *Seven Champions of Christendom*. Philip took up this last, which he had never seen before. In it he read how Sir Guy, Earl of Warwick, went to fight the Paynim in his own country, and was away for seven long years; and when he came back his own wife Phillis, the countess in her castle, did not know the poor travel-worn hermit, who came daily to seek his dole of bread at her hands along with many beggars and much poor. But at last, when he lay a-dying in his cave in the rock, he sent for her by a secret sign known but to them twain. And she came with great speed, for she knew it was her lord who had sent for her; and they had many sweet and holy words together before he gave up the ghost, his head lying on her bosom.

The old story known to most people from their childhood was all new and fresh to Philip. He did not quite believe in the truth of it, because the fictitious nature of the histories of some of the other Champions of Christendom was too patent. But he could not help thinking that this one might be true; and that Guy and Phillis might have been as real flesh and blood, long, long ago, as he and Sylvia had even been. The old room, the quiet moonlit quadrangle into which the cross-barred casement looked, the quaint aspect of everything that he had seen for weeks and weeks; all this predisposed Philip to dwell upon the story he had just been reading as a faithful legend of two lovers whose bones were long since dust. He thought that if he could thus see Sylvia, himself unknown, unseen—could live at her gates, so to speak, and gaze upon her and his child—some day too, when he lay a-dying, he might send for her, and in soft words of mutual forgiveness breathe his life away in her arms. Or perhaps—and so he lost himself, and from thinking, passed on to dreaming. All night long Guy and Phillis, Sylvia and his child, passed in and out of his visions; it was impossible to make the fragments of his dreams cohere; but the impression made upon him by them was not the less strong for this. He felt as if he were called to Monkshaven, wanted at Monkshaven, and to Monkshaven he resolved to go; although when his reason overtook his feeling, he knew perfectly how unwise it was to leave a home of peace and tranquillity and surrounding friendliness, to go to a place where nothing but want and wretchedness awaited him unless he made himself known; and if he did, a deeper want, a more woeful wretchedness, would in all probability be his portion.

In the small oblong of looking-glass hung against the wall, Philip caught the reflection of his own face, and laughed scornfully at the sight. The thin hair lay upon his temples in the flakes that betoken long ill-health; his eyes were the same as ever, and they had always been considered the best feature in his face; but they were sunk in their orbits, and looked hollow and gloomy. As for the lower part of his face, blackened, contracted, drawn away from his teeth, the outline entirely changed by the breakage of his jaw-bone, he was indeed a fool if he thought himself fit to go forth to win back that love which Sylvia had forsworn. As a hermit and a beggar, he must return to Monkshaven, and fall perforce into the same position which Guy of Warwick had only assumed. But still he should see his Phillis, and might feast his sad hopeless eyes from time to time with the sight of his child. His small pension of sixpence a day would keep him from absolute want of necessaries.

So that very day he went to the warden and told him he thought of giving up his share in the bequest of Sir Simon Bray. Such a relinquishment had never occurred before in all the warden's experience; and he was very much inclined to be offended.

'I must say that for a man not to be satisfied as a bedesman of St Sepulchre's argues a very wrong state of mind, and a very ungrateful heart.'

'I'm sure, sir, it's not from any ingratitude, for I can hardly feel thankful to you and to Sir Simon, and to madam, and the young ladies, and all my comrades in the hospital, and I niver expect to be either so comfortable or so peaceful again, but——'

'But? What can you have to say against the place, then? Not but what there are always plenty of applicants for every vacancy; only I thought I was doing a kindness to a man out of Harry's company. And you'll not see Harry either; he's got his leave in March!'

'I'm very sorry. I should like to have seen the lieutenant again. But I cannot rest any longer so far away from—people I once knew.'

'Ten to one they're dead, or removed, or something or other by this time; and it'll serve you right if they are. Mind! no one can be chosen twice to be a bedesman of St Sepulchre's.'

The warden turned away; and Philip, uneasy at staying, disheartened at leaving, went to make his few preparations for setting out once more on his journey northwards. He had to give notice of his change of residence to the local distributor of pensions; and one or two farewells had to be taken, with more than usual sadness at the necessity; for Philip, under his name of Stephen Freeman, had attached some of the older bedesmen a good deal to him, from his unselfishness, his willingness to read to them, and to render them many little services, and, perhaps, as much as anything, by his habitual silence, which made him a convenient recipient of all their garrulousness. So before the time for his departure came, he had the opportunity of one more interview with the warden, of a more friendly character than that in which he gave up his bedesmanship. And so far it was well; and Philip turned his back upon St Sepulchre's with his sore heart partly healed by his four months' residence there.

He was stronger, too, in body, more capable of the day-after-day walks that were required of him. He had saved some money from his allowance as bedesman and from his pension, and might occasionally have taken an outside place on a coach, had it not been that he shrank from the first look of every stranger upon his disfigured face. Yet the gentle, wistful eyes, and the white and faultless teeth always did away with the first impression as soon as people became a little acquainted with his appearance.

It was February when Philip left St Sepulchre's. It was the first week in April when he began to recognize the familiar objects between York and Monkshaven. And now he began to hang back, and to question the wisdom of what he had done—just as the warden had prophesied that he would. The last night of his two hundred mile walk he slept at the little inn at which he had been enlisted nearly two years before. It was by no intention of his that he rested at that identical place. Night was drawing on; and, in making, as he thought, a short cut, he had missed his way, and was fain to seek shelter where he might find it. But it brought him very straight face to face with his life at that time, and ever since. His mad, wild hopes—half the result of intoxication, as he now knew—all dead and gone; the career then freshly opening shut up against him now; his youthful strength and health changed into premature infirmity, and the home and the love that should have opened wide its doors to console him for all, why in two years Death might have been busy, and taken away from him his last feeble chance of the faint happiness of seeing his beloved without being seen or known of her. All that night and all the next day, the fear of Sylvia's possible death overclouded his heart. It was strange that he had hardly ever thought of this before; so strange, that now, when the terror came, it took possession of him, and he could almost have sworn that she must be lying dead in Monkshaven churchyard. Or was it little Bella, that blooming, lovely babe, whom he was never to see again? There was the tolling of mournful bells in the distant air to his disturbed fancy, and the cry of the happy birds, the plaintive bleating of the new-dropped lambs, were all omens of evil import to him.

As well as he could, he found his way back to Monkshaven, over the wild heights and moors he had crossed on that black day of misery; why he should have chosen that path he could not tell—it was as if he were led, and had no free will of his own.

The soft clear evening was drawing on, and his heart beat thick, and then stopped, only to start again with fresh violence. There he was, at the top of the long, steep lane that was in some parts a literal staircase leading down from the hill-top into the High Street, through the very entry up which he had passed when he shrank away from his former and his then present life. There he stood, looking down once more at the numerous irregular roofs, the many stacks of chimneys below him, seeking out that which had once been his own dwelling—who dwelt there now?

The yellower gleams grew narrower; the evening shadows broader, and Philip crept down the lane a weary, woeful man. At every gap in the close-packed buildings he heard the merry music of a band, the cheerful sound of excited voices. Still he descended slowly, scarcely wondering what it could be, for it was not associated in his mind with the one pervading thought of Sylvia.

When he came to the angle of junction between the lane and the High Street, he seemed plunged all at once into the very centre of the bustle, and he drew himself up into a corner of deep shadow, from whence he could look out upon the street.

A circus was making its grand entry into Monkshaven, with all the pomp of colour and of noise that it could muster. Trumpeters in parti-coloured clothes rode first, blaring out triumphant discord. Next came a gold-and-scarlet chariot drawn by six piebald horses, and the windings of this team through the tortuous narrow street were pretty enough to look upon. In the chariot sate kings and queens, heroes and heroines, or what were meant for such; all the little boys and girls running alongside of the chariot envied them; but they themselves were very much tired, and shivering with cold in their heroic pomp of classic clothing. All this Philip might have seen; did see, in fact; but heeded not one jot. Almost opposite to him, not ten yards apart, standing on the raised step at the well-known shop door, was Sylvia, holding a child, a merry dancing child, up in her arms to see the show. She too, Sylvia, was laughing for pleasure, and for sympathy with pleasure. She held the little Bella aloft that the child might see the gaudy procession the better and the longer, looking at it herself with red lips apart and white teeth glancing through; then she turned to speak to some one behind her—Coulson, as Philip saw the moment afterwards; his answer made her laugh once again. Philip saw it all; her bonny careless looks, her pretty matronly form, her evident ease of mind and prosperous outward circumstances. The years that he had spent in gloomy sorrow, amongst wild scenes, on land or by sea, his life in frequent peril of a bloody end, had gone by with her like sunny days; all the more sunny because he was not there. So bitterly thought the poor disabled marine, as, weary and despairing, he stood in the cold shadow and looked upon the home that should have been his haven, the wife that should have welcomed him, the child that should have been his comfort. He had banished himself from his home; his wife had forsworn him; his child was blossoming into intelligence unwitting of any father. Wife, and child, and home, were all doing well without him; what madness had tempted him thither? an hour ago, like a fanciful fool, he had thought she might be dead—dead with sad penitence for her cruel words at her heart—with mournful wonder at the unaccounted-for absence of her child's father preying on her spirits, and in some measure causing the death he had apprehended. But to look at her there where she stood, it did not seem as if she had had an hour's painful thought in all her blooming life.

Ay! go in to the warm hearth, mother and child, now the gay cavalcade has gone out of sight, and the chill of night has succeeded to the sun's setting. Husband and father, steal out into the cold dark street, and seek some poor cheap lodging where you may rest your weary bones, and cheat your more weary heart into forgetfulness in sleep. The pretty story of the Countess Phillis, who mourned for her husband's absence so long, is a fable of old times; or rather say Earl Guy never wedded his wife, knowing that one she loved better than him was alive all the time she had believed him to be dead.

584

CHAPTER XLIII

THE UNKNOWN

A few days before that on which Philip arrived at Monkshaven, Kester had come to pay Sylvia a visit. As the earliest friend she had, and also as one who knew the real secrets of her life, Sylvia always gave him the warm welcome, the cordial words, and the sweet looks in which the old man delighted. He had a sort of delicacy of his own which kept him from going to see her too often, even when he was stationary at Monkshaven; but he looked forward to the times when he allowed himself this pleasure as a child at school looks forward to its holidays. The time of his service at Haytersbank had, on the whole, been the happiest in all his long monotonous years of daily labour. Sylvia's father had always treated him with the rough kindness of fellowship; Sylvia's mother had never stinted him in his meat or grudged him his share of the best that was going; and once, when he was ill for a few days in the loft above the cow-house, she had made him possets, and nursed him with the same tenderness which he remembered his mother showing to him when he was a little child, but which he had never experienced since then. He had known Sylvia herself, as bud, and sweet promise of blossom; and just as she was opening into the full-blown rose, and, if she had been happy and prosperous, might have passed out of the narrow circle of Kester's interests, one sorrow after another came down upon her pretty innocent head, and Kester's period of service to Daniel Robson, her father, was tragically cut short. All this made Sylvia the great centre of the faithful herdsman's affection; and Bella, who reminded him of what Sylvia was when first Kester knew her, only occupied the second place in his heart, although to the child he was much more demonstrative of his regard than to the mother.

He had dressed himself in his Sunday best, and although it was only Thursday, had forestalled his Saturday's shaving; he had provided himself with a paper of humbugs for the child—'humbugs' being the north-country term for certain lumps of toffy, well-flavoured with peppermint—and now he sat in the accustomed chair, as near to the door as might be, in Sylvia's presence, coaxing the little one, who was not quite sure of his identity, to come to him, by opening the paper parcel, and letting its sweet contents be seen.

'She's like thee—and yet she favours her feyther,' said he; and the moment he had uttered the incautious words he looked up to see how Sylvia had taken the unpremeditated, unusual reference to her husband. His stealthy glance did not meet her eye; but though he thought she had coloured a little, she did not seem offended as he had feared. It was true that Bella had her father's grave, thoughtful, dark eyes, instead of her mother's gray ones, out of which the childlike expression of wonder would never entirely pass away. And as Bella slowly and half distrustfully made her way towards the temptation offered her, she looked at Kester with just her father's look.

Sylvia said nothing in direct reply; Kester almost thought she could not have heard him. But, by-and-by, she said,—

'Yo'll have heared how Kinraid—who's a captain now, and a grand officer—has gone and got married.'

'Nay!' said Kester, in genuine surprise. 'He niver has, for sure!'

'Ay, but he has,' said Sylvia. 'And I'm sure I dunnot see why he shouldn't.'

'Well, well!' said Kester, not looking up at her, for he caught the inflections in the tones of her voice. 'He were a fine stirrin' chap, yon; an' he were allays for doin' summut; an' when he fund as he couldn't ha' one thing as he'd set his mind on, a reckon he thought he mun put up wi' another.'

'It 'ud be no "putting up,"' said Sylvia. 'She were staying at Bessy Dawson's, and she come here to see me—she's as pretty a young lady as yo'd see on a summer's day; and a real lady, too, wi' a fortune. She didn't speak two words wi'out bringing in her husband's name,—"the captain", as she called him.'

'An' she come to see thee?' said Kester, cocking his eye at Sylvia with the old shrewd look. 'That were summut queer, weren't it?'

Sylvia reddened a good deal.

'He's too fause to have spoken to her on me, in t' old way,—as he used for t' speak to me. I were nought to her but Philip's wife.'

'An' what t' dickins had she to do wi' Philip?' asked Kester, in intense surprise; and so absorbed in curiosity that he let the humbugs all fall out of the paper upon the floor, and the little Bella sat down, plump, in the midst of treasures as great as those fabled to exist on Tom Tiddler's ground.

Sylvia was again silent; but Kester, knowing her well, was sure that she was struggling to speak, and bided his time without repeating his question.

'She said—and I think her tale were true, though I cannot get to t' rights on it, think on it as I will—as Philip saved her husband's life somewheere nearabouts to Jerusalem. She would have it that t' captain—for I think I'll niver ca' him Kinraid again—was in a great battle, and were near upon being shot by t' French, when Philip—our Philip—come up and went right into t' fire o' t' guns, and saved her husband's life. And she spoke as if both she and t' captain were more beholden to Philip than words could tell. And she come to see me, to try and get news on him.'

'It's a queer kind o' story,' said Kester, meditatively. 'A should ha' thought as Philip were more likely to ha' gi'en him a shove into t' thick on it, than t' help him out o' t' scrape.'

'Nay!' said Sylvia, suddenly looking straight at Kester; 'yo're out theere. Philip had a deal o' good in him. And I dunnot think as he'd ha' gone and married another woman so soon, if he'd been i' Kinraid's place.'

'An' yo've niver heared on Philip sin' he left?' asked Kester, after a while.

'Niver; nought but what she told me. And she said that t' captain made inquiry for him right and left, as soon after that happened as might be, and could hear niver a word about him. No one had seen him, or knowed his name.'

'Yo' niver heared of his goin' for t' be a soldier?' persevered Kester.

'Niver. I've told yo' once. It were unlike Philip to think o' such a thing.'

'But thou mun ha' been thinkin' on him at times i' a' these years. Bad as he'd behaved hissel', he were t' feyther o' thy little un. What did ta think he had been agait on when he left here?'

'I didn't know. I were noane so keen a-thinking on him at first. I tried to put him out o' my thoughts a'together, for it made me like mad to think how he'd stood between me and—that other. But I'd begun to wonder and to wonder about him, and to think I should like to hear as he were doing well. I reckon I thought he were i' London, wheere he'd been that time afore, yo' know, and had allays spoke as if he'd enjoyed hissel' tolerable; and then Molly Brunton told me on t' other one's marriage; and, somehow, it gave me a shake in my heart, and I began for to wish I hadn't said all them words i' my passion; and then that fine young lady come wi' her story—and I've thought a deal on it since,—and my mind has come out clear. Philip's dead, and it were his spirit as come to t' other's help in his time o' need. I've heard feyther say as spirits cannot rest i' their graves for trying to undo t' wrongs they've done i' their bodies.'

'Them's my conclusions,' said Kester, solemnly. 'A was fain for to hear what were yo'r judgments first; but them's the conclusions I comed to as soon as I heard t' tale.'

'Let alone that one thing,' said Sylvia, 'he were a kind, good man.'

'It were a big deal on a "one thing", though,' said Kester. 'It just spoilt yo'r life, my poor lass; an' might ha' gone near to spoilin' Charley Kinraid's too.'

'Men takes a deal more nor women to spoil their lives,' said Sylvia, bitterly.

'Not a' mak' o' men. I reckon, lass, Philip's life were pretty well on for bein' spoilt at after he left here; and it were, mebbe, a good thing he got rid on it so soon.'

'I wish I'd just had a few kind words wi' him, I do,' said Sylvia, almost on the point of crying.

'Come, lass, it's as ill moanin' after what's past as it 'ud be for me t' fill my eyes wi' weepin' after t' humbugs as this little wench o' thine has grubbed up whilst we'n been talkin'. Why, there's not one on 'em left!'

'She's a sad spoilt little puss!' said Sylvia, holding out her arms to the child, who ran into them, and began patting her mother's cheeks, and pulling at the soft brown curls tucked away beneath the matronly cap. 'Mammy spoils her, and Hester spoils her——'

'Granny Rose doesn't spoil me,' said the child, with quick, intelligent discrimination, interrupting her mother's list.

'No; but Jeremiah Foster does above a bit. He'll come in fro' t' Bank, Kester, and ask for her, a'most ivery day. And he'll bring her things in his pocket; and she's so fause, she allays goes straight to peep in, and then he shifts t' apple or t' toy into another. Eh! but she's a little fause one,'—half devouring the child with her kisses. 'And he comes and takes her a walk oftentimes, and he goes as slow as if he were quite an old man, to keep pace wi' Bella's steps. I often run upstairs and watch 'em out o' t' window; he doesn't care to have me with 'em, he's so fain t' have t' child all to hissel'.'

'She's a bonny un, for sure,' said Kester; 'but not so pretty as thou was, Sylvie. A've niver tell'd thee what a come for tho', and it's about time for me t' be goin'. A'm off to t' Cheviots to-morrow morn t' fetch home some sheep as Jonas Blundell has purchased. It'll be a job o' better nor two months a reckon.'

'It'll be a nice time o' year,' said Sylvia, a little surprised at Kester's evident discouragement at the prospect of the journey or absence; he had often been away from Monkshaven for a longer time without seeming to care so much about it.

'Well, yo' see it's a bit hard upon me for t' leave my sister—she as is t' widow-woman, wheere a put up when a'm at home. Things is main an' dear; four-pound loaves is at sixteenpence; an' there's a deal o' talk on a famine i' t' land; an' whaten a paid for my victual an' t' bed i' t' lean-to helped t' oud woman a bit,—an' she's sadly down i' t' mouth, for she cannot hear on a lodger for t' tak' my place, for a' she's moved o'er to t' other side o' t' bridge for t' be nearer t' new buildings, an' t' grand new walk they're makin' round t' cliffs, thinkin' she'd be likelier t' pick up a labourer as would be glad on a bed near his work. A'd ha' liked to ha' set her agait wi' a 'sponsible lodger afore a'd ha' left, for she's just so soft-hearted, any scamp may put upon her if he nobbut gets houd on her blind side.'

'Can I help her?' said Sylvia, in her eager way. 'I should be so glad; and I've a deal of money by me—-'

'Nay, my lass,' said Kester, 'thou munnot go off so fast; it were just what I were feared on i' tellin' thee. I've left her a bit o' money, and I'll mak' shift to send her more; it's just a kind word, t' keep up her heart when I'm gone, as I want. If thou'd step in and see her fra' time to time, and cheer her up a bit wi' talkin' to her on me, I'd tak' it very kind, and I'd go off wi' a lighter heart.'

'Then I'm sure I'll do it for yo', Kester. I niver justly feel like mysel' when yo're away, for I'm lonesome enough at times. She and I will talk a' t' better about yo' for both on us grieving after yo'.'

So Kester took his leave, his mind set at ease by Sylvia's promise to go and see his sister pretty often during his absence in the North.

But Sylvia's habits were changed since she, as a girl at Haytersbank, liked to spend half her time in the open air, running out perpetually without anything on to scatter crumbs to the poultry, or to take a piece of bread to the old cart-horse, to go up to the garden for a handful of herbs, or to clamber to the highest point around to blow the horn which summoned her father and Kester home to dinner. Living in a town where it was necessary to put on hat and cloak before going out into the street, and then to walk in a steady and decorous fashion, she had only cared to escape down to the freedom of the sea-shore until Philip went away; and after that time she had learnt so to fear observation as a deserted wife, that nothing but Bella's health would have been a sufficient motive to take her out of doors. And, as she had told Kester, the necessity of giving the little girl a daily walk was very much lightened by the great love and affection which Jeremiah Foster now bore to the child. Ever since the day when the baby had come to his knee, allured by the temptation of his watch, he had apparently considered her as in some sort belonging to him; and now he had almost come to think that he had a right to claim her as his companion in his walk back from the Bank to his early dinner, where a high chair was always placed ready for the chance of her coming to share his meal. On these occasions he generally brought her back to the shop-door when he returned to his afternoon's work at the Bank. Sometimes, however, he would leave word that she was to be sent for from his house in the New Town, as his business at the Bank for that day was ended. Then Sylvia was compelled to put on her things, and fetch back her darling; and excepting for this errand she seldom went out at all on week-days.

About a fortnight after Kester's farewell call, this need for her visit to Jeremiah Foster's arose; and it seemed to Sylvia that there could not be a better opportunity of fulfilling her promise and going to see the widow Dobson, whose cottage was on the other side of the river, low down on the cliff-side, just at the bend and rush of the full stream into the open sea. She set off pretty early in order to go there first. She found the widow with her house-place tidied up after the midday meal, and busy knitting at the open door—not looking at her rapid-clicking needles, but gazing at the rush and recession of the waves before her; yet not seeing them either,—rather seeing days long past.

She started into active civility as soon as she recognized Sylvia, who was to her as a great lady, never having known Sylvia Robson in her wild childish days. Widow Dobson was always a little scandalized at her brother Christopher's familiarity with Mrs. Hepburn.

She dusted a chair which needed no dusting, and placed it for Sylvia, sitting down herself on a three-legged stool to mark her sense of the difference in their conditions, for there was another chair or two in the humble dwelling; and then the two fell into talk—first about Kester, whom his sister would persist in calling Christopher, as if his dignity as her elder brother was compromised by any familiar abbreviation; and by-and-by she opened her heart a little more.

'A could wish as a'd learned write-of-hand,' said she; 'for a've that for to tell Christopher as might set his mind at ease. But yo' see, if a wrote him a letter he couldn't read it; so a just comfort mysel' wi' thinkin' nobody need learn writin' unless they'n got friends as can read. But a reckon he'd ha' been glad to hear as a've getten a lodger.' Here she nodded her head in the direction of the door opening out of the house-place into the 'lean-to', which Sylvia had observed on drawing near the cottage, and the recollection of the mention of which by Kester had enabled her to identify widow Dobson's dwelling. 'He's a-bed yonder,' the latter continued, dropping her voice. 'He's a queer-lookin' tyke, but a don't think as he's a bad un.'

'When did he come?' said Sylvia, remembering Kester's account of his sister's character, and feeling as though it behoved her, as Kester's confidante on this head, to give cautious and prudent advice.

'Eh! a matter of a s'ennight ago. A'm noane good at mindin' time; he's paid me his rent twice, but then he were keen to pay aforehand. He'd comed in one night, an' sate him down afore he could speak, he were so done up; he'd been on tramp this many a day, a reckon. "Can yo' give me a bed?" says he, panting like, after a bit. "A chap as a met near here says as yo've a lodging for t' let." "Ay," says a, "a ha' that; but yo' mun pay me a shilling a week for 't." Then my mind misgive me, for a thought he hadn't a shilling i' t' world, an' yet if he hadn't, a should just ha' gi'en him t' bed a' t' same: a'm not one as can turn a dog out if he comes t' me wearied o' his life. So he outs wi' a shillin', an' lays it down on t' table, 'bout a word. "A'll not trouble yo' long," says he. "A'm one as is best out o' t' world," he says. Then a thought as a'd been a bit hard upon him. An' says I, "A'm a widow-woman, and one as has getten but few friends:" for yo' see a were low about our Christopher's goin' away north; "so a'm forced-like to speak hard to folk; but a've made mysel' some stirabout for my supper; and if yo'd like t' share an' share about wi' me, it's but puttin' a sup more watter to 't, and God's blessing 'll be on 't, just as same as if 't were meal." So he ups wi' his hand afore his e'en, and says not a word. At last he says, "Missus," says he, "can God's blessing be shared by a sinner—one o' t' devil's children?" says he. "For the Scriptur' says he's t' father o' lies." So a were puzzled-like; an' at length a says, "Thou mun ask t' parson that; a'm but a poor faint-hearted widow-woman; but a've allays had God's blessing somehow, now a bethink me, an' a'll share it wi' thee as far as my will goes." So he raxes his hand across t' table, an' mutters summat, as he grips mine. A thought it were Scriptur' as he said, but a'd needed a' my strength just then for t' lift t' pot off t' fire—it were t' first vittle a'd tasted sin' morn, for t' famine comes down like stones on t' head o' us poor folk: an' a' a said were just "Coom along, chap, an' fa' to; an' God's blessing be on him as eats most." An' sin' that day him and me's been as thick as thieves, only he's niver telled me nought of who he is, or wheere he comes fra'. But a think he's one o' them poor colliers, as has getten brunt i' t' coal-pits; for, t' be sure, his face is a' black wi' fire-marks; an' o' late days he's ta'en t' his bed, an' just lies there sighing,—for one can hear him plain as dayleet thro' t' bit partition wa'.'

As a proof of this, a sigh—almost a groan—startled the two women at this very moment.

'Poor fellow!' said Sylvia, in a soft whisper. 'There's more sore hearts i' t' world than one reckons for!' But after a while, she bethought her again of Kester's account of his sister's 'softness'; and she thought that it behoved her to give some good advice. So she added, in a sterner, harder tone—'Still, yo' say yo' know nought about him; and tramps is tramps a' t' world over; and yo're a widow, and it behoves yo' to be careful. I think I'd just send him off as soon as he's a bit rested. Yo' say he's plenty o' money?'

'Nay! A never said that. A know nought about it. He pays me aforehand; an' he pays me down for whativer a've getten for him; but that's but little; he's noane up t' his vittle, though a've made him some broth as good as a could make 'em.'

'I wouldn't send him away till he was well again, if I were yo; but I think yo'd be better rid on him,' said Sylvia. 'It would be different if yo'r brother were in Monkshaven.' As she spoke she rose to go.

Widow Dobson held her hand in hers for a minute, then the humble woman said,—

'Yo'll noane be vexed wi' me, missus, if a cannot find i' my heart t' turn him out till he wants to go hissel'? For a wouldn't like to vex yo', for Christopher's sake; but a know what it is for t' feel for friendless folk, an' choose what may come on it, I cannot send him away.'

'No!' said Sylvia. 'Why should I be vexed? it's no business o' mine. Only I should send him away if I was yo'. He might go lodge wheere there was men-folk, who know t' ways o' tramps, and are up to them.'

Into the sunshine went Sylvia. In the cold shadow the miserable tramp lay sighing. She did not know that she had been so near to him towards whom her heart was softening, day by day.

CHAPTER XLIV

FIRST WORDS

It was the spring of 1800. Old people yet can tell of the hard famine of that year. The harvest of the autumn before had failed; the war and the corn laws had brought the price of corn up to a famine rate; and much of what came into the market was unsound, and consequently unfit for food, yet hungry creatures bought it eagerly, and tried to cheat disease by mixing the damp, sweet, clammy flour with rice or potato meal. Rich families denied themselves pastry and all unnecessary and luxurious uses of wheat in any shape; the duty on hair-powder was increased; and all these palliatives were but as drops in the ocean of the great want of the people.

Philip, in spite of himself, recovered and grew stronger; and as he grew stronger hunger took the place of loathing dislike to food. But his money was all spent; and what was his poor pension of sixpence a day in that terrible year of famine? Many a summer's night he walked for hours and hours round the house which once was his, which might be his now, with all its homely, blessed comforts, could he but go and assert his right to it. But to go with authority, and in his poor, maimed guise assert that right, he had need be other than Philip Hepburn. So he stood in the old shelter of the steep, crooked lane opening on to the hill out of the market-place, and watched the soft fading of the summer's eve into night; the closing of the once familiar shop; the exit of good, comfortable William Coulson, going to his own home, his own wife, his comfortable, plentiful supper. Then Philip—there were no police in those days, and scarcely an old watchman in that primitive little town—would go round on the shady sides of streets, and, quickly glancing about him, cross the bridge, looking on the quiet, rippling stream, the gray shimmer foretelling the coming dawn over the sea, the black masts and rigging of the still vessels against the sky; he could see with his wistful, eager eyes the shape of the windows—the window of the very room in which his wife and child slept, unheeding of him, the hungry, broken-hearted outcast. He would go back to his lodging, and softly lift the latch of the door; still more softly, but never without an unspoken, grateful prayer, pass by the poor sleeping woman who had given him a shelter and her share of God's blessing—she who, like him, knew not the feeling of satisfied hunger; and then he laid him down on the narrow pallet in the lean-to, and again gave Sylvia happy lessons in the kitchen at Haytersbank, and the dead were alive; and Charley Kinraid, the specksioneer, had never come to trouble the hopeful, gentle peace.

For widow Dobson had never taken Sylvia's advice. The tramp known to her by the name of Freeman—that in which he received his pension—lodged with her still, and paid his meagre shilling in advance, weekly. A shilling was meagre in those hard days of scarcity. A hungry man might easily eat the produce of a shilling in a day.

Widow Dobson pleaded this to Sylvia as an excuse for keeping her lodger on; to a more calculating head it might have seemed a reason for sending him away.

'Yo' see, missus,' said she, apologetically, to Sylvia, one evening, as the latter called upon the poor widow before going to fetch little Bella (it was now too hot for the child to cross the bridge in the full heat of the summer sun, and Jeremiah would take her up to her supper instead)—'Yo' see, missus, there's not a many as 'ud take him in for a shillin' when it goes so little way; or if they did, they'd take it out on him some other way, an' he's not gotten much else, a reckon. He ca's me granny, but a'm vast mista'en if he's ten year younger nor me; but he's gotten a fine appetite of his own, choose how young he may be; an' a can see as he could eat a deal more nor he's getten money to buy, an' it's few as can mak' victual go farther nor me. Eh, missus, but yo' may trust me a'll send him off when times is better; but just now it would be sendin' him to his death; for a ha' plenty and to spare, thanks be to God an' yo'r bonny face.'

So Sylvia had to be content with the knowledge that the money she gladly gave to Kester's sister went partly to feed the lodger who was neither labourer nor neighbour, but only just a tramp, who, she feared, was preying on the good old woman. Still the cruel famine cut sharp enough to penetrate all hearts; and Sylvia, an hour after the conversation recorded above, was much touched, on her return from Jeremiah Foster's with the little merry, chattering Bella, at seeing the feeble steps of one, whom she knew by description must be widow Dobson's lodger, turn up from the newly-cut road which was to lead to the terrace walk around the North Cliff, a road which led to no dwelling but widow Dobson's. Tramp, and vagrant, he might be in the eyes of the law; but, whatever his character, Sylvia could see him before her in the soft dusk, creeping along, over the bridge, often stopping to rest and hold by some support, and then going on again towards the town, to which she and happy little Bella were wending.

A thought came over her: she had always fancied that this unknown man was some fierce vagabond, and had dreaded lest in the lonely bit of road between widow Dobson's cottage and the peopled highway, he should fall upon her and rob her if he learnt that she had money with her; and several times she had gone away without leaving the little gift she had intended, because she imagined that she had seen the door of the small chamber in the 'lean-to' open softly while she was there, as if the occupant (whom widow Dobson spoke of as never leaving the house before dusk, excepting once a week) were listening for the chink of the coin in her little leathern purse. Now that she saw him walking before her with heavy languid steps, this fear gave place to pity; she remembered her mother's gentle superstition which had prevented her from ever sending the hungry empty away, for fear lest she herself should come to need bread.

'Lassie,' said she to little Bella, who held a cake which Jeremiah's housekeeper had given her tight in her hand, 'yon poor man theere is hungry; will Bella give him her cake, and mother will make her another to-morrow twice as big?'

For this consideration, and with the feeling of satisfaction which a good supper not an hour ago gives even to the hungry stomach of a child of three years old, Bella, after some thought, graciously assented to the sacrifice.

Sylvia stopped, the cake in her hand, and turned her back to the town, and to the slow wayfarer in front. Under the cover of her shawl she slipped a half-crown deep into the crumb of the cake, and then restoring it to little Bella, she gave her her directions.

'Mammy will carry Bella; and when Bella goes past the poor man, she shall give him the cake over mammy's shoulder. Poor man is so hungry; and Bella and mammy have plenty to eat, and to spare.'

The child's heart was touched by the idea of hunger, and her little arm was outstretched ready for the moment her mother's hurried steps took her brushing past the startled, trembling Philip.

'Poor man, eat this; Bella not hungry.'

They were the first words he had ever heard his child utter. The echoes of them rang in his ears as he stood endeavouring to hide his disfigured face by looking over the parapet of the bridge down upon the stream running away towards the ocean, into which his hot tears slowly fell, unheeded by the weeper. Then he changed the intention with which he had set out upon his nightly walk, and turned back to his lodging.

Of course the case was different with Sylvia; she would have forgotten the whole affair very speedily, if it had not been for little Bella's frequent recurrence to the story of the hungry man, which had touched her small sympathies with the sense of an intelligible misfortune. She liked to act the dropping of the bun into the poor man's hand as she went past him, and would take up any article near her in order to illustrate the gesture she had used. One day she got hold of Hester's watch for this purpose, as being of the same round shape as the cake; and though Hester, for whose benefit the child was repeating the story in her broken language for the third or fourth time, tried to catch the watch as it was intended that she should (she being the representative of the 'hungry man' for the time being), it went to the ground with a smash that frightened the little girl, and she began to cry at the mischief she had done.

'Don't cry, Bella,' said Hester. 'Niver play with watches again. I didn't see thee at mine, or I'd ha' stopped thee in time. But I'll take it to old Darley's on th' quay-side, and maybe he'll soon set it to rights again. Only Bella must niver play with watches again.'

'Niver no more!' promised the little sobbing child. And that evening Hester took her watch down to old Darley's.

This William Darley was the brother of the gardener at the rectory; the uncle to the sailor who had been shot by the press-gang years before, and to his bed-ridden sister. He was a clever mechanician, and his skill as a repairer of watches and chronometers was great among the sailors, with whom he did a very irregular sort of traffic, conducted, often without much use of money, but rather on the principle of barter, they bringing him foreign coins and odd curiosities picked up on their travels in exchange for his services to their nautical instruments or their watches. If he had ever had capital to extend his business, he might have been a rich man; but it is to be doubted whether he would have been as happy as he was now in his queer little habitation of two rooms, the front one being both shop and workshop, the other serving the double purpose of bedroom and museum.

The skill of this odd-tempered, shabby old man was sometimes sought by the jeweller who kept the more ostentatious shop in the High Street; but before Darley would undertake any 'tickle' piece of delicate workmanship for the other, he sneered at his ignorance, and taunted and abused him well. Yet he had soft places in his heart, and Hester Rose had found her way to one by her patient, enduring kindness to his bed-ridden niece. He never snarled at her as he did at too many; and on the few occasions when she had asked him to do anything for her, he had seemed as if she were conferring the favour on him, not he on her, and only made the smallest possible charge.

She found him now sitting where he could catch the most light for his work, spectacles on nose, and microscope in hand.

He took her watch, and examined it carefully without a word in reply to her. Then he began to open it and take it to pieces, in order to ascertain the nature of the mischief.

Suddenly he heard her catch her breath with a checked sound of surprise. He looked at her from above his spectacles; she was holding a watch in her hand which she had just taken up off the counter.

'What's amiss wi' thee now?' said Darley. 'Hast ta niver seen a watch o' that mak' afore? or is it them letters on t' back, as is so wonderful?'

Yes, it was those letters—that interlaced, old-fashioned cipher. That Z. H. that she knew of old stood for Zachary Hepburn, Philip's father. She knew how Philip valued this watch. She remembered having seen it in his hands the very day before his disappearance, when he was looking at the time in his annoyance at Sylvia's detention in her walk with baby. Hester had no doubt that he had taken this watch as a matter of course away with him. She felt sure that he would not part with this relic of his dead father on any slight necessity. Where, then, was Philip?—by what chance of life or death had this, his valued property, found its way once more to Monkshaven?

'Where did yo' get this?' she asked, in as quiet a manner as she could assume, sick with eagerness as she was.

To no one else would Darley have answered such a question. He made a mystery of most of his dealings; not that he had anything to conceal, but simply because he delighted in concealment. He took it out of her hands, looked at the number marked inside, and the maker's name—'Natteau Gent, York'—and then replied,—

'A man brought it me yesterday, at nightfall, for t' sell it. It's a matter o' forty years old. Natteau Gent has been dead and in his grave pretty nigh as long as that. But he did his work well when he were alive; and so I gave him as brought it for t' sell about as much as it were worth, i' good coin. A tried him first i' t' bartering line, but he wouldn't bite; like enough he wanted food,—many a one does now-a-days.'

'Who was he?' gasped Hester.

'Bless t' woman! how should I know?'

'What was he like?—how old?—tell me.'

'My lass, a've summut else to do wi' my eyes than go peering into men's faces i' t' dusk light.'

'But yo' must have had light for t' judge about the watch.'

'Eh! how sharp we are! A'd a candle close to my nose. But a didn't tak' it up for to gaze int' his face. That wouldn't be manners, to my thinking.'

Hester was silent. Then Darley's heart relented.

'If yo're so set upo' knowing who t' fellow was, a could, mebbe, put yo' on his tracks.'

'How?' said Hester, eagerly. 'I do want to know. I want to know very much, and for a good reason.'

'Well, then, a'll tell yo'. He's a queer tyke, that one is. A'll be bound he were sore pressed for t' brass; yet he out's wi' a good half-crown, all wrapped up i' paper, and he axes me t' make a hole in it. Says I, "It's marring good king's coin, at after a've made a hole in't, it'll never pass current again." So he mumbles, and mumbles, but for a' that it must needs be done; and he's left it here, and is t' call for 't to-morrow at e'en.'

'Oh, William Darley!' said Hester, clasping her hands tight together. 'Find out who he is, where he is—anything—everything about him—and I will so bless yo'.'

Darley looked at her sharply, but with some signs of sympathy on his grave face. 'My woman,' he said 'a could ha' wished as you'd niver seen t' watch. It's poor, thankless work thinking too much on one o' God's creatures. But a'll do thy bidding,' he continued, in a lighter and different tone. 'A'm a 'cute old badger when need be. Come for thy watch in a couple o' days, and a'll tell yo' all as a've learnt.'

So Hester went away, her heart beating with the promise of knowing something about Philip,—how much, how little, in these first moments, she dared not say even to herself. Some sailor newly landed from distant seas might have become possessed of Philip's watch in far-off latitudes; in which case, Philip would be dead. That might be. She tried to think that this was the most probable way of accounting for the watch. She could be certain as to the positive identity of the watch—being in William Darley's possession. Again, it might be that Philip himself was near at hand—was here in this very place—starving, as too many were, for insufficiency of means to buy the high-priced food. And then her heart burnt within her as she thought of the succulent, comfortable meals which Sylvia provided every day—nay, three times a day—for the household in the market-place, at the head of which Philip ought to have been; but his place knew him not. For Sylvia had inherited her mother's talent for housekeeping, and on her, in Alice's decrepitude and Hester's other occupations in the shop, devolved the cares of due provision for the somewhat heterogeneous family.

And Sylvia! Hester groaned in heart over the remembrance of Sylvia's words, 'I can niver forgive him the wrong he did to me,' that night when Hester had come, and clung to her, making the sad, shameful confession of her unreturned love.

What could ever bring these two together again? Could Hester herself—ignorant of the strange mystery of Sylvia's heart, as those who are guided solely by obedience to principle must ever be of the clue to the actions of those who are led by the passionate ebb and flow of impulse? Could Hester herself? Oh! how should she speak, how should she act, if Philip were near—if Philip were sad and in miserable estate? Her own misery at this contemplation of the case was too great to bear; and she sought her usual refuge in the thought of some text, some promise of Scripture, which should strengthen her faith.

'With God all things are possible,' said she, repeating the words as though to lull her anxiety to rest.

Yes; with God all things are possible. But ofttimes He does his work with awful instruments. There is a peacemaker whose name is Death.

CHAPTER XLV

SAVED AND LOST

Hester went out on the evening of the day after that on which the unknown owner of the half-crown had appointed to call for it again at William Darley's. She had schooled herself to believe that time and patience would serve her best. Her plan was to obtain all the knowledge about Philip that she could in the first instance; and then, if circumstances allowed it, as in all probability they would, to let drop by drop of healing, peacemaking words and thoughts fall on Sylvia's obdurate, unforgiving heart. So Hester put on her things, and went out down towards the old quay-side on that evening after the shop was closed.

Poor little Sylvia! She was unforgiving, but not obdurate to the full extent of what Hester believed. Many a time since Philip went away had she unconsciously missed his protecting love; when folks spoke shortly to her, when Alice scolded her as one of the non-elect, when Hester's gentle gravity had something of severity in it; when her own heart failed her as to whether her mother would have judged that she had done well, could that mother have known all, as possibly she did by this time. Philip had never spoken otherwise than tenderly to her during the eighteen months of their married life, except on the two occasions before recorded: once when she referred to her dream of Kinraid's possible return, and once again on the evening of the day before her discovery of his concealment of the secret of Kinraid's involuntary disappearance.

After she had learnt that Kinraid was married, her heart had still more strongly turned to Philip; she thought that he had judged rightly in what he had given as the excuse for his double dealing; she was even more indignant at Kinraid's fickleness than she had any reason to be; and she began to learn the value of such enduring love as Philip's had been— lasting ever since the days when she first began to fancy what a man's love for a woman should be, when she had first shrunk from the tone of tenderness he put into his especial term for her, a girl of twelve—'Little lassie,' as he was wont to call her.

But across all this relenting came the shadow of her vow—like the chill of a great cloud passing over a sunny plain. How should she decide? what would be her duty, if he came again, and once more called her 'wife'? She shrank from such a possibility with all the weakness and superstition of her nature; and this it was which made her strengthen herself with the re-utterance of unforgiving words; and shun all recurrence to the subject on the rare occasion when Hester had tried to bring it back, with a hope of softening the heart which to her appeared altogether hardened on this one point.

Now, on this bright summer evening, while Hester had gone down to the quay-side, Sylvia stood with her out-of-door things on in the parlour, rather impatiently watching the sky, full of hurrying clouds, and flushing with the warm tints of the approaching sunset. She could not leave Alice: the old woman had grown so infirm that she was never left by her daughter and Sylvia at the same time; yet Sylvia had to fetch her little girl from the New Town, where she had been to her supper at Jeremiah Foster's. Hester had said that she should not be away more than a quarter of an hour; and Hester was generally so punctual that any failure of hers, in this respect, appeared almost in the light of an injury on those who had learnt to rely upon her. Sylvia wanted to go and see widow Dobson, and learn when Kester might be expected home. His two months were long past; and Sylvia had heard through the Fosters of some suitable and profitable employment for him, of which she thought he would be glad to know as soon as possible. It was now some time since she had been able to get so far as across the bridge; and, for aught she knew, Kester might already be come back from his expedition to the Cheviots. Kester was come back. Scarce five minutes had elapsed after these thoughts had passed through her mind before his hasty hand lifted the latch of the kitchen-door, his hurried steps brought him face to face with her. The smile of greeting was arrested on her lips by one look at him: his eyes staring wide, the expression on his face wild, and yet pitiful.

'That's reet,' said he, seeing that her things were already on. 'Thou're wanted sore. Come along.'

'Oh! dear God! my child!' cried Sylvia, clutching at the chair near her; but recovering her eddying senses with the strong fact before her that whatever the terror was, she was needed to combat it.

'Ay; thy child!' said Kester, taking her almost roughly by the arm, and drawing her away with him out through the open doors on to the quay-side.

'Tell me!' said Sylvia, faintly, 'is she dead?'

'She's safe now,' said Kester. 'It's not her—it's him as saved her as needs yo', if iver husband needed a wife.'

'He?—who? O Philip! Philip! is it yo' at last?'

Unheeding what spectators might see her movements, she threw up her arms and staggered against the parapet of the bridge they were then crossing.

'He!—Philip!—saved Bella? Bella, our little Bella, as got her dinner by my side, and went out wi' Jeremiah, as well as could be. I cannot take it in; tell me, Kester.' She kept trembling so much in voice and in body, that he saw she could not stir without danger of falling until she was calmed; as it was, her eyes became filmy from time to time, and she drew her breath in great heavy pants, leaning all the while against the wall of the bridge.

'It were no illness,' Kester began. 'T' little un had gone for a walk wi' Jeremiah Foster, an' he were drawn for to go round t' edge o' t' cliff, wheere they's makin' t' new walk reet o'er t' sea. But it's but a bit on a pathway now; an' t' one was too oud, an' t' other too young for t' see t' water comin' along wi' great leaps; it's allays for comin' high up again' t' cliff, an' this spring-tide it's comin' in i' terrible big waves. Some one said as they passed t' man a-sittin' on a bit on a rock up above—a dunnot know, a only know as a heared a great fearful screech i' t' air. A were just a-restin' me at after a'd comed in, not half an hour i' t' place. A've walked better nor a dozen mile to-day; an' a ran out, an' a looked, an' just on t' walk, at t' turn, was t' swish of a wave runnin' back as quick as t' mischief int' t' sea, an' oud Jeremiah standin' like one crazy, lookin' o'er int' t' watter; an' like a stroke o' leeghtnin' comes a man, an' int' t' very midst o' t' great waves like a shot; an' then a knowed summut were in t' watter as were nearer death than life; an' a seemed to misdoubt me that it were our Bella; an' a shouts an' a cries for help, an' a goes mysel' to t' very edge o' t' cliff, an' a bids oud Jeremiah, as was like one beside hissel', houd tight on me, for he were good for nought else; an' a bides my time, an' when a sees two arms houdin' out a little drippin' streamin' child, a clutches her by her waist-band, an' hauls her to land. She's noane t' worse for her bath, a'll be bound.'

'I mun go—let me,' said Sylvia, struggling with his detaining hand, which he had laid upon her in the fear that she would slip down to the ground in a faint, so ashen-gray was her face. 'Let me,—Bella, I mun go see her.'

He let go, and she stood still, suddenly feeling herself too weak to stir.

'Now, if you'll try a bit to be quiet, a'll lead yo' along; but yo' mun be a steady and brave lass.'

'I'll be aught if yo' only let me see Bella,' said Sylvia, humbly.

'An' yo' niver ax at after him as saved her,' said Kester, reproachfully.

'I know it's Philip,' she whispered, 'and yo' said he wanted me; so I know he's safe; and, Kester, I think I'm 'feared on him, and I'd like to gather courage afore seeing him, and a look at Bella would give me courage. It were a terrible time when I saw him last, and I did say—'

'Niver think on what thou did say; think on what thou will say to him now, for he lies a-dyin'! He were dashed again t' cliff an' bruised sore in his innards afore t' men as come wi' a boat could pick him up.'

She did not speak; she did not even tremble now; she set her teeth together, and, holding tight by Kester, she urged him on; but when they came to the end of the bridge, she seemed uncertain which way to turn.

'This way,' said Kester. 'He's been lodgin' wi' Sally this nine week, an' niver a one about t' place as knowed him; he's been i' t' wars an' getten his face brunt.'

'And he was short o' food,' moaned Sylvia, 'and we had plenty, and I tried to make yo'r sister turn him out, and send him away. Oh! will God iver forgive me?'

Muttering to herself, breaking her mutterings with sharp cries of pain, Sylvia, with Kester's help, reached widow Dobson's house. It was no longer a quiet, lonely dwelling. Several sailors stood about the door, awaiting, in silent anxiety, for the verdict of the doctor, who was even now examining Philip's injuries. Two or three women stood talking eagerly, in low voices, in the doorway.

But when Sylvia drew near the men fell back; and the women moved aside as though to allow her to pass, all looking upon her with a certain amount of sympathy, but perhaps with rather more of antagonistic wonder as to how she was taking it—she who had been living in ease and comfort while her husband's shelter was little better than a hovel, her husband's daily life a struggle with starvation; for so much of the lodger at widow Dobson's was popularly known; and any distrust of him as a stranger and a tramp was quite forgotten now.

Sylvia felt the hardness of their looks, the hardness of their silence; but it was as nothing to her. If such things could have touched her at this moment, she would not have stood still right in the midst of their averted hearts, and murmured something to Kester. He could not hear the words uttered by that hoarse choked voice, until he had stooped down and brought his ear to the level of her mouth.

'We'd better wait for t' doctors to come out,' she said again. She stood by the door, shivering all over, almost facing the people in the road, but with her face turned a little to the right, so that they thought she was looking at the pathway on the cliff-side, a hundred yards or so distant, below which the hungry waves still lashed themselves into high ascending spray; while nearer to the cottage, where their force was broken by the bar at the entrance to the river, they came softly lapping up the shelving shore.

Sylvia saw nothing of all this, though it was straight before her eyes. She only saw a blurred mist; she heard no sound of waters, though it filled the ears of those around. Instead she heard low whispers pronouncing Philip's earthly doom.

For the doctors were both agreed; his internal injury was of a mortal kind, although, as the spine was severely injured above the seat of the fatal bruise, he had no pain in the lower half of his body.

They had spoken in so low a tone that John Foster, standing only a foot or so away, had not been able to hear their words. But Sylvia heard each syllable there where she stood outside, shivering all over in the sultry summer evening. She turned round to Kester.

'I mun go to him, Kester; thou'll see that noane come in to us, when t' doctors come out.'

She spoke in a soft, calm voice; and he, not knowing what she had heard, made some easy conditional promise. Then those opposite to the cottage door fell back, for they could see the grave doctors coming out, and John Foster, graver, sadder still, following them. Without a word to them,—without a word even of inquiry—which many outside thought and spoke of as strange—white-faced, dry-eyed Sylvia slipped into the house out of their sight.

And the waves kept lapping on the shelving shore.

The room inside was dark, all except the little halo or circle of light made by a dip candle. Widow Dobson had her back to the bed—her bed—on to which Philip had been borne in the hurry of terror as to whether he was alive or whether he was dead. She was crying—crying quietly, but the tears down-falling fast, as, with her back to the lowly bed, she was gathering up the dripping clothes cut off from the poor maimed body by the doctors' orders. She only shook her head as she saw Sylvia, spirit-like, steal in—white, noiseless, and upborne from earth.

But noiseless as her step might be, he heard, he recognized, and with a sigh he turned his poor disfigured face to the wall, hiding it in the shadow.

He knew that she was by him; that she had knelt down by his bed; that she was kissing his hand, over which the languor of approaching death was stealing. But no one spoke.

At length he said, his face still averted, speaking with an effort.

'Little lassie, forgive me now! I cannot live to see the morn!'

There was no answer, only a long miserable sigh, and he felt her soft cheek laid upon his hand, and the quiver that ran through her whole body.

'I did thee a cruel wrong,' he said, at length. 'I see it now. But I'm a dying man. I think that God will forgive me—and I've sinned against Him; try, lassie—try, my Sylvie—will not thou forgive me?'

He listened intently for a moment. He heard through the open window the waves lapping on the shelving shore. But there came no word from her; only that same long shivering, miserable sigh broke from her lips at length.

'Child,' said he, once more. 'I ha' made thee my idol; and if I could live my life o'er again I would love my God more, and thee less; and then I shouldn't ha' sinned this sin against thee. But speak one word of love to me—one little word, that I may know I have thy pardon.'

'Oh, Philip! Philip!' she moaned, thus adjured.

Then she lifted her head, and said,

'Them were wicked, wicked words, as I said; and a wicked vow as I vowed; and Lord God Almighty has ta'en me at my word. I'm sorely punished, Philip, I am indeed.'

He pressed her hand, he stroked her cheek. But he asked for yet another word.

'I did thee a wrong. In my lying heart I forgot to do to thee as I would have had thee to do to me. And I judged Kinraid in my heart.'

'Thou thought as he was faithless and fickle,' she answered quickly; 'and so he were. He were married to another woman not so many weeks at after thou went away. Oh, Philip, Philip! and now I have thee back, and—'

'Dying' was the word she would have said, but first the dread of telling him what she believed he did not know, and next her passionate sobs, choked her.

'I know,' said he, once more stroking her cheek, and soothing her with gentle, caressing hand. 'Little lassie!' he said, after a while when she was quiet from very exhaustion, 'I niver thought to be so happy again. God is very merciful.'

She lifted up her head, and asked wildly, 'Will He iver forgive me, think yo'? I drove yo' out fra' yo'r home, and sent yo' away to t' wars, wheere yo' might ha' getten yo'r death; and when yo' come back, poor and lone, and weary, I told her for t' turn yo' out, for a' I knew yo' must be starving in these famine times. I think I shall go about among them as gnash their teeth for iver, while yo' are wheere all tears are wiped away.'

'No!' said Philip, turning round his face, forgetful of himself in his desire to comfort her. 'God pities us as a father pities his poor wandering children; the nearer I come to death the clearer I see Him. But you and me have done wrong to each other; yet we can see now how we were led to it; we can pity and forgive one another. I'm getting low and faint, lassie; but thou must remember this: God knows more, and is more forgiving than either you to me, or me to you. I think and do believe as we shall meet together before His face; but then I shall ha' learnt to love thee second to Him; not first, as I have done here upon the earth.'

Then he was silent—very still. Sylvia knew—widow Dobson had brought it in—that there was some kind of medicine, sent by the hopeless doctors, lying upon the table hard by, and she softly rose and poured it out and dropped it into the half-open mouth. Then she knelt down again, holding the hand feebly stretched out to her, and watching the faint light in the wistful loving eyes. And in the stillness she heard the ceaseless waves lapping against the shelving shore.

Something like an hour before this time, which was the deepest midnight of the summer's night, Hester Rose had come hurrying up the road to where Kester and his sister sate outside the open door, keeping their watch under the star-lit sky, all others having gone away, one by one, even John and Jeremiah Foster having returned to their own house, where the little Bella lay, sleeping a sound and healthy slumber after her perilous adventure.

Hester had heard but little from William Darley as to the owner of the watch and the half-crown; but he was chagrined at the failure of all his skilful interrogations to elicit the truth, and promised her further information in a few days, with all the more vehemence because he was unaccustomed to be baffled. And Hester had again whispered to herself 'Patience! Patience!' and had slowly returned back to her home to find that Sylvia had left it, why she did not at once discover. But, growing uneasy as the advancing hours neither brought Sylvia nor little Bella to their home, she had set out for Jeremiah Foster's as soon as she had seen her mother comfortably asleep in her bed; and then she had learnt the whole story, bit by bit, as each person who spoke broke in upon the previous narration with some new particular. But from no one did she clearly learn whether Sylvia was with her husband, or not; and so she came speeding along the road, breathless, to where Kester sate in wakeful, mournful silence, his sister's sleeping head lying on his shoulder, the cottage door open, both for air and that there might be help within call if needed; and the dim slanting oblong of the interior light lying across the road.

Hester came panting up, too agitated and breathless to ask how much was truth of the fatal, hopeless tale which she had heard. Kester looked at her without a word. Through this solemn momentary silence the lapping of the ceaseless waves was heard, as they came up close on the shelving shore.

'He? Philip?' said she. Kester shook his head sadly.

'And his wife—Sylvia?' said Hester.

'In there with him, alone,' whispered Kester.

Hester turned away, and wrung her hands together.

'Oh, Lord God Almighty!' said she, 'was I not even worthy to bring them together at last?' And she went away slowly and heavily back to the side of her sleeping mother. But 'Thy will be done' was on her quivering lips before she lay down to her rest.

The soft gray dawn lightens the darkness of a midsummer night soon after two o'clock. Philip watched it come, knowing that it was his last sight of day,—as we reckon days on earth.

He had been often near death as a soldier; once or twice, as when he rushed into fire to save Kinraid, his chances of life had been as one to a hundred; but yet he had had a chance. But now there was the new feeling—the last new feeling which we shall any of us experience in this world—that death was not only close at hand, but inevitable.

He felt its numbness stealing up him—stealing up him. But the head was clear, the brain more than commonly active in producing vivid impressions.

It seemed but yesterday since he was a little boy at his mother's knee, wishing with all the earnestness of his childish heart to be like Abraham, who was called the friend of God, or David, who was said to be the man after God's own heart, or St John, who was called 'the Beloved.' As very present seemed the day on which he made resolutions of trying to be like them; it was in the spring, and some one had brought in cowslips; and the scent of those flowers was in his nostrils now, as he lay a-dying—his life ended, his battles fought, his time for 'being good' over and gone—the opportunity, once given in all eternity, past.

All the temptations that had beset him rose clearly before him; the scenes themselves stood up in their solid materialism— he could have touched the places; the people, the thoughts, the arguments that Satan had urged in behalf of sin, were reproduced with the vividness of a present time. And he knew that the thoughts were illusions, the arguments false and hollow; for in that hour came the perfect vision of the perfect truth: he saw the 'way to escape' which had come along with the temptation; now, the strong resolve of an ardent boyhood, with all a life before it to show the world 'what a Christian might be'; and then the swift, terrible now, when his naked, guilty soul shrank into the shadow of God's mercy-seat, out of the blaze of His anger against all those who act a lie.

His mind was wandering, and he plucked it back. Was this death in very deed? He tried to grasp at the present, the earthly present, fading quick away. He lay there on the bed—on Sally Dobson's bed in the house-place, not on his accustomed pallet in the lean-to. He knew that much. And the door was open into the still, dusk night; and through the open casement he could hear the lapping of the waves on the shelving shore, could see the soft gray dawn over the sea—he knew it was over the sea—he saw what lay unseen behind the poor walls of the cottage. And it was Sylvia who held his hand tight in her warm, living grasp; it was his wife whose arm was thrown around him, whose sobbing sighs shook his numbed frame from time to time.

'God bless and comfort my darling,' he said to himself. 'She knows me now. All will be right in heaven—in the light of God's mercy.'

And then he tried to remember all that he had ever read about, God, and all that the blessed Christ—that bringeth glad tidings of great joy unto all people, had said of the Father, from whom He came. Those sayings dropped like balm down upon his troubled heart and brain. He remembered his mother, and how she had loved him; and he was going to a love wiser, tenderer, deeper than hers.

As he thought this, he moved his hands as if to pray; but Sylvia clenched her hold, and he lay still, praying all the same for her, for his child, and for himself. Then he saw the sky redden with the first flush of dawn; he heard Kester's long-drawn sigh of weariness outside the open door.

He had seen widow Dobson pass through long before to keep the remainder of her watch on the bed in the lean-to, which had been his for many and many a sleepless and tearful night. Those nights were over—he should never see that poor chamber again, though it was scarce two feet distant. He began to lose all sense of the comparative duration of time: it seemed as long since kind Sally Dobson had bent over him with soft, lingering look, before going into the humble sleeping-room—as long as it was since his boyhood, when he stood by his mother dreaming of the life that should be his, with the scent of the cowslips tempting him to be off to the woodlands where they grew. Then there came a rush and an eddying through his brain—his soul trying her wings for the long flight. Again he was in the present: he heard the waves lapping against the shelving shore once again.

And now his thoughts came back to Sylvia. Once more he spoke aloud, in a strange and terrible voice, which was not his. Every sound came with efforts that were new to him.

'My wife! Sylvie! Once more—forgive me all.'

She sprang up, she kissed his poor burnt lips; she held him in her arms, she moaned, and said,

'Oh, wicked me! forgive me—me—Philip!'

Then he spoke, and said, 'Lord, forgive us our trespasses as we forgive each other!' And after that the power of speech was conquered by the coming death. He lay very still, his consciousness fast fading away, yet coming back in throbs, so that he knew it was Sylvia who touched his lips with cordial, and that it was Sylvia who murmured words of love in his ear. He seemed to sleep at last, and so he did—a kind of sleep, but the light of the red morning sun fell on his eyes, and with one strong effort he rose up, and turned so as once more to see his wife's pale face of misery.

'In heaven,' he cried, and a bright smile came on his face, as he fell back on his pillow.

Not long after Hester came, the little Bella scarce awake in her arms, with the purpose of bringing his child to see him ere yet he passed away. Hester had watched and prayed through the livelong night. And now she found him dead, and Sylvia, tearless and almost unconscious, lying by him, her hand holding his, her other thrown around him.

Kester, poor old man, was sobbing bitterly; but she not at all.

Then Hester bore her child to her, and Sylvia opened wide her miserable eyes, and only stared, as if all sense was gone from her. But Bella suddenly rousing up at the sight of the poor, scarred, peaceful face, cried out,—

'Poor man who was so hungry. Is he not hungry now?'

'No,' said Hester, softly. 'The former things are passed away—and he is gone where there is no more sorrow, and no more pain.'

But then she broke down into weeping and crying. Sylvia sat up and looked at her.

'Why do yo' cry, Hester?' she said. 'Yo' niver said that yo' wouldn't forgive him as long as yo' lived. Yo' niver broke the heart of him that loved yo', and let him almost starve at yo'r very door. Oh, Philip! my Philip, tender and true.'

Then Hester came round and closed the sad half-open eyes; kissing the calm brow with a long farewell kiss. As she did so, her eye fell on a black ribbon round his neck. She partly lifted it out; to it was hung a half-crown piece.

'This is the piece he left at William Darley's to be bored,' said she, 'not many days ago.'

Bella had crept to her mother's arms as a known haven in this strange place; and the touch of his child loosened the fountains of her tears. She stretched out her hand for the black ribbon, put it round her own neck; after a while she said,

'If I live very long, and try hard to be very good all that time, do yo' think, Hester, as God will let me to him where he is?'

Monkshaven is altered now into a rising bathing place. Yet, standing near the site of widow Dobson's house on a summer's night, at the ebb of a spring-tide, you may hear the waves come lapping up the shelving shore with the same ceaseless, ever-recurrent sound as that which Philip listened to in the pauses between life and death.

And so it will be until 'there shall be no more sea'.

But the memory of man fades away. A few old people can still tell you the tradition of the man who died in a cottage somewhere about this spot,—died of starvation while his wife lived in hard-hearted plenty not two good stone-throws away. This is the form into which popular feeling, and ignorance of the real facts, have moulded the story. Not long since a lady went to the 'Public Baths', a handsome stone building erected on the very site of widow Dobson's cottage, and finding all the rooms engaged she sat down and had some talk with the bathing woman; and, as it chanced, the conversation fell on Philip Hepburn and the legend of his fate.

'I knew an old man when I was a girl,' said the bathing woman, 'as could niver abide to hear t' wife blamed. He would say nothing again' th' husband; he used to say as it were not fit for men to be judging; that she had had her sore trial, as well as Hepburn hisself.'

The lady asked, 'What became of the wife?'

'She was a pale, sad woman, allays dressed in black. I can just remember her when I was a little child, but she died before her daughter was well grown up; and Miss Rose took t' lassie, as had always been like her own.'

'Miss Rose?'

'Hester Rose! have yo' niver heared of Hester Rose, she as founded t' alms-houses for poor disabled sailors and soldiers on t' Horncastle road? There's a piece o' stone in front to say that "This building is erected in memory of P. H."—and some folk will have it P. H. stands for t' name o' th' man as was starved to death.'

'And the daughter?'

'One o' th' Fosters, them as founded t' Old Bank, left her a vast o' money; and she were married to distant cousin of theirs, and went off to settle in America many and many a year ago.'

THE END.

THE HALF-BROTHERS
by Elizabeth Gaskell

My mother was twice married. She never spoke of her first husband, and it is only from other people that I have learnt what little I know about him. I believe she was scarcely seventeen when she was married to him: and he was barely one-and-twenty. He rented a small farm up in Cumberland, somewhere towards the sea-coast; but he was perhaps too young and inexperienced to have the charge of land and cattle: anyhow, his affairs did not prosper, and he fell into ill health, and died of consumption before they had been three years man and wife, leaving my mother a young widow of twenty, with a little child only just able to walk, and the farm on her hands for four years more by the lease, with half the stock on it dead, or sold off one by one to pay the more pressing debts, and with no money to purchase more, or even to buy the provisions needed for the small consumption of every day. There was another child coming, too; and sad and sorry, I believe, she was to think of it. A dreary winter she must have had in her lonesome dwelling, with never another near it for miles around; her sister came to bear her company, and they two planned and plotted how to make every penny they could raise go as far as possible. I can't tell you how it happened that my little sister, whom I never saw, came to sicken and die; but, as if my poor mother's cup was not full enough, only a fortnight before Gregory was born the little girl took ill of scarlet fever, and in a week she lay dead. My mother was, I believe, just stunned with this last blow. My aunt has told me that she did not cry; aunt Fanny would have been thankful if she had; but she sat holding the poor wee lassie's hand and looking in her pretty, pale, dead face, without so much as shedding a tear. And it was all the same, when they had to take her away to be buried. She just kissed the child, and sat her down in the window-seat to watch the little black train of people (neighbours—my aunt, and one far-off cousin, who were all the friends they could muster) go winding away amongst the snow, which had fallen thinly over the country the night before. When my aunt came back from the funeral, she found my mother in the same place, and as dry-eyed as ever. So she continued until after Gregory was born; and, somehow, his coming seemed to loosen the tears, and she cried day and night, till my aunt and the other watcher looked at each other in dismay, and would fain have stopped her if they had but known how. But she bade them let her alone, and not be over-anxious, for every drop she shed eased her brain, which had been in a terrible state before for want of the power to cry. She seemed after that to think of nothing but her new little baby; she had hardly appeared to remember either her husband or her little daughter that lay dead in Brigham churchyard—at least so aunt Fanny said, but she was a great talker, and my mother was very silent by nature, and I think aunt Fanny may have been mistaken in believing that my mother never thought of her husband and child just because she never spoke about them. Aunt Fanny was older than my mother, and had a way of treating her like a child; but, for all that, she was a kind, warm-hearted creature, who thought more of her sister's welfare than she did of her own and it was on her bit of money that they principally lived, and on what the two could earn by working for the great Glasgow sewing-merchants. But by-and-by my mother's eye-sight began to fail. It was not that she was exactly blind, for she could see well enough to guide herself about the house, and to do a good deal of domestic work; but she could no longer do fine sewing and earn money. It must have been with the heavy crying she had had in her day, for she was but a young creature at this time, and as pretty a young woman, I have heard people say, as any on the country side. She took it sadly to heart that she could no longer gain anything towards the keep of herself and her child. My aunt Fanny would fain have persuaded her that she had enough to do in managing their cottage and minding Gregory; but my mother knew that they were pinched, and that aunt Fanny herself had not as much to eat, even of the commonest kind of food, as she could have done with; and as for Gregory, he was not a strong lad, and needed, not more food—for he always had enough, whoever went short—but better nourishment, and more flesh-meat. One day—it was aunt Fanny who told me all this about my poor mother, long after her death—as the sisters were sitting together, aunt Fanny working, and my mother hushing Gregory to sleep, William Preston, who was afterwards my father, came in. He was reckoned an old bachelor; I suppose he was long past forty, and he was one of the wealthiest farmers thereabouts, and had known my grandfather well, and my mother and my aunt in their more prosperous days. He sat down, and began to twirl his hat by way of being agreeable; my aunt Fanny talked, and he listened and looked at my mother. But he said very little, either on that visit, or on many another that he paid before he spoke out what had been the real purpose of his calling so often all along, and from the very first time he came to their house. One Sunday, however, my aunt Fanny stayed away from church, and took care of the child, and my mother went alone. When she came back, she ran straight upstairs, without going into the kitchen to look at Gregory or speak any word to her sister, and aunt Fanny heard her cry as if her heart was breaking; so she went up and scolded her right well through the bolted door, till at last she got her to open it. And then she threw herself on my aunt's neck, and told her that William Preston had asked her to marry him, and had promised to take good charge of her boy, and to let him want for nothing, neither in the way of keep nor of education, and that she had consented. Aunt Fanny was a good deal shocked at this; for, as I have said, she had often thought that my mother had forgotten her first husband very quickly, and now here was proof positive of it, if she could so soon think of marrying again. Besides as aunt Fanny used to say, she herself would have been a far more suitable match for a man of William Preston's age than Helen, who, though she was a widow, had not seen her four-and-twentieth summer. However, as aunt Fanny said, they had not asked her advice; and there was much to be said on the other side of the question. Helen's eyesight would never be good for much again, and as William Preston's wife she would never need to do anything, if she chose to sit with her hands before her; and a boy was a great charge to a widowed mother; and now there would be a decent steady man to see after him. So, by-and-by, aunt Fanny seemed to take a brighter view of the marriage than did my mother herself, who hardly ever looked up, and never smiled after the day when she promised William Preston to be his wife. But much as she had loved Gregory before, she seemed to love him more now. She was continually talking to him when they were alone, though he was far too young to understand her moaning words, or give her any comfort, except by his caresses.

At last William Preston and she were wed; and she went to be mistress of a well-stocked house, not above half-an-hour's walk from where aunt Fanny lived. I believe she did all that she could to please my father; and a more dutiful wife, I have heard him himself say, could never have been. But she did not love him, and he soon found it out. She loved Gregory, and she did not love him. Perhaps, love would have come in time, if he had been patient enough to wait; but it just turned him sour to see how her eye brightened and her colour came at the sight of that little child, while for him who had given her so much, she had only gentle words as cold as ice. He got to taunt her with the difference in her manner, as if that would bring love: and he took a positive dislike to Gregory,—he was so jealous of the ready love that always gushed out like a spring of fresh water when he came near. He wanted her to love him more, and perhaps that was all well and good; but he wanted her to love her child less, and that was an evil wish. One day, he gave way to his temper, and cursed and swore at Gregory, who had got into some mischief, as children will; my mother made some excuse for him; my father said it was hard enough to have to keep another man's child, without having it perpetually held up in its naughtiness by his wife, who ought to be always in the same mind that he was; and so from little they got to more; and the end of it was, that my mother took to her bed before her time, and I was born that very day. My father was glad, and proud, and sorry, all in a breath; glad and proud that a son was born to him; and sorry for his poor wife's state, and to think how his angry words had brought it on. But he was a man who liked better to be angry than sorry, so he soon found out that it was all Gregory's fault, and owed him an additional grudge for having hastened my birth. He had another grudge against him before long. My mother began to sink the day after I was born. My father sent to Carlisle for doctors, and would have coined his heart's blood into gold to save her, if that could have been; but it could not. My aunt Fanny used to say sometimes, that she thought that Helen did not wish to live, and so just let herself die away without trying to take hold on life; but when I questioned her, she owned that my mother did all the doctors bade her do, with the same sort of uncomplaining patience with which she had acted through life. One of her last requests was to have Gregory laid in her bed by my side, and then she made him take hold of my little hand. Her husband came in while she was looking at us so, and when he bent tenderly over her to ask her how she felt now, and seemed to gaze on us two little half-brothers, with a grave sort of kindness, she looked up in his face and smiled, almost her first smile at him; and such a sweet smile! as more besides aunt Fanny have said. In an hour she was dead. Aunt Fanny came to live with us. It was the best thing that could be done. My father would have been glad to return to his old mode of bachelor life, but what could he do with two little children? He needed a woman to take care of him, and who so fitting as his wife's elder sister? So she had the charge of me from my birth; and for a time I was weakly, as was but natural, and she was always beside me, night and day watching over me, and my father nearly as anxious as she. For his land had come down from father to son for more than three hundred years, and he would have cared for me merely as his flesh and blood that was to inherit the land after him. But he needed something to love, for all that, to most people, he was a stern, hard man, and he took to me as, I fancy, he had taken to no human being before—as he might have taken to my mother, if she had had no former life for him to be jealous of. I loved him back again right heartily. I loved all around me, I believe, for everybody was kind to me. After a time, I overcame my original weakness of constitution, and was just a bonny, strong-looking lad whom every passer-by noticed, when my father took me with him to the nearest town.

At home I was the darling of my aunt, the tenderly-beloved of my father, the pet and plaything of the old domestics, the "young master" of the farm-labourers, before whom I played many a lordly antic, assuming a sort of authority which sat oddly enough, I doubt not, on such a baby as I was.

Gregory was three years older than I. Aunt Fanny was always kind to him in deed and in action, but she did not often think about him, she had fallen so completely into the habit of being engrossed by me, from the fact of my having come into her charge as a delicate baby. My father never got over his grudging dislike to his stepson, who had so innocently wrestled with him for the possession of my mother's heart. I mistrust me, too, that my father always considered him as the cause of my mother's death and my early delicacy; and utterly unreasonable as this may seem, I believe my father rather cherished his feeling of alienation to my brother as a duty, than strove to repress it. Yet not for the world would my father have grudged him anything that money could purchase. That was, as it were, in the bond when he had wedded my mother. Gregory was lumpish and loutish, awkward and ungainly, marring whatever he meddled in, and many a hard word and sharp scolding did he get from the people about the farm, who hardly waited till my father's back was turned before they rated the stepson. I am ashamed—my heart is sore to think how I fell into the fashion of the family, and slighted my poor orphan step-brother. I don't think I ever scouted him, or was wilfully ill-natured to him; but the habit of being considered in all things, and being treated as something uncommon and superior, made me insolent in my prosperity, and I exacted more than Gregory was always willing to grant, and then, irritated, I sometimes repeated the disparaging words I had heard others use with regard to him, without fully understanding their meaning. Whether he did or not I cannot tell. I am afraid he did. He used to turn silent and quiet—sullen and sulky, my father thought it: stupid, aunt Fanny used to call it. But every one said he was stupid and dull, and this stupidity and dullness grew upon him. He would sit without speaking a word, sometimes, for hours; then my father would bid him rise and do some piece of work, maybe, about the farm. And he would take three or four tellings before he would go. When we were sent to school, it was all the same. He could never be made to remember his lessons; the school-master grew weary of scolding and flogging, and at last advised my father just to take him away, and set him to some farm-work that might not be above his comprehension. I think he was more gloomy and stupid than ever after this, yet he was not a cross lad; he was patient and good-natured, and would try to do a kind turn for any one, even if they had been scolding or cuffing him not a minute before. But very often his attempts at kindness ended in some mischief to the very people he was trying to serve, owing to his awkward, ungainly ways. I suppose I was a clever lad; at any rate, I always got plenty of praise; and was, as we called it, the cock of the school. The schoolmaster said I could learn anything I chose, but my father, who had no great learning himself, saw little use in much for me, and took me away betimes, and kept me with him about the farm. Gregory was made into a kind of shepherd, receiving his training under old Adam, who was nearly past his work. I think old Adam was almost the first person who had a good opinion of Gregory. He stood to it that my brother had good parts, though he did not rightly know how to bring them out; and, for knowing the bearings of the Fells, he said he had never seen a lad like him. My father would try to bring Adam round to speak of Gregory's faults and shortcomings; but, instead of that, he would praise him twice as much, as soon as he found out what was my father's object.

One winter-time, when I was about sixteen, and Gregory nineteen, I was sent by my father on an errand to a place about seven miles distant by the road, but only about four by the Fells. He bade me return by the road, whichever way I took in going, for the evenings closed in early, and were often thick and misty; besides which, old Adam, now paralytic and bedridden, foretold a downfall of snow before long. I soon got to my journey's end, and soon had done my business; earlier by an hour, I thought, than my father had expected, so I took the decision of the way by which I would return into my own hands, and set off back again over the Fells, just as the first shades of evening began to fall. It looked dark and gloomy enough; but everything was so still that I thought I should have plenty of time to get home before the snow came down. Off I set at a pretty quick pace. But night came on quicker. The right path was clear enough in the day-time, although at several points two or three exactly similar diverged from the same place; but when there was a good light, the traveller was guided by the sight of distant objects,—a piece of rock,—a fall in the ground—which were quite invisible to me now. I plucked up a brave heart, however, and took what seemed to me the right road. It was wrong, nevertheless, and led me whither I knew not, but to some wild boggy moor where the solitude seemed painful, intense, as if never footfall of man had come thither to break the silence. I tried to shout—with the dimmest possible hope of being heard—rather to reassure myself by the sound of my own voice; but my voice came husky and short, and yet it dismayed me; it seemed so weird and strange, in that noiseless expanse of black darkness. Suddenly the air was filled thick with dusky flakes, my face and hands were wet with snow. It cut me off from the slightest knowledge of where I was, for I lost every idea of the direction from which I had come, so that I could not even retrace my steps; it hemmed me in, thicker, thicker, with a darkness that might be felt. The boggy soil on which I stood quaked under me if I remained long in one place, and yet I dared not move far. All my youthful hardiness seemed to leave me at once. I was on the point of crying, and only very shame seemed to keep it down. To save myself from shedding tears, I shouted—terrible, wild shouts for bare life they were. I turned sick as I paused to listen; no answering sound came but the unfeeling echoes. Only the noiseless, pitiless snow kept falling thicker, thicker—faster, faster! I was growing numb and sleepy. I tried to move about, but I dared not go far, for fear of the precipices which, I knew, abounded in certain places on the Fells. Now and then, I stood still and shouted again; but my voice was getting choked with tears, as I thought of the desolate helpless death I was to die, and how little they at home, sitting round the warm, red, bright fire, wotted what was become of me,—and how my poor father would grieve for me—it would surely kill him—it would break his heart, poor old man! Aunt Fanny too—was this to be the end of all her cares for me? I began to review my life in a strange kind of vivid dream, in which the various scenes of my few boyish years passed before me like visions. In a pang of agony, caused by such remembrance of my short life, I gathered up my strength and called out once more, a long, despairing, wailing cry, to which I had no hope of obtaining any answer, save from the echoes around, dulled as the sound might be by the thickened air. To my surprise I heard a cry—almost as long, as wild as mine—so wild that it seemed unearthly, and I almost thought it must be the voice of some of the mocking spirits of the Fells, about whom I had heard so many tales. My heart suddenly began to beat fast and loud. I could not reply for a minute or two. I nearly fancied I had lost the power of utterance. Just at this moment a dog barked. Was it Lassie's bark—my brother's collie?—an ugly enough brute, with a white, ill-looking face, that my father always kicked whenever he saw it, partly for its own demerits, partly because it belonged to my brother. On such occasions, Gregory would whistle Lassie away, and go off and sit with her in some outhouse. My father had once or twice been ashamed of himself, when the poor collie had yowled out with the suddenness of the pain, and had relieved himself of his self-reproach by blaming my brother, who, he said, had no notion of training a dog, and was enough to ruin any collie in Christendom with his stupid way of allowing them to lie by the kitchen fire. To all which Gregory would answer nothing, nor even seem to hear, but go on looking absent and moody.

Yes! there again! It was Lassie's bark! Now or never! I lifted up my voice and shouted "Lassie! Lassie! for God's sake, Lassie!" Another moment, and the great white-faced Lassie was curving and gambolling with delight round my feet and legs, looking, however, up in my face with her intelligent, apprehensive eyes, as if fearing lest I might greet her with a blow, as I had done oftentimes before. But I cried with gladness, as I stooped down and patted her. My mind was sharing in my body's weakness, and I could not reason, but I knew that help was at hand. A gray figure came more and more distinctly out of the thick, close-pressing darkness. It was Gregory wrapped in his maud.

"Oh, Gregory!" said I, and I fell upon his neck, unable to speak another word. He never spoke much, and made me no answer for some little time. Then he told me we must move, we must walk for the dear life—we must find our road home, if possible; but we must move, or we should be frozen to death.

"Don't you know the way home?" asked I.

"I thought I did when I set out, but I am doubtful now. The snow blinds me, and I am feared that in moving about just now, I have lost the right gait homewards."

He had his shepherd's staff with him, and by dint of plunging it before us at every step we took—clinging close to each other, we went on safely enough, as far as not falling down any of the steep rocks, but it was slow, dreary work. My brother, I saw, was more guided by Lassie and the way she took than anything else, trusting to her instinct. It was too dark to see far before us; but he called her back continually, and noted from what quarter she returned, and shaped our slow steps accordingly. But the tedious motion scarcely kept my very blood from freezing. Every bone, every fibre in my body seemed first to ache, and then to swell, and then to turn numb with the intense cold. My brother bore it better than I, from having been more out upon the hills. He did not speak, except to call Lassie. I strove to be brave, and not complain; but now I felt the deadly fatal sleep stealing over me.

"I can go no farther," I said, in a drowsy tone. I remember I suddenly became dogged and resolved. Sleep I would, were it only for five minutes. If death were to be the consequence, sleep I would. Gregory stood still. I suppose, he recognized the peculiar phase of suffering to which I had been brought by the cold.

"It is of no use," said he, as if to himself. "We are no nearer home than we were when we started, as far as I can tell. Our only chance is in Lassie. Here! roll thee in my maud, lad, and lay thee down on this sheltered side of this bit of rock. Creep close under it, lad, and I'll lie by thee, and strive to keep the warmth in us. Stay! hast gotten aught about thee they'll know at home?"

I felt him unkind thus to keep me from slumber, but on his repeating the question, I pulled out my pocket-handkerchief, of some showy pattern, which Aunt Fanny had hemmed for me—Gregory took it, and tied it round Lassie's neck.

"Hie thee, Lassie, hie thee home!" And the white-faced ill-favoured brute was off like a shot in the darkness. Now I might lie down—now I might sleep. In my drowsy stupor I felt that I was being tenderly covered up by my brother; but what with I neither knew nor cared—I was too dull, too selfish, too numb to think and reason, or I might have known that in that bleak bare place there was nought to wrap me in, save what was taken off another. I was glad enough when he ceased his cares and lay down by me. I took his hand.

"Thou canst not remember, lad, how we lay together thus by our dying mother. She put thy small, wee hand in mine—I reckon she sees us now; and belike we shall soon be with her. Anyhow, God's will be done."

"Dear Gregory," I muttered, and crept nearer to him for warmth. He was talking still, and again about our mother, when I fell asleep. In an instant—or so it seemed—there were many voices about me—many faces hovering round me—the sweet luxury of warmth was stealing into every part of me. I was in my own little bed at home. I am thankful to say, my first word was "Gregory?"

A look passed from one to another—my father's stern old face strove in vain to keep its sternness; his mouth quivered, his eyes filled slowly with unwonted tears.

"I would have given him half my land—I would have blessed him as my son,—oh God! I would have knelt at his feet, and asked him to forgive my hardness of heart."

I heard no more. A whirl came through my brain, catching me back to death.

I came slowly to my consciousness, weeks afterwards. My father's hair was white when I recovered, and his hands shook as he looked into my face.

We spoke no more of Gregory. We could not speak of him; but he was strangely in our thoughts. Lassie came and went with never a word of blame; nay, my father would try to stroke her, but she shrank away; and he, as if reproved by the poor dumb beast, would sigh, and be silent and abstracted for a time.

Aunt Fanny—always a talker—told me all. How, on that fatal night, my father,—irritated by my prolonged absence, and probably more anxious than he cared to show, had been fierce and imperious, even beyond his wont, to Gregory; had upbraided him with his father's poverty, his own stupidity which made his services good for nothing—for so, in spite of the old shepherd, my father always chose to consider them. At last, Gregory had risen up, and whistled Lassie out with him—poor Lassie, crouching underneath his chair for fear of a kick or a blow. Some time before, there had been some talk between my father and my aunt respecting my return; and when aunt Fanny told me all this, she said she fancied that Gregory might have noticed the coming storm, and gone out silently to meet me. Three hours afterwards, when all were running about in wild alarm, not knowing whither to go in search of me—not even missing Gregory, or heeding his absence, poor fellow—poor, poor fellow!—Lassie came home, with my handkerchief tied round her neck. They knew and understood, and the whole strength of the farm was turned out to follow her, with wraps, and blankets, and brandy, and every thing that could be thought of. I lay in chilly sleep, but still alive, beneath the rock that Lassie guided them to. I was covered over with my brother's plaid, and his thick shepherd's coat was carefully wrapped round my feet. He was in his shirt-sleeves—his arm thrown over me—a quiet smile (he had hardly ever smiled in life) upon his still, cold face.

My father's last words were, "God forgive me my hardness of heart towards the fatherless child!"

And what marked the depth of his feeling of repentance, perhaps more than all, considering the passionate love he bore my mother, was this: we found a paper of directions after his death, in which he desired that he might lie at the foot of the grave, in which, by his desire, poor Gregory had been laid with OUR MOTHER.

THE MANCHESTER MARRIAGE

Elizabeth Gaskell

(*Household Words*, Christmas 1858)

Mr and Mrs Openshaw came from Manchester to settle in London. He had been, what is called in Lancashire, a salesman for a large manufacturing firm, who were extending their business, and opening a warehouse in the city; where Mr Openshaw was now to superintend their affairs. He rather enjoyed the change; having a kind of curiosity about London, which he had never yet been able to gratify in his brief visits to the metropolis. At the same time, he had an odd, shrewd contempt for the inhabitants, whom he always pictured to himself as fine, lazy people, caring nothing but for fashion and aristocracy, and lounging away their days in Bond Street, and such places; ruining good English, and ready in their turn to despise him as a provincial. The hours that the men of business kept in the city scandalized him too, accustomed as he was to the early dinners of Manchester folk and the consequently far longer evenings. Still, he was pleased to go to London, though he would not for the world have confessed it, even to himself, and always spoke of the step to his friends as one demanded of him by the interests of his employers, and sweetened to him by a considerable increase of salary. This, indeed, was so liberal that he might have been justified in taking a much larger house than the one he did, had he not thought himself bound to set an example to Londoners of how little a Manchester man of business cared for show. Inside, however, he furnished it with an unusual degree of comfort, and, in the winter-time, he insisted on keeping up as large fires as the grates would allow, in every room where the temperature was in the least chilly. Moreover, his northern sense of hospitality was such that, if he were at home, he could hardly suffer a visitor to leave the house without forcing meat and drink upon him. Every servant in the house was well warmed, well fed, and kindly treated; for their master scorned all petty saving in aught that conduced to comfort; while he amused himself by following out all his accustomed habits and individual ways, in defiance of what any of his new neighbours might think.

His wife was a pretty, gentle woman, of suitable age and character. He was forty-two, she thirty-five. He was loud and decided; she soft and yielding. They had two children; or rather, I should say, she had two; for the elder, a girl of eleven, was Mrs Openshaw's child by Frank Wilson, her first husband. The younger was a little boy, Edwin, who could just prattle, and to whom his father delighted to speak in the broadest and most unintelligible Lancashire dialect, in order to keep up what he called the true Saxon accent.

Mrs Openshaw's Christian name was Alice, and her first husband had been her own cousin. She was the orphan niece of a sea-captain in Liverpool; a quiet, grave little creature, of great personal attraction when she was fifteen or sixteen, with regular features and a blooming complexion. But she was very shy, and believed herself to be very stupid and awkward; and was frequently scolded by her aunt, her own uncle's second wife. So when her cousin, Frank Wilson, came home from a long absence at sea, and first was kind and protective to her; secondly, attentive; and thirdly, desperately in love with her, she hardly knew how to be grateful enough to him. It is true, she would have preferred his remaining in the first or second stages of behaviour; for his violent love puzzled and frightened her. Her uncle neither helped nor hindered the love affair, though it was going on under his own eyes. Frank's stepmother had such a variable temper, that there was no knowing whether what she liked one day she would like the next, or not. At length she went to such extremes of crossness that Alice was only too glad to shut her eyes and rush blindly at the chance of escape from domestic tyranny offered her by a marriage with her cousin; and, liking him better than any one in the world, except her uncle (who was at this time at sea), she went off one morning and was married to him, her only bridesmaid being the housemaid at her aunt's. The consequence was that Frank and his wife went into lodgings, and Mrs Wilson refused to see them, and turned away Norah, the warm-hearted housemaid, whom they accordingly took into their service. When Captain Wilson returned from his voyage he was very cordial with the young couple, and spent many an evening at their lodgings, smoking his pipe and sipping his grog; but he told them, for quietness' sake, he could not ask them to his own house; for his wife was bitter against them. They were not, however, very unhappy about this.

The seed of future unhappiness lay rather in Frank's vehement, passionate disposition, which led him to resent his wife's shyness and want of demonstrativeness as failures in conjugal duty. He was already tormenting himself, and her too in a slighter degree, by apprehensions and imaginations of what might befall her during his approaching absence at sea. At last, he went to his father and urged him to insist upon Alice's being once more received under his roof; the more especially as there was now a prospect of her confinement while her husband was away on his voyage. Captain Wilson was, as he himself expressed it, 'breaking up', and unwilling to undergo the excitement of a scene; yet he felt that what his son said was true. So he went to his wife. And before Frank set sail, he had the comfort of seeing his wife installed in her old little garret in his father's house. To have placed her in the one best spare room was a step beyond Mrs Wilson's powers of submission or generosity. The worst part about it, however, was that the faithful Norah had to be dismissed. Her place as housemaid had been filled up; and, even if it had not, she had forfeited Mrs Wilson's good opinion for ever. She comforted her young master and mistress by pleasant prophecies of the time when they would have a household of their own; of which, whatever service she might be in meanwhile, she should be sure to form a part. Almost the last action Frank did, before setting sail, was going with Alice to see Norah once more at her mother's house; and then he went away.

Alice's father-in-law grew more and more feeble as winter advanced. She was of great use to her stepmother in nursing and amusing him; and although there was anxiety enough in the household, there was, perhaps, more of peace than there had been for years, for Mrs Wilson had not a bad heart, and was softened by the visible approach of death to one whom she loved, and touched by the lonely condition of the young creature expecting her first confinement in her husband's absence. To this relenting mood Norah owed the permission to come and nurse Alice when her baby was born, and to remain and attend on Captain Wilson.

Before one letter had been received from Frank (who had sailed for the East Indies and China), his father died. Alice was always glad to remember that he had held her baby in his arms, and kissed and blessed it before his death. After that, and the consequent examination into the state of his affairs, it was found that he had left far less property than people had been led by his style of living to expect; and what money there was, was settled all upon his wife, and at her disposal after her death. This did not signify much to Alice, as Frank was now first mate of his ship, and, in another voyage or two, would be captain. Meanwhile he had left her rather more than two hundred pounds (all his savings) in the bank.

It became time for Alice to hear from her husband. One letter from the Cape she had already received. The next was to announce his arrival in India. As week after week passed over, and no intelligence of the ship having got there reached the office of the owners, and the captain's wife was in the same state of ignorant suspense as Alice herself, her fears grew most oppressive. At length the day came when, in reply to her inquiry at the shipping office, they told her that the owners had given up hope of ever hearing more of the *Betsy-Jane* and had sent in their claim upon the underwriters. Now that he was gone for ever, she first felt a yearning, longing love for the kind cousin, the dear friend, the sympathizing protector, whom she should never see again;—first felt a passionate desire to show him his child, whom she had hitherto rather craved to have all to herself—her own sole possession. Her grief was, however, noiseless and quiet—rather to the scandal of Mrs Wilson who bewailed her stepson as if he and she had always lived together in perfect harmony, and who evidently thought it her duty to burst into fresh tears at every strange face she saw; dwelling on his poor young widow's desolate state, and the helplessness of the fatherless child, with an unction as if she liked the excitement of the sorrowful story.

So passed away the first days of Alice's widowhood. By and by things subsided into their natural and tranquil course. But, as if the young creature was always to be in some heavy trouble, her ewe-lamb began to be ailing, pining, and sickly. The child's mysterious illness turned out to be some affection of the spine, likely to affect health but not to shorten life—at least, so the doctors said. But the long, dreary suffering of one whom a mother loves as Alice loved her only child, is hard to look forward to. Only Norah guessed what Alice suffered; no one but God knew.

And so it fell out, that when Mrs Wilson, the elder, came to her one day, in violent distress, occasioned by a very material diminution in the value of the property that her husband had left her—a diminution which made her income barely enough to support herself, much less Alice—the latter could hardly understand how anything which did not touch health or life could cause such grief; and she received the intelligence with irritating composure. But when, that afternoon, the little sick child was brought in, and the grandmother—who, after all, loved it well—began a fresh moan over her losses to its unconscious ears—saying how she had planned to consult this or that doctor, and to give it this or that comfort or luxury in after years, but that now all chance of this had passed away—Alice's heart was touched, and she drew near to Mrs Wilson with unwonted caresses, and, in a spirit not unlike to that of Ruth, entreated that, come what would, they might remain together. After much discussion in succeeding days, it was arranged that Mrs Wilson should take a house in Manchester, furnishing it partly with what furniture she had, and providing the rest with Alice's remaining two hundred pounds. Mrs Wilson was herself a Manchester woman, and naturally longed to return to her native town; some connexions of her own, too, at that time required lodgings, for which they were willing to pay pretty handsomely. Alice undertook the active superintendence and superior work of the household; Norah—willing, faithful Norah—offered to cook, scour, do anything in short, so that she might but remain with them.

The plan succeeded. For some years their first lodgers remained with them, and all went smoothly—with that one sad exception of the little girl's increasing deformity. How that mother loved that child, it is not for words to tell!

Then came a break of misfortune. Their lodgers left, and no one succeeded to them. After some months, it became necessary to remove to a smaller house; and Alice's tender conscience was torn by the idea that she ought not to be a burden to her mother-in-law, but to go out and seek her own maintenance. And leave her child! The thought came like the sweeping boom of a funeral-bell over her heart.

By and by, Mr Openshaw came to lodge with them. He had started in life as the errand-boy and sweeper-out of a warehouse; had struggled up through all the grades of employment in it, fighting his way through the hard, striving Manchester life with strong, pushing energy of character. Every spare moment of time had been sternly given up to self-teaching. He was a capital accountant, a good French and German scholar, a keen, far-seeing tradesman—understanding markets and the bearing of events, both near and distant, on trade; and yet, with such vivid attention to present details, that I do not think he ever saw a group of flowers in the fields without thinking whether their colour would, or would not, form harmonious contrasts in the coming spring muslins and prints. He went to debating societies, and threw himself with all his heart and soul into politics; esteeming, it must be owned, every man a fool or a knave who differed from him, and overthrowing his opponents rather by the loud strength of his language than the calm strength of his logic. There was something of the Yankee in all this. Indeed, his theory ran parallel to the famous Yankee motto—'England flogs creation, and Manchester flogs England.' Such a man, as may be fancied, had had no time for falling in love, or any such nonsense. At the age when most young men go through their courting and matrimony, he had not the means of keeping a wife, and was far too practical to think of having one. And now that he was in easy circumstances, a rising man, he considered women almost as encumbrances to the world, with whom a man had better have as little to do as possible. His first impression of Alice was indistinct, and he did not care enough about her to make it distinct. 'A pretty, yea-nay kind of woman', would have been his description of her, if he had been pushed into a corner. He was rather afraid, in the beginning, that her quiet ways arose from a listlessness and laziness of character, which would have been exceedingly discordant to his active, energetic nature. But, when he found out the punctuality with which his wishes were attended to, and her work was done; when he was called in the morning at the very stroke of the clock, his shaving-water scalding hot, his fire bright, his coffee made exactly as his peculiar fancy dictated (for he was a man who had his theory about everything based upon what he knew of science, and often perfectly original)—then he began to think: not that Alice had any particular merit, but that he had got into remarkably good lodgings; his restlessness wore away, and he began to consider himself as almost settled for life in them.

Mr Openshaw had been too busy, all his days, to be introspective. He did not know that he had any tenderness in his nature; and if he had become conscious of its abstract existence he would have considered it as a manifestation of disease in some part of him. But he was decoyed into pity unawares; and pity led on to tenderness. That little helpless child— always carried about by one of the three busy women of the house, or else patiently threading coloured beads in the chair from which, by no effort of its own, could it ever move—the great grave blue eyes, full of serious, not uncheerful, expression, giving to the small delicate face a look beyond its years—the soft plaintive voice dropping out but few words, so unlike the continual prattle of a child—caught Mr Openshaw's attention in spite of himself. One day—he half scorned himself for doing so—he cut short his dinner-hour to go in search of some toy, which should take the place of those eternal beads. I forget what he bought; but, when he gave the present (which he took care to do in a short abrupt manner, and when no one was by to see him), he was almost thrilled by the flash of delight that came over that child's face, and he could not help, all through that afternoon, going over and over again the picture left on his memory, by the bright effect of unexpected joy on the little girl's face. When he returned home, he found his slippers placed by his sitting-room fire; and even more careful attention paid to his fancies than was habitual in those model lodgings. When Alice had taken the last of his tea-things away—she had been silent as usual till then—she stood for an instant with the door in her hand. Mr Openshaw looked as if he were deep in his book, though in fact he did not see a line; but was heartily wishing the woman would go, and not make any palaver of gratitude. But she only said:

'I am very much obliged to you, sir. Thank you very much,' and was gone, even before he could send her away with a 'There, my good woman, that's enough!'

For some time longer he took no apparent notice of the child. He even hardened his heart into disregarding her sudden flush of colour and little timid smile of recognition, when he saw her by chance. But, after all, this could not last for ever; and, having a second time given way to tenderness, there was no relapse. The insidious enemy having thus entered his heart, in the guise of compassion to the child, soon assumed the more dangerous form of interest in the mother. He was aware of this change of feeling—despised himself for it—struggled with it; nay, internally yielded to it and cherished it, long before he suffered the slightest expression of it, by word, action, or look to escape him. He watched Alice's docile, obedient ways to her stepmother; the love which she had inspired in the rough Norah (roughened by the wear and tear of sorrow and years); but, above all, he saw the wild, deep, passionate affection existing between her and her child. They spoke little to anyone else, or when anyone else was by; but, when alone together, they talked, and murmured, and cooed, and chattered so continually, that Mr Openshaw first wondered what they could find to say to each other, and next became irritated because they were always so grave and silent with him. All this time he was perpetually devising small new pleasures for the child. His thoughts ran, in a pertinacious way, upon the desolate life before her; and often he came back from his day's work loaded with the very thing Alice had been longing for, but had not been able to procure. One time, it was a little chair for drawing the little sufferer along the streets; and, many an evening that following summer, Mr Openshaw drew her along himself, regardless of the remarks of his acquaintances. One day in autumn, he put down his newspaper, as Alice came in with the breakfast, and said, in as indifferent a voice as he could assume:

'Mrs Frank, is there any reason why we two should not put up our horses together?'

Alice stood still in perplexed wonder. What did he mean? He had resumed the reading of his newspaper, as if he did not expect any answer; so she found silence her safest course, and went on quietly arranging his breakfast, without another word passing between them. Just as he was leaving the house, to go to the warehouse as usual, he turned back and put his head into the bright, neat, tidy kitchen, where all the women breakfasted in the morning:

'You'll think of what I said, Mrs Frank' (this was her name with the lodgers), 'and let me have your opinion upon it tonight.'

Alice was thankful that her mother and Norah were too busy talking together to attend much to this speech. She determined not to think about it at all through the day; and, of course, the effort not to think made her think all the more. At night she sent up Norah with his tea. But Mr Openshaw almost knocked Norah down as she was going out at the door, by pushing past her and calling out, 'Mrs Frank!' in an impatient voice, at the top of the stairs.

Alice went up, rather than seem to have affixed too much meaning to his words.

'Well, Mrs Frank,' he said, 'what answer? Don't make it too long; for
I have lots of office work to get through tonight.'

'I hardly know what you meant, sir,' said truthful Alice.

'Well! I should have thought you might have guessed. You're not new at this sort of work, and I am. However, I'll make it plain this time. Will you have me to be thy wedded husband, and serve me, and love me, and honour me, and all that sort of thing? Because, if you will, I will do as much by you, and be a father to your child—and that's more than is put in the prayer-book. Now, I'm a man of my word; and what I say, I feel; and what I promise, I'll do. Now, for your answer!'

Alice was silent. He began to make the tea, as if her reply was a matter of perfect indifference to him; but, as soon as that was done, he became impatient.

'Well?' said he.

'How long, sir, may I have to think over it?'

'Three minutes!' (looking at his watch). 'You've had two already—that makes five. Be a sensible woman, say Yes, and sit down to tea with me, and we'll talk it over together; for, after tea, I shall be busy; say No' (he hesitated a moment to try and keep his voice in the same tone), 'and I shan't say another word about it, but pay up a year's rent for my rooms tomorrow, and be off. Time's up! Yes or no?'

'If you please, sir—you have been so good to little Ailsie—'

'There, sit down comfortably by me on the sofa, and let's have our tea together. I am glad to find you are as good and sensible as I took you for.'

And this was Alice Wilson's second wooing.

Mr Openshaw's will was too strong, and his circumstances too good, for him not to carry all before him. He settled Mrs Wilson in a comfortable house of her own, and made her quite independent of lodgers. The little that Alice said with regard to future plans was in Norah's behalf.

'No,' said Mr Openshaw. 'Norah shall take care of the old lady as long as she lives; and, after that, she shall either come and live with us, or, if she likes it better, she shall have a provision for life—for your sake, missus. No one who has been good to you or the child shall go unrewarded. But even the little one will be better for some fresh stuff about her. Get her a bright, sensible girl as a nurse; one who won't go rubbing her with calf's-foot jelly as Norah does; wasting good stuff outside that ought to go in, but will follow doctors' directions; which, as you must see pretty clearly by this time, Norah won't; because they give the poor little wench pain. Now, I'm not above being nesh for other folks myself. I can stand a good blow, and never change colour; but, set me in the operating room in the infirmary, and I turn as sick as a girl. Yet, if need were, I would hold the little wench on my knees while she screeched with pain, if it were to do her poor back good. Nay, nay, wench! keep your white looks for the time when it comes—I don't say it ever will. But this I know, Norah will spare the child and cheat the doctor, if she can. Now, I say, give the bairn a year or two's chance, and then, when the pack of doctors have done their best—and, maybe, the old lady has gone—we'll have Norah back or do better for her.'

The pack of doctors could do no good to little Ailsie. She was beyond their power. But her father (for so he insisted on being called, and also on Alice's no longer retaining the appellation of Mamma, but becoming henceforward Mother), by his healthy cheerfulness of manner, his clear decision of purpose, his odd turns and quirks of humour, added to his real strong love for the helpless little girl, infused a new element of brightness and confidence into her life; and, though her back remained the same, her general health was strengthened, and Alice—never going beyond a smile herself—had the pleasure of seeing her child taught to laugh.

As for Alice's own life, it was happier than it had ever been before. Mr Openshaw required no demonstration, no expressions of affection from her. Indeed, these would rather have disgusted him. Alice could love deeply, but could not talk about it. The perpetual requirement of loving words, looks, and caresses, and misconstruing their absence into absence of love, had been the great trial of her former married life. Now, all went on clear and straight, under the guidance of her husband's strong sense, warm heart, and powerful will. Year by year their worldly prosperity increased. At Mrs Wilson's death, Norah came back to them as nurse to the newly-born little Edwin; into which post she was not installed without a pretty strong oration on the part of the proud and happy father, who declared that if he found out that Norah ever tried to screen the boy by a falsehood, or to make him nesh either in body or mind, she should go that very day. Norah and Mr Openshaw were not on the most thoroughly cordial terms; neither of them fully recognizing or appreciating the other's best qualities.

This was the previous history of the Lancashire family who had now removed to London.

They had been there about a year, when Mr Openshaw suddenly informed his wife that he had determined to heal long-standing feuds, and had asked his uncle and aunt Chadwick to come and pay them a visit and see London. Mrs Openshaw had never seen this uncle and aunt of her husband's. Years before she had married him, there had been a quarrel. All she knew was, that Mr Chadwick was a small manufacturer in a country town in South Lancashire. She was extremely pleased that the breach was to be healed, and began making preparations to render their visit pleasant.

They arrived at last. Going to see London was such an event to them, that Mrs Chadwick had made all new linen fresh for the occasion—from night-caps downwards; and as for gowns, ribbons, and collars, she might have been going into the wilds of Canada where never a shop is, so large was her stock. A fortnight before the day of her departure for London, she had formally called to take leave of all her acquaintance; saying she should need every bit of the intermediate time for packing up. It was like a second wedding in her imagination; and, to complete the resemblance which an entirely new wardrobe made between the two events, her husband brought her back from Manchester, on the last market-day before they set off, a gorgeous pearl and amethyst brooch, saying, 'Lunnon should see that Lancashire folks knew a handsome thing when they saw it.'

For some time after Mr and Mrs Chadwick arrived at the Openshaws' there was no opportunity for wearing this brooch; but at length they obtained an order to see Buckingham Palace, and the spirit of loyalty demanded that Mrs Chadwick should wear her best clothes in visiting the abode of her sovereign. On her return she hastily changed her dress; for Mr Openshaw had planned that they should go to Richmond, drink tea, and return by moonlight. Accordingly, about five o'clock, Mr and Mrs Openshaw and Mr and Mrs Chadwick set off.

The housemaid and cook sat below, Norah hardly knew where. She was always engrossed in the nursery in tending her two children, and in sitting by the restless, excitable Ailsie till she fell asleep. By and by the housemaid Bessy tapped gently at the door. Norah went to her, and they spoke in whispers.

'Nurse! there's someone downstairs wants you.'

'Wants me! who is it?'

'A gentleman—'

'A gentleman? Nonsense!'

'Well! a man, then, and he asks for you, and he rang at the front-door bell, and has walked into the dining-room.'

'You should never have let him,' exclaimed Norah. 'Master and missus out—'

'I did not want him to come in; but, when he heard you lived here, he walked past me, and sat down on the first chair, and said, "Tell her to come and speak to me." There is no gas lighted in the room, and supper is all set out.'

'He'll be off with the spoons!' exclaimed Norah, putting the housemaid's fear into words, and preparing to leave the room; first, however, giving a look to Ailsie, sleeping soundly and calmly.

Downstairs she went, uneasy fears stirring in her bosom. Before she entered the dining-room she provided herself with a candle, and, with it in her hand, she went in, looking around her in the darkness for her visitor.

He was standing up, holding by the table. Norah and he looked at each other; gradual recognition coming into their eyes.

'Norah?' at length he asked.

'Who are you?' asked Norah, with the sharp tones of alarm and incredulity. 'I don't know you'; trying, by futile words of disbelief, to do away with the terrible fact before her.

'Am I so changed?' he said pathetically. 'I dare say I am. But, Norah, tell me!' he breathed hard, 'where is my wife? Is she—is she alive?'

He came nearer to Norah, and would have taken her hand; but she backed away from him; looking at him all the time with staring eyes, as if he were some horrible object. Yet he was a handsome, bronzed, good-looking fellow, with beard and moustache, giving him a foreign-looking aspect; but his eyes! there was no mistaking those eager, beautiful eyes—the very same that Norah had watched not half an hour ago, till sleep stole softly over them.

'Tell me, Norah—I can bear it—I have feared it so often. Is she dead?' Norah still kept silence. 'She is dead!' He hung on Norah's words and looks, as if for confirmation or contradiction.

'What shall I do?' groaned Norah. 'Oh, sir! why did you come? how did you find me out? where have you been? We thought you dead, we did indeed!' She poured out words and questions to gain time, as if time would help her.

'Norah! answer me this question straight, by yes or no—Is my wife dead?'

'No, she is not,' said Norah, slowly and heavily.

'Oh, what a relief! Did she receive my letters? But perhaps you don't know. Why did you leave her? Where is she? Oh, Norah, tell me all quickly!'

'Mr Frank!' said Norah at last, almost driven to bay by her terror lest her mistress should return at any moment and find him there—unable to consider what was best to be done or said—rushing at something decisive, because she could not endure her present state: 'Mr Frank! we never heard a line from you, and the shipowners said you had gone down, you and everyone else. We thought you were dead, if ever man was, and poor Miss Alice and her little sick, helpless child! Oh, sir, you must guess it,' cried the poor creature at last, bursting out into a passionate fit of crying, 'for indeed I cannot tell it. But it was no one's fault. God help us all this night!'

Norah had sat down. She trembled too much to stand. He took her hands in his. He squeezed them hard, as if, by physical pressure, the truth could be wrung out.

'Norah.' This time his tone was calm, stagnant as despair. 'She has married again!'

Norah shook her head sadly. The grasp slowly relaxed. The man had fainted.

There was brandy in the room. Norah forced some drops into Mr Frank's mouth, chafed his hands, and—when mere animal life returned, before the mind poured in its flood of memories and thoughts—she lifted him up, and rested his head against her knees. Then she put a few crumbs of bread taken from the supper-table, soaked in brandy, into his mouth. Suddenly he sprang to his feet.

'Where is she? Tell me this instant.' He looked so wild, so mad, so desperate, that Norah felt herself to be in bodily danger; but her time of dread had gone by. She had been afraid to tell him the truth, and then she had been a coward. Now, her wits were sharpened by the sense of his desperate state. He must leave the house. She would pity him afterwards; but now she must rather command and upbraid; for he must leave the house before her mistress came home. That one necessity stood clear before her.

'She is not here: that is enough for you to know. Nor can I say exactly where she is' (which was true to the letter if not to the spirit). 'Go away, and tell me where to find you tomorrow, and I will tell you all. My master and mistress may come back at any minute, and then what would become of me, with a strange man in the house?'

Such an argument was too petty to touch his excited mind.

'I don't care for your master and mistress. If your master is a man, he must feel for me—poor shipwrecked sailor that I am—kept for years a prisoner amongst savages, always, always, always thinking of my wife and my home—dreaming of her by night, talking to her though she could not hear, by day. I loved her more than all heaven and earth put together. Tell me where she is, this instant, you wretched woman, who salved over her wickedness to her, as you do to me!'

The clock struck ten. Desperate positions require desperate measures.

'If you will leave the house now, I will come to you tomorrow and tell you all. What is more, you shall see your child now. She lies sleeping upstairs. Oh, sir, you have a child, you do not know that as yet—a little weakly girl—with just a heart and soul beyond her years. We have reared her up with such care! We watched her, for we thought for many a year she might die any day, and we tended her, and no hard thing has come near her, and no rough word has ever been said to her. And now you come and will take her life into your hand, and will crush it. Strangers to her have been kind to her; but her own father—Mr Frank, I am her nurse, and I love her, and I tend her, and I would do anything for her that I could. Her mother's heart beats as hers beats; and, if she suffers a pain, her mother trembles all over. If she is happy, it is her mother that smiles and is glad. If she is growing stronger, her mother is healthy: if she dwindles, her mother languishes. If she dies—well, I don't know; it is not everyone can lie down and die when they wish it. Come upstairs, Mr Frank, and see your child. Seeing her will do good to your poor heart. Then go away, in God's name, just this one night; tomorrow, if need be, you can do anything—kill us all if you will, or show yourself a great, grand man, whom God will bless for ever and ever. Come, Mr Frank, the look of a sleeping child is sure to give peace.'

She led him upstairs; at first almost helping his steps, till they came near the nursery door. She had wellnigh forgotten the existence of little Edwin. It struck upon her with affright as the shaded light fell over the other cot; but she skilfully threw that corner of the room into darkness, and let the light fall on the sleeping Ailsie. The child had thrown down the coverings, and her deformity, as she lay with her back to them, was plainly visible through her slight nightgown. Her little face, deprived of the lustre of her eyes, looked wan and pinched, and had a pathetic expression in it, even as she slept. The poor father looked and looked with hungry, wistful eyes, into which the big tears came swelling up slowly and dropped heavily down, as he stood trembling and shaking all over. Norah was angry with herself for growing impatient of the length of time that long lingering gaze lasted. She thought that she waited for full half an hour before Frank stirred. And then—instead of going away—he sank down on his knees by the bedside, and buried his face in the clothes. Little Ailsie stirred uneasily. Norah pulled him up in terror. She could afford no more time, even for prayer, in her extremity of fear; for surely the next moment would bring her mistress home. She took him forcibly by the arm; but, as he was going, his eye lighted on the other bed; he stopped. Intelligence came back into his face. His hands clenched.

'His child?' he asked.

'Her child,' replied Norah. 'God watches over him,' she said instinctively; for Frank's looks excited her fears, and she needed to remind herself of the Protector of the helpless.

'God has not watched over me,' he said, in despair; his thoughts apparently recoiling on his own desolate, deserted state. But Norah had no time for pity. Tomorrow she would be as compassionate as her heart prompted. At length she guided him downstairs, and shut the outer door, and bolted it—as if by bolts to keep out facts.

Then she went back into the dining-room, and effaced all traces of his presence, as far as she could. She went upstairs to the nursery and sat there, her head on her hand, thinking what was to come of all this misery. It seemed to her very long before her master and mistress returned; yet it was hardly eleven o'clock. She heard the loud, hearty Lancashire voices on the stairs; and, for the first time, she understood the contrast of the desolation of the poor man who had so lately gone forth in lonely despair.

It almost put her out of patience to see Mrs Openshaw come in, calmly smiling, handsomely dressed, happy, easy, to inquire after her children.

'Did Ailsie go to sleep comfortably?' she whispered to Norah.

'Yes.'

Her mother bent over her, looking at her slumbers with the soft eyes of love. How little she dreamed who had looked on her last! Then she went to Edwin, with perhaps less wistful anxiety in her countenance, but more of pride. She took off her things, to go down to supper. Norah saw her no more that night.

Beside having a door into the passage, the sleeping-nursery opened out of Mr and Mrs Openshaw's room, in order that they might have the children more immediately under their own eyes. Early the next summer's morning, Mrs Openshaw was awakened by Ailsie's startled call of 'Mother! mother!' She sprang up, put on her dressing-gown, and went to her child. Ailsie was only half awake, and in a not unusual state of terror.

'Who was he, mother? Tell me!'

'Who, my darling? No one is here. You have been dreaming, love. Waken up quite. See, it is broad daylight.'

'Yes,' said Ailsie, looking round her; then clinging to her mother, 'but a man was here in the night, mother.'

'Nonsense, little goose. No man has ever come near you!'

'Yes, he did. He stood there. Just by Norah. A man with hair and a beard. And he knelt down and said his prayers. Norah knows he was here, mother' (half angrily, as Mrs Openshaw shook her head in smiling incredulity).

'Well! we will ask Norah when she comes,' said Mrs Openshaw, soothingly. 'But we won't talk any more about him now. It is not five o'clock; it is too early for you to get up. Shall I fetch you a book and read to you?'

'Don't leave me, mother,' said the child, clinging to her. So Mrs Openshaw sat on the bedside talking to Ailsie, and telling her of what they had done at Richmond the evening before, until the little girl's eyes slowly closed and she once more fell asleep.

'What was the matter?' asked Mr Openshaw, as his wife returned to bed.

'Ailsie wakened up in a fright, with some story of a man having been in the room to say his prayers—a dream, I suppose.' And no more was said at the time.

Mrs Openshaw had almost forgotten the whole affair when she got up about seven o'clock. But, by and by, she heard a sharp altercation going on in the nursery—Norah speaking angrily to Ailsie, a most unusual thing. Both Mr and Mrs Openshaw listened in astonishment.

'Hold your tongue, Ailsie! let me hear none of your dreams; never let me hear you tell that story again!'

Ailsie began to cry.

Mr Openshaw opened the door of communication, before his wife could say a word.

'Norah, come here!'

The nurse stood at the door, defiant. She perceived she had been heard, but she was desperate.

'Don't let me hear you speak in that manner to Ailsie again,' he said sternly, and shut the door.

Norah was infinitely relieved; for she had dreaded some questioning; and a little blame for sharp speaking was what she could well bear, if cross-examination was let alone.

Downstairs they went, Mr Openshaw carrying Ailsie; the sturdy Edwin coming step by step, right foot foremost, always holding his mother's hand. Each child was placed in a chair by the breakfast-table, and then Mr and Mrs Openshaw stood together at the window, awaiting their visitors' appearance and making plans for the day. There was a pause. Suddenly Mr Openshaw turned to Ailsie, and said:

'What a little goosy somebody is with her dreams, wakening up poor, tired mother in the middle of the night, with a story of a man being in the room.'

'Father! I'm sure I saw him,' said Ailsie, half-crying. 'I don't want to make Norah angry; but I was not asleep, for all she says I was. I had been asleep—and I wakened up quite wide awake, though I was so frightened. I kept my eyes nearly shut, and I saw the man quite plain. A great brown man with a beard. He said his prayers. And then looked at Edwin. And then Norah took him by the arm and led him away, after they had whispered a bit together.'

'Now, my little woman must be reasonable,' said Mr Openshaw, who was always patient with Ailsie. 'There was no man in the house last night at all. No man comes into the house, as you know, if you think; much less goes up into the nursery. But sometimes we dream something has happened, and the dream is so like reality, that you are not the first person, little woman, who has stood out that the thing has really happened.'

'But, indeed, it was not a dream!' said Ailsie, beginning to cry.

Just then Mr and Mrs Chadwick came down, looking grave and discomposed. All during breakfast-time they were silent and uncomfortable. As soon as the breakfast things were taken away, and the children had been carried upstairs, Mr Chadwick began, in an evidently preconcerted manner, to inquire if his nephew was certain that all his servants were honest; for, that Mrs Chadwick had that morning missed a very valuable brooch, which she had worn the day before. She remembered taking it off when she came home from Buckingham Palace. Mr Openshaw's face contracted into hard lines; grew like what it was before he had known his wife and her child. He rang the bell, even before his uncle had done speaking. It was answered by the housemaid.

'Mary, was anyone here last night, while we were away?'

'A man, sir, came to speak to Norah.'

'To speak to Norah! Who was he? How long did he stay?'

'I'm sure I can't tell, sir. He came—perhaps about nine. I went up to tell Norah in the nursery, and she came down to speak to him. She let him out, sir. She will know who he was, and how long he stayed.'

She waited a moment to be asked any more questions, but she was not, so she went away.

A minute afterwards Mr Openshaw made as though he were going out of the room; but his wife laid her hand on his arm.

'Do not speak to her before the children,' she said, in her low, quiet voice. 'I will go up and question her.'

'No! I must speak to her. You must know,' said he, turning to his uncle and aunt, 'my missus has an old servant, as faithful as ever woman was, I do believe, as far as love goes,—but at the same time, who does not speak truth, as even the missus must allow. Now, my notion is, that this Norah of ours has been come over by some good-for-nothing chap (for she's at the time o' life when they say women pray for husbands—"any, good Lord, any") and has let him into our house, and the chap has made off with your brooch, and m'appen many another thing beside. It's only saying that Norah is soft-hearted and doesn't stick at a white lie—that's all, missus.'

It was curious to notice how his tone, his eyes, his whole face was changed, as he spoke to his wife; but he was the resolute man through all. She knew better than to oppose him; so she went upstairs, and told Norah that her master wanted to speak to her, and that she would take care of the children in the meanwhile.

Norah rose to go, without a word. Her thoughts were these:

'If they tear me to pieces, they shall never know through me. He may come—and then, just Lord have mercy upon us all! for some of us are dead folk to a certainty. But *he* shall do it; not me.'

You may fancy, now, her look of determination, as she faced her master alone in the dining-room; Mr and Mrs Chadwick having left the affair in their nephew's hands, seeing that he took it up with such vehemence.

'Norah! Who was that man that came to my house last night?'

'Man, sir!' As if infinitely surprised; but it was only to gain time.

'Yes; the man that Mary let in; that she went upstairs to the nursery to tell you about; that you came down to speak to; the same chap, I make no doubt, that you took into the nursery to have your talk out with; the one Ailsie saw, and afterwards dreamed about; thinking, poor wench! she saw him say his prayers, when nothing, I'll be bound, was further from his thoughts; the one that took Mrs Chadwick's brooch, value ten pounds. Now, Norah! Don't go off. I'm as sure as my name's Thomas Openshaw that you knew nothing of this robbery. But I do think you've been imposed on, and that's the truth. Some good-for-nothing chap has been making up to you, and you've been just like all other women, and have turned a soft place in your heart to him; and he came last night a-lovyering, and you had him up in the nursery, and he made use of his opportunities, and made off with a few things on his way down! Come, now, Norah; it's no blame to you, only you must not be such a fool again! Tell us,' he continued, 'what name he gave you, Norah. I'll be bound, it was not the right one; but it will be a clue for the police.'

Norah drew herself up. 'You may ask that question, and taunt me with my being single, and with my credulity, as you will, Master Openshaw. You'll get no answer from me. As for the brooch, and the story of theft and burglary; if any friend ever came to see me (which I defy you to prove, and deny), he'd be just as much above doing such a thing as you yourself, Mr Openshaw—and more so, too; for I'm not at all sure as everything you have is rightly come by, or would be yours long, if every man had his own.' She meant, of course, his wife; but he understood her to refer to his property in goods and chattels.

'Now, my good woman,' said he, 'I'll just tell you truly, I never trusted you out and out; but my wife liked you, and I thought you had many a good point about you. If you once begin to sauce me, I'll have the police to you, and get out the truth in a court of justice, if you'll not tell it me quietly and civilly here. Now, the best thing you can do is quietly to tell me who the fellow is. Look here! a man comes to my house; asks for you; you take him upstairs; a valuable brooch is missing next day; we know that you, and Mary, and cook, are honest; but you refuse to tell us who the man is. Indeed, you've told me one lie already about him, saying no one was here last night. Now, I just put it to you, what do you think a policeman would say to this, or a magistrate? A magistrate would soon make you tell the truth, my good woman.'

'There's never the creature born that should get it out of me,' said Norah. 'Not unless I choose to tell.'

'I've a great mind to see,' said Mr Openshaw, growing angry at the defiance. Then, checking himself, he thought before he spoke again:

'Norah, for your missus' sake I don't want to go to extremities. Be a sensible woman, if you can. It's no great disgrace, after all, to have been taken in. I ask you once more—as a friend—who was this man that you let into my house last night?'

No answer. He repeated the question in an impatient tone. Still no answer. Norah's lips were set in determination not to speak.

'Then there is but one thing to be done. I shall send for a policeman.'

'You will not,' said Norah, starting forward. 'You shall not, sir! No policeman shall touch me. I know nothing of the brooch, but I know this: ever since I was four-and-twenty, I have thought more of your wife than of myself: ever since I saw her, a poor motherless girl, putupon in her uncle's house, I have thought more of serving her than of serving myself! I have cared for her and her child, as nobody ever cared for me. I don't cast blame on you, sir, but I say it's ill giving up one's life to anyone; for, at the end, they will turn round upon you, and forsake you. Why does not my missus come herself to suspect me? Maybe, she is gone for the police? But I don't stay here, either for police, or magistrate, or master. You're an unlucky lot. I believe there's a curse on you. I'll leave you this very day. Yes! I'll leave that poor Ailsie, too. I will! No good ever will come to you!'

Mr Openshaw was utterly astonished at this speech; most of which was completely unintelligible to him, as may easily be supposed. Before he could make up his mind what to say, or what to do, Norah had left the room. I do not think he had ever really intended to send for the police to this old servant of his wife's; for he had never for a moment doubted her perfect honesty. But he had intended to compel her to tell him who the man was, and in this he was baffled. He was, consequently, much irritated. He returned to his uncle and aunt in a state of great annoyance and perplexity, and told them he could get nothing out of the woman; that some man had been in the house the night before; but that she refused to tell who he was. At this moment his wife came in, greatly agitated, and asked what had happened to Norah; for that she had put on her things in passionate haste, and left the house.

'This looks suspicious,' said Mr Chadwick. 'It is not the way in which an honest person would have acted.'

Mr Openshaw kept silence. He was sorely perplexed. But Mrs Openshaw turned round on Mr Chadwick, with a sudden fierceness no one ever saw in her before.

'You don't know Norah, uncle! She is gone because she is deeply hurt at being suspected. Oh, I wish I had seen her—that I had spoken to her myself. She would have told me anything.' Alice wrung her hands.

'I must confess,' continued Mr Chadwick to his nephew, in a lower voice, 'I can't make you out. You used to be a word and a blow, and oftenest the blow first; and now, when there is every cause for suspicion, you just do nought. Your missus is a very good woman, I grant; but she may have been put upon as well as other folk, I suppose. If you don't send for the police, I shall.'

'Very well,' replied Mr Openshaw, surlily. 'I can't clear Norah. She won't clear herself, as I believe she might if she would. Only I wash my hands of it; for I am sure the woman herself is honest, and she's lived a long time with my wife, and I don't like her to come to shame.'

'But she will then be forced to clear herself. That, at any rate, will be a good thing.'

'Very well, very well! I am heart-sick of the whole business. Come, Alice, come up to the babies; they'll be in a sore way. I tell you, uncle,' he said, turning round once more to Mr Chadwick, suddenly and sharply, after his eye had fallen on Alice's wan, tearful, anxious face, 'I'll have no sending for the police, after all. I'll buy my aunt twice as handsome a brooch this very day; but I'll not have Norah suspected, and my missus plagued. There's for you!'

He and his wife left the room. Mr Chadwick quietly waited till he was out of hearing, and then said to his wife, 'For all Tom's heroics, I'm just quietly going for a detective, wench. Thou need'st know nought about it.'

He went to the police-station and made a statement of the case. He was gratified by the impression which the evidence against Norah seemed to make. The men all agreed in his opinion, and steps were to be immediately taken to find out where she was. Most probably, as they suggested, she had gone at once to the man, who, to all appearance, was her lover. When Mr Chadwick asked how they would find her out, they smiled, shook their heads, and spoke of mysterious but infallible ways and means. He returned to his nephew's house with a very comfortable opinion of his own sagacity. He was met by his wife with a penitent face.

'Oh, master, I've found my brooch! It was just sticking by its pin in the flounce of my brown silk, that I wore yesterday. I took it off in a hurry, and it must have caught in it; and I hung up my gown in the closet. Just now, when I was going to fold it up, there was the brooch! I am very vexed, but I never dreamt but what it was lost!'

Her husband, muttering something very like 'Confound thee and thy brooch too! I wish I'd never given it thee,' snatched up his hat, and rushed back to the station, hoping to be in time to stop the police from searching for Norah. But a detective was already gone off on the errand.

Where was Norah? Half mad with the strain of the fearful secret, she had hardly slept through the night for thinking what must be done. Upon this terrible state of mind had come Ailsie's questions, showing that she had seen the Man, as the unconscious child called her father. Lastly came the suspicion of her honesty. She was little less than crazy as she ran upstairs and dashed on her bonnet and shawl; leaving all else, even her purse, behind her. In that house she would not stay. That was all she knew or was clear about. She would not even see the children again, for fear it should weaken her. She dreaded above everything Mr Frank's return to claim his wife. She could not tell what remedy there was for a sorrow so tremendous, for her to stay to witness. The desire of escaping from the coming event was a stronger motive for her departure, than her soreness about the suspicions directed against her; although this last had been the final goad to the course she took. She walked a way almost at headlong speed; sobbing as she went, as she had not dared to do during the past night for fear of exciting wonder in those who might hear her. Then she stopped. An idea came into her mind that she would leave London altogether, and betake herself to her native town of Liverpool. She felt in her pocket for her purse as she drew near the Euston Square station with this intention. She had left it at home. Her poor head aching, her eyes swollen with crying, she had to stand still, and think, as well as she could, where next she should bend her steps. Suddenly the thought flashed into her mind that she would go and find out poor Mr Frank. She had been hardly kind to him the night before, though her heart had bled for him ever since. She remembered his telling her, when she inquired for his address, almost as she had pushed him out of the door, of some hotel in a street not far distant from Euston Square. Thither she went: with what intention she scarcely knew, but to assuage her conscience by telling him how much she pitied him. In her present state she felt herself unfit to counsel, or restrain, or assist, or do aught else but sympathize and weep. The people of the inn said such a person had been there; had arrived only the day before; had gone out soon after arrival, leaving his luggage in their care; but had never come back. Norah asked for leave to sit down, and await the gentleman's return. The landlady—pretty secure in the deposit of luggage against any probable injury—showed her into a room, and quietly locked the door on the outside. Norah was utterly worn out, and fell asleep—a shivering, starting, uneasy slumber, which lasted for hours.

The detective, meanwhile, had come up with her some time before she entered the hotel, into which he followed her. Asking the landlady to detain her for an hour or so, without giving any reason beyond showing his authority (which made the landlady applaud herself a good deal for having locked her in), he went back to the police-station to report his proceedings. He could have taken her directly; but his object was, if possible, to trace out the man who was supposed to have committed the robbery. Then he heard of the discovery of the brooch; and consequently did not care to return.

Norah slept till even the summer evening began to close in, Then started up. Someone was at the door. It would be Mr Frank; and she dizzily pushed back her ruffled grey hair which had fallen over her eyes, and stood looking to see him. Instead, there came in Mr Openshaw and a policeman.

'This is Norah Kennedy,' said Mr Openshaw.

'Oh, sir,' said Norah, 'I did not touch the brooch; indeed I did not. Oh, sir, I cannot live to be thought so badly of'; and very sick and faint, she suddenly sank down on the ground. To her surprise, Mr Openshaw raised her up very tenderly. Even the policeman helped to lay her on the sofa; and, at Mr Openshaw's desire, he went for some wine and sandwiches; for the poor gaunt woman lay there almost as if dead with weariness and exhaustion.

'Norah,' said Mr Openshaw, in his kindest voice, 'the brooch is found. It was hanging to Mrs Chadwick's gown. I beg your pardon. Most truly I beg your pardon, for having troubled you about it. My wife is almost broken-hearted. Eat, Norah—or, stay, first drink this glass of wine,' said he, lifting her head, and pouring a little down her throat.

As she drank, she remembered where she was, and who she was waiting for. She suddenly pushed Mr Openshaw away, saying, 'Oh, sir, you must go. You must not stop a minute. If he comes back, he will kill you.'

'Alas, Norah! I do not know who "he" is. But someone is gone away who will never come back: someone who knew you, and whom I am afraid you cared for.'

'I don't understand you, sir,' said Norah, her master's kind and sorrowful manner bewildering her yet more than his words. The policeman had left the room at Mr Openshaw's desire, and they two were alone.

'You know what I mean, when I say someone is gone who will never come back. I mean that he is dead!'

'Who?' said Norah, trembling all over.

'A poor man has been found in the Thames this morning—drowned.'

'Did he drown himself?' asked Norah, solemnly.

'God only knows,' replied Mr Openshaw, in the same tone. 'Your name and address at our house were found in his pocket; that, and his purse, were the only things that were found upon him. I am sorry to say it, my poor Norah; but you are required to go and identify him.'

'To what?' asked Norah.

'To say who it is. It is always done, in order that some reason may be discovered for the suicide—if suicide it was. I make no doubt, he was the man who came to see you at our house last night. It is very sad, I know.' He made pauses between each little clause, in order to try and bring back her senses, which he feared were wandering—so wild and sad was her look.

'Master Openshaw,' said she, at last, 'I've a dreadful secret to tell you—only you must never breathe it to anyone, and you and I must hide it away for ever. I thought to have done it all by myself, but I see I cannot. Yon poor man—yes! the dead, drowned creature is, I fear, Mr Frank, my mistress's first husband!'

Mr Openshaw sat down, as if shot. He did not speak; but, after a while, he signed to Norah to go on.

'He came to me the other night, when—God be thanked!—you were all away at Richmond. He asked me if his wife was dead or alive. I was a brute, and thought more of your all coming home than of his sore trial; I spoke out sharp, and said she was married again, and very content and happy. I all but turned him away: and now he lies dead and cold.'

'God forgive me!' said Mr Openshaw.

'God forgive us all!' said Norah. 'Yon poor man needs forgiveness, perhaps, less than any one among us. He had been among the savages—shipwrecked—I know not what—and he had written letters which had never reached my poor missus.'

'He saw his child!'

'He saw her—yes! I took him up, to give his thoughts another start; for I believed he was going mad on my hands. I came to seek him here, as I more than half promised. My mind misgave me when I heard he never came in. Oh, sir, it must be him!'

Mr Openshaw rang the bell. Norah was almost too much stunned to wonder at what he did. He asked for writing materials, wrote a letter, and then said to Norah:

'I am writing to Alice, to say I shall be unavoidably absent for a few days; that I have found you; that you are well, and send her your love, and will come home tomorrow. You must go with me to the police court; you must identify the body; I will pay high to keep names and details out of the papers.'

'But where are you going, sir?'

He did not answer her directly. Then he said:

'Norah! I must go with you, and look on the face of the man whom I have so injured—unwittingly, it is true; but it seems to me as if I had killed him. I will lay his head in the grave as if he were my only brother: and how he must have hated me! I cannot go home to my wife till all that I can do for him is done. Then I go with a dreadful secret on my mind. I shall never speak of it again, after these days are over. I know you will not, either.' He shook hands with her; and they never named the subject again, the one to the other.

Norah went home to Alice the next day. Not a word was said on the cause of her abrupt departure a day or two before. Alice had been charged by her husband, in his letter, not to allude to the supposed theft of the brooch; so she, implicitly obedient to those whom she loved both by nature and habit, was entirely silent on the subject, only treated Norah with the most tender respect, as if to make up for unjust suspicion.

Nor did Alice inquire into the reason why Mr Openshaw had been absent during his uncle and aunt's visit, after he had once said that it was unavoidable. He came back grave and quiet; and from that time forth was curiously changed. More thoughtful, and perhaps less active; quite as decided in conduct, but with new and different rules for the guidance of that conduct. Towards Alice he could hardly be more kind than he had always been; but he now seemed to look upon her as someone sacred, and to be treated with reverence, as well as tenderness. He throve in business, and made a large fortune, one half of which was settled upon her.

Long years after these events—a few months after her mother died—Ailsie and her 'father' (as she always called Mr Openshaw) drove to a cemetery a little way out of town, and she was carried to a certain mound by her maid, who was then sent back to the carriage. There was a headstone, with F.W. and a date upon it. That was all. Sitting by the grave, Mr Openshaw told her the story; and for the sad fate of that poor father whom she had never seen, he shed the only tears she ever saw fall from his eyes.

Made in the USA
Las Vegas, NV
30 April 2022